The Aquitaine Progression
The Chancellor Manuscript

Robert Ludlum

Diamond Books,
An Imprint of HarperCollins*Publishers*,
77–85 Fulham Palace Road
Hammersmith, London W6 8JB

This Diamond Books Omnibus edition first published 1993
9 8 7 6 5 4 3 2 1

Published in the UK by Grange Books
An Imprint of Grange Books plc,
The Grange, Grange Yard, London SE1 3AG

The Aquitaine Progression © Robert Ludlum 1984
The Chancellor Manuscript © Robert Ludlum 1977

ISBN 1 85627 (UK)
ISBN Diamond Books 0261 66160–4 (international edition)

Phototypeset in Ehrhardt by Intype, London

Printed in France by Maury-Eurolivres

The Author asserts the moral right to be identified as the author of this work

Contents

By the same author

The Scarlatti Inheritance

The Osterman Weekend

The Matlock Paper

The Gemini Contenders

The Bourne Identity

The Matarese Circle

The Road to Gandolfo

The Parsifal Mosaic

The Bourne Supremacy

The Icarus Agenda

Trevayne

The Bourne Ultimatum

The Road to Omaha

The Scorpio Illusion

The Aquitaine Progression

For Jeffrey Michael Ludlum
Welcome, friend. Have a great life.

Part I

1

Geneva. City of sunlight and bright reflections. Of billowing white sails on the lake – sturdy, irregular buildings above, their rippling images on the water below. Of myriad flowers surrounding blue-green pools of fountains – duets of exploding colours. Of small quaint bridges arching over and beneath the glassy surfaces of man-made ponds to man-made sanctuaries that are tiny islands for lovers and friends and quiet negotiators. Reflections.

Geneva, the old and the new. City of high medieval walls and glistening tinted glass, of sacred cathedrals and less holy institutions. Of sidewalk cafés and lakeside concerts, of miniature piers and gaily-painted boats that chug around the vast shoreline, the guides extolling the virtues – and the estimated value – of the lakefront estates which surely belonged to another time – ogled by tourists very much of the present.

Geneva. City of purpose, dedicated to the necessity of dedication, frivolity tolerated only as it is intrinsic to the agenda or the deal. Laughter is measured, controlled glances conveying approval of sufficiency or silently admonishing excess. The canton by the lake knows its soul. Its beauty coexists with industry, the balance not only accepted but jealously guarded.

Geneva. City also of the unexpected, predictability in conflict with sudden unwanted revelation, the violence of the mind accompanied by striking bolts of personal lightning.

Cracks of thunder follow; the skies grow dark and the rains come. A deluge, pounding the angry waters taken by surprise, distorting vision, crashing down on the giant spray, Geneva's trademark on the lake, the *Jet d'Eau*, that geyser designed by man to dazzle man. When sudden revelations come, the gigantic fountain dies. All the fountains die and the flowers wither without the sunlight. The bright reflections are gone and the mind is frozen.

Geneva. City of inconstancy.

Joel Converse, attorney at law, walked out of the Hotel Richemond into the blinding morning on the Jardin Brunswick. Squinting, he turned left, shifting his attaché case to his right hand, conscious of the value of the contents, but thinking primarily about the man he was to meet for coffee and croissants at *Le Chat Botté*, a sidewalk café across from the waterfront. Re-meet was more accurate, thought Converse, if the man had not confused him with someone else.

A. Preston Halliday was Joel's American adversary in the current negotiations, the finalizing of last minute details for a Swiss-American merger that had brought both men to Geneva. Although the remaining work was minimal – formalities, really, discoveries having established that the agreements were in accord with the laws of both countries and acceptable to the International Court in the Hague – Halliday was an odd choice. He had not been part of the American legal team fielded by the Swiss to keep tabs on Joel's firm. That, in itself, would not have excluded him, fresh observation was frequently an asset, but to elevate him to the position of point, or chief spokesman, was to say the least unorthodox. It was also unsettling.

Halliday's reputation – what little Converse knew of it – was as a trouble-shooter, a legal mechanic from San Francisco who could spot a loose wire, rip it out and short an engine. Negotiations covering months and costing hundreds of thousands had been aborted by his presence, that much Converse recalled about A. Preston Halliday. But that was all he recalled. Yet Halliday said they knew each other.

"It's Press Halliday," the voice had announced over the hotel phone. "I'm pointing for Rosen in the Comm Tech-Bern merger."

"What happened?" Joel had asked, a muted electric razor in his left hand, his mind trying to place the name; it had come to him by the time Halliday replied.

"The poor bastard had a stroke, so his partners called me in." The lawyer had paused. "You must have been mean, counsellor."

"We rarely argued, counsellor. Christ, I'm sorry, I like Aaron. How is he?"

"He'll make it. They've got him in bed and on a dozen versions of chicken soup. He told me to tell you he's going to check your finals for invisible ink."

"Which means *you're* going to check because I don't have any and neither did Aaron. This marriage is based on pure greed, and if you've studied the papers you know that as well as I do."

"The larceny of investment write-offs," agreed Halliday, "combined with a large chunk of technological market. No invisible ink. But since I'm the new boy on the block, I've got a couple of questions. Let's have breakfast."

"I was about to order room service."

"It's a nice morning, why not get some air? I'm at the Président so let's split the distance? Do you know the *Chat Botté?*"

"American coffee and croissants. Quai du Mont Blanc."

"You know it. How about twenty minutes?"

"Make it a half hour, okay?"

"Sure." Halliday had paused again. "It'll be good to see you again, Joel."

"Oh? Again?"

"You may not remember. A lot's happened since those days . . . more to you than to me, I'm afraid."

"I'm not following you."

"Well, there was Vietnam and you were a prisoner for a pretty long time."

"That's not what I meant, and it was years ago. Where do we know each other? What case?"

"No case, no business. We were classmates."

"Duke? It's a large law school."

"Farther back. Maybe you'll remember when we see each other. If you don't, I'll remind you."

"You must like games . . . Half an hour. *Chat Botté*."

As Converse walked towards the Quai du Mont Blanc, the vibrant boulevard fronting the lake, he tried to fit Halliday's name into a time frame, the years to a school, a forgotten face to match an unremembered classmate. None came, and *Halliday* was not a common name, the short form *Press* even less so . . . unique, actually. If he had known someone named "Press Halliday", he could not imagine forgetting it. Yet the tone of voice had implied familiarity, even closeness.

It'll be good to see you again, Joel. He had spoken the words warmly, as he had the gratuitous reference to Joel's POW status. But then those words were always spoken softly, sympathy implied if not overtly expressed. Also, Converse understood why under the circumstances Halliday felt he had to bring up the subject of Vietnam, even fleetingly. The uninitiated assumed that all men imprisoned in the North Vietnamese camps for any length of time had been mentally damaged, *per se*, that a part of their minds had been altered by the experience, their recollections muddled. To a degree, some aspects were undeniable, but not with respect to memory, that was a false assumption. Memories were sharpened because they were searched, compulsively, often mercilessly. The accumulated years, the layers of experience . . . faces with eyes and voices, bodies with sizes and shapes; scenes flashing across the inner screen, the sights and sounds, images and smells – touching and the desire to touch . . . nothing of the past was too inconsequential to peel away and explore. Frequently it was all they had, especially at night – *always* at night, with the cold, penetrating dampness stiffening the body and the infinitely colder fear paralysing the immediate – memories were everything. They helped block out the distant screams in the dark, mute the sharp reports of small-arms fire, gratuitously explained in the mornings as necessary executions of the uncooperative and unrepentant. Or of even more unfortunate prisoners forced to play games too obscene to describe, demanded by captors in search of amusement.

Like most men kept isolated for the greater part of their imprisonment, Converse had examined and re-examined every stage of his life, trying to piece them together, to understand . . . to *like* . . . the cohesive whole. There was much that he did not understand – or like – but he could live with the product of those intensive investigations. Die with it, if he had to; that was the peace he had to reach for himself. Without it the fear was intolerable.

And because these self-examinations went on night after night and required the discipline of accuracy, Converse found it easier than most men to remember whole segments of his life. Like a spinning disc attached to a computer that suddenly stops, his mind could isolate a place or a person or a name, given only basic information. Repetition had simplified and accelerated the process, and that was what bewildered him now. Unless Halliday was referring to a time so far back as to have been only a brief, forgotten childhood acquaintance, no one of that name belonged to his past.

It'll be good to see you again, Joel. Were the words a ruse, a lawyer's trick?

Converse rounded the corner, the brass railing of *Le Chat Botté* glistening, hurling back tiny explosions of sunlight. The boulevard was alive with gleaming small cars and spotless buses; the pavements were washed clean, the strollers in various stages of hurried but orderly progress. Morning was a time for benign energy in Geneva. Even the newspapers above the tables in the sidewalk cafés were snapped with precision, not crushed or mutilated into legible positions. And vehicles and pedestrians were not at war; combat was supplanted by looks and nods, stops and gestures of acknowledgment. As Joel walked through the open brass gate of *Le Chat Botté*, he wondered briefly if Geneva could export its mornings to New York. But then the City Council would vote the import down, he concluded, the citizens of New York could not stand the civility.

A newspaper snapped directly below him on the left, the precision apparently contagious, as the paper was lowered revealing a face Converse knew. It was a . . . coordinated face, unlike his own, the features compatible and in place. The hair straight and dark, neatly parted and brushed, the nose sharp, above sharply defined lips. The face belonged to his past, thought Joel, but the name he remembered did not belong to the face.

The familiar-looking man raised his head; their eyes met and "A. Preston Halliday" rose, his short compact body obviously muscular under the expensive suit.

"Joel, how are you?" said the now-familiar voice, a hand outstretched above the table.

"Hello . . . Avery," replied Converse staring, awkwardly taking the necessary steps and shifting his attaché case once again to grip the hand. "It *is* Avery, isn't it? Avery Fowler. Taft, early 'sixties. You never came back for the senior year, and no one knew why; we all talked about it. You were a wrestler."

"Twice All New England," said the attorney, laughing, gesturing at the chair across from his own. "Sit down and we'll catch up. I guess it's sort of a surprise for you. That's why I wanted us to meet before the conference this morning. I mean, it'd be a hell of a note for you to get up and scream 'impostor!' when I walked in, wouldn't it?"

"I'm still not sure I won't, but I won't scream." Converse sat down, attaché case at his feet, studying his legal opponent. "What's this Halliday routine? Why didn't you say something on the phone?"

"Oh, come on, what was I going to say? By the way, old sport, you used to know me as Tinkerbell Jones. You never would have showed up."

"Is Fowler in jail somewhere?"

"He would have been if he hadn't blown his head off," answered Halliday, not laughing.

"You're full of surprises. Are you a clone?"

"No, the son."

Converse paused. "Maybe I should apologize."

"No need to, you couldn't have known. It's why I never came back for the senior year . . . and, goddamn it, I wanted that trophy. I would have been the only mat-jock to win it three years in a row."

"I'm sorry. What happened . . . or is it privileged information, counsellor? I'll accept that."

"Not for you, counsellor. Remember when you and I broke out to New Haven and picked up those pigs at the bus station?"

"We said we were Yalies . . ."

"And only got taken, never got laid."

"Our eyebrows were working overtime."

"Preppies," said Halliday. "They wrote a book about us. Are we really that emasculated?"

"Reduced in stature, but we'll come back. We're the last minority, so we'll end up getting sympathy . . . What happened, Avery?"

A waiter approached, the moment broken. Both men ordered American coffee and croissants, no deviation from the stated norm. The waiter folded two red napkins into cones, placing them in front of each.

"What happened?" said Halliday quietly, rhetorically after the waiter left. "The beautiful son of a bitch who was my father embezzled four hundred thousand from the Chase Manhattan while he was a trust officer, and when he was caught, went bang. Who was to know a respected, if transplanted, commuter from Greenwich, Connecticut, had two women in the city, one on the upper East Side, the other on Bank Street. He was beautiful."

"He was busy. I still don't understand the Halliday."

"After it happened – the suicide covered up – mother raced back to San Francisco with a vengeance. We were from California, you know . . . but then why would you? With even more vengeance she married my step-father, John Halliday, all traces of Fowler assiduously removed during the next few months."

"Even to your first name?"

"No, I was always 'Press' back in San Francisco. We Californians come up with catchy names. Tab, Troy, Crotch . . . The 1950s Beverly Hills syndrome . . . At Taft, my student ID read Avery Preston Fowler so you all just started calling me Avery or that awful 'Ave'. Being a transfer student I never bothered to say anything. When in Connecticut follow the gospel according to Holden Caulfield."

"That's all well and good," said Converse, "but what happens when you run into someone like me? It's bound to happen."

"You'd be surprised how rarely. After all, it was a long time ago, and the people I grew up with in California understood. Kids out there have their names changed according to matrimonial whim, and I was in the East for only a couple of years, just long enough for the fourth and fifth forms at school. I didn't know anyone in Greenwich to speak of, and I was hardly part of the old Taft crowd."

"You had friends there. We were friends."

"I didn't have many. Let's face it, I was an outsider and you weren't particular. I kept a pretty low profile."

"Not on the mats, you didn't."

Halliday laughed. "Not very many wrestlers become lawyers, something about mat-burns on the brain. Anyway, to answer your question, maybe five or six times

11

over the past ten years has anyone said to me, 'Hey, aren't you so-and-so and not whatever you said your name was?' When they do, I tell them the truth. My mother remarried when I was sixteen and the questions stop."

The coffee and croissants arrived. Joel broke his pastry in half. "And you thought I'd ask the question at the wrong time, specifically when I saw you at the conference. Is that it?"

"Professional courtesy. I didn't want you dwelling on it – or me – when you should be thinking about your client. After all, we tried to lose our virginities together that night in New Haven."

"Speak for yourself," Joel smiled.

Halliday grinned. "We got pissed and both admitted it, don't you remember? Incidentally, we swore each other to secrecy while throwing up in the can."

"Just testing you, counsellor, I remember. So you left the grey-flannel crowd for orange shirts and gold medallions?"

"All the way. Berkeley, then across the street to Stanford."

"Good school . . . How come the international field?"

"I liked travelling and figured it was the best way of paying for it. That's how it started, really . . . How about you? I'd think you would have had all the travelling you ever wanted."

"I had early delusions of the foreign service, diplomatic corps, legal section. That's how it started . . . really."

"After all that travelling you did?"

Converse levelled his pale blue eyes at Halliday, conscious of the coldness in his look. It was unavoidable, if misplaced – as it usually was. "Yes, after all that travelling. There were too many lies and no one told us about them until it was too late. We were conned and it shouldn't have happened."

Halliday leaned forward, his elbows on the table, hands clasped, his gaze returning Joel's. "I couldn't figure it," he began softly. "When I read your name in the papers, then saw you paraded on television, I felt awful. I didn't really know you that well, but I liked you."

"It was a natural reaction. I'd have felt the same way if it had been you."

"I'm not sure you would. You see, I was one of the honchos of the protest movement."

"You burned your draft card while extolling the Yippie label," said Converse gently, the ice gone from his eyes. "I wasn't that brave."

"Neither was I. It was an out-of-date library card."

"I'm disappointed."

"So was I . . . in myself. But I was visible." Halliday leaned back in his chair and reached for his coffee. "How did *you* get so visible, Joel? I didn't think you were the type."

"I wasn't. I was squeezed."

"I thought you said conned."

"That came later." Converse raised his cup and sipped his black coffee, uncomfortable with the direction the conversation had taken. He did not like discussing those years and all too frequently he was called upon to do so. They

12

had made him out to be someone he was not. "I was a sophomore at Amherst and not much of a student."

"Not much, hell, I was borderline-negative, and whatever deferment I had was about to go down the tube. But I'd been flying since I was fourteen."

"I didn't know that," interrupted Halliday.

"My father wasn't beautiful and he didn't have the benefit of concubines, but he *was* an airline pilot, later an executive for Pan Am. It was standard in the Converse household to fly a plane before you got your driver's licence."

"Brothers and sisters?"

"A younger sister. She soloed before I did and she's never let me forget it."

"I remember. She was interviewed on television."

"Only twice," broke in Joel, smiling. "She was on your turf and didn't give a damn who knew it. The White House bunker put the word out to stay away from her. Don't tarnish the cause, and check her mail while you're at it."

"That's why I remember her," said Halliday. "So a lousy student left college and the Navy gained a hot pilot."

"Not very hot, none of us were. There wasn't that much to be hot against. Mostly we burned."

"Still you must have hated people like me back in the States. Not your sister, of course."

"Her, too," corrected Converse. "Hated, loathed, despised . . . furious. But only when someone was killed, or went crazy in the camps. Not for what you were saying – we all knew Saigon – but because you said it without any real fear. You were safe, and you made us feel like assholes. Dumb, frightened assholes."

"I can understand that."

"So nice of you."

"I'm sorry, I didn't mean it the way it sounded."

"How did it sound, counsellor?"

Halliday frowned. "Condescending, I guess."

"No guess," said Joel. "Right on."

"You're still angry."

"Not at you, only the, dredging. I hate the subject and it keeps coming back up."

"Blame the Pentagon PR. For a while you were a *bona fide* hero on the nightly news. What was it, three escapes? On the first two you got caught and put on the racks, but on the last one you made it all by yourself, didn't you? You crawled through a couple of hundred miles of enemy jungle before you reached the lines."

"It was barely a hundred and I was goddamned lucky. With the first two tries I was responsible for killing eight men. I'm not very proud of that. Can we get to the Comm Tech-Bern business?"

"Give me a few minutes," said Halliday, shoving his croissant aside. "Please. I'm not trying to dredge. There's a point in the back of my mind, if you'll grant I've got a mind."

"Preston Halliday has one, his rep confirms it. You're a shark, if my colleagues are accurate. But I knew someone named Avery, not Press."

13

"Then it's Fowler talking, you're more comfortable with him."

"What's the point?"

"A couple of questions first. You see, *I* want to be accurate because you've got a reputation, too. They say you're one of the best on the international scene, but the people I've talked to can't understand why Joel Converse stays with a relatively small if entrenched firm when he's good enough to get flashier. Or even go out on his own."

"Are you hiring?"

"Not me, I don't take partners. Courtesy of John Halliday, attorney at law, San Francisco."

Converse looked at the second half of his croissant and decided against it. "What was the question, counsellor?"

"Why are you where you're at?"

"I'm paid well and literally run the department; no one sits on my shoulder. Also I don't care to take chances. There's a little matter of, alimony, amiable but demanding."

"Child support, too?"

"None, thank heavens."

"What happened when you got out of the Navy? How did you feel?" Halliday again leaned forward, his elbow on the table, chin cupped in his hand – the inquisitive student. Or something else.

"Who are the people you've talked to?" asked Converse.

"Privileged information, for the moment, counsellor. Will you accept that?"

Joel smiled. "You *are* a shark . . . Okay, the gospel according to Converse. I came back from that disruption of my life wanting it all. Angry to be sure, but wanting everything. The non-student became a scholar of sorts, and I'd be a liar if I didn't admit to a fair amount of preferential treatment. I went back to Amherst and raced through two and a half years in three semesters and a summer. Then Duke offered me an accelerated programme and I went there, followed by some specializations at Georgetown while I clerked."

"You clerked in Washington?"

Converse nodded. "Yes."

"For whom?"

"Clifford's firm."

Halliday whistled softly, sitting back. "That's golden territory, a passport to Blackstone's heaven as well as the multinationals."

"I told you I had preferential treatment."

"Was that when you thought about the foreign service? While you were at Georgetown? In Washington?"

Again Joel nodded, squinting as a passing flash of sunlight bounced off a grill somewhere on the lakefront boulevard. "Yes," he replied quietly.

"You could have had it," said Halliday.

"They wanted me for the wrong reasons, *all* the wrong reasons. When they realized I had a different set of rules in mind, I couldn't get a twenty cent tour of the State Department."

"What about the Clifford firm? You were a hell of an image, even for them."

The Californian raised his hands above the table, palms forward. "I know, I know. The wrong reasons."

"Wrong numbers," insisted Converse. "There were forty-plus lawyers on the masthead and another two hundred on the payroll. I'd have spent ten years trying to find the men's room and another ten getting the key. That wasn't what I was looking for."

"What were you looking for?"

"Pretty much what I've got. I told you, the money's good and I run the international division. The latter's just as important to me."

"You couldn't have known that when you joined," objected Halliday.

"But I did. At least I had a fair indication. When Talbot, Brooks and Simon – as you put it, that small but entrenched firm I'm with – came to me we reached understanding. If after four or five years I proved out, I'd take over for Brooks. He was the overseas man and was getting tired of adjusting to all those time zones." Again Converse paused. "Apparently I proved out."

"And just as apparently somewhere along the line you got married."

Joel leaned back in the chair. "Is this necessary?"

"It's not even pertinent, but I'm intensely interested."

"Why?"

"It's a natural reaction," said Halliday, his eyes amused. "I think you'd feel the same way if you were me and I were you, and I'd gone through what you went through."

"Shark dead ahead," mumbled Converse.

"You don't have to respond, of course, counsellor."

"I know, but oddly enough I don't mind. She's taken her share of abuse because of that what-I've-been-through business." Joel broke the croissant but made no effort to remove it from the plate. "Comfort, convenience, and a vague image of stability," he said.

"I beg your pardon?"

"Her words," continued Joel. "She said that I got married so I'd have a place to go and someone to fix the meals and do the laundry, and eliminate the irritating, time-consuming foolishness that goes with finding someone to sleep with. Also by legitimizing her, I projected the proper image . . . 'and, Christ, did I have to play the part' . . . also her words."

"Were they true?"

"I told you, when I came back I wanted it all and she was part of it. Yes, they were true. Cook, maid, laundress, bedmate, and an acceptable, attractive appendage. She told me she could never figure out the pecking order."

"She sounds like quite a girl."

"She was. She is."

"Do I discern a note of possible reconciliation?"

"No way." Converse shook his head, a partial smile on his lips but only a trace of humour in his eyes. "She was also conned and it shouldn't have happened. Anyway, I like my current status, I really do. Some of us just weren't meant for a hearth and roast turkey, even if we sometimes wish we were."

"It's not a bad life."

"Are you into it?" asked Joel quickly so as to shift the emphasis.

"Right up with orthodontists and scholastic aptitude tests. Five kids and one wife. I wouldn't have it any other way."

"But you travel a lot, don't you?"

"We have great homecomings." Halliday again leaned forward, as if studying a witness. "So you have no real attachments now, no one to run back to."

"Talbot, Brooks and Simon might find that offensive. Also my father. Since mother died we have dinner once a week when he's not flying all over the place, courtesy of a couple of lifetime passes."

"He still gets around a lot?"

"One week he's in Copenhagen, the next in Hong Kong. He enjoys himself; he keeps moving. He's sixty-eight and spoiled rotten."

"I think I'd like him."

Converse shrugged, again smiling. "You might not. He thinks all lawyers are piss ants, me included. He's the last of the white-scarved fly-boys."

"I'm sure I'd like him . . . But outside of your employers and your father, there are no – shall we say – priority entanglements in your life."

"If you mean women, there are several and we're good friends, and I think this conversation has gone about as far as it should go."

"I told you, I had a point," said Halliday.

"Then why not get to it, counsellor? Interrogations are over."

The Californian nodded. "All right, I will. The people I spoke with wanted to know how free you were to travel."

"The answer is that I'm not. I've got a job and a responsibility to the company I work for. Today's Wednesday; we'll have the merger tied up by Friday, I'll take the weekend off and be back on Monday . . . when I'm expected."

"Suppose arrangements could be made that Talbot, Brooks and Simon found acceptable?"

"That's presumptuous."

"And you found very difficult to reject."

"That's preposterous."

"Try me," said Halliday. "Five hundred thousand for accepting on a best-efforts basis, one million if you pull it off."

"Now you're insane." A second flash of light blinded Converse, this one remaining stationary longer than the first. He raised his left hand to block it from his eyes as he stared at the man he had once known as Avery Fowler. "Also, ethics notwithstanding because you haven't a damn thing to win this morning, your timing smells. I don't like getting offers – even crazy offers – from attorneys I'm about to meet across a table."

"Two separate entities, and you're right, I don't have a damn thing to win or lose. You and Aaron did it all, and I'm so ethical. I'm billing the Swiss only for my time – minimum basis – because no expertise was called for. My recommendation this morning will be to accept the package as it stands, not even a comma changed. Where's the conflict?"

16

"Where's the sanity?" asked Joel. "To say nothing of those arrangements Talbot, Brooks and Simon will find acceptable. You're talking roughly about two and a half top years of salary *and* bonuses for nodding my head."

"Nod it," said Halliday. "We need you."

"*We?* That's a new wrinkle, isn't it? I thought it was *they*. *They* being the people you spoke with. Spell it out, *Press*."

A. Preston Halliday locked his eyes with Joel's. "I'm part of them, and something is happening that shouldn't be happening. We want you to put a company out of business. It's bad news and it's dangerous. We'll give you all the tools we can."

"What company?"

"The name wouldn't mean anything, it's not registered. Let's call it a government in exile."

"A what?"

"A group of like-minded men who are in the process of building a portfolio of resources so extensive it'll guarantee them influence where they shouldn't have it . . . authority where they shouldn't have it."

"Where is that?"

"In places this poor inept world can't afford. They can do it because no one expects them."

"You're pretty cryptic."

"I'm frightened. I know them."

"But you have the tools to go after them," said Converse. "I presume that means they're vulnerable."

Halliday nodded. "We think they are. We have some leads, but it'll take digging, piecing things together. There's every reason to believe they've broken laws, engaged in activities and transactions prohibited by their respective governments."

Joel was silent for a moment, studying the Californian. "Governments?" he asked. "Plural?"

"Yes." Halliday's voice dropped. "They're different nationalities."

"But one company?" said Converse. "One corporation?"

"In a manner of speaking, yes."

"How about a simple yes?"

"It's not that simple."

"I'll tell you what is," interrupted Joel. "You've got leads, so you go after the big bad wolves. I'm currently and satisfactorily employed."

Halliday paused, then spoke. "No, you're not," he said softly.

Again there was silence, each man appraising the other. "What did you say?" asked Converse, his eyes blue ice.

"Your firm understands. You can have a leave of absence."

"You presumptuous son of a bitch! Who gave you the right even to *approach* . . ."

"General George Marcus Delavane," broke in Halliday. He delivered the name in a monotone.

It was as if a bolt of lightning had streaked down through the blinding sunlight burning Joel's eyes, turning the ice into fire. Cracks of thunder followed, exploding in his head.

The pilots sat around the long rectangular table in the wardroom, sipping coffee and staring down into the brown liquid or up at the grey walls, no one caring to break the silence. An hour ago they had been sweeping over Pak Song, firing the earth, interdicting the advancing North Vietnamese battalions, giving vital time to the regrouping ARVN and American troops who soon would be under brutal siege. They had completed the strike and returned to the carrier – all but one. They had lost their commanding officer. Lieutenant Senior Grade Gordon Ramsey had been hit by a fluke rocket that had winged out of its trajectory over the coastline and zeroed in on Ramsey's fuselage; the explosion had filled the jet streams, death at 600 miles an hour in the air, life erased with the blinking of an eye. A severe weather front had followed hard upon the squadron; there would be no more strikes, perhaps for several days. There would be time to think and that was not a pleasant thought.

"Lieutenant Converse," said a sailor by the open wardroom door.

"Yes?"

"The captain requests your presence in his quarters, sir."

The invitation was so nicely phrased, mused Joel, as he got out of his chair, acknowledging the sombre looks of those around the table. The request was expected, but unwelcome. The promotion was an honour he would willingly have forgone. It was not that he held longevity or seniority or even age over his fellow pilots; it was simply that he had been in the air longer than anyone else and with that time came the experience necessary for the leader of a squadron.

As he climbed the narrow steps up toward the bridge he saw the outlines of an immense army Cobra helicopter in the distant sky stuttering its way toward the carrier. In five minutes or so it would be hovering over the threshold and lower itself to the pad; someone from land was paying the navy a visit.

"It's a terrible loss, Converse," said the captain standing over his chart table, shaking his head sadly. "And a letter I hate like hell to write. God knows they're never easy, but this one's more painful than most."

"We all feel the same way, sir."

"I'm sure you do." The captain nodded. "I'm also sure you know why you're here."

"Not specifically, sir."

"Ramsey said you were the best and that means you're taking over one of the crack squadrons in the South China Sea." The telephone rang, interrupting the carrier's senior officer. He picked it up. "Yes?"

What followed was nothing Joel expected. The captain at first frowned, then tensed the muscles of his face, his eyes both alarmed and angry. "What?" he exclaimed, raising his voice. "Was there any advance notice – anything in the radio room?" There was a pause, after which the captain slammed down the phone, shouting, "Jesus Christ!" He looked at Converse. "It seems we have the dubious honour of an unannounced visitation by Command-Saigon, and I do mean visitation!"

"I'll return below, sir," said Joel, starting to salute.

"Not just yet, Lieutenant," shot back the captain quietly but firmly. "You are

receiving your orders and as they affect the air operations of this ship, you'll hear them through. At the least, we'll let Mad Marcus know he's interfering with navy business."

The next thirty seconds were taken up with the ritual of command-assignment, a senior officer investing a subordinate with new responsibilities. Suddenly, there was a sharp two-rap knock, as the captain's door opened and the tall, broad-shouldered General of the Army, George Marcus Delavane, intruded, breaking the space in front of him with the sheer force of his presence.

"Captain?" said Delavane courteously, saluting the ship's commander first despite the navy man's lesser rank. The somewhat high-pitched voice was courteous, but not the eyes; they were intense, instantly hostile.

"General," replied the captain, saluting back along with Converse. "Is this an unannounced inspection by Command-Saigon?"

"No, it's an urgently-demanded conference between you and me – between Command-Saigon and one of its lesser forces."

"I see," said the four-striper, anger showing through his calm. "At the moment I'm delivering urgent orders to this man . . ."

"You saw fit to countermand mine!" broke in Delavane vehemently. "General, this has been a sad and trying day," said the captain. "We lost one of our finest pilots barely an hour ago."

"Running away?" Again Delavane interrupted, the tastelessness of his remark compounded by the nasal pitch of his voice. "Was his goddamned tail shot off?"

"For the record, I resent that!" said Converse, unable to control himself. "I'm replacing that man and I resent what you just said – General!"

"You? Who the hell are you?"

"Easy, Lieutenant. You're dismissed."

"I respectfully request to answer the general, sir!" shouted Joel, in his anger refusing to move.

"You what, prissy flyboy?"

"My name is . . ."

"Forget it, I'm not interested!" Delavane whipped his head back toward the captain. "What I want to know is why you think you can disobey my orders – the orders from Command-Saigon! I called a strike for fifteen hundred hours! You 'respectfully declined' to implement that order!"

"A weather front's moved in and you should know it as well as I do."

"My meteorologists say it's completely flyable!"

"I suspect if you asked for that finding during a Burma monsoon they'd deliver it."

"That's gross insubordination!"

"This is my ship and military regulations are quite clear as to who's in command here."

"Do you want to connect me to your radio room? I'll reach the Oval Office and we'll see just how long you've got this ship!"

"I'm sure you'll want to speak privately – probably over a scrambler. I'll have you escorted there."

"Goddamn you, I've got four thousand troops – maybe twenty per cent seasoned –

19

moving up into Sector Five! We need a low-altitude combined strike from land and sea and we'll have it if I have to get your ass out of here within the hour! And I can do it, Captain! . . . We're over here to win, win, and win it all! We don't need sugar-coated Nellies hedging their goddamned bets! Maybe you never heard it before, but all war is a risk! You don't win if you don't risk, Captain!"

"I've been there, General. Common sense cuts losses and if you cut enough losses you can win the next battle."

"I'm going to win this one, with or without you, Blue Boy!"

"I respectfully advise you to temper your language, General."

"You what?!" Delavane's face was contorted in fury, his eyes the eyes of a savage wild animal. "You advise me? You advise Command-Saigon! Well, you do whatever you like — Blue Boy in your satin pants — but the incursion up into the Tho Valley is on."

"The Tho," interrupted Converse. "That's the first leg of the Pak Song route. We've hit it four times. I know the terrain."

"You know it?" shouted Delavane.

"I do, but I take my orders from the commander of this ship — General."

"You prissy shit-kicker, you take orders from the President of the United States! He's your commander-in-chief! And I'll get those orders!"

Delavane's face was inches from Joel's, the maniacal expression challenging every nerve ending in his body; hatred was matched with loathing. Barely realizing the words were his, Converse spoke. "I, too, would advise the General to be careful of his language."

"Why, shit-kicker? Has Blue Boy got this place wired?"

"Easy, Lieutenant! I said you were dismissed!"

"You want me to watch my language, big fella with your little gold bar? No, sonny boy, you watch it, and you read it! If that squadron of yours isn't in the air at fifteen hundred hours, I'll label this carrier as the biggest yellow streak in Southeast Asia! You got that, satin-pantsed Blue Boy, third class?"

Once more Joel replied, wondering as he spoke where he found the audacity. "I don't know where you come from, sir, but I sincerely hope we meet under different circumstances sometime. I think you're a pig."

"Insubordination! Also, I'd break your back."

"Dismissed, Lieutenant!"

"No, Captain, you're wrong!" shouted the general. "He may be the man to lead this strike after all. Well, what'll it be, Blue Boys? Airborne, or the President of the United States — or the label?"

At 1520 hours Converse led the squadron off the carrier deck. At 1538, as they headed at low altitude into the weather, the first two casualties occurred over the coastline; the wing planes were shot down — fiery deaths at 600 miles an hour in the air. At 1546, Joel's right engine exploded; his altitude made the direct hit easy. At 1546.30, unable to stabilize, Converse ejected into the downpour of the storm clouds, his parachute instantly swept into the vortex of the conflicting winds. As he swung violently down toward the earth, the straps digging into his flesh with each whipping buffet, one image kept repeating its presence within the darkness. The maniacal face of General George Marcus Delavane. He was about to begin an indeterminate stay in hell courtesy of a madman. And as he learned, the losses were infinitely greater on the ground.

Delavane! The Butcher of DaNang and Pleiku. Waster of thousands, throwing battalion after battalion into the jungles and the hills with neither adequate training nor sufficient fire power. Wounded, frightened children had been marched into the camps, bewildered, trying not to weep and, finally understanding, weeping out of control. The stories they told were a thousand variations on the same sickening theme. Inexperienced, untried troops had been sent into battle within days after disembarkation, the weight of sheer numbers expected to vanquish the often unseen enemy. And when the numbers did not work, more numbers were sent. For three years command headquarters listened to a maniac. *Delavane!* The warlord of Saigon, fabricator of body-counts, denyer of blown-apart faces and severed limbs, liar and extoller of death without a cause! A man who had proved to be too lethal even for the Pentagon zealots – a zealot who had outdistanced his own, in the end revolting his own, recalled and retired only to write diatribes read by fanatics in search of their own personal furies.

Men like that can't be allowed any more, don't you understand? He was the enemy, OUR enemy! Those had been Converse's own words, shouted in a fever of outrage in front of a panel of uniformed questioners who had looked at one another, avoiding him, not wanting to respond to those words. They had thanked him perfunctorily, told him that the nation owed him and thousands like him a great debt, and with regard to his final comments, he should try to understand that there were often many sides to an issue, and that the complex execution of command frequently was not what it appeared. In any event, the President had called upon the nation to bind its wounds; what good was served by fuelling old controversies? And then the final kicker, the threat.

"You yourself briefly assumed the terrible responsibility of leadership, Lieutenant," said a pale-faced Army lawyer, barely glancing at Joel, his eyes scanning the pages of a file folder. "Before you made your final and successful escape – by yourself, from a pit in the ground away from the main camp – you led two previous attempts involving a total of seventeen prisoners of war. Fortunately you survived, but eight men did not. I'm sure that you, as their leader, their tactician, never anticipated a casualty risk of nearly fifty per cent. It's been said often, but perhaps not often enough: command is awesome, Lieutenant."

Translation: *Don't join the freaks, soldier. You survived but eight were killed. Were there circumstances the military is not aware of, tactics that protected some more than others, one more than others? One man who managed to break out – by himself – eluding guards that shot loose prisoners on sight at night. Merely to raise the question by reopening a specific file will produce a stigma that will follow you for the rest of your life. Back off, soldier. We've got you by simply raising a question we all know should not be raised, but we'll do it because we've taken enough flak. We'll cut it off wherever we can. Be happy you survived and got out. Now, get out.*

At that moment, Converse had been as close to consciously throwing away his life as he would ever think possible. Physically, hysterically, assaulting that panel of sanctimonious hypocrites had not been out of the question ... until he studied the face of each man, his peripheral gaze taking in rows of tunic ribbons, battle stars on most. Then a strange thing had happened: an odd admixture of disgust, revulsion ... and compassion swept over him. These were panicked men, a number having committed their lives to the call of their country's practice of war ... only to have been conned, as he had been conned. If to protect what was decent meant protecting the worst, who was to say they were wrong? Where were the saints? Or the sinners? Could there be any of either when all were victims?

Disgust, however, won out. Lieutenant Joel Converse, USNR, could not bring himself to give a final salute to that aggregate council of his superiors. In silence, he had turned, with no military bearing whatsoever, and walked out of the room as if he had pointedly spat on the floor.

A flash of light again from the boulevard, a blinding echo of the sun from the Quai du Mont Blanc. He was in Geneva, not in a North Vietnamese camp holding children who vomited while telling their stories, or in San Diego being separated from the United States Navy. He was in Geneva ... and the man sitting across the table knew everything he was thinking and feeling.

"Why *me?*" asked Joel.

"Because, as they say," said Halliday. "You could be motivated. That's the simple answer. A story was told. The Captain of an aircraft carrier refused to put his planes in the air for a strike demanded by Delavane. Several storms had moved in; he called it suicidal. But Delavane forced him to, threatened to call the macho White House and have the Captain removed of command. You led that strike. It's where you got it."

"I'm alive," said Converse, flatly. "Twelve hundred kids never saw the next day and maybe a thousand more wished they never had."

"And you were in the Captain's quarters when Mad Marcus Delavane made his threats and called the shots."

"I was there," agreed Converse, no comment in his voice. Then he shook his head in bewilderment. "Everything I told you – about myself – you've heard it before."

"Read it before," corrected the lawyer from California. "Like you – and I think we're the best in the business under fifty – I don't put a hell of a lot of stock in the written word. I have to hear a voice, or see a face."

"I didn't answer you."

"You didn't have to."

"But *you* have to answer *me. Now* ... You're not here for Comm Tech-Bern, are you?"

"Yes, that part's true," said Halliday. "Only the Swiss didn't come to me, I went to them. I've been watching you, waiting for the moment. It had to be the right one, perfectly natural, geographically logical."

"Why? What do you mean?"

"Because I'm being watched ... Rosen did have a stroke. I heard about it, contacted Bern, and made a plausible case for myself."

"Your reputation was enough."

"It helped, but I needed more. I said we knew each other, that we went way back – which God knows was true – and much as I respected you, I implied that you were extremely astute with finals . . . and that I was familiar with your methods. I also put my price high enough."

"An irresistible combination for the Swiss," said Converse.

"I'm glad you approve."

"But I don't," contradicted Joel. "I don't approve of you at all, least of all *your* methods. You haven't told me anything, just made cryptic remarks about an unidentified group of people you say are dangerous, and brought up the name of a man you knew would provoke a response. Maybe you're just a freak after all, still pushing that safe, Yippee label."

"Calling someone a 'freak' is subjectively prejudicial in the extreme, counsellor, and would be stricken from the record."

"Still the point's been made with the jury, lawyer-man," said Converse in quiet anger. "And I'm making it now."

"Don't prejudge the safety," continued Halliday, with equally quiet sincerity. "I'm not safe, and outside of a proclivity for cowardice, there's a wife and five children back in San Francisco I care deeply about."

"So you come to me because I have no such . . . what was it? Priority entanglements?"

"I came to you because you're invisible, you're not involved, and because you're the best and I can't do it! I *legally* can't do it, and it's got to be done *legally*."

"Why don't you say what you mean?" demanded Converse. "Because if you don't, I'm getting up and we'll see each other later across a table."

"I represented Delavane," said Halliday quickly. "God help me I didn't know what I was doing, and very few people approved, but I made a point we used to make all the time. Unpopular causes and people also deserve representation."

"I can't argue with that."

"You don't know the cause. I do. I found out."

"What cause?"

Halliday leaned forward. "The generals," he said, his voice barely audible. "They're coming back."

Joel looked closely at the Californian. "From where? I didn't know they'd been away."

"From the past," said Halliday. "From years ago."

Converse sat back in the chair, his own eyes now amused. "Good Lord, I thought your kind were extinct. Are you talking about the Pentagon menace, *Press* . . . it is 'Press', isn't it? The San Francisco short-term, or was it from Haight Ashbury, or the Beverly Hills something or other? You're a little behind the times; you already stormed the Presidio."

"Please, don't make jokes. I'm not joking."

"Of course not. It's *Seven Days in May*, or is it *Five Days in August*? It's August now, so let's call it *The Old Time Guns of August*. Nice ring, I think."

"Stop it!" whispered Halliday. "There's nothing remotely funny, and if there were, I'd find it before you did."

"That's a comment, I suppose," said Joel.

"You're goddamned right it is, because I *didn't* go through what you went through. I stayed out of it, I wasn't conned, and that means I can laugh at fanatics because they never hurt me and I still think it's the best ammunition against them. But not now. There's nothing to laugh at now!"

"Permit me a small chuckle," said Converse without smiling. "Even in my most paranoid moments I never subscribed to the conspiracy theory that had the military running Washington. It couldn't happen."

"It might be less apparent than in other countries, but that's all I'll grant you."

"What does that mean?"

"It would undoubtedly be much more obvious in Israel, certainly in Johannesburg, quite possibly in France and Bonn, even the UK – none of them takes its pretences that seriously. But I suppose you've got a point. Washington will drape the constitutional robes around itself until they become threadbare and fall away . . . revealing a uniform, incidentally."

Joel stared at the face in front of him and heard the voice that shot quietly, intensely across the table. "You're *not* joking, are you? And you're too bright to try to snow me."

"Or con you," added Halliday. "Not after that label I wore while watching you in pyjamas halfway across the world. I couldn't do it."

"I think I believe you . . . You mentioned several countries, specific countries. Some aren't speaking, others barely; a few have bad blood and worse memories. On purpose?"

"Yes," nodded the Californian. "It doesn't make any difference because the group I'm talking about thinks it has a cause that will ultimately unite them all. And run them all . . . their way."

"The generals?"

"And admirals, and brigadiers, and field marshals . . . old soldiers who pitched their tents in the right camp. So far right there's been no label since the Reichstag."

"Come *on*, Avery!" Converse shook his head in quiet consternation. "A bunch of tired old warhorses."

"Recruiting and indoctrinating young, hard, capable new commanders," interrupted Halliday.

" . . . coughing their last bellows . . ." Joel stopped. "Have you proof of that?" he asked, each word spoken slowly.

"Not enough . . . but with some digging . . . maybe enough."

"Goddamn it, stop being elliptical."

"Among the possible recruits, twenty or so names at the State Department and the Pentagon," said Halliday. "Men who clear export licences and who spend millions upon millions because they're allowed to spend it, all of which, naturally, widens any circle of friends."

"And influence," stated Converse. "What about London, Paris, and Bonn . . . Johannesburg and Tel Aviv?"

"Again names."

"How firm?"

"They were there, I saw them myself. It was an accident. How many have

24

taken an oath I don't know, but they were there and their stripes fit the philosophical pattern."

"The Reichstag?"

"All they need is a Hitler."

"Where does Delavane fit in?"

"He may appoint one. He may designate the Führer."

"That's ridiculous. Who'd take him seriously?"

"He was taken seriously before. You saw the results."

"That was then, not now. You're not answering the question."

"Men who thought he was right before, and don't fool yourself, they're out there by the thousands. What's mind-blowing is that there are a few dozen with enough seed money to finance his and their delusions – which, of course, they don't see as delusions at all, only as the proper evolution of current history, all other ideologies having failed miserably."

Joel started to speak, then stopped, his thoughts suddenly altered. "Why haven't you gone to someone who can stop them? Stop him."

"Who?"

"I shouldn't have to tell you that. Any number of people in the government – elected and appointed – and more than a dozen departments. For starters, there's Justice."

"I'd be laughed out of Washington," said Halliday. "Beyond the fact that we have no proof – as I told you, just names, suppositions – don't forget that Yippy label I once wore. They'd pin it on me again and tell me to get lost."

"But you *represented* Delavane."

"Which only compounds the legal aspects, I shouldn't have to tell you that."

"The lawyer-client relationship," completed Converse. "You're in a morass before you can make a charge. Unless you've got hard evidence against your client, proof that he's going to commit further crimes and that you're aiding the commission of those crimes by keeping silent."

"Which proof I don't have," interrupted the Californian.

"Then no one will touch you," added Joel. "Especially ambitious lawyers at Justice; they don't want their post-government avenues cut off. As you say, the Delavanes of this world have their constituencies."

"Exactly," agreed Halliday. "And when I began asking questions and tried to reach Delavane, he wouldn't see me or talk to me. Instead, I got a letter telling me I was fired ... that if he had known what I was he never would have retained me. 'Smoking dope and screaming curses while brave young men answered their country's call'."

Converse whistled softly. "And you think you weren't conned? You provide legal services for him, a structure he can use for all intents and purposes within the law, and if anything smells, you're the last person who can blow the whistle. He drapes the old soldier's flag around himself and calls you a vindictive freak."

Halliday nodded. "There was a lot more in that letter – nothing that could damage me except where *he* was concerned – but it was brutal."

"I'm certain of it." Converse took out a pack of cigarettes; he held it forward as Halliday shook his head. "How did you represent him?" asked Joel.

"I set up a corporation, a small consulting firm in Palo Alto specializing in imports and exports. What's allowed, what isn't, what are the quotas, and how to legitimately reach the people in DC who will listen to your case. Essentially it was a lobbying effort, trading in on a name, if anyone remembered. At the time, it struck me as kind of pathetic."

"I thought you said it wasn't registered," remarked Converse, lighting a cigarette.

"It's not the one we're after. It'd be a waste of time."

"But it's where you first got your information, isn't it? Your leads?"

"That was the accident and it won't happen again. It's so legitimate it's legal Clorox, clean as a whistle."

"Still it's a front," insisted Joel. "It has to be if everything – or anything – you've said is true."

"It's true, and it is. But nothing's written down. It's an instrument for travel, an excuse for Delavane and the men around him to go from one place to another, carrying on legitimate business. But while they're in a given area, they do their real thing."

"The gathering of the generals and the field marshals?" said Converse.

"We think it's a spreading missionary operation. Very quiet and very intense."

"What's the name of Delavane's firm?"

"Palo Alto International."

Joel suddenly crushed out his cigarette. "Who's *we*, Avery? Who's putting up this kind of money when amounts like that mean they're people who can reach anyone they want to in Washington?"

"Are you interested?"

"Not in working for someone I don't know ... or approve of. No, I'm not."

"Do you approve of the objectives as I've outlined them to you?"

"If what you've told me is true, and I can't think of any reason why you'd lie about it, of course I do. You knew I would. That still doesn't answer my question."

"Suppose," went on Halliday rapidly, "I were to give you a letter stating that the sum of five hundred thousand dollars to be allocated to you from a blind account on the island of Mykonos was provided by a client of mine whose character and reputation are of the highest order. That his ..."

"Wait a minute, *Press*," broke in Converse harshly.

"Please don't interrupt me, *please!*" Halliday's eyes were riveted on Joel, a manic intensity in his stare. "There's no other way, not *now*. I'll put my name – my professional life on the line. You've been hired to do confidential work within your specialization by a man known to me to be an outstanding citizen who insists on anonymity. I endorse both the man and the work he's asked you to do, and swear not only to the legality of the objectives but to the extraordinary benefits which would be derived by any success you might have. You're covered, you've got five hundred thousand dollars – and I expect just as important to you, perhaps more so – you have the chance to stop a maniac – *maniacs*—from carrying

26

out an unthinkable plan. At the least, they'd create widespread unrest, political crises everywhere, enormous suffering – both individual and group. At the worst, they might change the course of history to the point where there wouldn't *be* any history."

Converse sat rigid in his chair, his gaze unbroken. That's quite a speech. Practise it long?"

"No, you son of a bitch! It wasn't necessary to practise. Any more than you rehearsed that little explosion of yours twelve years ago in San Diego. 'Men like that can't be allowed any more, don't you understand? He was the enemy, *our* enemy.' . . . Those were the words, weren't they?"

"You did your homework, counsellor," said Joel, his anger controlled. "Why does your client insist on being anonymous? Why doesn't he take his money, make a political contribution, and talk to the Director of the CIA, or the National Security Council, or to the White House, any of which he could do easily. A half a million dollars isn't chopped chicken liver even today."

"Because he can't be involved officially in any way whatsoever." Halliday frowned as he expelled his breath. "I *know* it sounds crazy, but that's the way it is. He *is* an outstanding man and I went to him because I was concerned. Frankly, I thought he'd pick up the phone and do what you just said. Call the White House, if it came to it, but he wanted to go this route."

"With *me?*"

"Sorry, he didn't know you. He said a strange thing to me. He told me to find someone to shoot down the bastards without giving them the dignity of the government's concern, even its recognition. At first I couldn't understand, but then I did. It fitted in with my own theory that laughing at the Delavanes of this world renders them impotent more thoroughly than any other way."

"It also eliminates the spectre of martyrdom," added Converse. "Why would this . . . outstanding citizen . . . do what he's doing? Why is it worth the money to him?"

"If I told you, I'd be breaking the confidence."

"I didn't ask you his name. I want to know why."

"By telling you," said the Californian, "you'd know who he is. I can't do that. Take my word for it, you'd approve of him."

"Next question," said Joel, a sharp edge to his voice. "Just what the *hell* did you say to Talbot-Brooks that they found so acceptable?"

"Resigned to finding acceptable," explained Halliday. "I had help. Do you know Judge Lucas Anstett?"

"Second Court of Appeals," said Converse, nodding. "He should have been tapped for the Supreme Court years ago."

"That seems to be the general consensus. He's also a friend of my client, and as I understand it, he met with John Talbot and Nathan Simon – Brooks was out of town – and without revealing my client's name, told them there was a problem that might well erupt into a national crisis if immediate legal action wasn't taken. Several US firms were involved, he explained, but the problem basically lay in Europe and required the talents of an experienced international lawyer. If their junior partner, Joel Converse, was selected and he accepted, would they consent to a leave of absence so he could pursue the matter on a confidential basis. Naturally, the judge strongly endorsed the project."

"And naturally Talbot and Simon went along," said Joel. "You don't refuse Anstett. He's too damned reasonable, to say nothing of the power of his court."

"I don't think he'd use that lever."

"It's there."

Halliday reached into his jacket pocket and took out a long white business envelope. "Here's the letter. It spells out everything I said. There's also a separate page defining the schedule in Mykonos. Once you make arrangements at the bank – how you want the money paid or where you want it transferred – you'll be given the name of a man who lives on the island; he's retired. Phone him; he'll tell you when and where to meet. He has all the tools we can give you. The names, the connections as we think they are, and the activities they're most likely engaged in that violate the laws of their respective governments, sending arms, equipment, and technological information where they shouldn't be sent. Build just two or three cases that are tied to Delavane – even circumstantially – and it'll be enough. We'll turn it all into ridicule. It *will* be enough."

"Where the *hell* do you get your nerve?" said Converse angrily. "I haven't agreed to anything! You don't make decisions for me, and neither do Talbot or Simon' or the holy Judge Anstett, *or* your goddamned client! What did you think you were doing? Appraising me like a piece of horseflesh, making arrangements about me behind my back! Who do you people think you are?"

"Concerned people who think we've found the right man for the right job at the right time," said Halliday, dropping the envelope in front of Joel. "Only there's not that much time left. You've been where they want to take us and you know what it's like." Suddenly the Californian got up. "Think about it. We'll talk later. By the way, the Swiss know we were meeting this morning. If anyone asks what we talked about, tell them I agreed to the final disposition of the Class A stock. It's in our favour even though you may think otherwise. Thanks for the coffee. I'll be across the table in an hour.. It's good to see you again, Joel."

The Californian walked swiftly into the aisle and out through the brass gate of the *Chat Botté* into the sunlight of the Quai du Mont Blanc.

The telephone console was built into the far end of a long, dark conference table. Its muted hum was in keeping with the dignified surroundings. The Swiss *arbitre*, the canton of Geneva's legal representative, picked it up and spoke softly, nodding his head twice, then replaced the phone in its cradle. He looked around the table; seven of the eight attorneys were in their chairs talking quietly with one another. The eighth, Joel Converse, stood in front of an enormous window flanked by drapes and overlooking the Quai Gustave Ador. The giant *Jet d'eau* erupted beyond, its pulsating spray filling the corridor above, cascading to the left under the force of a north wind. The sky was growing dark; a summer storm was on its way from the Alps.

"Messieurs," said the *arbitre*, as conversations trailed off and faces were turned to the Swiss. "That was Monsieur Halliday. He has been detained, but urges

28

you to proceed. His associate, Monsieur Rogeteau has his recommendations and it is understood that he met with Monsieur Converse earlier this morning to resolve one of the last details. Is that not so, Monsieur Converse?"

Heads turned again, now in the opposite direction toward the figure by the window. There was no response. Converse continued to stare down at the lake.

"Monsieur *Converse?*"

"I beg your pardon?" Joel turned, a frown creasing the upper regions of his face, his thoughts far away, nowhere near Geneva."

"It is so, Monsieur?"

"What was the question?"

"You met earlier with Monsieur Halliday?"

Converse paused. "It is so," he replied.

"*And?*"

"And . . . he agreed to the final disposition of the Class A stock."

There was a quiet but audible expression of relief on the part of the Americans, and a silent acceptance from the Bern contingent, their eyes non-committal. Neither reaction was lost on Joel, and under different circumstances he might have tabled the item for additional consideration. Halliday's judgment of Bern's advantage notwithstanding, the acceptance was too easily achieved; he would have postponed it anyway, at least for an hour's worth of analysis. Somehow it did not matter. *Goddamn him!* thought Converse.

"Then let us proceed as Monsieur Halliday suggested," said the *arbitre*, glancing at his watch.

An hour stretched into two, then three, the hum of voices mingling in counterpoint as pages were passed back and forth, points clarified, paragraphs initialled. And still Halliday did not appear. Lamps were turned on as the darkness filled the midday sky outside the huge windows; there was talk of the approaching storm.

Then suddenly like an unexpected bolt of lightning, screams came from beyond the thick oak door of the conference room, swelling in volume until images of horror filled the minds of all who heard the prolonged, terrible sounds. Some around the enormous table lunged beneath it, others got out of their chairs and stood in shock, in stunned bewilderment, and a few rushed to the door, among them Converse. The *arbitre* twisted the knob and yanked it back with such force that the door crashed into the wall. What they saw was a sight none of them would ever forget. Joel lashed out his hands, gripping, pulling, parting the bodies in front of him as he raced into the anteroom.

Avery Fowler's striped jacket fell away from his chalk white fingers, his white shirt covered with blood, his chest a mass of tiny, bleeding holes. He fell, grabbing a secretary's desk, his upturned collar separating, revealing more blood on his throat. The expulsions of breath were too well known to Joel; he had held the heads of children in the camps as they had wept in anger and the ultimate fear. He held Avery Fowler's head now, lowering him to the floor.

"My God, what *happened?*" cried Converse, cradling the dying man in his arms."

"They're . . . back," coughed the classmate from long ago. "The elevator. They trapped me in the elevator! . . . They said it was for Aquitaine, that was the name they used . . . *Aquitaine.* Oh, Christ! Meg . . . the *kids* . . . !" Avery Fowler's head twisted spastically into his right shoulder, then the final eruption of air came from his bloodied throat.

A. Preston Halliday was dead.

Converse stood in the rain, his clothes drenched, staring at the unseen place on the water where only an hour ago the fountain had shot up to the sky proclaiming *this* was Geneva. The lake was angry, an infinity of whitecaps had replaced the graceful white sails. There were no reflections anywhere. But there was distant thunder from the north. From the Alps.

And Joel's mind was frozen.

2

He walked past the long, marble counter of the Hotel Richemond's front desk and headed for the winding staircase on the left. It was habit; his suite was on the second floor and the brass-grilled elevators with their wine-coloured velvet interiors were things of beauty, but not swiftness. Also, he enjoyed passing the casement displays of outrageously priced, brilliantly-lighted jewels that lined the walls of the elegant staircase – shimmering diamonds, blood-red rubies, webbed necklaces of spun gold. Somehow they reminded him of change, of extraordinary change. For him. For a life he had thought would end violently, thousands of miles away in a dozen different yet always the same rat-infested cells, with muted gunfire and the screams of children in the dark distance. Diamonds, rubies, and spun gold were symbols of the unattainable and unrealistic, but they were there, and he passed them, observed them, smiling at their existence . . . and they seemed to acknowledge him, large shining eyes of infinite depth staring back, telling him they were there, he was there. Change.

But he did not see them now, nor did they acknowledge him. He saw nothing, felt nothing; every tentacle of his mind and body was numbed, suspended in airless space. A man he had known as a boy under one name had died in his arms years later under another, and the words he had whispered at the brutal moment of death were as incomprehensible as they were paralysing. *Aquitaine. They said it was for Aquitaine.* . . . Where was sanity, where was reason? What did the words mean and why had he been drawn into that elusive meaning? He *had* been drawn in, he knew it, and there was reason in that terrible manipulation.

The magnet was a name, a man. George Marcus Delavane, warlord of Saigon.

"*Monsieur!*" The suppressed shout came from below; he turned on the stairs and saw the formally-attired *directeur* rushing across the lobby and up the steps. The man's name was Henri, and they had known each other for nearly five years. Their friendship went beyond that of hotel executive and hotel guest; they had gambled together frequently at Divonne, across the French border.

"Hello, Henri."

"*Mon Dieu*, are you all right, Joel? Your office in New York has been calling you repeatedly. I heard it on the radio, it is all over Geneva! *Narcotiques!* Drugs, crime, guns . . . *murder!* It touches even us now!"

"Is that what they say?"

"They say small packages of cocaine were found under his shirt, a respected *avocat international* a suspected connection."

"It's a lie," Converse broke in.

"It's what they say, what can I tell you? Your name was mentioned; it was reported that he died as you reached him . . . You were not implicated, of course; you were merely there with the others. I heard your name and I've been worried sick! Where have you *been?*"

"Answering a lot of unanswerable questions down at police headquarters." *Questions that were answerable, but not by him, not to the authorities in Geneva. Avery Fowler – Preston Halliday – deserved better than that. A trust had been given, accepted in death.*

"Christ, you're drenched!" cried Henri, intense concern in his eyes. "You've been walking in the rain, haven't you? There were no taxis?"

"I didn't look, I wanted to walk."

"Of course, the shock, I understand. I'll send up some brandy, some decent Armagnac. And dinner, perhaps; I'll release your table at the *Gentilshommes.*"

"Thanks. Give me thirty minutes and have your switchboard get New York for me, will you? I never seem to dial it right."

"Joel?"

"What?"

"Can I help? Is there something you should tell me? We have won and lost together over too many bottles of *grand cru classé* for you to go alone when you don't have to. I know Geneva, my friend."

Converse looked into the wide brown eyes beneath him, at the lined, concerned face, rigid in its concern. "Why do you say that?"

"Because you so quickly denied the police reports of cocaine, what else? I watched you. There was more in what you said than what you said."

Joel blinked, and for a moment shut his eyelids tight, the strain in the middle of his forehead acute. He took a deep breath and replied. "Do me a favour, Henri, and don't speculate. Just get me an overseas line in a half hour, okay?"

"*Mais oui, Monsieur,*" said the Frenchman, nodding his head on the staircase. "*Le directeur du Richemond* is here only to serve her guests, special guests accorded special service, of course . . . I'm here if you need me, my friend."

"I know that. If I turn a wrong card, I'll let you know."

"If you have to turn *any* card in Switzerland, call me. The suits vary with the players."

"I'll remember that. Thirty minutes? A line?"

"*Certainement, Monsieur.*"

The shower was as hot as his skin could tolerate, the steam filling his lungs, cutting short the breath in his throat. He then forced himself to endure an ice-cold spray until his head shivered, the cold pain real. He reasoned that the shock of extremes might clear his mind, at least reduce the numbness. He had to think; he had to decide; he had to listen.

He came out of the bathroom, his white terry-cloth robe blotting the residue of the shower, and shoved his feet into a pair of slippers on the floor beside the bed. He removed his cigarettes and lighter from the bureau top, and walked out into the sitting room. The concerned Henri had been true to his word; on the coffee table a floor-steward had placed a bottle of expensive Armagnac, the two glasses for appearance, not function. He sat down on the soft, pillowed couch, poured himself a drink, and lighted a cigarette. Outside, the heavy August rain pounded the casement windows, the tattoo harsh and unrelenting. He looked at his watch; it was a few minutes past six – shortly past noon in New York. Joel wondered if Henri had been able to get a clear trans-Atlantic line. The lawyer in Converse wanted to hear the words spoken from New York, words that would either confirm or deny a dead man's revelation. It had been twenty-five minutes since Henri had stopped him on the staircase; he would wait another five and call the switchboard.

The telephone rang, the blaring, vibrating European bell unnerving him. He reached for the phone on the table next to the couch; his breath was short and his hand trembled. "Yes? Hello?"

"New York calling, Monsieur," said the hotel operator. "It's your office. Should I cancel the call listed for six-fifteen?"

"Yes, please. And thank you."

"Mr *Converse?*" The intense, high-pitched voice belonged to Lawrence Talbot's secretary.

"Hello, Jane."

"Good God, we've been trying to reach you since ten o'clock! Are you all *right?* We got the news then, around ten. It's all so horrible!"

"I'm fine, Jane. Thanks for your concern."

"Mr Talbot's beside himself. He can't believe it!"

"Don't believe what they're saying about Halliday. It's not true. May I speak with Larry, please?"

"If he knew you were on the phone talking to me, I'd be fired."

"No, you wouldn't. Who'd write his letters?"

The secretary paused briefly, her voice calmer when she spoke. "Oh, God, Joel, you're the end. After what you've been through, you still find something funny to say."

"It's easier, Jane. Let me have Bubba, will you?"

"You *are* the limit!"

Lawrence Talbot, senior partner of Talbot, Brooks and Simon, was a perfectly competent attorney but his rise in law was as much due to his having been one of the few All American football players from Yale as from any prowess in the courtroom. He was also a very decent human being, more of a coordinating coach than the driving force of a conservative yet highly competitive law firm. He was also eminently fair and fair-minded; he kept his word. He was one of the reasons Joel had joined the firm; another was Nathan Simon, a giant of a man and an attorney. Converse had learned more about the law from Nate Simon than from any other lawyer or professor he had ever met. He felt closest to Nathan yet Simon was the most difficult to get close to; one approached this uniquely private man with equal parts of fondness and reserve. Lawrence Talbot burst over the phone.

"Good *Lord*, I'm appalled! What can I *say?* What can I *do?*"

"To begin with, strike that horseshit about Halliday. He was no more a drug connection than Nate Simon."

"You haven't heard, then? They've backed off on that. The story now is violent robbery; he resisted and the packets were stuffed under his shirt after they shot him. I think Jack Halliday must have burned the wires from San Francisco, threatened to beat the crap out of the whole Swiss government . . . He played for Stanford, you know."

"You're too much, Bubba."

"I never thought I'd enjoy hearing that from you, young man. I do now."

"Young man and not so young, Larry . . . Clear something up for me, will you?"

"Whatever I can."

"Anstett. Lucas Anstett."

"We talked. Nathan and I listened, and he was most persuasive. We understand."

"*Do* you?"

"Not the particulars certainly; he wouldn't elaborate. But we think you're the best in the field, and granting his request wasn't difficult. T, B and S *has* the best and when a judge like Anstett confirms it through such a conversation we have to congratulate ourselves, don't we?"

"Are you doing it because of his bench?"

"Christ, *no*. He even told us he'd be harder on us in appeals if we agreed. He's one rough cookie when he wants something. He tells you you'd be worse off if you give it to him."

"Did you believe him?"

"Well, Nathan said something about billy-goats having certain identifiable markings that were not removed without a great deal of squealing, so we should go along. Nathan frequently obfuscates issues, but goddamnit, Joel, he's usually right."

"If you can take three hours to hear a five-minute summation," said Converse.

"He's always thinking, young man."

"Young and not so young. Everything's relative."

"Your wife called . . . Sorry, your ex-wife."

"Oh?"

"Your name came up on the radio or television or something, and she wanted to know what happened."

"What did you tell her?"

"That we were trying to reach you. We didn't know any more than she did. She sounded very upset."

"Call her and tell her I'm fine, will you, please? Do you have the number?"

"Jane does."

"I'll be leaving then."

"On full pay," said Talbot from New York.

"That's not necessary, Larry. I'm being given a great deal of money, so save the bookkeeping. I'll be back in three or four weeks."

"I could do that, but I won't," said the senior partner. "I know when I've got the best and I intend to hold him. We'll bank it for you." Talbot paused, then spoke quietly, urgently. "Joel, I have to ask you. Did this thing a few hours ago have anything to do with the Anstett business?"

Converse gripped the telephone with such force his wrist and fingers ached. "Nothing whatsoever, Larry," he said. "There's no connection."

Mykonos, the sun-drenched, white-washed island of the Cyclades, neighbouring worshipper of Delos. Since Barbarossa's conquest it had been host to successive brigands of the sea who sailed on the Meltemi winds – Turks, Russians, Cypriots, finally Greeks – placed and displaced over the centuries, a small land mass alternately honoured and forgotten until the arrival of sleek yachts and shining aircraft, symbols of a different age. Low-slung automobiles – Porsches, Maseratis, Jaguars – now sped over the narrow roads past starched-white windmills and alabaster churches; a new type of inhabitant had joined the laconic, tradition-bound residents who made their livings from the sea and the shops. Free-spirited youths of all ages, with their open shirts and tight pantsuits, their sunburned skins serving as backdrops for adornments of heavy gold, had found a new playground. And ancient Mykonos, once a major port to the proud Phoenicians, became the St Tropez of the Aegean.

Converse had taken the first Swiss Air flight out of Geneva to Athens, and from there a smaller Olympic plane to the island. Despite the fact that he had lost an hour in the time zones, it was barely four o'clock in the afternoon when the airport taxi crawled through the streets of the hot, blinding white harbour and pulled up in front of the smooth white entrance of the bank. It was on the waterfront, and the crowds of flowered shirts and wild print dresses, and the sight of launches chopping over the gentle waves towards the slips on the main pier, were proof that the giant cruise ships far out in the harbour were managed by knowledgeable men. Mykonos was a dazzling snare for tourists; money would be left on the white-washed island; the *tavernas* and the shops would be full from the early sun to burning twilight. The ouzo would flow and Greek fishermen's caps would disappear from the shelves, placed on the swaying or embarrassed heads of suburbanites from Grosse Pointe and Short Hills. And when night came and the last *efharisto* and *parakalo* had been awkwardly uttered by the visitors, other games would begin, the courtiers and courtesans, the beautiful, ageless, self-indulgent children of the blue Aegean would start to play. Peals of laughter would be heard as *drachmas* were counted and spent – especially spent – in amounts that would stagger those who had opulent suites on the highest decks of the most luxurious ships. Where Geneva was contrary, Mykonos was accommodating . . . in ways the long-ago Turks might have envied.

Joel had called the bank from the airport, not knowing its business hours, but knowing the name of the banker he was to contact. Kostas Laskaris greeted him cautiously over the phone, making it clear that he expected not only a passport that would clear a spectograph, but the original letter from A. Preston Halliday with his signature, said signature to be subjected to scanner, matching the signature the bank had been provided by the deceased Mr A. Preston Halliday.

"We hear he was killed in Geneva. It is most unfortunate."

"I'll tell his wife and children how your grief overwhelms me."

Converse paid the taxi and climbed the short, white steps of the entrance, carrying his suitcase and attaché case, grateful that the door was opened by a uniformed guard whose appearance brought to mind a long-forgotten photograph of a mad sultan who whipped his harem's women in a courtyard when they failed to arouse him.

Kostas Laskaris was not at all what Joel had expected from the short, disconcerting conversation over the phone. He was a balding, pleasant-faced man in his late fifties, with warm dark eyes and relatively fluent in English but certainly not comfortable with the language. His first words upon rising from his desk and indicating a chair in front of it for Converse contradicted Joel's previous impression.

"I apologize for what might have appeared as a cal*loos* statement on my part regarding Mr Halliday. However, it *was* most unfortunate, and I don't know how else to phrase it. And it is difficult, sir, to grieve for a man one never knew."

"I was out of line. Forget it, please."

"You are most kind, but I'm afraid I cannot forget the arrangements . . . mandated by Mr Halliday and his associate here on Mykonos. I must have your passport and the letter, if you please?"

"Who is he?" asked Joel, reaching into his jacket pocket for his passport billfold; it contained the letter. "The associate, I mean."

"You are an attorney, sir, and surely you are aware that the information you desire cannot be given to you until the barriers . . . have been leaped, as it were. At least I think that's right."

"It'll do. I just thought I'd try." He took out his passport and the letter, handing them to the banker.

Laskaris picked up his telephone and pressed a button. He spoke in Greek and apparently asked for someone. Within seconds the door opened and a bronzed, stunning dark-haired woman entered and walked gracefully over to the desk. She raised her downcast eyes and glanced at Joel, who knew the banker was watching him closely. A sign from Converse, another glance – from him directed at Laskaris

35

– and introduction would be forthcoming, accommodation silently promised, and a conceivably significant piece of information would be entered in a banker's file. Joel offered no such sign; he wanted no such entry. A man did not pick up a half a million dollars for nodding his head, and then look for a bonus. It did not signify stability; it signified something else.

Inconsequential banter about flights, customs and the general deterioration of travel covered the next ten minutes, at which time his passport and the letter were returned. However, not by the striking, dark-haired woman but by a young, blond Adonis who was slightly balletic as he moved toward the desk. The pleasant-faced Laskaris was not missing a trick; he was perfectly willing to supply one, whichever route his wealthy visitor required.

Converse looked into the Greek's warm eyes, then smiled, the smile developing into quiet laughter. Laskaris smiled back and shrugged, dismissing the beach boy.

"I am chief manager of this branch, sir," he said, as the door closed, "but I do not set the policies for the entire bank. This is, after all, Mykonos."

"And a great deal of money passes through here," added Joel. "Which one did you bet on?"

"Neither," replied Laskaris, shaking his head. "Only on exactly what you did. You'd be a fool otherwise, and I do not think you are a fool. In addition to being chief manager on the waterfront, I am also an excellent judge of character."

"Is that why you were chosen as the intermediary?"

"No, that is not the reason. I am a friend of Mr Halliday's associate here on the island. His name is Beale, incidentally. Dr Edward Beale . . . You see, everything is in order."

"A doctor?" asked Converse leaning forward and accepting his passport and the letter. "He's a doctor?"

"Not a medical man, however," clarified Laskaris. "He's a scholar, a retired professor of history from the United States. He has an adequate pension and he moved here from Rhodes several months ago. A most interesting man, most knowledgeable. I handle his financial affairs – in which he is not very knowledgeable, but still interesting." The banker smiled again, shrugging again.

"I hope so," said Joel. "We have a great deal to discuss."

"That is not my concern, sir. Shall we get to the disposition of the funds? How and where would you care to have them paid?"

"A great deal in cash. I bought one of those sensorized money belts in Geneva – the batteries are guaranteed for a year. If it's ripped off me, a tiny siren goes off that splits your eardrums. I'd like American currency – except for a few thousand, of course.

"Those belts are effective, sir, but not if you are unconscious, or if there is no one around to hear them. Might I suggest traveller's cheques?"

"You could and you'd probably be right, but I don't think so. I may not care to write out a signature."

"As you wish. The denominations for yourself, please?" said Laskaris, pencil in hand, pad below. "And where would you like the remainder to be sent?"

"Is it possible," asked Converse slowly, "to have accounts set up, not in my name, but accessible to me?"

"Of course, sir. Frankly, it is often standard in Mykonos . . . as well as in Crete, Rhodes, Athens, Istanbul, and also much of Europe. A description is wired, accompanied by words written out in your handwriting – another name, or numbers . . . one man I knew used a nursery rhyme – and they are matched. One must use a sophisticated bank, of course."

"Of course. Name a few."

"Where?"

"In London . . . Paris . . . Bonn . . . maybe Tel Aviv," said Joel, trying to remember Halliday's words.

"Bonn is not easy; they are so inflexible. A wrong apostrophe and they summon whomever they consider their authorities . . . Tel Aviv is simple; money is as freewheeling and as serpentine as the Knesset. London and Paris are standard and, of course, their greed is overwhelming. You will be heavily taxed for the transfers because they know you will not make an issue over covert funds. Very proper, very mercenary, and very much thievery."

"You know your banks, don't you?"

"I've had experience, sir. Now, as to the disbursements?"

"I want a hundred thousand for myself – nothing larger than five hundred dollar bills. The rest you can split up and tell me how I can get it if I need it."

"It is not a difficult assignment, sir. Shall we start writing names, or numbers . . . or nursery rhymes?"

"Numbers," said Converse. "I'm a lawyer. Names and nursery rhymes are in dimensions I don't want to think about right now."

"As you wish," said the Greek, reaching for a pad. "And here is Dr Beale's telephone number. When we have concluded our business, you may call him . . . Or not, as you wish. It is not my concern."

Dr Edward Beale, resident of Mykonos, spoke over the telephone in measured words and the slow, thoughtful cadence of a scholar. Nothing was rushed, nothing accelerated for the moment; everything was deliberated and deliberate.

"There is a beach – more rocks than beach, and not frequented at night – about seven kilometres from the waterfront. Walk to it. Take the west road along the coast until you see the lights of several buoys riding the waves. Come down to the water's edge. I'll find you."

The night clouds sped by, propelled by high altitude winds, letting the moonlight penetrate rapidly, sporadically, illuminating the desolate stretch of beach that was the meeting ground. Far out on the water, the red lamps of four buoys bobbed up and down. Joel climbed over the rocks and into the soft sand, making his way to the water's edge; he could both see and hear the small waves lapping forward and receding. He lit a cigarette, assuming the flame would announce his presence. It did; in moments a voice came out of the darkness behind him, but the greeting was hardly what he expected from an elderly, retired scholar.

"Stay where you are and don't move," was the first command, spoken with quiet authority. "Put the cigarette in your mouth and inhale, then raise your arms and hold them straight out in front of you . . . Good. Now smoke; I want to see the *smoke*."

"Christ, I'm choking!" shouted Joel, coughing, the smoke, blown back by the ocean breeze, stinging his eyes. Then suddenly he could feel the sharp, quick movements of a single hand stabbing about his clothes, reaching across his chest and up and down his legs. "What are you *doing?*" he cried, spitting the cigarette out of his mouth involuntarily.

"You don't have a weapon," said the voice.

"Of *course* not!"

"I do. You may lower your arms and turn around now."

Converse spun, still coughing, and rubbed his watery eyes. "You crazy son of a bitch!"

"It's a dreadful habit, those cigarettes. I'd give them up if I were you. Apart from the terrible things they do to your body, now you see how they can be used against you in other ways."

Joel blinked and stared in front of him. The pontificator was a slender, white-haired old man of medium height, but standing very erect in what looked like a white canvas jacket and trousers. His face – what could be seen of it in the intermittent moonlight – was deeply lined and there was a partial smile on his lips. There was also a gun in his hand, held in a firm grip, levelled at Converse's head. "You're *Beale?*" asked Joel. "Dr *Edward* Beale?"

"Yes. Are you calmed down now?"

"Considering the shock of your warm welcome, I guess so."

"Good. I'll put this away then." The scholar lowered the gun and knelt down on the sand next to a canvas satchel. He shoved the weapon inside and stood up again. "I'm sorry, but I had to be certain."

"Of what? Whether or not I was a commando?"

"Halliday's dead. Could a substitute have been sent in your place? Someone to deal with an old man in Mykonos? If so, that person would most certainly have a gun."

"Why?"

"Because he would have had no idea that I *was* an old man. *I* might have been a commando."

"You know, it's possible – just *possible*—that I could have had a gun. Would you have blown my goddamned head off?"

"A respected attorney coming to the island for the first time, passing through Geneva's airport security? Where would you get it? Whom would you know on Mykonos?"

"Arrangements could have been made," protested Converse with little conviction, realizing it was useless.

"I've had you followed since you arrived. You went directly to the bank, then to the Kouneni hotel where you sat in the garden and had a drink before going to your room. Outside of the taxi driver, my friend Kostas, the desk clerk, and the waiters in the garden, you spoke to no one. As long as you *were* Joel Converse I was safe."

"For a product of an ivory tower, you sound more like a hit man from Detroit."

"I wasn't always in the academic world, but yes, I've been cautious. I think we must all be very cautious. With a George Marcus Delavane it's the only sound strategy."

"Sound strategy?"

"Approach, if you like." Beale reached between the widely-separated buttons of his jacket and withdrew a folded page of paper. "Here are the names, he said, handing it to Joel. "There are five key figures in Delavane's operation over here. One each from France, West Germany, Israel, South Africa and England. We've identified four – the first four – but we can't find the Englishman."

"How did you get these?"

"Originally from notes found among Delavane's papers by Halliday when the General was his client."

"That was the accident he mentioned, then? He said it was an accident that wouldn't happen again."

"I don't know what he told you, of course, but it certainly was an accident. A faulty memory on Delavane's part, an affliction I can personally assure you touches the aging. The General simply forgot he had a meeting with Halliday and when Preston arrived, his secretary let him into the office so he could prepare papers for Delavane, who was expected in a half hour or so. Preston saw a file folder on the General's desk; he knew that folder, knew it contained material he could cross check. Without thinking twice, he sat down and began working. He found the names and knowing Delavane's recent itinerary in Europe and Africa, everything suddenly began to fall into place – very ominously. For anyone politically aware those four names are frightening – they dredge up frightening memories."

"Did Delavane ever learn that he'd found them?"

"In my judgment, he could never be certain. Halliday wrote them down and left before the General returned. But then Geneva tells us something else, doesn't it?"

"That Delavane did find out," said Converse grimly.

"Or he wasn't going to take any further chances, especially if there was a schedule, and we're convinced there is one. We're in the countdown now."

"To what?"

"From the pattern of their operations – what we've pieced together – a prolonged series of massive, orchestrated conflagrations designed to spin out of control destabilizing governments."

"That's a tall order. In what way?"

"Guesswork," said the scholar, frowning. "Probably widespread, coordinated eruptions of violence led by terrorists everywhere – terrorists fuelled by Delavane and his people. When the chaos becomes intolerable, it's their excuse to march in with military units and assume the controls, initially with martial law."

"It's been done before," said Joel. "Feed and arm a presumed enemy, then send out provocateurs . . ."

"With massive sums of money and material," interrupted Beale.

"And when they rise up," completed Converse, "pull out the rug, crush them, and take over. The citizens give thanks and call the heroes saviours, as they start marching to their drums. But how could they *do* it?"

"That's the all-consuming question. What are the targets? Where are they, *who* are they? We have no idea. If we had an inkling, we might approach from that end, but we don't and we can't waste time hunting for unknowns. We must go after what we do know."

"Again time," Joel broke in. "Why are you so sure we're in a countdown?"

"Increased activity everywhere – in many cases frantic. Shipments originating in the States are funnelled out of warehouses in England, Ireland, France, and Germany to groups of insurgents in all the troubled areas. There are rumours out of Munich, the Mediterranean and the Arab states. The talk is in terms of final preparations but no one seems to know what exactly for – except that they must be ready. It's as though such groups as Baader Meinhoff, the Brigate Rosse, the PLO, and the red legions of Paris and Madrid are all in a race with none knowing the course, only the moment when it begins."

"When is that?"

"Our reports vary but they're all within the same time span. Between three to five weeks."

"Oh, my *God!*" Joel felt the rush of anger and fear. Suddenly, he remembered. "Avery – *Halliday* whispered something to me just before he died. Words that were spoken by the men who shot him. 'Aquitaine . . . They said it was for Aquitaine'. Those were the words he whispered. What do they mean, Beale?"

The old scholar was silent, his eyes alive in the intermittent moonlight. He slowly turned his head and stared out at the water in thought. "It's *madness*," he whispered.

"That doesn't tell me anything."

"No, of course not," said Beale quickly, apologetically, turning back to Converse. "It's simply the magnitude of it all. It's so incredible."

"I'm not reading you."

"Aquitaine . . . Aquitania as Julius Caesar called it . . . was the name given to a region in southern France that at one time in the first centuries after Christ was said to have extended from the Atlantic, across the Pyrenees to the Mediterranean, and as far north as the mouth of the Seine west of Paris on the coast"

"I'm vaguely aware of that," Joel broke in, too impatient for an academic dissertation.

"If you are, you're to be commended. Most people are only aware of the later centuries, say from the eighth on, when Charlemagne conquered the region, formed the kingdom of Aquitaine and bestowed it on his son Louis, and *his* sons Pepins One and Two. Actually, these and the following three hundred years are the most pertinent."

"To what?"

"The *legend* of Aquitaine, Mr Converse. Like many ambitious generals, Delavane sees himself as a student of history – in the tradition of Caesar, Napoleon, Von Clausewitz . . . even Patton. I was rightly or wrongly considered a scholar, but he remains a student, and that's as it should be. Scholars can't take liberties without substantive evidence – or they shouldn't – but students can and usually do."

"What's your point?"

"The legend of Aquitaine becomes convoluted, the What-If syndrome riding over the facts until theoretical assumptions are made that distort the evidence. You see, the story of Aquitaine is filled with sudden, massive expansions and abrupt contractions. To simplify, an imaginative student of history might say that had there not been political, marital and military miscalculations on the part of Charlemagne and his son, the two Pepins, and later Louis the Seventh of France and Henry the Second of England, *both* of whom were married to the extraordinary Eleanor, the kingdom of Aquitaine might have encompassed most if not all of Europe." Beale paused. "Do you begin to understand?" he asked.

"Yes," said Joel. "Christ, *yes*."

"That's not all," continued the scholar. "Since Aquitaine was once considered a legitimate possession of England, it might have in time enveloped all of her foreign colonies, including the original thirteen across the Atlantic. Later the United States of America . . . Of course, miscalculations or not, it could never have happened due to a fundamental law of western civilization, valid since the deposition of Romulus Augustulus and the collapse of the Roman Empire. You cannot crush, then unite by force and rule disparate peoples and their cultures – not for any length of time."

"Someone's trying to now," said Converse. "George Marcus Delavane."

"Yes. In his mind he's constructed the Aquitaine that never was, never could be. And it's profoundly terrifying."

"Why? You just said it couldn't happen."

"Not according to the old rules, not in any period since the fall of Rome. But you must remember, there's never *been* a time in recorded history like this one. Never such weapons, such anxiety. Delavane and his people know that, and they will play upon those weapons, those anxieties. They *are* playing upon them." The old man pointed to the sheet of paper in Joel's hand. "You have matches. Strike one and look at the names."

Converse unfolded the page, reached into his pocket and took out his lighter. He snapped it' the flame illuminating the paper, as he studied the names. "My *God*," he said, frowning in the sharp spill of light. "They fit in with Delavane. It's a gathering of warlords if they're the men I think they are." Joel extinguished the flame.

"They are," replied Beale, "starting with General Jacques Louis Bertholdier in Paris, a remarkable man, quite extraordinary. A Resistance fighter in the War, given the rank of major before he was twenty, but later an unreconstructed member of Salan's OAS. He was behind an assassination attempt on de Gaulle in August of '62, seeing himself as the true leader of the Republic. He nearly made it. He believed then as he believes now that the Algerian generals were the salvation of an enfeebled France. He has survived not only because he's a legend, but because his voice isn't alone – only he's more persuasive than most. Especially with the élite crowd of promising commanders produced by St Cyr. Quite simply, he's a fascist, a fanatic hiding behind a screen of eminent respectability."

"And the one named Abrahms," said Converse. "He's the Israeli strong man who struts around in a safari jacket and boots, isn't he? The screecher who holds rallies in front of the Knesset and in the stadiums, telling everyone there'll be a blood bath in Judea and Samaria if the children of Abraham are denied. Even the Israelis can't shut him up."

"Many are afraid to; he's become electrifying, like lightning, a symbol. Chaim Abrahms and his followers make the Begin regime seem like reticent, self-effacing pacifists. He's a Sabra tolerated by the European Jews because he's a brilliant soldier, proven in two wars, and has enjoyed the respect – if not the affection – of every Minister of Defence since the early years of Golda Meir. They never know when they might need him in the field."

"And this one," said Joel, again using his lighter. "Van Headmer. South African, isn't it? The 'hangman in uniform' or something like that."

"Jan van Headmer, also the 'slayer of Soweto', as the Blacks call him. He executes *offenders* with alarming frequency and government tolerance. His family is oldline Afrikaner, all generals going back to the Boer War, and he sees no reason on earth to bring Pretoria into the twentieth century. Incidentally, he's a close friend of Abrahms and makes frequent trips to Tel Aviv. He's also one of the most erudite and charming general officers ever to attend a diplomatic conference. His presence denies his image and reputation."

"And Leifhelm," completed Converse, again shutting down the flame. "A mixed bag, if I'm accurate. Supposedly a great soldier who followed too many orders, but still respected. I'm weakest on him."

"Entirely understandable," said Beale, nodding in the moonlight. "In some ways his is the oddest story – the most monstrous, really, because the truth has been consistently covered up so as to use him and avoid embarrassment. Field Marshal Erich Leifhelm was the youngest general ever commissioned by Adolf Hitler. He foresaw Germany's collapse and made a sudden about face. From brutal killer and a fanatic super Aryan to a contrite professional who abhorred the Nazis' crimes as they were 'revealed' to him. He fooled everyone and was absolved of all guilt; he never saw a Nuremberg courtroom. During the cold war the Allies used his services extensively, granting him full security clearances, and later, in the 'fifties. when the new German divisions were mounted for the NATO forces, they made sure he was put in command."

"Weren't there a couple of newspaper stories about him a few years ago? He had several run-ins with Helmut Schmidt, didn't he?"

"Exactly," agreed the retired soldier. "But those stories were soft and carried only *half* the story. Leifhelm was quoted as saying merely that the German people could not be expected to carry the burden of past guilt into future generations. It had to stop. Pride should once more be established in the nation's heritage. There was some sabre-rattling aimed at the Soviets, but nothing substantively beyond that."

"What was the other half?" asked Converse.

"He wanted the *Bundestag's* restrictions on the armed forces lifted completely, and fought for the expansion of the intelligence services, patterned after the

Abwehr, including rehabilitation sentences for political troublemakers. He also sought widespread deletions in German text books throughout the school systems. 'Pride has to be restored,' he kept saying, claiming everything in the name of virulent anti-communism."

"The Third Reich's first strategy in everything when Hitler took over."

"You're quite right. Schmidt saw through him and knew there'd be chaos if he had his way – and he *was* influential. Bonn could not afford the spectre of painful memories. Schmidt forced Leifhelm to resign and literally removed his voice from all government affairs."

"But he keeps speaking."

"Not openly. However, he's rich and retains his friends and contacts."

"Among them Delavane and his people."

"Foremost among them now."

Joel once more snapped his lighter, as if remembering something he had seen, and scanned the lower part of the page. There were two lists of names, the row on the left under the title of *State Department*, the right beneath the word *Pentagon*. There were perhaps twenty-five people in all. "Who are the Americans?" He released the lever; the flame died and he put the lighter back in his pocket. "The names don't mean anything to me."

"Some should, but it doesn't matter," said Beale elliptically. "The point is that among those men are disciples of George Delavane. They carry out his orders. How many of them is difficult to say, but at least several from each grouping. You see, these are the men who make the decisions – or conversely, do not oppose decisions – without which Delavane and his followers would be stopped in their tracks."

"Spell that out."

"Those on the left are key figures in the State Department's Office of Munitions Control. They determine what gets cleared for export, who under the blanket of 'national interest' can receive weapons and technology withheld from others. On the right are the senior officers at the Pentagon on whose word millions upon millions are spent for armament procurements. All are decision makers . . . and a number of those decisions have been questioned, a few openly, others quietly by diplomatic and military colleagues. We've learned that much."

"Questioned why?" interrupted Converse.

"There were rumours – there always *are* rumours – of large shipments improperly licensed for export. Then there's surplus military equipment – excess supplies – lost in transfers, using temporary warehouses and out-of-the-way storage depots. Surplus equipment is easily unaccounted for; it's an embarrassment in these days of enormous budgets and cost overruns. Get rid of it and don't be too particular. How fortunate in these instances and coincidental – if a member of this Aquitaine shows up, willing to buy and with all his papers in order. Whole depots and warehouses are sent where they shouldn't be sent."

"A *Libya* connection!"

"There's no doubt of it. A great many connections."

"Halliday mentioned it and you said it a few moments ago. Laws broken – arms, equipment, technological information – sent to people who shouldn't have them. They break loose on cue and there's disruptions, terrorism . . ."

"Justifying military responses," broke in old Beale. "That's part of Delavane's concept. Justifiable escalation of armed might, the commanders in charge, the civilians helpless, forced to listen to them, obey them."

"But you just said questions were raised."

"And answered with such worn out phrases as 'national security' and 'adversarial disinformation' to stop or throw off the curious."

"That's obstruction. Can't they be caught at it?"

"By whom? With what?"

"Damn it, the questions themselves!" replied Converse. "Those improper export licences, the military transfers that got lost, merchandise that can't be traced."

"By people without the clearances to go around security classifications, or lacking the expertise to understand the complexities of export licensing."

"That's nonsense," insisted Joel. "You said some of those questions were asked by diplomatic personnel. military colleagues, men who certainly had the clearances *and* the expertise."

"And who suddenly, magically, didn't ask them any longer. Of course, many may have been persuaded that the questions were, indeed, beyond their legitimate purviews; others may have been too frightened to penetrate for fear of involvement, others still, forced to back off – frankly threatened. Regardless, behind it all there are those who do the convincing, and they're growing in numbers everywhere."

"Christ, it's a . . . a *network*," said Converse softly.

The scholar looked hard at Joel, the night light off the water reflecting across the old man's pale, lined face. "Yes, Mr Converse, a 'network'. That word was whispered to me by a man who thought I was one of them. 'The network,' he said. 'The network will take care of you.' He meant Delavane and his people."

"Why did they think you were part of them?"

The old man paused. He looked briefly away at the shimmering Aegean, then back at Converse. "Because *that* man thought it was logical . . . Thirty years ago I took off a uniform, trading it for the Harris tweeds and unkempt hair of a university professor. Few of my colleagues could understand, for you see I was one of the élite, perhaps a later, American version of Erich Leifhelm – a brigadier-general at thirty-eight, the Joint Chiefs were conceivably my next assignment. But where the collapse of Berlin and the disembodiment of the bunker had one effect on Leifhelm, the evacuation of Korea and the disembowelment of Panmunjong had another effect on me. I saw only the waste, not the cause I once saw, only the futility where once there'd been sound reasons. I saw death, Mr Converse, not heroic death against animalistic hordes, or even on a Spanish afternoon with the crowds shouting '*Olé*', but just plain death. Ugly death, shattering death, and I knew I could no longer be a part of those strategies that called for it . . . Had I been qualified in belief, I might have become a priest."

"But your colleagues who couldn't understand," said Joel, mesmerized by Beale's words, words that meant so very much to him. "They thought it was something else?"

44

"Of course they did. I'd been praised in evaluation reports by the holy MacArthur himself. I even had a label: The Red Fox of Inchon – my hair was red then. My commands were marked by quick, decisive moves and countermoves, all reasonably well thought out and swift in execution. And then one day, south of Chunchon, I was given an order to take three adjacent hills that comprised dead high-ground – vantage points that served no strategic purpose – and I radioed back that it was useless real estate, that whatever casualties we sustained were not worth it. I asked for clarification, a field officer's way of saying 'You're crazy, why should I?' . . . The reply came in something less than fifteen minutes. 'Because it's there, General.' That was all. 'Because it's there.' A symbolic point was to be made for someone's benefit or someone else's macho news briefing in Seoul . . . I took the hills, and I also wasted the lives of over three hundred men – and for my efforts I was awarded another cluster of the Distinguished Service Cross."

"Is that when you quit?"

"Oh, Lord no, I was too confused, but inside, my head was boiling. The end came, and I watched Panmunjong, and was finally sent home, all manner of extraordinary expectations to be considered my ordinary rewards. However, a minor advancement was denied me for a very good reason: I didn't speak the language in a sensitive European post, but another did. By then my head had exploded; I used the rebuke and I took my cue. I resigned quietly and went my way."

It was Joel's turn to pause and study the old man in the night light. "I've never heard of you," he said finally. "Why haven't I ever heard of you?"

"You didn't recognize the names on the two lower lists, either, did you? 'Who are the Americans?' you said. 'The names don't mean anything to me.' Those were your words, Mr Converse."

"They weren't young decorated generals – heroes – in a war."

"Oh, but several *were*," interrupted Beale swiftly, "in several wars. They had their moments in a fleeting sun, and then they were forgotten, the moments only remembered by them, relived by them. Constantly."

"That sounds like an apology for them."

"Of course it is! You think I have no feelings for them? For men like Chaim Abrahms, Bertholdier, even Leifhelm? We call upon these men when the barricades are down, we extol them for acts beyond our abilities . . ."

"*You* were capable. You performed those acts."

"You're right and that's why I *understand* them. When the barricades are rebuilt, we consign them to a very dull oblivion. Worse, we force them to watch inept civilians strip the gears of reason, and through oblique vocabularies plant the explosives that will blow those barricades apart again. Then when they're down once more, we summon our commanders."

"Jesus. whose side are you on?"

Beale closed his eyes tightly, reminding Joel of the way he used to shut his own when certain memories came back to him. "Yours, you idiot," said the scholar quietly. "Because I know what they can do when we ask them to do it. I meant what I said before. There's never been a time in history like this one. Far better that inept, frightened civilians are still talking, still searching, than one of us . . . Forgive me, one of them."

A gust of wind blew off the sea; the sand spiralled about their feet. "That man," said Converse, "the one who told you the network would take care of you. Why did he say it?"

"He thought they could use me. He was one of the field commanders I knew in Korea, a kindred spirit then. He came to my island – for what reason I don't know, perhaps a vacation, perhaps to find me, *who* knows – and found me on the waterfront. I was taking my boat out of the Plati Harbour when suddenly he appeared, tall, erect and very military in the morning sun. 'We have to talk,' he said, with that same insistence we always used in the field . . . I asked him aboard and we slowly made our way out of the bay. Several miles out of the Plati he presented his case, *their* case. *Delavane's* case."

"What happened then?"

The scholar paused for precisely two seconds, then answered simply. "I killed him. With a scaling knife, dropping his body over a cluster of sharks beyond the shoals of the Stephanos."

Stunned, Joel stared at the old man, the iridescent light of the moon contributing to the macabre revelation. "Just like that?" he said in a monotone.

"It's what I was trained to do, Mr Converse. I was the Red Fox of Inchon. I never hesitated when the ground could be gained. or an adversarial advantage eliminated."

"You *killed* him?"

"It was a necessary decision, not a wanton taking of life. He was a recruiter and my response was in my eyes, in my silent outrage. He saw it, and I understood. He could not permit me to live with what he'd told me. One of us had to die, and I simply reacted more swiftly than he did."

"That's pretty cold reasoning."

"You're a lawyer, you deal every day with options. Where was the alternative?"

Joel shook his head, not in reply but in astonishment. "How did Halliday find you?"

"We found each other. We've never met, never talked, but we have a mutual friend."

"In San Francisco?"

"He's frequently there."

"Who is he?"

"It's a subject we won't discuss. I'm sorry."

"Why not? Why the secrecy?"

"It's the way he prefers it. Under the circumstances, I believe it's a logical request."

"Logic? Find me logic in any of this! Halliday reaches a man in San Francisco who just happens to know you, a former general thousands of miles away on a Greek island who just *happens* to have been approached by one of Delavane's people. Now that's coincidence, but damned little logic!"

"Don't dwell on it. Accept it."

"Would you?"

"Under the circumstances, yes, I would. You see, there's no alternative."

"Sure there is. I could walk away five hundred thousand dollars richer, paid by an anonymous stranger who could only come after me by revealing himself."

"You could but you won't. You were chosen very carefully."

"Because I could be motivated? That's what Halliday said."

"Frankly, yes."

"You're off the wall, all of you!"

"One of us is dead. You were the last person he spoke with."

Joel felt the rush of anger again, the sight of a dying man's eyes burned into his memory. Aquitaine," he said softly. "*Delavane* . . . All right, I was chosen carefully. Where do I begin?"

"Where do you think you should begin? You're the attorney, everything must be done legally."

"That's just it. I'm an attorney, not the police, not a detective."

"No police in any of the countries where those four men live could do what you can do, even if they agreed to try, which frankly I doubt. More to the point, they would alert the Delavane network."

"All right, I'll try," said Converse, folding the page with the list of names and putting it in his inside jacket pocket. "I'll start at the top. In Paris. With this Bertholdier."

"Jacques Louis Bertholdier," added the old man, reaching down into his canvas bag and taking out a thick manila envelope. "This is the last thing we can give you. It's everything we could learn about those four men, perhaps it can help you. Their addresses, the cars they drive, business associates, cafés and restaurants they frequent, sexual preferences where they constitute vulnerability . . . anything that could give you an edge. Use it, use everything you can. Just bring us back briefs against men who have compromised themselves, broken laws – above all, evidence that shows they are not the solid, respectable citizens their lifestyles would indicate. Embarrassment, Mr Converse, *embarrassment*. It leads to ridicule, and Preston Halliday was profoundly right about that. Ridicule is the first step."

Joel started to reply, to agree, then stopped, his eyes riveted on Beale. "I never told you Halliday said anything about ridicule."

"Oh?" The scholar blinked several times in the dim light, he was momentarily unsure of himself, caught by surprise. "But, naturally, we discussed . . ."

"You never met, you never *talked!*" broke in Converse.

" . . . through our mutual friend the strategies we might employ," completed the old man, his eyes now steady, unblinking. "The aspect of ridicule is a keystone. Of course, we discussed it."

"You just hesitated."

"You startled me with a meaningless statement. My reactions are not what they once were."

"They were in a boat beyond the Stephanos," corrected Joel.

"An entirely different situation, Mr Converse. Only one of us could leave that boat. Both of us will leave this beach tonight."

"All right, I may be reaching. You would, too, if you were me." Converse withdrew a pack of cigarettes from his shirt pocket, shook one up nervously to his lips and took out his lighter. "A man I knew as a kid under one name approaches me years later calling himself something else." Joel snapped his lighter and held the flame under the cigarette, inhaling. "He tells a wild story that's just credible enough so I can't dismiss it. The believable aspect is a maniac named Delavane. He says I can help stop him – stop *them* – and there's a great deal of money for nodding my head – provided by a man in San Francisco who won't say who he is, expedited by a former general on a fashionably remote island in the Aegean. And for his efforts, this man I knew under two names is murdered in daylight, shot a dozen times in an elevator, dying in my arms, whispering the name 'Aquitaine'. And then this other man, this ex-soldier, this doctor, this *scholar* tells me another story that ends with a 'recruiter' from Delavane killed with a scaling knife, his body thrown overboard into a school of sharks beyond the Stephanos – whatever that is."

"The Aghios Stephanos," said the old man. "A lovely beach, far more popular than this one."

"Goddamn it, I *am* reaching, Mr Beale, or Professor Beale, or *General* Beale! It's too much to absorb in two lousy days! Suddenly I don't have much confidence. I feel way beyond my depth – let's face it, overwhelmed and underqualified . . . and damned frightened."

"Then don't overcomplicate things," said Beale. "I used to say that to students of mine more often than I can remember. I would suggest they not look at the totality that faced them, but rather each thread of progression, following each until it met and entwined with another thread, and then another, and if a pattern did not become clear, it was not their failure but mine. One step at a time, Mr Converse."

"You're one hell of a Mr Chips. I would have dropped the course."

"I'm not saying it well, I used to say it better. When you teach history, threads are terribly important."

"When you practise law, they're everything."

"Go after the threads then, one at a time. I'm certainly no lawyer, but can't you approach this as an attorney whose client is under attack by forces that would violate his rights, cripple his manner of living, deny his pursuit of peaceful existence – in essence, destroy him?"

"Not likely," replied Joel. "I've got a client who won't talk to me, won't see me, won't even tell me who he is."

"That's not the client I had in mind."

"Who else? It's his money."

"He's only a link to your real client."

"Who's that?"

"What's left of the civilized world, perhaps."

Joel studied the old scholar in the shimmering light. "Did you just say something about not looking at totalities, but at threads? You scare the hell out of me."

Beale smiled. "I could accuse you of misplaced concretion, but I won't."

"That's an antiquated phrase. If you mean out-of-context, say it, and I'll deny it. You're securely in *well-placed* contradiction, Professor."

"Good heavens, you were chosen carefully. You won't even let an old man get away with an academic bromide."

Converse smiled back. "You're a likeable fellow, General . . . or Doctor. I'd hate to have met you across a table if you'd taken up law."

"That could truly be misplaced confidence," said Edward Beale, his smile gone. "You're only about to begin."

"But now I know what to look for. One thread at a time . . . until the threads meet and entwine, and the pattern's there for everyone to see. I'll concentrate on export licences, and whoever's shuffling the controls, then connect three or four names with one another and trace them back to Delavane in Palo Alto. At which point we blow it apart *legally.* No martyrs, no causes, no military men-of-destiny crucified by traitors, just plain bloated, ugly profiteers who've professed to be super patriots when all the while they were lining their unpatriotic pockets. Why *else* would they have done it? Is there another *reason? . . .* That's ridicule, Dr Beale. Because they *can't answer.*"

The old man shook his head, his lined brows indicating bewilderment. "The professor becomes a student," he said, hesitantly. "How can you do this?"

"The way I've done it dozens of times in corporate negotiations . . . only I'll take it a step farther. In those sessions, I'm like any other lawyer, I try to figure out what the fellow across the table is going to ask for and then why he wants it. Not just what *my* side wants, but what *he* wants. What's going through his mind? . . . You see, Doctor, I'm trying to think like him; I'm putting myself in his place, never for a second letting him forget that I'm doing just that. It's very unnerving, like making notes on margins whenever your opponent says anything, whether he's saying anything or not . . . But this time it's going to be different. I'm not looking for opponents. I'm looking for allies. In a cause, *their* cause. I'll start in Paris, then on to Bonn, or Tel Aviv, then probably Johannesburg. Only when I reach these men I won't try to think like them, I'm going to *be* one of them."

"That's a very bold strategy, I compliment you."

"Talking of options, it's the only one open. Also, I've got a lot of money I can spend around, not lavishly but effectively, as befits my unnamed client. Very unnamed, very much in the background, but always there." Joel stopped, a thought striking him. "You know, Doctor Beale, I take it back. I don't want to know who my client is – the one in San Francisco, I mean. I'm going to create my own, and knowing him might distort the portrait I've got in mind. Incidentally, tell him he'll get a full accounting of my expenses: the rest will be returned to him the same way I got it. Through your friend Laskaris at the bank here on Mykonos."

"But you've accepted the money," objected Beale. "There's no reason . . ."

"I wanted to know if it was real. If *he* was real. He is, and he knows exactly what he's doing. I'll need a great deal of money because I'm going to have to become someone I'm not, and money is the most convincing way to do it . . .

No, Doctor, I don't want your friend's money, I want Delavane. I want the warlord of Saigon . . . But I'll use his money, just as I'm using him – the way I want him to be. To get inside that network."

"If Paris is your first stop and Bertholdier is going to be your initial contact, there's a specific munitions transfer we think is directly related to him. It might be worth a try. If we're right, it's a microcosm of what they intend doing everywhere."

"It is in here?" asked Converse, tapping the thick manila envelope containing the dossiers.

"No, it came to light only this morning – early this morning. I don't imagine you listened to the news broadcasts."

"I don't speak any language but English. If I heard a news programme I wouldn't know it. What happened?"

"All Northern Ireland is on fire, the worst riots, the most savage killing in fifteen years. In Belfast and Ballyclare, Dromora and in the Mourne Mountains, outraged vigilantes – on *both* sides – are roaming the streets and the hills, firing indiscriminately, slaughtering in their anger everything that moves. It's utter chaos. The Ulster government is in panic, parliament tied down, emotionally disrupted, everyone trying to find a solution. That solution will be a massive infusion of troops and their commanders."

"What's it got to do with Bertholdier?"

"Listen to me carefully," said the scholar, taking a step forward. "Eighty days ago a munitions shipment containing three hundred cases of cluster bombs and two thousand cartons of explosive was air freighted out of Beloit, Wisconsin. Its destination was Tel Aviv by way of Montreal, Paris and Marseilles. It never arrived and an Israeli trace – employing the Mossad – showed that only the cargo's paperwork reached Marseilles, nothing else. The shipment disappeared in either Montreal or Paris, and we're convinced it was diverted to provisional extremists – again on both sides – in Northern Ireland."

"Why do you think so?"

"The first casualties – over three hundred men, women and children – were killed or severely wounded, ripped to shreds by cluster bombs. It's not a pleasant way to die, perhaps worse to be hurt; the bombs tear away whole sections of the body. The reactions have been fierce and the hysteria's spreading. Ulster's out of control, the government paralysed. All in the space of one day, *one single day*, Mr Converse!"

"They're proving to themselves they can do it," said Joel quietly, the fear in his throat.

"Precisely," agreed Beale. "It's a test case, a microcosm of the full scale horror they can bring about."

Converse frowned. "Outside of the fact that Bertholdier lives in Paris, what ties him to the shipment?"

"Once the plane crossed into France, the French insurers were a firm in which Bertholdier is a director. Who would be less suspect than a company that had to pay for the loss, a company, incidentally, which has access to the merchandise it covers? The loss was upward of four million francs, not so immense to create

50

headlines, but entirely sufficient to throw off suspicion. And one more lethal delivery is made – death, mutilation, and chaos to follow."

"What's the name of the insurance company?"

"*Compagnie Solidaire*. It would be one of the operative words, I'd think. *Solidaire*, and perhaps Beloit and Belfast."

"Let's hope I get to confront Bertholdier with them. But if I do, I've got to say them at the right time. I'll catch the plane from Athens in the morning."

"Take the urgent good wishes of an old man with you, Mr Converse. And urgent is the appropriate word. Three to five weeks, that's all you've got before everything blows apart. Whatever it is, wherever it is, it will be Northern Ireland ten thousand times more violent. It's real and it's coming."

Valerie Charpentier woke up suddenly, her eyes wide, her face rigid, listening intently for sounds that broke the dark silence around her and the slap of the waves in the distance. Any second she expected to hear the shattering bell of the alarm system which was wired into every window and door of the house.

It did not come, yet there had been other sounds, intrusions on her sleep, penetrating enough to wake her. She pulled the covers back and got out of bed, walking slowly, apprehensively to the glass doors that opened onto her balcony – the rocky beach, the jetty, and the Atlantic Ocean beyond.

There it was *again*. The bobbing, dim lights were unmistakably the same, washing over the boat which was moored exactly where it had been moored before. It was the sloop that for two days had cruised up and down the coastline, always in sight, with no apparent destination other than this particular stretch of the Massachusetts' shore. At twilight on the second evening it had dropped anchor no more than a quarter of a mile out in the water in front of her house. It was back. After three days it had returned.

Three nights ago she had called the police, who in turn reached the Cape Ann Coast Guard patrols, who came back with an explanation that was no more lucid than it was satisfactory. The sloop was a Maryland registry, the owner an officer in the United States Army, and there were no provocative or suspicious movements that warranted any official action.

"I'd call it damned provocative *and* suspicious," Val had said firmly. "When a strange boat sails up and down the same stretch of beach for two days in a row, then parks in front of my house within shouting distance – shouting distance being swimming distance."

"The water rights of the property you leased don't extend beyond two hundred feet, mam," had been the official reply. "There's nothing we can do."

At the first light of the next morning, however, Valerie knew that *something* had to be done. She had focused her binoculars on the boat, only to have gasped and moved back away from the glass doors. Two men had been standing on the deck of the sloop, their own binoculars – far more powerful than hers – directed at the house, at the bedroom upstairs. At her.

A neighbour down the beachside *cul-de-sac* had recently installed an alarm system. She was a divorced woman, too, but with a hostile ex-husband and three children; she deemed the alarm necessary. Two phone calls and Val was speaking to the owner of Watchguard Security. A temporary system had been hooked up that day while a permanent installation was designed.

A bell – not shattering but instead soft and gentle. It was the quiet clanging of a ship's bell out on the dark water, its clapper swinging with the waves. It was the sound that had awakened her and it was both a relief, yet strangely disturbing. Men out on the water at night who intended harm did not announce their presence. On the other hand, those same men had come back to her house, the boat only several hundred yards off shore. They had returned in the darkness, the moon blocked by a sky thick with clouds, no moonlight to guide them. It was as if they wanted her to know they were there and they were watching. They were waiting.

For what? What was happening to her? A week ago her phone had gone dead for seven hours and when she had called the telephone company from her friend's house, a supervisor in the service department told her he could find no malfunctions. The line was operative.

"Maybe for you, but not for me, and you're not paying the bills."

She had returned home; the line was still dead. A second, far angrier call brought the same response. No malfunctions. Then two hours later the dial tone was inexplicably there, the phone working. She had put the episode down to less than the best equipment over at the rural telephone complex. She did not know what to ascribe to the sloop now eerily bobbing in the water in front of her house.

Suddenly, in the boat's dim light, she could see a figure crawl up out of the cabin. For a moment or two it was hidden in the shadows, then there was a brief flare of intense light. A match. A cigarette. A man was standing motionless on the deck smoking a cigarette. He was facing her house, as if studying it. Waiting.

Val shivered as she dragged a heavy chair in front of the balcony door – but not too close, away from the glass. She pulled the light blanket off the bed and sat down, wrapping it around her, staring out at the water, at the boat, at the man. She knew that if the man or that boat made the slightest move toward the shore she would press the buttons she had been instructed to press in the event of an emergency. When activated, the huge circular alarm bells – both inside and outside – were ear-piercing, erupting in concert, drowning out the surf and the waves crashing on the jetty, heard thousands of feet away – the only sound on the beach, frightening, overwhelming. She wondered if she would cause them to be heard tonight – this morning.

She would not panic. Joel had taught her not to panic, even when she thought a well-placed scream was called for on the dark streets of Manhattan. Every now and then the inevitable had happened. They had been confronted by drug addicts or punks and Joel would remain calm – icily calm – moving them both back against a wall and offering a cheap, spare wallet he kept in his hip pocket with a few bills in it. *God*, he was ice! Maybe that was why no one had ever actually assaulted them, not knowing what was behind that cold, brooding look.

"I should have screamed!" she once had cried.

52

"No," he had said. "Then you would have frightened him, panicked him. That's when those bastards can be lethal."

Was the man on the boat lethal – were the *men* on the boat deadly? Or were they simply novice sailors hugging the coastline, practising tacks, anchoring near the shore for their own protection – curious, perhaps concerned, that the property owners might object? An Army officer was not likely to be able to afford a captain for his sloop, and there were marinas only miles away north and south – marinas without available berths but with men who could handle repairs.

Was the man out on the boat smoking the cigarette merely a land-locked young officer getting his sailing legs, comfortable at a familiar anchor away from deep water? It was possible, of course – anything was possible, and summer nights held a special kind of loneliness that gave rise to strange imaginings. One walked the beach alone and thought too much.

Joel would laugh at her and say it was all those demons racing around her artist's head in search of regimen and logic. And he would undoubtedly be right. The men out on the boat were probably more up-tight than she was. In a way they were trespassers who had found a haven in sight of hostile natives; one inquiry of the Coast Guard proved it. And that clearance, as it were, was another reason why they had returned to the place where, if not welcome, at least they were not harassed. If Joel were with her she knew exactly what he would do. He would go down to the beach and shout across the water to their temporary neighbours and ask them to come in for a drink.

Dear Joel, foolish Joel, ice-cold Joel. There were times you were comforting – when you were comfortable. And amusing, so terribly amusing – even when you weren't comfortable. In some ways I miss you, darling. But not enough, thank you .

And yet why did the feeling – the instinct, perhaps persist? The small boat out on the water was like a magnet, pulling her toward it, drawing her into its field, taking her where she knew she did not want to go.

Nonsense! Demons in search of logic! She was being foolish – *Foolish Joel, ice-cold Joel* – stop it, for God's sake! Be *reasonable!*

Then the shiver passed through her again. Novice sailors did not navigate around strange coastlines at night.

The magnet held her until her eyes grew heavy and troubled sleep came.

She woke up again, startled by the intense sunlight streaming through the glass doors, its warmth enveloping her. She looked out at the water. The boat was gone – and she wondered for a moment whether it had really been there.

Yes, it had. But it was gone.

3

The 747 lifted off the runway at Athen's Hellikon Airport, soaring to the left in its rapid ascent. Below in clear view, adjacent to the huge field, was the US Naval Air Station, permitted by treaty although reduced in size and in the number of aircraft during the past several years. Nevertheless, far-reaching, jet-streamed American eyes still roamed the Mediterranean, Ionian and Aegean seas, courtesy of a resentful yet nervous government all too aware of other eyes to the north. Staring out of the window, Converse recognized the shapes of familiar equipment on the ground. There were two rows of Phantom F-4T's and A-6E's on opposite sides of the dual strip, updated versions of the F-4G's and A-6A's he had flown years ago.

It was so easy to slip back, thought Joel, as he watched three Phantoms break away from the ground formation; they would head for the top of the runway, and another patrol would be in the skies. Converse could feel his hands tense, in his mind he was manipulating the thick, perforated shaft, reaching for switches, his eyes roaming the dials, looking for right and wrong signals. Then the power would come, the surging force of pressurized tons beside him, behind him, himself encased in the centre of a sleek, shining beast straining to break away and soar up into its natural habitat. *Final check, all in order; cleared for take off. Release the power of the beast, let it free. Roll! Faster, faster; the ground is a blur, the carrier deck a mass of passing grey, blue sea beyond, blue sky above. Let it free! Let me free!*

He wondered if he could still do it, if the lessons and the training of boy and man still held. After the Navy, during the academic years in Massachusetts and North Carolina, he had frequently gone to small airfields and taken up small insignificant single-engined aircraft just to get away from the pressures, to find a few minutes of blue freedom, but there were no challenges, no taming of all-powerful beasts. Later still, it had all stopped . . . for a long, long time. There were no airfields to visit on weekends, no playing around with sleek company planes; he had given his promise. His wife had been terrified of his flying. Valerie could not reconcile the hours he had flown – civilian and in combat – with her own evaluation of the averages. And in one of the few gestures of understanding in his marriage, he had given his word not to climb onto a wing and into a cockpit. It had not bothered him until he knew – they knew – the marriage had gone sour, at which point he began driving out to a field called Teterboro in New Jersey every chance he could find and had flown whatever was available, any time, any hour, in search of the blue freedom. Still, even then – especially then – there had been no challenges, no beasts . . . other than himself.

The ground below disappeared as the 747 stabilized and began to climb to its assigned altitude. Converse turned away from the window and settled back in his seat. The lights were abruptly extinguished on the *No Smoking* sign, and Joel took out a pack of cigarettes from his shirt pocket, extracting one to his lips. He snapped his lighter, the smoke diffusing instantly in the rush of air from the vents above. He looked at his watch; it was 12.20. They were due in Orly Airport at 3.35, French time. Allowing for the zones, it was a three hour flight, and during those three hours he would commit to memory everything he could about General Jacques Louis Bertholdier – if Beale and the dead Halliday were right, the arm of Aquitaine in Paris.

At Hellikon he had done something he had never done before, something that had never occurred to him, an indulgence that was generally attributed to romantic fiction or movie stars or idols of the rock mania. Fear and caution had joined with an excess of money and he had paid for two adjoining seats in First Class. He wanted no one's eyes straying to the pages he would be reading. Old Beale had made it frighteningly clear on the beach last night. If there was the remotest possibility that the materials he carried might fall into other hands – *any* other hands – he was to destroy them at all costs. For they were in-depth dossiers on men who could order multiple executions by placing a single phone call.

He reached down for his attaché case, the leather handle still dark from the sweat of his grip since Mykonos early that morning. For the first time he understood the value of a device he had seen and read about in films and novels. Airport security aside, had he been able to chain the handle of his attaché case to his wrist, he would have breathed far more comfortably.

Jacques Louis Bertholdier, age 59, only child of Alphonse and Marie Therese Bertholdier, was born at the military hospital in Dakar. Father a career officer in the French army, reputedly autocratic and a harsh disciplinarian. Little is known about the mother, significance perhaps to be found in that Bertholdier never speaks of her, as if dismissing her existence. He retired from the army four years ago at the age of 55, and is now a director of Juneau et Cie, a conservative firm on the *Bourse des Valeurs*, Paris's Stock Exchange.

Early years appear to be typical of a commanding officer's son, moving from post to post, accorded the privileges of the father's rank and influence. He was used to servants and fawning military personnel. If there was a difference, it was in the boy himself. It is said that he could execute the full dress manual-of-arms by the time he was five and at ten could recite by rote the entire book of regulations.

In 1938, the Bertholdiers were back in Paris, the father a member of the General Staff. They were chaotic times, as the war with Germany was imminent and the elder Bertholdier one of the few commanders aware that the Maginot could not hold. His outspokenness so infuriated his fellow officers that he was transferred to the field, commanding the 4th Army, stationed along the north-eastern border.

The war came and the father was killed in the fifth week of combat. Young Bertholdier was then 16 years old and going to school in Paris.

The fall of France in June of 1940 could be called the beginning of our subject's adulthood. Joining the Resistance first as a courier, he fought for four years, rising in the underground's ranks until he commanded the Calais-Paris sector. He made frequent undercover trips to England coordinating espionage and sabotage operations with the Free French and British Intelligence. In February of 1944, de Gaulle conferred on him the temporary rank of Major. He was 20 years of age.

Several days prior to the Allied occupation of Paris, Bertholdier was severely wounded in a street skirmish between the Resistance fighters and the retreating

German troops. Hospitalization relieved him from further activity for the remainder of the European war. Following the surrender he was appointed to the national military academy at St Cyr, a compensation deemed proper by de Gaulle for the young hero of the underground. Upon graduation he was elevated to the permanent rank of captain. He was 24 and given successive commands in the Dra Hamada, French Morocco; Algiers; then across the world to the garrisons at Haiphong, and, finally, the Allied Sectors in Vienna and West Berlin. (Note this last post with respect to following information on Field Marshal Erich Leifhelm. It's where they first met and became friends, at first openly, subsequently denying the relationship after both had resigned from military service.)

Setting Erich Leifhelm aside for the moment, Converse thought about the young legend that was Jacques Louis Bertholdier. Though Joel was as unmilitary as a man could be, in an odd way he could identify with the military phenomenon described in these pages. Although no hero, he had been accorded a hero's return from a war in which very few were so acclaimed, these generally from the ranks of those who had endured capture more than they had fought. Nevertheless, the attention – the sheer *attention* – that led to privileges was a dangerous indulgence. Although initially embarrassed, one came to accept it all ... then expect it all. The recognition could be heady, the privileges soon taken for granted. And when the attention began to dwindle away a certain anger came into play; one wanted it all back.

These were the feelings of someone with no hunger for authority – success, yes; power, no. But what of a man whose whole being was shaped by the fabric of authority *and* power, whose earliest memories were of privilege and rank, and whose meteoric rise came at an incredibly young age? How does such a man react to recognition and the ever increasing spectrum of his own ascendancy? One did not lightly take away much from such a man; anger could turn into fury. Yet Bertholdier had walked away from it all at fifty-five, a reasonably young age for one so prominent. It was not consistent. Something was missing from the portrait of this latter-day Alexander. At least so far.

Timing played a major part in Bertholdier's expanding reputation. After posts in the Dra Hamada and pre-crisis Algiers, he was transferred to French Indochina where the situation was deteriorating rapidly for the colonial forces, then in violent guerilla warfare. His exploits in the field were instantly the talk of Saigon and Paris. The troops under his command provided several rare but much needed victories, which although incapable of altering the course of the war convinced the hard-line militarists that the inferior Asian forces could be defeated by superior Gallic courage and strategy; they needed only the materials withheld by Paris. The surrender at Dienbienphu was bitter medicine for those men who claimed that traitors in the Quai d'Orsay had brought about France's humiliation. Yet out of the defeat Colonel Bertholdier emerged as one of the few heroic figures, but he was wise enough or cautious enough to keep his own counsel, and did not, at least in appearance, join the "hawks". Many say that he was waiting for a signal that never came. Again he was transferred, serving tours in Vienna and West Berlin.

Four years later, however, he broke the mould he had so carefully constructed. In his own words, he was "infuriated and disillusioned" by de Gaulle's accords with the independence-seeking Algerians; he joined General Raoul Salan's rebellious OAS, which violently opposed policies it termed betrayals. During this revolutionary interim of his life, he was implicated in an assassination attempt on de Gaulle. With Salan's capture in April of 1962, and the insurrectionists' collapse, once again Bertholdier emerged stunningly intact out of defeat. In what can only be described as an extraordinary move – and one which has never really been understood – de Gaulle had Bertholdier released from prison and brought to the Quai d'Orsay. What was said between the two men has never been revealed, but Bertholdier was returned to rank. De Gaulle's only comment of record was given during a press conference on 4 May, 1962. In reply to a question regarding the reinstated rebel officer, he said (verbatim translation): "A great soldier-patriot must be permitted and forgiven a single misguided interlude. We have conferred. We are satisfied." He said no more on the subject.

For seven years Bertholdier was stationed at various influential posts, rising to the rank of general, more often than not the chief military *chargé d'affaires* at major embassies during France's participation in the NATO Alliance. He was frequently recalled to the Quai d'Orsay, accompanying de Gaulle to international conferences, always visible in newspaper photographs, usually within several feet of the great man himself. Oddly enough, although his contributions appear to have been considerable, after these conferences – or summits, if you will – he was invariably sent back to his previous station while internal debates continued and decisions were reached without him. It was as though he was constantly being groomed but never permanently summoned. Was that ultimate summons the signal he had been waiting for seven years before at Dienbienphu? It is a question for which we have no answer here, but we believe it's vital to pursue it.

With de Gaulle's dramatic resignation over his demands for constitutional reform in 1969, Bertholdier's career went into an eclipse. His assignments were far from the centres of power and remained so until his resignation. Research into bank and credit card references as well as passenger manifests shows that during the past eighteen months our subject made trips to the following: London, 3; New York, 2; San Francisco, 2; Bonn, 3; Johannesburg, 1; Tel Aviv, 1 (combined with Johannesburg). The pattern is clear. It is compatible with the rising geographical pressure points of General Delavane's operation.

Converse rubbed his eyes and rang for a drink. While waiting for the Scotch he scanned the next few paragraphs, his memory of the man now jogged; they were familiar history and not terribly relevant. Bertholdier's name had been put forward by several ultra-conservative factions, hoping to pull him out of the military into the political wars, but nothing came of the attempts. The ultimate summons had passed him by; it never came. At fifty-five, he resigned from the army to become a director of a large firm on the Paris stock exchange, basically a figurehead capable of overwhelming the wealthy, and keeping the socialistically-inclined at bay by the sheer weight of his own legend

He travels everywhere in a company limousine (read: staff car) and wherever he goes his arrival is expected, the proper welcome arranged. The vehicle is a dark blue American Lincoln Continental, Licence Plate 100–1. The restaurants he frequents are: Taillevent, The Ritz, Julien and Lucas Carton. For lunches, however, he consistently goes to a private club called Les Étalons Blancs three to four times a week. It is a very off-the-track establishment whose membership is restricted to the highest-ranking military, what's left of the rich nobility, and wealthy fawners who, if they can't be either, put their money on both so as to be in with the crowd.

Joel smiled; the author of the report was not without humour. Still, something was missing. His lawyer's mind looked for the lapse that was not explained. What was the signal Bertholdier had not been given at Dienbienphu? What had the imperious de Gaulle said to the rebellious officer, and what had the rebel said to the great man? Why was he consistently accommodated – but only accommodated – never summoned to power? An Alexander had been primed, forgiven, elevated, then dropped? There was a message buried in these pages, but Joel could not find it.

Converse reached what the writer of the report considered relevant only in that it completed the portrait, adding little, however, to previous information.

Bertholdier's private life appears barely pertinent to the activities that concern us. His marriage was one of convenience in the purest La Rochefoucauld sense: It was socially, professionally and financially beneficial for both parties. The marriage itself, however, appears to be solely a business arrangement. There have been no children, and although Madame Bertholdier appears frequently at her husband's side for state and social occasions, they have rarely been observed in close conversation. Also, as with his mother, Bertholdier has never been known to discuss his wife. There might be a psychological connection here, but we find no evidence to support it. Especially since Bertholdier is a notorious womanizer, supporting at times as many as three separate mistresses as well as numerous peripheral assignations. Among his peers there is a soubriquet which has never found its way into print: Le Grand Timon, and if the reader here needs a translation, we recommend drinks on the Montparnasse.

On that compelling note the report was finished. It was a dossier that raised more questions than it answered. In broad strokes it described the *whats* and the *hows* but few of the *whys*; these were buried and only imaginative speculation could unearth even the probabilities. But there were enough concrete facts to operate on. Joel glanced at his watch; an hour had passed. He had two more to reread, think, and absorb as much as possible. He had already made up his mind who he would contact in Paris.

René Mattilon was not only an astute lawyer frequently called upon by Talbot, Brooks and Simon when they needed representation in the French courts, he was also a friend. Although he was older than Joel by a decade, the roots of their friendship were traced back to a common experience, common in the sense of global geography, futility and waste. Thirty years ago Mattilon was a young attorney in his twenties conscripted by his government and sent to French Indochina as a legal officer. He witnessed the inevitable and could never understand why it cost so much for his proud, intractable nation to perceive it. Also, he could be scathing in his comments about the subsequent American involvement.

58

"*Mon Dieu!* You thought you could do with arms what we could not do with arms *and* brains? *Déraisonnable!*"

It had become standard that whenever Mattilon flew to New York or Joel to Paris, they found time for dinner and drinks. Also, the Frenchman was amazingly tolerant of Converse's linguistic limitations; Joel simply could not learn another language. Even Val's patient tutoring had fallen on deaf and dead ears and an unreceptive brain. For four years his ex-wife, whose father was French and mother German, tried to instil in him the simplest phrases but found him hopeless.

"How the hell can you call yourself an international lawyer when you can't be understood beyond Sandy Hook?" she had asked.

"Hire interpreters trained by Swiss banks and put them on a point system," he had replied. "They won't miss a trick."

Whenever he came to Paris, he stayed in a suite of two rooms at the opulent George V Hotel, an indulgence permitted by Talbot, Brooks and Simon he had assumed more to impress clients than to satisfy a balance sheet. The assumption was only half right, as Nathan Simon had made clear.

"You have a fancy sitting room," Nate had told him sepulchrally. "Use it for conferences and you can avoid those ridiculously expensive French lunches and – God forbid – the dinners."

"Suppose they want to eat?"

"You have another appointment. Wink and say it's personal; no one in Paris will argue."

The impressive address could serve him now, mused Converse, as the taxi maniacally weaved through the mid-afternoon traffic on the Champs-Elysées toward the Avenue George V. If he made any progress – and he intended to make progress – with men around Bertholdier or Bertholdier himself, the expensive hotel would fit the image of an unknown client who had sent his personal attorney on a very confidential search. Of course, he had no reservation, an oversight to be blamed on a substituting secretary.

He was greeted warmly by the assistant manager, albeit with surprise and, finally, apologies. No telexed request for reservations had come from Talbot, Brooks and Simon in New York, but, naturally, accommodation would be found for an old friend. They were; the standard two-room suite on the second floor, and before Joel could unpack, a steward brought a bottle of the Scotch whisky he preferred, substituting it for the existing brand on the small bar. He had forgotten the accuracy of the copious notes such hotels kept on recurrent guests. Second floor, the right whisky, and no doubt during the evening he would be reminded that he usually requested a wake up call for seven o clock in the morning. It would be the same.

But it was close to five o'clock in the afternoon now. If he was going to reach Mattilon before the lawyer left his office for the day, he had to do so quickly. If

René could have drinks with him, it would be a start. Mattilon either was his man or he was not, and the thought of losing even an hour of any kind of progress was disturbing. He reached for the Paris directory on a shelf beneath the phone on the bedside table; he looked up the firm's number and dialled.

"Good *Christ*, Joel!" exclaimed the Frenchman. "I read about that terrible business in Geneva! It was in the morning papers and I tried to call you – Le Richemond, of course – but they said you'd checked out. Are you all right?"

"I'm fine. I was just there, that's all."

"He was American. Did you know him?"

"Only across the table. By the way, that crap about his having something to do with narcotics was just that. Crap. He was cornered, robbed, shot and set up for post-mortem confusion."

"And an overzealous *préfet* leapt at the obvious, trying to protect his city's image. I know; it was made clear. It's all so horrible. Crime, killing, terrorism; it spreads everywhere. Less so here in Paris, thank God."

"You don't need muggers, the taxi drivers more than fill the bill. Except nastier, maybe."

"You are, as always, *impossible*, my friend! When can we get together?"

Converse paused. "I was hoping tonight. After you left the office."

"It's very short notice, *mon ami*. I wish you had called before."

"I just got in ten minutes ago."

"But you left Geneva."

"I had business in Athens," interrupted Joel.

"Ah, yes, the money flees from the Greeks these days. Precipitously, I think. Just as it was here."

"How about drinks, René? It's important."

It was Mattilon's turn to pause; it was obvious he had caught the trace of urgency in Converse's brevity, in his voice. "Of course," said the Frenchman. "You're at the George V, I assume?"

"Yes."

"I'll be there as soon as I can. Say forty-five minutes."

"Thanks very much. I'll get a couple of chairs in the gallery."

"I'll find you."

That area of the immense marble-arched lobby outside the tinted glass doors of the George V Bar was known informally as the "gallery" by habitués, its name derived from the fact that there *was* an art gallery narrowly enclosed within a corridor of clear glass on the left. However, just as reasonably, the name fitted the opulent room itself. The deeply-cushioned, cut velvet chairs, settees and polished, low dark tables that lined the marble walls were beneath works of art – mammoth tapestries from long-forgotten chateaux and huge, heroic canvases by artists, both old and new. And the smooth, quarried stone of the floor was covered by giant Oriental rugs, while affixed to the high ceiling was a series of intricate chandeliers, throwing soft light through filigrees of lacelike gold.

Quiet conversations took place between men and women of wealth and power at these upholstered enclaves, in calculated shadows under spotlit paintings and woven cloth from centuries ago. Frequently they were opening dialogues, testing questions that as often as not were finalized in boardrooms, peopled by chairmen and presidents, treasurers, and prides of lawyers. The movers and the shakers felt comfortable with the initial informality – the uncommitted explorations – of first meetings in this very formal room. The ceremonial environs somehow lent an air of ritualized disbelief; denials were not hard to come by later. The "gallery" also lived up to its caveat: within the fraternity of those who had achieved success on the international scene, it was said that if such a person spent any length of time in these elegant surroundings sooner or later he would invariably run into almost everyone he knew. Therefore, if one did not care to be seen, one should go somewhere else.

The room was filling up, waiters from the discreetly raucous bar roving outside and taking orders, knowing where the real money was. Converse found two chairs at the far end, the dim light more pronounced. He looked at his watch, barely able to read it – seen and not seen; he had settled for the middle ground. Forty minutes had passed since his call to René, a shower taking up the time and the sweat-stained dirt of his all-day journey from Mykonos. Placing his cigarettes and lighter on the table, he ordered a drink from an alert waiter, his eyes on the marble entrance to the room.

Twelve minutes later he saw him: Mattilon walked energetically out of the harsh glare of the street lobby into the soft light of the gallery. He stopped for a moment, squinting, then nodded. He started down the centre of the carpeted floor, his eyes levelled at Joel from a distance, a broad, genuine smile on his face. René Mattilon was in his mid to late fifties, but his stride, like his outlook, was that of a younger man. There was about him that aura peculiar to successful trial lawyers; his confidence was apparent because it was the essence of his success, yet it was born of diligence, not merely ego and performance. He was the secure actor comfortable in his role, his greying hair and blunt, masculine features all part of his considered appearance. Beyond that appearance, however, there was also something else, thought Joel, as he rose from his chair. René was a thoroughly decent man; it was a disarming conclusion. God knew they both had their flaws, but they were both decent men; perhaps that was why they enjoyed each other's company.

A firm handshake preceded a brief embrace. The Frenchman sat down across from Converse, as Joel signalled an attentive waiter. "Order in French," he said. "I'd end up getting you a hot fudge sundae."

"This man speaks better English than either of us. Campari and ice, please."

"*Merci, Monsieur.*" The waiter left.

"Thanks again for coming over," said Converse. "I mean it."

"I'm sure you do . . . You look well, Joel, tired but well. That shocking business in Geneva must give you nightmares."

"Not really, I told you, I was simply there."

"Still, it might have been *you*. The newspapers said he died while you held his head."

"I was the first one to reach him."

"How horrible."

"I've seen it happen before, René," said Converse quietly, no comment in his voice.

"Yes, of course. You were better prepared than most, I imagine."

"I don't think anyone's ever prepared . . . But it's over. How about you? How are things?"

Mattilon shook his head, pinching his rugged, weather-beaten features into a sudden look of exasperation. "France is madness of course, but we survive. For months and months now, there are more plans than are stored in an architect's library, but the planners keep colliding with each other in government hallways. The courts are full, business thrives."

"I'm glad to hear it." The waiter returned with the Campari; both men nodded silently, Mattilon's eyes on Joel. "No, I really am," Converse continued, as the waiter walked away. "You hear so many stories."

"Is that why you're in Paris?" The Frenchman studied Joel. "Because of the stories of our so-called upheavals? They're not so earth-shaking, you know, not so different from before. Not *yet*. Most private industry here was publicly financed through the government. But naturally not managed by government incompetents, and for that we may pay. Is that what's bothering you or, more to the point, your clients?"

Converse drank. "No, that's not why I'm here. It's something else."

"You're troubled, I can see that. Your customary glibness doesn't fool me. I know you too well. So tell me, what's so important? That was the word you used on the telephone."

"Yes, I guess it was. It may have been too strong." Joel drained his glass and reached for his cigarettes.

"Not from your eyes, my friend. I see them and I don't see them. They're filled with clouds."

"You've got it wrong. As you said, I'm tired. I've been on planes all day, with some ungodly layovers." He picked up his lighter, snapping it twice until the flame appeared.

"We haggle over foolishness. What is it?"

Converse lit a cigarette, consciously trying to sound casual as he spoke. "Do you know a private club called *Les Étalons Blancs?*"

"I know it, but I couldn't get in the door," replied the Frenchman laughing. "I was a young, inconsequential lieutenant – worse, attached to the *juge-avocat* – essentially with our forces to lend an appearance of legality, but mind you only an appearance. Murder was a misdemeanour, and rape to be congratulated. *Les Étalons Blancs* is a refuge for *les grands militaires* . . . and those rich enough or foolish enough to listen to their trumpets."

"I want to meet someone who lunches there three or four times a week."

"You can't call him?"

"He doesn't know me, doesn't know I want to meet him. It's got to be spontaneous."

"Really? For Talbot, Brooks and Simon? That sounds most unusual."

"It *is*. We may be dealing with someone we don't want to deal with."

"Ahh, missionary work. Who is he?"

"Will you keep it confidential? I mean that, not a word to anyone?"

"Do I breathe? If the name is in conflict with something on our schedule, I will tell you and, frankly, be of no help to you."

"Fair enough. Jacques Louis Bertholdier."

Mattilon arched his brows in mock astonishment, less in mockery than astonishment. "The emperor has all his clothes," said the Frenchman, laughing quietly. "Regardless of who claims otherwise. You start at the top of the line, as they say in New York. No conflict, *mon ami*; he's not in our league – as you also say."

"Why not?"

"He moves with saints and warriors. Warriors who would be saints, and saints who would be warriors. Who has time for such façades?"

"You mean he's not taken seriously?"

"Oh no, he *is*. Very seriously, by those who have the time and the inclination to move abstract mountains. He is a pillar, Joel, grounded in heroic marble and himself immovable. He was the de Gaulle who never followed and some say it is a pity."

"What do you say?"

Mattilon frowned, then cocked his head in a Gallic shrug. "I'm not sure. God knows the country needed someone, and perhaps Bertholdier could have stepped in and steered a far better course than the one we embarked upon, but the times were not right. The Elysée had become an imperial court, and the people were tired of royal edicts, imperial sermons. Well, we don't have *those* any longer; they've been supplanted by the dull, grey banalities of the workers' credo. Perhaps it *is* a pity, although he could still do it, I imagine. He began his climb up Olympus when he was very young."

"Wasn't he part of the OAS? Salan's rebels in Algeria? They were discredited, called a national disgrace."

"*That* is a judgment even the intellectuals must reluctantly admit could be subject to revision. The way all of North Africa and the Middle East has gone, a French Algeria could be a trump card today." Mattilon paused and brought his hand to his chin, his frown returning. "Why on earth would Talbot, Brooks and Simon walk away from Bertholdier? He may be a monarchist at heart, but God knows he's honour personified. He's regal, perhaps even pompous, but a very acceptable client for all of that."

"We've heard things," said Converse quietly, shrugging now himself, as if to lessen the credibility of hearsay evidence.

"*Mon Dieu*, not his *women?*" exclaimed Mattilon laughing. "Come now, when will you grow up?"

"Not women."

"What then?"

"Let's say some of his associates, his acquaintances."

"I hope you make the distinction, Joel. A man like Bertholdier can choose his associates certainly, but not his acquaintances. He walks into a room and everyone wants to be his friend, most claim he is a friend."

"That's what we want to find out. I want to bring up some names, see whether they *are associates* . . . or unremembered acquaintances."

"*Bien*. Now you're making sense. I can help; I *will* help. We shall have lunch at *Les Étalons Blancs* tomorrow and the next day. It is the middle of the week and Bertholdier will no doubt choose one or the other to dine there. If not, there's always the day after."

"I thought you couldn't get in the door?"

"Not by myself, no. But I know someone who can, and he will be most obliging, I can assure you."

"Why?"

"He wishes to talk with me whenever and wherever he can. He's a dreadful bore and unfortunately speaks very little English – numbers mainly, and words like 'In and Out', or 'Over and Out', and 'Dodger-Roger' or 'Rodger-Dodger' and 'Runway Six' or 'Lift-off-Five' and all manner of incomprehensible phrases."

"A *pilot?*"

"He flew the first *Mirages*, brilliantly I might add, and never lets anyone forget it. I shall have to be the interpreter between you, which at least eliminates my having to initiate conversation. Do you know anything about the *Mirage?*"

"A jet's a jet," said Joel. "Pull and sweep out, what else is there?"

"Yes, he's used that one, too. Pull and, sweep something. I thought he was cleaning a kitchen."

"Why does he always want to talk with you? I gather he's a member of the club."

"Very much so. We're representing him in a futile case against an aircraft manufacturer. He had his own private jet, and lost his left foot in one of your crash landings . . ."

"Not mine, pal."

"The door was jammed. He couldn't ground-eject where he wished to, when the plane's speed was sufficiently reduced for him to avoid a final collision."

"He didn't slap the right buttons."

"He says he did."

"There are at least two back-ups, including an instant manual, even on your equipment."

"We've been made aware of that. It's not the money, you understand; he's enormously wealthy. It's his pride. To lose brings into question his current – or if you will, latter day – skills."

"They'll be a lot more in question under cross examination. I assume you've told him that."

"Very gently. It's what we're leading up to."

"But in the meantime every conference is a hefty fee."

"We're also saving him from himself. If we did it swiftly or too crudely, he'd simply dismiss us and be driven to someone far less principled. Who else would take such a case? The government owns the plant now, and God knows it won't pay."

"Good point. What'll you tell him about me? About the club?"

Mattilon smiled. "That as a former pilot *and* an attorney you can bring an expertise to his suit that might be helpful. As to *Les Étalons Blancs*, I shall suggest it, tell him you'd be impressed. I shall describe you as something of an Attila the Hun of the skies. How does that appeal to you?"

"With very little impact."

"Can you carry it off?" asked the Frenchman. The question was sincere. "It would be one way to meet Bertholdier. My client and he are not simply acquaintances, they *are* friends."

"I'll carry it off."

"Your having been a prisoner of war will be most helpful. If you see Bertholdier enter, and express a desire to meet him, such requests are not lightly refused former POWs."

"I wouldn't press that too hard," said Converse.

"Why not?"

"A little digging could turn up a rock that doesn't belong in the soil."

"Oh?" Mattilon's brows arched again, neither in mockery nor astonishment, simply surprise. " 'Digging', as you use it, implies something more than a spontaneous meeting with odd names spontaneously thrown about."

"Does it?" Joel revolved his glass, annoyed with himself, knowing that any argument would only enlarge the lapse. "Sorry, it was an instinctive reaction. You know how I feel about that topic."

"Yes, I do, and I forgot. How careless of me. I apologize."

"Actually, I'd just as soon not use my own name. Do you mind?"

"You're the missionary, not I. What shall we call you?" The Frenchman was now looking hard at Converse.

"It doesn't matter."

Mattilon squinted. "How about the name of your employer, Simon? If you meet Bertholdier, it might appeal to him. *Le duc de St Simon* was the purest chronicler of the monarchy . . . Henry Simon. There must be ten thousand lawyers named Henry Simon in the States."

"Simon it is."

"You've told me everything, my friend?" asked René, his eyes non-committal.

"Everything you care to."

"Yes, I have," said Joel, his own eyes a blue-white wall. "Let's have another drink."

"I think not. It's late and my current wife has *malaise if* her dinner is cold. She's an excellent cook, incidentally."

"You're a lucky man."

"Yes, I am." Mattilon finished his drink, placed the glass on the table and spoke casually. "So was Valerie. I shall never forget that fantastic duck a *l'orange* she fixed for us three or four years ago in New York. Do you ever hear from her?"

"Hear and see," answered Converse. "I had lunch with her in Boston last month. I gave her the alimony cheque and she picked up the tab. By the way, her paintings are beginning to sell."

"I never doubted that they would."

"She did."

"Unnecessarily . . . I always liked Val. If you see her again, please give her my affectionate best."

"I will."

Mattilon rose from the upholstered chair, his eyes no longer non-committal. "Forgive me, I thought so often you were such a . . . matched pair, I believe is the expression." The passions dwindle, of course, but not the *de suite*, if you know what I mean."

"I think I do, and speaking for both of us, I thank you for the misplaced concretion."

"*Je ne comprends pas.*"

"Forget it, it's antiquated – doesn't mean anything. I'll give her your affectionate best."

"*Merci.* I'll phone you in the morning."

Les Étalons Blancs was a pacifist's nightmare. The club's heavy dark wood walls were covered with photographs and prints, interspersed with framed citations and glistening medals – red ribbons and gold and silver discs cushioned on black velvet, throwing back the light, drawing all eyes, which then strayed to the pictures. They were a visual record of heroic carnage going back two centuries. The linear drawings evolved into products of film, as the horses and caissons and sabres became motorcycles, tanks, planes and guns, but the scenes were not all that different, the themes constant. Victorious men in uniform were depicted in moments of glory; whatever suffering there might have been was strangely absent, only stern purpose and awareness shining in their eyes and apparent in their postures. These men did not lose, no missing limbs or shattered faces here; these were the privileged warriors, somehow unscathed yet scathing, genuine arrogance found in their life-long missions. And Joel felt a profound fear as he studied the martial array. These were not ordinary men, nor did they care to be; they scorned the ordinary as unthinkable for them, perhaps only to be commanded by them. They were hard and strong and the word "capability" was written across their countless faces. What had Beale said on Mykonos? What had been the judgment of the Red Fox of Inchon, a man who knew whereof he spoke?

. . . I know what they can do when we ask them to do it. Yet how much more could they do if they asked it of themselves, wondered Joel. Without the searching, vacillating impediments of civilian authorities?

"Luboque has just arrived," said Mattilon quietly, coming up behind Converse. "I heard his voice in the lobby. Remember, you don't have to overdo it – I'll translate what I think is appropriate anyway – but nod profoundly when he makes one of his angry remarks. Also laugh when he tells jokes; they're dreadful, but he likes it."

"I'll do my best."

"I'll give you an incentive. Bertholdier has a reservation for lunch. At his usual place, table eleven, by the window."

"Where are *we?*" asked Joel, seeing the pressed lips of minor triumph on the Frenchman's face.

"Table twelve. Now."

"If I ever need a lawyer, I'll call you."

"We're terribly expensive. Come now, as they say in all those wonderful films of yours. 'You're on, Monsieur Simon.' Play the role of Attila but don't overplay it."

"You know, René, for someone who speaks English as well as you do, you gravitate to the tritest phrases."

"The English language and American phrases have very little in common, Joel, trite or otherwise."

"Smart ass."

"Need I say more? . . . *Ahh*, Monsieur Luboque, Serge, *mon ami!*"

Mattilon's third eye had spotted the entrance of Serge Luboque; he pivoted in place as the thumping became louder on the floor – lending also a certain credibility to the lawyer's hearing. Luboque was a short, slender man, his physique giving rise to the images of those early jet pilots when compactness was a requirement. He was also very close to being a caricature of himself. His short, waxed moustache was affixed to a miniaturized face that was pinched in vaguely hostile dismissal. It was directed both at no one and everyone. The effect was important, not the content. Whatever he had been before, Luboque was now a *poseur* who knew his postures; it was all he had to know. A brilliant and exciting past had disappeared for him; he had only the memories, the rest was anger.

"*Et voici l'expert légal des compagnies aériennes,*" he said, looking at Converse, extending his hand for Joel's grasp.

"Serge is delighted to meet you and is sure you can help us," explained Mattilon.

"I'll do what I can," said Converse. "And apologize for my not speaking French."

The lawyer obviously did so, as Luboque shrugged, speaking rapidly, incomprehensibly; the word *anglais* repeated several times.

"He, too, apologizes for not speaking English," said Mattilon, glancing at Joel, mischievousness in his look, as he added, "If he's lying, Monsieur Simon, we may both be placed against these decorated walls and shot?"

"No way," said Converse, smiling. "Our executioners might dent the metals and blow up the pictures. Everybody knows you're lousy shots."

"*Qu'est-ce que vous dites?*"

"*Monsieur Simon tient à vous remercier de ce déjeuner,*" said Mattilon, turning to his client. "*Il en est très fier car il estime que l'officier français est le meilleur du monde.*"

"What did you say?"

"I explained," said the lawyer, turning again, "that you were honoured to be here as you believe the French military – especially the officer corps – to be the finest on earth."

"Not only lousy shots but rotten pilots," said Joel, smiling and nodding profoundly.

"*Est-il vrai que vous avez pris part à de nombreuses missions dans l'Asie du Sud?*" asked Luboque, his eyes fixed on Converse.

"I beg your pardon?"

"He wants it confirmed that you are really an Attila of the skies, that you flew many missions."

"Quite a few," answered Joel.

"*Beaucoup,*" said Mattilon.

Luboque again spoke rapidly, even more incomprehensibly, as he snapped his fingers for a steward.

"What now?"

"He'd rather tell you, about *his* exploits – in the interests of the case, of course."

"Of course," said Converse, his smile now fixed. "Lousy shots, rotten pilots and insufferable egos."

"Ah, but our food, our women, our incomparable understanding of life."

"There's a very explicit word in French – one of the few I learned from my ex-wife – but I don't think I should use it." Joel's smile was now cemented to his lips.

"That's right, I forgot," said Mattilon. "She and I would converse in *la belle langue*; it used to irritate you so . . . Don't use it. Remember your incentive."

"*Qu'est-ce que vous dites encore? La belle langue?*" Luboque spoke as a steward stood by his side.

"*Notre ami, Monsieur Simon, suivra un cours à l'école Berlitz et pourra ainsi s'entretenir directement avec vous.*"

"*Bien!*"

"What?"

"I told him you would learn the Berlitz French so you could dine with him whenever you flew into Paris. You're to ring him up. Nod . . . smart ass."

Converse nodded.

And so it went. Point, non-counter point, *non sequitur*. Serge Luboque held forth during drinks in the warrior's playroom, Mattilon translating, in each case advising Joel as to the expression that should appear on his face as well as suggesting an appropriate reply, which he would deliver in any event.

Finally Luboque stridently described the crash which had cost him his left foot and the obvious equipment failures for which he should be compensated. Converse looked properly pained and indignant, and offered to write a legal opinion for the court, based on his expertise as a pilot of jet aircraft. Mattilon translated; Luboque beamed and rattled off a barrage of consonated vowels that Joel took for thanks.

"He's forever in your debt," said René.

"Not if I write that opinion," replied Converse. "He locked himself in the cockpit and threw away the key."

"Write it," countered Mattilon, smiling. "You've just paid for my time. We'll use it as a wedge to open the door of retreat. Also, he'll never ask you to dinner when you're in Paris."

"When's lunch? I'm running out of expressions."

It came, or more precisely, they marched in hesitant lock-step into it, matching Luboque's thumping foot against the hard, ornate parquet floor. The ridiculous, three-sided conversation continued as wine was proffered – a bottle sent back by the sneering *poseur* – and Converse's eyes kept straying to the dining room's entrance.

The moment came. Bertholdier arrived. He stood in the open archway, his head turned slightly to his left as another man in a light brown gabardine topcoat spoke without expression. The general nodded his head and the subordinate retreated. Then the soldier walked in with a quiet vitality, with a grandiosity borne of his own self-understood impact, no flourishes required. Heads turned and they were acknowledged, the man's eyes piercing into each, accepting each as a great dauphin, who will soon be king, accepts the attention of the ministers of a failing monarch. The effect was extraordinary, for there were no kingdoms, no monarchies, no lands to be divided through conquest to the knights of Crécy or anybody else, but this *man* was quietly being accorded the arrival of . . . *goddamn it*, thought Joel . . . an *emperor* of his own.

Jacques Louis Bertholdier was of medium height, between 5,9' and 5' 11', certainly no more, but his bearing – the sheer straight shaft of his posture, the breadth of his shoulders and the length of his strong slender neck made him appear much taller, much more imposing than another might to a less anticipatory group. He was among his own, and here, indeed, he was above the others, elevated by their own consensus.

"Say something reverential," said Mattilon, as Bertholdier approached, heading for the table next to theirs. "Glance up at him and look suitably awed. I'll do the rest."

Converse did as he was told, uttering Bertholdier's full name under his breath, but loud enough to be heard. He followed this quiet exclamation by leaning toward Mattilon and saying, "He's a man I've always wanted to meet."

There followed a brief exchange in French between René and his client, whereupon Luboque nodded, his expression that of an arrogant man pleased to dispense a favour to a new friend.

Bertholdier reached his chair, the *mâtre* and his head waiter hovering on either side. The pavane took place less than four feet away.

"*Mon Général*," said Luboque, rising.

"*Serge*," replied Bertholdier, stepping forward, hand extended, a superior officer aware of a worthy subordinate's disability. "*Comment ça va?*"

"*Bien, Jacques. Et vous?*"

The greetings were brief, the direction of the conversation changed quickly by Luboque, who gestured at Converse, as he continued speaking. Instinctively, Joel got to his feet, posture straight, his eyes level, unblinking, staring at Bertholdier, his look as piercing as the general's, professional but without awe . . . He had been right – in an unexpected way. The South-east Asian connection had validity for Jacques Louis Bertholdier. And why not? He, too, had his memories. Mattilon was introduced almost as an afterthought, the soldier nodding, as he crossed behind René to shake hands with Joel.

"A pleasure, Monsieur Simon," said Bertholdier, his English precise, his grip firm, a comrade acknowledging another comrade, the man's imperious charm instantly apparent.

69

"I'm sure you've heard it thousands of times, sir," said Joel, maintaining the steady, professional burn in his eyes, "but this is an occasion I never expected. If I may, General, it's an honour to meet you."

"It is an honour to meet *you*," rejoined Bertholdier. "You gentlemen-of-the-air did all you could, and I know something about the circumstances. So many missions! I think it was easier on the ground!" The general laughed quietly, the celebrated now acknowledging a worthy uncelebrated comrade-in-arms.

Gentlemen-of-the-air; the man's unreal, thought Converse. But the connection was firm; *it* was real, he felt it, he *knew* it. The combination of words and looks had brought it about. So simple; a lawyer's ruse, taming an adversary – in this case an enemy. The enemy.

"I couldn't agree with that, General; it was a lot cleaner in the air. But if there'd been more like you on the ground in Indochina, there never would have been a Dienbienphu."

"A flattering statement, but I'm not sure it could stand the test of reality."

"I'm sure," said Joel quietly, clearly. "I'm convinced of it."

Luboque, who had been engaged in conversation by a knowing Mattilon, interrupted. "*Mon Général, voulez vous vous joindre à nous?*"

"*Je m'excuse. Je suis occupé . . . mes invités,*" answered Bertholdier, turning back to Converse. "I must decline Serge's invitation, I'm expecting guests. He tells me you are an attorney, a specialist in aircraft litigation."

"It's part of the broader field, yes. Air, ground, oceangoing craft . . . we try to represent the spectrum. Actually, I'm fairly new at it – not the expertise, I hope – but the representation."

"I see," said the general, obviously bewildered. "Are you in Paris on business?"

This was it, thought Joel. The words, the eyes, and the voice had to join in subtle evocation. Especially the eyes; they had to convey the unspoken. "No, I'm just here to catch my breath. I flew from San Francisco to New York and on to Paris. Tomorrow I'll be in Bonn for a day or so, then off to Tel Aviv."

"How tiring for you." Bertholdier was now returning his stare.

"Not the worst, I'm afraid," said Converse, a half smile on his lips. "After Tel Aviv, there's a night flight to Johannesburg."

"Bonn, Tel Aviv, Johannesburg . . ." The soldier spoke softly, his eyes much louder. "A most unusual itinerary."

"Productive, we think. At least, we hope so."

"We?"

"My client, General. My new client."

"*Déraisonnable!*" cried Mattilon, laughing at something Luboque had said, and, just as obviously, telling Joel he could no longer keep his impatient litigant in conversation.

Bertholdier, however, did not take his eyes off Converse. "Where are you staying, my young fighter-pilot friend?"

"Young and not so young, General."

"Where?"

"The George V. Suite two-three-five."

"A fine establishment."

"It's habit. My previous firm always posted me there."

"Posted? As in garrisoned?" asked Bertholdier, a half smile now on his lips.

"An unconscious slip," said Joel. "But then again, it says it, doesn't it, sir?"

"It does, indeed . . . Ah ha, my guests arrive!" The soldier extended his hand. "It's been a pleasure, Monsieur Simon."

Swift *au revoirs* accompanied nods and rapid handshakes, as Bertholdier returned to his table to greet his luncheon companions. Through Mattilon, Joel thanked Luboque for the introduction; the disabled pilot gestured with both hands, palms in the giving position, and Converse had the distinct feeling that he had been baptized. The insane, three-sided dialogue then resumed at high speed, and it was all Joel could do to maintain even minimum concentration.

Progress had been made; it was in Bertholdier's eyes, and he could feel those eyes straying over to him through the animated conversation taking place at both tables. The General was diagonally to Converse's left; the slightest turning of either face and the line of sight between them was direct. Twice it happened. The first time, Joel felt the forceful gaze resting on him as if two shafts of magnified sunlight were burning the flesh at his temple. He shifted his head barely inches; their eyes locked, the soldier's penetrating, questioning, severe. The second occasion took place a half hour later, this exchange prompted by Converse himself. Luboque and Mattilon were discussing legal strategy and, as if drawn by a magnet, Joel slowly turned to his left and watched Bertholdier, who was quietly, emphatically making a point with one of his guests. Suddenly, as a voice replied across the adjacent table, the General snapped his head in Converse's direction, his eyes no longer questioning, only cold and ice-like. Then just as abruptly, there was warmth in them; the celebrated soldier nodded, a half-smile on his face.

Joel sat in the soft leather chair by the window in the dimly-lit sitting room; what light there was came from a fringed lamp on the desk. Alternately, he stared at the telephone in front of the lamp, and then turned and looked out of the window at the weaving night traffic of Paris, and the lights on the wide boulevard below – but not for long the night outside. He kept returning to the phone, his focus isolating it, framing it, giving it a substance he so frequently gave telephones when waiting for a call from a legal adversary he expected to capitulate, knowing that man or woman *would* capitulate. It was simply a question of time.

He expected no capitulation now, only communication, a connection, *the* connection. In what form it would take, he had no idea, but it would come. It had to come.

It was nearly 7.30, four hours since he had left *Les Étalons Blancs*, and a final, firm handshake exchanged with Jacques Louis Bertholdier. The look in the soldier's eyes was unmistakable: If nothing else, Converse reasoned, Bertholdier would have to satisfy his sheer curiosity.

Joel had covered himself with the hotel's front desk, distributing several well-placed 100-franc notes. The device was not at all unusual in these days of national and financial unrest – had not been for years, actually, unrest notwithstanding. Visiting businessmen frequently chose to use *noms de commerce* for any number of reasons, ranging from negotiations best kept quiet to amorous engagements best left untraceable. In Converse's case, the use of the name, Simon, made it appear logical, if not eminently respectable. If Talbot, Brooks and Simon preferred that all communications be made in the surname of one of the senior partners, who could question the decision? Joel, however, carried the ploy one step farther. After telephoning New York, he explained, he was told that his own name was not to be used at all; no one knew he was in Paris and that was the way his firm wanted it. Obviously, the delayed instructions accounted for the mix up in the reservation, which was void at any rate. There was to be no billing; he would pay in cash, and since this was Paris, no one raised the slightest objection. Cash was infinitely preferable, delayed payment a national anathema.

Whether anyone believed this nonsense or not was irrelevant. The logic was sufficiently adequate and the franc notes persuasive; the original registration card was torn up and another placed in the hotel file. H. Simon replaced J. Converse. The permanent address of the former was a figment of Joel's imagination, a numbered house on a numbered street in Chicago, Illinois, said house and said street most likely non-existent. Anyone asking or calling for Mr Converse – which was highly unlikely – would be told no guest of that name was currently at the George V. Even René Mattilon was not a problem for Joel had been specific. Since he had no further business in Paris, he was taking the 6 o'clock shuttle to London and staying with friends for several days before flying back to New York. He thanked René profusely, telling the Frenchman that his firm's fears about Bertholdier had been groundless. During their quiet conversation he had brought up three key names with the general, each greeted with a blank look from Bertholdier, who proceeded to apologize if his memory was faulty.

"He wasn't lying," Joel had said.

"I can't imagine why he would," Mattilon had replied.

I can, Converse had thought to himself. They call it *Aquitaine*.

A crack! There was a sudden intrusion of sound, a harsh metallic snap then another, and another . . . the tumblers of a lock falling out of place, a knob being turned. It came from beyond the open door to the bedroom. Joel bolted forward in his chair; then, looking at his watch, just as rapidly he expelled his breath and relaxed. It was the hour when the floor maid turned down the bed; the tension of the expected call and what it represented had frayed his nerves. Again he leaned back, his gaze resting on the telephone. When would it ring? *Would* it ring? The minutes were passing so slowly, the hours too quickly.

"*Pardon, Monsieur,*" said a feminine voice, accompanied by light tapping on the open door frame. Joel could not see the speaker.

"Yes?" Converse forced his eyes away from the silent phone.

What greeted him, however, was not the appearance of a uniformed maid, but instead a sight that caused him to silently gasp. It was the figure of Jacques Louis Bertholdier, his posture erect, his angled head rigid, his eyes a strange mixture of cold appraisal, condescension, and – if Joel was not mistaken – a trace of fear.

He walked through the door and stood motionless; when he spoke his voice was a rippling sheet of ice.

"I was on my way to a dinner engagement on the fourth floor, Monsieur Simon. By chance, I remembered you were in this very hotel. You did give me the number of your suite. Do I intrude?"

"Of course not, General," said Converse, on his feet.

"Did you expect me?"

"Not this way."

"But you did expect me?"

Joel paused. "Yes."

"A signal sent and received?"

Again Joel paused. "Yes."

"You are either a provocatively subtle attorney or a strangely obsessed man. Which is it, Monsieur Simon?"

"If I provoked you into coming to see me and I was subtle about it, I'll accept that gladly. As to being obsessed, the word implies an exaggerated or unwarranted concern. Whatever concerns I have, I know damned well they're neither exaggerated nor unwarranted. No obsession, General. I'm too good a lawyer for that."

"A pilot cannot lie to himself. If he does so blindly, he crashes to his death."

"I've been shot down. I've never crashed through pilot error."

Bertholdier walked slowly to the brocaded couch against the wall. "Bonn, Tel Aviv and Johannesburg," he said quietly as he lowered himself, sitting down and crossing his legs. "The signal?"

"The signal."

"My company has interests in those areas."

"So does my client," said Converse.

"And what do *you* have, Monsieur Simon?"

Joel stared at the soldier. "A commitment, General."

Bertholdier was silent, his body immobile, his eyes searching. "May I have a brandy?" he said finally. "My escort will remain in the corridor outside this door."

4

Converse walked to the small bar against the wall, conscious of the soldier's gaze, wondering which tack the conversation would take. He was oddly calm, the way he frequently was before a merger conference, or a pre-trial examination, knowing he knew things his adversaries were not aware of – buried information that had surfaced through long hours of hard work. In the present circumstances, there had been no work at all on his part, but the results were the same. He knew a great deal about the legend across the room named Jacques Louis

Bertholdier. In a word, Joel was prepared, and over the years he had learned to trust his on-the-feet instincts . . . as he had once trusted those that had guided him through the skies years ago.

Also, as it was part of his job, he was familiar with the legal intricacies of import-export manipulations. They were a maze of often disconnected authorizations, easily made baffling for the untrained ear, and during the next few minutes he intended to baffle this disciple of George Marcus Delavane – warlord of Saigon – until the soldier's trace of fear became something far more pronounced.

Clearances for foreign shipments came in a wide variety of shapes and colours, from the basic export licence with specific bills of lading, to those with the less specific generic limitations. Then up – or out – to the more coveted licences entailing a wide variety of products subject to governmental reviews and usually shunted back and forth between vacillating departments until deadlines forced bureaucratic decisions – often based on whose influence was the strongest, or whom among the bureaucrats were the weakest.

Finally, there was the most lethal authorization of all, a document too frequently received in corruption and delivered in blood. It was called the *End-User's Certificate*, an innocuously-named permit that was a licence to ship the most abusive merchandise in the nation's arsenals into air and sea lanes beyond the controls of those who should have them.

In theory, this deadly equipment was intended solely for allied governments with shared objectives, thus the "use' at the discretion of the parties at the receiving "end' – calculated death legitimized by a "certificate" that obfuscated everyone's intentions. But once *en route*, diversion was the practice. Shipments destined for the Bay of Haifa or Alexandria would find their way to the Gulf of Sidra and a precocious madman in Libya, or to an assassin named Carlos training killer teams anywhere from Beirut to the Sahara. Fictional corporations with non-existent – yet strangely influential – officers operated through obscure brokers in shadows and out of hastily-constructed or out-of-the-way warehouses in the US and abroad. Millions upon millions were to be made; death was merely a consequence and there was a phrase for it all. Boardroom terrorism. It fitted, and it would be the way of Aquitaine. There was no other.

These were the thoughts, the methods of operation that rapidly, like flashes of cards, leaped through Converse's mind as he poured the drinks. He was ready; he turned and walked across the room.

"What are you seeking, Monsieur Simon?" asked Bertholdier, taking the brandy from Converse.

"Information, General."

"About what?"

"World markets – expanding markets that my client might service." Joel crossed back to the chair by the window and sat down.

"And what sort of service does he render?"

"He's a broker."

"Of what?"

"A wide range of products." Converse brought his glass to his lips; he drank, then added, "I think I mentioned them in general terms at your club this afternoon. Planes, vehicles, ocean-going craft, munitions material. The spectrum."

"Yes, you did. I'm afraid I did not understand."

"My client has access to production and warehouse sources beyond anyone I've ever known or ever heard of."

"Very impressive. Who is he?"

"I'm not at liberty to say."

"Perhaps I know him."

"You might, but not in the way I've described him. His profile is so low in this area, it's non-existent."

"And you won't tell me who he is," said Bertholdier.

"It's privileged information."

"Yet in your own words, you sought me out, sent a signal to which I responded, and now say you want information concerning expanding markets for all manner of merchandise, including Bonn, Tel Aviv, and Johannesburg. But you won't divulge the name of your client who will benefit if I have this information – which I probably do not. Surely you can't be serious."

"*You have* the information, and yes, I'm very serious. But I'm afraid you've jumped to the wrong conclusion."

"I have no fear of it at all. My English is fluent and I heard what you said. You came out of nowhere, I know nothing about you; you speak elusively of this unnamed influential man."

"You *asked* me, General," interrupted Joel firmly, without raising his voice. "What I was seeking."

"And you said information."

"Yes, I did, but I didn't say I was seeking it from you."

"I beg your pardon?"

"Under the circumstances – for the reasons you just mentioned – you wouldn't give it to me anyway, and I'm well aware of that."

"Then what is the point of this . . . shall I say induced conversation? I do not like my time trifled with, Monsieur."

"That's the last thing on earth we'd do – *I'd do.*"

"Please be specific."

"My client wants your trust. *I* want it. But we know it can't be given until you feel it's justified. In a few days – a week at the outside – I hope to prove that it is."

"By trips to Bonn, Tel Aviv . . . Johannesburg?"

"Frankly, yes."

"Why?"

"You said it a few minutes ago. The signal."

Bertholdier was suddenly wary. He shrugged too casually; he was pulling back. "I said it because my company has considerable investments in those areas. I thought was entirely plausible you had a proposition, or propositions, to make relative to those interests."

"I intend to have."

"Please be specific," said the soldier, controlling his irritation.

"You know I can't," replied Joel. "Not yet."

"When?"

"When it's clear to you – all of you – that my client, and by extension myself, have as strong motives for being a part of you as the most dedicated among you."

"A part of my company? *Juneau et Cie?*"

"Forgive me, General, I won't bother to answer that."

Bertholdier glanced at the brandy in his hand, then back at Converse. "You say you flew from San Francisco."

"I'm not based there," broke in Joel.

"But you came from San Francisco. To Paris. Why *were* you there?"

"I'll answer that if for no other reason than to show you how thorough we are . . . and how much more thorough others are. We traced – *I* traced – overseas shipments back to export licences originating in the northern California area. The licencees were companies with no histories and warehouses with no records – chains of four walls erected for brief, temporary periods of convenience. It was a mass of confusion leading nowhere and everywhere. Names on documents where no such people existed, documents themselves that came out of bureaucratic labyrinths virtually untraceable – rubber stamps, official seals, and signatures of authorization where no authority was granted. Unknowing medium-level personnel told to expedite departmental clearances . . . That's what I found in San Francisco. A morass of complex, highly questionable transactions that could not bear intense scrutiny."

Bertholdier's eyes were fixed, too controlled. "I would know nothing about such things, of course," he said.

"Of course," agreed Converse. "But the fact that my client does – through me – and the additional fact that neither he nor I have any desire whatsoever to call attention to them must tell you something."

"Frankly, not a thing."

"Please, General. One of the first principles of free enterprise is to cripple your competition, step in, and fill the void."

The soldier drank, gripping the glass firmly. He lowered it and spoke. "Why did you come to me?"

"Because you were there."

"What?"

"Your name was there – among the morass, way down deep, but there."

Bertholdier shot forward. "Impossible! *Preposterous!*"

"Then why am I here? Why are *you* here?" Joel placed his glass on the table by the chair, the movement that of a man not finished speaking. "Try to understand me. Depending upon which government department a person's dealing with, certain recommendations are bound to be helpful. You wouldn't do a damn thing for someone appealing to Housing and Urban Development, but over at the State Department's Munitions Controls or at Pentagon procurements, you're golden."

"I have never lent my name to any such appeals."

"Others did. Men whose recommendations carried a lot of weight, but who perhaps needed extra clout."

"*Quest ce que vous dites?* This clout."

"A final push for an affirmative decision ... without any apparent personal involvement. It's called support for an action through viable second and third parties. For instance, a memo might read: 'We – the department, not a person – don't know much about this, but if a man like General Bertholdier is favourably disposed, and we are informed that he is, why should, we argue?' "

"*Never.* It could not happen."

"It did," said Converse softly, knowing it was the moment to bring in reality to support his abstractions. He would be able to tell instantly if Beale was right, if this legend of France was responsible for the slaughter and chaos in the cities and towns of a violently upended Northern Ireland. "You were there, not often but enough for me to find you ... Just as you were there in a different way when a shipment was air freighted out of Beloit, Wisconsin, on its way to Tel Aviv. Of course it never got there, somehow diverted to maniacs on both sides in Belfast. I wonder where it happened? Montreal? Paris? Marseilles? The Separatists in Quebec would certainly follow your orders, as would men in Paris and Marseilles. It's a shame a company named Solidaire had to pay off the insurance claim. Oh, yes, you're a director of the firm, aren't you? And it s so convenient that insurance carriers have access to the merchandise they cover."

Bertholdier was frozen to the chair, the muscles of his face pulsating, his eyes wide and staring at Joel. His guilt was suppressed, but no less for that control. "I cannot believe what you are implying. It's shocking and incredible!"

"I repeat, why am I here?"

"Only you can answer that, Monsieur," said Bertholdier, abruptly getting to his feet, the brandy in his hand. Then slowly, with military grace, he leaned over and lowered the glass to the coffee table; it was a gesture of finality; the conference was over. "Quite obviously I made a foolish error," he continued, straightening up, shoulders square again, head rigid again, but now with a strained yet oddly convincing smile on his lips. "I am a soldier, not a businessman; it is a late direction in my life. A soldier tries to seize an initiative and I attempted to do just that, only there was – there *is* – no initiative. Forgive me, I misread your signal this afternoon."

"You didn't misread anything, General."

"Am I contradicted by a stranger – I might even say a devious stranger – who arranges a meeting under false pretences and proceeds to make outrageous statements regarding my honour and my conduct? I think not." Bertholdier strode across the room toward the hallway door; Joel rose from his chair. "Don't bother, Monsieur, I'll let myself out. You've gone to enough trouble, for what purpose I haven't the faintest idea."

"I'm on my way to Bonn," interrupted Converse. "Tell your friends I'm coming. Tell them to expect me. And please, General, tell them not to prejudge me. I mean that."

"Your elliptical references are most annoying ... Lieutenant. It was 'lieutenant' wasn't it? Unless you also deceived poor Luboque as well."

"Whatever deception I employed to meet you can only be for his benefit. I've offered to write a legal opinion for his case. He may not like it, but it'll save him a lot of pain and money. And I have not deceived you."

"A matter of judgment, I think." Bertholdier turned and reached for the outsized brass knob.

"*Bonn*, Germany," pressed Joel.

"I heard you. I haven't the vaguest notion what you . . ."

"Leifhelm," said Converse quietly. "Erich Leifhelm."

The soldier's head turned slowly; his eyes were banked fires, the coals glowing, about to erupt with a gust of wind. "A name known to me, but not the man."

"Tell him I'm coming."

"Good night, Monsieur," said Bertholdier, opening the door, his face ashen, his eyes inflamed by that sudden uncontrollable wind.

Joel raced into the bedroom, grabbed his suitcase which was against the wall and threw it on the luggage rack. He had to get out of Paris immediately, tonight. Within hours, perhaps minutes, Bertholdier would have him watched, and if he was followed to an airport, his passport would expose the name Simon as a lie. He could not let that happen, not yet.

It was so strange, so unsettling. He had never had any reason to leave a hotel surreptitiously, on short notice, *without* notice. He was not sure he knew how to do it, only that it had to be done. The altering of the registration card came instinctively; there were occasions when legal negotiations had to be kept quiet for everyone's benefit – not the least, in reverse, the stock manipulators – but this was different. It was so . . . abnormal. He had said to Beale on Mykonos that he was going to become someone he was not. It was an easy thing to say, not at all easy to do.

His suitcase packed, he checked the battery charge on his electric razor and absently turned it on, moving it around his chin, as he walked to the bedside telephone. He shut the switch off as he dialled, unsure of what he would say to the assistant *directeur* nevertheless instinctively orienting his mind to a business approach. After initial remarks, mutually flattering, the words came.

"There's an extremely sensitive situation, and my firm is anxious that I leave for London just as soon as possible . . . and as discreetly as possible. Frankly, I would prefer not to be seen checking out."

"Discretion, Monsieur, is honoured here, and haste is a normal request. I shall come up and present your bill myself. Say, ten minutes?"

"I've only one piece of luggage. I'll carry it, but I'll need a cab. Not in front."

"Not in front, of course. The freight elevator, Monsieur. It connects below with our corridor for deliveries. Arrangements will be made."

"I've made arrangements!" said Jacques Louis Bertholdier harshly into the limousine's mobile phone, the glass partition between him and the chauffeur tightly shut. "One man remains in the gallery in sight of the elevators, another in the

78

cellars where the hotel supplies are brought in. If he attempts to leave during the night, it is the only other exit available to him. I've used it myself on several occasions."

"This . . . is all most difficult to absorb." The voice on the line spoke with a clipped British accent, the speaker obviously astonished, his breathing audible, a man suddenly afraid. "Are you sure? Could there be some other linkage?"

"Imbecile! I repeat. He knew about the munitions shipment from Beloit! He knew the routing, even the method of theft, going so far as to identify *Solidaire* and my position as a board member! He made a *direct* reference to our business associate in *Bonn! Then* to Tel Aviv . . . *Johannesburg! What* other linkage *could* there be?"

"Corporate entanglements, perhaps. One can't rule them out. Multinational subsidiaries, munitions investments, our associate in West Germany also sits on several boards . . . and the locations – money *pours into* them."

"What in the name of God do you think I'm talking about? I can say no more now, but what I've told you, my English *flower*, take it to be the worst!"

There was a brief silence from London. "I understand," said the voice of a subordinate rebuked.

"I hope you do. Get in touch with New York. His name is Seemón, Henri Seemón."

"What?"

"*Henree Seemón*. He's an attorney from Chicago. I have the address; it's from the hotel's registration file." Bertholdier squinted under the glare of the reading lamp, haltingly deciphering the numbers and the numbered street written down by a senior page, well paid by one of the general's men to go into the office and obtain information on the occupant of Suite two-three-five. "Do you have that?"

"Yes," was the reply, the voice now speaking sharply, a subordinate about to redress a grievance. "Was it wise to get it that way? A friend or a greedy employee might tell him someone was inquiring about him."

"*Really*, my British *daffodil*? An innocuous page checking the registry so as to post a lost garment to a recent guest?"

Again the brief silence. "Yes, I see. You know, Jacques, we work for a great cause – a *business* cause, of course – more important than either of us, as we did once years ago. I must constantly remind myself of that, or I don't think I could tolerate your insults."

"And what would be your recourse, *Anglais?*"

"To cut your arrogant Frog balls off in Trafalgar Square and stuff them in a lion's mouth. The repository wouldn't have to be large; an ancient crack would do . . . I'll ring you up in an hour or so." There was a click and the line went dead.

The soldier held the mobile phone in his hand. He lowered it in front of his eyes, a smile slowly emerging on his lips. They were the *best, all* of them! They were the hope, the only hope of a very sick world.

Then the smile faded, the blood again draining from his face, arrogance turning into fear. What did this Henry Simon want, *really* want? Who was the unknown man with access to extraordinary sources . . . planes, vehicles, *munitions*? *What* in God's name did they know? What were they *doing*?

The padded elevator descended slowly, its interior designed for moving furniture and luggage, its speed adjusted for room service deliveries. The assistant *directeur* stood beside Joel, his face pleasantly impassive; in his right hand was the leather *bourse* containing a copy of Converse's bill and the franc notes covering it – as well as a substantial gratuity for the Frenchman's courtesy.

A slight whirring sound preceded the stop; the panel light shone behind the letters *Sous-sol* and the heavy doors parted. Beyond in the wide hallway was a platoon of white-jacketed waiters, maids, porters, and a few maintenance personnel, commandeering tables, racks of linens, luggage and assorted cleaning materials. Loud, rapid chatter, heightened by bursts of laughter and guttural expletives, accompanied the bustling activity. At the sight of the assistant *directeur*, there was a perceptible lessening of volume and an increase of concentrated movement, nods and fawning smiles directed at the man who, with the flick of a pen, could eliminate their jobs.

"If you'll just point me in the right direction, I'll be on my way," said Joel, not wishing to call further attention to himself in the company of the *directeur*. "I've taken up too much of your time."

"*Merci*. If you will follow that corridor, it will lead to the service exit," replied the Frenchman, pointing to a hallway on the left, beyond the bank of elevators. "The guard is at his desk and is aware of your departure. Outside in the alley, turn right and walk to the street; your taxi is waiting for you."

"I appreciate – my *firm* appreciates – your cooperation. As I mentioned upstairs, there's nothing really that secretive, or unusual . . . just sensitive."

The hotel man's impassive countenance did not change, except for a slightly sharper focus in his eyes. "It is of no matter, Monsieur, an explanation is not required. I did not request it and, if you'll forgive me, you should not feel an obligation to offer one. *Au'voir*, Monsieur Simon."

"Yes, of course," said Converse, maintaining his composure despite the fact he felt like a schoolboy admonished for speaking out of turn, for offering an answer when he had not been called upon. "See you next time I'm in Paris."

"We await the day, Monsieur. *Bon soir*."

Joel turned quickly, making his way through the uniformed crowd toward the hallway, apologizing whenever his suitcase made contact with a body. He had just been taught a lesson, one he should not have had to learn. He knew it in a courtroom and in conference: Never explain what you don't have to. Shut up. But this was not a court, or a conference. It was, it suddenly dawned on him, something quite different. It was an escape, and the realization was a little frightening, certainly very strange. Or was it? Escape was in his vocabulary, in his experience. He had tried it three times before in his life – years ago. And death had been everywhere. He put it out of his mind and walked down the corridor toward the large metal door in the distance.

He slowed down; something was wrong. Ahead, standing in front of the security desk talking to the guard, was a man in a light coloured topcoat. Joel had seen him before but he did not know where; then the man moved and Converse began to remember; an image came back to him. Another man had moved the same way – taking several steps backward before turning – in the previous instance to disappear from an archway, now to cross the corridor to lean against the wall. Was it the same man? Yes, it *was!* It was the one who had accompanied Bertholdier to the dining-room entrance of *Les Étalons Blancs.* Joel had thought at the time that a subordinate was taking leave of a superior. He was here now under orders from that same superior.

The man looked up, the flash of recognition instantly in his eyes. Stretching, he raised himself to his full height and turned away, his hand slowly moving toward the fold in his coat. Converse was stunned. Was the man actually reaching for a *gun?* With an armed guard barely ten feet away? It was insane! Joel stopped; he considered racing back into the crowd by the elevators but knew it was pointless. If Bertholdier had posted a watchdog in the basement, others would be upstairs, in the corridors, in the lobby. He could not turn and run; there was no place to go, nowhere to hide. So he kept walking, now faster, directly toward the man in the light brown topcoat, his mind confused, his throat tight.

"*There* you are!" he cried out loud, not sure the words were his. "The general told me where to find you!"

If Converse was stunned, the man was in shock, numbed speechless but still in shock. "*Le général?*" he said, barely above a whisper. "He . . . tell you . . . ?"

The man's English was not good and that was very good. He could understand, but not well. Rapidly spoken words, persuasively delivered, might get them both out the door. Joel turned to the guard, while angling his attaché case into the small man's back. "My name's Simon. I believe the *directeur* spoke to you about me."

The juxtaposition of the name and the title was sufficient for the bewildered guard. He glanced at his papers, nodding. "*Oui, Monsieur. Le directeur.*"

"Come on!" Converse shoved the attaché case into the man in the light brown topcoat, propelling him toward the door. "The general's waiting for us outside. Let's go! Hurry *up!*"

"*Le général . . . ?*" The man's hands instinctively shot out at the crash bar of the exit door; in less than five seconds he and Joel were alone in the alley. "*Qu'est-ce que ça? Ou est le général? . . .* Where?"

"Here! He said to wait here. You. You're to wait here! *Ici!*"

"*Arrétez!*" The man was recovering. He stood his ground, thrusting his left hand out, pushing Converse back against the wall, his right hand surging into his overcoat.

"Don't!" Joel dropped his attaché case, gripping his suitcase and pulling it up in front of him, about to rush forward. He stopped. The man did not pull out a gun; instead, it was a thin, rectangular object bound in black leather. An unseen switch was pressed and a long metallic needle rose from the narrow flat top. An antenna . . . a *radio!*

All thought was blurred for Converse, only motion counted. He could not permit the man to use the radio, no second switch or button could be pressed, emitting a signal, alerting those with other radios elsewhere in the hotel. With a sudden, uncontrollable surge of strength, he rammed his suitcase into the man's knees, tearing the radio away with his left hand, whipping his right arm out and over the man's shoulder. He cracked his elbow, vicing the Frenchman's neck, as he spun on the pavement. Then without thinking, he yanked Bertholdier's soldier forward, both bodies rushing toward the wall, and crashed the man's head into the stone. Blood spread throughout the Frenchman's skull, matting his hair and streaking down his face in deep red rivulets. Joel could not think, he could not *allow* himself to think. If he did, he would be sick and he knew it. Motion, *motion!*

The man went limp. Converse angled the unconscious body by the shoulders, propelling it against the wall, shoving it away from the metal door and letting it drop in the farther shadows. He leaned down and picked up the radio, snapping off the antenna, and shoving the case into his pocket. He stood up, confused, frightened, trying to orient himself; then he saw what he had to see and rushed forward. Grabbing his attaché case and suitcase off the ground, he raced breathlessly out of the alley, conscious of the blood that had somehow erupted over part of his face. The taxi was at the kerb, the driver smoking a cigarette in the darkness, oblivious to the violence that had taken place only thirty yards away.

"De Gaulle Airport!" shouted Joel, opening the door, and throwing his luggage inside. "Please, I'm in a hurry! *Pressé!*" He lurched into the seat, gasping, his neck stretched above the cushioned rim, swallowing the air that would not fill his lungs.

The rushing lights and shadows that bombarded the interior of the cab served only to coil out his suspended thought, allowing his racing pulse to decelerate and the air to reach him, slowly drying the perspiration that had broken out at his temples and his neck. He leaned forward, wanting a cigarette but afraid he would vomit from the smoke trapped in his throat. He shut his eyes, his lids pressing against one another so tightly a thousand specks of white light assaulted the dark screen of his mind. He felt ill, nauseatingly ill, and he knew it was not simply fear alone. It was something quite apart, something that was in and of itself as paralysing as fear. He had committed an act of utter brutality and it both shocked and appalled him. He had actually, *physically* attacked a man, wanting to punish him, cripple him, perhaps kill him which he might very well have done. No matter why, he may have *killed* another human being! Did the presence of a hand-held radio justify a shattered skull? Did it constitute self-defence? *Goddamn it*, he was a man of words, of logic, not blood! *Never* blood, that was in the past, so long ago and so painful.

Those memories belonged to another time, to an uncivilized time, when men became what they were not – in order to survive. Converse never wanted to go back. Above all things, he had promised himself he never would, a promise he made when the terror and the violence were all around him, at their shattering worst. He remembered so vividly, with such pain the final hours before his last escape – and the quiet, generous man without whom he would have died twenty feet down in the earth, a shaft in the ground designed for troublemakers.

Colonel Sam Abbott, US Air Force, would always be a part of his life no matter how many years might separate them. At the risk of death preceded by torture, Sam had crawled out at night and had thrown a crudely-fashioned metal wedge down the "punishment hole"; it was that primitive tool that allowed Joel to build a crude ladder out of earth and rock and finally to freedom. Abbott and he had spent the last twenty-seven months in the same camp, both officers trying to hold what sanity there was together. But Sam understood the burning inside him; the Colonel had stayed behind, and during those final hours before break-out, Joel was racked by the thoughts of what might happen to his friend.

Don't worry about me, sailor. Just keep your minimum wits about you and get rid of that wedge.

Take care, Sam.

You take care. This is the last shot you've got.

I know.

Joel moved over toward the door and rolled down the window several inches, letting the rush of wind from the highway cool him. Christ, he needed Sam Abbott's quiet objectivity now! His lawyer's mind told him to get hold of himself; the brain had to give rise to thought, thought to whatever imagination of which he was capable. First things first. Think! The radio; he had to get rid of the *radio*. But not at the airport . . . it might be found in the airport; it was evidence, worse a means of tracing him. He rolled the window down several more inches and threw it out, his eyes on the rear-view mirror above the windscreen. The driver glanced up at him, briefly concerned; Joel took repeated deep breaths – a man wanting air to suspend the discomfort of acid or anxiety – and then rolled the window back up. Think. He had to *think!* Bertholdier expected him to go from Paris to Bonn and when the general's soldier was found – and he had undoubtedly been found by now – all flights to Bonn would be watched . . . whether or not the man was alive or dead.

He would buy a ticket for somewhere else, some place where connections to Köln-Bonn were accessible on a regular basis. As the stream of air brushed his face he thought, composing himself sufficiently to remove the handkerchief from his breast pocket and wipe away the moist blood that covered his right cheek and lower chin.

"Scandinavian Air Lines," he said raising his voice to the driver. "*SAS*. Do you . . . *comprenez?*"

"Very clearly, Monsieur," said the bereted man behind the wheel in well-spoken English. "Do you have a reservation for Stockholm, Oslo, or Copenhagen? They are different gates."

"I'm . . . I'm not sure."

"We have time, Monsieur. At least fifteen minutes."

The voice over the telephone from London was frigid, the words and the delivery an impersonal rebuke, made extremely personal because of familiarity. "There is no attorney by that name in Chicago, and certainly not at the address you gave me. In fact, the address does not exist. Do you have something else to offer, or do we put this down as one of your most paranoid fantasies, *mon general?*"

"You are a fool, *Anglais*, with no more comprehension than a frightened rabbit. *I heard* what I *heard!*"

"From whom? A non-existent man?"

"A non-existent man who has put my guard in a hospital! A fractured skull with a great loss of blood and severe brain damage. He may not live, and if he does, it will no doubt be as a vegetable. Speak to me not of fantasies, *daffodil. The* man is real."

"Are you serious?"

"Call the hospital! *L'hôpital de St Jérôme.* Let the doctors tell you."

"All right, all right, compose yourself. We must think."

"I am perfectly composed," said Bertholdier, getting up from the desk of his study, and carrying the phone to the window, the extension cord snaking across the floor. He looked out; it had begun to rain, the street lights diffused in the spattered glass. "He's on his way to Bonn," continued the, general. "It was his next stop, he was very clear about it."

"Intercept him. Call Bonn, reach Köln, give them his description. How many flights can there be from Paris with a lone American on board? Take him at the airport."

Bertholdier sighed audibly into the phone, his tone one of discouragement bordering on disgust. "It was never my intention to *take* him. It would serve no purpose and probably cut us off from what we have to learn. I want him followed, I want to know where he goes, whom he calls, whom he meets with; these are the things we must learn."

"You said he made a direct reference to our associate. That he was going to reach him."

"Not *our* people. *His* people."

"I'll say it again," insisted the voice from London. "Call Köln, reach Bonn. Listen to me, Jacques, he can be found, and once he is, surveillance can be put in place."

"Yes, yes, I'll do as you say, but it may not be as easy as you think. Three hours ago I would have thought otherwise, but that was before I knew what he was capable of. Someone who can take another man and rush that man's head into a stone wall at full force is either an animal, a maniac, or a zealot who will stop at nothing. In my judgment, he is the last. He said he had a commitment . . . and it was in his eyes. And he'll be clever; he's already proved he can be clever."

"You say *three* hours?"

"Yes."

"Then he may already be in Bonn."

"I know."

"Have you called our associate?"

"Yes, he's not at home and the maid could not give me another number. She doesn't know where he is, or when he's expected."

"Probably in the morning."

"No doubt . . . *Attendez!* There was another man at the club this afternoon.

84

With Luboque and this Simon whose name is not Simon. He *brought* him to Luboque! Good bye, *Anglais*. I'll keep you informed."

René Mattilon opened his eyes. The streaks of light on the ceiling seemed to shimmer, myriad tiny clots bursting, breaking up the linear patterns. Then he heard the sound of the rain on the windows and understood. The shafts of light from the streetlamps had been intercepted on their journeys through the glass, distorting the images he knew so well. It was the rain, he concluded; that was what had awakened him. That and perhaps the weight of his wife's hand between his legs. She stirred and he smiled, trying to make up his mind – or find the energy – to reach for her. She had filled a void for him he never thought could be filled after his first wife had died. He was grateful, and along with his feeling of gratitude came excitement, two emotions satisfyingly compatible. He was becoming aroused; he rolled over on his side and pulled down the covers, revealing the swell of her breasts encased in laced silk, the diffused light and the pounding on the windows heightening his sensuality. He reached for her.

Suddenly, there was another sound, not the rain, yet intruding on the rain, and from within the mists of sleep he recognized it. Quickly, he withdrew his hand and turned away from his wife. He had heard that noise only moments before; *it* was sound that had awakened him, an insistent tone that had broken the steady rhythm of the downpour. It was the chimes of his apartment doorbell.

Mattilon climbed out of bed as carefully and as silently as he could, reaching for his bathrobe on a nearby chair and sliding his feet into the slippers beneath. He walked out of the bedroom, closing the door quietly behind him, and found the wall switch that turned on the lamps in the living room. He glanced at the ornate clock on the fireplace mantel; it was nearly 2.30 in the morning. Who could possibly be calling on them at this hour? He tied the sash around his robe and walked to the door.

"Yes, who is it?"

"*Sûreté*, Monsieur. Inspector Prudhomme. My state identification is zero-five-seven-two-zero." The man's accent was Gascon, not Parisian. It was often said they made the best police officials. "I shall wait while you call my station, Monsieur. The telephone number is . . ."

"No need," said Mattilon, alarmed, unlatching the door. He knew the man was genuine not only from the information offered, but anyone from the *Sûreté* calling on him at this hour would know he was an attorney. The *Sûreté* was legally circumspect.

There were two men, both in raincoats spotted by the downpour, their hats drenched; one was older than the other and shorter. Each held out an open identification card for René's inspection. He waved the cards aside and gestured the two men to come in, adding, "It's an odd time for visitors, gentlemen. You must have pressing business."

"Very pressing, Monsieur," said the older man entering first. He was the one who had spoken through the door, giving his name as Prudhomme, and was obviously the senior. "We apologize for the inconvenience, of course. Both men removed their hats."

"Of course. May I take your coats?"

"It won't be necessary, Monsieur. With your cooperation we'll only be a few minutes."

"And I shall be most interested to know how I can cooperate with the *Sûreté* at this time of night."

"A matter of identification, sir. Monsieur Serge Antoine Luboque is a client of yours, we are informed. Is this so?"

"My God, has something happened to Serge? I was with him only this afternoon!"

"Monsieur Luboque appears in excellent health. We left his country house barely an hour ago. And to the point, it is your meeting with him this afternoon – *yesterday* afternoon – that concerns the *Sûreté*."

"In what way?"

"There was a third party at your table. As yourself, an attorney, introduced to Monsieur Luboque as a man named Simon. Henry Simon, an American."

"And a pilot," said Mattilon warily. "With considerable expertise in aircraft litigation. I trust Luboque explained that; it was the reason he was there at my request. Monsieur Luboque is the plaintiff in just such a lawsuit. That of course, is all I can say on the subject."

"It is not the subject that interests the *Sûreté*."

"What is then?"

"There is no attorney by the name of Henry Simon in the city of Chicago, Illinois, in the United States."

"I find that hard to believe."

"The name is false. At least, it is not his. The address he gave the hotel does not exist."

"The address he *gave* the hotel?" asked René, astonished. Joel did not have to give an address to the George V; it knew him well, knew the firm of Talbot, Brooks and Simon very well, indeed."

"In his own handwriting, Monsieur," added the younger man stiffly.

"Has the hotel management confirmed this?"

"Yes," said Prudhomme. "The assistant *directeur* was very cooperative. He told us he escorted Monsieur Simon down the freight elevator to the hotel cellars."

"The cellars?"

"Monsieur Simon wished to leave the hotel without being seen. He paid his bill in his room."

"A minute, please," said Mattilon, perplexed, his hands protesting, as he turned and walked aimlessly around an armchair, stopping, his hands on the rim. "What *precisely* do you want from me?"

"We want you to help us," answered Prudhomme. "We think you know who he is. You brought him to Monsieur Luboque."

"On a confidential matter entailing a legal opinion. He agreed to listen and to evaluate on the condition that his identity should be protected. It's not unusual when seeking expertise if one is involved with, shall we say, an individual as wealthy and as temperamental as Monsieur Luboque. You've spoken with him; need I say more?"

"Not on that subject," said the older man from the *Sûreté*, permitting himself a smile. "He thinks all government personnel work for Moscow. We were surrounded by dogs in his foyer, all salivating, I might add."

"Then you can understand why my American colleague prefers to remain unnamed. I know him well, he's a splendid man."

"Who is he? And do you know where we can find him?"

"Why do you want him?"

"We wish to question him about an incident that took place at the hotel."

"I'm sorry. As Luboque is a client, so by extension is Simon."

"That is not acceptable to us under the circumstances, Monsieur."

"I'm afraid it will have to be, at least for a few hours. Tomorrow I shall try to reach him through his office in . . . in the United States . . . and I'm sure he'll get in touch with you immediately."

"We don't think he will."

"Why not?"

Prudhomme glanced at his starchly-postured associate and shrugged. "He may have killed a man," he said matter-of-factly.

Mattilon stared at the *Sûreté* officer in disbelief. "He . . . *what?*"

"It was a particularly vicious assault, Monsieur. A man's head was rammed into a wall; there are extensive cranial injuries and the prognosis is not good. His condition as of midnight was critical, the chances of recovery less than half. He may be dead by now, which one doctor said could be a blessing."

"No . . . *no!* You are mistaken! You're wrong!" The lawyer's hands gripped the rim of the chair. "A terrible error has been made!"

"No error. The identification was positive – that is Monsieur Simon was identified as the last person seen with the man who was beaten. He forced the man out into an alley; there were sounds of scuffling and minutes later that man was found, his skull fractured, bleeding, near death."

"Impossible! You don't *know* him! What you suggest is inconceivable. He *couldn't.*"

"Are you telling us he is disabled, physically incapable of assault?"

"No," said Mattilon, shaking his head. Then suddenly he stopped all movement. "*Yes,*" he continued thoughtfully, his eyes pensive, now nodding, rushing ahead. "He's incapable, yes, but not physically. *Mentally.* In that sense he is disabled. He could not do what you say he did."

"He's mentally deranged?"

"My *God*, no! He's one of the most lucid men I've ever met. You have to understand. He went through a prolonged period of extreme physical stress and mental anguish. He endured punishment, both to his body and his mind. There was no permanent damage but there are indelible memories. As so many men like him – men who've been subjected to such treatment – he avoids all forms of physical confrontation or abuse. It is repugnant to him. He can't inflict punishment because too much was inflicted on him."

"You mean he would not defend himself, his own? He would turn the other cheek if he, or his wife, or his children were attacked?"

"Of course not, but that's not what you described. You said 'a particularly vicious assault' implying something quite different. And if it were otherwise – if he were threatened or attacked and defended himself – he most certainly would not have left the scene. He's too fine a lawyer." Mattilon paused. "*Was* that the case? Is that what you're saying? Is the injured man known to you from the police files? Is he . . ."

"A limousine chauffeur," interrupted Prudhomme. "An unarmed man who was waiting for his assigned passenger of the evening."

"In the *cellars?*"

"Apparently it is a customary service and not an unfamiliar one. These firms are discreet. This one sent another driver to cover before inquiring as to their employee's condition. The client would not know."

"Very chic, I'm sure. What do they say happened?"

"According to a witness, a guard who's been with the hotel for eighteen years, this Simon approached in a loud voice, speaking English – the guard thinks angrily, although he does not understand the language – and forced the man outside."

"The guard is wrong! It must have been someone else."

"Simon identified himself. The assistant *directeur* had cleared his departure. The description fits; it was the one who called himself Simon."

"But *why?* There has to be a reason!"

"We should like to hear it, Monsieur."

René shook his head in bewilderment; nothing made sense. A man could register at any hotel under any name he wished, of course, but there were charges, credit cards, people calling; a false name served no purpose. Especially at a hotel where one was presumably known, and if one *was* known and chose to travel incognito, that status would not be protected if a front desk was questioned by the *Sûreté*. "I must ask you again, Inspector, have you checked thoroughly with the hotel?"

"Not personally, Monsieur," replied Prudhomme, looking at his associate. "My time was taken up interrogating those in the vicinity of the assault."

"I checked with the *concierge* myself, Monsieur," said the younger, taller man, speaking like a programmed robot. "Naturally, the hotel is not anxious for the incident to receive attention, but the management was cooperative. The night *directeur* is newly employed from the Hotel Meurice and wished to minimize the incident, but he himself showed me the registration form."

"I see." And Mattilon did, at least insofar as Joel's identity was concerned. Hundreds of guests at a large hotel and a nervous night *directeur* protecting his new employer's image. The obvious source was accepted as truth, another truth no doubt forthcoming in the morning from more knowledgeable men. But that was all René understood – nothing else. He needed a few moments to think, to try and understand. "I'm curious," he said, reaching for words. "At worst, this is an assault with severe results, but nevertheless an assault. Why isn't it a simple police matter? Why the *Sûreté?*"

"My first question, Monsieur," said the plain-spoken Prudhomme. "The reason given us was that the incident involved a foreigner, obviously a wealthy foreigner. One does not know these days where such things lead. We have certain controls not available to the *arrondissement* police."

"I see."

"Do you?" asked the man from the *Sûreté*. "May I remind you that as an attorney you have an obligation to uphold the courts and the law? You have been offered our credentials and I have suggested you call my station for any further verification you might wish. Please, Monsieur, who is Henry Simon?"

"I have other obligations, as well, Inspector. To my word, to a client, to an old friendship."

"You put these above the law?"

"Only because I know you're *wrong*."

"Then where is the harm? If we are, we shall find this Simon undoubtedly at an airport and he will tell us himself. But if we are not wrong, we may find a very sick man who needs help. Before he harms others. I am no psychiatrist, Monsieur, but you have described a troubled man – a once-troubled man, in any event."

Mattilon was uncomfortable with the blunt official's logic . . . and also something else he could not define. Was it Joel? Was it the clouds in his old friend's eyes, the unconscious verbal slip about a blemished rock in the dirt? René looked again at the clock on the mantel; a thought occurred to him. It was only 8.42 in New York.

"Inspector, I'm going to ask you to wait here while I go into my study and make a phone call on my private line. The line, incidentally, is not connected to the telephone on the table."

"That was unnecessary, Monsieur."

"Then I apologize."

Mattilon walked rapidly to a door on the opposite side of the room, opened it, and went inside. He crossed to his desk, sat down and opened a red leather telephone index. He flipped the pages to the letter T, scanning the names until he reached *Talbot, Lawrence*. He had both the office and the house number; it was necessary as the courts in Paris were in operation before the East Coast of America was out of bed. If Talbot was not there, he would try Nathan Simon, then Brooks, if he had to. Neither was necessary. Lawrence Talbot answered the phone.

"I'll be damned, how are you, René? You in New York?"

"No, Paris."

"Sounds like you're down the block."

"So do you. It's always startling."

"It's also late where you are, if I'm not mistaken."

"It's very late, Larry. We may have a problem, that's why I'm calling."

"A problem? I didn't even know we had any business going. What is it?"

"Your missionary work."

"Our what?"

"Bertholdier. His friends."

"*Who?*"

"Jacques Louis Bertholdier."

"Who is he? I've heard the name but I can't place him."

"You can't . . . place him?"

"Sorry."

"I've been with Joel. I arranged the meeting."

"Joel? How is he? Is he in Paris now?"

"You weren't aware of it?"

"Last time I spoke with him was two days ago in Geneva – after that awful business with Halliday. He told me he was all right, but he wasn't. He was shaken up."

"Let me understand you, Larry. Joel is not in Paris on business for Talbot, Brooks and Simon, is that what you're saying?"

Lawrence Talbot paused before answering. "No, he's not," said the senior partner softly. "Did he say he was?"

"Perhaps I just assumed it."

Again Talbot paused. "I don't think you'd do that. But I do think you should tell Joel to call me."

"That's part of the problem, Larry. I don't know where he is. He said he was taking the 6 o'clock plane for London, but he didn't. He checked out of the George V quite a bit later under very odd circumstances."

"What do you mean?"

"His hotel registration was altered, changed to another name – a name I suggested, incidentally, as he didn't wish to use his own at lunch. Then he insisted on leaving by way of some basement delivery entrance."

"That's strange."

"I'm afraid it's the least of the oddities. They say he assaulted a man. He may have killed him."

"*Jesus!*"

"I don't believe it, of course," said Mattilon quickly. "He wouldn't, he couldn't."

"*I hope* not."

"Certainly you don't think."

"I don't know *what* to think," interrupted Talbot. "When he was in Geneva and we talked, I asked him if there was any connection between Halliday's death and what he was doing. He said there wasn't, but he was so remote, so distant; his voice sounded hollow."

"What he's *doing* . . . ? What *is* he doing?"

"I don't know. I'm not even sure I can find out, but I'll do my damnedest. I tell you, I'm worried. Something's happened to him. His voice was like an echo chamber, do you know what I mean?"

"Yes, I do," said Mattilon quietly. "I heard him, I saw him. I'm worried, too."

"Find him, René. Do whatever you can. Give me the word and I'll drop everything and fly over. He's hurting somewhere, somehow."

"I'll do what I can."

* * *

90

Mattilon walked out of his study and faced the two men from the *Sûreté*.

"His name is Converse, Joel Converse," he began.

"His name is Converse, first name Joel," said the younger, taller man from the *Sûreté*, speaking into the mouthpiece of a pay phone on the Boulevard Raspail, as the rain pounded the booth. "He's employed by a law firm in New York: Talbot, Brooks and Simon; the address is on Fifth Avenue. The assumed name Simon, however, was apparently a convenience, and not related to the firm."

"I don't understand."

"Whatever this Converse is involved with has nothing to do with his employers. Mattilon spoke to one of the partners in New York and it was made clear to him. Also both men are concerned, worried; they wish to be kept informed. If Converse is found, Mattilon insists on immediate access to him as the attorney of record. He may be holding back, but in my judgment he's genuinely bewildered. In shock, might be more accurate. He knows nothing of consequence, I could tell if he did."

"Nevertheless, he *is* holding back. The name Simon was used for my benefit, so that I would not learn the identity of this Converse. Mattilon knows that; he was there and they are friends and he brought him to Luboque."

"Then he was manipulated, General. He did not mention you."

"He might if he's questioned further. I cannot be involved in any way."

"Of course not," agreed the man from the *Sûreté* with quiet emphasis.

"Your superior, what's his name? The one assigned to the incident."

"Prudhomme. Inspector First Grade Prudhomme."

"Is he frank with you?"

"Yes. He thinks I'm something of a mechanical ex-soldier whose instincts may outdistance his intellect, but he sees that I'm willing. He talks to me."

"You'll be kept with him for a while. Should he decide to go back and see Mattilon, let me know immediately. Paris may lose a respected attorney. My name must not surface."

"He would only go back to Mattilon if Converse was found. And if word came to the *Sûreté* as to his whereabouts, I'd reach you instantly."

"There could be another reason, Colonel. One that might provoke a persistent man into re-examining his progress – or lack of it – in spite of orders to the contrary."

"Orders to the contrary, sir?"

"They will be issued. This Converse is solely our concern now. All we needed was a name. We know where he's heading. We'll find him."

"I don't understand, General."

"News has come from the hospital. Our chauffeur has taken a turn for the better."

"Good news indeed."

"I wish it were. The sacrifice of a single soldier is abhorrent to any field commander, but the broader tactics must be kept in view, they must be served. Do you agree?"

"Yes, of course."

"Our chauffeur must not recover. The larger strategy, Colonel."

"If he dies, the efforts to find Converse will be intensified. And you're right, Prudhomme will re-examine everything, including the lawyer, Mattilon."

"Orders to the contrary will be issued. But watch him."

"Yes, sir."

"And now we need your expertise, Colonel. The talents you developed so proficiently while in the service of the Legion before we brought you back to a more civilized life."

"My gratitude isn't shallow. Whatever I can do."

"Can you get inside the hospital of St Jérôme with as little notice as possible?"

"With no notice. There are fire escapes on all sides of the building and it's a dark night, heavy with rain. Even the police stay in doorways. It's child's play."

"But man's work. It has to be done."

"I don't question such decisions."

"A blockage in the windpipe, a convulsion in the throat."

"Pressure applied through cloth, sir. Gradually and with no marks, a patient's self-induced trauma . . . But I would be derelict if I didn't repeat what I said, General. There'll be a search of Paris, then a large scale manhunt. The killer will be presumed to be a rich American, an inviting target for the *Sûreté*."

"There'll be no search, no manhunt. Not yet. If it is to be, it will come later, and if it does, a convicted corpse will be trapped in the net . . . Go into the field, my young friend. The chauffeur, Colonel; the broader strategy must be served."

"He's dead," said the man in the telephone booth, hanging up.

5

Erich Leifhelm . . . born 15 March 1912, in Munich to Dr Heinrich Leifhelm and his mistress, Marta Stoessel. Although the stigma of his illegitimacy precluded a normal childhood in upper-middle-class, morality-conscious Germany of those years, it was the single most important factor in his later pre-eminence in the National Socialist movement. At birth, he was denied the name of Leifhelm; until 1931 he was known as Erich Stoessel.

Joel sat at a table in the open café in Copenhagen's Kastrup Airport, trying to concentrate. It was his second attempt within the past twenty minutes, the first he abandoned when he realized he was absorbing nothing, being only black letters forming an unending string of vaguely recognizable words relating to a figure in the outer reaches of his mind. He could not focus on that man; there were too many interferences, real and imagined. Nor had he been able to read on the two-hour flight from Paris, having opted for economy class, hoping to melt in with the greater number of people in the larger section of the aircraft. The concept at least was valid; the seats were so narrow and the plane so fully occupied that elbows and forearms were virtually immobile. The conditions prohibited his taking out the report, both for reasons of space and for fear of the proximity to straying eyes.

Heinrich Leifhelm moved his mistress and their son to the town of Eichstatt, 50-odd miles north of Munich, visiting them now and then, and providing an adequate but not over comfortable standard of living. The doctor was apparently torn between maintaining a successful practice – with no social blemishes – in Munich, and a disinclination to abandon the stigmatized mother and child. According to close acquaintances of Erich Stoessel-Leifhelm, these early years had a profound effect on him. Although too young to grasp the full impact of World War I – a memory that was later to haunt him – the small household's subsistence level fell as the elder Leifhelm's ability to contribute lessened with the burden of wartime taxes. Also, his father's visits served to heighten the fact that he could not be acknowledged as a son and was not entitled to the privileges accorded two stepbrothers and a stepsister, strangers he was never to know and whose home he could not enter. Through the absence of proper lineage, certified by hypocritical documents and more hypocritical church blessings, he felt he was denied what was rightfully his, and so there were instilled in him a furious sense of resentment, competitiveness, and a deep-seated anger at existing social conditions. By his own admission, his first conscious longings were to get as much as he could for himself – both materially and in the form of recognition – through the strengths of his own abilities, and by doing so strike out at the status quo which had tried to emasculate him. By his mid-teens, Stoessel-Leifhelm's anger consumed him.

Converse stopped reading, suddenly aware of the woman across the half-deserted café; she was seated alone at a table, looking at him. Their eyes met and she turned away, placing her arm on the low white railing that enclosed the restaurant, studying the thinning, late night crowds in the terminal, as if waiting for someone. Startled, Joel tried to analyse the look she had given him. Was it recognition? Did she know him? Know his face? Or was it appraisal? A well-dressed whore cruising the airport in search of a mark, seeking out a lonely businessman far away from home. Airports at night frequently served as sexual meeting grounds, appetites born of distance and loneliness, monies exchanged as often as not for conversation as for copulation, foreplay extended, vacuums filled. She turned her head slowly and looked at him again, now obviously upset that his eyes were still on her. Then abruptly, in two swiftly defined motions, she glanced at her watch, tugged at her wide-brimmed hat, and opened her purse. She took out a Krone note, placed it on the table, got up, and walked rapidly toward the entrance of the café. Beyond the open gate she walked faster, her strides longer, heading for the arch that led to the baggage claim area. Converse watched her, shaking his head, annoyed at his alarm; he was seeing shadows in the dull white neon light of the terminal. With his attaché case and leather-bound report, the woman had probably thought he was some kind of airport official. Who was the mark then?

He was seeing too many shadows, he thought, as he followed the graceful figure nearing the arch. Too many shadows that held no surprises, or alarms. There had been a man on the plane from Paris sitting several rows in front of him. Twice the man had got up and gone to the toilet, and each time he came back to his seat he had looked hard at Joel, studied him, actually. Those looks had been enough to prime his adrenalin. Had he been spotted at the de Gaulle airport? Was the man an employee of Jacques Louis Bertholdier? . . . As a man in an alley had been – *don't think about that!* He had flicked off an oval of dried blood on his shirt as he had given himself the command.

"I can always tell a good ole Yank! Never miss!"

That had been the antiquated salutation in Copenhagen, as both Americans waited for their luggage.

"Well, I missed once. Some son of a bitch on a plane in Geneva. Sat right next to me. A real guinea in a three-piece suit, that's what he was! He spoke English to the stewardess, so I figured he was one of those rich Cuban spicks from Florida, you know what I mean?"

An emissary in salesman's clothes. One of the diplomats.

Geneva. It had started in Geneva.

Too many shadows. No surprises, no alarms. The woman went through the arch and Joel pulled his eyes away, forcing his attention back to the report on Erich Leifhelm. Then a slight, sudden movement stopped him; he looked back at the woman. A man had stepped out of an unseen recess; his hand had touched her elbow. They exchanged words briefly, swiftly, and parted as abruptly as they had met, the man continuing into the terminal as the woman disappeared. Did the man glance over in his direction? Converse watched closely; *had* that man looked at him? It was impossible to tell; his head was turning in all directions, looking at or *for* something. Then, as if he had found it, the man hurried toward a bank of airline counters. He approached the Japan Air Lines desk, taking out his wallet as he began speaking to an oriental clerk.

No surprises, no alarms. A harried traveller had asked directions; the interferences were more imagined than real. Yet even here his lawyer's mentality intervened. Interferences were real whether based in reality or not. *Oh, Christ! Leave it alone! Concentrate!*

At the age of 17, Erich Stoessel-Leifhelm had completed his studies at the Eichstatt II Gymnasium, excelling both academically and on the playing field where he was known as an aggressive competitor. It was a time of universal financial chaos, the American stock market crash of '29 further aggravating the desperate economy of the Weimar Republic, and few but the most well-connected students went on to universities. In a move he later described to friends as one of youthful fury, Stoessel-Leifhelm travelled to Munich to confront his father and demand assistance. What he found was not only a shock, but turned out to be a profound opportunity, strangely arrived at. The doctor's staid, placid life was in shambles. His marriage, from the beginning unpleasant and humiliating, had caused him to drink heavily with increasing frequency until the inevitable errors of judgment occurred. He was censured by the medical community (with a high proportion of Jews therein), charged with incompetence and barred from the Karlstor Hospital. His practice was in ruins; his wife had ordered him out of the house; an order expedited by an old but still *powerful father-in-law, also a doctor and member of the hospital's board of directors. When Stoessel-Leifhelm found his father, he was living in a cheap apartment house in the poorer section of the city picking up pfennigs by dispensing prescriptions (drugs) and Deutschemarks by performing abortions.*

In what apparently (again according to friends from the time) was a watershed of pent-up emotions, the elder Leifhelm embraced his illegitimate son and told him the story of his tortured life with a disagreeable wife and tyrannical in-laws. It was the classic syndrome of an ambitious man of minimal talents and maximum connections. But withal, the doctor claimed he had never abandoned his beloved mistress and their son. And during this prolonged and undoubtedly drunken confession, he revealed a fact Stoessel-Leifhelm had never known. His father's wife was Jewish. It was all the teenager needed to hear.

The disenfranchised boy became the father to the ruined man.

There was an announcement in Danish over the airport's loudspeakers and Joel looked at his watch. It came again, now in German. He listened intensely for the words, he could barely distinguish them, but they were there. Hamburg-Köln-Bonn. It was the first boarding call for the last flight of the night to the capital of West Germany by way of Hamburg. The flying time was less than two hours, the layover in Hamburg justified for those executives who wanted to be at their desks by the start of the business day. Converse had checked his suitcase through to Bonn, making a mental note as he did so to replace the heavy black leather bag with a carry-on. He was no expert in such matters but common sense told him that the delays required by waiting for one's luggage – in the open for anyone to see – was no way to travel swiftly or to avoid eyes that might be searching for him. He put Erich Leifhelm's dossier in his attaché case, closed it and spun the brass combination discs. He then got up from the table, walked out of the café, and across the terminal toward the Lufthansa gate.

Sweat matted his hairline; the tattoo inside his chest accelerated until it became a hammering fugue for kettle-drums. He *knew* the man sitting next to him, but from where or from what period in his life he had no idea. The crag-lined face, deep ridges that creased the sun-tanned flesh, the intense blue-grey eyes beneath the thick, wild brows and brown hair streaked with white; he *knew* him, but no name came, no clue to the man's identity.

Joel kept waiting for some sign of recognition directed at himself. None came, and involuntarily he found himself looking at the sun-tanned man out of the corner of his eye – "stealing glances" was the embarrassing phrase that came to him. The man did not respond; instead his attention was on a bound sheaf of typewritten pages, the type larger than the print normally associated with legal briefs or even summonses. Perhaps, thought Converse, the man was half blind, wearing contact lenses to conceal his infirmity. But was there something else? Not an infirmity, but a connection being concealed. Had he seen this man in Paris – as he had seen another wearing a light brown topcoat in a hotel basement corridor? Had this man beside him also been at *Les Étalons Blancs?* Had he been part of a stationary group of ex-soldiers in the warriors' playroom . . . in a corner, innocuous because of the numbers? Or at Bertholdier's table, his back to Joel, presumably unseen by the American he was now following? *Was* he following him at this moment? wondered Converse, gripping his attaché case. He turned his head barely inches and studied his seatmate.

Suddenly the man looked up from the bound, typewritten pages and over at Joel. His eyes were non-committal, expressing neither concern nor curiosity.

"Sorry," said Converse, awkwardly.

"Sure, it's okay . . . why not?" was the strange, laconic reply, the accent American, the dialect distinctly Texas-Western. The man returned to his pages.

"Do we know each other?" asked Joel, unable to back off from the question.

Again the man looked up. "Don't think so," he said tersely, once more going back to his report, or whatever it was.

Converse looked out the window, at the black sky beyond, flashes of red light illuminating the silver metal of the wing. Absently he tried to calculate the digital degree heading of the aircraft but his pilot's mind would not function. He *did* know the man, and the oddly-phrased "why not?" served only to disturb him further. Was it a signal, a warning? As his words to Jacques Louis Bertholdier had been a signal, a warning that the general had better contact him, recognize him.

The voice of a Lufthansa stewardess interrupted his thoughts. "Herr Dowling, it is a pleasure, indeed, to have you on board."

"Thank you, darlin'," said the man, his lined face creasing into a gentle grin. "You find me a little bourbon over ice and I'll return the compliment."

"Certainly, sir. I'm sure you've been told so often you must be tired of hearing it, but your television show is enormously popular in Germany."

"Thanks again, honey, but it's not my show. There are a lot of pretty little fillies runnin' around that screen."

An actor. *A goddamned actor!* thought Joel. No alarms, no surprises. Just intrusions, far more imagined than real.

"You're too modest, Herr Dowling. They're all so alike, so disagreeable. But you are so kind, so manly . . . so understanding."

"Understandin'? Tell you somethin', I saw an episode in Cologne last week while on this picture and I didn't understand a word I was sayin'."

The stewardess laughed. "Bourbon over ice, is that correct, sir?"

"That's correct, darlin'."

The woman started down the First Class aisle toward the galley as Converse continued to look at the actor. Haltingly, he spoke. "I am sorry. I should have recognized you, of course."

Dowling turned his sun-tanned head, his eyes roaming Joel's face, then dropping to the hand-tooled leather attaché case. He looked up with an amused smile. "I could probably embarrass you if I asked you where you knew me from. You don't look like a *Sante Fe* groupie."

"A *Sante Fe* . . . ? Oh, sure, that's the name of the show." And it was, reflected Converse. One of those phenomena on television that by sheer force of incredible ratings and extraordinary network profits had been featured on the covers of *Time* and *Newsweek*. He had never seen it.

"And, naturally," continued the actor. "You follow the tribal rites . . . and wrongs . . . the dramatic vicissitudes of the imperious Ratchet family, owners of the biggest spread north of Santa Fe as well as the historic Chimaya Flats, which they stole from the impoverished Indians."

"The who? What?"

Dowling's leathery face again laminated itself into a grin. "Only Pa Ratchet, the Indians' friend, doesn't know about the last part, although he's being blamed by his red brothers. You see, Pa's no-good sons heard there was oil shale beneath the Chimayas and did their thing . . . Incidentally, I trust you catch the verbal associations inherent in the name Ratchet; you can take your choice. There's just plain 'rats', or Ratchet as in 'wretched', or Ratchet as in the tool – screwing everything in front of it by merely pressing forward."

There was something different about the actor now, thought Joel, bewildered. Was it his words . . . ? No, not the words, his voice. The Western inflections were greatly diminished. "I don't know what you're talking about, but you sound different."

"Wal, Ah'll jes' be *hornswoggled!*" said Dowling, laughing. Then he returned to the unaccented tones he had begun to display. "You're looking at a renegade teacher of English and college dramatics who said a dozen years ago to hell with old age tenure, let's go after a very impractical dream. It led to a lot of funny and not very dignified jobs, but the god Thespis moves in mysterious ways. An old student of mine, on one of those undefinable jobs like 'production–coordinator' spotted me in a crowd scene; it embarrassed the hell out of him. Nevertheless, he put my name in for several small parts. A few panned out and a couple of years later an accident called *Sante Fe* came along. That's when my perfectly respectable name of Calvin was changed to Caleb. 'Fits the image better,' said a pair of Gucci loafers who never got closer to a horse than a box at Santa Anita . . . It's crazy, isn't it?"

"Crazy," agreed Converse, as the stewardess walked back up the aisle toward them.

"Crazy or not," added Dowling, under his breath. "This good old rancher isn't going to offend *anyone*. They want Pa Ratchet, they've got him."

"Your bourbon, sir," said the woman, handing the actor a glass.

"Why, *thank you*, li'l darlin'! My oh my, you're purtier than any filly on the show!"

"*Mein Herr,* you're too kind."

"May I have a Scotch, please," said Joel.

"That's better, son," said Dowling, grinning again as the stewardess left. "And now that you know my crime, what do you do for a living?"

"I'm an attorney."

"At least you've got something legitimate to read. This screenplay sure as hell isn't."

Although considered by most of Munich's respectable citizens to be a collection of misfits and thugs, the National Socialist Workers Party, with its headquarters in Munich, was making itself felt throughout Germany. The radical-populist movement was taking hold by basing its inflammatory message on the evil, un-German "them'. It blamed the ills of the nation on a spectrum of targets ranging from the Bolsheviks to the ingrate Jewish bankers; from the foreign plunderers who had raped an Aryan land to, finally, all things not "Aryan', namely-in-focus, the Jews and their ill-gotten-wealth.

Cosmopolitan Munich and its Jewish community laughed at the absurdities; they were not listening. The rest of Germany was; it was hearing what it wanted to hear. And Erich Stoessel-Leifhelm heard it, too. It was his passport to recognition and opportunity.

In a matter of weeks, the young man literally whipped his father into shape. In later years he would tell the story with heavy doses of cruel humour. Over the dissolute physician's hysterical objections, the son removed all alcohol and smoking materials from the premises, never letting his father out of his sight. A harsh regimen of exercise and diet was enforced. With the zeal of a puritannical athletic trainer, Stoessel-Leifhelm started taking his father out to the countryside for "Gewaltmär-sche" – forced marches – gradually working up to all-day hikes through the exhausting trails of the Bavarian mountains, continuously shouting at the older man to keep moving, to rest only at his son's commands, to drink water only with permission.

So successful was the rehabilitation that the doctor's clothes began to hang on him like seedy, old-fashioned garments purchased for a much fatter man. A new wardrobe was called for, but good clothing in Munich in those days was beyond the means of all but the wealthy, and Stoessel-Leifhelm had only the best in mind for his father – not out of filial devotion but, as we shall see, for a quite different purpose.

Money had to be found, which meant it had to be stolen. He interrogated his father at length about the house the doctor had been forced to leave, learning everything there was to learn. Several weeks later Stoessel-Leifhelm broke into the house on the Luisenstrasse at three o'clock one morning, stripping it of everything of value, including silver, crystal, oil paintings, gold place-settings, and the entire contents of a wall safe. Sales to "fences" were not difficult in Munich of 1930, and when everything was disposed of, father and son had the equivalent of nearly eight thousand American dollars, virtually a fortune in those times.

The restoration continued; clothes were tailored in the Maximilienstrasse, the best footwear purchased at bootsmiths on the Odeonsplatz and, finally, cosmetic changes were effected. The doctor's unkempt hair was trimmed and heightened by colouring into a masculine Nordic blond, and his shabby inch-long beard shaved off, leaving only a small, unbroken, well-manicured moustache above his upper lip. The trans-formation was complete; what remained was the introduction.

Every night during the long weeks of rehabilitation, Stoessel-Leifhelm had read aloud to his father whatever he could get his hands on from the National Socialists' headquarters, and there was no lack of material. There were the standard inflammatory pamphlets, pages of ersatz biological theory purportedly proving the genetic superior-ity of Aryan purity and, conversely, the racial disintegration resulting from indiscrimi-nate breeding – all the usual Nazi diatribes – plus generous excerpts from Hitler's *Mein Kampf.*

The son read incessantly until the doctor could recite by rote the salient outrages of the National Socialists' message. Throughout it all, the seventeen-year old kept telling his father that this was the way to get back everything that had been stolen from him, to avenge the years of humiliation and ridicule. As Germany itself had been humiliated by the rest of the world, the Nazi party was the avenger, the restorer of all things truly

German. It was, indeed, the New Order for the Fatherland, and it was waiting for men of stature to recognize the fact.

The day came, a day when Stoessel-Leiflielm had learned that two high-ranking party officials would be in Munich. They were the crippled Josef Goebbels, and the would-be aristocrat, Rudolph Hess. The son accompanied the father to the National Socialist headquarters where the well-tailored, imposing, obviously rich and Aryan Doktor requested an audience with the two Nazi leaders on an urgent and confidential matter. It was granted, and according to early party historical archives, his first words to Hess and Goebbels were the following.

"Gentlemen, I am a physician of impeccable credentials, formerly head surgeon at the Karlstor Hospital and for years I enjoyed one of the most successful practices in Munich. That was in the past. I was destroyed by Jews who stole everything from me. I am back, I am well, and I am at your service."

The Lufthansa plane began its descent into Hamburg and Joel, feeling the drag, dog-eared the page of Leifhelm's dossier and reached down for his attaché case. Beside him, the actor Caleb Dowling stretched, script in hand, then jammed his screenplay into an open flight bag at his feet.

"The only thing sillier than this movie," he said, "is the amount of money they're paying me to be in it."

"Are you filming tomorrow?" asked Converse.

"Today," corrected Dowling, looking at his watch. "It's an early shoot, too. Have to be on location by five-thirty – dawn over the Rhine, or something equally inspiring. Now if they'd just turn the damn thing into a travelogue, we'd all be better off. Nice scenery."

"But you were in Copenhagen."

"Yep."

"You're not going to get much sleep."

"Nope."

"Oh."

The actor looked at Joel, the crow's feet around his generous eyes creasing deeper with his smile. "My wife's in Copenhagen and I had two days off. This was the last plane I could get."

"Oh? You're married?" Converse immediately regretted the remark; he was not sure why, but it sounded foolish.

"Twenty-six years, young fella. How do you think I was able to go after that impractical dream? She's a whiz of a secretary; when I was teaching, she'd always be this or that dean's Gal Friday."

"Any children?"

"Can't have everything. Nope."

"Why is she in Copenhagen? I mean why isn't she staying with you . . . on location?"

The grin faded from Dowlings sun-tanned face; the lines were less apparent, yet somehow deeper. "That's an obvious question, isn't it? That is, you being a lawyer would pick it up quickly."

"It's none of my business, of course. Forget I asked it."

"No, that's okay. I don't like to talk about it – rarely do – but friendly seatmates on airplanes are for telling things. You'll never see them again, so why not slice off a bit and feel better." The actor tried haltingly to smile; he failed. "My wife's name was Muhlstein – it means a mill-stone. She's Jewish. Her story's not much different from a few million others, but for her it's . . . well, it's hers. She was separated from her parents and her three younger brothers in Auschwitz. She watched them being taken away – away from her – while she screamed, not understanding. She was lucky; they put her in a barracks, a fourteen-year-old sewing uniforms until she showed other endowments that could lead to other work. A couple of days later, hearing the rumours, she got hysterical and broke out, racing all over the place trying to find her family. She ran into a section of the camp they called the *Abfall*, the garbage, corpses hauled out of the gas chambers. And there they were, the bodies of her mother and her father and her three brothers, the sight and the stench so sickening it's never left her. It never will. She won t set foot in Germany and I wouldn't ask her to."

No alarms, just surprises . . . and another Iron Cross for the Erich Leifhelms of the past, retroactively presented.

"Christ, I'm sorry," murmured Converse. "I didn't mean to . . ."

"You didn't. I did . . . You see, she knows it doesn't make sense."

"Doesn't make *sense*? Maybe you didn't hear what you just described."

"I heard, I know, but I didn't finish. When she was sixteen, she was loaded into a truck with five other girls, all on their way to that different type of work, when they did it. Those kids took their last chance and beat the hell out of a *Wehrmacht* corporal who was guarding them in the van. Then with his gun they got control of the truck from the driver and escaped." Dowling stopped, his eyes on Joel.

Converse, silent, returned the look, unsure of its meaning, but moved by what he had heard. "That's a marvellous story," he said quietly. "It really is."

"And," continued the actor, "for the next two years they were hidden by a succession of German families, who surely knew what they were doing and what would happen to them if they got caught. There was a pretty frantic search for those girls – a lot of threats made, more because of what they could tell than anything else. Still, those Germans kept moving them around, hiding them, until one by one they were taken across the border into occupied France where things were easier. They were smuggled across by the underground, the *German* underground." Dowling paused, then added. "As Pa Ratchet would say, 'Do you get my drift, son?' "

"I'd have to say it's obvious."

"There's a lot of pain and a lot of hate in her and God knows I understand it. But there should be some gratitude, too. Couple of times clothing was found, and some of those people – those German people – were tortured, a few shot for what they did. I don't push it, but she could level off with a little gratitude. It might give her a bit more perspective." The actor snapped on his seat belt.

Joel pressed the locks on his attaché case, wondering if he should reply. Valerie's mother had been part of the German underground. His ex-wife would tell him amusing stories her mother had told her about a stern, inhibited French Intelligence officer forced to work with a high-spirited, opinionated German girl, a

100

member of the *Untergrundbewegung*. How the more they disagreed, and the more they railed against each other's nationality, the more they noticed one another. The Frenchman was Val's father; she was proud of him, but in some ways prouder of her mother. There had been pain in that woman too. And hate. But there had been a reason, and it was unequivocal. As there had been for one Joel Converse years later.

"I said it before and I mean it," began Joel slowly, not sure he should say anything at all. "It's none of my business, but I wouldn't ever push it, if I were you."

"Is this a lawyer talkin' to ole Pa?" asked Dowling in his television dialect, his smile false, his eyes far away. "Do I pay a fee?"

"Sorry, I'll shut up." Converse adjusted his seat belt and pushed the buckles in place.

"No, *I'm* sorry. I laid it on you. Say it. Please."

"All right. The horror came first, then the hate. In sidewinder language that's called *prima facie* – the obvious, the first sighting . . . the real, if you like. Without these, there'd be no reason for the gratitude, no call for it. So, in a way, the gratitude is just as painful because it never should have been necessary."

The actor once again studied Joel's face, as he had done before their first exchange of words. "You're a smart son of a bitch, aren't you?"

"Professionally adequate. But I've been there . . . that is, I *know* people who've been where your wife has been. It starts with the horror."

Dowling looked up at the ceiling light, and when he spoke his words floated in the air, his harsh voice quietly strained. "If we go to the movies, I have to check them out; if we're watching television together, I read the TV section . . . sometimes on the news – with some of those fucking nuts – I tense up, wondering what she's going to do. She can't see a swastika, or hear someone screaming in German, or watch soldiers marching in a goosestep; she can't stand it. She runs and throws up and shakes all over . . . and I try to hold her . . . and sometimes she thinks I'm one of them and she screams. After all these years . . . *Christ!*"

"Have you tried professional help – not my kind – but the sort she might need?"

"Oh, hell, she recovers pretty quick," said the actor defensively, as if slipping into a role, his teacher's grammar displaced for effect. "Also, until a few years ago we didn't have the money for that kind of thing," he added sombrely, without effect.

"What about now? That can't be a problem now."

Dowling dropped his eyes to his flight bag at his feet. "If I'd found her sooner . . . maybe. But we were both late bloomers; we got married in our forties – two oddballs looking for something. It's too late now."

"I'm sorry."

"I never should have made this goddamn picture. Never."

"Why did you?"

"She said I should. To show people I could play something more than a drivelling, south-forty dispenser of fifth-rate bromides. I told her it didn't matter . . . I was in the war, in the Marine Corps. I saw some crap in the South

Pacific but nothing to compare with what she went through, not a spit in the proverbial bucket. *Jesus!* Can you imagine what it must have been like?"

"Yes, I can."

The actor looked up from the flight bag, a half-drawn smile on his lined, sun-tanned face. "You, good buddy? Not unless you were caught in Korea . . ."

"I wasn't in Korea."

"Then you'd be hard put to imagine it any more than I. You were too young and I was too lucky."

"Well, there was . . ." Converse fell silent; it was pointless. It had happened so often he did not bother to think about it anymore. 'Nam had been erased from the national conversational psyche. He knew that if he reminded a man like Dowling, a decent man, the air would be filled with apologies, but nothing was served by a jarring remembrance. Not as it pertained to Mrs Dowling, born Muhlstein. "There's the no smoking sign," said Joel, covering. "We'll be in Hamburg in a couple of minutes."

"I've taken this flight a half-dozen times over the past two months," said Caleb Dowling, "and let me tell you, Hamburg's a bitch. Not German customs, that's a snap, especially this late. Those rubber stamps fly and they push you through in ten minutes tops. But then you wait. Twice, maybe three times, it was over an hour before the plane to Bonn even got here. By the way, care to join me or a drink in the lounge?" The actor suddenly switched to is Southern dialect. "Between you and me, they make it mighty pleasant for ol' Pa Ratchet. They Telex ahead and Ah got me my own gaggle of cowpokes, all ridin' hard to git me to the waterin' hole."

"Well . . . ?" Joel felt flattered. Not only did he like Dowling, but being the guest of a celebrity was a pleasant high. He had not had many pleasant things happen to him recently.

"I should also warn you," added the celebrity, "that even at this hour the groupies crawl out of the walls, and the airline PR people manage to roust out the usual newspaper photographers, but none of it takes too long."

Converse was grateful for the warning. "I've got some phone calls to make," he said casually, "but if I finish them on time, I'd like very much to join you."

"Phone calls? At this hour?"

"Back to the States. It's not this hour back in . . . Chicago."

"Make them from the lounge; they keep it open for me."

"It may sound crazy," said Joel, reaching for words, "but I think better alone. There are some complicated things I have to explain. After customs I'll find a phone booth."

"Nothing sounds crazy to me, son. I work in Holl–eeewood." Suddenly, the actor's amused exuberance faded. "In the States," he said softly, his words floating again, eyes distant again. "You remember that crap in Skokie, Illinois? They did a television show on it . . . I was in the study learning lines when I heard the screams and the sound of a door crashing open. l ran out and saw my wife racing down to the beach. I had to drag her out of the water. Sixty-seven years old, and she was a little girl again, back in that goddamn camp, seeing the lines of hollow-eyed prisoners, knowing which lines were which . . . seeing her mother and father,

102

her three kid brothers. When you think about it, you can understand why those people say over and over . . . 'never again'. It can't ever happen again. I wanted to sell that fucking house; I won't leave her alone in it."

"Is she alone now?"

"Nope," said Dowling, his smile returning. "That's the good part. After that night we faced it; we both knew she couldn't be. Got her a sister, that's what we did. Bubbly little thing with more funny stories about Cuckooburg than ever got into print. But she's tough as they come; she's been bouncing around the studios for forty years."

"An actress?"

"Not so's anyone could tell, but she's a great face in the crowd. She's a good lady, too, good for my wife."

"I'm glad to hear it," said Joel, as the aircraft's wheels made bouncing contact with the runway, and the jet engines screeched into reverse thrust. The plane rolled forward, then started a left turn toward its dock.

Dowling turned to Converse. "If you finish your calls, ask someone for the VIP lounge. Tell them you're a friend of mine."

"I'll try to get there."

"If you don't," added the actor in his Santa Fe dialect, see y'awl back in the steel corral. We got us another leg on this here cattle drive, pard'ner. Glad you're ridin' shotgun."

"On a cattle drive?"

"What the hell do I know? I hate horses."

The plane came to a stop and the forward door opened in less than thirty seconds as a number of excited passengers rapidly jammed the aisle. It was obvious from the whispers and the stares and the few who stood up on their toes to get clearer views, that the reason for the swift exodus of this initial crowd was the presence of Caleb Dowling. And the actor was playing his part, dispensing Pa Ratchet benedictions with warm smiles, broad infectious winks and deep-throated laughter, all with good old wrangler humility. As Joel watched, he felt a rush of compassion for this strange man, this actor, this risk-taker with a private hell he shared with the woman he loved.

Never again. It can't ever happen again. Words.

Converse looked down at the attaché case he held with both hands on his lap. Inside was another story, one that held the sound of distant thunder far off bolts of lightning filling the air with deadly electricity.

I am back, I am well, and I am at your service. Also words – from another time – but also swollen with thunder for the present, for they were part of the story of a living man's silent return. A spoke in the wheel of Aquitaine.

The first rush of curious passengers filed through the exit door after the television star, and Joel slipped into the less harried line. He would go through customs as rapidly and as unobtrusively as possible, then find a dark corner of the airport and wait in the deepest shadows until the loudspeakers announced the plane for Köln-Bonn.

Goebbels and Hess accepted Dr Heinrich Leifhelm's offer with enthusiasm. One can easily imagine Goebbels visualizing the image of this blond, Aryan physician of "impeccable credentials" spread across thousands of pamphlets confirming the specious theories of Nazi genetics, as well as his all-too-willing condemnation of the inferior, avaricious Jew; he was heaven-sent. Whereas for Rudolph Hess, who wanted more than his little boys to be accepted by the Junkers and the monied class, the Herr Doktor was his answer; the physician was obviously a true aristocrat, and in time, quite possibly a lover.

The confluence of preparation, timing and appearance turned out to be more than young Stoessel-Leifhelm could have imagined. Adolph Hitler returned from Berlin for one of his Marienplatz rallies, and the imposing *Doktor*, along with his intense, well-mannered son, was invited to dinner with the Fuhrer. The national proclivity was consistent; Hitler heard everything he wanted to hear, and from that day until his death in 1934, Heinrich Leifhelm was Hitler's personal physician.

There was nothing that the son could not have, and in short order he had everything he wanted. In June of 1931, a ceremony was held in the *Heiligtum Hof* at the National Socialists' headquarters where Heinrich Leifhelm's marriage to "a Jewess" was held to be invalid due to a "concealment of Jewish blood" on the part of an "opportunistic Hebrew family", and all rights, claims and inheritances of the children of that "insidious union" were deemed void. A civil marriage was performed between Leifhelm and Marta Stoessel, and the true inheritor, the only child who could claim the name of Leifhelm, was an eighteen-year-old called Erich.

Munich and the Jewish community still laughed, but not as loudly, at the absurd announcement the Nazis inserted in the legal columns of the newspapers. It was considered nonsense; the Leifhelm name was a discredited name, and certainly no paternal inheritance was involved; finally it was all outside the law. What they were only beginning to understand was that the laws were changing in changing Germany; they were not to remain constant. In two short years there would be only one law: Nazi determination.

Erich Leifhelm had arrived and his ascendancy in the party was swift and assured. At eighteen he was *Jugenaführer* of the Hitler Youth movement, photographs of his strong, athletic face and body challenging the children of the New Order to join the national crusade. During his tenancy as a symbol, he was sent to the University of Munich where he completed his courses of study in three years with high academic honours. By this time, Adolf Hitler had been swept into power; he controlled the Reichstag which gave him dictatorial powers. The Thousand Year Reich had begun and Erich Leifhelm was sent to the Officers' Training Centre in Magdeburg.

In 1935, a year after his father's death, Erich Leifhelm, now a youthful favourite of Hitler's inner circle, was promoted to the rank of Oberstleutnant in the Vergeltungswaffen Korps, the youngest field commander in the *Wehrmacht*. He was deeply involved in the vast military expansion that was taking place in Germany, and as the war drew nearer he entered what we can term the third phase of his complicated life, one that ultimately brought him to the centre of Nazi power and at the same time provided him with an extraordinary means of separating himself from the leadership of which he was an intrinsic and influential part. This is briefly covered in the following final pages, a prelude to the fourth phase which we know is his fanatic allegiance to the theories of George Marcus Delavane.

But before we leave the young Erich Leifhelm of Eichstatt, Munich and Magdeburg, two events should be recorded here that provide insights into the man's psychotic mentality. Mentioned above was the robbery at the Luisenstrasse house and the resulting profits of the theft. Leifhelm to this day does not deny the incident,

104

taking pleasure in the tale because of the despicable images he paints of his father's first wife and her overbearing parents. What he does not speak of – nor does anyone in his presence – is the original police report in Munich, which as near as can be determined was destroyed some time in August, 1934, a date corresponding to Hindenburg's death and Hitler's rise to absolute power as both President and Chancellor of Germany with the title of *Der Führer* raised to official mandatory status.

All copies of the police report were removed from the files, but two elderly pensioners from the Munich department remember it clearly. They are both in their late seventies, have not seen each other in years, and were questioned separately.

Robbery was the lesser crime that early morning on the Luisenstrasse; the more serious one was never spoken of at the insistence of the family. The fifteen-year-old Leifhelm daughter was raped and severely beaten, her face and body battered so violently that upon admission to the Karlstor Hospital the doctors gave her little chance of recovery. She did recover physically, but remained emotionally disturbed for the rest of her short life. The man who committed the assault must have been familiar with the interior of the house, had to know there was a back staircase that led to the girl's room, which was separated from her two brothers and her mother in the front. Erich Leifhelm had questioned his father in depth regarding the inside design of that house; he was there by his own admission, and was aware of the fierce pride and strict moral code held by the "tyrannical in-laws". There is no question; his compulsion was such that he had to inflict the most degrading insult he could imagine, and he did so, knowing the influential family would and could insist on official silence.

The second event took place during the months of January or February, 1939. The specifics are sketchy insofar as there are few survivors of the time who knew the family well, and no official records, but from those who were found and interviewed, certain facts surfaced. Heinrich Leifhelm's legal wife, his children and her family tried without success for several years to leave Germany. The official party line was that the old patriarch's medical skills – having been acquired in German universities – were owed to the State. Also, there were unresolved legal questions arising from the disbanded union between the late Doktor Heinrich Leifhelm and a member of the family, questions specifically relating to commonly-shared assets and the rights of inheritance as they affected an outstanding officer of the *Wehrmacht*.

Erich Leifhelm was taking no chances. His father's "former' wife and children were virtually held prisoners, their movements restricted, the house on the Luisenstrasse watched, and for weeks following any renewed applications for visas, they were all kept under full "political surveillance" on the chance that they had plans of vanishing. This information was revealed by a retired banker who recalled that orders came from the Finanzministerium in Berlin instructing the banks of Munich to immediately report any significant withdrawals by the former Frau Leifhelm and/or her family.

During what week or on what day it happened, we did not learn, but some time in January or February of 1936, Frau Leifhelm, her children and her father disappeared.

However, the Munich court records, impounded by the Allies on 23 April 1945, give a clear, if incomplete, picture of what took place. Obviously driven by his compulsion to validate his seizure of the estate in the eyes of the law, a brief was filed on behalf of Oberstleutnant Erich Leifhelm listing the articles-of-grievance suffered by his father, Dr Heinrich Leifhelm, at the hands of a family cabal, said family of criminals having fled the Reich under indictment. The charges, as expected, were outrageous lies: from outright theft of huge non-existent bank accounts to character assassination in order to usurp a great doctor's practice. There was the legal certificate of the "official" divorce, and a copy of the elder Leifhelm's last will and testament. There was only one true union and one true son, all rights, privileges and inheritances passed on to him: Oberstleutnant Erich Stoessel Leifhelm.

Possessing reasonably accurate dates, survivors were found. It was confirmed that Frau Leifhelm, her three children and her father perished at Dachau, ten miles outside of Munich.

The Jewish Leifhelms were gone; the Aryan Leifhelm was now the sole inheritor of considerable wealth and property that would have been confiscated. Before the age of thirty, he had wiped his personal slate clean and avenged the wrongs he was convinced had been visited on his superior birth and talents. A killer had matured.

"You must have one hell of a case there," said Caleb Dowling, grinning and poking Joel with his elbow. "Your butt burned up in the ashtray a while ago. I reached over to close the goddamned lid and all you did was raise your hand like I was out of order."

"I'm *sorry*. It's . . . it's a complicated brief. Christ, I wouldn't raise my hand to you, you're a celebrity." Converse laughed because he knew it was expected.

"Well, my second bit of news for you, good buddy, is that celebrity or no, the smoking lamp's been on for a couple of minutes now and you still got a reefer in your fingers. Now, I grant you, you didn't light it, but we're getting a lot of Nazi looks over here."

"Nazi . . . ?" Joel spoke the word involuntarily, as he pressed the unlighted cigarette into the receptacle; he was not aware that he had been holding it.

"A figure of speech and a bad line," said the actor. "We'll be in Köln before you put all that legal stuff away. Come on, good buddy, he's going in for the approach."

"No, countered Joel without thinking. "He's making a pitch-out until he gets the tower's instructions. It's standard; we've got at least three minutes."

"You sound like you know what the hell you're talking about."

"Vaguely," said Converse, putting the Leifhelm dossier into his attaché case. "I used to be a pilot."

"No kidding? A *real* pilot?"

"Well, I got paid."

"For an airline? I mean, one of these *real* airlines?"

"Larger than this one, I think."

"Goddamn, I'm impressed. I wouldn't have thought so. Lawyers and pilots somehow don't seem compatible."

"It was a long time ago." Joel closed his case and snapped the locks.

The plane rolled down the runway, the landing having been so unobtrusive that a smattering of applause erupted from the rear of the aircraft. Dowling spoke as he unfastened his seat belt. "I used to hear some of that after a particularly good class."

"Now you hear a lot more," said Converse.

"For a hell of a lot less. By the way, where are you staying. counsellor?"

Joel was not prepared for the question. "Actually, I'm not sure," he replied, again reaching for words, for an answer. "This trip was a last-minute decision."

"You may need help. Bonn's crowded. Tell you what, I'm at the Konigshof and I suspect I've got a little influence. Let's see what we can do."

"Thanks very much but that won't be necessary." Converse thought rapidly. The last thing he wanted was the attention focused on anyone in the actor's company. "My firm's sending someone to meet me and he'll have seen to the accommodation. As a matter of fact, I'm supposed to be one of the last people off the plane, so he doesn't have to try and find me in the crowd."

"Well, if you've got any time and you want a couple of laughs with some actor types, call me at the hotel and leave a number."

"I probably will. I enjoyed riding shotgun."

"On a cattle drive, pard'ner?"

Joel waited. The last stragglers were leaving the plane nodding at the flanking stewardesses, some yawning, others in awkward combat with shoulder bags, camera equipment, and suit-carriers. The final passenger exited through the aircraft's concave door and Converse got up, gripping the handle of his attaché case and sliding into the aisle. Instinctively, without having a conscious reason to do so, he glanced to his right, into the rear section of the plane.

What he saw – and what saw him – caused him to freeze, his breath exploding silently within his chest. Seated in the last row of the long fuselage was a woman. The pale skin under the wide brim of the hat, and the frightened, astonished eyes that abruptly looked away – all formed an image he vividly remembered. She was the woman in the café at the Kastrup Airport in Copenhagen! When he last saw her she was walking rapidly into the baggage claim area, *away* from the row of airline counters. She had been stopped by a man in a hurry; words had been exchanged – and now Joel knew they had concerned him.

The woman had doubled back, unnoticed in the last-minute rush for boarding. He felt it, he *knew* it! She had followed him from Denmark!

6

Converse rushed up the aisle and through the metal door into the carpeted tunnel. Fifty feet down the passageway the narrow walls opened into a waiting area, the plastic seats and the roped-off stanchions designating the gate. There was no one; the place was empty, the other gates shut down, the lights off. Beyond, suspended from the ceiling were signs in German, French, and English directing passengers to the main terminal and the downstairs baggage claim. There was no time for his luggage; he had to run; he had to get away from the airport as fast as possible, get away without being seen. Then the obvious struck him, and he felt sick. He *had* been seen; they knew he was on the flight from Hamburg – whoever *they* were. The instant he walked into the terminal, he would be spotted, and there was nothing he could do about it. They had found him in Copenhagen; the woman had found him and she had been ordered on board to make certain he did not stay in Hamburg, or switch planes to another destination.

How? How did they *do* it?

There was no time to think about it; he would think about it later – if there was a later. He passed the arches of the closed-down metal detectors and the black conveyor belts where hand luggage was X-rayed. Ahead, no more than 75 feet were the doors to the terminal. What was he going to do, what *should* he do?

Nur für hier Beschäftigte Männer

Joel stopped. The sign on the door was emphatic, the German print forbidding. Yet he had seen those words before. Where? What was it? Zurich! He had been in a department store in Zurich when a stomach attack had descended to his bowels. He had pleaded with a sympathetic clerk who had taken him to a nearby employees' men's room. In one of those odd moments of gratitude and relief, he had focused on the strange words as they had drawn nearer. *Nur fur hier Beschäftigte Männer*.

No further memory was required. He pushed the door open and went inside, not sure what he would do other than collect his thoughts. A man in green overalls was at the far end of the line of sinks against the wall; he was combing his hair while inspecting a blemish on his face in the mirror. Converse walked to the row of urinals beyond the basins, his demeanour that of an airline executive. The affectation was accepted; the man mumbled something courteously and left. The door swung shut and he was alone.

Joel stepped back from the urinal and studied the tiled enclosure, hearing for the first time the sound of several voices ... outside, somewhere outside, beyond ... the *windows*. Three-quarters up from the floor and recessed in the far wall were three frosted glass windows, the painted white frame melting into the whiteness of the room. He was confused. In these security-conscious days of airline travel with the constant emphasis on guarding against smuggled arms and narcotics, a room inside a gate area that had a means of getting *outside before* entering customs did not make sense. Then the obvious fact occurred to him. It could be his way out! The flight from Hamburg was a *domestic* flight, this part of the Köln-Bonn airport a *domestic* terminal – there were no customs. Of *course* there were exterior windows in an enclosure like this. What difference did it make? Passengers still had to pass through the electronic arches, and conversely, authorities wanting to pick up a passenger flying domestically would simply wait by a specific gate.

But no one waited for him. He had been the last – the *second* to last – passenger off the late night flight. The roped-off gate had been deserted; anyone sitting in one of the plastic chairs or standing beyond the counter would be obvious. Therefore, those who were keeping him in their sights did not want to be seen themselves. Whoever they were, they were waiting, watching for him from some remote spot inside the terminal. They could wait.

108

He approached the far right window and lowered his attaché case to the floor. Standing erect, the sill was only inches above his head. He reached for the two white handles and pushed; the window slid easily up several inches. He poked his fingers through the space; there was no screen. Once the window was raised to its full height, there would be enough room for him to crawl outside.

There was a clattering behind him, rapid slaps of metal against wood. He spun around as the door opened revealing a hunched-over old man in a white maintenance uniform carrying a mop and pail. Slowly, with deliberation, the old man took out a pocket watch, squinted at it, said something in German, and waited for an answer. Joel was not only aware that he was expected to speak, he assumed that he had been told the employees' men's room was being closed until morning. He had to think; he could not leave; the only way out of the airport was through the terminal. If there was another, he did not know where and it was no time to be running around a section of an airport shut down for the remainder of the night. Patrolling guards might compound his problems.

His eyes dropped, centring on the metal pail, and in desperation he knew what he had to do, but not whether he could do it. With a sudden grimace of pain, he moaned and grabbed his chest, falling to his knees. He cried louder, his face contorted, and sank further to the floor.

"Doctor, doctor . . . *Doctor!*" he shouted over and over again in muted tones of pain.

The old man dropped the mop and the pail; a guttural stream of panicked phrases accompanied several cautious steps forward. Converse rolled to his right against the wall; he gasped for breath as he watched the German with wide, blank eyes.

"Doctor . . . !" he whispered.

The old man trembled and backed away toward the door; he turned, opened it, and ran out, his frail voice raised for help.

There would only be seconds! The gate was no more than two hundred feet to the left, the entrance to the terminal perhaps a hundred to the right. Joel got up quickly, raced to the pail, turned it upside down, and brought it back to the window. He placed it on the floor and stepped up with one foot, his palms making contact with the base of the window; he shoved. The glass rose about four inches and stopped, the frame lodged against the sash. He pushed again with all the strength he could manage in his awkward position. The window would not budge; breathing hard he studied it, his intense gaze zeroing in on two small steel objects he wished to God were not in place, but they were. Two protective braces were screwed into the opposing sashes, preventing the window from being opened more than six inches. Köln-Bonn might not be an international airport with a panoply of sophisticated security devices, but it was not without its own.

There were distant shouts from beyond the door; the old man had reached someone. The sweat rolled down Converse's face as he stepped off the pail and reached for his attaché case on the floor. Movement and decision were intertwined, neither preceding the other, only instinct unconsciously governing both. Joel picked up the leather case, stepped forward, and crashed it repeatedly into the window, shattering the glass, finally breaking away the lower wooden frame. He stepped back up on the pail and looked out. Beyond – below – was a cement path bordered by a guardrail, floodlights in the distance, no one in sight. He threw the attaché case out of the window, and pulled himself up, his left knee kicking fragments of glass and what was left of the frame to the concrete below. Awkwardly, he hunched his whole body, pressing his head into his shoulder blades, and plunged through the opening. As he fell to the ground, he heard the shouts from inside: they grew in volume, all in counterpoint, mixtures of anger and bewilderment. He ran.

Minutes later, at a sudden curve in the cement path, he saw the floodlit entrance of the terminal and the line of taxis waiting for the passengers of Flight 817 from Hamburg to collect their luggage before the drivers collected their inflated night prices to Bonn and Köln. There were entrance and exit roads leading to the platform, broken by pedestrian crosswalks, and beyond these an immense parking lot with several lighted booths still operating for those driving their own cars. Converse slipped over the guardrail and ran across the intersecting lawn until he reached the first road, racing into the shadows at the first blinding glare of a floodlight. He had to reach a taxi, a taxi with a driver who spoke English; he could not remain on foot . . . he had been captured on foot once, years ago. On a jungle trail, where if he had only been able to commandeer a jeep – an enemy jeep – he might have . . . *Stop it!* This is not 'Nam, it's a goddamn airport with a million tons of concrete poured between flowers, grass, and asphalt! He kept moving in and out of the shadows, until he had made a complete semi-circle – one-eight zero. He was in darkness, the last of the taxis in the line ahead if him. He approached the first, which was the last.

"English? Do you speak English?"

"*Englisch? Nein.*"

The second cab driver was equally negative, but the third was not.

"As you Americans say, only the asshole would drive a taxi here wizzout the English reasonable. Is so?"

"It's reasonable," said Joel, opening the door.

"*Nein!* You cannot do that!"

"Do what?"

"Come in the taxi."

"Why not?"

"The line. Allviss is the line."

Converse reached into his jacket pocket and withdrew a folded layer of Deutschemarks. "I'm generous. Can you understand that?"

"Is also urgent sickness. Get in, *Mein Herr.*"

The cab pulled out of the line and sped toward the exit road. "Bonn or Köln?" asked the driver.

"Bonn," replied Converse, "but not yet. I want you to drive into the other lane and stop across the way in front of that parking lot."

"*Vas . . . ?*"

"The other lane. I want to watch the entrance back there. I think there was someone on the Hamburg plane I know."

110

"Many have come out. Only those with luggage."

"She's still inside," insisted Joel. "*Please*, just do as I say."

"She . . . Ach, *ein Fräulein*. Is your Deutschemarks, *Mein Herr*."

The driver swung the cab into the cut off that led to the incoming road and the parking lot. He stopped in the shadows beyond the second booth; the terminal doors were on the left, no more than a hundred yards away. Converse watched as weary passengers, carrying assorted suitcases, golfbags, and the ever-present camera equipment, began to file out of the terminal's entrance, most raising their hands for taxis, a few walking across the pedestrian lanes toward the parking lot.

Twelve minutes passed and still there was no sign of the woman from Copenhagen. She could not have been carrying luggage, so the delay was voluntary, or instructed. The driver of the cab had assumed the role of non-observer; he had turned off the lights, and with a bowed head appeared to be dozing. Silence . . . Across the parallel roads, the travellers from Hamburg had dwindled down. Several young men, undoubtedly students, two in scissored jeans, their companions drinking from cans of beer, were laughing as they counted the bills of Deutschemarks between them. A yawning businessman in a three-piece suit struggled with a bulging suitcase and an enormous cardboard box wrapped in a floral print, while an elderly couple argued, their dispute emphasized by two shaking heads of grey hair. Five others, men and women, were by the kerb at the far end of the platform apparently waiting for prearranged transportation. But where . . . ?

Suddenly, she was there, but she was not alone. Instead, she was flanked by two men, a third directly behind her. All four walked slowly, casually out of the automatic glass doors, moving to the left, their pace quickening until they reached the dimmest area of the canopied entrance. Then the three men angled themselves in front of the woman, as if mounting a wall of protection, their heads turning, talking to her over their shoulders while studying the crowd. Their conversation became animated but controlled, anger joining confusion, tempers held in check. The man on the right broke away and crossed to the corner of the building, then walked beyond into the shadows. He pulled an object out of an inside pocket and Joel instantly knew what it was; the man raised it to his lips. Someone in or around the airport was being contacted by radio.

Barely seconds passed when the beams of powerful headlights burst through the glass over Converse's right shoulder, filling the back of the taxi. He pressed himself into the seat, his head turned, neck arched, his face at the edge of the rear window. Beyond, by the exit booth of the parking lot, a dark red limousine had stopped, the driver's arm extended, a bill clutched in his hand. The attendant took the money, turned to give change, when the large car lurched forward leaving the man in the booth bewildered. It careened around the taxi and headed for the curve in the road that led to the airport terminal's entrance. The timing was too precise; radio contact had been made and Joel spoke to the driver.

"I told you I was generous," he said, startled by the words he was forming in his head. "I can be *very* generous if you'll do as I ask you."

"I am an honest man, *Mein Herr*," replied the German, uncertainty in his voice, his eyes looking at Joel in the rear-view mirror.

"So am I," said Converse. "But I'm also honestly curious, and there's nothing wrong with that. You see the dark red car over there, the one that's stopping at the corner of the building?"

"*Ja.*"

"Do you think you could follow it without being seen? You'd have to stay pretty far behind, but keep it in sight. Could you do it?"

"Is not a reasonable request. How generous is the *Amerikaner?*"

"Two hundred Deutschemarks over the fare."

"You are generous, *Mein Herr*, and I am a superior driver."

The German did not underestimate his talents behind the wheel. Skilfully, he weaved the cab unobtrusively through a cut off, swinging abruptly left into the parallel exit road and bypassing the entrance to the terminal.

"What are you doing?" asked Joel, confused. "I want you to follow."

"Is only way out," interrupted the driver, glancing back at the airport platform while maintaining moderate speed. "I shall let him pass me. I am just one more insignificant taxi on the *Landstrasse.*"

Converse sank back into the corner of the seat, his head away from the windows. "That's reasonably good thinking," he said.

"Superior, *Mein Herr.*" Again the driver looked briefly back out of the window, then concentrated on the road and the rear view mirror. Moments later he gradually accelerated his speed; it was not noticeable; there was no breaking away, instead merely a faster pace. He eased to the left, passing a Mercedes coupé, staying in the lane to overtake a Volkswagen, then returning to the right.

"I hope you know what you're doing," muttered Joel.

No reply was necessary as the dark red vehicle streaked by on the left.

"Directly ahead the road separates," said the driver. "One way to Köln, the other to Bonn. You say you are going to Bonn, *Mein Herr*, but what if your friend goes to Köln?"

"Stay with him."

The limousine entered the road for Bonn and Converse lighted a cigarette, his thoughts on the reality of having been found, which meant his name was known from the passenger manifest. So be it; he would have preferred otherwise but once the initial contact had been made with Bertholdier, it was not a vital point. He could operate as himself; his past might even be an asset. Also, there was a positive side to the immediate situation; he had learned something, several things. Those following him – who now had lost him – were no part of the authorities; they were not connected with either the German or the French police, or the coordinating Interpol. If they were, they would have taken him at the gate or on the plane itself, and that told him something else. Joel Converse was not wanted for assault or – God forbid – murder back in Paris. And this assumption could only lead to a third probability: the violent, bloody struggle in the alley was being covered up. Jacques Louis Bertholdier was taking no chances that because of his severely wounded aide his own name might surface in any connection whatsoever with a wealthy guest of the hotel who had made such alarming insinuations to the revered general. The protection of Aquitaine was paramount.

There was a fourth possibility, so realistically arrived at it could be considered fact. The men in the dark red limousine who had met the Hamburg plane were also part of Aquitaine, underlings of Erich Leifhelm, the spoke of Aquitaine in West Germany. Some time during the last five hours, Bertholdier had learned the identity of the ersatz Henry Simon – probably through the management of the George V – and contacted Leifhelm. Then, both alarmed that no passenger manifest listed an American named Converse flying from Paris to Bonn, they checked the other airlines and found he had gone to Copenhagen. The alarms must have been strident. Why Copenhagen? He said he was going to Bonn. Why did this strange man with his extraordinary information go to Copenhagen? Who are his contacts, who will he meet? Find him. Find *them!* Another phone call had been made, a description given, and a woman had stared at him in a café in the Kastrup Airport. It was all so through-the-looking-glass.

He had flown to Denmark for one reason, but another purpose had been served. They had found him, but in the finding they revealed their own panic. An agitated reception committee, the use of a radio at night to reach an unseen vehicle only a few hundred feet away, a racing limousine; these were the ingredients of anxiety. The enemy was off-balance and the lawyer in Converse was satisfied. At this moment, that enemy was a quarter of a mile down the road, speeding into Bonn, unaware that a taxi behind them, skilfully manoeuvred by a driver slipping around the intermittent traffic was keeping them in sight.

Joel crushed out his cigarette as the driver slowed down to let a pick-up truck pass, the large dark red car seen clearly ahead on the long curve. The German was no amateur; he knew the beneficial moves to make, and Converse understood. Whoever was in that limousine might well be an influential owner, and even two hundred Deutschemarks were not worth the probable enmity of a powerful man.

Probabilities . . . everything was probabilities. He had built his legal reputation on the study of probabilities and it was a simpler process than most of his colleagues believed. The approach, that is, was simple, not the work; that was never easy. It demanded the dual discipline of both concentrating on the minute, and prodding the imagination to expand until the minutiae were arranged and rearranged into dozens of different equations. The exhaustive what-if syndrome was the keystone of legal thinking; it was as simple as that. It was also a verbal trap, Joel reflected, as he thought back several years, an uncomfortable smile forming. In one of her moments of pique, Val had told him that if he would spend one iota of the time on the two of them that he spent on his "goddamned probabilities", he would "probably" come to realize that the "probability" of their surviving together was "very probably nil".

She had never lacked for being succinct, nor sacrificed her humour in the pursuit of candour. Her striking looks aside, Valerie Carpentier Converse was a very funny lady. Unable not to, he had smiled at her explosion that night years ago, then they had both laughed quietly until she turned away and left the room, too much sadness in the truth she had spoken.

Large picturesque buildings gradually replaced the quiet countryside, so many somehow reminding Converse of huge Victorian houses with filigreed borders and overlapping eaves and grilled balconies beneath large rectangular windows – geometric shapes starkly defined. These in turn gave way to a contradictory stretch of attractive but perfectly ordinary residential homes, the sort that could be found in any traditional wealthy suburb on the outskirts of a major American city. Scarsdale, Chevy Chase, Grosse Pointe, or Evanston. Then came the centre of Bonn where narrow, gas-lit streets ran into wider avenues with modern lighting, quaint squares only blocks away from banks of contemporary stores and boutiques. It was an architectural anachronism – old world ambience coexisting with up-to-the-minute structure – but with no sense of a city, no sense of electricity or grandeur. Instead it appeared to be a large town, growing rapidly larger, the town fathers uncertain of its direction. The birthplace of Beethoven and the gateway to the Rhine Valley was the most unlikely capital of a major government imaginable. It was anything but the seat of a hard-nosed Bundestag, and a series of astute, sophisticated prime ministers who faced the Russian bear across the borders.

"*Mein Herr!*" cried the driver. "They take the road to Bad Godesberg. *Das Diplomatenviertel.*"

"What does that mean?"

"Embassies. They have *Polizeistreifen!* We could be, how do you say, *known?*"

"Spotted," explained Joel. "Never mind. Do what you've been doing, you're great. Stop, if you have to; park, if you have to. Then keep going. You now have three hundred Deutschemarks over the fare. I want to know where they stop."

It came six minutes later, and Converse was stunned. Whatever he had thought, wherever his imagination had led him, he was not prepared for the driver's words.

"That is the American Embassy, *Mein Herr.*"

Joel tried to focus his thoughts. "Take me to the Hotel Konigshof," he said, remembering, not knowing what else to say.

"Yes, I believe Herr Dowling left a note to that effect," said the desk clerk, reaching below the counter.

"He *did?*" Converse was astonished. He had used the actor's name in the outside hope of some possible preferential treatment. He expected nothing else, if, indeed, that.

"Here it is." The clerk extracted two small telephone memos from the thin stack in his hand. "You are John Converse, an American attorney."

"Close enough. That's me."

"Herr Dowling said you might have difficulty finding appropriate accommodation here in Bonn. Should you come to the Konigshof tonight, he requested that we be as helpful as possible. It is possible, Herr Converse. Herr Dowling is a very popular man."

"He deserves to be," said Joel.

"I see he also left a message for you."

The clerk turned and retrieved a sealed envelope from one of the mailboxes behind him. He handed it to Converse, who opened it.

Hi, pard'ner.

If you don't pick this up, I'll get it back in the morning. Forgive me, but you sounded like too many of my less fortunate colleagues who say no when they want to say yes. Now collectively in their case, it's some kind of warped pride because they think I'm suggesting a handout – it's either that or they don't want to meet someone who may be where they're going. By the looks of you, I'd have to rule out the former and stick with the latter. There's someone you don't want to meet here in Bonn, and you don't have to. The room's taken care of and in my name – change that if you like – but don't argue about the bill. I owe you a fee, counsellor, and I always pay my debts. At least during the last four years I have.

Incidentally, you'd make a lousy actor. Your pauses aren't at all convincing.

Pa Ratchet

Joel put the note back in the envelope, resisting the temptation to go to a house phone and call Dowling. The man would have little enough sleep before going to work; thanks could wait until morning. Or evening.

"Mr Dowling's arrangements are generous and completely satisfactory," he said to the clerk behind the counter. "He's right. If my clients knew I'd come to Bonn a day early, I'd have no chance to enjoy your beautiful city."

"Your privacy will be respected, sir. Herr Dowling is a most thoughtful man, as well as generous, of course. Your luggage is outside with a taxi, perhaps?"

"No, that's why I'm so late. It was put on the wrong plane out of Hamburg and will be here in the morning. At least that's what I was told at the airport."

"*Ach*, so inconvenient, but all too familiar. Is there anything you might require?"

"No thanks," replied Converse, raising his attaché case slightly. "The bare necessities travel with me ... Well, there is one thing. Would it be possible to order a drink?"

"Of course."

Joel sat up in bed, the dossier at his side, the drink in his hand. He needed a few minutes to think before going back into the world of Field Marshal Erich Leifhelm. With the help of the switchboard, he had called the all-night number for Lufthansa and had been assured that his suitcase would be held for him at the airport. He gave no explanation other than the fact that he had been travelling for two days and nights and simply did not care to wait for his luggage. The attendant could read into his words whatever she liked; he did not care. His mind was on other things.

The American Embassy! What appalled him was the stark reality of old Beale's words ... *Behind it all are those who do the convincing, and they're growing in numbers everywhere ... We're in the countdown – three to five weeks, that's all you've got ... It's real and it's coming.* Joel was not prepared for the reality. He could accept Delavane and Bertholdier, certainly Leifhelm, but the shock of knowing that ordinary embassy personnel – *American* personnel – were on the receiving end of orders from Delavane's network was paralysing. How far *had* Aquitaine progressed? How widespread were its followers, its influence? Was tonight the frightening answer to both questions? He would think about it all in the morning. First, he had to be prepared for the man he had come to find in Bonn. As he reached for the dossier, he remembered the sudden deep panic in Avery Fowler's eyes – Preston Halliday's eyes. How long had he known? How much had he known?

It is pointless to recount Erich Leifhelm's exploits in the early to middle years of the war other than to say his reputation grew, and – what is most important that he was one of the very few superior officers to come up through Nazi party ranks to be accepted by the old line professional generals. Not only did they accept him but they sought him out for their commands. Men like Rundstedt and von Falkenhausen, Rommel and von Treskow; at one time or another each asked Berlin for Leifhelm's services. He was unquestionably a brilliant strategist and a daring officer, but there was something else. These generals were aristocrats, part of the ruling class of pre-war Germany and by and large loathed the National Socialists, considering them thugs, exhibitionists and amateurs. It is not difficult to imagine Leifhelm, sitting among these men, modestly expounding on what was clearly noted in his military record. He was the son of the late prominent Munich surgeon Dr Heinrich Leifhelm, who had left him considerable wealth and property. We need no conjecture, however, to understand how much further he went to ingratiate himself, for the following is extracted from an interview with General Rolf Winter, Standortkommandant of the Wehrbereichskommando in the Saar sectors.

"We would sit around having coffee after dinner, the talk quite depressing. We knew the war was lost. The insane orders from Berlin – most we agreed we would never carry out – guaranteed wholesale slaughter of troops and civilians. It was madness, a *Gotterdammerung*. And always, this young Leifhelm would say things like, 'Perhaps the fools will listen to me. They think I'm one of them, they've thought so from the early days in Munich.' . . . And we would wonder. Could he bring some sanity to the collapsing front? He was a fine officer, highly regarded, and the son of a well-known doctor, as he constantly reminded us. After all, young men's heads were turned in those early days – the cavernous roars of *Sieg Heil*, the fanatic crowds; the banners and drums and marching beside ten thousand torches at night; it was all so melodramatic, so Wagnerian. But Leifhelm was different; he wasn't one of the gangsters; patriotic, of course, but not a hoodlum . . . So we sent dispatches with him to our closest comrades in Berlin, dispatches that would have resulted in our execution if they fell into the wrong hands. We were told he tried very hard, but he could not pull sanity out of the minds of men who lived in daily fear of death from rumour and gossip. But he maintained his own sanity – and loyalty – which were constant. We were informed by one of his adjutants, not him, mind you, that he was confronted by an SS colonel who had followed him in the street and demanded the contents of his briefcase. He refused, and when threatened with immediate arrest, he shot the man so as not to betray us. He was one of us. It was a noble risk and only a night bombing raid saved his own life."

It is clear what Leifhelm was doing and equally clear that the dispatches were never shown to anyone, nor was there an SS colonel shot in the streets during a bombing raid. According to Winter, those dispatches from Saar were so explosive in content someone would have remembered them; no one does. Once again, Leifhelm saw an opportunity. The war was lost, and the Nazis were about to become the ultimate twentieth century villains. But not the élite, German general corps – there was a distinction. He wiped another slate clean and joined the "Prussians". He was so successful that he was rumoured to have been part of the plot to assassinate Adolf Hitler at Wolfsschanze, and called upon to be a member of Doenitz's surrender team.

During the cold war, Allied Central Command asked him to join other key elements of the *Wehrmacht* officer corps in the *Bundes Polizei*. He became a privileged military consultant with full security clearance. A mature killer had survived and history, with the Kremlin's help, took care of the rest.

In May 1949 the Federal Republic was established, and the following September the Allied occupation formally came to an end. As the cold war escalated and West Germany began its remarkable recovery, the NATO forces demanded material and personnel support from their former enemies. The new German divisions were formed under the command of ex-Field Marshal Erich Leifhelm.

No one had dredged up the questionable decisions of the Munich courts from nearly two decades past; there were no other survivors and his services were desired by the victors. During the post-war reconstruction when countless settlements and labyrinthine legal resolutions were being sought throughout Germany, he was quietly awarded all assets and property previously decreed, including some of the most valuable real estate in Munich. So ends the third phase of Erich Leifhelm's story. The fourth phase – which concerns us most – is the one we know least about. The only certainty is that he has become as deeply entrenched in General Delavane's operation as any name on the primary list.

There was a rapping on the door. Joel lunged off the bed, the Leifhelm dossier cascading to the floor. He looked at his watch, fear paramount, confusion not far behind. It was nearly four o'clock. Who wanted him at *this* hour? Had they *found* him? Oh, *Christ!* The *dossier!* The *brief-case!*

"Joe . . . ? *Joe, you up?*" The voice was both a whisper and a shout . . . an actor's *sotto voce.* "It's me, Cal Dowling."

Converse ran to the door and opened it, his breath coming in gasps. Dowling was fully dressed, holding up both his hands for silence, as he glanced up and down the corridor. Satisfied, he walked rapidly inside, pushing Joel back and closing the door.

"I'm *sorry*, Cal," said Converse. "I was asleep. I guess the sound startled me."

"You always sleep in your trousers with the lights on?" asked the actor quietly. "Keep your voice down. I checked the hallways, but you can never be clear about what you didn't see."

"Clear about what?"

"One of the first things we learned on Kwajalein in 'forty-four. A patrol doesn't mean shit unless you've got something to report. All it means is that they were better than you were."

"I was going to call you, to thank you . . ."

"*Cut* it, *good* buddy," broke in the lined, sun-tanned Dowling, his expression serious. "I'm timing this down to the last couple of minutes, which is about all we've got. There's a limo downstairs waiting to take me out to the cameras over an hour away. I didn't want to come out of my room before in case anyone was hanging around, and I didn't want to call you because a switchboard can be watched or bribed – ask anyone in Cuckooburg. I don't worry about the desk; they're not too fond of our crowd over here." The actor sighed and shook his head. "When I got to my room, all I wanted was sleep, and all I got was a visitor.

117

I'm down the hall and I was hoping to Christ – *if* you came here – he wouldn't see you."

"A visitor?"

"From the embassy. The *US* embassy. Tell me, Joe."

"Joel," interrupted Converse. "Not that it matters."

"Sorry, I've an obstruction in my left ear and that doesn't matter, either . . . He spent damn near twenty-five minutes with me asking questions about you. He said we were seen talking together on the plane. Now, you *tell* me, counsellor, are you okay, or are my instincts all fucked up?"

Joel returned Dowling's steady gaze. "Your instincts are perfectly fine," he said without emphasis. "Did the man from the embassy say otherwise?"

"Not exactly. As a matter of fact, he didn't *say* a hell of a *lot*. Just that they wanted to talk to you, wanted to know why you'd come to Bonn, where you were."

"But they knew I was on the plane?"

"Yep, said you'd flown out of Paris."

"Then they knew I was on that plane."

"That's what I just said – what he said."

"Then why didn't they meet me at the gate and ask me themselves?"

Dowling's face creased farther, his eyes narrowing within the wrinkles of bronzed flesh. "Yeah, why didn't they?" he asked himself.

"Did he say?"

"No, but then Paris didn't come up until he was about to leave."

"What do you mean?"

"It was like he figured I was holding back something – which I certainly was – but he couldn't be sure. I'm pretty good at what I do, Joe . . . Joel."

"You also took a risk," said Converse, remembering that he was talking to a risk-taker.

"No, I covered myself. I specifically asked if there were charges against you or anything like that. He said there weren't."

"Still, he was . . ."

"Besides, I didn't like him. He was one of those pushy official types. He kept repeating things, and when he couldn't come up with anything, he said, 'We know he flew out of Paris,' as if challenging me. I said *I* didn't."

"There's not much time, but can you tell me what else he asked you?"

"I told you, he wanted to know everything we talked about. I said I didn't have a tape recorder in my head, but it was mainly small talk, the kind of chatter I get all the time from people I meet on planes. About the show, the business. But he didn't want to settle for that; he kept pushing, which gave me the opportunity to get a little pissed off myself."

"How so?"

"I said, yes, we did talk about something else but it was very personal, and none of his damn business. He got pretty upset at that, and that let me get even angrier. We exchanged a few barbs but his weren't very sharp; he was too uptight. Then he asked me for about the tenth time if you'd said anything about Bonn, especially where you were staying. So I told him for the tenth time the truth –

118

at least what you said. That you were a lawyer and here to see clients and I didn't know where the hell you were. I mean I didn't actually know you were here."

"That's fine."

"Is it? Instincts are okay for first reactions, counsellor, but then you have to wonder. An aggravating Ivy League government man, waving an embassy ID and acting obnoxious, may be very annoying in the middle of the night, but he *is* from the Department of State. What the hell's this all about?"

Joel turned and walked to the foot of the bed; he looked down at the Leifhelm dossier on the floor. He turned again and spoke clearly, hearing the exhaustion in his voice. "Something I wouldn't for the life of me involve you in. But for the record, those instincts of yours were right on, pard'ner."

"I'll be honest," said the actor, his clear eyes amused, peering out from behind the crag-lines. "I thought as much. I said to that bastard if I remembered anything else, I'd phone Walter what's-his-name – except I called him Walt – and let him know."

"I don't understand."

"He's the ambassador here in Bonn. Can you imagine. with all the troubles they've got over here, that diplomatic yo-yo had a luncheon for *me*, a lousy television actor? . . . Well, that bit of volunteerism on my part made our Preppie more upset than anything else; he didn't expect it. He said – three times, as I recall – that the ambassador wasn't to be bothered with this problem. It wasn't that important, and he had enough on his mind, and actually he wasn't even aware of it. And catch this, Mr Lawyer. He said you were an in-house, State Department 'queery', as if a simple-minded actor couldn't possibly understand bureaucratic jingoism. I think that's when I said 'bullshit'."

"Thank you," said Converse, not knowing what else to say, but knowing what he wanted to find out.

"That's also when I figured my instincts weren't so bad." Dowling looked at his watch, then hard at Converse, his eyes now penetrating. "I was a Marine, but I'm no flag-waver, good buddy. However, I *like* the flag. I wouldn't live under any other."

"Neither would I."

"Then you make it plain. Are you working for it?"

"Yes, the only way I know how and that's all I can tell you."

"Are you looking into something here in Bonn? Is that why you didn't want to be seen with me? Why you stayed away from me in Hamburg . . . and even getting off the plane here?"

"Yes."

"And that son of a bitch didn't want me to call the ambassador."

"No, he didn't. He doesn't. He can't afford it. And, please, I ask you not to."

"Are you – oh, *Christ!* Are you one of those undercover people I read about? I walk into a guy on a plane who can't be seen when he gets to an airport."

"It's not that melodramatic. I'm a lawyer and simply following up on some alleged irregularities. Please accept that. And I appreciate what you did for me. I'm kind of new at this myself."

"You're cool, good buddy. *Man*, are you cool." Dowling turned and walked to the door. He stopped and looked back at Converse. "Maybe I'm crazy," he said. "At my age it's allowed, but there's a streak in you, young fella. Part go-ahead, part stay-where-you-are. I saw it when I talked about my wife. Are you married?"

"I was."

"Who isn't? *Was* married, that is. Sorry."

"I'm not. We're not."

"Who is? Sorry, again. My instincts were right. You're okay." Dowling reached for the knob.

"Cal?"

"Yes?"

"I have to know. It's terribly important. Who was the man from the embassy? He must have identified himself."

"He did," said the actor. "He pushed an ID in front of my face when I opened the door, but I didn't have my glasses on. But when he was leaving I made it clear I wanted to know who the hell he was."

"Who was he?"

"He said his name was Fowler. Avery Fowler."

7

"*Wait!*"

"What?"

"*What did* you say!?" Converse reeled under the impact of the name. He physically had to steady himself, grabbing the nearest solid object, a bedpost, to keep from buckling.

"What's the matter, Joe? What's wrong with you?"

"That name! Is this some kind of joke – a bad joke – a bad *line!* Were you *put* on *the* plane? Did I walk into *you!* Are you part of it, Mr *Actor?* You're damned good at what you do!"

"You're either juiced or sick. What are you talking about?"

"This *room,* your *note! Everything! That name!* Is this whole goddamned night a set up?"

"It's morning, young man, and if you don't like this room you can stay wherever you like as far as I'm concerned."

"Wherever . . . ?" Joel tried to push the blinding flashes of light from the Quai du Mont Blanc from his eyes and clear the searing blockage in his throat. "No . . . I *came* here," he said hoarsely. "There's no way you could have known I'd do that. In Copenhagen, on the plane . . . I got the last ticket in First Class; the seat next to me had been sold, an aisle seat."

"That's where I always sit. On the aisle."

"Oh, *Jesus!*"

"Now you're rambling." Dowling glanced at the empty glass on the bedside table, then over at the bureau top where there was a silvery tray and a bottle of Scotch whisky provided by an accommodating desk clerk. "How much sauce have you had?"

Converse shook his head. "I'm not drunk . . . I'm sorry. *Christ, I'm sorry!* You had nothing to do with it. They're using you – trying to use you to find me! You *saved my* . . . my job . . . and I went after you. Forgive me. You've been so helpful."

"And you don't look like someone who's that worried about a job," said the actor, his scowl more one of concern than anger.

"It's not the employment, it's . . . pulling it off." Joel silently took a deep breath, imposing control, postponing the moment when he would have to confront the awesome implications found in what he had just heard. *Avery Fowler!* "I want to succeed in what I'm doing; I want to win," he added limply, hoping to conceal the slip he saw Dowling, had spotted. "All lawyers want to win."

"Sure."

"I *am* sorry, Cal."

"Forget it," said the actor, his voice casual, his look not casual at all. "Where I'm at these days screeching's an hourly occurrence, only they don't say anything. I think you just did."

"No, I over-reacted, that's all. I told you I was new at this. Not the law, just this . . . not talking directly, I guess says it."

"Does it?"

"Yes. Please believe that."

"All right, if you want me to." Dowling again looked at his watch. "I've got to go, but there's something else that might be helpful in saving that . . ." The actor paused convincingly. "That job of yours."

"What is it?" asked Converse tightly, trying not to leap at the question.

"As this Fowler was leaving I had a couple of thoughts. One was that I'd been pretty hard on a fellow who was simply doing *his* job, and the other was just plain selfish. I hadn't cooperated and that could come back and snap me in the ass. Of course if you never showed up here, I'd get my note back and it wouldn't matter. But if you did, and you wore a black hat, my tail could be in a bucket of boiling lead."

"That should have been your first concern," said Joel truthfully.

"Maybe it was, I don't know. At any rate, I told him that in the course of our conversation I asked you for drinks, to come out on location if you wanted to. He seemed puzzled at the last part, but he understood the first. I asked whether I should call him at the embassy if you took me up on either invitation, and he said no, I shouldn't do that."

"*What?*"

"In short words, he made it very plain that my calling him would only louse up this 'in-house queery". He told me to wait for *his* call. He'd phone me around noon."

"But you're filming. You're on location."

"That's the beauty part, but the hell with it. There are mobile telephone hookups; the studios insist on them these days. It's another kind of screeching called budgetary controls. We get our calls."

"You're losing me."

"Then find me. When he calls me, I'll call *you*. Should I tell him you reached me?"

Surprised, Converse stared at the aging actor, the risk-taker. "You're way ahead of me, aren't you?"

"You're pretty obvious. So was he, when I put it together – which I just did. This Fowler wants to reach you, but he wants to do it solo, away from those people you don't want to meet. You see, when he was at the door and we had our last words, I was bothered by something. He couldn't sustain the role – anymore than you did on the plane – but I couldn't be certain. He kind of fell apart on his exit, and that you never do even if you've got to hold in a sudden attack of diarrhoea . . . What do I tell him, Joe?"

"Get a telephone number, I guess."

"Done. You get some sleep. You look like a coked-up starlet who's just been told she's going to play Medea."

"I'll try."

Dowling reached into his pocket, taking out a scrap of paper. "Here," he said approaching Converse and handing it to him. "I wasn't sure I was going to give this to you but I damn well want you to have it now. It's the mobile number where you can reach me. Call me after you've talked to this Fowler. I'm going to be a nervous wreck until I hear from you."

"I give you my word . . . Cal, what did you mean when you mentioned 'the beauty part' and forgetting about it?"

The actor's head shifted back in perfect precision, at just the right angle for any in the audience. "The son of a bitch asked me what I did for a living . . . As they say in the Polo Lounge, 'Ciao, baby.' "

Converse sat on the edge of the bed, his head pounding, his body tense. Avery Fowler! *Jesus!* Avery Preston Fowler *Halliday! Press* Fowler . . . *Press Halliday!* The names bombarded him, piercing his temples and bouncing off the walls of his mind, screaming echoes everywhere. He could not control the assault; he began to sway back and forth, his arms supporting him, a strange rhythm emerging, the beat accompanying the name – names – of the man who had died in his arms in Geneva. A man he had known as a boy, the adult a stranger who had manipulated him into the world of George Marcus Delavane and a spreading disease called Aquitaine.

This Fowler wants to reach you, but he wants to do it solo, away from those people you don't want to meet . . . The judgment of a risk-taker.

Converse stopped, his eyes on the Leifhelm dossier on the floor. He had assumed the worst because it was beyond his comprehension, but there was an alternative, and outside possibility, perhaps under the circumstances even a probability. The geometrics were there; he could not trace them but they *were there! The* name Avery Fowler meant nothing to anyone but him – at least not in Bonn, not as it pertained to a murder in Geneva. Was Dowling right? Joel's

122

request to the actor to get the man's telephone number had been made without conviction, the stigma of the American Embassy on his mind, the sight of a dark red limousine driving through the embassy's gates refusing to leave him. *That* was the connection that had enveloped the shock of Avery Fowler's name. The man using it was from the *embassy* and at least part of the embassy was part of *Aquitaine*, therefore the impostor was part of the *trap*. That was the logic; it was simple arithmetic . . . but it was not geometry. Suppose there was a break in the line, an insertion from another plane that voided the arithmetic progression? If there was, it was in the form of an explanation he could not possibly perceive unless it was given to him.

The shock was receding; he was finding his equilibrium again. As he had done so many times in courtrooms and boardrooms, he began to accept the totally unexpected, knowing he could do nothing about it until something happened, something over which he had no control. The most difficult part of the process was forcing himself to function until it *did* happen, whatever it was. Conjecture was futile; all the probabilities were beyond his understanding.

He reached down for the Leifhelm dossier.

Erich Leifhelm's years with the *Bundes Polizei* were unique and require a word about the organization itself. In the aftermath of all wars, a subjugated national police force is required in an occupied country for reasons ranging from simple language to the understanding of local customs and traditions. There must be a buffer between the occupation troops and a vanquished people to maintain order. There is also a side issue rarely elaborated upon or analysed in the history books, but no less important for that lack. Defeated armies possess talent and unless that talent is utilized, the humiliation of defeat can ferment, at the minimum distilling itself into hostilities that are counterproductive to a stabilized political climate, or at the maximum, into internal subversion that can lead to violence and bloodshed at the expense of victors and whatever new government that is being formed. To put it bluntly, the Allied General Staff recognized that it had on its hands another brilliant and popular military man who would not suffer the anonymity of early retirement or a corporate boardroom. The *Bundes Polizei* – literally translated: Federal Police – like all police organizations was, and is, a paramilitary force, and as such the logical repository for men like Erich Leifhelm. They were the leaders; better to use them than be abused by them. And as always among leaders, there are those few who surge forward, leading the pack. During these years foremost among those few was Erich Leifhelm.

His early work with the *Polizei* was that of a military consultant during the massive German demobilization, then afterwards as the chief liaison between the police garrisons and the Allied occupation forces. Following demobilization, his duties were mainly concentrated in the trouble-spots of Vienna and Berlin where he was in constant touch with the commanders of the American, British and French sectors. His zealous anti-Soviet feelings were spread rapidly by Leifhelm throughout the command centres and duly noted by the senior officers. More and more he was taken into their confidence until – as had happened before with the Prussians – was literally considered one of them.

It was in Berlin that Leifhelm first came in contact with General Jacques Louis Bertholdier. A strong friendship developed but it was not an association either one cared to parade due to the age-old animosities between the German and French militaries. We were able to trace only three former officers from Bertholdier's command post who remembered – or would speak of – seeing the two men frequently at dinner together in out-of-the-way restaurants and cafés, deep in conversation, obviously comfortable with one another. Yet during those occasions when Leifhelm was summoned to French headquarters in Berlin, the formalities were icily proper, names rarely used and certainly never first names, only ranks and titles. In recent years, as noted above, both men have denied knowing each other personally, albeit admitting their paths may have crossed.

Whereas previously acknowledgment of their friendship was discouraged because of traditional prejudices, the current reasons are far more understandable. Both are spearheads in the Delavane organization. Their names are on the primary list with good reason. They are influential men who sit on the boards of multinational corporations which deal in products and technology ranging from the building of dams to the construction of nuclear plants; in between are a hundred likely subsidiaries throughout Europe and Africa which could easily expedite sales of armaments. As detailed in the following pages, it can be assumed that Leifhelm and Bertholdier communicate through a woman named Ilse Fishbein in Bonn. Fishbein is her married name, the marriage itself questionable in terms of motive insofar as it was dissolved years ago when Yakov Fishbein, a survivor of the camps, emigrated to Israel. Frau Fishbein, born in 1942, is the youngest illegitimate daughter of Hermann Goering.

Converse lowered the dossier and reached for a memo pad next to the telephone on the bedside table. He then unclipped the gold Cartier ballpoint pen Val had given him years ago from his shirt pocket and wrote down the name "Ilse Fishbein". He looked at both the pen and the name, having singular thoughts about each. The Cartier status symbol was a remembrance of better days – no, not really better, he considered, but at least more complete. Valerie, at his insistence, had finally quit the New York advertising agency with its insane hours, and gone freelance. On her last day of formal work, she had walked across town to Cartier and spent a considerable portion of her last pay cheque on his gift. When he asked her what he had done outside of his meteoric rise in Talbot, Brooks and Simon to deserve such impractical opulence she had replied: "For making me do what I should have done a long time ago. On the other hand, if free-lancing doesn't pay off, I'll steal-it back and pawn it . . . What the hell, you'll probably lose it."

Free-lancing had paid off very well, indeed, and he had never lost the pen.

Ilse Fishbein gave rise to another kind of thought. Much as he would like to confront her, it was out of the question. Whatever Erich Leifhelm knew had been provided by Bertholdier in Paris and relayed by Frau Fishbein here in Bonn. And it obviously contained a detailed description as well as a warning; the American was dangerous. Ilse Fishbein, as a trusted confidante in Aquitaine, could undoubtedly lead him to others in Germany who were part of Delavane's network, but to approach her was to ask for his own . . . whatever it was they intended for him at the moment, and he was not ready for that. Still, it was a name, a piece of information, a fact he was not expected to have, and experience had taught him to keep such details up front and reveal them, spring them quietly when the moment was right. Or use them himself when no one was looking. He was a lawyer and the ways of adversary law were labyrinthian; whatever was withheld was no man's land. On either side; to the more patient, the spoils.

Yet the temptation was so damned *inviting*. The bloodline of Hermann Goering involved with the contemplated resurrection of the generals! In *Germany*. Ilse Fishbein could be an immediate threat to unlock a floodgate of unwanted memories. He held in his hand a spiked club; the moment would come when he would swing it.

Leifhelm's commanding duties in the field with the West German NATO divisions lasted seventeen years, whereupon he was elevated to SHAPE headquarters, near Brussels, as military spokesman for Bonn's interests.

Again his tenure was marked by extreme anti-Soviet postures, frequently at odds with his own government's pragmatic approach to coexistence with the Kremlin, and throughout his final months at SHAPE, he was more often appreciated by the Anglo-American right-wing factions than by the political leadership in Bonn.

It was only when the Chancellor concluded that American Foreign Policy had been taken out of the hands of professionals and usurped by bellicose ideologies that he ordered Leifhelm home, creating an innocuous post for the soldier to keep him at bay.

Leifhelm, however, had never been a gullible fool, nor was he one now in his new, improvised status. He understood why the politicians had recreated it and, thereby, his own subtle strengths. People everywhere were looking to the past, to men who spoke clearly, with candour, and did not obfuscate the problems facing their countries and the world, especially the western world.

So he began to speak. At first to veterans' groups, and splinter organizations where military pasts and preformed partisan politics guaranteed him a favourable reception. Spurred by the enthusiastic response he evoked, Leifhelm began to expand, seeking larger audiences, his position more strident, his statements more provocative.

One man listened and was furious. The Chancellor learned that Leifhelm had carried his quasi-politicking into the Bundestag itself, implying a constituency far beyond what he really had, but by the sheer force of his personality swaying members who should not have been swayed. Leifhelm's words came back to the Chancellor of the Federal Republic: An enlarged army in far greater numbers than the NATO commitments; an intelligence service patterned after the once-extraordinary *Abwehr*; a general revamping of textbooks, deleting injurious and slanderous materials; rehabilitation camps for political trouble-makers and subversives pretending to be "liberal thinkers". It was all there.

The Chancellor had had enough. He summoned Leifhelm to his office where he demanded his resignation in the presence of three witnesses. Further, he ordered Leifhelm to remove himself from all aspects of German politics, accepting no further speaking engagements, neither lending his name nor his presence to any cause whatsoever. He was to retire totally from public life. We have reached one of those witnesses whose name is not pertinent to this report. The following is his recollection.

"The Chancellor was furious. He said to Leifhelm: "Herr General, you have two choices, and, if you'll forgive me, a final solution. Number one you may do as I say. Or you can be stripped of your rank and all pensions and financial accruals afforded therein, as well as the income from some rather valuable real estate in Munich, which in the opinion of any enlightened court would be taken from you instantly. That is your second choice.'

I tell you, the field marshal was apoplectic! He demanded his rights, as he called them, and the chancellor shouted. 'You've had your rights, and they were wrong! They're still wrong!' Then Leifhelm asked what was the final solution, and I swear to you, as crazy as it sounds, the Chancellor opened a drawer of his desk, took out a pistol, and aimed it at Leifhelm. 'I myself, will kill you right now,' he said. 'You will not, I repeat, *not* take us back.'

I thought for a moment that the old soldier was going to rush forward and accept the bullet, but he didn't. He stood there staring at him, such hatred in his eyes, matched by the other man's cold appraisal. Then Leifhelm did a stupid thing. He shot his arm forward – not at the Chancellor, but away from him – and cried 'Heil Hitler'. Then he turned in military fashion and walked out the door.

We were all silent for a moment or two. Then the Chancellor broke our silence. 'I should have killed him,' he said. 'I may regret it. We may all regret it.' "

Five days after this confrontation, Jacques Louis Bertholdier made the first of his two trips to Bonn following his retirement. On his initial visit he stayed at the Schlosspark Hotel. As hotel records are kept for a period of three years, we were able to obtain copies of his billing charges. There were numerous calls to various firms doing business with *Juneau et Cie*, too numerous to examine individually, but one number kept being repeated, the name having no apparent business connections with Bertholdier or his company. It was Ilse Fishbein. However, upon checking Erich Leifhelm's telephone bills for the dates in question, it was found that he too had placed calls to Ilse Fishbein, identical in number to those placed by Bertholdier. Inquiries and brief surveillance further established that Frau Fishbein and Leifhelm have known each other for a number of years. The conclusion is apparent: She is the conduit between Paris and Bonn in Delavane's apparatus.

Converse lighted a cigarette. There was the name again, the temptation again. Ilse Fishbein could be the shortcut. Threatened with exposure, this daughter of Hermann Goering could reveal a great deal. Not only could she confirm that she was the liaison between Leifhelm and Bertholdier, but conceivably much more, for the two ex-generals had to transmit information to each other. The names of companies, of buried subsidiaries, firms doing business related to Delavane in Palo Alto might surface, names he could pursue legally, looking for the illegalities that had to be there. If there only was a way, his presence felt, not seen.

An intermediary. He had used intermediaries in the past, often enough to know the value of the procedure. It was relatively simple. A third party was employed to make contact with an adversary carrying information that could be of value to the latter insofar as it might be deemed damaging to his interests – and was in the hands of his opponent. If the facts were strong enough, an equitable solution was usually forthcoming. The ethics were questionable, but contrary to accepted belief, ethics were in three dimensions, if not four. The ends did not justify the means, but justifiable means that brought about a fair and necessary conclusion were not to be dismissed.

And nothing could be fairer or more necessary than the dismantling of Aquitaine. Old Beale was right that night on the moonlit beach of Mykonos. His client was not an unknown man in San Francisco, but instead a large part of this so-called civilized world. Aquitaine had to be stopped, aborted.

An intermediary? It was another question he would put off until the morning. He picked up the dossier, his eyes heavy.

> Leifhelm has few intimate friends that appear to be constant, probably due to his awareness that he is under watch by the government. He sits on the boards of several prominent corporations which have stated frankly that his name justifies his stipend . . .

Joel's head fell forward. He snapped it back, widened his eyes, and scanned the final pages rapidly, impressions made, not really absorbed; his concentration was waning. There were several restaurants, the names meaningless; a marriage during the war that ended when Leifhelm's wife disappeared in November 1943, presumed killed in a Berlin bombing raid, no subsequent wife or wives, his private life extraordinarily private, if not austere. The exception here was his proclivity for small dinner parties, the guest lists always varied, again names, again meaningless. The address of his residence on the outskirts of Bad Godesberg . . . Suddenly, Converse's neck stiffened, his eyes briefly alive and steady.

> The house is in the remote countryside, on the Rhine River and far from any shopping areas or suburban concentration. The grounds are fenced and guarded by attack dogs who bark viciously at all approaching vehicles except Leifhelm's dark red Mercedes limousine.

A dark red Mercedes! It was Leifhelm himself who had been at the airport! Leifhelm who had driven directly to the embassy! How could it happen? *How?*

It was too much to absorb, too far beyond his understanding. The darkness was closing in, Joel's brain telling him it could no longer accept further input; it simply could not function. The dossier fell to his side; he closed his eyes and sleep came.

He was plunging headlong down through a cavernous hole in the earth, jagged black rocks on all sides, infinite darkness below. The walls of irregular stone kept screaming in frenzy, screeching at him like descending layers of misshapen gargoyles, sharp beaks and raised claws lunging at his flesh. The hysterical clamour was unbearable. Where had the silence gone? Why was he falling into black nothingness?

He flashed his eyes open; sweat lined his sockets, his forehead drenched, his breath coming in gasps. The telephone by his head was ringing, the erratic bell jarring, panic in its dissonance. He tried to shake the sleep and the fear from his semi-consciousness; he reached for the blaring instrument, glancing at his watch as his hand shot out above the bedside table. It was 12.15, a quarter past noon, the sun streaking through the hotel window.

"Yes? Hello . . . ?"

"Joe? *Joel?*"

"Yes."

"If's Cal Dowling. Our boy called."

"What? Who?"

"This Fowler. Avery Fowler."

"Oh, *Jesus!*" It was coming back, it was *all* coming back. He was seated at a table in the *Chat Botté* on the Quai du Mont Blanc, flashes of sunlight bouncing off the grills from the lakeside boulevard. No . . . he was not in Geneva. He was in a hotel room in Bonn and only hours ago he had been plunged into madness by that name. "Yes," he choked, catching his breath. "Did you get a telephone number?"

"He said there wasn't time for games, and besides, he doesn't have one. You're to meet him at the east wall of the Alter Zoll as fast as you can get there. Just walk around; he'll find you."

"That's not good enough!" cried Converse. "Not after Paris! Not after the airport last night! I'm not stupid!"

"I didn't get the impression he thought you were, replied the actor. "He told me, to tell you something; he thought it might convince you."

"What is it?"

"I hope I get this right; I don't even like saying it . . . He said to tell you a judge named Anstett was killed last night in New York. He thinks you're being cut loose."

8

The Alter Zoll, that ancient bulwark once Bonn's southern fortress on the Rhine only to be razed to the ground three centuries ago, a toll house now standing where the last of the great fortification's towers stood. Antique cannons were dotted about the green lawns, remembrances of a might that had slipped away under the squabblings of emperors and kings, priests and princes. A winding mosaic wall of red and grey stone overlooked the massive river below where boats of varied descriptions ploughed furrows in the open water, caressing the shorelines on both sides, diligent and sombre in their appointed rounds; no Lake Geneva here, far less the blue-green waters of the mischievous Como.

Joel stood by the low wall, trying to focus on the view, trying to accept it really, hoping it would calm him, but the exercise was futile. The beauty before him was lost, it would not penetrate his thoughts; nothing could. Lucas Anstett, Second Circuit Court of Appeals, judge extraordinary and intervening negotiator between one Joel Converse and his employers and an unknown man in San Francisco. Apart from that unknown man and a retired scholar on the island of Mykonos, the only other person who knew what he was doing and why. How in the space of eighteen hours or less could he have been *found?* Found and killed!

"Converse?"

Joel turned, whipping his head over his shoulder, his body rigid. Standing twenty feet away on the far edge of a gravel path was a sandy-haired man several years younger than Converse, in his early to mid-thirties, his face a boyish face that would grow old slowly, giving the illusion of youth long after its time. He was also shorter than Joel, but not much, perhaps 5'10" or 11", and dressed in light grey trousers and a cord jacket, his white shirt open at the neck.

"Who are you?" asked Converse hoarsely.

A couple strolled between them on the path as the younger man moved his head to his left, gesturing for Joel to follow him onto the lawn beyond. Converse did so, joining him by the huge iron wheel of a bronze cannon.

"All right, who are you?" repeated Joel.

"My sister's name is Meagen," said the sandy-haired man. "And so neither one of us makes a mistake, you tell me who I am."

"How the *hell* . . . ?" Converse stopped, the words coming back to him, words whispered by a dying man in Geneva. *Oh, Christ! Meg, the kids* . . . "Meg, the kids," he said out loud. "Fowler called his wife Meg."

"Short for Meagen, and she was Halliday's wife, only you knew him as Fowler."

"You're Avery's brother-in-law."

"Press's brother-in-law," corrected the man, his hand extended – in seriousness not conviviality. "Connal Fitzpatrick," he added.

"Then we're on the same side."

"I hope so."

"I've got a lot of questions to ask you, Connal."

"No more than I've got for you, Converse."

"Are we going to start off belligerently?" asked Joel, noting the harsh use of his own last name and releasing Fitzpatrick's hand.

The younger man blinked, then reddened, embarrassed. "Sorry," he said. "I'm one angry brother – on both sides – and I haven't had much sleep. I'm still on San Diego time."

"San Diego? Not San Francisco?"

"Navy. I'm a lawyer stationed at the naval base there."

"Whew," whistled Converse softly. "It's a small world."

"I know all about the geography," agreed Fitzpatrick. "And also you, Lieutenant. How do you think Press got his information? Of course, I wasn't in San Diego then, but I had friends."

"Nothing's sacred then."

"You're wrong; everything is. I had to pull some very thick strings to get that stuff. It was about five months ago when Press came to me and we made our . . . I guess you'd call it the contract between us."

"Clarification, please."

The naval officer placed his right hand on the barrel of the cannon. "Press Halliday wasn't just my brother-in-law, he came to be my best friend, closer than any blood brother, I think."

"And you with the militaristic hordes?" asked Joel, only half joking, a point of information on the line.

Fitzpatrick smiled awkwardly, boyishly. "That's part of it, actually. He stood by me when I wanted to go for it. The services need lawyers too, but the law schools don't tell you much about that. It's not where they're going to get any endowments from. Me, I happen to like the Navy, and I like the life; and the challenges, I guess you'd call them."

"Who objected?"

"Who didn't? In both our families the pirates – who go back to skimming the earthquake victims – have always been attorneys. The two current old men knew Press and I got along and saw the writing they wrote on their own wall. Here's this sharp Wasp, and this Catholic boy; now if they ring in a Jew and a light-skinned black and maybe even a not-too-offensive gay, they've got half the legal market in San Francisco in their back pockets."

"What about the Chinese and the Italians?"

"Certain country clubs still have remnants of the old school ties in their lockers. Why soil the fabric? Deals are made on the fairways, the accent on 'ways', not 'fair'."

"And you didn't want anything to do with that, counsellor?"

"Neither did Press, that's why he went international. Old Jack Halliday pissed bright red when Press began corralling all those foreign clients; then purple when he added a lot of US sharks who wanted to operate overseas. But old Jack couldn't complain; his wild-eyed stepson was adding considerably to the bottom line."

"And you went happily into uniform," said Converse, watching Fitzpatrick's eyes, impressed by the candour he saw in them.

"*Back* into uniform, and very happy – with Press's blessings, legal and otherwise."

"You were fond of him, weren't you?"

Connal lifted his hand off the cannon. "I loved him, Converse. Just as I love my sister. That's why I'm here. That's the contract."

"Incidentally," said Joel kindly, "speaking of your sister, even if I were somebody else I could easily have found out her name was Meagen."

"I'm sure you could; it was in the papers."

"Then it wasn't much of a test."

"Press never called her Meagen in his life, except for that one phrase in the wedding ceremony. He wasn't averse to talking about her, but it was always 'Meg'. I would have asked you about that somehow, and if you were lying I'd have known it. I'm very good on direct."

"I believe you. What's the contract between you and . . . Press?"

"Let's walk," said Fitzpatrick, and as they strolled toward the wall with the winding river below and the seven hills of Westerwald in the distance, Connal began. "Press came to me and said he was into something pretty heavy and he couldn't let it go. He'd come across information that tied a number of well-known men – or once well-known men – together in an organization that could do a lot of harm to a lot of people in a lot of countries. He was going to stop it,

130

stop them, but he had to go outside the usual courtroom ballparks to do it – do it legally.

"I asked the normal questions: Was he involved, culpable, that sort of thing, and he said no, not in any indictable sense, but he couldn't be sure whether or not he was entirely safe. Naturally, I said he was crazy; he should take his information to the authorities and let them handle it."

"Which is exactly what I told him," interrupted Converse.

Fitzpatrick stopped walking and turned to Joel. "He said it was more complicated than that."

"He was right."

"I find that hard to believe."

"He's dead. Believe it."

"That's no answer!"

"You didn't ask a question," said Converse. "Let's walk. Go on. Your contract."

Bewilderment on his face, the naval officer began. "It was very simple," he continued. "He told me he would keep me up to date whenever he travelled, letting me know if he was seeing anyone related to his major concern – that's what we called it, his 'major concern'. Also anything else that could be helpful if . . . if . . . goddamn it, *if!*"

"If what?"

Fitzpatrick stopped again, his voice harsh. "If anything *happened* to him!"

Converse let the emotion of the moment pass. "And he told you he was going to Geneva to see me. The man who knew Avery Preston Fowler Halliday as Avery Fowler roughly twenty-odd years ago in school."

"Yes. We'd been over that before when I got him the security material on you. He said the time was right, the circumstances right. By the way, he thought you were the best." Connal permitted himself a brief uncomfortable smile. "Almost as good as he was."

"I wasn't," said Joel, a half smile returned. "I'm still trying to figure out his position on some Class A stock in the merger."

"What?"

"Nothing. What about Lucas Anstett? I want to hear about that."

"It's in two parts. Press said they'd worked through the judge to spring you if you'd agree to take on the . . ."

"*They?* Who's they?"

"I don't know. He never told me."

"Goddamn it! Sorry, go ahead."

"That Anstett had talked to your firm's senior partners and they said okay if you said okay. That's part one. Part two is a personal idiosyncrasy; I'm a news freak and like most of my ilk I'm tuned into the hourly AFR."

"Clarification."

"Armed Forces Radio. Oddly enough it's probably got the best news coverage on the air; it pools all the networks. I have one of those small transistorized jobs with a couple of shortwave bands I pack when I'm travelling."

"I used to do that," offered Converse. "For the BBC, mainly because I didn't speak French – or anything else for that matter."

"They've got good coverage but they shift bands too much. Anyway I had AFR on early this morning and heard the story, such as it was."

"What was it?"

"Short on details. His apartment on Central Park South was broken into around two in the morning, New York time. There were signs of a struggle and he was shot in the head."

"That's it?"

"Not quite. According to a housekeeper nothing was taken so robbery was ruled out. *That's it.*"

"*Jesus.* I'll call Larry Talbot. He may have more information. There wasn't anything else?"

"Only a quick sketch of a brilliant jurist. The point is nothing was *taken.*"

"I understand that," broke in Joel. "I'll talk to Talbot." They started walking again south along the wall. "Last night," continued Converse, "why did you tell Dowling you were an embassy man? You must have been at the airport."

"I'd been at the airport for seven hours going from counter to counter asking for passenger information, trying to find out what plane you were on."

"You knew I was on my way to Bonn?"

"Beale thought you were."

"*Beale?*" asked Joel, startled. "Mykonos?"

"Press gave me his name and the number but said I wasn't to use either unless the worst happened." Fitzpatrick paused. "The worst happened," he added.

"What did Beale tell you?"

"That you went to Paris, and, as he understood it, you were going to Bonn next."

"What else?"

"Nothing. He said he accepted my credentials, as he called them, because I had his name and knew how to reach him; only Press could have given me that information. But anything else I'd have to learn from you, if you felt there was something to tell me. He was pretty damned cold."

"He had no choice."

"Although he did say that in case I couldn't find you, he wanted to see me on Mykonos before I began raising my voice . . . 'for everything Mr Halliday stood for'. That's the way he put it. I was going to give you two more days to get here, if I could hold up."

"Then what? Mykonos?"

"I'm not sure. I figured I'd call Beale again but he'd have to tell me a lot more than he did to convince me."

"And if he didn't? Or couldn't?"

"Then I'd have flown straight to Washington and gone to whoever the top floor of the Navy Department suggested. If you think for one goddamned minute I'm going to let this thing pass for what it isn't, you're wrong and so is Beale."

"If you'd have made that clear to him, he would have come up with something. You'd have gone to Mykonos. Converse reached into his shirt pocket for his cigarettes; he offered one to Fitzpatrick, who shook his head. "Avery didn't smoke either," said Joel aimlessly as he snapped his lighter. "Sorry ... Press." He inhaled.

"It's okay; that name's how I got you to see me."

"Let's go back to that a minute. There's a slight inconsistency in your testimony, counsellor. Let's clear it up – just so neither one of us makes a mistake."

"I don't know what you think you're crowding in on, but go ahead."

"You said you were going to give me two more days to get here, is that right?"

"Yes, if I could make arrangements, get some sleep and hold-up."

"How did you know I didn't get here two days *before* you did?"

Fitzpatrick glanced at Joel. "I've been a legal officer in the Navy for the past eight years, both as defence counsel and judge advocate in any number of situations – not always court martials. They've taken me to most of the countries where Washington has reciprocal legal agreements."

"That's a mouthful, but I'm not in the Navy."

"You were, but I wasn't going to use it if I didn't have to, and I didn't. I flew into Dusseldorf, showed my naval papers to the *Inspektor* of immigration, and asked for his operation. There are seven international airports in West Germany. It took roughly five minutes with the computers to find out that you hadn't entered any of them during the past *three* days, which was all I was concerned about."

"But then you had to get to Köln-Bonn."

"I was there in forty minutes and called him back. No Converse had been admitted and unless you were crossing the border incognito – which I suspect I know more about than you do – you had to fly in sooner or later."

"You're tenacious."

"I've given you my reasons."

"What about Dowling and that embassy routine at the hotel?"

"Lufthansa had you listed on the passenger manifest from Hamburg – you'll never know how relieved I was. I hung around the counter in case there was a delay or anything like that when these three embassy guys showed up flashing their IDs, the head man speaking rotten German."

"You could tell?"

"I speak German ... and French, Italian and Spanish. I have to deal with different nationalities."

"I'll let that pass."

"I suppose that's why I'm a lieutenant–commander at thirty-four. They move me around a lot."

"Pass again. What caught you about the embassy people?"

"Your name, naturally. They wanted confirmation that you were on Flight Eight–eleven. The clerk sort of glanced at me and I shook my head; he cooperated without a break in his conversation. You see, I'd given him a few Deutschemarks but that wasn't it. These people don't really dig the official US over here."

"I heard that last night. From Dowling. How did he come up?"

"Dowling himself, but later. When the plane arrived I stood at the rear of the baggage claim; the embassy boys were by the entrance to the gates about fifty feet away. We all waited until there was only one piece of luggage on the conveyor belt. It was yours but you never showed up. Finally a woman came out and the embassy contingent surrounded her, everyone excited, upset. I heard your name mentioned, but that's all I heard because by that time I'd decided to go back and speak to the clerk."

"To see if I'd really been on the plane?" asked Converse. "Or whether I turned out to be a no-show."

"Yes," agreed Fitzpatrick. "He was cute; he made me feel like I was suborning a juror. I paid him and he told me this Caleb Dowling – who I think I was expected to know – had stopped at the desk before going out to the platform."

"Where he left instructions," said Joel, interrupting quietly.

"How did you know?"

"I picked up a set at the hotel."

"That was it, the *hotel*. Dowling told him he'd met this lawyer on the plane, a fellow American named Converse who'd sat with him since Copenhagen. He was worried that his new friend might not have accommodation in Bonn and, if he asked Lufthansa for suggestions, the clerk should send him to the Konigshof Hotel."

"So you totalled up the figures and decided to become one of the embassy people who'd lost me," said Converse, smiling. "To confront Dowling. Who among us hasn't taken advantage of a hostile witness?"

"Exactly. I showed him my naval ID and told him I was an attaché. Frankly, he wasn't very cooperative."

"And you weren't very convincing, according to his theatrical critique. Neither was I. Strangely enough that's why he got us together." Joel stopped, crushed out his cigarette against the wall and threw it over the stone. "All right, Commander, you've passed muster or roster or whatever the hell you call it. Where do we stand? You speak the language and you've got government connections I don't have. You could help."

The naval officer stood motionless; he looked hard at Joel, his eyes blinking in the glare of the sunlight, but not from any lack of concentration. "I'll do whatever I can," he began slowly, "as long as it makes sense to me. But you and I have to understand each other, Converse. I'm not backing away from the two days. That's all you've got – *we've* got if I come on board."

"Who made the deadline?"

"I did. I do now."

"It can't work that way."

"Who says?"

"I did. I do now." Converse started walking along the wall.

"You're in Bonn," said Fitzpatrick, catching up, neither impatience nor supplication in either his gait or his voice, only control. "You've been to Paris and you came to *Bonn*. That means you have names, areas of evidence, both concrete or hearsay. I want it all."

"You'll have to do better than that, Commander."

"I made a *promise*."

"To whom?"

"My sister. You think she doesn't know? It was tearing Press apart! For a

134

whole goddamned year he'd get up in the middle of the night and wander around the house, talking to himself but shutting her out. He was obsessed and she couldn't crack the shell. You'd have to know them to appreciate this, but they were good, I mean *good* together. I know it's not very fashionable these days to have two people with a passel of kids who really like each other, who can't wait to be with each other when they're apart, but that's the way they were."

"Are you married?" asked Joel, without breaking his stride.

"No," answered the Navy man, obviously confused by the question. "I expect to be. Perhaps. I told you, I move around a lot."

"So did Press . . . Avery."

"What's your point, *counsellor?*"

"Respect what he was doing. He knew the dangers and he understood what he could lose. His life."

"That's why I want the facts! His body was flown back yesterday. The funeral's tomorrow and I'm not there because I gave Meagen a promise! I'm coming back, too, but with everything I need to blow this whole fucking thing apart!"

"You'll only *implode* it, sending it way down deep if you're not stopped before that."

"That's *your* judgment."

"It's all I've got."

"I don't buy it!"

"Don't. Go back and talk about rumours, about a killing in Geneva that nobody will admit was anything but a robbery, or a murder in New York that remains, and probably will remain something it wasn't. If you mention a man on Mykonos, believe me, he'll disappear. Where are you, Commander? Are you just a freak, after all, a philosophical blood brother of Press Halliday who stormed the Presidio and burned his draft card in the good old days of muscatel and grass?"

"That's a crock of shit!"

"It's on the record, Commander. By the way, as a judge-advocate how many officers did you prosecute?"

"What . . . ?"

"And as defence counsel how many cases did you lose?"

"I've had my share of wins and losses, mostly wins, frankly."

"Mostly? Frankly? You know there are certain people who can take fifteen numbers, insert what they call variables, and make the statistics say anything they want them to say."

"What's that got to do with anything? How is it connected to Press' death, his *murder?*"

"Oh, you'd be surprised, Commander Fitzpatrick. Beneath that brass could be a very successful infiltrator, perhaps even an *agent-provocateur* in a uniform you shouldn't be wearing."

"What the *hell* are you talking about . . . Forget it, I don't want to know. I don't have to listen to you but you have to listen to me! You've got two days, Converse. Am I on board or not?"

Joel stopped and studied the intense young face beside him – young and not so young. There were hints of creases around the angry eyes. "You're not even in the same fleet," said Converse wearily. "Old Beale was right. It's my decision and I choose to tell you nothing. I don't want you on board, sailor. You're a hotheaded piss ant and you bore me."

Joel turned and walked away.

"All right, *cut!* That's a print! Nice work, Cal, I almost believed that drivel." The director, Roger Blynn, checked the clipboard thrust in front of him by a script girl and issued instructions to the camera crew's interpreter before heading over to the production table.

Caleb Dowling remained seated on the large rock on the slope of the hill above the Rhine; he patted the head of an odoriferous goat which had just defecated on the toe of his boot. "I'd like to kick the rest of the shit out of you, li'l partner," he said quietly, "but it wouldn't be congruous with my well-developed image."

The actor got up and stretched, aware that the onlookers beyond the roped-off set were staring at him, chattering away like tourists in a zoo. In a few minutes he would walk over – no, not walk, amble over – and pull the rope off the carriage of an arc light so that he could mingle with the fans. He never tired of it, probably because it came so late in his life and was, after all, symbolic of what he and his wife currently could afford. Also every now and then there was a bonus: One of his former students, who usually approached him cautiously, obviously wondering if the good-natured rapport he had established in the class-room had survived the onslaught of national recognition or been drowned in the tidal wave of so-called stardom. Cal was good at remembering faces, and not too bad with at least one of a person's two names, so when these occasions arose, he invariably would eye his former charge and ask him if he had completed yesterday's assignment. Or walk up to him – or her – and pedagogically inquire something like: "Of the chronicles Shakespeare drew from for his histories, which had the greatest impact on his language, Daniel, Hollinshed, or Froisart?" If the answer came back naming the last, he would slap his thighs and exclaim words akin to: "Hot damn, l'il wrangler, you busted a tough bronc there!" Laughter followed, and frequently drinks and reminiscences later.

It was a good life these days, almost perfect. If only some sunlight would reach into the painfully dark corners of his wife's mind. If it could, she'd be here on a hillside in Bonn chatting in her quietly vivacious way with the people beyond the rope – mostly women, mostly those around her age – telling them that her husband was really quite like their own. He never picked up his socks and was a disaster in the kitchen; people liked to hear that even if they didn't believe it. But the sunlight did not reach those far, dark corners. Instead, his Frieda remained in Copenhagen, walking along the beaches of Sjaelland Island, having tea in the botanical gardens, and waiting for a call from her husband saying that he had a few days off and would come out of hated Germany. Dowling looked around at the efficiently enthusiastic crew and the curious spectators; laughter punctuated their conversations, a certain respect as well. These were not hateful people.

"Cal?" the voice belonged to Blynn, the film's director, who was walking rapidly across the slope of the hill. "There's someone here to see you."

"I hope more than one, Roger, otherwise the men who go under the dubious title of our employers are grossly overpaying me."

"Not for this pile of kitsch." The director's smile disappeared, as he approached the actor. "Are you in any trouble, Cal?"

"Constantly, but not so it's noticeable."

"I'm serious. There's a man here from the German police – the Bonn police. He says he has to talk to you, claims it's urgent."

"What about?" Dowling felt a rush of pain in his stomach; it was the fear he lived with.

"He wouldn't tell me. Just that it was an emergency and he had to see you alone."

"Oh, *Christ!*" whispered the actor. "Freddie! . . . where is he?"

"Over in your trailer."

"*In* my . . ."

"Rest easy," said Blynn. "That stunt-jock Moose Rosenberg's with him. If he moved an ashtray, I think that gorilla would throw him through the wall."

"Thanks, Roger."

"He meant it when he said 'alone'!"

Dowling did not hear this; he had started running across the hill toward the small camper he used for brief periods of relaxation. He prayed to no one in particular for the best, preparing himself for the worst.

It was neither, simply another complication in an enigma. Frieda Dowling was not the subject; instead it was Joel Converse, an American attorney at law. The stunt man climbed out of the trailer, leaving Caleb and the police officer alone. The man was in civilian clothes, his English fluent, his manner vaguely officious yet courteous.

"I'm sorry to have upset you, Herr Dowling," said the German in response to Caleb's initial, intense inquiry about his wife. "We know nothing of Frau Dowling. Is she ill, perhaps?"

"She's had a few spells lately, that's all. She's in Copenhagen."

"Yes, so we understand. You fly there frequently, don't you?"

"Whenever I can."

"She does not care to join you here in Bonn?"

"Her name was Muhlstein and the last time she was in Germany she wasn't considered much of a human being. Her memories are, let's say memorable in the extreme. They come back with a lot of acid."

"Yes," said the police officer, his eyes as steady as Caleb's. "We will live with that for generations."

"I hope so," said the actor.

"I wasn't alive, Herr Dowling. I'm very happy she survived, I mean that."

Dowling was not sure why but he lowered his voice, the words nearly inaudible, if not involuntary. "Germans helped her."

"I would hope so," said the German quietly. "*My* business, however, concerns a man who sat next to you last night on the planes from Copenhagen to Hamburg

137

and from Hamburg to Bonn. His name is Joel Converse, an American attorney."

"What about him? By the way, may I see your identification?"

"Certainly." The police officer reached into his pocket, removed his plastic ID case and handed it to the actor who had his glasses firmly in place. "I trust everything is in order," added the man.

"What's this '*Sonder Dezernat'?*" asked Dowling, squinting at the small print on the card.

"It is best translated as 'special branch' or 'department'. We are a unit of the *Bundes Polizei*, the Federal Police. It is our job to look into matters the government feels are more sensitive than the normal jurisdictional complaints."

"That doesn't say a damn thing, and you know it," said the actor. "We can use lines like that in movies and get away with it because we write in all those reactions, but you're not Helmut Dantine or Martin Kosleck and I'm not Elisa Landi. Spell it out."

"Very well, I shall spell it out. Interpol. A man died in a Paris hospital as a result of head injuries inflicted by the American, Joel Converse. His condition was diagnosed as improving, but unfortunately it was only temporary; he was found dead this morning, his death attributed to an unprovoked attack by Herr Converse. We know he flew into Köln-Bonn, and according to the airline stewardesses you sat with him for three and a half hours. We want to know where he is. Perhaps you can help us."

Dowling removed his glasses, lowering his chin and swallowing as he did so. "And you think I know?"

"We have no idea, but you talked with him. And we hope you *do* know that there are severe penalties for withholding information about a fugitive, especially one sought for a killing."

The actor fingered the stems of his glasses, his instincts in conflict, erupting. He walked over to the bed against the wall and sat down, looking up at the police officer. "Why don't I trust you?" he asked.

"Because you think of your wife and will trust no German," replied the German. "I am a man of law and *peace*, Herr Dowling. Order is something the people decide for themselves, myself among them. The report we have received states, clearly that this Converse may be a very disturbed man."

"He didn't sound disturbed to me. In fact, I thought he had a damned good head on his shoulders. He said a lot of very perceptive things."

"That you wanted to hear?"

"Not all of them."

"But a good percentage, leading up to all of them."

"What does that mean?"

"A madman is convincing; he plays on all sides, eventually weighing everything in his favour. It's the essence of his madness, his psychosis, his *own* convictions."

Dowling dropped the glasses on the bed, exhaling audibly, feeling the pain of fear again in his stomach. "A madman?" he said – without conviction. "I don't believe that."

"Then let us have a chance to disprove it. Do you know where he is?"

The actor squinted at the German. "Give me a card or a number where I can reach you. He may get in touch with me."

"Who was responsible?" The man in the red velvet jacket behind the large desk sat in semi-darkness, a brass lamp serving only to throw a harsh circle of light on the surface in front of him. Beyond, the light was dim. Yet the glow was sufficient to reveal the outlines of a huge map centred on the wall behind the man and the desk. It was a strange map, not of the global world, but instead fragmented. The shapes of nations were clearly defined yet oddly shadowed, eerily coloured, as if an attempt had been made to create a single land mass out of disparate geographical areas. They included all of Europe, most of the Mediterranean and selected portions of Africa. And, as if the wide expanse of the Atlantic Ocean was merely a pale blue connector, Canada and the United States of America were part of this arcane entity.

The man stared straight ahead, his lined, square-jawed face with its aquiline nose and thin, stretched lips seemed moulded from parchment, his close-cropped salt-and-pepper hair a proper garland for a head set atop such a rigidly framed torso. He spoke again; his voice was rather higher in the vocal register than lower, with no resonance, but with a secure sense of command. One could easily imagine this voice raised in volume – even to fever pitch, like a tom cat screeching across a frozen lake. It was not raised now, however; it was the essence of quiet urgency. "Who was responsible?" he repeated. "Are you still on the line, London?"

"Yes," replied the caller from Great Britain. "Yes, of course. I'm trying to think, trying to be fair."

"I admire that, but decisions have to be made. In all likelihood the responsibility will be shared, we simply have to know the sequence. The man paused; when he continued his voice suddenly took on an intensity that was a complete departure from his previous tone. It was the shrill call of the cat across the ice-bound lake. "How was Interpol involved?"

Startled, the Englishman answered quickly, his phrases clipped, the words rushing headlong over one another. "Bertholdier's aide was found dead at four in the morning, Paris time. Apparently he was to receive hospital medication at that hour. The nurse called the *Sûreté*."

"The *Sûreté*?" shouted the man behind the desk in front of the fragmented map. "Why the *Sûreté*? Why not Bertholdier? It was *his* employee, not the *Sûreté's*!"

"That was the lapse," said the Britisher. "No one realized instructions to that effect had been left at the hospital desk ... apparently by an inspector named Prudhomme, who was awakened and told of the man's death."

"And *he was* the one who called in Interpol?"

"Yes, but too late to intercept Converse at German immigration."

"For which we can be profoundly grateful," said the man lowering his voice.

"Normally, of course, the hospital would have waited and reached Bertholdier in the morning, telling him what happened. As you say, the patient was an employee, not a member of the family. After that undoubtedly the *arrondissement* police would have been informed and finally the *Sûreté*. By then our people would have been in place and fully capable of preventing Interpol's involvement. We can still stop them but it will take several days. Personnel transfers, new evidence, amendments to the case file; we need time."

"Then don't waste any."

"It was those *damned* instructions."

"Which no one had the brains to look for," said the man in front of the shadowed map. "This Prudhomme's instincts were aroused. Too many rich people, too much influence, the circumstances too bizarre. He smells something."

"We'll get him off the case, just a few days," said the Englishman. "Converse is in Bonn, we know that. We're closing in."

"So may Interpol and the German police. I don't have to tell you how tragic that would be."

"We have certain controls through the American Embassy. The fugitive is American."

"The *fugitive* has information!" insisted the man behind the desk, his fist clenched in the circle of light. "How much and supplied by whom we don't know and we *must* know."

"Nothing was learned in New York? The judge?"

"Only what Bertholdier suspected and what I knew the moment I heard his name. After forty years Anstett came back, still hounding me, still wanting my neck. The man was a bull, but only a go-between; he hated me as much as I hated him, and up to the end he shielded those behind him. Well, he's gone and his holy righteousness with him. The point is, Converse is *not* what he pretends to be. Now, *find* him!"

"As I say, we're closing in. We have more sources, more informers than Interpol. He's an American fugitive in Bonn who, we understand, doesn't speak the language. There are only so many places he can hide. We'll find him; we'll break him and learn where he comes from. After which, we'll terminate immediately, of course."

"*No!*" The sleek male cat again shrieked across the frozen lake. "We play *his* game! We welcome him, embrace him. In Paris he talked about Bonn, Tel Aviv, Johannesburg; therefore you'll accommodate him. Bring him to Leifhelm – even better have Leifhelm go to him. Fly in Abrahms from Israel, van Headmer from Africa, and, yes, Bertholdier from Paris. He obviously knows who they are anyway. He'll claim ultimately to want a council meeting, to be a part of us. So we'll hold a conference and listen to his lies. He'll tell us more with his lies than he can with the truth."

"I really don't understand."

"Converse is a *point*, but *only* a point. He's exploring, studying the forward terrain, trying to understand the tactical forces ahead of him. If he were anything else, he'd deal directly through legitimate authorities and legitimate methods. There'd be no reason for him to use a false name, or give false information . . . or to run away, forcibly overcoming a man he thinks is trying to stop him. He's an infantry point who has certain information but doesn't know where he's going. Well, a point can be sucked into a trap, the advancing company ambushed. Oh, yes, we must give him his conference."

"I submit that's extraordinarily dangerous. He *must* know who recruited him, who gave him the names, his sources. We can break him physically or chemically and get that information."

"He probably doesn't have it," explained the man patiently. "Infantry points are not privileged to command decisions; frankly, they might turn back. We have to know more about this Converse, and by six o'clock tonight I'll have every report, every résumé, every word ever written about him. There's something here we can't see."

"We already know he's resourceful," said the Britisher. "From what we can piece together in Paris, he's considered an outstanding attorney. If he sees through us, or gets away from us, it could be catastrophic. He will have met with our people, *spoken* with them."

"Then once you find him don't let him out of your sight. By tomorrow I'll have other instructions for you."

"Oh?"

"Those records that are being gathered from all over the country. For a man to do what Converse is doing he had to be manipulated very carefully, very thoroughly, a driving intensity instilled in him. It's the manipulators we have to find. They're not even who we think they are. I'll be in touch tomorrow."

George Marcus Delavane replaced the telephone in its cradle and slowly, awkwardly twisted his upper body around in the chair. He gazed at the strange, fragmented map as the first light of dawn fired the eastern sky, its orange glow filling the windows. Then, with effort, his hands gripping the arms of the steel chair, he pivoted himself around again, his eyes on the stark pool of light on the desk. He moved his hands to his waist and carefully, trembling, unbuttoned his dark red velvet jacket, forcing his gaze downward, ordering himself to observe the terrible truth once more. He stared past the 5-inch-wide leather strap that diagonally held him in place, now *commanding* his eyes to focus, to accept with loathing what had been done to him.

There was nothing but the edge of the thick, steel seat, the polished wood of the floor the next plane of vision. The long, sturdy legs that had carried his trained, muscular body through battles in the snow and the mud, and triumphant parades in the sunlight, through ceremonies of honour and defiance had been stolen from him, said by the doctors to have been diseased, instruments of death that would kill the rest of him. He clenched his fists and pressed them slowly down on the desk, his throat filled with a silent scream.

9

"*Goddamn you*, Converse, who do you think you are?" cried Connal Fitzpatrick, his voice low, furious, as he caught up with Joel who was walking rapidly between the tall trees of the Alter Zoll.

"Someone who knew Avery Fowler as a boy and watched a man named Press Halliday die a couple hundred years later in Geneva," replied Converse, quickening his pace, heading toward the gates of the national landmark where there were taxis.

"Don't pull that crap on me! I knew Press far better and far longer than you *ever* did. For Christ's sake, he was married to my sister! We were close friends for fifteen years!"

"You sound like a little kid playing one-upmanship. Get lost."

Fitzpatrick rushed forward, pivoting in front of Joel, blocking him. "It's true! Please, I can help, I want to help! I know the language; you don't! I have connections here; you don't."

"You also have your own idea about a deadline which *I* don't. Get out of my way, sailor."

"*Come* on," pleaded the naval officer. "So I didn't get everything I wanted. Don't crowd me out."

"I beg your pardon?"

Fitzpatrick shifted his weight awkwardly. "You've come on strong before yourself, haven't you, counsellor?"

"Not if I didn't know the circumstances."

"Sometimes it's a way of finding them out."

"Not with me it isn't."

"Then my error was in not knowing you; the circumstances were beyond that scope. With someone else it might have worked."

"Now you're talking tactics, but you meant it when you said two days."

"You're damned right I did," agreed Connal, nodding. "Because I want whatever it is exposed. I want *whoever it* is to *pay!* I'm mad, Converse, I'm mad as hell. I don't want this thing to linger and die away. The longer nothing is done the less people care; you know that as well as I do and probably better. Have you ever tried to reopen an old case? I have with a few courts-martial where I thought things had been screwed up. Well, I learned something: the system doesn't like it! You know why?"

"Yes, I do," said Joel. "There are too many new cases in the dockets, too many rewards in going after the current ones."

"Bingo, counsellor. Press deserves better than that. Meagen deserves better."

"Yes, he does – they do. But there's a complication that Press Halliday understood better than either of us. Put simply – and cruelly – his life wasn't terribly important compared to what he was going after."

"That's pretty damned cruel," said the officer.

"It's very damned accurate," said Converse. "Your brother-in-law would have wrestled you to the mat for walking into this and trying to call the shots. Back off, Commander. Go back to the funeral."

"*No*. I want to come on board. I withdraw the deadline."

"How considerate of you."

"Oh, Christ, you know what I mean."

"No, I don't know what you mean."

"You call the shots," said Fitzpatrick, nodding again, exhaling in defeat. "I'll do what you tell me to do."

"Why?" asked Joel, their eyes locked.

The Navy lawyer did not flinch; he spoke simply. "Because Press trusted you. He said you were the best."

"Except for him," completed Converse, permitting his expression to relax slightly, a hint of a smile apparent. "All right, I believe you, but there are ground rules. You either accept them or, as you put it, on board you're not."

"Let's hear them. I'll wince inside so you can't see it."

"Yes," agreed Joel, "you'll wince. To begin with I'll tell you only what I think you have to know in a given situation. Whatever you develop will be on your own; that way it's free-wheeling, no way can you tip the evidence we've compiled."

"That's rough."

"That's the way it is. I'll give you a name now and then when I think it will open a door, but it will *always* be a name you heard second or third hand. You're inventive; figure out your own unidentifiable sources so as to protect yourself."

"I've done that on quite a few waterfronts."

"You have? How good are you at play acting?"

"What?"

"Never mind, I think you just answered that. You didn't go down to those waterfronts in your dress whites as a lieutenant-commander."

"Hell, no."

"You'll do."

"You've got to tell me *something*."

"I'll give you an overview, a lot of abstractions and a few facts. As we progress – *if we* progress – you'll learn more. If you think you've put it together, tell me. That's essential. We can't risk blowing everything while you operate under wrong assumptions."

"Who's we?"

"I wish to hell I knew."

"That's comforting."

"Yes, it isn't."

"Why don't you tell me everything now?" asked Fitzpatrick.

"Because Meagen Halliday lost a husband. I don't want to see her lose a brother."

"I'll accept that."

"By the way, how long have you got? I mean you're on active duty."

"My initial leave is thirty days, with extensions as warranted. Christ, an only sister with five kids and her husband is killed. I could probably write my own ticket."

"We'll stick to the thirty days, Commander. It's more than we're allowed."

"Start talking, Converse."

"Let's walk," said Joel, heading back to the Alter Zoll wall and the view of the Rhine below.

The "overview" delivered by Converse described a current situation in which like-minded individuals in various countries were coming together and using their considerable influence to get around the laws and ship armaments and technology to hostile governments and organizations.

"For what purpose?" asked Fitzpatrick.

"I could say profits but you'd see through it."

"As the only motive, yes," said the Navy lawyer pensively. "Influential people – as I understand the word 'influential' as related to existing laws – would operate singly or at best in small groups within their own countries. That is if profits were the primary objective. They wouldn't coordinate outside; it isn't necessary. It's a sellers' market; they'd only water down the profits."

"Bingo, counsellor."

"So?" Fitzpatrick looked at Joel as they strolled toward a break in the stone wall where a bronzed cannon was in place.

"Destabilization," said Converse. "Mass destabilization. A series of flashpoints in highly volatile areas that will call into question the status quo's ability to cope with the violence."

"I've got to ask you again, for what purpose?"

"You're quick," said Joel, "so I'll let you answer that. What happens when an existing political structure is crippled by disorder, when it can no longer function because things have got out of control?"

The two men stopped by the cannon, the naval officer's eyes following the line of the huge, threatening barrel. "It's restructured or replaced," he said, pulling his gaze back to look at Converse.

"Bingo again," said Converse softly. "That's the overview."

"It doesn't make sense." Fitzpatrick creased his eyes in the sunlight, as well as in thought. "Let me recap. Am I allowed?"

"You're allowed."

" 'Influential individuals' connotes people in pretty good standing in very high places. Assuming we're not talking about an out-and-out criminal element – which the lack of a pure profit motive would seem to eliminate we're talking about reasonably respectable citizens. Is there another definition I'm not aware of?"

"If there is I'm not aware of it, either."

"Then why would they want to destabilize the political structures that guarantee them their influence? It *doesn't* make sense."

"Ever hear of the phrase 'everything's relative'?"

"To a fare-thee-well. So what?"

"So think."

"About what?"

"Influence." Joel took out his cigarettes, shook one to his lips, and lighted it. The younger man stared at the seven hills of Westerwald in the distance.

"They want *more*," said Fitzpatrick slowly, turning back to Converse.

"They want it all," said Joel. "And the only way they can get it is to prove that their solutions are the only solutions, all others having proved worthless against the eruptions of chaos suddenly everywhere."

Connal's expression was fixed, immobile, as he absorbed Converse's words. "Holy *Mary* . . ." he began, his voice a whisper, yet still a cry. "An international plebiscite – the peoples' will – for the almighty state. Fascism. It's multinational *fascism*."

"I'm sick of saying 'bingo', so I'll say 'right–on', counsellor. You've just said it better than any of us."

"*Us?* Which is '*we*', but you don't know who you are!" added Fitzpatrick, bewilderment and anger coming together with his creased, linked eyebrows.

"Live with it," said Joel. "I have. I do."

"*Why?*"

"Avery Fowler. Remember him?"

"Oh, *Jesus!*"

"And an old man on the island of Mykonos. That's all we have. But what they said is true. It's real. I've seen it, and that's all I need to know. In Geneva, Avery said there was very little time left. Beale refined it; he called it a countdown. Whatever's going to happen will happen before your leave is up – two weeks and four days is the earliest report. That's what I meant before."

"Oh my God," whispered Fitzpatrick. "What else can you tell me – *will you* tell me?"

"Very little."

"The embassy," Connal interrupted. "It's been a couple of years, but I *was there*. I worked with the military attaché. I don't need any introductions. We can get help there."

"We can also get killed there."

"*What?*"

"It's not clean. Those three men you saw at the airport, the ones from the embassy . . ."

"What about them?"

"They're on the other side."

"I don't believe you!"

"Why do you think they were at the airport?"

"To meet you, talk to you. There could be a dozen different reasons. Whether you know it or not you're considered a hot shot lawyer on the international scene. Foreign service personnel frequently want to touch base with guys like you."

"I've had this conversation before," said Converse, irritated.

"What does *that* mean?"

"If they wanted to see me why didn't they go to the gate?"

"Because they thought you'd come into the terminal like everybody else."

"And when I didn't – according to you – they were upset, angry. That's what you said."

"They were."

"All the more reason to meet me at the gate."

Fitzpatrick frowned. "Still, that's kind of flimsy . . ."

"The woman. Do you remember the woman?"

"Of course."

"She spotted me in Copenhagen. She followed me. Also, there's something else. Later, on the platform, all four were picked up by a car belonging to a man we know – we *know* – is part of everything I've described to you. They drove to the embassy and you'll have to take my word for that. I saw them."

Connal fixed his gaze on Joel, accepting what he had heard. "Oh, *Jesus*," he said, astonished. "Okay, no embassy. What about Brussels, SHAPE? There's a Navy Intelligence unit; I've dealt with those people before."

"Not yet. Maybe not at all."

"I thought you wanted to use the uniform, my connections."

"Maybe I will. It's nice to know they're there."

"Well, what do you want me to do? I've got to do *something*."

"Are you really fluent in German?"

"*Hochdeutsch, Schwäbisch, Bayerisch* and several dialects in between. I told you, I can handle five languages . . ."

"You've made it obnoxiously clear," interrupted Converse. "There's a woman named Fishbein here in Bonn. That's the first name I'm going to give you. She's involved; we're not sure how, but she's suspected of being what they call a conduit – a relayer of information. I want you to meet her, talk with her, establish a relationship. We'll have to think of something that'll be convincing in order for you to do it. She's in her forties, and she's the youngest daughter of Hermann Goering. She married a survivor of the holocaust for obvious reasons; he's long gone. Any ideas?"

"Sure," said Fitzpatrick without hesitating. "Inheritance. There are a couple of thousand last wills and testaments every year that the deceased want processed through the military. They're from crazies who leave everything they've got to the *other* survivors. The true Aryan Germanic stock and all that horseshit. We bounce them back to the civil courts who don't know what to do with them, so they end up in limbo and eventually in the Treasury Department's coffers."

"No kidding?"

"*Ein, zwei, drei*. Believe me, those people mean it."

"Can you use the device?"

"How about a million-plus legacy from a small Midwest brewer of lager beer?"

"You'll do," said Joel. "You're on board."

There was no mention of Aquitaine or of George Marcus Delavane or Jacques Louis Bertholdier or Erich Leifhelm, or of twenty-odd names at the State

Department and the Pentagon. Nor was there any detailed analysis of the "network" progress as it appeared in the dossiers in Converse's possession, or as described by Dr Edward Beale on Mykonos. Connal Fitzpatrick was given the barest bones of the body of information. Joel's reasoning was far less benign than he had stated. If the navy lawyer was taken and interrogated – no matter how brutally – there was little of substance he could reveal.

"You're not really telling me a hell of a lot," said Fitzpatrick.

"I've told you enough to get your head blown off, and that's not a phrase normally in my lexicon."

"Nor mine."

"Then consider me a nice fellow," said Converse, as the two men headed for the entrance gate of the Alter Zoll.

"On the other hand," continued Halliday's brother-in-law, "you've been through a lot more than I ever have. I read that stuff about you in the security files – files, not file – they were cross-correlated with the files of a lot of other prisoners. You were something else. According to most of the men in those camps, you held them together . . . until they put you into solitary."

"They were wrong, sailor. I was shaking and scared to death and would have fucked a Peking duck to save my skin."

"That's not what the files say. They say . . ."

"I'm really not interested, Commander," said Joel, as they passed through the ornate gate. "But I've got an immediate problem you can help solve."

"What is it?"

"I gave my word I'd call Dowling on some mobile phone line. I wouldn't know how to ask for it."

"There's a booth over there," said Connal, pointing to a white plastic bubble that protruded from a concrete pylon on the pavement abutting the drive. "Do you have the number?"

"It's here somewhere," replied Converse, crawling through various pockets. "Here it is," he said as he separated the scrap of paper from several credit card charges.

"*Vermittlung, bitte.*" The naval officer sounded authentic as he spoke crisply into the telephone. "*Fräulein, geben Sie mir bitte sieben, drei, vier, zwei, zwei.*" Fitzpatrick then inserted a series of coins into the metal box and turned to Joel. "Here you are. They're ringing."

"Stay there. Ask for him . . . say it's his lawyer calling, the one at the hotel."

"*Guten Tag, Fräulein. Ist Herr* . . . Oh, no, I speak English. Do you speak English? No, I'm not calling from California, but it's an emergency . . . Dowling, I have to reach . . ."

"*Caleb,*" said Joel quickly.

"Caleb Dowling." The Navy man covered the mouthpiece. "What kind of name is that?"

"Something to do with Gucci shoes."

"What? . . . *Oui, ja* – yes, thanks. They're getting him. Here take it." Fitzpatrick handed the phone to Converse.

"*Joe?*"

"Yes, Cal. I said I'd call you after I met with Fowler. Everything's okay."

"No, it's not, Mister Lawyer," said the actor quietly. "You and I had better have a very serious talk, and I don't mind telling you a hunk of beef named Rosenberg will be just a few feet away."

"I don't understand."

"A man died in Paris. Does that clear things up for you?"

"Oh, *God*." Converse felt the blood draining from his head and a hollowness in his throat. For a moment he thought he was going to be sick. "They came to you?" he whispered.

"A man from the German police a little over an hour ago and this time I didn't have any doubts about my visitor. He was the real item."

"I don't know what to say," stammered Joel.

"Did you do it?"

"I . . . I guess I did." Converse stared at the telephone dial, seeing the bloodied face of the man in the alleyway, feeling the blood on his own fingers.

"You *guess?* That's not something you guess about."

"Then yes . . . The answer is yes. I did it."

"Did you have a reason?"

"I thought I did."

"I want to hear it, but not now. I'll tell you where to meet me."

"No!" exclaimed Joel, confused but emphatic. "I can't involve you. You can't be involved!"

"This fellow gave me a card and wants me to call him if you got in touch with me. He was very specific about withholding information; how it's considered aiding a fugitive."

"He was right, *absolutely* right! For God's sake, tell him everything, Cal! The truth. You got me a room for the night because you thought I might not have a reservation and we had a pleasant few hours on the plane. You put it in your name because you didn't want me to pay. Don't hide *anything!* Not even this call."

"Why didn't I tell him before?"

"That's all right, you're telling him now. It was a shock and I'm a fellow American and you're in a foreign country. You wanted time to think, to reflect. My phone call shook you into behaving rationally. Tell him you confronted me with the accusation and I didn't deny it. Be honest with him, Cal."

"How honest? Should I include my session with Fowler?"

"That's all right, too, but it's not necessary. Let me back up and clarify. Fowler's a false name and he's not relevant to Paris, I give you my word. Bringing him in is only volunteering an unnecessary complication."

"Should I tell him you're at the Alter Zoll?"

"It's where I'm calling you from. I just admitted it."

"You won't be able to go back to the Konigshof."

"It doesn't matter," said Joel, speaking rapidly, wanting to get off the phone and start thinking. "My luggage is at the airport and I can't go back there either."

"You had a briefcase."

"I've taken care of that. It's where I can get it."

The actor paused, then spoke slowly. "So your advice to me is to level with the police, to tell them the truth."

"Without volunteering extraneous and unrelated material. Yes, that's my advice, Cal. It's the way you can stay clean and you *are* clean."

"It sounds like fine advice, Joe – Joel, and I certainly wish I could take it, but I'm afraid I can't."

"What? *Why?*"

"Because bad men like thieves and killers don't give advice like that. It's not in any script I ever read."

"That's nonsense! For Christ's sake, do as I tell you!"

"Sorry, partner, it's not good dramaturgy. So you do as I tell *you*. There's a big stone building at the university – beautiful place, a restored palace actually – with a layout of gardens you don't see very often. They're on the south side with benches here and there on the main path. It's a nice place on a summer's night, kind of out of the way and not too crowded. Be there at ten o'clock."

"Cal, I won't involve you in this!"

"I'm already involved. I've withheld information and I've aided a fugitive." Dowling paused again. "There's someone I want you to meet," he said.

"*No.*"

There was a click and the line went dead.

10

Converse hung up the phone and braced himself on the sides of the plastic booth, trying to clear his head. He had killed a man, not in a war anyone knew about, and not in the heat of survival in a South-east Asian jungle, but in a Paris alleyway because he had to make an instant decision based on probabilities. Rightly or wrongly the act had been done and he could not dwell on it. The German police were looking for him, which meant that Interpol had entered the picture, transmitting from Paris information somehow supplied by Jacques Louis Bertholdier, who remained out of sight, beyond the scope of the hunt. Joel recalled his own words spoken only minutes ago. If Press Halliday's life was not terribly important compared to what he was going after, neither was the life of a minion who worked for Bertholdier, Delavane's disciple, Aquitaine's arm in France. There were no options, thought Converse. He had to go on; he had to stay free.

"What's the matter?" asked Fitzpatrick, standing anxiously several feet to Joel's left. "You look like you got kicked by a mule."

"I got kicked," agreed Converse.

"What happened to Dowling? Is he in trouble?"

"He *will be!*" exploded Joel, "because he's a misguided idiot who thinks he's in some kind of goddamned movie!"

"That wasn't your opinion a little while ago."

"We met; it came out all right. This can't, not for him." Converse pushed himself away from the booth and looked at the Navy lawyer, his mind now trying desperately to concentrate on the immediate. "I may tell you and I may not," he said glancing around for an available taxi. "Come on, we're going to put your awesome linguistic abilities to work. We need shelter, expensive but not showy, especially *not* a place where the well-heeled tourists go who don't speak German. If there's one thing they'll spread about me is that I can't talk my way through the five boroughs of New York. I want a rich hotel that doesn't need foreigners, doesn't cater to them. Do you know the kind of place I mean?"

Fitzpatrick nodded. "Exclusive, clubby, German business oriented. Every large city has them and they're always twenty times my *per diem* for breakfast."

"That's okay, I've got money here in Bonn. I might as well try to get it out."

"You're full of surprises," said Connal. "I mean *real* surprises."

"Do you think you can handle it? Find a hotel like that?"

"I can explain what I want to a cab driver; he'll probably know. Bonn's small, nothing like New York or London or Paris . . . There's a taxi letting people out." The two men hurried to the kerb and the cab with a quartet of discharging passengers, balancing camera equipment and outsized Louis Vuitton handbags.

"How will you do it?" asked Converse, as they nodded to the tourists, two couples in the midst of an argument, male versus female, Nikon versus Vuitton.

"A combination of what we both said," answered Fitzpatrick, "A quiet, nice hotel away from the *Ausländerlärm.*"

"What?"

"The clamour of tourists – and worse. I'll tell him we're calling on some very important German businessmen – bankers, say – and we'd like a place they'd be most comfortable in for confidential meetings. He'll get the drift."

"He'll see we don't have any luggage," objected Joel.

"He'll see the money in my hand first," said the naval officer, holding the door for Converse.

Lieutenant-Commander Connal Fitzpatrick, USN, member of the military bar and limited thereby, impressed Joel Converse, vaunted international attorney, to the point where the latter felt foolish. Effortlessly, the Navy lawyer got them situated in a two-bedroom suite at an inn on the banks of the Rhine called *Das Rektorat.* It was one of those converted pre-war estates where most of the guests seemed to have at least a nodding acquaintance with several others and the clerks rarely looked anyone in the eye, as if silently announcing their subservience – or confirming the fact that they would certainly not acknowledge having seen Herr So-and-So should someone ask them.

Fitzpatrick had begun his campaign with the taxi driver, leaning forward. in the seat and speaking in rapid, quiet phrases. Their exchanges seemed to grow more confidential as the cab sped toward the heart of the city; then it abruptly veered away, crossing the railroad tracks that intersected the capital and entered a smooth road paralleling the river north. Joel had started to speak, to ask what was happening, but the Navy lawyer had held up his hand, telling Converse to be quiet.

Once they had stopped at the entrance of the inn, reached by an interminably long, manicured drive, Fitzpatrick got out.

"Stay here," he said to Joel. "I'll see if I can get us a couple of rooms . . . And don't say anything."

Twelve minutes later Connal returned, his demeanour stern, his eyes, however, lively. His mission had been accomplished. "Come on, Chairman of the Board, we're going straight up." He paid the driver handsomely and once again held the door for Converse – now a touch more deferentially, thought Joel.

The lobby of *Das Rektorat* was unmistakably German with odd overtones of the more delicate Victorian; thick heavy wood and sturdy leather chairs were beside and below filigrees of brass ornamentation forming arches over doorways, elegant borders for large mirrors, and valances above thick bay windows where none were required. One's first impression was of a quiet, expensive spa from decades ago, its initial solemnity lightened by the flashes of reflecting metal and glass. It was a strange mixture of the old and the very old, money its underpinnings.

Fitzpatrick led Converse to a panelled elevator recessed in the panelled corridor, no bellboy – or manservant – in attendance. It was a small enclosure, room for no more than four people, the walls of tinted, marbled glass; they vibrated as the elevator ascended two storeys.

"I think you'll approve of the accommodation," said Connal. "I checked it out; that's why it took me so long."

"We're back in the nineteenth century, you know," countered Joel. "I trust they have telephones and not just the Hessian express."

"All the most modern communications, I made sure of that, too." The elevator door opened. "This way," said Fitzpatrick, gesturing to the right. "The suite's at the end of the hall."

"The suite?"

"You said you had money in Bonn."

Two bedrooms flanked a tastefully furnished sitting room, with French doors that opened onto a small balcony overlooking the Rhine. The rooms were sunlit and airy, the decor of the walls again an odd mixture: Impressionist reproductions of floral arrangements were beside dramatic prints of past champion horses from leading German tracks and breeding farms.

"All right, wonder boy," said Converse, looking out of the open French doors, then turning back to Connal Fitzpatrick who stood in the middle of the room, the key still in his hand. "How did you do it?"

"It wasn't hard," replied the Navy lawyer, smiling. "You'd be surprised what a set of military papers will do for a person in this country. The older guys sort of stiffen up and look like boxer puppies smelling a pot roast, and there aren't that many people here much under sixty."

"That doesn't tell me anything unless you're enlisting us."

"It does when I combine it with the fact that I'm an aide assigned by the US Navy to accompany an important American financier over here to hold confidential meetings with his German counterparts. While in Bonn, naturally, incognito is the best means for my eccentric financier to travel. Everything's in *my* name."

"What about reservations?"

"I told the manager that you'd rejected the hotel reserved for us as having too many people you might know. I also hinted that those countrymen of his you're going to meet might be most appreciative of his cooperation. He agreed that I might have a point there."

"How did we hear about this place?" asked Joel, still suspicious.

"Simple. I remembered it from several conversations I had at the International Economic Conference in Dusseldorf last year."

"You were *there?*"

"I didn't know there was one," said Fitzpatrick, heading for the door on the left. "I'll take this bedroom, okay? It's not as large as the other one and that's the way it should be since I'm an aide – which Jesus, Mary, and Joseph all know is the truth."

"*Wait* a minute," broke in Converse, stepping forward. "What about our luggage? Since we don't have any, didn't that strike your friend downstairs as a little odd for such important characters?"

"Not at all," said Connal, turning. "It's still in the city at that unnamed hotel you rejected so emphatically after twenty minutes. But only I can pick it up."

"Why?"

Fitzpatrick brought his index finger to his lips. "You also have a compulsion for secrecy. Remember, you're eccentric."

"The manager *bought* all that swill?"

"He calls me *Kommandant*."

"You're quite a bullshitter, sailor."

"I remind you, sir, that in the land of *Erin go Bragh* it's called good healthy blarney. And although you lack certain qualifications, Press said you were a master of it in negotiations." Connal's expression became serious. "He meant it in the best way, counsellor, and that's not bullshit."

As the Navy lawyer turned again and walked through the door to the bedroom, Joel felt an odd sense of recognition but could not define it. What was it about the younger man that struck a chord in him? Fitzpatrick had that boldness that came with the untried, that lack of fear in small things that caution would later teach him often led to larger things. He tested waters bravely; he had never come close to drowning.

Suddenly, Converse understood the recognition. What he saw in Connal Fitzpatrick was himself . . . before things happened. Before he knew the meaning of fear, raw terrible fear. And finally the loneliness.

* * *

152

It was agreed that Connal would return to the Köln-Bonn airport, not for Joel's luggage but for his own, which was stored in a locker in the baggage claim area. He would then go into Bonn proper, buy an expensive suitcase and fill it with half a dozen shirts, underwear, socks, and the best off-the-rack clothing he could find in Joel's sizes, namely three pairs of trousers, a jacket or two and a raincoat. It was further agreed that casual clothes were most appropriate; an eccentric financier was permitted such lapses of sartorial taste, and also such attire more successfully concealed its non-custom made origins. Finally the last stop he would make before returning to *Das Rektorat* was at a second locker in the railroad station where Converse had left his attaché case. Once the case was in the Navy lawyer's possession and the taxi waiting outside, there were to be no further stops. He was to drive directly to the countryside inn.

"I wanted to ask you something," said Fitzpatrick just before leaving. "Back at the Alter Zoll you said something about how 'they' would spread the word that you couldn't talk your way through the five boroughs of New York. I gathered that referred to the fact that you don't speak German."

"That's right. Or any other language, adequate English excepted. I tried but it never took. I was married to a girl who spoke fluent French and German and even she gave up. I don't have the ear, I guess."

"Who did '*they*' refer to?" asked Connal, barely listening to Converse's explanation. "The embassy men?"

Joel hesitated. "A little wider, I'm afraid," he said choosing his words carefully. "You'll have to know but not now, not yet. Later."

"Why later? Why not now?"

"Because it wouldn't do you a damned bit of good, and it might raise questions you wouldn't want raised under shall we say, adverse circumstances."

"That's elliptical."

"It certainly is."

"Is that it? Is that all you'll say?"

"No. There's one other thing. I want my briefcase."

Fitzpatrick had assured him that the switchboard of *Das Rektorat* was eminently capable of handling telephone calls in English – as well as at least six other languages including Arabic – and he should have no qualms about placing a call to Lawrence Talbot in New York.

"Christ, where *are* you, Joel?" Talbot shouted into the phone.

"Amsterdam," replied Converse, not wanting to say Bonn and having had the presence of mind to make the call station-to-station. "I want to know what happened to Judge Anstett, Larry. Can you tell me anything?"

"I want to know what's happened to *you!* René called last night . . ."

"Mattilon?"

"You told him you were flying to London."

"I changed my mind."

"What the hell *happened*? The police were with him; he had no choice. He had to tell them who you were." Talbot suddenly paused, then spoke in a calmer voice, a false voice. "Are you all right, Joel? Is there something you want to tell me, something bothering you?"

"Something bothering me?"

"Listen to me, Joel. We all know what you went through, and we admire you, *respect you.* You're the finest we've got in the international division . . ."

"I'm the *only* one you've got," Converse broke in, trying to think, trying to buy time as well as information. "What did René say? Why did he call you?"

"You sound like your old self, fella."

"I *am* my old self, Larry. What did René call you about? Why were the police with him?" Joel could feel the slippage; he was entering another sphere and he knew it, accepted it. The lies would follow, guile joining deceit, time and freedom of movement paramount. He had to *stay* free; there was so much to do, so little time.

"He called me back after the police left to fill me in incidentally, they were from the *Sûreté.* As he understood it, the driver of a limousine was assaulted outside the George V's service entrance . . ."

"The driver of a limousine . . . ?" interrupted Converse involuntarily. "They said he was a *chauffeur?*"

"From one of those high-priced services that ferry around people who make odd stops at odd hours. Very posh and very confidential. Apparently the fellow was pretty well smashed up and they say you did it. No one knows why but you were identified and they say the man may not live."

"Larry, this is preposterous!" objected Joel, his protestation accompanied by feigned personal outrage. "Yes, I *was* there – in the area – but it had nothing to do with *me!* Two hot heads got into a fight and since I couldn't stop them I wasn't going to get my head handed to me. I got out of there and before I found a taxi I yelled at the doorman to call for help. The last thing I saw he was blowing his whistle and running toward the alley."

"You weren't even involved then," said Talbot. The statement was a lawyer's positive fact.

"Of course not! Why would I be?"

"That's what we couldn't understand. It didn't make sense."

"It *doesn't* make sense. I'll call René and fly back to Paris, if I have to."

"Yes, do that," agreed Talbot haltingly. "I should tell you I may have aggravated the situation."

"You? How?"

"I told Mattilon that perhaps you were . . . well, not yourself. When I spoke with you in Geneva you sounded awful, Joel. Just plain *awful.*"

"Good God, how did you think I'd feel? A man I was negotiating with dies in front of me bleeding from a dozen bullet wounds. How would *you* feel?"

"I understand," said the lawyer in New York, "but then René thought he saw something in you – heard something – that disturbed him, too."

"Oh, come on, will you people get off it!" Converse's thoughts raced; every word he spoke had to be credible, his now diminished outrage rooted in believability. "Mattilon saw me after I'd been flying in and out of airports for damn near fourteen hours. Christ, I was exhausted!"

"Joel?" Talbot began, obviously not quite ready to get-off-it. "Why did you tell René you were in Paris for the firm?"

Converse paused, not for lack of a response, but for effect. He was ready for the question; he had been ready when he first approached Mattilon. "A white lie, Larry, and no harm to anyone. I wanted some information and it seemed the best way to get it."

"About this Bertholdier? He's the general, isn't he?"

"He turned out to be the wrong source. I told René as much and he couldn't have agreed with me more." Joel lightened his tone of voice. "Also it would have appeared strange if I said I was in Paris for somebody else, wouldn't it? I don't think it would have done the firm any good. Rumours and speculation run rampant down our corridors; you told me that once."

"Yes, and it's true. You did the right thing . . . Damn it, Joel, why the *hell* did you leave the hotel, the way you did? From the basement, or wherever it was."

It was the moment for total conviction, a small inconsequential untruth that if not carried off would lead to the larger, far more dangerous lie. Connal Fitzpatrick could do it well, reflected Converse. The Navy lawyer had not learned to fear the small things; he did not know they were spoors that could lead one back to a rat cage in the Mekong River.

"Bubba, my friend and sole support," said Joel, as cavalierly as he could muster. "I owe you many things, but not the intimacies of my private life."

"The what of your what?"

"I am approaching middle age – at least it's not far off and I have no matrimonial encumbrances or guilt by reasons of fidelity."

"You were avoiding a *woman?*"

"Fortunately for the firm not a man."

"Jee-sus! I'm so well into middle age I don't think about those things. Sorry, young fella."

"Young and not so young, Larry."

"We were all off-base then. You'd better call René right away and get this thing cleared up. I can't tell you how relieved I am."

"You can tell me about Anstett. That's why I called you."

"Of course." Talbot lowered his voice. "A terrible thing, a tragedy. What did the papers over there say?"

Converse was caught; he had not anticipated the question. "Very little," he replied, trying to remember what Fitzpatrick had told him. "Just that he was shot and apparently nothing was taken from his apartment."

"That's right. Naturally, the first thing Nathan and I thought of was you, and whatever the hell you're involved with, but that wasn't the case. It was a Mafia vendetta, pure and simple. You know how rough Anstett was on appeals from those people; he'd throw them out as fast as he'd call their attorneys a disgrace to the profession."

"It was a confirmed Mafia killing?"

"It will be, and that's straight from O'Neil down at the commissioner's office. They know their man; he's an executioner for the Delvecchio family and last month Anstett threw the key away on Delvecchio's eldest son. He's in for twelve years with no appeals left, The Supreme Court won't touch him."

"They *know* the man?"

"It's only a matter of picking him up."

"How come it's so clear-cut?" asked Joel, confused.

"The usual way," said Talbot. "An informer who needs a favour. And since everything's happened so fast and so quietly it's assumed that the ballistics will prove out."

"So fast? So quietly?"

"The informer reached the police first thing this morning. A special hunt was dispatched and only they know the man's identity. They figure the gun will still be in his possession. He'll be picked up any time now; he lives in Syosset."

Something was wrong, thought Converse. There was an inconsistency but he could not spot the flaw. Then it came to him. "Larry, if everything's so quiet, how do you know about it?"

"I was afraid you'd ask that," said Talbot uneasily. "I might as well tell you: it'll probably be in the newspaper follow-ups anyway. O'Neil's keeping me posted; call it courtesy, and also because I'm nervous."

"Why?"

"Except for the man who killed him, I was the last person to see Anstett alive."

"*You?*"

"Yes. After René's second call I decided to phone the judge, after conferring with Nathan, of course. When I finally reached Anstett, I said I had to see him. He wasn't happy about it but I was adamant. I explained that it concerned you. All I knew was that you were in terrible trouble and something had to be done. I went over to his apartment on Central Park South and we talked. I told him what had happened and how frightened I was for you, frankly letting him know that I held him responsible. He didn't say much but I think he was frightened, too. He said he'd get in touch with me in the morning. I left, and according to the coroner's report, he was killed approximately three hours later."

Joel's breath was short, his head splitting, his concentration absolute. "Let me get this straight, Larry. You went over to Anstett's apartment after René's call — his second call. *After* he told the *Sûreté* who I was."

"That's right."

"How long was it?"

"How long was what?"

"Before, you left for Anstett's. After you spoke with Mattilon."

"Well, let me see. Naturally, I wanted to talk to Nathan first but he was out to dinner, so I waited. Incidentally, he concurred and offered to join me . . ."

"How *long*, Larry?"

"An hour and a half, two hours at the outside."

Two hours plus three hours totalled five hours. More than enough time for the puppets to be put in place. Converse did not know how it had been done, only that it *had* been done. Things had suddenly erupted in Paris, and in New York an agitated Lawrence Talbot had been followed to an apartment on Central Park South, where someone, somewhere, recognized a name and a man and the part

156

he had played against Aquitaine. Were it otherwise, Talbot would be the corpse, not Lucas Anstett. All the rest was a smoke screen behind which the disciples of George Marcus Delavane manipulated the puppets.

" . . . and the courts owed so much to him, the country owed so much." Talbot was speaking but Joel could no longer listen.

"I have to go, Larry," he said, hanging up.

The killing was obscene, and the fact that it was carried out so quickly, so efficiently and with such precise deception was as frightening as anything Converse could imagine.

Joseph (Joey the Nice) Albanese drove his Pontiac down the quiet, tree-lined street in Syosset, Long Island, waving to a couple in a front yard. The husband was trimming a hedge under his wife's guidance. They stopped what they were doing, smiled and waved back. Very nice. His neighbours liked him, thought Joey. They considered him a sweet guy and very generous, what with letting the kids use his pool, and serving their parents only the best booze when they dropped over, and the biggest steaks money could buy when he had weekend barbecues – which he did often, rotating the neighbours so that no one should feel left out.

He *was* a sweet guy, mused Joey. He was always pleasant and never raised his voice in anger to anyone, offering only a glad hand, a nice word and a happy smile to everybody, no matter how lousy he really felt. That was it, *goddamn it!* thought Joey. Irre – fuckin' – gardless of how upset he was he never let it show! Joey-the-Nice was what they called him and they were right. Sometimes he figured he had to be some kind of saint – may Jesus Christ forgive him for having such thoughts. He had just waved to neighbours but in truth he felt like smashing his fist through the windscreen and shoving the glass down their throats.

It wasn't them, it was last *night* that did it! A crazy night, a crazy *hit*, everything *crazy!* And that *gumbar* they brought in from the West Coast, the one they called "Major", he was the nuttiest fruitcake of them all! And a sadist to boot, the way he beat the shit out of that old man and the crazy questions he asked, and shouting all the time. *Tutto pazzo!*

One minute he's playing cards in the Bronx, and the next the phone is ringing. Get down to Manhattan *in fretta e furia!* A bad heat is needed *subito!* So he goes and what does he find? It's that iron-balled judge, the one who closed the steel doors on Delvecchio's boy! What craziness! They'll trace it back to the old man for sure. He'll know such *afflizione* from the cops and the courts he'll be lucky to own a small whorehouse in Palermo – if he ever gets back.

Then maybe . . . just maybe . . . thought Joey at the time, there was a turning muscle in the organization. Old Delvecchio was losing his grip; just maybe it was being called for, this *afflizione* that surely would follow. And possibly – just possibly – Joey himself was being tested. Maybe he was *too* nice, too *suave*, to put the bad heat on someone like the old judge who gave them all such a hard time. Well, he wasn't. No sirree, the nice stopped with the handle of a gun. It was his job, his profession. The Lord Jesus decided who should live and who should die, only He spoke through mortal men on earth who told people like Joey whom to hit. There was no moral dilemma for Joey the Nice. It was important, however, that the orders always came from a man with respect; that was necessary.

They did last night; the order came from a man with great respect. Although Joey did not know him personally, he had heard for years about the powerful *padrone* in Washington, DC. The name was whispered, never spoken out loud.

Joey touched the brakes of his car, slowing down so to swing into his driveway. His wife, Angie, would be pissed off at him, maybe shout a little because he didn't come home last night. One more irritation on top of all the craziness, but what the hell was he going to say? Sorry, Angie, but I was gainfully employed throwing six bullets into an old guy who definitely discriminated against Italians. So you see, Angie, I had to stay across the bridge in Jersey where one of the *paesani* I played cards with and who'll swear I was there all night happens to be the chief of police.

But, of course, he would never go into such details with his wife. That was his own law. No matter how aggravated he was he never brought his job home. More husbands should be like him and there would be happier households in Syosset.

Shit! One of the fucking kids had \ left a bicycle in front of the attached garage; he wouldn't be able to open the automatic door and drive inside. He'd have to get out. Shit! One more aggravation. He couldn't even park by the Millers' kerb next door; some creep's car was there but it wasn't the Millers' Buick. Double shit!

Joey brought the Pontiac to a stop halfway into the sloping driveway and got out. He went up to the bike and leaned down. The rotten kid didn't even use the kickstand and Joey hated bending over what with his heavy gut and all.

"Joseph Albanese!"

Joey the Nice spun around, crouching, reaching under his jacket. That tone of voice was used by only one type of slime! He pulled out his .38 and dived toward the grill of his car.

The explosions reverberated throughout the neighbourhood. Birds fluttered out of trees and there were screams along the block in the bright afternoon sunlight. Joseph Albanese was sprawled against the grill of the Pontiac, rivulets of blood slowly rolling down the shiny chrome. Joey the Nice had been caught in the vectored fire, and gripped in his hand was the gun he had used so effectively the night before. Ballistics would prove out. The killer of Lucas Anstett was dead. The judge had been victim of a gangland assassination, and so far as the world was concerned, it had nothing to do with events taking place eight thousand miles away in Bonn, Germany.

Converse stood on the small balcony, his hands on the railing, looking down at the majestic river beyond the forest of trees that formed the banks of the Rhine. It was past seven o'clock; the sun was going below the mountains in the west, its orange rays shooting up, creating blocks of shadows over the earth – moving shadows that floated across the waters in the descending distance. The vibrant colours were hypnotic, the breezes cooling, but nothing could stop the pounding echo in his chest. *Where was Fitzpatrick? Where was his attaché case? The dossiers?* He tried to stop thinking, to stop his imagination from catapulting into frightening possibilities.

There was a sudden harsh echo, not from his chest, but from inside the room. He turned quickly as the door opened and Connal Fitzpatrick stood there, removing his key from the lock. He stepped aside letting a uniformed porter enter with two suitcases, instructing the man to leave them on the floor while he reached into his pocket for a tip. The porter left and the Navy lawyer stared at Joel. There was no attaché case in his hand.

"Where is it?" said Converse, afraid to breathe, afraid to move.

"I didn't pick it up."

"Why *not?*" cried Joel, rushing forward.

"I couldn't be sure . . . maybe it was just a feeling, I don't know."

"What are you talking about?"

"I was at the airport for seven hours yesterday, going from counter to counter asking about you," said Connal softly. "This afternoon I passed the Lufthansa desk and the same clerk was there. When I said hello he didn't seem to want to acknowledge me; he looked nervous, and I couldn't understand. I came back out of the baggage claim with my suitcase and watched him. I remembered how he had glanced at me last night, and as I passed him I swore his eyes kept shooting to the centre of the terminal, but there were so many people, so much confusion, I couldn't be certain."

"You think you were picked up? *Followed?*"

"That's just it, I don't *know*. When I was shopping in Bonn I went from store to store and every now and then I'd turn around, or shift my head, to see if I could spot anyone. A couple of times I thought I saw the same people twice, but then again it was always crowded, and – again – I couldn't be sure. But I kept thinking about that Lufthansa clerk; something was wrong."

"What about when you were in the taxi? Did you."

"Naturally. I kept looking out of the rear window. Even during the drive out here. Several cars made the same turns we did, but I'd tell the driver to slow down and they passed us."

"Did you watch where they went after they passed you?"

"What was the point?"

"There is one," said Joel, recalling a clever driver who followed a deep red Mercedes limousine.

"All I knew was that you're pretty uptight about that attaché case. I don't know what's in it and I figure you don't want anyone else to know, either."

"Bingo, counsellor."

There was a knocking at the door, and although it was soft, it had the intrusion of a staccato burst of thunder. Both men stood motionless, their eyes riveted on the door.

"Ask who it is," whispered Converse.

"*Wer ist da, bitte?*" said Fitzpatrick, loud enough to be heard. There was a brief reply in German and Connal breathed again. "It's okay. It's a message for me from the manager. He probably wants to sell us a conference room. The Navy lawyer went to the door and opened it."

However, it was not the manager, or a bellboy, or a porter bringing a message from the manager. Instead, standing there, was a slender, elderly man in a dark suit with erect posture and very broad shoulders. He glanced first at Fitzpatrick, then looked beyond at Converse.

"Excuse me, please, Commander," he said courteously, walking through the door and approaching Joel, his hand outstretched. "Herr Converse, may I introduce myself? The name is Leifhelm. Erich Leifhelm."

11

Stunned, Joel took the German's hand, too paralysed to do anything else. "Field Marshal . . . ?" he uttered, instantly regretting it – he could have had the presence at least to say "General". It was Leifhelm's dossier, that incredible story of an incredibly polished monster. The pages flashed across Converse's mind as he looked at the man – his straight hair, still more blond than white, his pale blue eyes glacial, his pinkish skin lined, waxen, set it seemed for decades.

"An old title and one thankfully I have not heard in many years. But you flatter me. You were sufficiently interested to learn something of my past."

"Not very much."

"I suspect enough." Leifhelm turned to Fitzpatrick. "I apologize for my little ruse, Commander. I felt it was best."

Fitzpatrick shrugged, bewildered. "You know each other, apparently."

"*Of* one another," corrected the German. "Mr Converse came to Bonn to meet with me, but I imagine he's told you that."

"No, I haven't told him that," said Joel.

Leifhelm turned back, studying Converse's eyes. "I see. Perhaps we should talk privately."

"I think so," Joel looked over at Fitzpatrick. "Commander, I've taken up too much of your time. Why not go downstairs to dinner and I'll join you in a while?"

"Whatever you say, sir," said Connal, an officer assuming the status of an aide. He nodded and left, closing the door firmly behind him.

"A lovely room," said Leifhelm, taking several steps toward the open French doors. "And with such a lovely view."

"How did you find me?" asked Converse.

"Him," replied the former field marshal, looking at Joel. "*Ein Offizier*, according to the front desk. Who is he?"

"How?" repeated Converse.

160

"He spent hours last night at the airport inquiring about you; many remembered him. He was obviously a friend."

"And you knew he'd checked his luggage? That he'd be back for it?"

"Frankly no. We thought he might come for yours. We knew you wouldn't. Now, please, who is he?"

Joel understood that it was vital he maintain a level of arrogance, as he had done with Bertholdier in Paris. It was the only route he could take with such men; to be accepted by them they had to see something of themselves in him. "He's not important and he knows nothing. He's a legal officer in the Navy who's worked in Bonn before and is over here now I gather on personal business. A prospective fiancée, I think he mentioned. I saw him the other week; we chatted and I told him I was flying in today or tomorrow and he said he'd make it a point to meet me. He's obsequious, and persistent. I'm sure he has delusions of a civilian practice. Naturally – under the circumstances – I used him. As you did."

"Naturally." Leifhelm smiled; he *was* polished. "You gave him no arrival time?"

"Paris changed any possibility of that, didn't it?"

"Oh, yes, Paris. We must discuss Paris."

"I spoke to a friend who deals with the *Sûreté*. The man died."

"Such men do. Frequently."

"They said he was a driver, a chauffeur. He wasn't."

"Would it have been wiser to say he was a trusted associate of General Jacques Louis Bertholdier?"

"Obviously not. They say I killed him."

"You did. We gather it was an uncontrollable miscalculation, no doubt brought on by the man himself."

"Interpol's after me."

"We, too, have friends; the situation will change. You have nothing to fear – as long as *we* have nothing to fear." The German paused, glancing around the room. "May I sit down?"

"Please. Shall I ring for a drink?"

"I drink only light wine and very sparingly. Unless you wish . . . it's not necessary."

"It's not necessary," said Converse, as Leifhelm sat in a chair nearest the balcony doors. Joel would sit when he felt the moment was right, not before.

"You took extraordinary measures at the airport to avoid us," continued the youngest field marshal ever to be so designated by Adolf Hitler.

"I was followed from Copenhagen."

"Very observant of you. You understand no harm was intended."

"I didn't understand anything. I just didn't like it. I didn't know what effect Paris would have on my arrival in Bonn, what it meant to you."

"What Paris meant?" asked Leifhelm rhetorically. "Paris meant that a man, an attorney using a false name, said some very alarming things to a most distinguished figure many consider a brilliant statesman. This attorney, who called himself Simon, said he was flying to Bonn to see me. On his way – and I'm sure with provocation – he kills a man, which tells us something; he's quite ruthless and very capable. But that is all we know; we would like to know more. Where he goes, who he meets? In our position, would you have done otherwise?"

It was the moment to sit down. "I would have done it better."

"Perhaps if we'd known how resourceful you were we might have been less obvious. Incidentally, what happened in Paris? What did that man do to provoke you?"

"He tried to stop me from leaving."

"Those were not his orders."

"Then he grossly misunderstood them. I've a few bruises on my chest and neck to prove it. I'm not in the habit of physically defending myself, and I certainly had no intention of killing him. In fact, I didn't know I had. It was an accident purely in self-defence."

"Obviously. Who would want such complications?"

"Exactly," agreed Converse bluntly. "As soon as I can rearrange my last hours in Paris so as to eliminate any mention of my seeing General Bertholdier, I'll return and explain what happened to the police."

"As the adage goes, that may be easier said than done. You were seen talking together at *Les Étalons Blancs*. Undoubtedly, the general was recognized later when he came to the hotel; he's a celebrated man. No, I think you'd be wiser to let us handle it. We *can*, you know."

Joel looked hard at the German, his eyes cold yet questioning. "I admit there are risks doing it my way. I don't like them and neither would my client. On the other hand I can't go around being hunted by the police."

"The hunt will be called off. It will be necessary for you to remain out of sight for a few days, but by then new instructions will be issued from Paris. Your name will disappear from the Interpol lists; you'll no longer be sought."

"I'll want assurances, guarantees."

"What better could you have than my word? I tell you nothing when I tell you that we could have far more to lose than you."

Converse controlled his astonishment. Leifhelm had just told him a great deal whether he knew it or not. The German had as good as admitted he was part of a covert organization that could not take any chance of exposure. It was the first concrete evidence Joel had heard. Somehow it was too easy. Or were these elders of Aquitaine simply frightened old men?

"I'll concede that," said Converse, crossing his legs. "Well, General, you found me before I found you, but then, as we agreed, my movements are restricted. Where do we go from here?"

"Precisely where you wanted to go, Mr Converse. When you were in Paris you spoke of Bonn, Tel Aviv, Johannesburg. You knew whom to reach in Paris and whom to look for in Bonn. That impresses us greatly; we must assume you know more."

"I've spent months in detailed research – on behalf of my client, of course."

"But who are you? Where do you come from?"

Joel felt a sharp, sickening ache in his chest. He had felt it many times before; it was his own response to imminent danger and very real fear. "I am who I want people to think I am, General Leifhelm. I'm sure you can understand that."

"I see," said the German, watching him closely. "A sworn companion of the prevailing winds, but with the power beneath to carry you to your own destination."

"That's a little heavy, but I guess it says it. As to where I come from I'm sure you know that by now."

Five hours. More than enough time to put the puppets in place. A killing in New York; it had to be dealt with.

"Only bits and pieces, Mr Converse. And even if we knew more, how could we be certain it's true? What people think you are you may not be."

"Are you, General?"

"*Ausgezeichnet!*" said Leifhelm, slapping his knee and laughing. It was a genuine laugh, the man's waxen face creasing with humour. "You are a fine lawyer, *Mein Herr.* You answer – as they say in English – a pointed question with another question that is both an answer and an indictment."

"Under the circumstances, it's merely the truth. Nothing more."

"Also modest. Very commendable, very attractive."

Joel uncrossed his legs, then crossed them again impatiently. "I don't like compliments, General. I don't trust them – under the circumstances. You were saying before about where I wanted to go, about Bonn, Tel Aviv, and Johannesburg. What did you mean?"

"Only that we have complied with your wishes," said Leifhelm, spreading his hands in front of him. "Rather than your making such tedious trips we have asked our representatives in Tel Aviv and Johannesburg, as well as Bertholdier, of course, to fly to Bonn for a conference. With you, Mr Converse."

He had *done it!* thought Joel. They *were* frightened, *panicked* perhaps the better description. Despite the pounding and the pain in his chest, he spoke slowly, quietly. "I appreciate your consideration, but in all frankness, my client isn't ready for a summit. He wanted to understand the parts before he looked further at the whole. The spokes support the wheel, sir. I was to report, how strong they were – how strong they appeared to me."

"Oh, yes, your client. Who is he, Mr Converse?"

"I'm sure General Bertholdier told you I'm not at liberty to say."

"You were in San Francisco, California . . ."

"Where a great deal of my research was done," interrupted Joel. "It's not where my client lives. Although I readily admit there's a man in San Francisco – Palo Alto, to be exact – whom I'd like very much to *be* a client."

"Yes, yes, I see," Leifhelm put the ends of his fingers together, as he continued. "Am I to understand that you reject the conference here in Bonn?"

Converse had taken a thousand such questions in opening gambits with attorneys seeking accommodation between corporate adversaries. Both parties wanted the same thing; it was simply a question of flattening out the responsibility so that no one party would be the petitioner.

"Well, you've gone to a lot of trouble," Joel began. "And as long as it's understood that I have the option of speaking to each individually should I wish, I can't see any harm." Converse permitted himself a strained smile – as he had done a thousand times. "In the interests of my client, of course."

"Of course," said the German. "Tomorrow, say four o'clock in the afternoon. I'll send a car for you. I assure you, I set an excellent table."

"A table?"

"Dinner, naturally. After we have our talk." Leifhelm rose from the chair. "I wouldn't think of your coming to Bonn and forgoing the experience. I'm known for my dinner parties, Mr Converse. And if it concerns you, make whatever ... security arrangements ... you like. A platoon of personal guards, if you wish. You'll be perfectly safe. *Mein Haus ist dein Haus.*"

"I don't speak German."

"Actually, it's an old Spanish saying. *Mi casa, su casa.* 'My house is your house'. Your comfort and well-being are my most urgent concerns."

"Mine, too," said Joel, rising. "I wouldn't think of having anyone accompany me, *or* follow me. It'd be counterproductive. Of course, I'll inform my client as to my whereabouts, telling him approximately when he can expect my subsequent call. He'll be anxious to hear from me."

"I should think so." Leifhelm and Converse walked to the door; the German turned and once more offered his hand. "Until tomorrow then. And may I again suggest while you're here you be careful, at least for several days."

"I understand."

The puppets in New York. The killing that had to be dealt with – the first of two obstacles, two sharp, sickening aches in his chest.

"By the way," said Joel, releasing the field marshal's hand. "There was a news item on the BBC this morning that interested me – so much that I phoned an associate. A man was killed in New York, a judge. They say it was a revenge killing, a contract put out by organized crime. Do you know anything about it?"

"*I?*" asked Leifhelm, his blond-white eyebrows raised, his wax-like lips parted. "It seems people are killed by the dozens every day in New York, judges included, I presume. Why should I know anything about it? The answer, obviously, is no."

"I just wondered. Thank you."

"But ... but you. You must have a ..."

"Yes, General?"

"Why does this judge interest you? Why did you think I would know him?"

Converse smiled, but without a trace of humour. "I *won't* be *telling* you anything when I tell you he was our mutual adversary – enemy, if you like."

"Our ... ? You really must explain yourself!"

"As you, and as I said, I am what I want people to think I am. This man knew the truth. I'm on leave of absence from my firm, working confidentially for a personal client. He tried to stop me, tried to get the senior partner to cancel my leave and call me back."

"By giving him *reasons?*"

"No, just veiled threats of corruption and impropriety. He wouldn't go any farther; he's on the bench and couldn't back it up; his own conduct would be suspect. My employer is completely ignorant – angry as hell and confused – but I've calmed him down. It's a closed issue, the less explored the better for us all."

164

Joel opened the door for Leifhelm. "Till tomorrow . . ." He paused for a brief moment, loathing the man standing in front of him, but with only respect in his eyes. "Field Marshal," he added.

"*Gute Nacht*," said Erich Leifhelm, nodding his head sharply once in military acknowledgment.

Converse persuaded the switchboard operator to send someone into the dining room for the American, Commander Fitzpatrick. The task was not easy for the naval officer was neither in the dining room nor the bar, but outside on the *Spanische Terrasse* having a drink with friends, watching the Rhine in twilight.

"What goddamned friends?" demanded Joel over the phone.

"Just a couple I met out there. He's a nice guy – an executive type, pretty much into his seventies, I think."

"And she?" asked Converse, his lawyer's antennae struck by a vocal signal.

"Maybe . . . thirty, forty years younger," replied Connal with less elaboration.

"Get up here, sailor!"

Fitzpatrick leaned forward on the couch, his elbows on his knees, his expression a mixture of concern and astonishment as he looked over at Joel, who was smoking a cigarette in front of the open balcony doors. "Let me run this again," he said warily. "You want me to stop someone from getting your service record?"

"Not all of it, just part of it."

"Who the hell do you think I am?"

"You did it for Avery – for *Press*. You can do it for me. You *have to!*"

"That's backwards. I *opened* those files for him, I didn't keep them closed."

"Either way it's control. You've got access; you've got a key."

"I'm *here*, not there. I can't scissor out something you don't like eight thousand miles away. Be reasonable!"

"Somebody can, somebody *has* to! It's only a short segment, and it's got to be at the end. The final interview."

"An *interview?*" said Connal, startled, getting to his feet. "In a service record? You mean some kind of operational report? Because if you do, I wouldn't be . . ."

"Not a report," interrupted Converse, shaking his head. "The discharge . . . my *discharge* interview. That stuff Press Halliday quoted to me."

"Wait a minute, *wait* a minute!" Fitzpatrick held up his hands. "Are you referring to the remarks made at your discharge *hearing?*"

"Yes, that's it. The hearing!"

"Well, relax. They're not part of your service record, or anyone else's."

"Halliday had them – *Avery* had them! I just told you, he quoted my words verbatim!" Joel walked to a table where there was an ashtray; he crushed out his cigarette. "If they're not part of the record, how did he get them? How did *you* get them for him?"

"That's different," said Connal, obviously remembering as he spoke. "You were a POW and a lot of those hearings were put under a debriefing classification, and I *do* mean classified. Even after all these years, many of those sessions are still touchy. A lot of things were talked about that no one to this day wants made public – for everyone's good, not just the military's."

"But *you* got them! I heard my own words, goddamn it!"

"Yes, I got them," admitted the Navy lawyer without enthusiasm. "I got the transcript, and I'd be busted to a Seaman 3rd Class if anyone knew about it. You see, I believed Press. He swore to me he needed it, needed everything. He couldn't make any mistakes."

"How did you do it? You weren't even in San Diego at the time, that's what you said!"

"By calling the vaults and using my legal release number to have a photostat made. I said it was a Four-Zero emergency and I'd take responsibility. The next morning when the authorization came in by pouch for counter signature, I had the Chief Legal Officer at the base sign it with a lot of other things. It simply got buried in the paper work."

"But how did you know about it in the first place?"

"Selected POW records have flags on their discharge sheets."

"Clarification, please?"

"Just what I said, flags. Small blue seals that denote additional information still held under tight security. No flags, everything's clean; but if there is one, that means there's something else. I told Press and he said he had to have whatever it was, so I went after it."

"Then anyone else could, too."

"No, not anyone. You need an officer with a legal release number and there aren't many of us. Also there's a minimum forty-eight hour delay so the material can be vetted. That's almost always in the area of weapons and technology data that still might be classified."

"*Forty-eight* . . . ?" Converse swallowed. as he tried to count the hours since Paris, since the first moment his name had surfaced. "There's still time!" he said, his voice taut, his words clipped. "If you can do it there's still *time*. And if you can I'll tell you everything I know because you'll deserve it. No one will deserve it more."

"Spell it out."

Joel turned aimlessly, shaking his head. "That's funny. I said the same thing to Avery. I said 'spell it out, Avery.' . . . Sorry, his name was Press." Converse turned back to the Navy lawyer, a military lawyer with a mystifying military privilege called a legal-release-number. "Listen to me and hear me clearly. A few minutes ago something happened that I wasn't sure would or *could* happen – something your brother-in-law was killed to prevent. Tomorrow at four o'clock in the afternoon I'm going to walk into the middle of those men who are coming together to promote the kind of violence that'll stun this world, toppling governments, allowing *these* people to step in and fill the voids, running things their way, shaping the *laws* their way. One big Supreme Court, each chair owned by a fanatic with specific convictions as to who and what has value and who and

166

what doesn't, and those who don't can go to hell, no appeals on the agenda . . . I'm going to meet them face to face! I'm going to *talk* with them, *hear* their *words!* I admit I'm the most amateurish fox you've ever heard of in a chicken coop – only in this case it's a vultures' nest, and I mean the type that swoop down and tear the flesh off backs with one pass . . . But I've got something going for me: I'm one hell of a good lawyer and I'll learn things they won't know I've learned. Maybe enough to piece together a couple of cases that will blow it all apart – blow *them* apart. Before I told you I rejected your deadline. I still reject it, but *now* it doesn't seem so far out of the ballpark. Certainly not two days, but perhaps not ten! But, you see I thought I was going to have to fly to Tel Aviv, then Johannesburg. Prime everyone, frighten them. Now I don't! We've already done it! They're coming to me because they're frightened *now!* They don't know what to think and that means they're panicked." Converse paused, sweat forming on his hairline; then he added. "I don't have to tell you what a good lawyer can do with panicked hostile witnesses. The materials he can collect for evidence."

"Your plea's accepted, counsellor," said Fitzpatrick, not without awe. "You're convincing. Now tell me why my intercession can help? What does it accomplish?"

"I want those men to think I'm one of them! I can live with everything they can put together about me – I'm not proud of it all; I've made my compromises – but I *can't* live with that transcript of my discharge! . . . Don't you *see?* It's what Avery – Press – understood! I understand now. He knew me nearly twenty-five years ago, and when I think back we were actually pretty damned good friends. And no matter what happened to us individually, he was banking on the fact that I hadn't really changed that much, not in the deeper things. By the time we reach the voting age we're pretty well set, all of us. The real changes come later, much later, dictated by such things as acceptance and rejection and the state of our wallets – the prices we pay for our convictions, or to support our talents – defending success or explaining failure. That transcript confirmed what Halliday believed, at least enough so for him to want to meet me, talk with me, and finally to recruit me. Only he did it – finally – by dying with me holding his head. I couldn't walk away after that."

Connal Fitzpatrick was silent as he walked out on the balcony. He leaned over and gripped the railing, Converse watching him. Then he stood up, raised both his hands, and pulled back the sleeve of his left wrist; he turned. "It's 12.15 in San Diego. No one in legal goes to lunch before one o'clock; the Coronado's bar doesn't begin to jump until then."

"Can you *do* it?"

"I can try," said the naval officer, crossing through the French doors toward the telephone. "No, damn it, if you've got your times straight, I can do better than try, I can issue an order. That's what rank's all about."

The first five minutes were excruciating for Joel. There were delays on all overseas calls, but somehow the bi-, tri- or quadri-lingual Fitzpatrick, speaking urgently, unctuously in German, managed to get through, the phrase *dringende Not* repeated frequently.

"Lieutenant Senior Grade Remington, David. Legal Division, SAND PAC.

This is an emergency, sailor, Commander Fitzpatrick calling. Break in if the lines are occupied." Connal covered the mouthpiece and turned to Converse. "If you'll open my suitcase, there's a bottle of bourbon in the middle."

"I'll open your suitcase, Commander."

"*Remington?* . . . Hello, David, it's Connal . . . Yes, thanks very much, I'll tell Meagen . . . No, I'm not in San Francisco, don't call me there. But something's come up I want you to handle, something on my calendar that I didn't get to. For openers, it's a Four-Zero emergency. I'll fill you in when I get back, but until I do you have to take care of it. Got a pencil? . . . There's a POW service record under the name of Converse, Joel . . . Lieutenant, one and a half stripes, Air Arm, pilot – carrier-based, Vietnam duty. He was discharged in the sixties . . ." Fitzpatrick looked down at Converse, who held up his right hand and three fingers of his left. " . . . Nineteen sixty-eight, to be exact . . ." Joel stepped forward, his spread right hand still raised, his left now showing only the index finger. " . . . June of 'sixty-eight," added the Navy lawyer, nodding. "Point of separation our old home town, San Diego. Have you got all that? Read it back to me, please, David."

Connal nodded sporadically, as he listened. "C-O-N-V-E-R-S-E, That's right . . . June "sixty-eight, Air Arm, pilot, Vietnam, POW section, San Diego separation; that's it, you've got it. Now here's the wicket, David. This Converse's SR is flag status; the flag pertains to his discharge hearing, no weapons of high tech involved . . . Listen carefully, David. It's my understanding that there may be a request pending accompanied by a legal release code for the discharge transcript. Under *no* circumstances is that transcript to be released. The flag stays fixed and can't be removed by anyone without my authorization. And if the release *has* been processed it'll still be within the forty-eight hour vet-delay. *Kill it.* Understood?"

Again Fitzpatrick listened, but instead of nodding, he shook his head. "No, not under any circumstances. I don't care if the secretaries of State, Defense and the Navy all sign a joint petition on White House stationery, the answer is no. If anyone questions the decision tell him I'm exercising my authority as Chief Legal Officer of SAND PAC. There's some goddamned article in the 'shoals' that says a station CLO can impound materials on the basis of conceivably-privileged information relative to the security of the sector, *et cetera, et cetera.* I don't recall the time element – seventy-two hours or five days or something like that – but find that statute. You may need it."

Connal listened further, his brows creasing, his eyes straying to Joel. He spoke slowly, as Converse felt the sickening ache again in his chest. "Where can you reach me . . . ?" said the naval officer, perplexed. Then suddenly he was no longer bewildered. "I take back what I said before; call Meagen in San Francisco. If I'm not with her and the kids, she'll know where to reach me . . . Thanks again, David. Sweep your decks and get right on this, okay? Thanks . . . I'll tell Meg." Fitzpatrick hung up the phone and exhaled audibly. "There," he said, slouched in relief, pushing his hand through his loose, light brown hair. "I'll phone Meagen and give her this number, tell her to say I've gone up to the Sonoma hills, if Remington calls – Press had some property there."

"Give her the telephone number," said Joel, "but don't tell her anything else."

"Don't worry, she's got enough on her mind." The naval officer looked at Converse, frowning. "If your hourly count is right, you've got your time now."

"My count's all right. Is Lieutenant Remington? I mean that only in the sense that he wouldn't let anyone override your order, would he?"

"Don't mistake my officiousness where he's concerned," replied Connal. "David isn't easily pushed around. The reason I chose him and not one of four other senior lawyers in the department is that he's got a reputation for being a stickler-prick. He'll find that statute and nail it to the forehead of any four-striper who tries to countermand that order . . . I like Remington; he's very useful. He scares the hell out of people."

"We all have case-partners like that. It's called the good guy-bad guy routine."

"David fits. He's got an eye that keeps straying to the right." Fitzpatrick suddenly stood erect, his bearing military. "I thought you were going to get the bourbon, *Lieutenant?*"

"Yes, *sir*, Commander!" shot back Joel, heading for Fitzpatrick's suitcase.

"And if I remember correctly, after you pour us a drink, you're going to tell me a story I want very much to hear."

"*Aye, aye*, sir!" said Converse, lifting the suitcase off the floor and putting it on the couch. "And if I may suggest, sir," continued Joel. "A room-service dinner might be in order. I'm sure the Commander needs nourishment after his trying day at the wheel."

"Good thinking, Lieutenant. I'll phone down to the *Empfang.*"

"Before calling your bookie, may I also suggest that you first call your sister?"

"Oh, Christ, I forgot!"

Chaim Abrahms walked down the dark street in Tel Aviv, his stocky frame draped in his usual safari jacket, boots beneath his khaki trousers, and a beret covering his nearly bald head. The beret was the only concession he made to the night's purpose; normally he enjoyed being recognized, accepting the adulation shouted at him with well-rehearsed humility. In daylight, his head uncovered and held erect, his familiar safari stared at and the heavy sound of his boots heard, he would listen to the words and respond with a nod, his eyes boring in on the speakers, acknowledgment in his looks.

"*First a Jew!*" was the phrase with which he was always greeted, whether in Tel Aviv or Jerusalem, sections of Paris and most of New York.

The phrase had been born years ago when as a young terrorist for the Irgun, he had been condemned to death *in absentia* by the British for the slaughter of a Palestinian village, the Arab corpses put on display for *Nakama!* He had then issued a cry heard around the world.

"I am first a Jew, a son of Abraham! All else follows, and rivers of blood will follow if the children of Abraham are denied!"

The British, in 1948, not caring to create another martyr, commuted his sentence and he joined a kibbutz. Yet the acreage of the settlement could not confine the militant Sabra. Three wars had unleashed his agricultural shackles as well as his ferocity – and his brilliance in the field. It was a brilliance developed and refined through the early years of racing with a fugitive, fragmented army. Where the tactics of surprise, shock, hit and melt away were constant, when out-manned and out-gunned were the accepted odds, but only victory the acceptable outcome. He later applied the strategies and the philosophy of those years to the ever-expanding war machine that became the Army, Navy and Air Force of a mighty Israel. Mars was in the heavens of Chaim Abrahms's vision and, the prophets aside, the god of war was his strength, his reason for being. From Ramat Aviv to Har Hazeytim, from Metullah to Masada of the Negev, *Nakama!* was the cry. *Retribution* to the enemies of Abraham's children!

If only the Poles and the Czechs, the Hungarians and the Romanies, as well as the haughty Germans and the impossible Russians had not immigrated by such tens of thousands. They arrived and the complications came with them. Faction against faction, culture against culture, each screaming louder than the last, all trying to prove they were more entitled to the name *Jew* than the others. It was all nonsense! They were there because they had to be; they had succumbed to Abraham's enemies, permitted – yes *permitted* – the slaughter of millions rather than rising as millions and slaughtering in return. Well, they found out what their *civilized* ways brought them, and how much their Talmudic convolutions earned them. So they came to the Holy Land – *their* Holy Land, so they proclaimed. Well, it wasn't theirs. Where were they when it was being clawed out of rock and arid desert by strong hands with primitive tools – biblical tools? Where were they when the hated Arab and the despised English first felt the wrath of the tribal Jew? They were in the capitals of Europe, in their banks and their fancy drawing rooms, making money and drinking expensive brandy out of crystal goblets. No, they came here because they had to; they came to the Holy Land of the Sabra.

They brought with them money and dandy ways and elegant words and confusing arguments and influence and the guilt of the world. But it was the Sabra who taught them how to fight. And it was a Sabra who would bring all Israel into the orbit of a mighty new alliance.

Abrahms reached the intersection of Ibn Guirol and Arlosoroff streets. There was a mist in the air; the street lamps were haloed, their lights constricted. It was just as well; he should not be seen. He had another block to go, to an address on Jabotinsky, an unprepossessing apartment house where there was an undistinguished flat leased by a man who appeared to be no more than an unimportant bureaucrat. What few realized, however, was that this man, this specialist who operated sophisticated computer equipment with communications throughout most of the world, was intrinsic to the global operations of the Mossad, Israel's intelligence service which many considered the finest on earth. He, too, was a Sabra. He was one of them.

Abrahms spoke his name quietly into the mouthpiece above the mail slot in the outer lobby; he heard the click in the lock of the heavy door, and walked inside. He began the climb up the three flights of steps that would take him to the flat.

"Some wine, Chaim?"

170

"Whisky," was the curt reply.

"Always the same question and always the same answer," said the specialist. "I say 'Some wine, Chaim?' and you say one word. 'Whisky' you say. You would drink whisky at the Seder, if you could get away with it."

"I can and I do." Abrahms sat in a cracked leather chair, looking around the plain, dishevelled room with books everywhere, wondering, as he always did, why a man with such influence lived this way. It was rumoured that the Mossad officer did not like company, and larger, more attractive quarters might invite it. "I gathered from your grunts and coughs over the telephone that you have what I need."

"Yes, I have it," said the specialist, bringing a glass of very good Scotch to his guest. "I have it, but I don't think you're going to like it."

"Why not?" asked Abrahms, drinking, his eyes alert over the rim of the glass, holding them on his host as the latter sat down opposite him.

"Basically because it's confusing, and what's confusing in this business is to be approached delicately. You are not a delicate man, Chaim Abrahms, forgive the indelicacy of my saying it. You tell me this Converse is your enemy, a would-be infiltrator, and I tell you I find nothing to support the conclusion. Before anything else there must be a deep personal motive for a non-professional to engage in this kind of deception, this kind of behaviour, if you will. There has to be a driving compulsion to strike out at an image of a cause he loathes . . . Well, there is a motive, and there is an enemy for which he must have great hatred, but neither is compatible with what you suggest. The information, incidentally, is completely reliable. It comes from the *Quang Dinh* . . ."

"What in hell is that?" interrupted the general.

"A specialized branch of North Vietnamese – now, of course, Vietnamese – intelligence."

"You have sources *there?*"

"We fed them for years – nothing terribly vital, but sufficient to gain a few ears . . . and voices. There were things we had to know, weapons we had to understand; they could be turned against us."

"This Converse was in North Vietnam?"

"For several years as a prisoner of war; there's an extensive file on him. At first, his captors thought he could be used for propaganda, radio broadcasts, television . . . imploring his brutal government to withdraw and stop the bombing – all the usual garbage. He spoke well, presented a good picture, and was obviously very American. Initially they televised him as a murderer from the skies, saved from the angry mobs by humane troops, then later while eating and exercising; you see, they were programming him for a violently sudden reversal. They thought he was a soft, privileged young man who could be broken rather easily to do their bidding in exchange for more comfortable treatment – after having experienced a period of harsh deprivation. What they learned, however, was quite different. Under that soft shell the inner lining was made of hard metal, and the odd thing was that as the months went by it grew harder, until they realized they had created – created was their word – a hellhound of sorts, somehow forged in steel."

"Hellhound? Was that their word, too?"

"No, they called him an ugly troublemaker, which considering the source is not without irony. The point is they recognized the fact that they *had* created him. The harsher the treatment the more volatile he became, the more resilient."

"Why not?" said Abrahms sharply. "He was angry. Prod a desert snake and watch him strike."

"I can assure you, Chaim, it is not the normal human response under such conditions. A man can go mad and strike in crazed fury, or he can become reclusive to the point of catatonia, or fall apart weeping, willing to compromise anything and everything for the smallest kindness. He did none of these things. His was a calculated and inventive series of responses drawing on his own inner resources to survive. He led two escapes – the first lasting three days and the second five – before the groups were recaptured. As the leader, he was placed in a cage in the Mekong River and devised a way to kill the water rats by grabbing them from beneath the surface like a shark. He was then thrown into solitary confinement, a pit in the ground twenty feet deep with barbed wire anchored across the top. It was from there, during a heavy rainstorm at night, that he clawed his way up, bent the wire back and escaped alone. He made his way south through the jungles and in the river streams for over a hundred miles until he reached the American lines. It was no easy feat. They created a savagely obsessed man who won his own personal war."

"Why didn't they simply kill him before that?"

"I wondered myself," said the specialist, "so I phoned my source in Hanoi, the one who provided the information. He said a strange thing, something quite profound in its way. He said he wasn't there, of course, but he thought it was probably respect."

"For an ugly troublemaker?"

"Captivity in war does odd things, Chaim, to both the captured and the captors. There are so many factors at work in a vicious game. Aggression, resistance, bravery, fear, and not the least, curiosity – especially when the players come from such diverse cultures as the Occident and the Orient. An abnormal bond is often formed, as much from the weariness of the testing-game as anything else, perhaps. It doesn't lessen the national animosities, but a subtle recognition sets in that tells these men, these players, that they are not really in the game by their own choosing. In depth analyses further show us that it is the captors not the captured that first perceive this commonality. The latter is obsessed with freedom and survival, while the former begin to question their absolute authority over the lives and conditions of other men. They start to wonder what it would be like to be in the other player's shoes. It's all part of what the psychiatrists call the Stockholm syndrome."

"What in the name of *God* are you trying to say? You sound like one of those bores in the Knesset reading a position paper. A little of this, a little of that and a lot of wind!"

"You are definitely not delicate, Chaim. I'm trying to explain to you that while this Converse nurtured his hatreds and his obsessions, his captors wearied of the game, and as our source in Hanoi suggests, they grudgingly spared his life out of respect, before he made his final and successful escape."

172

To Abrahms' bewilderment the specialist had apparently finished. "And?" said the Sabra.

"Well, there it is. There is the motive and the enemy, but they are also *your* motive and *your* enemy – arrived at from different routes, of course. Ultimately, you wish to smash insurgentism wherever it erupts, curb the spread of Third World revolutions, especially Islamic because you know they're being fostered by the Marxists – read Soviets – and are a direct threat to Israel. One way or another it's the global threat that's brought you all together and in my judgment rightfully so. There is a time and a place for a military-industrial complex, and it is now. It must run the governments of the free world before that world is buried by its enemies."

Again the specialist stopped. Chaim Abrahms squinted and tried not to shout. "*And?*"

"Can't you see? This Converse is one of you. Everything supports it. He has the motive and an enemy he's seen in the harshest light. He is a highly regarded attorney who makes a great deal of money with a very conservative firm, and his clients are among the wealthiest corporations and conglomerates. Everything he's been and everything he stands for can only benefit from your efforts. The confusion lies in his unorthodox methods and I can't explain them except to say that perhaps they are not unorthodox in the specialized work he does. Markets can plummet on rumours; concealment and diversion are surely respected. Regardless, he doesn't want to destroy you, he wants to join you."

The Sabra put his glass down on the floor and struggled out of the chair. With his chin tucked into his breastbone and his hands clasped behind his back, Abrahms paced back and forth in silence. He stopped and looked down at the specialist.

"Suppose, just *suppose*," he said, "the almighty Mossad has made a mistake, that there's something you didn't find?"

"I would find that hard to accept."

"But it's a possibility!"

"In light of the information we've gathered, I doubt it. Why?"

"Because I have a sense of smell, *that's* why!"

The man from the Mossad kept his eyes on Abrahms, as if studying the soldier's face – or thinking – from a different viewpoint. "There is only one other possibility, Chaim. If this Converse is not who and what I've described, which would be contrary to all the data we've compiled, then he is an agent of his government."

"That's . . . what I smell," said the Sabra softly.

It was the specialist's turn to be silent. He breathed deeply, then responded. "I respect your nostrils, old friend. Not always your conduct but certainly your sense of smell. What do the others think?"

"Only that he's lying, that he's covering for others he may or may not know, who are using him as a scout, an 'infantry point' was the term used by Palo Alto."

The Mossad officer continued to stare at the Sabra, but his eyes were no longer focused; he was seeing abstract, twisted patterns, convolutions few men would comprehend. They came from a lifetime of analysing seen and unseen, legitimate and racial enemies, parrying dagger thrusts with counter-thrusts in the blackest darkness. "It's possible," he whispered, as if replying to an unspoken question heard only by himself. "Almost inconceivable, but possible."

"What is? That Washington is behind him?"

"Yes."

"Why? You just said it."

"As an outrageous alternative I did not subscribe to, but the only one left that has the slightest plausibility. Simply put, he has too much information."

"And?"

"Not Washington in the usual sense, not the government in the broader sense, but within a *branch of* the government a *section* that has heard whispers but cannot be sure. If there is such an organization, they must invade it to expose it. So they choose a man with the right history, the right memories, even the right profession, to do the job. He might even believe everything he says."

The Sabra was transfixed but impatient. "That has too many complications for me," he said bluntly.

"Try it my way first. Try to accept him; he may be genuine. He'll have to give you *something* concrete; you can force that. Then again he may not because he cannot."

"*And?*"

"And if he can't you'll know you're right. Then put as much distance between him and his sponsors as is humanly and brutally possible. He must become a pariah, a man hunted for crimes so insane his madness is unquestioned."

"Why not just kill him?"

"By all means, but not before he's been labelled so mad that no one will step forward to claim him. It will buy you the time you need. The final phase of Aquitaine is when? Three, four weeks away?"

"That's when it begins, yes."

The specialist got up from the chair and stood pensively in front of the soldier. "I repeat, first try to accept him, see if what I said before is true. But if that sense of smell of yours is provoked further, if there's the slightest possibility he has been willingly or unwillingly, wittingly or unwittingly, made a *provocateur* by men in Washington, then build your case against him and throw him to the wolves. Create that pariah as the North Vietnamese created a hellhound. Then kill him quickly, before anyone else reaches him."

"A Sabra of the Mossad speaks?"

"As clearly as I can."

The young Army captain and the somewhat older civilian came out of the Pentagon from adjacent glass doors and glanced briefly at each other, no recognition in their looks. They walked separately down the short bank of steps and turned left on the cement path that led to the enormous parking lot; the army officer was perhaps ten feet ahead of the civilian. Upon reaching the huge asphalt area, each veered in a different direction toward his car. If these two men had been the subjects of photographic surveillance during the past fifty seconds, there was no indication whatsoever that they knew each other.

The green Buick coupé turned right in the middle of the block, going through the open chasm that was the entrance to the hotel's underground parking lot. At the bottom of the ramp the driver showed his room key to the attendant, who raised the yellow barrier and waved him along. There was an empty space in the third column of stationary automobiles. The Buick eased into it and the Army captain got out.

He circled through the revolving door and walked to a bank of elevators in the hotel's lower lobby. The panels of the second elevator opened, revealing two couples who had not intended to reach the underground level; they laughed as one of the men repeatedly pressed the Main Lobby button. The officer, in turn, touched the button for the fourteenth floor. Sixty seconds later he walked out into the corridor toward the Exit staircase. He was heading for the eleventh floor.

The blue Toyota station wagon came down the ramp, the driver's hand extended, a room key held out, the number visible. Inside the parking area the driver found an empty space in the sixth column and carefully steered the small station wagon into it.

The civilian stepped out and looked at his watch. Satisfied, he started toward the revolving door and the elevators. The second elevator was empty and the civilian was tempted to press the button for the eleventh floor; he was tired and did not relish the additional walk. However, there would be other occupants on the way up; he held to the rules and placed his index finger over the button opposite the number *nine*.

Standing in front of the hotel room door, the civilian raised his hand, rapped once, waited several beats, then rapped twice more. Seconds later the door was opened by the Army captain. Beyond him was a third man, also in uniform, the colour and the insignia denoting a Lieutenant, junior grade, in the Navy. He stood by the desk, above a telephone.

"Glad you got here in time," said the Army officer. "The traffic was rotten. Our call should be coming through in a few minutes."

The civilian entered, nodding to the Navy man as he spoke. "What did you find out about Fitzpatrick?" he asked.

"He's where he shouldn't be," replied the Lieutenant.

"Can you bring him back?"

"I'm working on it, but I don't know where to begin. I'm a very low man on a very big totem pole."

"Aren't we all?" said the captain.

"Who'd have thought Halliday would have *gone to* him?" asked the naval officer, frustration in his voice. "Or if he was going to bring him in why didn't he go to him *first*? Or tell him about us?"

"I can answer the last two questions," said the Army man. "He was protecting him from a Pentagon backlash. If we go down his brother-in-law stays clean."

"And I can answer the first question," said the civilian. "Halliday went to Fitzpatrick because, in the final analysis, he didn't trust us. Geneva proved he was right."

"*How?*" asked the captain defensively – but without apology. "We couldn't have prevented it."

"No, we couldn't," agreed the civilian. "But we couldn't do anything about it afterwards, either. That was part of the trust and there was no way we could live up to it. We couldn't afford to."

The telephone rang. The lieutenant picked it up and listened. "It's Mykonos," he said.

Part II

12

Connal Fitzpatrick sat opposite Joel at the room service table drinking the last of his coffee. The dinner was finished, the story completed, and all the questions the Navy lawyer could raise answered by Converse because he had given his word; he needed a complete ally.

"Except for a few identities and some dossier material," said Connal, "I don't know an awful lot more than I did before. Maybe I will when I see those Pentagon names. You say you don't know who supplied them?"

"No. Like Topsy, they're just there. Beale said a number of them are probably mistakes, but others aren't; they have to be linked to Delavane."

"They had to be supplied by someone, too. There had to be reasons why they were listed."

"Beale called them 'decision makers' in military procurements."

"Then I *have to* see them. I've dealt with those people."

"*You?*"

"Yes. Not very often, but enough to know my way around."

"Why *you?*"

"Basically, translating legal nuances from language to language where navy tech was involved. I think I mentioned that I speak . . ."

"You did," broke in Joel.

"*Goddamn* it!" cried Fitzpatrick, crushing his napkin in a fist.

"What's the matter?"

"Press *knew* I had dealings with those committees, with the technology and armaments boys! He even asked me about them. Who I saw, who I liked . . . who I trusted. *Jesus!* Why didn't he come to me? Of all the people he knew, I was the logical one! I'm down the pike and his closest friend."

"That's why he didn't come to you," said Converse.

"Stupid *bastard!*" Connal raised his eyes. "And I hope you hear that, Press. You might still be around to see Connal Two win the Bay Regatta."

"I think you really believe he might hear you."

Fitzpatrick looked across the table at Joel. "Yes, I do. You see, I believe, counsellor. I know all the reasons why I shouldn't – Press enumerated them to a fare-thee-well when we were in our cups – but I believe. I answered him once with a quote from one of his laid-back Protestant forebears."

"What was that?" asked Joel, smiling kindly.

" 'There's more faith in honest doubt than is held by all the archangels in the mind of God'."

"It's very nice. I've never heard it before."

"Maybe I didn't get it right . . . I've got to see those names!"

"And I have to get my attaché case, but I can't go myself."

"Then I'm elected," said the Navy man. "Do you think Leifhelm's right? You think he can really call off Interpol?"

"I'm of two thoughts about it. For my immediate manoeuvrability I hope he can. But if he does, it'll scare the hell out of me."

"I'm on your side about that," agreed Connal, getting out of the chair. "I'll call the desk and get a taxi. Give me the key to the locker."

Converse reached into his pocket and pulled out the small, rounded key with the German numerals. "Leifhelm's seen you. He could have you followed; he did before."

"I'll be ten times more careful. If I see the same pair of headlights twice, I'll go to a *Bierkeller*. I know a few here."

Joel looked at his watch. "It's twenty minutes to ten. Do you think you could swing around to the university first?"

"Dowling?"

"He said he had someone he wanted me to meet. Just walk by him – or them – and say everything's under control, nothing else. I owe him that much."

"Suppose he tries to stop me?"

"Then pull out your ID and say it's high priority, or ultrasecret, or whatever bullshit security phrases that come to that very inventive mind of yours."

"Do I sense a touch of legal envy?"

"No, just recognition. I know where you're coming from. I've been there."

Fitzpatrick walked slowly along the wide path on the south façade of the immense University Building, once the great palace of the all powerful Archbishops of Köln. The unimpeded moonlight swelled over the area, reflecting off the myriad rows of cathedral windows and lending a luminous dimension to the light stone walls of the majestic structure. Beyond the path the winding gardens of August seemed to possess an eerie night elegance – sleeping circles of floral wonder totally unaware of their beauty. Connal was so struck by the tranquil loveliness of the nocturnal setting that he nearly forgot why he was there.

The reason was brought sharply back into focus when he saw the figure of a long, slender man slouched alone on a bench. The man's legs were extended and crossed at the ankles, his head covered by a soft cloth hat, but not sufficiently to hide the flowing grey-blond hair that protruded slightly over his temples and the back of his neck. So this Caleb Dowling was an actor, thought the Navy lawyer, amused by the fact that Dowling had feigned protestations of shock when he realized Connal did not know him. But then neither had Converse; they were obviously a minority in a world of television addicts. A College professor who had fulfilled the fantasies of youth, a risk-taker, according to Joel, who had won a battle against astronomical odds was a nice thing to think about, saddened by the knowledge of a haunted wife he loved dearly. Also a marine who had fought in the bloody mess that was Kwajalein was a man to be reckoned with; he was not to be underestimated.

Fitzpatrick walked over to the bench and sat down several feet away from Dowling. The actor glanced at him, then did a perfectly natural double-take, his head snapping, no rehearsal required.

"*You?*"

"I'm sorry about last night," said Connal. "I gather I wasn't very convincing."

"You lacked a certain finish, young fella. Where the hell is Converse?"

"Sorry again. He couldn't make it, but not to worry. Everything's A-okay and under control."

"Whose okay and whose control?" countered the actor, annoyed. "I told Joel to come here, not a cub scout interlocutor."

"I resent that. I'm a lieutenant-commander in the United States Navy and the Chief Legal Officer at a major naval base. Mr Converse accepted an assignment from us which has an element of personal risk for him and the highest priority of classification for us. Back off, Mr Dowling. We appreciate – and I speak for Converse as well as myself – your interest and your generosity, but it's time for you to recede. For your own benefit, incidentally."

"What about Interpol? He killed a man."

"Who tried to kill *him*," added Fitzpatrick quickly, a lawyer rejoining a negative statement by a witness on the stand. "That will be clarified internally and the charges dropped."

"You're pretty smooth, Commander," said Dowling, sitting up. "Better than you were last night – this morning, actually."

"I was upset. I'd lost him and I had to find him. I had to deliver vital information."

The actor now crossed his legs at the knees and leaned back, his arm slung casually over the slatted rim of the bench. "So this thing Converse and you are involved with is a real hush-hush operation?"

"It's highly classified, yes."

"And you and he being lawyers it's got something to do with legal irregularities over here that somehow reach into the military, is that right?"

"In the broadest sense, again yes. I'm afraid I can't be any more specific. Converse mentioned that there was someone you wanted him to meet."

"Yes, there is. I said a couple of harsh things about him, but I take them back; he was doing his thing. He didn't know who the hell I was anymore than you did; his wife told him. He's one smart man, tough but fair."

"I hope you understand that under the circumstances Converse can't comply with your request."

"You'll do," said Dowling calmly, removing his arm from the back of the bench.

Connal was suddenly alarmed. There was movement behind him in the shadowed moonlight; he whipped his head around, peering over his shoulder. Out of the protective darkness of the building from within the pitch black cover of a doorway, the figure of a man began walking across the dark green lawn . . .

An *arm* thrown casually over the rim of the bench! Then just as casually removed. Both movements had been signals! Identity confirmed; move in.

"What the hell have you *done?*" asked the Navy lawyer harshly.

"Bringing you two bucks to your senses," replied Dowling. "If my celebrated instincts are valid, I did the right thing. If they're wrong, I still did the right thing."

"*What?*"

The man crossing the lawn entered the spill of clear moonlight. He was heavy-set and in a dark suit and tie, his scowling, late-middle-aged face and straight grey hair giving him the air of a prosperous businessman, who at the moment was intensely angry. Dowling spoke, as he got up from the bench.

"Commander, may I introduce the Honourable Walter Peregrine, United States Ambassador to the Federal Republic of Germany?"

Lieutenant David Remington wiped his steel-rimmed glasses with a silicone-treated tissue, then threw the tissue into a waste basket and got up from his desk. Returning the glasses to his face, he walked to a mirror secured to the back of his office door and checked his appearance. He smoothed his hair, shoved the knot of his tie in place, and looked down at the failing crease of his trousers. All things considered, considering it was 1730 hours and he had been harassed at his desk since 0800 in the morning, including that crazy Four-Zero emergency from Fitzpatrick, he looked as presentable as possible. And anyway, Rear-Admiral Hickman was not a stickler for spit-'n'polish where the desk corps were concerned. He knew damn well most of the legal execs would bolt in a minute for much higher paying jobs in the civilian sector if the dress and other disposable codes were taken too seriously. Well, David Remington wouldn't. Where the hell else could a man travel all over the world, housing a wife and three kids in some of the nicest quarters imaginable, with all the medical and dental bills paid for, and not have the terrible pressures of rising in private or corporate practice? His father had been an attorney for one of the biggest insurance companies in Hartford, Connecticut, and his father had had ulcers at forty-three, a nervous breakdown at forty-eight, his first stroke at fifty-one, and a final, massive coronary at fifty-six – when everyone said he was so terrific at his job he might even be in line for the presidency. But then people always said things like that when a man died in the line of corporate duty – which men did too goddamned frequently.

None of that for David Remington, no sir! He was simply going to be one of the best lawyers in the US Navy, serve his thirty years, get out at fifty-five with a generous pension, and become a well-paid legal-military consultant at fifty-six. At the precise age when his father died, he would start living very nicely, indeed. It was simply a matter of building a reputation as a man who knew more about naval and maritime law – and stuck to it – than any other lawyer in the Navy. If he stepped on toes in his performance, so be it; it could only enhance that reputation. He didn't give a damn about being popular, only right. And he never made a decision until he was certain of its correct legal position. Consultants like that were prized commodities in civilian practice.

Remington wondered why Admiral Hickman wanted to see him, especially at this hour when most of the desk corps had gone for the day. There was a court martial pending that could become a sensitive issue. A black officer, an Annapolis graduate, had been caught selling cocaine off a destroyer berthed in the Philippines; that was probably it. Remington had pre-prepared the case for the judge-advocate, who frankly did not care to prosecute; the amount was not that large, and certainly others were selling far more, and they were probably white. That was not the point, Remington had insisted. If there were others, they had not been caught; if there was evidence, it had not been found. The law was colour-blind.

He would say the same thing to Hickman. The "stickler-prick", a derisive nickname Remington knew was used behind his back, would stand firm. Well, at fifty-six – the age at which his father had been killed by company policy – a stickler-prick would have all the comforts of an exclusive country club without paying the corporate price. Lieutenant Remington opened the door, walked out into the grey hallway, and started for the elevator that would take him to the floor of the office of the highest ranking man at the San Diego naval base.

"Sit down, Remington," said Rear-Admiral Brian Hickman, shaking the rigidly-postured lieutenant's hand and indicating a chair in front of the large desk. "I don't know about you but this has been what I used to call at your age one fucked-up day. Sometimes I wish Congress wouldn't appropriate so damn much money down here. Everyone gets on such a high you'd think they'd smoked everything in Tijuana. They forget they're supposed to have architects before they start bribing the contractors."

"Yes, sir, I know what you mean, sir," said Remington, sitting down with proper deference as Hickman stood several feet to his left. The mere reference to Tijuana and drugs confirmed his suspicions; the admiral was about to launch into the everybody-does-it routine, so why should the navy stir up a racial controversy with something that took place in the Philippines. Well, he was prepared. The law – naval law – was colour blind.

"I'm going to have a well-deserved drink, Lieutenant," said Hickman, heading for a copper bar against the wall. "Can I get you something?"

"No, thank you, sir."

"Hey, look, Remington, I appreciate your staying late for this . . . conference, I guess you'd call it, but I don't expect any version of corporate military behaviour. Frankly, I'd feel foolish drinking by myself, and what we've got to talk about isn't so almighty important. I just want to ask you a couple of questions."

"Corporate behaviour, sir? I'll have some white wine, if you have it, sir."

"I always have it," said the admiral with resignation. "It's usually for personnel who are about to get divorced."

"I'm happily married, sir."

"Glad to hear it. I'm on my third wife – should have stuck with the first."

The drinks poured, the seating arrangements in order, Hickman spoke from behind the desk, his tie loosened, his voice casual. But what he said evoked anything but casualness in David Remington.

"Who the hell is Joel Converse?" asked the admiral.

"I beg your pardon, sir?"

The admiral sighed, the sound indicating that he would begin again. "At twelve hundred hours, twenty-one minutes today, you placed a CLO negative on all inquiries regarding a flag on one Lieutenant Joel Converse's service record. He was a pilot in the Vietnam action."

"I know what he was, sir," said Remington.

"And at fifteen hundred hours, two minutes," continued Hickman looking at a note on his desk. "I get a teletype from the Fifth Naval District requesting that the flag be removed in their favour and the material released immediately. The basis for their request was – and it always is – national security." The admiral paused to sip his drink; he appeared to be in no hurry, simply weary. "I ordered my adjutant to call you and ask why you did it."

"And I answered him completely, sir," broke in Remington. "It was at the instructions of the Chief Legal Officer of SAND PAC and I cited the specific regulation that states clearly that the CLO of a naval base can withhold files on the basis that his own inquiries can be compromised by the entrance of a third party. It's standard in civil law, sir. The Federal Bureau of Investigation rarely gives a local or metropolitan police force the information it's collected in an investigation for the simple reason that the investigation could be compromised by leaks or corrupt practices."

"And our Chief Legal Officer, Lieutenant Commander Fitzpatrick, is currently carrying out an investigation of an officer who left the service *eighteen years* ago?"

"I don't know, sir," said Remington, his eyes noncommittal. "I only know those were his orders. They're in force for seventy-two hours. After that, you, of course, can sign the order of release. And the President, naturally, can do so anytime in a national emergency."

"I thought it was forty-eight hours," said Hickman.

"No, sir. The forty-eight hours is standard with the release of every flag regardless of who asks for it – except, of course, the President. It's called the vet delay. Naval Intelligence cross checks with the CIA, the NSA and G-Two to make sure there's no material being released that's still considered classified. That procedure has nothing to do with the prerogatives of a Chief Legal Officer."

"You know your law, don't you?"

"I believe as well as any attorney in the United States Navy, sir."

"I see." The admiral leaned back in his upholstered swivel chair and placed his legs on the corner of the desk. "Commander Fitzpatrick's off the base, isn't he? Emergency leave, if I recall."

"Yes, sir. He's in San Francisco with his sister and her children. Her husband was killed in a robbery in Geneva; the funeral's tomorrow morning, I believe."

"Yes, I read about it. Goddamned lousy . . . But you know where to reach him."

"I have the telephone number, yes, sir. Do you want me to call him, Admiral? Apprise him of the Fifth Naval request."

"No, no," said Hickman, shaking his head. "Not at a time like this. They can dry their mops at least until tomorrow afternoon. I've got to assume they also know the regulations; if security's so damned jeopardized they know where the Pentagon is – and the latest rumour out of Arlington is that they found out where the White House is." The Admiral stopped, frowned, and looked over at the lieutenant. "Suppose you didn't know where to reach Fitzpatrick?"

"But I do, sir."

"Yes, but suppose you didn't? And a legitimate request was received – below presidential involvement, but still pretty damned urgent – *you* could release that flag, couldn't you?"

"Theoretically, as next in authority yes I could. As long as I accepted the legal responsibility for my judgment."

"The what?"

"That I believed the request was sufficiently urgent to override the Chief Legal Officer's prior order which granted him seventy-two hours for whatever action he deemed necessary. He was adamant, sir. Frankly, short of presidential intervention, I'm legally bound to uphold the CLO's privilege."

"I'd say morally, too," agreed Hickman.

"Morality has nothing to do with it sir. It's a clear legal position. Now, shall I make that call, Admiral?"

"No, the hell with it." Hickman removed his feet from the desk. "I was just curious and, frankly, you've convinced me. Fitz wouldn't have given you the order unless he had a reason. The Fifth D can wait three days, unless those boys want to run up telephone bills to Washington."

"May I ask, sir, who specifically made the request?"

The admiral looked pointedly at Remington. "I'll tell you in three days. You see, I've got a man's privilege to uphold, too. You'll know them anyway because in Fitz's absence you'll have to countersign the transfer." Hickman finished his drink and the lieutenant understood. The conference was over. Remington got up and returned the half-filled wine glass to the copper bar; he stood at attention and spoke.

"Will that be all, sir?"

"Yes, that's it," said the admiral, his gaze straying to the window and the ocean beyond.

The lieutenant saluted sharply as Hickman brought a casual hand to his forehead. The lawyer then did an about-face and started for the door.

"Remington?"

"Yes, sir?" replied the lieutenant, turning.

"Who the hell *is* this Converse?"

"I don't know, sir. But Commander Fitzpatrick said the status of the flag was a Four-Zero emergency."

"*Jesus . . .*"

Hickman picked up his phone and touched a combination of buttons on the console. Moments later he was speaking to a fellow ranking officer in the Fifth Naval District.

"I'm afraid you'll have to wait three days, Scanlon."

"Why is that?" asked the admiral named Scanlon.

"The CLO negative holds on the Converse flag as far as SAND PAC is concerned. If you want to go the DC route, be my guest. We'll cooperate."

"I told you, Brian, my people don't want to go through Washington. You've had these things happen before. DC makes waves and we don't want waves."

"Well then, why don't you tell me why you want the Converse flag? Who is he?"

"I'd tell you if I could, you know that. Frankly, I'm not all that clear on it myself, and what I do know I've sworn to keep secure."

"Then go to Washington. I'm standing behind my Chief Legal, who, incidentally, isn't even here."

"He isn't . . . ? But you talked to him."

"No, to his next in line, a lieutenant named Remington. He took the direct order from the CLO. Believe me, Remington won't budge. I gave him the chance and he covered himself with legalities. Around here he's known as a sticklerprick."

"Did he say why the negative was put out?"

"He didn't have any idea. Why don't you call him yourself? He's probably still downstairs and maybe you can . . ."

"You didn't use my *name*, did you?" interrupted Scanlon, apparently agitated.

"No, you asked me not to, but he'll know it in three days. He'll have to sign the release and I'll have to tell him who requested it." Hickman paused, then without warning exploded. "What the *hell* is this all about, Admiral? Some pilot who was discharged over eighteen years ago is suddenly on everybody's mostwanted list. I get a departmental priority teletype from the big Fifth D and you follow it up with a personal call, playing the old Annapolis memory game, but you won't tell me anything. Then I find out my own CLO without my knowing about it has put a negative on this Converse flag and labelled it a Four-Zero emergency status! Now I know he's got personal problems and I won't bother him until tomorrow, and I realize you've given your word to stay secure, but goddamn it, somebody had better start telling me *something!*"

There was no response from the other end of the line. But there was the sound of breathing; and it was tremulous.

"Scanlon!"

"What did you just say?" said the voice of the admiral 3,600 miles away.

"I'm going to find out anyway. . . ."

"No, the status. The status of the flag." Scanlon could barely be heard.

"Four-Zero emergency, that's what I said!"

The interruption was abrupt; there was only an echoing click. Admiral Scanlon had hung up the phone.

Walter Peregrine, United States Ambassador to the Federal Republic of Germany, was an angry man. "What's your name, Commander?"

"Fowler, sir," answered Fitzpatrick, glancing briefly but hard at Dowling.

"Lieutenant-Commander Avery Fowler, United States Navy." Again Connal looked at the actor, who stared at him through the moonlight.

"I understand there's some question about that," said Peregrine, his glare as hostile as Dowling's. "May I see your identification, please?"

"I'm not carrying identification, sir. It's the nature of my assignment not to do so, sir." Fitzpatrick's words were rapid, precise, his posture squared and erect.

"I want verification of your name, your rank, and your branch of service! *Now!*"

"The name I've given you is the name I was instructed to give should any beyond the scope of the assignment inquire."

"*Whose* instructions?" barked the diplomat.

"My superior officers, sir."

"Am I to infer that Fowler is not your correct name?"

"With respect, Mr Ambassador. My name is Fowler, my rank is lieutenant-commander, my branch of service is the United States Navy."

"Where the *hell* do you think you are? Behind the lines, captured by the enemy? 'Name, rank, and serial number – that's all I'm required to say under the Rules of the Geneva Convention!' "

"It's all I'm *permitted* to say, sir."

"We'll damn well find out about that, Commander – if you are a commander. Also about this Converse, who appears to be a very odd liar – one minute the soul of propriety, the next a very strange man on the run."

"Please try to understand, Mr Ambassador, our assignment is classified. In no way does it involve diplomacy or will it impair your efforts as the chief American representative of our government, but it *is* classified. I will report this conversation to my superiors and you will undoubtedly hear from them. Now, if you gentlemen will forgive me, I'll be on my way."

"I don't think so, Commander – or whoever you are. But if you are who you say, nothing's compromised. I'm not a damn fool. Nothing will be said to anyone on the embassy staff. Mr Dowling insisted on that and I accepted the condition. You and I will be locked in a communications room with a phone on a scrambler and you're going to place a call to Washington. I didn't take this job at a loss of three-quarters of a million a year to find shoe clerks running an investigation of my own company without my knowing about it. If I want an outside audit, I'll damn well order it myself!"

"I wish I could comply, sir; it sounds like a reasonable request. But I'm afraid I can't."

"I'm afraid you will!"

"Sorry."

"Do as he says, Commander," interjected Dowling. "As he told you, nothing's been said to anyone, and nothing will be. But Converse needs protection; he's a wanted man in a foreign country and he doesn't even speak the language. Take Ambassador Peregrine's offer. He'll keep his word."

"With respect, sirs, the answer is negative." Connal turned away and started up the wide path.

"*Major!*" shouted the ambassador, his voice furious. "Stop him! *Stop* that man!"

Fitzpatrick looked behind him; for reasons he could not explain to himself he saw what he never expected to see, and the instant he did, he knew he should have expected it. From out of the distant shadows of the immense, majestic building, a man rushed forward, a man who was obviously a military aide to the ambassador – a member of the *embassy staff!* Connal froze, Joel's words coming back to him.

Those men you saw at the airport, the ones from the embassy . . . they're on the other side.

Under almost any other circumstances, Fitzpatrick would have remained where he was and weathered it out. He hadn't actually done anything wrong; there was nothing illegal, no laws broken of which he was cognizant, and no one could force him to discuss personal matters where no law had been violated. Then he realized how wrong he was! The generals of George Marcus Delavane would force him, *could* force him! He spun around and ran.

Suddenly, gunfire erupted. Two shots – splitting cracks of broken air above him! He dived to the ground and rolled into the shadows of the bushes, as a man's voice roared over the already disturbed stillness of the peaceful night and the sleeping gardens.

"You goddamned son of a *bitch!* What do you think you're *doing!*"

There were further shouts, a further barrage of obscenities, and the sounds of struggle filled the quiet enclave of the university.

"You don't *kill* a man . . . ! Besides, you *bastard*, there could be other people! Don't say a *word*, Mr Ambassador!"

Connal scrambled across the gravel path, raising his hands to spread the bordering foliage. In the clear, unimpeded moonlight of the distant bench, the actor, Caleb Dowling – the former marine from Kwajalein – stood over the figure of the major who had run out of the shadow, his boot on the supine man's throat, his hand grasping the man's extended arm, the weapon wrenched free of the major's offending grip.

"You are one dumb son of a bitch, Major! Or, goddamn you, maybe you're something else!"

Fitzpatrick got to his knees, then his feet, and, crouching, raced into the receding darkness of the wide path toward the exit.

13

"I didn't have any choice!" said Connal, the attaché case on the couch, the Navy lawyer in an adjacent chair, leaning forward, still shaking, still intense.

"Calm down, try to relax." Converse walked to the elegant antique hunt table against the wall where there was a large silver tray with whisky, ice and glasses. Joel had learned to make use of room service in England. "You need a drink," he said, pouring Fitzpatrick's bourbon.

"Do I *ever!* I've never been shot at. You have. Christ, is that what it's *like?*"

"That's what it's like. You can't believe it. It's unreal, just mind-blowing sounds that can't really have anything to do with you, until – until you see the evidence for yourself. It's real, it's meant for you, and you're sick. There's no swelling music, no brass horns, just vomit." Converse brought the naval officer his drink.

"You're omitting something," said Connal, taking the glass and looking up at Joel.

"No, I'm not. Let's think about tonight. If you heard Dowling right, the ambassador won't say anything around the embassy . . ."

"I remember," interrupted Fitzpatrick, taking several swallows of the bourbon, his eyes still on Converse. "It was in one of the other flags. During your second escape a man got killed; it was sundown. You reached him when it happened and the flag said you went crazy for a couple of minutes. Somehow, according to this guy – a sergeant, I think – you circled around in the jungle, caught the North Vietnamese, killed him with his own knife and got his repeating rifle. Then you blew away three other Viets in the area."

Joel held his place in front of the Navy lawyer. He answered the younger man, his voice quiet, his look angry. "I hate descriptions like that," he said flatly. "It raises all the images I loathe . . . Let me tell you the way it was – like it was, counsellor. A kid, no more than nineteen, had to relieve himself, and although we stuck together he had the dignity to go ten or fifteen feet away to take care of his private functions, using leaves because squeezable toilet paper wasn't available. The maniac – I won't use the word soldier – who killed him waited for the precise moment, then fired off a burst that cut that kid's face apart. When I reached him, half of that face in my hands, I heard the cackle, the obscene laughter of an obscene man who personified for me everything I found despicable – whether North Vietnamese or American. If you want to know the truth, whatever I did I did against both – because both were guilty, all of us turned into animals, myself included. Those other three men, those enemies, those uniformed robots probably with wives and children back in villages somewhere up north, had no idea I got behind them. I shot them in the back, counsellor. What would Johnny Ringo say about that? Or John Wayne?"

Connal was silent as Joel walked over to the hunt table to pour himself a whisky. The Navy lawyer drank, then spoke. "A few hours ago you said you knew where I was coming from because you'd been there. Well, I haven't been where you were, but I'm beginning to see where *you're* coming from. You really despise everything that Aquitaine stands for, don't you? Especially those running it."

Converse turned. "With everything that's in me," he said. "That's why we've got to talk about tonight."

"I told you, I had no choice. You said the embassy people I saw at the airport were with Delavane. I couldn't take the chance."

"I know. Now we're both running, hunted by our own people and protected by the men we want to trap. We've got to *think* Commander."

The telephone rang; two abrasive, static-like bells. Fitzpatrick leaped from the chair, his initial reaction one of shock. Joel watched him, calming him with his look. "Sorry," said Connal. "I'm still edgy. I'll get it; I'll be all right." He crossed to the phone and picked it up. "*Ja?*" He listened for several seconds, covered the mouthpiece and looked at Converse. "It's the overseas operator. San Francisco. It's Meagen."

"Which means Remington," said Joel, his throat suddenly dry, his pulse accelerating.

"Meagen? Yes, I'm here. What is it?" Fitzpatrick stared straight ahead as his sister talked; he nodded frequently, the muscles of his jaw working as he concentrated. "Oh, *Christ!* . . . No, it's all right. I *mean* it, everything's okay. Do you have the number?" Connal looked down at the small telephone table, there was a message pad but no pencil He glanced over at Joel, who had already started for the desk and a hotel pen. Fitzpatrick held out his hand, took the pen, and wrote out a series of numbers. Converse stood aside, conscious that he was barely breathing, his fingers gripping the glass which remained immobile. "Thanks, Meagen. I know it's a hell of a time for you; you don't need this, but if you have to call again, make it station-to-station, okay? . . . I will, Meg. I give you my word. Goodbye." The Navy lawyer hung up, his hand for a moment remaining on the telephone.

"Remington called, didn't he?" said Joel.

"Yes."

"What *happened?*"

"Someone tried to get the flag on your service record released," said Fitzpatrick, turning, looking at Converse.

"It's okay. Remington stopped it."

"Who was it?"

"I don't know, I'll have to reach David. Meagen doesn't have any idea what a flag is, much less who you are. The message was only that 'a release was sought for the flag' but he stopped it."

"Then everything's all right."

"That's what I said, but it's not."

"Clarification, goddamn it!"

"There's a time limit on how long my order stands. It's only a day or two after the vetting process."

"Which is forty-eight hours," interrupted Joel.

"Yes, I'm sure of that; it's *after* that. You see, you thought this would happen, but frankly I didn't. Whoever's asking for that flag isn't small potatoes. You could walk out of that meeting and a few hours later your new associates could have that stuff in their hands. Converse the Delavane-hater. Is he now the Delavane-hunter?"

"Call Remington." Joel went to the French doors, opened them, and walked out on the small balcony. Drifting wisps of cloud filtered the moonlight, and far to the east there were flashes of heat lightning reminding Converse of the silent artillery fire he and the other escaping prisoners would see in the hills, knowing

188

it was both sanctuary and unreachable. He could hear Fitzpatrick inside; from the sound of his voice he was getting a line through to San Diego. Joel reached into a pocket for his cigarettes; he lighted one. Whether it was the bright glow of the flame that illuminated the movement, he did not know, but he looked in the direction of that movement. Two balconies away, about thirty feet to his right, a man stood watching him. The figure was a silhouette in dark light; he nodded in that dim light and went back inside. Was the man simply another guest who had coincidentally gone outside for a breath of air? Or had Aquitaine posted a guard? Converse could hear the Navy lawyer talking conversationally; he turned and walked back into the room.

Connal was seated in the chair on the other side of the table. He held the phone to his ear with his left hand, his right held the pen above the message pad. He made a note, interrupting.

"Wait a minute. You say Hickman told you to let it ride but he wouldn't tell you who specifically made the request? . . . I see. All right, David, thanks very much. Are you going out tonight? . . . So if I need you I can reach you at this number . . . Yes, I know, it's these damn phones up in Sonoma. One heavy rain in the hills and you're lucky to get a line, forget a clear one. Thanks again, David. Goodbye." Fitzpatrick hung up the phone and looked strangely, almost guiltily at Joel. Instead of speaking, he shook his head, breathing out and frowning.

"What is it? What's the matter?"

"You'd better get everything you can at that meeting tomorrow. Or is it today?"

"It's past midnight. It's today. Why?"

"Because twenty-four hours later that flag will be released to a section in the Fifth Naval District – that's Norfolk, and it's powerful. They'll know everything you don't want them to know about you. The time limit is seventy-two hours."

"Get an extension!"

Connal stood up, helplessness in his expression. "On what basis?"

"What else? National security."

"I'd have to spell out the reasons, you know that."

"I *don't* know that. Extensions are granted for all sorts of contingencies. You need more time to prepare. A source or a witness has been postponed – illness or an injury. Or personal matters – goddamn it, your brother-in-law's funeral, your sister's grief – they've delayed your progress!"

"Forget it, Joel. If I tried that, they'd tie you in with Press and goodbye Charlie. They killed him, remember?"

"No," said Converse firmly. "It's the other way around. It separates us farther."

"What are you talking about?"

"I've thought about this, tried to put myself in Avery's shoes. He knew his every move was being watched, his telephone probably tapped. He said the geography, the Comm Tech-Bern merger, the breakfast, Geneva itself, everything had to be logical; it couldn't be any other way. At the end of that breakfast he said if I agreed we'd talk later."

"So?"

"He knew we'd be seen together – it was unavoidable – and I think he was going to give me the words to say if someone in Aquitaine asked me about him.

He was going to turn everything around and give me the push I needed to reach these men."

"What the hell are you talking about?"

"Avery was going to stamp me with the label I had to wear to get inside Delavane's network. We'll never know, but I have an idea he was going to tell me to say that he, A. Preston Halliday, suspected me of being one of *them*, that he had inserted himself in the Comm Tech-Bern merger to threaten me with exposure, to *stop me*."

"Wait a minute." Connal shook his head. "Press didn't know what you were going to do or how you were going to do it."

"There was only one way *to* do it, he knew that! He also knew I'd reach the same conclusion once I understood the particulars. The only way to stop Delavane and his field marshals is to infiltrate Aquitaine. Why do you think all that money was put up front? I don't need it and he knew he couldn't buy me. But he knew it could be used – would *have to* be used to get inside and start talking, start gathering evidence... Call Remington again. Tell him to prepare an extension."

"It's not Remington, it's the commander of SAND PAC, an admiral named Hickman. David said I could expect a call from him tomorrow. I'll have to figure that one out and phone Meagen back. Hickman's uptight; he wants to know who you are and why all the interest."

"How well do you know this Hickman?"

"Fairly well. I was with him in New London and Galveston. He requested me as his CLO in San Diego, that's what gave me the stripe."

Converse studied Fitzpatrick's face, then without any apparent reason kept silent as he turned and walked to the open balcony doors. Connal did not interrupt; undoubtedly he understood. He had seen too many attorneys, himself included, struck by a thought they had to define for themselves, an idea upon which a case might hinge. Joel turned around slowly, haltingly, the dim, abstract shadows of a possibility coming into focus.

"Do it," he began. "Do what I think your brother-in-law might have done. Finish what he might have said but never got a chance to say it. Assume he and I had that meeting after the merger conference. Give me the springboard I need."

"In your words, clarification, please, counsellor."

"Present Hickman with a scenario as it might have been written by A. Preston Halliday. Tell him that flag's got to remain in place because you have reason to believe I was connected with your brother-in-law's murder. Explain that before Halliday flew to Geneva he came to see you – as he did – and told you he was meeting me, an opposing attorney he suspected of being involved with corrupt export licensing, a legal front for some boardroom profiteers. Say he said he was going to confront me. Preston Halliday had a history of causes."

"Not for the past ten or twelve years, he didn't," corrected Fitzpatrick. "He joined the establishment with a vengeance and with a healthy respect for the dollar."

"It's the history that counts. He knew that; it was one of the reasons he came to me. Say you're convinced he did confront me, and since millions are made out of that business, you think I methodically had him removed, covering myself by being there when he died ... I have a certain reputation for being methodical."

Connal lowered his head and ran his hand through his hair, then walked in thought toward the antique hunt table. He stopped, raising his gaze to one of the racehorse prints and turned back to Converse.

"Do you know what you're asking me to do?"

"Yes. Give me the springboard that'll catapult me right in the middle of those, would-be Genghis Khans. To do it you'll have to go farther with Hickman. Because you're so personally involved and so goddamned angry – which again is the truth – tell him to explain your position to whoever wants the flag released. It's a non-military matter, so you're taking what you know to the civilian authorities."

"I understand all that," said Fitzpatrick. "Everything I say *is* the truth, as I saw it when I flew over here to find you. Except that I reverse the targets. Instead of being the one who can help me, you're now the one I want nailed."

"Right on, counsellor. And I'm met by a welcoming committee at Leifhelm's estate."

"Then I guess you don't see."

"What?"

"You're asking me to go on record implicating you in first degree murder. I'll be branding you a killer. Once I say it, I can't take the words back."

"I know that. Do it."

George Marcus Delavane twisted his torso in his chair behind the desk in front of the strangely coloured fragmented map on the wall. It was not a controlled movement; it was an action in search of control. Delavane did not care for obstructions and one was being explained to him now by an admiral in the Fifth Naval District.

"The status of the flag is Four-Zero," said Scanlon. "To get it released we'd have to go through Pentagon procedures and I don't have to tell you what that means. Two senior officers, one from Naval Intelligence, plus a supporting signature from the National Security Agency; all would have to appear on the request sheet, the level of the inquiry stated, thus escalating the request to a sector demand. Now, General, we can do all this, but we run the risk ..."

"I know the risk," interrupted Delavane. "The signatures are the risk, the identities a risk. Why the Four-Zero? Who placed it and *why?*"

"The Chief Legal Officer of SAND PAC. I checked him out. He's a lieutenant-commander named Fitzpatrick, and there's nothing in his record to give us any indication as to why he did it."

"I'll tell you why," said the warlord of Saigon. "He's hiding something. He's protecting this Converse."

"Why would a Chief Legal Officer in the navy protect a civilian under these circumstances? There's no connection. Furthermore, why would he exercise a Four-Zero condition? It only calls attention to his action."

"It also clamps a lid down on that flag." Delavane paused, then continued before the admiral could interrupt. "This Fitzpatrick," he said. "You've checked the master list?"

"He's not one of us."

"Has he ever been considered? Or approached?"

"I haven't had time to find out." There was the sound of a buzzer, not part of the line over which the two men spoke. Scanlon could be heard punching a button, his voice clear, officious. "Yes?" Silence followed and seconds later the admiral returned to Palo Alto. "It's Hickman again."

"Maybe he has something for us. Call me back."

"Hickman wouldn't give us anything if he had the slightest idea we existed," said Scanlon. "In a few weeks, he'll be one of the first to go. If it were up to me he'd be shot."

"Call me back," said George Marcus Delavane, looking at the map of the new Aquitaine on the wall.

Chaim Abrahms sat at the kitchen table in his small stone Mediterranean villa in Tzahala, a suburb of Tel Aviv favoured by the retired military and those with adequate incomes or influence to live there. The windows were open and the breezes from the garden stirred the oppressive summer's night air. There was air conditioning in two other rooms, and ceiling fans in three more, but Chaim liked the kitchen. In the old days they would sit in primitive kitchens and plan raids; ammunition was often passed about while desert chicken boiled on a wood stove in the Negev. The kitchen was the soul of the house. It gave warmth and sustenance to the body, clearing the mind for tactics – so long as the women left after performing their chores and did not interrupt the men with their incessant trivialities. His wife was asleep upstairs; so be it. He had little to say to her any more, or she to him; she could not help him now. And if she could, she would not. They had lost a son in Lebanon, *her* son she said, a teacher, a scholar, not a soldier, not a killer by choice. Too many sons were lost on both sides, she said. For old men, she said, old men who infected the young with their hatreds and who used biblical legends to justify death by questionable real estate. Death, she cried. Death before *talk!* She had forgotten the early days; too many forgot too quickly. Chaim Abrahms did not forget, nor would he ever.

And his sense of smell was as acute as ever. This lawyer, this Converse, this talk! It was all too clever; it had the stench of cold, analytical minds, not the heat of believers. The Mossad specialist was the best, but even the Mossad made mistakes. The specialist looked for a motive, as if one could dissect the human brain and say this action caused that reaction; this punishment that commitment to vengeance. Too damned *clever!* A believer was fuelled by the heat of his convictions. They were his only motive, and they did not call for clever manipulations.

Chaim knew he was a plain-spoken man, a direct man, but it was not because he was unintelligent or lacked subtle perceptions; his prowess on the battlefield proved otherwise. He was direct because he knew what he wanted, and it was a waste of time to pretend to be clever. In all the years he had lived with his convictions he had never met a fellow believer who allowed himself to waste time.

This Converse knew enough to reach Bertholdier in Paris. He showed how much more he knew when he mentioned Leifhelm in Bonn, and specifically named the cities of Tel Aviv and Johannesburg. What more did he have to prove? *Why* should he prove it if his belief was there? Why did he not plead his case with his first connection and not waste time? . . . No, this lawyer, this Converse, was from somewhere else. The Mossad specialist said the motive was there for affiliation. He was wrong. The redhot heat of the believer was *not* there. Only cleverness, only talk.

And the specialist had not dismissed Chaim's sense of smell. As well he should not, for the two Sabras had fought together for years, as often as not against the Europeans and their conniving ways – those immigrants who held up the Old Testament as if they had written it – calling the true inhabitants of Israel uneducated, ruffian clowns. The Mossad specialist *respected* his Sabra brother; it was in his look, that respect. No one could dismiss the instincts of Chaim Abrahms, son of Abraham, archangel of darkness to the enemies of Abraham's children. Thank God his wife was asleep.

It was time to call Palo Alto.

"My General, my friend."

"Shalom, Chaim," said the warlord of Saigon. "Are you on your way to Bonn?"

"I'm leaving in the morning – we're leaving. Van Headmer is in the air now. He'll arrive at Ben Gurion at eight-thirty and together we'll take the ten o'clock flight to Frankfurt where Leifhelm's pilot will meet us with the Cessna."

"Good. You can talk."

"*We* must talk now," said the Israeli. "What more have you learned about this Converse?"

"He becomes more of an enigma, Chaim."

"I smell a fraud."

"So do I, but perhaps not the fraud I thought. You know what my assessment was. I thought he was no more than an infantry point, someone being used by more knowledgeable men – Lucas Anstett among them – to learn far more than they knew or heard rumours about. I don't discount a degree of minor leaks; they're to be anticipated and managed, scoffed at as paranoia."

"Get to the point, Marcus," said the impatient Abrahms, who always called Delavane by his middle name. He considered it a Hebrew name, in spite of the fact that Delavane's father had insisted on it for his first son in honour of the Roman Caesar-philosopher, Marcus Aurelius, a proselytizer of moderation.

"Three things happened today," continued the former general in Palo Alto. "The first infuriated me because I could understand it, and frankly disturbed me because it portended a far greater penetration than I thought possible from a sector I thought *impossible*."

"What was it?" broke in the Israeli.

"A firm prohibition was placed on getting part of Converse's service record."

"Yes!" cried Abrahms, in his voice the sound of triumph.

"What?"

"Go on, Marcus! I'll tell you when you're finished. What was the second calamity?"

"Not a calamity, Chaim. An explanation so blatantly offered it can't be turned aside. Leifhelm called me and said Converse himself brought up Anstett's death, claiming to be relieved, but saying little else except that Anstett was his enemy – that was the word he used."

"So instructed!" Abrahms' voice reverberated around the kitchen. "What was the third gift, my General?"

"The most bewildering as well as enlightening – and, Chaim, do not shout into the phone. You are not in one of your stadium rallies or provoking the Knesset."

"I am in the field, Marcus. Right *now!* Please continue my friend."

"The man who clamped the lid down on Converse's military record is a naval officer who was the brother-in-law of Preston Halliday."

"Geneva! Yes!"

"*Stop* that!"

"My apologies, my dear friend. It's just all so perfect!"

"Whatever you have in mind," said Delavane, "may be negated by the man's reason. This naval officer, this brother-in-law, believes Converse engineered Halliday's murder."

"Of course! *Perfect!*"

"You *will* keep your *voice* down!" The cry of the cat on a frozen lake was heard.

"Again my deepest and most sincere apologies, my General . . . Was that all this naval officer said?"

"No, he made it clear to the commander of his base in San Diego that Halliday had come to him and told him he was meeting a man in Geneva he believed was involved with illegal exports to illegal destinations. An attorney for profiteers in armaments. He intended to confront this man, this international lawyer named Converse, and threaten to expose him. What do we have?"

"A *fraud!*"

"But on whose *side*, Sabra? The volume of your voice doesn't convince me."

"Be convinced. I'm right. This Converse is the desert scorpion!"

"What does that mean?"

"Don't you *see?* The Mossad sees!"

"The Mossad?"

"Yes! I talked with our specialist and he senses what I smell – he admits the possibility! I grant you, my General, my honoured warrior, that he has information that led him to think this Converse might be genuine, that he wanted truly to be with us, but when I said I smelled bad meat, he granted one other, exceptional possibility. Converse may or may not be programmed, but he could be an agent for his government!"

"A *provocateur?*"

"Who knows, Marcus? But the pattern is so perfect. First, a prohibition is placed on his military record – it will tell us something, we know that. Then he

194

responds in the negative about the death of an enemy – not his, but *ours* – and he claims it is his enemy too – so simple, so instructable. Finally, this Converse is insinuated to be the killer in Geneva – so orderly, so precisely to his advantage . . . We are dealing with very analytical minds who watch every move in the chess game, and match every pawn with a king."

"Yet everything you say can be reversed. He could be . . ."

"He *can't* be!" cried Abrahms.

"Why, Chaim? Tell me why?"

"There is no *heat*, no *fire* in him! It is not the way of a believer! We are not clever, we are adamant!"

George Marcus Delavane said nothing for several moments, and the Israeli knew better than to speak. He waited until the quiet cold voice came back on the line.

"Have your meeting tomorrow, General. Listen to him and be courteous; play the game he plays. But he must not leave that house until I give the order. He may never leave it."

"Shalom, my friend."

"Shalom, Chaim."

14

Valerie approached the glass doors of her studio – identical to the doors of her balcony upstairs – and looked out at the calm, sunwashed waters of Cape Ann. She thought briefly of the boat that had dropped anchor so frighteningly in front of her house several nights ago. It had not come back; whatever had happened was past, leaving questions but no answers. If she closed her eyes she could still see the figure of a man crawling up out of the cabin light, and the glow of the cigarette, and she still wondered what that man was doing, what was he thinking. Then she remembered the sight of the two men in the early light, framed in the dark rims of her binoculars – staring back at her with far more powerful lenses. Questions. No answers. Were they novices finding a safe harbour? Amateurs navigating the dark waters of a coastline at night? Questions, no answers.

Whatever, it was past. A brief, disturbing interlude that gave rise to black imaginings – demons in search of logic, as Joel would say.

She tossed her long, dark hair aside and returned to her easel, picking up a brush and putting the final dabs of burnt umber beneath the shadowed sand dunes of wild grass. She stepped back, studied her work, and swore to herself for the fifth time that the oil painting was finished. It was another seascape; she never tired of them and fortunately she was beginning to get a fair share of the market. Of course there were those painters in the Boston-Boothbay axis who claimed she had virtually cornered the market but that was rubbish. It was true that her prices had risen satisfactorily as a result of the critical approval accorded her two showings at the Copley Galleries, but if the truth were known she could hardly afford to live where she lived and how she lived without at least a part of Joel's cheque every month.

Then again not too many artists had a house on the beach with an attached twenty by twenty foot studio enclosed by full-length glass doors and with a ceiling that was literally one entire skylight. The rest of the house, the original house, on the northern border of Cape Ann was more rambling-quaint than functional. The initial architecture was early-coast-confusion, with lots of heavy bleached wood and curlicues, the balustraded balcony and outsized bay windows in the front room that were charming to look at and look out of, but leaked something fierce when the winter winds came off the ocean. No amount of putty or sashing compound seemed to work; nature was extracting a price for observing her beauty.

Still it was Val's dream house, the one she had promised herself years ago she would some day afford. She had come back from the École des Beaux Arts in Paris prepared to assault New York's art world via the Greenwich Village-Woodstock route only to have stark reality alter her plans. The family circumstances had always been sufficiently healthy for her to live comfortably, albeit not lavishly, throughout three years in college and two more in Paris. Her father was a passably good, if excessively enthusiastic amateur painter who always complained that he had not taken the risk and gone totally into the fine arts rather than architecture. As a result, he supported his only child both morally and financially, in a very real sense living through her progress and devoted to her determination. And her mother – slightly mad, always loving, *always* supportive in anything and everything – would take terrible photographs of Val's crudest work and send the pictures back to her sister and cousins in Germany, writing outrageous lies that spoke of museums and galleries and insane commissions.

"The crazy *Berlinerin*," her father would say fondly, in his heavy Gallic accent. "You should have seen her during the war. She frightened us all to death! We half expected she would return to headquarters some night with a drunken Goebbels or a doped-up Goering in tow, then tell us if we wanted Hitler to give her the word!"

Her father had been the Free French liaison between the Allies and the German-Berlin underground. A rather stiff Parisian autocrat who happened to speak German had been assigned to the cell in the Charlottenburg, which coordinated all of Berlin's underground's activities. He frequently said that he had more trouble with the wild *Fräulein* with the impetuous ideas than he had avoiding the Nazis. Nevertheless they married each other two months after the end of the war. In Berlin. Where neither his family would talk to hers, nor hers to his. "We had two small orchestras," her mother would say. "One played pure, beautiful Viennese *Schnitzel*, the other some white cream sauce with deer droppings."

Whether family animosities had anything to do with it, neither ever said, but the Parisian and the Berliner emigrated to St Louis, Missouri, in the United States of America, where the Berliner had distant relations.

The stark reality. A frightened, tearful father had flown to New York and told

196

Val a terrible truth. His beloved crazy Berliner had been ill for years; it was the cancer and it was about to kill her. In desperation, he had spent nearly all the money he had, including unpaid second and third mortgages on the rambling house in Bellefontaine, to stem the disease. Among the profiteers were clinics in Mexico; there was nothing else he could say. He could only weep and his losses had nothing to do with his tears. And she could only hold her father and ask him why he had not told her before.

"It was not your battle, *ma chérie*. It was ours. Since Berlin, it was always we two. We fought then together; we fight now as always – as one."

Her mother died six days later, and six months after that her father lighted a Gaulois on the screened-in-porch and mercifully fell asleep, not to wake up. Valerie could not cry. It was a shock but not a tragedy. Wherever he was he wanted to be there, not alone.

So Valerie Charpentier looked for a job, a paying job that did not rely on the sales of an unknown artist. What astonished her was not the fact that employment was so easy to find, but that it had very little to do with the thick portfolio of sketches and line drawings she presented. The second advertising agency she applied to seemed more interested in the fact that she spoke both German and French fluently. It was the time of corporate take-overs, of multi-national alliances where profits could be made on both sides of the Atlantic by single entities. Valerie Charpentier, artist-in-residence inside, became a company hack on the outside. Someone who could draw and sketch rapidly and make presentations and speak the languages and she hated it. Still, it was a remarkable living for a woman who had anticipated a period of years before her name meant something on a canvas.

Then a man came into her life who made whatever affairs she had had totally forgettable. A nice man, a *decent* man – even an exciting man – who had his own problems but did not talk about them, *would* not talk about them, and that should have given her a clue. Joel, her Joel, effusive one moment, withdrawn the next, but always with that shield, that façade of quick humour which was as often biting as it was amusing. For a while they had been good for each other. Both were ambitious for entirely different reasons – she for the independence that came with recognition, he for the wasted years he could never reclaim – and each acted as a buffer when the other faced disappointment or delay. But it all began to fall apart. The reasons were painfully clear to her but not to him. He became mesmerized by his own progress, by his own determination to the exclusion of everything else, starting with her. He never raised his voice or made demands, but the words were ice and the demands were increasingly there. If there was a specific point when she recognized the downhill slide it was a Friday night in November. The agency had wanted her to fly to West Berlin; a *Telefunken* account required some fast personal service and she was elected to calm the churning waters. She had been packing when Joel came home from work. He had walked into the bedroom of their apartment and asked her what she was doing, where she was going. She told him and he had replied.

"You can't. We're expected at Brooks' house in Larchmont tomorrow night.

Talbot and Simon'll be there, too. I'm sure they'll talk international. You've got to be there."

She had looked at him, at the quiet desperation in his eyes. She did not go to Germany. It was the turning point, the downhill race had begun and, within a brief few months, she knew it was irreversible. She quit the agency, giving up authority for the dog days of free-lancing, hoping the extra time she had to devote to him might help. It did not; he seemed to resent any overt act of sacrifice, no matter how she tried to conceal it. His periods of withdrawal and disinterest multiplied and in a way she felt sorry for him. His furies were driving him and it was so obvious that he disliked what was happening; he disliked himself but could not help himself. He was on his way to a burn-out and she could not help him, either.

If there had been another woman she could have fought, staking out her claim and insisting on the right to compete fiercely, but there was no one else, only himself and his silent compulsions. Finally she could not penetrate his shield; he had nothing left for anyone else emotionally. That was what she had hurled at him. "Emotional burn out!" she had cried. He had agreed in that quiet, kind voice and the next day he was gone.

So she took him. Four years, she demanded, the exact amount of time he had taken from her. Those four years of heady generosity were about to come to an end, Val reflected, as she cleaned her brushes and scraped the palette. In January they were over, the last cheque as always posted by the fifteenth. Five weeks ago during lunch at the Ritz in Boston Joel had offered to continue the payments. He claimed he was used to them and was making more in salary and bonuses than he could spend soberly. The money was no hardship and besides it gave him a certain stature among his peers and was a marvellous ploy to avoid prolonged entanglements. She had declined, borrowing words from her father or more likely her mother, saying that things were far better than they were. He had smiled that half-sad, yet still infectious smile and said.

"If they turn out otherwise, I'm here."

Goddamn him!

Poor Joel. Sad Joel. He was a good man caught in the vortex of his conflicts. And Val had gone as far as she could go – to go farther was to deny her own identity. She would not do that; she had not done it.

She placed her brushes in the tray and walked to the glass doors that looked over the dunes and the ocean. He was out there, far away, still somewhere in Europe. Valerie wondered if he had given a thought to the day. It was the anniversary of their marriage.

To summarize, Chaim Abrahms was moulded in the stress and chaos of fighting for daily survival. They were years of never ending violent skirmishes, of out-thinking and out-living enemies bent on killing not only whole Sabra settlements but on the destruction of the desert Jew's aspirations for a homeland as well as political freedom and religious expression. It is not difficult to understand where Abrahms came from and why he is what he is, but it is frightening to think about where he is going. He is a fanatic with no sense of balance or compromise where other peoples with identical aspirations are concerned. If a man has a different stripe, whether of the same species or not, he is the enemy. Armed force takes precedence over negotiations in all matters, and even those in Israel who plead for more moderate stands based on totally secure borders are branded traitors. Abrahms is an imperialist who sees an ever-expanding Israel as the ruling kingdom of the entire Middle East. An appropriate ending to this report is a comment he made after the well-known statement issued by the Prime Minister during the Lebanon invasion: "We covet not one inch of Lebanon." Abrahms' reply in the field to his troops – by no means the majority sympathetic – was the following.

"Certainly not an inch! The whole damned country! Then Gaza, the Golan, and the West Bank! And why not Jordan, then Syria, and Iraq! We have the means and we have the will! We are the mighty children of Abraham!"

He is Delavane's key in the volatile Middle East.

It was nearly noon, the overhead sun beating down on the small balcony beyond the french doors. The late-breakfast remnants had been cleared away by room service; only a silver pot remained on the hunt table. They had been reading for hours, since the first coffee was brought to the suite at 6.30. Converse put down the dossier, and reached for his cigarettes on the table by the armchair. *It is not difficult to understand where Abrahms came from . . . but frightening to think about where he is going.* Joel looked over at Connal Fitzpatrick who was seated on the couch, leaning forward over the coffee table and reading a single page while making notes on the telephone message pad; the Bertholdier and Leifhelm dossiers were in two neat piles on his left. The Navy lawyer had said practically the same words to him, thought Converse, lighting a cigarette. *I'm beginning to see where you're coming from . . .* The inherent question put to Joel's legal mind was simple: Where was he himself going? He hoped to hell he knew. Was he an inept gladiator marching into a Roman arena facing far stronger, better armed and superior talent? Or were the demons from his own past turning him into his own sacrifice, leading him into the arena's hot sand where huge angry, half-starved cats waited for him, ready to pounce and tear him apart. So many questions, so many variables he was incapable of addressing. He just knew he could not turn back.

Fitzpatrick looked up. "What's the matter?" he asked, obviously aware that Converse was staring in his direction. "You worried about the Admiral?"

"Who?"

"Hickman, San Diego."

"Among other things. In the clear light of day you're sure he bought the extension?"

"No guarantees, but I told you he said he'll call me if any emergency heat came down. I'm damn sure he won't do anything before consulting me. If he tries to reach me, Meagen knows what to do and I'll lean harder. If need be, I'll claim point of personal privilege and demand a meeting with those unnamed people in the Fifth District, maybe go so far as to imply they could be part of Geneva. *That'd* be a full circle. We could end up with a stand-off – the release of that flag only with a full-scale investigation of the circumstances. Irony and stand-off."

"You won't have a stand-off if he's with them. He'll override you."

199

"If he was *with* them he wouldn't have told Remington he was going to call me. He wouldn't have said anything; he'd have waited the extra day and let it go. I know him. He wasn't just non-plussed, he was mad. He stands by his people and he doesn't like outside pressures, especially Navy pressures. We're on hold, and as long as it's hold, the flag's in place. I told you, he's a lot angrier with Norfolk than with me. They won't even *give* him a reason; they claim they can't."

Converse nodded. "All right," he said. "Call it a case of nerves on my part. I just finished the Abrahms' dossier. That maniac could blow up the whole Middle East all by himself and drag the rest of us in with him . . . What did you think of Leifhelm and Bertholdier?"

"As far as the information goes they're everything you said and then some. They're more than just influential ex-generals with fistfuls of money, they're powerful rallying symbols for what a lot of people think are justifiable extremes. That's as far as the information goes – but the operative word for *me* is the information itself."

"That's a step back. It's there."

"It sure is, but how come? You say Beale gave it to you, that Press used the phrase 'we' – 'the ones *we're* after', 'the tools *we* can give you', 'the connections as *we* think they are'."

"And we went over this," insisted Joel. "The man in San Francisco, the one he went to who provided the five hundred thousand and told him to build cases against these people legally, and together they'd turn them into plain-and-simple profiteers. It's the ultimate ridicule for super-patriots. It's sound reasoning, counsellor, and that's the *we*."

"Press and this unknown man in San Francisco?"

"Yes."

"And they could pick up a phone and hire someone to put together *these?*" Fitzpatrick gestured at the two dossiers on his left.

"Why not? This is the age of the computer. Nobody today lives on an unmapped island or in an undiscovered cave."

"*These*," repeated Connal, "are not computer print-outs. They're well-researched, detailed, in-depth dossiers that take in the importance of political nuances and personal idiosyncrasies."

"You have a way with words, sailor. Yes, they are. A man who can forward half a million dollars to the right bank on an Aegean island can hire just about anyone he likes."

"He can't hire these."

"What does that mean?"

"Let me take a real step back," said the Navy lawyer, getting to his feet and reaching down for the single page he had been reading. "I won't reiterate my relationship with Press because right now it hurts a little to think about it." Fitzpatrick paused, seeing the look in Converse's eyes that rejected this kind of sentimentality in their discussion. "Don't mistake me," he continued. "It's not his death, not the funeral; it's the other way around. It's not the Press Halliday I knew. You see, I don't think he told us the truth, either you or me."

"Then you know something I don't know," said Converse quietly.

"I know there's no man in San Francisco that even vaguely fits the description or the image he gave you. I lived all my life there, including Berkeley and Stanford, just like Press. 1 knew everyone he knew, especially the wealthiest and the more exotic ones; we never held back on those with each other. I was legal worlds away and he always filled me in if new ones came along. It was part of the fun for him."

"That's tenuous, counsellor. I'm sure he kept certain associations to himself."

"Not those kinds," said Connal. "It wouldn't be like him. Not with me."

"Well, I . . ."

"Now let me step forward," interrupted Fitzpatrick. "These dossiers — I haven't seen them before, but I've seen hundreds like them, maybe a couple of thousand on their way to becoming full-fledged versions of them."

Joel sat up. "Please explain that, Commander."

"You just hit it, Lieutenant. The rank says it."

"Says *what?*"

"Those dossiers are the reworked, finished products of intelligence probes. They've been bounced around the community each branch contributing its input — from straight biographical data to past surveillances to psychiatric evaluation — and put together by teams of specialists. They were taken from way down in the government vaults and rewritten with current additions and conclusions, then shaped to appear as the work of an outside, non-government authority. But they're not. They've got *Classified, Top Secret* and *Eyes Only* written all over them."

From simply sitting up, Converse sat forward. "That could be a subjective judgment based on limited familiarity. I've seen some very detailed, very in-depth reports put together by high-priced firms specializing in that sort of thing."

"Describing precise military incidents during time of war? Pin-pointing bombing raids and specifying regiments and battalions and the current strategies employed? Detailing through *interviews* the internal conflicts of ranking enemy officers, and the tactical reasons for shifting military personnel into civilian positions after the cessation of hostilities? No firm would have access to that material."

"They could be researched," said Joel, suddenly not convinced himself.

"Well, *these* couldn't," Connal broke in, holding up the page of typewritten names, his thumb on the lower two columns listing the "decision-makers" from the Pentagon and the State Department. "Maybe five or six — three from each side at maximum — but not the rest. These are people *above* the ones I've dealt with, men who do their jobs under a variety of titles so they can't be reached — bribed, blackmailed, or threatened. When you said you had names I assumed I'd know most of them, or at least half of them. I don't. I only know the departmental execs, upper-echelon personnel who have to go even higher, who obviously report to these people. Press couldn't have gotten these names himself or through others on the outside. He wouldn't know where to look and they wouldn't know where to look — *I* wouldn't know."

Converse rose. "Are you sure you know what you're talking about?"

"Yes. Someone – probably more than one – deep in the Washington cellars provided these names just as he or they provided the material for those dossiers."

"Do you know what you're saying?"

Connal stood still and nodded his head. "It's not easy for me to say," he began grimly. "Press lied to us. He lied to you by what he said, and to me by what he didn't say. You're tied to a string and it goes right back to Washington. And I wasn't to know anything about it."

"The puppet's in place . . ." Joel spoke so softly he could barely be heard as he walked aimlessly across the room toward the bright sunlight streaming through the balcony doors.

"What?" asked Fitzpatrick.

"Nothing, just a phrase that kept running through my head when I heard about Anstett." Converse turned. "But if there's a string why have they hidden it? Why did *Avery* hide it? For what purpose?"

The Navy lawyer remained motionless, his face without expression. "I don't think I have to answer that. You answered it yourself yesterday afternoon when we were talking about me – and don't kid yourself, Lieutenant, I knew exactly what you were saying. 'I'll give you a name now and then that may open a door . . . but that's all.' Those were your words. Freely translated, you were telling yourself that the sailor you took on board might stumble on to something, but in case he was taken by the wrong people, they couldn't beat out of him what he didn't know."

Joel accepted the rebuke, not merely because the essence was accurate, but because it made clear a larger truth, one he had not understood on Mykonos. Beale told him that among those raising questions in Washington had been military men who for one reason or another had not pursued their inquiries; they had kept silent. They had kept silent where they might be overheard, perhaps, but they had not kept their silence. They had talked in quiet voices until another quiet voice from San Francisco – a man who knew whom to reach courtesy of his close friend and brother-in-law in San Diego – made contact. They had talked together and out of their secret conversations had come a plan. They needed an infiltrator, a man with the expertise who had a loathing they could fuel, and once fired send out into the labyrinth.

The realization was a shock, but oddly enough Joel could not fault the strategy. He did not even fault the silence that remained even after Preston Halliday's murder; loud accusing voices would have rendered that death meaningless. Instead, they had stayed quiet, knowing their puppet had the tools to make his way through the maze of illegalities and do the job they could not do themselves. He understood that, too. But there was one thing Converse could not accept and that was his own expendability as the puppet. He had tolerated being left unprotected under the conditions outlined by Avery Fowler-Preston Halliday. Not under these. If he was on a string he wanted the puppeteers to know he knew it. He also wanted the name of someone in Bonn he could call, someone who was a part of them. The old rules did not apply any longer, a new dimension had been added.

202

In four hours he would be driven through the iron gates of Erich Leifhelm's estate; he wanted someone on the outside, a man Fitzpatrick could reach if he did not come out by midnight. The demons were pressing hard – even furiously, thought Joel. Still he could not turn back. He was so close to trapping the warlord of Saigon, so close to making up for so much that had warped his life in ways no one would ever understand . . . No, not "no one", he reflected. One person did, and she had said she could not help him any longer. Nor had it been fair any longer to seek her help.

"What's your decision?" said Connal.

"Decision?" asked Joel, startled.

"You don't have to go this afternoon. Throw it all *back!* This belongs stateside with the FBI in conjunction with the Central Intelligence Agency overseas. I'm appalled they didn't take that route."

Converse breathed the start of a reply, then stopped. It had to be clear, not only to Fitzpatrick but to himself. He thought he understood. He had seen the look of profound panic in Avery Fowler's eyes – Preston Halliday's eyes – and he had heard the cry in his voice. The lies were his strategy, but the look and the cry were his innermost feelings.

"Has it occurred to you, Commander, that they can't take that route? That, perhaps, we're not talking about men who can pick up a phone – as you said before – and put those wheels in motion? Or if they tried, they'd have their heads cut off, perhaps literally with an official rebuke and a bullet in the back of their skulls? Let me add that I don't think they're afraid for themselves any more than I believe they chose the best man for the job, but I *do* think they came to a persuasive conclusion. They couldn't work from the inside because they didn't know whom they could trust."

"Christ, you're a cold son of a bitch."

"Ice, Commander. We're dealing with a paranoid fantasy called Aquitaine, and it's controlled by proven, committed, highly intelligent and resourceful men who if they achieve what they've set out to do will appear as the voices of strength and reason in a world gone mad. They'll control that world – our world – because all other options will pale beside their stability. *Stability*, Counsellor, as opposed to destabilization and chaos. What would you choose if you were an everyday nine-to-fiver with a wife and kids, and you could never be sure when you went home at night whether or not your house had been broken into, your wife raped, your kids strangled? You'd opt for tanks in the street."

"With justification," said the Navy lawyer, the two words spiralling quietly off into the air of the sunlit room.

"Believe that, sailor. They're banking on it and that's just what they're planning to do on an international scale. It's only a few days or a few weeks away – whatever it is, wherever it is. If I can just get an inkling . . ." Converse turned and started for the door of his bedroom.

"Where are you going?" asked Connal.

"Beale's telephone number on Mykonos; it's in my briefcase. He's my only contact and I want to talk to him. I want him to know the puppet was just granted some unexpected free will."

Three minutes later Joel stood over the table, the phone to his ear as the Greek operator in Athens routed his call to the island of Mykonos. Fitzpatrick sat on the couch, Chaim Abrahms' dossier in front of him on the coffee table, his eyes on Converse.

"Are you getting through all right?" asked the Navy lawyer.

"It's ringing now." The erratic, stabbing signals kept repeating – four, five, six times. On the seventh the telephone in the Aegean was picked up.

"*Kherete?*"

"Dr Beale, please. Dr Edward Beale."

"*Tee thelate?*"

"Beale. The owner of the house. Get him for me, *please!*" Joel turned to Fitzpatrick. "Do you speak Greek?"

"No, but I've been thinking about taking it up."

"You do that." Converse listened again to the male voice in Mykonos. Greek phrases were spoken rapidly, none comprehensible. "Thank you! Goodbye." Joel tapped the telephone bar several times hoping the overseas line was still open and that the English-speaking Greek operator was still there. "Operator? Is this the operator in Athens? . . . Good! I want to call another number on Mykonos, the same billing in Bonn." Converse reached down on the table for the instructions Preston Halliday had given him in Geneva. "It's the Bank of Rhodes. The number is . . ."

Moments later the waterfront banker, Kostas Laskaris, was on the line. "*Kherete.*"

"Mr Laskaris, this is Joel Converse. Do you remember me?"

"Of course . . . Mr Converse?"

The banker sounded distant, somehow strange, as if wary or bewildered. "I've been trying to call Dr Beale at the number you gave me, but all I get is a man who can't speak English. I wondered if you could tell me where Beale is."

A quiet expulsion of breath could be heard over the phone. "I wondered," said Laskaris quietly. "The man you reached was a police officer, Mr Converse. I had him placed there myself. A scholar has many valuable things."

"*Why?* What do you mean?"

"Shortly after sunrise this morning, Dr Beale took his boat out of the harbour accompanied by another man. Several fishermen saw them. Two hours ago Dr Beale's boat was found crashed on the rocks beyond the Stephanos. There was no one on board."

I killed him. With a scaling knife, dropping his body over a cluster of sharks beyond the shoals of the Stephanos.

Joel hung up the phone. Halliday, Anstett, Beale, all of them gone – all his contacts dead. He was a puppet on the loose, his strings gone haywire, leading only to shadows.

15

Erich Leifhelm's wax-like skin paled further as his eyes narrowed and his starched, white lips parted. There followed a rush of blood to his head as he sat forward in his chair at the desk in his library and spoke into the telephone.

"What was that name again, London?"

"Admiral Hickman. He's the. . . ."

"*No*," interrupted the German sharply. "The other one! The officer who has refused to release the information."

"Fitzpatrick, an Irish name. He's the ranking legal officer at the naval base in San Diego."

"A Lieutenant-Commander Fitzpatrick?"

"Yes, how did you know?"

"*Unglaublich! Diese Stümper!*"

"*Wieso?*" asked the Englishman. "In what sense?"

"He may be what you say he is in San Diego, *Engländer*, but he is not *in* San Diego! He's here in Bonn!"

"Are you mad? No, of course, you're not. Are you *certain?*"

"He's *with* Converse! I spoke to him myself. The two are registered in *his* name at *Das Rektorat!* He is how we found Converse!"

"There was no attempt to conceal the name?"

"On the contrary, he used his papers to gain entrance!"

"How bloody third-rate," said London, bewildered. "Or how downright sure of himself," added the Britisher, his tone changing. "A signal? No one dares touch him?"

"*Unsinn!* It's not so."

"Why not?"

"He spoke to Peregrine, the ambassador. Our man was there. Peregrine wanted to take him, wanted him brought forcibly to the embassy. There were complications; he got away."

"Our man wasn't very good, then."

"An obstruction. Some *Schauspieler* – an actor. Peregrine will not discuss the incident. He says nothing."

"Which means no one will touch this naval officer from California," concluded London. "There's a very good reason."

"What is it?"

"He's the brother-in-law of Preston Halliday."

"Geneva! *Mein Gott*, they are onto us!"

"Someone is, but not anyone with a great deal of information. I agreed with Palo Alto, who also agrees with our specialist in the Mossad – with Abrahms, as well."

"The Jew? What does the Jew say? What does he *say?*"

"He claims this Converse is an agent flying blind out of Washington."

"What more do you *need?*"

"He is not to leave your house. Instructions will follow."

Stunned, Undersecretary of State Brewster Tolland hung up the phone, sank briefly back in his chair then shot forward, his hand rushing toward his console, his fingers pressing the appropriate buttons.

"Chesapeake," said the female voice. "Code, please?"

"Six Thousand," said Tolland. "May I speak with Consular Operations, Station Eight,, please?"

"Station Eight requires . . ."

"Plantagenet," interrupted the Undersecretary.

"Right away, sir."

"What is it, Six Thousand?"

"Cut the horseshit, Harry, this is Brew. What have you got running in Bonn we don't know about?"

"Off the top of my head, nothing."

"How far off the top is that?"

"No, it's straight. You're current on everything we're doing. There was an FRG review yesterday morning and I'd remember if there was anything that excluded you."

"You might remember but if I'm excluded, I'm out."

"That's right and I'd tell you as much if only to keep you out, you know that. What's your problem?"

"I just got off the scrambler with a very angry ambassador, who may just call a very old friend at Sixteen Hundred."

"Peregrine? What's *his* problem?"

"If it's not you, then someone's playing Cons-Op. It's supposedly a covert investigation of the embassy – his embassy – somehow connected with the Navy Department."

"The *Navy* . . . ? That's crazy – I mean *dumb* crazy! Bonn's a port?"

"Actually, I suppose it is."

"I never heard of the *Bismarck* or the *Graf Spee* steaming around the Rhine. No way, Brew. We don't have anything like that and we wouldn't have. Do you have any names?"

"Yes, one," replied Tolland, looking down at a pad with hastily scribbled notes on it. "An attorney named Joel Converse. Who is he, Harry?"

"For Christ's sake, I never *heard* of him. What's the naval angle?"

"Someone who claims to be the Chief Legal Officer of a major Navy base with the rank of Lieutenant-Commander."

"*Claims* to be?"

"Well, before that he passed himself off as a military attaché working at the embassy."

"Somewhere the inmates broke out of a home."

"This isn't funny, Harry. Peregrine's no fool. He may be a vanity appointment

206

but he's damned good and he's damned smart. He says these people aren't only real but may know something he doesn't."

"What does he base that on?"

"First, the opinion of a man who's met this Converse . . ."

"Who?" interrupted Harry of Station Eight.

"He won't say, just that he trusts him, trusts his judgment. This person with no name says Converse is a highly qualified, very troubled man, not a black hat."

"A what?"

"That was the term Peregrine used. Obviously someone who's okay."

"What else?"

"What Peregrine calls isolated odd behaviour in his personnel ranks. He wouldn't elaborate; he says he'll discuss it with the Secretary or Sixteen Hundred if I can't satisfy him. He wants answers fast and we don't want to rock the boat over there."

"I'll try to help," said Harry. "Maybe it's something from Langley or Arlington – the *bastards!* I can run a check on the navy's chief legals in an hour, and I'm sure the American Bar Association can tell us who Converse is – *if* he is. At least narrow him down if there's more than one."

"Get back to me. I haven't got much time and we don't want the White House raising its voice."

"The last thing ever," agreed the Director of Consular Operations, the State Department's branch of foreign clandestine activities.

"Try *that* on for legal size!" shouted Rear-Admiral Hickman, standing by the window, angrily addressing a rigid, pale-faced David Remington. "And tell me with as few goddamned details as possible how it fits!"

"I find it impossible to believe, sir. I spoke with him yesterday – at noon – and then again last evening. He was in Sonoma!"

"So did *I*, Lieutenant. And whenever there was a scratching or an echo, what were the words? All that rain in the hills screwed up the telephone lines!"

"Those were the words, sir."

"He passed through Düsseldorf immigration two *days* ago! He's now in Bonn, Germany, with a man he swore to me had something to do with his brother-in-law's death. The *same* man he's protecting by putting a clamp on that flag. This *Converse!*"

"I don't know what to say, sir."

"Well, the State Department does and so do I. They're pushing through that vet-delay or whatever the hell you called it in your legalese."

"It's vetted material, sir. It simply means . . ."

"I don't want to *hear*, Lieutenant," said Hickman, heading back to his desk, adding under his breath. "Do you know how much you bastards cost me for the two divorces?"

"I beg your pardon, sir?"

"Never mind. I want that flag released. I brought Fitz on board here. I gave him his striper and the son of a bitch lied to me. He not only *lied*, he did it ten thousand miles away – lying about where he was when he knew he shouldn't be there without my authorization! He *knew* it! . . . Do you have any objections, Lieutenant? Something you can put into a sentence or two that won't require my bringing in three other legals to translate?"

Lieutenant Remington, one of the finest lawyers in the United States Navy, knew when to put the engines in reverse. Legal ethics had been violated by misinformation; the course was clear. Aggressive retreat with full boilers – or nuclear power, he supposed, although he did not really know. "I'll personally accelerate the vet-delay, Admiral. As the officer responsible for the secondary CLO statute, I'll make it clear that the direct order is now subject to immediate cancellation. No such order can or should originate under questionable circumstances. Legally . . ."

"*That* will be all, Lieutenant," said the Admiral, cutting off his subordinate and sitting down.

"Yes, sir."

"No, that *isn't* all!" continued Hickman, abruptly leaning forward. "How's that transcript released and how soon can you expect it?"

"With State's input it'll only be a matter of hours, sir, noon or shortly afterwards, I'd guess. A classified teletype will be sent to those requesting the flag. However, since SAND PAC has only placed a restriction and not a request . . ."

"*Request* it, Lieutenant. Bring it up to me the minute it gets here and don't leave the base until it does."

"Aye, aye, sir!"

The deep red Mercedes limousine weaved down the curving road inside the massive gates of Erich Leifhelm's estate. The late afternoon orange sun filtered diagonally through the tall trees, which not only bordered the road but were everywhere beyond on both sides. The drive might have been restful, even awesomely so – shafts of sunlight bursting down through immense, verdant foliage – except for a sight that made the whole scene grotesque. For racing alongside the car were at least half a dozen giant Dobermanns, not one of them making a sound. There was something unearthly about their running furiously in silence, black eyes flashing up at the windows, their jaws wide with rapid, erratic breathing, teeth bared, but no sound emerging from their throats. Somehow Converse knew that if he stepped out of the car without the proper commands being issued, the huge dogs would tear him to pieces.

It was true. The limousine pulled into a long circular drive that fronted wide brown marble steps leading to an arched doorway, the heavy panels in dark *bas relief* – a remnant of some ancient pillaged cathedral. Standing in the centre on the lower step was a man with a silver whistle raised to his lips. Again there was no sound, but suddenly the animals abandoned the car and ran to him, flanking him, facing forward on their haunches, jaws slack, bodies pulsating.

"Please wait, sir," said the chauffeur, in Germanic English, climbing out and running round to Joel's door. He opened it. "If you will step out, please, and take two paces away from the car. Only two paces, sir." The chauffeur now held in his hand a black object with a rounded metal tube extending from the front of the instrument, not unlike a miniaturized electric charcoal starter.

"What's that?" asked Converse, not kindly.

"Protection, sir. For you, sir. The dogs, sir. They are trained to sense heavy metal."

Joel stood there as the German moved the electronic detector over his clothes, including his shoes, his inner thighs and the back of his waist. "Do you people really think I'd come out here with a gun?"

"I do not think, sir. I do as I am told."

"How original," mumbled Converse, as he watched the man on the marble step raise the silver whistle again to his lips. As one, the phalanx of Dobermanns suddenly lurched forward. In panic, Joel grabbed the chauffeur, spinning the German in front of him. There was no resistance; the man simply turned his head and grinned as the dogs veered to the right and raced around the circular drive into the approach road cut out of the forest.

"Don't apologize, *Mein Herr*," said the chauffeur. "It happens often."

"I wasn't going to apologize," said Converse flatly, as he released the man. "I was going to break your neck." The German moved away as Joel remained motionless, stunned by his own words. He had not spoken words like that in over fifteen years. Before then, yes, but he tried never to remember.

"This way, sir," said the man on the steps, his accent oddly yet distinctly British.

Inside, the great hall was lined with medieval banners hanging down from an interior balcony. The hall led into an immense sitting room, the motif again medieval, made comfortable by soft leather, gaily fringed lamps and silver salvers everywhere on thin polished tables. It was also made ugly by the profusion of protruding animals' heads on the upper walls; large cats, elephants and boar looked down in defiant anger. It was a field marshal's lair.

But it was not the trimmings that absorbed him, it was the sight of the four men who stood beside four separate chairs facing him.

The next few seconds were like extended minutes, his mind racing as he defined them – two really. He knew Bertholdier and Leifhelm; they stood beside each other on the right. It was the two on the left he stared at. The medium-sized, stocky man with the fringe of close-cropped hair beneath a balding head and wearing a rumpled safari jacket, the ever-present boots beneath his khaki trousers, could be no one but Chaim Abrahms. His pouched, angry face with its slits of glaring eyes was the face of an avenger. The very tall man with the gaunt, aquiline features and the straight grey hair was General Jan van Headmer, the *Slayer of Soweto*. Joel had read the van Headmer dossier quickly: fortunately it was the briefest, the final summary saying it all.

In essence, van Headmer is a Capetown aristocrat, an Afrikaner who has never really accepted the British, say nothing of the tribal blacks. His convictions are rooted in a reality that for him is unshakable. His forebears carved out a savage land under savage conditions and at a great loss of life brutally taken by savages. His thinking is unalterably late nineteenth and early twentieth centuries. He will not accept the sociological and political inroads made by the more educated Bantu because he will never consider them anything more than bush primitives. When he orders austere deprivations and mass executions, he thinks he is dealing only with semi-verbalizing animals. It is this thinking that led him to be jailed along with Prime Ministers Verwoerd and Vorster during World War II. He concurred wholeheartedly with the Nazi concept of superior races. His close association with Chaim Abrahms is his single difference with the Nazis, and not a contradiction for him. The Sabras carved a land out of a primitive Palestine; they are one in that parallel history, and both take pride in their strength and respective accomplishments. Van Headmer, incidentally, is one of the most charming men one could meet. On the surface, he is cultured, extremely courteous and always willing to listen. Underneath he is an unfeeling killer and he is Delavane's key figure in South Africa with its vast resources.

"*Mein Haus ist dein Haus,*" said Leifhelm, walking towards Joel, his hand outstretched.

Converse stepped forward to accept the German's hand. Their hands clasped. "That was an odd greeting outside for such a warm sentiment," said Joel, releasing Leifheim's hand and immediately, abruptly, walking past the former field marshal to Bertholdier. "Good to see you again, General. My apologies for the unfortunate incident in Paris the other night. I don't mean to speak lightly of a man's life but in those few split seconds I didn't think he had much regard for mine."

Joel's boldness had the desired effect. Bertholdier stared at him, momentarily unsure of what to say. And Converse was aware that the other three men were watching him intently, without question struck by his audacity, both in manners and words.

"To be sure, Monsieur," said the Frenchman, pointlessly but with composure. "As you know, the man disregarded his orders."

"Really? I was told he misunderstood them."

"It is the same!"

The sharp, deep, heavily accented voice came from behind. Joel turned. "Is it?" he asked coldly.

"In the field, yes," said Chaim Abrahms. "Either one is an error, and errors are paid for with lives. The man paid with his."

"May I introduce General Abrahms?" broke in Leifhelm, touching Converse's elbow and leading him across the room. Hands were extended.

"General Abrahms, it's a privilege," said Joel sincerely. "Like everyone here, I've admired you tremendously, although perhaps your rhetoric has been excessive at times."

The Israeli's face reddened as soft, throated laughter crept quietly around the large room. Suddenly, van Headmer stepped forward, Converse's eyes drawn to his strong face, the brows frowning, his muscles taut.

"You are addressing one of my closest associates, sir," he said: the rebuke was unmistakable. Then he stopped, a thin smile creasing his gaunt, chiselled face. "And I could not have said it better myself. A pleasure to know you, young man."

The Afrikaner's hand was stretched out towards Joel, who accepted it as the laughter swelled.

"I am insulted!" cried Abrahms, his thick eyebrows raised, his head bobbing in mock despair. "By *talkers*, I'm insulted! Frankly, Mr Converse, they agree with you because none of them has had a woman in a quarter of a century. They may tell you otherwise – others may tell you otherwise – but believe me they hire whores to play cards with them or read stories into their old grey ears just to fool their friends!" The laughter grew louder and the Israeli, with an audience went on, leaning forward and pretending to speak *sotto voce* to Joel. "But, you see, *I* hire the whores to tell me the truth while I *shtup* them! They tell me these fancy talkers nod off by nine o'clock, whining for warm milk. With the *Ovaltine*, if it's possible.'

"My dear Sabra,' said Leifhelm, talking through his laughter. "You read your own romantic fiction too assiduously."

"You see what I mean, Converse?" asked Abrahms, palms extended, his thick neck and head shrugging. "You hear that? 'Assiduously'. Now you know why the Germans lost the war. They forever spoke so dramatically of the *Blitzkrieg* and the *Angriffe*, but actually they were talking – *assiduously* – about what to do next!"

"They should have given you a commission, Chaim," said Bertholdier, enjoying himself. "You could have changed your name, called Rommel and von Rundstedt Jews and taken over both fronts."

"The High Command could have done worse," agreed the Israeli.

"I wonder, though," continued the Frenchman, "if you would have stopped there? Hitler was a fine orator, as you are a fine orator. Perhaps you would have claimed he, too, was a Jew and moved into the Chancellery."

"Oh, I have it on good authority that he *was* a Jew. But from a *very* bad family. Even we have them: of course they're all from Europe."

The laughter grew again and then rapidly began to subside. Joel took the cue.

"Sometimes I speak too frankly, General," he said, addressing the Israeli. "I should learn better, but believe me no insult was intended. I have nothing but admiration for your stated positions, your policies."

"And that's precisely what, we shall discuss," said Erich Leifhelm, drawing everyone's attention. "Positions, policies, overall philosophy, if you will. We will stay as far away from specifics as we can, although a few will undoubtedly intrude. However, it is our approach to the larger abstractions that count. Come, Mr Converse, have a chair. Let us begin our conference, the first of many I trust."

Rear-Admiral Hickman put the transcript slowly down on his desk and looked aimlessly past his propped-up feet at the window and the ocean under a grey sky beyond. He crossed his arms, lowered his head and frowned, the combined gestures matching his thoughts. He was as bewildered now as he had been when he first read the transcript, as convinced now as he was then that Remington's conclusion was off the mark. But then the legal officer was too young to have any real knowledge of the events as they had actually happened: no one who had not been there could really understand. Too many others did: it was the reason for the flag, but it made no sense to apply that reasoning to this Converse eighteen years later. It was exhuming a corpse that had died from a fever, whether the shell of a man lived on or not. It had to be something else.

Hickman looked at his watch, unfolded his arms and removed his feet from the edge of the table. It was 3.10 in Norfolk; he reached for the telephone.

"Hello, Brian," said Rear-Admiral Scanlon of the Fifth Naval District. "I want you to know how much we appreciate SAND PAC's help in this thing."

"SAND PAC's?" asked Hickman, bemused that no credit was given to the State Department.

"All right, Admiral, *your* help. I owe you one, old Hicky."

"Start paying by dropping that name."

"Hey, come on, don't you remember the hockey games? You'd come racing up the ice and the whole cadet corps would shout: 'Here comes *Hicky!* Here comes *Hicky!* "

"May I unblock my ears now?"

"I'm just trying to thank you, pal."

"That's just it, I'm not sure for what? Have you read the transcript?"

"Naturally."

"What the hell's *there?*"

"Well," answered Scanlon tentatively. "I read it pretty quickly. It's been an awful day and frankly I just passed it on. What do *you* think is there? Between you and me, I'd like to know, because I barely had time to skim through it."

"What do I think is there? Absolutely *nothing*. Oh, sure we kept flags on stuff like that back then because the White House passed the order to put a lid on officially-recorded criticism and we all went along. Also we were pretty sick and tired of it ourselves. But there's nothing in that transcript that hasn't been heard before, or that has any value for anyone but military historians a hundred years from now as a very small footnote."

"Well . . ." repeated Scanlon, even more tentatively, "this Converse had some pretty harsh things to say about Command–Saigon."

"About *Mad Marcus?* Christ, I said worse during the Force-Tonkin conferences and *my* CO did me ten times better. We ferried in those kids up and down the coast when all they were ready for was a day at the beach with hot dogs and Ferris wheels . . . I don't get it. You and my legal zero in on the same thing, and I think it's old hat and discredited. Mad Marcys is a relic."

"Your who?"

"My legal exec. I told you about him, Remington."

"Oh, yes. The stickler-prick."

"He picked up on the Saigon thing, too. 'That's it,' he said. 'It's in those remarks. It's Delavane.' He wasn't around to know Delavane was fair game for every anti-war group in the country. Hell, *we* gave him the name 'Mad Marcus'. No, it's not Delavane, it's something else. Perhaps it's in those escapes, specifically Converse's last escape. Maybe there's some MIA input we don't know about."

"Well," repeated the Admiral in Norfolk for the third time, but now far less tentatively. "You may have something there but it doesn't concern us. Look, I'll be honest with you. I didn't want to say anything because I didn't want you to think you went to a lot of trouble for nothing, but the word I get is that the whole thing is a bust-negative."

"Oh?" said Hickman, suddenly listening very carefully. "How so?"

"It's the wrong man. Apparently an over-enthusiastic junior grade officer was doing some digging in the same time period, the same general circumstances. He saw the flag and drew six wrong conclusions. I hope he enjoys taking five a.m. muster."

"And that's it?" asked SAND PAC's admiral, controlling his astonishment.

"That's the feedback we get here. Whatever your CLO had in mind hasn't anything to do with our people."

Hickman could not believe what he was hearing. Of course Scanlon had not mentioned the State Department's efforts. He knew nothing about them! He was quickly putting as much distance between himself and the Converse flag as he could, lying because he had not been told. State was working quietly – probably through Cons Op – and Scanlon had no reason to think "old Hicky" knew a damn thing about Bonn or Converse or Connal Fitzpatrick's whereabouts. Or about a man named Preston Halliday who had been murdered in Geneva. What was *happening*? He would not find out from Scanlon. Nor did he care to.

"To hell with it then. My CLO will be back in three or four days and maybe I'll learn something."

"Whatever it is, it's back in your sandbox, Admiral. My people had the wrong man."

"Your people couldn't navigate a row boat in the DC Reflecting Pool."

"Can't blame you for that, Hicky."

Hickman hung up the phone and resumed his standard position when in thought, gazing beyond his propped-up shoes to the window and the ocean beyond. The sun was trying to break through the overcast without much success.

He had never liked Scanlon for reasons too petty to examine. Except one: he knew Scanlon was a liar. What he had not known was that he was such a stupid liar.

Lieutenant David Remington was flattered by the call. The well-known four-striper had invited him to lunch, not only invited him but had apologized for the lateness of the invitation and told him that it was perfectly understandable if it was not convenient. Further the captain wanted him to know that the call was of a personal nature, having nothing to do with naval business. The high-ranking officer, although a resident of La Jolla, was in port for only a few days and needed legal advice. He had been told that Lieutenant Remington was just about the best lawyer in the United States Navy. Would the lieutenant accept?

Of course Remington had made it perfectly clear that whatever advice he might offer would be offered on the basis of *amicus-curiae*; no remuneration could possibly be considered as that would be a violation of Statute . . .

"May I buy you lunch, Lieutenant, or do we have to split the cheque?" the four-striper had asked, somewhat impatiently, thought Remington.

The restaurant was high in the hills above La Jolla, an out-of-the-way roadside inn that apparently catered to diners of the area and those from San Diego and University City who did not care to be seen together in the usual places. Remington had not been too pleased: he would have preferred being seen at the Coronado with the captain than travelling ten miles north so as not to be seen in the hills of La Jolla. Nevertheless, the four-striper had been politely adamant: it was where he wanted to meet. David had checked him out. The much-decorated captain was not only in line for promotion, but was considered a potential candidate for the Joint Chiefs of Staff. Remington would have ridden a bicycle on the exposed Alaskan pipeline to keep the appointment.

Which was exactly what he thought he was doing, as he spun the steering wheel right, then left, then right and right again as he made his way up the steep narrow roads. It was important to keep in mind, he thought, as he whipped the car to the left, that *personal* advice was nevertheless *professional* advice, and *without* payment of any sort whatsoever constituted a *debt* that would one day be acknowledged. And if a man was elevated to the Joint Chiefs ... Remington could not help it. In a glow of self-importance he had let it drop to a fellow legal officer – the one who had coined the name "stickler-prick" – that he was lunching with a highly-regarded four-striper in La Jolla and might be late returning to the office. Then to drive his point home, he asked his associate for directions.

Oh, my *God!* What *was* it!? Oh, my *God!*

In the apex of the hairpin curve was an enormous black rig, thirty feet in length, and out of control. It weaved right and left on the narrow incline, its speed gathering with every fool, measured in racing yards, a black behemoth swerving, crashing down on everything in front of it, a wild beast gone mad!

Remington whipped his head to his right as he spun the wheel to avoid impact. There were only thin trunks of young trees and saplings in late summer bloom; beneath was a floral abyss. These were the last images he saw as the car careened on its side and began to plunge.

Far above on another hill, a man knelt, binoculars in his hands, raised to his face as the explosion below confirmed the kill. His expression was neither one of joy nor sadness, merely acceptance. A mission had been accomplished. After all, it was war.

And Lieutenant David Remington, whose life was so ordered and orderly, who knew exactly where and how he was going in this world, who knew above all that he would never be trapped by the forces that had killed his father in the name of corporate policy, was put to death by the policy of a company he had never heard of. An enterprise called Aquitaine. He had seen the name, Delavane.

Their view is that it's the proper evolution of current history, all other ideologies having failed ... The words spoken by Preston Halliday in Geneva kept repeating themselves in Converse's inner ear as he listened to the four voices of Aquitaine. The frightening thing was that they believed those words without equivocation, morally and intellectually, their convictions rooted in observations going back decades, their arguments persuasive, illuminating past global mistakes of judgment that resulted in horrible suffering and unnecessary loss of life.

The simple objective of their coming together – allies and former enemies alike – was to bring benevolent order to a world in chaos, to permit the industrial states to flourish, their economies strong for the benefit of all people, spreading the strengths and benefits of multinational trade to the impoverished, uncommitted Third World and by so doing secure its commitment. Only in this way, in this coming together, could the tide of Communism be stopped – stopped and reversed until its systems collapsed under the sheer force of superior armed might and financial resources.

To bring all this about required a shift of values and priorities. Industrial decisions everywhere must be coordinated to bring about the total strength of the free states. Government treasuries, multinational corporations and giant conglomerates must look to a stratum of interlocking committees, agree to be directed by these committees, to accept their decisions – which would in effect be their respective governments' decisions, each keeping the others apprised of its current agenda. What was this stratum of ultimate negotiators? Who comprised these committees which would in effect speak for the free nations and set their policies?

Throughout history only one class of people remained constant in its excellence, who when called upon in times of crisis performed far beyond human expectations – even in defeat. The reasons for their segment's unique contributions in war and, unfortunately, less so in peace, were historically clear: They were selfless. They belonged to a class that was trained to serve without thought of reward except *by* excellence. Wealth was irrelevant because their needs were furnished and prerequisites granted only through the outstanding performance of duty. This class of people was not subject to the corruption of the market place. In reality it was unusually equipped to deal with such corruption for it could not be touched by them. The mere presence of any excessive benefactions within its ranks would instantly be recognized and condemned, resulting in courts-martial. This class of society, this novel branch of the human race was not only incorruptible at the highest levels, it was the ultimate saviour of mankind as we know it today.

It was the military. The world over, even encompassing one's enemies. Together – even as enemies – they best understood the catastrophic results of weakness.

To be sure, certain minor liberties would perforce have to be withheld from the body politic but these were small sacrifices for survival. Who could argue?

None of the four spokesmen for Aquitaine raised his voice. They were the quiet prophets of reason, each with his own history, his own identity . . . allies and enemies together in a world gone mad.

Converse replied in the affirmative to everything that was said – it was not difficult to do so – and asked abstract questions of philosophy – as he was expected to ask. Even the court jester, Chaim Abrahms, became deeply serious and answered quietly.

"You think we Jews are the only ones in the Diaspora, my friend? You are wrong. The whole human race is dispersed everywhere, all of us locking rams' horns and not knowing where to go. Certain rabbis claim we Jews shall not see salvation until the Messianic era, the time of divine redemption when a god will appear to show us the way to our own promised land. He was far too late arriving: we could not wait for Him any longer. We created Israel. Do you see the lesson? We – we *here* – are now the divine intervention on earth. And I – even *I*, a man of accomplishment and ego – will give up my life in silence so we may succeed."

Jacques Louis Bertholdier. "You must understand, Mr Converse, that Rousseau said it best in his *Essay on Human Understanding*. Essentially he wrote that man attained his highest freedom only when he understood the parameters of his behaviour. We will establish those parameters. Is anything more logical?"

Erich Leifhelm. "Goethe said it perhaps better when he insisted that the *Romantik* of politics was best used to numb and quell the fears of the uninformed. In his definitive *Aus Meinem Leben* he states clearly that all governing classes must be imbued above all with discipline. Where is it more prevalent?"

Jan van Headmer. "My own country, sir, is the living embodiment of the lesson. We took the beast out of the savage and formed a vast, productive nation. The beast returns and my nation is in turmoil."

And so it went for several hours. Quiet dissertations delivered thoughtfully, reflectively, passions apparent only in the deep sincerity of their convictions. Twice Joel was pressed to reveal the name of his client and twice he demurred, stating the legal position of confidentiality – which could change in a matter of days, perhaps less.

"I'd have to offer my client something concrete. An approach, a strategy that would warrant his immediate involvement, his commitment, if you will."

"Why is that necessary at this juncture?" asked Bertholdier. "You've heard our reasoning. Certainly an approach can be discerned."

"All right, scratch approach. A strategy then. Not the 'why' but the 'how'."

"You ask for a plan?" asked Abrahms. "On what basis?"

"Because you'll be asking for an investment surpassing anything in our experience."

"That's an extraordinary statement," interjected van Headmer.

"He has extraordinary resources," replied Converse.

"Very well," said Leifhelm, glancing at each of his associates before he continued. Joel understood; permission was being sought based on prior discussions. It was granted. "What would you say to the compromising of certain powerful individuals in specific governments?"

"Blackmail?" asked Joel. "Extortion? It wouldn't work. There are too many checks and balances. A man's threatened, the threat's discovered and he's out anyway. Then the purification rites set in and where there was one weakness, suddenly there's a great deal of strength."

"That's an extremely narrow interpretation," said Bertholdier.

"You do not take into consideration the time element!" cried Abrahms defiantly, for the first time raising his voice. "*Accumulation*, Converse! Rapid *acceleration!*"

Suddenly Joel was aware that the three other men were looking at the Israeli, but not simply watching him. Within each composed pair of eyes was a glare, a warning. Abrahms shrugged. "It's merely a point."

"Well taken," said Converse, without emphasis.

"I'm not even sure it applies," added the Israeli, compounding his error.

"Well, *I'm* sure it's time for dinner," said Leifhelm, unobtrusively removing his hand from the side of his chair. "I've boasted so about my table to our guest that I admit to a shortness of breath – concern, of course. I trust the chef has upheld my honour." As if answering a signal – which Joel knew was the case – the British manservant appeared beneath an archway at the far end of the room. "I am clairvoyant!" Leifhelm rose. "Come, come, my friends. Saddle-of-lamb *cicatrisé*, a dish created by the gods for themselves and stolen by the irrepressible thief who rules my kitchen."

The dinner was, indeed, superb, each dish an isolated effort into which had gone great concentration, both in taste and setting. Converse was more gourmand than gourmet, his culinary education having been force-fed in expensive restaurants where his mind was only mildly distracted by the food, but he knew when a dish was the best in its class. There was nothing second-rate about Leifhelm's table, including the table itself, an enormous solid mass of mahogany perched on two huge, delicately carved tripods that swept out, legs surging for their grips on the intricate parquet floor in the high-ceilinged room with oils of hunting scenes on the deep red velour walls. Low candelabra were placed in front of the silver-mirrored placemats, but the flames of the candles did not obstruct one's view of another person, a feat Joel wished could be mastered by most of the hostesses in New York, London and Geneva.

The talk veered away from the serious topics explored in the sitting room. It was as if a recess had been called, a diversion to ease the burdens of statesmanship and replenish the reservoirs of thought. If that was the aim, it was eminently successful, and it was the Afrikaner, van Headmer, who led the way. In his soft-spoken, charming way (the dossier had been accurate; the "unfeeling killer" *was* charming) he described a safari he had taken Chaim Abrahms on in the Veldt.

"Do you realize, gentlemen, that I bought this poor Hebrew his first jacket at Safarics' in Johannesburg and there's never been a day I haven't regretted it. It's become our great general's trademark! Of course, you know why he wears it. It absorbs perspiration and requires very little washing, simply large applications of bay rum. This *is* a different jacket, isn't it, great general?"

"Bleach, *bleach*, I tell my wife!" replied the Sabra court jester, grimacing. "It takes out the smell of the godless slave traders!"

"Talking of slaves, let me tell you," said the Afrikaner, warming to his story with a glass of wine, changed with each new course.

The story of Chaim Abrahms' first and only safari was worthy of good vaudeville. Apparently the Israeli had been stalking a male lion for hours with his gun bearer, a Bantu he constantly abused, not realizing the black understood and spoke English as well as he. Abrahms had zeroed-in each of his four rifles prior to the hunt, but whenever he had the lion in his sights, he missed. This supposedly superb marksman, this celebrated general with the rifle-eye of the

217

hawk, could not hit eight feet of flesh a hundred yards away. At the end of the day, an exhausted Chaim Abrahms bribed the gun bearer, using broken English and a multiplicity of hand gestures, not to tell the rest of the safari of his misses. The hunter and the Bantu returned to camp, the hunter crying the woes of non-existent cats and stupid gun bearers. The native had gone to van Headmer's tent and as the Afrikaner told it in perfectly mimicked Bantu English, said the following.

"I liked the lion more than the Jew, sir. I altered his sights, sir, but apparently I will be forgiven my indiscretion, sir. Among other enticements, he has offered to have me *bar mitzvahed*."

The diners collapsed in laughter, Abrahms to his credit loudest of all. Obviously he had heard the story before and relished the telling. It occurred to Joel that only the most secure could hear such telling tales of themselves and respond with genuine laughter. The Israeli was a rock in the firmament of his convictions and could easily tolerate a laugh at himself. That, too, was frightening.

The British servant intruded, walking silently on the hard wood floor and spoke into Erich Leifhelm's ear.

"Forgive me, please," said the German, rising to take the call. "A nervous broker in Munich who consistently picks up rumours from Riyadh. A sheik goes to the toilet and he hears thunder from the east."

The ebullient conversation went on without a break in the flow, the three men of Aquitaine behaving like old comrades sincerely trying to make a stranger feel welcome. This appearance, too, was frightening. Where were the fanatics who wanted to destroy governments, ruthlessly grabbing controls and shackling whole societies, channelling "body-politics" into their vision of the military state? These were men of intellect. They spoke of Rousseau and Goethe, and had compassion for suffering and pain and unnecessary loss of life. They had humour and could laugh at themselves, and talk quietly of sacrificing their own lives for the betterment of a world gone mad. Joel understood. These were persuaders assuming the mantles of statesmen. What had Leifhelm said, quoting Goethe? "The romance of politics was best used to numb and quell the fears of the uninformed."

Frightening.

Leifhelm returned, followed by the British servant carrying two open bottles of wine. If the call from Munich brought unfavourable news, the German gave no indication of it. His spirits were as before, his waxen smile at the ready and his enthusiasm for the next course unbridled. "And now, my friends, the lamb *cicatrisé* – medallions of ambrosia and, hyperbole aside, actually rather good. Also, in honour of our guest we have a bonus this evening. My astute English friend and companion was in Siegburg the other day and ran across several bottles of Östreicher Lenchen Beerenauslese, 'Seventy-one. What could be a more fitting tribute?"

The men of Aquitaine glanced at one another, then Bertholdier spoke. "Certainly a find, Erich. It's one of the more acceptable German varieties."

"The 'Eight-two Klausberg Riesling in Johannesburg promises to be among the finest in years," said van Headmer.

"I doubt it will rival the Richon Zion Carmel," added the Israeli.

"You are all impossible!"

A be-hatted chef rolled in a silver service trolley, uncovered the saddle of lamb and, under appreciative looks, proceeded to carve and serve. The Englishman presented the various side dishes to each diner, then poured the wine.

Erich Leifhelm raised his glass, the flickering light of the candles reflecting off the carved crystal and the edges of the silver-mirrored placemats. "To our guest and his unknown client both of whom we trust will soon be in our fold."

Converse nodded his head and drank.

He took the glass from his lips and suddenly was aware of the four men of Aquitaine. They were staring at him, their own glasses firmly on the table. None had drunk the wine.

Leifhelm spoke again, his voice nasal, cold, a fury held in check by an intellect in control.

" 'General Delavane was the enemy, *our* enemy! Men like that can't be allowed any more, can't you understand!' Those were the words, were they not, Mr Converse?"

"*What?*" Joel heard his voice but was not sure it was his. The flames of the candles suddenly erupted; fire filled his eyes and the burning in his throat became an unbearable pain. He grabbed his neck as he struggled out of the chair, hurling it back, hearing the crash, yet not hearing it, hearing only a succession of echoes. He was falling, layers of black earth passed his eyes broken by flashes of lightning. The pain surged into his stomach; it was intolerable; he clutched his groin trying to force the pain back up and out of his body. Then he felt his own movement on a hard surface and somehow knew he was writhing wildly on the floor, held in check by overpowering arms.

"The gun. Step back. Hold him." The voice, too, was a series of echoes, sharply enunciated in a searing British accent. "Now. *Fire!*"

An explosion blew up the universe. The rest was silence.

16

The telephone rang, jolting Connal Fitzpatrick out of a deep sleep. He had fallen back on the couch, the van Headmer dossier in his hand, both feet still angled on the floor. Shaking his head and rapidly blinking and widening his eyes, he tried to orient himself. Where *was* he? What *time* was it? The phone rang again, now a prolonged, shattering bell. He lurched off the couch, his legs unsteady, his breathing erratic – his exhaustion too complete to shake off in a few seconds. He had not really slept since California; his body and mind could barely function. He grabbed the phone, nearly dropping it as he momentarily lost his balance.

"Yes . . . *hello!*"

"Commander Fitzpatrick, if you please," said a male voice in a clipped British accent.

"This is he."

"Philip Dunstone here, Commander. I'm calling for Mr Converse. He wanted me to tell you that the conference is going extremely well, far better than he thought possible."

"You're *who?*"

"Dunstone Major Philip Dunstone. I'm senior aide to General Berkeley-Greene."

"Berkeley-Greene . . . ?"

"Yes, Commander. Mr Converse said to tell you that along with the others he's decided to accept General Leifhelm's hospitality for the night. He'll be in touch with you first thing in the morning."

"Let me talk to him. Now."

"I'm afraid that's not possible. They've all gone out on the motor launch for a spin down river. Frankly, they're a secretive lot, aren't they? Actually, I'm not permitted to attend their discussions any more than you are."

"I'm not settling for this, Major!"

"Really, Commander, I'm simply relaying a message . . . Oh yes, Mr Converse did mention that if you were concerned I should also tell you that, if the admiral called, you were to thank him and give him his regards."

Fitzpatrick stared at the wall. Converse would not bring up the Hickman business unless he was sending a message. The request made no sense to anyone but the two of them. Everything *was* all right. Also there could be several reasons why Joel didn't care to talk directly on the phone. Among them, thought Connal resentfully, was probably the fact that he didn't trust his "aide" to say the proper words in the event their conversation was being overheard.

"All right, Major . . . what was the name again? Dunstone?"

"That's right, Philip Dunstone. Senior aide to General Berkeley-Greene."

"Leave word for Mr Converse that I'll expect to hear from him by eight o'clock."

"Isn't that a little harsh, old boy? It's nearly two A.M. now. The breakfast buffet usually starts about nine-thirty out here."

"Nine o'clock then," said Fitzpatrick firmly.

"I'll tell him myself, Commander. Oh, one final thing. Mr Converse asked me to apologize for his not having reached you by midnight. They've really been at it hammers and tongs in there."

That was it, thought Connal. Everything was under control. Joel certainly would not have made that remark otherwise. "Thanks, Major, and by the way I'm sorry I was rude. I was asleep and tried to get it together too fast."

"Lucky chap. You can head back to the pillows while I stand watch. Next time you can take my place."

"If the food's good, you're on."

"It's not, really. A lot of pansy cooking, to tell you the truth. Good night, Commander."

"Good night, Major."

Relieved, Fitzpatrick hung up the phone. He looked over at the couch, thinking briefly of going back to the dossiers but decided against it. He felt hollow all over, hollow legs, hollow chest, a hollow ache in his head. He needed sleep badly.

He gathered up the papers and took them into Converse's room, placing them in the attaché case, locking it and turning the combination tumblers. Gripping the handle he went back into the sitting room, checked the door, turned off the lights and headed for his own bedroom. He threw the case on the bed and removed his shoes, then his trousers, but that was as far as he got. He collapsed on the pillows, somehow managing to wrap part of the bedspread around him. The darkness was welcome.

"*That* was hardly necessary," said Erich Leifhelm to the Englishman, as the latter replaced the phone. " 'Pansy cooking' is not the way I would describe my table."

"He undoubtedly would," said the man who had called himself Philip Dunstone. "Let's check the patient."

The two walked out of the library and down the hall to a bedroom. Inside were the three other men of Aquitaine along with a fourth, his black bag and the exposed hypodermic needles denoting a physician. Below on the bed was Joel Converse, his eyes wide and glass-like, saliva oozing from the sides of his mouth, his head moving back and forth as if in a trance, unintelligible sounds emerging from his lips. The doctor glanced up and spoke.

"There's nothing more he can give us because there *is* nothing more," said the physician. "The chemicals don't lie. Quite simply, he's a blind sent out by men in Washington but he has no idea who they are. He didn't even know they existed until this naval officer convinced him they had to exist. His only referrals were Anstett and Beale."

"Both dead," interrupted van Headmer. "Anstett is public and I can vouch for Beale. My employee on Santorini flew into Mykonos and confirmed the kill. There can be no trace, incidentally. The Greek is back on the chalk cliffs selling laces and inflated whisky in his *taverna*."

"Prepare him for his odyssey," said Chaim Abrahms, looking down at Converse. "As our specialist in the Mossad put it so clearly, distance is now the necessary requirement. A vast separation between this American and those who would send him out."

Fitzpatrick stirred, the bright morning sunlight from the windows piercing the darkness – expanding shades of white forcing his eyelids open. He stretched, his shoulder digging into a hard corner of the attaché case, the rest of him constricted by the bedspread which was tangled about his legs. He kicked it off and flung his arms on both sides of the bed, breathing deeply, feeling the relaxed swelling of his chest. He swung his left hand above his head, twisted his wrist and looked at his watch. It was 9.20; he had slept for seven and a half hours, but the uninterrupted sleep seemed much longer. He got out of bed and took several steps; his balance was steady, his mind clearing. He looked at his watch again, remembering. The major named Dunstone had said breakfast at Leifhelm's estate was served from 9.30 on, and if the conference had moved to a boat on the river at 2.00 A.M. Converse probably would not call before ten o'clock.

Connal walked into the bathroom; there was a phone on the wall by the toilet if he was wrong about the call. A shave followed by a hot and cold shower and he would be fully himself again.

Eighteen minutes later Fitzpatrick walked back into the bedroom, a towel around his waist, his skin still smarting from the harsh sprays of water. He crossed to his open suitcase on a luggage rack next to the closet where he had hung his clothes. He took out his miniaturized radio, placed it on the bureau and deciding against the Armed Forces band, dialled into what was left of a German newscast. There were the usual threats of strikes in the industrial south, as well as charges and counter charges hurled around the Bundestag, but nothing earthshaking. He selected comfortable clothes – lightweight slacks, an oxford blue shirt and his cord jacket. He got dressed and walked out into the sitting room, heading for the phone; he would call room service for a small breakfast and a great deal of coffee.

He stopped. Something was Wrong. What was it? The pillows on the couch were still rumpled, a glass half filled with stale whisky still on the coffee table, as were pencils and a blank telephone message pad. The balcony doors were closed, the curtains drawn, and across the room the silver ice bucket remained in the centre of the silver tray on the antique hunt table. Everything was as he had last seen it, yet there was something . . . The *door!* The door to Converse's bedroom was shut. Had he closed it? No, he had *not!*

He walked rapidly over, twisted the knob and pushed the door open. He studied the room, conscious of the fact that he had stopped breathing. It was immaculate, cleaned and smoothed to a fare-thee-well, no indication whatsoever that it was occupied. The suitcase was gone, the few articles Converse had left on the bureau no longer there. Connal rushed to the closet, yanking it open. It was empty. He went into the bathroom; it was spotless, new soap in the receptacles, the glasses wrapped in clinging paper ready for incoming guests. He walked out of the bathroom stunned. There was not the slightest sign that anyone except a maid had been in that bedroom for days.

Fitzpatrick ran out to the sitting room and the telephone. Seconds later the manager was on the line; it was the same man Connal had spoken with yesterday.

"Yes, indeed, your businessman was even more eccentric than you described, Commander. He checked out at three-thirty this morning, paying all the bills, incidentally."

"He was *here?*"

"Of course."

"You *saw* him?"

"Not personally. I don't come on duty until eight o'clock. He spoke with the night manager and settled your account before going up to pack."

"How could your man know it was *him?* He never saw him before!"

"Really, Commander, he identified himself as your associate and paid the bill. He also had his key; he left it at the desk."

Fitzpatrick paused, astonished, then spoke harshly. "The room was cleaned! Was that also done at three-thirty this morning?"

"No, *Mein Herr*, at seven o'clock. By the first housekeeping shift."

"But not the outer room?"

"The commotion might have disturbed you. Frankly, Commander, that suite must be prepared for an early afternoon arrival. I'm sure the staff felt it would not bother you if they got a head start on the task. Obviously it did not."

"Early afternoon . . . ? *I'm* here!"

"And welcome to stay until twelve noon; the bill has been paid. Your friend has departed and the suite has been reserved."

"And I don't suppose you have another room."

"I'm afraid there's nothing available, Commander."

Connal slammed down the phone. *Really, Commander* . . . Those same words had been spoken by another over the same telephone at two o'clock in the morning. There were three directories in a wicker rack by the table; he pulled out the one for Bonn and found the number.

"*Guten Morgen. Hier bei General Leifhelm.*"

"*Herrn Major Dunstone, bitte.*"

"*Wen?*"

"Dunstone," said Fitzpatrick, then continuing in German. "He's a guest. Philip Dunstone. He's the senior aide to . . . to a General Berkeley-Greene. They're English."

"English? There are no Englishmen here, sir. There's no one here – that is to say there are no guests."

"He was there last night! They both were. I *spoke* with Major Dunstone."

"The General had a small dinner party for a few friends, but no English people, sir."

"Look, I'm trying to reach a man named Converse."

"Oh, yes, Mr Converse. *He* was here, sir."

"Was?"

"I believe he left . . ."

"Where's *Leifhelm?*" shouted Connal.

There was a pause before the German replied coldly. "Who should I say is calling *General* Leifhelm?"

"Fitzpatrick. Lieutenant-Commander Fitzpatrick!"

"I believe he's in the dining room. If you'll stay on the telephone." The line was put on hold, the dead, suspended silence unnerving. Finally there was a click and Leifhelm's voice reverberated over the phone.

"Good morning, Commander. Bonn has provided a lovely day, no? The seven hills are as clear as in a picture postcard. I believe you can see them . . ."

"Where's Converse?" interrupted the Navy lawyer.

"I would assume at *Das Rektorat* . . ."

"He was supposed to be staying at your place."

"No such arrangements were made. They were neither requested nor offered. He left rather late, but he did leave, Commander. My car drove him back."

"That's not what I was told! A Major Dunstone called me around two this morning . . ."

"I believe Mr Converse left shortly before then . . . *Who* did you say called?"

"Dunstone. A Major Philip Dunstone. He's English. He said he was the senior aide to General Berkeley-Greene."

"I don't know this Major Dunstone; there was no such person here. However, I'm familiar with just about every general in the British Army and I've never heard of anyone named Berkeley-Greene."

"Stow it, Leifhelm!"

"I beg your pardon."

"I *spoke to* Dunstone! He . . . he said the right words. He said Converse was staying at your place – with the *others!*"

"I think you should have spoken directly with Herr Converse, because there was no Major Dunstone or General Berkeley-Greene at my home last night. Perhaps you should check with the British Embassy, certainly they'd know if these people were in Bonn. Perhaps you heard the words incorrectly: perhaps they met later at a café."

"I *couldn't* speak to him! Dunstone said you were out on the river in a boat." Fitzpatrick's breath was now coming in short gasps.

"Now that's ridiculous, Commander. It's true I keep a small launch for guests, but it's a well-known fact that I am not partial to the water." The General paused, adding with a short laugh. "The great field marshal gets seasick in a flat boat six feet from shore."

"You're *lying!*"

"I resent that, sir. Especially about the water. I never feared the Russian Front, only the Black Sea. And if we had invaded England, I assure you I would have crossed the Channel in a plane." The German was toying: he was enjoying himself.

"You know exactly what I mean!" Again Connal shouted. "They said Converse checked out of here at three-thirty this morning! I say he never came *back!*"

"And I say this conversation is pointless. If you are truly alarmed, call me back when you can be civil. I have friends in the *Staats Polizei.*" Again a click; the German had hung up.

As Fitzpatrick replaced the phone, another thought suddenly struck him, frightening him. He walked quickly into the bedroom, his eyes instantly zeroing in on the attaché case. It was half under the pillow; oh *God*, he had been in such a sound sleep! He went to the bed, yanked the case out and examined it. Breathing again, he saw that it was the same case, the combination locks secure, no amount of pressure on the small brass buttons would release the plates. He lifted the case up and shook it; the weight and the sounds were proof that the papers were inside and intact, proof also that Converse had not returned to the inn and checked out. All other considerations aside and regardless of whatever emergencies that might have arisen, he never would have left without the dossiers and the list of names.

Connal carried the case back into the sitting room, trying to collect his thoughts, putting them in numerical sequence so as to impose some kind of order. *A.* He had to assume the flag on Joel's service record had been lifted or the damaging information unearthed in some other way and that Converse was now being held by Leifhelm and the contingent from Aquitaine that had flown in from Paris, Tel Aviv and Johannesberg. *B.* They would not kill him until they had used every means possible to find out what he knew – which was far less than they imagined and could take several days. *C.* The Leifhelm estate, according to his dossier, was a fortress, thus the chances of going in and bringing Converse out were nil. *D.* Fitzpatrick knew he could not appeal to the American Embassy. To begin with Walter Peregrine would place him under territory-arrest and those doing the arresting might put a bullet in his head. One had tried. *E.* He could not risk seeking help from Hickman in San Diego, which under different circumstances might be a logical course of action. Everything in the admiral's make-up ruled out any connection with Aquitaine; he was a fiercely independent officer whose conversations were laced with scepticism about the Pentagon's policies and mentality. But if that flag had been officially released – whether with his consent or over his objections – Hickman would have no choice but to call him back to the base for a full inquiry. Any contact at all could result in the immediate cancellation of his leave, but if there was no contact and no way to reach him the order could not be given.

Connal sat down on the couch, the attaché case at his feet, and picked up a pencil; he wrote out two words on the telephone message pad: *Call Meagen.* He would tell his sister to say that after Press's funeral he had left for parts unknown without explanation. It was consistent with what he had said to the admiral, that he was taking his information to "the authorities" investigating Preston Halliday's death.

F. He could go to the Bonn police and tell them the truth. He had every reason to believe that an American colleague was being held against his will inside the gates of General Erich Leifhelm's estate. Then, of course, the inevitable question would arise: Why didn't the Lieutenant-Commander contact the American Embassy? The unspoken was just below the surface: Regardless of one's opinion General Leifhelm was a prominent figure and such a serious charge should have diplomatic support. The embassy again. Strike out. Then again if Leifhelm said he had "friends" in the *Staats Polizei*, he probably owned key men in the Bonn Police. If he was alarmed Converse could be moved. Or killed. *G.* . . . was insane, thought the Navy lawyer as a legal phrase crept slowly into his consciousness, suddenly taking on a blurred viability. *Trade off.* It was a daily occurrence in pre-trial examinations, both civilian and military. *We'll drop this if you accept that. We'll stay out of this area if you stay out of that one.* Standard practice. Trade off. Was it possible? Could it even be considered? It was crazy and it was desperate, but then nothing was sane, nothing sanguine. Since force was out of the question . . . could an exchange be made? Leifhelm for Converse. A general for a lieutenant.

Connal did not dare analyse; there were too many negatives. He had to act on instinct because there was nothing else left, nowhere he could turn that did not

225

lead to a blank wall or a bullet. He got up from the couch and went to the table with the telephone, sitting down in the chair and reached for the directory on the floor. What he had in mind was insane but he could not think about that. He found the name. *Fishbein, Ilse.* The illegitimate daughter of Hermann Goering.

The rendezvous was set: a back table at the Hansa-Keller café on the Kaiserplatz, the reservation in the name of Parnell. Fitzpatrick had had the presence of mind in California to pack a conservative civilian suit; he wore it now as the American attorney, Mr Parnell, who was fluent in German and sent by his firm in Milwaukee, Wisconsin, to make contact with one Ilse Fishbein in Bonn, West Germany. He also had the presence of mind in Bonn, West Germany, to have managed a single room at the Schlosspark on the Venusbergweg and he had placed Converse's attaché case where it was safe for a considerable length of time, a trail left for Converse should everything blow apart. A trail he would recognize.

Connal arrived ten minutes early, not merely to secure the table but to familiarize himself with the surroundings and silently practise his approach within them. He had done the same thing many times before, walking into military courtrooms before a trial, testing the chairs, the height of the tables, the scan of vision of the tribunal on the dais. It all helped.

He knew it was she when the woman arrived and spoke to the *maître* at his lectern. She was tall and full-formed, not obese but fleshed out, statuesque in a way, conscious of her mature sensuality, but smart enough not to parade it. She was dressed in a light grey summer suit, the jacket buttoned above her generous breasts, a wide white collar demurely angled over the fabric. Her face too was full but not soft, the cheekbones high, lending an appearance of character that might not otherwise have been there; her hair was dark and shoulder length, with slight streaks of early grey. She was escorted to the table by the head waiter. Fitzpatrick rose as she approached.

"*Guten Tag, Frau Fishbein,*" he said, extending his hand. "*Bitte, setzen Sie sich.*"

"It's not necessary for you to speak German, Herr Parnell," said the woman, releasing his hand and sliding into the chair under the guidance of the waiter who bowed and left. "I make my living as a translator."

"Whatever you feel most comfortable with," said Connal.

"I think under the circumstances I should prefer English, and spoken softly, if you please. Now what is this incredible thing you alluded to over the telephone, Mr Parnell?"

"Quite simply an inheritance, Mrs Fishbein," replied Fitzpatrick, his expression sincere, his eyes steady. "If a few technical questions can be settled, and I'm sure they can be, as a rightful legatee you will receive a substantial sum of money."

"From someone in America I never knew?"

"He . . . knew your father."

"I did not," said Ilse Fishbein quickly, her eyes darting about at the adjacent tables. "Who is this man?"

"He was a member of your father's staff during the war," answered Connal, lowering his voice still further. "With your father's help – certain contacts in Holland – he got out of Germany before the Nuremberg trials with a great deal of money. He came to the United States by way of London, his funds intact, and started a business in the Midwest. It became enormously successful. He died recently, leaving sealed instructions with my firm, his attorneys."

"But why me?"

"A debt. Without your father's influence and assistance our client would probably have withered for years in jail instead of flourishing as he did in America. As far as anyone was concerned he was a Dutch immigrant from the Netherlands whose family business was destroyed in the war and who sought his future in America. That future included considerable real estate holdings and a very successful meat packing plant – all in the process of being sold. Your inheritance is in excess of two million American dollars. Would you care for an aperitif, Mrs Fishbein?"

The woman could not at first reply. Her eyes had grown wide, her full jaw slackened, her stare trance-like. "I believe I will, Herr Parnell," she said in a monotone, finding her voice. "A large whisky, if you please."

Fitzpatrick signalled the waiter, ordered drinks and tried several times to make idle conversation, commenting on the beautiful weather and asking what sites he should see while in Bonn. It was no use. Ilse Fishbein was as close to being in a catatonic state as Connal could imagine. She had gripped his wrist, clutching it in silence with extremely strong fingers, her lips parted, her eyes two blank glass agates. The drinks came, the waiter left, and still she would not let go of him. Instead, she drank somewhat awkwardly, lifting the glass with her left hand.

"What are these questions to be settled, *Mein Herr?* Ask anything, *demand* anything. Do you have a place to stay? Things are so crowded in Bonn."

"You're very kind; yes, I do. Try to understand, Mrs Fishbein, this is an extremely sensitive matter for my firm. As you can well imagine it's not the sort of legal work American attorneys are too happy with, and frankly had our client not made certain provisos connecting the successful completion of this aspect of his last will and testament to the full execution of other aspects we might have . . ."

"The questions! What are the *questions?*"

Fitzpatrick paused before answering, the thoughtful lawyer permitting the interruption but still intent on making his point. "Everything will be handled confidentially, the probate court operating *in camera* . . ."

"With *photographs?*"

"In private, Mrs Fishbein. For the good of the community, in exchange for specific state and local taxes which might not be paid in the event of confiscation. You see, the higher courts might decide the entire estate is open to question."

"Yes, the questions! What *are* they?"

"Really quite simple. I've prepared certain statements which you will sign and to which I can swear to your signature. They establish your bloodline. Then there is a short deposition required substantiating the claim. We need only one but it must be given by a former high-ranking member of the German forces, preferably a man whose name is recognizable, whom the recent history books or war accounts establish as a working colleague of your natural father. Of course, it would be advantageous to have someone known to the American military in the event the judge decides to call the Pentagon and ask 'who is this fellow?' "

"I know the man!" whispered Ilse Fishbein. "He was a Field Marshal, a brilliant *General!*"

"Who is he?" asked the Navy lawyer, then instantly shrugging, dispensing with the question of identity as irrelevant. "Never mind. Just tell me why you think he's the right man, this field marshal."

"He is greatly respected, although not everyone agrees with him. He was one of the *grossmächtigen* young commanders, once decorated by my father himself for his brilliance!"

"But would anyone in the American military establishment know him?"

"*Mein Gott!* He worked for the Allies in Berlin and Vienna after the war!"

"Yes?"

"And at SHAPE Headquarters in Brussels!"

Yes, thought Connal, we're talking about the same man. "Fine," he said, casually but seriously. "Don't bother giving me his name. It doesn't matter and I probably wouldn't know it anyway. Can you reach him quickly?"

"In minutes! He's here in Bonn."

"Splendid. I should catch the plane back to Milwaukee by tomorrow noon."

"You will come to his house and he will dictate what you need to his secretary."

"I'm sorry I can't do that. The deposition must be countersigned by a notary. I understand you have the same rules over here – and why not, you invented them – and the Schlosspark Hotel has both typing and notary services. Say this evening, or perhaps early in the morning? I should be more than happy to send a taxi for your friend. I don't want this to cost him a *Pfennig.* Any expenses he incurs my firm will be happy to repay."

Ilse Fishbein giggled – a silent, hysterical giggle, but a giggle never the less. "You do not know my friend, *Mein Herr.*"

"I'm sure we'll get along. Now how about lunch?"

"I have to go to the toilet," said the German woman, her eyes glass agates again. As she rose, Connal rising with her, her whisper could be heard. "*Mein Gott! Zwei Millionen Dollar!*"

"He does not even care to know your *name!*" cried Ilse Fishbein into the phone. "He's from a place called Milwaukee, Wisconsin, and is offering me *two million dollars American!*"

"He did not even ask who I was?"

"He said it didn't matter! He probably wouldn't know you, in any event. Can you imagine? He offered to send a taxi for you! He said you should not spend a penny!"

"It's true Goering was excessively generous during the last weeks," mused

228

Leifhelm. "Of course he was more often drugged than not, and those who supplied him with narcotics which were difficult to obtain were rewarded with the whereabouts of priceless art treasures. The one who later smuggled him the poisoned suppositories still lives like a Roman emperor in Luxembourg."

"So you see, it's true! Goering *did* these things!"

"Rarely knowing what he was doing, however," agreed the general reluctantly. "This is really most unusual and very inconvenient, Ilse. Did this man show you any documents, any proof of his assignment?"

"*Naturally!*" lied Fishbein close to panic, picking remembered words out of the air. "There was a formal page of legal statements and a . . . *deposition* – all to be handled by the courts confidentially! In *private!* You see there is a question of taxes which would not be paid if the estate was confiscated . . ."

"I've heard it all before, Ilse," Leifhelm broke in wearily. "There are no statutes for so-called war criminals and expatriated funds. So the hypocrites choke on their hypocritical rules the instant they cost money."

"You are always so perceptive, my general, and I have always been so loyal. I've never refused you a single request whether it was professional in nature or far more intimate. *Please*. Two million American! It will take but ten or fifteen minutes!"

"You've been like a good niece, I can't deny it, Ilse. And there is no way anyone could know about you in other matters . . . Very well, this evening then. I'm dining at the Steigenberger at nine o'clock. I'll stop at the Schlosspark at eight-fifteen or thereabouts. You can buy me a gift with your – shall we say, ill-conceived new riches."

"I'll meet you in the lobby."

"My driver will accompany me."

"*Ach*, bring twenty men!"

"He's worth twenty-five," Leifhelm said.

Fitzpatrick sat in the chair in the small conference room on the first floor of the hotel and examined the gun, the manual of instructions on his lap. He tried to match what the clerk had told him to the diagrams and words below his eyes, satisfied that he knew enough. There were basic similarities to the standard Navy issue Colt .45, the only handgun he was familiar with, and the technical information was extraneous to his needs. The weapon he had purchased was a *Heckler und Koch PGS auto pistol*, about six inches long, its calibre nine millimetres, and with a nine-shell magazine clip. The instructions emphasized such points as "polygonal rifling" and "sliding roller lock functions'; he let the manual slip to the floor, and practised removing the clip and slapping it back into place. He could load the weapon, aim it and fire it; those movements were all that was necessary and he trusted the last would *not* be necessary.

He glanced at his watch; it was almost eight o'clock. He shoved the automatic into his belt, reached down for the instructions and stood up, looking around the room, mentally checking off the movements and the locations he had designed for himself. As he expected, the Fishbein woman had told him Leifhelm would be accompanied by someone, a "driver" in this case, and it could be assumed the man had other functions. If so, he would have no chance to practise them.

The room – one of twenty-odd conference rooms in the hotel and which he had reserved under the name of a fictitious company – was not large but there were structural arrangements that could be put to advantage. The usual rectangular table was in the centre, three chairs on each side and two at the ends, one with a telephone. There were additional chairs against the walls for stenographers and observers – all this was normal. However, in the centre of the left wall was a doorway that led to a very small room apparently used for private conversations. Inside was another telephone which when off the hook caused a button on the first telephone on the conference table to light up; confidentiality had its limits in Bonn. Further, the hallway door opened into a short foyer, thus prohibiting those entering from scanning the room while standing in the corridor.

Connal folded the Heckler and Koch instructions, put them in his jacket pocket, and walked over to the table surveying his set pieces. He had gone to an office supply store and purchased the appropriate items. On the far end of the table by the telephone – which was placed parallel to the edge, the buttons in clear view – were several file folders next to an open brief case (from a distance its dark plastic looked like expensive leather). Scattered about were papers, pencils and a yellow legal pad, the top pages looped over. The setting was familiar to anyone who had ever kept an appointment with an attorney, said learned counsel having put his astute observations down on paper prior to the conference.

Fitzpatrick retraced his steps to the chair, moved it forward several feet, and crossed to the door of the small side room. He had turned on the lights – two table lamps flanking a short couch; now he went to the nearest with the telephone and turned it off. He then walked back to the open door and stood between it and the wall, peering through the narrow vertical space broken up by upper and lower hinges. He had a clear view of the foyer's entrance; three people would pass into the conference room and he would come out.

There was a knock on the hallway door, the rapid, impatient tapping of an heiress unable to control herself. He had told the Fishbein woman the location of the room, but nothing else. No name or number and, in her anxiety, she had not asked about either. Fitzpatrick took the necessary steps to the telephone table in the small room; he lifted the phone out of its cradle and placed it on its side. He returned to his position behind the door, angling himself so as to look through the crack, his body in the shadows. He took the pistol from his belt, held it in front of his mouth and shouted loud enough to be heard outside in the hotel corridor, but pleasantly, not angrily.

"*Bitte, kommen Sie herein! Die Tür ist offen. Ich telefoniere gerade.*"

The sound of the door as it opened preceded Ilse Fishbein as she walked rapidly into the room, her eyes directed at the conference table. She was followed by Erich Leifhelm, who glanced about then turned slightly, nodding his head. A third man in the uniform of a chauffeur came into view, his hand in the pocket of his black jacket. Connal then heard the second sound he needed to hear. The hallway door was slammed shut.

230

The Navy lawyer yanked back the small door and quickly stepped around it, the gun extended, aimed directly at the chauffeur.

"*You!*" he cried in German. "Take your hand out of your pocket! *Slowly!*" The woman gasped, then began the start of a scream. Fitzpatrick interrupted harshly. "Be *quiet!* As your friend will tell you, I haven't anything to lose. I can kill the three of you and be out of the country in an hour, leaving the police to look for a Mr Parnell who doesn't exist."

The chauffeur, the muscles of his jaw rippling, removed his hand from his pocket, his fingers rigid. Leifhelm stared in anger and fear at Connal's gun, his face no longer ashen but flushed.

"You *dare* . . . ?"

"I dare, Field Marshal," said Fitzpatrick. "Just as you dared forty years ago to rape a young kid and make damned sure that she and her whole family never walked out of the camps. You bet your ass I dare and, if I were you, I wouldn't give me the slightest cause to be any angrier than I am." Connal spoke to the woman. "*You.* Inside that briefcase on the table are eight strands of rope. Start with the driver. Bind his hands and feet, I'll tell you how. Now! *Quickly!*"

Four minutes later the chauffeur and Leifhelm sat in two conference chairs, their ankles and wrists bound, the driver's weapon removed from his pocket. The Navy lawyer checked the ropes, the knots having been tied under his instructions. Everything was secure; the more one writhed the tighter the knots would become. Fitzpatrick ordered the panicked Fishbein woman into a third chair; he lashed her hands to the arms and her feet to the legs.

Rising, Connal picked up the automatic from the table and approached Leifhelm who was sitting in the chair next to the lighted telephone. "Now," he said, the gun pointed at the German's head. "As soon as I hang up the phone in the other room we're going to make a call from here." The Navy lawyer walked quickly into the small side room, hung up the telephone, and returned. He sat down next to the bound Leifhelm and took a scrap of paper out of the open briefcase. On it was written the phone number of the general's estate on the Rhine beyond Bad Godesberg.

"What do you think you'll accomplish?" asked Leifhelm.

"Trade off," replied Fitzpatrick, the barrel of the gun, pressed against the German's temple. "You for Converse."

"*Mein Gott!*" whispered Ilse Fishbein, petrified, as the chauffeur winced, his hands straining against the ropes which were now biting into the flesh of his wrists.

"You believe anyone will listen to you, much less carry out our orders?"

"They will if they want to see you alive again. You know I'm right, General. This gun isn't so loud, I made sure of that. I can turn on the radio and kill you and be on a plane out of Germany before you're found. This room is reserved for the night with instructions that we're not to be disturbed for any reason whatsoever."

Connal shifted the weapon to his left hand, picked up the telephone, and dialled the number written on the scrap of paper.

"*Guten Tag. Hier bei General Leifhelm.*"

"Put someone in authority on this phone," said the Navy lawyer in perfect high-German. "I have a gun less than a foot away from General Leifhelm's head and I'll kill him right now unless you do as I say."

There were muffled shouts over the line while a hand was held against the mouthpiece. In seconds a crisp British accent was speaking slowly, deliberately in English.

"Who is this and what do you want?"

"Well, what do you know? This sounds like Major Philip Dunstone – that *was* the name, wasn't it? You don't sound half so friendly as you did last night."

"Don't do anything rash, Commander. You'll regret it."

"And don't you do anything stupid or Leifhelm will regret it sooner – that is until he can't regret anything any longer. You've got one hour to get Converse to the airport and inside the Lufthansa security gate. He has a reservation on the ten o'clock flight to Washington, DC, by way of Frankfurt. I've made arrangements. I'll be calling a number in a room where he'll be taken and I'll expect to talk with him. After I do, I'll leave here and call you on another phone, telling you where your employer is. Just get Converse to that security gate. One hour, Major!" Fitzpatrick shoved the phone in front of Leifhelm's face, and once again pressed the barrel of the gun into the German's temple.

"Do as he says," said the General, choking on the words.

The minutes went by slowly, stretching into a quarter of an hour, then thirty, the silence finally broken by Leifhelm.

"So you found her," he said, gesturing his head at Ilse Fishbein, who trembled as tears of fear and gargantuan loss streaked down her full-blown cheeks.

"Just as we found out about Munich forty years ago, and a hell of a lot of other things. You're all on your way to that great big war room in the sky, Field Marshal, so don't worry about whether I'll go back on my word to your English butler, I wouldn't miss seeing you bastards paraded for everyone to see what you really are. People like you give the military everywhere a goddamned rotten name."

There was a slight commotion from the hallway beyond the door. Connal looked up, raising the gun and holding it directly a Leifhelm's head.

"*Was ist?*" said the German, shrugging.

"*Keine Bewegung!*"

From beyond the door the strains of a melody filled the hotel corridor sung by several male voices more off key than on. Another conference in one of the other rooms had broken up, obviously as much due to the intake of alcohol as from the completion of a business agenda. Raucous laughter pierced a refrain as unsuccessful harmony was attempted. Fitzpatrick relaxed, lowering the automatic; no one on the outside knew the name or number of the room.

"You say men like me give your profession – which is my profession as well – a seriously bad name," said Leifhelm. "Has it occurred to you, Commander, that we might elevate that profession to one of indispensable greatness in a world that needs us badly?"

"Needs us?" asked Connal. "We need the world first and not your kind of world. You tried it once and blew it, don't you remember?"

"That was one nation led by a madman trying to impose his imprimatur over the globe. This is many nations with one class of self-abnegating professionals coming together for the good of all."

"Whose definition? Yours? You're a funny fellow, General Municher. Somehow I question your benevolent tendencies."

"Indiscretions of a deprived youth whose name and rightful opportunities were stolen from him should not be held against the man a half century later."

"Deprived or depraved? I think you made up for lost time pretty quickly, and as brutally as you could. I don't like your remedies."

"You have no vision."

"Thanks be to Jesus, Mary and Joseph it's not yours." The singing out in the corridor faded briefly, then swelled again, the harmony and the volume more discordant and louder than before. "Maybe that's some of your old Dachau playboys having a beer bust."

Leifhelm shrugged.

Suddenly, shatteringly, the door burst open, crashing into the wall as three men raced in, spits filling the air as silenced guns fired, hands jerking back and forth, the surface of the table chewed up, splinters of wood flying everywhere. Fitzpatrick felt the searing repetitions of pain in his arm as the automatic was blown out of his grip. He looked down and saw the blood rising to the surface, drenching the fabric of his right sleeve. In his shock he winced, glancing to his left. Ilse Fishbein was dead, her bleeding skull shattered by a fusillade of bullets; the chauffeur was smiling obscenely.

The door was closed as if nothing had happened, the last moments a faded, unremembered incident. Leifhelm spoke.

"*Stümper*," he said, as one of the invaders cut the ropes around his wrists. "I used that term only yesterday, Commander, but I did not know how right I was. Did you think a single telephone call could not be traced to a single room? . . . It was all too coincidentally symmetrical. Converse is ours and suddenly this poor whore comes into immense riches – *American* riches. I grant you it was entirely possible – such bequests are made frequently by sausage-soaked idiots who don't realize the harm they do – but the timing was too perfect, too . . . amateurish."

"You're one son of a bitch." Connal briefly closed his eyes, trying to force the pain out of his mind, unable to move his fingers.

"Why, Commander," said the general getting out of the chair, "do I sense the bravado of fear? Do you think I'm going to have you killed?"

"You sense it. I won't give you any more than that."

"You're quite wrong. Considering the nature of your military leave, you can be of minor but unique service to us. One more statistic to disrupt a pattern. You'll be our guest, Commander, but not in Germany proper. You are going on a trip."

17

Converse opened his eyes, dead, flat iron weighed on his lids, nausea in his throat, blurred darkness everywhere. And there was a terrible stinging at his side – on his arm – flesh separated from flesh, stretched and inflamed. Blindly he tried to touch the offending spot, but gasped, pulling back in pain. Then somewhere light was creeping around the dark space above him, picking its way through moving obstructions, peering into the shadows. Objects slowly came into focus – the metal rim of the cot-like bed next to his face, two wooden chairs opposite each other at a small table in the distance, a door also in the distance, but farther away and shut ... then another door, this one open, a white basin with a pair of dull taps on the left in a far away cubicle. The light? It was still moving, now dancing, flickering. Where was it?

He found it; he found them. High in the wall on either side of the closed door were two rectangular windows, the short curtains billowing in the breezes. The windows were open, but oddly not open, not clear, the spaces interrupted. Joel raised his head, supporting himself on his forearm and squinted, trying to see more clearly. He focused on the interruptions behind the swelling curtains – thin black metal shafts vertically connecting the window frames. They were bars. He was in a cell.

He fell back on the bed, swallowing repeatedly to lessen the burning in his throat, and moving his arm in circles trying to lessen the pain of the ... wound? Yes, a wound, a gunshot! The realization jarred his memory: a dinner party had turned into a battleground filled with hysteria. Blinding lights and sudden jolts of pain were accompanied by low, strident voices bombarding him, incessant echoes pounding in his ears as he tried desperately to repel the piercing assaults. Then there were moments of peaceful calm, the drone of a single voice in the mists. Converse closed his eyes, pressing his lids tightly together with all his strength as another realization struck him and disturbed him deeply. That voice in the swirling mists was *his* voice; he had been drugged and he knew he had given up secrets.

He had been drugged before, a number of times in the North Vietnamese camps, and as always there was the sickening feeling of numbed outrage. His mind had been stripped and violated, his voice made to perform obscenities against the last vestiges of his will.

And, again as always, there was the empty hole in his stomach, a vacuum that ran deep and produced only weakness. He felt starved and probably was. The chemicals usually induced vomiting, the linings of the intestines screaming for a coating of density that could not be found. It was strange, he reflected, opening his eyes and following the moving shafts of light, but those memories from years ago evoked the same protective instincts that had helped him then – so many years ago. He could not waste energy; he had to conserve what strength he had. Regain new strength. Otherwise there was nothing but the numbed outrage and neither his mind nor his body could do anything about it.

There was a sound across the room! Then another and another after that. The sliding, grating metal told him that a bolt was being released; the sharp sound of a key followed by the twisting of a knob meant that the door in the far distant wall was about to be opened. It was, and a wide, blinding burst of sunlight filled the room that was his cell. Converse shielded his eyes, peering between his fingers. The blurred, frazzled silhouette of a man stood in the doorframe carrying a flat object in his left hand, bracing it from beneath. The figure walked in and Joel, blinking, saw it was the chauffeur who had electronically searched him in the driveway.

The uniformed driver crossed to the table and deftly lowered the flat object; it was a tray, its contents covered by cloth. It was only then that Converse's attention was drawn back to the sunlit doorway. Outside, milling about in anxious contempt, was the pack of Dobermanns, their shining black eyes continuously shifting towards the door, their lips curled, teeth bared in unending quiet snarls.

"*Guten Morgen, Mein Herr,*" said Leifhelm's chauffeur, shifting instantly to English. "Another beautiful day on the northern Rhine, no?"

"It's bright out there, if that's what you mean," replied Joel, his hand still cupping his eyes. "I suppose I should be grateful to notice after last night."

"Last night?" The German paused, then added quietly, "It was two nights ago, Amerikaner. You've been here for the past thirty-three hours."

"*Thirty* ... ?" Converse pushed himself up and swung his legs over the side of the bed. He had to stop all motion; the dizziness was too much, too much strength had been drained. *Oh Christ! He remembered so clearly! Don't waste movement. They'll be back. The bastards!* "You bastards," he said out loud but without any real meaning. Then for the first time he realized he was shirtless, and noticed the bandage on his left arm between his elbow and his shoulder. It covered the gunshot wound. "Did somebody miss my head?" he asked.

"I'm told you inflicted the injury yourself. You tried to kill General Leifhelm, when the others took your gun away."

"I tried to kill ... ? With my non–existent gun? The one you made sure I didn't *have?*"

"You were too clever for me, *Mein Herr.*"

"What happens now?"

"Now? Now you eat. I have instructions from the doctor. You begin with the *Hafergrütze* ... how do you say? The porridge."

"Hot mush or cereal," completed Joel. "With skim or powdered milk. Then some kind of soft–boiled eggs taken with pills. And if it all goes down a little ground meat, and if *that* stays down a few spoonfuls of crushed turnips or potatoes or squash. Whatever's available."

"How do you know this?" asked the uniformed man, genuinely surprised.

"It's a basic diet," said Converse cynically. "Variations with the territory and the supplies. I once had some comparatively good meals ... You're planning to put me under again."

The German shrugged. "I do what I'm told. I bring you food. Here, let me help you."

Joel looked up as the chauffeur approached the bed. "Under other circumstances I'd spit in your goddamned face. But if I did I wouldn't have that slight, *slight* possibility of spitting in it some other time. You may help me. Be careful of my arm."

"You are a very strange man, *Mein Herr.*"

"And you're all perfectly normal citizens catching the early train to Larchmont so you can put down ten martinis before going to the PTA meeting."

"*Was?* I know of no such meeting."

"They're keeping it secret; they don't want you to know. If I were you, I'd get out of town before they make you president."

"*Mich? Präsident?*"

"Just help me to the chair, like a good ole' Aryan boy, will you?"

"Hah, you are being amusing, *ja?*"

"Probably not," said Converse easing into the wooden chair. "It's a terrible habit I wish I could break." He looked up at the bewildered German. "You see, I keep trying," he said in utter seriousness.

Three more days passed, his only visitor the chauffeur accompanied by the sullen, high-strung pack of Dobermanns. His well-searched suitcase was given to him, scissors and a nail file removed from the travelling kit – his electric razor intact. It was their way of telling him that his presence had been removed from Bonn, leaving to painful speculation the whereabouts and the life or death of Connal Fitzpatrick. Yet there was an inconsistency and as such the basis for hope. No allusions were made to his attaché case, either with visual evidence – the page of a dossier, perhaps – or through his brief exchanges with Leifhelm's driver. The generals of Aquitaine were men of immense egos; if they had those materials in their possession, they would let him know it.

As to his conversations with the chauffeur, they were limited to questions on his part and disciplined pleasantries on the German's part, no answers at all – at least none that made any sense.

How long is this going to go on? When am I going to see someone other than you?

There is no one here, sir, except the staff. General Leifhelm is away – in Essen, I believe. Our instructions are to feed you well and restore your health.

Incommunicado. He was in solitary.

But the food was not like that given to prisoners anywhere else. Roasts of beef and lamb, chops, poultry and fresh fish; vegetables that must have come directly from a nearby garden . . . and wine – which at first Joel was reluctant to drink – but when he did even he knew was superior.

On the second day, as much to keep from thinking as anything else, he had begun to perform mild exercises – as he had done so many years ago. By the third day he had actually worked up a sweat during a running-in-place session, a healthy sweat, telling him the drugs had left his body. The wound on his arm was still there but he thought about it less and less. Curiously, it was not serious.

On the fourth day questions and reflections were no longer good enough.

Confinement and the maddening frustration of having no answers forced him to turn elsewhere, to the practical, to the most necessary consideration facing him. Escape. Regardless of the outcome the attempt had to be made. Whatever plans Delavane and his disciples in Aquitaine had for him, they obviously included parading a drugless man – more than likely a dead man with no narcotics in his system. Otherwise they would have killed him at once, disposing of his body in any number of untraceable ways. He had done it before. Could he do it again?

He was not rotting in a rat-infested cell and there was no terrible gunfire in the distant darkness, but it was far more important that he succeed now than it ever was eighteen years ago. And there was an extraordinary irony: eighteen years ago he had wanted to break out and tell whomever would listen to him about a madman in Saigon who sent countless children to their deaths – and worse, to broken minds and hollow feelings that would follow them for the rest of their lives. Now he had to tell the world about that same madman.

He had to get out. He had to tell the world what he knew. He had to escape!

Converse stood on the wooden chair, the short curtain pulled back, and peered through the black metal bars outside. His cabin, or cottage, or jailhouse, whatever it was, seemed to have been lowered from above into a cleared-out patch of the forest. There was a wall of tall trees and thick foliage as far as he could see in either direction, a dirt path angling to the right beneath the window. The clearing itself extended no more than twenty feet in front of the structure before the dense greenery began; he presumed it was the same on all sides – as it was from the other window to the left of the door, except that there was no path below, only a short, coarse stubble of brown grass. The two front windows were the only views he had. The rest of this isolated jailhouse consisted of unbroken walls, a small ceiling vent in the bathroom, but no other openings.

All he could be certain of, since the chauffeur and the dogs and the warm meals indicated he was still within the grounds of Leifhelm's estate, was that the river could not be far away. He could not see it but it was there and it gave him hope – more than hope, a sense of morbid exhilaration rooted in his memory. Once before the waters of a river had been his friend, his guide, ultimately the lifeline that had taken him through the worst of his journey. A tributary of the Huong Khe south of Duc Tho had rushed him silently at night under bridges and by patrols and past the encampments of three battalions. The waters of the Rhine, like the currents of the Huong Khe years ago, were his way out.

The multiple sounds of animal feet clawing the earth preceded the streaking dark coats of the Dobermanns as they raced below the window, instantly stopping and crowding angrily in front of the door. The chauffeur was on his way with a breakfast no prisoner in isolation should expect. Joel climbed off the chair and quickly carried it back to the table, setting it in place and going to his bed. He sat down, kicked off his shoes, and lay back on the pillow, his legs stretched out over the rumpled blanket.

The bolt was slid back, the key inserted and the heavy knob turned; the door opened. As he did every time he entered, the German pushed the centre of the door with his right hand as he supported the tray with his left. However, this morning he was gripping a bulging object in his right hand, the blinding sunlight obscuring it for Converse. The man walked in and, more awkwardly than usual, placed the tray on the table.

"I have a pleasant surprise for you, *Mein Herr*. I spoke with General Leifhelm on the telephone last night and he asked about you. I told him you were recovering splendidly and that I had changed the bandage on your unfortunate injury. Then it occurred to him that you had nothing to read and he was very upset. So an hour ago I drove into Bonn and purchased three days of the *International Herald Tribune*." The driver placed the rolled-up newspapers next to the tray on the table.

But it was not the issues of the *Herald Tribune* that Joel stared at. It was the German's neck and the upper outside pocket of his uniform jacket. For looped around that neck and angled over to that pocket was a thin silver chain, the top of a tubular silver whistle protruding, clearly visible against the dark fabric. Converse shifted his eyes to the door; the huge Dobermanns were sitting on their haunches, each breathing breathlessly, salivating, but reasonably quiet, for all intents and purposes immobile. Converse remembered his arrival at the general's monumental lair, and the strange Englishman who had controlled the dogs with a silver whistle.

"Tell Leifhelm I appreciate the reading material but I'd be even more grateful if I could get out of this place for a few minutes."

"*Ja*, with a plane ticket to the beaches in the south of France, *nein?*"

"For Christ's sake, just to take a walk and stretch my legs! What's the matter? Can't you and that drooling band of mastiffs handle one unarmed man getting a little air? . . . No, you're probably too frightened to try." Joel paused, then added in an insulting mock-German accent. " 'I do vot I am tolt'."

The driver's smile faded. "The other evening you said you would not apologize but instead break my neck. That was a joke, *Mein Herr*. Do you understand? A joke I find so amusing I can laugh at it."

"Hey, come on," said Converse, changing his tone as he swung his legs off the bed and sat up. "You're ten years younger than I am and twenty times stronger. I felt insulted and reacted stupidly, but if you think I'd raise a hand against you you're out of your mind. I'm sorry. You've been decent to me and I was stupid again."

"*Ja*, you were stupid," said the German without rancour. "But also you were right. I do as I am told. And why not? It is a privilege to take orders from General Leifhelm. He has been *gut* to me."

"Have you been with him long?"

"Since Brussels. I was a sergeant in the Federal Republic's border patrols. He heard about my problem and took an interest in my case. I was transferred to the Brabant garrison and made his chauffeur."

"What was your problem? I'm a lawyer, you know."

"The charge was that I strangled a man. With my arm."

"Did you?"

"*Ja*. He was trying to put a knife in my stomach – and lower. He said I took advantage of his daughter. I took no advantage; it was not necessary. She was a whore – it was in the clothes she wore, the way she walked – *es ist klar!* The father was a pig."

Joel looked at the man, at the clouded malevolence in his eyes. "I can understand General Leifhelm's sympathies," he said.

"Now you know why I do as I am told."

"Clearly."

"He is calling for his messages at noon. I shall ask him about your walking. You understand that one word from me and the Dobermanns will rip your body from its bones."

"Nice puppies," said Converse, addressing the pack of dogs outside.

Noon came and the privilege was granted. The walk was to take place after lunch, when the driver returned to remove the tray. He returned and after several severe warnings Joel ventured outside, the Dobermanns crowding around him, black nostrils flared, white teeth glistening, bluish-red tongues flattened out in anticipation. Converse looked around; for the first time he saw that the small house was made of thick, solid stone. The unique squad began its constitutional up the path, Joel growing bolder as the dogs lost a degree of interest in him under the harsh admonitions of the German's commands. They began racing ahead and regrouping in circles, snapping at one another, but always whipping their huge heads back or across at their master and his prisoner. Converse walked faster.

"I used to jog a lot back home," he lied.

"*Was ist?* 'Jog?' "

"Run. It's good for the circulation."

"You run now, *Mein Herr*, you will have no *Zirkulation*. The Dobermanns will see to it."

"I've heard of people getting coronaries from jogging, too," said Joel, slowing down, but not reducing the speed with which his eyes darted in all directions. The sun was directly overhead; it was no help in determining direction.

The dirt path was like a marked single line in an intricate network of hidden trails. It was bordered by thick foliage, more often than not roofed by low-hanging branches, then breaking open into short stretches of wild grass that might or might not lead to other paths. They reached a fork, the leg to the right curving sharply into a tunnel of greenery. The dogs instinctively raced into it, stopped by the chauffeur who shouted commands in German. The Dobermanns spun around, bouncing off each other, and returned to the fork, then raced into the wider path on the left. It was an incline and they started up a steep hill, the trees shorter and less full, the bramble bushes wilder, coarser, lower to the ground. Wind, thought Converse. A valley wind; a wind whipping up from a trough, a long narrow slice in the earth, the kind of wind a pilot of a small plane avoided at the first sign of weather. A river.

It was there. To his left; they were travelling east. The Rhine was below, perhaps a mile beyond the lower line of tall trees. He had seen enough. He began breathing audibly. The exhilaration inside him was intense; he could have walked for miles. He was back on the banks of the Huong Khe, the dark watery lifeline that would take him away from the Mekong cages and the cells and the chemicals. He had done it before; he *was* going to do it again!

"Okay, Field Marshal," he said to Leifhelm's driver, looking at the silver whistle in the German's pocket. "I'm not in as good shape as I thought I was. This is a mountain! Don't you have any flat pastures or grazing fields?"

"I do as I am told, *Mein Herr*," replied the man grinning. "Those are nearer the main *Haus*. This is where you must walk."

"This is where I say thank you and no thank you. Take me back to my little grass shack and I'll play you a simple tune."

"*Wie bitte?*"

"I'm bushed and I haven't finished the newspapers. Seriously, I want to thank you. I really needed the air."

"*Sehr gut*. You are a pleasant fellow."

"You have no idea, good ole Aryan boy."

"*Ach*, so amusing. *Der Jude ist in Israel, nicht wahr?* Better than in Germany, *Mein Herr.*"

"Nate Simon would love you. He'd take your case for nothing just to blow it . . . No, he wouldn't. He'd probably give you the best defence you ever had."

Converse stood on the wooden chair under the window to the left of the door. All he had to hear and see was the sound and the sight of the dogs; after that he had twenty or thirty seconds. The taps in the bathroom were turned on, the door open; there was sufficient time to run across the room, flush the toilet, close the door and return to the chair. But he would not be standing on it. Instead, it would be gripped in his hands, laterally. The sun was descending rapidly; in an hour it would be dark. Darkness had been his friend before – years ago – as the waters of a river had been his friend – years ago. They had to be his friends again. They *had* to be!

The sounds came first – racing paws and nasal explosions – then the sight of gleaming dark coats of animal fur rushing in circles in front of the jailhouse. Joel ran to the bathroom, concentrating on the instants as he waited for the sliding of the bolt. It came and he flushed the toilet, pivoting in the small space, closing the bathroom door, and racing back to the chair. He raised it and stood in place, his legs and feet locked to the floor. The door was opened several inches – only seconds now – then the German's right hand pushed it back.

"Herr Converse? *Wo ist . . . ? Ach, die Toilette.*"

The chauffeur walked in with the tray, and Joel swung the chair with all his strength into the German's head. The driver arched back off his feet, tray and dishes crashing to the floor. He was stunned, nothing more. Converse kicked the door shut and brought the heavy chair repeatedly down on the chauffeur's skull until the man went limp, blood and saliva pouring down his eyes and face.

The phalanx of dogs had lurched as one at the suddenly closed door, the roars of fury and protest and clawing, scratching feet-on-wood, the sounds of maniacal behemoths.

Joel grabbed the silver chain, slipped it over the unconscious German's head, and pulled the silver whistle out of the pocket. There were four tiny holes on the tube: each meant something. He pulled the remaining chair to the window at the right of the door, climbed up and put the whistle to his lips. He covered the first hole and blew into the mouthpiece. There was no sound but it made no difference.

The Dobermanns went mad! They began to attack the door in suicidal assaults. He removed his finger, placed it over the second hole and blew.

The dogs were confused; they circled around each other, snapping, yelping, snarling, but still they would not take their concentration off the door. He tried the third tiny hole and blew into the whistle with all the breath he had.

Suddenly, the dogs stopped all movement, their tapered, close-cropped ears upright, shifting – they were waiting for a second signal. He blew again, again with all the breath that was in him. It was the second they were waiting for, and again, as one, the pack raced to the right beneath the window, pounding to some other place where they were meant to be by command.

Converse leaped down from the chair and knelt by the unconscious German. He went rapidly through the driver's pockets, taking his billfold and all the money he had, as well as his wristwatch . . . and his gun. For an instant Joel looked at the weapon, loathing the memories it evoked. He shoved it under his belt and went to the door.

Outside, he pulled the heavy door shut, heard the click of the lock and slid the bolt in place. He ran up the dirt path estimating the distance to the fork where the right leg was *verboten* and the left led to the steep hill and the sight of the Rhine below. It was actually no more than two hundred yards away, but the winding curves and the thick bordering foliage made it seem longer. If he remembered accurately – and on the walk back he had been like a pilot without instruments relying on sightings – there was a flat stretch of about eighty feet below the fork.

He reached it, the same flat area, the same diverging paths up ahead. He ran faster.

Voices! Angry, questioning? Not far away and coming nearer! He dived into the brush to his right, rolling over the needle-like bushes until he could barely see through the foliage. Two men walked rapidly into his limited view, talking loudly, as if arguing but somehow not with each other.

"*Was haben die Hunde?*"

"*Die sollten bei Heinrich sein!*"

Joel had no idea what they were saying; he only knew that as they passed him that they were heading for the isolated cabin. He also knew that they would not spend much time trying to raise anyone inside before they took more direct methods. And once they did all the alarms in Leifhelm's fortress would be activated. Time was measured for him in minutes and he had a great deal of ground to cover. He crept cautiously out of the brush on his hands and feet. The Germans were out of sight, beyond a rounding curve. He got up and raced for the fork and the steep hill to the left.

The three guards at the immense iron gate that was the entrance to Leifhelm's estate were bewildered. The pack of Dobermanns were circling around impatiently in the rough grass, obviously confused.

"*Was haben die Hunde denn?*" asked one man.

"*Ich verstehe das nicht,*" replied a second.

"*Heinrich hat sie losgelassen, aber warum?*" said the third.

"*Das werden wir schon noch hören,*" muttered the first guard, shrugging. "*Sonst rufen wir in ein paar Minuten an.*"

"*Mir gefällt das nicht!*" shouted the second guard. "*Ich rufe jetzt an!*"

The first guard walked into the gate house and picked up the telephone.

Converse ran up the steep hill, his breath short, his lips dry, his heartbeat thundering in his chest. There it was! He had a clear line of sight, pilotage confirmed! He could take the equipment that was his body into the huge watery airstrip below, no contact with a tower necessary. He started running down, gathering speed, the wind sweeping his face, stinging in exhilaration. He *was* back! He was racing through the sudden, open clearings of another jungle, no fellow prisoners to worry about, only the numbed outrage within himself to prod him, to make him break through the barriers and somehow, somewhere strike back at those who had stripped him naked and raped an innocence and . . . *goddamn it* . . . turned him into an animal! A reasonably pleasant human being without hatred had been turned into a half-man with more hatreds than a person should live with. He would get back at them all, all enemies, all *animals!*

He reached the bottom of the open slope of gnarled grass and bush, the trees and intertwining underbrush once more a wall to be penetrated. But he had his bearings; no matter how dense the woods he simply had to keep the last rays of the sun on his left, heading due north, and he would reach the river.

Rapid explosions made him spin around. Five gunshots followed one upon the other in the distance. It was easy to imagine the target: a circle of wood around the cylinder of a lock in the door of an isolated cabin in the forest. His jailhouse was being assaulted, entrance gained. The minutes were growing shorter.

And then two distinctly different sounds pierced the twilight, interwoven in dissonance. The first was a series of short, staccato bursts of a high-pitched siren. The second, between and under the repeated blasts, was the hysterical yelping of running dogs. The alarms had been set off; scraps of discarded clothing and slept-on sheets would be pressed into inflamed nostrils and the Dobermanns would come after him, no quarter considered – no cornered prey – only animal teeth ripping human flesh a satisfactory reward.

Converse plunged into the wall of green and ran as fast as he could, dodging, crouching, lurching from one side to the other, his arms outstretched, his hands working furiously against the strong, supple impediment of the woods. His face and body were repeatedly whipped by slashing branches and obstinate limbs, his feet continuously tripped by fallen debris and exposed roots. He stumbled more than he could count, each time – each brief instant of surrounding silence – serving only to emphasize the sound of the dogs somewhere between the fork and the hill and the lower forest. They were no farther away, perhaps nearer. They *were* nearer! They had entered the woods, the echoes of their hysteria all around him, punctuated by howling yelps of animal frustration as one or another or several were caught in the tangled ground cover, straining and roaring maniacally to be free to pursue the hated object implanted in their nostrils.

The *water!* He could see the water through the trees! Sweat was now rolling down his face, the salt blinding his eyes, stinging the scrapes on his neck and chin, his shirt drenched, his hands bleeding from the sharp briars and the coarse bark everywhere.

He fell, his foot plunging into a hole burrowed by some river bank animal, his ankle twisted and in pain.

He got up, pulling at his leg, freeing his foot, and, limping badly, tried to resume running. The Dobermanns were gaining, the yelping and the harsh barking louder and more furious; they had picked up his direct scent, the trail of undried sweat maddening them, preparing them for the kill.

The river bank! It was filled with soft mud and floating debris, a webbing of nature's garbage caught in a cavity, whirling slowly, waiting for a strong current to pull it all away. Joel grabbed the handle of the chauffeur's gun, not to pull it out but to secure it as he limped down the bank, selecting the quickest way into the water.

He heard nothing until the last instant when the massive roar came out of the shadows and the huge body of an animal flew through the air over the river bank directly at him. The monstrous face of the dog was a contorted study in fury, the eyes on fire, the enormous jaws wide, all teeth and a gaping, shining black mouth. Converse fell to his knees as the Dobermann whipped past his right shoulder, ripping his shirt with its upper eye teeth and flipping over on its back in the mud. The momentary defeat was more than the animal could stand. It writhed furiously, rolling over, snarling, then literally raising itself on its hind legs, simultaneously lunging up from the mud for Joel's groin.

The gun was in his hand. Converse fired, blowing the top of the attack dog's head off, blood and tissue spraying the shadows. The slack, huge jaws fell into his crotch.

The rest of the pack was now racing towards the bank – ear-shattering crescendos of animal violence announcing its arrival. Joel threw himself into the water and swam as rapidly as he could away from the shoreline; the weapon was an impediment but he knew he could not let it go.

Years ago – centuries ago – he had desperately needed a weapon, knowing it could be the difference between survival and death, and for five days none could be had. But on that fifth day, he had found one on the banks of the Huong Khe. He had floated half under water past a squad on patrol, and found the point ten minutes later down river – too far from the scout's unit to be logical – a man perhaps thinking angry thoughts that made him walk faster, or bored with his job and wanting to find a few moments to be by himself and out of it all. Whichever, it made no difference to that soldier. Converse had killed him with a rock from the river and had taken his gun. He had fired that gun twice, twice saved his life before he reached an advance unit south of Phu Loc.

As he pushed against the shoreline currents of the Rhine, Joel suddenly remembered. This was the fifth day of his imprisonment in Leifhelm's compound, no jungle cell to be sure, but no less imprisonment. He had done it! And on the fifth day a weapon was his! There were omens wherever one wished to find them; he did not believe in omens but for the moment he accepted the possibility.

He was in the shadows of the river now, the surrounding mountains blocking the dying sun. He paddled in place and turned. Back on shore, at the cavity in the bank that had been his plank to the water, the dogs were circling in confused anger, snarling, yelping, as several ventured down to sniff their slain leader, each urinating as it did so – territory and status were being established. The beams of powerful flashlights suddenly broke through the trees. Converse swam farther out; he had survived searchlights in the Mekong. He had no fear of them now; he had been there – here – and he knew when he had won.

He let the outer currents carry him east along the river. Somewhere there would be other lights, lights that would lead him to shelter and a telephone. He had to get everything in place and build his brief quickly but he could do it. Yet the attorney in him told him that a man with a bandaged gunshot wound in soaked clothing and screaming a foreign language in the streets was no match for the disciples of George Marcus Delavane; they would find him. So it would have to be done another way – with whatever artifices he could muster. He had to get to a telephone. He had to place an overseas call. He could do it; he would do it! The Huong Khe faded; the Rhine was now his lifeline.

Swimming breaststroke, the gun still gripped in his hand, his arm smarting in the water, he saw the lights of a village in the distance.

18

Valerie frowned as she listened on the phone in her studio, the spiralling cord outstretched as she reached over and placed a brush in the track of her easel. Her eyes scanned the sunlit dunes outside the glass doors, her thoughts, however, were on the words she was hearing, words that implied things without saying them. "Larry, what's *wrong* with you?" she interrupted, unable to hold herself in check any longer. "Joel's not just an employee or a junior partner, he's your friend! You sound like you're trying to build a case against him. What's that term you all use? . . . Circumstantial, that's it. He was here, he was there; someone said this and somebody else said that."

"I'm trying to *understand*, Val," protested Talbot from his office in New York. "You've got to try to understand, too. There's a great deal I can't tell you because I've been instructed by people whose offices I have to respect to say very little or preferably nothing at all. I'm bending those instructions because Joel *is* my friend and I want to help."

"All right, let's go back," said Valerie. "What exactly were you leading up to?"

"I know it's none of my damned business and I wouldn't ask it if I didn't think I had to . . ."

"I'll accept that," agreed Val. "Now what is it?"

"Well, I know you and Joel had your problems," continued the senior partner of Talbot, Brooks and Simon, as though he were referring to an inconsequential spat between children. "But there are problems and there are problems."

"Larry," interrupted Val again. "There were problems. We're divorced. That means the problems were serious."

"Was physical abuse one of them?" asked Talbot quickly in a low voice, the words obviously repugnant to him.

Valerie was stunned; it was a question she would never have considered. "*What?*"

"You know what I mean. In fits of anger did he strike you? Cause you bodily harm?"

"You're not in a courtroom, and the answer is no, of course not. I might have welcomed it – at least the anger."

"I beg your pardon?"

"Nothing," said Valerie, recovering from her astonishment. "I don't know what prompted you to ask, but it couldn't be farther from the truth. Joel had far more effective ways to deflate my ego than hitting me. Among them, dear Larry, was his dedication to the career of one Joel Converse in Talbot, Brooks and Simon."

"I'm aware of that, my dear, and I'm sorry. Those complaints are perennial in the divorce courts and I'm not sure there's anything we can do about them – not in this day and age, perhaps not ever. But that's different. I'm talking about his black moods – we knew he had them."

"Do you know any rational person who doesn't?" asked the former Mrs Converse. "This isn't really the best of all possible worlds, is it?"

"No, it isn't. But then Joel lived through a period of time in a far worse world than most of us will ever know or could imagine. I can't believe he emerged from it without a scar or two."

Valerie paused, touched by the older man's unadorned directness; it did have its basis in concern. "You're sweet, Larry, and I suspect you're right – in fact I know it. So I think you should tell me more than you have. The term 'physical abuse' is what you lawyers call a leading some-thing-or-other. It's not fair because it could also be misleading. Come on, Larry, be fair. He's not my husband any more, but we didn't break apart because he chased girls or bashed my head in. I may not want to be married to him but I respect him. He's got his problems and I've got mine, and now you're implying his are a lot bigger. What's happened?"

Talbot was silent for a moment, then blurted out the words, again quickly, quietly; once more they were obviously repugnant to him. "They say he assaulted a man in Paris without provocation. The man died."

"*No*, that's impossible! He didn't, he *couldn't!*"

"That's what he told me, but he lied. He told me he was in Amsterdam, but he wasn't. He said he was going back to Paris to clear things up but he didn't.

He was in Germany – he's *still* somewhere in Germany. He hasn't left the country and Interpol has a warrant for him; they're searching everywhere. Word reached him to turn himself into the American Embassy but he refused. He's disappeared."

"Oh, my God, you're all so *wrong!*" exploded Valerie. "You don't *know* him! If what you say happened, he was attacked first – *physically* attacked – and had no choice but to hit back!"

"Not according to an impartial witness who didn't know either man."

"Then he's not impartial, he's lying! . . . Listen to me. I lived with that man for four years and, except for a few trips, all of them here in New York City. I've seen him accosted by drunks and street garbage – punks he could have pushed through the pavements, and perhaps some of them he should have – but I never saw him so much as take a step forward. He'd simply raise the palms of his hands and walk away . . . A few times some damn fools would call him names and he'd just stand there and look at them. And let me tell you, Larry, that look was enough to make you feel cold all over. But that's all he'd do, never anything more."

"Val, I want to believe you. I want to believe it was self-defence, but he ran away, he's disappeared. The embassy can help him, protect him, but he won't come in."

"Then he's frightened. That *can* happen, but it was always for only a few minutes, usually at night when he'd wake up. He'd bolt up, his eyes shut so tight his whole face was a mass of wrinkles. It never lasted long and he said it was perfectly natural and not to worry about it – he didn't, he said. And I don't think he really did; he wanted all that in the past, none of it was ever mentioned."

"Perhaps it should have been," said Talbot softly.

Valerie replied with equal softness. "*Touché*, Larry. Don't think I haven't thought about that these last couple of years. But whatever's happened he's acting this way only because he's afraid – or you know it's quite possible he's been hurt. Or, oh my *God* . . ."

"All the hospitals and registered doctors have been checked," broke in Talbot.

"Well, damn it, there's got to be a *reason!* This isn't like him and you know it!"

"That's just it, Val. Nothing he's done is like the man I know."

The ex-Mrs Converse stiffened. "To use one of Joel's favourite expressions," she said apprehensively. "Clarification, please?"

"Why not?" answered Talbot, the question was directed as much at himself as her. "Perhaps you can shed some light, nobody else can."

"What about this man in Paris, the one who died?"

"There's not much to tell; apparently he was a chauffeur for one of those limousine services. According to the witness, a basement guard in the hotel, Joel approached him, yelled something at him and pushed him out the door. There were sounds of a scuffle and a few minutes later the man was found severely beaten in an alley."

"It's *ridiculous!* What did Joel say?"

"That he walked out the door, saw two men fighting and ran to tell the doorman on the way to his taxi."

"That's what he'd have done," said Val firmly.

"The doorman at the George V says it didn't happen. The police say follicles of hair found on the beaten man matched those in Joel's shower."

"Utterly unbelievable!"

"Let's say there was provocation we don't know about," went on Talbot rapidly. "It doesn't explain what happened later, but before I tell you I want to ask you another question. You'll understand."

"I don't understand a single thing! What is it?"

"During those periods of depression, his dark moods, did Joel ever fantasize? I mean did he indulge in what psychiatrists call role-playing?"

"You mean did he assume other personalities, other kinds of behaviour?"

"Exactly."

"Absolutely not."

"Oh."

"Oh what? Let's have it, Larry."

"Talking about what's believable and what isn't, you're in for a jolt, my dear. According to those people who don't want me to say very much – and you'll have to take my word they know – Joel flew into Germany claiming he was involved in an undercover investigation of the embassy in Bonn."

"Perhaps he was! He was on a leave of absence from T, B and S, wasn't he?"

"On an unrelated matter in the private sector, that much we know. There *is* no investigation – undercover or otherwise – of the embassy in Bonn. Frankly, the people who reached me were from the State Department."

"Oh, my *God* . . ." Valerie fell silent, but before the lawyer could speak, she whispered. "*Geneva*. That horrible business in Geneva!"

"If there's a connection – and both Nathan and I considered it first – it's so buried it can't be followed."

"It's there. It's where it all started."

"Assuming your husband's rational."

"He's not my husband and he *is* rational!"

"The scars, Val. There had to be scars. You agreed with me."

"Not the kind you're talking about. Not killing, and lying and running away! That's *not* Joel! That isn't – *wasn't* – my husband!"

"The mind is a highly complex and delicate instrument. The stresses of the past can leap forward from years ago . . ."

"Get off it, Larry!" shouted Valerie. "Save it for a jury, but don't pin that nonsense on Converse!"

"You're upset."

"You're damned right I am. Because you're looking for explanations that don't fit the man! They fit what you've been *told*. By those people you say you have to respect."

"Only in the sense that they're knowledgeable – they have access to information we don't have. Then there's the overriding fact that they hadn't the faintest idea who Joel Converse was until the American Bar Association gave them the address and telephone number of Talbot, Brooks and Simon."

"And you *believed* them? With everything you know about Washington you simply accepted their word? How many times did Joel come back from a trip to Washington and say the same thing to me? 'Larry says they're lying. They don't know what to do so they're lying.'"

"Valerie," said the attorney sternly. "This wasn't a case of bureaucratic clearance, and after all these years I think I can tell the difference between someone playing games and a man who's genuinely angry – angry and frightened, I should add. The man who reached me was an Undersecretary of State, Brewster Tolland – I had a call-back confirmation – and he wasn't putting on an act. He was appalled, furious, and, as I say, a very worried man."

"What did you tell him?"

"The truth, of course. Not only because it was the right thing to do, but it wouldn't help Joel to do anything else. If he's ill he needs help, not complicity."

"And you deal with Washington every week."

"Several times a week, and of course it was a consideration."

"I'm sorry, Larry, that was unfair."

"But realistic, and I meant what I said. It wouldn't help Joel to lie for him. You see, I really believe something's happened. He's not himself."

"Wait a minute," cried Valerie, the obvious striking her. "Maybe it's *not* Joel!"

"It's him," said Talbot simply.

"Why? Just because people you don't know in Washington say it is?"

"No, Val," replied the lawyer. "Because I spoke with René in Paris before Washington entered the picture."

"*Mattilon?*"

"Joel went to Paris to ask for René's help. He lied to him just as he lied to me, but it was more than the lies – Mattilon and I agreed on that. It was something he saw in Joel's eyes, something I heard in his voice. An unhinging, a form of desperation; René saw it and I heard it. He tried to conceal it from both of us but he couldn't . . . When I last spoke to him, he hung up before we'd finished talking, in the middle of the sentence, his voice echoing like a zombie's."

Valerie stared at the harsh, dancing reflections of sunlight off the waters of Cape Ann. "René agreed with you?" she asked, barely above a whisper.

"Everything I've just told you we said to each other."

"Larry, I'm frightened."

Chaim Abrahms walked into the room, his heavy boots pounding the floor. "So he did it!" shouted the Israeli. "The Mossad was right, he's a hellhound!"

Erich Leifhelm sat behind his desk, the only other person in the book-lined study. "Patrols, alarms, *dogs!*" cried the German, slamming his frail hand on the red blotter. "How did he *do* it?"

"I repeat – a hellhound – that's what our specialist called him. The longer he's restricted, the angrier he gets. It goes back a long time. So our *provocateur* starts his odyssey before we planned. Have you been in touch with the others?"

"I've called London," said Leifhelm, breathing deeply. "He'll reach Paris and Bertholdier will have the units flown up from Marseilles, one to Brussels, the other here to Bonn. We can't waste an hour."

"You're looking for him now, of course."

"*Natürlich!* Every inch of the shoreline for miles in both directions. Every back road and path that leads up from the river and into the city."

"He can elude you, he's proved it."

"Where can he go, Sabra? To his own embassy? There he's a dead man. To the Bonn police or the *Staats Polizei?* He'll be put in an armoured van and brought back here. He goes nowhere."

"I heard that when he left Paris and I heard it again when he flew into Bonn. Errors were made in both places, both costing a great *many* hours. I tell you I'm more concerned now than at any moment in three wars and a lifetime of skirmishes."

"Be reasonable, Chaim, and try to be calm. He has no clothes but what he wears in the river and the mud; he possesses no identification, no passport, no money. He doesn't speak the language . . ."

"He *has* money!" yelled Abrahms, suddenly remembering. "When he was under the needle he spoke of a large sum of money promised in Geneva and delivered on Mykonos."

"And where is it?" asked Leifhelm. "In this desk, *that's* where it is. Nearly seventy thousand American dollars. He hasn't got a Deutschemark in his pocket, or a watch or a piece of jewellery. A man in filthy, soaked clothing, with no identification, no money, no coherent use of the language, and telling an outlandish tale of imprisonment involving The General Leifhelm, would undoubtedly be put in jail as a vagrant or a psychopath or both. In which case, we shall be informed instantly and our people will bring him to us. And bear in mind, Sabra, by ten o'clock tomorrow morning it won't make any difference. That was *your* contribution, the Mossad's ingenuity. We simply had the resources to make it come to pass . . . as is said in the Old Testament."

Abrahms stood in front of the enormous desk, arms akimbo above the pockets of his safari jacket. "So the Jew and the Field Marshal set it all in motion. Ironical, isn't it, Nazi?"

"Not as much as you think, *überlegener Jude.* Impurity (as with beauty) is in the eye of the frightened beholder. You are not my enemy, you never were. If more of us in the old days had your commitment, your audacity, we never would have lost the war."

"I know that," said the Sabra. "I watched and listened when you reached the English Channel. You lost it then. You were weak."

"It was not *us!* It was the frightened *Debutant* in Berlin!"

"Then keep them away when we create a *truly* new order, German. We can't afford weakness."

"You do try me, Chaim."

"I mean to."

The chauffeur felt the bandages on his face, the swelling around his eyes and his lips painful to the touch. He was in his own room, the doctor having put on the television – probably as an insult as he could barely see it.

He was disgraced. The prisoner had escaped in spite of his own formidable talents and the supposedly impassable pack of Dobermanns. The American had used the silver whistle, that much the other guards had told him, and the fact that it had been removed from his neck was a further embarrassment.

He would not add to his disgrace. With blurred vision he had gone through his pockets – which no one in the panic of the chase had thought to do – and found that his billfold, his expensive Swiss watch and all his money had been taken. He would say nothing about them. He was embarrassed enough and any such revelations might be cause for dismissal, conceivably his death.

Joel headed for the shoreline as fast as he could, submerging his head underwater whenever the beam of the searchlight swept towards him. The boat was a large motor launch, its bass-toned engines signifying power, its sudden turns and circles evidence of rapid manoeuvrability. It hugged the overgrown banks then would sweep out towards the open water at the slightest object in the river.

Converse felt the soft mud below; he half swam, half trudged towards the darkest spot on the shore, the chauffeur's gun securely in his belt. The boat approached, its penetrating beam studying every foot, every moving branch or limb or cluster of river weeds. Joel took a deep breath and slowly lowered himself beneath the water, his face angled up towards the surface, his eyes open, his vision a muddy dark blur. The searchlight grew brighter and seemed to hover above him for an eternity; he inched his way to the left and the beam moved away. He rose to the surface, his lungs bursting, but suddenly realized he could make no sound; he could not fill his chest with gasps of air. For directly above him, less than five feet away loomed the broad stern of the motor launch, bobbing in the water as if idling. The dark figure of a man was peering through very large binoculars at the river bank.

Converse was bewildered; it was too dark now to see anything even with magnification. Then he remembered and the memory accounted for the size of the binoculars. The man was focusing through infra-red lenses; they had been used by patrols in South-east Asia and often made the difference, he had been told, between search-and-destroy, and search-and-be-destroyed. They revealed objects in the darkness, soldiers in the darkness.

The boat moved forward, but the idle increased only slightly, entering the slowest of trawling speeds. Again Joel was confused. What had brought Leifhelm's searching party to this particular spot on the river front? There were several other boats behind and out in the distance, their searchlights sweeping the water, but they kept moving, circling. Why did the huge motor launch concentrate on this stretch of the shore? Could they have spotted him through infra-red binoculars? If they had, they were proceeding very strangely; the North Vietnamese had been far swifter – more aggressive, more effective.

Silently, Converse lowered himself beneath the surface and breast-stroked out beyond the boat. Seconds later he raised his head above the water, his vision clear, and he began to understand the odd manoeuvrings of Leifhelm's patrol. Beyond the darkest part of the river bank into which he had lurched for conceal-ment were the lights he had seen eight or nine minutes ago, before the launch and its searchlight monopolized his attention. He had thought they were the lights of a small village but he was in the wrong part of the world. Instead they were the inside lights of four or five small houses, a river colony with a common dock, summer homes perhaps of those fortunate enough to own waterfront property.

If there were houses and a dock, there had to be a drive – an open passage up to the road or roads leading into Bonn and the surrounding towns. Leifhelm's men were combing every inch of the riverbank, cautiously, quietly, the searchlights angled down so as not to alarm the inhabitants or forewarn the fugitive in case he had reached the cluster of cottages and was on his way up to the unseen road or roads. A ship's radio would be activated, its frequency aligned to those in cars roaming above, ready to spring the trap. In ways it was the Huong Khe again for Joel, the obstacles far less primitive, but no less lethal. And then as now there was a time to wait, wait in the black silence and let the hunters make their moves.

They made them quickly. The launch slid into the dock, the powerful twin screws quietly churning in reverse, as a man jumped off the bow with a heavy line and looped it around a pile. Three others followed, instantly racing off the short pier up onto the sloping lawn, one heading diagonally to the right, the other two towards the first house. What they were doing was obvious: one man would position himself in the bordering woods of the downhill entrance drive while his colleagues checked the houses, looking for signs of entry – nervousness, eyes filled with fear, mud on the floors.

Converse's arms and legs began to feel like weights, each an anvil he could barely support much less keep moving, but there was no choice. The beam of the searchlight kept moving up and down the base of the riverbank, its spill illuminating everything in its vicinity. A head surfacing at the wrong moment would be blown out of the water. *Huong Khe. Tread water in the reeds. Do it! Don't die!*

He knew the waiting was no longer than thirty minutes, but it seemed more like thirty hours or thirty days suspended in a floating torture rack. His arms and legs were now in agony; sharp pains shot through his body everywhere; muscles formed cramps that he dispersed by holding his breath and floating in a foetal position, his thumbs pressing relentlessly into the core of the knotted muscles. Twice, gasping for air, he swallowed water, coughing it out below the surface, his nostrils drowning, and twice finding the air silently again. There we e moments when it crossed his inner consciousness that it would be so simple to drift away. *Huong Khe. Don't do it! Don't die!*

Finally through water-logged eyes he saw the men returning. One, two . . .

three? . . . they ran down to the dock, to the man with the rope. *No!* The man with the rope had rushed forward! His eyes were playing blurred tricks! Only two men had run onto the dock, the first man joining them, asking questions. The line man returned to the pile and released the rope; the other two jumped on board. The first man once again joined his companions, now on the bow of the launch – leaving another on shore, a lone observer somewhere unseen between the riverbank and the road above. *Huong Khe. An infantry scout separated from his patrol.*

The motor launch swung away from the dock and sped within feet past Joel, who was buffeted under water by its wake. Once more the boat veered towards the shoreline and slowed down, its searchlight peering into the dense foliage of the bank, heading west, back towards Leifhelm's estate. Converse held his head above the surface, his mouth wide open swallowing all the air he could as he made his way slowly – very slowly – into the mud. He pulled himself up through the wet reeds and branches until he felt dry ground. *Huong Khe.* He pulled the undergrowth over him as best he could, finally covering his upturned face. He would rest until he felt the blood flowing steadily if painfully through his limbs; until the muscles of his neck lost their tension – it was always the neck; the neck was the warning signal – and then he would consider the man on the dark hill above him.

He dozed, a slapping wave below stirring him. He pushed the branches and the leaves away from his face and looked at the chauffeur's watch on his wrist, squinting at the weak radium dial. He had slept for nearly an hour – fitfully to be sure, the slightest sounds forcing his eyelids briefly open, but he had rested. He rolled his neck back and forth, then moved his arms and his legs. Everything still hurt but the excruciating pain was gone. And now he faced a man on a hill above him. He tried to examine his thoughts. He was frightened, of course, but his anger – his outrage – would control that terrible fear; it had done so before, it would do so now. The objective was all that mattered – some kind of sanctuary, a place where he could think and put things together and somehow make the most important telephone call in his life. To Larry Talbot and Nathan Simon in New York. Unless he could do these things he was dead . . . as Connal Fitzpatrick was undoubtedly dead. *Jesus!* What had they *done* to him? A man with the purity of vengeance purely sought caught in a diseased web called Aquitaine! It was a very unfair world . . . He could not think about it; he had a man on the hill to think about.

He crept on his hands and knees. Stretch by stretch he crawled through the woods bordering the dirt road that wound up the hill from the lawn and the riverbank. Whenever a twig crunched or a rock was displaced he stopped, waiting for the moment to dissolve back into the sounds of the forest. He kept telling himself he had the advantage; he was the unexpected. It helped counteract the fear of the darkness and the knowledge that a physical confrontation was before him. Like the patrol scout years ago in the Huong Khe, that man above him now had things he needed. The combat could not be avoided, so it was best not to think about it, simply force his mind into a time-set without feelings, and do it. But do it completely, his mind had to understand that, too. There could be no hesitation, no intrusions of conscience – and no sound of a gun, only the use of the steel.

He saw him, oddly enough silhouetted in the distant glare of a single street lamp far above on a road. The man was standing – leaning actually – against the trunk of a tree facing down, his sweep of vision taking in everything below. The stretches between Joel's hands and knees became inches, the stops more frequent, silence more vital. Slowly he made his way in an arc above the tree and the man and started down, a large cat descending on its prey, his mind in a time-set, no feeling, only the instinct for survival. He was the predator he had once been long ago, everything blocked out but the requirement of the lifeline.

He was within six feet; he could hear the man's breathing. There was a snap beneath him! A branch! The scout turned, his eyes alive in the dim glare of light. Converse lunged, the barrel of the gun gripped in his hand. He crashed the steel handle into the German's temple, withdrew his arm and smashed it up into the scout's throat. The man fell backward, dazed but not unconscious; he started to scream. Joel sprang, the fingers of his left hand spread, surging for his enemy's neck, the weapon aimed accurately, the handle impacting directly into the German's forehead, blood and red tissue erupting.

Silence. No movement. Another scout separated from his patrol had been taken out. And, as he had years ago, Converse permitted himself no feeling. It was done and he had to go on.

The man's dry clothes fitted reasonably well including the dark leather jacket. Like most small or medium-sized commanders, Leifhelm surrounded himself with tall men, as much for protection as to proclaim his superiority over his larger compatriots. There was also another gun; Joel struggled with the clip, removed it, and threw it along with the weapon into the woods. The bonus came with the German's billfold; it contained a sizeable sum of money as well as a frayed, much-stamped passport. Apparently, this trusted employee of Leifhelm travelled widely for Aquitaine – probably knowing nothing and very expendable – but always available at the moment of decision. The man's shoes did not fit; they were too small. So Converse used his drenched clothing to wipe his own, the German's dry socks absorbing some of the soft, wet moisture of the leather. He covered the man with branches and walked up the hill to the road.

He stayed out of sight between the trees as five cars passed by, all sedans, all possibly belonging to Erich Leifhelm. Then he saw a bright yellow Volkswagen come into view, weaving slightly. He stepped out and held up his hands, the gesture of a man in trouble.

The small car stopped, a blonde girl in the passenger seat, the driver no more than eighteen or twenty, another young man in the back, also blonde; he looked as though he might be the girl's brother.

"*Was ist Los, Opa?*" asked the driver.

"I'm afraid I don't speak German. Can you speak any English?"

"I speak some English," said the boy in the back, slurring his words. "Better than these two! All they want to do is get to our place and make love. See! I do speak English?"

"You certainly do, and very well, indeed. Would you explain to them, please?

Frankly, I've had a fight with my wife at a party down there – you know, at those cottages – and I want to get back to Bonn. I'll pay you, of course."

"*Ein Streit mit seiner Frau! Er will nach Bonn gehen. Er wird uns bezahlen.*"

"*Warum nicht? Sie hat mich heute sowieso schon zu viel gekostet,*" said the driver.

"*Nicht für was du kriegst, du Drecksack!*" cried the girl, laughing.

"Get in, *Mein Herr!* We are your chauffeurs. Just pray he stays on the road, *ja!* What hotel are you staying at?"

"Actually, I'd rather not go back there. I'm really very angry. I'd like to teach her a lesson by staying away tonight. Do you think you could find me a room? I'll pay you even more, of course. Frankly, I've been drinking a bit myself."

"*Ein betrunkener Tourist. Er will ein Hotel. Fahren wir ihn ins Rosencafé?*"

"*Dort sind mehr Nutten als der alte Knacker schafft.*"

"We are your guides, *Amerikaner,*" said the young man beside Converse. "We are students from the university who will not only find you a room, but with excellent prospects of getting back at your wife with some pleasure! There's also a café. You'll buy us a lager or six, *ja?*"

"All you want. But I'd also like to make a telephone call. To the United States – it's business. Will I be able to?"

"Most everyone in Bonn speaks English, *Mein Herr.* If they don't at this *Rosencafé*, I, myself, will take care of it. Six lagers, though, remember that!"

"Twelve, if you like."

"*Da wird es im Pissoir eine Überschwemmung geben!*"

He knew the rate of exchange and once inside the raucous café – actually a run-down bar favoured by the university crowd – he counted the money he had taken from the two Germans. It was roughly five hundred dollars, over three from the man on the hill. The seedy clerk at the registration desk explained in convoluted English that, indeed, the switchboard could place a call to America, but it might take several minutes. Joel left fifty dollars in Deutschemarks for his youthful Good Samaritans and excused himself, heading up to his room – such as it was. An hour later the call came through.

"Larry?"

"Joel?"

"Thank *God* you're there!" cried Converse in relief. "You'll never know how I kept hoping you weren't out of town. Getting a call through from here is a bitch."

"I'm here," said Talbot, his voice suddenly calm and in control. "Where are *you*, Joel?" he asked quietly.

"Some poor excuse for a hotel in Bonn. I just got here. I didn't get the name."

"You're in a hotel in Bonn but you don't know which one?"

"It doesn't matter, Larry! Get Simon on the line. I want to talk to you both. Quickly."

"Nathan's in court. He should be back here by four o'clock – our time. That's about an hour from now."

"*Goddamn it!*"

"Take it easy, Joel. Don't upset yourself."

"Don't *upset* . . . ? For Christ's sake, I've been locked up in a stone cabin with bars in the windows for five days! I broke out a couple of hours ago, and ran like hell through the woods with a pack of dogs and lunatics carrying guns chasing me. I spent an hour in the water damn near drowning before I could reach land without getting my head shot off, and then I had to – I had to . . ."

"You had to what, Joel?" asked Talbot, a strange passivity in his voice. "What did you have to do?"

"Goddamn it, Larry. I may have *killed* a man to get out of there!"

"You had to kill someone, Joel? Why did you think you had to do that?"

"He was Waiting for me! They were searching for me! On the land, in the woods along the river banks – he was a scout separated from his patrol. *Scouts, patrols!* I had to get out, get *away!* And you tell me not to be upset!"

"Calm down, Joel, try to get hold of yourself . . . You escaped before, didn't you? A long time ago . . ."

"What's that got to do with anything?" broke in Converse.

"You had to kill people then, didn't you? Those memories must always be with you."

"Larry, that's bullshit! Listen to me and take down everything I say – the names I give you, the facts – get it all down."

"Perhaps I should bring Janet on the line. Her shorthand . . ."

"No! Only you, no one else! They can trace people, anyone who knows anything. It's not that complicated. Are you ready?"

"Of course."

Joel sat down on the narrow bed and took a deep breath. "The best way to put it – as it was put to me, but you don't have to write this down, just understand – is that they've come back."

"Who?"

"The generals . . . field marshals, admirals, colonels . . . allies and enemies, all field and fleet commanders and above. They've come together from everywhere to change things, change governments and laws and foreign policies, everything to be based on military priorities and decisions . . . It's crazy, but they could do it. We'd live out their fantasies because they'd be in control, believing they're right and selfless and dedicated – as they've always believed."

"Who are these people, Joel?"

"Yes, write this down. The organization is called Aquitaine. It's based on an historical theory that the region in France once known as Aquitaine might have become all of Europe and by extension – as colonies – the North American continent as well."

"Whose theory?"

"It doesn't *matter*, it's just a theory. The organization was conceived by General George Delavane – he was known as 'Mad Marcus' in Vietnam – and I saw only a fraction of the damage that son on a bitch did! He's pulled in military personnel from all over the place, all commanders, and they're fanning out recruiting their own kind, fanatics who believe as they do, that theirs is the only way. For the past year or so, they've been shipping illegal weapons and armaments to terrorist groups, encouraging destabilization wherever they can, the ultimate purpose being that they'll be called in to restore order, and when they do, they'll take over . . . Five days ago I met with Delavane's key men from France and Germany, Israel and South Africa – and I think possibly England."

"You met with these people, Joel? Did they invite you to a meeting?"

"They thought I was one of them, that I believed in everything they stood for. You see, Larry, they didn't know how much I hated them. They hadn't been where I'd been, hadn't seen what I saw . . . as you said, years ago."

"When you *had* to escape," added Talbot sympathetically. "When you had to kill people – times you'll never forget. They must have been terrible for you."

"Yes, they were. Goddamn it, *yes!* Sorry, let's stay on course. I'm so tired – still frightened, too, I think."

"Relax, Joel."

"Sure. Where was I?" Converse rubbed his eyes. "Oh, yes, I remember. They got information on me, information from my service record, my status as a POW, which wasn't actually part of the record but they got it and they found out what and who I was. They heard the words that told them how much I hated them, hated what Delavane had done, what they all had done. They drugged me, got whatever they could and threw me into a godforsaken stone house set in the middle of the woods above the Rhine. While under the chemicals I must have told them everything I knew . . ."

"Chemicals?" asked Talbot, obviously never having heard the term.

"Amatols, Pentothals, scopolamine. I've been the route, Larry. I've been there and back."

"You *have?* Where?"

"In the camps. It's immaterial."

"I'm not sure it is."

"It is. The point is they found out what I know. That means they'll move up their schedule."

"Schedule?"

"We're in the countdown. *Now!* Two weeks, three weeks, four at the outside! No one knows how or where or what the targets are but there'll be eruptions of violence and terrorism all over the place, giving them the excuse to move in and take over. 'Accumulation' . . . 'rapid acceleration', those were the words they used! Right now in Northern Ireland – everything's blown apart, nothing but chaos – whole armoured divisions are moving in. *They* did it, Larry! It's a test, a trial run for them! . . . I'm going to give you the names." Converse did so, both surprised and annoyed that Talbot produced no reaction to any of the men of Aquitaine. "Have you got them?"

"Yes, I have."

"Those are the salient facts and the names I can vouch for. There's a lot more – people in the State Department and the Pentagon, but the lists are in my briefcase and it's been stolen, or hidden somewhere. I'll get some rest and start writing out everything I know then call you in the morning. I have to get out of here. I'm going to need help."

"I agree, so may I talk now," said the lawyer in New York in that odd flat voice. "First, where are you, Joel? Look on the phone or read the print on an ashtray – or check the desk; there must be stationery."

"There's no desk and the ashtrays are chipped glass . . . Wait a minute, I picked up some matches from the bar when I bought cigarettes." Converse reached into the pocket of the leather jacket and pulled out the book of matches. "Here it is. '*Riesendrinks*'."

"Look below that. My German is limited but I think it means 'big drinks' or something."

"Oh? Then it must be this. *Rosencafé*."

"That sounds more like it. Spell it for me, Joel."

Converse did, an undefined feeling disturbing him. "Have you got it?" he asked. "Here's a telephone number." Joel read off the numbers printed on the cover.

"Good, that's splendid," said Talbot. "But before you get off the line – and I know you need rest badly – I have a couple of questions."

"I would hope to hell you do!"

"When we spoke after that man was hurt in Paris, after that fight you saw in the alley, you told me you were in Amsterdam. You said you were going to fly back to Paris and see René, straighten everything out. Why didn't you, Joel?"

"For God's sake, Larry, I just told you what I've been through! It took every minute I had to set things up. I was going after these people – this goddamned Aquitaine – and it could only be done one way. I had to work myself in, I couldn't waste time!"

"That man died. Did you have anything to do with his death?"

"Christ, yes, I killed him! He tried to stop me, they all tried to stop me! They found me in Copenhagen and had me followed. They were waiting for me at the airport here. It was a trap!"

"To stop you from reaching these men, these generals and field marshals?"

"Yes!"

"Yet you just told me these same men invited you to meet with them."

"I'll spell it all out for you in the morning," said Converse wearily, the tension of the last hours – days really – culminating in exhaustion and a racking headache. "By then I'll have everything down on paper, but you may have to come over here to get it – and me. The main thing is we're in touch. You've got the names, the overview, and you know where I am. Talk with Nathan, think about everything I've said and the three of us will figure out what to do. We have contacts in Washington, but we'll have to be careful. We don't know who's with whom. But there's a plus here. Some of the material I have – I *had* – could only have come from people down there. One view is that I was set in motion by them, that men I don't know are watching every move I make because I'm doing what they can't do."

"By yourself," said Talbot, agreeing. "Without Washington's help. Without their help."

"That's right. They can't show themselves; they have to stay in the background until I bring out something concrete . . . That was the plan. When you and

Nathan talk, if you have questions call me. I'm just going to lie down for an hour or so anyway."

"I've got another question now, if you don't mind. You know Interpol has an international warrant for you."

"I do."

"And the American Embassy is looking for you."

"I know that, too."

"I was told that word reached you to come into the embassy."

"*You* were told . . . ?"

"Why haven't you done it, Joel?"

"Jesus, I *can't!* Don't you think I would if I could? The place is crawling with Delavane's people. Well, that's an exaggeration, but I know of three. I saw them."

"It's my understanding that Ambassador Peregrine himself got word to you, guaranteeing you protection, confidentiality. Wasn't that enough?"

"Your *understanding* . . . The answer is *no!* Peregrine hasn't any idea what he's got inside that place . . . Or maybe he does. I saw Leifhelm's car go through those gates like he had a lifetime pass. At three o'clock in the morning. Leifhelm's a Nazi, Larry, he's never been anything else! So what does that make Peregrine?"

"Come on, Joel. You're maligning a man by implication who doesn't deserve it. Walter Peregrine was one of the heroes of Bastogne. His command at the Battle of the Bulge is a legend of the war. And he was a reserve officer, not part of the regular army. I doubt that Nazis are his favourite guests."

"His command? Another *commander*? Then maybe he knows *exactly what* he's got in that embassy!"

"That's not fair. His outspoken criticisms of the Pentagon are a documented part of his post-war career. He's called them megalomaniacs with too damn much money feeding their egos at the taxpayers' expense. No, you're not being fair, Joel. I think you should listen to him. Call him on the phone, talk to him."

"Not being fair?" said Converse softly, the undefined feeling coming into focus, now a warning. "Wait a minute! You're the one who's not being fair. '*I* was told' . . . 'It's *my* understanding?' What oracle have you been in touch with? Who's imparting these pearls of wisdom about me? On what basis and where from?"

"All right, Joel, all right . . . calm down. Yes, I have talked to people – people who want to help you. A man is dead in Paris, and now you say there's another in Bonn. You talk of scouts and patrols and those horrible chemicals, and how you ran through the woods and had to hide in the river. Don't you understand, son? Nobody's blaming you or even holding you responsible. Something happened; you're living it all over again."

"My God!" broke in Converse, stunned. "You don't believe a word I've *said!*"

"You believe it and that's all that matters. I saw my share in North Africa and Italy, but nothing to compare with what you went through later. You have a deep, understandable hatred for war and all things military. You wouldn't be human if you didn't, not with the suffering you experienced and the terrible things you endured."

"Larry, everything I've told you is *true!*"

"Fine, splendid. Then reach Peregrine, go to the embassy and tell them. They'll listen to you. *He'll* listen."

"Are you denser than I think?" shouted Joel. "I just told you, I can't! I'd never get to *see* Peregrine! I'd get my head blown away!"

"I spoke to your wife – sorry, your ex-wife. She said you'd have these moments at night . . ."

"You spoke to *Val?* You brought *her* into this! Christ, are you out of your mind! Don't you know they trace everyone *down?* It was right under your nose, counsellor! *Lucas Anstett!* Stay away from her! Stay away or I'll . . . I'll . . ."

"You'll what, son?" asked Talbot quietly. "Kill me, too?"

"Oh, *Jesus!*"

"Do as I say, Joel. Call Peregrine. Everything will be all right."

Suddenly Converse heard an odd sound over the line, odd in context but one he had heard hundreds of times before. It was a short buzz, barely significant but there was significance to it. It was Lawrence Talbot's courteous signal to his secretary to come into his office and pick up a revised letter or a corrected brief or a dictation tape. Joel knew what it was now. The address of a seedy hotel in Bonn.

"All right, Larry," he said, feigning an exhaustion that was all too real. "I'm so *damned* tired. Let me lie down for a while and maybe I will call the embassy. Maybe I should get in touch with Peregrine. Everything's so confused."

"That's the way, son. Everything's going to be fine now. Just splendid."

"Goodbye, Larry."

"Goodbye for now, Joel. See you in a couple of days."

Converse slammed down the phone and looked around the dimly-lit room. What was he checking for? He had come with nothing and he would leave with nothing but what was on his back – what he had stolen. And he had to leave quickly. He had to run. In minutes men would be speeding in cars from the embassy, and at least one of those men would have a gun and a bullet meant for him!

What in hell was *happening to* him? The truth was a fantasy bolstered by lies and the lies were his only means of survival. *Insanity!*

19

He ran past the elevator to the staircase, descending the steps two and three at a time, his hand on the iron railing as he lurched around the landings, and reached the lobby door four storeys below. He swung it open, suddenly gripping the edge and slowing his pace so as not to call attention to himself; he need not have been concerned. The small band of people milling about in front of the benches against the wall and wandering around the warm tile floor were the neighbourhood elderly looking for nightly companionship and a few drunks walking in and out of the neon-lighted door to the noisy café. Oh, *Christ!* His mind was in a frenzy! He could walk around in the night, hiding in alleys, but a lone man in unfamiliar streets was too easily spotted by unofficial hunters or by the official police. He had to get inside somewhere, somehow. Out of sight.

The café! His Samaritans! He pulled up the collar of the leather jacket, and forced the belt of the trousers lower, inching down the gap around his ankles. He then approached the door casually, permitting himself a slight stagger as he pushed it open. He was greeted by floating levels of smoke – not all of it tobacco by any means – and adjusted his stinging eyes to the erratically flashing lights, as he tried to block out the offending noise – a combination of guttural roars and disco music blaring from hi-tech speakers. His Good Samaritans were gone; he looked for the young blonde girl as his focal point but she was not there. The table they had occupied was taken by another foursome – no, not four *different* people, only three – they had joined the English-speaking student who had sat beside him in the car, three other young men in various stages of collegiate release. Joel approached them, passing an empty chair in his path; he gripped the rim and unobtrusively pulled it behind him to the table. He sat down and smiled at the blond-haired student.

"I didn't know if I'd left enough money for those twelve beers I promised," he said pleasantly.

"*Ach!* I was just talking about you, *Mein Herr Amerikaner!* These are my friends – like me, all dreadful students!" The three newcomers were introduced rapidly the names lost in the music and the smoke. Everyone nodded; the American was welcome.

"Our other two friends left?"

"I told you," shouted the blond youngster through the noise. "They wished to drive to our house and make love. That's all they *do!* Our parents went to Bayreuth for the music festival, so they shall make their own music on her bed and I shall come home late!"

"Nice arrangement," said Converse, trying to think of how to broach the subject that had to be broached quickly. He had very little time.

"Very *good*, sir!" said a dark-haired young man on his right. "Hans would have missed that; his English is understandably inferior. I was an exchange student in the state of Massachusetts for two years. 'Arrangement' is also a musical term. You combined the two! *Very* good, sir!"

"I keep trying," said Joel aimlessly, looking at the student. "You really speak English?" he asked sincerely.

"Very well, *Mein Herr*. My scholarship depends upon it. My friends here are good people, make no mistake, but they are rich and come here for amusement. As a boy, I lived two streets away from this place. But they protect the lads here, and why not? Let them have fun; nobody is hurt and money is spread."

"You're sober," said Converse, the statement bordering on a question.

The young man laughed, as he nodded. "Tonight, yes. Tomorrow afternoon I have a difficult exam and need a clear head. The summer session examinations are the worst. The professors would rather be on holiday."

"I was going to talk to *him*," said Joel, nodding at the blond student, who was arguing with his two companions, his hands waving in the smoke, his voice strident. "But that doesn't make sense. You do."

"In *what* sense, sir, if you will forgive the redundancy of the expression?"

" 'Redundancy'? What's your major?"

"Preliminary law, sir."

"I don't need that."

"It is a difficulty, sir?"

"Not for me . . . Listen, I haven't much time and I have a problem. I have to get out of here. I need to find another place to stay – just until tomorrow morning. I assure you I've done nothing wrong, nothing illegal – in case my clothes or my appearance give another impression. It's strictly a personal matter. Can you help me?"

The dark-haired young German seemed to hesitate, as if reluctant to answer, nevertheless doing so, leaning forward to be heard. "Since you bring up the subject, *Mein Herr*, I'm sure you can understand that it would not be seemly for a student of the law to help a man under questionable circumstances."

"That's exactly why I brought it up," said Converse rapidly, speaking into the student's ear. "I'm an attorney and under these clothes a reasonably respectable one. I simply took on the wrong American client over here and can't wait to get a plane out tomorrow morning."

The young man listened, studied Joel's face and nodded. "Then these are not lodgings you would normally seek?"

"To be avoided wherever possible. I just thought it would be a good idea to be inconspicuous for the night."

"There are very few places such as this in Bonn, sir."

"To Bonn's credit, counsellor." Glancing about the café and its predominant clientele, Converse had another thought. "It's summer!" he said urgently to the student through the bedlam. "Are there any youth hostels around here?"

"Those in the vicinity of Bonn or Köln are filled, sir, mostly with Americans and the Dutch. The others which might have spaces are quite far north towards Hanover. However, there is another solution, I think."

"What?"

"Summer, sir. The rooming houses usually filled by those attending the university have many spaces during the summer months. In the house where I stay there are two empty rooms on the second floor."

"I thought you lived around here."

"That was long ago. My parents are retired and live with my sister in Mannheim."

"I'm in a great hurry. May we go? I'll pay you what I can tonight and more tomorrow morning."

"I thought you said you were taking the plane in the morning."

"I have two stops to make first. You can come with me: you can show me where they are."

The young man and Joel excused themselves, knowing they would not be missed. The student started towards the lobby door, but Converse grabbed his elbow, gesturing at the street entrance.

"Your luggage, sir!" shouted the German through the din and the flashing lights.

"You can lend me a razor in the morning!" yelled back Converse, pulling the young man through the mingling bodies towards the door. Several tables before the entrance was an empty chair, on the seat a soft, rumpled cloth cap. He reached down and picked it up, holding it in front of him as he reached the door and walked outside to the pavement, the student behind him. "Which way?" he asked, pulling the cap over his head.

"This way, sir," replied the young German, pointing beneath the shabby canopy of the adjacent hotel entrance.

"Let's go," said Joel, stepping forward.

They stopped – that is Converse stopped first, gripping the student's shoulder and turning him into the building. A black sedan had come speeding down the street, swerving into the open space in front of the canopy. Two men got out of the back doors and rushed towards the entrance, the second man running around the car to catch up with the first. Joel angled his head as the young German stared at him. He recognized both men; both were Americans. They had been at the Köln–Bonn airport eight nights ago hoping to trap him then as they were coming to trap him now. The black car moved forward out of the glare of the lights, into the shadows. It pulled into the kerb and waited, a hearse prepared to receive its cargo.

"*Was ist los?*" asked the German youth, unable to conceal his fear.

"Nothing really." Converse removed his hand and gave the student two friendly claps on the shoulder. "Just let this be a lesson to you, counsellor. Know who your client is before you get greedy and accept too large a retainer."

"*Ja,*" said the young German, attempting a smile but not succeeding, his eyes on the black sedan.

They walked rapidly past the parked automobile with the driver inside, the glow of a cigarette seen in the darkness of the front seat. Joel pulled down the cloth cap and again angled his head, now away from one of his countrymen.

The truth was a fantasy bolstered by lies . . . Survival was in running and concealment. Insanity!

The early morning was mercifully uneventful except for his thoughts, which were raging. The student, whose name was Johann, had secured him a room at the boarding house, the proprietress delighted with a hundred Deutschemarks for the rental. It more than made up for the gauze, tape and antiseptic she gave him to rebandage his wound. Converse had slept soundly if intermittently, awakened by fears transposed into macabre dreams. By seven o'clock sleep was impossible.

There was an urgent piece of business that had to be taken care of; he understood the risk but the money was necessary, now more than ever. On Mykonos, the knowledgeable if serpentine Laskaris had forwarded $100,000 to banks in Paris, London, Bonn and New York, using the accepted practice of written-out numbers as a signature to withdraw the funds. Laskaris had suggested further that Joel should not attempt to carry with him or try to memorize four sets of lengthy and entirely different digits. Instead the banker would wire the American Express travel offices in the four cities to hold for a period of three months a message for – *who, Mr Converse? It should be a name meaningful to you but not to others. It will be your code, no other identification necessary – as with certain telephone banking facilities in your own country . . . Make it Carpentier. J. Carpentier.*

Joel understood that he might have revealed the device while under narcotics. Also he might not; his mind was not on money. He had a great deal in his possession and the chemicals tended to elicit only feverish priorities. He had learned that in the camps a lifetime ago, twice astonished that he had not mentioned far-off tactics down the roads of escape. There was also a back-up, ethics notwithstanding. The young German, Johann, would be his intermediary. The risks could not be avoided, only minimized; he had also learned that a lifetime ago. If the boy was taken, his conscience would be stricken, but then what could be the worst that would happen to him? There was no point in thinking about it.

"Go inside and ask if there's a message for J. Carpentier," said Joel to the student. They were in the back seat of a taxi across the street from the American Express office. "If the answer is yes, say the following words. 'It must be a wire from Mykonos',," he added, recalling Laskaris' precise instructions.

"That is necessary, sir?" asked the dark-haired Johann, frowning.

"Yes, it is. Without mentioning Mykonos and the fact that the message is a cable, they won't give it to you. Also it identifies you. You won't have to sign anything."

"This is all very strange, *Mein Herr.*"

"If you're going to be a lawyer, get used to odd forms of communication. There's nothing illegal, simply a means of protecting your client's and your firm's confidentiality."

"I have much to learn, it seems."

"You're not doing anything wrong," continued Joel quietly, his eyes level with Johann's. "On the contrary, you're doing something very right and I'll pay you very well for doing it."

"*Sehr gut,*" said the young man.

Converse waited in the taxi, his eyes scanning the street, concentrating on stationary automobiles and those pedestrians walking too slowly or not at all, or anyone whose glances even seemingly strayed to American Express' storefront. Johann went inside and Joel swallowed repeatedly, a tightness in his throat: the waiting was awful, made worse by the knowledge that he was using the student in a high-risk situation. Then he thought briefly of Avery Fowler-Halliday and Connal Fitzpatrick; they had lost. The young German had an infinitely far greater chance of living for many years.

The minutes went by as the sweat crawled through Converse's hair and down his neck; time was suspended in fear. Finally, Johann came outside, blinking in the sunlight, innocence personified. He crossed the street and climbed into the taxi.

"What did they say to you?" asked Joel, trying to sound casual, his eyes still roaming the street.

"Only if I had been waiting long for the message. I replied that I expected it was a cablegram from Mykonos. I didn't know what else to say."

"You did fine." Joel tore open the envelope and unfolded the wire. There was an unbroken series of written out numbers, well over twenty he judged at a glance. Again he remembered Laskaris' instructions: *Pick every third number beginning with the third and ending with the third from the last. Think merely in terms of three. It's quite simple — these things usually are — and in any event no one else can sign for you. It's merely a precaution.*

"Is everything all right?" asked Johann.

"So far we're ahead one step and you're one step nearer a bonus, counsellor."

"I'm also nearer my examination."

"What time do you take it?"

"Three-thirty this afternoon."

"Good omen. Think in terms of three."

"I beg your pardon?"

"Nothing. Let's find a pay telephone. You've only got one more thing to do and tonight you can buy your friends the biggest dinner in Bonn."

The taxi waited at the corner while Converse and the young German stood outside the booth, Johann having written down the bank's number from the telephone book. The student was reluctant to go any farther; the exotic chores asked of him now were more than he cared to accept.

"All you have to do is tell the truth!" insisted Joel. "*Only* the truth. You met an American attorney who doesn't speak German and he's asked you to make a call for him. This attorney has to withdraw funds for a client from a confidential accounts-transfer and wants to know whom he should see. That's all. No one will ask your name, or mine, either, for that matter."

"And when I do this there will be something else, *Mein Herr? Nein*, I think not. You call yourself . . ."

"I can't make a mistake! I can't misunderstand a word. And there is nothing else. Just wait wherever you like around the bank or near the bank. When I come out I'll give you two thousand Deutschemarks, and, as far as I'm concerned — as far as *anyone's* concerned — we never met."

"So much for so little, sir. You can understand my fears."

"They're nothing compared to mine," said Converse, quietly yet urgently. "Please, do this. I need your help."

264

As he had done the night before through the noise and the smoke and the flashing lights of the raucous bar, the young German looked hard at Joel, as if trying to see something he could not be sure was there. Finally, he nodded once without enthusiasm. "*Sehr gut*," he said, stepping into the booth with several coins in his hand.

Converse watched through the glass as the student dialled and obviously had brief conversations with two or three different people before reaching the correct party. The one-sided dialogue as observed by Joel seemed interminable – far too long and too complicated for the simple request of a name in the transferred accounts department. At one point, as he wrote something down on the scrap of paper with the bank's number on it, Johann appeared to object and Converse had to restrain himself from opening the door and terminating the call. The German youth hung up and came out, his expression confused and angry.

"What happened? Was there a problem?"

"Only with the hour and institutional policy, sir."

"What does that mean?"

"Such accounts are serviced only after twelve noon. I made it clear that you had to be at the airport by then but *Herr Direktor* said the bank's policy would stand." Johann handed Converse the slip of paper. "You're to see a man named Lachmann on the first floor."

"I'll catch a later plane." Joel looked at the chauffeur's watch on his wrist. It was 10.35; an hour and a half to go.

"I was hoping to be at the university library long before noon."

"You can still be there," said Converse sincerely. "We can stop, get a stamped envelope, and you can write out your name and address. I'll mail the money to you."

Johann glanced at the pavement, his hesitation all too obvious. "I think, perhaps . . . the examination is not so difficult for me. It's one of my better subjects."

"Of course," agreed Joel. "There's no reason on earth why you should trust me."

"You mistake me, sir. I believe you would mail the money to me. It's just that I'm not sure it's such a good idea for me to receive the envelope."

Converse smiled; he understood. "Fingerprints?" he asked kindly. "Accepted rules of evidence?"

"It's also one of my better subjects."

"Okay, you're stuck with me for another couple of hours. I've got about seven hundred Deutschemarks left until I reach the bank. Do you know some clothing store away from the main shopping district where I can buy a pair of trousers and a jacket?"

"Yes, sir. And if I may suggest, if you are going to withdraw enough funds to give me two thousand Deutschemarks, perhaps a clean shirt and a tie might be in order."

"Always check your client's appearance. You may go far, counsellor."

The ritual at the *Bonner Sparkasse* was a study in awkward but adamant efficiency. Joel was ushered into Herr Lachmann's office on the first floor, where neither a handshake nor small talk was offered. Only the business at hand was addressed.

"Origin of transfer, please?" asked the blunt, corpulent executive.

"Bank of Rhodes, Mykonos branch, waterfront office. The name of the . . . 'dispatcher', I guess you'd call him . . . is Laskaris. I don't recall his first name."

"Even his last is unnecessary," said the German, as though he did not care to hear it. The transaction itself seemed somehow to offend him.

"Sorry, I just wanted to be helpful. As you know, I'm in a great hurry. I have a plane to catch."

"Everything will be done according to the regulations, *Mein Herr*."

"Naturally."

The banker shoved a sheet of paper across the desk. "You will write out your numerical signature five times, one below the other, as I read you the regulations which constitute the policy of the *Bonner Sparkasse* as they pertain to the laws of the Federal Republic of Germany. You will then be required to sign – again in your numerical signature – an affidavit that you thoroughly understood and accept these prohibitions."

"I thought you said 'regulations'."

"One and the same, *Mein Herr*."

Converse took the cablegram out of the inside pocket of his newly-purchased sports jacket and placed it beside the blank page of stationery. He had underlined the correct numbers and began writing.

" 'You, the numerically undersigned, traceable from the origin of transfer,' " droned the obese Lachmann, leaning back in his chair and reading from a single page, " 'swear to the fact that whatever funds withdrawn from the *Bonner Sparkasse* from this confidential account have been subject to all taxes, individual and corporate, from whatever sources of revenue. That they are not being processed through differing currencies to avoid said taxes, or for the purpose of making unlawful payments to individuals, companies, or corporations trafficking in illegal and . . .' "

"Forget it," broke in Joel. "I know it; I'll sign it."

" ' . . . egregious activities outside the laws of the Federal Republic of Germany or the laws of the nation of which the undersigned is a legal resident with full citizenship.' "

"Ever tried half-full or resident alien status?" said Converse, starting the last line of numbers. "I know a law student who could punch holes in that affidavit."

"There is more, but you say you'll sign?"

"I'm sure there's more and of course I'll sign." Joel pushed the page with the handwritten numbers back to the banker. "There. Just get me the money. One hundred thousand American, minus your fee. Split it two-thirds and a third. US and German, no bills over a thousand Deutschemarks or five hundred American."

"That is quite a bit of paper, *Mein Herr*."

266

"I'll handle it. Please, as quickly as possible."

"Is that amount the entire account? I would not know, of course, until the scanners verify your 'signature'."

"It's the entire account."

"It could take several hours, *natürlich*."

"What?"

"The regulations, the *policy, mein Herr*." The fat man extended his arms in supplication.

"I don't *have* several hours!"

"What can I do?"

"What *can* you do? A thousand American ... for *you*."

"One hour, *Mein Herr*."

"Five thousand?"

"Five minutes, my good friend."

Converse walked out of the elevator, the abrasive newly-acquired money belt far less comfortable than the one he had purchased in Geneva. However, it was pointless to refuse it. It was a courtesy of the bank, according to Lachmann, as the German pocketed nearly twelve thousand Deutschemarks for himself. The "five minutes" had been a persuasive exaggeration, thought Joel as he glanced at the clock on the wall; it was nearly 12.45. The ritual had taken over half an hour, from his "indoctrination" to the verification of his "signature" by electronic scanners capable of picking the slightest "fundamental" variation in the writing characteristics. Apparently no one dared make any mistakes in the German banks where questionable practices were concerned. The regulations were followed right to the borders of illegality, everyone covered by following orders that placed the burden of innocence solely on the recipients.

Converse started for the bronze-bordered doors of the entrance when he saw the student, Johann, sitting on a marble bench, looking out of place but not uncomfortable. The young man was reading some sort of pamphlet put out by the bank. Or more precisely he was pretending to read it, his eyes, however, darting above the paper, watching the crowds criss-crossing the marble floor. Converse nodded as Johann saw him; the student got up from the bench and waited until Joel reached the entrance before he began to follow.

Something had happened. Outside on the pavement people were rushing in both directions, but mainly to the right; voices were raised, questions shouted, replies blurred with anger and angry ignorance.

"What the hell is it?" asked Converse.

"I don't know," replied Johann, next to him. "Something ugly, I think. People are running to the kiosk on the corner. The newspapers."

"Let's get one," said Joel, touching the young man's arm, as they started towards the growing crowd on the block.

"Attentat! Mord! Amerikanischer Botschafter ermordet!"

The news-stand vendors were shouting, handing out papers as they grabbed coins and bills with little or no attempt to give change. There was a sense of the swelling panic that comes with sudden unexplained events that presage greater disasters. All around them people were snapping papers, their eyes riveted on the headlines and the stories beneath.

"*Mein Gott!*" cried Johann, glancing at a folded newspaper on his left. "The American ambassador has been assassinated!"

"*Christ!* Get one of those!" Converse threw a number of coins into the kiosk as the young German grabbed a paper from the extended hand of a news vendor. "Let's get out of here!" yelled Joel, gripping the student's arm.

But Johann did not move. He stood there in the middle of the shouting crowd, staring at the newspaper, his eyes wide, his lips trembling. Converse shoved two men away with his shoulders as he pulled the young man forward, now both of them surrounded by anxious, protesting Germans obsessed with getting papers.

"*You!*" Johann's scream was muted by some intolerable fear.

Joel ripped the newspaper from the student's hands. In the upper centre of the front page were photographs of two men. On the left was the murdered Walter Peregrine, American ambassador to the Federal Republic. On the right was the face of an American *Rechtsanwalt* – one of the few words in German Converse knew; it meant attorney. The photograph was of himself.

20

"*No!*" roared Joel, crushing the paper in his left fist, his right hand gripping Johann's shoulder. "Whatever it says, it's a *lie!* I'm not any part of this! Don't you see what they're trying to *do?* Come on with me!"

"*Nein!*" screamed the young German, looking frantically around, realizing his voice was lost in the enveloping bedlam.

"I said *yes!*" Converse shoved the newspaper inside his jacket and threw his right arm around Johann's neck, vicing the student into him. "You can think and do what you like but first you come with *me!* You're going to read me every goddamned word!"

"*Da ist es! Der Attentäter,*" shrieked the young German, reaching out, clutching the trousers of a man in the crowd who cursed and swung his arm down on the offending hand.

Joel wrenched the student's neck to his left, pulling him away while shouting into the student's ear, his words stunning himself as much as they did the young man. "You want it this way you can *have* it! I've got a gun in my pocket and if I have to use it I will! Two decent men have been killed already – now three – why should you be the exception? Because you're *young?* That's no reason! When you come right down to it, who the hell are we *dying* for?"

Converse yanked the youth back and forth, dragging him out of the crowd. Once on the clear pavement he released his armlock, replacing it with a strong grip on the back of Johann's neck. He propelled the student forward, his eyes roving the street, trying to find a secluded area where they could talk – where Johann could talk, reading a string of lies put out by the men of Aquitaine. The newspaper slipped down beneath his jacket; he reached in and grabbed it by the edge, pulling the paper out intact. He could not just keep walking, pushing his reluctant captive down the pavement; several people had glanced at them, fuel for the curious. Oh, *Christ!* The photograph – his *face!* Anyone might recognize him, and he was calling attention to himself by keeping the boy in tow.

Up ahead, on the right, there was a bakery or a coffee shop or a combination of both with tables under umbrellas on the sidewalk; several were empty at the far end. He would have preferred a deserted alley or a cobblestoned side street too narrow for vehicles, but he could not keep doing what he was doing, walking so rapidly with a prisoner in his grip.

"Over there! That table in the rear. You sit facing out. And remember, I wasn't joking about the gun; my hand will be in my pocket."

"*Please*, let me *go!* You've done enough to me! My friends know we left together last night; my landlady knows I got you a room! The police will *question* me!"

"Get in there," said Converse, shoving Johann between the chairs to the table at the rear of the pavement. Both sat down, the young German no longer trembling; instead his eyes were pivoting in all directions. "Don't even think about it," continued Joel. "And when a waiter comes over speak in English. *Only* English!"

"There are no waiters. Customers go inside and bring out their own sweet rolls and coffee."

"We'll do without – you can get something later. I owe you money and I pay my debts."

. . . I always pay my debts. At least during the last four years I have. Words from a note left by a risk-taker. An actor named Caleb Dowling.

"I want no money from you," said Johann, his English guttural with fear.

"You think it's tainted, makes you a true accessory, is that right?"

"You are the lawyer, I am merely a student."

"Let me set you straight. It's not tainted because I didn't do whatever they said I did and there's no such thing as an accessory to innocence."

"You are the lawyer, sir."

Converse pushed the newspaper in front of the young German and with his right hand reached into his pocket where he had put ten thousand Deutschemarks in ascending denominations for his immediate use. He counted out seven thousand and reached over, placing it in front of Johann. "Put that away before I shove it down your throat."

"I will not take your money!"

"You'll take it and tell them I gave it to you, if you want to. They'll have to give it back."

"*Was ist?*"

"The truth, counsellor. You'll find out one day that it's the best shield you've got. Now, read what the paper *says!*"

"The ambassador was killed some time last night," began the student haltingly, as he awkwardly put the Deutschemarks in his pocket. " . . . the approximate time of death is difficult to establish until further examinations," he continued, translating the words in the article in fits and starts, trying to find the appropriate meanings. " . . . The fatal wound was . . . *Schädel* – cranial, a head wound – the body in the water for many hours, washed up on the riverbank in the Plittersdorf and found early this morning . . . The military *chargé d'affaires* was quoted as saying that the last person known to have been with the ambassador was an American by the name of Joel Converse. When that name appeared there were . . ." The young German squinted, shaking his head nervously. "How do you *say* it?"

"I don't know," said Joel coldly, his voice flat. "What am I trying to say?"

" . . . very excited – frantic – communications between the governments of Switzerland, France and the Federal Republic, all in coordination with the International Criminal Police, otherwise known as Interpol, and the . . . pieces of the tragic . . . *Rätsel* . . . puzzle fell into place – became clear, it means. Unknown to Ambassador Peregrine, the American Converse had been the object of an Interpol . . . *Suche* . . . search as a result of killings in Geneva and Paris as well as several attempted murders not yet clarified." Johann looked up at Converse. There was a throbbing in his throat.

"Go on," ordered Joel. "You don't know how enlightening this is. Go *on!*"

"According to the ambassador's office a confidential meeting was arranged at the request of this man Converse, who claimed to have information injurious to American interests and which has subsequently proven to be false. The two men were to meet at the entrance of the Adenauer Bridge, between 7.30 and 8 o'clock last evening. The *chargé d'affaires* who accompanied Ambassador Peregrine confirmed that the two men met at 7.51 P.M. and started across the bridge on the pedestrian walkway. It was the last time anyone from the embassy saw the ambassador alive." Johann swallowed, his hands trembling. He took several deep breaths and went on, his eyes rushing forward across the print, beads of perspiration breaking out on his hairline. "Below are more complete . . . *eingehendere* . . . details as they are known, but a statement issued by Interpol described the suspect, Joel Converse, as an apparently normal man who is in reality a . . . *wandernde* . . ." The young German lowered his voice to a whisper. " . . . a walking explosive with severe mental disturbances. He is judged by several behavioural experts in the United States to be psychopathically ill as a result of nearly four years as a prisoner of war during the Vietnam conflict . . ."

As Johann stammered on, frightened by his own voice, the telling words and damning phrases came with staccato regularity, backed up by hastily-contacted departmental "sources" and unnamed, faceless "authorities'. The portrait was that of a mentally deranged man who had been thrown back in time, his derangement triggered by some violent event that left him with his intelligence intact but without moral or physical control. In addition, Interpol's search for him was spoken of in clouded terms, implying a secret manhunt that had been in progress for a number of days, if not weeks.

" . . . His homicidal tendencies are channelled," continued the now near-panicked student, the article quoting another "authoritative" source. " . . . He has a pathological hatred for present or former high-ranking military personnel, especially those who had gained prominent public stature . . . Ambassador Peregrine was a celebrated battalion commander in World War II's Bastogne campaign during which many American lives were lost . . . Authorities in Washington have speculated that the disturbed man, who after several harrowing attempts finally escaped from a maximum security camp in North Vietnam years ago, travelling over a hundred miles through enemy . . . *Dschungel* . . . jungle to reach his lines, is reliving his own experiences . . . His justification for survival – according to a military psychiatrist – is the killing of superior officers, past or present, who gave orders in combat, or in the extreme even civilians who in his imaginings bore some responsibility for the suffering he and others endured. Yet he is outwardly a normal man, as so many like him . . . Guards have been placed in Washington, London, Brussels, and here in Bonn . . . As an international lawyer, he is presumed to have access to numerous criminal elements who deal in illegal passports . . ."

It was a brilliantly executed trap, the crucial lies supported by truths, half truths, distortions and complete false-hoods. Even the precise timing of the evening was considered. The *chargé d'affaires* at the embassy stated unequivocally that he had seen Joel at the Adenauer Bridge "at 7.51 P.M.", approximately twenty-five minutes after he had broken out of the stone jailhouse on Leifhelm's estate, and less than ten minutes after he had plunged into the Rhine. Every fragment of the hour was accounted for. That he was "officially" placed at the bridge by "7.51" denied his story of capture and escape any credibility.

The incident in Geneva – the death of A. Preston Halliday – was introduced as a possible explanation for the violent act that had hurled him back in time, triggering Joel's maniacal behaviour. " . . . It has been learned that the attorney who was shot to death had been a well-known leader in the American protest movement in the 'sixties . . ." The veiled conclusion was that Converse might have hired the killers. Even the death of the man in Paris was given a much different and far more important dimension – oddly enough based in reality. " . . . Initially the victim's true identity was withheld in hopes of aiding the manhunt, as suspicions were aroused as a result of an interview the *Sûreté* had with a French lawyer who has known the suspect for a number of years. The attorney, who had lunched with the suspect that day, indicated that his American friend was in 'serious trouble' and needed "medical attention' . . ." The dead man in Paris, of course, was an outstanding colonel in the French army, and an aide successively to several "prominent generals".

Finally, as if to convince any remaining unbelievers in this public trial by "authoritative" journalism, references were made not only to his conduct but to the remarks he made upon his separation from service over a decade and a half ago. These were released by the United States Department of the Navy, Fifth Naval District, which included its own recommendation at the time that one Lieutenant Converse be placed under voluntary psychiatric observation; it was refused. His conduct had been insulting in the extreme to the panel of officers who wished only to help him, and his remarks were nothing short of violent threats against numerous high-ranking military personnel whom, as a carrier pilot, he could have known nothing about.

It all completed the portrait as painted by the artists of Aquitaine. Johann finished the article, the newspaper now clutched in his hands, his eyes wide and frightened. "That's all there is . . . sir."

"I'd hate to think there's any more," said Joel. "Do you believe it?"

"I have no thoughts. I'm too frightened to think."

"That's an honest answer. Uppermost in your mind is the fact that I might kill you, so you can't face what you think. That's what you're really saying. You're afraid that by a look or a wrong word I could take offence and pull a trigger."

"*Please*, sir, I am not adequate!"

"Neither was I."

"Let me *go*."

"*Johann*. My hands are on the table. They've been on the table since we sat down."

"*Was* . . . ?" The young German blinked and looked at Converse's forearms, both of which were in front of him, his hands clasped on the white metal surface. "You have no gun?"

"Oh, yes, I have a gun. I took it from a man who would have killed me if he'd had the chance." Joel reached into his pocket as Johann stiffened. "Cigarettes," said Converse, taking out a pack and a book of matches. "It's a terrible habit. Don't start if you haven't."

"It's very expensive."

"Among other things . . . We've talked off and on since last night." Joel struck a match, lighting a cigarette, his eyes remaining on the student. "Except for a few moments back there in the crowd when you could have had me lynched, do I look or sound like the man described in that newspaper story?"

"I am no more a doctor than a lawyer."

"Two points for the opposition. The burden of sanity's on me. Besides, it said I appeared perfectly normal."

"It said you suffered a great deal."

"Several hundred years ago, but no more than thousands of others and far, far less than some fifty-eight thousand who never came back. I don't think an insane man is capable of making a rational remark like that under these circumstances, do you?"

"I don't know what you're talking about."

"I'm trying to tell you that everything you just read to me is an example of a man being tried by negative journalism. Truths mixed with half-truths, distortions and implausible judgments were slanted to support the lies that are meant to convict me. There's not a court in any civilized country that would admit that kind of testimony or permit a jury to hear it."

"Men have been killed," said Johann, again his words whispered. "The ambassador was killed."

"Not by me. I wasn't anywhere near the Adenauer Bridge at eight o'clock last night. I don't even know where it is."

"Where were you?"

"Not where anyone saw me, if that's what you mean. And those who know I couldn't have been at the bridge would be the last people on earth to say so."

"There has to be some evidence of where you were." The young German nodded at the cigarette in Converse's hand. "Perhaps one of those. Perhaps you finished a cigarette."

"Or finger or footprints? Pieces of clothing? There's all of that but they don't tell the time."

"There are methods," corrected Johann. "The advances in the technology of . . . *Forschung* . . . the investigation techniques have been rapid."

"Let me finish that for you. I'm not a criminal lawyer but I know what you're saying. Theoretically, for example, the ground depression of a footprint matched with the scrapings off my shoes could put me where I was within the hour."

"*Ja!*"

"No. I'd be dead before a scrap of evidence reached a laboratory."

"*Why?*"

"I can't tell you. I wish to God I could but I can't."

"Again, I must ask why?" The fear in the young man's eyes was joined by disappointment, the last glimpse of believability, perhaps, gone with Joel's refusal to explain.

"Because I can't, I won't. You said a few minutes ago that I'd done enough to you and without meaning to, I have. But I won't do this. You're not in a position to do anything but get yourself killed. That's as frankly as I can put it, Johann."

"I see."

"No you don't, but I wish there was a way to convince you that I have to reach others. People who *can* do something. They're not here; they're not in Bonn, but I'll reach them if I can get away."

"There's something else? You would have me do something *else?*" The young German stiffened again and again his hands trembled.

"No. I don't want you to do anything. I'm asking you *not* to do anything – at least for a while. Nothing. Give me a chance to get out of here and somehow get in touch with people who can help me – help all of us."

"All of us?"

"I mean that and it's all I'll say."

"These people are not to be found in your own embassy, *Amerikaner?*"

Converse looked hard at Johann, has eyes as steady as he could manage in light of the snapping newspapers at most of the nearby tables. "Ambassador Walter Peregrine was killed by one or more men at that embassy. They came to kill me last night at the hotel."

Johann breathed deeply, taking his eyes off Joel and staring down at the table. "Back at the kiosk, in the crowd, when you threatened me . . . you said three men had been killed already – three decent men."

"I'm sorry. I was desperate."

"It wasn't simply that, it was what you said right afterwards. You said why should I be the exception? Because I was young? That was no reason, you claimed, and then you shouted very strange words – I remember them precisely.

You said: 'When you come right down to it, who the hell are we dying for?' It was more than a question, I think."

"I won't discuss the implications of that remark, counsellor. And I can't tell you what to do. I can only tell you what I've told dozens of clients over the years. When a decision is reduced to several strong opposing arguments – mine included – and you've listened to them all, put them behind you and follow your own gut instinct. Depending upon who and what you are, it'll be the right one for you. Converse paused, pushing back his chair. "Now I'm going to get up and walk out of here. If you start screaming, I'll run and try to hide somewhere where I'll be safe before anyone recognizes me. Then I'll do whatever I can do. If you don't set off an alarm, I'll have a better chance, and in my view that would be best . . . for all of us. You could go to the university library and come out in an hour or so, buy a paper, and go to the police. I'd expect you to do that, if you felt you had to. That's my view. I don't know what yours is. Goodbye, Johann."

Joel rose from the table, bringing his hand instantly to his face, his fingers spread, touching his eyebrows. He turned and walked through the tables to the pavement, veering right, heading for the first intersection. He barely took a breath, his lungs bursting for air but he dared not let even a breath impair his hearing. He waited as he walked, his pulse accelerating, his ears so alive that the slightest dissonance would have burned them.

There were only the sounds of the excited street conversations in counterpoint with the blaring horns of taxis – but these were not the dissonance he was prepared for; that would come with the screams of a young male voice raising an alarm. It did not come; he walked faster, entering the flow of pedestrians crossing the square – faster, *faster* – passing strollers who saw no need to rush. He reached the kerb of the opposite pavement and slowed down – a rapidly walking man called attention to himself; he dared not do that either. Yet the impulse to break into a run was almost uncontrollable the farther he distanced himself from the tables of the sidewalk bakery café. His ear had picked up no alarm and every split second of that absence told him to race into whatever secluded side streets he could find.

Nothing. Nothing broke the excitable discordant sounds of the square – no hysterical voice raised above the din – but there *was* a change, a discernible change, and it had nothing to do with strident alarms provoked by a single screaming voice. The discordant sounds *themselves* had been lowered, replaced by a growing symphony of shrugs and gestures of incomprehensibility and obvious relaxation. The words *Amerikaner – Amerikaner* were repeated everywhere. The panic of the first news had passed. An American had killed an American; it was not a German assassin, or a communist, or even a terrorist who had eluded the Federal Republic's security arrangements. Life could go on; Deutschland could not be held responsible for the death – and a sigh of relief could be felt among the citizens of Bonn.

Converse spun around the corner of a brick building and stared across the square at the tables of the bakery-café. The student, Johann, remained in his chair, his head bowed, supported by both hands, reading the newspaper. Then he got up and walked into the bakery itself. *Was there a telephone inside? Would he talk to someone?*

How long can I wait? thought Converse, prepared to run, as instinct held him back.

Johann came out of the bakery carrying a tray of coffee and rolls. He sat down and meticulously separated the plates from the tray and once again stared at the newspaper in front of him. Then he looked up at nothing in particular – as if he knew he was being watched by unseen eyes – and nodded once.

Another risk-taker, thought Joel, as he turned and looked and listened to the unfamiliar sights and sounds of the side street he had entered. He had been given a few hours; he wished he knew how to use them – he wished he knew what to *do*.

Valerie ran to the phone. If it was another reporter, she would say the same thing she had said to the last five. *I don't believe a word of it and I've nothing more to say!* And if it was one more person from Washington – from the FBI or the CIA or the VA or any other combinations of the alphabet, she would scream! She had spent three hours being interviewed that morning until she had literally ordered the crucifiers out of the house. They were liars trying to force her to support their lies. It would be far easier to take the phone off the hook but she could not do that. She had called Lawrence Talbot in New York twice, telling his office to trace him wherever he was and have him call her back. It was all madness. *Insanity!* as Joel used to say with such quiet intensity she thought his voice was a wild roar of protest.

"Hello?"

"*Valley?* It's Roger."

"*Dad!*" Only one person had ever called her by that name and that man was her former father-in-law. The fact that she was no longer married to his son had made no difference in their relationship. She adored the old pilot and knew he felt the same about her. "Where *are* you? Ginny didn't know and she's frantic. You forgot to turn on your answering machine."

"I didn't forget, Valley. Too damned many people to call back. I just flew in from Hong Kong when I got off the plane I was up-winded by fifty or sixty screaming newspaper people and so many lights and cameras I won't be able to see or hear for a week."

"Some enterprising airline clerk let out the word you were on board. Whoever it was will eat for a week off a generous expense account. Where are you?"

"Still at the airport – in the traffic manager's office. I'll say this for 'em, they got me out of there . . . Valley, I just read the papers. They got me the latest editions. What the *hell* is this all about?"

"I don't know, Dad, but I do know it's a lie."

"That boy's the sanest thing I ever had anything to do with! They're twisting everything, making the good things he did into something . . . I don't know, sinister or something. He's too damned *up-front* to be crazy!"

"He's not crazy, Roger. He's being taken, he's being put through a wringer."

"What *for?*"

"I don't know. But I think Larry Talbot does — at least more than he's told me."

"What *has* he told you?"

"Not now, Dad. Later."

"Why?"

"I'm not sure . . . Something I feel, perhaps."

"You're not making sense, Valley."

"I'm sorry."

"What did Ginny say? I'll call her, of course."

"She's hysterical."

"She always was — a little bit."

"No, not that way. She's blaming herself. She thinks people are striking out at her brother for the things *she* did in the 'sixties. I tried to tell her that was nonsense but I'm afraid I made it worse. She asked me perfectly calmly if I believed what was being said about Joel. I told her of course I didn't."

"The old paranoia. Three kids and an accountant for a husband and it still comes back. I never could handle that girl. Damned good pilot, though. Soloed before Joel, and she was two years younger. I'll phone her."

"You may not be able to reach her."

"Oh?"

"She's having her number changed and I think you should do the same thing. I know I'm going to the minute I hear from Larry."

"Valley . . ." Roger Converse paused. " . . . don't do that."

"Why not? Have you any idea what it's been *like* here?"

"Look, you know I've never asked what happened between you and Joel, but I usually have dinner with that piss ant lawyer once a week when I'm in town. He thinks it's some kind of filial necessity but I'd knock it off in a minute if I didn't like him. I mean he's a likeable guy, kind of funny sometimes."

"I know all that, Roger. What are you trying to say?"

"*They* say he disappeared, that no one can find him."

"And?"

"He may call you. I can't think of anyone else he would call."

Valerie closed her eyes; the afternoon sun through the skylight was blinding. "Is that based on your weekly dinner conversations?"

"It's not intuition. I never had any except in the air . . . Of course it is. It was never said outright, but it was always just below the cloud cover."

"You're impossible, Dad."

"Pilot error's like any other. There are times when you can't afford it . . . Don't change your number, Valley."

"I won't."

"Now what about me?"

"Ginny's husband had a good idea. They're referring all questions to their attorney. Maybe you should do the same. Do you have one?"

"Sure," said Roger Converse. "I got three. Talbot, Brooks and Simon. Nate's the best, if you want to know the truth. Did you know at the age of sixty-seven that son of a bitch took up flying? He's qualified in multi-engines now – can you imagine?"

"*Dad!*" broke in Valerie, suddenly. "You're at the airport?"

"That's what I said. Kennedy."

"Don't go home. Don't go to your apartment. Take the first plane you can to Boston. Use another name. Call me back and let me know what flight you're on. I'll pick you up."

"*Why?*"

"Just do as I say, Roger. *Please!*"

"What for?"

"You're staying here. I'm leaving."

21

Converse hurried out of the clothing store on the crowded Bornheimer Strasse and studied his reflection in the window. He surveyed the overall effect of his purchases, not as he had done inside in front of the full length mirror for fit and appearance, but as one of the strolling pedestrians on the sidewalk. He was satisfied; there was nothing about the clothes that called attention to him. The photograph in the papers – the only one in the past fifteen years that would be in a wire service or newspaper file – was taken about a year ago when he was one of several merger attorneys interviewed by Reuters. It was a head-and-shoulders shot, showing him in his lawyer's wardrobe – a dark suit and waistcoat, white shirt and a striped tie, the image of a rising international specialist. It was also the image everyone who read the papers had of him, and since it would not change, only spread, then he was the one who had to change.

Also, he could not continue to wear the clothes he had worn to the bank. A panicked Lachmann would undoubtedly give a complete description to the police, but even if his panic rendered him silent, those clothes were dark, the shirt white, the tie striped. Unconsciously or not, thought Joel, he had sought a patina of respectability. Perhaps all men running for their lives did so, their essential dignity stolen from them. Regardless, dressed in those clothes he was the man in the newspaper photograph.

The appearance he had in mind belonged to a history professor at college, a man whose various articles of clothing were all related. His jackets were always subdued tweeds with elbow patches, the trousers grey – heavy and light flannel, never anything else – and his shirts were button-down Oxford blue, again without exception. Above his thick horn-rimmed glasses was perched a soft Irish walking hat, the brim sloped downward front and back. Wherever that man went, whether down a street in Boston or on New York's Fifth Avenue or Beverly Hills' Rodeo

Drive – which Joel was sure he never saw – one would know he belonged to academic New England.

Converse had managed to duplicate the outward appearance of the man in his memory, tinted glasses replacing the horn-rims, but only for a while. He had passed a large variety store, Bonn's equivalent of an American Five-and-Dime, and he knew that there would be a counter with different sizes and shapes of glasses, a few slightly magnified for reading, others clear.

For reasons that were only beginning to come into focus, those glasses were now vital to him. Then he understood. He was preoccupied with what he knew he *could* do – change his appearance. He was procrastinating, uncertain what to do next, not sure he was capable of doing anything.

He looked at his face in the oval mirror of the variety store, again satisfied with what he saw. The ersatz tortoiseshell rims were thick, the glass clear; the effect was owlish, scholarly. He was no longer the man in the newspaper photograph and, equally important, the concentration he had devoted to his appearance, had begun to clear his mind. He could think again, sit down somewhere and sort things out. He also needed food and a drink.

The café was crowded, the stained glass windows muting the summer sunlight into shafts of blue and red piercing the smoke. He was shown to a table against the black-leathered upholstered banquette, assured by the *maître*, or whoever he was, that all he had to do was request a menu in English; the items were numbered. Whisky on the Continent, however, was universally accepted as Scotch; he ordered a double, and took out the pad and ballpoint pen he had picked up at the variety store. His drink came and he proceeded to write.

Connal Fitzpatrick?
Briefcase?
$93,000.00 plus
Embassy out
No Larry Talbot et al
No Beale
No Anstett
No man in San Francisco
Men in Washington. Who?
Caleb Dowling? No.
Hickman, Navy, San Diego? Possible.
. . . Mattilon?

René! Why hadn't he thought of Mattilon *before?* He understood why the Frenchman made the remarks attributed to him anonymously in the newspaper story. René was trying to be protective. If there was no defence, or if it was so weak as not to be viable, the most logical back-up was temporary insanity. Joel circled Mattilon's name and wrote the number 1 on the left, circling it also. He would find a telephone exchange in the street, the kind where operators assigned booths to bewildered tourists, and call René in Paris. He drank two swallows of whisky, relaxing as the warmth spread through him then went back to his list, starting at the top.

Connal . . . ? The presumption that he had been killed was inevitable but it was not conclusive. If he was alive, he was being held for whatever information could be pried out of him. As the Chief Legal Officer of the West Coast's largest and most powerful naval base, and a man who had a history of meetings with the State Department's Office of Munitions Control as well as its counterparts at the Pentagon, Fitzpatrick could be an asset to the men of Aquitaine. Yet to call attention to him was to guarantee his execution if he had not been killed already. If he *was* still alive, the only way to save him was to find him, but not in any orthodox or official manner; it had to be done secretly. Connal had to be rescued secretly. Suddenly, Joel saw the figure of a man in the uniform of the United States Army across the café talking with two civilians at the bar. He did not know the man. It was the uniform that struck him. It brought to mind the military *chargé d'affaires* at the embassy, that extraordinarily observant and precise officer who was capable of seeing a man who was not at a bridge at the exact moment he was not there. A liar for Aquitaine, someone whose lies identified him. If that liar did not know where Fitzpatrick was, he could be made to find out. Perhaps there was a way, after all. Converse drew a line on the right side of his list, connecting Connal Fitzpatrick with Admiral Hickman in San Diego. He did not give it a number; there was too much to consider.

Briefcase? He was still convinced that Leifhelm's men had not found it. If the generals of Aquitaine had that attaché case, they would have let him know. It was not like those men to conceal such a prize, not from the prisoner who had thought he was a match for them. No, they would have told him one way or the other, if only to make clear to him how totally he had failed. If he was right, Connal had hidden it. At the inn called *Das Rektorat?* It was worth a try. Joel circled the word *Briefcase* and numbered it 2.

"*Speisekarte, Mein Herr?*" said a waiter who had come up to the table before Converse knew it.

"English, please?"

"Certainly, sir." The waiter separated his menus as though they were an outsize deck of cards. He selected one and handed it to Joel as he spoke. "The *Spezialität* for today is *Wienerschnitzel* – it is the same in English."

"That's fine. Keep the menu, I'll take it."

"*Danke.*" The man swept away before Joel could order another drink. It was just as well, he thought.

$93,000.00 plus. There was nothing more to be said; the irritating bulge around his waist said it all. He had the money; it was to be used.

Embassy out . . . No Larry Talbot, et al . . . No Beale . . . No Anstett . . . No man in San Francisco. Throughout the meal he thought about each item, each statement, wondering how it all could have happened. Every step had been considered carefully, facts absorbed, dossiers memorized, caution uppermost. But everything had been blown away by complications far beyond the simple facts provided by Preston Halliday in Geneva.

Build just two or three cases that are tied to Delavane – even circumstantially – and it'll be enough.

In the light of the revelations on Mykonos, then in Paris, Copenhagen and

Bonn, the simplicity of that remark was almost criminal. Halliday would have been appalled at the depth and breadth of influence Delavane's legions had attained, at the penetrations they had made at the highest levels of the military, the police, Interpol and, obviously now, those who controlled the flow of news from so-called "authoritative sources" in western governments! It *was* appalling.

Converse abruptly checked his racing thoughts. He suddenly realized that he was thinking about Halliday in the context of a man who saw only a pair of eyes at night in the jungle, unaware of the size or the ferocity of the unseen animal in the darkness. That was wrong. Halliday knew the materials Beale was handing over to him on an island in the Aegean; he knew about the connections between Paris, Bonn, Tel Aviv and Johannesburg; he knew about the decision-makers in the State Department and the Pentagon – he knew it *all!* He had *arranged* it all with unknown men in Washington! Halliday had lied in Geneva. A Californian wrestler he had befriended years ago in school named Avery Fowler was the manipulator, and in the name of A. Preston Halliday, he had lied.

Where were those subterranean men in Washington who had the audacity to raise half a million dollars for an incredible gamble but were too frightened to come out in the open? What kind of men *were* they? Their scout had been killed, their puppet accused of being a psychopathic assassin. How long could they *wait? What* were they?

The questions enraged Converse, so much so that he tried not to pursue them as they led only to fury. They blinded his reason. He needed reason and, above all, the protection that came with awareness. He could not risk blindness. It was time to find a telephone exchange and reach Mattilon in Paris. René would believe him, René would help him. It was unthinkable that his old friend would do anything else.

The civilian walked in silence to the hotel window, knowing he was expected to deliver a pronouncement that would form the basis of a miracle – not a solution but a miracle, and there were no such things in the business he knew so well. Peter Stone was by all the rules a relic, a castaway who had seen it all, and in the final years of seeing had finally fallen apart. Alcohol had taken the place of true audacity, at the end rendering him a professional mutant, a part of him still proud of past accomplishments, another part sickened by the waste, by the knowledge of wasted lives, wasted strategies – morality thrown into a gargantuan wastebasket of a collective non-conscience.

Still, he had once been one of the best – he could not forget that. And when it was all over he had faced the fact that he was killing himself with a plethora of bourbon and self-pity; he had pulled out. But not before he had gained the enmity of his past employers in the Central Intelligence Agency, not for speaking out publicly but for telling them privately who and what they were. Fortunately, as sobriety returned, he learned that his past employers had other enemies in Washington, enemies having nothing to do with foreign entanglements or competition. Simply men and women serving the Republic who wanted to know what the hell was going on when Langley wouldn't tell them. He had survived

– was surviving. He thought about these things knowing that the two other men in the room believed he was concentrating on the issue at hand.

There was no issue. The file was closed, the border rimmed in black. They were so young – God, so *damned* young! – they would find it too terrible to accept. He remembered – vaguely – when such a conclusion appalled him. But that was nearly forty years ago; he was almost sixty now and he had heard such conclusions repeated too often to sweat the bullets of regret. The regret – the sadness was there – but time and repetition had dulled his senses; clear evaluation was everything. Stone turned and spoke.

"We can't *do anything*," he said with quiet authority. The Army captain and the Navy lieutenant were visibly upset. Peter Stone continued. "I spent twenty-three years in the tunnels, including a decade with Angleton, and I'm telling you there's absolutely nothing we can do. We have to let him hang out, we can't touch him."

"Because we can't *afford* to?" asked the naval officer scathingly. "That's what you said when Halliday was killed in Geneva. We can't *afford* to!"

"We can't. We were outmanoeuvred."

"That's a *man* out there," insisted the lieutenant. "We *sent* him out . . ."

"And they set him up," broke in the civilian, his voice calm, his eyes sadly knowledgeable. "He's as good as dead. We'll have to start looking elsewhere."

"Why is that?" asked the Army captain. "Why is he as good as dead?"

"They have too many controls, we can see that now. If they don't have him locked up in a cellar, they know pretty much where he is. Whoever finds him will kill him. A riddled body of a crazed killer is delivered up and there's a collective sigh of relief. That's the scenario."

"And that's the most cold-blooded analysis of a murder I've ever heard! *Murder*, an unwarranted execution!"

"Look, Lieutenant," said Stone, stepping away from the window. "You asked me to come with you – convinced me I should – because you wanted some experience in this room. With that experience comes the moment when you recognize and accept the fact that you've been beaten. It doesn't mean you're finished, but you've been punched out of the round. We've been punched out, and it's my guess the punches haven't stopped yet."

"Maybe . . ." began the captain haltingly. "Maybe we should go to the Agency, tell them everything we know – everything we *think* we know – and what we've done. It might get Converse out alive."

"Sorry," countered the former CIA man. "They want his head and they'll get it. They wouldn't have gone to all this trouble if 'dead' wasn't written all over him. That's the way it works."

"What kind of world do you live in?" asked the naval officer quietly, shaking his head.

"I don't live in it any more, Lieutenant, you know that. I think it's one of the reasons you came to me. I did what you two – and whoever else is with you – are doing now. I blew a whistle, only I did it with two months of bourbon in my veins and ten years of disgust in my head. You say you might go to the Company?

Good, go ahead, but you'll do it without me. No one worth a quarter in Langley will touch me."

"We can't go to G-2 or Naval Intelligence," said the Army officer. "We know that, we've all agreed. Delavane's people are there; they'd shoot us down."

"Aptly put, Captain. Would you believe with real bullets?"

"I do now," said the naval man, nodding at Stone. "The report out of San Diego is that the legal, Remington, was killed in an automobile accident in La Jolla. He's the one who last spoke to Fitzpatrick, and before he left the base, he asked another legal the directions to a restaurant in the hills. He'd never been there – and I don't think it was an accident."

"Neither do I," agreed the civilian. "But it takes us to the somewhere-else we can look."

"What do you mean?" said the Army captain.

"Fitzpatrick. SAND PAC can't find him, right?"

"He's on leave," interjected the naval officer. "He's got another twenty days or so. He wasn't ordered to list his itinerary."

"Still they've tried to find him but they can't."

"And I still don't understand," objected the captain.

"We go after Fitzpatrick," said Stone. "Out of San Diego, not Washington. We find a reason to *really* want him back. A SAND PAC emergency, routed strictly through Eyes-Only, a base problem – nobody else's."

"I hate to repeat myself," said the Army man, "but you've lost me. Where do we start? Whom do we start with?"

"With one of your own, Captain. Right now he's a very important person. The *chargé d'affaires* at the Mehlemer House."

"The what?"

"The American Embassy in Bonn. He's one of them. He lied when it counted most," said Stone. "His name is Washburn. Major Norman Anthony Washburn, the Fourth."

The telephone complex was off the lobby of an office building. It was a large square room with five enclosed booths built into three walls and a high, squared counter in the centre where four operators sat in front of consoles, each woman obviously capable of speaking two or more languages. Telephone directories of the major European cities and their suburbs were on racks to the left and right of the entrance, small pads with attached ballpoint pens on ledges above for the convenience of those seeking numbers. The routine was familiar: A caller delivered a written-out number to an operator, specified the manner of payment – cash, credit card, or collect – and was assigned a booth. There were no lines; a half dozen booths were empty.

Joel found the number of Matillon's law firm in the Paris directory. He wrote it out, brought it to an operator and said he would pay cash. He was told to go to booth number seven and wait for the ring. He entered it quickly, the soft cloth brim of his hat falling over his forehead above the tortoiseshell glasses. Any enclosure, whether a toilet stall or a glass booth, was preferable to being out in the open. He felt his pulse accelerating; it seemed to explode when the bell rang.

"*Saint Pierre, Nelli et Matillon,*" said the female voice in Paris.

"Monsieur Mattilon, please – *s'il vous plaît.*"

"*Votre . . . ?*" The woman stopped, undoubtedly recognizing an American's abysmal attempt at French. "Who may I say is calling, please?"

"His friend from New York. He'll know. I'm a client."

René did know. After several clicks his strained voice came on the line. "Joel?" he whispered. "I don't believe it!"

"Don't," said Converse. "It's not true – not what they say about Geneva or Bonn, not even what *you* said. I had nothing to do with those killings, and Paris was an accident. I had every reason to think – I *did* think – that man was reaching for a gun."

"Why didn't you stay where you were then, my friend?"

"Because they wanted to stop me from going on. It's what I honestly believed, and I couldn't let them do that. Let me talk . . . At the George V you asked me questions and I gave you evasive answers and I think you saw through me. But you were kind and went along. You have nothing to be sorry about, take my word for it – my very *sane* word. Bertholdier came to me that evening in my room; we talked and he panicked. Six days ago I saw him again here in Bonn – only this time it was different. He was ordered to be there, along with three other very powerful men, two generals and a former field marshal. It's a cabal, René, an international cabal, and they can pull it off. Everything's secret and moving fast. They've recruited key military personnel all over Europe, the Mediterranean, Canada, and the US. There's no way to tell who's with them and who isn't – and there isn't time to make a mistake. They've got millions at their disposal, warehouses all over filled with munitions ready to ship to their people when the moment comes."

"The moment?" broke in Mattilon. "What moment?"

"Please," insisted Joel, rushing ahead. "They've been funnelling weapons and explosives to maniacs everywhere – terrorists, provos, certified lunatics – with one purpose only: Destabilization through violence. It's their excuse to move in. Right now they're blowing up Northern Ireland."

"The madness in *Ulster?*" interrupted the Frenchman again. "The horrors going on . . ."

"It's *their* horror! It's a trial run. They did it with one massive shipment from the States – to prove they *can* do it! But Ireland's only a test, a minor exercise. The big explosion's coming in a matter of days, a few weeks at most. I've got to reach the people who can stop them and I can't do that if I'm dead!" Converse paused, only to catch his breath, giving Mattilon no chance to speak. "These are the men I was after, René – after *legally,* to build a few cases against them, expose them in the courts before they got anywhere. But then I found out. They're already there. I was too late."

"But why *you?*"

"It started in Geneva – with Halliday, the man who was shot to death. He was killed by their gunmen, but not before he recruited me. You asked me about

Geneva and I lied to you, but that's the truth ... Now you'll either help me, or try to help me, or you won't. Not for me – I'm insignificant – but what I got roped into isn't. And I *was* roped into it, I know that now. But I've seen them, *talked* to them, and they're so goddamned logical, so fucking persuasive, they'll turn all Europe fascist; they'll set up a military federation with my country the progenitor. Because it started in my country; it started in San Francisco with a man named Delavane."

"Saigon? The Mad Marcus of *Saigon?*"

"Alive and well and living in Palo Alto, pushing his military buttons all over the place. He's still a magnet and they're drawn to him like flies to a pig."

"Joel, are you ... are you ... all *right?*"

"Let's put it this way, René. I took a lousy watch off a man who guarded me – a paranoid who nevertheless was nice to me – and it's got a sweep hand. You've got thirty seconds to think about what I've told you, then I'll hang up. *Now*, old friend, twenty-nine seconds."

Ten passed and Mattilon spoke. "An insane man does not deliver such a precise explanation so precisely. Nor does he use such words as 'progenitor'; it is not in his vocabulary ... Very well, perhaps I am mad, too, but what you speak of – God knows the times are right, what else can I say? *Everything* is crazy!"

"I've got to get back to the States alive, to Washington. I know people there. If I can reach them and show myself for what I am, they'll listen to me. Can you help?"

"I have contacts in the Quai d'Orsay. Let me go to them."

"No," objected Converse strenuously. "They know we're friends. One word to the wrong person and you'd be killed. Forgive me, but more important, your talking would set off alarms. We can't afford that."

"Very well," said Mattilon. "There is a man in Amsterdam – don't ask me how I know him – who can arrange such things. I assume you have no passport."

"I have one but it's not mine. It's German. I took it off a guard who was ready to put a bullet in my head."

"Then I'm sure he's not in a position to complain to the authorities."

"He's not."

"In your mind you really did go back, didn't you, my friend?"

"Let's not talk about it, okay?"

"*Bien*. You are you. Keep that passport; it will be useful."

"Amsterdam. How do I get there?"

"You are in Bonn, no?"

"Yes."

"There is a train to Emmerich on the Dutch border. In Emmerich switch to local transport – streetcars, autobuses, whatever. The customs are lax, especially during the peak hours when workers go back and forth. No one looks, so just show the passport you have quickly, partially covering the photograph, perhaps. It's good that it's German. You should have no trouble."

"Suppose I do?"

"Then I can't help you, my friend. I'm being honest. And then I *must* go to the Quai d'Orsay."

"All right. I get across, then what?"

"You'll reach Arnhem. From there you take the train to Amsterdam."

"And then?"

"The man. His name is on a card in my bottom drawer. Do you have something to write on – write with?"

"Go ahead," said Converse, reaching for the notepad and the ballpoint pen on the ledge beneath the telephone.

"Here it is. Thorbecke. Cort Thorbecke. The apartment house is on the southwest corner of Utrechtse and Kerk Straats. The telephone number is zero-two-zero, four-one-one-three-zero. When you call for an appointment, tell him you are a member of the Tatiana family. Do you have that? *Tatiana*."

"René . . . ?" said Joel, writing. "I never would have guessed. How come you know someone like this?"

"I told you not to ask but on the other hand he may probe and you should have at least vague answers – everything was always vague. Tatiana is a Russian name, one of the Czar's daughters reputedly executed at Ekaterinburg in 1918. I say reputedly because many believe she was spared along with her sister Anastasia and smuggled out with a nurse who had a fortune of jewels on her. The nurse favoured Tatiana and once free gave everything to the child and nothing to her sister. It's said she lived anonymously in great wealth – may even be living today – but no one knows where."

"That's what I have to know?" asked Converse.

"No, it's merely the origins of its present meaning. Today it is a symbol of trust given to very few people in recent years, people who themselves are trusted by the most suspicious men on earth, men who cannot afford to make mistakes."

"Good Lord, who?"

"Russians, powerful Soviet commissars who have a fondness for Western banking, who broker money out of Moscow for investments. You can understand why the circle is small. Few are called and fewer chosen. Thorbecke is one of them and he does an extensive business in passports. I'll reach him and tell him to expect your call. Remember, no name, just Tatiana. He'll have you on a KLM to Washington in short order. You'll need money, however, so we must think how I can . . . "

"Money's one thing I don't need," interrupted Converse. "Just a passport and a plane ticket to Dulles Airport without being picked up."

"Get to Amsterdam. Thorbecke will help."

"Thank you, René. I wanted to count on you and you came through. It means a lot to me. It means my life."

"You're not in Washington yet, my friend. But call me when you get there, no matter the hour."

"I will. Thanks, again."

Joel hung up, put the notepad and the pen into his pocket, and went out of the booth to the counter. He asked for his charges and, while the English-speaking operator was getting them, he remembered the item he had marked 2 on his list. His attaché case with the dossiers and the names of the decision-makers at the Pentagon and the State Department. *Das Rektorat*. Through some extraordinary oversight on Leifhelm's part, had Connal managed to hide it somewhere? Could it have been found perhaps by an employee at the country inn? Converse spoke to the operator who was handing him his bill.

"There's a place called *Das Rektorat*. It's a hotel in the countryside – where I'm not sure, but I'd like to call it and reach the manager. I'm told he speaks English."

"Yes, sir. *Das Rektorat* has splendid accommodation, if any is available."

"I'm not looking for a reservation. A friend of mine stayed there last week and thinks he may have left a valuable item in his room. He called me and asked me to check for him, to speak with the manager. If I find the number, would you place the call for me and get him on the line? I'm sorry to say I don't speak German; I'd probably reach the chef."

"Certainly, sir," replied the woman, smiling. "It would be easier for me to get the number. Return to booth seven and I'll ring you. You can pay for both calls when you are finished."

Inside the glass enclosure Joel lighted a cigarette, thinking about what he was going to say. He barely had time to formulate his words when the ring came.

"This is the *Vorsteher* – the manager – of *Das Rektorat*, sir," said the operator. "And he does speak English."

"Thank you." The operator broke off her connection. "Hello?"

"Yes, may I help you, sir?"

"I hope so. I'm an American friend of Commander Connal Fitzpatrick, Chief Legal Officer of the San Diego Naval Base in California. I understand he stayed there last week."

"Indeed he did, sir. We were so sorry we could not have extended his visit with us but there was a prior reservation."

"Oh? He left unexpectedly?"

"I shouldn't put it that way. We spoke in the morning and I believe he understood our situation. I myself made arrangements for a taxi."

"He was alone when he left?"

"Yes, sir."

"Oh. Then if you'll tell me which hotel he went to, I can check there as well."

"Check, sir?"

"The Commander misplaced one of his briefcases, a flat leather type with two combination locks. The contents are of no value except to him, but he very much wants to find it. It was a present from his wife, I think. Have you come across it?"

"No, *Mein Herr*."

"Are you *sure*? The Commander has a habit of concealing his legal papers, sometimes under a bed or in the back of a closet."

"He left nothing here, sir. The room was thoroughly examined and cleaned by our staff."

286

"Perhaps someone came to see him and took the wrong case." Converse knew he was pressing but there was no reason not to.

"He had no visitors . . ." The German paused. "Just one moment, I do recall now."

"Yes?"

"You say a flat briefcase, what is generally referred to as an attaché case?"

"Yes!"

"He carried it with him. It was in his hand when he left."

"Oh . . ." Joel tried to recover quickly. "Then if you'll just tell me what forwarding address he left, what hotel he went to."

"I'm sorry sir. There were no such instructions."

"Somebody had to make a reservation for him! Rooms are tight in Bonn!"

"Please, *Mein Herr*. I myself offered to try but he refused my aid, somewhat discourteously I might add."

"I'm sorry." Joel was annoyed that he had lost control. "Those legal papers were important. Then you have no idea where he went?"

"But I do, sir, if one wishes to be humoured. I made a point of asking. He said he was going to the *Bahnhof*, the train station. If anyone asked for him, we were to say he was sleeping in a baggage locker. I'm afraid it was also meant discourteously."

The *train* station? A locker! It was a *message!* Fitzpatrick was telling him where to look! Without speaking further, Converse hung up the phone, left the booth, and went to the counter. He paid for both calls and thanked the operator, wanting to leave her a tip but knowing it would only call attention to him. "You've been very kind and, if I may, one last favour."

"Sir?"

"Where is the train station?"

"You can't miss it. Turn left out of the building and walk four streets, then left again for two more. It is one of the more uncertain prides of Bonn."

"You've been very kind."

Joel hurried down the pavement constantly reminding himself to check his speed. Everything depended on control now, *everything*. Every move he made had to be normal, even casual, nothing to cause anyone to take a second glance at him. It was another omen! He was beginning to think they *did* exist. Mattilon had told him to take a train; Fitzpatrick had told him to go to the train station. A locker!

He walked through the large open doors of the entrance and turned to his right towards the row of lockers where he had left the attaché case before heading out to the Alter Zoll to meet "Avery Fowler". He reached the locker itself; there was a key in it, nothing inside. He began scrutinizing the lockers around it, on both sides, below, not at all sure what he was looking for but knowing he was looking for *something*. He found it! Two rows above on the left! The initials were small but clear, scratched into the metal by a strong, precise hand. *C.F.* Connal Fitzpatrick!

The Navy lawyer had done it! He had put the explosive papers back where only the two of them knew where they would be. Suddenly Converse felt sick.

How could he get them out? How could he get *inside?* He looked around the station, peering between the summer crowds. The huge clock read 2.30; in two and a half hours the offices would be closed, the business day over, the crowds fuller. Mattilon had told him to reach Emmerich during the busiest time, when workers travelled back and forth across the border at the end of the day, and it took nearly two hours to reach Emmerich, *if* there was a train. He had less than a half hour to get inside the locker.

There was an information booth at the far end of the cavernous station. He walked towards it, his mind again racing, choosing words that might produce a key. The abrasive weight of the money belt around his waist gave him a glimpse of hope.

"Thank you very much," he said to the clerk, his tortoiseshell glasses perched on his nose, the cloth hat falling over his forehead. He had been assigned an English-speaking, middle-aged information-dispenser with a pinched face and bored, irritated expression. "Quite simply I've lost the key to the locker in which I stored my luggage and I have to get a train to Emmerich. By the way, when is the next one?"

"*Ach*, it is always ze case," replied the cat-faced clerk, thumbing a schedule. "Nozzing but trouble wiz zer sommer people. You lose ziss, you lose zat; and you expect everyone to help you! Zer train for Emmerich left twenty-seven minutes ago. Zer iss another in nineteen *minuten*, but nozzing after that for an hour."

"Thank you. I have to be on it. Now, about the locker?" Joel removed a hundred Deutschemark note below the counter, and raised it slowly above the ledge. "It's very important that I get my luggage and take that train. May I shake your hand for helping me?"

"It will be done!" exclaimed the clerk quietly, looking to his right and left as he grasped Converse's hand and the money. He picked up the phone at his side and dialled abusively. "*Schnell! Wir müssen ein Schliessfach öffnen. Standort zehn Auskunft!*" He slammed down the phone and looked up at Joel, a smile sculpted onto his rigid lips. "A man will be here instantly to be of service, *Mein Herr*. We are always eager to be of service. The *Amerikaner*, so thoughtful."

The man came, bulging out of his railroad uniform, his eyes dull, his authority questionable. "*Was ist los?*"

The clerk explained in German, then looked again at Converse. "He speaks some English, not well, of course, but adequately, and he will assist you."

"Zer are regulations," said the official keeper of the locker keys. "Come, show me."

"Happy Birthday," said Joel to the clerk behind the information booth.

"It is not my birthday, *Mein Herr*."

"How would you know?" asked Converse, smiling, taking the fat man's arm.

"Zer are procedures," said the railroad bureaucrat, opening the locker with a master key. "You will sign for zer contents at zer office."

It was *there!* His attaché case was on its side, nothing broken or slashed. He reached into his pocket and took out his money. "I'm in a great hurry," he said as he slipped out first a hundred Deutschemarks, then, with hesitation, another.

288

"My train leaves in a few minutes." He shook the German's hand, passing the money, and asked calmly but with enthusiasm in his eyes. "Couldn't you say it was a mistake?"

"It *was* a mistake!" answered the uniformed man enthusiastically. "You must catch a train!"

"Thank you. You're a nice person. Happy Birthday."

"*Was?*"

"I know, don't bother. Thank you again."

Glancing around rapidly, subtly, hoping against hope that no one was watching him, Joel walked to an unoccupied wooden bench against the wall, sat down, and opened the attaché case, everything was there. But he could not keep it. Again he looked around the station, knowing what he had to find; he saw it. A drug store, or its equivalent; there would be envelopes somewhere inside. He closed the briefcase and got up, starting towards the store, trusting someone would speak English.

"Nearly all of us speak English, *Mein Herr*," said the matronly woman behind the counter near the stationery section. "It is practically a requirement, especially during the summer months. What are your needs?"

"I have to send a business report back to the United States," answered Converse, a large, thick envelope and a roll of tape in his right hand, the attaché case in his left, "but my train leaves in a few minutes and I don't have time to get to a post office."

"There are several post-collection boxes in the *Bahnhof*, sir."

"I need stamps, postage. I don't know how much," said Joel helplessly.

"If you will put your materials in the envelope, seal it and address it, I shall weigh the package and suggest the appropriate amount of stamping. We keep sheets here for convenience, but they are more expensive than in the *Postamt*."

"It doesn't matter. I'd like it to go air mail, and more postage rather than less." Five minutes later Converse handed the accommodating clerk the heavily sealed package for weighing. He had written a note on the top of the first dossier, and printed the address clearly on the front of the envelope. The woman returned with the appropriate postage. He paid her and placed the envelope on the counter in front of him.

"Thank you," he said, looking at his watch, as he began frantically licking the stamps and securing them. "Would you by any chance know where I can buy a ticket to . . . Emmerich, or Arnhem, I guess?"

"Emmerich is *deutsch*, Arnhem is *holländisch*. Any stall, sir."

"I may not have time," said Joel, in the last three stamps. "I suppose I could buy one on the train."

"They will not stop it if you have money."

"There." He had finished. "Where's the nearest mail box – collection box?"

"At the other end of the *Bahnhof*, *Mein Herr*."

Again Joel looked at his watch, again the pounding in his chest as he ran out into the station, instantly checking himself again, watching the crowds for any who might be watching him. He had less than eight minutes to mail the envelope, buy a ticket and find the train. Depending on the complications, perhaps he could eliminate the second step. But to pay his fare on board would mean engaging in conversation, conceivably finding someone to translate – the possibilities and the possible consequences were frightening.

As he feverishly looked for the mail box, he kept repeating to himself the exact words he had scribbled on the top of the first dossier's cover: *Do not – repeat do not – let anyone know you have this. If you don't hear from me within five days, send it to Nathan S. I'll call him if I can. Your once and obedient HUSBAND. Love, J.* He then looked down at the name and the address he had written on the envelope in his hand and wondered, a dull, sickening pain of concern spreading through him.

> *Ms Valerie Charpentier*
> *R.F.D.16*
> *Dunes Ridge*
> *Cape Ann, Massachusetts*
> *USA*

Three minutes later he found a mail box and deposited the envelope, opening and closing the slot several times to make sure it had fallen inside. He looked around at the signs everywhere, the Germanic lettering confusing him, the lines in front of the windows discouraging him. He felt so goddamned *helpless*, wanting to ask questions but afraid of stopping anyone, afraid that someone would study his face.

There was a window across the station, far away on the other side; two couples had left the line – four people with a sudden change of plans. Only one person was left. Converse hurried through the crowds, once again trying to hold himself in check, minimizing his movements, gliding, as it were.

"Emmerich, please," he said to the clerk, as the lone customer finally left the window.

The attendant briefly turned and looked at the clock on the wall behind him. Then he spoke in German, the phrases fast and guttural. "*Verstehen Sie?*" he asked, the word a question.

"*Nein* . . . Here!" Converse put three one-hundred Deutschemark notes on the ledge of the counter, shaking his head, shrugging. "Please, a ticket! I know, I've only got a few minutes."

The man took two of the bills, shoving the third back. He made change and pressed several buttons beneath him; a ticket spewed out and he handed it to Joel. "*Danke. Zwei Minuten!*"

"The track. What *track*? Can you understand? Where?"

"*Wo?*"

"Yes, yes that's it! Where?"

"*Acht.*"

"What?" Then Converse held up his right hand, raising and lowering the fingers, as if indicating numbers.

The attendant responded by holding up both hands, a five-finger spread and three middle fingers. "*Acht*," he repeated, pointing across the station to Joel's left.

"Eight! Thank you." Gripping his attaché case Converse walked as fast as possible without breaking into a run. He saw the gate through the throngs of people; a conductor was making an announcement while looking at his watch and backing into the archway.

A woman carrying packages collided with him, careening into his left shoulder, the bundles plummeting out of her arms, scattering on the floor. He tried to apologize through the abuse she hurled at him, loud words that caused the surrounding travellers to stop and gape. He picked up several shopping bags as the woman's barking voice reached a crescendo.

"Up yours, lady," he mumbled, dropping the packages and turning, now running to the closing gate. The conductor saw him and pushed it open.

He got to his seat, gasping, trying not to, his soft hat pulled down over his forehead, the wound in his left arm aching sharply. He thought he might have ripped it open in the collision. He felt under his jacket, past the handle of the gun he had taken from Leifhelm's chauffeur, to his shirt. There was no blood and he closed his eyes briefly in relief.

He was oblivious of the man across the aisle who stared at him.

In Paris, the secretary sat at her desk, the telephone held against her head, her voice low, muted further by her cupped hand over the mouthpiece.

"That is everything," she said quietly. "Do you have it?"

"Yes," said the man on the other end of the line. "It's extraordinary."

"Why? It's the reason I'm here."

"Of course. I should say *you're* extraordinary."

"Of course. What are your instructions?"

"The gravest. I'm afraid."

"I thought so. You have no choice."

"Can you?"

"It's done. I'll see you at Taillevent. Eight o'clock?"

"Wear your black Galanos. I adore it so."

"The Great Spike anticipates."

"It is ever so, my dearest. Eight o'clock."

The secretary hung up the phone, rose from the chair, and smoothed her dress. She opened a drawer and took out a bag with long straps, unlatching the snaps as she slipped it over her shoulder and walked to her employer's closed door. She knocked.

"Yes?" asked Mattilon inside.

"It is Suzanne, Monsieur."

"Come in, come *in*," said René, leaning back in his chair as the woman entered. "The last letter is filled with incomprehensible language, no?"

"Not at all, Monsieur. It's just that I . . . well I'm not sure it's proper to say."

"What could be improper? And if it is, at my age I'd be so flattered I'd probably tell my wife."

"Oh, Monsieur . . ."

"No, really, Suzanne, you've been here what now, a week, ten days? One would think you had been here for months. Your work is excellent and I appreciate your filling in."

"Your secretary is a dear friend, Monsieur. I could do no less."

"Well, I thank you. I hope the good Lord sees His way to pull her through. Young people today, they drive so fast – so terribly fast and so dangerously. I'm sorry, what is it, Suzanne?"

"I've had no lunch, sir. I was wondering."

"My *God*, I'm inconsiderate! I'm afraid it goes with two partners who take August seriously and go on holiday! Please, as long as you like, and I insist you bring the bill to me and let me reimburse you."

"That's not necessary, but thank you for the offer."

"Not an offer, Suzanne, an order. Have lots of wine and let's both of us make messes of my partners' clients. Now, off you go."

"Thank you, Monsieur." Suzanne turned towards the door, opened it slightly, and then stopped. She turned her head and saw that Mattilon was absorbed in reading. She closed the door silently, reached into her bag, and withdrew a large pistol with the perforated cylinder of a silencer attached to the barrel. She pivoted slowly and walked towards the desk.

The lawyer looked up as she approached. "*What?*"

Suzanne fired four times in rapid succession. René Mattilon sprang back in his chair, his skull pierced from his right eye to his left forehead. Blood streaked down his face and over his white shirt.

22

"Where in God's name have you been?" cried Valerie into the phone. "I've been trying to reach you since early this morning!"

"Early this morning," said Lawrence Talbot, "when the news broke, I knew I had to get the first plane to Washington."

"You don't *believe* what they're saying? You *can't!*"

"I do, and worse, I feel responsible. I feel as if I'd unwittingly pulled the trigger myself, and in a way that's exactly what happened."

"Goddamn you, Larry, explain that."

"Joel called me from a hotel in Bonn, only he didn't know which one. He wasn't rational, Val. He was calm one moment, shouting the next, finally admitting to me that he was confused and frightened. He rambled on – most of the time incoherently – telling some incredible story of having been captured and thrown into a stone house in the woods, and how he escaped, hiding in the river, eluding guards and patrols and killing a man he called a "scout". He kept screaming that he had to get away, that men were searching for him, in the woods, along the riverbank . . . Something's happened to him. He's gone back to those terrible days when he was a prisoner of war. Everything he says, everything he describes is a variation of those experiences – the pain, the stress, the tensions of running for his life through the jungle and down rivers. He's sick, my dear, and this morning was the horrible proof."

Valerie felt the hollowness in her throat, the sudden, awful vacuum below. She was beyond thinking; she could only react to words. "Why did you say you were responsible, that in some way you pulled the trigger?"

"I told him to go to Peregrine. I convinced him that Peregrine would listen to him, that he wasn't the man Joel thought he was."

". . .'Thought he was?' What did Joel say?"

"Very little that made sense. He ranted about generals and field marshals and some obscure historical theory that brought all the commanders from various wars and armies together in a combined effort to take control of governments. He wasn't lucid. He'd pretend to be but the minute I questioned a statement he made or a point in his story, he'd blow up and tell me it didn't matter, or I wasn't listening, or I was too dense to understand. But at the end he admitted he was terribly tired and confused and how badly he needed sleep. That was when I made my last pitch about Peregrine, but Joel didn't trust him. He was actually hostile towards him because he said he saw a former German general's car go through the embassy gates and, as you may or may not know, Peregrine was an outstanding officer during the Second World War. I explained as patiently and as firmly as I could that Peregrine was not one of 'them', that he was no friend of the military . . . Obviously I failed. Joel reached him, set up a rendezvous and killed him. I had no *idea* how sick he was."

"Larry," began Valerie slowly, her voice weak. "I hear everything you say but it doesn't ring true. It isn't that I don't believe you – Joel once said you were an embarrassingly honest man – but something's missing. The Converse I know and lived with for four years never bent the facts to support abstractions he wanted to believe. Even when he was angry as hell he couldn't do that. I told him he'd make a lousy painter because he couldn't bend a shape to fit a concept. It wasn't in him and I think he explained it. At five hundred miles an hour, he said, you can't mistake a shadow on the ocean for a carrier if your instruments are out."

"You're telling me he doesn't lie."

"I'm sure he does – I'm sure he did – but never about important things. It simply isn't in him."

"That was before he became ill, violently ill . . . He killed that man in Paris, he admitted it to me."

Valerie gasped. "*No!*"

"Yes, I'm afraid. Just as he killed Walter Peregrine."

"Because of some obscure historical *theory?* It's all wrong, Larry!"

"Two psychiatrists at the State Department explained it, but in phrases I'm sure I'd mangle if I tried to repeat them. 'Progressive latent retrogression', I think was one of them."

"Bullshit!"

"But you may be right about one thing. Geneva. Remember you said it all had something to do with Geneva?"

"I remember. What about Geneva?"

"It's where it started, everyone in Washington agrees with that. I don't know if you've read the papers . . ."

"Only *The Globe*; it's delivered. I haven't left the phone."

"It was Jack Halliday's son – stepson, actually. He was the lawyer who was killed in Geneva. It seems he was a prominent leader of the anti-war movement in the 'sixties and he was Converse's opponent in the merger. It was established that they met for breakfast before the conference. The theory is that he baited Joel, and we can assume it was brutal as he had a reputation of going for the jugular."

Why would he do that?" asked Val, her frayed nerves now suddenly alert.

"To throw Joel off. To distract him. Remember, they were dealing in millions and the attorney who came off best could do very well for himself – clients lining up all over Wall Street to retain him. There's even evidence that Halliday succeeded."

"What evidence?"

"The first part's technical so I won't try to explain it except to say that there was a subtle transfer of voting stock which under certain isolated market conditions might give Halliday's clients more say in management than the merger intended. Joel accepted it; I don't think he would have normally."

"Normally? What's the other part?"

"Joel's behaviour at the conference itself. According to the reports – interviews with everyone in that room – he wasn't himself, he *was* distracted, some said agitated. Several lawyers on both sides commented on the fact that he kept to himself, standing by a window most of the time, looking out as if he expected something. His concentration was so lax that questions addressed to him had to be repeated and, when they were, he appeared as though he didn't understand them. His mind was somewhere else, on something that consumed him."

"Larry!" shouted Valerie. "What are you *saying?* That Joel had something to do with this Halliday being *killed?*"

"It can't be ruled out," said Talbot sadly. "Either psychologically or in light of what people saw in the anteroom when Halliday died."

"What they *saw?*" whispered Valerie. "The paper said he died with Joel holding his head."

"I'm afraid there's more, my dear. I've read the reports. According to a receptionist and two other attorneys, there was a violent exchange between them just before Halliday died. No one's sure what was said, but they all agree it seemed vicious, with Halliday clutching Joel's lapels, as though accusing him. Later, when questioned by the Geneva police, Joel claimed there was no coherent conversation, only the hysterical words of a dying man. The police report added that he was not a cooperative witness."

"My God, he was probably in *shock!* You know what he went through – the sight of that man dying literally in his arms must have been traumatic for him!"

"Admittedly this is hindsight, Valerie, but everything must be examined, above all his behaviour."

"What do they think he did? What's the theory *now?* That Joel went out into the street, saw someone who fitted the bill and hired him to *kill* a man? Really, Larry, this is ludicrous."

"There are more questions than there are answers, certainly, but what's happened – what we know has happened – isn't ludicrous at all. It's tragic."

"All right, all right," said Valerie, her words rushed, "But why would he do it? Why would he want Halliday killed? *Why?*"

"I think that's obvious. How he must have despised someone like Halliday. A man who stayed safely at home, who condemned and ridiculed everything men like Joel went through, calling them goons and murderers and lackeys . . . and unnecessary sacrifices. Along with his hated 'commanders', the Hallidays of this world must have stood for everything else he loathed. One group ordering them into battle – to be maimed, killed, captured . . . tortured, the other making a mockery of everything they endured. Whatever Halliday said at that breakfast table must have made something snap in Joel's head."

"And you think," said Valerie, quietly, the words echoing in her throat, "that's why he wanted Halliday dead?"

"Latent vengeance. It's the prevalent theory, the consensus, if you will."

"I don't 'will'. Because it's not true, it couldn't be true."

"These are highly qualified experts, Val, doctors in the behavioural sciences. They've analysed everything in the records and they feel the pattern is there. Shock-induced, instant pathological schizophrenia."

"That's very impressive. They should embroider it on their Snoopy baseball caps because that's where it belongs."

"I don't think you're in a position to dispute . . ."

"I'm in a hell of a position," interrupted the ex-Mrs Converse. "But nobody bothered to ask me, or Joel's father, or his sister – who just happened to have been one of those wild-eyed protesters you all speak of. There's no way Halliday could have provoked Joel the way they say he did – at breakfast, lunch *or* dinner."

"You can't make such a statement, my dear. You simply don't know that."

"I *do* know, Larry. Because Joel thought the Hallidays of this world, as you put it, were *right*. He wasn't always crazy about the way they did things but he thought they *were right!*"

"I don't believe that. Not after what he went through."

"Then go to another source – if that's what you call it. To some of those records your high priests of the behavioural sciences conveniently overlooked . . . When Joel came back, there was a parade for him at Travis Air Force Base in California, where he was given everything but the keys to every starlet's apartment in Los Angeles. Am I right?"

"I recall there was a military welcome for a man who had escaped under extraordinary circumstances. The Secretary of State greeted him at the plane, in fact."

"In absolute fact, Larry. Then what? Where else was he paraded?"

"I don't know what you mean?"

"Look at the records. Nowhere. He wouldn't do it. How many invitations did he get? From how many towns and cities and companies and organizations – all pushed like *hell* by the White House? A hundred, five hundred, five *thousand*? At least that many, Larry. And do you know how many he accepted? Tell me, Larry, do you know? Did those high priests talk about this?"

"It wasn't an issue."

"Of course it wasn't. It warped the pattern, it bent the shapes Joel Converse wouldn't bend! The answer is *zero*, Larry. He wouldn't do it, any of it! He thought one day more of that war was one more day in hell too long. He refused to lend his name."

"What are you trying to say?" said Talbot sternly.

"Halliday wasn't his enemy, not the way you're trying to paint him. The brush strokes aren't there. They're not on the canvas."

"Your metaphors are more than I can handle, Val. What are you trying to tell me?"

"That something smells, Larry. It's so rotten I can hardly breathe, but the stench isn't coming from my former husband. It's coming from all of you."

"I have to take exception to that. All I want to do is help, I thought you knew that."

"I do, really I do. It's not your fault. Goodbye, Larry."

"I'll call you the minute I learn anything."

"Do that. Goodbye." Valerie hung up the phone and looked at her watch. It was time to get down to Logan Airport in Boston to pick up Roger Converse.

"*In Köln um zehn nach drei!*" shouted the voice over the loudspeaker.

Converse sat by the window, his face next to the glass, as the towns sped by on the way to Köln: Bornheim, Wesel, Brühl. The train was perhaps three-quarters full, which was to say that each double seat had at least one occupant, many two, but certainly not all. When they pulled out of the station a woman had been sitting where he sat now, a fashionably dressed suburbanite. Several seats behind them another woman – a friend – spotted her. His seatmate spoke to Joel. The brief attention she had called to both of them when he could not reply unnerved him. He shrugged and shook his head; she exhaled impatiently, got up in irritation and joined her friend.

She had left a newspaper behind, the same newspaper with his photograph on the front page, which remained flat out on the seat. He stared at it until he realized what he was doing and instantly shifted seats, picking up the paper and folding it so that the picture would be out of sight. He glanced around cautiously, holding his hand casually above his lips, frowning, pensive, trying to seem a man in thought whose eyes saw nothing. But he had seen another pair of eyes and they were studying him – staring at him while the owner was engaged in what appeared to be a lively conversation with an elderly woman next to him. The man had looked away, and Converse had a brief half second to observe the face before he turned to the window. He knew that face; he had talked to that man

296

but he could not remember where it was or when it was, only that they had spoken. The realization was as maddening as it was frightening. *Where* was it? *When* was it? Did the man know him, know his *name?*

If the face did, he had done nothing about it. He had returned his concentration to the woman, the conversation still lively. Joel tried to picture the whole man; perhaps it would help. He was large, not so much in height as in girth, and on the surface jovial, but Converse sensed a meanness to him. Was that now or before? When was before? *Where?* Ten minutes or so had passed since the exchange of looks, and Joel was no further ahead in peeling away the layers of memory. He was stymied and afraid.

"Wir kommen in zwei Minuten in Köln an. Bitte achten Sie auf Ihr Gepäck!"

A number of passengers got up from their seats, tugging at their jackets and skirts, reaching for luggage. As the train began to slow down Converse literally pressed himself into the window, the glass cooling the right side of his forehead. He let his mind go slack, unfocused, expecting the next few minutes to tell him what to do.

The minutes passed, the suspension on hold, his mind blank as passengers got off and others got in, many carrying briefcases – attaché cases – several very much like his own which he had left in a trash can in Bonn. He had wanted to keep it but he could not. It had been a gift from Valerie, as his gold pen was a gift, both initialled in those better days ... No, not better, he told himself, simply different. Nothing was better or worse; there were no comparisons where commitments were concerned. They either stuck or they did not. Theirs came unstuck.

Then why, he asked himself, as the train ground its wheels to a stop at Köln, had he sent the contents of his briefcase to Val? His answer was the essence of logic, he thought. She would know what to do: the others would not. Talbot, Brooks and Simon were out. His sister, Virginia, was even farther out. His father? The fly-boy with a sense of responsibility that went as far as his last wing dip? It could not be the pilot. He loved old Roger, more than he suspected Roger loved him, but the pilot could never come to grips with the ground. Hard earth meant relationships and old Roger never knew how to handle them, even with a wife he claimed to have loved dearly. The doctors said she had died of a coronary occlusion; her son thought it was from neglect. Roger was not on the scene, had not been for several weeks. So that left Valerie ... his once and former Valerie.

"Entschuldigen Sie. Ist der Platz frei?" The intruding voice came from a man about his own age, carrying an attaché case.

Joel nodded, assuming the words referred to the empty seat beside him.

"Danke," said the man, sitting down, the attaché case at his feet. He withdrew a newspaper from under his left arm and snapped it open. Converse tensed as he saw his photograph, his own serious face staring at him. He turned again to the window, pulling the soft brim of the hat lower, his face down, hoping he looked like an exhausted traveller wishing only to catch a few minutes' sleep. Moments later, as the train started forward, he had an inkling that he had succeeded.

"Verrückt, nicht wahr?" said the man with the attaché case reading the newspaper.

Joel stirred and blinked open his eyes beneath the brim of the hat. "Umm?"

"Traurig," added the man, his right hand separated from the paper in a gesture of apology.

Converse settled back into the window, the coolness of the glass an anchor, his eyes closed, the darkness more welcome than he could ever remember . . . No, that was not true; he remembered to the contrary. In the camps there were moments when he was not sure he could keep up the façade of strength and revolt. When everything in him wanted to capitulate, to hear even a few kind words, to see a smile that had meaning. Then the darkness would come and he would cry, the tears drenching his face. And when they stopped the anger was inexplicably restored. Somehow the tears had cleansed him, purged the doubts and the fears and made him whole again. And angry again. The darkness was so inviting.

"Wir kommen in fünf Minuten in Düsseldorf an!"

Joel bolted forward, his neck painfully stiff, his head cold. He had dozed for a considerable distance judging from the stiffness above his shoulder blades. The man beside him was reading and marking a report of some kind, the attaché case on his lap, the newspaper folded neatly between himself and Converse, folded maddeningly so that his photograph stared up at the ceiling of the train in clear view. The man opened his case, put the report inside, and snapped it shut. He turned to Converse.

"Der Zug ist pünktlich," he said, nodding his head.

Joel nodded back, suddenly aware that the passenger across the aisle had got up with the elderly woman, shaking her hand and replying to something she said. But he was not looking at her; his eyes had strayed over to Converse. Joel slumped back into the seat and the window, resuming the appearance of a weary traveller, the soft brim of his hat pulled down to the rims of his glasses. Who *was* that man? If they knew each other how could he be silent under the circumstances? How could he simply look over now and then and casually return to his conversation with the woman? At the very least, he would have to betray some sense of alarm or fear, or at the minimum, excited recognition.

The train began to slow down, the metallic grinding of the steel plates against the huge wheels swelling; soon the whistles would commence for their arrival in Düsseldorf. Converse wondered whether the German next to him would get off. He had closed his attaché case but he made no preliminary moves to rise and join the line forming at the forward door. Instead, he picked up the newspaper, mercifully opening it to an inside page.

The train stopped, passengers disembarked and others got on board – mostly women with shopping boxes and plastic bags emblazoned with the logos of expensive boutiques and recognizable names in the fashion industry. The train to Emmerich was a suburban "mink run", as Val used to call the afternoon trains from New York to Westchester and Connecticut. Joel saw that the man from across the aisle had walked the elderly woman up to the rear of the line, again shaking her hand solicitously before sidestepping his way back towards his seat.

Converse turned his face to the glass, his head bowed, and closed his eyes.

"*Bitte, können wir die Plätze tauschen? Dieser Herr ist ein Bekannter. Ich sitze in der nächsten Reihe.*"

"*Sicher, aber er schläft ja doch nur.*"

"*Ich wecke ihn,*" said the German next to Converse, while laughing and getting up. The man from across the aisle had changed seats. He sat down next to Joel.

Converse stretched, covering a yawn with his left hand, his right slipping under his jacket to the handle of the gun he had taken from Leifhelm's chauffeur. If it became necessary he would show that gun to his new yet familiar companion. The train started, the noise below growing in volume; it was the moment. Joel turned to the man, his eyes knowing but conveying nothing.

"I *figured* it was you," said the man, obviously an American, grinning broadly but not attractively.

Converse had been right, there was a meanness about the obese man; he heard it in the voice as he had heard it before – but where he did not remember. "Are you sure?" asked Joel.

"Sure I'm sure. But I'll bet you're not, are you?"

"Frankly, no."

"I'll give you a hint. I can always spot a good ole Yank! Only made a couple of mistakes in all the years of hopping around selling my li'l ole line of look-alike, almost originals."

"Copenhagen," said Converse, remembering with distaste, waiting for his luggage with the man. "And one of your mistakes was in Rome when you thought an Italian was an Hispanic from Florida."

"You *got* it! That guinea bastard had me buffaloed, figured him for a spic with a lot of bread – probably from running dope, you know what I mean? You know how they are, how they cornered the market from the Keys up . . . Say, what's your name again?"

"Rogers," replied Joel for no other reason than the fact he had been thinking about his father a while ago. "You speak German," he added, making a statement.

"Shit, I'd better. West Germany's just about our biggest market. My old man was a Kraut; it's all he spoke."

"What do you sell?"

"The best imitations on Seventh Avenue, but don't get me wrong, I'm not one of the Jew boys. You take a Balenciaga, right? You change a few buttons and a few pleats, put a ruffle maybe where the Latino doesn't have one. Then farm the patterns out to the Bronx and Jersey, lower Miami and Pennsylvania, where they sew in a label like 'Valenciana'. Then you wholesale the batch at a third of the price and everybody's happy – except the Latino. But there's not a fucking thing he can do that'd be worth his time in court because for the most part it's legal."

"I wouldn't be so sure about that."

"Well, a guy would have to plough through a road of *hazzerai* to prove it *wasn't* legal."

"Sadly, that's true."

"Hey, don't get me wrong! We provide the merchandise and a service for thousands of nice l'il ole housewives who can't afford that Paris crap. And I earn my bread, ole Yankee Doodle. Take that wrinkled old broad I was with; she owns a half dozen speciality shops in Köln and Düsseldorf, and now she's looking into Bonn. Let me tell you, I waltz her . . ."

The towns and small cities went by. Leverkusen . . . Lagenfeld . . . Hilden, and still the salesman went on, one tasteless anecdote leading to the next, his voice grating, repetitive.

"Wir kommen in fünf Minuten in Essen an!"

It happened in Essen.

The commotion came first but it was not sudden. Instead, it grew in volume as an immense rolling wave gathers force approaching a ragged coastline, a sustained crescendo arriving with its crash over the rocks, the sound sustained because of the unseen wave behind it. The embarking passengers all seemed to be talking with one another, heads turned, voices excited, necks craned to hear a stranger's words. Several carried small transistor radios, some held against ears, others held out, the volumes turned up at the request of those nearby. The more crowded the train became, the louder and more electric the conversations, heightened by the shrill, metallic tones from the radios. A thin young girl in the uniform of a private school, her books in a canvas beach bag, and a blaring radio in her left hand sat down in the seat in front of Joel and the salesman. Passengers gathered around, shouting, apparently asking the girl if she could make the radio louder.

"What's it all about?" asked Converse, turning to the obese man.

"Wait a minute!" replied the salesman, leaning forward with difficulty, and in greater discomfort rising partially up from the seat. "Let me listen."

There was a perceptible lull, but only among the crowd around the seat where the girl now held the radio in the air. Suddenly there was a burst of static and Converse could hear two voices, in addition to that of the newscaster, a remote report from somewhere away from the radio. And then Joel heard the words spoken in English; they were nearly impossible to pick out as an interpreter kept rushing in to give the German translation.

"A full inquiry . . . *Eine gründliche Untersuchung* . . . entailing all security forces . . . *die alle Sicherheitsbelagschaften* . . . *efordert* . . . has been ordered . . . *wurde veranlasst.*"

Converse grabbed the salesman's coat. "What is it – tell me what happened?" he asked rapidly.

"That *nut* hit again! . . . Wait, they're going back. Lemme hear this." Again there was a short burst of static and the excited newscaster came back on the air. A terrible sense of dread spread through Joel as the onslaught of German crackled out of the small radio, each phrase more breathless than the last. Finally the guttural diatribe ended. The passengers straightened their backs. Some stood up, turning to one another, their voices raised in counterpoint, excited conversations resumed. The salesman lowered himself into the seat, breathing hard, not apparently because of the alarming news he had heard but out of sheer physical discomfort.

"Would you *please* tell me what this is all about?" asked Converse, controlling his anxiety.

"Yeah, sure," said the heavy set man, taking a handkerchief from his breast pocket and mopping his forehead. "This mother-loving world is filled with crazies, you know what I mean? For Christ's sake, you can't tell who the fuck you're talking to! If it was up to me, every kid who was born cross-eyed or couldn't find a tit would be buried in dirt. I'm just sick of the weirdos, you know what I mean?"

"That's very enlightening, now what *happened?*"

"Yeah, okay." The salesman put the handkerchief back in his pocket, then loosened his belt and undid the buttons above his zippered fly. "The soldier boy, the one who runs the headquarters in Brussels . . ."

"The Supreme Commander of NATO," said Joel, his dread complete.

"Yeah, that one. He was shot, his head blown off right in the goddamned street when he was leaving some little restaurant in the old section. He was in civilian clothes, too."

"When?"

"A couple of hours ago."

"Who do they say did it?"

"The same creep who knocked off that ambassador in Bonn. The *nut!*"

"How do they know that?"

"They got the gun."

"The what?"

"The gun. It's why they didn't release the news right away: they wanted to check the fingerprints with Washington. It's his, and they figure the ballistics will show it's the same gun that was used to kill what's-his-name."

"Peregrine," said Converse quietly, aware that his dread was not complete. The worst part was only coming into focus. "How did they get the gun?"

"Yeah, well that's where they've marked the bastard. The soldier boy had a guard with him who shot at the nut and hit him – they think on the left arm. When the weirdo grabbed his arm the gun dropped out of his hand. The hospitals and the doctors have been alerted and all the borders all over the place are being checked, every fucking American male passport made to roll up his sleeves, and anyone looking anywhere's near like him hauled off to a customs tank."

"They're being thorough," said Joel, not knowing what else to say, feeling only the pain of his wound.

"I'll say this for the creep," continued the salesman, eyes wide and nodding his head in some obscene gesture of respect. "He's got 'em chasing their asses from the North Sea to the Mediterranean. They got reports he was seen on planes in Antwerp, Rotterdam and back there in Düsseldorf. It only takes forty-five minutes to get from Düsseldorf to Brussels, you know. I got a friend in Munich who flies a couple times a week to have lunch in Venice. Every place over here's a short hop. Sometimes we forget that, you know what I mean?"

"Yes, I do. Short flights . . . Did you hear anything else?"

"They said he could be heading for Paris or London or maybe even Moscow – he could be a Commie, you know. They're checking the private airfields, too, figuring he's got friends who are helping him – some friends, huh? A regular happy group of drooling psychos. They're even comparing him to that Carlos, the one they call "the jackal', what do you think of that? They say if he does go to Paris, the two of them might link up and there could be a few more executions. This Converse, though, he's got his own regular trademark. He puts bullets in their heads. Some kind of Boy Scout, huh?"

Joel stiffened, feeling the tension throughout his slumped body, a sharp hollow pain in the centre of his chest. It was the first time he had heard his name spoken casually by a stranger, identifying him as the psychopathic killer, an assassin hunted by governments whose border patrols were scrutinizing everyone at every checkpoint, private airfields watched, a dragnet in progress. The generals of Aquitaine had done their job with precision, right down to his fingerprints on a gun and a flesh wound in his arm. But the timing – how could they *dare?* How did they know he was not in an embassy somewhere asking for temporary asylum until he could make a case for himself? How could they take the *chance?*

Then the realization came to him and he had to dig his fingers into his wrist to control himself, to contain his panic. The call to *Mattilon!* How easily René's phone could have been tapped, by either the *Sûreté* or Interpol and how quickly would Aquitaine's informers spread the word! Oh, *Christ!* Neither one of them had thought of it! They *did* know where he was, and no matter where he went he was trapped! As the offensive salesman accurately phrased it "every place over here's a short hop". A man could fly from Munich to Venice to lunch and be back in his office for a 3.30 appointment. Another man could kill in Brussels and be on a train in Düsseldorf forty-five minutes later. Distances were measured in half hours. From ground-zero in Brussels, "a couple of hours ago" covered a wide circle of cities and a great many borders. Were his hunters on the train? They might be but there was no way they could know which train he had taken. It would be easier and far less time-consuming to wait for him in Emmerich. He had to think, he had to *move.*

"Excuse me, said Converse, getting up. "I have to use the men's room."

"You're lucky." The salesman moved his heavy legs, holding his trousers as he let Joel pass. "I can hardly squeeze into those boxes. I always take a leak before . . ."

Joel made his way up the aisle, abruptly stopping, swallowing, trying to decide whether to continue or turn around. He had left the newspaper on his seat, the photograph easily revealed by unfolding the top page. He had to continue; any change of movement, however minor, might attract attention. His objective was not the men's room, it was the passageway between the cars; he had to see it. A number of people had opened the door and gone through, several apparently looking for someone they expected to find on the train. He would look down at the lock on the toilet door and proceed.

He stood in the swerving, vibrating passageway studying the metal door. It was a standard two-tiered exit; the top opened first before the lower part could be unlocked and pulled back, revealing the steps. It was all he had to know.

He returned to his seat and to his relief the salesman was splayed back, his thick lips parted, his eyes closed, a high-pitched wheeze emanating from his throat. Converse cautiously lifted one foot after the other over the fat man's legs and manoeuvred himself into his seat. The newspaper had not been touched. Another relief.

Diagonally above and in front of him, he saw a small receptacle in the curved wall with what appeared to be a sheaf of railroad schedules fanned out by disuse. Limp, bent pieces of paper ignored because these commuters knew where they were going. Joel raised himself off the seat, reached out, and took one, apologizing with several nods of his head to the young girl below. She giggled.

Oberhausen . . . Dinslaken . . . Voerde . . . Wesel . . . Emmerich.

Wesel. The last stop before Emmerich. He had no idea how many miles Wesel was from Emmerich but he had no choice. He would get off the train at Wesel, not with whatever departing passengers there were, but by himself. He would disappear in Wesel.

He felt a slight deceleration beneath him, his pilot's instincts telling him it was the outer perimeter of an approach, the final path to touchdown in the scope. He stood up and carefully manoeuvred both feet between the fat man's legs, pivoting at the last second as the salesman snorted, shifting his position. Squinting under the brim of his hat, Joel casually glanced around, as if he were momentarily unsure of which way to go. He moved his head slowly, his eyes recording rapidly; as far as he could see no one was paying the slightest attention to him.

He walked wearily up the aisle, a tired passenger in search of relief. He reached the toilet door and was greeted by an ironic sign of that relief. The white slot below the handle spelled out *Besetzt*. His first manoeuvre had its basis in reality. The toilet was in use. He turned towards the heavy passageway door, pulled it open and stepped outside, crossing the vibrating, narrow coupling area to the opposite door. He pushed it open, but instead of going inside he took a single stride forward, then lowered his body, turning as he did so and stepped back into the passageway, into the shadows. He stood up, his back against the external bulkhead and inched his way to the edge of the thick glass window. Ahead was the inside of the rear car and by turning he had a clear view of the car in front. He waited, watching, turning, at any moment expecting to see someone lowering a newspaper, or breaking off a conversation and looking over at his empty seat.

None did. The excitement at the news of the assassination in Brussels had tapered, as had the rush of near panic in Bonn when the streets learned that an ambassador had been killed. A number of people were obviously still talking about both incidents, shaking their heads and grappling with the implications and the future possibilities, but their voices were lowered: the crisis of the first reports had passed. After all, it was not fundamentally the concern of these citizens. It was American against American. There was even a certain gloating in the air; the gunfight at OK Corral had new significance. The colonists were, indeed, a violent breed.

"Wir kommen in . . ." The rapid clacking of the wheels below, echoing in the metal chamber, obscured the distant announcement over the loudspeakers. Only moments now, thought Converse as he turned and looked at the exit door. When the train slowed sufficiently and the lines began to form at both inner doors, he would make his moves.

"*Wir kommen in drei Minuten in Wesel an!*"

Several passengers in both cars got out of their seats, adjusted their briefcases and shopping bags and started up the aisle. The grinding of the huge wheels underneath signified the approach to touchdown. *Now.*

Joel turned to the exit door and finding the upper latch snapped it open, pulling the upper section back: the rush of air was deafening. He spotted the handle of the lower release and gripped it, prepared to yank it up as soon as the ground beyond slowed down. It would be in only seconds. The sounds below grew louder and the sunlight outside created a racing silhouette of the horizontal train. Then the sharp, abusive words broke through the dissonance and he froze.

"*Very* well thought out, Herr Converse! Some win, some lose. You *lost.*"

Joel spun around. The man yelling at him in the metal chamber was the passenger who had got on the train at Düsseldorf, the apologetic commuter who sat next to him until the obese salesman had asked him to exchange seats. In his left hand was a gun held far below his waist, in his right the ever-respectable attaché case.

"You're a surprise," said Converse.

"I would hope so. I barely made the train in Düsseldorf. *Ach,* three cars I walked through like a madman – but not the madman you are, *ja?*"

"What happens now? You fire that gun and save the world from a madman?"

"Nothing so simplistic, pilot."

"Pilot?"

"Names are immaterial, but I am a colonel in the West German Luftwaffe. Pilots only kill one another in the air. It is embarrassing on the ground."

"You're comforting."

"I also exaggerate. One disconcerting move on your part and I shall be a hero of the Fatherland, having cornered a crazed assassin and killed him before he killed me."

" 'Fatherland'? You still call it that?"

"*Natürlich.* Most of us do. From the father comes the strength, the female is the vessel."

"They'd love you in a Vassar biology class."

"Is that meant to be amusing?"

"No, just disconcerting – in a very minor way, nothing serious." Joel had moved in inches until his back was against the bulkhead, his whole mind, his entire thinking process, on pre-set. He had no choice except to die, now or a matter of hours from now. "I suppose you have an itinerary for me," he asked, as he swung his left arm forward with the question."

"Quite definitely, pilot. We will get off the train at Wesel and you and I will share a telephone, my gun firmly against your chest. Within a short time a car will meet us and you will be taken . . ."

Converse slammed his concealed right elbow into the bulkhead, his left arm in plain sight. The German glanced at the door of the forward car. *Now!*

Joel lunged for the gun, both hands surging for the black barrel as he crashed his right knee with all the force he could command into the man's testicles. As

304

the German fell back, he grabbed his hair and smashed the man's head down onto a protruding hinge of the opposite door.

It was over. The German's eyes were wide, alarmed, glassy. Another scout was dead, but this man was no ignorant conscript from an impersonal government, this was a soldier of Aquitaine.

A stout woman screamed in the window, her lips separated by her screams, her face hysterical.

"*Dies ist Wesel* . . . !"

The train had slowed down and other excited faces appeared at the window, the frenzied crowd now blocking those who tried to open the door.

Converse lunged across the vibrating metal enclosure to the exit panel. He grasped the latch and pulled it open, crashing the door into the bulkhead. The steps were below, gravel and tar beyond. He took a deep breath and plunged outside, curling his body to absorb the hard ground, and when he made contact he rolled over, and over, and over.

23

He careened off a rock and into a cluster of bushes. Nettles and coarse tendrils enveloped him, scraping his face and his hands. His body was a mass of bruises, the wound in his left arm stinging and moist – unbearable, untouchable – but there was no time even to acknowledge pain. He had to get away: in minutes the whole area would be swarming with men searching for him, hunting for the murderer of an officer in the Federal Republic's air arm. It took no imagination to foresee what would happen next. The passengers would be questioned – including the salesman – and suddenly a newspaper would be in someone's hand, a photograph studied, the connection made. A crazed killer last seen in a back street in Brussels was not on his way to Paris or London or Moscow. He was on a train out of Bonn, passing through Köln, Essen, and Düsseldorf – and he killed again in a town called Wesel.

Suddenly he heard the high-pitched wail of a horn. He looked up the small hill towards the tracks; a southbound train was gathering speed out of the station several thousand feet away. His *hat*. It was upturned half way down the hill. Joel crept out of tangling brush, staggered to his feet, and ran to it, refusing to listen to that part of his mind which told him he could barely walk. He grabbed the hat off the ground, and began running to his right. The southbound train passed; he raced up the hill and across the tracks, heading for an old building, apparently deserted. More of its windows were shattered than intact. He might rest there for a few moments but no longer: it was too obvious a hiding place. In ten or fifteen minutes, it would be surrounded, men with guns aimed at every exit, every window.

He tried desperately to remember. How had he done it before? How had he eluded the patrols in the jungles north of Phu Loc? . . . Vantage points! Get where you can see them but they can't see you! But there were tall trees then and he was younger and stronger and could climb them, concealing himself behind green screens of full branches on firm limbs. There was nothing like that here on the outskirts of a railroad yard . . . or maybe there was! To the right of the building was a landfill dump, tons of earth and debris piled high in several pyramids; it was his only choice.

His arms and legs aching, gasping, his wound inflamed, he ran towards the last of the pyramids. He reached it, propelled his way around the mass, and started climbing the rear side, his feet slipping into soft earth, and wood and cardboard and patches where garbage had been layered. The sickening smells were oddly distracting: they took his mind off the pain. He kept crawling, clawing with each slipping foot. If he had to, he could burrow himself into the stinking mess. There were no rules for survival, and if sinking himself into the putrid hill kept a spray of bullets from ending his life, so be it.

He reached the top and lay prone below the ridge, dirt and protruding debris all around him. Sweat rolled down his face, stinging the scrapes on his face, his legs and arms heavy with stabbing pain, his breathing erratic from the trembling caused by unused muscles and fear. He looked down at the outskirts of the railroad yard, then up ahead at the station. The train had stopped, its journey halted, the platform filled with people milling around, bewildered. Several uniformed men were shouting orders, trying to separate passengers – apparently those in the two cars flanking the scene of the killing or anyone else who knew anything. In the parking lot surrounding the station house was a blue and white striped police car, its red roof light spinning, the signal of emergency. There was a rapid clanging in the distance and seconds later a long white ambulance streaked into the lot, whipped into a horseshoe turn and plunged back, stopping close to the platform. As the rear doors opened, two attendants jumped out carrying a stretcher; a police officer above them on the steps shouted at them, gesturing with his arm. They ran up the metal staircase and followed him.

A second patrol car swerved into the lot, tyres screeching as it stopped next to the ambulance. Two police officers got out and walked up the steps: the previous officer joined them, two civilians, a man and woman beside him. The five talked and moments later the two patrolmen returned to their vehicle. The driver backed up and spun to his left, gunning the engine, heading for the south end of the parking lot, directly towards Converse. Again they stopped and got out, now with weapons drawn; they raced across the tracks and down the slope of gravel and tar into the wild grass. They would be coming back in minutes, thought Joel, absently clawing the ragged surface by his shoulders. They would stop and check out the deserted building, perhaps call for assistance, but sooner or later they would examine the huge mounds of landfill.

Converse looked behind him: there was a dirt road marked with the tracks of heavy trucks leading to a tall link fence, the gate held in place with a thick chain. A man running up that road and climbing that fence would be seen; he had to stay where he was, hidden in the putrid rubble.

Another sound interrupted his frantic calculations . . . a sound like one he had heard only moments before. On his right, in the parking lot. A third patrol car came speeding in, its klaxon howling, but instead of heading for the ambulance and the first police vehicle by the platform, it veered to its left, racing over to join the striped car at the south end of the lot. The two policemen in the field *had* radioed for assistance and Joel felt a numbing sense of despair. He was looking at his own executioners . . . Executioner. The newly-arrived patrol car contained only a driver . . . or did it? Did the policeman turn his head and speak? No, he was disengaging something, a seat belt probably.

A grey-haired uniformed man got out, looked around, then started walking rapidly towards the tracks. He crossed them and stood on the top of the slope, shouting down at the police officers in the brown, sun-drenched grass. Converse had no idea what the man was saying but the scene appeared strangely out of place.

The two policemen came racing into view, their guns no longer in their hands but holstered. There was a brief heated conversation. The older officer was pointing to a distant area south of the landfill; his words by their volume were commands. Joel looked back at his patrol car; on the panel of the front door was an insignia that was absent on the other car. The man held a superior rank to his young associates; he was issuing orders.

The younger policemen ran back across the tracks to their vehicle, their superior following, but not running. They swung back the doors, literally jumped in, and in the burst of an engine's roar, swerved to the right and sped out the parking lot. The older man reached his patrol car, but he made no movement to open the door or get inside. Instead, he spoke – at least his lips moved – and five seconds later the rear doors opened and two men emerged. One man Converse knew well. His gun was in Joel's pocket. It was Leifhelm's chauffeur, a taped bandage across his forehead, another on the ridge of his nose. He pulled out a gun and barked a command to the other man, in his voice the fury of an injured fanatic combat soldier.

Peter Stone left the hotel in Washington. He had told the young Navy lieutenant and the slightly older Army captain that he would contact them in the morning. *Children*, he thought. Idealistic amateurs were the worst because their righteousness was usually as valid as their actions were impractical. Their childish disdain for duplicity and deceit did not countenance the fact that to rip the maniacal bastards out frequently required greater malevolence and far more venal deception than they could imagine.

Stone got into a taxi – leaving his car in the basement parking area – and gave the driver the address of an apartment building on Nebraska Avenue. It was a lovely apartment but it did not belong to him: it was leased by an Albanian diplomat at the United Nations who was rarely there; naturally based in New York. But the former intelligence officer had worked hard and turned the Albanian several years ago, not merely with ideological pleas to a fine scholar's conscience, but also with photographs of this same scholar in all manner of sexual indulgences with very strange women. They were in their sixties and seventies, bag ladies off the streets, who, after carnal abuse, were subject to sheer physical abuse. He was a winner, the scholar-diplomat. A psychiatrist in Langley had said something about wish-fulfilling – sexually-repressed matricide. Stone did not need that nonsense: he had the photographs of a son of a bitch sadist. But it was the children that occupied his mind now, not the excesses of a fool that permitted him access to a luxury apartment far beyond his consultation fees.

The *children. Jesus!* They were so right, their sensibilities so correctly on target, but they did not understand that when they took on the George Marcus Delavanes of today's world it was war in all its shades of brutality, because that was the way these men fought. Righteousness had to join with a commitment to crawl in the gutter if it was necessary, no quarter sought for none would be given. This was the last fifth of the twentieth century and the generals were going for it all; the paranoia of their disgust and frustration had come to the end of endurance.

Stone had seen it coming for years and there were times when he had come close to applauding, throwing his hands up in frustration, willing to sell what was left of his soul. Strategies had been aborted – men *lost* – because of the maddening bureaucratic restraints that led back to laws and a constitution which were never written with anything like Moscow in mind. The "Mad Marcuses" of this planet – this part of the planet – had a number of very plausible points. There were those in the Company years ago who were adamant and not squirrelly about it. They said: *Bomb* the nuclear plants in Tashkent and Tselinograd! Blow them the hell up in Chengdu and Shenyang! Don't let them begin! We are responsible and they are *not!*

Who knew? Would the world have been better off?

Then Peter would wake up in the morning and that part of his soul he had not sold would tell him, no, we cannot do that. There had to be another way, a way without confrontation and wholesale death. He still clung to that alternative, but he could not dismiss the Delavanes as megabomb off-the-wallers. Where were we heading now?

He knew where *he* was heading – had been heading for years. It was why he had joined the children. Their righteousness was justified, their indignation valid. He had seen it all before in too many places – always at the extremes of the political spectrum. The Delavanes of the planet would turn everyone into robots. In many ways, death was preferable.

Stone unlocked the door of the apartment, closed it, took off his jacket and made himself the only drink he would permit himself for the evening. He walked to the leather chair by the telephone and sat down, taking several swallows before putting the glass on the table beneath the floor lamp. He picked up the phone and dialled seven digits, then three more, and one more after that. A very faint dial tone replaced the original and he dialled again. Everything was in order. The call was being routed through a KGB diplomatic scrambler-cable on an island in the Cabot Strait south-west of Newfoundland. Only Dzerzhinsky Square would be confused. Peter had paid six negatives for the service. Five rings preceded the sound of a male voice in Bern, Switzerland.

"*Allo?*"

"This is your old friend from Bahrain, also the vendor in Lisbon and a buyer in the Dardanelles. Do I have to sing *Dixie?*"

"Well, *mah wuhd*," said the man in Bern stretching out the phrase in a dialect bred in the American deep south, the French pretence dropped. "You go back a long time, don't you, suh?"

"I do, sir."

"I hear you're one of the bad guys now."

"Unloved, mistrusted, but still appreciated," said Stone. "That's more accurate. The Company won't touch me but it's got its share of unfriendlies in town who throw me consultations pretty regularly. I wasn't as smart as you. No deposits from Uncle No-Name in Swiss accounts."

"I was told you had a little juice problem."

"A big one but it's over."

"Never negotiate a release from people worse than you if you can't pass a Breathalyser test. You've got to scare them, not make 'em laugh."

"I found that out. I hear you do some consulting yourself."

"On a limited basis and only with clients who could pass Uncle No-Name's muster. That's the agreement and I stick to it. Either I do or some Boom Boom Botticelli is flown over and massa's in de cole, cole ground."

"Where the threats don't do you any good," completed the civilian.

"That's the stand-off, Pearlie May. It's our little *détente*."

"Would I pass muster? I give you my word I'm working with good people. They're young and they're on to something and they haven't got an evil thought in their heads, which under the circumstances is no recommendation. But I can't tell you anything substantive. For your sake as well as mine and theirs. Is that good enough?"

"If the consultation doesn't take place in outer space it's more than enough, and you know it. You saved Johnny Reb's ass three times, only y'awl got the sequence backwards. In the Dardanelles and Lisbon you got me out before the guns came in. Over in Bahrain you rewrote a report about a little matter of missing contingency funds that probably kept me from five years in a Leavenworth stockade."

"You were too valuable to lose over a minor indiscretion. Besides, you weren't the only one, you merely got caught – or nearly did."

"Regardless, Johnny Reb owes. What is it?"

Stone reached for his glass and took a drink. He spoke, choosing his words carefully. "One of our commanders is missing. It's a Navy problem, SAND PAC based, and the people I'm with want to keep it contained. No Washington input at this stage."

"Which is part of what you can't tell me," said the Southerner. "Okay. SAND PAC – that's San Diego and points west and wet until the date-line, right?"

"Yes, but it's not relevant. He's the chief legal out there – maybe *was*, by now. If he's not past tense, *if* he's alive, he's nearer you than me. Also if I get on a plane, my passport ignites the computers and things can't go that way."

"Which is also part of what you can't tell me."

"Check."

"What *can* you tell me?"

"You know the embassy in Bonn?"

"I know it's in trouble. Just like the security units in Brussels. That psycho's cutting one hell of a path. What about Bonn?"

"It's all related. Our commander was last seen there."

"He's got something to do with this *Converse?*"

Stone paused. "You can probably fill in more spaces than is good for any of us, but the bones of the scenario are as follows. Our commander was a very upset man. His brother-in-law – who, incidentally was his closest friend – was killed in Geneva . . ."

"Down the road from here," interrupted the expatriate in Bonn. "The American lawyer whose demise was engineered by Converse, at least that's what I've read."

"That's what our commander believed. How or from whom he got the information no one knows, but apparently he found out that Converse was heading for Bonn. He went on leave to go after him."

"Commendable but dumb," said the Southerner. "A one-man lynching mob?"

"Actually, no. By simple equations we can assume he went to the embassy, at least he met someone *from* the embassy to explain why he was there, perhaps to warn them, who knows? But the rest speaks for itself. This Converse struck and our commander disappeared. We'd like to find out whether he's alive or dead."

It was the Southerner's turn to pause, his breathing, however, clearly heard on the line. Finally. "Brer Rabbit, you've simply *got* to put a little flesh on those bones."

"I'm about to, General Lee."

"Much obliged, Yankee."

"It's also related. If you were a lieutenant commander in the United States Navy and wanted to reach someone at the embassy in Bonn, someone who would accord you the attention your rank deserved, who would you call?"

"The military *chargé d'affaires*, who else?"

"That's the man, Uncle Remus. Among other things, he's a liar, but I can't go into that. It's our thinking that the commander spoke with him and the *chargé* dismissed him as a fringe case, probably didn't even give him an appointment with Ambassador Peregrine. And when it happened, to save his ass and his career . . . well, people do strange things."

"What you're suggesting is awful damned strange."

"I won't back away from it," said the civilian.

"Okay, what's his name?"

"Washburn. He's a . . ."

"*Norman* Washburn?! Major Norman Anthony Washburn, the Third, Fifth, or Sixth?"

"That's the one."

"*Don't* back away. You left the field too early. Washburn was in Beirut, then Athens and after that Madrid. He gave every Company flack in the territories the business! He'd nail his Park Avenue mama to a velvet wall for a good

310

evaluation report. He figures by forty-five he'll be heading the Joint Chiefs – and he intends to."

"By forty-five?"

"I've been out of touch for a couple of years, but he can't be any more than thirty-six, thirty-seven. The last I heard they were going to jump the light-colonel status and make him a full bird, then a brigadier soon after that. He is *loved*, Yankee!"

"He's a liar," said the civilian in the dimly-lit apartment on Nebraska Avenue.

"Sure 'nuff," agreed the man in Bern, "but I never figured anything this radical. I mean, he's got to be scratchin' mule shit for oil to do something so far out."

"I still won't back away," repeated the civilian, drinking his bourbon.

"Which means you know."

"Check."

"And you can't talk about that, either." A statement.

"Check again."

"Are you firm?"

"No room for error. He knows where the commander is – if he's alive."

"Holy *Jesus!* What *are* you Northern boys *into?*"

"Will you track? Starting yesterday?"

"With pleasure, Yankee. How do you want it?"

"In the twilight zone. Only words that come with needles – that's important. He has to wake up thinking he ate a bad piece of meat."

"Women?"

"I don't know. You probably have a better fix on that than I do. Would he risk his image?"

"With two or three *Fräuleins* I've got in Bonn, Jesuits would risk the papacy, suh. The name of the commander, please?"

"Fitzpatrick, Lieutenant-Commander Connal Fitzpatrick... And, Uncle Remus, whatever you hear under the needles, give only to me. No one else. *No one.*"

"Which is the last part of what you can't tell me, right?"

"Check."

"My blinders are in place. One objective only with only one target. No side trips and no curiosity, just a tape recorder in my head or my hand."

Again Stone paused filling the silence with a tentative whisper. "*Tape...?*" Then he continued. "The latter's not a bad idea. Mini-micro, of course."

"Naturally. Those little mothers are so small you can hide them in the most embarrassing places. Where do I reach you? My quill is poised."

"All right, the area code's eight-zero-four." The former CIA man gave the expatriate in Bern a telephone number in Charlotte, North Carolina. "A woman will answer. Tell her you're from the Tatiana family and leave a number."

Their brief goodbyes concluded, Peter hung up the phone, got out of the chair and carried his drink to the window. It was a hot, still night in Washington, the air outside barely moving, the hint of a summer storm. If the rains came they would wash the streets and cleanse at least part of the pollution.

The former deep-cover agent wished there was some balm on earth or from the skies that could wash his hands and cleanse that part of his soul he had not put on the auction block – or for a disastrous period of time into a bottle of bourbon. Maybe all he had done was hammer another nail in Converse's coffin, one more scrap of credibility that labelled the lawyer something he was not. Stone realized that instead of casting reasonable doubts based on his own certain knowledge, he had compounded the fiction that Converse was the psychopathic killer the international media described. Worse, he had attributed that credibility to a responsible missing man, a naval officer who was most likely dead. There were two justifications for the lie, and only one was remotely feasible: the other, however, was probably the most productive move they could make. The first assumed that Fitzpatrick *might* be alive, a weak premise. But if he was dead, the missing commander provided the reason to call in an old debt and go after a *chargé d'affaires* named Washburn and do so without any connection to George Marcus Delavane. Even if "Johnny Reb" was caught – and every man in a grey to black operation had to assume the possibility – no mention could be made of an international conspiracy of generals . . . Major Norman Washburn, IV, might or might not know the fate of Connal Fitzpatrick, but everything else he might say under the needles especially about the commander would be of value.

What surprised the civilian was Converse himself in the matter of the lying military attaché. If Converse was running and not under lock and key he certainly must have learned about the lie that had condemned him. If so, why hadn't the attorney done something about it? The major's lie was the chain's weakest link; it could be snapped with a minimum of effort – the man's a liar. I was here, or there, or anywhere except where he placed me when he placed me. Stone drank sparingly from the glass; he knew the futility of speculating because he knew the answer. It was why he did not feel that yet another part of his soul had been clipped away. Converse was not in a position to do anything. He was either trapped or taken, soon to be offered up as a sacrificial corpse by the generals. There was nothing anyone could do for him. He was a dead man, a sacrifice in the truest sense of the word – given up even by his own.

Peter walked back to the chair and sat down, loosening his tie and kicking off his shoes. He had learned years ago to cut losses in the field wherever possible. If it meant disowning pawns or plants or blinds, one took the statistical approach and let the executions follow. It was better than losing more. But what was even better was to make a significant progress with whatever the loss. He was doing that now with Converse's death and "Johnny Reb" in Bern . . . and a liar named Washburn.

Oh, *Christ!* He was playing *God* again with charts and diagrams – pluses and minuses of human value! Yet the objective was worth more than anything he had ever faced before. Delavane and his legions had to be stopped, and they would not be stopped in Washington. There were too many watchful eyes, too many ears, too many men in unknown corners who believed in the myth; men who had nothing else. The children were right about that. And there would be no empty bottles of bourbon on the floor now, or blurred memories of nights past, or words passed. Despite advancing age, he was ready; he was primed.

It was odd, thought the civilian. He had not used the *Tatiana family* in years.

Joel watched from the ridge of the landfill as Leifhelm's chauffeur and his companion approached the deserted building. Both were experienced; one raced before the other, stopping behind displaced rocks from the fill and barrels used for early morning fires. Almost simultaneously they reached separate doors, each door off its hinges, angling into the dirt. The chauffeur gestured with his weapon and both men disappeared inside.

Converse again looked behind him. The fence was about two hundred yards away. Could he slide down the stinking hill, race to the interwoven wire and climb over the fence before his executioners came out of the decrepit building? Why *not?* He could *try!* He raised himself off his stomach, hands sinking into the debris, spun to his right, and plunged downward.

A distant crash came first and then a scream. He spun around again and scrambled up the ten odd feet his lunge had carried him. The chauffeur was racing out of his door, around the corner to where his companion had entered, his gun levelled, prepared to fire. He approached cautiously then, seeing something, exploded in disgust as he entered the shadows. Seconds later he emerged holding the other man; obviously a staircase or a floorboard had collapsed. The second man held his leg and limped.

Two piercing blasts came from the station; the platform was empty, the milling passengers back on board. The panic had subsided and the train would make a Teutonic effort to be on time. The last police car and the ambulance were gone.

Below, the chauffeur slapped his companion repeatedly in fury, shoving him backwards to the ground. The man got up, gesturing, pleading for no more, and the chauffeur relented, ordering his subordinate to a position between the building, the landfill and the fence and, when the man was in place, the chauffeur went back into the deserted building.

A half hour passed, the descending sun intercepted by low-flying clouds in the west, creating long, lateral shadows over the outskirts of the railroad yard. Finally the chauffeur came into view, emerging from an unseen exit on another side of the building. He stood for a moment and looked west across the tracks, to the expanse of wild grass and marshland beyond. Then he turned and stared at the mounds of landfill and made up his mind.

"*Rechts über Ihnen!*" he screamed at his companion, pointing to the second mound. "*Hinter Ihnen! Er schiept!*"

Joel crawled, racing down the debris like a panicked sand crab. Halfway to the bottom his left hand was snared; he yanked at the looping entrapment, pulled it free and was about to discard it when he saw it was a length of ordinary, electric cord. He bunched it up in his hand and frantically continued downward. When he was within six feet of the ground, he whipped his whole body into frenzy and clawed at the dirt and garbage. He stabbed his legs repeatedly into the rubbish and loose earth and he sank his body into the mass, pulling debris around his head. The stench was overpowering and he could feel the insects penetrating his clothes, crawling over his skin. But he was hidden, of that he was certain. He began to comprehend what his fragmented mind was trying to tell him. He was back in the jungle about to spring on a scout from an unseen place.

Minutes passed and the shadows became longer, then permanent as the sun's trajectory dropped below the top of the landfill. Converse remained immobile, straining every muscle, grinding his teeth to stop himself from thrashing his arms and scratching his clothes and his exposed skin to rip away the maddening insects. But he knew he could not move. It would happen any moment, any second.

The prelude came. The limping man was in view, peering up at the hill of refuse and dirt, squinting against the residue of sunlight at the top, his gun held out, angled diagonally, prepared to fire. He side-stepped slowly, cautiously, apprehensive of what he could not see. He passed directly in front of Joel, the extended gun no more than three feet away from Converse's face. Another step and the line of contact would be clear.

Now! Joel lunged out, grabbing the barrel of the gun, instantly and violently twisting it clockwise and downward. As the German fell forward Converse crashed his knee up into the bridge of the man's nose, stunning him before he could scream. The weapon spiralled off into the debris. The man staggered, about to find his voice, and Joel lunged again, a section of the wire cord stretched out in both hands; he whipped it over the scout's head, pulling it taut around the scout's throat. The *scout* had to die because the *scout* would kill him! It was as simple as that! No, it was *not* that simple. This was a soldier of Aquitaine, *garbage* from Aquitaine. He killed on command – he followed *orders!* He would never kill again.

The man went limp, and Converse bent over the body, about to roll it into the base of the landfill and conceal it, but then he stopped. There had to be another way because there was another option, one he had taken a hundred years ago with another scout in a jungle. He looked around; there was a pile of carelessly dumped railroad ties thirty-odd yards away on his right – old ties, several broken . . . forming a low wall. A *wall*.

It was a risk. If Leifhelm's chauffeur finished his examination of the first mound of landfill and stepped out towards the second one at any three of the four angles, he would have a clear line of sight. The man had been sent to the Emmerich train for two reasons – one, he knew the quarry by sight, and, two, the quarry had disgraced him; Joel's corpse would be his redemption. Such a man was an expert with weapons . . . which the quarry was not. What was the point of thinking! Since Geneva, *everything* was a risk, a gamble against death when he did not know it.

He gripped the German's body under the armpits, and breathing hard – for some reason foolishly counting off *one, two, three* – he lurched backwards, hauling the dead man across a dead man's zone.

He reached the railroad ties and swung the corpse around them, the heels of its shoes digging an arc into the dirt as he dragged the dead German into the base of his wall. Then, without thinking, acting only on instinct, Converse did what he had been wanting to do for the last hour. Concealed by the ties, he ripped off his jacket and shirt and rolled on the ground, scattering the insects like an infested dog in a field, scratching them out of his hair, away from his face. It was all he could do for the moment. He crawled into the bank of railroad ties and found a space between two separated logs.

"*Werner! Wo sind Sie?*"

The shouts preceded the figure of Leifhelm's chauffeur. He appeared at the far end of the second mound, moving slowly, his gun raised, each step taken cautiously, his head shifting in all directions, a soldier experienced in combat patrol. Converse thought how much better off the world would be if he were an expert shot. He was not. In pilot training he had gone through the obligatory small arms course, and at twenty-five feet had rarely hit the target. This second soldier of Aquitaine had to be sucked in much closer.

"*Werner! Antworten Sie doch!*"

Silence.

The chauffeur was alarmed; he walked backwards, now crouching, scanning the hill of refuse, kicking away any object in his backward path, his head pivoting. Joel knew what he had to do; he had done it before. Divert the killer's attention, pulling him closer to the encounter, then move away.

"*Auughh* . . . !" Converse let the wail come out of his throat. Then added in clear English, "Oh, my *God!*" Instantly he crawled to the far end of the wall of railroad ties. He peered around the side, his head in shadows.

"*Werner! Wo sind* . . . !" The German stood erect, his eyes following his line of hearing. Suddenly he broke into a run, his weapon thrust in front of him like a man cornering a hated object, an escaped sound in English leading him to that loathed enemy.

The chauffeur lunged prone across the railroad ties, his expression alert, his gun in front of him. He fired into the shadowed corpse below, a roar of vengeance accompanying the explosions.

Joel got to his knees, aimed his automatic, and pulled the trigger once. The German spun off the ties, a trickle of blood erupting in his chest.

"Some win," whispered Converse rising to his feet, remembering the man on the train to Emmerich.

He was down in the marshlands, the clothes in his arms. He had scrambled across the railroad tracks, down through the wild grass into the swampy dampness of the marsh. It was water, and that was all he had to know. Water was cleansing, whether as an escape route or to bathe one's racking body – also lessons he had learned years ago. He sat naked on a sloping marsh bank, taking his inhibiting money belt off, wondering if the paper bills inside were soaked but not caring enough to examine them.

He did, however, examine every pocket of the clothes he had stripped from his would-be executioners. He was not sure what was of value and what was not. The money was irrelevant, except for the small bills; and the drivers' licences had photographs embedded in plastic – neither was worth the risk of scrutiny. There was an ominous-looking knife, the long blade released through the head

315

by the touch of a button on the handle; he kept it. Also a cheap butane lighter and a comb and for the drinking man, two breath fresheners. The rest were personal effects – keys, a 4-leaf clover good luck charm . . . photographs in the wallets – he did not care to look at them. Death was death, enemy and friend fundamentally equalized. The only things he was interested in were the clothes. *They* were the option, the option he had used in the jungle a lifetime ago. He had crammed himself inside a scout's tattered uniform and twice across a narrow riverbank he had not been shot by the enemy who had spotted him. Instead, they had waved.

He selected the articles of clothing that fitted best and put them on; the rest he threw into the marsh. Whatever he looked like, there was little or no resemblance to the tweedy academic he had tried to be in Bonn. If anything, he could be mistaken for a man who worked on the Rhine, a rough-hewn mate or a foreman of a barge crew. He had chosen the chauffeur's coat, a dark, coarse-woven jacket cut to the hips, with the man's blue denim shirt underneath – both bullet holes washed clean of blood. The trousers were those of the subordinate executioner; brown creaseless corduroys, flared slightly at the ankles, which thankfully they reached. Neither man had worn a hat and his was somewhere in the landfill; he would find one or buy one or steal one. He had to; without a hat or a cap covering part of his face, he felt as naked, as exposed and as frightened as he felt without his clothes.

He lay back in the dry wild grass as the sun disappeared over an unseen horizon and stared up at the sky.

24

"Well, *Ah'll be* . . . !" exclaimed the distinguished-looking man with the flowing mane of white hair, his full, nearly white eyebrows arched in astonishment. "You're Molly Washburn's boy?"

"I beg your pardon?" said the Army officer at the adjacent table along the banquette in Bonn's *Am Tulpenfeld* restaurant. "Have we met, sir?"

"Not so's you'd remember, Major . . . Please forgive my intruding." The Southerner addressed the apology to the officer's companion across the table, a balding middle-aged man who had been speaking English with a pronounced German accent. "But Molly would never forgive this poor old Georgia cracker if he didn't say hello to her son and insist on buyin' him a drink."

"I'm afraid I'm at a loss," said Washburn pleasantly but without enthusiasm.

"I would be, too, young fella. I know it sounds corn-pone but you were just barely in long pants back then. The last time I saw you, you were in a blue blazer jacket and madder 'n hell at losing a soccer game. I think you blamed it on your left wing, which in my opinion then and now is a logical place to blame *anything*."

The major and his companion laughed appreciatively. "Good Lord, that does go back a long time – to when I was at Dalton."

"And captain of the team, as I recall."

"How did you ever recognize me?"

"I dropped in on your momma the other week at the house in Southampton. Proud girl that she is, there were a few real handsome photographs of you in the living room."

"Of course, on the piano."

"That's where they were, silver frames and all."

"I'm afraid I've forgotten your name."

"Thayer. Thomas Thayer, or just plain old 'T.T.' as your momma calls me." The two shook hands.

"Good to see you again, sir," said Washburn, gesturing at his companion. "This is Herr Schindler. He handles a great deal of our press relations with the West German media."

"How do you do, Mr Schindler."

"A pleasure, Herr Thayer."

"Speaking of the embassy and I assume you were, I promised Molly I'd ring you up over there when I got here. Mah word on it, I was going to do just that tomorrow – I'm fightin' jet lag today. One hell of a coincidence, isn't it? You bein' here and my bein' here, right *next* to each other!"

"Herr Major," interrupted the German courteously. "Two people who go back so many years must have a great deal to reminisce about. And since our business is fundamentally concluded, I think I shall press on."

"Now hold on, Mr Schindler," objected Thayer. "Ah simply couldn't allow you to do that!"

"No, really, it's perfectly all right." The German smiled. "Truthfully, Major Washburn felt he should insist on taking me to dinner this evening after the terrible things we've had to deal with during the past few days – he far more than I – but to be quite honest, I'm exhausted. Also I am far older than my young friend and nowhere near as resilient. The bed cries out, Herr Thayer. Believe me when I tell you that."

"Hey, Mr Schindler, Ah've got an idea. You're fanned out and I'm droppin' from the jet stream, so why don't we leave the young skunk here and *both* hit the pillows?"

"But I couldn't allow *you* to do that." The German got up from the table and extended his hand to Thayer. They shook, and Schindler turned to Washburn, shaking his hand also. "I'll call you in the morning, Norman."

"All right, Gerhart . . . Why didn't you just say you were tired?"

"And conceivably offend one of my largest clients? Be reasonable, Norman. Good night, gentlemen." The German smiled again, and walked away.

"Ah guess we're stuck with each other, young man," said the Southerner. "Why not move over here and let me save the embassy a couple of dollars?"

"All right," replied Washburn, getting up with his drink and sidling between the tables to the chair opposite Thayer. He sat down. "How is mother? I haven't called her in a couple of weeks."

"Molly is always Molly, my boy. She came forth and they broke the mould, but I don't have to tell *you* that. She looks the same as she did twenty years ago. I swear I don't know how she *does* it!"

"And she's not going to tell you, either."

Both men laughed as the Southerner raised his glass, pressing it forward for the touch. The glasses met, the gentle ring heard. It was the beginning.

Converse waited, watching from a dark storefront on the shabby street in Emmerich. Across the way were the dim lights of a cheap hotel, the entrance uninviting, sleazy. Yet with any luck he would have a bed there in the next few minutes. A bed with a basin in the corner of the room and, with even more luck, hot water with which he could bathe his wound and change the bandage again. During the last two nights he had learned that such places were his only stops of refuge. No questions were asked and a false name on a registration card was to be expected. But even the most sullen greeting was a menace for him. He opened his mouth and whatever came out identified him as an American who could not speak German.

He felt like a deaf-mute careening off walls of people in a labyrinth designed as a gauntlet. He was so helpless, so goddamned *helpless!* The killings in Bonn, Brussels and Wesel somehow made every American male over thirty and under fifty suspect. The melodramatic suspicions were compounded by speculations that the obsessed man was being aided, perhaps manipulated, by terrorist organizations – Baader Meinhof, the PLO, Libyan splinter groups, even KGB destabilization teams sent out by the dreaded *Voennaya*. He was being hunted everywhere and as of yesterday, the *International Herald Tribune* had printed further reports that the assassin was heading for Paris – which meant that the generals of Aquitaine wanted the concentration to be *on* Paris, not where they knew he was, where their soldiers could run him down, take him, kill him.

To get off the streets he had to move with the flotsam and jetsam, and a run-down hotel like the one across the street was more appealing than the Waldorf Astoria. And he *had* to get off the streets; there were too many traps outside. So on the first night in Wesel he remembered the student, Johann, and looked for ways to recreate vaguely similar circumstances. Young people were less prone to be suspicious, the promise of immediate reward quelling doubts for pockets and appetites more in need.

It was odd but that first night in Wesel was both the most difficult and the easiest. Difficult because he had no idea where to look, easy because it happened so rapidly, so logically. He had stopped at a drug store, buying gauze, adhesive tape, antiseptic and an inexpensive cap with a visor. Then he went to a café, to the men's room, where he had washed his face and stung the wound, binding it tight, skin joining skin, the bandage firmly in place. Suddenly, as he finished his ministrations, he heard the familiar words and emphatic melody, young raucous voices in song.

"*On Wisconsin... On Wisconsin... on to victoreee... we shall...*"

A group of students from the German Society at the University of Wisconsin were bicycling through the northern Rhineland. Casually approaching a young man getting more beers from the bar, and introducing himself as an exhausted and ashamed fellow American, he told an outrageous story of having been taken by a whore and rolled by her pimp – who stole his passport but never thought of a money belt. He was a respected businessman who had to sleep it off, gather his wits together, and reach his firm back in New York. However, he spoke no German; would the student consider the payment of a hundred dollars for helping him out?

He would and did. Down the block was a dingy hotel where no questions were asked; the young man paid for a room and brought Converse his receipt and his key outside.

All yesterday he had walked, following the roads in sight of the railroad tracks until he reached a town named Halden. It was smaller than Wesel, but there was a rundown, industrial section east of the railroad yards. The only "hotel" he could find, however, was a large, shoddy house at the end of a row of shoddy houses with signs in two ground-floor windows and a larger one over the front door all proclaiming the same message. *Zimmer. 20 Mark.* It was a boarding house, and several doors beyond in the spill of the street lamps, a heated argument was taking place between an older woman and a young man. Above, a few neighbours sat in their windows, arms on the sills, obviously listening. Then Joel heard the words, shouted in heavily accented English.

" ... 'I hate it here!' *Das habe ich ihm gesagt.* "I do not care to stay, Onkel! I vill go back to Germany! Maybe join Baader-Meinhof!' *Das habe ich ihm gesagt.*"

"*Narr!*" screamed the woman, turning and going up the steps. "*Schweinehund!*" she roared, as she opened the door, went inside and slammed it shut behind her.

The young man had looked up at his audience in the windows and shrugged. A few clapped, so he made an exaggerated, elaborate bow.

Converse approached the young man; there was no harm in trying, he thought, as he spoke.

"You speak very good English," he said.

"Vye not?" replied the German. "They spend bags of groceries for five years to give me lessons. I must go to her brother in America. I say *Nein!* They say *Ja!* I go. I *hate* it!"

"I'm sorry to hear that. I'm an American and I like the German people. Where were you?"

"In Yorktown."

"Virginia?"

"*Nein!* The city of New York."

"Oh, *that* Yorktown."

"*Ja*, my uncle has two butcher shops in New York, in what they call Yorktown. *Shit*, as you say in America!"

"I'm sorry. Why?"

"The *Schwarzen* and the *Juden!* If you speak like me, the black people steal from you with knives, and the Jews steal from you with their cash registers. *Heinie*, they call me, and *Nazi.* I told a Jew he cheated me – I was nice, I was not impolite – and he told me to get out of his shop or he would call the 'cops'! I was *shit*, he said! . . . You wear a good German suit and spend good German money, they don't say those things. You are a delivery boy trying to learn, they kick the shit out of you! "What do *I* know! My father was too young to be anything but a fourteen-year-old soldier. *Shit!*"

"Again, I'm telling you I'm sorry. I mean it. It's not in our nature to blame children."

"*Shit!*"

"Perhaps I can make up for a little of what you went through. I'm in trouble – because I was a *stupid* American. But I'll pay you a hundred American dollars . . ."

The young German happily got him a room at the boarding house. It was no better than the one in Wesel, but the water was hotter, the toilet nearer his door.

But tonight was different, thought Joel, as he looked across the street at the time-worn old hotel in Emmerich with no significance in its past. Tonight could lead to his passage into Holland. To Cort Thorbecke and a plane to Washington. The man he had recruited was somewhat older than the others. He was a merchant seaman out of Bremerhaven, in Emmerich to make a duty call on his family with whom he felt ill at ease. He had made the obligatory call, been soundly rebuked by his mother and father, and had returned to the environs and the people he loved best – a bar on the bend of the riverbank.

Again, as it had been in Wesel, it was a song and the lyrics of a song that caused Joel to stare at the young seaman standing at the bar, a guitar in his hands. What he played was no college football anthem, but the words were in English, albeit Germanically anglicized, and the melody was an odd, haunting mixture of slow biting rock and a sad madrigal.

"When you finally came down . . . when your feet hit the ground, did you know where you were? . . . When you finally were real, could you touch what you feel, were you there in the know?"

The men around the bar were caught up by the precise beat of the minor key music. When the seaman finished there was respectful applause, followed by fast talk and faster refilled mugs of beer. Minutes later Converse was standing next to the sea-going troubadour, the guitar now slung over his shoulder, held in place by a wide strap like a weapon. Joel wondered if the man really knew English or only lyrics. He would find out in seconds. The seaman laughed at a companion's remark; when the laughter subsided, Converse spoke.

"I'd like to buy you a drink," he said. "For reminding me of home. It was a nice song."

The man looked at him quizzically. Joel stammered. thinking that the seaman had no idea what he was talking about; the German spoke only lyrics, not the language. Then, to Converse's relief, the man answered.

"*Danke.* It is a good song. Sad but good, like some of ours. You are *Amerikaner?*"

"Yes. And you speak English."

"Okay. I don't read no good, *aber* I speak okay. I'm on merchant ship. We sail Boston, New York, Baltimore – sometimes ports, Florida."

"What'll you have?"

"*Ein Bier*," said the seaman, shrugging.

"Why not whisky?"

"*Ja?*"

"Certainly."

"*Ja.*"

Minutes later they were at a table. Joel told his story about a non-existent whore and a fictional pimp. He told it slowly, not because he felt he had to pace the narrative to his listener's understanding, but because another option was coming sharply into focus. The guitar-playing merchantman was young but there was a patina about him that indicated he knew the docks and the waterfront and the various businesses that flourished in that very special world.

"You should go to the *Polizei*," said the man when Converse had finished. "They know the whores and they will not print your name." The German smiled. "We want you back to spend more money."

"I can't take the chance. In spite of the way I look, I deal with a lot of important people – here and in America."

"Which makes *you* important, *ja?*"

"And very stupid. If I could just get over into Holland, I could handle everything."

"*Der Niederlande?* What is problem?"

"I told you, my passport was taken. And it's just my luck that every American crossing any border is looked at very carefully. You know, that crazy bastard who killed the ambassador in Bonn and the NATO commander."

"*Ja*, and in Wesel two, three days ago," completed the German. "They say he goes to Paris."

"I'm afraid that doesn't help me . . . Look, you know the river people, the men who have boats going out every day. I told you I'd pay you a hundred dollars for the hotel . . ."

"I agreed, *Mein Herr*. You are generous."

"I'll pay you a great deal more if you can somehow get me over into Holland. You see my company has an office in Amsterdam. They can help me. Will *you* help me?"

The German grimaced and looked at his watch. "Is too late for such arrangements tonight and I leave for Bremerhaven on the morning train. My ship sails at fifteen hundred."

"That was the amount I had in mind. Fifteen hundred."

"*Deutschemarks?*"

"Dollars."

"You are more crazy than your *Landsmann* who kills soldiers. If you knew the language, it would cost no more than fifty."

"I don't know the language. Fifteen hundred American dollars – for you if you can arrange it."

The young man looked hard at Converse, then moved back his chair. "Wait here. I will make a phone call."

"Send over more whisky on your way."

"*Danke.*"

The waiting was neither pleasant nor unpleasant; it was time spent in a vacuum of anxiety. Joel looked at the weathered guitar lying below across an extra chair. What were the words? . . . "*When you finally came down, when your feet hit the ground . . . did you know where you were? When . . . you were real, could you touch . . . what you feel, were you there in the know? . . .*"

"I will stop for you at five o'clock in the morning." The announcement came from the merchant seaman who sat down with two glasses of whisky. "The captain will accept two hundred dollars, *aber* only if there are no drugs. If there are drugs, you don't come on board."

"I have no drugs," said Converse, smiling, controlling his elation. "That's done and you've earned your money. I'll pay you at the dock or pier or whatever it is."

"*Natürlich.*"

It had all happened less than an hour ago, thought Joel, watching the hotel entrance across the street. Tonight *was* different. At five o'clock in the morning he would be on his way to Holland, to Amsterdam, to a man named Cort Thorbecke, Mattilon's broker of illegal passports. All the passenger manifests on all aircraft heading to the United States would be watched by Aquitaine, but a hundred years ago he had learned that there were ways to elude the watchers. He had done it before from a deep, cold shaft in the ground and a barbed wire fence in the darkness. He could do it again.

A figure emerged under the dimly-lit marquee of the hotel. It was the young merchant seaman. Grinning, he beckoned Converse to join him.

"Hell's fire and Jeesus *H*, what *is* it, Norman?" cried the Southerner, as Washburn suddenly began an erratic series of convulsions, his lips trembling as he gasped for air.

"I . . . don't . . . know." The major's eyes grew wide, the pupils now dancing and out of control.

"Maybe it's that Heimlich thing!" said Thomas Thayer, rising from the banquette and quickly side-stepping his way between the table on the left and Washburn. "Hell no, it *can't* be! Our food's not here; you haven't *eaten!*"

The couples on both sides expressed alarm, talking loudly, rapidly in German. At one of the diner's remarks, the Southerner turned and spoke to the man. "*Das glaube ich nicht,*" said Johnny Reb. "*Mein Wagen steht draussen. Ich kenne einen Arzt.*"

The *maître* came rushing over and, seeing that the commotion involved the Americans, addressed his concern in English. "Is the major ill, *Mein Herr?* Shall I ask if there is . . ."

"No doctor I'm not familiar with, thanks," interrupted Thayer, bent over the embassy's *chargé d'affaires*, who was now inhaling deeply, his eyes half-closed, his head swaying back and forth. "This here is Molly Washburn's boy and I'll see he gets the best! My car's outside. Maybe if a couple of your waiters will give a hand we can put him in the limo and I'll take him right over to my man. He's a specialist. At my age you gotta have 'em everywhere."

"*Bestimmt*. Certainly!" The *maître* snapped his fingers; three waiters responded instantly.

"The embassy . . . the *embassy!*" choked Washburn as the three men half carried the officer to the door of the restaurant.

"Don't you worry, Norman-boy!" said the Southerner, hearing the plea, walking behind with the *maître*. "I'll phone 'em from the car, tell 'em to meet us at Rudi's place." Thayer turned to the German beside him. "You know what Ah think? Ah think this fine soldier is jest plumb wore out. He's been workin' from sunrise to sunrise with nary a break. I mean, can you imagine everything he's had to contend with these last couple of days? That crazy mongrel goin' around shootin' up a feud, killin' the ambassador then that honcho in Brussels! You know, Molly's boy here is the *char-jay d'affaires.*"

"Yes, the major is our guest frequently – an honoured guest."

"Well, even the most honourable among us has a right and a time to say 'the hell with it, I'll sit this one out'."

"I'm not sure I understand?"

"Ah have an idea this fine young man who I knew as a mere saplin' lad never learned about the quantitative effects of old demon whisky."

"Ohh?" The *maître* looked at Johnny Reb as might a carrier of fashionable gossip hearing a new rumour.

"He had several mites too much, that's all – and *that's* jest between *us.*"

"He vas not in focus . . ."

"He started bustin' corks before the sun hit the roof of the west barn." They reached the front entrance, the unit of busboys manoeuvring Washburn out the door. "Who was more entitled? That's what I say." Thayer removed his wallet.

"*Ja*, I agree."

"Here," said the Southerner, removing bills. "I haven't had time to convert, so there's a hundred American – that should cover the tab and plenty for the boys outside . . . And here's a hundred for you – for not talkin' too much, *verstehen?*"

"Completely, *Mein Herr!*" The German pocketed both hundred dollar bills, smiling and nodding his head obsequiously. "I vill say absolutely nozzing!"

"Well, I wouldn't go that far. It might be a good thing for Molly's boy to learn that it ain't the end of the world if a few people know he's had a drink or two. Might loosen him up a bit, and in mah Georgia judgment, he needs a little loosenin'. Maybe you might wink at him when he next comes in."

"*Vink?*"

"Give him a friendly smile, like you know and it's okay. *Verstehen Sie?*"

"*Ja*, I agree! He vas entitled!"

Outside at the kerb, Johnny Reb instructed the waiters just how to place Major Norman Anthony Washburn, IV, into the back seat. Stretched out, facing up, supine. The Southerner gave each man a twenty-dollar American bill and dis-

323

missed them. He then spoke to the two men in front, pressing a button so they could hear his voice beyond the glass partition.

"Ah got the jump seats down," he said, pulling the velvet backs out of the velvet wall. "He's out. Come on and join me, Witch Doctor. And you, Klaus, you entertain us with a long drive in your beautiful countryside."

Minutes later, as the limousine entered a back country road, the overhead light switched on, the doctor unbuckled Washburn's belt, slid the trousers down, and rolled the *chargé d'affaires* over and into the seat. He found the area he wanted at the base of the spine the needle held above in his steady hand.

"Ready, chap?" asked the dark-skinned Palestinian, yanking down the elastic top of the unconscious man's shorts.

"You got it, Pookie," answered Johnny Reb, holding a small recorder over the edge of the jump seat. Right where he won't find it for a week, if he ever does. Take him up, Arab. I want him to *fly*."

The doctor inserted the long hypodermic needle, slowly pressing his thumb on the plunger. "It will be quick," said the Palestinian. "It is a heavy dose and I've seen it happen when the patient began babbling before the interrogator was ready."

"I'm ready."

"Put him on track instantly. Ask direct questions, centre his concentration immediately."

"Oh, Ah will, indeed. This is a bad man, Pookie. A nasty little boy who tells tall tales that ain't got nothin' to do with a big catfish that broke off a hook." The Southerner gripped the unconscious Washburn's left shoulder and yanked him forward, face up on the seat. "All right, Molly's boy, let's you and me talk. How come you got the *audacity* to mess around with an officer of the United States Navy named Fitzpatrick? Connal Fitzpatrick, boy! Fitzpatrick, Fitzpatrick, *Fitzpatrick!* C'mon, baby, talk to daddy, "cause you've got nobody else *but* daddy! Everyone you think you got is gone! They set you up, Molly's boy! They made you lie in print so the whole world *knows* you lied! But daddy can make it right. Daddy can straighten it all out and put you on top – right on the very *top!* The joint chiefs – the *big* chief! Daddy's your tit, boy! Grab it or suck air! Where'd you put Fitzpatrick? Fitzpatrick, *Fitzpatrick!*"

The whisper came, as Washburn's body writhed on the seat, his head whipping back and forth, saliva oozing out of the edges of his mouth. "Scharhörn, the isle of Sharhörn . . . The Heligoland Bight."

Caleb Dowling was not only angry, he was bewildered. Despite a thousand doubts he could not let it go; too many things did not make sense, not the least of which was the fact that for three days he had been unable to get an appointment with the acting-ambassador. The scheduling *attaché* claimed there was too much confusion resulting from Walter Peregrine's assassination to permit an audience at this time. Perhaps in a week . . . In short words, *actor get lost, we have important things to do and you're not one of them.* He was being checked, shoved into a corner, and given the lip service one gave to a well-known but insignificant person. His motives as well as his intelligence were undoubtedly questioned out loud by arrogant, harried diplomats. Or someone else.

Which was why he was sitting now at a back table in the dimly lit bar of the Königshof Hotel. He had learned the name of Peregrine's secretary, one Enid Heathley, and had sent the stunt man, Moose Rosenberg, to the embassy with a sealed letter purportedly from a close friend of Miss Heathley's in the States. Moose's instructions had been to deliver the envelope personally, and as Rosenberg's size was formidable, no one in the reception room had argued. Heathley had come down in person. The message was short and to the point.

Dear Miss Heathley:
I believe it to be of the utmost importance that we talk as soon as possible. I will be in the bar of the Königshof at 7.30 this evening. If it is convenient, please have a drink with me, but I urge you not to speak to anyone about our meeting. Please, no one.
Sincerely,
C. Dowling

It was 7.38 and Caleb was growing anxious. For the past several years he was used to people being on time for appointments and interviews; it was one of the minor perks of being Pa Ratchet. But there could be several reasons why the secretary might not wish to meet him. She knew he and Peregrine had become friends of sorts and there were actors and then there were actors – some were known to seek publicity from events they had nothing to do with, posturing with statesmen and politicians when they couldn't spell out a position on slavery. He hoped to hell . . .

There she *was*. The middle-aged woman had come through the door, squinting in the dim light. The *maître* approached her and moments later she was escorted to Dowling's table.

"Thank you for coming," said Caleb, rising as Enid Heathley took her chair. "I wouldn't have asked you if I didn't think it was important," he added, sitting down again.

"I gathered that from your note," said the pleasant-faced woman with signs of grey in her hair and very intelligent eyes. Her drink ordered, casual talk covered its arrival.

"I imagine it's been very difficult for you," said Dowling.

"It hasn't been easy," agreed Miss Heathley. "I was Mr Peregrine's secretary for nearly twenty years. He used to call us a team, and Jane and I – Mrs Peregrine – are quite close. I should be with her now, but I told her I had some last minute things to do at the office."

"How is she?"

"Still in shock, of course. But she'll make it. She's strong. Walter wanted the women around him strong. He thought they were worthwhile and they shouldn't hide their worth."

"I like that kind of thinking, Miss Heathley."

Her drink came, the waiter left, and the secretary looked quizzically at Caleb. "Forgive me, Mr Dowling, I can't say I'm a devoted follower of your television show, but, of course, I've seen it a number of times. It seems that whenever I'm asked to dinner and the magic hour arrives, meals are suspended."

"I'd suggest those people upgrade their kitchens."

The woman smiled. "You're too modest but that's not what I mean. You don't sound at all like the man on the television screen."

"Because I'm not he, Miss Heathley," said the former university professor, his expression serious, his intelligent eyes level with hers. "I assume we share certain traits because I've the physical instrument through which his fictions are filtered, but that's the extent of any similarity."

"I see. That's very well put."

"I've had practice saying it. But I didn't ask you here to expound on theories of acting. It's a subject with limited appeal."

"Why did you ask me?"

"Because I don't know who else to go to. Well, I do but I can't get near him."

"Who's that?"

"The acting-ambassador the one who flew over from Washington."

"He's up to his ears . . ."

"He should be told," interrupted Caleb. "Warned."

"Warned?" The woman's eyes grew wide. "An attempt on his *life?* Another killing – that maniac, *Converse?*"

"Miss Heathley," began the actor, his posture rigid, his voice quiet. "What I'm about to say may shock you, even offend you, but as I said, I don't know another person I can go to at the embassy. However, I *do* know there are people over there I *can't* go to."

"What are you talking about?"

"I'm not convinced that Converse is either a maniac or that he killed Walter Peregrine."

"*What?* You can't be serious! You've heard what they say about him, how unbalanced he is. He was the last person *with* Mr Peregrine. Major Washburn established that!"

"Major Washburn is one of those people I'd rather not see."

"He's considered one of the finest officers in the United States Army," objected the secretary.

"Then for an officer he has a strange concept of taking orders from a superior. Last week I brought Peregrine to meet someone. The man ran and Walter told the major to stop him. Instead, Washburn tried to kill him."

"Oh, *now* I understand," said Enid Heathley, her tone unpleasant. "That was the night you arranged a meeting with Converse – it *was* you, I remember now! Mr Peregrine told me. What *is* this, Mr Dowling? A Hollywood actor protecting his image? Afraid he'll be held responsible and his ratings, or whatever they are, will plummet – that *is* the word, isn't it? This conversation is despicable." The woman moved her chair back, prepared to leave.

"Walter Peregrine was a man of his word, Miss Heathley," said Caleb, still immobile, staring at the secretary. "I think you'll agree with that."

"*And?*"

"He made a promise to me. He told me that if Converse reached him and asked to meet with him, I'd come along. *Me*, Miss Heathley. Specifically *not* Major Washburn, whose actions that night at the university were as bewildering to him as they were to me."

The middle-aged woman held her place, her eyes narrowed, concerned. "He *was* upset the next morning," she said softly.

"Damned angry better describes him, I think. The man who ran away wasn't Converse – and he also wasn't crazy. He was deadly serious, with the speech of someone used to authority. There was – or is – some kind of confidential investigation going on involving the embassy. Peregrine didn't know what it was but he intended to find out. He mentioned that he was going to call Washington on a scrambler phone. I'm not up on the technology but I don't think a person places a call like that unless he's worried that someone might try to tap the line."

"He *did* place a scrambler call. He told you that?"

"Yes, he did. And there's something else, Miss Heathley. As you correctly stated, I'm the one responsible for Walter Peregrine ever having heard of Converse, and I don't feel very good about it. But isn't it odd that in spite of the fact that it wasn't a secret – *you* knew, Washburn knew – nobody has come to question me since Walter was killed."

"No one?" asked the woman incredulously. "But I included your name in my report."

"Who did you give it to?"

"Well, Norman was handling everything . . ." Enid Heathley stopped.

"Washburn?"

"Yes."

"Didn't you speak to anyone else? Weren't you questioned?"

"Yes, of course. An inspector from the Bonn police. I'm sure I mentioned your name – I'm *positive* I did."

"Was anybody else in the room?"

"Yes," said the murdered ambassador's secretary. "Norman," she whispered.

"Strange behaviour for a police department, isn't it?" Caleb leaned forward, but only slightly. "Let me reemphasize something you just said, Miss Heathley. You asked me if I was a Hollywood actor trying to protect his image. It's a logical question and if you ever saw the unemployment lines in Los Angeles you'd understand just how logical it is. Don't you think other people believe the same thing? I haven't been questioned because *specific* people here in Bonn think I'm shaking in Pa Ratchet's boots, keeping silent so to protect that late-coming image and the ratings that make it possible. Oddly enough, that reasoning is my best physical protection. You don't kill off a Pa Ratchet unless you want the wrath of millions of viewers who, in my judgment, would latch on to the flimsiest connection to raise hysterical questions. *National Inquirer*, you are there."

"But you're not keeping silent," said Enid Heathley.

"I'm not talking loudly, either," corrected the actor. "But not for the reasons I've described. I owe Walter Peregrine – I know that better than anyone else. And I can't pay that debt if a man I think is innocent is hung for his murder.

But here's where I step back into my own confusion. I can't be certain. I could be wrong."

The woman returned Dowling's stare, then slowly frowned, keeping her eyes on him. "I'm going to leave now but I'd like you to stay here for a while, if you wouldn't mind. I'm going to call someone I think you should see. You'll understand. He'll reach you here – no paging, of course. Do as he says, go where he wants you to go."

"Can I trust him?"

"Mr Peregrine did," said Enid Heathley, nodding. "And he didn't like him."

"That's trust," said the actor.

The phone call came and Caleb wrote out the address. The doorman at the Königshof secured him a taxi, and eight minutes later he got out in front of an ornate Victorian house on the outskirts of Bonn. He walked up to the door and rang the bell.

Two minutes later he was ushered into a large room – once a library, perhaps – but now with shades covering the obvious bookshelves. Shades that were detailed maps of East and West Germany. A man wearing glasses got up from behind a desk. He nodded perfunctorily and spoke.

"Mr Dowling?"

"Yes."

"I appreciate your coming out here, sir. My name is not important – why not call me George?"

"All right, George."

"But for your own confidential information – and I must stress *confidential* – I am the Station Chief for the Central Intelligence Agency here in Bonn."

"All right, George."

"What do you do, Mr Dowling? What's your line of work?"

"*Ciao*, baby," said the actor, shaking his head.

25

The first indefinite light of dawn crept up the lower wall of the eastern sky, and along the river pier boats bobbed in their slips, straining their lines, composing an eerie symphony of creaks and thumps. Joel walked beside the young merchant seaman, his right arm bent at the elbow, his hand unconsciously straying to his face, to the new soft hair that was the outgrowth of a stubble. He had not shaved in four days, since Bonn, and now he had the beginnings of a short, neat beard, not yet full but no longer a shabby bristle. One more day and he would have to begin clipping it, shaping it, another plane of removal from the photograph in the newspapers.

And in one more day he would have to decide whether or not to phone Val at Cape Ann. Actually, he had made his decision – negative. His instructions had been clear enough and the possibility that her telephone was tapped was more than he could handle. Yet he wanted so terribly to hear her voice, to hear the support he knew he would find in it. Negative. To hear it was to involve her. *Negative!*

"It is the last boat on the right," said the seaman, slowing his pace. "I must ask you again as I have given my word. You carry no drugs."

"I carry no drugs."

"He may care to search you."

"I can't permit that," broke in Converse, thinking of his money belt. What could be mistaken for a cache for narcotics would reveal many times the amount of money for which most of the dregs on the river front would kill.

"Perhaps he will want to know why. Drugs bring bad penalties, long prison terms."

"I'll explain to him privately," said Joel, thinking again. He would do so with his gun in one hand and an additional five hundred dollar bill in the other. "But I give you my word, no drugs."

"It is not my boat."

"But you made the arrangements, and you know enough about me to come after me if they came after you."

"*Ja*, I remember. Connect-teecut – I been to visit friends in Bridge-port. A broker house, a vice-president. I find you, if I have to."

"I wouldn't want that. You're a nice fellow who's helping me out and I'm grateful. I won't get you in trouble."

"*Ja*," said the young German, nodding his head. "I believe you. I believe you last night. You talk very good, very high class, but you were stupid. You did a stupid thing and your face is red. A red face costs more than you want to pay, so you pay much more to make it go away."

"Your homilies are getting to me."

"*Was ist?*"

"Nothing. You're right. It's the story of upper-level management. Here." Joel had the bills in his left-hand pocket; he pulled them out. "I promised you fifteen hundred dollars. Count it, if you like."

"*Vye?* If is not there I talk loud and you stay here. You are too afraid to risk that."

"You're a natural born lawyer."

"Come, I bring you to the captain. That is all he is to you, only 'captain'. You will be dropped off where he says . . . And a caution, *Mein Herr*. Watch the men on the boat. They will suspect you have money."

"That's why I don't want to be searched," admitted Converse.

"I know. I do my best for you."

The seaman's best was not quite good enough. The captain of the filthy barge, a short hulk of a man with very poor teeth, brought Joel up to the wheelhouse where he told him in broken but perfectly clear English to remove his jacket.

"I explained to my friend on the dock that I can't do that."

"Two hundred dollars *Amerikaner*," said the captain.

Converse had the money in his right-hand pocket. He reached down for it, his eyes briefly glancing at the portside window where he saw two other men climb on board below in the dim light. They did not glance up: they had not seen him in the wheelhouse shadows.

The blow came suddenly, without warning, the impact such that Joel doubled over expunging his breath, gripping his stomach. In front of him the surly bull of a captain was shaking his right hand, the grimace on his face indicating sharp pain. The German's fist had crashed into the gun lodged in Converse's belt. Joel staggered back into the bulkhead, leaned against it, and lowered himself to the floor as he reached under his jacket and took out the weapon. On his haunches, his legs bracing him against the wall, he aimed the automatic at the captain's huge chest.

"That was a rotten thing to do," said Converse, breathing hard, still holding his stomach. "Now, you bastard, *your* jacket!"

"*Was* . . . ?"

"You heard me! Take it off, hold it upside down, and shake the goddamned thing!"

The German slowly, reluctantly slid off his waist-length coat, twice darting his eyes to the left of Joel, towards the wheelhouse door. "I look only for drugs."

"I'm not carrying any, and if I were, I suspect whoever sold them to me would have a better way to get across the river than with you. Turn it upside down! *Shake* it!"

The captain held his coat by the bottom edge and let it fall away. A short, ugly revolver plummeted to the floor, clacking on the wood, followed by the lighter sound of a long knife encased in a flat bone handle, flared at the end. As it struck the deck, the blade shot out.

"This is the river," said the German without elaboration.

"And I just want to cross it without any trouble – and trouble to someone as nervous as I am is anyone walking through that door." Converse angled his head, gesturing at the wheelhouse entrance on his left. "In my state of mind, I'd fire this gun. I'd probably kill you and whoever else came in here. I'm not as strong as you, Captain, but I'm afraid, and that makes me much more dangerous. Can you understand that?"

"*Ja*. I not hurt you. I look only for drugs."

"You hurt me plenty," corrected Joel. "And that frightens me."

"*Nein. Bitte* . . . please."

"When do you take the boat out?"

"When I say."

"How many crew?"

"One man, that is all."

"*Liar!*" whispered Converse sharply, the gun thrust forward.

"*Zwei*. Two men . . . *today*. We pick up heavy crates in Elten. On my word, is normal only one man. I can't pay more."

"Start the engine," ordered Joel. "Or engines. I only know Chris Crafts and Bertrams, which is a silly fucking thing to say."

"*Was?*"

"Do it!"

"*Die Mannschaft*. The . . . crew. I must give *Befehle*."

"Wait!" Converse crawled sideways past the wheelhouse door, glancing above to his left at the thick wooden panelling of the pilot's window, his gun never once wavering from its line of fire into the German's chest. Again, he used the bulkhead and his braced legs to shinny himself up the wall; he was in shadows, with a clear view of the bow, and through both wheelhouse windows behind him, the stern of the boat. In sight were the fore and aft piles on both sides, the lines looped around the thick protrusions of weather-beaten logs. The two crewmen were sitting on a storage hatchway, smoking cigarettes, one drinking from a can of beer. "All right," said Joel, clicking the hammer back on the automatic – a weapon with which he was not sure he could be accurate within ten feet. "Open that door and give your orders. And if either of those men down there does anything but free those ropes, I'll kill you. Can you understand that?"

"I understand . . . everything you say, but you do not understand me. I search you for drugs – not a *grosse Mann* – the *Polizei* do not go after such people, they leave them alone. They go after the *Kleine*, the small people who use the river boats. It makes them look good, you see. I would not hurt you, *Mein Herr*. I only protect myself. I want to believe what my *Neffe* – nephew – told me, but I must be sure."

"Your *nephew?*"

"The seaman from Bremerhaven. How you think he got his job? *Ach, mein Bruder* sells flowers! It is his *Frau's* shop! He once sailed the oceans as I did. Now, he is a *Blumenhändler!*"

"I swear to Christ I don't understand anything," said Joel, partially lowering his gun.

"Would it help to tell you that he offered to pay me one half of the fifteen hundred dollars you pay him?"

"Absolutely nothing. A consortium of thieves."

"*Nein*, I not take. I tell him buy a new *Gitarre*."

Converse sighed. "I have no drugs. Do you believe me?"

"*Ja*, you are only a fool, he told me. Rich fools pay more. They cannot afford to admit their foolishness. The poor do not care."

"Do those little bromides run in the family?"

"*Was?*"

"Forget it. Give the orders. Let's get out of here."

"*Ja*. Watch through the windows, please. I would not want you to be more afraid. You are right. A man afraid is much more dangerous."

Joel leaned back against the bulkhead as the captain shouted his orders. The engines started and the lines were released from their pilings. It was so contrary, he thought. Hostile, belligerent men who struck out in anger were not always his enemies, while pleasant, seemingly friendly people wanted to kill him. It was a world he knew nothing about, a long stretch from a courtroom or a boardroom where courtesy and "killing" could mean a variety of things. There were no such grey areas a hundred years ago in the camps and the jungles. One knew who the enemy was: the definitions were clear on all sides. But during the past four days he had learned that there were no defined lines for him now. He *was* in a labyrinth, a gauntlet, its deceptive walls lined with progressively more grotesque people he could not understand. Converse stared out the window, at the pockets of mist rising out of the water, a few spiralling up to catch the early light in their clouds of vapour. His mind went blank. He did not care to think for a while.

"Five, perhaps six minutes, *Mein Herr*," said the captain, swinging the wheel to his left.

Joel blinked; he had been in a peaceful, rest-filled void, for how long he was not sure. "What are the procedures?" he asked, conscious of the rising orange sun firing what was left of the river mists. "I mean what do I do?"

"As little as you can," answered the German. "Just walk as if you walked the pier every morning and go through the repair yard to the street. You will be in the south section of the city of Gendringen. You will be in *Die Niederlande* and we have never seen each other."

"I understand that, but how?"

"You see that *Bootshafen?*" said the captain, pointing to a complex of docks with heavy winch machinery and hoisting devices across the water.

"It's a marina."

"*Ja*, marina. My second petrol tank is empty – I say I test. I stall the engines three hundred metres off shore and go in. I yell at the Dutchman's price but I pay, for I do not buy from the *Deutsche* thief this far down river. You get off with one of my crew, have a cigarette and laugh at your stupid captain – then you walk away."

"Just like that?"

"*Ja.*"

"It's so easy."

"*Ja.* No one said it was difficult. You have only to keep your eyes clear."

"For the police?"

"*Nein*," said the captain, shrugging. "If there is *Polizei* they come to boat, you stay on board."

"Then who am I looking for?"

"Men who may watch you, may see you walk away."

"What men?"

"*Gesindel, Gauner* – what you call scum. They come each morning to the piers to look for work, most still drunk. Watch for such men. They will think you have drugs or money. They will break your head and steal."

"Your nephew told me to watch the men on your own boat."

"Only the new man, he is a *Gauner*. He chokes on his *Bier* hoping it will clear his head. He thinks he fools me but he does not. I keep him on board, tell him to scrape the rail, something. The other is no problem for you. He is loyal to me, an *Idiot* with a strong back and no head. The river boats do not hire him. I do. *Verstehen Sie?*"

"I think so. You're quite a guy, Captain."

"I once sailed the oceans, not a stinking river. Fifteen years of age I ship out with *mein Bruder*. By twenty-three I am *Obermaat* – 'petit' officer – good money, good life . . . Very happy." The German lowered his voice as he throttled back the engines and spun the wheel to starboard; the boat skidded on the water. "Why talk? It is over," he added angrily.

"What happened?"

"It is not for you, *Amerikaner*." The captain pushed the throttle forward; the engines coughed.

"I'm interested."

"*Warum?* Why?"

"I don't know. Maybe it takes my mind off my own problems," said Converse honestly.

The German looked briefly at him. "You ask? Okay. We never see each other . . . I stole money, much money. It took the company purser nine months to find me. *Aber, ach*, he *find* me! It was many years ago. No more oceans, only the river."

"But you said you were making good money. Why did you steal?"

"Why do most men steal, *Mein Herr?*"

"They need it – the money – or they want things they can't have normally, or they're just basically dishonest – which I don't think you are."

"Go back. Adam stole the apple, *Amerikaner*."

"Not exactly. You mean a woman?"

"Many years ago, *Mein Herr*. She was with child and she did not want her man on the seas and the ships. She wanted more." The captain permitted himself the slightest glint in his eyes and a touch of a smile on his lips. "She wanted a flower shop."

From the core of his stomach, his pain momentarily forgotten, Joel laughed. "You're *quite* a guy, Captain."

"I never see you again."

"Then your nephew . . ."

"Never *see* you again!" broke in the German, now laughing out loud himself, his eyes on the water as he headed into the Dutch marina.

Converse leaned against a pile smoking a cigarette, the visor of his cheap cap angled over his forehead, his eyes roaming up and down the pier and beyond to the repair yard in the Dutch marina. The men milling about the huge machinery were mechanically going about their tasks while those around the boats seemed more intent on inspecting than doing, shaking their heads over solemn pronouncements of disrepair The captain argued with the dispenser of fuel, making obscene gestures at the rapidly climbing figures on the glass-encased face of the pump while his soft-headed deck hand grinned several feet away. On board, the *Gauner* alternately leaned over the railing, a large wire brush in his hands, abruptly turning back to his scraping whenever his employer glanced over at him.

The time was right, thought Joel as he pushed himself away from the piling. No one anywhere had the slightest interest in him; the despondent chores and the early morning dissatisfactions took precedence over the insignificant and unfamiliar.

He started walking up the pier, his pace casual to the point of being slovenly, his eyes, however, alert. He proceeded to the edge of the repair yard approaching a row of hulls in dry dock. Beyond the last elevated boat, no more than three hundred feet away, was an inordinately tall hurricane fence and an open gate. A uniformed guard sat on the left drinking coffee and reading a newspaper, his chair angled back into the criss-crossing wire mesh. Seeing him, Joel stopped, his breath suspended, an internal alarm going off – for no reason. Men passed back and forth through the gate, but the guard did not so much as glance at anyone, his eyes devouring only the tabloid angled on his lap.

Converse turned, a last look at the river. Suddenly, he was aware of the captain. The German had run to the base of the pier and was gesturing wildly, pressing his hands forward in short, rapid strokes. He was trying to warn his smuggled cargo. Then he shouted at the top of his lungs; men stared at him and turned away, none caring to be involved. They had seen too much in the early hours on the waterfront, slashing hooks too frequently the language of the docks.

"*Lauf!* Run! *Get out!*"

Joel was mystified; he looked around. Then he saw them. Two – no *three* – burly men were lurching up from the pier, their glassy eyes focused on him. The first man staggered forward to the left of the captain. The German grabbed his shoulder, swinging him around, stopping him, but only for seconds as the other two men crashed their fists into the captain's neck and spine. They were animals – *Gauner* – their nostrils inflamed by the scent of trapped fat quarry who might keep them in food and drink for days.

Converse dived under the row of dry-docked boats, smashing his head on several hulls as he scrambled towards the other side and the shafts of light beyond. He could see frantic legs pounding the earth behind him; they were gaining on him; they were running, he was crawling. He reached the end of the suspended row of hulls, sprang out and started for the gate. He pulled out his shirt, tore off the lower section and held it against the cuts on his head as he walked rapidly past the guard and through the gate. He looked around. The three men were arguing furiously, drunkenly among themselves, two crouching, peering unsteadily under the boats. Then the man standing saw him. He shouted to the others; they stood up and started after Joel. He ran faster, until he could see them no longer; the animals had given up.

He was in the Netherlands, the welcome less than gracious, but he was there, one step closer to Amsterdam. On the other hand he had no idea where he was right now except that the town was named Lobith. He had to catch his breath and think. He stepped into a deserted storefront where a dark shade behind the entrance served as a dim mirror: it was enough. He was a mess. Think. For God's sake, *think!*

Mattilon had told him to take the train from Arnhem to Amsterdam, he remembered that clearly. And the captain of the barge had said he had to take an "omnibus" from Lobith to Arnhem; there was no train in Lobith. The first thing he had to do was reach the railroad station in Arnhem and clean himself up, then study the crowds and judge whether to risk becoming part of them. And relative to this consideration, his mind darted in several directions at once. The plain-lensed glasses had long since disappeared, undoubtedly during the insane events in Wesel; he would replace them with dark glasses. There was little he could do about the scrapes on his face but they would appear less menacing after soap and water, and certainly in or around a railroad station something could be done about his torn clothing . . . and a *map*. Goddamn it, he was a pilot! He could reach Point A from Point B – and he had to do so quickly. He had to reach Amsterdam and find a way to make contact with a man named Cort Thorbecke . . . and call Nathaniel Simon in New York. There was so much to *do!*

He walked out of the storefront suddenly aware of what was happening to him. It had happened before – a lifetime ago, in the jungle – when the fears of the night sounds had passed and he could watch the dawn and accurately plot his directions, his lines of march, his survival. He was thinking, his mind functioning again. All things considered, he was far less than what he had been, but he could be better than he was – he *had* to be. Every day that passed brought the generals of Aquitaine closer to whatever madness they were planning. Everywhere. He and they had to reverse roles. The hunted had to become the hunter. Delavane's disciples had convinced the world he was a psychopathic assassin, and so they had to find him, take him, kill him and hold him up as one more example of the spreading insanity that could be contained only with *their* solutions. Aquitaine had to be exposed and destroyed before it was too late. The countdown was in progress, the commanders surely, inexorably, moving into their positions, consolidating their powers.

Move! shouted Converse silently to himself, as he walked faster down the pavement.

He sat in the last car of the train, still wary but satisfied by the progress he had made. He had done everything cautiously but without wasting motion, his concentration absolute, aware of a dozen possible malfunctions – eyes that stared at him, a man or a woman seen twice in too short a time, a clerk delaying him by being more helpful than the hour and the crowds would normally permit. These calculated possibilities were his read-outs, his dials, his gauges; without clearance he would abort all forward motion, take-off cancelled, the escape hatch sprung, safety found in the streets. His equipment was not an aircraft that was an extension of himself, it *was* himself, and he had never flown with such precision in his life.

English Spoke, had read the sign tacked to the roof of the busy corner newsstand in Lobith. He had asked directions to the "omnibus" to Arnhem while buying a map and a newspaper, holding both close to his face. The owner was too preoccupied with customers to notice his appearance and shouted rapid instructions, useful in the pointed finger more than in the words. Joel found the bus stop some four blocks away. He sat in the crowded vehicle, his face buried in a newspaper he could not read, and forty-odd minutes later he got off at the railroad station in Arnhem.

First on his checklist was a trip to the farthest wash basin in the men's room where he cleaned himself up. He had brushed his clothes as best he could and looked in the mirror. He was still a mess but somehow he looked more like a man who had been injured than one who had been beaten; there was a difference. The checklist had continued.

Outside in the station he converted his Deutschemarks and five hundred American dollars into florin and guilder. He then bought a pair of wide-rimmed dark glasses at a pharmacy several doors from the currency exchange. As he got into the cashier's line, his hand casually covering the bruises on his face, his eyes fell on a cosmetics counter across the far side. It triggered a memory. He stepped out of the line and made his way around the cases to the display of creams and colognes, shampoos, and nail polish.

He had remembered. Shortly after they were married, in one of those maddening accidents that only happen at the most inopportune times, Valerie had slipped on a foyer rug and fell, hitting her head against the corner of an antique hallway table. By 7 o'clock that night she had what Joel had described as "one hell of a mouse". The black eye was an almost perfect oval, arcing from the bridge of her nose to the edge of her left temple, and at ten the next morning she was leading a bi-lingual presentation for agency clients from Stuttgart. She had sent him out to the drug store for a small bottle of liquid make-up which, except at close range, had covered the bruise remarkably well.

"I don't want people to think my brand new husband beat the hell out of me for not fulfilling his wildest sexual fantasies."

"Which one did you miss?"

He recognized the bottle, chose a darker shade, and returned to the cashier's line.

A second trip to a wash basin had taken ten minutes but the results justified the time. He applied the make-up carefully; the scrapes and bruises faded. Unless someone stood very close to him, he was no longer a battered brawler but a man who had perhaps suffered a serious fall. Converse had congratulated himself in that men's room in the railroad station. Under other circumstances, he might not have dressed a client so well before a trial for assault and battery. The checklist continued.

It had taken him to where he was now, in the last car on the straight-through train from Arnhem to Amsterdam. After buying his ticket on what he inferred was a low-priced excursion train that made numerous stops, he had walked out on the platform prepared to run back at the slightest negative read-out, the first steady glance that held him in focus. Instead he saw a group of men and women, couples around his own age, talking and laughing together, friends more than likely off for a short summer's holiday, perhaps leaving the river for the sea. The men carried worn, dented suitcases, most held together with rope, while a number of the women held wicker baskets looped over their arms. Their luggage and their clothing denoted working class – factories for the men, home and children or the less-demanding clerical jobs for the women – all within that part of the spectrum that suited Joel's own appearance. He had walked behind them, laughing quietly when they laughed, climbing on board as though he were part of the group, sitting in an aisle seat across from a burly man with a slender woman who, despite her thin frame, proudly wore a pair of enormous breasts. Converse's eyes could hardly avoid them and the man grinned at Joel, no malice in his look as he had raised a bottle of beer to his lips.

Somewhere Converse had read or heard that in the northern countries people going on summer vacations – or on holiday, as was the term – gravitated to the last cars in the Trans-Europa-Express. It was a custom that somehow signified their status, producing a general camaraderie, the working man's junket. Joel observed the none-too subtle transformation. Men and women got out of their seats and walked up and down the aisle talking to friends and strangers alike, cans and bottles in their hands. From the front of the car a few people broke into a song, obviously a familiar country song; others took up the words and melody only to be drowned out by Converse's group who raised their voices in an entirely different chorus until both camps dwindled away in laughter. Conviviality, indeed, was the order of the morning in the last car on the train to Amsterdam. The stations went by, a few passengers getting off at each, more getting on, suitcases, baskets, and broad smiles accompanying the arrivals, boisterous greetings welcoming them on board. A number of men wore tee-shirts emblazoned with the names of town and district teams – soccer, assumed Converse. Catcalls and amiably derisive shouts were hurled at them by age-old competitors. The railroad car was turning into an odd Dutch version of a trainload of suddenly freed adults going off to a summer camp. The volume grew.

The towns were announced, the brief stops made as Joel remained in his seat, motionless and unobtrusive, now and then glancing at his adopted group, half-smiling or laughing softly when it seemed appropriate. Otherwise he looked like someone of limited intelligence poring over a map as a child might, equal parts wonderment and confusion. Neither was the case; he was studying the streets and canals of Amsterdam. There was a man who lived on the southwest corner of Utrechtsestraat and Kerkstraat, a man he had to identify by sight, isolate and make contact with . . . his springboard to Washington found as a "member of the Tatiana family". He had to pull Cort Thorbecke away from his base of operations without alerting the hunters of Aquitaine. He would pay an English-speaking intermediary to use a telephone, the words sufficiently plausible to draw the broker out to some other location, with no mention of the Tatiana connection or its source in Paris. Those words would have to be found; he would find them somehow, he *had* to. He was psychologically on his way back towards friendly fire – in terms of actual time less than seven hours from Washington – and men who would listen to him with Nathan Simon's help and an extraordinary file that would persuade them to hide him and protect him until the soldiers of Aquitaine were exposed. It was not the way envisioned by a man he had once known in Connecticut as Avery Fowler, hardly the legal tactics whose roots were in ridicule as prescribed by A. Preston Halliday in Geneva, but there was no time now. Time was running out for manipulated webs of legality.

The train slowed down, jerking as it did so, as if the engineer far up ahead was trying to send another kind of message to a rowdy car in the rear which felt the shocks most severely. If that was his intent, it, too, backfired. The pitching motion served only to accelerate the laughter and provoke insults shouted at an unseen incompetent.

"*Amstel!*" screamed a conductor, opening the forward door between the cars. "*Amsterdam! Amst . . . !*" The poor man did not finish, instead pulling the door shut to avoid a barrage of rolled-up newspapers thrown at him.

Summer camp in the Netherlands.

The train pulled into the station and a contingent of tee-shirted chests and breasts announced their entrance with shouts of recognition. Five or six people at the front of Joel's group rose as one to welcome their friends, again cans and bottles extended in the air, laughter bouncing off the narrow walls, nearly drowning out the whistles of departure outside. Bodies fell over bodies, hugs exchanged, breasts playfully grabbed at.

Beyond the new arrivals, walking unsteadily, was the illogically logical capstone for the juvenile antics taking place in front of Converse. An old woman, obviously drunk, made her way down the aisle, her flowing dishevelled clothes matching the large, tattered canvas bag she clutched in her left hand, while she steadied herself with her right on the edge of the seats as the train accelerated. Grinning, she accepted a bottle of beer, as another was thrown into her satchel, followed by several sandwiches wrapped in wax paper. Again, there were greetings of welcome as two men in the aisle bowed to the waist as if to a queen. A third slapped her behind and whistled. For several minutes the ritual continued, a new mechanical toy for the children off to summer camp. The old woman drank and danced a jig and made playfully suggestive gestures at men and women alike, sticking out her tongue and rolling it around, her ancient eyes bulging, rolling, her ragged shawl twirling in circles like some macabre Scheherazade. She amused everyone with her drunken antics as she accepted all that was dropped into her offering cloth, including coins. The Dutch vacationers were kind, thought Joel: they took care of someone less fortunate than themselves, someone who would be barred from another class of car on another train. The woman approached him, her canvas bag now held in front of her so to accept alms from both sides. Converse reached into his pocket for a few guilder, letting them slip from his hand into the bag.

"*Goedemorgen,*" said the old woman, weaving. "*Dank U wel, beste man, erg, vriendelijk van U!*"

Joel nodded, returning to his map, but the bag lady remained.

"*Uw hoofd! Ach, heb je een ongeluk gehad, jongen?*"

Again Converse nodded, reaching again into his pocket and giving the inebriated old hag more money. He pointed to his map, waving her away, as yet another raucous chorus erupted from the front, now rolling back, the words picked up and sung with enormous enthusiasm by everyone around him.

"*Spreekt U Engels?!*" shouted the bag lady, leaning over unsteadily.

Joel shrugged, sinking back into the seat, his eyes riveted on the map.

"I think you *do*." The old woman spoke hoarsely, clearly, soberly, her right

338

hand no longer steadying herself on the edge of the seat, but instead in the canvas bag. "We've been looking for you every day, on every train. Don't *move!* The gun is equipped with a silencer. With all this noise, if I pull the trigger no one would know the difference, including the man beside you who wants only to join the party and the big-breasted woman. I think we shall let him. We *have* you, *Mijnheer* Converse!"

There was no summer camp after all. Only death minutes away from Amsterdam.

26

"*Mag ik u even lastig vallen?*" shouted the old woman, once more weaving unsteadily as she spoke to the passenger beside Converse. The man took his eyes off the raucous festivities in the aisle and glanced up at the harridan. She shouted again, her right hand still in the bag, her mass of grey, dishevelled hair springing back and forth as she nodded to her right, towards the front of the car. "*Zou ik op uw plaats mogen zitten?*"

"*Mij best!*" The man got up, grinning, as Joel instinctively moved his legs to let him pass. "*Dank U wel,*" the man added, heading for a single empty seat seen beyond a couple discoing in the aisle.

"Move over!" commanded the old woman harshly, swaying – not drunkenly – but with the rhythm of the racing train.

If it was going to happen, thought Converse, it was going to happen *now.* He started to rise, his eyes straight ahead, his right elbow inches from the bulging bag. Suddenly, his elbow slipped on the arm rest and he lashed out and downward, plunging his hand into the open canvas, gripping the fat wrist that held the unseen gun. Straining, pressing farther down, clutching flesh and metal, he swung violently to his left, yanking the old woman through the narrow space, twisting her, crashing her down into the seat next to the window. There was a sharp spit as the gun exploded, burning a hole in the heavy cloth, smoke billowing, the bullet embedding itself somewhere below. The hag's strength was maniacal, unlike anything he might have imagined. She fought viciously, clawing at his face until he pulled her arm above her head, twisting it, clamping it behind her, their two hands still struggling below in the bag. She would not let go of the weapon and he could not pry it loose, only hold it downward, his grip immobilizing her fingers, force against force, her contorted face telling him she would not surrender.

The mid-morning revels of the railroad car reached a crescendo; a cacophony of rising voices in countering melodies filled out the swelling echoes of laughter. And no one paid the slightest attention to the savage struggle that was literally one of life and death taking place in the narrow seat. Suddenly, within the panic of that struggle, within the violent impasse, Joel was aware that the train was slowing down, if only imperceptibly. Once again his pilot's instincts told him a descent was imminent. He jammed his elbow into the old woman's right breast, trying to jolt her so to free the gun. Still she held on, bracing herself against the seat, her arm pinned, her fat legs stretched below, angled like thick pylons anchored beneath the forward seat, her obese body twisted, locking his own arm in place so he could not dislodge the weapon from her grip.

"Let go!" he whispered hoarsely. "I won't hurt you – I won't kill you. Whatever you're being paid, I'll pay you more!"

"*Nee!* I would be found at the bottom of a canal! You can't escape, *Mijnheer!* They wait for you in Amsterdam, they wait for the *train!*" Grimacing, the old woman kicked out, briefly freeing her left arm. She swung her hand around, clawing his face, her nails sliding down his beard until he grabbed her wrist, pulling her arm across the seat and cracking it into her own knee, twisting her hand clockwise, forcing her to be still. It made no difference. Her right hand had the strength of an aging lioness protecting its pride; she would not release the gun below.

"You're lying!" cried Converse. "No one knows I'm on this train! *You* just got on twenty minutes ago!"

"Wrong, *Amerikaan!* I've been on since Arnhem – I start in the front, walk back. I found you out at Utrecht and a telephone call was made."

"*Liar!*"

"You will see."

"Who hired you?"

"Men."

"*Who?*"

"You will see."

"*Goddamn* you, you're not part of them! You *can't* be!"

"They pay. Up and down the railroad they pay. On the piers, in the airports. They say you speak nothing but English."

"What else do they say?"

"Why should I tell you? You're caught. It is you who should let *me* go. It could be easier for you."

"How? A quick bullet in the head instead of a Hanoi rack?"

"Whatever it is, the bullet could be better. You are too young to know, *Mijnheer.* You were never under occupation."

"And you're too old to be so goddamned strong, I'll give you that."

"*Ja*, I learn that, too."

"Let *go!*"

The train was braking and the heavily-drinking crowd in the car roared its approval, as men grabbed suitcases from the upper racks. The passenger who had been sitting next to Joel hastily yanked his from above the seat, his stomach pressing into Converse's shoulder. Joel tried to appear as though he were in a deep conversation with his grimacing half-prisoner; the man fell back, suitcase in hand, laughing.

The old woman lurched forward, sinking her mouth into Converse's upper arm, millimetres from his wound. She bit him viciously, her yellow teeth penetrating his flesh, blood bursting out of his skin, trickling down the woman s grey chin.

He pulled back in pain. She freed her hand from his grip in the canvas bag; the gun was hers! She fired; the muted spit was accompanied by a splintering, shattering section of the floor in the aisle, missing Joel's feet by inches. He grabbed the unseen barrel, twisted it, pulled it, trying with all his strength to wrench it away. She fired again.

Her eyes grew wide as she arched back into the seat. They remained open as she slumped into the window, blood spreading quickly through the thin fabric of her dress in the upper section of her stomach. She was dead, and Joel felt ill, nauseous – so thoroughly sick he had to swallow air to keep from vomiting. Trembling, he wondered briefly who this old woman was, why she was – what had she lived through that made her become what she was. *You were too young to know . . . You were never under occupation.*

No time! She had wanted to kill him, that was all he had to know, and that men were waiting for him only minutes away. He had to think, *move!*

He twisted the gun from her rigid fingers inside the canvas bag, quickly lifting it up and shoving it beneath his coarse jacket, inserting it under his belt, feeling the weight of the other weapon in his pocket. He reached over and bunched the woman's dress in folds, layering her shawl over the blood stains, and pushing her mass of dishevelled grey hair over her right cheek, concealing the wide, dead eyes. Experience in the camps told him not to try to close the eyes; too often they would not respond. The action might only call attention to him – to her. The last thing he did was to pull a can of beer out of the bag, open it, and place it on her lap; the liquid spilled out, drenching her lap.

"Amsterdam! De volgende halte is Amsterdam-Centraal!"

A roar went up from the vacationing crowd as the line began to form towards the door. Oh, *Christ!* thought Converse. *How?* The old woman said a telephone call was made. A telephone call, which implied she had not made it herself. It was logical: there was too little time. She had undoubtedly paid one of her sister bag ladies who plied the trains at the station in Utrecht to make it. The information therefore would be minimal, simply because there *was* no time. She was a special employee, one who had been researched as only Aquitaine could research, an old woman who was strong and who could use a weapon and who would not shrink from taking a life – who would not say too much to anyone. She would merely give a telephone number and instruct the hired caller to repeat the time of the train's arrival. Again . . . therefore . . . he had a chance. Every male passenger would be scrutinized, every face matched against the face in the newspapers. But he was and he was *not* that face. And he did not speak any other language but English, that information had been spread with emphasis.

Think!

"Ze is dronken!" The words were shouted by the burly man with the enormously endowed wife at his side as he pointed to the dead woman. Both were laughing, and Joel did not need an interpreter to understand. They thought the old woman had passed out. Converse nodded, grinning broadly as he shrugged. He had found his way out of the station in Amsterdam.

For Converse understood there was a universal language employed when the decibel of noise was such that one could neither hear nor be heard. It was also used when one was bored at cocktail parties, or when one watched football games on television with clowns who were convinced they knew a great deal more than coaches or quarterbacks, or when one was gathered and trapped into an evening in New York with the "beautiful people" – most of whom qualified as neither in the most rudimentary sense, egos far outdistancing either talent or humanity, the ability to make a productive dollar very much in question. In such situations one nodded; one smiled; one occasionally placed a friendly hand on a shoulder, the touch signifying communication – but one said nothing.

Joel did all of these things as he got off the train with the burly man and the excessively-breasted wife. He became almost manic, playing the role as one who knew there was nothing left between death and survival but a certain kind of controlled madness. The lawyer in him provided the control; the child pilot tested the winds, knowing his aircraft would respond to the elemental pressures because it was sound and he was good and he enjoyed the craziness of a stall forced by a downdraught; he could easily pull out.

He had removed his dark glasses, his cap was now perched far over his forehead, his hand on the burly man's shoulder. They walked up the platform, the Dutchman laughing as he spoke, Joel nodding, slapping his companion's shoulder, laughing in return whenever there was a break in the man's monologue. Since the couple had been drinking, neither took much notice of his incomprehensible replies; he seemed like a nice person, and in their state nothing else really mattered.

As they walked along the platform towards the terminal Converse's constantly roving eyes were drawn to a man standing in a crowd of welcomers beyond the archway at the end of the ramp. Joel first noticed him because, unlike those around him – whose faces were lit up in varying degrees of anticipation – this man's expression was serious to the point of being solemn. He was aware; he studied the column of arrivals but he was not there to offer welcome. Then suddenly Converse knew there was another reason why this man caught his attention. He recognized the face, and the instant he realized the fact he also knew exactly where he had seen it. Walking rapidly down a path surrounded by thick foliage with another man, another guard. The man up ahead was one of the patrols from Erich Leifhelm's compound above the Rhine.

As they approached the arch, Joel laughed a little louder and made it a point to clap the burly Dutchman's shoulder a little harder, his cap still angled down over his forehead, the movements of his head fluid and precise. He followed several nods with a shrug or two, then a good- humoured negative; he shook his head, his brows furrowed, his lips constantly moving, obviously in fluent conversation. Through the squinting flesh of his eyelids Converse saw that Leifhelm's guard was staring at him; then the man looked away. They passed through the arch and in the corner of his vision Joel was abruptly aware of a head snapping, whipping around; then of a figure pushing other figures out of his path, remaining on the sidelines, as it were, but propelling himself forward. Converse turned, looking over the Dutchman's shoulder. It happened. His eyes locked with those of Leifhelm's guard. The moment of recognition was instant and for that instant the German panicked, turning his head back towards the ramp. He started to shout, then stopped. He reached under his jacket and moved forward.

Joel broke away from the couple and began racing, threading his way through succeeding walls of bodies, heading for a series of arch-like ascending exits through which sunlight streamed into the ornate terminal. Twice he looked behind him as he ran; the first time he could not see the man, the second time he did. Leifhelm's guard was screaming orders to someone across the way, rising on the balls of his feet to see and be seen, gesturing at the exit doors in the distance. Converse ran faster, pulling his way through the crowd towards the steps that led to the massive exit. He climbed the staircase swiftly but within the rhythm of the most hurried departing passengers, holding to the centre, trying to call as little attention to himself as possible.

He bolted through a door into the sunlight, into total confusion. Below was water and piers and glass-covered boats bobbing up and down, people rushing past them, others ushered on board under the watchful eyes of men in white and blue uniforms. He had come off a train only to emerge on some kind of strange waterfront. Then he remembered; the railroad station in Amsterdam was built on an island facing the centre of the city; thus it was known as the Central Station. Yet there was a street – two streets, *three* streets bridging the water towards other streets and trees and buildings . . . no *time!* He was out in the open and those streets in the distance were his caves of survival; they were the ravines and the thick, impenetrable acres of bush and swamp that would hide him from the enemy! He ran as fast as he could along the wide boulevard bordered by water reaching an even wider thoroughfare clogged with traffic, buses, trams and automobiles, all at their own starting gates, anxious for bells to release them. He saw a dwindling line at the door of an electric tramway, the final two passengers climbing on board; he raced ahead, stopping abruptly, turning before the door swung shut. He stepped up into the tram entrance and was the last fare.

He walked quickly to the back of the huge vehicle spotting an empty seat in the last row. He sat down, breathing hard, desperately, the sweat matting his hairline and his temples, rolling down his face, the shirt under his jacket drenched. It was the first moment he realized how exhausted he was, how loud and rapid the tattoo was in his chest, how blurred his vision and his thoughts. Fear and pain had combined into a form of hysteria. The desire to stay alive and the hatred of Aquitaine had kept him going. Pain? He was suddenly aware of the ache in his arm above his wound, an old woman's last act of vengeance – against what? For what? An enemy? Money? No time!

The tram started up and he turned in his seat to look out the rear window. He saw what he wanted to see. Leifhelm's guard racing across the intersection, a second man running to join him from the waterfront quay. They met and the words they exchanged were obviously shouted in near panic. Another joined them, from where Joel could not see; he was suddenly just there. The three men spoke rapidly, Leifhelm's guard apparently the leader; he pointed in several directions, issuing orders. One man ran down the street, below the kerb, and

343

began checking the half-dozen or so taxis in the traffic jam; a second stayed on the pavement, slowly making his way around the tables of a sidewalk café, then going inside. Finally, Leifhelm's guard ran back across the intersection, dodging cars, reaching the kerb and signalling. A woman walked out of a store and met him at the corner.

No one had thought of the tram. It was his first cave of survival. He sat back and tried to collect his thoughts, knowing they would be difficult to face. Aquitaine would penetrate all of Amsterdam, canvass it, tear it apart until they found him. Was there conceivably a way to reach Thorbecke or had he been fooling himself, reaching into the past where too often accidents and misplaced arrogance led to success? No, he could not think for a while. He had to lie down in the cave and rest and, if sleep came, hope the nightmares did not come with it. He looked out the window and saw a sign. It read *Damrak*.

He remained on the tram for well over an hour. The lively streets, and the lovely architecture of the centuries-old buildings and the endless canals calmed him. His arm still ached from the old woman's teeth but not severely, and thoughts of cleansing it faded. She probably had been more hygienic than most lawyers in New York, whose teeth were whiter but whose grips paled beside the old hag's. He could not weep for the old woman but, as with certain, strange witnesses at a trial, he wished he knew her story.

Hotels were out. The foot soldiers of Aquitaine would scour them, offering large sums for any information about any American of his general description – which they now specifically had. Thorbecke would be watched, his telephone tapped, his every move and conversation scrutinized. Even the embassy, or consulate – whichever it was in Amsterdam – would have another military *chargé d'affaires* or his equivalent on the prowl for a signal that a non-assassin wanted to come in and start the process of rectification. If his perceptions were right, that left him with only one escape hatch. Nathan Simon.

Nathan-the-Wise, Joel had dubbed him once, only to be told that a gentile with his intelligence should certainly come up with something more original. Then after a particularly long session at the office in which Nate expounded in excruciating detail why they should not take on a client named Liebowitz, who in his opinion would put too great a burden on the obligation to respect a client's confidence, and during which Lawrence Talbot had dozed off, Converse suggested that he alter his soubriquet to Nathan, the Talmudic-pain-in-the-ass. Nate had roared, shocking Talbot awake, and proclaiming: "I love it! And Sylvia will love it better!"

Joel had learned more about the law from Nathan Simon than from anyone else, but there was always a distance between them. It was as though Nate never really wanted them to be too close in spite of the obvious affection the older man had for the younger. Converse thought he understood; it was a question of loyalty. Simon had two sons who, in the properly guarded phrase were in business for themselves in California and Florida". One sold insurance in Santa Barbara and the other ran a bar in Key West. Nate Simon was a tough act to follow, and Joel was given a hint of just how hard it was one late afternoon when Simon had offered to buy him a drink at "21" after a harrowing conference on Fifth Avenue.

"I like your father, Converse. I like Roger. He has minimal legal requirements, of course, but he's a good man."

"He has *no* legal requirements, and I tried to stop him from coming to us."

"You couldn't. It was the gesture he had to make. Put some business where the son is. Very touching."

"With an unnecessary will that you much too generously charged him only two hundred dollars for, and some crazy disposition of his war medals to three different institutions – *for* which you refused to bill him on patriotic grounds?"

"We were in the same theatre of operations."

"Where?"

"Europe."

"Come on, Nate. He's my father and I love him but I also know he's off-the-wall. Take him out of a vintage prop and he's not sure where he is. Pan Am got their money's worth, not in any administrative sense, but because he was a pistol at conventions."

Nathan Simon had gripped his glass that late afternoon at "21", and when he spoke, the quiet thunder of a deeply troubled man poured forth. "You have respect for your father, do you hear me, Joel? My friend Roger offered a gesture to his son for it was all he had, all he could imagine. I had a great deal more and I didn't know how to make such gestures. I only gave commands . . . He said I could still do it. I'm going to take up flying."

Simon would help him, but only if he were convinced there was substance to his case. But he would legally lean over backwards in the negative if he thought a relationship or personal sentimentality were being used to manipulate him. Of course, if an indictment followed, he would rush in for the defence after the fact. That was professional; those were his ethics. And by now Valerie would have sent him the envelope with the dossiers and their awesome implications. *They* were one substance Simon required. Knowing Val, she would have sent them down by car, the great American postal service having given rise to a score of competitors who eschewed the tax payer's dollar. Joel's decision was made. Since there was a five hour time difference, he would wait until early evening and then call Nathan Simon. He was functioning again.

The tram came to the last stop before its return run. At least he was the only one left on board; he walked up the aisle, got off and saw another tram. He got on. Sanctuary.

A hundred streets and a dozen criss-crossed canals later, he looked out the window, encouraged by the seedy neighbourhood he saw, washed clean on the surface, but with the promise of far more interesting bacteria below. There was a row of pornography shops, their wares in magnified displays in the store-fronts. Above, in open windows, garishly painted girls stood provocatively, brass-ieres slipped on and off lethargically, faced bored but pelvises churning, disassociated from the feelings of their owners. The crowds in the streets were animated, some curious, some feigning shock, others interested in buying. There

345

was a carnival atmosphere, one into which he could melt, thought Converse, as he got out of his seat and went to the door.

He wandered around the streets, quite frankly astonished, even embarrassed, as he always was when sex was paraded so publicly.

Joel enjoyed sexual encounters and never lacked for them but the privacy of the acts was intrinsic to their fulfilment. He could no more walk into one of those neon-lighted doors up-to-heaven than he could have performed a bowel movement on the kerb.

There was a café across the street; it was above a canal, tables on the sidewalk, dark within. He crossed the crowded thoroughfare, wove his way between the tables and went inside. Sleep might be out of the question but he needed food. He had not eaten a real meal in nearly three days. He found a small empty table in the back of the room, annoyed that a television set, clamped above on the wall to his right, kept blaring its afternoon inanities. At least the language was Dutch; that helped but not much.

Straight whisky helped, too, but again not much. The anxiety of the hunted came back and he kept turning his head towards the entrance, at any moment expecting to see one of the foot soldiers of Aquitaine walk through the door, out of the sunlight and into the cave to find him. He went to the men's room at the rear of the café, removed his jacket, placed the gun with the silencer in the inside pocket, and tore the left sleeve of his shirt. He filled one of the two basins with cold water, and then he plunged his face into it, pouring the water through his hair over the back of his neck. He felt a vibration, a sound! He whipped his head up, gasping, frightened, his hand instinctively reaching for his coat on a hook to his left. A portly middle-aged man nodded and went to a urinal. Quickly, Joel looked at the teeth marks on his arm; they were like a dog bite. He drained the basin, turned on the hot water tap and, with a paper towel, squeezed and blotted the painful area until blood emerged from the broken skin. It was the best he could do; he had done much the same thing a lifetime ago when attacking water rats swam through the bars of his bamboo cage. Then, in another kind of panic, he learned that rats could be frightened. And killed. The man at the urinal turned and went out the door, glancing uncomfortably at Converse.

Joel layered a paper towel over the teeth marks, put on his coat and combed his hair. He opened the door and went back to his table, once again annoyed by the blaring television on the wall.

The menu was in four languages, the last Oriental, undoubtedly Japanese. He was tempted to go for the largest, rarest piece of meat he could find but here his pilot's control dictated otherwise. He'd had no solid sleep in days, oddly enough since his imprisonment at Leifhelm's compound, where the sleep itself had been greatly induced by the huge quantities of excellent food the healing process for a defecting pawn. A heavy meal would make him drowsy and one did not fly a jet going 600 miles an hour in that condition. At the moment his air speed was approaching Mach I. He ordered fillet of sole and rice: he could always order twice. And one more whisky.

The voice! Oh, Christ. The *voice!* He was hallucinating! He was going mad!

He was hearing a voice – an echo of a voice – he could not *possibly* be *hearing!*

" . . . Actually, I think it's a national disgrace, but like so many others I speak only English."

"*Frau* Converse . . ."

"Miss . . . *Fräulein* . . . I think that's right . . . Charpentier, if you don't mind."

"*Dames en heren* . . ." a third voice broke in quietly, authoritatively, speaking Dutch.

Converse gasped for the air he could not find, gripping his wrist, closing his eyes with such intensity every muscle in his face was in pain, twisting his neck away from the source of the terrible, horrible hallucination.

"I'm in Berlin on business – I'm a consultant for a firm in New York . . ."

"*Mevrouw Converse, of Juffrouw Charpentier, zoals we . . .*"

Joel felt the madness complete – he *was* mad; he was *insane!* Hearing and listening . . . ! *Hearing! Listening!* He spun around and looked up, The television screen! It was *she!* It was *Valerie!* She was *there!*

"Whatever you say, *Fräulein* Charpentier, will be accurately translated, I can assure you."

"*Zoals Juffrouw Charpentier zojuist zei . . .*" The third voice, the voice in Dutch.

"I haven't seen my former husband in several years three or four, I'd say. Actually we're strangers. I can only express the shock my whole country feels."

"*Juffrouw Charpentier, de vroegere Mevrouw Converse . . .*"

" . . .he was a deeply disturbed man, subject to extreme depressions, but I never imagined anything like this."

"*Hij moet mentaal gestoord zijn . . .*"

"There's no connection between us and I'm surprised you learned I was flying to Berlin. But I appreciate the chance to clear the air, as we say."

"*Mevrouw Converse gelooft . . .*"

"In spite of the dreadful circumstances over which, of course, I had no control, I'm delighted to be in your beautiful city. Half city, I guess, but yours is the beautiful part. And I hear the Bristol-Kempinski . . . I'm terribly sorry, that's what we call a 'plug' and I shouldn't."

"It is a landmark, *Fräulein* Charpentier. It is not *verboten* over here. Do you feel at all threatened?"

"*Mevrouw Converse, voelt u zich bedreigd?*"

"No, not really. We've had nothing to do with each other for so long."

My *God!* Val had come over to *find* him! She was sending him a signal – signals! She spoke every bit as fluent German as the interviewer! They kept in touch every month; they had lunch together six weeks ago in Boston! Everything she was saying was a lie and in those lies was the code. *Their* code! *Reach me!*

Part III

27

Stunned, he tried to isolate the words, the phrases. The message was in them! The Bristol-Kempinski was a hotel in West Berlin, he knew that. It was something else she said, something that should trigger a memory – one of *their* memories. What *was* it?

I haven't seen my former husband in years . . . No, only one of the lies. *He was a deeply disturbed man* . . . Less a lie, but not what she was trying to tell him. *Actually we're strangers* . . . *There's no connection between us* . . . Another lie but hardly a fraudulent assertion in terms of interpretive context – *stop it!* What *was* it?! . . . Before, earlier . . . *I'm a consultant* . . . That was it!

"May I speak with Miss Charpentier, please? My name is Mr Whistletoe, Bruce Whistletoe. I'm the confidential consultant for Springtime Anti-perspirant for which your agency is doing some artwork, and it's urgent, *most* urgent!" *Con vibrato.*

Val's secretary had been a talker, a marvellous spreader of in-house gossip, and whenever Joel and Valerie had wanted an extra hour for lunch or even a day, he would make such a phone call. It never failed. If a demanding vice-president (of which there were dozens) wanted to know where she was the excitable secretary would tell of an urgent call from one of those outside watchdogs of a *very* large account. It was enough for any ulcer-prone executive, and Valerie's understated professionalism took care of the rest. She would say "things" were under control and rarely did a relieved account man pursue what might give him an acid attack.

She was telling him to use the tactic in case the police were monitoring her calls. He would have done so in any event; she was simply reminding him, warning him.

The interview was over, the last few minutes obviously a recap in Dutch, the camera frozen on a still frame of Valerie's face. *Still* frame! The interview was taped, not live! When had the tape been made! How long had she been in Berlin? *Goddamn* it, why couldn't he understand anything unless it was spoken in English? In the lie proclaiming her own inability to speak German, Val said it was a national disgrace. She was right, but she might have gone farther; it was a national disorder rooted in arrogance. He looked around the café for a telephone; there was one on the rear wall several feet from the door to the men's room and he hadn't the vaguest idea of how to use it! His frustrations grew, swirling up into circles of panic. It was only the beginning. Suddenly, he heard his name.

"De Amerikaanse moodenaar Converse is advocaat en was piloot en de Vietttam-orloog. Een andere advocaat Franz, een vriend van Converse . . ."

Joel looked up at the screen bewildered, at once shocked, then paralysed. There was a film clip, a hand-held camera entered an office door centring in on a body slumped over a desk, streams of blood spreading out from the head like a hideous Medusa wig over the shiny wooden surface. Oh, *Christ!* It was René!

As the recognition came an insert appeared on the upper left of the screen. It was a photograph of Mattilon – then another photograph was suddenly, dramatically, inserted on the right. It was he, the *Amerikaanse moodenaar*, Joel Converse. Neither language nor diagrams were necessary. René had been killed and he had been named the killer. It answered the question; it was the reason Aquitaine had put out the word that an assassin was heading for Paris.

He was a giver of death; it was his gift to new and old friends. René Mattilon, Edward Beale . . . Avery Fowler. And to enemies he did not know, could not evaluate, either as enemies or as individuals – a man in a tan overcoat in a Paris cellar, a guard above a river bank on the Rhine, a pilot on a train, a memorably unmemorable face at the base of a landfill pyramid, a chauffeur moments later who had actually befriended him in a stone house with bars in the windows . . . an old woman who had played her role brilliantly in a raucous railway car. *Death.* He was either the distant observer or the executioner, all in the unholy name of Aquitaine. He *was* back, back in the camps and the jungles that he had sworn never to visit again. He could only survive and hope that someone better than himself would provide the solutions. But at that moment, death was his closest ally and his most hostile adversary. He was not capable of accepting the responsibility of recognition; he was not equipped. He wanted to collapse into nothingness, let someone else take up the cause no one knew had been given him in Geneva.

Jesus! The tape! If it was even twelve or twenty-four hours old, Val could not – probably *had* not – received the envelope he had sent from Bonn! She could *not* have. She would not have flown to Europe if she *had!*

Oh, my God! thought Joel, swallowing the last of the whisky as he rubbed his forehead, his confusion complete. Without the envelope in Nathan Simon's hands, no plea to him made sense! No call to him would evoke anything but a demand that Joel turn himself in and a telephone trace would be put on the line. Nate would not disobey the law; he would fight violently for a client afterwards, but not before that client obeyed the law. It was his religion, far more important to him than his temple, for the law allowed mistakes: it was essentially human, not esoterically metaphysical. Converse's hands began to tremble; he *had* to find out!

"Your fillet of sole, *Mijnheer.*"

"What?"

"Your sole, sir," repeated the waiter.

"You speak English?"

"But, of course," said the gaunt, bald-headed man with detached courtesy. "We spoke before, but you were very excited. This district can do that to a man, I understand."

"Listen . . . to . . . me." Joel brought his hand across his lips emphasizing each word. "I will pay you a lot of money if you will place a phone call for me. I . . . I don't speak Dutch, or French, or German or anything but English. Can you understand that?"

"I understand, *Mijnheer*."

"To West Berlin."

"It is not difficult, sir."

"Will you do it for me?"

"But, of course, *Mijnheer*. You have a telephone credit card?"

"Yes . . . no. I don't want to use it."

"Of course."

"I mean I don't . . . I don't want it recorded anywhere. I have money."

"I understand. In a few minutes I shall be off my shift. *Mijnheer*. I shall come for you. We shall place your call and I shall know the amount from the operator. You shall pay."

"Absolutely."

"And 'a lot of money', *ja?* Fifty guilder, *ja?*"

"You're on. Yes."

Twenty minutes later Converse sat behind a small desk in a very small office. The waiter handed him the phone. "They speak English, *Mijnheer*."

"Miss Charpentier, please," said Joel, his voice choking, overwhelmed by a kind of paralysis. If he heard her voice he was not sure he could handle his own reaction. For an instant he thought about slamming down the phone. He could not *involve* her!

"Hello?"

It was *she* and as a part of him died, another part came alive. A thousand pictures flashed across his mind, memories of happiness and anger, of love and of hate. He could not speak, but she was *there!*

"Hello? Who's this?"

"Oh . . . there you are. Sorry, it's a lousy connection. This is Jack Talbot from . . . Boston Graphics. How are you, Val?"

"Fine . . . Jack. How are you? It's been a couple of months. Since lunch at the Four Seasons, if I remember."

"That's right. When did you get in?"

"Last night."

"Staying long?"

"Just for the day. I've been in crisis meetings all morning with another one this afternoon. If I'm not too bushed I'll catch the plane back tonight. When did you get to Berlin?"

"Actually, I'm not. I saw you on a Belgian broadcast. I'm in . . . Antwerp, but I'm going to Amsterdam this afternoon. Christ, I'm sorry about all that crap you had to take. Who would ever have guessed it? About Joel, I mean."

"I should have guessed it, Jack. It's all so horrible. He's so very sick. I hope they catch him quickly for everyone's sake. He needs help."

"He needs a firing squad, if you don't mind my saying so."

"I'd rather not discuss it."

"Did you get the sketches I sent you when we lost the Gillette account? I figured it was a way to your sack."

"Sketches? . . . No, Jack, I never got anything like that. But thanks for the thought, the sack notwithstanding."

Christ! "Oh? I thought you might have looked at your mail."

"I did . . . until the day before yesterday. It doesn't matter – you'll be in Amsterdam?"

"For a week. I wondered if you were going to check any of the agency's accounts up there before heading back to New York."

"I should, but I don't think so. There's no time. If I do, I'll be at the Amstel Hotel. If not, I'll see you back in New York. You can buy me lunch at Lutece, and we'll swap trade secrets."

"I've got more of them. You buy. Take care, youngster."

"Take care . . . Jack."

She was *magnificent*. And she had not received the envelope from Bonn.

He roamed the streets, afraid of walking too fast, frightened of staying in one place too long, knowing only that he had to keep moving, watching, finding the shadows and letting them envelop him. She would be in Amsterdam by evening; he knew that, it was in her voice, and she had told him to reach her at the Amstel Hotel. *Why?* Why had she come? What did she think she was *doing?* Suddenly, the face of René Mattilon came to him. It was in sharp focus, filling his inner eye, surrounded by sunlight, the face a mask – a death mask. René had been killed by Aquitaine for sending him to Amsterdam. Valerie would not be spared if the disciples of George Marcus Delavane thought she had flown over to find him, help him.

He would *not* reach her! He *could* not! It was signing another death warrant! *Her* death warrant. He had taken so much from her, giving so little. The last gift could not be the taking of her life. Yet . . . yet there was Aquitaine and he meant what he had said to Larry Talbot on the phone. He, one Joel Converse, was inconsequential where the gathering of the generals was concerned. So was A. Preston Halliday and Edward Beale and Connal Fitzpatrick. If Val could help he had no right to let his feelings stop her – the lawyer in him told him that, the outraged man confirmed it. And it was possible she *could* help, do the things he could not do himself. She could fly back, get the envelope and go to Nathan Simon herself, saying that she had seen him, talked to him, *believed* him.

It was 3.30; it would be dark by 8 o'clock or so. He had roughly five hours to remain unseen and stay alive. And somehow find a car.

He stopped on the pavement and looked up at an overly made-up, extremely bored whore in a window on the second floor of a colourful brick house. Their eyes made contact and she smiled a bored smile at him, the thumb and forefinger of her right hand meeting, the wrist motion leaving little to the imagination.

Why not? thought Converse. The only certain thing in a very uncertain world was the fact that there was a bed beyond that window.

The "*concierge*" was a clerk, a man in his middle fifties with the pink face of an aging cherub, who explained in perfectly fluent English that payment was based on twenty-minute sessions, two sessions paid in advance, one to be refunded should the guest come downstairs during the final five minutes of the first period. It was a loan shark's dream, thought Converse, glancing at the various clocks on the counter – placed on numbered squares – as an elderly man walked down the staircase. The clerk grabbed one of the clocks hastily and pushed the second hand forward.

Joel calculated rapidly, converting guilder to dollars, the rate of acceleration based on roughly $30.00 per session. He gave the astonished "*concierge*" the equivalent of $275.00 accepted his number and headed for the staircase.

"She is a friend, sir?" asked the stunned custodian-of-revels, as Converse reached the first step. "An old lover, perhaps?"

"She's a Dutch cousin I haven't seen in years," replied Joel, sadly. "We have to have a long talk." With heavy shoulders, he continued up the staircase.

"*Slapen?*" exclaimed the woman with the spangled dark hair and heavily rouged cheeks. She was as astonished as her keeper below. "You want *slapen?*"

"It doesn't translate well, but yes," said Converse, removing his glasses and his cap and sitting on the bed. "I'm very tired and sleep would be terrific, but I suspect I'll just rest. Read one of your magazines. I won't bother you."

"What is the matter? You think I am not pretty? Not clean? You yourself are no fine picture, *Mijnheer!* Cuts on your face, a bruise here and there, red eyes. Perhaps it is you who are not clean!"

"I fell down. Come on, I think you're adorable and I love your deep-purple eye shadow but I really want to rest."

"Why here?"

"I don't want to go, back to the hotel. My wife's lover is there. He's my boss."

"*Amerikaans!*"

"You speak our language very well," Joel took off his shoes and stretched out on the bed.

"Ach, I start with is *Amerikaanse* college boys. All talk, most are too afraid for nothing but talk. Those who get on the bed – *poof!* . . . Is over. Then talk, too goddamn much talk. Then your soldiers and your sailors and your businessmen. Most drunk; they behave like giggle-children. All talk. Twelve years, *I* learn."

"Don't write a book. They're probably all senators and congressmen and priests by now." Converse placed his hands behind his head and stared at the ceiling. There was a glimmer of peace. He softly whistled the tune first, then found the words. " 'Yankee Doodle' came to Holland nothing in his pistol . . ."

"You are amusing, *Minjheer*," said the whore, laughing coarsely and picking up a thin blanket off a chair. She carried it to the bed and spread it over him. "You don't tell the truth but you are amusing."

"How do you know I'm not telling you the truth?"

"If your wife had a lover, you would kill him."

"Not so."

"Then she would not be your wife. I see many men, *Mijnheer*. It's in your face. You are a good man, perhaps, but you would kill."

"I'll have to think about that," said Joel, uncomfortably.

"Sleep, if you wish. You paid. I am here." The woman walked to the chair against the wall and sat down with a magazine.

"What's your name?" asked Converse.

"Emma," replied the whore.

"You're a nice person, Emma."

"No, *Mijnheer*, I am not."

He awoke, startled by the touch, bolting upright on the bed, his hand instinctively rushing to his waist to make sure his money belt was in place. He had been so deep in sleep that for a moment he had no idea where he was, then he saw the garishly made-up woman standing beside him, her hand on his shoulder as she spoke.

"*Mijnheer*, are you hiding from people?" she asked softly.

"What?"

"Word goes up and down the *Leidseplein*. Men are asking questions."

"What?" Converse whipped the blanket off the bed and swung his legs to the floor. "What men? Up and down *where?*"

"*Het Leidseplein* – This district. Men ask questions. They look for an American."

"Why *here?*" Joel moved his right hand from the money belt up to the outline of the weapon above.

"People who wish not to be seen often come down to the Leidseplein."

Why not? thought Converse. If he thought of it, why wouldn't the enemy? "Do they have a description?"

"It is you," answered the whore frankly.

"*And?*" Joel looked into the woman's eyes.

"Nothing was said."

"I can't believe our friend downstairs felt so charitable towards me. I'm sure they offered money."

"It was given," corrected the whore. "More promised with additional information. A man remains behind down the street. In a café next to a telephone. He is to be called and will bring back the others. Our . . . friend downstairs thought you might want to match the funds."

"I see. An auction. One head on the block."

"I do not understand."

"What are we talking about? How much?"

"A thousand guilder. Much more if you are taken."

"Our friend still sounds too charitable. I'd think he'd grab it and close up shop."

"He owns the building. Also, the man was German and spoke like a soldier giving orders, that's what our friend downstairs said."

"He was right. The man is a soldier but not in any army Bonn knows about."

"*Zo?*"

"Nothing. Find out if our friend will take American money."

"Of course he will."

"Then I'll match the offer and double it."

The whore hesitated. "Now it is my turn, *Mijnheer*."

"I beg your pardon?"

"*En?* As you say . . . "*and*"?"

"Oh. You?"

"*Ja*."

"I have something special for you. Can you drive a car, or do you know someone who can?"

"I do myself, *natuurlijk*. In bad weather I drive my children to school."

"Oh, Jesus . . . I mean, that's good."

"Without my face like *so*, of course."

The stories. Oh, God, the stories! thought Converse. "I want you to rent a car and bring it around here to the front door. Then get out and leave the keys inside. Can you do that?"

"*Ja*, but nothing is for nothing."

"Three hundred dollars – eight hundred guilder, give or take."

"Five hundred – fourteen hundred, take or give," countered the woman. "And the money to rent the automobile."

Joel nodded as he unbuttoned his jacket and pulled out his shirt. The handle of the gun with the short barrel and the extended silencer was clearly visible beneath the wide canvas belt. The whore saw it, a short gasp emerging from her throat. "It's not mine," said Converse quickly. "Whether you believe it or not doesn't matter to me, but I took it from someone who tried to kill me."

The woman stared at him, her look partially one of fear, but it was not hostile, only curious. "The man – this soldier from no German army – the others who ask questions in the street. They wish to kill you?"

"Yes." Joel unzipped the belt and counted off the money with his thumb. He pulled out the bills and closed the pocket.

"You have done them much harm?"

"Not yet, but I hope to." Converse held out the money. "There's enough for our friend downstairs and the rest is for you. Just bring me the car along with one of those tourist maps of Amsterdam that show where all the major stores and hotels and restaurants are."

"Perhaps I can tell you where it is you wish to go."

"No, thank you."

"*Ja*." The whore nodded knowingly and took the money. "These people are bad people?" she asked, counting out the bills.

"The pits, lady."

"They do those things to your face?"

"Yes. Mostly."

"Go to the *politie*."

"The police? It's not practical. They wouldn't understand."

"They want you also," concluded the woman.

"Not for anything I did."

The whore shrugged. "It is no problem for me," she said, going to the door.

"I will say the auto is stolen. There is a *Tromp* garage twelve blocks from here; they know me. I have rented there when my Peugeot has troubles and I must get home. *Ach, kinderen!* Recitals, dance classes! Be downstairs in twenty minutes."

"Recitals? . . ."

"Don't look so, *Mijnheer*. I do my job and call it what it is. Most people do the same and call it something else. Twenty minutes." The spangled-haired woman went out the door, closing it behind her.

Joel approached the sink against the wall without enthusiasm, then saw it was spotless, a can of cleanser and a bottle of bleach below on the floor next to a roll of paper towels. Naturally. Dance lessons and recitals were part of the whore's life, as well as a car that often gave her trouble, just like any other commuter. Converse looked in the mirror; the woman was right, he was "no fine picture", but one had to be quite close to him to notice the severity of the bruises. He splashed water on his face, then blotted it, put on the dark glasses and made himself as presentable as possible.

It had happened. Val had come to find him, and despite the horrors surrounding their seeing each other again, a part of him wanted to sing – silently, or shout silently into the mists of his imagination. He wanted so much to look at her, to touch her, hear her voice close to him – and he knew it was for all the wrong reasons. He was the hunted and in pain and vulnerable, all the things he never was when they were together, and because he was what he had become, he permitted her to find him. It was hardly admirable. He did not care to be a hungry dog in a cold rain; it did not fit his part of their past dual image, the *de suite*, as René Mattilon had phrased it . . . René. A telephone call had signed the order for his execution. *Aquitaine.* How in God's name could he let Val even come near him? thought Joel, a terrible pain in his throat. The answer was the same: Aquitaine. And the fact that he thought he knew what he was doing. Every move he made in the streets, and on the trains, and in the cafés, was as carefully thought out as the steps he had taken in the jungle; in the routes he had chosen, in the rivers and streams he had forged and used as watery tunnels to bypass an enemy time and again. He would use an automobile in Amsterdam, and a map of Amsterdam.

He looked at his watch; it was almost five-thirty. He had roughly two and a half hours to find the Amstel Hotel and drive around again and again until he knew every foot of the area, every stop light, every side street and canal. And then the route to one other place – the American Embassy, or the consulate. It was part of his plan, the only protection he could give her – if she followed his instructions. And somewhere an airline schedule; that, too, was part of the plan.

Twelve minutes had passed and he wanted to be at the doorway when Emma, the honest commuter, drove up in front of the house on the crowded street. If there was no place to park at the kerb he would walk out on the pavement and signal her to leave the car, quickly replacing her behind the wheel so as not to hold up traffic. He left the small room, went to the staircase, and started down, aware of the feigned groans of ecstasy behind several closed doors. He wondered briefly if the girls had thought of using cassette recorders; they could push buttons while reading magazines. He reached the second landing; below in clear view was the cherub-faced, middle-aged owner of the establishment behind his counter. He was on the telephone. Joel continued down the steps, in his hand a hundred dollar bill he had decided to give the man – an additional gratuity in exchange for his life.

As he set foot on the lobby floor, he suddenly was not at all sure he should let the "*concierge*" have anything but a cage in the Mekong River. The pink-faced man looked over at Converse, his eyes wide, staring in place, the blood draining from his cherubic cheeks. He trembled as he hung up the phone and pretended first a smile, then spoke in a high-pitched voice.

"Problems! There are always problems, *Mijneer*. Scheduling is so difficult I should buy a computer."

The *bastard* had done it! He had made the call to a man down the street in a café! "Keep your hands on the counter!" shouted Joel.

The command did not come in time; the Dutchman raised a gun from below. Converse rushed forward, lunging to his right, his hand tearing at the buttons of his jacket, finding the handle of the gun in his belt. The "*concierge*" fired wildly as Joel crashed his left shoulder up into the flimsy counter; it collapsed and Converse saw the extended arm, the hand holding the gun. He swung the barrel of his own weapon into the Dutchman's wrist; the gun went flying, clattering over the lobby floor.

"You bastard!" cried Joel, grabbing the man by the front of his shirt, pulling him up. "You *bastard! I paid you!*"

"Don't kill me! *Please!* I am a poor man in much debt! They said they only wished to talk to you! What *harm* is there in that? Please! Don't do this!"

"You're not worth the price – to me, you son of a bitch." Converse crashed the barrel of the gun into the Dutchman's head and ran to the door. The street was crowded with traffic, then suddenly there was a break and the cars and buses and open tourist vans lurched forward. Where *was* she? Where was Emma-the-Practical?

"*Theodoor! Deze kerel is onmogelijk! Hij wil . . . !*" The hysterical words came from a bare-breasted woman rushing down the staircase, a thin, short slip covering the essentials of her trade. She stopped on the next to last step, saw the carnage and the unconscious Theodoor and screamed. Joel ran to her, clamping his left hand over her mouth, his right – with the gun, pressing against her shoulder, pushing her into the railing.

"Be quiet!" whispered Converse – intending to whisper, instead shouting. "Shut up!" He slammed his elbow into the prostitute's neck; it careened off her throat, the weapon now in front of her face. She screamed again and kicked viciously out at his groin, her two fingers in his nostrils, scratching, pushing him away. There was nothing else; he pummelled his fist with the handle of the gun into the base of her jaw. Her red lips parted and remained open; she went limp.

Doors crashed everywhere above, beyond the staircase, metal and wood smashing into walls. Shouts descended, angry, frightened, questioning. The words were incomprehensible to him, but not the alarms. A horn suddenly intruded, blaring from the street beyond the open front door. He ran to the doorframe, his right arm supporting him, the gun out of sight.

It was Emma-the-whore, the car in the middle of the street, unable to crawl into the kerb. He shoved the weapon under his jacket, under his belt, and ran outside. She understood his gestures and got out of the car; he raced around the hood, meeting her briefly.

"*Thank* you!" he said.

"It was stolen!" she replied shrugging. "Good fortune, *Mijnheer*. I think you will need it, but it is not my problem."

He jumped into the seat, behind the wheel, his eyes studying the panel as if he were approaching Mach I and had to understand the read-outs of every dial. He did; they were primitive; he pulled the gear into D and started up with the surrounding traffic.

Without warning, the figure of an immense man slammed into the window on his right. Joel lurched, slapping the lock on the window, taking advantage of another break in the traffic, spurting forward. The killer held on, as he yanked a gun from some unseen place in his body. Converse careened into the side of an automobile parked at the kerb, and still the man held on. Joel reached under his jacket as the killer, holding on to God-knew-what, brought his weapon up, levelling it into the glass, aiming at Converse. Joel ducked, smashing his head into the window frame as the explosion shattered the glass, fragments entering his skin above his eyes. But his gun was free; he pointed it at the figure hugging the window and pulled the trigger. Twice.

Two muted spits echoed in the darkness of the car as two holes appeared in the area of the glass that had not been shattered. Screaming, both hands covering his throat, the man fell away, rolling into the gutter between two trucks. Converse turned right into a wide, empty alleyway. *One man remains behind, down the street . . . He will bring back the others.* He was free again – for a while – thought Joel. A dead man could not identify an automobile. He parked the car in shadows and pulled out a cigarette, trying to steady his hand as he struck the match. Inhaling deeply, he felt his forehead, and slowly, carefully removed the particles of glass.

He now prowled the streets like a mechanized animal, with each hesitation, each stop, employing the eyes and nostrils of a primitive thing, knowing only it had to survive in a violently hostile environment. He had made the run four times from the Amstel Hotel on the Tulpplein, across the streets and over the canals to the American consulate on the city square called Museumplein. He had learned the alternate approaches; he knew the side streets that would bring him back to the main route without interruption. Lastly, he drove east and crossed the Schellingwouder Brug, the bridge over the IJ River Sea-Canal and took the road along the coast until he found a stretch of deserted fields above the water. They would do; they were isolated. He turned around and headed back to Amsterdam.

It was 8.30; the sky dark; he was ready. He had studied the tourist map, which included a paragraph on the use of pay phones. He had once been a pilot; instructions were second nature. They were the difference between blowing an aircraft apart and landing it on a carrier. He parked the car across the street from the Amstel Hotel and walked into a booth.

"Miss Charpentier, please."

"*Dank U*," said the operator, shifting instantly to English. "One moment please . . . Oh, yes *Mejnffrouw* Charpentier arrive only an hour ago. I have her room now."

"Thank you."

"Hello?"

Oh *God*, should he speak? *Could* he speak? *Aquitaine*. "Val, it's Jack Talbot. I took a chance you might fly in. Glad you did. How are you youngster?"

"Totally exhausted, you awful man. I talked to New York this afternoon and mentioned our accounts in Amsterdam – courtesy of one Jack Talbot. The orders were for me to get to Canal City and spend tomorrow morning hold-ing hands."

"Why not hold mine?"

"They're too cold. You can, however, buy me dinner."

"Be delighted, but first I need a favour. Can you grab a cab and pick me up at the consulate on Museumplein?"

"*What* . . . ?" The pause was filled with fear. "Why, Jack?" The question was a whisper.

Converse lowered his voice. "I've been here for a couple of hours taking too damn much abuse and I'm afraid I blew my cork."

"What . . . happened?"

"It was dumb. My passport expired today and I needed a temporary extension. Instead I got a half a dozen lectures and told to come back in the morning. I was very loud and not too benign."

"And now it would be embarrassing for you to ask them to call you a cab, is that it?"

"That's it. If I knew this part of the city I'd walk and try to find one, but I've never been over here before."

"I'll straighten my face and pick you up. Say in about twenty minutes?"

"Thanks, I'll be outside. If I'm not, wait in the cab; I'll only be a few minutes. You've got yourself a good dinner, youngster." Joel hung up the phone, left the booth and went back to the rented car. The waiting had begun, the watching would soon follow.

Ten minutes later he saw her and the pounding in his chest accelerated. A mist clouded his eyes. She walked out the glass doors of the Amstel, carrying a large, dark cloth bag, her posture erect, her stride long and graceful, bespeaking the dancer she might have been, breaking the space in front of her, announcing her presence without pretence, telling anyone who watched her that she was herself; no artifices were necessary. He had once loved her so, as much for the person she appeared to be, as the woman she was. But he had not loved her enough; she had slipped away from him because he had not cared enough. There was not that much love or care in him. *Burn out!* she had shouted. *Emotional burn out!*

There had been nothing left to say; he could not dispute her. He had been running so fast, so furiously, wanting it all yet not wanting to remember the reasons why – wanting only to get even. He had concealed the intensity of his feelings with flippancy and a casualness that bordered on disdain, but he was not casual at all, and there was little room for the time consumed in being disdainful. There was also very little room for people, for Val. Being together demanded the responsibility that was part of any relationship and, as the months stretched into a year then two and three, he knew it was not in him to live up to that responsibility. As much as he profoundly disliked himself for it, he could not be dishonest – with either himself or Valerie. He had nothing left to give; he could only take. It was better to break clean.

The waiting was over; the watching began. The Amstel doorman hailed her a cab and she climbed in, immediately leaning forward in the seat giving instructions. Twenty tense seconds later, during which his eyes scanned the street and the pavements in every direction, he started the car and switched on the head-lights. No automobile had crept out from the kerb after the taxi; still, he had to be certain. Joel swung the wheel and drove into the street heading for the most direct route to the consulate. A minute later he saw Val's cab take the correct right turn over a canal. There were two cars behind her; he concentrated on their shapes and sizes; but instead of following, he continued straight ahead, pressing down on the accelerator, using an alternate route on the bare chance that he himself had been picked up by a hunter from Aquitaine. Three minutes later, after two right turns, and a left, he entered the Museumplein. The taxi was directly ahead, the two other automobiles no longer in sight. His strategy was working. The possibility that Val's phone was being tapped was real – René's had been, and his death was the result – so in Val's case he assumed the worst. If it was relayed that the Charpentier woman was heading over to the American consulate to pick up a business acquaintance, one Joel Converse would be ruled out. The consulate was no place for the fugitive assassin; he would not go near it. He was a killer of Americans.

The taxi pulled into the kerb in front of number 19 Museumplein, the stone building that was the consulate. Converse remained a half a block behind, waiting again, watching again. Several ears went by, none stopping or even slowing down. A lone cyclist pedalled down the street, an old man who braked and turned around and disappeared in the opposite direction. The tactic *had* worked. Val was alone in the cab sixty yards away and no one had followed her from the Amstel. He could make his final move to her, his hand under his coat, gripping the gun with the perforated silencer attached to the barrel.

He got out of the car and walked up the pavement, his gait slow, casual, a man taking a summer night's stroll. There were perhaps a dozen people – couples mainly also walking, strolling in both directions. He studied them as a rigid but frenzied cat studies the new mounds of mole holes in a field; no one in the street had the slightest interest in the stationary taxi. He approached the rear door and knocked once on the window. She rolled it down.

They stared at each other for a brief moment, then Val brought her hand to her lips, stifling a gasp. "Oh, my God," she whispered.

"Pay him and walk back to a grey car about two hundred feet behind us. The last three numbers of the licence are one, three, six. I'll be there in a few minutes." He tipped his hat, as if he had just answered a question from a bewildered tourist, and proceeded down the pavement. Thirty feet past the taxi, at the end of the block, he turned and crossed the Museumplein, reaching the other side with his head angled to the left, a pedestrian watching for traffic; in reality he was apprehensively watching a lone woman make her way down the sidewalk towards an automobile. He went swiftly into the shadows of a doorway and stood there watching, breathing erratically, peering into every pocket of darkness along the opposite pavement. Nothing. No one. He walked out of the doorway, suppressing a maddening desire to run, and ambled casually down the block until he was directly across from the rented car. Again he paused, now lighting a cigarette, the flame cupped in his hand, again waiting, watching . . . No one. He threw the cigarette to the kerb, and unable to contain himself any longer, ran across the street, opened the door and climbed in behind the wheel.

She was inches from him, her long, dark hair framing her face in the dim light, that lovely face, taut, filled now with anxiety, her piercing wide eyes burning into his. "*Why*, Val? Why did you *do* it?" he asked, a cry in the question.

"I didn't have a choice," she answered quietly, enigmatically. "Drive away from here, please."

28

They drove for several minutes. Neither of them spoke. Joel was concentrating on the streets, knowing the turns he wanted to make – knowing, too, he wanted to *shout*. It was all he could do to control himself, to keep from stopping the car and grabbing her, demanding to know why she had done what she did, furiously replying to whatever she said that she was a goddamned *fool*! Why had she come back into his life? He was *death*! . . . Above all he wanted to hold her in his arms, his face against hers, and thank her and tell her how sorry he was – for so much, for now.

"Do you know where you're going?" asked Val, breaking the silence.

"I've had the car since six o'clock. A map of the city came with it and I've spent the time driving around, learning what I thought I had to learn."

"Yes, you'd do that. You were always methodical."

"I thought I *should*", he said defensively. "I followed you from the hotel just in case anybody else did. Also I'm better off in a car than on the streets."

"I wasn't insulting you."

Converse glanced at her; she was studying him, her eyes roving over his face in the erratic progressions of light and shadow. "Sorry. I guess I'm a little sensitive these days. Can't imagine why."

"Neither can I. You're only wanted on two continents and in some eight countries. They say you're the most talented assassin since that maniac they call Carlos."

"Do I have to tell you it's all a lie? All a huge lie with a very clear motive – purpose is better."

"No," replied Valerie simply. "You don't have to tell me that because I know it. But you've got to tell me everything else. *Everything*."

He looked at her again, searching her eyes in the flashes of light, trying to penetrate, trying to peel away the layers of clouded glass that held her thoughts, her reasons. Once he had been able to do that, in love and in anger. He could not do it now; what she felt was too deep inside her, but it was not love, he knew that. It was something else, and the lawyer in him was cautious, oblique. "What made you think I'd see you on television? I almost missed you."

"I didn't think about television, I was counting on the newspapers. I knew my face would be on the front pages all over Europe. I assumed your memory was not so dulled that you wouldn't recognize me, and reporters always pick up on hotels or addresses – it lends authenticity."

"I can't read anything but English."

"Your memory *is* dulled. I made three trips with you to Europe, two to Geneva and one to Paris. You wouldn't have coffee in the morning unless the *Herald Tribune* was on the room service table. Even when we went skiing in Chamonix – from Geneva – you made an awful fuss until the waiter brought the *Tribune*."

"You were in the *Tribune?*"

"Class acts aside, it's their kind of story. With all the details. I assumed you'd pick one up and realize what I was doing."

"Because we were strangers and hadn't seen each other in years, and, of course, you couldn't speak German or French or anything else."

"Yes. It was an acceptable explanation for those who knew I did. A cover, I guess. A lot of people who speak several languages do it all the time. It's common practice; it cuts conversations short or at least keeps them to basic statements, and you always know if you're misquoted."

"I forgot, that's your business in a way."

"It's not where the idea came from. It came from Roger."

"*Dad?*"

"Yes. He flew in from Hong Kong a few days ago and some hungry clerk alerted the newspapers that he was on the flight. When he got into Kennedy it was a media blitz. He hadn't read a newspaper or listened to a radio or seen a television screen in two days. He was in a panic and called me. I simply made sure the wire services in West Berlin knew I was flying in."

"How *is* Dad? He can't handle this."

"He's handling it. So's your sister – less so than your father but her husband stepped into the breach and took over. He's a better man than you thought, Converse."

"What's happening to them? How *are* they taking it?"

"Confused, angry, bewildered. They've changed their telephone numbers. They speak through attorneys, supporting you, incidentally. You may not realize it but they love you very much, although I'm not sure you gave them much reason to."

"I think we're closer to home," said Joel quietly, as they approached the Schellingwouder Brug. "Our once and former home." They entered the dark span of the bridge, diaphanous lights above, speckled dots far below on the water. Valerie did not respond to his statement; it was not like her to avoid a provocation. He could not *stand* it. "*Why*, Val?" he cried. "I asked you before, and I have to *know!* Why did you fly over?"

"I'm sorry, I was thinking," she said, her eyes leaving his face, staring straight ahead through the windscreen. "I guess it's better I say it now while you're driving and I don't have to look at you. You look awful, you're a mess, and your face tells me what you've gone through, and I don't *want* to look at you."

"I'm hurt," said Converse gently, trying genuinely to lessen the impact of his appearance. "Helen Gurley Brown called and wants me for *Cosmopolitan's* centrefold."

"*Stop* that! It's not remotely funny and you know it – worse you don't even feel like saying it!"

"I retreat. There were times when you never did read me right."

"I *always* read you right, Joel!" Valerie continued to focus on the road and the beams of the headlights; she did not move her head. "Don't play the serious fool any longer. We haven't time for that; we haven't time for your flip remarks. It was always a little sad to watch you put people off who really wanted to talk to you, but it's finished now."

"Glad to hear it. Then *talk!* Why the hell did you walk *into* this?"

Their eyes met in anger, in abrupt recognition, in a love once remembered, perhaps. She turned away as Converse steered the car into the right exit off the bridge, then peeled into the road that ran along the coastline.

"All right," said Valerie, hesitant but in complete control. "I'll spell it out as best I can. I say as best I can because I'm not entirely sure – there are too many complications to be absolutely sure . . . You may be a rotten husband and careless beyond stoning where another person's feelings are concerned, but you're not what they say you are. You didn't kill those men."

"I know that. You said you knew it, too. Why did you come *over* here?"

"Because I had to," said Val, her voice firm, still staring straight ahead. "The other night after the news – your picture was on every channel, so different from what it was years ago – I walked along the beach and thought about you. They weren't pleasant thoughts, but they were honest ones . . . You put me through my own personal hell, Joel. You were driven by terrible things in your past, and I tried to understand because I knew what had happened to you. But you never tried to understand *me*. I, too, had things I wanted to do, but they faded, they weren't important . . . Okay, I thought. Someday it'll pass and the nightmares will go away for him and he'll stop and look at me and say, "Hey, you're *you*". Well, the nightmares went away and it never happened."

"I concede my adversary's logic," said Converse painfully. "I still don't understand."

"I needed you, Joel, but you couldn't respond. You were amusing as hell, even when I knew you didn't feel like it, and you were terrific in bed, but your only real concerns were for you, always you."

"Conceded again, learned counsellor. *And?*"

"I remembered something I said to myself that afternoon when you left the apartment, said it silently as I watched you leave. I promised myself that if ever a person I was close to needed me as much as I needed you then, I wouldn't walk away. Call it the one moral commitment I've ever made in my life. Only the irony is that that person turned out to be you. You're not a madman and you're not a killer but someone wants the world to think you are. And whoever it is, has done it very well. Even your friends who've known you for years believe what's being said about you. I don't, and I can't walk away."

"Oh *Christ*, Val . . ."

"No strings, Converse. No playing an old sweet song and hopping into bed. That's out. I came here to help you, not console you. And over here I can. My roots go back several generations. They may be withering underground but they *were* the underground – undergrounds – and they're willing to help. For once you need *me*, and that's a twist, isn't it, friend?"

"A veritable twist," said Joel, understanding her last statement, but little else, speeding down the coast road towards the deserted fields. "Only a few minutes," he added. "I can't be seen in the city and neither can you – and you not a chance with me."

"I wouldn't worry so much. We're being watched by friends."

"*What?* What . . . 'friends'?"

"Keep your eyes on the road. There were people in front of the Amstel, didn't you see them?"

"I suppose so. No one got in a car and went after you."

"Why should they? There were others on the streets and over the canals to the consulate."

"What the hell are you talking about?"

"And an old man on a bicycle on the Museumplein."

"I saw *him*. Was he . . . ?"

"Later," said Valerie, shifting the large cloth bag at her feet into another position and stretching her long legs. "They may follow us out here but they'll stay out of sight."

"Who *are* you, lady?"

"The niece of Hermione Geyner, my mother's sister. You never knew my father, of course, but if you had he would have regaled you with tales of mom during the war, but he would have choked at the mention of my aunt. Even according to the French she went too far. The Dutch and German undergrounds worked together. I'll tell you all about it later."

"You'll tell me *later! Following* us?"

"You're new at this. You won't see them."

"*Shit!*"

"That's expressive."

"All right, all right! . . . What about Dad?"

"He's weathering it. He's staying at my place."

"Cape Ann?"

"Yes."

"I sent the envelope there! The "sketches" I mentioned on the phone. It's everything! Everything about what's happened. It names the names, gives the reasons. Everything!"

"I left three days ago. It hadn't arrived by then. But Roger's there." Valerie's face paled. "Oh, my God!"

"What?"

"I've been trying to call him! Two days ago, then yesterday and again today!"

"*Goddamn it!*" In the distance there were the lights of a bay front café. Joel spoke rapidly, giving an order that could not be disobeyed. "I don't care how you do it but you call Cape Ann! You come back here and tell me my father's all right, do you *understand?*"

"Yes. Because I want to hear it, too."

Converse skidded to a stop in front of the café, knowing he should not have done so, but not caring, not seeing, really. Valerie rushed out of the car, her purse open, her telephone credit card in her hand. If there was a phone on the premises, she would use it; no one could stop her. Joel lighted a cigarette; the smoke was acrid, stinging his throat; it was no relief. He stared out at the dark water, at the lights spanning the bridge in the distance, trying not to think. It was no use. What had he *done?* His father knew his handwriting and the instant he recognized it he would rip open the envelope. He would be looking for exculpation for his son and he would find it. He would undoubtedly call Nathan Simon immediately – and therein was the horrible possibility. Val would know enough from the material itself to say little or nothing on the phone, but not his father, not Roger. He would blurt out everything in a frenzy of anger and defence. And if others were listening on that line . . . Where was Val! She was taking too *long!*

Converse could not stop himself. He cracked the handle of the door and leaped out of the car, his feet hitting the ground, instantly propelling him around the hood. He raced towards the entrance of the café, stopping abruptly on the gravel. Valerie walked out, gesturing for him to back away. He could see the tears rolling down her cheeks.

"Get in the car," she said, approaching him.

"No. Tell me what happened. *Now.*"

"Please, Joel, get back in the car. Two men in there kept watching me while I was on the phone. I spoke German but they knew I was placing a call to the States, and they saw I was upset. I think they recognized me. We have to get out of here."

"Tell me what *happened!*"

"In the car." Valerie tossed her head to the side, her dark hair flying over her shoulder as she brushed away several tears, and walked past Converse to the automobile. She opened the door and got in, sitting motionless in the seat.

"*Goddamn you!*" Trembling, Converse ran to the car, jumped in behind the wheel and started the engine, slamming the door shut as he pulled on the gearshift. Turning the wheel, he backed up, then shot forward into the road, the tyres spinning on the border of gravel. He kept his foot on the accelerator until the dark scenery outside was a racing blur.

"Slow down," said Val, simply, without emphasis. "You'll only call attention to us.

He could barely hear her through his panic, but he heard the order. He eased his foot off the pedal. "He's dead, isn't he?"

"Yes."

"Oh, *Christ!* What happened? What did they tell you? Whom did you talk to?"

"A neighbour, the name's not important. We have keys to each other's house. She volunteered to take in the newspapers and check the place until the police reached me. She happened to be there when I called. I asked her if there was a large envelope sent from Germany in the pile of mail. She said there wasn't."

"The police? What *happened?*"

"You know my house is on the beach. There's a jetty of rocks about a hundred yards up-water. It's not large or long really, just some kind of marking from years ago . . ."

"Tell me!" shouted Joel, gripping the wheel.

"They say he must have gone for a walk last night, went out on the jetty and slipped on the wet rocks. There was a large bruise on his head. His body was washed up on shore and found this morning."

"Lies! *Lies!* They heard him! They went after him!"

"My telephone? On the plane over here I thought about that."

"You would, he *wouldn't!* I killed him. Goddamn it, I *killed* him!"

"No more than I did, Joel," insisted the ex-Mrs Converse, touching his arm, wincing at the sight of tears in his eyes. "And I loved him very much. You and I left each other but he was still a very close friend, perhaps my closest."

"He called you "Valley"," said Joel, choking, trying to push back the pain of his feelings. "The bastards! *Bastards!*"

"Do you want me to drive?"

"*No!*"

"The telephone. I have to ask you – I thought the police or the FBI or people like that might get a court order."

"Of course they would! It's why I, knew I couldn't call you. I was going to call Nate Simon."

"But you're not talking about the police or the FBI. You're talking about someone else, some *thing* else."

"Yes. No one knows who they are – where they are. But they're there. And they can do whatever they want to do. Jesus! Even *Dad!* That's what's so goddamned frightening."

"And that's what you're going to tell me about, isn't it?" said Valerie, gripping his arm.

"Yes. A few minutes ago I was going to hold back and *not* tell you everything, instead try to persuade you to get Nate to fly over here so we could meet and he could see I wasn't crazy. But not now. There's no time now; they're cutting off every outlet. They've got the envelope – it was all I *had*! . . . I'm sorry, Val, but I *am* going to tell you everything. I wish to God I didn't have to – for your sake but like you, I don't have a choice any more."

"I didn't come over here to give you a choice."

He drove into the field near the water's edge and stopped the car. The grass was high, the moon a bright crescent over the bay, the lights of Amsterdam in the distance. They got out and he led her to the darkest spot he could find, holding her hand, suddenly realizing that he had not held her hand in years – the touch, the grip, so comfortable, so much a part of them. He repelled the thought; he was a provider of death.

"Here, I guess," he said, releasing her hand.

"All right." She lowered herself gracefully, like a dancer and sat down on the soft grass, pushing the reeds aside. "How do you feel?" she asked.

"Awful," said Joel, looking up at the dark sky. "I meant what I said. I killed him. All the years of trying – his trying, my trying – and I end up killing him. If I'd only let him alone, let him be himself, not someone I wanted him to be, he'd probably be drinking up a storm somewhere thousands of miles away, telling his crazy stories, making everyone laugh. But not in your house at Cape Ann yesterday."

"You didn't force him to fly back from Hong Kong, Joel."

"Oh, hell, not by pleading or giving him an order, if that's what you mean. But the order was there nevertheless. After mother died it was the unspoken words between us. 'Grow up, Dad. Have your little trips but don't stay away so long, people worry. Be responsible, father mine.' Christ, I was so *fucking* holier-than-thou! And I end up killing him."

"You *didn't* kill him! *Others* did! Now tell me about them."

Converse swallowed, brushing the tears from his eyes. "Yes, you're right – there isn't time, even for old Roger."

"There'll be time later."

"If there's a later," said Joel, breathing deeply, finding control. "You know about René, don't you?"

"Yes, I read about it yesterday. I was sick . . . Larry Talbot told me that you saw him in Paris. How even René thought you were disturbed, as Larry did when you talked to him. And René was killed for seeing you. Larry must be going out of his mind."

"That's not the reason René was killed. Let's talk about Larry. The first time I reached him I needed information without asking him directly. He was being used because of me, followed, and he didn't know it. If I'd told him, the jock in him would have reacted, and he'd have been shot down in the street. But the last time I spoke with him I walked into it. I'd broken away from the people who'd caught me – I was exhausted, still frightened, and I was open with him. I told him everything."

"He mentioned it to me," interrupted Val. "He said you were reliving your experiences in North Vietnam. There was a psychiatric term for it."

Converse shook his head, a short, derisive laugh emerging from his throat. "Isn't there always? I suppose there were similarities and I'm sure I alluded to them, but that's all they were, similarities . . . Larry didn't hear what I was saying. He was listening for words that confirmed what others had said about me, what he believed was true. He pretended to be the friend I knew but he wasn't. He was a lawyer trying to convince a client that he was sick, that for everyone's safety the client should turn himself in. When I realized what he was doing and that I'd told him where I was, I knew he'd spread the word, thinking he was doing the right thing. I just wanted to get out of there, so I halfway agreed with him, hung up, and ran . . . I was lucky. Twenty minutes later I saw a car drive up in front of the hotel with two of my would-be executioners."

"You're sure of that?"

Joel nodded. "The next day one of them stated for the record that he'd seen me at the Adenauer Bridge with Walter Peregrine. I wasn't anywhere near that bridge, at least I don't think so. I don't know where it is."

"I read that story in the *Times*. The man was an army officer, a major from the embassy named Washburn."

"That's right." Converse broke off a long blade of grass, twisting it, tearing it in his fingers. "They're great at manipulating the media – newspapers, radio, television. Every word they put out is cleansed through channels, branded authentic, official. They take out lives as if people were pieces in a chess game, including their own. They don't care; they only want to win. And it's the biggest game in modern history. The terrifying thing is that they can win it."

"Joel, do you know what you're *saying?* An American ambassador, the Supreme Commando of NATO, René, your father . . . *you*. Then killers in the embassy, a manipulated press, lies out of Washington, Paris, Bonn – all given official status. You're describing some kind of *Anschluss*, some demonic, political *take over!*"

Converse looked at her in the moonlight, the breezes off the water bending the tall grass. "That's exactly what it is, conceived by one man and run by a handful of others, all completely sincere in their beliefs and as persuasive as any group of professionals I've ever heard. But the bottom line is that they're fanatics, killers in a quest they consider nothing less than holy. They've recruited – *are* recruiting – like-minded men everywhere, other frustrated professionals who think there's nowhere else to turn. They grab at the theories and the promises, accepting – accepting, hell, extolling – the myths of efficiency and discipline and self-sacrifice, because they know it leads to power. Power to replace the inefficient, the undisciplined, the corruptors and the corrupted. They're blind; they can't see beyond their own distorted image of themselves . . . If that sounds like a summation it probably is. I haven't slept much but I do a lot of thinking."

"The jury's still in place, Joel," said Valerie, her eyes alive, again levelled at his. "I don't want a summation, I want it all. I think you should begin at the beginning – where it began for you."

"Okay. It started in Geneva . . ."

"I *knew* it," interrupted Val, whispering.

"What?"

"Nothing. Go on."

"With a man I hadn't seen in twenty-three years. I knew him by one name then, but in Geneva he was using another. He explained it and it didn't matter. Except that it was a little eerie . . . I didn't know how eerie it was, or how much he didn't explain, or how many lies he told me in order to manipulate me. The hell of it is he did what he did for all the right reasons. I was the man they needed. *They.* And I don't know who they are, only that they're there, somewhere . . . As long as I live – however long I'm permitted – I'll never forget the words he used when he reached the core of why he had come to Geneva. "They're back," he said. "The generals are back"."

He told her everything, allowing his mind and his thoughts to wander, to include every detail he could recall. The countdown was in progress. In a matter of days, or at best a week or two there would be eruptions of violence everywhere – like what was taking place in Northern Ireland right now. "Accumulations," they said. "Rapid acceleration!" Only no one knew who or what or where the targets were. George Marcus Delavane was the madman who conceived it all, and other powerful madmen were listening to him, following his orders, moving into positions from which they would leap for the controls. *Everywhere.*

Finally he was finished, a part of him in anguish, knowing that if she were caught by the soldiers of Aquitaine, the narcotics inserted in her body would reveal the information that would result in her death. He said as much when he had finished, wanting desperately to breach the space between them and hold her, telling her how much he hated himself for doing what he knew he had to do. But he made no move towards her; her eyes told him not to; she was evaluating, thinking things out for herself.

"Sometimes," she said quietly, "when the dreams would come, or you drank too much, you'd talk about this Delavane. You'd become so panicked you'd tremble and close your eyes and every now and then you'd scream. You hated that man so. You were also frightened to death of him."

"He *caused* a lot of death, unnecessary death. Kids . . . children in grown-up uniforms who didn't know that *gungho* meant search-and-destroy and get blown apart."

"There's no way you could be – what do they call it – transferring your emotions?"

"If you believe that, I'll drive you back to the Amstel and you can fly home in the morning and go back to your easels. I'm not crazy, Val. I'm here and it's happening."

"All right, I had to ask. You didn't live through some of those nights, I did. You were either crashing into the bed or so scratched by a bottle you didn't know where you were."

"It didn't happen often."

"I'll grant you that, but when it did you were *there*. And hurting."

"Which is exactly, why I was reached in Geneva – recruited in Geneva."

"And this Fowler, or Halliday, knew the exact words to use. Your own."

"Fitzpatrick got it all for him. He thought he was doing the right thing, too."

"Yes, I know, you told me. What do you think happened to him? Fitzpatrick, I mean."

"For days I've tried to come up with a reason for them to keep him alive. I can't. He's more dangerous to them than I am. He's worked the streets they're undermining; he knows his way around Pentagon procurements and export clearances so well he could nail them with half the evidence. They've killed him."

"You liked him, didn't you?"

"Yes, I did, and just as important I was almost in awe of that mind of his. He was quick and perceptive and had one hell of an imagination which he wasn't afraid to use."

"He sounds like someone I was married to," said Val gently.

Converse kept his eyes on her for a moment, then looked away at the water. "If I get out of this alive – and I don't really think I will – I'm going hunting. I'm going to find out who did it, who pulled the trigger. There won't be any trial, no witnesses for the prosecution or the defence, no circumstances, mitigating or otherwise. Just me – and a gun."

"Sorry to hear that, Joel. I always admired your principles. They were a constant, like your attraction – your reverence, I think – for the law. It wasn't all conceit and ambition, I knew that. It gave you the only real roots you ever had. You could look at the law and argue, as a child does with a parent, knowing the parent is some kind of absolute . . . Your father never gave you that – by his own admission, incidentally."

"I think that's pretty tasteless."

"I'm sorry. He brought it up once. I *am* sorry."

"It's all right. We're talking. We didn't do much of that the last year or so together, did we?"

"I didn't think you wanted to."

"You're on target. Forget it. There's now."

"And there's so much you can deny! All they have is words against you! I said the same thing to Larry – they say you were here, you were there, you did this and you did that, but you *weren't* where they said you were and you *didn't* do what they say! You're the lawyer, Converse. For God's sake, stand up and defend yourself!"

"I'd never get near a courtroom, can't you understand that? Wherever and whenever I showed up someone would be there, someone ordered to kill me even if it meant losing his own life – considering the consequences, an insignificant sacrifice. My idea was to use the envelope – the dossiers and all the information they contained, the information that could only have come from government sources, which means I have partners somewhere in Washington. With all of that I could reach people I knew the firm knew – and with Nathan's help get them to listen to me, see I wasn't crazy. Hear from *me* what I saw, what I heard, what I *learned*. But without that envelope, even Nate couldn't help. Besides, he'd insist I go by the book and come *in*, telling me he had guarantees of full protection. There *is* no protection, not from them. They're in embassies and naval stations and army bases; in the Pentagon, police departments, Interpol, and the Department of State. They're bag ladies on a train and commuters with attaché cases – you don't know who they are but they're there. And they can't afford to let me live. I've heard their almighty credo first hand."

"Checkmate," said Val, softly.

"Check," agreed Converse.

"Then we have to find somebody else."

"What?"

"Someone those people you want to reach would listen to. Someone whose presence might force those men in Washington who sent you out from Geneva to say who they are – to show themselves."

"Who are you thinking of? John the Baptist?"

"Not John. Sam. Sam Abbott."

"*Sam?* My God, I thought about him that night in Paris! How did you . . . ?"

"Like you, I've had a lot of time to think. In New York, on the plane, last night after I saw my aunt in Berlin."

"Your aunt?"

"I'll get to that . . . I knew that if you were alive there had to be a reason why you stayed in hiding, why you didn't come out shooting, denying all those insane things they were saying about you. It didn't make sense; it wasn't *you.* And if you'd been killed or captured it would have been on the front pages everywhere, on all the broadcasts. Since there was no such story, I assumed you had to be alive. But why did you keep running, hiding? Then I thought, 'my God, if Larry Talbot doesn't believe him, who will?' And if Larry didn't, it meant that the people around him, men like him, all your friends and your so- called contacts had been reached and convinced that you were the maniac everyone in Europe was talking about. No one would touch you and you needed someone. Not me, heaven knows. I'm your ex-wife and I don't carry any weight and you needed someone who did . . . So I thought about everyone you'd ever talked about, everyone we knew. One name kept on coming back to me. Sam Abbott. Brigadier-General Abbott now, according to the papers about six months ago."

" 'Sam the Man'," said Joel, shaking his head in approval. "He was shot down three days after I was, and we were both shoved around from one camp to another. Once he was in the cell next to mine and we'd tap out Morse on the walls until they moved me. He stayed in the Air Force for all the right reasons. He knew he could be his best there."

"He thought the world of you," said Val, her voice a mixture of conviction and quiet enthusiasm. "He said you did more for morale than anyone in the camps, that your last escape gave everyone hope."

"That's a crock. I was a trouble-maker – that's what they called me – who could afford to take chances. Sam had the roughest job. He could have done what I did, but he was the ranking officer. He knew there'd be reprisals if he ever tried. He held everyone together, I didn't."

"He said otherwise. I think he's the reason you never thought much of your sister's husband. Remember when Sam flew into New York and you tried to match him up with Ginny? We all had dinner at the restaurant we couldn't afford."

"Ginny scared the hell out of him. He told me later that if she'd been drafted and put in charge of Command-Saigon it never would have fallen. He wasn't going to re-fight that war for the rest of his life."

"And you lost a desirable brother-in-law." Valerie smiled: then the smile faded and she leaned forward. "I can reach him, Joel. I'll find him and talk to him, tell him everything you've told me. Above all that you're no more insane than I am, than *he* is. That you were manipulated by people you don't know, men who lied to you so you'd do the work they either couldn't do or were afraid to do."

"That's unfair," said Converse. "If they started digging around State and the Pentagon, there could be a rash of accidents – very fatal and very dead . . . No, they were right. It had to start over here and be traced back. It was the only way."

"If you can say that after all you've been through, you're saner than any of us. Sam will know that. He'll help."

"He *could*," said Joel slowly, pensively, breaking off another blade of grass. "He'd have to be careful – none of the usual channels – but he could do it. Three or four years ago – after you and I broke up – he found out I was in Washington for a few days and called me. We had dinner and later too many drinks; he ended up spending the night on the sofa in my hotel room. We talked – both of us too much. Me about me – and you – and Sam about his newest monumental frustration."

"Then you're still close. It wasn't that long ago."

"That isn't my point. It's what he was doing. He'd worked his ass off to get into the NASA programme, but they turned him down. They said he was too valuable where he was. No one was in his class when it came to all-altitude, sub-mach manoeuvres. He designed more patterns in the sky than any designer on Seventh Avenue ever did on the ground. He could look at an aircraft – specs aside – and tell you what it could do."

"I don't understand."

"Oh, sorry. He'd been brought to Washington from wherever he was stationed as a consultant to the National Security Agency, cross-pollinating with the CIA. It was his job to evaluate the capabilities of the new Soviet and Chinese equipment."

"What?"

"Airplanes, Val. He worked over at Langley and at a dozen different safe-houses in Virginia and Maryland, appraising photographs brought out by agents, questioning defectors – especially pilots, mechanics and technicians. He knows the people I have to reach, he's worked with them."

"You're talking about the intelligence service, or services, I gather."

"Not just services," corrected Joel. "Men who crawl around in the shadows of those paintings of yours. People trained to cut down bastards like Delavane and his tribe, cut them out silently by using methods and techniques you and I know nothing about – drugs and whores and little boys. They should have been brought in at the beginning. Not Geneva, not me. They kill when it's the pragmatic thing to do, and justify the killing because it's in the ultimate interests of the country. And Lord, how I railed against them, the righteous attorney in me demanding that they be held accountable. Well, Mr Naive has changed – been changed –

because I've seen the enemy and he isn't us – not the us I think we are. If it takes a garrotte to choke off a cancer when legal medicine can't do it, hand me the wire, pal, and I'll read the manual."

"I thought you loathed fanatics."

"I do. I . . . do."

"Sam," persisted Valerie. "I'll go home tomorrow and find him."

"No," said Converse. "I want you to fly back tonight. You always carried your passport in your purse – still the same?"

"Of course. But I have . . ."

"I don't want you going back to the Amstel. You've got to get out of Amsterdam. There's a KLM night flight to New York at 11.45."

"But my things . . ."

"They're not worth it. Call the hotel when you get back. Wire them money and say it was an emergency. They'll mail everything to you."

"You're serious, aren't you?"

"Never more so in my life. I think you should know the truth about René. He wasn't killed because we met in Paris; nothing had happened then. I called him from Bonn four days ago and we talked. He believed me. He was shot to death because he sent me to Amsterdam, to reach a man who might have gotten me on a plane to Washington. That's out now and it doesn't matter. You do. You came here and you found me and the people who are looking for me all over the city will know it soon if they don't know it already."

"I never said I was going to Amsterdam," broke in Valerie. "I specifically left word at the Kempinski that I was flying directly home, that if I got any calls to refer them to New York."

"Did you have a reservation on the plane?"

"Naturally. I Just never showed up."

"Good, but not good enough. Delavane's people are efficient. Leifhelm has connections at every airport and immigration point in Germany. They'll find out otherwise. We might have fooled them once tonight, not twice. My guess is there's a German waiting for you at the Amstel now, probably in your room. I want him to think you're coming back, that you're still here."

"If someone like that goes to my room – *into* my room – he's in for a shock."

"What do you mean?"

"Someone else is there. An old man with a long memory, who's been given instructions I'd rather not repeat."

"Your aunt's doing?"

"She sees things in black and white, no greys. There *is* the enemy and there is *not* the enemy. And anyone who would harm her sister's daughter is very definitely the enemy. You don't know these people, Joel. They live in the past; they never forget. They're old now and not what they once were, but they remember what they were and why they did the things they did. It was so simple for them. Good and evil. They live with those memories – frankly, it's a little scary, *they're* a little scary, to tell you the truth. Nothing in their lives since has been so alive, so important to them. I honestly think they'd all prefer going back to those days, the horror and all."

"What about your aunt, though? After everything that's been said about me in the newspapers and on television, she went along with you? She didn't ask any questions? The fact that you were her sister's daughter was *enough?*"

"Oh, no, she asked one very specific question and I answered it. *That* was enough. I must tell you, though. She'd odd – very odd – but she can do what has to be done and that's all that matters."

"Okay . . . You will go back tonight?"

"Yes," said Val, nodding. "It's reasonable and I can do more from New York in the morning than from here. From everything you've said, every hour's important."

"Vital. Thanks . . . Also you may have trouble reaching Sam. I don't have any idea where he is and the services aren't cooperative when it comes to a woman trying to locate an officer – especially one with high rank. It's too complicated – an overseas love affair, a child the man never knew about, probably not his – they're very circumspect."

"Then I won't ask them to tell me where he is. I'll say I'm a relative *he's* been trying to reach, that I travel a great deal and if he wishes to call me, I'll be at the so-and-so hotel for the next twenty-four hours. Certainly they have to relay that kind of message to a general."

"Certainly," agreed Joel. "But if you leave your name, you're risking too much. For you *and* Sam."

"I'll use a variation, one he'll recognize." Valerie blinked, staring at the ground. "Like Parquet only I'll feminize it – Parquette. A floor, wood – something associated with a Charpentier. Then I'll add Virginia he'd remember Ginny because of you. Virginia Parquette, he'll figure it out."

"He probably will. So might others. When you don't show up tonight, Leifhelm will have the airports checked. They could pick you up at Kennedy."

"Then I'll lose them at LaGuardia. I'll go to a motel where I stay when I take the plane to Boston. I'll check in and get out without their knowing it."

"You're very quick."

"I told you, my roots go back; I've heard the stories . . . Now what about you?"

"I'll stay out of sight. I'm getting pretty good at it and I can pay for anything I need."

"Your words, Converse: Not good enough. The more money you spread the more of a trail you leave. They'll find you. You have to get out of Amsterdam, too."

"Well, I could slip across a few borders and head down to Paris for my old suite at the George V. Of course it might be a little obvious but then if I tipped high enough, they *are* French."

"Don't try to be funny."

"I don't feel remotely amusing. Also, I'd like a private toilet and a shower – even a second-hand bath. The rooms I find you *can't* find in the most esoteric travel guides."

"You haven't had a shower in God knows how long, that much I can tell you in the open air."

374

"Oh, beware the wife who's offended by her husband's hygiene. It's a sign of something."

"Cut it out, Joel, I'm not your wife . . . I've got to be able to reach you."

"Let me think, I'm also getting *very* inventive. I'll figure out something. I could . . ."

"I've already figured it out," interrupted Val firmly. "Before I flew over I talked with my aunt."

"From your house?"

"From the mid-town hotel in New York where I registered under a different name."

"You *were* thinking about your phone."

"Not the way you were . . . I told her what I thought had happened, what I was going to try to do. She came to see me in Berlin last night. She talked up a storm – how she could do this, do that – but it all boiled down to the fact that she'll help. She'll hide you. So will others."

"In *Germany?*"

"Yes. She lives in the countryside, on the outskirts of Osnabrück. It's the safest place you could go, the last place those people would think to look for you."

"How do I get *back* into Germany? It was rough enough getting out! Delavane's people aside, every border's on the alert, my photograph on every wall."

"I talked to Hermione this afternoon, after you called from a pay phone; she was staying with a friend. She started making arrangements right away and when I flew in here a few hours ago, an old man met me at the airport, the same man you'll be staying with tonight. You don't know him but you've seen him, he was riding the bicycle in the Museumplein. I was taken to a house on the Lindengracht where I was to call my aunt; the phone was what they term *unaangeroerd*, clean, untouched."

"My God, they are back in the 'forties."

"Not much has changed, has it?"

"No, I guess not. What did she say?"

"Only your instructions. Late tomorrow afternoon, when the terminal's full, you're to go to the Central Station here in Amsterdam and walk around by the information booth. A woman will come up to you and say hello, saying she recognized you as someone she met in Los Angeles. Respond to her, and during the conversation she'll hand you an envelope. Inside will be a passport, a letter and a train ticket."

"A passport? *How?*"

"All they needed was a photograph. I knew that much when I left your father in Cape Ann."

"You *knew?*"

"I told you, I've heard the stories all my life. How they got Jews and Gypsies and all the men who parachuted down from planes out of Germany and into neutral or occupied countries. The false papers, the photographs, they became an art form."

"And you brought a photograph?"

"It seemed logical. Roger thought so, too. Remember, he was in that war."

"Logical . . . a photograph."

"Yes. I found one in an album. Do you remember when we went to the Virgin Islands and you scorched yourself that first day in the sun?"

"Sure. You made me wear a tie to dinner and my neck was killing me."

"I was trying to teach you a lesson. That picture's a close-up. I wanted your sunburn in all its agony."

"It's still my *face*, Val."

"That photograph was taken eight years ago and the burn softened your features. It'll do."

"Don't I have to *know* anything?"

"If you're detained for that kind of questioning, you'll probably be caught. My aunt doesn't think you will be."

"Why is she so confident?"

"The letter. It spells out what you're doing."

"Which is?"

"A pilgrimage to Bergen-Belsen, later to Auschwitz in Poland. It's written in German and you're to hand it to anyone who stops you because you speak only English."

"But why would that . . . ?"

"You're a priest," interrupted Valerie. "The pilgrimage was financed by an organization in Los Angeles called The Coalition of Christians and Jews for World Peace and Repentance. Only a German very sure of himself will call attention to you. I've got a dark suit in your size in my tote bag, along with a black hat, shoes and a clerical collar. The instructions will be with your ticket. You'll take the northern express to Hanover where you're supposed to switch trains for Celle and be driven to Bergen-Belsen in the morning, but of course you won't. When you reach Osnabrück, get off. My aunt will be waiting for her priest. And by then I'll be back in New York getting in touch with Sam."

Converse shook his head. "Val, it's all very impressive but you weren't listening to me. Leifhelm's men have seen me – in that station, as a matter of fact. They know what I look like."

"They saw a pale-faced man with a beard and a battered face. Shave off the beard tonight."

"And apply for cosmetic surgery?"

"No, apply a generous amount of lotion called *Instant Sun* – it's in the clothes I brought you. It'll darken your face more like the photograph on the passport and also cover the bruises; they won't be that noticeable. The black hat and the clerical collar will take care of the rest."

"Omens," said Joel, touching his bruises on his face, noting that they were less painful to the touch. "Do you remember when you fell and hit the table in the foyer, the black eye?"

"I was in panic; I had a presentation the next day. You went out and got the make-up for me."

"I bought the same stuff this morning. It helped."

"I'm glad."

They looked at each other across the short distance between them in the moonlit field. "I'm sorry about everything, Val. I wish you weren't part of this. If there was any other way I wouldn't let you be, you know that."

"I know it, but it doesn't matter to me one way or the other. I came over here because of a promise I made to myself – a promise I meant. Not you. I'm *over* you, Joel, believe that."

"The promise you made to yourself was provoked by me. As the offending party of the second part that should have cancelled it."

"That's probably a rotten legal opinion" said Val, shifting her legs and looking away. "There's also the obvious. Everything you've told me terrifies me – not fact *A* and fact *B*, or who's conspiring with whom; I'm a landscape painter; I can't deal with such things. But I'm so terribly afraid because I can personalize. I can see how these people – this Aquitaine – *can* win, can take control of our lives, turning us all into complacent flocks of sheep. Good *God*, Joel, we'd *welcome* them!"

"I missed something."

"Then you're blind. I don't think it's just women, or women who live alone like me, I think it's most of the people walking around in the streets, trying to earn a living, trying to make the rent or a mortgage or a car payment, trying to *make* it through life. We're *sick* of everything around us! We're told one minute we may be blown up in a nuclear war unless we're taxed out of our houses to pay for bigger bombs, and that our water's contaminated, or that we can't buy this or that because it might be poisoned. Children disappear, and people are killed walking into a store for a quart of milk, and addicts and muggers with guns and knives cut people down on the streets. I live in a small town and I won't go there after dark, and if I'm in the city – any city – I look behind me in broad daylight, and I'll be damned if I'll get into an elevator unless it's crowded . . . I couldn't afford it but I put in a burglar alarm system in a house I don't own because there was a boat out in the water one day that stayed there overnight. In my mind I saw men crawling up the beach to my windows. We all see such things, whether out on the water, or down city blocks, or in a field like this. We're frightened; we're sick of the problems, sick of the *violence*. We want someone strong to *stop* it – and I'm not sure it even matters who they are. And if the men you're talking about push things any farther – believe me they know what they're doing. They can walk in and be crowned, no votes required . . . And in spite of everything I've said, that's even more frightening. Which is why you're going to take me to the airport."

"Why did I ever let you go?" whispered Joel, more to himself than to her.

"Cut it out, Converse. It's over. *We're* over."

He watched from the darkest area of the parking lot at Amsterdam's Schiphol airport as the plane sped down the runway and lifted off into the night sky. He had driven up to a crowded platform where Val had got out, giving him the scrap of paper with the address that was to be his refuge for the night. So that he would know she had been able to get on the flight, she was to come out the glass doors, look at her watch and go back inside. If the plane was overbooked, she was to continue on the pedestrian walk to the temporary lot a hundred yards away from the entrance where he would be waiting for her. She had come outside, glanced at her watch and returned to the terminal. A part of him had felt relief, another part a quiet, hollow emptiness.

He watched the huge silver plane bank to the left and disappear, its fading lights a trajectory in the dark sky.

He stood naked in front of the mirror in the small bathroom in the house on the Lindengracht. The car was some twenty streets away. He had made the return journey cautiously on foot. The old man who owned the flat was pleasant and spoke in haltingly clear English, but his eyes were far away and never really made contact. His mind was in another place, another time.

Joel had shaved carefully, showered far longer than a guest should, and had finished applying the deep red lotion to his face, neck and hands. In moments his skin was bronzed. The result was far more authentic than he remembered the earlier products, when anyone who used them stood out with a mask of sickly brown, too smooth and cosmeticized to be anything but unnatural. The new colouring further concealed the bruises on his face: he looked almost normal. He would discard the tinted glasses: they would only call attention to him, especially from anyone who had seen him or had been given his description. He washed his hands repeatedly, kneading them together to remove the stains from his fingertips.

He gasped silently, his body stiffening. From somewhere beyond the door came the sound of an erratic bell. He quickly turned off the water and listened, his breathing suspended, his eyes on the gun he had placed on the narrow window sill. He heard the sound again; it stopped. Then he heard a single voice, a man on a telephone. He dried his hands and slipped on the short cotton bathrobe that had been left on the bed in his small, immaculate room. He put the gun in his pocket, went out the door and down the dark, narrow hallway that led to the old man's "study", a former bedroom filled with old magazines, a few books, and tabloid newspapers on tables and chairs opened to the bloodiest sections, red crayon marks circling articles and pictures. On the walls were prints and photographs of long-past wartime accomplishments – including corpses in various poses of death. In an odd way it reminded Converse of *Les Étalons Blancs* in Paris, except that here there were no glories of war, only the ugliness of death. It was more honest, he thought, if nothing else.

"Ah, *Mijnheer*," said the old man, sitting forward in a huge leather chair that engulfed his frail body, the telephone beside him. "You are safe, *quite* safe! That was Kabel – code name, Kabel, *natuurlijk*. He has left the hotel and reports his progress." Fragile, in his seventies, the Dutchman struggled out of the chair and stood erect, his thin shoulders back, his body rigid – a foolish old man playing soldier. "Operation Osnabrück proceeds!" he said, as if reporting to a commanding officer. "As contemplated by underground intelligence reports, the enemy infiltrated the area and has been compromised."

"He's been what?"

"Executed, *Mijnheer*. A wire around the throat, taken from behind. The blood stays on the clothes as the neck is pulled back, thus there are no signs of combat and the enemy is removed from the place of compromise."

"*What* did you say?"

"Kabel is strong for one of his age," said the old man grinning, his weathered face a thousand creases, his posture now relaxed. "He took the body from the room, dragged it to the fire exit and down into the alley. From there he gained access to the cellars and put the corpse back by the furnaces. It is summer; the man may not be found for days – unless the stench becomes too much."

Converse heard the words, but his concentration was only on one. *Compromise.* In this odd language of another time it meant . . . execution. Execution . . . murder . . . assassination!

What would you say to compromising certain powerful individuals in specific governments . . . ? Leifhelm's words.

It wouldn't work. His own.

You do not take into consideration the time element! Accumulation! Rapid acceleration! Chaim Abrahms.

My God! thought Joel. Was that what the generals of Aquitaine meant? *Assassinations?* Was it the reason for the glaring, disapproving looks directed at the Israeli and Abrahms' sudden retreat into qualification then voidance.

It's merely a point . . . I'm not sure it even applies.

Accumulation, rapid acceleration, one after another – national leaders cut down *everywhere.* Presidents and prime ministers, ministers of state and vice-presidents, powerful men and women from all shades of the narrow, acceptable political spectrum violently eliminated – governments in chaos. All to take place in a matter of hours, savagery erupting in the streets, fuelled by hysteria, victims and violators blurred until the commanders were summoned to restore order, not to leave until the controls were theirs. The climate was established, the day was coming. *Assassinations!*

He had to get back into Germany. He had to reach Osnabrück and be there when Val called. Sam Abbott had to be told.

29

His hands manacled and chained, his wounded right forearm encased in a filthy bandage, Connal Fitzpatrick gripped the ledge of the small window and peered out beyond the bars at the strange, violent activity taking place in the huge concrete parade ground. That it was a parade ground had been clear on the second morning of his capture when, along with the other prisoners, he was granted an hour's exercise outside the concrete barracks – and they *were* barracks, once part of an old refuelling station for submarines was his guess. The slips along the water as well as the winching machinery were far too small and too obsolete for today's nuclear marauders – no Trident could fit in any space along the concrete and steel piers – but once, he judged, the base had served the German undersea navy well.

Now, however, it was being used to the great *disservice* of the Federal Republic of Germany and of free governments everywhere. It was Aquitaine's training ground, the place where strategies were being refined, manoeuvres perfected, and the final preparations made for the massive assaults that would propel Delavane's military commanders to power over paralysed civilian authorities. Everything was reduced to killing – swift and brutal, the shock of the acts themselves intrinsic to the wave of violence.

Beyond the window, units of four and five men raced separately, and in succession around and between a crowd of perhaps a hundred others, taking their turns at the sickening exercise they were perfecting. For at the end of the parade ground was a concrete platform, 7 feet high and perhaps 30 feet long, where mannequins were lined up in a row – some standing, others in chairs – their inanimate figures rigid, their lifeless glass eyes staring straight ahead. They were the targets. At the centre of each clothed chest, "male" and "female", was an encased circle of bullet-proof wire mesh; within each was a high-intensity orange light, seen clearly in the afternoon sun. At the discretion of the compound's trainer, it flashed on. It was the signal that this particular mannequin was the particular unit's specific target or, if more than one, targets. Hits were recorded electronically by other lights on the high stone wall above each figure on the platform. Red was a kill, blue merely a wound. Red was acceptable, blue was not.

The screaming admonitions over the loud speakers did not vary except in terms of numbers – of time. They were delivered in nine languages, four of which Connal understood. The words were the same.

Thirteen days to Ground Zero! Accuracy is uppermost! Escape is with the diversion of a kill! Otherwise there is only death!

Eleven days to Ground Zero! Accuracy is uppermost . . . !

Eight days to Ground Zero! Accuracy is . . . !

Individual members of the killer teams fired at their targets – exploding stuffed skulls and pulverizing chests and stomachs – sometimes by themselves, at other times in unison with their comrades. Each "kill" was greeted with vocal exuberance, as the men raced through the crowd, melting into it, finally becoming part of it as their manoeuvre was completed. Another team was then instantly formed from within the ranks of the spectators; and another exercise in assassination was mounted, executed swiftly. And so it went on, hour after hour, the crowd reacting to the "kills" with shouts of approval as weapons were reloaded for up-coming assaults against the eerily marked mannequins. Every twenty minutes or so, as sections of the lifeless figures on the platform were progressively blown apart, they would be replaced with fresh heads and torsos. All that was missing were rivers of blood and mass hysteria.

In anger and frustration, Connal spread his manacled wrists apart, snapping the unbreakable chain, yanking with all his might, as the rusted, circular braces dug into his flesh, the scrapes red, his wrist bones bruised. There was nothing he could do, no way to get out! He knew the secret of Aquitaine! The enigma of its ultimate strategy was right there before his eyes! Assassinations! The mass killing of political figures in nine different nations – eight days away! Something was going to happen in eight days, something he knew nothing about, but widespread enough and provocative enough to demand the appearances of statesmen the world over. He did not know what it was, but others would – if he could *reach* them! What tore him apart was the simple truth: There was nothing he could do – *absolutely nothing!*

He turned away from the window, arms and wound aching, wrists stinging, and looked around at the barracks full of prisoners, forty-three men trying not to fail but failing fast. Many were lying listlessly on their beds, others stared forlornly out of various windows; a number talked quietly in small groups against the blank walls. All were manacled, as he was, all pathetic, as he was rapidly becoming pathetic, the abysmally short rations and the now-prolonged brutal periods of "exercise" designed to weaken them swiftly in both body and in mind. Whispering among themselves, when languages were understood, they had come to several conclusions, but their unique captivity eluded reason. They were part of a strategy none could understand, and only Connal understood who the strategists were. In unwatched corners he tried to explain, only to be met with blank stares and expressions of bewilderment.

Several points were established – for whatever they signified. To begin with, they were all military officers ranging in rank from the middle to the higher echelons. Secondly, all were bachelors or divorced, none with children or currently involved in serious relationships that demanded constant communication. Lastly, all were on 30- to 45-day leaves, only one other with emergency status like Connal, the rest on normal summer holidays. There was a pattern, but what did it mean?

There *was* a clue to that meaning only it, too, was beyond understanding. Every other day or so the prisoners were brought postcards from widely diverse locations – resort areas in Europe and North America – and instructed to write specific messages to specific individuals they all recognized as various fellow officers at the posts or bases from which they were on leave. The messages were always in the vein of *Having-wonderful-time; Wish-you-were-here; Off-to-(another location)*. To refuse to write these peripatetic greetings in their own hands was to be denied the scant food they were given and driven out to the parade ground where the objectors ran as fast as they could in laps, under guns until they dropped.

They agreed among themselves that the reason behind the near-starvation level of daily rations had a purpose. They were all trained, competent officers. Such men in decent physical and mental condition were capable of attempting escapes or, at the least, creating serious disturbances. But that was all they could understand. All but Connal had been there for a minimum of twenty-two to a maximum of thirty-four days. With a specific regimen of repeated punishment and a disastrously insufficient diet, the times of imprisonment were sufficient to inflict severe physical and psychological damage rapidly. They were in a concentration camp somewhere on some undetermined coastline, not knowing their crimes, real or imagined by their captors.

"*Qué pasa?*" asked a prisoner named Enrique from Madrid.

"*Afuera en el campo de maniobras es lo mismo,*" replied Fitzpatrick, nodding his head at the window and continuing in Spanish. "They're killing stuffed dummies out there, figuring each hit makes them heroes or martyrs or both."

"It's crazy!" cried the Spaniard. "It's crazy and it's sick in the head! What do they accomplish? Why this madness?"

"They're going to cut down a lot of important people eight days from now. They're going to kill them during some kind of international holiday or celebration or something like that. What the *hell* is happening eight days from now? Have you any idea?"

"I am only a major at the garrison at Zaragoza. I make my reports on the Basque provisionals, and read my books. What do I know of such things? Whatever it is, it would not reach Zaragoza – barbarous country, but I would wear corporal's stripes to return to it."

"*Vite! Contre le mur!*"

"*Schnell! Gegen die Mauer!*"

"Move! Against the wall!"

"*Fa presto! Contro il muro.*"

Four guards burst through the barracks doors, others following, repeating the same order in different languages. It was a manacles-and-chain inspection, carried out at whim day and night, never less than once an hour during the daylight, as frequently as four times at night. The slightest evidence of any prisoner having attempted to break or weaken his chain or crack his manacles by filing against the concrete or smashing into rock was met with immediate punishment. The sentences were the same for each prisoner: Running naked – preferably in the rain – until collapse, remaining in chains where he fell with no food or water for thirty-six hours. Of the forty-three men, twenty-nine of the strongest among them had been "convicted", a number more than twice and three times until they had little strength left. Connal had run the gauntlet only once, thanks apparently to his bi-lingual guard, an Italian who seemed to appreciate the fact that his *americano* had taken the trouble to learn *italiano*. The man from Genoa was a bitter, cynical former paratrooper – and probably a convict – who referred to himself as a *rifiut* coming into his own, garbage soon to be rewarded. But like most men from his part of the world, there was an instinctive response to a foreigner's reference to *bella Italia, bellissima Roma*.

It was from their short, quiet yet staccato conversations that Fitzpatrick had learned as much as he had, his legal military mind operating on the level of addressing a malcontented military client. He had pushed the buttons he had pushed so often before.

"What's in it for *you*? They *know* you're garbage!"

"They promise me. They pay me much money to teach what I know. Without people like me – many of us here – they will not accomplish."

"Accomplish what?"

"That is for them to say. I am, as *you* say, employed."

"To show them how to kill?"

"And to run and not be seen. That is our life – the lives of many of us here."

"You could lose everything."

"Most of us have nothing. We were used and discarded."

"These men will do the same to you."

"Then we will kill again. We are experienced, *Signore*."

"Suppose their enemies find this place?"

"They will not. They cannot."

"Why not?"

"It's an island no one thinks of."

"They know that."

"Impossible! No planes fly over, no boats approach. We would know if they did."

"Why don't you think about what *was* here?"

"*Che cosa volete dire?*"

"Submarines. Surrounding your island."

"If such were the case, *americano*, the – how you say? – the *custode* . . ."

"The warden."

"He would explode everything away. Everything on this side of the island would be *fumo* – smoke, nothing. It is part of our *contratto*. We understand."

"The warden – the *custode* – he's the big German with the short grey hair, isn't he?"

"Enough talk. Have your drink of water."

"I have information for you," whispered Connal, as the guard checked his manacles and chain. "Information that will guarantee you a big reward and might possibly save my life."

"What kind of information?"

"Not here. Not now. There isn't time. Come back tonight; everyone's so exhausted they're asleep before they reach their beds. I'll stay awake. Come and get me, but come alone. You don't want to share this."

"My head is filled with *zucchini*? I come alone to a barracks filled with condemned men?"

"What can any of us do? What can *I* do? I'll stay by the door; you open it and I'll step out, your gun no doubt at my head. I don't want to die, that's why I'm talking to you!"

"You will die. May you go with God."

"You're a fool, a *buffone!* You could have a fortune instead of a bullet in your chest."

The Italian looked guardedly at Fitzpatrick, then around at the others; the inspections were nearly finished. "For me to do such a thing, I need more than what you have told me."

"Two of your guards are traitors," whispered Connal.

"*Che cosa?*"

"That's all you get until tonight."

Fitzpatrick lay in the darkness, waiting, listening for the sound of footsteps, the sweat of anxiety drenching his face. All around him were the sleep-induced moans of hungry, punished men. He pushed his own pains out of his mind; he had other things to think about. If he could reach the water the manacles would slow him down but not stop him; he could side-stroke nearly indefinitely – and some where down the coastline, away from "this side of the island", there would be a beach or a dock, a place where he could crawl out of the sea. There was nothing else left; he had to try it. He also had to make sure his Italian guard could raise no alarms.

The bolt in the door was quietly sliding back! He had missed the footsteps; his thoughts had intruded. He got up silently and started up the aisle, each step on the balls of his feet, flexing his hands but keeping the chain taut. He could not make any noise whatsoever; several prisoners had begun to have nightmares, provoked by the slightest disturbance. He reached the door and somehow understood he was to push it open, not the other way around; the guard would stay back, his weapon aimed at the informer.

It was so. The Italian gestured with his gun for Connal to move forward as he side-stepped to the door and secured the bolt. He then pointed with the barrel of his weapon, ordering Fitzpatrick to walk ahead. Moments later both men stood in the shadows in front of the barracks, the old refuelling station still visible in the darkness, the ocean waves lapping at the pilings.

"Now we talk, *Signore*," said the guard. "Who are these traitors and why should I believe you?"

"I want your word that you'll tell your superiors I turned them in. I don't say anything until I have your word!"

"My word, *americano?*" said the Italian, laughing softly. "Very well, *amico*, you have my word."

The guard's quiet, cynical laughter covered the seconds. Connal suddenly whipped out the chain, crashing it down on the man's weapon, grabbing the barrel of the gun with his right hand and wrenching it free; it fell to the grass beneath. He then raised the chain, as he kicked the guard in the groin, and slammed the heavy links into the man's face, smashing the manacles into the Italian's skull until the guard's eyes grew wide and then closed in unconsciousness. Fitzpatrick crouched, finding his bearings.

It was directly ahead – an old submarine slip, its long pier extending out to the middle water. He got up and ran, the air exhilarating, the breezes from the sea telling him to run faster, *faster!* Escape was seconds away!

He plunged over the dock into the water, knowing he would find the strength to do *anything*, swim *anywhere!* He was *free!*

Suddenly, he was blinded, the floodlights everywhere. Then a fusillade of bullets exploded from all sides, ripping up the water around him, cracking the air overhead, but none entering his body or blowing apart his head. And words over a loudspeaker filled the night.

"You are most fortunate, Prisoner Number Forty-three, that we still might have need of your handwriting or your voice over a telephone. Otherwise, your corpse would be food for the North Sea fishes."

30

Joel walked out of the bright afternoon sun into Amsterdam's cavernous Central Station. The dark suit and hat fitted comfortably; the clerical collar and the black shoes pinched but were bearable, and the small suitcase was an impediment he could discard at any time, although it was a correct accessory and held odd bits of clothing, none of which was likely to fit. His déja *vu* being no illusion, he walked cautiously, every sudden movement – no matter how inconsequential – observed, studied, faces explored. He expected at any instant to see men rushing toward him, their eyes alert, filled with purpose, and the intent to kill.

None came, but even if they did he had done his best. He had written the most complete brief of his legal career, written it with painstakingly clear handwriting, organizing the material, pulling together the facts to support his judgments and conjectures. He had recalled the salient points of each dossier to lend credibility to his own conclusions. Regarding his own painful experiences and first-hand observations he weighed every statement, discarding those that might seem too emotional, reshaping the rest to reflect the cold objectivity of a trained, *sane*, legal mind. He had lain awake for hours during the night, allowing the organizational blocks to fall into place, then started writing in the early morning, ending with a personal letter that dispelled any misconceptions of madness on his part. He was a pawn who had been manipulated by frightened, unseen men who had supplied the tools and knew exactly what they were doing. In spite of everything that had happened, he understood, and felt that perhaps there had not been any other way to do it. He had finished it all an hour ago and sealed the pages in a large envelope supplied by the old man who said he would post it on the Damrak after dropping Converse off. Joel had sent it to Nathan Simon.

"*Pastoor* Wilcrist! It is *you*, is it not?"

Converse spun round at the touch on his arm. He saw that the shrill greeting came from a gaunt, slightly bent woman in her late seventies. Her wizened face was dominated by intense eyes, her head framed by a nun's crown, her slender body encased in a black habit. "Yes," he said, startled, briefly looking around. "Hello, Sister?"

"I can tell you don't remember me, *Pastoor*," exclaimed the woman, her English heavily – loudly – accented. "No, don't fib, I can see you have no idea who I am!"

"I might if you'd keep your voice down, Sister." Joel spoke softly, leaning down and trying to smile. "You'll call attention to us, lady."

"The religious always greet each other *zo*," said the old woman confidentially, her eyes wide and direct, too direct. "They wish to appear like normal people."

"Shall we walk over here so we can talk quietly?" Converse took the woman by the arm and led her toward a crowded area of a gate. "You have something for me?"

"Where are you from?"

"Where am I from? What do you mean?"

"You know the rules. I have to be certain."

"Of what?"

"That you are the proper contact. There can be no substitutes, no deviations. We are not fools, *Mijnheer*. Now, where are you *from?* Quickly! Hesitation itself is a lie."

"Wait a minute! You were told to meet me here; you were given a description. What more do you want?"

"To know where you're from."

"*Christ*, how many sunburned priests did you expect to see at the information booth?"

"They are not *zo* un-normal. Some swim, I am told. Others play tennis. The pope himself once skied in the mountain sun! You see I am a good Catholic, I know these things."

"You were *given* a description! Am I that man?"

"You all look alike. The father last week at confession was not a good man. He told me I had too many sins for my age and he had others waiting. He was not a patient man of God."

"Neither am I."

"All alike."

"*Please*," said Joel, looking at the thick, narrow envelope in the woman's hands, knowing that if he took it forcibly from her she would scream. "I have to reach Osnabrück, you know that!"

"You are from *Osnabrück?*" The "nun" clutched the envelope to her chest, her body bent further, protecting a holy thing.

"No, not Osnabrück!" Converse tried to remember Val's words. He was a priest on a pilgrimage . . . to Auschwitz and Bergen-Belsen . . . from, from . . . "*Los Angeles!*" he whispered harshly.

"*Ja, goed*. What country?"

"Jesus!"

"*Wat?*"

"The United States of America."

"*Goed!* Here you are, *Mijnheer*." The old woman handed him the envelope, now smiling sweetly. "We all must do our jobs, must we not? Go with God, my fellow servant of the Lord . . . I do like this costume. I was on the stage, you know. I don't think I'll give it back. Everyone smiles, and a gentleman who came out of one of those dirty houses, stopped and gave me fifty guilder."

The old woman walked away, turning once and smiling again, discreetly showing him a pint of whisky she had taken from under her habit.

It might have been the same platform, he could not tell, but his fears were the same as when he arrived in Amsterdam twenty-four hours ago. He had come to the city as an innocuous-looking labourer with a beard and a pale, bruised face. He was leaving as a priest, erect, clean-shaven, sunburned, a properly-dressed man of the cloth on a pilgrimage of repentance and reaffirmation. Gone was the outraged lawyer in Geneva, the manipulating supplicant in Paris, the captured dupe in Bonn. What remained was the hunted, and to survive he had to be able to stalk the hunters before they stalked him; that meant spotting them before they spotted him. It was a lesson he had learned eighteen years ago when his eyes were sharper and his body more resilient. To compensate he had to use whatever other talents he had developed; all were reduced to concentration – without appearing to concentrate. Which was how and why Joel saw the man.

He was standing by a concrete pillar up ahead on the platform, reading an unfolded train schedule in the dim light. Converse glanced at him – as, indeed, he glanced briefly at nearly everyone in sight – then seconds later he looked again. Something was odd, incongruous. There could be several reasons why a man remained outside a well-lighted railroad car to read a schedule – a last cigarette in the open air, waiting for someone – but that same man could hardly read the very small print while casually holding the schedule midway between his head and his waist without any evidence of a squint. It was like trying to read a page from a telephone directory in a car stuck in traffic in the Lincoln Tunnel; it took observable effort. The man showed none.

Converse continued down the platform, approaching the two open doors that signified the end of one railway car and the beginning of the next. He purposely let his suitcase catch on a protruding window ledge, pivoting as it did so, apologizing to a couple behind him. Courteously he let them pass and courteously, as each saw his collar, they smiled and nodded. But whilst his head remained facing them, his eyes strayed to the man diagonally to the left by the pillar. He clutched the schedule in his hand – another forgotten accessory. The man was concentrating now on Joel. It was enough.

Converse entered the second door, his gait casual again, but altered the instant he could no longer see the man by the pillar. He rushed ahead inside the railroad car and tripped, falling to the floor by the first seat, again apologizing to those behind him – a divine undone by profane luggage. He looked out the window, past the two passengers in the seat, both of whom paid attention to his collar before his face.

The man by the pillar had dropped the schedule and was now signalling with quick, short beckoning gestures, his right hand moving frantically. In seconds he was joined by another man; their conversation was rapid, each separating, one to the door at the front of the car, the other heading for the entrance Joel had just passed through.

They had found him. He was trapped.

Valerie paid the driver and climbed out of the cab, acknowledging the assistance of the doorman. It was the second hotel reservation she had made in the space of two hours, having left a dead end trail in case anyone was following her. She had taken a cab from Kennedy to LaGuardia, buying a ticket to Boston on a mid-morning shuttle, then registering at the airport motel, both under the name of Charpentier. She had left the motel thirty minutes later, having paid the cab driver to return for her at a side exit and calling the hotel in Manhattan to see if a reservation was possible at that hour. It was. The St Regis would welcome Mrs DePinna, who had flown in from Tulsa, Oklahoma, on a sudden emergency.

At the all-night Travellers Shop in Schiphol Airport, Val had purchased a carry-on bag, filling it with toiletries and whatever more subdued articles of clothing she could find on the all too colourful racks. It was still the height of the summer – the heat of the summer – and, depending upon the circumstances, such clothes might come in handy. Also she had something to show customs.

She registered at the hotel desk, using a "Cherrywood Lane" without a number she remembered from her childhood in St Louis. Indeed, the name DePinna came from those early days as well, a neighbour down the street, the face a blur now, only the memory of a sad, vituperative woman who loathed all things foreign, including Val's parents. "Mrs R. DePinna"; she had no idea where the R came from – possibly Roger for balance.

In the room she turned on the radio to the all-news station, a habit she inherited from her marriage, and proceeded to unpack her clothing and toiletries. She undressed, took a shower, washed out her underthings, and slipped into the out-sized T-shirt. This last was another habit; "T-sacks", as she called them, had replaced bathrobes and morning coats on her patio in Cape Ann although none had a sunburst emblazoned on the front with words above and below heralding: *Tot Ziens – Amsterdam!*

She resisted calling Room Service for a pot of tea; it would be calming but it was an unnecessary act that at 3 o'clock in the morning had to call even minor attention to the woman in *714*. She sat in the chair staring absently at the window wishing she hadn't given up cigarettes; it would give her something to do while thinking, and she had to think. She had to rest too, but first she had to think, organize herself. She looked around the room, her eyes centring on her purse which she had placed on a bedside table. She was rich, if nothing else. Joel had insisted she take the risk of getting through customs with more than the $5,000 legal limit. So she had rolled up an additional twenty five-hundred dollar bills and shoved them into her brassiere. He had been right; she could not use credit cards or anything that carried her name.

She lowered her gaze to the two telephone directories on the shelf of the table, got out of the chair and went to the bed. Sitting on the edge she removed both volumes. One read, *New York County, Business to Business*; the other, *Manhattan* – and in the upper left-hand corner, printed across a blue diagonal strip: *Government*

Listings. See Blue Pages. It was the place to start. She returned the Business directory to the shelf and carried the Manhattan book over to the desk. She sat down, opened to the blue pages and found her beginning. *Department of the Air Force . . . Command Post ARPC.* It was an 800 number, the address on York Street in Denver, Colorado. If it was not the number she needed, whoever she reached could supply the correct one. She wrote it down on a page of St Regis stationery.

Suddenly Val heard the words. Her head snapped around toward the television set, her eyes on the vertical radio dial.

" . . . And now the latest update on the search for the American attorney, Joel Converse, one of the most tragic stories of the decade. The former Navy pilot, once honoured for outstanding bravery in the Vietnam war, whose dramatic escape electrified the nation, and whose subsequent tactical reports shocked the military, leading, many believed, to basic changes in Washington's South-east Asian policies, is still at large, hunted not for the man he was, but for the homicidal killer he has become. Reports are that he may still be in Paris. Although not official, word has been leaked from unnamed but authoritative sources within the *Sûreté* that fingerprints found on the premises where the French lawyer, René Mattilon, was slain are definitely those of Converse, thus confirming what the authorities believed – that Converse killed his French acquaintance for cooperating with Interpol and the *Sûreté*. The manhunt is spreading out from Paris and this station will bring you . . ."

Valerie sprang from the chair and ran to the television set, furiously pushing several buttons until the radio was silent. She stood for a moment, trembling with anger – and fear. And something else she could not define – did not care to define. It tore her apart and she had to stay together.

She lay on the bed staring at the ceiling, seeing the reflections of light from moving things below in the street, hearing the sounds of the city. None of it was comforting, only abrasive intrusions that kept her mind alert, rejecting sleep. She had not slept on the plane; but had dozed intermittently, repeatedly jarred awake by half-formed nightmares, not helped by excessive turbulence over the North Atlantic. She needed sleep now . . . she needed Joel now. The first came; the latter was out of reach.

There was a shattering dissonance accompanied by a burst of sunlight that remained constant, blinding her as she shot up from the bed, kicking away the sheet, throwing her feet on the floor. It was the telephone. The telephone? She looked at her watch; it was 7.25, the sun streaming through the windows, the phone once again ringing, piercing the mists of sleep but not clearing them away. The telephone? How . . . ? *Why?* She reached over and picked it up, gripping it with all her strength, trying to find herself before speaking.

"Hello?"

"Mrs DePinna?" inquired a male voice.

"Yes."

"We trust everything is satisfactory."

"Are you in the habit of waking up your guests at seven o'clock in the morning to ask if they're comfortable?"

"I'm terribly sorry, but we were anxious for you. This *is* the Mrs DePinna from Tulsa, Oklahoma, isn't it?"

"Yes."

"We've been looking for you all night . . . since the flight from Amsterdam arrived at one-thirty this morning."

"Who are you?" asked Val, petrified, holding her wrist below the phone.

"Someone who wants to help you, Mrs Converse," said the voice, now relaxed and friendly. "You've given us quite a run around. We must have woken up a hundred and fifty women who checked in at hotels since two A.M. . . . the "plane from Amsterdam" did it; you didn't ask me what I was talking about. Believe me, we want to help, Mrs Converse. We're both after the same thing."

"Who *are* you?"

"The United States Government covers it. Stay where you are. I'll be over in fifteen minutes."

The hell the United States Government covers it! thought Val shivering, as she hung up the phone. The United States Government had cleaner ways of identifying itself . . . She had to get *out!* What did the fifteen minutes mean? Was it a trap? Were men downstairs waiting for her now — waiting to see if she would run? She had no *choice!*

She ran to the bathroom, grabbing the carry-on case off a chair and throwing her things into it. She dressed in seconds, stuffing what clothes remained into the bag, snatching the room key off the bureau, and running to the door. She stopped. Oh, *Lord*, the stationery with the Air Force number! She raced back to the desk, picked up the page beside the open telephone book and shoved it into her purse. She glanced wildly about; was there anything *else?* No. She left the room and walked rapidly down the hall to the elevators.

Maddeningly, the elevator stopped at nearly every floor, men and women getting on, most of the men with puffed circles under their eyes, a few of the women looking drawn, sheepish. Several apparently knew one another, others nodded absently, gazes straying to lapels and upper blouses. Then Valerie understood; the majority of the passengers had plastic name plates affixed to the fronts of their jackets and dresses; it was some sort of convention.

The doors opened to a crowded bank of elevators; the ornate lobby to the right was swarming with people, voices raised in greetings, questions and instructions. Cautiously, Val approached the gilded arch that led to the lobby-proper, looking around in controlled panic to see if anyone was looking at her. A large gold-framed sign with block letters arranged in black felt under glass was on the wall; it explained the commotion.

Welcome: Micmac Distributors.

There followed a descending list of meetings and activities.

Buffet Breakfast 7.30 – 8.30 A.M.
Regional Conferences 8.45 – 10.00 A.M.
Advertising Symposium Q and A 10.15 – 11.00 A.M.

"Hey, sweet face," said a burly, red-eyed man standing next to Val. "That's a no-no."

"I beg your pardon?"

"We are *marked*, princess!"

Valerie stopped breathing; she stared at the man, gripping the handles of her carry-on, prepared to smash it into his face and bolt for the glass doors thirty feet away. "I have no idea what you mean?"

"The *name*, princess! Where's your Micmac spirit? How can I ask you to have breakfast with me if I don't know your name?"

"Oh . . . the name tag. I'm sorry."

"What's your region, beautiful creature?"

"Region?" Again Valerie understood; she suddenly smiled. "Actually, I'm new – just hired yesterday. They said my instructions would be at the desk, but it's so crowded I'll never get over there. Of course, with *your* shoulders I might make it before I'm fired."

"Grab hold, princess! These shoulders used to play semi-pro ball." The heavy-set salesman was an effective blocking back; they reached the counter and the man growled appropriately, a lion preening before its conquest. "Hey, fella! This lady's been trying to get your attention. Need I say more, fella?" The salesman grinned at Val, holding in his stomach.

"No, sir – yes, mam?" said the perplexed clerk who was not at all busy. The activity was taking place in front of the counter, not *at* the counter.

Valerie leaned forward, ostensibly to be heard through the noise. She placed her key on the counter and opened her purse, taking out three fifty-dollar bills. "This should cover the room. I've been here one night, and there are no charges. What's left is yours."

"Thank *you*, mam."

"I need a favour."

"Of course!"

"My name is Mrs DePinna – but of course the key tells you that."

"What, mam?"

"I'm visiting a friend who's just had an operation. Could you tell me where the . . . Lebanon Hospital is?"

"The Lebanon . . . ? It's in the Bronx, I think. Somewhere on the Grand Concourse. Any cab driver will know, mam."

"Mrs DePinna's the name."

"Yes, Mrs DePinna. *Thank* you."

Valerie turned to the heavy-set, red-eyed salesman, again smiling. "I'm sorry. Apparently I'm at the wrong hotel, the wrong company, can you imagine? It would have been nice. Thanks for your help." She turned and quickly dodged her way through the crowd toward the revolving doors.

The street was only beginning to come alive. Valerie walked rapidly down the pavement, stopping almost immediately in front of a small, elegant bookstore; she decided to wait in the doorway. The stories she had heard all her life included not only tales of leaving false information, but lessons involving the necessity of knowing what the enemy looked like; it was often the difference.

A taxi drove up in front of the St Regis and, before it had come to a stop, the rear door opened. She could see the passenger clearly, his hand extended over the front seat paying the fare without thought of change. He climbed out swiftly and started running toward the glass doors. He was hatless, with unkempt, nearly blond hair, and dressed in a madras jacket and light-blue summer jeans. He was the enemy, Valerie knew that and accepted it. What she found hard to accept was his youth. He was in his twenties, hardly more than a boy. But the face was hard and set in anger, the eyes cold – distant flashes of steel in the sunlight. *Wie ein Hitlerjunge*, thought Val, walking out of the bookstore doorway.

A car streaked past her, heading west toward the hotel and within seconds she heard screeching tyres, expecting a crash to follow. She turned, as any pedestrian might turn, hearing the sudden, hysterical sound in the street. But the hysteria belonged to her. Fifty feet away, a brown sedan had come to a stop, on its door panels and trunk in clear black lettering: *US Army*. A uniformed officer got out quickly. He was staring at her.

She broke into a run.

Converse sat in an aisle seat roughly in the middle of the railway car. His palms perspired as he turned the pages of the small, black prayer book. It had been placed in the envelope along with his passport, the letter of pilgrimage and a typewritten sheet of instructions which included a few basic facts about Father William Wilcrist, should they be necessary. At the bottom of the page was a final order: *Commit to memory, tear up, and flush down toilet before immigration at Oldenzaal.*

The instructions were unnecessary, even distracting. Quite simply, he was to get off at Osnabrück, coincidentally taking a stroll through the railway cars twenty minutes out of a station called Rheine, leaving the suitcase behind as if he intended to return to his seat. The details of his supposedly changing trains at Hanover for Celle and the subsequent morning drive north to Bergen-Belsen could have been said in one sentence rather than the complicated paragraphs entailing deep motivations and past successes. They were irrelevant. The facts about Father William Wilcrist, however, were succinct and he had memorized them after the second reading. Wilcrist was thirty-eight years old, a graduate of Fordham with theological degrees from Catholic University in Washington, and ordained at St Ignatius in New York. He was an "activist priest" and currently assigned to the Church of the Blessed Sacrament in Los Angeles. In Valerie's words, if he was asked to recite more than that he was probably caught.

For all practical purposes he was caught now, thought Joel, gazing at the back of a man's head in the front of the car, the same man who had joined another standing by a pillar on the platform in Amsterdam. Undoubtedly that first man was now looking at the back of *his* head from a seat in the rear, mused Converse, turning another page in the prayer book. On the surface, the odds against him were overwhelming but there was a fact and a factor just below the surface. The fact was that he knew who his executioners were and they did not know he knew. The factor was a state of mind he had drawn upon in the past – he was desperate.

The train travelled north, then east; there were two stops before Oldenzaal, after which he presumed they would cross the Rhine into West Germany. They had pulled in and out of the Deventer station; that left one more, a city named Hengelo. The announcement came and Joel got out of his seat before any of the Hengelo commuters rose from theirs; he turned in the aisle and walked back to the rear of the car. As he passed the man who stood by the pillar, he saw that Aquitaine's hunter stared straight ahead, his body so rigid it barely moved with the movement of the train. Converse had seen such postures many times before, at trials and in boardrooms; they invariably belonged to insecure witnesses and unsure negotiators. The man was tense, frightened perhaps of failing an assignment or of the people who had sent him to Amsterdam – whatever it was, his anxiety was showing and Joel could use it. *He was crawling out of a deep shaft in the ground, one tenuous grasp of earth after another, the indentations preformed after nights of preparation. The wire fence was in the distance, the rain falling, the patrols concerned, anxious – frightened by every sound they could not quickly identify. He needed only one and he had it . . . he could reach the fence!*

Reach Osnabrück . . . alone.

The toilet was unoccupied; he opened the door, went inside, and took out the page of instructions. He folded it, tore it in shreds, and dropped the pieces into the bowl, pressing the foot button as he did so. They disappeared with the flush; he turned back to the door and waited.

A second announcement blared from the speakers outside as the train slowed down; the sound of gathering feet was inches away beyond the door. The train came to a stop; he could feel the vibration of moving bodies, determined commuters thinking of home and relief and undoubtedly the Dutch equivalent of a martini. The vibrations stopped; the sounds faded away. Converse opened the door no more than half an inch. The rigid hunter was not in his seat. *Now.*

Joel slid out of the door and stepped quickly into the open separation between cars, excusing himself between the stragglers getting off from the car behind, walking rapidly inside and down the aisle. As he approached the last rows he saw an empty seat – two seats, facing the platform – and swung in, sitting beside the window, his hand in front of his face, peering through his fingers.

Aquitaine's hunter raced back and forth, sufficiently aggressive to stop three men who were walking away, their backs to him; rapid apologies followed. The hunter turned to the train, the exiting possibilities exhausted. He got back on board, his face a creased map falling apart – valleys of anxiety.

More, thought Converse. *I want more, I want you stretched, as patrols before you were stretched. Until you can't stand it!*

Oldenzaal arrived, then was left behind. The train crossed the Rhine, the clattering of the bridge below like snares – hammering tympany, kettledrums to follow. The hunter had crashed the forward door open, too panicked to do anything but quickly look around and return to his companion, or to a lone suitcase, perhaps. Joel's head was below the back of the seat in front of him.

Minutes later the heavy drums came in the form of *Sonderpolizei* checking the border, scrutinizing every male of a vague description, dozens of uniformed men walking through the railway cars. They were courteous to be sure, but nevertheless they gave rise to ugly vestiges of a time past. Converse showed his passport and the letter written in German for the conscience of Germans. A policeman grimaced sadly, then nodded in acquiescence and went on to the next seat. The uniforms left; the minutes became quarter hours. He could see through the windows into the forward car; the two hunters met several rows behind where he had been sitting. Again they separated; one fore, one aft. *Now.*

Joel got up from his seat and side-stepped into the aisle, checking his schedule and bending down to look out of the darkened window, meaningless motions. But he would stay there for as long as he had to, until one of the hunters spotted him. It took less than ten seconds. As Converse pitched his head down supposedly to see a passing sign outside, he caught a glimpse of a figure moving into the upper panel of glass on the forward door. Joel stood up. The man behind the glass spun out of sight. It was the sign he was waiting for, the moment to move quickly.

He turned and walked to the rear of the car, went out the door and across the dark clattering space to the car behind. He went inside and swiftly made his way down the aisle, again to the rear and again into the next car, turning in the intervening darkness to see what he expected to see, what he wanted to see. The man was following him. *A guard was taking himself out of position in the downpour. Only seconds and he could reach the barbed wire.*

He ran through the third car aware that a number of passengers looked up at him, looked up at a running priest. Most turned in their seats to see if there was an emergency, and seeing none shook their heads in bewilderment. He reached the door, pulled it open, and stepped into the shadows, suddenly startled by what he saw, by what he physically felt. In front of him, instead of another railroad car door, the upper part of a window, there was a solid panel of heavy wood, the word *FRACHT* printed across the midsection above a large steel knob. Then he heard the announcement over the loud speakers.

"*Bad Bentheim! Nachste Station, Bad Bentheim!*"

The train was slowing down, the first of the two stops before Osnabrück. Joel moved forward into the darkest area and inched his head in view of the window behind him, confident that he would not be seen by a man facing reflected light off a panel of glass. What he saw again startled him – not by the activity, but by the *inactivity.* The hunter made no move toward the door; instead, he sat down – sat *down* facing forward, a commuter finding a more comfortable seat, nothing else on his mind. The train came to a stop, those passengers getting off forming a line in front . . . in *front.*

There had been a sign above this last door but since he could not read it, he had simply gone outside. He looked now at the exit doors; there were no handles. Obviously that incomprehensible sign had informed any who approached the door that it was not an exit. If he had been facing a trap before, he was in a cage now, a steel cage that began moving again, as the wheels gathered speed against the tracks. A racing jail from which there was no escape. Converse reached into his shirt pocket and took out his cigarettes. *He was so close to the barbed wire; he had to think!*

A rattle? A key . . . a *bolt*. The door of heavy wood with the word *FRACHT* stencilled on it opened and the figure of a stout man emerged, preceded by his stomach.

"*Eine Zigarette für Sie, während ich zum Pinkeln gehe!*" said the railroad guard, laughing, as he crossed through the short, dark corridor to the door. "*Dann ein Whisky, ja?*"

The German was going for a drink, and although he had pulled the door of his domain nearly shut, he had not closed it; he was an untroubled man, a guard with nothing he felt worth guarding. Joel pushed the heavy panel open and went inside, knowing what would happen; it *had* to happen the instant the guard walked by the hunter on his way to "ein Whisky".

There were half a dozen sealed crates and roughly ten cages holding animals – dogs mostly and several cats, cowering in corners, claws extended at the sound of growls and coughing barks. The only light came from a naked bulb swaying on a thick wire from the ceiling beyond another cage, this one built for man with wire mesh at the end of the freight car. Converse concealed himself behind a crate near the door. He reached under his priestly coat and pulled out the gun with the perforated cylinder, the silencer.

The door opened – cautiously, millimetre by millimetre – the weapon appeared before the hand or the arm. Finally there was the man, the hunter, the foot soldier from Aquitaine.

Joel fired twice, not trusting a single shot. The arm crashed back into the edge of the half-open door, the gun spinning out of the killer's hand, a single spurt of blood erupting near the executioner's wrist. Converse sprang from behind the crate – *the patrol was his, and so was the stretch of barbed wire fence! He could climb it and crawl over now! The rock had smashed the window in the barracks! The staccato barrage of machine gun fire was spraying where he was not! Seconds, only seconds, and he was out!*

Joel pinned the man to the floor, gripping the hunter's throat, his knee pressed into the executioner's chest – one enormous plunge and the soldier from Aquitaine was dead. He held the barrel of the gun against the man's temple.

"You speak any *English?*"

"Ja!" coughed the German. "*Ich spreche Englisch!*"

"*What?*"

"I . . . speak English."

"What were your orders?"

"Follow you. Only follow you. Don't shoot! I am *Angestellte!* I know not a thing!"

"A *what?*"

"A hired man!"

"*Aquitaine!*"

"*Was . . . ?*"

The man was not lying; there was too much panic in his eyes. Converse raised the gun and abruptly shoved it into the German's left eye the perforated cylinder pressed deep into the socket.

"You tell me exactly what you were told to do! The truth – and I'll know a lie – and if you lie your skull will be all over this wall! Talk to me!"

"To follow you!"

"*And?*"

"If you left the train we were to phone the *Polizei*. Wherever. Then . . . we were to kill you before they came. But I would not *do* that! I swear by my *Christ* I would *never* do that! I am a good Christian. I even love the Jews! I am unemployed, *Mein Herr!*"

Joel crashed the weapon into the man's skull – *the patrol had been taken out! He could climb the fence now!* He pulled the German behind a crate and waited. How long it was impossible to tell; his heartbeat was too rapid consider time. The railway guard came back, somewhat more drunk than sober, and took refuge behind his wire meshed office with the single light bulb.

The other cages were not so serene. The smell of human blood and sweat was more than the dogs could take; they began to react, viciousness the cousin of fear. Within minutes the railway car labelled *FRACHT* became a madhouse, the animals were now incensed – the dogs snarling, barking, hurling themselves against their cages; the cats screeching, hissing, backs arched, fur extended, provoked by the dogs. The guard was perplexed and frightened, anchoring himself to the chair in his sanctuary of wire mesh, drinking whisky from a bottle. He stared at the cages, his eyes wide within the folds of puffed flesh. Twice he looked at a glass-encased lever on the wall inches above the desk, above his hand. He had only to lift the casing and pull it.

"*Rheine! Nächste Station, Rheine!*"

The last stop before Osnabrück. Before long the German would revive and unless Joel's eyes were on him at that instant the man would scream and an emergency lever would be pulled. Too, there was another man only cars behind who was also hired to follow him, to kill him. To remain where he was any longer was to let the trap close. He had to get off.

The train stopped and Converse lunged for the door, his movement causing a dozen caged animals to vent their anger and confusion. He pushed back the bolt, opened the heavy door and raced into the forward car. He ran up the aisle – a priest perhaps on an errand of mercy – and excused himself past the departing passengers, intent only on getting off before an unconscious body was found, a lever pulled, an alarm sounded. He reached the exit and leaped from the second step to the platform; he looked around and ran into the shadows of the station. He would have to keep running.

He was free. He was alive. But he was miles away from an old woman waiting for her priest.

31

Valerie kept running, afraid to look behind but she was not a fool. She did so and saw that the Army officer was arguing with the driver of the Army car. Seconds later she looked again as she reached the corner of Madison Avenue; she tried not to panic. The officer was now running after her, shortening the distance between them with each stride. She raced across the street as the light turned, the blaring of horns signifying the anger of several drivers.

Thirty feet away a taxi heading north pulled to the kerb and a grey-haired man lethargically stretched himself out to the pavement, tired, unwilling to accept the morning. Val ran back into the street, into the traffic, and raced to the cab's outer door; she opened it and climbed in as the startled grey-haired man was accepting change.

"Hey, lady, you *crazy?*" yelled the black driver. "You're supposed to use the kerb! You'll get flattened by a bus!"

"I'm *sorry!*" cried Val, unable to control herself, sinking low and back on the seat. *What the hell?* "My husband is running up the street after me and I *will* not be hit again! I hurt. He's . . . he's an Army officer."

The grey-haired man sprang out of the cab like a decathlon contender, slamming the door behind him. The taxi driver turned around and looked at her, his large black face suspicious, curious.

"You tellin' the truth?"

"I threw up all morning from the punches last night."

"An officer? In the Army?"

"Yes! Will you please get *out* of here?" Val sank lower. "He's at the corner now! He'll cross the street – he'll see me!"

"Fret not, mam," said the driver, calmly reaching over the seat and pressing down the locks on the rear doors. "Oh, you were right on! Here he comes runnin' across like a crazy man. And would you look at them ribbons! Would you believe that horseshit – excuse me, mam. He's kind'a skinny, ain't he? Most of the real bad characters were skinny. They compensated – that's a psychiatric term, you know."

"Get out of here!"

"The law's precise, mam. It's the duty of every driver of a medallion vehicle to protect the well-being of his fare . . . And I was an infantry grunt, mam, and I've waited a hell of a long time for this particular opportunity. Having a real good reason and all that. I mean, you sure can't deny the words you said to me." The driver climbed out of the cab; he matched his face; he was a very large man, indeed. Val watched in horrified astonishment as the black walked around the car to the kerb and shouted.

"Hey, Captain! Over here, on the sidewalk! You lookin' for a very pretty lady? Like maybe your wife?"

"*What?*" The officer ran up·on the pavement to the black man.

"Well, Captain-baby, I'm afraid I can't salute 'cause my uniform's in the attic – if I had an attic – but I want you to know that this search-and-destroy has successfully been completed. Would you step over to my jeep, sir?"

The officer started to run toward the taxi, but he was suddenly grabbed by the driver who spun him around and punched him first in the stomach, then brought his knee crashing up into the army man's groin, and finally "completed" the assignment by hammering a huge fist into the officer's mouth. Val gasped; blood spread over the captain's entire face as he fell to the pavement. The driver ran back to the cab, climbed in, shut the door and pulled the gear; the taxi shot forward in the traffic.

"Lawdy, *lawdy!*" said the driver in a caricatured dialect. "That felt *real* good! Is there an address, mam? The meter's running."

"I . . . I'm not sure."

"Let's start with the basics. Where do you want to go?"

"To a telephone . . . Why did you *do that?*"

"That's my business, not yours."

"You're *sick!* You could have been arrested!"

"For what? Protecting a fare from assault? That bad character was actually runnin' toward my cab and the vibes were not good, not good at all. Also there weren't no cops around."

"I presume you were in Vietnam," said Val, after a period of silence, looking at the large head of black hair in front of her.

"Ohm yes, I was accorded that privilege. Very scenic, mam."

"What did you think of General Delavane? General George Marcus Delavane?"

The cab suddenly, violently swerved as the driver gripped the wheel and slammed his heavy foot on the brake, causing the taxi to bolt to a stop, throwing Val into the rim of the front seat. The huge black head whipped around, the coal-black eyes filled with fury and loathing and that deep unmistakable core of fear Valerie had seen so many times in Joel's eyes. The driver swallowed, his piercing stare somehow losing strength, turning inward, the fear taking over. He turned back to the wheel and answered simply. "I didn't do much thinking about the General mam. What's the address, Mrs? The meter's running."

"I don't know . . . A telephone, I have to get to a telephone. Will you wait?"

"Do you have money? Or did the captain take it all? There are limits to my concern, lady. I don't get no compensation for good deeds."

"I have money. You'll be well paid."

"Show me a bill."

Valerie reached into her purse and pulled out a hundred dollars. "Will that do?" she asked.

"It's fine, but don't do that with every cab you want in a hurry. You could end up in Bed-Stuy a damn good lookin' corpse."

"I don't want to believe that."

"Oh, my, we have a liberal! Stick to it, mam, until they stick it to you. Me, I want 'em all to *fry!* Your kind don't really get it – *we* do. You only get the *periphery*, you *dig?* A couple of rapes in the classy suburbs – and some of *them* might be open to dispute – and a few heists of silver and jewellery – *hell*, you're covered by insurance! Where I come from we're covered by a gun under the pillow, and God help the son of a bitch who tries to take it from me."

"A telephone, please."

"Your meter, lady."

They stopped at a booth on the corner of Madison and 78th Street. Valerie got out, opening her purse and removing the page of St Regis stationery with the Air Force telephone number. She inserted a coin, and dialled.

"Air Force, Recruit Command, Denver," announced the female operator.

"I wondered if you could help me, miss," said Val, her eyes darting about at the traffic, looking for a roving brown sedan with *US Army* printed across its doors. "I'm trying to locate an officer, a relative, actually."

"One minute, please. I'll transfer you."

"Personnel, Denver Units, came a second voice, now male. "Sergeant Porter."

"Sergeant, I'm trying to locate an officer," repeated Valerie. "A relative of mine who left word with an aunt he wanted to reach me."

"Where in Colorado, mam?"

"Well, I'm not sure."

"The Springs? The Academy? Lowrey field or possibly Cheyenne Mountain?"

"I don't know that he *is* in Colorado, Sergeant."

"Why did you call Denver then?"

"You were in the telephone book."

"I see." The Army man paused, then continued, his words spoken by rote. "And this officer left word that he wanted to reach you?"

"Yes."

"But he didn't leave an address or a telephone number."

"If he did, my aunt lost it. She's quite elderly."

"The procedure is as follows, miss. If you will write a letter to the MPC – Military Personnel Centre – at the Randolph Air Force Base, San Antonio, Texas, stating your request and the officer's name and rank, the letter will be processed."

"I don't have time, Sergeant! I travel a great deal . . . I'm calling from an airport now, as a matter of fact."

"I'm sorry, miss, those are the regulations."

"I'm not a "Miss" and my cousin's a general and he really does want to speak to me! I just want to know where he is, and if you can't tell me, certainly you can call him and give him my name. I'll call *you* back with a number where he can reach me. That's reasonable, isn't it, Sergeant. Frankly, this is an emergency."

"A general, mam?"

"Yes, Sergeant Potter. A General Abbott."

"Sam Abbott? I mean, Brigadier General Samuel Abbott?"

"That's the one, Sergeant Potter."

"Porter, mam."

"I'll remember that."

"Well, I can't see any security breach here, miss – mam. Everybody knows where General Abbott is stationed. He's a popular officer and in the newspapers a lot."

"Where is that, Sergeant? I'll personally tell him you've been most helpful – to both of us."

"Nellis Air Force Base in Nevada, mam, just outside Las Vegas. He commands the advanced tactical manoeuvre squadrons. All the squadron commanders get their final training at Nellis. He's the *man* . . . May I have your name, please?"

"Oh, good Lord! There's the last boarding call for my plane! Thank you, Sergeant." Valerie hung up the phone, her eyes still scanning the street, trying to decide what to do – whether to call Sam now or wait. Suddenly she realized she could *not* call; it would mean using a credit card, origin of call and destination listed. She went out of the booth and returned to the taxi.

"Lady, I'd just as soon get out of here, if you don't mind," said the driver, a quiet urgency in his voice.

"What's the matter?"

"I keep a police scanner in my cab in case there's problems in my neighbourhood, and I just heard the word. An army captain was clobbered on Fifty-fifth and Madison by a black driver of a taxi heading north. Lucky for me they didn't get the licence or the company, but the description's pretty good. "A big black son of a bitch with a size twelve fist", was the way those mothers put it."

"Let's go," said Val. "I hate to say this, and I mean that, but I can't get involved." The cab sped forward, the driver turning east on Eighty-first Street. "Is . . . my husband pressing charges?" she asked, suddenly bewildered.

"No, I'm off the hook there," replied the driver. "He must have punched you real bad. He just fled and had nuthin' to say. Bless his white heart. Where to?"

"Let me think."

"It's your meter."

She had to get to Las Vegas but the idea of going back to Kennedy or LaGuardia Airports frightened her. They seemed too logical, too easily anticipated. Then she remembered. About five or six years ago she and Joel were week-ending with friends in Short Hills, New Jersey, when Joel got a call from Nathan Simon, telling him he had to fly to Los Angeles on Sunday for a Monday morning meeting. All the legal papers would be sent to the Beverly Hills Hotel by air express. Joel had taken the plane from Newark Airport.

"Can you drive me to Newark?"

"I can drive you to Alaska, lady, but *Newark?*"

"The airport."

"That's better. It's one of the best. I guess Newark's okay, too. I got a brother there and, hell, he's still alive. I'll swing through the Park at Sixty-sixth and head down to the Lincoln Tunnel. Do you mind if I turn on the scanner again?"

"No, go right ahead."

The voices went in and out, then the driver pushed a button and the phrases were steady. *"Incident at Fifty-fifth and Madison is a negative. Precinct Ten has called it off as the victim refused assistance and did not identify himself. So patrols, onward and upward. We helps them what helps themselves. On, brothers."*

"Oh, he's a *brother!*" shouted the driver in relief, as he turned off the radio. "You catch that 'incident is a negative?' They could'a used him in 'Nam, in those

400

big body-count press conferences . . . Come to think of it, he was probably there – not with the press, just one of the bodies. They never did get it right."

Valerie leaned forward on the seat. "I asked you about . . . Nam. About General Delavane. Would you tell me about him?"

It was nearly a minute before the black replied, and when he did so, his voice was soft, even mellifluous. And somewhere at the base of it was abject defeat. "My driver's identification is lookin' at you, lady. I'm driving you to Newark Airport – that's what you're payin' for, and that's what you'll get."

The rest of the ride was made in silence, an oppressive sense of fear pervading the cab. *After all these years*, thought Val. *Oh, God.*

They hit heavy traffic at the Tunnel and then on the Turnpike; it was the start of the weekend and vacationers were heading for the Jersey shore. The airport was worse; it was jammed, cars backed up for a quarter of a mile in the departure lanes. Finally, they edged up into a parking space and Valerie got out. She paid the driver a hundred dollars above the fare and thanked him. "You've been much more than helpful, you know that. I'll never really know why but I'll think about it."

"Like I said, it's my business. I got my reasons."

"I wish I could say something, something that could help."

"Don't try, lady. The green is enough."

"No, it's not."

"Sure it is until something better comes along, and that ain't gonna be in my lifetime . . . You take care, Mrs, I think you got bigger problems than most of us. You said too much, which I don't recall, of course."

Valerie turned and went into the terminal. The lines in front of the counters were horrendous and before joining one she had to know which one. Twenty minutes later she was in the proper line and nearly an hour after that she had a ticket to Las Vegas on American's 12.35 flight, another hour before boarding. It was time to see if it all made sense. If Sam Abbott made sense, or whether she was grasping desperately at a man she once remembered who might not be that man any longer. She had exchanged $20.00 in bills for two $10.00 rolls of quarters. She hoped it would be enough. She took an escalator up to the first floor and went to a telephone at the far end of the wide corridor past the shops. Nevada information gave her the number of main switchboard at Nellis Air Force Base. She dialled and asked to be put through to Brigadier General Samuel Abbott.

"I don't know if he's on the base yet," said the operator.

"Oh?" she had forgotten. There was a three hour time difference.

"Just a minute, he's checked in. Early morning flight schedule."

"General Abbott's office."

"May I speak to the General, please. The name is Parquette, Mrs Virginia Parquette."

"May I ask what this is in reference to?" asked the secretary. "The general's extremely busy and is about to head down to the field."

"I'm a cousin he hasn't seen in a long time, actually. There's been a tragedy in the family."

"Oh, I'm terribly sorry."

"Please tell him I'm on the line. He may not recall my name; it's been so many years. But you might remind him that in the old days we had some wonderful dinners in New York. It's really most urgent. I wish someone else were making this call, but I'm afraid I was elected."

"Yes . . . yes, of course."

The waiting put Valerie in the last circle of hell. Finally there was a click, followed by the voice she remembered.

"Virginia . . . Parquette?"

"Yes."

"*Ginny* – from New York? Dinner in New York?"

"Yes."

"You're the wife, not the sister."

"*Yes!*"

"Give me a number. I'll call you back in ten minutes."

"It's a pay phone."

"*Stay* there. The number."

She gave it to him and hung up, frightened, wondering what she had done, but knowing that she could not have done anything else. She sat in the plastic chair by the phone, watching the escalators, looking at the people going into and walking out of the various shops, the bar, the fast-food restaurant. She tried not to look at her watch; twelve minutes passed. The phone rang.

"Yes?"

"Valerie . . ."

"*Yes!*"

"I wanted to get out of the office – too many interruptions. Where are you? I know the area code's New Jersey."

"Newark Airport. I'm on the twelve-thirty flight to Las Vegas. I've got to see you."

"I tried to call *you*. Talbot's secretary gave me your number."

"*When?*"

"Starting two days ago. I was in the Mojave on manoeuvres and too bushed to turn on a radio – we didn't have newspapers. A man answered and when he said you weren't there I hung up."

"That was Roger, Joel's father. He's dead."

"I know. They say it might have been suicide."

"*No!* . . . I've seen him, Sam. I've seen Joel! It's all lies!"

"That's what we have to talk about," said the general. "Call me when you get in. Same name. I don't want to pick you up at the airport; too many people know me over there. I'll figure out a place where we can meet."

"*Thank* you, Sam!" said Valerie. "You're all we have left."

"We?"

"For the time being, yes. I'm all *he* has left."

Converse watched from the far dark corner of the railroad station as the train for Osnabrück started up, its huge wheels pressing into the tracks, groaning for momentum. At any moment he expected whistles to pierce the quiet night and the train to stop, a bewildered half-drunken guard running from the freight car, screaming.

None of it happened. Why? Was the man more than half drunk? Had the sounds of the enraged animals driven him further into the bottle, strengthening his resolve to remain in the safety of his cage? Had he seen only a blur racing to the door in the dim light, or perhaps nothing, an unconscious body subsequently not discovered? Then Joel saw that there was another possibility, a brutal one. He could see a figure running forward through the second to last car, twice lunging between the seats, his face pressed against the glass. Moments later the man was leaning out above the lower door of the first exit, the steps below blocked off by the heavy solid gate. In his hand was a gun, held laterally across his forehead as he squinted against the station lights, peering into the shadows.

Suddenly the killer made his decision. He gripped the metal rim and leaped over the guardrail, dropping to the ground, rolling over in the gravel away from the gathering speed of the train. The hunter from Aquitaine was in panic; he dared not lose the quarry, dared not fail to carry out his assignment.

Converse spun around the corner and raced along the dark side of the building to a parking area. The passengers who had got off the train were starting automobiles or climbing into them; two couples were chatting on the near platform, obviously waiting to be picked up. A car came curving in off the road beyond; the two men waved and in moments all four were inside, laughing as the car sped away. The parking area was deserted, the station shut down for the night. A single floodlight from the roof illuminated the emptiness, a border of tall trees beyond the wide expanse of coarse gravel gave the appearance of a huge impenetrable wall.

Staying as best he could in the shadows, Joel darted from one space of darkness to another, remaining in the last, a solid, indented arch at the end of the building, his back pressed into the brick. He waited, his hand gripping the gun at his side, wondering if he would have to use it, even perhaps if he would have a chance to use it. He had been lucky on the train and he knew it; he was no match for professional killers. And no matter how strongly he tried to convince himself, he was not in the jungle a lifetime ago, not the younger man he had been then. But when he thought about it – as he was thinking about it now – those memories were all he had to guide him. He ducked out of the shadowed arch and quickly dashed to the corner.

The explosion came, blowing out the stone to the left of his head! He lunged to his right, rolling on the gravel, rising, and running away from the spill of the floodlight. Three more shattering explosions tore up the rock and earth around his feet. He reached a dark row of foliage and dived into the bushes, suddenly, instinctively, knowing exactly what he had to do!

"*Augh! Aughhh.*" His final scream ended in expelled agony.

He then crawled through the undergrowth as fast as he could penetrate the tangled nets of scraping greenery. He was at least ten feet away from where he had shouted; he stopped and pivoted on his knees, remaining still, facing the floodlit expanse beyond the bushes.

It happened, as it had happened before when three children in official pyjamas had killed another child indelicately in the jungle. Anxious men were drawn to the last sounds they heard – as this hunter from Aquitaine was drawn now. The man stalked out of the darkness of the railroad station's rear platform, his gun extended, held steady with both hands. He walked directly, cautiously to that small section in the overgrowth where the two screams had come from.

Converse scratched the ground silently until he found a rock larger than his fist. He gripped it, waiting, staring. In his throat he could feel the drumming in his chest. The killer was within eight feet of the border of greenery. Joel lobbed the rock, arcing it in the air to his right.

The crunching thud was loud and Aquitaine's soldier crouched, firing one round after another – *two, three, four!* Converse raised his weapon and pulled the trigger twice. The man spun to his left, gasping, the start of a roar aborted as he clutched his upper stomach and fell to the ground.

There was no time to think or feel or consider what had happened. Joel crawled out to the gravel, raced over to his would-be executioner, grabbing him by the arms and dragging him back into the bushes. Still, he had to find out. He knelt down and held his fingers against the base of the man's throat. He was dead, another scout taken out in the war of the modern Aquitaine, the military confederation of George Marcus Delavane.

There was no one around – if there had been the gunshots would have provoked screams and running feet; the police would have been summoned; they would have been there by now. How far away was Osnabrück? He had read the schedule and tried to figure out the times, but everything had happened so swiftly, so brutally, he had not absorbed what he read. It was less than an hour, that much he knew. Somehow he had to get word to the station at Osnabrück. Christ, *how?*

He walked out on the platform, glancing up at the sign: *Rheine*. It was a start; he had only counted the stops, not the names. Then he saw it – a glow of light? There was something in the distance – above the ground, high above – with lights on the inside. a tower! He had seen them dozens of times in Switzerland and France . . . signal depots! They dotted the Eurorail landscape, controlling the trains that sped across their sectors. He started running along the tracks, suddenly wondering what he looked like. His hat was gone, his clothes soiled, but his clerical collar was still in place – he was still a priest. He would *be* a priest.

He reached the base of the tower, brushed off his clothes, and tried to smooth his hair. He composed himself and began climbing the metal steps. At the top he saw that the steel door to the tower itself was bolted, the inch-thick bulletproof glass a sign of the terrorist times; speeding trains were vulnerable targets. He approached the door and rapped on the metal frame. Three men were inside, huddled over electronic consoles; and elderly man turned from the numerous green screens and came to the door. He peered through the glass and crossed himself, but was not sufficiently religious to open the door. Instead. there was a sudden echoing sound projected into the air. and the man's voice emerged from a speaker.

"*Was ist, Hochwürden?*"

"I don't speak German. Do you speak English?"

"*Engländer?*"

"Yes – *ja.*"

The old man turned to his associates and shouted something. Both shook their heads, but one held up his hand, and came to the door.

"*Ich spreche* ... a little, Mister *Engländer. Nicht* come enter here, *verstehen?*"

"I have to call Osnabrück! A woman is waiting for me ... a *Frau!*"

"Ohh? *Hochwürden! Fine Frau?*"

"No, *no!* You don't understand! Can't anybody here speak *English?*"

"*Sie sprechen Deutsch?*"

"No!"

"*Warten Sie.*" said the third man from the console. There was a rapid exchange between the two men. The one who spoke "a little" turned back to the door.

"*Eine Kirche,*" said the man groping for words. "Church! *Ein Pfarrer* – priest! *Er spricht nur Englisch. Drie* ... *t'ee strattes* ... *there!*" The German pointed to his left; Joel looked down over his shoulder. There was a street in the distance. He understood; there was a church three blocks away and a priest who spoke English, presumably a priest who had a telephone.

"The train to Osnabrück. *When?* When does it *get* there?" Converse pointed to his watch. "When? *Osnabrück?*"

The man looked over at the console, seeing what, Converse could not tell. He turned back to Joel and smiled; why he smiled was beyond understanding. "*Zwölf Minuten, Hochwürden!*"

"How? *What?*"

"*Zwölf* ... Tvelf."

"*Twelve?*"

"*Ja.*"

Converse turned and clattered down the steps; on the ground he ran as fast as he could toward the street lamps in the distance. Once there, he raced in the middle of the street, clutching his chest, vowing for the five hundredth time to give up cigarettes. He had persuaded Val to throw them away; why hadn't he taken his own advice'? He was invulnerable, that's why. Or did he simply care for her more than he cared for himself? *Enough!* Where was the goddamned *church?*

It was there, on the right. A small church with fake spires. a silly-looking church with what looked like a decorated Quonset hut for a rectory beside it. Joel ran up the short path to the door, a door with a hideously bejewelled crucifix in the centre – a rhinestone Jesus; rockalong with Christ – and knocked. Moments later an overweight, cherubic-looking man with very little white hair – albeit perfectly groomed – Opened the door.

"*Ah, Guten Tag, Herr Kollege.*"

"Forgive me." said Converse, out of breath, "I don't speak German. I was told you speak English."

"Ah, yes, indeed, I should hope so. I spent my novitiate in the Mother Country – as opposed to the Fatherland – you understand the difference in gender, of course. Come in, come *in!* A visit from a fellow priest calls for a *Schnapps.* 'A touch of wine' sounds better, doesn't it? Again the Mother Country – so soft, so understanding. My, you're an attractive young man!"

"Not so young, Father," said Joel, stepping inside.

"That's relative, isn't it?" The German priest walked unsteadily into what was obviously his living room. Again there were jewelled figures on the walls, the cheap stones set in black velvet, the faces of the saints unmistakably feminine. "What would you like? I have Sherry and Muscatel and for rare occasions a Port I've been saving for very special visitors . . . Who sent you? That wicked novice from Lengerich?"

"I need *help,* Father."

"Great Jesus, who *doesn't?* Is this to be a confessional? If so, for God's sake give me until morning. I love the Lord my God with all my soul and all my strength – and if there are sins of the flesh – they are *Satan's.* Not I, but the *Archangel of Darkness!"*

The man was drunk; he fell over a hassock, tumbling to the floor. Converse ran to him and lifted him up, lowering him into a chair – a chair by the only telephone in the room.

"Please understand me, Father. Or don't *mis*understand me. I have to reach a woman who's waiting for me at Osnabrück. It's *important!"*

"A woman? *Satan!* He is *Lucifer* with the eyes of fire! You think you're better than *me?"*

"Not at all. *Please.* I need *help!"*

It took ten minutes of pleading, but finally the priest calmed down and got on the telephone. He identified himself as a man of God and moments later Joel heard the words that allowed him to breathe steadily again.

"Frau Geyner? Es tut mir leid . . ." The old priest and the old woman talked for several minutes, the priest nodding for the last thirty seconds. He hung up and turned to Converse. "She waited for you," he said, frowning in bewilderment. "She thought you might have got off in the freight yards . . . What freight yards?"

"I understand."

"I do not. But she knows the way here and will pick you up in thirty minutes or so . . . You have sobered me, Father. Was I disgraceful?"

"Not at all," said Joel. "You welcomed a man in trouble, there's nothing wrong with that."

"Let's have a drink. Forget *Schnapps* and 'a glass of wine'; they're a bore, aren't they? I have some American bourbon in the refrigerator. You *are* American, are you not?"

"Yes, and a glass of bourbon would be just fine."

"Good! Follow me into my humble kitchen. It's right through here, mind the sequinned curtain, dear boy. It *is* too much, isn't it? . . . Oh, well, for all of that

406

– whatever it is – I'm a good man. I believe that. I give comfort."

"I'm sure you do."

"Where were you schooled, Father," asked the priest.

"Catholic University in Washington," replied Converse, pleased with himself that he remembered and answered so quickly.

"Good Lord, I was there *myself!*" exclaimed the German prelate. "They shunted me around,, you understand. Do you remember what's his name."

Oh, my God! thought Joel.

Frau Hermione Geyner arrived and took Converse in tow – commandeered him, in fact. She was a small woman, far older than Joel had imagined, her face withered, reminding him of the woman in the Amsterdam station . . . dominated by wide, intense eyes that shot out bolts of electricity. He got into the car as she closed the door for him, pushing the lock in place. She climbed behind the wheel and sped up the street, reaching what had to be sixty miles an hour in a matter of seconds.

"I appreciate everything you're doing for me," said Converse, bracing his feet against the floor.

"It is *nothing!*" exclaimed the old woman. "I have myself taken out officers from airplanes that crashed in Bremerhaven and Stuttgart and Mannheim! I spat in *soldiers'* eyes, and crashed through barricades! I never failed! The pigs could not touch me!"

"I only meant that you're saving my life, and I want you to know I'm grateful. I'm aware that Valerie – your niece, and my . . . my former wife – told you I didn't do the things they said I did, and she was right. I didn't."

"*Ach*, Valerie! A sweet child, but not very reliable, *ja?* You got rid of her, *ja?*"

"That's not exactly the way it happened."

"How *could* she be?" continued Hermione Geyner, as if he had not spoken. "She is an artist and we all know how unstable they are. And, of course, her father was a Frenchman. I ask you, *Mein Herr*, could she have a greater disadvantage? *Franzose!* The worms of Europe! As untrustworthy as their wine, which is mostly in their stomachs. They're drunkards, you know. It's in their blood."

"But you believed her where I was concerned. You're helping me, you *are* saving my life."

"Because we *could, Mein Herr!* We *knew* we could!"

Stunned, Joel stared at the road ahead, at the rapidly oncoming curves, taken as the tyres screeched. Hermione Geyner was not at all what he expected, but then nothing was any more. She was so old and it was late at night and she had been through a great deal these last two days; it must have taken its toll on her. Old prejudices came to the surface when very old people were tired. Perhaps in the morning they could have a clear-headed conversation. The morning – it was the start of the second day and Valerie had promised to call him in Osnabrück with news of Sam Abbott and the progress she was making to reach the pilot. She *had* to make that call! Sam had to be told about the strange language Joel had heard from an old man in Amsterdam, where a word meaning one thing, also meant something else entirely. Assassination! *Val, call me. For God's sake, call me!*

Converse looked out of the window. The minutes passed, the countryside peaceful, the silence awkward.

"Here we are *Mein Herr!*" shouted Hermione Geyner, turning crazily into the drive that led to a large, old, three storey house set back off the country road. From what Converse could see, it was a house that once had a certain majesty, if only by its size and the proliferation of roofed windows and gables everywhere. In the moonlight now, the majesty was gone; like its owner, it was very old, its grandeur frayed and shabby.

They walked up the worn wooden steps of the huge porch and crossed to the door. Frau Geyner knocked rapidly, insistently; in seconds an old woman – another old woman – opened it, nodding solemnly as they went inside.

"It's very lovely," began Joel. "I want you to know . . ."

"Sshh!" Hermione Geyner dropped her car keys in a red-lacquered bowl on a hall table and held up her hand. "*Diese Richtung!*"

Converse followed her to a pair of double doors; she opened them and Joel walked in behind her. He stopped, confusion and astonishment coming together. For in front of them in the large Victorian room with the subdued lighting was a row of high-backed chairs and seated in each was an old woman – nine old women! Mesmerized, he looked closely at them. Some smiled weakly, several trembled with age and infirmity, obviously senile; a few wore stern, intense expressions, and one seemed to be humming to herself.

There was an eruption of fragile applause – hands thin and veined, others swollen with flesh, flesh striking flesh with obvious effort. Two chairs had been placed in front of the women; Valerie's aunt indicated that they were for Joel and herself. They sat down as the applause dwindled off to silence.

"*Meine Schwestern Soldaten,*" cried Hermione Geyner, rising. "*Heute Nacht . . .*"

The old woman spoke for nearly ten minutes, interrupted occasionally by scattered applause and audible expressions of wonder and respect. Finally, she sat down, acknowledging the barely animated ovation. "*Nun. Fragen!*"

As if in reply, the women one after another began to speak – frail, halting voices for the most part, yet several were emphatic, almost hostile. And then Converse realized that most were looking at him. They were asking him questions, one or two crossing themselves as they spoke, as if the fugitive they had saved were actually a priest.

"Come, *Mein Herr!*" cried Hermione Geyner. "Answer the ladies. They deserve the courtesy of your replies."

"I can't answer what I can't understand," protested Joel quietly.

Suddenly, without any indication or sign of warning, Valerie's aunt rose quickly out of the chair, turned to him and struck him across the face. "Such evasive tactics will not serve you *here!*" she screamed, striking him again, the ring on her finger breaking his skin. "We know you understand every word that's been spoken! Why do you Czechs and Poles always think you can fool us? You *collaborated!* We have *proof!*"

The old women began to shout, their lined, contorted faces filled with hate. Converse got to his feet; he understood. Hermione Geyner and everyone in that

408

room was mad or senile or both. They were living in a violent time that was forty years in the past.

And then, as if on some demented cue, a door opened across the room and two men came out, one in a raincoat, his right hand in his pocket, some kind of package in his left. The second man held a topcoat over his arm, that arm extended, a weapon without doubt concealed under the fabric. And then a third man appeared and Joel closed his eyes, pressing them shut, the pain in his chest unbearable. The third man had a bandage across his forehead, his arm in a sling. Converse had caused those wounds; he had last seen the man in a freight car filled with incensed animals on a train.

The first man came up to him and held out the package. It was a thick manila envelope with no stamps on the cover. It was the brief he had sent to Nathan Simon in New York.

"General Leifhelm sends you his regards, even his respects," said the man, pronouncing the word general with the hard German *G*.

32

Peter Stone watched as the CIA-approved doctor put the third and final stitch into the corner of the Army officer's mouth as the captain sat straining in the chair.

"The bridge will have to be repaired," said the doctor. "I have a man in the laboratory who'll do it in a few hours and a dentist on Seventy-second Street; he'll do the rest. I'll call you later when I've made the arrangements."

"Son of a *bitch!*" roared the captain, as loud as he could with half his mouth novacained. "He was a tank, a fucking black *tank!* He couldn't have been working for her, he was just a goddamned cab driver! Why the *hell?*"

"Maybe you triggered him," said the civilian, walking away, reading several pages of notes. "It happens."

"*What* happens?" yelled the officer.

"Cut it out, captain. You'll break the stitches." The doctor held up a hypodermic needle; it was a threat.

"Okay, okay." The officer spoke in a softer voice. "What does 'trigger' mean in that esoteric language of yours?"

"It's perfectly clear English." Stone turned to the doctor. "You know I'm not employed any longer, so you'd better give me a bill."

"When you're in town a dinner will do. The lab and the dentist are different, though. I'd suggest cash. And get him out of uniform."

"Will do."

"What does . . . ?" The captain stopped, seeing the civilian's hand held unobtrusively up in front of his chest.

The doctor put his instruments in the black bag and went to the door. "By the way, Stone," he said turning, addressing the former CIA agent, "thanks for the Albanian. His wife is spending Moscow's roubles like mad for every ache I can find a name for."

"The ache is her husband. He has an apartment in DC she doesn't know about and some very strange sex habits."

"I'll never tell."

The doctor left and Stone turned back to the captain. "When you're with men like that, don't say any more than you have to and that includes questions. They don't want to hear and they don't want to know."

"Sorry. What did you mean – *I* triggered that hulk?"

"Come on. An attractive woman being chased down the street by a be-ribboned Army officer. How many memories – black memories – do you think are out there with less than fondness for your ilk?"

"Ilk? I never thought of myself as an ilk, but I see what you mean . . . You were on the phone when I got here, and then there were two other calls. What is it? Any line on the Converse woman?"

"No." Stone again looked down at his notes, shuffling the pages. "We can assume she came back to reach someone – someone she and her ex-husband trust."

"He knows his way around Washington. Maybe someone on the Hill, or even in the administration, or State."

"I don't think so. If he knew anyone like that and thought his story would get out before his head was shot off, he would have surfaced days ago. Remember he's been tried, convicted, and condemned. Can you think of anyone in Washington who wouldn't play it – play *him* strictly by the rules? He's contaminated. Too many authoritative sources have confirmed it, even diagnosed the disease."

"And by now he's learned what we found out months ago. You don't know where they are or who you're talking to."

"Or whom they've hired," added Stone. "Or whom they've blackmailed into doing what they want without giving away any trade secrets." The civilian sat down opposite the Army officer. "But a couple of other things have fallen into place. We're getting a pattern and a few additional names. If we could pull Converse out and combine what he's learned with what we've got . . . it might just possibly be enough."

"*What?*" The captain shot forward in the chair.

"Take it easy. I said just possibly. I've been calling in some old debts and if we could put it all together, there are one or two left I can trust."

"That's why we called *you* in," said the officer quietly. "Because you know what to do, we don't . . . What have you got?"

"To begin with, have you ever heard of an actor named Caleb Dowling – actually, it's Calvin but that's not important except for the computers."

"I know who he is. He plays the father on a television show called *Santa Fe*. Don't shout it from the rooftops, but my wife and I watch it now and then. What about him?"

Stone looked at his watch. "He'll be here in a few minutes."

"No kidding? I'm impressed."

"You may be more impressed after we've talked to him."

"Jesus, fill me in!"

"It's one of those odd breaks we all look for that seem to come out of left field but are perfectly logical. It's the timing that's not logical . . . Dowling was in Bonn filming a picture and struck up a friendship with Peregrine. American celebrity, *et cetera*. He also met Converse on a plane and got him a hotel room when they were tough to find. Most significant, Dowling was the initial contact between Peregrine and Converse – which didn't work out because Fitzpatrick stepped in."

"So?"

"When Peregrine was killed, Dowling called the embassy a number of times trying to get an appointment with the acting-ambassador, but he was put on hold. Finally he sent a note to Peregrine's secretary saying he had to see her, that it was important. The secretary met with him and this Dowling dropped a clap of thunder in her lap. Apparently he and Peregrine had an agreement that if Converse called the embassy and contact was to be made, Dowling would go along. He didn't think Peregrine would go back on his word. Secondly, Peregrine told Dowling that something was rotten in the embassy ranks, some very odd behaviour. One incident Dowling witnessed himself. He said there were too many things that didn't make sense – from Converse's sane and lucid conversations to the fact that he, Dowling, hadn't been officially questioned, as if people were avoiding one of the last people to see Converse. The bottom line was that he didn't think Converse had anything to do with Peregrine's murder. The secretary damn near fainted but told him he would be contacted. She knew the Agency's Station Chief in Bonn and called him . . . So did I, two days ago, telling him I was brought in deep-down by State."

"He confirmed all of this?"

"Yes. He called Dowling in, listened to him, and has begun digging himself. He's coming up with names, one of which we know but there'll be others. I was on the phone with him when you got here. Dowling flew in yesterday; he's at the Pierre and will be here by eleven-thirty."

"That's movement," said the captain, nodding. "Anything else?"

"Two other things. You know how stymied we were when Judge Anstett caught it and how strong the case was made for a mob killing. Hell, we weren't even sure why Halliday used Anstett in the first place. Well, the computer boys at the Army data banks have come up with the answer. It goes back to October 1944. Anstett was a legal officer in Bradley's first Army, where Delavane held a battalion command. Delavane railroaded a sergeant who'd cracked through a court martial. The charge was desertion under fire, and Colonel Delavane wanted an example both for his own troops and the Germans, to let the first know they were being led by a ramrod, and the second that they were fighting one. The verdict was guilty, the sentence execution."

"Oh, my God," exclaimed the Army officer. "Slovic all over again."

"Exactly. Except that a lowly lieutenant named Anstett heard about it and came rolling in with all his legal barrels smoking. By using psychiatric evaluation reports he not only got the sergeant sent home for treatment, but literally turned the proceedings around and put Delavane himself on trial. Using the same kind of psychological evaluations – stress mainly – he called into question Delavane's fitness for command. It damned near ruined an illustrious military career, and would have if it hadn't been for the colonel's friends in the War Department. They buried the report so well it was under another Delavane's name and wasn't picked up until all the records were computerized in the "sixties."

"That's one hell of an explanation, Stone."

"It's only part of it," said the civilian, shaking his head. "I didn't explain Anstett's killing itself. And make no mistake, it was the Mafia down to the man with the gun." Stone paused and turned a page. "So there had to be a connection somewhere, somehow a link, probably going back years. The boys with the discs looked farther and I think we've got it. Guess who was Colonel Delavane's chief aide in the First Army? No, don't bother, you couldn't. He was a Captain Parelli, Mario Alberto Parelli."

"Good Christ! The senator?"

"The five-term senator, thirty years in that august body. Up-from-the-boots-traps Mario, with a slight push from the GI Bill, some early benefactors and a few lucrative legal retainers."

"Wow . . . , said the captain softly, without enthusiasm as he leaned back in the chair. "That's pretty heavy, isn't it?"

"It's there. It fits. And I don't mind telling now that in "sixty-two and three, during the let's-get-Fidel days, Parelli was a frequent visitor at the White House, courtesy of both the Kennedy boys."

"Even in the Senate. He's one of the biggest cannons on the Hill."

"While you're staring, let me give you the last item. We've found Commander Fitzpatrick."

"*What?*"

"At least we know where he is," completed Stone. "As to whether we can bring him out, or even want to try, that's another question."

Valerie got in the cab at McCarran Airport in Las Vegas and gave the driver the address of a restaurant on Route 93, repeated twice by Sam Abbott over the phone. The driver looked at her in his rearview mirror, creases across his forehead. Val was used to men scrutinizing her; she was neither flattered nor annoyed any more. Frankly, she was just bored by the childishness of it all, by the fantasies of grown up children abusing themselves with their eyes.

"Are you sure, miss?" asked the driver.

"I beg your pardon?"

"That isn't a restaurant – like I mean a *restaurant*. It's a diner, a pit stop for trucks."

"It's where I wish to go," said Val coolly.

"Sure, okay, fine." The taxi pulled out into the departing traffic.

The driver was right. A half acre of asphalt surrounded the long, low, L-shaped diner, housing a dozen huge trucks that dwarfed the cars, the latter parked at respectful distances from their mammoth cousins. Val paid the driver and went inside; she looked around and walked past the cashier's counter toward the L-shaped section. Sam had told her he would be in one of the booths in that area.

He was, at the rear of the second aisle. As Valerie approached she looked at the man she had not seen in nearly seven years. He had not changed much; the brown hair had a fringe of grey around the temples, but the strong relaxed face was not very different – perhaps the eyes were a little deeper, a few more lines at the sides and the cheekbones a touch more pronounced. It was a better face for a portrait now, she thought; the character beneath was emerging. Their eyes met and the brigadier general got out of the booth, his clothes denying his rank and profession. He was dressed in an open sports shirt, tan summer slacks and dark loafers. He was somewhat shorter than Joel, but not much. He was a welcome sight; it was in his grey eyes.

"*Val*." Abbott held her briefly, obviously not wanting to call attention to them.

"You look well, Sam," she said, sitting down across from him, putting the carry-on case beside her.

"You look merely outstanding, which is military for all those other adjectives." Abbott smiled. "It's funny, but I come out here a lot because no one pays any attention to me, so I thought, hell, it's the perfect place. I should have remembered – you walk through that arcade of gorillas and eggs get put in ears with coffee spoons."

"Thanks. I could use some confidence."

"I could probably use a strong alibi. If someone does recognize me, word will go back that the brigadier's pulling outside duty."

"You're *married*, Sam?"

"Five years ago. Late but with all the fixings. A lovely bride and two beguiling daughters."

"I'm so happy for you. I hope I get a chance to meet her, meet them – but not on this trip. Definitely not this trip."

Abbott paused, looking into her eyes, a touch of sadness in his. "Thank you for understanding," he said.

"There's nothing to understand, or rather, there's everything to understand. The fact that you're willing to meet me after all that's happened is more than we had a right to expect. Both Joel and I know the risks you're taking – legally, as a general, all of it – and if there was any other way we wouldn't involve you. We just don't know one, and after you hear what I have to say, you'll understand why we can't wait any longer, why Joel agreed to let me try and find you . . . You were my idea, Sam, but Joel wouldn't have heard of it unless he felt he had to – not for himself; he doesn't expect to live. That's what he said and he believes it."

A waitress brought coffee and Abbott thanked her. We'll order later," he said, staring at Valerie. "You'll have to trust my judgment, you understand that, don't you?"

"Yes. Because I trust you."

"When I couldn't reach you I made a few phone calls to people I worked with a couple of years ago in Washington. They're men who're deep into these kind of things, who have answers long before most of us know the questions."

"Those are the people Joel wants you to reach!" interrupted Val. "You saw him then; you spent the night at his hotel, don't you remember? He said you both drank too much."

"We did," agreed Sam. "And talked too much."

"You were evaluating aircraft – 'equipment', Joel called it – with specialists from various intelligence units."

"That's right."

"They're the ones he has to contact! He has to see them, talk to them, tell them everything he knows! I'm getting ahead of myself, Sam, but Joel thinks those people should have come in at the beginning – the beginning for him. He understands why he was chosen and, incredibly, he doesn't even now fault that decision! But *they* should have been there!"

"You're way ahead of yourself."

"I'll go back."

"Let me finish first. I talked to them, telling them I didn't believe what I was reading and hearing; it wasn't the Converse I knew, and to a man they told me to back off. It was hopeless and I could get badly tarnished. It *wasn't* the Converse I knew, they said. He'd psyched out; he was another person. There was too much evidence to support the blow out."

"But you took *my* call. Why?"

"Two reasons. The first is obvious – I knew Joel; we went through a lot together and none of this makes sense to me, maybe I don't want it to make sense. The second reason is a lot less subjective. I know a lie when I hear one – when I know it can't be the truth – and a lie was fed to me just as it was fed to the people who delivered it." Abbott sipped his coffee, as if telling himself to slow down and be clear. The leader of the squadron was in control; he had to be. "I spoke to three men I knew, men I trust, and each checked with his own sources. They all came back to me, each telling me essentially the same thing but in different language, different viewpoints depending on their priorities – that's the way it works with these people. But one item didn't vary so much as a syllable and it was the lie. The label is drugs. Narcotics."

"*Joel?*"

"Their words were practically identical. 'Evidence is pouring in from New York, Geneva, Paris, that Converse was a heavy buyer.' That was one phrase; the other was: 'Medical opinion has it that the hypodermics finally blew him up and blew him back'."

"That's crazy! It's *insane!*" cried Valerie, as Abbott grabbed her hand, silencing her. "I'm sorry, but it's such a *terrible* lie," she whispered. "You don't know."

"Yes, Val, I do know. Joel was pumped five or six times in the camps with substances sent down from Hanoi and no one fought it harder or hated it more than he did. The only chemicals he'd allow in his body after that were tobacco and alcohol. I've seen us both with third degree hangovers and while I tore medicine cabinets apart for a Bromo or an aspirin, he wouldn't touch them."

"Whenever his passport shots came up, he had to have four martinis before he went to the doctor," said Valerie. "Good God, who would spread a thing like that?"

"When I tried to find out I was told that even I couldn't have that information."

The former Mrs Converse now stared at the brigadier-general. "You *have* to find out, Sam, you know that, don't you?"

"Tell me why, Val. Put it together for me."

"It began in Geneva, and for Joel the operative name – the *operative* name was George Marcus Delavane."

Abbott closed his eyes, pressing them shut, as his face became suddenly older.

The cry of the cat on a frozen lake became a scream as the man in the wheelchair fell to the floor, his two stumps that once were legs scissoring maniacally to no avail, his strong arms pushing his torso up from the rug.

"Adjutant! *Adjutant!*" roared General George Marcus Delavane, as the dark red telephone kept ringing on the desk below the fragmented map.

A large, muscular middle-aged man in full uniform ran out of a door and rushed to his superior. "Let me help you, sir," he said emphatically. pulling the wheelchair toward them both.

"Not me!" yelled Delavane. "The *phone!* Get the phone! Tell whoever it is I'll be right there!" The old soldier began crawling pathetically toward the desk.

"Just one minute, please," said the adjutant into the phone. "The general will be with you in a moment." The lieutenant-colonel placed the red telephone on the desk and ran first to the chair and then to Delavane. "Please, sir, let me *help* you."

A look of loathing on his face, the half-man permitted himself to be manoeuvred back into the wheelchair. He propelled himself forward. "Give me the phone!" he ordered. It was given. "Palo Alto International. You're red! What is the day's code?"

"Charing Cross," was the reply, spoken in a clipped British accent.

"What is it, England?"

"Radio relay from Osnabrück. We've got him."

"*Kill him!*"

Chaim Abrahms sat in his kitchen, tapping his fingers on the table, trying to take his eyes off the telephone and the clock on the wall. It was the fourth time span and still there was no word from New York. The orders had been clear: the calls were to be placed within thirty minute periods every six hours commencing twenty-four hours ago, the estimated arrival time of the plane from Amsterdam. Twenty-four hours and nothing! The first omission had not troubled him; transatlantic flights were rarely on schedule. The second he had rationalized; if the woman was in transit, travelling somewhere else either in a car or by plane, the surveillance might find itself in a difficult position to place an overseas call to Israel. The third omission was unacceptable, this fourth intolerable! It was nearly the end of the thirty-minute span, six minutes to go. When in the name of God would it *ring?*

It rang. Abrahms leaped from the chair and picked it up.

"Yes?"

"We lost her," was the flat statement.

"You *what?*"

"She took a taxi to LaGuardia Airport and bought a ticket for a morning flight to Boston. Then she checked into a motel and must have left minutes later."

"Where were our *people?*"

"One parked in a car outside, the other in a room down the hall. There was no reason to suspect she would leave. She had a ticket to Boston."

"Idiots! *Garbage!*"

"They will be disciplined . . . Our men in Boston have checked every flight, every train. She hasn't shown up."

"What makes you think she *will?*"

"The ticket. There was nothing else."

"*Imbeciles!*"

Valerie had finished; there was nothing more to say. She looked at Sam Abbott who seemed far older than he had been an hour ago.

"There are so many questions," said the brigadier-general. "So much I want to ask Joel. The lousy thing is I'm not qualified, but I know someone who is. I'll talk to him tonight and tomorrow the three of us will fly to Washington. Like today, I have an early A.M. squadron run but I'll be finished by ten. I'll take the rest of the day off — one of the kids is sick, but nothing serious, nothing out of the ordinary. Alan will know whom we should go to, whom we can trust."

"Can you trust *him?*"

"Metcalf? With my life."

"Joel says you're to be careful. He warns that they can be anywhere — where you least expect them."

"But somewhere there's got to be a list. *Somewhere.*"

"Delavane? San Francisco?"

"Probably not. It's too simple, too dangerous. It's the first place anyone would look; he'd consider that . . . This countdown? Joel thinks it's tied into massive riots taking place in various cities?"

"On a vast scale, larger and more violent than anything we can imagine. Eruptions, total destabilization, spreading from one place to another, fuelled by the same people who are called in to restore order."

Abbott shook his head. "It doesn't sound right. It's too complicated and there are too many built-in controls. Police, troops from the National Guard; they have separate commands. The chain would break somewhere."

"It's what he believes. He says he can't think of anything else, and they could do it. He's convinced they have warehouses everywhere stocked with weapons and explosives, even armoured vehicles and conceivably planes in out-of-the-way airfields."

416

"Val, that's *crazy* – sorry, wrong word. The logistics are simply too over-whelming."

"Newark, Watts, Miami. They were also overwhelming."

"They were different. They were essentially racial and economic."

"The cities burned, Sam. People were killed and order came with guns. Suppose there were more guns than either of us could count? On both sides. Just like what's happening in Northern Ireland right now."

"Ireland? The slaughter in Belfast? It's a war no one can stop."

"It's *their* war! *They* did it! Joel called it a test, a trial run!"

"It's *wild*," said the pilot.

" 'Accumulation, rapid acceleration'. Those were the words Abrahms used in Bonn. Joel tried to figure them out. He couldn't buy Leifhelm's state-ment that they referred to blackmail or extortion. That wouldn't work, he said."

"Extortion?" Abbott frowned. "I don't remember your mentioning it."

"I probably didn't because Joel discounted it. Leifhelm asked him what he thought about powerful figures in various governments being compromised, and Joel said it wouldn't work. The cleansing process was too certain, the reactions too quick."

"Compromised . . . ?" Sam Abbott leaned forward in the booth. "*Compromised*, Val?"

"Yes."

"Oh, my *God*."

"What do you mean?"

"Mean? . . . Meaning, that's what I mean. 'Compromised' has more than one meaning. Like 'neutralize' and 'take-out', and probably a dozen others I don't know about."

"You're beyond me, Sam."

"In one context, the word 'compromise' means *killing*. Pure and simple murder. Assassination."

Valerie checked into the MGM-Grand Hotel giving the bewildered clerk three days' advance payment for the room in lieu of a credit card. Key in hand, she took the elevator up to the ninth floor and let herself into a pleasantly garish opulence found only in Las Vegas. She stood briefly out on the balcony, watching the setting orange sun, thinking about the insanity of everything. She would call Joel first thing in the morning – noon or thereabouts in Osnabrück, West Germany.

She ordered from room service, ate what she could, watched an hour or so of mind-numbing television, and finally lay down on the bed. She had been right about Sam Abbott. Dear Sam, straight-as-the-proverbial-arrow Sam, direct and uncomplicated. If anyone would know what to do Sam would, and if he did not know he would find out. For the first time in days, Val felt a degree of relief. Sleep came and this time there were no horrible dreams.

She awoke to the sight of the early sun firing the mountains beyond the balcony doors in the distance. For a moment or two while she emerged through the layers of vanishing sleep she thought she was back at Cape Ann, the sunlight streaming into her bedroom from the balcony outside, a distant nightmare vaguely recalled. Then the bold floral drapes came into focus and the far away mountains and the slightly stale odour of thick hotel carpeting, and she knew the nightmare was very much with her.

She got out of the oversized bed and navigated to the bathroom, stopping on the way at the television set to switch on the radio. She reached the door and suddenly stopped, gripping the edge, bracing herself, her head detonating with a thousand explosions, her eyes and throat on fire.

She could only scream. And scream again and again as she fell to the floor.

Peter Stone turned up the radio in the New York apartment, then walked quickly to the table where there was an open telephone directory, the pages blue, the book itself having been taken from "Mrs DePinna's" room in the St Regis Hotel. Stone listened to the news report as he scanned the opposing blue pages of government listings.

> It has now been confirmed that the earlier reports of the crash of an F\18 jet fighter plane at Nellis Air Force Base in Nevada are accurate. The accident took place this morning at seven-forty-two, Pacific time, during first-light manoeuvres over the desert thirty-eight miles northwest of the Nellis field. The pilot, Brigadier-General Samuel Abbott, was Chief of Tactical Operations and considered one of the finest pilots in the Air Force as well as a superb aerial tactician. The press officer at Nellis said a full enquiry will be launched, but stated that according to the other pilots the lead plane of the squadron, flown by General Abbott, plunged to the ground after executing a relatively low altitude manoeuvre. The explosion could be heard as far away as Las Vegas. The press officer's remarks were charged with emotion as he described the downed pilot. 'The death of General Abbott is a tragic loss for the Air Force and the nation,' he told reporters. A few minutes ago the President . . .

"That's it," said Stone turning to the Army captain across the room. "That's where she was heading . . . Shut that damn thing off, will you? I knew Abbott; worked with him out of Langley a couple of years ago."

The Army officer stared at the civilian as he turned off the radio. "Do you know what you're saying?" he asked.

"Here it is," replied Stone, his right hand extended, his index finger pointing to the lower left hand corner of a page in the thick telephone directory. "Blue thirteen, three pages from the end of the book. 'United States Government offices.' 'Air Force, Department of the – ' "

"There are dozens of other listings, too, including your former employer. 'Central Intelligence – New York Field Office'. Why not it? Them? It fits better."

"He can't go that route and he knows it."

"He didn't go," corrected the captain. "He sent her."

"*That* doesn't fit – with everything we know about him. She'd be sent to Virginia and come out a basket case. No, she came back here to find a particular person, not a faceless department or a section or an agency. An individual they both knew and trusted. Abbott. She found him, told him everything Converse told her and he talked to others – the wrong others. *Goddamn it!*"

"How can you be sure?" pressed the Army man.

"*Christ*, Captain, what do you want, a *diagram?* Sam Abbott was shot down over the coast of the Tonkin Gulf. He was a POW and so was Converse. I have an idea that if we put it through the computers, we'd find out they knew each other. I'm so sure I won't use up another debt. *Fuckit!*"

"You know," said the Army officer. "I've never seen you lose your temper. The cold can get hot, can't it, Stone. I believe you."

The former intelligence officer looked hard at the captain and when he spoke his voice was flat – and cold. "Abbott was a good man – even an exceptional man for someone in uniform – but don't mistake me, Captain. He was killed – and he *was* killed – because whatever that woman told him was so conclusive he had to be compromised hours later."

"Compromised?"

"Figure it out . . . I'm angry at Sam's death, yes you're damned right. But I'm a lot angrier that we don't have the woman. Among other things, with us she has a chance, without us I judge very little and I don't want her on my conscience – what little I've got left. Also to get Converse out we have to find her, there's no other way."

"But if you're right she's somewhere near Nellis, probably Las Vegas."

"Undoubtedly Las Vegas, and by the time we reach anyone who could check around for us, she'll be on her way somewhere else . . . You know, I'd hate to be her now. The only avenue she had was neutralized. Whom can she turn to, where can she go? It's what Dowling said about Converse yesterday, what he didn't tell Peregrine's secretary. Our man was systematically isolated and more afraid of US Embassy personnel than anyone else. He would never have agreed to a meeting with Peregrine because he knew it'd be a trap, therefore he couldn't have killed him. He was set up, everywhere he looked another trap to keep him running and out of sight." The civilian paused, then added firmly. "The woman's finished, Captain. She's at the end of a bad road – their road. And that may be the best part of it for us. If she panics, we could find her. But we're going to have to take some risks. How's that neck of yours? Have you made out a will?"

Valerie wept quietly by the glass doors overlooking the gaudy strip of Las Vegas. Her tears were not only for Sam Abbott and his wife and children, but for herself and Joel. It was permitted under the circumstances and she could not lie to herself. She had no idea what to do next. No matter whom she went to the answer would be the same. *Tell him to come out of hiding and we'll listen to him.* And the minute he did, Joel would be dead, fulfilling his own prophecy. And if through a bureaucratic miracle she was granted a meeting with someone of power and influence, how strong would her case be? What words would she use?

I was married to this man for four years and I divorced him – let's call it incompatibility – but I know him! I know he couldn't have done what they say he

*did, he didn't kill those men . . . What proof? I just told you, I know him! . . . What
does incompatibility mean? I'm not sure, we didn't get along – he was remote, distant.
What difference does it make? What are you implying? Oh, God! You're so wrong! I
have no interest in him that way. Yes, he's successful but I don't need his money.
I don't want it! . . . You see, he told me about this . . . this incredible plot to put the
military establishments of the United States and the countries of Western Europe in
virtual control of their governments, that they could do it by massive rioting in key
cities, terrorism, destabilization everywhere. He's met them and talked with them;
there's a plan already in progress! They see themselves as a dedicated international
organization, as a strong alternative to the weak governments of the West who won't
stand up to the Soviet bloc. But they're not a reasonable alternative, they're fanatics!
They're killers; they want total control of all of us! . . . My former husband wrote it
all up, everything he's learned, and sent it to me but it was stolen, his own father
killed because he undoubtedly read it. No, it was not suicide! . . . He calls it a
conspiracy of generals conceived by a general who'd been labelled a madman. General
George Delavane – "Mad Marcus" Delavane . . . Yes, I know what the police in
Paris and Bonn and Brussels say, what Interpol says, what our own embassy has
reported – finger-prints and ballistics and seeing him in this place and that place, and
drugs, and meeting with Peregrine – but can't you understand, they're all lies! . . .
Yes, I know what happened when he was a prisoner of war – what he went through,
the things he said when he was discharged. None of that is relevant! His feelings aren't
relevant! He told me that! He told me – he looks so terrible . . . he's been so hurt.*

Who would believe her?

Tell him to come in. We'll listen.

He can't! He'll be killed! . . . You'll kill him!

The telephone rang, for a moment paralysing her. She stared at it, terrified
but forcing herself to stay in control. Sam Abbott was dead and he told her only
he would call – only he. My God, thought Val, they'd *found* her, just as they'd
found her in New York. But they would not repeat the mistakes they had made
in New York. She had to remain calm and think – and out-think. The ringing
stopped and she approached the phone, lifting it up and pressing the button
marked *O.*

"Operator, this is Room Nine-one-four. Please send the Security police up
here right away. It's an emergency."

She had to move quickly, be ready to leave the instant the security men arrived.
She had to get out and find a telephone that was . . . *unberührt*. She had heard
the stories; she knew what to do. She had to reach Joel in Osnabrück.

Colonel Alan Metcalf, Chief Intelligence Officer, Nellis Air Force Base, walked
out of the telephone booth and looked around the shopping mall, his hand in
the pocket of his sports jacket, gripping the small revolver inside. He glanced at
his watch; his wife and children would be in Los Angeles soon, then reach
Cleveland by late afternoon. The four of them would stay with her parents until
he said otherwise. It was better this way – since he had no idea what the "way"
would be like.

420

He only knew that Sam Abbott had run that sub-mach manoeuvre a thousand times; he knew every stress point and PSI throughout the entire aircraft, and he never flew a jet that had not been scanned electronically. To ascribe that crash to pilot error was ludicrous; instead, someone had lied to that pilot, a circuit and back-up shorted. Sam was killed because his friend, Metcalf, had made a terrible mistake. After talking with Abbott for nearly five hours, Metcalf had called a man in Washington, telling him to prepare a conference the following afternoon with two ranking members each from the NSC, G\2, and Naval Intelligence. The reason-of-record: Brigadier-General Samuel Abbott had pertinent and startling information about the fugitive Joel Converse.

And if they could kill the man who had the information so readily, so efficiently, they might easily go after the messenger, the intelligence officer bringing him in. It was better this way, with Doris and the kids in Cleveland. He had a great deal to do and a terrible debt to repay.

The Converse woman! Oh, Christ, why had she *done* it, why had she run so quickly? He expected it, of course, but he had hoped against hope that he could reach her in time, but it was not possible. First there was Doris and the kids and plane reservations and the call to her folks; they had to get out; he could be next. Then racing to the field, his revolver beside him in the car, and ransacking Sam's office – as Nellis' intelligence officer, a particularly loathsome duty, but in this case vital – and questioning Abbott's distraught secretary. A name had emerged: Parquette.

"I'll pick her up," Sam had said last night. "She's staying at the Grand and I promised only I'd phone her. She's a cool lady but she had a close call in New York. She wants to hear a voice she knows and I can't blame her."

Cool lady, thought Alan Metcalf, as he climbed into his car, *you made the biggest mistake of your shortened life. With me you had a chance to live – perhaps – but now as they say in this part of Nevada, the odds are heavily against.*

Nevertheless she would be on his conscience, reasoned the intelligence officer, now speeding into the cut-off toward Route 15 and points south.

Conscience. He wondered if those silent bastards in Washington had Joel Converse on their collective conscience. They had sent a man out and abandoned him, not even having the grace to make sure he was killed quickly, mercifully. The programmers of the kamikaze were saints beside such people.

Converse. Where *was* he?

33

Joel stood silently as Leifhelm's man removed his gun and turned to speak to the assembled row of senile old women in the high-backed chairs. He spoke for less than a minute, then grabbed Converse by the arm – his and their trophy – forcing Joel to face Hermione Geyner, whose true prisoner he was. It was a mystical ritual of triumph from a time long past.

"I have just told these brave women of the Underground," said the German looking at Converse, "that they have uncovered a traitor to our cause. Frau Geyner will confirm this, *Ja, Meine Dame?*"

"*Ja!*" spat out the intense old woman, her face alive with arrogance and victory. "Betrayal!" she screamed.

"The telephone calls have been made and our instructions received," continued Leifhelm's soldier. "We shall leave now, *Amerikaner*. There's nothing you can do, so let us go quietly."

"If you had this whole thing so organized, why those two men on the train, including that one?" asked Joel, nodding at the man with his arm in the sling, instinctively stalling for time, an attorney allowing an adversary to compliment himself.

"Observed, not organized," answered the German. "We had to be sure you did everything expected of you. Everyone here agrees, *Stimmt das, Frau Geyner?*"

"*Ja!*" exploded Valerie's aunt.

"The other one is dead," said Joel.

"A loss for the cause and we shall mourn him. Come!" The German bowed to the ladies, as did his two companions, and led Converse through the large double doors to the front entrance. Outside on the huge decrepit porch, Leifhelm's hunter gave the thick envelope to the man with the sling and issued orders. Both nodded and walked rapidly down the steps, the wounded man steadying himself on an unsteady railing. Below on the long circular drive they hurried to the right. Down at the far exit, near the country road, Joel could see the shape of a long sedan in the darkness.

The three prison guards led him out of the compound. It was the middle of the night and he was either being transferred to another camp or to his own execution, the killing ground somewhere in the dense jungle where his screams would be muted. The head guard barked a command to his two subordinates who bowed and began running down the road toward a captured American jeep several hundred yards away in the darkness. He was alone with the man, thought Converse, knowing the moment would not come again except as a corpse. If it was going to happen, it had to happen now. He moved his head slightly, lowering his gaze to the dark outline of the gun in the guard's hand . . .

The German's hand was steady, the weapon in it rigid, angled up at Joel's chest. Inside the timeworn house, the old women had broken into a song, frail

422

voices growing louder in some pathetic victory anthem heard through the large casement windows open for the summer breezes. Converse inched his right foot around the floorboards at his side, testing several and finding one weaker than the others. He pressed down with his full weight; the resulting creak was loud and sharp. Startled, the German turned at the echo all around them.

Now. Joel grabbed the barrel of the gun, twisting hand and steel back and clockwise, hammering the man across the porch into the wall, gripping the weapon with all his strength, twisting farther, fuller, shoving it into the man's stomach . . . The gunshot was partially muffled by the cloth and flesh, by an engine starting and the sound of excited senile voices raised in song, louder now through the open windows. The German collapsed, his head snapping to the right, his eyes bulging, the stench of burnt fabric and intestines floating up; he was dead. Converse crouched, whipping around and looked down at the long U-shaped drive, half expecting to see the other two men racing toward him, guns extended. Instead, he saw the lights of the car in the distance; it was on the country road outside, now turning into the entrance gate on the left. It would be at the porch in moments.

Prying the weapon out of the German's hand, Joel dragged him across the floorboards into the shadows to the right of the steps. Seconds now.

Get the jeep. Use the jeep. The nearest vehicle check was five miles down the road – they had seen it on work details. Get the jeep! Cover the ground! The jeep!

The long sedan pulled up in front of the porch and the man with his arm in the sling got out of the right front door. Converse watched him from behind the thick corner pillar as the wounded German stood on the pavement, looking up into the shadows.

"Koenig?" he asked softly, questioning. "*Wo ist* Koenig?" He started up the steps, his left hand awkwardly, tentatively going inside his jacket.

Joel spun around the pillar, rushing down the old staircase and grabbed the wounded man by the sling. He jammed the pistol into the foot soldier's throat, turning him and rushing him back to the car, crashing his head into the roof, again crouching, thrusting the weapon through the open front window.

The astonished driver was quicker than the foot soldier; he was yanking his gun out of an unseen holster. He fired wildly, shattering the windscreen. Converse fired back, blowing the man's head half out of the window.

Take the bodies into the jungle! Don't leave them here near the compound! Every second counts, every minute!

Joel sprang up and pulled the wounded German away from the car as he opened the front door. "You're going to help me, you good Christian!" he whispered, remembering the whining supplications of a killer in a freight car. "You do as I tell you or you'll join your friends. *Capisce*, or is it *verstehen Sie?* Whatever the hell it is, you do as I say, do you understand me? I'm a panicked man, mister – on the *edge*, and I'll argue that position in front of the Supreme Court! . . . What the hell am *I saying?* I've got the gun and I've killed again – it gets easier when you don't want to be killed yourself. *Move!* That lousy Son-of-Gestapo on the porch! Bring him down here! In the back!"

Perhaps a minute later, Joel would never know the time, the wounded man was behind the wheel, driving with difficulty, the two corpses in the back seat, a tableau of horror, and Converse thought he would vomit. Illness aside – and it was not easily surmounted – he watched every landmark in the countryside as he directed the driver to take this turn and that, pilotage indelibly imprinted on the mind for the flight back without a radio or a map or a means to obtain either. They reached what looked like a series of rocky pastures at the base of a mountain and Converse told the German to get off the road. They clambered over several hundred yards until there was a sharp decline, ending at a row of full-blown trees. He ordered the driver out.

He had given the last guard a chance. He was a kid in a mismatched uniform, his eyes intense but his face in question. How much was felt, how much indoctrinated? He had given the boy – the child – a simple exam, and a believer had failed the examination.

"Listen to me," said Joel. "You told me on the train that you were *hired* – I didn't understand the German word but that you didn't want to kill anybody. You were just unemployed and needed a job, is that right?"

"Yes, *Mein Herr!* I kill *no one!* I only watched, followed!"

"All right. I'll put the gun away and I'm going to walk out of here. You go wherever you want to go, okay?"

"Ich verstehe! Yes, of course!"

Converse shoved the weapon in his belt and turned, his fingers still gripping the handle as he started up the slope. The *scratch!* The rocks displaced! He pivoted, dropping to his knees as the German lunged.

He fired once at the body above him. The footsoldier screamed as he arced in the air and rolled down the hill in silence. *A believer had failed the examination.*

Joel walked up the incline with the envelope addressed to Nathan Simon and across the rocky field to the road. He knew the landmarks; the pilot in him would make no mistakes. He knew what he had to do.

He was concealed far back in the bushes on the edge of Hermione Geyner's property, thirty yards from the decaying house, twenty from the U-shaped drive which was filled with ruts and bordered by brown, overgrown grass, dead from the heat and a lack of water. He had to stay awake, for if it was going to happen, it would happen soon. Human nature could take only so much anxiety; he had played upon the truism too often as a lawyer. Answers had to be given to anxious men – panicked men. The sun was up, the birds foraging in the early light, myriad noises replacing the stillness of the night. But the house was silent, the large casement windows, through which only hours ago the voices of demented old women helped muffle gunshots, were closed, more panes cracked than clear. And through all the madness, the insanity of violent events, he still wore the clerical collar, still had his priestly passport and the letter of pilgrimage. The next few hours would tell him whether or not they were of any value.

The roar of an engine came first and then the sight of a black Mercedes swerving off the country road into the drive. It sped up to the porch, jolting to a stop; two men climbed out, the driver racing around the back to join his companion. They stood for a moment looking up at the porch and the windows of the house, then turned and scanned the grounds, walking over to Hermione Geyner's car and peering inside. The driver nodded and reached under his jacket, pulling out a gun; they went back to the steps, taking them rapidly, heading across the porch to the door. Finding no bell, the man without a gun in his hand knocked harshly, repeatedly, finally pounding with a closed fist while twisting the knob to no avail.

Guttural shouts came from inside as the door swung back revealing an angry Frau Geyner dressed in a tattered bathrobe. Her voice was that of a shrewish teacher lambasting two students for cheating when in fact they had not. Each time one of the men tried to speak her voice rose to new, shrill heights; the man with the gun put it away. His companion, however, apparently moved by a far greater fear, suddenly grabbed Valerie's aunt by the shoulders and spoke harshly, directly, forcing her to listen.

Whatever change the man sought, it was minor. Hermione Geyner did listen but when she replied her answers were equally harsh, equally direct, and delivered with authority. She pointed down at the overgrown drive and apparently described what she had witnessed in the dark, early morning hours – what she herself had accomplished. The men looked at each other, their eyes questioning and afraid, but not questioning what the old woman had told them, only what she could not tell them. They raced across the porch and down the steps to their car. The driver started the engine with a vengeance so pronounced the ignition mechanism flew into a high-pitched, grinding scream. The Mercedes plunged forward, skirting past Frau Geyner's car, and in a sudden attempt to avoid a hole in the overgrown pavement, the driver swung briefly to his left, then to his right, skidding on the surface, the tyres sliding on the crawling vine weeds until the side of the car careened into the disintegrating stone gate. Roars of abuse from both men filled the morning air as the Mercedes was straightened and raced through the exit. It swung left and sped down the country road, as Hermione Geyner slammed the door up on the porch.

There was nothing any longer without risk, thought Joel, as he crawled out of the foliage, but the risk for him now was one he faced with a degree of confidence. Aquitaine had used up Frau Geyner; there was nothing more to be learned. To return to a madwoman held a greater risk for them. Envelope in hand he walked across the ugly drive, up the creaking steps, and across the sagging porch to the door. He knocked and ten seconds later a screeching Hermione Geyner opened it. He then did something so totally unpredictable, so completely out of character, he did not believe it himself as he followed through with the sudden impulse.

He punched the old woman squarely in the centre of her lower jaw. It was the beginning of the longest eight hours of his life.

The bewildered Security Police from the MGM-Grand Hotel reluctantly refused Valerie's offer of a gratuity, especially as she had raised it from $50 to $100, thinking that the economy of Las Vegas was somewhat different from New York and certainly Cape Ann. They had driven around the streets of the old and the new city for nearly forty-five minutes, until both men, both professionals in their work, assured her that no one was following their car. And they would put a special patrol on the Ninth floor in an attempt to catch the man who had harassed her, who had attempted to gain entrance to the room. They were, of course, naturally chagrined that she took a room across the boulevard at Caesar's Palace.

Val tipped the bellman, took her small overnight bag from him, and closed the door. She ran to the phone on the table by the bed.

"*I haff* to go to the toilet!" shouted Hermione Geyner, holding an ice pack under her chin.

"Again?" asked Converse, his eyes barely open, sitting across from the old woman, the envelope and the gun in his lap.

"You make me nervous. You struck me."

"You did the same and a hell of a lot more to me last night," said Joel, getting up from the chair and shoving the gun under his belt, the envelope in his hand.

"I vill see you hanging from a rope! *Betrayer!* How many hours now? You think our operatives in the *Untergrundbewegung* will not *miss* me?"

"I think they're probably feeding pigeons in the park, cooing along with the best of them. Go on, I'll follow."

The telephone rang, the hours suddenly meaningless. Converse grabbed the old woman by the back of her neck and propelled her to the antique desk and the phone. "Just as we practised," he whispered, holding her firmly. "Do it!"

"*Ja?*" said Hermione Geyner into the telephone, Joel's ear next to hers.

"*Tante! Ich bin's*, Valerie!"

"*Val!*" shouted Converse, pushing the old woman away. "It's *me!* I'm not sure the phone's clean; she was set up, I was set up! Quickly! Tell Sam I was *wrong* – I *think* I was wrong! The countdown could be *assassinations* – all over the goddamned place!"

"He knew that!" shouted Valerie in reply. "He's dead, Joel! He's *dead!* They *killed* him!"

"Oh, *Christ!* There's no time, Val, no *time!* The *phone!*"

"*Meet me!*" screamed the ex-Mrs Converse.

"Where? Tell me *where?*"

The pause was less than several seconds, an eternity for both. "Where it began, my darling!" cried Valerie. "Where it began but *not* where it began . . . The clouds, darling! The patch and the clouds!"

Where it began. Geneva. But not Geneva. Clouds, a patch. A patch!

"Yes, I *know!*"

"Tomorrow! The next day! I'll be there!"

"I have to get out of here . . . Val . . . I love you so much! *So* much!"

426

"The clouds, my darling – my only darling – oh, *God* stay alive!"

Joel ripped the telephone out of the wall, as Hermione Geyner came rushing at him, swinging a heavy brass handled poker from the fireplace. The iron hook glanced off his cheek; he grabbed her arm and shouted.

"I haven't got time for you, you crazy *bitch!* My *client* doesn't have time!" He spun her around and pushed her forward, picking up the envelope from the table. "You were on your way to the bathroom, remember?"

It was in the hall and Converse saw what he hoped he would see in the red-lacquered bowl on the wall table; the old woman had dropped them there last night – the keys to her car. The bathroom door pulled out; it was the solution. Once she was inside, Joel grabbed a heavy chair from against the wall, dragged it over and jammed the thick rim under the knob, kicking the legs in place, wedging them into the floor. Valerie's aunt heard the commotion and tried to open the door; it held. The harder she pressed, the firmer the legs were embedded.

"We convene again tonight!" she roared. "We will send out our best people! The *best!*"

"God help Eisenhower when you meet," muttered Converse, inwardly relieved. If Aquitaine did not have the phone covered, the old woman would be found in a few hours. He took the keys from the lacquered bowl, the envelope under his arm, and pulled the gun from his belt. He ran to the front door, opening it cautiously. There was no one, nothing, only Hermione Geyner's car parked on the weed-ridden drive. He went outside, pulling the door shut, leaving it unlocked, and raced down the steps to the stationary automobile. He started the engine; there was half a tank of gas, enough to get him far away from Osnabrück before refilling. Until he could get a map, he would go by the sun, heading south.

Valerie made arrangements at the travel office in Caesar's Palace, paying cash and using her mother's maiden name, hoping perhaps that some of the facile woman's wartime expertise might find its way to the daughter. There was a 6 P.M.. Air France flight to Paris from Los Angeles. She would be on it the hour's trip to LAX made on a chartered plane to which she would be chauffeured, thus avoiding the terminal at McCarran Airport. Such courtesies were always available, usually for celebrities and casino winners. There was no basic problem with a false name on the Air France passenger manifest – at worst only embarrassment, in her case easily explained; her former husband, now a stranger, was an infamous man, a hunted man; she preferred anonymity. She would not legally be required to produce her passport until she arrived at Immigration in Paris, and once through, she could travel anywhere she wished, under any name she gave, for she would not be leaving the borders of France. It was why she had thought of Chamonix.

She sat in the chair, looking out of the window, thinking of those days – in Chamonix. She had flown over with Joel to Geneva where he had three days of conferences with the promise of five days off to go skiing at Mont Blanc, a bonus from John Brooks, the brilliant international negotiator of Talbot, Brooks and Simon, who flatly refused to give up some reunion dinner for what he termed "lizardshit meetings between idiots – our boy can do it. He'll charm their asses off while emptying their corporate pockets." It was the first time Joel really knew that he was on his way, yet oddly enough he was almost as excited about the skiing. They both enjoyed it so much. Together. Perhaps because they both were good.

But Joel had not enjoyed the skiing at Chamonix that trip. On the second day he had taken a terrible fall and sprained his ankle. The swelling was enormous, the pain as acute in his head as in his foot. She had knighted him "Sir Grump"; he demanded his *Herald Tribune* in the morning, childishly refusing to have his breakfast before the paper arrived, and even more childishly playing the martyr as his wife went off to the slopes. When she had suggested that she really did not care to go without him, it was worse, he had charged her with trying to be some kind of saint. He would be perfectly fine – he had things to read, which artists would not understand. Reading, that was.

Oh, what a little boy he had been, thought Val. But during the nights it was so different, he was so different. He became the man again, loving and tender, at once the generous lion and the sensitive lamb. They made love, it seemed, for hours on end, the moonlight on the snow outside, finally the hint of the sun's earliest rays on the mountains until they fell – together – into exhausted sleep.

On their last day before heading back to Geneva for the night flight to New York, she had surprised him. Instead of going out for a few final hours of skiing, she went downstairs at the hotel and bought him a sweater, to which she had sewn a large patch on the sleeve. It read: *Downhill Racer – Chamonix*. She had presented it to him while a porter waited outside the door with a wheelchair – she had made arrangements through the influential manager of the hotel. They were taken to the centre of Chamonix, to the cable car that scaled 13,000 feet to the top of Mont Blanc – through the clouds to the top of the world, it seemed. When they reached the final apex, where the view was breathtaking, Joel had turned to her, that silly, oblique look in his eyes that belied everything he was and everything he had been through – again, as always, his way of thanking her.

"Enough of this foolish scenery," he had said. "Take off your clothes. It's not really that cold."

They had hot coffee, sitting on a bench outside, the magnificence of natural grandeur all around them. They held hands, and *Christ!* she had held back the tears of love she felt.

She felt them now and got out of the chair, rejecting the imposition. It was the wrong time for such reflections. Whatever clarity of mind she could summon, she needed it now. She had to travel halfway across the world avoiding God knew how many people who were looking for her.

He had said he loved her–so *much*. Was it love or was it need . . . support? She had replied with the words *my darling* – no, she had said more than that;

she had been far more specific. She had said *my only darling*. Was it a response born of the panic?

Not knowing was the worst of it, thought Converse, studying the road signs in the wash of the headlights. He had been driving for nearly seven hours, having picked up a map in the city of Hagen while refilling the tank – seven hours and according to the map he was still a long way from the border crossing he had chosen. The reason lay in his ignorance, in not knowing whether Hermione Geyner's car had been the object of a search in the first few hours out of Osnabrück. It undoubtedly was now – officially by the police – but during those early hours he could have made better time on the highways he dared not use in case Aquitaine had raced to Geyner's house with Val's call. He had travelled circuitous back country roads, his pilot's eye on the sun, veering always south until he reached Hagen. Now the back roads were a necessity; whether they were before he would never know. Now, however, Hermione Geyner and her band of lunatics must have gone to the police to report her stolen car. Joel had no idea what they could possibly say that would convince the *Polizei* Valerie's aunt was an injured party, but a stolen car was a stolen car, whether driven by St Francis of Assisi or Jack the Ripper. He would stay on the back roads.

Lennestadt to Krentzel, crossing the Rhine at Bendorf and following the west bank of the river through Koblenz, Oberwessel and Bingen, then south to Neustadt and east to Speyer and the Rhine again. And again south through the border towns of Alsace-Lorraine, finally to the city of Kehl. It was where he would cross into France, a decision based on the fact that several years ago John Brooks had sent him to Strasbourg, the French city across the river border, to a terribly dull conference at which eight lawyers argued continuously with one another over minor aspects of language and translation to the point where nothing of substance was accomplished. As a result, Joel had walked the city and driven out to the countryside, awed by its beauty. He had taken several boat trips up and down the Rhine and remembered the ferries that shuttled back and forth between the piers of Germany and France. Above all, he remembered the crowds in Strasbourg – always the crowds, especially now.

It would take another three to four hours of driving, but somewhere he would have to stop and sleep for a while. He was exhausted; he had not slept for so long he could not accurately remember when. But there was Chamonix and Val ahead. He told her he loved her – he had *said* it. He had got it out after so many years, the relief was incredible – the response more incredible. *My darling – my only darling*. Did she mean it? Or was she supporting him again, the artist's emotions riding over reason and experience?

Aquitaine! Push everything out of your mind and get into France!

The polar flight from Los Angeles to Paris was uneventful, the moonscapes of ice over the northernmost regions of the world hypnotically peaceful, suspending thought by the sheer expanse of their cold infinity. Nothing seemed to matter to

Val as she looked down from the sub–stratosphere. But whatever tranquillity the flight produced, it came to an end in Paris.

"Are you in France on business or on holiday, Madame?" asked the Immigration official, taking Valerie's passport and typing her name into the computer.

"*Les deux.*"

"*Vous parlez français?*"

"*Je le préfère. Mes parents étaient de Paris,*" explained Val, continuing in French. "I'm an artist and I'll be talking with several galleries. Naturally, I'll want to travel . . ." She stopped, seeing the official's eyes glance up from his screen, studying her. "Is anything the matter?" she asked.

"Nothing of concern, Madame," said the man, picking up his telephone and talking in a low voice, the words indistinguishable under the hum of the huge customs hall. "There is someone who wishes to speak with you."

"That's of considerable concern to *me*," objected Valerie, suddenly frightened. "I'm not travelling under my own name for a very good reason – which I suspect that machine of yours has told you, and I will *not* be subjected to interrogations or the indignity of the press! I've said all I have to say. Please reach the American Embassy for me."

"There is no need for that, Madame," said the man, replacing the phone. "It is not an interrogation and no one of the press will know you are in Paris unless you tell them. Also, there is nothing in this machine but the name on your passport – and a request."

A second uniformed official hurriedly entered the roped off aisle from a nearby office. He bowed politely. "If you will come with me, Madame," he said quietly in English, obviously noticing the fear in her eyes, and assuming her objections. "You may, of course, refuse, as this is in no way official, but I hope you will not. It is a favour between old friends."

"Who are you?"

"Chief Inspector of Immigration, Madame."

"And who wishes to speak with me?"

"It would be up to him to tell you that – his name does not appear on the request. However, I'm to give you another name. Mattilon. He says you, too, were old friends and he respected him a great deal."

"*Mattilon?*"

"If you will be so kind as to wait in my office, I will personally clear your luggage."

"This is my luggage," said Val, her thoughts on someone who would bring up René's name. "I'll want a police officer nearby, one who can watch through a glass door."

"*Pourquoi? . . .* Why, Madame?"

"*Sécurité,*" replied Valerie.

"*Oui, bien sûr, mais ce n'est pas nécessaire.*"

"*J'insiste, ou je pars tout de suite.*"

"*D'accord.*"

It was explained that the person who wished to speak with her was driving out to de Gaulle Airport from the centre of Paris; it would take thirty-five minutes, during which time she had coffee and a small glass of Calvados. The man walked through the door. He was late middleaged and dressed in rumpled clothing, as if his appearance did not matter any longer. His face seemed lined as much from weariness as from age, and when he spoke his voice was tired but nevertheless precise.

"I will keep you but a few minutes, Madame. I'm sure you have places to go, people to see."

"As I explained," said Val, looking hard at the Frenchman, "I'm in Paris to talk with several galleries . . ."

"That is no concern of mine," interrupted the man, holding up his hands. "Forgive me, I do not care to hear. I care to hear nothing unless Madame wishes to speak after I've spoken to her."

"Why did you use the name of Mattilon?"

"An introduction. You were friends. May I go back before Monsieur Mattilon?"

"Go back by all means."

"My name is Prudhomme. I am with the *Sûreté*. A man died in a hospital here in Paris several weeks ago. It is said your former husband, Monsieur Converse, was responsible."

"I'm aware of that."

"It was not possible," said the Frenchman calmly, sitting down and taking out a cigarette. "Have no fear, this office is not 'tapped' or 'bugged'. The Chief Inspector and I go back to the *Résistance*."

"That man died after a brutal fight with my former husband," said Val cautiously. "I read it in the newspapers, heard it on the radio. Yet you're telling me he wasn't responsible for his death. How can you say that?"

"The man did not *die* in the hospital, he was killed. Between 2.15 and 2.45 in the morning. Your husband was on a flight from Copenhagen to Hamburg during those hours. It has been established."

"You *know* this?"

"Not officially, Madame. I was removed from the case. A subordinate, a man with little police experience but with the Army – later in the Foreign Legion, no less – was given the assignment while I was shifted to more 'important' matters. I asked questions; I will not bore you with details but the man's lungs collapsed – a sudden trauma unrelated to his wounds. The man was suffocated. It was not in the report. It was removed."

Valerie controlled herself, keeping her voice cool and distant despite her anxiety. "Now," she said, "what about Mattilon? My *friend*, Mattilon."

"Fingerprints," replied the Frenchman, wearily. "They suddenly are discovered twelve hours after the *arrondissement* police – who are *very* good – have examined that office? And yet there was a death in Wesel, West Germany, within the rising and the setting of the same sun. Your former husband's countenance was described, his identity all but confirmed. And an old woman on a train to Amsterdam – the same routing – who is found with a gun in her hand – again a description given. Has this Converse wings? Does he fly over borders by himself? Again it is not possible."

"What are you trying to tell me, Monsieur Prudhomme?"

The man from the *Sûreté* inhaled on his cigarette as he tore off a page from his notepad and wrote something out on the edge of the table. "I'm not certain, Madame, since I am no longer officially privileged in these matters. But if your former husband did not cause the man in Paris to die and could not have shot your old friend, Monsieur Mattilon . . . how many others did he *not* kill, including the American ambassador in Bonn and the Supreme Commander of NATO? And who are these people who can tell government sources to confirm this and confirm that, to change assignments of senior police personnel at will, to alter medical reports removing – suppressing – evidence? . . . There are things I do not understand, Madame, but I am certain those are the very things I am not *meant* to understand. And that is why I'm giving you this telephone number. It is not my office; it is my flat in Paris – my wife will know where to reach me. Simply remember, in an emergency say that you are from the *Tatiana* family."

Stone sat at the desk, the ever-present telephone in his hand. He was alone – had been alone when the call came from Charlotte, North Carolina, from a woman he had once loved very dearly years ago in the field. She had left the "terrible game", as she called it; he had stayed, their love not strong enough.

The connection was completed to Cuxhaven, West Germany, to a telephone the civilian was sure would be sterile. That certainty was one of the pleasures in dealing with Johnny Reb.

"Bobbie-Jo's Chicken Fry," was the greeting over the line. "We deliver."

"I gather that. It's Stone."

"*Mah wuhd*, the Tatiana re-route!" exclaimed the Southerner. "Someday you must tell me about this here fascinating family of yours, Brer Rabbit."

"Someday I will."

"I seem to recollect having heard the name somewheres around the late 'sixties, but I didn't know what it meant."

"Trust whoever used it."

"Why should I do that?"

"Because whoever it was was trusted by the hangingest judges in the world."

"Who might that be?"

"The enemy, Rebel."

"If that's a parable, Yankee, you lost me."

"Someday, Johnny, not now. What have you got?"

"Well, let me tell you. I saw the damnedest little island over here you ever did see. It's not twenty miles off the coast near the mouth of the Elbe, right where it's supposed to be. In the Heligoland Bight, they call it, which is a section of the North Sea."

"Scharhörn," said the civilian, making a statement. "You found it."

"It wasn't tough to find – everybody seems to know about it – but nobody goes near a certain south-west shoreline. It used to be a U-boat refuelling station in World War II. The security was so tight most of the German High Command didn't know about it, and the Allies never got a clue. The old concrete and steel structures are still there and it's supposed to be deserted except for a couple of caretakers, who, I'm told, wouldn't pick you out of the water if your boat crashed into one of the old submarine winches." Johnny Reb paused, then continued softly. "I went out there last night and saw lights, too many lights in too many places. There are people out there on that old base, not just a couple of watchmen, and you can bet a Yankee pot roast your lieutenant commander is one of them. Also around two o'clock in the morning after the lights went out, the tallest mother-lovin' antenna this side of Houston slid up like a bionic cornstalk, but there was no corn on the top. Instead, it bloomed like a regular flower. It was a disc, the kind they use for satellite transmissions . . . You want me to mount a team? I can do it there is a lot of unemployment these days. Also the cost will be minimal, because the more I think about it the more I appreciate your swinging me out of the Dardanelles before those guns got there. That was really more important than getting me off the hook with those contingency funds in Bahrain."

"Thanks, but not yet. If you go in for him now, we show cards we can't show."

"How long can you wait? Remember I taped that prick Washburn."

"How much did you put together?"

"More than this old brain can absorb, if you want the truth. But not more than I can accept. It's been a long time coming, hasn't it? The eagles think they're gonna catch the goddamned sparrows after all, don't they? 'Cause they're gonna turn everyone *into* sparrows . . . You know, Stone, I shouldn't say this because in your old age you became a bit softer than I did in mine, but if they get it off the ground, a lot of people everywhere may just lie back in their hammocks, or go fishin', and say the hell with it – let the big, uniformed daddys do it. Let 'em straighten things out – get the pot-heads with their guns and switchblades off the streets and out of the parks. Show the Ruskies and the oil boys in bathrobes we don't take their crap any more. Let's show Jesus we're the good guys with a lot of clout. Those soldiers, they got the guts and the guns, the corporations and the conglomerates, so what does it mean to me? Where do *I* change, says the Joe in the hammock, except maybe for the better?"

"Not better," said Stone icily. "Those same people become robots. We all become robots, if we live. Don't you understand that?"

"Yeah, *I* do," answered Johnny Reb. "I guess I always have. I live on a hog-high in Bern while you scratch in DC. Yes, old buddy, I understand. Maybe better than you do . . . Forget it, I'm enlisted. But what in all-fire hell are you going to do about this Converse? I don't think he's going to get out."

"He *has* to. We think he has the answers – the *first-hand* answers – that give us the proof."

"In my opinion he's dead," said the Southerner. "Maybe not now but soon – soon's they find him."

"We have to find him first. Can you help?"

"I started the night I needled Major Norman Anthony Washburn, the Fourth, Fifth, or Sixth – I keep losin' track of the numerals. You got the computers – the ones you have access to – and I've got the streets where they sell things you're not supposed to buy. So far, nothing."

"Try to find something because you were right before we don't have much time. And, Johnny, do you have the same feeling I have about that island, about Scharhorn?"

"Like Appomattox, way down deep in the stomach. I can taste the bile, Brer Rabbit, which is why I'm going to possum down here for a few days. We found ourselves a beehive, boy, and the drones are restless, I can sense it."

34

Joel put the map and the thick envelope on the grass and began pulling branches down from the small tree in the field to cover Hermione Geyner's car. Every snap of wood, each yanking of a limb, filled him with pain, as much from fatigue as from the strain in his arms. Finally, he bunched together reeds of tall grass and threw them everywhere over the frame. The result in the moonlight was an immense mound of hay under an innocuous tree in an orchard. He picked up the map and the envelope and started walking toward the road two hundred yards away. According to the map, he was on the outskirts of a city or town called Appenweier, ten miles from the border at Kehl, directly across the Rhine from Strasbourg.

He walked along the road, running into the grass whenever he saw the head-lights of a car in either direction. He had travelled perhaps five or six miles there was no way to tell – and knew that he could go no further.

In the jungles he had rested, knowing that rest was as much a weapon as a gun, the eyes and the mind far more lethal when alert than a dozen steel weapons strapped to his body.

He found a short ravine that bordered a country brook, the rocks his fortress, and fell asleep.

Valerie walked out of the Charles de Gaulle Airport on the arm of the Sûreté's Prudhomme, having accepted the scrap of paper with his telephone number but volunteering nothing. They approached the cab stand on the platform and Prudhomme spoke.

"I will make myself clear, Madame. You may take a taxi here and I shall bid you *adieu*, or you may permit me to drive you wherever you like – perhaps to another taxi stand in the city, to go wherever you wish and I will know if anyone is following you."

"You would?"

"In thirty-two years, even a fool learns something. My wife keeps telling me she has no lovers only because I have learned the rudiments of my profession."

434

"I accept your invitation," interrupted Val, smiling. "I'm terribly tired. A small hotel, perhaps. *Le Pont Royal*, I know it."

"An excellent choice, but I must say that my wife would welcome you – without any questions."

"My time must be my own, Monsieur," said Valerie, climbing into the car. "*D'accord*."

"*Why* are you doing this?" she asked, as Prudhomme got behind the wheel. "My husband was a lawyer – *is* a lawyer. The rules can't be that different. Aren't you some kind of accessory – assuming what I know damned well you're assuming?"

"I only wish that you will call me, saying that you are from the Tatiana family. That is my risk and that is my reward."

Converse looked at his watch – a watch taken from a collapsed body so long ago he could not remember – and saw that it was 5.45 in the morning, the sun abruptly illuminating his fortress-ravine. The stream was below and so he took care of his necessities – downstream – and he plunged his face into the flow of water – upstream. He had to move; he had five miles to walk to the border, as he remembered.

He remembered well. He reached Kehl and bought a razor, reasoning that a priest would maintain his appearance as best he could even under the duress of poor travel accommodation. He shaved at the river depot then took the ferry across the scenic Rhine to Strasbourg. The customs officials were so deferential to his collar and his passport, as well as his somewhat shabby presence – undoubtedly taken for the vow of poverty that he found himself blessing a number of men, and by extension their entire families, as he was passed through the building.

Out on the bustling streets he knew that the first thing he had to do was to get into a hotel room, shower off two days of fear and violence, and have his clothes cleaned or replaced. An impoverished-looking priest did not travel to the expensive wonders of Chamonix; it would be unseemly. A normally-dressed priest, however, was perfectly acceptable, even desirable, a figure of respectability among the crowds. And a priest he would remain, Converse had decided – the decision here again based on legal experience. Think out – anticipate – what your adversary expects you to do, then do not conform unless you retain the advantage. The hunters of Aquitaine would expect him to shed his priestly habit as it was his last known means of disguise; he would not do that; there were too many priests in France and too much advantage in being one.

He registered at the Sofitel on the Place St Pierre-leJeune and, without elaboration, explained to the *concierge* that he had been through a dreadful three days of travelling and would the kind man see to several items he needed rather desperately. He was from a very well-endowed parish in Los Angeles and – an American $100 bill took care of the rest. His suit was cleaned and pressed within the hour, his muddy shoes shined, and two new shirts with clerical collars purchased from a shop "unfortunately quite a distance away on the Quai Kellermann", thus necessitating an additional charge. The gratuities, the expenses and the surcharges for *Rush* – all were a hotelman's dream. The sun-tanned priest with a blemish or two on his face, and odd demands based on time, certainly had to come from a "well-endowed" parish. It was worth it. He had checked in at 8.30 in the morning and by 9.55 he was ready to make his final arrangements for Chamonix.

He could not risk taking a plane or going by rail; too much had happened to him at airports and on trains – they would be watched. And sooner or later Hermione Geyner's car would be found and his direction if not his destination would be known. Aquitaine's alarms would go out across the three borders of Germany, France and Switzerland; again the safest way was by automobile. The eagerly-accommodating *concierge* was summoned; a fine rental car was arranged for the youngish monsignor, and a route planned to Geneva, some 238 miles south.

Of course, he would not cross over into Geneva, but round the border roads and head for Chamonix, an hour-plus away. His estimated travel time was between five and six hours; he would reach the base of the majestic Mont Blanc by 4.30 in the afternoon, five o'clock at the latest. He wasted no time speeding out of Strasbourg on the Alpine Autoroute marked *83* on his map.

Valerie dressed as the first light silhouetted the irregular-shaped buildings of Paris outside her windows on the Boulevard Raspail. She had not slept nor had she made any attempt to; she had lain awake pondering the words of the strange Frenchman from the *Sûreté* who could not speak officially. She had been tempted to tell him the truth but knew she would not, not yet, perhaps not at all, for the possibility of a trap was considerable, revelations based in truth too easily employed to corner the one being hunted. Still, his plea had the ring of truth, his own truth, not someone else's . . . *Call and say you are from the Tatiana family. That is my wish and my reward.*

Joel would have an opinion. If the man was not simply bait put out by Aquitaine, it was a crack in their strategy the generals knew nothing about. She hoped it was and he was not, but to trust such a man at this point was impossible.

She had read the domestic schedules provided by Air France on the plane from Los Angeles and knew the routing she would take to Chamonix. Touraine Air had four flights daily to Annecy, the nearest airport to Chamonix and Mont Blanc. She had hoped to make reservations on the 7.00 A.M. flight last night but the sudden, unnerving intrusion of Prudhomme had ruled it out, and by the time she called Touraine from the Pont Royal there were no seats – it was summer and Mont Blanc was a tourist attraction. Nevertheless, she was on standby for the 11 o'clock flight. It was better to be at Orly Airport, better to be in the crowds, as Joel insisted.

She took the open, brass-grilled elevator down to the lobby, paid her bill, and asked for a taxi.

"*A quelle heure, Madame?*"

"*Maintenant, s'il vou plaît.*"

"*Dans quelques minutes.*"

"*Merci.*"

The taxi arrived and Val went outside, greeted by a surly, sleepy-eyed driver through the window, who had no intention of getting out of the cab, only vaguely willing to accept her patronage.

"*Orly, s'il vous plaît.*"

The driver started up, reached the corner and swung his wheel to the left, making a rapid U-turn so as to head back into the Boulevard Raspail toward the expressway that led to the airport. The intersection appeared to be deserted. It was not.

The crash behind them was close by and sudden – metal crashing against metal as glass shattered and tyres screeched. The driver slammed on his brakes, screaming in shock and fear as the taxi veered into the kerb. Val was thrown against the front seat, her knees scraping the floor. Awkwardly, she started to get up as the driver leaped from the cab yelling at the offending parties behind.

Suddenly, the right rear door opened and the lined, weary face of Prudhomme was above her, a trickle of blood rolling down from a gash in his forehead. He spoke quickly, quietly.

"Go, Madame – wherever it is you go. No one will follow you now."

"*You?* . . . You've been here all night! You were waiting for me, watching. It was you who crashed into that car!"

"There is no time. I will send your driver back. I must make out my tedious report while scattering a few items in the man's car, and you must leave. Now – before others learn."

"That name!" cried Val. "It was *Tatiana?*"

"Yes."

"Thank you!"

"*Bonjour. Bonne chance.*" The man from the Sûreté ducked away, closing the door, and ran back to the two Frenchmen shouting at one another behind the tax,.

It was 3.20 in the afternoon when Converse saw the sign: *St Julien en Genevois* – 15 km. He had rounded the border of Switzerland, the autoroute to Chamonix directly ahead, east of Geneva, just south of Annemasse. He would reach Mont Blanc in something over an hour; he had done it! He had also driven as he had never driven in his life before, the powerful Citröen responding to his pilot's touch, his pilot's mind oblivious to everything but the sweep in front of him, the equipment around him – the feel of the hard road beneath as he took the Alpine curves. He had stopped to refuel once at Pontarlier, where he drank steaming hot tea from a vending machine. Since he had left the expressway for the shorter distance of the mountain roads, his speed depended on his every reaction being instantaneous and accurate. An hour now. *Be there, Val. Be there, my love!*

Furious, Valerie looked at her watch ready to scream – as she had wanted to scream since 6.30 in the morning at Orly Airport. It was 4.10 in the afternoon and the entire day had been filled with one crisis after another, from the crash in the Boulevard Raspail and Prudhomme's revelation that she was being followed to her arrival at Annecy on the 1 o'clock flight from Paris – itself delayed by a malfunctioning luggage door. Her nerves were stretched to the outer limits yet she knew above all – had known throughout the day – that she could not lose her control. Doing so would only rivet attention on her; it briefly had.

There were no seats on the 7 o'clock flight and the 11 o'clock plane had been overbooked. Only those with tickets in their hands were permitted through the gate. She had so angrily protested that people began staring at her. Then she retreated to the soft-spoken bribe which only served to irritate the clerk – not that he was morally offended, only that he could not accommodate her and accept the money. Again passengers behind and on both sides, in both lines, had looked over as the clerk admonished her in true Gallic *hauteur*. It was no way to get to Chamonix alive, thought Val, accepting a ticket on the 1 o'clock flight.

The plane landed at Annecy over a half-hour late, several minutes after 3.00, and the subsequent crush at the taxi platform caused her to behave in a way she generally tried to avoid. Being a relatively tall woman – tall in appearance, certainly – she knew the effect she provoked when she looked disdainfully down at those around her: A genetic preordination had made her privileged, didn't they know? Foolishly, too many people accepted the posturing as proof of some sort of preordained fact; the women were intimidated, the men both intimidated and sexually aroused. It had gained her a few forward places in the taxi line, but the line was still long. Then she had glanced to her right; at the far end of the platform were the limousines, several chauffeurs leaning against their glistening vehicles, smoking cigarettes, picking their teeth and chattering. *What in heaven's name was she doing?* She had broken away from the line, opening her purse as she ran.

Her final frustration now was the result of something she should have remembered. There was a point in the theatrical setting that was the wondrous "village" of Chamonix where automobiles could not pass, only small official vehicles, and tourist minibuses. She got out of the limousine; she was on her own, as she walked rapidly down the wide, crowded boulevard. She could see the large red terminal of the cable car in the distance. Somewhere above, above the clouds, was Joel. Her Joel. She could not stop herself; she did not try to impose the control she had imposed all day. She began to run – faster, faster! *Be up there, my darling! Be alive, my darling – my only darling!*

It was ten minutes to five when Converse literally screeched into the parking lot, slamming on the brakes as he crashed himself out of the car. There had been traffic on the Mont Blanc autoroute, a holdover at the new construction over the vast gorge bridge. Every muscle in his right leg had been cramped with every anticipation, every opportunity seized to swing around the lethargic traffic. He was *here!* He was in Chamonix, the majestic splendour of the Alps in front of

438

him, the village below. He started running, his breath gone, taking swallows of breath from the clear air of the clean mountains, forgetting the pain – welcoming it for she *had* to be there! *Please, Val, make it! I love you so . . . goddamn it, I need you so! Be there!*

She stood outside the cable lift, the clouds below on the mountains forming a barrier from the peaks beneath, a wall of mist from any concerns of the earth they knew. She shivered in the Alpine cold but she could not leave. She stood by the stone railing, by a thick mountain telescope through which tourists could observe the wonders of the Alpine world for a few francs. She was frightened to death he would not come – could not come. *Death.*

It was the last cable car, none were permitted after the sun descended over the western peaks – cables were suddenly frozen with shadows. Except for the bartender and several customers inside the glass doors of the bar, she was the only one outside. *Joel! I told you to stay alive! Please do what I said, my darling – my only darling! My only love!*

The cable car ground into a thousand grinding aberrations then screechingly came to a stop. There was no one *there!* It was empty, without people! *Death.*

And then he walked into view, a tall man in a clerical collar, and the top of the world made sense again. He stepped down out of the car and she ran to him as he ran to her. They embraced, both holding each other as they had never held each other as man and wife.

"I love you!" he whispered. "Oh, *God*, I love you."

She pulled back, holding his shoulders, tears filling her eyes. "You're alive, you're here! You did what I asked you to do."

"What I had to do," he said. "Because it was you."

35

They slept naked, their bodies together, their arms around each other, for a while pushing out the world as they knew it to be, a world they would face in the morning. But for a time there had to be something for themselves, for each other, giving and receiving, precious hours alone, speaking in whispers, trying to understand what they had lost and why, each telling the other it would never be lost again.

When morning came, they both wanted to deny its arrival, yet not completely. There *was* the world as they knew it, and there was another world, as the generals of Aquitaine would have it. They ordered Continental breakfast and an extra pot of coffee.

While Val combed her hair, Joel went to the window and looked down at the colourfully vibrant town of Chamonix. Hoses pouring out water were seemingly everywhere, as the streets were washed down. The storefronts were splashed until they glistened. Chamonix was preparing for the onslaught of summer tourists – thinking of which, mused Converse, they had been lucky to find rooms. They had gone to three hotels – the first was nearly a disaster before they reached the desk. "For God's sake, get rid of that *collar!*" Valerie had whispered. None of the three had anything available, but the fourth, the *Croix Blanche Inn*, had just received a cancellation.

"I'll go out and get you some clothes later," said Val, coming up behind him, placing her head on his shoulder.

"I've missed that," he said, turning, putting his arms around her. "I've missed you. So much."

"We've found each other, darling. That's all that matters." There was a knock on the door, the polite knock of a waiter. "That'll be the coffee. Go use my toothbrush."

They sat across from each other at the small marble table in front of the window. It was time and they both knew it. Joel placed a page of hotel stationery beside his coffee, a hotel pen on top.

"I still can't get over my aunt!" said Val, suddenly. "How could I have *done* it? How could I not have *known?*"

"A couple of times I asked myself the same question." Converse smiled gently. "About you, I mean."

"I'm surprised you didn't throw me out of the cable car."

"Only crossed my mind twice."

"God, I was *stupid!*"

"No, you were desperate," corrected Joel. "Just as she was desperate. You were clutching for possibilities, for help. She was desperately trying to go back to the only meaningful days of her life. A person can be terribly convincing feeling like that. She had the proper words, all those esoteric phrases you'd heard all your life. You believed her. I would have believed her, too."

"You're devastating when you're kind, darling. Go easy, it's morning."

"Tell me about Sam Abbott," he said.

"Yes, of course, but before I do I want you to know we're not alone. There's a man in Paris, an inspector from the *Sûreté*, who knows you didn't kill René and you couldn't have killed the one they called a chauffeur at the George V."

Startled, Joel leaned forward over his coffee. "But I did kill that man. God knows I didn't mean to – I thought at first he was reaching for a gun, not a radio – but I fought him, I smashed his head into the wall; he died from a cranial something-or-other."

"No, he didn't. He was killed in the hospital. He was suffocated; his lungs were collapsed by suffocation. It was unrelated to his injuries, that's what Prud-homme said. As he put it, if you didn't kill the driver and you didn't kill René, how many others didn't you kill? He thinks you've been set up; he doesn't know why any more than he can understand why evidence has been suppressed, or suddenly found when it should have been found earlier if it existed – in this case your fingerprints in Mattilon's office. He wants to help; he gave me a telephone number where we can reach him."

"Can we trust him?" asked Joel, writing a note on the stationery.

"I think so. He did something remarkable this morning, but I'll get to that."

"The man at the George V," said Converse softly. "Bertholdier's aide. It's where the running began. It's as though the moment was suddenly seized upon, someone recognizing a possible strategy, not wanting to let the opportunity slip away. 'Brand him a killer now, maybe we can use it, build on it. All it costs is a life.' *Jesus!*" Joel struck a hotel match and lit a cigarette. "Go on," he continued. "Go back. What about Sam?"

She told him everything, starting with the madness at the St Regis in New York – the frightening telephone call that led to an intense young man racing up the steps and an Army officer running after her down the street.

"The odd thing here," interrupted Converse, "is that those men, that call, might have been legitimate."

"*What?* How? The first one looked like a Hitler youth and the other was in uniform!"

"Most people in uniform would be the first ones to want the generals of Aquitaine cut loose in a typhoon. Remember Fitzpatrick said those four dossiers came from way down deep in official vaults and, judging from much of the material, Connal thought there was heavy military input. Maybe my silent partners in Washington are beginning to crawl out of their sewers. Sorry. Go on."

She told him of meeting Sam at the diner in Las Vegas, the married Sam, Sam the father of two young girls. Wincing, Joel listened, all his antennae revolving, catching every turn of phrase, every meaning that might have more than one meaning, trying desperately to find a clue, a way – something, *anything* they might use or act upon. And then he held up his hand, only inches above the table but it was a signal for Val to stop.

"The *three* of you were going to Washington?"

"Yes."

"You and Sam and this third person he was going to see, going to talk to – the one he said would know what to do."

"Yes. The man who had Sam killed. He was the *only* one Sam talked to."

"But Abbott said he trusted him. With 'his life', I think you said."

"Sam said," corrected Valerie. "He was wrong."

"Not necessarily. Sam was easy-going but not easily conned. He chose his friends carefully; he didn't have too many because he knew his rank was vulnerable."

"But he didn't talk with anyone else."

"I'm sure he didn't but this other man had to. I know something about crisis conferences in Washington – and that's exactly what Sam meant when he said you were going there. Those meetings don't just happen, some strong words are used to cut a path through the bureaucratic mess. Certainly Sam's name would be put forward first – he had the status and the rank – and just possibly my name, or yours, or even Delavane's, any of which would have been enough." Converse picked up the pen. "What was his name?"

"Oh, Lord," said Val, closing her eyes, her fingers massaging her forehead. "Let me think.... Alan, the first name was Alan.... Alan Metzger? Metland ...?"

"Was there a rank, a title of some kind?"

"No. *Metcalf!* Alan Metcalf, that was it."

Joel wrote down the name. "Okay, let's get to Paris, the man from the *Sûreté*."

She began with the odd behaviour of the immigration officials which led to the strange meeting with the lined, weary, rumpled Prudhomme. She reached the end of the Frenchman's startling revelations, repeating herself but filling in all the details she had omitted previously. When she had finished Converse held up his palm for the second time, his mouth open in astonishment, his eyes wide and alive.

"The *Tatiana* family?" he asked incredulously. "Are you certain?"

"Completely. I asked him again yesterday."

"Yesterday? Yes, you said he did something remarkable yesterday. What happened?"

"He stayed up all night outside the hotel in his car and when I left in a taxi shortly after the sun was up he crashed – and I mean crashed – into the car behind us. I was being followed. He told me to hurry up and get out of there. That's when I asked him to repeat the name. It was Tatiana."

"That was the name René told me to use with Cort Thorbecke in Amsterdam. 'Say you're a member of the Tatiana family'. Those were his instructions."

"What does it mean?"

"René didn't go into it too deeply but I got the drift. Apparently it means some kind of trust, a litmus test that clears someone for a level of information that would be withheld from ninety-nine per cent of the people wanting it."

"Why?" ·

"It sounds crazy but Mattilon said it was because whoever was part of Tatiana was trusted by the most suspicious people on earth – men who couldn't afford to make a mistake."

"My God, *who?*"

"Russians. Commissars in the Kremlin who floated money out to brokers in the West who invested it."

"You're right," said Val. "It's crazy."

"But it works, don't you see? Decent men who for one reason or another found themselves in a world they probably hated, never knowing whom they could trust, figured out a code among themselves. To be a member of the Tatianas is some kind of clearance. It's not only a signal of emergency, it's more than that. It means that whoever sends that signal Is all right – in spite of what he may have to do. I'll bet it's one hell of a small circle. Rene, this Prudhomme, they'd fit into it. And for us it's a key; we can trust it."

"You're in court, aren't you?" said the now and former Mrs Converse, reaching across the table for his free hand.

"I don't know any other way to do it. Facts, names, tactics; somewhere there's a crack, a road we can take – we *have* to take. Quickly."

"I'd start with Prudhomme," said Val.

"We'll call in his hand but maybe not first. Let's take things in sequence. Are there two phones in here? A certain – ex-wife had me too preoccupied to notice last night."

"She's probably pregnant."

"Wouldn't that be *wonderful?*"

"Down, boy. Yes, there's another phone. It's in the bathroom."

"I want you to call this Metcalf, Alan Metcalf in Las Vegas. We'll get the number from information. I'll listen."

"What do I say?"

"What name did you and Sam use?"

"The one I told you. Parquette."

"Say that's who's calling, nothing else. Let him make the first move. If it's wrong, I'll know – we'll both know – and I'll hang up. You'll hear me and you hang up, too."

"Suppose he's not there? Suppose I get a wife or a girl friend or a child?"

"Leave your name quickly and say you'll call back in an hour."

The civilian sat in the sofa, his feet up on the coffee table. Across, in two arm chairs, were the Army captain – out of uniform and the young Navy lieutenant, also in street clothes.

"We agree, then," said Stone. "We try this Metcalf and hope for the best. If we're wrong – if *I'm* wrong – we could be traced and don't fool yourselves, you've been seen here, you could be identified. But as I told you before, there comes a time where you have to take a risk you'd rather not take. You're out of safe-territory and you hope to Christ you get through it fast. I can't promise that you will. This phone is tapped into another number, a hotel across town, so any trace would be delayed, but only delayed while everyone registered was checked, every room checked. Once that's over with, any experienced telephone repairman could go down in the cellars and find the intercept."

"How much time would that give us?" asked the Army officer.

"It's one of the largest hotels in New York," replied the civilian. "With luck, twenty-four to thirty-six hours."

"Go for it!" ordered the Navy man.

"Oh, for God's sake," said the captain, running his hand through his hair. "Yes, of course, try it, try *him*. But I'm still not sure *why?*"

"Scat-patterns. It was routine information and easy to get. Abbott wrote out his schedules every day and he was precise about them. There was a predominance of lunches alone with Metcalf, and dinners with both families at either the Abbott or the Metcalf homes. I think he trusted the man, and as a long-time intelligence officer Metcalf was the logical one to go to. Also, there's something else. Along with Converse, all three were prisoners of war in Vietnam."

"Go for it!" cried the Navy lieutenant.

"For Christ's sake, find another phrase," said the captain.

"It's an answering machine!" shouted Val, gripping the mouthpiece of the telephone.

Joel came out of the bathroom. "One hour," he whispered.

"One hour," she said. "Miss Parquette will call back in an hour." She hung up.

"And every hour after that," added Converse, staring down at the phone. "I don't like this. It's one o'clock in the morning back there, and if there's a wife or children around, someone should have been there."

"Sam didn't mention a wife or children, except his own."

"No reason why he would."

"There could be a dozen explanations, Joel."

"I just hope it's not the one I keep thinking about."

"Let me call Prudhomme," said Valerie. "Let's use this Tatiana family."

"Not yet."

"Why *not?*"

"We need something else – *he* needs something else."

Suddenly, Converse's gaze fell on the thick envelope addressed to Nathan Simon. It was on the bureau, his false passport on top. "My God, we may *have* it," he said quietly. "It's been right there all the time and I didn't see it."

Val followed his eyes. "The analysis you wrote for Nathan?"

"I called it the best brief I ever wrote, but of course it's not a brief at all. It doesn't address points of law except in the widest, most abstract sense, without acceptable evidence to support the accusations. What it does address is the perverted ambitions of powerful men who want to *change* the laws, altering governments, supplanting them with raw, military controls, all in the name of maintaining the *law* and preserving the *order* they themselves will be called upon to maintain and preserve. And if 'compromise' means killing – if they intend mounting wholesale assassinations – they can do it."

"What's your *point*, Joel?"

"If I'm going to build a case, I'd better do it the only way I know how – from premise to conclusion based on affidavits – depositions – starting with my own and ending with pre-trial examinations."

"What the hell are you talking about?"

"The law, Mrs Converse," said Joel, picking up the envelope. "And what it's meant to do. I can use most of what's in here – just in a different form. Naturally, I'll want other corroborating depositions, the farther afield the better. That's when you'll call this Prudhomme and join the Tatiana family. Then hopefully we'll reach Sam's friend, Metcalf goddamn it, he'll have *something* to give us . . . Finally, I'm going to want to examine at least two of the alleged defendants orally – Leifhelm, for one, and probably Abrahms, maybe Delavane himself."

"You're *mad!*" cried Valerie.

"No, I'm not," said Converse simply. "I'll need help, I know that. But I've got enough money to hire a couple of squads of miscreants – and once Prudhomme understands, I have an idea he'll know where the union hall is. We've got a lot of work to do, Val. All courts like immaculate manuscripts."

"For Christ's sake, Joel, speak English."

444

"You're a romantic, Mrs Converse," he said approaching her. "These are the nuts and bolts you don't find in seascapes."

"They *do* have to be sketched, my darling. And balanced or unbalanced, the colours deliberate . . . What *are* you talking about?"

"A stenographer – a legal secretary, if you can find one. Someone who's willing to stay here all day and half the night, if need be. Offer three times the going rate."

"Say I find one," said Val. "What in heaven's name are you going to tell her? Or him?"

Joel frowned as he crossed aimlessly to the window. "A novel," he said, turning. "We're writing a novel. The first twenty or thirty pages are to be read as an upcoming court case, a trial."

"Based on real people, men everyone's read about?"

"It's a new kind of fiction, but it's only a novel. That's all it is."

Morning came to New York and Stone was alone again. The Navy lieutenant and the Army captain back at their desks in Washington. It was better this way; they could not help him and the less they were seen around the apartment the more likely they might escape detection if the hammer came down. And the hammer could come down, Stone knew it. It was as clear as the fact that Colonel Alan Metcalf was the chord they needed to start the music. "Without him," as Johnny Reb might have said in the old days, "the tune ain't gonna get out of the fiddle – no stompin' unless he shows up." But could he show up? wondered the former operations officer for Central Intelligence. For all intents and purposes he had disappeared, that was the word from Nellis, and the investigating unit did not pretend to understand or appreciate his absence. That, too, was the word and it was delivered harshly.

But Stone understood. Metcalf now knew what he knew – what they knew – and the colonel would not play by any rules written in the regulations, not if he was any good. Not if he was alive. And the ex-agent also understood something else when it came to telephone answering machines and intelligence personnel. The equipment was adaptable and sophisticated, courtesy of the American tax-payer and one of the better investments he made considering the extraordinary waste. Metcalf would play it well – if he was alive and any good. He would use a remote, programming it and reprogramming it, hearing what he wanted to hear, erasing what he wanted to erase, and leaving in certain information, preferably misleading. There would also be a code, probably changed daily, that if not-inserted accurately would melt the tape with a ten second burst of microwaves – all standard. If he was any good. If he was alive.

Stone counted on both – that the colonel was both good and that he was alive. There was no point in thinking otherwise; that only led to staying in Johnny Reb's hammock or "goin" fishin', doing whatever one did as a robot. Which was why Stone had left a message on Metcalf's machine an hour ago at 6.35. He had chosen a name Converse's wife – former wife – must have relayed to the dead Samuel Abbott. *Marcus Aurelius ascending. Respond and erase, please.* Then Stone had given the telephone number at the apartment, which, if traced, would lead the tracers to the Hilton Hotel on Fifty-Second Street.

There was only one other person in the world Stone wished he could reach, but that man was "on holiday we have no means of getting in touch". The words were patently a lie, but to intrude on that lie would mean Peter would have to say more than he wanted to say. The man was Derek Belamy, Chief of Clandestine Operations for Britain's MI6 and one of the only real friends Stone ever had in all his years with the Central Intelligence Agency. Belamy was such a good friend that when Peter was Station Chief in London, the Englishman told him bluntly to get out for a while before the whisky took over all together and his ass was nailed to an alcoholic cross.

I have a doctor who'll certify a minor breakdown, Peter. I've a guest cottage on the grounds in Kent. Stay there, get well, old boy.

Stone had refused, and it was the most destructive decision he had ever made. The rest was the drunken nightmare Belamy had predicted.

But it was not Derek's concerns for a friend that caused Peter to want to reach him. It was Belamy's brilliance, his perceptions quietly concealed behind a pleasant, even prosaic exterior. And the fact that Derek Belamy had the pulse of Europe in his head, he could smell out a Delavane operation given the most basic facts. And, in fact, thought Stone hopefully, he was smelling them out now in Ireland – certainly where he was now. Sooner or later – preferably sooner – Belamy would return his call. When he did, a munitions shipment from Beloit, Wisconsin, would be described in full. Derek Belamy loathed the Delavanes of this world. His old friend would become an ally against the generals.

The telephone rang; the civilian looked at it and let it ring again. *Metcalf* He reached over and picked it up.

"Yes?"

"Aurelius?"

"Somehow I knew you'd come through, Colonel."

"Who the hell *are* you?"

"The name's Stone and we're on the same side, at least I think we are. However, you wear a uniform and I don't, so I need a little more confidence in you. Can you understand that?"

"You're one of those *bastards* in DC who sent him out!"

"You're warmer, Colonel. I came on late, but yes, I am one of those bastards. What happened to General Abbott?"

"He was killed, you son of a bitch! . . . I assume this phone is clean."

"For at least twenty-four hours. Then we all disappear, just like you disappeared."

"No remorse? No conscience? Do you know what you've *done?*"

"We don't have time for that, Colonel. Perhaps later, if there's a later for us . . . Get *off* it, soldier! I've *lived* with this! *Now.* Where do we meet? Where are you?"

"Okay, okay," said the obviously exhausted Air Force officer. "I took a dozen different flights. I'm in – where the hell am I? – in Knoxville, Tennessee. I've got a flight to Washington in twenty minutes."

"Why?"

"To blow this fucking thing out of the air, what *else?*"

"Forget it, you're a dead man. I'd think you'd have learned that by now. You set up something on the information Abbott gave you, right?"

"Yes."

"And *he* was blown out of the air, right?"

"Goddamn you, shut up!"

"You should have learned. They're where you can't see them or find them. But the wrong word to the wrong person and they can find you."

"I *know* that!" shouted Metcalf. "But I've been in this business for twenty years. There's got to be *someone* I can trust!"

"Let's talk about it, Colonel. Scratch DC and fly up to New York. I'll get a room at the Algonquin – actually I've already reserved one.'

"What name?"

"What else? Marcus."

"You're on, but since we're in this deep I should tell you. The woman's been trying to reach me since one o'clock this morning."

"Converse's *wife?*"

"Yes."

"We need her. We need *him!*"

"I'll re-program the machine. The Algonquin?"

"That's it."

"He's from New York, isn't he? I mean he's a New Yorker."

"Whatever that means, yes. He's lived here for years."

"I hope he's bright – they're bright."

"Neither of them would be alive now if they weren't very bright, Colonel."

"See you in a few hours, Stone."

The civilian hung up the phone, his hands shaking, his eyes on a bottle of bourbon across the room. *No!* There would be no drinks, he had *promised* himself! He got out of the chair and went to the bed where his small suitcase was open, a gaping mouth waiting to be filled. He filled it, leaving the bottle of whisky on the table, and went outside to the elevators down the hall.

I, Joel Harrison Converse, an attorney admitted to practise before the bar of the State of New York and employed by the firm of Talbot, Brooks and Simon, 666 Fifth Avenue, New York City, New York, arrived in Geneva, Switzerland, on 9 August for legal conferences on behalf of our client, the Comm Tech Corporation, for the purpose of finalizing a contemplated business association referred to hereafter as the Comm Tech-Bern merger. On the morning of 10 August, at approximately 8 o'clock, I was contacted by the chief counsel representing the Bern Group, Mr Avery Preston Halliday of San Francisco, California. As he was an American only recently retained by the Swiss companies, I agreed to meet with him to clarify the existing points of argument and our positions with respect to them. When I arrived at the café on the Quai du Mont Blanc, I recognized Mr Halliday as a student and close friend I had known years ago at The Taft School in Watertown, Connecticut. His name then was Avery P. Fowler. Mr Halliday readily confirmed this fact, explaining that his surname had been changed upon the death of his father and the remarriage of his mother to a John Halliday of San Francisco. The explanation was acceptable, the circumstances, however, were not. Mr Halliday had ample prior time and opportunity to apprise me of his identity – the identity with which I was familiar – but did not do so. There was a reason. On that morning of 10 August, Mr Halliday sought a confidential meeting with the undersigned regarding a matter totally unrelated to the Comm Tech-Bern merger. This meeting was the primary reason for his being in Geneva. It was the first of many disturbing revelations . . .

If the very proper and distant British stenographer had the slightest interest in the material she transcribed in segments from dictation to the typewritten page, she did not show it. Her thin lips pursed, her grey hair knotted into a forbidding bun on the top of her head, she performed like a machine, as if everything was accepted in rote and by rote. Valerie's somewhat guarded explanation that her husband was an American novelist intrigued by recent events in Europe was greeted with a cold stare and the gratuitous information that the legal secretary never watched television and rarely read the newspapers. She was a member of the Franco-Italian Alpine Society, which took up all her time and efforts in defence of natural endowments being eroded by man – when not earning a living so as to remain in her beloved mountains. She was an automaton putting in her time; one could dictate the book of Genesis and Val doubted the woman would know what she was typing.

It was the seventh hour and still no answer at Alan Metcalf's telephone in Las Vegas. Only a machine. It was time for the eighth call.

"If we don't get him now," said Converse grimly, under the quiet tapping of the typewriter across the room, "go ahead and reach Prudhomme. I wanted to talk to this Metcalf first but it's possible – that it may not be possible."

"What difference does it make? You need help quickly and he's willing to help."

"The difference is I know where Prudhomme's coming from, you've told me. I've got an idea what he can do and what he can't do, but I don't know anything about Metcalf – except that Sam put him way up on a high priority. Whoever I call first I've got to make specific statements to him, accusations and observations that'll blow his mind. Those are commitments, Val, and I have to go with the strongest . . . Try Metcalf again." Joel turned and headed for the telephone in the bathroom as Valerie dialled the international codes for Las Vegas, Nevada.

"Caller C, message received. Please re-identify yourself twice followed by a slow count to ten. Stay on the line."

Joel put the phone down on the edge of the basin and rushed out to the bedroom-sitting room. He walked over to Val, holding up his hand as he reached for a pencil on the desk. He wrote out the words on a page of stationery.

Go ahead. Stay calm. PSE.

"This is Miss Parquette speaking," said Valerie, frowning, bewildered. "This is Miss Parquette speaking. One, two, three, four . . ."

Converse returned to the bathroom, picked up the telephone and listened.

" . . . eight, nine, ten."

Silence. Finally, there were two sharp clicks and the metallic voice came back on the line.

"*Confirmed, thank you. This is the second tape and will be microed out when completed. Listen carefully. There is a place on an island well known for its tribal nights. The King will be in his chair. That's it. We are burning.*"

Joel hung up the phone and studied the only half-legible words he had hastily scribbled in soap on the mirror above the basin. The door opened and Valerie walked in, the page of hotel stationery in her hand.

"I wrote it down," she said, handing him the paper.

"I wrote it sideways – your way is better. Christ, a *riddle!*"

"No more than the one you gave me. What in heaven's name does PSE mean?"

" 'Psychological Stress Evaluator'," answered Converse, leaning against the wall and reading the words of Metcalf's message. He looked at her. "It's a voice scanner you can attach to a phone or a recording machine that supposedly tells you whether the person you're talking to is lying or not. Larry Talbot played around with one for a while but claimed he couldn't find anyone telling the truth including his ninety-two-year-old mother. He threw it away."

"Does it work?"

"They say it's much more accurate than a lie detector and I suppose it is if you know how to read it or use it. It worked in your case. Your voice was matched against the other calls you made, which means this Metcalf is into pretty high-tech equipment. That scanner tripped the second tape and it was all done by remote, from another phone, otherwise he would have answered himself after you passed the test."

"But if I passed, why the riddle? Why an island with tribal nights?"

"Because any machine like that can be beaten. It's why they're not admissible in court. Years ago Willie Sutton was wired into a lie detector and according to the results he never even broke into a piggy bank much less Chase Manhattan. Metcalf was willing to take a risk, but not all the way. He's running, too." Converse returned to the page of stationery.

"An island." Val spoke softly, reading the soaped words on the mirror. "Tribes . . . The Carib tribes; they were all through the Antilles. Or Jamaica – tribal nights, obeah rituals, voodoo rites in Haiti. Even the Bahamas – the Lucayan Indians – they held puberty rituals, they all did."

"You impress me," said Joel, looking up from the paper. "How come?"

"Art courses," she replied. "Those nuts and bolts you won't grant us that go into the make-up of a culture's visual work . . . And it doesn't fit. It's too loose."

"Why? It could mean some place in the Caribbean, some resort that's advertised a lot. The King is an emperor and that has to mean Delavane – Mad Marcus as in Aurelius . . . All those television commercials, the newspaper ads – pictures of people doing the limbo under torches with costumed blacks smiling down benignly, counting the dollars. Which *one?*"

"Too loose," repeated Val. "Too abstract – blocks and geometric shapes without specifics – no representational images."

"Now what the hell are *you* talking about," objected Converse.

"It's too wide, Joel, too many places to choose from, places you might not know anything about. It has to be closer, more familiar to you or to me, something we can recognize. Like Bruegel or Vermeer, littered with specific detail."

"They sound like dentists."

Valerie took the paper from him. "*Manhattan's* an island," she said softly, reading and frowning again.

"If there are torches and tribal puberty rites, it's not my part of town."

"Not tribal rites, tribal nights," corrected Val. "Tribal – not black but red? 'The King will be in his chair' – chair . . . table. His *table*. Tribal . . . nights. Nights! That's where we're misreading it. *Nights!*"

"How else can you read it?"

"Not nights but *knights!* With a K!"

"And a table," broke in Converse. "Knights of the Round Table."

"But *not* the King Arthur legend, not Camelot. Much nearer, much closer. Tribal – *American* natives. American *Indians*."

"Algonquins. The Roundtable!"

"The Algonquin Hotel," cried Valerie. "That's it, that's what he meant!"

"We'll know in a few minutes," said Joel. "Go inside and place the call."

The wait was both intolerable and interminable. Converse looked at his face in the mirror; perspiration began to drench his face, the salt stinging his scrapes and burning his eyes. Far more telling, his hand shook and his breath was short. The Algonquin switchboard answered and Val asked for a Mr Marcus. There was a stretch of silence and when the operator came back on the line, Joel thought he would smash the telephone into the mirror.

"There are two Marcuses registered, Mam. Which one did you wish to speak to?"

"*Already* it's a rotten day!" Val broke in suddenly over the phone, startling Converse with her words. "My boss, the *clown*, told me to call Mr Marcus at the Algonquin right away and give him the time and place for lunch. Now the clown's disappeared to a meeting somewhere outside and I'm left holding it. Sorry, dear, I didn't mean to take it out on you."

"It's okay, hon, we got a few like that around here."

"Maybe you can help me. Which Marcus is which. Maybe I'll recognize the first name or a company."

"Sure. Lemme plug into Big Reggie. We all gotta stick together when it comes to the clowns, right? . . . Okay, here they are. Marcus, Myron. Sugarman's Original Replicas, Los Angeles. And Marcus, Peter . . . not much help here, sweetie. Just says Georgetown, Washington, DC."

"That's the one. Peter. I'm sure of it. Thanks, dear."

"Glad to be of help, hon. I'll ring now."

The folded *New York Times* resting on his knee, Stone inked in the last two words of the crossword puzzle and looked at his watch. It had taken him nine minutes, nine minutes of relief; he wished it had been longer. One of the joys of having been Station Chief in London was *The Times* crossword. He could always count on at least a half hour when he could forget problems in the search for words and meanings.

450

The telephone rang. Stone whipped his head around, staring at it, his pulse accelerating, his throat suddenly dry. No one knew he had checked into the Algonquin under the name of Marcus. *No* one! . . . Yes, there was someone but he was in the air, flying up from Knoxville, Tennessee. What had gone *wrong?* Or had he been wrong about Metcalf? Was the supposedly angry, sermonizing Air Force intelligence officer one of *them?* Had his own instincts, honed over a thousand years of sorting out garbage, deserted him because he so desperately sought an opening, an escape from a steel net that was dropping down on him, a hammer descending within it? He got out of his chair and walked slowly, in fear, to the bedside table. He picked up the insistently ringing phone.

"Yes?"

"Alan Metcalf?" said the soft, firm voice of a woman.

"*Who?*" Stone was so thrown by the name he could barely concentrate, barely think!

"I beg your pardon, I have the wrong room."

"*Wait!* Don't hang up. Metcalf's on his way here."

"I'm sorry."

"Please! Oh Christ, *please!* I was tired, I was *asleep.* We've been up night and day . . . Metcalf. I talked with him two hours ago – he said he was going to reprogram his machine, that someone had been trying to reach him since one o'clock this morning. He had to get *out* of there. A man was killed, a pilot. It was *not* an *accident!* Am I making sense to you?"

"Why should I talk to you?" asked the woman. "So you can trace the call?"

"*Listen* to me," said Stone, his voice now in total control. "Even if I wanted to – and I don't – this is a hotel, not a private line, and to do what you suggest would take at least three men on the trunk lines and another controlling the switchboard. And even with such a unit it would be at least four minutes before they could isolate the wire and send out a tracer signal – which, incidentally, would only give us an area location, not a specific phone. *And* if you were calling from overseas we'd have to have another man, an expert, *in* that specific location to narrow it down to *perhaps a* twenty mile radius, but only if you stayed on *your* phone for at least eight minutes . . . Now, for God's sake, give me at least *two!*"

"Go on. Quickly!"

"I'm going to assume something. Maybe I shouldn't, but you're a clever woman, Mrs DePinna, and you could do it."

"*DePinna?*"

"Yes. You left a telephone book open to the blue pages, the government pages. When the *accident* happened in Nevada, I made a simple connection with a listing and two hours ago I learned I was right. Metcalf returned my call – from a pay phone at an airport. A pilot, a general, had talked to him at length. He's joining us . . . You ran from the wrong people, Mrs DePinna. But as for what I'm thinking, I think the man we want to find is listening on this phone."

"There's no one else here!"

"Please don't interrupt me, I've got to use every second." Stone's voice suddenly became stronger. "*Leifhelm, Bertholdier, van Headmer, Abrahms!* And a fifth man we can't identify, an Englishman who's down so deep he makes Burgess,

451

Maclean and Blunt look like amateurs. We don't know who he is but he's there, using warehouses in Ireland and off-shore cargo ships, and long-forgotten airfields to transport materials that shouldn't be going out. Those dossiers came from *us*, *Converse!* We sent them to you! You're a lawyer and you know that by using your name I'm incriminating myself or committing suicide if anyone's taping this. I'll go farther. We sent you out through Preston Halliday in Geneva. We sent you out to build a legal case – from left field – so we could abort this thing with a minimum of fallout, sending all those goddamned idiots back to reality. But we were wrong. They were much farther ahead than we ever suspected – *we* ever suspected – but not Beale on Mykonos. He was dead right and he's dead because he was right. Incidentally, he was the 'man from San Francisco'. It was his five hundred thousand dollars; he came from a rich family which, among other things, bequeathed him a conscience. Think back to Mykonos! To what he told you – what his life was all about. From celebrated soldier to a scholar – to a killing that must have killed a part of him to commit . . . He said you almost caught him up on a couple of things he didn't mean to say. He said you were a good lawyer, a good choice. Preston Halliday was a student of his at Berkeley, and when this broke a year and a half ago, when Halliday realized what Delavane was doing and how he was being used, he went to Beale who was about to retire. The rest you can figure out."

The woman's voice interrupted. "Say what I want to hear you say. *Say* it!"

"Of course I will. Converse didn't kill Peregrine and he didn't kill the commander of NATO. Both of them were marked by Delavane – George Marcus Delavane – because both those men would have taken him and his ilk to the mat! They were convenient, *very* convenient, targets. I don't know about the others – I don't know what you've been through – but we broke a liar in Bad Godesberg, the major from the embassy who put *you*, *Converse*, at the Adenauer Bridge! He doesn't know it, but we broke him, and we learned something. We think we know where Connal Fitzpatrick is. We think he's alive!"

A male voice intruded. "You *bastards*," said Joel Converse.

"Thank *God!*" said the civilian, sitting down on the hotel bed. "Now we can talk. We have to talk. Tell me everything you can. This phone is clean."

Twenty minutes later, his hands trembling, Peter Stone hung up the phone.

36

General Jacques Louis Bertholdier ceased the rushing pelvic thrusts of intercourse, withdrew himself from the moaning dark haired woman beneath him, and rolled over, grabbing the telephone.

"*Yes?*" he shouted angrily. And then he listened, his flushed face growing ashen as his organ collapsed. "Where did it happen?" he whispered, not in confidence but in sudden fear. "The Boulevard Raspail? The charges? . . . *Narcotics? Impossible!*"

Holding the phone, the general swung his legs over the side of the bed, listening carefully, concentrating as he stared at the wall. The naked woman rose to her knees and leaned into him, her breasts pressed into his back, her open mouth caressing his ear, her teeth gently biting his lobe.

Bertholdier suddenly, viciously, swung his arm back, cracking the phone into the woman's face, sending her reeling to the other side of the bed, blood erupting from her broken lower lip.

"Repeat that, please," he said into the phone. "It's obvious then, isn't it? The man cannot be questioned further, can he? There is always the larger strategy to consider, losses to be anticipated in the field, no? It is the hospital all over again, I'm afraid. See to it then, like the fine officer you are. The Legion's loss was our immense gain . . . Oh? What is it? The arresting officer was *Prudhomme?*" Bertholdier paused, his breathing steady and audible; then he spoke, rendering a command decision. "A stubborn bureaucrat from the *Sûreté* will not let go, will he? . . . He is your second assignment, to be carried out with your usual expertise before the day is over. Call me when both are accomplished, and consider yourself the aide to General Jacques Bertholdier."

The general hung up and turned to the dark-haired woman who was wiping her lips with a bed sheet, her eyes an admixture of anger, embarrassment and fear.

"Apologies, my dear," he said courteously. "But you must leave now. I have telephone calls to make, business to attend to."

"I will not come back!" cried the woman defiantly.

"You will come back," said the legend of France standing up, his body rigid in its nakedness. "If you are asked."

Erich Leifhelm walked rapidly into his study and directly over to the large desk, where he took the phone from a white-jacketed attendant, dismissing the man with the nod of his head. The instant the door was closed he spoke. "What is it?"

"The Geyner car was found, Herr General."

"Where?"

"Appenweier."

"And what is that?"

"A town fifteen or eighteen kilometres from Kehl. In the Alsace."

"*Strasbourg!* He crossed into France! He *was* a priest!"

"I don't understand, Herr."

"We never *thought* . . . ! Never mind! Who have you got in the sector?"

"Only one man, *Mein Herr*. The man with the police."

"Tell him to hire others. Send them into Strasbourg! Look for a priest!"

"Get *out* of here!" roared Chaim Abrahms, as his wife walked through the door into their kitchen. "This is no place for you now!"

"The Testaments say otherwise, my husband – yet not my husband," said the frail woman dressed in black, the circle of soft white hair framing her gentle features, her brown eyes dark, receding mirrors. "Will you deny the Bible you employ so readily when it suits you? It is not all thunder and vengeance. Must I read it to you?"

"Read *nothing! Say* nothing! These are matters for men!"

"Men who kill? Men who use the primitive savagery of the scriptures to justify the spilling of children's blood? My *son's* blood? I wonder what the mothers of the Masada would have said had they been permitted to speak their hearts ... Well, I speak now, *General*. You will not kill any more. You will not use this house to move your armies of death, to plot your tactics of death – always your holy tactics, Chaim, your holy vengeance."

Abrahms slowly got out of the chair. "What are you talking about?"

"You think I haven't heard you? Phone calls in the middle of the night, calls from men who sound like you, who speak of killing so easily ..."

"*You listened!*"

"Several times. You were breathing so hard you heard nothing but the sound of your own voice, your own orders to kill. Whatever you're doing will be done without you now, my husband – yet not my husband. The killing is over for you. It lost its purpose years ago but you could not stop. You invented new reasons until there was no reason left in you."

The Sabra's wife removed her right hand from the folds of her black dress. She was holding Abrahms' service automatic. The soldier slapped his holster in disbelief, then whipped to his right, suddenly lunging to his left, crashing into the woman he had lived with for thirty-eight years, grabbing her wrist, spinning her. She would not relent! She resisted him, clawing at his face as he crashed her back into the wall, twisting her hand, trying to disarm her.

The explosion filled the kitchen and the woman who had borne him four children, finally a son, fell to the floor at his feet. In horror, Chaim Abrahms looked down. Her dark brown eyes were wide, saying nothing, her black dress drenched with blood, half her chest torn away.

The telephone rang. Abrahms ran to the wall and grabbed it, screaming. "The children of Abraham *will not be denied!* A blood bath will follow – we will have the land delivered to us by God! Judea, Samaria – they are *ours!*"

"*Stop* it!" roared the voice over the line. "Stop it, *Jew!*"

"Who calls me *Jew* calls me *righteous!*" yelled Chaim Abrahms, the tears falling down his face as he stared at the dead woman with the wide brown eyes. "I have sacrificed with *Abraham!* No one could ask *more!*"

"*I* ask more!" came the cry of the cat. "I ask *always* more!"

"*Marcus?*" whispered the Sabra, closing his eyes and leaning, collapsing into the wall, turning away from the corpse below him. "Is it you ... my leader, my *conscience?* Is it you?"

"It is I, Chaim, my friend. We have to move fast. Are the units in place?"

"Yes. Scharhörn. Twelve units in place, all trained, prepared. Death is no consideration."

"That's what I had to know," said Delavane.

"They await your codes, my General." Abrahms gasped, then wept uncontrollably.

"What is it, Chaim? Get hold of yourself!"

"She's dead. My wife lies dead at my *feet!*"

"My God, what *happened?*"

"She overheard, she listened . . . she tried to kill me. We fought and she's dead."

"A terrible, terrible loss, my dear friend. You have my deepest affection and condolences in your bereavement."

"Thank you, Marcus."

"You know what you must do, don't you, Chaim?"

"Yes, Marcus. I know."

There was a knock at the door. Stone got out of the chair and picked up his gun awkwardly from the table. In all the years of sorting out garbage he had fired a weapon only once. He had blown the foot off a KGB informant in Istanbul for the simple reason that the man had been exposed while drunk and had lunged at him with a knife. That one incident was enough. Stone did not like guns.

"Yes?" he said, the automatic at his side.

"Aurelius," replied the voice behind the door.

Stone opened it and greeted his visitor. "Metcalf?"

"Yes. Stone?"

"Come in. And I think we'd better change the code."

"I suppose I could use 'Aquitaine'," said the intelligence officer, walking into the room.

"Somehow I'd rather you didn't."

"Somehow I don't think I will. Do you have coffee?"

"I'll get some. You look exhausted."

"I've looked better on a beach in Hawaii," said the slender, muscular middle-aged Air Force man. He was dressed in summer slacks and a white Izod jacket and his thin face matched his short, thinning brown hair, the dark circles prominent under his clear authoritative eyes. "At nine o'clock yesterday morning I drove south out of Las Vegas to Halloran and from there I began a series of cross-country flights a computer couldn't follow, hopping from airport to airport under more names than I can remember."

"You're a frightened man," said the civilian.

"If you're not, I'm talking to the wrong person."

"I'm not only frightened, Colonel, I'm petrified." Stone went to the phone, ordered coffee and before hanging up, turned to Metcalf. "Would you like a drink?" he asked.

"I would. Canadian on the rocks, please."

"I envy you." The civilian gave the order and both men sat down, for several moments the sounds of the street outside the only intrusion. They looked at each other, neither concealing the fact that each was silently evaluating the man across the way.

"You know who and what I am," said the Colonel, breaking the silence. Who are you? What?"

"CIA. Twenty-nine years. Station Chief in London, Athens, Istanbul and points east and north. A once-disciple of Angleton and coordinator of clandestine operations until I was fired. Anything else?"

"No."

"Whatever you did to your answering machine, you did it right. The Converse woman called."

Metcalf shot forward in the chair. "*And?*"

"It was touch and go for a while – I wasn't at my best – but he finally got on the line, or I should say he finally spoke. He was there all the time."

"Your second best must have been pretty good."

"All he wanted to hear was the truth. It wasn't hard."

"Where is he? Where are *they?*"

"The Alps, that's all he'd say."

"Goddamn it!"

"For now," completed the civilian. "He wants something from me first."

"What?"

"Affidavits. You could call them depositions."

"*What?*"

"You heard me. Affidavits from myself and the people I'm working with – working for, actually – stating what we know and what we did."

"He's out to hang you and I don't blame him."

"That's part of it and I don't blame him, either. but he says it's secondary and I believe that. He wants Aquitaine. He wants Delavane and his crowd of maniacs nailed to the wall before the whole damn thing erupts – before the killing begins."

"That was Sam Abbott's judgment. The killing – multiple assassinations, here and throughout Europe, the quickest and surest way to international chaos."

"The woman told him."

"No, he pieced it together from things Converse told *her*. Converse didn't understand the words."

"He does now," said Stone. "Did I say I was petrified? What's a stronger phrase?"

"Whatever it is it applies to both of us because we both know how simple it would be – so *simple*. We're not dealing with woolly-brained crazies or even your run-of-the-mill terrorists – we've got thirty years' experience and ninety per cent of them are in our computers. When the signals break out we know where they are and usually we can stop them. But here we're dealing with the roughest professionals in our own and in allied ranks, also with years of experience. They're walking around the Pentagon, and on Army and Navy bases – and at an Air Force base in Nevada. *Christ*, where *are* they? You open your mouth and you don't know whom you're talking to, who'll cut you down or program an aircraft to break apart in the sky. How can we stop what we can't see?"

"Perhaps Converse's way."

"With *affidavits?*"

"Maybe. Incidentally, he wants one from you. Your meeting with Abbott, everything he told you, as well as your evaluation of his mental capacities and stability. That means you'll have to stay here tonight. Half an hour ago I reserved three other rooms – I said I'd give the front desk the names later."

"Would you mind answering my question? What the hell are affidavits going to do? We're dealing with an army out there – how large and how wide-spread we don't know – but it is an *army!* At minimum, a couple of battalions, here and in Europe. Professional officers trained to carry out orders, believing in those orders and in the generals who are issuing them. Affidavits, depositions, for Christ's sake! Is this some kind of flaky legal handspring that doesn't mean anything? Do we have *time* for this?"

"You're not thinking anything I didn't think, Colonel. But then I'm not a lawyer and neither are you. Converse is, and I had a long conversation with him. He's taking the only route he knows. The legal route. Oddly enough, it's why we sent him out."

"Give me an answer, Stone," said Metcalf coldly.

"Protection," replied Stone. "What Converse wants is instant protection and for all of us to be taken seriously. Not as psychopaths or as cranks or as people with mental aberrations or diminished capacities – I think those were his words."

"Aren't they nice? What in the name of sweet Jesus do they mean? How?"

"With formal legal documents. Responsible men setting forth what they know and in the case of depositions, under qualified examination. Through the courts, Colonel. *A* court – it only takes one, only one judge. On the basis of the affidavits a petition is made to the court – *a* court, *a* judge – that protection be given under seal."

"Under what?"

"Under seal. It's completely confidential – no press, no divulging of information, simply an order from the court transmitted to the authorities most suited to carry out the order. In this case, all the branches of the Secret Service instructed by the court to provide *extraordinary* service."

"Extraordinary . . . ? For whom?"

"The President of the United States, the Vice President, the Speaker of the House, the Secretary of Defense, the Secretary of State – right on down the line. The law, Colonel. That's what the law can do – also his words, I think."

"*Jesus!*"

There was a rapping on the door, but this time Stone covered his automatic with the folded New *York Times.* He got up, crossed to the door, and admitted a waiter rolling in a table with a pot of coffee, two cups, a bottle of Canadian whisky, ice and glasses. He signed the bill and the man left.

"Coffee or a drink first?" asked Stone.

"My God, a drink. *Please.*"

"I envy you."

"You're not going to join me?"

"Sorry, I can't. I allow myself one in the evening; I'll join you then. You live in Las Vegas, so you'll understand. I'm trying to beat the odds, Colonel. I intend to beat them. I was fired, remember?" Stone brought the Air Force officer a drink and sat down.

"You can't beat the odds, don't you know that?"

"I've beaten a few. I'm still here."

"The courts," said Metcalf, shaking his head. "*A* court! It's an end run. He's using the law to go around the flanks of the government people he should reach but whom he can't trust. Can it *work?*"

"It buys time, a few days perhaps, it's hard to tell. 'Under seal' lasts only so long. The law also calls for full disclosure. But what's most important is that it legitimately tightens the security around potential targets, hopefully screwing up whatever tactics Aquitaine is mounting, forcing the generals to regroup, rethink. Again time."

"But that's only over here in the States."

"Yes. That's why Converse wants the time."

"What for?"

"He won't tell me and I'm in no position to make demands."

"I see," said the Colonel, his drink to his lips.

"You said three rooms. Who are the others?"

"You'll meet them and you won't like them. They're two kids who stumbled into this along with a few others I don't know and they won't say who they are. After Halliday reached them – or one of them – they provided the dossiers for Converse. They're young but they're all right, Colonel. If I ever had a son, I'd like to think he'd be one of them."

"I have a son and I expect he would be," said Metcalf. "Otherwise, I blew it. What are the procedures?"

Stone sat rigidly back in the chair and spoke slowly, his voice pitched in the static emphasis of a monotone. He was repeating instructions not of his own making and certainly not to his liking. "At three o'clock this afternoon I'm to call an attorney named Simon, Nathan Simon, one of the senior partners of Converse's firm here in New York. Presumably by then Converse's wife will have reached him, telling him to expect a call from me and to please do as I ask – apparently they believe he will. To be brief about it, Simon will come over here to the hotel accompanied by a stenographer and take all our depositions, along with our credentials, ranks and current responsibilities. He'll stay until he's finished."

"You were right on the phone," interrupted the military man. "We're dead."

"I said as much to Converse and he asked me how it felt. He was inquiring, of course, from first-hand knowledge."

"He wants all of you."

"But not you," said Stone. "He'd like your testimony – and by extension Abbott's – but he won't insist on it. He knows he can't ask you to walk in on this."

"I walked in when that plane went down. Also there's something else. If we can't stop Delavane and his generals, what the hell's left for people like us? . . . Converse wouldn't tell you what he was going to do?"

"Not in terms of what he calls the countdown, but yes, as far as tomorrow is concerned. He's sending over his own affidavit and, he expects, another from a man from the *Sûreté* who has information showing that most of the official reports out of Paris are lies . . . And we're not dead yet, Colonel. Converse made it clear that Nathan Simon was the best attorney we could have – as long as he believes us."

"What can a lawyer do?"

"I asked Converse the same thing and he gave me a strange answer. He said 'he can use the law, because the law isn't men, it's the law'."

"That's beyond me," said Metcalf, irritated. "Not in a philosophical context but how it applies now – right goddamned *now!* . . . Hell, it doesn't make any difference – *we* don't make any difference! Once those guns go off and the bodies fall in Washington and London, Paris or Bonn – wherever – they've got the controls and we won't get them back. I know that because I know how long so many people have wanted someone to *take* control. Stop the carnage, make things safe, piss on the Soviets. God help me, there were times I thought that way myself."

"So did I," said the civilian quietly.

"We were wrong."

"I know that. It's why I'm here."

Metcalf drank, holding the cold glass against his warm cheek. "I keep thinking about what Sam said to me. 'There's got to be a list', he said. 'A master list of everyone in this Aquitaine'. He ruled out all the obvious places – not in a vault, not on paper – probably electronically programmed, flashed on with codes, as his aerial tactics were frequently flashed on a screen inside a jet's cockpit. Someplace no one would ever think of, away from anything official or tied in with anyone remotely military. 'A list. There *has* to be a list!' he kept saying. For a pilot, he had a hell of an imagination. I guess it's why he was so good at that tactical stuff at forty thousand feet in the air. Come out of the sun where they don't expect you, or from a dark horizon where the radar can't pick you up. He knew it all. He was a tactical genius."

As Metcalf talked, Stone leaned forward in the chair, his eyes centring on the Air Force officer's face, his ears absorbing every word the man spoke.

"Scharhörn," he said, barely above a whisper. "It's *Scharhörn!*"

The twin engine Riems 406 circled the private airfield at St Gervais, fifteen miles east of Chamonix, the amber lights of the two runways throwing an orange glow up into the lower night sky. Inside, Prudhomme checked the straps of his seatbelt as the pilot on his left received clearance to make his final approach to the north-south strip.

Mon Dieu, what an incredible day! thought the man from the *Sûreté*, as he glanced at his right hand under the spill of the panel lights. The dark bruises on his fingers were at least less noticeable than the blood that had covered his entire hand only hours ago. *Formidable!* His ordained executioner had not even bothered to conceal his assignment, such was his arrogance – bred undoubtedly *as a Légionnaire!* And the sentence of death had been delivered right inside the car at the far end of the parking area in the Bois de Boulogne! The man had called him at the office and, in truth, it had entered Prudhomme's thoughts that this man might call him, and so it was less a surprise than it could have been – and certainly gave him cause to be prepared. The man had asked his recent superior to meet him at the Boulogne, in the parking lot; he had startling news. He would be driving his official Peugeot and, since he could not leave his radio phone, would the inspector mind joining him. Of course not.

But there had been no startling news other than the fundamental revelation. Only questions, asked very arrogantly.

Why did you do what you did this morning?

Shave? Go to the toilet? Eat breakfast? Kiss my wife goodbye? What are you talking about?

You know what I refer to! Earlier! The man on the Boulevard Raspail. You crashed into his car, stopping him. You threw narcotics inside. You arrested him falsely!

I didn't approve of what he was doing. Any more than I approve of this conversation. Prudhomme had awkwardly reached for the handle of the door with his left hand, his right having other business.

Stop! shouted his subordinate, grabbing his shoulder. *You were protecting the woman!*

Read my report. Let me go.

I'll let you go to hell! I'm going to kill you, meddler! Insignificant bureaucrat!

The former subordinate had yanked a gun from his jacket holster but he was too late. Prudhomme had fired twice, the small weapon under his coat gripped in his right hand. Unfortunately, it was a small calibre and the ex-colonel of the Legion was a very large man; he had lunged at Prudhomme in a final assault inside the automobile. However, the veteran of the *Résistance* had gone back to the old habit from the war – just in case. Along the lapels of his coat was threaded a long wire – a wire with two braided loops at each end. He had whipped it out, looping it over his subordinate's head, his wrists crossed, violently yanking it taut, until the flesh burst around his executioner's throat, drenching the condemned man's hands – condemned but very much alive.

"We're cleared for landing, Inspector" said the pilot, grinning. "I swear to Christ no one would *believe* this! Of course I have no intention of saying a thing, I swear on my mother's grave!"

"She's probably drinking brandy in Montmartre at this moment," interjected Prudhomme dryly. "Say nothing and you may have another six months flying in your foolish tobacco from Malta."

"Nothing else! *Never* anything else, Inspector. I am a father!"

"You are to be commended. Six months and then get out, do you understand?"

"On my father's grave, I swear!"

460

"He's very much alive and in jail – he'll be out in sixty days. Tell him to stop his presses – government relief cheques, *really*."

Joel and Valerie listened in silence as the man from the *Sûreté* told his story. He was finished now; there was nothing left to say. Interpol had been compromised, the *arrondissement* police manipulated, the *Sûreté* itself corrupted, and official government communiqués issued on the basis of lies – all lies. Why?

"I'll tell you because I want your help – much more help," said Converse, getting out of the chair and going to the desk where the typewritten pages of his affidavit were in the centre of the green blotter. "Better, you can read it yourself, but I'm afraid you'll have to read it here. In the morning I'll have copies made; until then I don't want it to leave this room. By the way, Val got you a reservation, a single – don't ask me how but a clerk downstairs will have a new wardrobe if not a new house by tomorrow."

"*Merci*, Madame."

"The name is French," added Joel.

"Yes?"

"No, I mean the *name* is French."

"*Oui.*"

"No, what I mean is . . ."

"*Pardon, monsieur*," interrupted Valerie. "*Le nom sur le registre est 'Monsieur French', c'est un nom anglais, pas français. French. Arthur French.*"

"But I will have to sign, talk. Surely they will know."

"You sign nothing and you say nothing," said Val, taking a key off the bedside table and handing it to Prudhomme. "The room is paid for – three days to be precise. After that – before, if possible, if you agree to help – the three of us will be someplace else."

"*Formidable.* I must read."

"*Mon ami – mon époux – est un avoué brilliant.*"

"*Je comprends.*"

"There are some forty pages here," said Converse, bringing the papers to Prudhomme. "To absorb it will take you at least an hour. We'll go downstairs and grab a bite to eat and leave you alone."

"*Bien.* There is much I wish to learn."

"What about you?" asked Joel, standing above the Frenchman. "I mean now. They'll find the body in the car."

"Most certainly," agreed Prudhomme. "I left it where it was. But for the *Sûreté* there will be no connection to me."

"Fingerprints? The fact that you were away from your office?"

"Another old habit from the war," said the man from the *Sûreté*, reaching into his pocket. He pulled out a pair of extremely thin rubberized gloves – surgical gloves – cut off above the fingers, before the wrist. "I washed these out at the Boulogne. The German occupation forces had all our fingerprints in a thousand files. There was no point in asking for our own executions. As for my absence at my desk, it is quite simple. I explained to an assistant that I would be in Calais for several days on a contraband investigation and would call in. My years permit a certain latitude and flexibility."

"That's the *Sûrete*, not the others. Not where the *Légionnaire* came from."

"I am aware of that, Monsieur. So I must be careful. It will not be the first time."

"Enjoy your reading," said Converse, nodding at Val to join him. "If you want anything, call room service."

"*Bon appétit*," said Prudhomme.

Chaim Abrahms lifted the stiffening wrist of his dead wife's hand, the weapon gripped fiercely in her white fingers, and angled the gun toward her chest, into the bloody cavern between her breasts.

The wide, brown eyes would not stay closed! They stared up at him, accusing — accusing!

"What do you *want* from me?!" he screamed. "I have seen the dead. I have *lived* with the dead! Leave me be, woman! You couldn't *understand!*"

Yet she had, for so many years. She had cooked the meat — the desert chicken and the lamb — caught in the outlying marshes — and fed the units of the Irgun and the Haganah, never questioning death then. Fighting for a hope, a simple hope that was the beginning of a dream. The land was *theirs*, rightfully, biblically, *logically* theirs! They had fought and they had won! Two thousand years of being outcasts — despised, reviled, scorned and spat upon by the almighty gentiles until the tribes were burned and gassed and told to eliminate themselves from the face of the earth — and yet they had survived. Now the tribes were strong! They were the *conquerors*, not the conquered!

"It's what we fought for! What we prayed for! Why do you insult me with your eyes!" Chaim Abrahms roared as he pressed his forehead against the dead flesh of his wife's face.

Hitabdut was among the most heinous crimes committed against the laws of the Talmud. It was *Ebude Atzmo*, the taking of one's own life against the wishes of almighty God in whose image man was created. A Jew who consigned his or her earthly being to *Hitabdut* was denied burial in the Hebrew cemetery. It would be so for Chaim Abrahms' wife, the most devout human being ever known.

"I have to do it!" he screamed, raising his eyes in supplication. "It is for the best, can't you *understand?*"

Prudhomme poured himself a cup of coffee and returned to his chair. Valerie sat opposite him as Converse stood by the window looking over at the man from the *Sûreté*, listening.

"I cannot think of any other questions," said the Frenchman, his troubled eyes darting about intensely above the cup in his hand, his lined face wearier than before. "Although it's possible I'm still too deep in shock to think at all. To say it's incredible serves no purpose; also it would not be true. It's all *too* credible. The world is so frightened it cries out for stability, for a place to hide, for protection – from the skies, from the streets, from each other. I believe the time has come when it will settle for sheer, absolute strength, no matter the cost."

"The operative word is absolute," said Joel, "as in controls and power. A confederation of military governments fuelling one another, interlocking policies and altering the laws all in the name of stability – until anyone who disagrees with them is declared unstable and silenced. And if too many disagree the chaos erupts again – stability wins, Aquitaine wins. All they need is that initial wave of terror, a *tidal* wave of killing and confusion. 'Key figures' were the words they used. 'Accumulation' . . . 'rapid acceleration' . . . chaos. Powerful men cut down as riots break out in half a dozen capitals and the generals march in with their commanders. That's the scenario, right from their own words."

"That also is the problem, Monsieur. They are only words, words you can pass along to very few people for they could be the wrong people. You could move up this countdown, as you call it trigger this holocaust yourself."

"The countdown's running out, make no mistake," broke in Converse. "But there *is* a way, 'Accumulation' and 'rapid acceleration' can be used in another manner, and. you're right, it's only with words – *accumulated* words, *accelerated* words. I can't come out, not yet. I can't show myself. There's no protection any court or government agency or the police could provide that would stop them from killing me, and then once I'm dead, calling whatever I said the ravings of a psychopath. Don't misunderstand me, I have no death wish but my death in itself isn't important. What is important is that the truth goes down with me because I'm the only one who's talked directly to Delavane's four Caesars over here, and probably the fifth, the Englishman."

"And these *declarations* – these affidavits you speak of can change that?"

"They can turn things around, maybe just enough."

"Why?"

"Because that's a real world out there, a practical complicated world that has to be penetrated as fast as possible – people have to be reached who can be trusted, who can do something. Quickly. It's what I wanted to do a couple of weeks ago but I was going about it the wrong way. I wanted to get everything I knew to someone I knew. Nathan Simon, the best attorney I've ever met. I wrote it all out – twice – not realizing that I was only tying his hands, probably killing him." Joel stepped away from the window, a lawyer in summation. "Who could he go to without me, without the presence of an obviously sane man and not simply the words of a 'psychopathic killer'? And if I did come out, as he would have rightfully insisted, we were both dead. Then Val told me about the man in New York who reached her on the phone and the other who chased her down the street and I guessed right. Those aren't the methods of people who want to kill you; they don't announce themselves. They were the men in Washington who had sent me out and were now trying to make contact with me. Then she described her meeting with Sam Abbott and his mentioning this Metcalf, a man he trusted and who had to be some kind of very-important-person for him to tell the story to . . . Finally, there was you in Paris – what you said, what you did, and how you offered to help, using the same code as René Mattilon – the

Tatiana family. Tatiana, a name or a word I think means trust, even among sharks."

"You are right, Monsieur."

"That's when it all came together for me. If I could somehow establish lines of communication and reach all of you, there was a way. You people knew the truth; some of you knew all of it, others like yourself, knew only fragments, but regardless, you understood the immensity, the reality of the generals and their Aquitaine and what they could do – what they're *doing*. Even you, Prudhomme. What did you say? Interpol is compromised, the police manipulated, the *Sûreté* corrupted – official reports all lies? Added to these, Anstett in New York, Peregrine, the commander of NATO, Mattilon, Beale, Sam Abbott ... Connal Fitzpatrick – the only question mark – and God knows how many others. All dead. The generals are marching – forget theories, they're *killing!* ... If I could persuade all of you to write out affidavits – or have depositions taken – and get them to Nathan Simon, he'd have the ammunition he needs. I fed legal mumbo-jumbo to Stone in New York; some of it applies, most of it doesn't, but he'll do his part and force the others to join me – he has no choice. The main point, the *only* point, is to get this material to Simon. Once he has written testimony, a series of events and observations all sworn to be true by diverse men of experience, he has a *case*. Believe me, he'll treat them like the plans of a neutron bomb. He'll have it all tomorrow and he'll reach the right people if he has to walk into the Oval Office – which he could do, but may not choose to." Joel paused and looked hard at the man from the *Sûreté*, nodding at the pages of his own affidavit on the table beside the Frenchman. "I've made arrangements for that to be flown to New York tomorrow. I'd like one from you."

"Certainly you may have it. But can you trust the courier?"

"The world could blow apart and she'd still be sitting in her house in the mountains and not know it. Or care. How's your English?"

"Adequate, I believe. We've talked for several hours."

"I mean written English. It'd save time if you wrote it out tonight."

"My spelling is probably no better than yours is in French."

"Make that English," corrected Valerie. "I'll straighten it out and if you're not sure of something – *écrivez en français.*"

"*Merci.* Tonight?"

The secretary will be here first thing in the morning," explained Converse. "She'll type it up. She's the one taking the flight from Geneva to New York tomorrow afternoon."

"She agreed to do this?"

"She agreed to accept a large donation to a nature organization that apparently runs her life."

"Very convenient."

"There's something else," said Joel, sitting on an arm of Valerie's chair and leaning forward. "You know the truth now, and beyond the material that has to reach Simon, there's one last thing I have to do. I've got a lot of money and a banker in Mykonos who'll confirm I have access to a great deal more – but you've read all that. With time to find the personnel and the equipment I might be able to pull it off myself, but we don't have the time. I need your help, I need the resources you have."

"For what, Monsieur?"

"The final depositions. The last part of the testimony. I want to kidnap three men."

37

I, Peter Charles Stone, age 58, a resident of Washington, DC, was employed by the Central Intelligence Agency for twenty-nine years during which time I attained the rank of Station Chief in various European posts and ultimately 2nd Director of Clandestine Operations, Langley, Virginia. My record is on file at the Central Intelligence Agency and may be obtained pursuant to the regulations governing such procedures. Since separation from the CIA, I have worked as a consultant and analyst for numerous intelligence departments, the specifics therein withheld from this statement pending government clearances should they be deemed pertinent to this document.

On or about 15 March last, I was contacted by Captain Howard Packard, United States Army, who asked if he might come to my apartment to discuss a confidential matter. When he arrived, he stated at the outset that he was speaking for a small group of men from both the military services and the State Department, the number and identities of which he would not divulge. He stated further that they sought professional consultation from an experienced intelligence officer no longer associated (permanently) with any branch of the intelligence community. He said he had certain funds available he believed would be adequate and would I be interested. It should be noted here that Captain Packard and his associates had made a thorough if not exhaustive search of my background – warts and alcohol and all, as is said . . .

I, Captain Howard N.M.I. Packard, US Army, 507538. age 31, currently residing in Oxon Hill, Maryland, and assigned to Section 27, Department of Technological Controls, the Pentagon, Arlington, Virginia. In December of last year, Mr A. Preston Halliday, an attorney from San Francisco with whom I had struck up a friendship as a result of his numerous petitions to our section on behalf of clients (all successful and above reproach), asked me to have dinner with him at a small restaurant in Clinton, approximately ten miles from my house. He apologized for not asking my wife, explaining that what he had to say would only disturb her, as, indeed, it would disturb me, but in this case it was my responsibility to be disturbed. He added that there was no conceivable conflict in our meeting as he had no business pending, only business that should be investigated and stopped.

I, Lieutenant (J.G.) William Michael Landis, US Navy, a bachelor, age 28; current address, The Somerset Garden Apartments, Vienna, Virginia, am a computer programmer for the Department of the Navy, Sea-Armament's Procurements Division, stationed at the Pentagon, Arlington, Virginia. Actually, in all but rank (due within 60 days), I'm in command of most programming for pentagon-Navy having received a doctorate in advanced computer technology from the University of Michigan, College of Engineering . . . I'm probably not saying this right, sir.

[Go ahead, young man.]

I state this because with the highly sophisticated equipment at my disposal as well as the classified micro-conversion codes available to me, I'm able to tap into a great many restricted computers with a tracing capacity that can circumvent – or penetrate, if you like – closures placed on extremely sensitive information.

Last February, Captain Howard Packard, US Army, and three other men – two from the Department of State, Office of Munitions Controls, and the third a Marine Corps officer I knew from the Amphibious Section, Navy Procurements – came out to see me on a Sunday morning. They said they were alarmed over a series of weapons and high-tech transfers that appeared to violate Department of Defense and State Department sanctions. They gave me the data they had concerning nine such incidents, impressing upon me the confidentiality of the inquiry.

The next afternoon I went to the maximum security computers and with the conversion codes inserted the data for the nine transfers. The initial entries were confirmed – those numbers never change so as to eliminate the possibility of duplication – but in each case, after confirmation, the remaining information was erased, wiped off the computer tapes. Six of those nine transfers were traced through the initial entries to a firm called Palo Alto International, owned by a retired Army general named Delavane. This was my first involvement, sir.

[Who were the three other men, Lieutenant?]

It wouldn't do any good to give their names, sir. It could only hurt their families.

[I'm not sure I understand – can possibly understand.]

They're dead. They went back and asked questions and they're dead, sir. Two supposedly in automobile accidents involving trucks – on back roads they never took home – and the third indiscriminately shot by a deranged sniper while jogging in Rock Creek Park. All those joggers and he was the one who got it.

As an Army captain with full security clearance and frequently dealing in top-secret procedures, I was able to set up a sterile telephone (i.e.: constantly scanned for taps or intercepts) so Mr Halliday could reach me any time of day or night without fear of being overheard. Also in concert with Mr Stone and Lieutenant Landis, we pooled our sources and obtained in-depth intelligence dossiers on the well-known names Halliday found among General Delavane s notes. Specifically, Generals Bertholdier, Leifhelm, Abrahms and van Headmer. Using funds provided by Dr Edward Beale, we secured the services of private firms in Paris, Bonn, Tel Aviv and Johannesburg to up-date the dossiers with all available current information about the subjects.

By now we had uncovered ninety-seven additional computer erasures directly related to export licensing and military transfers involving an estimated $45,000,000. A great many were initiated by Palo Alto International but without further data there was nothing to trace. It was like a series of blips disappearing from a radar screen.

My years in the CIA's Clandestine Operations taught me that the larger the pattern, the greater the numbers, and those areas with the heaviest concentration of activity invariably held the tightest and most ruthless security. Nothing terribly original here but the reverse application is frequently overlooked. Since Washington was the clearing house for illegal exports totalling millions upon millions in American merchandise and material, it stood to reason that there would be a range of safeguards, scores of Delavane's informants – both knowing and unknowing; that is ideologically involved or simply hired or threatened – in the government agencies and departments related to the activities of Palo Alto International. Without going into specifics, Captain Packard confirmed this judgment by telling me an incident had recently taken place that cost the lives of three men who tried to follow up on a number of computer erasures. We had moved from the realm of ideological extremists into one of fanatics and killers. Therefore it was my contention – and I hereby assume full responsibility for the decision – that safer and more rapid progress could be made by sending a man out into the peripheral sectors of Delavane's operation with enough information to trace connections back to Palo Alto International. By the nature of illegal export licensing itself there is more open territory at the receiving end. The obvious place to start was with the four generals whose names were found in Delavane's notes. I had no candidate with the expertise I felt was necessary for the assignment.

On or about 10 July, Mr Halliday called me on the sterile phone I'd set up for him and said he believed he'd found the proper candidate for the assignment as outlined by Mr Stone. An attorney whose field was international law, a man he had known years ago and a former prisoner of war in Vietnam who conceivably had the motivation to go after someone like General Delavane. His name was Joel Converse . . .

I, Alan Bruce Metcalf, age 48, am an officer in the US Air Force, holding the rank of Colonel and currently stationed at the Nellis Air Force Base, Clark County, Nevada, as Chief Intelligence officer. Thirty-six hours ago, as I dictate this statement, on 25 August at 4 o'clock in the afternoon, I received a telephone call from Brigadier General Samuel Abbott, Commanding Officer, Tactical Operations, Nellis Air Force Base. The general said it was urgent that we meet, preferably off-base, as soon as possible. He had new and extraordinary information regarding the recent assassinations of the Supreme Commander of NATO and the American Ambassador to Bonn, West Germany. He insisted that we be in civilian clothes and suggested the library at the University of Nevada, Las Vegas campus. We met at approximately 5.30 P.M. and talked for five hours. I will be as accurate as possible and that will be very accurate as the conversation is still fresh in my mind, indelibly heightened by the tragic death of General Abbott, a close friend for many years and a man I admired greatly.

The above then are the events as told to General Abbott by the former Mrs Converse, and as he related them to me, and the subsequent actions I took to convene an emergency meeting of the highest level intelligence personnel in Washington. General Abbott believed what he had been told, based on his knowledge and perceptions of the individuals involved. He was a brilliant and stable man, not given to bias where judgments were concerned. In my opinion, he was deliberately murdered because he had new and extraordinary information about a fellow prisoner of war, one Joel Converse.

Nathan Simon, tall, portly, sitting well back in his chair, removed the tortoiseshell glasses from his tired face and tugged at the small chin-beard that covered the scars of shrapnel embedded at Anzio years ago. His thick salt-and-pepper eyebrows were arched above his hazel eyes and sharp, straight nose. The only other person in the room was Peter Stone. The stenographer had been dismissed; Metcalf, exhausted, had retired to his room, and the other two officers, Packard and Landis, had opted to return to Washington – on separate planes. Simon carefully placed the typewritten affidavits on the table beside his chair.

"There was *no one* else, Mr Stone?" he asked, his deep voice gentle, far gentler than his eyes.

"No one I knew, Mr Simon," replied the former intelligence officer. "Everyone I've used since what we call pulling-in-old-debts – was lower level with access to upper level equipment, not decisions. Please remember, three men were killed when this thing barely started."

"Yes, I know."

"Can you do what Converse said? Can you get something 'under-seal' and move some mountains we can't move?"

"He told you that?"

"Yes. It's why I agreed to all of this."

"He had his reasons. And I have to think."

"There's no time to *think*. We have to act, we have to *do* something! Time's running out!"

"To be sure, but we cannot do the wrong thing, can we?"

"Converse said you had access to powerful people in Washington. I could trust you to reach them."

"But you've just told me I don't know whom to trust, isn't that right?"

"*Oh, Christ!*"

"A lovely and inspired prophet." Simon looked at his watch as he gathered up the papers and rose from the chair. "It's two-thirty in the morning, Mr Stone, and this weary body has come to the end of its endurance. I'll be in touch with you later in the day. Don't try to reach me. I'll be in touch."

"In *touch*? The package from Converse is on its way here. I'm picking it up at Kennedy Airport on the Geneva flight at 2.45 this afternoon. He wants you to have it right away. I want you to have it!"

"You'll be at the airport?" asked the lawyer.

"Yes, meeting our courier. I'll be back here by four or four-thirty depending on when the plane gets in and traffic, of course."

"No, don't do that, Mr Stone, stay at the airport. I'll want everything Joel has compiled for us in my hands as soon as possible, of course. As there is a courier from Geneva, you may be the courier from New York."

"Where are you going? Washington?"

"Perhaps, perhaps not. At this moment I'm going home to my apartment to think. Also I hope to sleep, which is doubtful. Give me a name I can use to have you paged at the airport."

Johnny Reb sat low in the small boat, the motor idling, the waves slapping the sides of the shallow hull in the darkness. He was dressed in black trousers, a black turtleneck sweater and a black knit hat, and he was as close as he dared drift into the south-west coast of the island of Scharhörn. He had spotted the bobbing green glows of the series of buoys the first night; they were trip lights, beams intersecting each other above the water, ringing the approach to the old U-boat base. They formed an impenetrable, unseen wall – to penetrate it would set off alarms. This was the third night and he began to feel vindicated.

Trust the gut, trust the stomach and the bile that crept up into the mouth. The bellies of the old-time whores of the community knew when things were going to happen – partly out of dread, partly because a score was near that would enlarge an account in Bern. There was no account in the offing now, of course, only a succession of outlays to pay back a considerable debt, but there was a score to be made. Against the Delavanes and the Washburns, and those German and French and Jewish catfish who would sweep the ponds and make it impossible for gentlemen like Johnny Reb to make a high-hog living. He didn't know much about the South African, except that those nigger-haters had better-the-hell wise up. The coloureds were coming along just fine and that was fine by Johnny; his current girlfriend was a lovely black singer from Tallahassee, who just happened to be in Switzerland for silly reasons involving a little cocaine – and a good-sized account in Bern.

But the other catfish were *bad*. *Real* bad. Johnny Reb had it in for men who would make it jailhouse for people to think the way they wanted to. *No sir*, those people had to go!

Johnny Reb was very seriously committed to that proposition.

It was happening! He focused his infra-red binoculars on the old concrete piers of the sub base. It was also flat-out crazy! The seventy-foot motor launch had pulled into a dock, and moving out on the pier was a long, double line of men 40,60,80 . . . nearly 100 – preparing to board. What was crazy was the way they were dressed. Dark suits and conservative summer jackets and ties; a number wore hats and every damned one of them carried luggage and a *briefcase*. They looked like a convention of bankers or a parade of lace-pants from the diplomatic corps. *Or*, thought The Rebel as he inched his binoculars backward along the line of passengers, ordinary businessmen, middle to upper-level management – nothing really out of the ordinary – men seen every day standing on railroad platforms and getting out of taxis and flying in planes. It was the very ordinariness of their collective appearance compared to the exotically macabre dark outlines of the old U-boat refuelling station that gnawed at Johnny's imagination. These men could go unnoticed almost anywhere yet they did not *come* from anywhere. They came from Scharhörn; they came from what was undoubtedly a highly sophisticated cell of this multinational military collusion that could put the goddamned catfish generals in the catbird seats. Ordinary people going wherever they were ordered to go – looking like everyone else, behaving like everyone else, their attaché cases open on planes and trains; reading company reports, sipping drinks but not too many, an occasional paperback novel permitted to ease the strain of business – *going wherever they were ordered to go*

That was it, thought The Rebel, as he lowered the binoculars. *That was it!* These were the *hit teams!* The stomach never lied; the bile was sent up for a reason, its acrid sickening taste an ugly alarm that came to those privileged enough to have survived. Johnny Reb turned and fingered the motor, cautiously pushing the rudder to the right and inching the throttle forward. The small boat spun in the water and the rogue intelligence officer – former intelligence officer – headed back to his berth in Cuxhaven, accelerating the engine with each fifty feet of distance.

Twenty-five minutes later he pulled into the slip, lashed the lines to the cleats, grabbed his small waterproof case, and with effort climbed up onto the pier. He had to move quickly, but very, *very* cautiously. He knew vaguely the area of the Cuxhaven waterfront where the motor launch would return for he had watched the lights of the vessel as it bobbed its way out of the harbour toward the island. Once in the vicinity he could determine the specific dock as the boat headed into port, and then he would have only minutes to scout the area and get into position. Carrying his unmarked waterproof case, he hurried to the base of the pier and turned left, walking rapidly through the shadows toward the area from which he judged the launch had departed. He passed a huge warehouse and reached an open space beyond; there were five short piers, one after the other, extending no more than two hundred feet out into the water. It was dockage for small and medium-sized craft; several trawlers and a few antiquated pleasure boats, long past their primes were lashed to the pilings on each of the piers except one. The fourth pier was empty. The Rebel knew it belonged to the launch; he could taste the bitterness in his mouth. He started out across the space; he would find a place to conceal himself.

"*Halt – Stehenbleiben!*" shot out the guttural command, as a man walked out of the darkness from around the hull of a trawler at the third pier. "*Was machen Sie hier? Wersind Sie?*"

Johnny Reb knew when to use his age; he stooped his shoulders and extended his head slightly forward, lowering his neck. "*Passen Sie auf diese alten Hasten auf?*" he asked, continuing in German. "I'm a fisherman on one of these relics and I lost my billfold this afternoon. Is it a crime to look for it?"

"Come back later, old man. You can't look for it now."

"*Eh?* What?" The Rebel raised his right hand to his ear, twisting the ring on his middle finger as he did so and pressing a catch on the band. "My hearing's not what it was, Mr Watchman. What did you say?"

The man stepped forward, first looking out at the water, as the sound of a powerful engine was heard in the distance. "Get out of here!" he shouted, his lips close to Johnny's ear. "*Now!*"

"Good heavens, you're Hans!"

"Who?"

"*Hans!* It's so good to *see* you!" The Rebel slapped his hand around the German's neck, prelude to an affectionate embrace – and plunged the surface of his ring into the man's flesh, the needle firmly, deeply embedded.

"Get your hands off me, you stinking old man! My name's not Hans and I never saw you before. Get out of here or I'll put a . . . a bullet . . . in your . . . *head!*" The German's hand plunged inside his jacket but did not come out. Instead the man collapsed.

"You younger catfish really ought to have more respect for your elders," mumbled Johnny, as he dragged the unconscious body into the shadows to the left of the trawler on the third pier. "Cause you don't know the flies we use. Your daddys do, but you little pricks don't. And I *want* your daddys, those mind-suckers!"

The Rebel climbed aboard the trawler and dashed across the deck to the gunrail. The motor launch was heading directly into the fourth pier. He opened his waterproof case, into which he had snapped the binoculars in place, and adjusted his eyes to the dim light, studying the tools of his trade. He unlatched a camera and then a lens, a Zeiss Icon telescopic, developed by conscientious Germans during World War II for photographing Allied installations at night; it was the best. He inserted it into the lens mount, locking it into position, and switched on the camera's motor, noting with satisfaction that the battery was at full capacity, but then he knew it would be. He had been too long in the deadly game to make amateurish mistakes.

The huge motor launch slid into the pier like a mammoth black whale, a killer whale. The lines were secured, and as the passengers disembarked, Johnny Reb began taking pictures.

"Honeychile, this is Tatiana. I've got to reach my boy."

"The Algonquin Hotel in New York City," said the calm female voice. "The number is Area Code two-one-two, eight-four-zero, six-eight-zero-zero. Ask for Peter Marcus."

"Subtle son of a bitch, isn't he?" said Johnny Reb. "Pardon my language, mam."

"I've heard it before, Rebel. This is Anne."

"*Goddamn*, little lady, why didn't you tell me *before!* How *are* you, sweet child?"

"Doing fine in my dotage, Johnny. I'm out, you know. This is just a courtesy for an old friend."

"An old *friend?* Fair girl, if it wasn't for Petey, I'd have made one hell of a play for you!"

"You should have, Reb. I wasn't in his cards, his terribly important cards. And you were one of the nicest – a little more subterranean than most but a nice person. What was it? 'Gentleman Johnny Reb'?"

"I've always tried to keep up appearances, Annie. May I request the privilege of calling you one day, if we ever get out of this mess?"

"I don't know what the mess is, Reb, but I do know you have my telephone number."

"You give me heart, fair girl!"

"We're older now, Johnny, but I guess you wouldn't understand that."

"Never, child. Never."

"Stay well, Reb. You're too good to lose."

The operator at the Algonquin Hotel was adamant. "I'm sorry, sir. Mr Marcus is not in his room and does not answer the page."

"I'll call back," said The Rebel.

* * *

"Sorry sir. There's no answer from Mr Marcus' room and no response to the page."

"I believe we spoke several hours ago, sir. There's still no answer from Mr Marcus' room so I took the liberty of calling the desk. He hasn't checked out and he didn't list an alternate number. Why not leave a message?"

"I believe I will. As follows, please. 'Stay put until I reach you. Or you reach me. Imperative. Signed, Z. Tatiana.' That's TATIA . . ."

"Yes, sir. Thank you, sir. 'Z', sir?"

"As in zero, miss." Johnny Reb hung up the phone in the flat in Cuxhaven. The taste in his mouth was overpoweringly sour.

Erich Leifhelm entertained his luncheon guests at his favourite table at the Ambassador restaurant on the eighteenth floor of the Steigenberger Hotel in Bonn. The huge, elegant room had a magnificent view of the city and the river and the mountains beyond, and this particular table was positioned to take advantage of that view. It was a clear, bright, cloudless afternoon and the natural wonders of the northern Rhineland were there for the fortunate to observe; none could help but be touched or awed or both.

"I never tire of it," said the former field marshal, addressing the three men at his table, gesturing with masculine grace at the enormous window behind him. "I wanted you to see it before returning to Buenos Aires indeed, one of the most beautiful cities in the world, I must add."

The *maître d'hôtel* intruded with deference, bowing as he spoke softly to Leifhelm. "*Herr General*, there is a telephone call for you."

"An aide is dining at Table fifty-five," said Leifhelm casually, in spite of his racing pulse. Perhaps there was word of a priest in Strasbourg! "I'm sure he can take it for me."

"The gentleman on the line specifically requested that I speak with you personally. He said to tell you he was calling from California."

"I see. Very well." Leifhelm got out of his chair, apologizing to his guests. "No surcease from the vagaries of commerce, is there? Forgive me, I shall only be a moment or two. Please, more wine."

The *mâtre* nodded, adding, "I've had the call put through to my private office, *Herr General*. It's right inside the foyer."

"That pleases me. Thank you."

Erich Leifhelm casually, even subtly, shook his head as he passed Table fifty-five near the entrance. The lone diner acknowledged the dismissal with a nod of his head. In all the years of strategies and tactics, military and political, that dismissal was among the field marshal's gravest errors.

Two men stood in the foyer, one looking at his watch, the other looking annoyed. By their expensive clothes they belonged to the Ambassador's clientele and were obviously waiting for late luncheon companions, probably their wives as they had not gone to their table. A third man stood outside the glass doors in the corridor; he was dressed in the maintenance uniform of the hotel and watched the two men inside.

Leifhelm thanked the *mâtre*, as the latter held the door open for the general to enter his modest office. The restaurateur closed the door and returned to the dining room. The two men – swiftly, as one – raced inside after the old soldier, who was at that moment picking up the telephone.

"*Was geht hier vor? Wer ist . . . !*"

The first man lunged across the desk, gripping Leifhelm's head, clamping the general's mouth with very strong hands. The second man pulled a hypodermic needle from his pocket and removed the rubber shield as he tore at Leifhelm's jacket, then the collar of his shirt. He plunged the needle into the base of the general's throat, released the serum, pulled out the syringe and immediately began massaging the flesh as he restored the collar and pulled the jacket in place.

"He'll be mobile for about five minutes," said the doctor in German. "But he can neither speak nor reason. His motor controls are now mechanical and have to be guided."

"And after five minutes?" asked the first man.

"He collapses, probably vomiting."

"A nice picture. Hurry! Get him up, *guide* him, for God's sake! I'll check outside and knock once."

Seconds later the knock came and the doctor, with Leifhelm firmly in his grip, propelled the general out of the office and through the glass doors into the hotel corridor.

"This way!" ordered the third man in the maintenance uniform, heading to the right.

"*Quickly!*" added the doctor.

Among the strollers in the plush hallway and the diners heading for the restaurant, a number recognized the legendary old soldier, not a few staring at his pale, comatose face with the lips trembling, trying to speak. Or scream.

"The great man has had terrible news," said the doctor reverentially and repeatedly. "It's terrible, simply terrible!"

They reached a service elevator, which was on *hold*, and went inside. A stretcher on wheels stood against the padded back wall. The third man took a key from his pocket, inserted it in the *hold* lock releasing the controls, as he pressed the non-stop switch for the basement. The other two lifted Leifhelm up on the stretcher covering him with a sheet – covering all of him.

"They'll start talking up there," said the first man. "His bulls will come running. They're never far away."

"The ambulance is downstairs now by the elevator door," said the man in the maintenance uniform. "The plane is waiting at the airfield."

The once great field marshal of the Third Reich threw up under the sheet.

Jacques Louis Bertholdier let himself into the apartment on the Boulevard Montaigne and removed his woven silk jacket, throwing it on a chair. He walked over to the mirrored bar against the wall, poured a vodka, threw in two cubes of ice from a sterling silver bucket, and strolled to the window beyond the elegantly upholstered couch. The tree-lined Montaigne was so peaceful at mid-afternoon, so spotlessly clean, and somehow so pastoral although very much part of the city. There were times when he thought it was the essence of the Paris he loved, the Paris of influence and wealth, whose inhabitants never had to soil their hands. It was why he had purchased the extravagant flat and installed his most extravagant and desirable mistress. He needed her now. My *God*, how he needed release!

The *Légionnaire* shot and garrotted in his own automobile! In the parking lot of the Bois de Boulogne! And Prudhomme, the filthy bureaucrat, supposedly in Calais! No fingerprints! *Nothing!* The once and foremost general of France needed an hour or so of tranquillity, of – release.

"*Elise!* Where *are* you? Come out, Egyptian! I trust you're wearing what I instructed you to wear. If you need reminding, it's the short black Givenchy, nothing underneath, you understand! Absolutely *nothing*."

"Of course, my general," came the words, strangely hesitant, from behind the bedroom door.

Bertholdier laughed silently to himself as he turned and walked back to the couch. *Le Grand Timon* was still an event to be reckoned with, even by highly sexual twenty-five year olds who loved money and fast cars and elegant apartments as much as they adored having their bodies penetrated. Well, he was too upset to disrobe, his nerves too frayed to go through any prolonged nonsense. He had something else in mind – release without effort.

The sound of the turning knob broke off his thoughts. The door opened and the raven-haired girl emerged, her elongated, perfectly proportioned face set in anticipation, her brown eyes wide in a distant wonder. Perhaps she had been smoking marijuana, thought Bertholdier. She was dressed in a short negligee of black lace, her breasts circled like diadems in grey, her hips revolving in sexual provocation as she approached the couch.

"Exquisite, you whore of the Nile. Sit down. It's been a dreadful day, a *horrible* day and it is not over. My driver will return in two hours and until then I need rest – and release. Give it to me, Egyptian." Bertholdier zipped down the fly of his trousers and reached for the girl. "Fondle it, as I will fondle you, and then do what you can do." He grabbed her breasts, forcing her, pulling her head down into his groin. "Now. *Now. Do* it!"

A blinding flash filled the room as two men walked out of the bedroom. The girl sprang back into the couch, as Bertholdier looked up in shock. The man in front put the camera in his pocket, as his companion, a short, middle-aged heavy-set man with a gun in his hand, walked slowly toward the legend of France.

"I admire your taste, General," he said in a gruff voice. "But then, I suppose I've always admired you, even when l disagreed with you. You don't remember me, but you court-martialled me in Algiers, sending me to the stockade for thirty-six months because I struck an officer. I was a sergeant-major and he had brutally abused my men with excessive penalties over minor offences. Three years for hitting a Paris-tailored pig. Three years in those filthy barracks for taking care of my men."

"Sergeant-Major LeFevre," said Bertholdier with authority, calmly replacing his pants and zipping up his fly. "I remember. I never forget. You were guilty of treasonable conduct: assaulting an officer. I should have had you shot."

"There were moments during those three years when I would have welcomed the execution, Monsieur. But I'm not here to discuss Algiers – it's when I knew you were all crazy. I'm here to tell you you're coming with me. You'll be returned unharmed to Paris in several days."

"Preposterous!" spat out the general. "You think your weapon frightens me?"

"No, it's merely to protect myself from you from the last gesture of a brave and famous soldier. I know you too well to think that threats of bodily harm, or even death, could move you. I have another persuasion, however, one you've just made quite irresistible." The ex-sergeant major withdrew a second, odd-shaped gun from his pocket. "This weapon does not hold bullets, instead it fires darts containing a chemical that accelerates the heart to bursting point. My thoughts were to threaten you with fielding the photograph after your death, showing that the great general died ignominiously at what he did best. Now, perhaps, there is another approach. The angle was advantageous for certain, expert brushwork – your position and the expression on your face would not be touched, of course – but your companion might easily become a *he* rather than a she, a little boy rather than a girl . . . There were rumours of your excesses once, and a hastily arranged marriage few could understand. Was this the secret *Le Grand Timon* ran from all his life? Was it the threat the great de Gaulle held over the head of his popular but all too ambitious and rebellious colonel? That the appetites of this pretender, this would-be successor, were so extensive they included anything he could get his hands on, his body on, the gender making no difference. Small boys when there were no women. The whispers of corrupted young lieutenants and captains, of rapes, conveniently called interrogations in your quarters."

"*Enough!*" cried Bertholdier, shooting up from the couch. "Further conversation is pointless. Regardless of how absurd and unfounded I will not permit my name to be dragged through filth! I want that film!"

"My God, it's true," said the ex-infantry sergeant. "All of it."

"The *film!*" shouted the general. "Give it to me!"

"You shall have it," replied LeFevre. "On the plane."

Chaim Yakov Abrahms walked with a bowed head out of the *Ihud Shivat Zion* synagogue on the Ben Yehuda in Tel Aviv. The solemn crowds outside formed two deep flanks of devoted followers, men and women who wept openly at the terrible suffering this great man, this patriot-soldier of Israel, had been forced to endure at the hands of his wife. *Hitabdut*, they spoke in hushed voices. *Ebude Atzmo*, they said to one another, cupping mouths to ears, out of Chaim's hearing. The rabbis would not relent; the sins of a despicable woman were visited upon this son of Sabras, this fierce child of Abraham, this biblical warrior who loved the land and the Talmud with equal fervour. The woman had been refused burial in a holy place; she was to remain outside the gates of the *beht Hakvahroht*, her soul left to struggle with the wrath of Almighty God, the pain of that knowledge an unbearable burden for the one left behind.

It was said she did it out of vengeance and a diseased mind. She had her daughters. It was the father's son — always the *father's* son — who had been slain on the father's battlefield. Who would weep more, who *could* weep more, or be in greater anguish than the father? And now this, the further agony of knowing that the woman he had given his life to had most heinously violated God's Talmud. The shame of it, the *shame!* Oh, Chaim, our brother, father, son and leader, we weep with you. For you! Tell us what to do and we will do it. You are our *king!* King of Eretz Israel, of Judea and Samaria, and all the lands you seek for our protection! Show us the way and we shall follow you, oh *King!*

"She's done more for him in death than she could ever do alive," said a man on the outskirts of the crowd and not part of it.

"What do you think really happened?" asked the man's companion.

"An accident. Or worse, far worse. She came to our temple frequently and I can tell you this. She never would have considered *Hitabdut* . . . We must watch him carefully before these fools and thousands like them crown him emperor of the Mediterranean and he marches us to oblivion."

An Army staff car, two flags of blue and white on either side of the hood, made its way up the street to the kerb in front of the synagogue. Abrahms, wearing his bereavement like a heavy mantle of sorrow only his strength could endure, bowing his lowered head to the crowds, his eyes opening and closing, his hands reaching out to touch and be touched, listened to the words of a young soldier at his side.

"Your car, General."

"Thank you, my son," said the legend of Israel, as he climbed inside and sank back in the seat, his eyes shut in anguish. Weeping faces pressed against the windows. The door closed and when he spoke, his eyes still closed, there was anything but anguish in his harsh voice. "Get me *out* of here! Take me to my cottage in the country. We'll all have whisky and forget this *crap*. Holy rabbinical bastards! They had the temerity to *lecture* me! The next war, I'll call up the rabbis and put those Talmudic chicken-shits in the front lines! Let them lecture while the shrapnel flies up their asses!"

No one spoke as the car gathered speed and left the crowds behind. Moments later Chaim opened his eyes and pulled his thick back from the seat; he stretched his barrel-chested frame and reclined again in a more comfortable — less anguished position. Then slowly, as if aware of the stares of the two soldiers beside him, he looked at both men, his head whipping back and forth.

"Who *are* you?!" he shouted. "You're not my men, not my *aides!*"

"They'll wake up in an hour or so," said the man in the front seat beside the driver. He turned facing Abrahms. "Good afternoon, General."

"You!"

"Yes, it is I, Chaim. Your goons couldn't stop me from testifying before the Lebanon Tribunal and nothing on earth could stop me from what I'm doing today. I told about the slaughter of women and children and quivering old men as they pleaded for their lives and watched you laugh. You call yourself a Jew? You can't begin to understand. You're just a man filled with hate, and I don't care for you to claim to be any part of what I am or what I believe. You're shit,

476

Abrahms. But you'll be brought back to Tel Aviv in several days."

One by one the planes landed, the propeller-driven aircraft from Bonn and Paris having flown at low altitudes, the jet from Israel, a Dassault-Bruguet Mystere 10/100, dropping swiftly from 28,000 feet to the private airfield at St Gervais. And as each taxied to a stop at the end of the runway, the same dark blue sedan waited to drive the "guest" and his escort to an Alpine château fifteen miles east in the mountains. It had been rented for two weeks from a real estate firm in Chamonix.

The arrivals had been scheduled carefully, as none of the three visitors was to know the others were there. The planes from Bonn and Paris landed at 4.30 and 5.45 respectively, the jet from the Mediterranean nearly three hours later at 8.27. And to each stunned guest, Joel Converse said the identical words.

"As I was offered hospitality in Bonn, I offer you mine here. Your accommodation will be better than I was given, although I doubt the food will be as good. However, I know one thing – your departure will be far less dramatic than mine."

But not your stay, thought Converse, as he spoke to each man. *Not your stay.* It was part of the plan.

38

The first light floated up into the dark sky above the trees in Central Park. Nathan Simon sat in his study and watched the new day's arrival from the large, soft leather chair facing the huge window. It was his thinking-seat, as he called it. Recently he had used it as much for dozing as for thought. But there were no brief interludes of sleep tonight – this morning. His mind was on fire; he had to explore and re-explore the options, stretching the limits of his perceptions of the dangers within each. To choose the wrong one would send out alarms that would force the generals to act immediately, and once underway, events would swiftly race out of control, the control of events solely in the hands of the generals – everywhere. Of course, they might start within hours quite by themselves but Nathan did not think so; the generals were not fools. All chaos had its visual beginnings, the initial turbulence that gave rise to the credibility of violence. If nothing else, confusion had to be established as the players moved into place without being seen. Abstractions, yes, but that was where ideas began, and the concept of military control over governments was a time-worn idea since the age of the Pharaohs. It bore early fruit in Peloponnisos and Sparta's conquest of Athens, later with the Caesars, and later still, was capitalized on by the emperors of the Holy Roman Empire, then exercised by the Renaissance princes and finally brought to totality by the Soviets and the Germans in the twentieth century. Unrest preceded violence and violence preceded take-over, whether it was a revolution entailing hundreds of thousands of oppressed Russians or the strangling inequities of a Versailles Treaty.

Therein lay the weakness of the generals' strategy: The unrest had to exist before the violence erupted. The people ordinary hordes of people – had to be worked into a frenzy, but for that to happen the hordes had to be there in the first place. That would be the sign, the prelude as it were, but where, *when?* And what could he do, what moves could he make that would escape the attention of Delavane's informers? He was an employer and friend of Joel Converse, the "psychopathic assassin" the generals had created. He had to presume he was being watched – at the very least any overt action he took would be scrutinized and if he became suspect he would be thwarted. His life was immaterial. In a sense he was trapped, as he and frightened, frustrated multitudes like him had been trapped on the beaches of Anzio, realizing there was a degree of safety in the foxholes behind the dunes, knowing that to rise out of them was to face screaming, unending barrages of bullets. Yet knowing, too, nothing was accomplished if they remained where they were, only more and more lives lost with each burst of mortar fire.

Contrary to what he had told Peter Stone, Nathan knew precisely whom he had to see – not one man, but three. The President, the Speaker of the House, and the Attorney General. The apex of the Executive, the leader of the Legislative, and the nation's chief law enforcement officer. He would see no one less and it was far more advantageous to see them all together rather than individually. In either case, he had to see them and that was his dilemma; it was the trap. One did not simply pick up a telephone and make appointments with such men. There were procedures, formalities, and screening processes to ensure the validity of the requests; men with their responsibilities could not waste time. The trap. As soon as his name was mentioned, the word would go out. Delavane himself would know within a matter of hours, if not minutes.

Despite Joel's gratuitous and highly dubious statements to Peter Stone, it was not easy to reach powerful government figures, any more than it was logical to have a judge issue a court order under-seal that somehow miraculously, *legally*, guaranteed extraordinary protection for those same people without informing the entire security apparatus as to why the protection was deemed vital. Ridiculous! Such court orders were reasonable where intimidated witnesses were concerned before a criminal trial and even afterwards in terms of fabricated rehabilitation, but that process hardly applied to the White House, the Congress, or the Justice Department. Joel had taken a legal manoeuvre, ballooned it way out of probability, and scaled it up into orbit – for a reason, of course. Stone and his colleagues had provided depositions.

And yet, thought Simon, there was an odd logic in Converse's misapplied exaggerations. Not in any way Joel had considered but as a means to reach these men. "A court, a single judge . . ." Converse had said to Stone. That was the logic, the rest was nonsense. *The Supreme Court*, a justice of that court. Not a request from one Nathan Simon who would have to be screened, if only in terms

478

of content not character, but an urgent message to the President from a venerated justice of the *Supreme Court!* No one would dare question such a man if he pronounced his business to be between the President and himself. Presidents were far more solicitous of the Court than of Congress and with good reason. The latter was a political battleground, and the former an arena of moral judgment, and no one lived his life in a deep freeze, not even – perhaps especially – presidents. And Nathan Simon knew the man he could call *and* see, a Justice in his late seventies. The Court was not in session, October was a month away. He was somewhere in New England, his private number was at the office.

Nathan blinked, then brought his hand up to shield his eyes. For a brief moment, the fireball of the early sun had careened a blinding ray through a geometric maze of glass and steel across the park and entered his window before being blocked by a distant building. And suddenly, at that instant of blindness, he was given the answer to the terrifying question of *where* and *when* – the unrest that had to be the prelude for the eruption of violence. There was scheduled throughout Free Europe, Great Britain, Canada and the United States, an internationally coordinated week-long series of anti-nuclear protests. Millions of concerned, frightened people joining hands and snarling up traffic in the streets of the major cities and capitals, making their voices heard at the expense of normality. Rallies were to be held in the parks and in the squares and in front of government buildings. Politicians and statesmen, perceiving as always the power of ground swells, had promised to address huge crowds everywhere in Paris and Bonn, Rome and Madrid, Brussels and London – Toronto, Ottawa, New York and Washington. And again, as always, these moulders and benefactors, these sincere advocates and posturing sycophants of the bodies politic would blame the lack of arms control progress on the intransigence of evil adversaries, never their own deficiencies. The genuine and the phony walked hand in hand across podiums, none sure of the other's stripes.

Crowds everywhere, espousing deeply-felt, deeply-divisive issues, pitting the believers of universal restraint against pockets of those who sincerely believed in the raw power of excessive strength, and the latter would surely be heard. No one thought the massive demonstrations would be without incidents . . . yet how far might these minor confrontations escalate if the incidents themselves were massive? Units of terrorist fanatics financed anonymously, persuaded to infiltrate and savagely disrupt so as to get their message across, messages of real and imagined grievances having nothing to do with the protests, creating chaos primarily because the crowds were not of their world or their fevers. The crowds – everywhere. *These* were the hordes of people who could be galvanized by sudden violence and worked into multiple frenzies! It was the prelude. Everywhere.

The demonstrations were scheduled to begin in three days.

Peter Stone walked down the wide dirt path toward the lake behind the A-frame house somewhere in lower New Hampshire he did not know precisely where, only that it was twenty minutes from the airport. It was close to dusk, the end of a day filled with surprises and apparently it was not over – they were not over, the surprises. Ten hours ago, in his room at the Algonquin, he had called Swissair to see if the flight from Geneva was on schedule, only to be told it was thirty-four minutes ahead of schedule and, barring landing delays, was expected a half hour early. It was the first surprise and inconsequential; the second was not. He had arrived at Kennedy shortly before 2 o'clock and within a few minutes he heard the page over the public address system for a "Mr Lackland", the name he had given Nathan Simon.

"Take Pilgrim Airlines to Manchester, New Hampshire," the lawyer had said. "There's a reservation for Mr Lackland on the 3.15 plane. Can you make it?"

"Easily. The flight from Geneva's early. I assume that's LaGuardia?"

"Yes. You'll be met in Manchester by a man with red hair. I've described you to him. See you around five-thirty."

Manchester, New Hampshire? Stone had been so sure Simon would ask him to fly to Washington he had not even bothered to put a toothbrush in his pocket. Surprise number Two.

Surprise number Three was the courier from Geneva. A prim, gaunt English-woman with a face of pale granite and the most uncommunicative pair of eyes he had seen outside of Dzerzhinsky Square. As arranged, she had met him in front of the Swissair Lounge, a copy of *The Economist* in her left hand. After studying the wrong side of his out-of-date government identification, she had given him the attaché case and made the following statement – in British high dudgeon.

"I don't like New York, I never have. I don't like flying either, but everyone's been so lovely and it's better to get the whole whack-a-doo over all at once, righto? They've arranged for me to take the next plane back to Geneva. I miss my mountains. They need me and I do try to give them my *very* all, righto?"

With that obtuse information she smiled wanly and turned, somewhat oddly, and started back toward the escalator. It was then that Stone began to understand. The woman's eyes were not uncommunicative, the whole person was. She was drunk – or, perhaps, pickled – having overcome her fear of flying with liquid courage. Converse had a strange concept of couriers, Stone had thought, instantly changing his mind. Who could be less suspect?

The fourth surprise came at the Manchester airport. An ebullient, middle-aged red-headed man had greeted him as though they were long-lost fraternity brothers from some mid-western university in the late thirties when such fraternal ties were deemed far deeper than blood. He was positively effusive to the point where Stone was not only embarrassed by the display of camaraderie, but seriously concerned that unwarranted attention would be drawn to them. But once in the parking lot, the red-head had suddenly slammed him into the doorframe of the car and shoved the barrel of a gun into the back of his neck while the man's free hand stabbed his clothes for a weapon.

"I wouldn't take the risk of going through metal detectors with a gun, damn it!" protested the ex-CIA agent.

"Just making sure, spook. I've dealt with you assholes, you think you're something else. Me, I was Federal."

"Which explains a great deal," said Stone, meaning it.

"You drive."

"Is that a question or an order?"

"An order. All spooks drive," replied the red-head.

Surprise number Five came in the car, as Stone took the sudden turns commanded by the red-headed man who casually replaced the gun in his jacket holster.

"Sorry about the horseshit," he said in a voice far less hostile than in the parking lot, but nowhere near the false ebullience in the terminal. "I had to be careful, piss you off, see where you stood, you know what I mean? And I was never Federal – I hated those turkeys. They always wanted you to know they were better than you were just because they came from DC. I was a cop in Cleveland, name's Gary Frazier. How are you?"

"Somewhat more comfortable," Stone had said. "Where are we going?"

"Sorry, pal. If he wants you to know, he'll tell you."

Surprise number Six awaited Stone when he drove the car up through the New Hampshire hills to an isolated house of wood and glass, surrounded by forests, the structure an inverted V, two narrowing storeys looking out in all directions on woods and water. Nathan Simon had walked down the stone steps from the front door.

"You've brought it?" he asked.

"Here it is," said Stone, handing the attaché case to the lawyer through the open window. "Where are we? Who are you seeing?"

"It's a very unlisted residence, but if everything is in order we'll call you. There are guest quarters attached to the boathouse down at the lake. Why not freshen up after your trip? The driver will point the way. If we need you for anything, we'll ring you on the phone. It's a separate number from the house, so just pick it up."

And now Peter Stone was walking down the wide dirt path that led to the boathouse by the lake, aware that eyes were following him. Surprise number Seven: He had no idea where he was and Simon wasn't going to tell him unless "everything was in order", whatever that meant.

The guest quarters alluded to by the attorney was a three-room cottage on the edge of the lake with an entrance to the adjacent boathouse, in which was berthed a small sleek motor boat and a nondescript catamaran that looked more like a raft with two canvas seats and fishing equipment for drift trawling. Stone wandered about trying to find some clue as to the owner's identity but there was nothing. Even the names on the boats were meaningless, but not lacking in humour. The cumbersome, raft-like sailcraft was named *Hawk*, while the aggressive-looking little speedboat was *Dove*.

The former deep cover intelligence officer sat on the porch and looked out at the peaceful waters of the lake and the rolling, darkening green hills of New Hampshire. Everything *was* peaceful. The cries of the loons were cushioned french horns proclaiming the permanence of tranquillity in this special place. But Stone's insides were not peaceful; his stomach churned and he remembered what Johnny Reb used to say in the field. "Trust the stomach, Br'er Rabbit, trust the bile. They never lie." He wondered what The Rebel was doing, what he was learning.

The phone rang, a strident, unnerving porch bell accompanying the softer ring from inside the cottage. As if jolted by an electric prod, Stone sprang from the chair, swung back the door and walked rapidly across the room to the telephone.

"Come up to the house, please," said Nathan Simon; adding, "if you were out on the porch, I apologize for not telling you about that damned bell."

"I accept your apology. I was."

"It's for guests who expect calls and may be out in one of the boats."

"The loons are quiet. I'll be right there."

Stone walked up the dirt path and saw the lawyer standing by a screen door that was the lake entrance to the house; it was on a patio reached by curving brick steps. He started climbing, prepared for surprise number Eight.

Supreme Court Justice Andrew Wellfleet, his thinning unkempt white hair falling in strands over his wide forehead, sat behind the large desk in his library. Converse's thick affidavit was in front of him and a floor lamp on his left threw light down on the pages. It was several moments before he looked up and removed his steel-rimmed glasses; his eyes were not pleasant. They were stern and disapproving, matching the nickname given him over two decades ago when he was summoned to the Court. "Irascible Andy" was the sobriquet the clerks had assigned to him, but temperament notwithstanding, no one ever questioned his awesome intelligence, his fairness, or his devotion to the law. All things considered, surprise number Eight was as welcome a shock as Stone could imagine.

"Have you read this?" asked Wellfleet, offering neither his hand nor a chair.

"Yes, sir," replied Stone. "On the plane. It's essentially what he told me over the phone, in far greater detail of course. The affidavit from the Frenchman, Prudhomme, was a bonus. It tells us how they operate – how they're *capable* of operating."

"And what in hell did you think you were going to do with all of this?" The elderly Justice waved his hand over the desk on which were scattered the other affidavits. "Petition the courts here and in Europe to please, if they'd be so kind, to issue injunctions restricting the activities of all military personnel above a certain rank on the conceivable possibility that they may be part of this?"

"I'm not a lawyer, sir, the courts never entered my mind. But I did think that once we had Converse's own words – along with what we knew – they'd be sufficient to reach the right people in the highest places who *could* do something. Obviously Converse thought the same thing insofar as he called in Mr Simon and, if you'll forgive me, Mr Justice, you're reading it all now."

"It isn't enough," said the Supreme Court Justice. "And damn the courts, I shouldn't have to tell you that, Mr Former CIA Man. You need names, a lot more names, not just five generals, three of whom are retired and one of them, the so-called instigator, a man who had an operation several months ago that left him without legs."

"Delavane?" asked Simon, stepping away from the window.

"That's right," said Wellfleet. "Kind of pathetic, huh? Not exactly the picture of a very imposing threat, is he?"

"It could drive him into being an extraordinary threat."

"I'm not denying that, Nate. I'm just looking at the collection you've got here. Abrahms? As anyone worth his kosher salt in Israel will tell you, he's a strutting, bombastic hothead – a brilliant soldier but with ten screws loose. Besides, his only real concerns are for Israel. Van Headmer? He's a relic of the nineteenth century, pretty fast with a hangman's rope but his voice doesn't mean doodly-shit outside South Africa."

"Mr Justice," said Stone, speaking more firmly than he had before. "Are you implying that we're wrong? Because if you are, there are other names – and I don't just mean a couple of attachés at the embassy in Bonn – names of men who have been killed because they tried to find answers."

"You weren't listening!" snapped back Wellfleet. "I just told Nate I wasn't denying anything. How in hell could I? Forty-five *million* in untraceable, *illegal* exports! An apparatus that can shape the news media here and in Europe, that can corrupt government agencies, and as Nate here puts it, 'create a psychopathic assassin' so that they can find *you*, or make you back *down*. Oh, no, Mister, I'm not saying you're wrong. I'm saying you better damn well do what I'm told you're pretty good at, and you'd better do it quickly. Haul in this Washburn and any others you can find in Bonn; pick a cross section of those people at State and the Pentagon and fill 'em full of dope or whatever the hell you use and get *names!* And if you ever mention that I suggested such wanton measures that violate our most sacred human rights, I'll say you're full of shit. Talk to Nate here. You don't have time for niceties, Mister."

"We don't have the resources, either," said Stone. "As I explained to Mr Simon, there are a few friends I can call upon for information but nothing like you suggest – like what you didn't suggest. I simply don't have the leverage, the men or the equipment. I'm not even employed by the government any longer."

"I can help you there." Wellfleet made a note. "You'll get whatever you need."

"There's the other problem," continued Stone. "No matter how careful we are, we'd send out alarms. These people are *believers*, not just mindless extremists. They're orchestrated; they have lines of fall-backs and know exactly what they're doing. It's a progression, a logical capitalizing on sequences until we're all forced to accept them – or accept the unacceptable, the continuation of violence, of wholesale rioting, of the killing."

"Very nice, Mister. And what are *you* going to do? *Nothing?*"

"Of course not. Rightly or wrongly I believed Converse when he told me that with our affidavits – with all the evidence we provided him – Mr Simon could reach people we couldn't reach. Why shouldn't I have believed him? It was an extension of my own thinking *without* a Nathan Simon but with Converse himself. Only my way would take longer. The precautions would be far more elaborate, but it *could* be done. We'd reach the right people and start the counter attack."

"Who'd you have in mind?" asked Wellfleet sharply.

"The President first, obviously. Then because we're dealing with half a dozen other countries, the Secretary of State. A maximum security screening process would be set up immediately – one undoubtedly using those chemicals you didn't speak of until we had unblemished personnel, men and women we were certain beyond doubt had no connections to this Aquitaine. We create cells, command posts here and abroad. Incidentally, there's a man who can help us immeasurably in this, a man named Belamy in Britain's MI6. I've worked with him and he's the best – knows the best – and he's done this sort of thing before. Once our cells are in place and in deep cover we then pull in Washburn and at least two others we know of by description in Bonn. Prudhomme can furnish us with the names of those in the *Sûreté* who approve transfers, and who furnished evidence against Converse when it didn't exist. And as you know from my own affidavit, we've got the island of Scharhörn under surveillance now – we think it's a nerve centre or a communications relay. With the proper equipment we could tap in. The whole point is we widen the circles of information. Once you know a strategy you can mount a counter-strategy without setting off alarms." Stone paused and looked at both men. "Mr Justice, Mr Simon. I was Station Chief in five vital posts in Great Britain and the Continent. I *know it* can be done."

"I don't doubt you," said Nathan Simon. "How long would it take?"

"If Justice Wellfleet can get me the cooperation and the equipment I need, with the people I select – here and abroad – Derek Belamy and I can mount a crash programme. We'd be operational in eight to ten days."

Simon looked at the Supreme Court Justice then back at Stone. "We don't have eight or ten days," he said. "We have three – less than three days now."

Peter Stone stared at the tall, portly attorney with the sad, penetrating eyes. He could feel the blood draining from his face.

The cry of the cat was muted in fury. General George Marcus Delavane slowly replaced the telephone on the console. His half body was propped into the wheelchair, his waist strapped to the steel poles, his arms as heavy as his breath was short, the veins in his neck protruding. He brought his hands together, entwining his fingers and pressing his knuckles against each other until the surrounding flesh was white. He raised his large head, his cold, angry eyes narrowing up at the uniformed aide standing in front of the desk.

"They've disappeared," he said, his high-pitched voice icily controlled. "Leifhelm was taken from a restaurant in Bonn. They say there was an ambulance that raced away, no one knows where. Abrahms' guards were drugged. Others took their places. He was driven off in his own staff car, picked up in front of a synagogue. Bertholdier did not come down from his apartment on the Montaigne so the driver went up to discreetly remind him of the time. The woman was bound naked on the bed, the word 'whore' written in lipstick across her breasts. She said two men took him away at gunpoint. There was talk of a plane she said."

"What about van Headmer?" asked the aide.

"Nothing. Our charming and oblivious Afrikaner dines at the Johannesburg Military Club and says he will put himself under extra guard. He's not part of the orbit; he's too far away to matter."

"What do you mean, General? What happened?"

"What happened? This *Converse* happened! We created our own most accomplished enemy, Colonel – and I can't say we weren't warned. Chaim said it, our man in the Mossad made it clear. The North Vietnamese created a hellhound – the Mossad's words – and we created a monster. He should have been killed in Paris, certainly in Bonn."

"You couldn't have ordered it then," said the aide, shaking his head. "You had to know where he came from and if you couldn't find out, you had to isolate him, make him – what was it? A pariah – so no one would come forth to claim him. It was sound strategy, General. It still remains sound. No one's come forth – no one's *coming* forth. You held them back and now it's too late."

Delavane's eyes widened as he appraised the colonel's face. "You've always been the best of adjutants, Paul. You tactfully remind a superior that, regardless of immediate set-backs, his decisions were based on sound reasons, and that those reasons will prevail."

"I've disagreed when I thought it was necessary, General, because whatever I learned, I learned from you, so I merely reminded you of yourself. Right now, at this moment, I'm right. You were right."

"Yes, I was – I am. Nothing matters now. Everything's set in motion and nothing can stop it. This Converse – this bold, resourceful enemy – was also held in check by having to keep running. And now *he's* too late. In any event, the men he's taken were merely symbols, magnets to attract others. That's the beauty of clean strategy, Colonel. Once it's set in motion, it rolls like the ocean wave. The power underneath is unseen but relentlessly propels it forward. Events will dictate the only acceptable solutions. It's my legacy, Colonel."

Nathan Simon had nearly finished his explanation. It had taken less than three minutes, during which time Peter Stone remained motionless, his eyes riveted on the older man, his face ashen, the taste in his mouth unbearable.

"You can see the pattern, can't you?" concluded the attorney. "The protests begin in the Middle East and follow the sun and the time zones across the Mediterranean, up through Europe, and over the Atlantic, culminating in Canada and the United States. They start with the *Peace Now* movement in Jerusalem, then Beirut, Rome, Paris, Bonn, London, Toronto, Washington, New York, Chicago, *et cetera*. Gigantic rallies in the major cities and capitals covering every nation and government Delavane and his people have infiltrated. Confrontations occur – the initial unrest – growing into major disruptions with the infusion of terrorist units. Bombs wired into cars, or under the streets in sewers, or simply rolled into the crowds – the second wave of greater violence – all leading to the mass confusion and disorder they require to put their leading players in position. Or more precisely, once in position to exercise their assignments."

"The final assaults," broke in Stone quietly. "Selected assassinations."

"Chaos," agreed Simon. "Men of awesome responsibilities suddenly dead, the descending mantles of authority unclear, too many men protesting, fighting one another, screaming that *they* are in charge. Total chaos."

"*Scharhörn!*" said the middle-aged, former intelligence officer. "We have no other choice now. We have to go in! May I use your telephone, Mr Justice?" Without waiting for a reply Stone walked to Wellfleet's desk as he removed his billfold and pulled out the small piece of paper with a number in Cuxhaven, West Germany, written on it. He turned the phone around under the harsh gaze of the Supreme Court Justice, picked it up and dialled. The sequence of trans-Atlantic relays was intolerable. It rang.

"Rebel?" The explosive invective over the line from half a world away could be heard throughout the library. Stone broke it off. "*Stop* it, Johnny! I haven't been near the hotel in hours and I haven't time for this! . . . You *what?*" The CIA man listened, his eyes growing wide, his breathing stopped. He covered the mouthpiece and turned to Nathan Simon. "My God, there's a breakthrough!" he whispered. "Photographs. Infra-red, taken last night and developed this morning – all clear. Ninety-seven men from Scharhörn getting off a boat, heading for the airport and train station. He thinks they're the hit teams."

"Get those photographs to Brussels and flown to Washington on the fastest goddamned military transport you can find!" ordered the venerated Justice of the Supreme Court.

39

"*Preposterous!*" shouted General Jacques Louis Bertholdier from the brocaded wing chair in the spacious study of the Alpine château. "I don't believe you for a minute!"

"That's a favourite word of yours, isn't it?" said Converse, standing by the open cathedral window across the room, the mountain fields beyond. He was dressed in a dark suit, white shirt and a regimental tie, all purchased in Chamonix. "The word 'preposterous', I mean," he continued. "You used it at least twice when we spoke in Paris, I think. It's as though whoever presents you with information you don't like is preposterous – absurd, unwarranted – the person as well as the information. Is that the way you look at people who don't accommodate you?"

"Certainly not! It is the way I treat liars." The legend of France began to rise. "And I see no reason . . ."

"*Stay in that chair!*" Joel's voice was a sudden, sharp command. "Or only your corpse will get back to Paris," he added simply, without hostility, merely a clarification. "I told you, all I wanted was this conversation with you. It won't take long and then you'll be free to go. That's more charity than any of you showed me."

"You were expendable. I apologize for being so blunt but it is the truth."

"If I was so expendable, why didn't you just kill me? Why the elaborate build-

486

up, all that trouble to make me a killer, an assassin, a man hunted all over Europe."

"The Jew gave us that."

"The Jew? Chaim Abrahms?"

"It makes no difference now," said Bertholdier. "Our man in the Mossad – incidentally, a brilliant analyst – made it clear that if we could not find where you came from – if you yourself did not know – then we had to put you in 'forbidden territory', I believe was the expression. And that was not preposterous. No one claims you. You were – you *are* – indeed, untouchable."

"Why doesn't it make any difference now – the fact that you've told me what you presume I already know?"

"You've lost, Monsieur Converse."

"I have?"

"Yes, and if you have delusions of drugging me – as we drugged you – let me spare you and me the discomfort of such procedures. I do not have the information. Actually, no one does. Only a machine that is set in motion and issues commands."

"To other machines?"

"Of course not. To men – men who will do what they have been trained to do, who believe in what they're doing. I have no idea who they are."

"That's the killing, isn't it? They're the killers."

"All war is reduced to killing, young man. And make no mistake. This *is* war. The world has had enough. We will put it to rights, as the English say. You will see; we will not be opposed. We are not only needed, we are wanted."

" 'Accumulation . . . rapid acceleration', those were the words, weren't they?"

"The Jew was precipitous. He talks too much."

"He says you're the pompous asshole of creation. He told me that he and van Headmer were going to put you in a glass room with little boys and girls and watch you screw yourself into a coronary."

"His conversations were always tasteless . . . But no, I *don't* believe you."

"So we're back to my original statement." Joel walked away from the window and sat down in an armchair diagonally across from Bertholdier. "Why do you find it so difficult to believe? Because you didn't think of it?"

"No, Monsieur. Because it's unthinkable."

Converse pointed to a telephone on the desk. "You know their private numbers," he said. "Call them. Call Leifhelm in Bonn and Abrahms in Tel Aviv. Also van Headmer, if you like, although I'm told he's in the States, probably California."

"California?"

"Ask each if he came to see me at that little stone house on Leifhelm's property. Ask them what we talked about. Go on, the phone's right over there."

Bertholdier looked sharply at the telephone as Joel held his breath. Then the soldier turned back to Converse, reluctance winning out over inclination. "What are you trying to do? What sort of trick is this?"

"What trick? There's the phone. I can't rig it, I can't make it dial numbers or hire people hundreds or thousands of miles away to impersonate those men."

The Frenchman looked again at the telephone. "What could I say?" he asked quietly, more to himself than Joel.

"Try the truth. You're very big on truth, as you see it, as it pertains to large global concepts and this is only a small matter of several minor omissions. *They're* omitting to tell you that each one of them came to see *me*. Or perhaps they weren't so minor."

"How would I know they came to see you?"

"You weren't listening to me. I said try the truth. I had you kidnapped, no one else. I did it because I didn't understand, and if push-comes-to-shove, I want to save my life. There's a huge world out there, General. Large parts of it you'll leave intact and I could live very nicely as long as I didn't have to worry about someone coming out of a doorway to blow my head off."

"You're not the man I thought you were – we thought you were."

"We're all what circumstances make us. I've had my share of sweat. I'm bowing out of the crusading business, or the lid-blowing business, or whatever you want to call it. Would you like to know why?"

"Very much so," said Bertholdier, staring at Joel, confusion and curiosity fighting each other in his eyes.

"Because I listened to you in Bonn. Maybe you're right, or maybe I just don't care anymore because I was left way out in the cold. Maybe the world really does need you arrogant bastards right now."

"It *does!* There's no other *way!*"

"It's the year of the generals then, isn't it?"

"No, not simply the *generals!* We are the consolidators, the symbols of strength and discipline and lawful order. Surely what follows in the aggregate – in the international market places, in joint foreign policies, and yes, in the legal processes themselves – will reflect our leadership, our example, and out of it all will come what is most lacking in today's world. *Stability*, Monsieur Converse! No more madmen like the senile Khomeini or the hollow braggard Gaddafi, or the insane Palestinians. Such men and such nations and would-be nations will be pincered by truly international forces, crushed by the overwhelming might of like-minded governments. Retribution will be swift and total. I am a military strategist of some reputation, so let me assure you the Russians will stand aside, appalled, not daring to interfere – knowing at last they cannot divide us any longer. They cannot rattle their sabres, frightening one segment while appeasing others, for we are all one!"

"Aquitaine," said Joel softly.

"An adequate codename, yes," agreed Bertholdier.

"You're as convincing as you were in Bonn," added Converse. "And maybe it could all work, but not this way, not with you people."

"I beg your pardon?"

"Nobody has to divide *you* – you're already oceans apart."

"I don't understand."

"Place those calls, General. Make it easy on yourself. Reach Leifhelm first. Tell him you just heard from Abrahms in Tel Aviv and you're appalled. Say Abrahms wants to meet with you because he has information about me, that he admitted he and van Headmer came to see me alone in Bonn. You could add that *I* told Abrahms he and his Afrikaner friend were my second and third visitors. Leifhelm was the first."

"Why would I tell him this?"

"Because you're angry as hell. No one told you about these separate meetings with me and you consider them highly improper – which, if you don't you damn well should. A little while ago you said I was expendable. Well, you're in for a shock, General."

"Explain that!"

"No. Use the phone. Listen to what he says, how he reacts, how they all react. You'll know. See if I'm telling you the truth."

Bertholdier placed both his hands on the arms of the brocaded chair and started to rise, his eyes on the telephone. Converse sat motionless, watching the Frenchman closely, barely breathing, his pulse racing. Suddenly, the general pushed himself violently back into the chair, pressing his spine into the fabric, his fingers now gripping the arms. "All *right!*" he shouted. "What was *said?* What did they *say?*"

"I think you should use that phone first."

"Pointless!" snapped Bertholdier. "As you say, you cannot make it dial other numbers – well, I suppose you could, but to what end? Imposters? Ridiculous! I could ask any of several hundred questions and know they were merely play-actors."

"All the more reason to call them," said Joel calmly. "You'd know I was telling the truth."

"And give an advantage where none was shown to me."

Converse breathed normally again. "It's up to you, General. I'm just looking for a safe way out."

"Then tell me what was said to you."

"Each asked me the obvious – as if he didn't trust the drugs or the one who administered them or each other. Whom did I really represent?" Joel paused; he was about to fish with a witness, but knew he had to pull back instantly if the pond was barren. "I guess I mentioned Beale on Mykonos," he offered hesitantly.

"You did," confirmed the general. "He was reached several months ago but our contact never returned. You explained that also."

"You thought he might be one of you, didn't you?"

"We thought he threw away a brilliant military career out of disgust. Apparently it was a different disgust, the very weakness we abhorred. But these are not the things I want to hear. You made reference to some aspect of expendability. That is what I want to hear. *Now.*"

"You want it straight. Without the frills?"

"No frills, Monsieur."

"Leifhelm said you'll be out in a matter of months, if not sooner. You give too many orders; the others are sick of them – and you want too much for France."

"*Leifhelm?* The hypocritical *weasel* who sold his very soul to deny everything he espoused?! Who betrayed his leaders in the dock at Nuremberg, furnishing the court with all manner of evidence so as to worm his way into the Allies' *bowels!* Everywhere, whatever our commitments, we cringed! He brought dishonour on the most honourable profession in this world. Let me tell you, Monsieur, it is not I who will be out, it is *he!*"

"Abrahms said you were a sexual embarrassment," continued Converse, as though Bertholdier's response was irrelevant. "That was the phrase he used, 'a sexual embarrassment'. He mentioned the fact that there was a record – one he obtained, in fact – that spelled out a string of rapes, female and male, that were covered up by the French army because you were damned good at what you did. But then he asked the question. Could a bi-sexual opportunist, one who ravaged women at will and who sodomized young men and boys, who corrupted the word 'interrogation' as well as whole sections of the officer corps, be truly considered the French leader of codename Aquitaine? He *also* said you wanted too many controls centred in your own government. But by the time there were such controls, you'd be gone."

"*Gone?*" cried the Frenchman, his eyes once more on fire as they had been weeks ago in Paris, his postured body trembling with rage. "Convicted by a *barbarian*, a smelly, uneducated *Jew?*"

"Van Headmer didn't go that far. He said you were simply too vulnerable."

"Forget van Headmer!" roared Bertholdier. "He's a fossil! He was courted solely on the basis that he might deliver raw materials. He's of no consequence."

"I didn't think he was," agreed Joel truthfully.

"But the strutting, foul-mouthed Israeli thinks he can move against *me?* Let me tell you, Monsieur, I have been threatened before – by a great man – and nothing ever came of those threats because, as you put it, I was 'damned good' at what I did. I *still* am! And there is another record, one of outstanding and brilliant service, that dwarfs any compilation of filthy rumours and barrack gossip. My record is unmatched by any in codename Aquitaine, and that includes the legless egomaniac in San Francisco. He believes it was all *his* idea! *Preposterous!* I refined it! He merely gave it a name based on a far-fetched reading of history."

"He also got the ball started by exporting one hell of a lot of hardware," interrupted Converse.

"Because it was *there*, Monsieur! And there were profits to be made!" The general paused, not finished, leaning forward in the chair. "I will be frank with you. As with any elite corps of leadership, one man rises above the others by the sheer strength of his character and his mind. Beside me the others – all the others – pale into mediocrity. Delavane is a deformed, hysterical caricature. Leifhelm is a Nazi and Abrahms is a bombastic polarizer; alone he could set off waves of anti-semitism, the worst sort of symbol of leadership. When the tribunals rise out of the confusion and the panic they will look to me. I shall be the true leader of codename Aquitaine."

Joel got out of the chair and walked back to the cathedral window, staring out at the mountain fields, feeling the soft breezes on his face. "This examination is finished, General," he said.

As if on cue the door opened and a former sergeant-major in the French army based in Algiers stood there waiting to escort the bewildered legend of France out of the room.

Chaim Abrahms sprang out of the brocaded chair, his barrel chest pressed against the seams of his black safari jacket. "He said those things about *me*? About *himself*?"

"I told you before we got into any of this to use the phone," broke in Converse, sitting across from the Israeli, a pistol on the newly-set table beside his chair. "Don't take my word for it. I've heard it said you've got good gut instincts. Call Bertholdier. You don't have to say where you are – as a matter of fact, I'd put a bullet in your head if you tried. Just tell him one of Leifhelm's guards, a man you bought to keep his eyes open for you because of a certain innate mistrust you have of Germans, told you that he, Bertholdier, came to see me alone on two separate occasions. Since I haven't been found, you want to know why. It'll work. You'll hear enough to know whether I'm telling you the truth or not."

Abrahms stared down at Joel. "But why *do* you tell me this truth – if it is the truth? Why do you abduct me to tell me these things? *Why?*"

"I thought I made that clear. My money's running out and although I'm not wild about saltfish or blintzes, I'd be better off living in Israel under a protective cover than being hunted and ultimately killed running around Europe. You can do that for me, but I know I've got to deliver something to you first. I'm delivering it now. Bertholdier intends to take over what he calls codename Aquitaine. He said you're a foul-mouthed Jew, a destructive symbol, you'll have to go. He said the same about Leifhelm; the spectre of a Nazi couldn't be tolerated, and van Headmer was a 'fossil', that was the word, 'fossil'."

"I can hear him," said Abrahms softly, his hands clasped behind his back, pacing toward the window. "Are you sure our military *boulevardier* with the cock of steel did not say 'smelly Jew'? I've heard our French hero use such words, always of course apologizing to me, saying I was exempt."

"He used them."

"But *why?* Why would he say such things to *you?* I don't deny part of his logic, for Christ's sake. Leifhelm will be shot once controls are established. A *Nazi* running the goddamned German government? Absurd! Even Delavane understands this, he will be eliminated. And poor old van Headmer is a relic, we all know that. Still there is gold in South Africa. He could deliver it. But why *you?* Why would Bertholdier come to *you?*"

"Ask him yourself. There's the phone. Use it."

The Israeli stood motionless, his narrow eyes encased in swells of flesh riveted on Converse. "I *will*," he said quietly, emphatically. "You are far too clever, Mr Lawyer. The fire inside you remains in your head – it has not reached your stomach. You think too much. You say you were manipulated? I say you manipulate." Abrahms turned and strode like a bulky. compact Coriolanus to the phone.

He stood for a moment, squinting, remembering, then picked up the phone and dialled the series of numbers long ago committed to memory.

Joel remained in the chair, every muscle in his body taut, his throat suddenly dry, as the pounding in his chest reached his temples. Slowly he inched his hand over the arm of the chair nearer the pistol. In seconds he might have to use it, his strategy – his *only* strategy blown apart by a phone call he never thought would be made. *What was wrong with him? Where were his vaunted examining tactics taking him? Had he forgotten who he was dealing with?*

"Code Isaiah," said Abrahms into the phone. his angry eyes again staring across the room at Converse. "Patch me through to Verdun-sur-Meuse. *Quickly!*" The Israeli's massive chest heaved with every breath, but it was the only part of his stocky frame that moved. He spoke again, furiously. "Yes, code *Isaiah!* I have no time to waste! Reach Verdun-sur-Meuse! *Now!*" Abrahms' eyes grew wide as he listened. He looked briefly away from Converse, then snapped his head back, his eyes filled with knowledge and loathing, Joel the object of both. "*Repeat* that!" he shouted. And then he slammed the telephone down with such force the desk shook. "*Liar!*" he screamed:

"You mean me?" asked Joel, his hand inches from the gun.

"They say he *disappeared!* They cannot *find him!*"

"*And?*" The dryness in Converse's throat was now a vacuum. He had lost.

"He *lies!* The cock of steel is no more than a whining coward! He's hiding – he *avoids* me! He will not *face* me!"

Joel swallowed repeatedly as he moved his hand away from the weapon. "Force the issue," he said, somehow managing to keep the tremor out of his voice. "Trace him down. Call Leifhelm, van Headmer. Say it's imperative you reach Bertholdier."

"*Stop* it! And let him know I *know?* He had to give you a reason! Why did he come to see you in the first place?"

"I wanted to wait until you'd spoken to him," said Converse, crossing his legs and picking up a pack of cigarettes next to the pistol. "He might have told you himself – then again he might not. He has this idea I was sent out by Delavane to test all of you. To see who might betray him."

"*Betray* him? Betray the legless one? *How?* Why? And if our French peacock believed that, again why would he say these things to you?"

"I'm an attorney. I provoked him. Once he understood how I felt about Delavane, what that bastard did to me, he knew I couldn't possibly have anything to do with him. His defences were down; the rest was easy. And as he talked I saw a way to save my own life." Joel struck a match, lighting a cigarette. "By reaching you," he said.

"At the end you bank on the morality of a Jew then? His acknowledgment of a debt."

"In part, yes, but not entirely, General. I know something about Leifhelm, about the way he's manoeuvred through the years. He'd have me shot, then send his men after the rest of you, leaving himself in the number one position."

"That's exactly what he'd do," agreed the Israeli.

"And I didn't think van Headmer had any real authority north of Pretoria."

"Right again," said Abrahms, walking back toward Converse. "So the hellhound created in South-east Asia is a survivor."

"Let's be more specific," countered Joel. "I was sent out by people I don't know who abandoned me without raising the slightest question as to my guilt or innocence. For all I know they joined in the hunt to kill me to save their own lives. Given these conditions I intend to survive."

"What about the woman? Your woman?"

"She goes with me." Converse put down the cigarette and picked up the gun. "What's your answer? I can kill you now, or leave that to Bertholdier, or Leifhelm, if he kills the Frenchman first . . . Or I can bank on your morality, your acknowledgment of a debt. What's it going to be?"

"Put away the gun," said Chaim Abrahms. "You have the word of a Sabra."

"What'll you do?" asked Joel, placing the weapon back on the table.

"*Do?*" shouted the Israeli in a sudden burst of anger. "What I've always *intended* to do! You think I give a horse's fart for this abstraction, this Aquitaine's infrastructure? Do you think I care one whit for titles or labels or chains of command? Let them have it all! I only care that it works and for it to work *respectability* must come out of the chaos *along* with strength. Bertholdier was right. I am too divisive a figure – as well as a Jew – to be so visible on the Euro-American scene. So I will be *invisible* – except in Eretz Israel, or Yisrael where my word will be the law of this new order. I, myself, will help the French bull get whatever medals he wants. I will not fight him, I will *control* him."

"How?"

"Because I can destroy his respectability."

Converse sat forward, suppressing his astonishment. "His *sex* life? Those buried scandals?"

"My God, no, you imbecile! You kick a man below his belt in public you ask for trouble. Half the people cry 'foul' thinking it could happen to them, and the other half applaud his courage to indulge himself – which they would very much like to do."

"Then how, General? How can you do this, destroy his respectability?"

Abrahms sat down again in the brocaded chair, his thick body squeezed dangerously between the delicately carved mahogany arms. "By exposing the role he played in 'codename, Aquitaine'. The roles we all played in this extraordinary adventure that forced the civilized world to summon us and the strengths of our professional leadership. It's entirely possible that all free Europe will turn to Bertholdier, as France nearly turned to him after de Gaulle. But one must understand a man like Bertholdier. He doesn't merely seek power, he seeks the *glory* of power – the trappings, the adulation, the mysticism. He would rather give up certain intrinsic authority than lose any part of the glory. *Me?* I don't give a shit about the glory. All I want is the power to get what I need, what I command. For the kingdom of Israel and its imprimatur in all of the Middle East."

"You expose him, you expose yourself. How can you win that way?"

"Because he'll blink first. He'll think of the, glory and submit. He'll do as I say, give me what I want."

"I think he'll have you shot."

"Not when he's told that if I die several hundred documents will be released describing every meeting we attended, every decision we made. Everything is scrupulously detailed, I assure you."

"You intended this from the beginning?"

"From the beginning."

"You play rough."

"I'm a Sabra. I play for the advantage – without it we would have been massacred decades ago."

"Among these documents is there a list of everyone in Aquitaine?"

"No. It has never been my intention to jeopardize the movement. Call it whatever you will, I believe truly in the concept. There *must* be a unified, international military–industrial complex. The world will not stay sane without it."

"But there is such a list."

"In a machine, a computer, but it must be programmed correctly, the proper codes used."

"Could you do it?"

"Not without help."

"What about Delavane?"

"You have certain perceptions yourself," said the Israeli, nodding. "What about him?"

Again Joel had to control his astonishment. The computer codes that released the master list of Aquitaine were with Delavane. At least the key symbols were. The remainder were provided by his spokes, the four leaders across the Atlantic. Converse shrugged. "You haven't really mentioned him. You've talked about Bertholdier, about the elimination of Leifhelm, and the impotence of van Headmer who could, however, bring in raw materials."

"I said gold," corrected Abrahms.

"Bertholdier said raw materials. . . . But what about George Marcus Delavane?"

"Marcus is finished," said the Israeli flatly. "He was coddled – we all coddled him – because he brought us the concept and he worked his end in the United States. We have equipment and *materiel* all over Europe, say nothing of the contraband we've shipped to insurgents, just to keep them occupied."

"Clarification," interrupted Joel. " 'Occupied' means killing?"

"All is killing. Disingenuous philosophers notwithstanding the ends *do* justify the means. Ask a man hunted by killers if he will jump into human excrement to conceal himself."

"I've asked him," said Converse. "I'm he, remember? What about Delavane?"

"He's a madman, a maniac. Have you ever heard his voice? He speaks like a man with testicles in a vice. They cut off his legs, you know, amputated only months ago for diabetes. The great general felled from an excess of *sugar!* He's tried to keep it a secret. He sees no one and no longer goes to his impressive office filled with photographs and flags and a thousand decorations. He operates out of his home where the servants come only when he's hidden in a darkened bedroom. How he wished it could have been a mortar shell or a bayonet charge, but no. Only sugar. He's become worse, a raving fool, but even fools can have flashes of brilliance. He had it once.

"What *about* him?"

"We have a man with him, an aide with the rank of colonel. When everything begins, when our commands are in place, the colonel will do as instructed. Marcus will be shot for the good of his own concept."

It was Joel's turn to get out of his chair. Once again he walked to the cathedral window across the room and felt the cool mountain breezes on his face. "This examination is finished, General," he said.

"*What?*" roared Abrahms. "You want your life. *I* want guarantees!"

"Finished," repeated Converse, as the door opened and a captain in the Israeli army walked inside, his gun levelled at Chaim Abrahms.

"There will be no discussion between us, Herr Converse," said Erich Leifhelm, standing by the door of the study, the doctor from Bonn having left, closing it behind him. "You have your prisoner. Execute him. Over many years and in many ways I have been waiting for this moment. In truth, I'm weary of the morbidity."

"Are you telling me you want to die?" asked Joel, by the table with the pistol on top.

"No one *wants* to die, least of all a soldier in the quiet of a strange room. Drums and sharp commands to a firing squad are preferable – there's a certain meaning in that. But I've seen too much death to go into hysterics. Pick up your pistol and get it over with. I would if I were you."

Converse studied the German's face, his strange noncommittal eyes that said nothing, accepting whatever was before him with only contempt. "You mean it, don't you?"

"Shall I give orders myself? There was a newsreel years ago. A black man did that against a blood-stained wall in Castro's Cuba. I've always admired that soldier." Leifhelm suddenly shouted. "*Achtung! Soldaten! Das Gewehr präsentieren! Vorbereiten . . .*"

"For Christ's sake, why not *talk?*" roared Joel, riding over the fanatical voice.

"Because I have nothing to say. My actions speak, my life has *spoken!* What is it, Herr Converse? You have no stomach for executions? You cannot give the order to yourself? A small, insignificant man's conscience will not permit him to kill? You are laughable!"

"I remind you, General, I've killed several people these past few weeks. Killed with less feeling than I ever thought possible."

"The lowliest coward running for his life will kill in panic. There is no character in that, merely survival. No, Herr Converse, you *are* insignificant, an impediment even your own forces care nothing about. You abound in this world. There is an odd phrase you have in your country that so readily applies to you, a phrase our associate uses frequently. You are a 'shit-kicker', Herr Converse, nothing more and probably less."

"What did you say? What did you call me?"

"You heard me clearly. A shit-kicker. A little man who steps in waste. Shit-kicker, Herr Converse. *Shit-kicker!*"

He was back a lifetime ago, on the bridge of a carrier, the face in front of him contorted, obscene, the voice shrill. Shit-kicker! Shit-kicker, shit-kicker, shit-kicker! Then other explosions followed, and he was blown into the dark clouds, the wind and the rain buffeting him, hammering him as he swung down toward the earth. Down to the ground and four years of madness and death and dying children weeping. Madness! Shit-kicker . . . shit-kicker. shit-kicker!

Converse reached down for the pistol on the table. He picked it up and levelled it at Erich Leifhelm, his index finger around the trigger, slowly, slowly squeezing it.

And then a sudden shock went through him. *What was he doing? He needed all three men of Aquitaine. Not one, not two, but three! It was the basis, the spine of what he had to do! But still there was something else. He had to kill, he had to destroy the deadly human virus staring at him, wanting death. Oh, Jesus! Had Aquitaine won after all? Had he become one of them? If he had, he had lost.*

"Your kind of courage is cheap, Leifhelm," he said softly, lowering the gun. "Better a quick bullet than other alternatives."

"I live by my code. I die by it gladly."

"Cleanly, you mean. Swiftly. No Dachau, no Auschwitz."

"You have the gun."

"I thought you had so much to offer."

"My successor has been chosen carefully. He will carry out details, every nuance of my agenda."

The opening was there, a strategy suddenly revealed. Joel pushed the button.

"Your successor?"

"*Ja.*"

"You have no successor, Field Marshal."

"What?"

"Any more than you have an agenda. You don't have anything without me. It's why I brought you here. Just you."

"What are you saying?"

"Sit down, General. I've several things to tell you, and for your own sake you'd better be seated. Your own execution might be more preferable to you than what I've got to say."

"*Liar!*" screamed Erich Leifhelm four minutes later, his hands gripping the arms of the brocaded chair. "Liar, liar, *liar!*" he roared, his eyes furious.

"I didn't expect you to believe me," said Joel calmly, standing halfway across the spacious, book-lined study. "Call Bertholdier in Paris and tell him you just heard some disturbing news and you'd like a clarification. Say it outright; you've learned that while you were in Essen, Bertholdier and Abrahms came to see me at your place in Bonn."

"How would I *know* that?"

"The truth. They paid a guard to open the door – I don't know which one, I didn't see him – but a guard did unlock the door and let them in."

"Because they believed you were an *informer*, sent out by Delavane, himself?"

"That's what they told me."

"You were drugged! There were no such indications!"

"They were suspicious. They didn't know the doctor and they didn't trust the Englishman. I don't have to tell you they don't trust you. They thought the whole thing might be a hoax. They wanted to cover themselves."

"*Incredible!*"

"Not when you think about it," said Converse sitting down opposite the German. "How did I really get the information I had? How did I know the exact people to reach – except through Delavane. That was their thinking."

"That Delavane would do this – *could* do it?" began the perplexed, astonished Leifhelm.

"I know what that means now," interrupted Joel quickly, centring in on the new opening presented him. "Delavane's finished, they both admitted it when they understood he was the last person on earth I'd work for. Maybe they were throwing me a few crumbs before setting me up for my own execution."

"That had to be done!" exclaimed the Third Reich's once youngest field marshal. "Certainly you can understand. Who *were* you? Where did you come from? You yourself did not know. You spoke of inconsequential names and lists and a great deal of money but nothing that made sense. Who had penetrated us? Since we could not find out you had to be turned into a *fauliger Abfall*."

"I beg your pardon?"

"Something rotten. A thing of rot no one would touch, the disease catching."

"You did it very well."

"For that I must take credit," said Leifhelm, nodding. "It was essentially my organization. Everything was mine."

"I didn't bring you here to discuss your achievements. I brought you here to save my life. You can do that for me – the people who sent me out either can't or won't – but you can. All I have to do is give you a reason."

"By implying Abrahms and Bertholdier conspire against me?"

"I won't imply anything, I'll give it to you straight in their own words. Remember, neither one of them thought I'd leave your place except as a corpse conveniently shot in the vicinity of some particularly gruesome assassination." Suddenly Converse got out of the chair, shaking his head. "*No!*" he said emphatically. "Call your trusted French and Israeli allies, your fellow *Aquitainians*. Say nothing if you like, just listen to their voices – you'll be able to tell. It takes an accomplished liar to spot other liars and you're the best."

"I find that offensive."

"Oddly enough I meant it as a compliment. It's why I reached you. I think you're going to be the winner over here and after what I've been through I want to go with a winner."

"Why do you say that?"

"Oh, come on, let's be honest. Abrahms is hated; he's insulted everyone in Europe, the UK and the US who doesn't agree with his expansionist policies for

Israel. Even his own countrymen can't shut him up. All they can do is censure him and he keeps on screaming. He'd never be tolerated in any kind of international federation."

The Nazi quickly, repeatedly shook his head. "*Never!*" he shouted. "He is the most loathsome, unattractive man to come out of the Middle East. And, of course, he's a Jew. But how is Bertholdier to be equated in this manner?"

Joel paused before answering. "His manner," he replied thoughtfully. "I'm not trying to be cute, I mean it. He's imperious, arrogant. He sees himself not only as a great military figure and a history-making power-broker, but also as some sort of god, above other men. There's no room on his Olympus for mortals. Also he's French. The English and the Americans wouldn't give him spit; one de Gaulle for them in a century is enough."

"There's clarity in your thoughts. He's the sort of abominable egotist only the French can suffer. He is, of course, a reflection of the entire country."

"Van Headmer doesn't count except where he can bring South Africa around for raw materials."

"Agreed," said the German.

"But you, on the other hand," went on Converse rapidly, again sitting down, "worked with the Americans and the English in Berlin and Vienna. You helped implement occupation policies, and in good conscience you turned over evidence to both the US and the UK prosecution teams in Nuremberg. Finally you became Bonn's spokesman in NATO. Whatever you were in the past, they like you." Again Joel paused, and when he continued there was a degree of simple deference in his voice. "Therefore, General, you're the winner, and you can save my life. All you need is a reason."

"Then give it to me."

"Use the phone first."

"Don't be an idiot and don't take *me* for one! You would not insist so unless you were sure of yourself, which means you are telling the truth. And if those *Schweinhunde* conspire against me, I will not inform them that I'm *aware* of it! What did they say?"

"You're to be killed. They can't risk the accusation that an old-line member of the Nazi Party has assumed vital controls in West Germany. Even under Aquitaine there'd be too many cries of 'foul!', too much fuel for the inescapable dissenters. A younger man or someone who thinks like they do but with no Party affiliations in his past will take your place. But no one you recommend."

Leifhelm was braced rigidly in the brocaded chair, his aged but still taut body immobile, his pallid face surrounding his piercing light-blue eyes like an alabaster mask. "*They* have made this most *holy* decision?" he said icily through lips that barely moved. "The vulgar Jew and the depraved French prince of maggots *dare* to attempt such a move against me?"

"Not that it matters, but Delavane agrees."

"Delavane! A raging, infantile clump of fantasies! The man we knew two years ago has disintegrated to a point beyond senility! He doesn't know it, but we give *him* orders, couched naturally as suggestions and beneficial possibilities. He has no more power of reason than Adolf Hitler had in his last years of madness."

"I don't know about that," said Converse. "Abrahms and Bertholdier didn't go into it other than to say he was finished. They talked about you."

"Really? Well, let *me* talk about *me!* Who do you think it was that made Aquitaine feasible throughout all Europe and the Mediterranean? Who fed the terrorists with weapons and millions of pounds of explosives – from the Baader-Meinhof to the Brigate Rosse to the Palestinians priming them for their final, let's say their *finest*, hours? *Who?* It was *I, Mein Herr!* Why are our conferences always in Bonn? Why are all directives funnelled, ultimately *issued* through *me?* Let me explain. *I* have the organization! *I* have the manpower dedicated men ready to do my bidding with a single order. *I* have the *money!* I created an advanced, highly sophisticated communications centre out of rubble; no one else in Europe could have done that ... I've known it all along. Bertholdier has nothing to speak of in Paris other than influence and the aura that hovers about him – in true battle, meaningless. The Jew and the South African are a continent away. When the chaos comes, it is *I* who will be the voice of Aquitaine in Europe. I never thought otherwise! My men will cut down Bertholdier and Abrahms at their toilets!"

"Scharhörn's the communications centre, isn't it?" asked Joel with no emphasis whatsoever.

"They told you that?"

"The name was dropped. The master list of Aquitaine's in a computer there, isn't it?"

"That, *also?*"

"It's not important. I don't care anymore. I was abandoned, remember? You must have figured out the computer, too – no one else could."

"A considerable accomplishment," admitted Leifhelm, his humility shining brightly on his waxen face. "I even assumed the catastrophe of death. There are sixteen letters; we each carry different sets of four, the remaining twelve are with the legless maniac. He thinks no one can activate the codes without his primary set but in truth a pre-coded combination of two sequences doubled will do it."

"That's ingenious," said Converse. "Do the others know?"

"Only my trusted French comrade," answered the German coldly. "The prince of traitors, Bertholdier. But, naturally, I never gave him the accurate combination, and an inaccurate insertion would erase everything."

"That was a winner thinking." Joel nodded approvingly, then frowned with concern. "What would happen, though, if your centre was assaulted?"

"Like Hitler's plans for the bunker, it would go up in flames. There are explosives everywhere."

"I see."

"But since you speak of winners, and in my judgment such men are prophets," continued Leifhelm, leaning forward in the brocaded chair, his eyes widening with enthusiasm. "Let me tell you about the isle of Scharhörn. Years ago, in 1945, out of the ashes of defeat, it was to be the site of the most incredible creation designed by true believers the world has ever known, only to be aborted by cowards and traitors. It was called *Operation Sonnenkinder* – the children of the sun – infants biologically selected and sent out all over the world to people

499

waiting for them, prepared to guide them through their lives to positions of power and wealth. As adults, the *Sonnenkinder* were to have but one mission across the globe. The rising of the Fourth Reich! You see now the symbolic choice of Scharhörn? From this inner complex of Aquitaine will come forth the *new order!* We will have *done* it!"

"Stow it," said Converse, getting out of the chair and walking away from Erich Leifhelm. "The examination's finished."

"*Was?*"

"You heard me, get out of here. You make me sick." The door opened and the young doctor from Bonn came in, his eyes on the once celebrated field marshal. "Strip him," ordered Converse. "Search him."

Joel entered the dimly lit room where Valerie and the *Sûreté's* Prudhomme flanked a man behind a tripodded video camera, its thick lens inserted in the wall. Ten feet away was a television monitor, showing only the deserted study, the brocaded wing-back chair now in the centre of the screen.

"Everything go all right?" he asked.

"Beautifully," said Valerie. "The operator didn't understand a word, but he claimed the lighting was exquisite. He can make as many copies as you like; they'll take about thirty-five minutes each."

"Ten and the original print will be enough," said Converse, looking at his watch, then up at Prudhomme, as Val spoke quietly in French to the cameraman. "You can take the first copy and still make the five o'clock flight to Washington."

"With the greatest of enthusiasm, my friend. I assume one of these prints will be for Paris."

"And every other head of government along with our affidavits. You'll bring back copies of the depositions Simon took in New York?"

"I'll go and make arrangements," said the Frenchman. "It is best my name does not appear on the passenger manifest." He turned and left the room, followed by the cameraman who headed for his duplicating equipment down the hall.

Valerie went to Joel, reaching for him, taking his face in both her hands and kissing him lightly on the lips. "For a few minutes in there you had me in knots. I didn't think you were going to make it."

"Neither did I."

"But you did. That was some display, Mister. I'm so very proud of you, my darling."

"A lot of lawyers'll cringe. It was the worst sort of entrapment. As an old, bewildering, but very bright law professor of mine would have put it, they were admissions elicited on the basis of false statements, those same admissions forming the basis of further entrapment."

"Stow it, Converse. Let's go for a walk. We used to walk a lot and I'd like to get back in the habit. It's not much fun alone."

Joel took her in his arms. They kissed, gently at first, feeling the warmth and

500

the comfort that had come back to them. He pulled his head away, his hands sliding to her shoulders, and looked into her wide, vibrant eyes, loving them so. "Will you marry me, Mrs Converse?" he said.

"Good Lord, again? Well, why not? As you said once before I wouldn't even have to change the initials on my lingerie."

"You never had initials on it."

"You found that out long before you made the remark."

"I didn't want you to think I stared."

"Yes, my darling, I'll marry you. But first we have things to do. Even before our walk."

"I know Peter Stone by way of the Tatiana family in Charlotte, North Carolina. He did terrible things to me but strange as it seems, I think I like him."

"I don't," said Valerie firmly. "I want to kill him."

40

It was the end of the second day in the countdown of three. The world-wide demonstrations against nuclear war were only ten hours away, to start at first light halfway across the world. The killings would begin, the chaos set in motion.

The group of eighteen men and fifteen women sat scattered about in the dark projection room in the underground strategy complex of the White House. Each had a small writing tray attached to his seat with a yellow pad lighted by a Tensor lamp. On the screen was flashed in thirty-second intervals one face after another, each with a number in the upper right hand corner. The instructions had been terse, in the language best understood by these people, and delivered by Peter Stone who had selected them. *Study the faces, make no audible comments, and mark down by number any you recognize, bearing in mind terminal-operations. At the end of the series the lights will be turned on and we'll talk. And, if need be, run the series again and again until we come up with something. Remember, we believe these men are killers. Concentrate on that.*

They were told nothing else. Except MI6's Derek Belamy, who had arrived within a half hour of the extraordinary session, looking haggard from his obviously exhausting journey. When Derek walked through the door, Peter had pulled him aside, their arms gripping each other, Stone never so happy or so relieved in his life to see a man. Whatever *he* might have missed, or could miss, Belamy would find it. The British agent had a tenth sense above anyone else's sixth, including Peter's, denied, of course with modesty by Derek.

"I need you, old friend," said Peter, as their hands gripped each other's arms. "I need you badly."

"It's why I'm here, old friend," replied Belamy his warm eyes reassuring. "Can you tell me anything?"

"There's no time now but I can give you a name. Delavane."

"Mad Marcus?"

"The same. It's his crisis and it's real."

"The *bastard!*" whispered the Englishman. "There's no one I'd rather see at the end of a barbed wire rope. Talk to you later, Peter. You've got your socializing to do. Incidentally, from what I can see, you've got the best here tonight."

"The best, Derek. We can't afford any less."

Beyond the American military personnel who had initially approached Stone, as well as Colonel Alan Metcalf, Nathan Simon, Justice Andrew Wellfleet, and the Secretary of State, the remaining audience was composed of the most experienced and secure intelligence officers Peter Stone had known in a lifetime of clandestine operations. They had been flown over by military transport from France, Great Britain, West Germany, Israel, Spain and the Netherlands. Among them were, of course, the extraordinary Derek Belamy, then François Villard, chief of France's highly secretive *Organisation Étrangere*; Yosef Behrens, the Mossad's leading authority on terrorism; Pablo Amandariaz, Madrid's specialist in KGB Mediterranean penetrations and Hans Vonmeer of the Netherlands' Secret State Police. The others, including the women, were equally respected in the caverns of deep-cover, beyond-salvage operations. They knew by name, face, or reputation the legions of killers-for-hire, killers-by-order, and killers-by-reason-of-ideology. Above all each was trusted, each a man or woman Stone had worked with; collectively they were the élite of the shadow world.

A face! He knew the face! It stayed on the screen and he wrote on his pad. *Dobbins, Number 27. Cecil or Cyril Dobbins. British Army. Transferred to British Intelligence . . . Personal aide to . . . Derek Belamy!*

Stone looked over at his friend across the aisle, fully expecting him to be writing on his yellow pad. Instead, the Englishman frowned and sat motionless in his chair, his pencil poised above the paper. The next face appeared on the screen. And the next, and the next, until the series was over. The lights came on and the first person to speak was the Mossad's Yosef Behrens.

"Number 17 is an artillery officer in the IDF recently transferred to the Security Branch, Jerusalem. His name is Arnold."

"Number 38," said François Villard, "is a colonel in the French Army attached to the guard of *Les Invalides*. It is the face; the name I do not recall."

"Number 26," said the man from Bonn, "is Oberleutnant Ernst Müller of the Federal Republic's Luftwaffe. He is a highly skilled pilot frequently assigned to fly ministers of state to conferences both within and without West Germany."

"Number 44," said a dark-skinned woman with a pronounced Hispanic accent, "has no such credentials as your candidates. He is a drug dealer, suspected of many killings and operates out of Ibiza. He was once a paratrooper. Name, Orejo."

"Son of a *gun*, I just don't believe it!" said the young lieutenant, William Landis, the computer expert from the Pentagon. "I know Number 51, I'm almost positive! He's one of the adjutants in Middle East procurements. I've seen him a lot but I don't know his name."

Six other men and two women volunteered twelve additional identities and positions, as everyone in the room silently looked for an emerging pattern. There was a preponderance of military personnel but by no means all, and the umbrella of the rest was puzzling. In the main they were ex-combat soldiers from high-casualty outfits who had drifted into crime – largely violent crime, the sort of men Peter Stone knew the generals of Aquitaine considered human garbage.

Finally Derek Belamy spoke in his hard, clipped distant voice. "There are four or five faces I associate with dossiers, but I'm not making connections." He looked over at Stone. "You'll run them again, won't you, old boy?"

"Of course, Derek," replied the former Station Chief in London. Then Stone, who had said nothing before, rose from his chair and addressed the gathering. "Everything you've given us will be fed immediately into computers and we'll see if we come up with any correlations. And to repeat what I said previously, I want to thank you all and apologize again for not giving you the explanations you deserve, not only for your help but for the trouble we've caused you. Speaking personally, my consolation is that you've all been here before and I know you understand. We'll break for fifteen minutes and start again. There are coffee and sandwiches in the next room." Stone nodded his thanks once more and started for the door. Derek Belamy intercepted him in the aisle.

"Peter, I'm dreadfully sorry it took me so long to get back to you. Truth is, the office had a devil of a time tracking me down. I was visiting friends in Scotland."

"I thought you might be in Northern Ireland. It's a hell of a mess, isn't it?"

"You were always better than you thought you were. I was in Belfast, of course. But right now I promise to do better – I'm sure I will—but the fact is I'm bushed; it was a perfectly terrible trip and, of course, no sleep whatsoever. All those faces began to look alike – I either knew them all or I didn't know a damned one!"

"Running them again will help," said Stone.

"Quite so," agreed Belamy. "And Peter, whatever this tangle is with that maniac, Delavane, I couldn't have been more delighted to see you in the control chair. We were all told you were out, rather firmly out."

"I'm back in. Very firmly."

"I can see that, old chap. That *is* your Secretary of State in the back row, isn't it?"

"Yes, it is."

"*Congratulations*, old boy. Well, off for coffee, black and hot. See you in a few minutes."

"Across the aisle, old friend."

Stone walked out of the door and turned right in the white corridor. He could feel the rapid acceleration of his heartbeat; it was a cousin to Johnny Reb's claims of a churning stomach and an acid taste in his mouth – bile, The Rebel called it. He had to get to a telephone quickly. Converse's courier, the Sûreté's Prud-homme, would be arriving within the hour; a Secret Service escort was waiting for him at Dulles Airport with instructions to bring him directly to the White House. But it was not the Frenchman who concerned Stone now, it was Converse himself. He had to reach him before the session began again. He *had* to!

When the lawyer had contacted him through the Tatiana relay, Peter had been astonished by the sheer audacity of what Converse had done. *Kidnapping* the three generals – video-taping the interrogations or the "oral examinations" or whatever the legal terminology was; it was insane! The only thing more insane was the fact that he had carried it off – due obviously to the resources of a very determined, very angry man from the *Sûreté*. The computer *was* in Scharhörn, the master list of Aquitaine buried somewhere in its intricate mechanism, only to be erased by inaccurate codes, the complex itself mined with explosives. *Jesus!*

And now the final insanity. The man no one could find, the source so deeply shrouded they frequently doubted his existence despite the fact that all logic insisted he was there. Aquitaine's man in England *had* to be, for there could be no Aquitaine without the British. Further, Stone knew he was the conduit, the primary communicator between Palo Alto and the generals overseas, for constant screenings of Delavane's telephone charges showed repeated calls to a number in the Hebrides, and such a relay device was all too familiar to the former intelligence agent. The calls disappeared at that number in the Scottish islands, just as the KGB calls processed through Canada's Prince Edward Island disappeared, and the Company's communications routed through Key West could not be traced.

Belamy! The man whose face never appeared in any publication – films were destroyed instantly by aides if he was even in the background of a photograph. The most guarded operations officer in England, with access to secrets culled over decades and scores of devices created by the best minds of MI6. And yet, was it *possible?* Derek Belamy, the quiet good-humoured chess player, the *friend* who gave good whisky and a fine ear to an American colleague who progressively had serious doubts about his calling in life. The *better* friend for having the wisdom and the courage to warn his colleague that he was drinking too much, that perhaps he should take a sabbatical and if money was a problem, surely some sort of quiet consultation agreement could be worked out with his own organization. *Was* it possible, this decent man, this *friend?*

Stone reached the door in the hallway marked simply by the number 14, *Occupied*. He walked inside the small room and went to the desk and the telephone. He did not sit down; his anxiety would not permit it. He picked up the phone and dialled the White House switchboard, as he took out the slip of paper in his pocket with Converse's number somewhere in France. He gave it to the operator, adding simply, "This should be scrambled. I'm talking from Strategy Fourteen, confirm by trace."

"Trace confirmed, sir. Scrambler will be in operation. Shall I call you back?"

"No, thanks, I'll stay on the line." Stone remained standing as he heard the hollow echo of numbers being punched and the faint hum of the scrambling machine. And then he heard an intruding sound, the sound of a door opening. He turned.

504

Put the phone down, Peter," said Derek Belamy quietly, as he shut the door. "There's no point to this."

"It *is* you, isn't it?" Stone slowly, awkwardly replaced the phone in its cradle.

"Yes, it is. And I want everything you want, my old friend. Neither of us could deny ourselves the parting shots, could we? I said I was visiting friends in Scotland and you said you thought I was in Ireland . . . We've learned over the years, haven't we? The eyes don't lie, Scotland – calls to the Hebrides; the glass fell over your eyes. And earlier, when that face came on the screen you looked across the aisle a bit too obviously, I think."

"Dobbins. He worked for you."

"You wrote frantically on your pad yet you said nothing."

"I was waiting for you to say something."

"Yes, of course, but I couldn't, could I?"

"Why, Derek? For Christ's sake, *why?*"

"Because it's right and you know it."

"*I don't* know it! You're a sane, reasonable man. They're *not!*"

"They'll be replaced, naturally. How often have you and l used drones we couldn't abide because their contributions were necessary to the objective?"

"*What* objective? An international totalitarian alliance? A military state without borders? All of us robots marching to the drums of fanatics?"

"Oh, come off it, Peter. Spare us both the liberal drivel. You left this business once, drinking yourself into a stupor because of the waste, the futility, the deceits we all practised – the *people* we killed – to maintain what we laughingly called the *status quo*. What *status quo*, old man? To be continuously harassed by our inferiors the world over? To be held hostage by screaming *mullahs* and hysterical fools who still live in the dark ages and would cut our throats over the price of a barrel of oil? To be manipulated at every turn by Soviet deceptions? No, Peter, there really *is* a better way. The means may be distasteful but the end result is not only desirable, it's also honourable."

"Whose definition? George Marcus Delavane's? Erich Leifhelm's? Chaim . . ."

"They'll be *replaced!*" broke in Belamy angrily."

"They *can't* be!" shouted Stone. "Once it starts, you can't stop it. The image becomes the reality. It's expected, *demanded!* To deviate is to be accused, to oppose is to be ostracized, penalized! It's lock-step and lock-jaw, and you damn well *know* that!"

The telephone rang.

"Let it ring," ordered the man from MI6.

"It doesn't matter now. *You* were the Englishman at Leifhelm's house in Bonn. A brief description of you would have confirmed it for me."

"That's *Converse?*" The phone rang again.

"Would you like to talk to him? I understand he's quite a lawyer, although he broke the fundamental rule – he took himself on as a client. He's coming out, Derek, and he's going after you, all of you. We all are – after all of you."

"You won't!" cried Belamy. "You *can't!* As you yourself put it, once it starts you can't *stop* it!"

Without the slightest indication that he was about to move, the Englishman suddenly lunged at Stone, the three middle fingers of his right hand rigid, zeroing in on the CIA man's throat like three steel projectiles. Stone took the agonizing blow, gasping for air as the room spiralled out of control, a thousand dazzling irregular spots of white light in his eyes. He could hear the door opening and closing, as the phone insistently rang again. But Peter could not see it; the white lights had turned into darkness. The ringing stopped as Stone wildly, blindly careened around the room, trying to trace the bell, trying to find the phone. The minutes passed in madness as he smashed into walls and fell over the desk. Then the door crashed open and Colonel Alan Metcalf shouted.

"Stone! What *happened?*" The Air Force officer raced to Peter, instantly recognizing the effects of the judo chop. He began massaging Stone's throat, pressing his knee into the CIA man's stomach to force up air. "The switchboard reached us, saying that Room Fourteen had placed a scrambler call but didn't pick up. *Christ*, who *was* it?"

Vague images came back to Stone, but still he could not speak; he was capable only of gasping coughs. He writhed under Metcalf's strong hands, pointing to a notepad that had fallen from the desk. The colonel understood; he reached for it, yanking out a ballpoint pen from his pocket. He rolled Stone over, placing the pen in his hand, guiding the hand to the pad.

Struggling for control Peter wrote.

BELMY. STP. AQUTAIN.

"Oh, my *God!*" whispered Metcalf, reaching for the phone and dialling *zero*. "Operator, this is an emergency. Give me Security ... Security? Colonel Alan Metcalf talking from Strategy Fourteen. *Emergency!* There's an Englishman named Belamy who may still be on the premises trying to leave. Stop him! Hold him! Consider him dangerous. And get word to the infirmary. Send a doctor to Strategy Fourteen. *Quickly!*"

The White House staff doctor removed the oxygen mask from Stone's face, placing it on the desk next to the cylinder. He then gently moved Peter's head back in the chair, inserting a tongue depressor and peering into the CIA man's throat with a pencil light.

"It was a nasty shot," he said, "but you'll feel better in a couple of hours. I'll give you some pills for the pain."

"What's in them?" asked Stone hoarsely.

"A mild analgesic with some codeine."

"No thanks, Doctor," said Peter, looking over at Metcalf. "I don't think I like what I see on your face."

"I don't either. Belamy got out. His pass was high priority and he told the East Gate he was needed urgently at the British Embassy."

"*Goddamn* it!"

"Try not to strain your voice," said the doctor.

"Yes, of course," replied Stone. "Thank you very much, and now if you'll excuse us." He got out of the chair, as the doctor nodded, picking up his medical bag and heading for the door. "I meant what I said, Doctor. Thanks very much."

"Sure. I'll send someone back for the air."

The telephone rang as the door closed. Metcalf picked it up. "Yes? Yes it is; he's right here." The colonel listened for several moments then turned to Stone. "Breakthrough," he said. "All those military who were identified have two things in common. Each is on a minimum thirty-day summer leave and every request was made five months ago, nearly to the day."

"Thus guaranteeing request-granted status because they were first in line," added the CIA man with difficulty. "And the plans for the anti-nuclear demonstrations were announced in Sweden *six* months ago."

"Clockwork," said Metcalf. "To identify and neutralize the others we'll send out the word. Every officer in half a dozen armies and navies who returns from summer leave is to be restricted to quarters. There'll be errors but that's rough. We can send out the photographs and correct them."

"It's time for Scharhörn." Stone got out of the chair, massaging his throat. "And I don't mind telling you it scares me to death. A wrong symbol and we erase Aquitaine's master list. Worse, a wrong move and that whole complex is blown away." The CIA man went to the phone.

"Are you going to call The Rebel?" asked the colonel.

"Converse first. He's working on the codes."

The three generals of Aquitaine sat stunned in their chairs, staring straight ahead, refusing to look at one another. The lights had been turned on, the large television screen turned off. Behind each soldier was a man with a gun and concise instructions *If he gets up, kill him.*

"You know what I want," said Converse, walking in front of the generals. "And as you've just seen there's really no reason why any of you shouldn't give it to me. Four little numbers or letters each of you has memorized in sequence. Of course, if you refuse there's a doctor here who I'm told has a bag of magic – the same sort of magic you administered to me in Bonn. What'll it be, gentlemen?"

Silence.

"Four, three, L, one," said Chaim Abrahms, looking down at the floor. "They're *filth*," he added quietly.

"Thank you, General." Joel wrote in a small notepad. "You're free to go now. You can get out of the chair."

"Go?" said the Israeli, getting up. "*Where?*"

"Wherever you like," replied Converse. "I'm sure you'll have no trouble at the airport in Annecy. You'll be recognized."

General Chaim Abrahms left the room accompanied by the Israeli Army captain.

"Two, M, zero, six," said Erich Leifhelm. "And, if you wish, I will submit to the drugs for verification. I will not be associated with such treacherous pigs."

"I want the combination," pressed Joel, writing. "And I won't hesitate to send you up into space to get it."

"Inversion," said the German. "Reverse the order of the symbols in the second sequence."

"He's yours, Doctor." Converse nodded to the man behind Leifhelm's chair. "We can't take the chance blowing this one."

General Erich Leifhelm, once the youngest field marshal of the Third Reich, got up and walked slowly out of the room, followed by the doctor from Bonn.

"You're all unworthy, all blind," said General Jacques Louis Bertholdier with imperious calm. "I prefer to be shot."

"I'm sure you would, but no such luck," answered Joel. "I don't need you now, and I want to know you're back in Paris where everyone can see you. Take him to his room."

"The room? I thought I was free to leave, or was that another lie?"

"Not at all. Just a matter of logistics – you know what logistics are, General. We're a little short of transportation and drivers here, so when the doctor's finished, I'm lending the three of you a car. You can draw straws for who drives."

"*What?*"

"Get him out of here," said Converse, addressing a former sergeant-major in the French army once stationed at Algiers.

"Move, *vache!*"

The door opened, only coincidentally for Bertholdier. It was Valerie and she looked at Joel. "Stone's on the telephone. He says hurry."

It was 2.05 A.M. when the Mystere jet dropped out of the night sky and landed at the airstrip eight miles from Cuxhaven, West Germany. It taxied to the north end of the runway where the stately, white-maned figure of Johnny Reb waited by a black Mercedes sedan.

The doors of the plane opened, the short steps swinging down in place, and Converse climbed out, taking Valerie's hand as she descended after him. Next came the former sergeant-major from Algiers, followed by a fourth passenger, a slender blond man in his mid-forties who wore tortoiseshell glasses. They walked away from the aircraft as the pilot retracted the steps and closed the automatic doors; the twin engines accelerated and the plane swerved around heading back toward the maintenance hangars. The Rebel came away from the car and met them, extending his hand to Joel.

"Ah've seen your picture here and there and it's a pleasure, sir. Frankly, I never thought I'd meet you, leastways not in this world."

"There were a number of times I had my doubts just how long I'd be here. This is my wife, Valerie."

"Ah'm enchanted, ma'am," said the southerner, bringing Val's hand to his lips as he bowed gallantly. "Your accomplishments have astonished some of the best minds in my former profession."

"I hope not *too* former," interjected Converse.

"Not at the moment, son."

"This is Monsieur LeFevre and Dr Geoffrey Larson. Stone said you've been briefed."

"A pleasure, sir," exclaimed The Rebel, shaking the Frenchman's hand. "My hat's off to you, to all of you for what you did with those three generals. Absolutely *remarkable!*"

"Such men have enemies," said LeFevre simply. "They are not hard to find and Inspector Prudhomme knew that. We are in many places with many memories. Let us hope they will be put to rest tonight."

"Let's hope," said The Rebel, turning to the fourth passenger. "Dr Larson, so nice to meet you, sir. I understand you know just about everything there is to know about every computer ever made."

"An exaggeration, I'm sure," said the Englishman, shyly. "But I suspect if it ticks I can make it hum. Actually, I was vacationing in Geneva."

The *non-sequitur* momentarily threw Johnny Reb. who could only utter, "Sorry about that," as he looked at Joel.

It had been the most difficult decision Peter Stone had made in all his years of agonizing decisions. To make the wrong move – to telegraph the incursion into the complex at Scharhörn – would result in its destruction by the setting off of explosives all over the communications centre. There would be nothing left of the old U-boat station but shattered concrete and twisted equipment. Stone had gone by instincts honed over a lifetime in the shadow world. There could be no élite commando units, no official special forces ordered up for an extraordinary assignment, for there was no telling who within the various government forces could be a member, an officer of Aquitaine. Such a man could make a telephone call and the complex at Scharhörn would be blown up. Therefore the incursion had to be made by rogue elements, men hired by outlaws who had no allegiance to anyone or anything but money and their immediate employers. Nothing was a secret any longer without the master list of Aquitaine. The President of the United States gave Stone twelve hours, after which he said he would convene an emergency session of the Security Council of the United Nations. Peter Stone could hardly believe he had replied to the most powerful man in the free world with the words: "That's meaningless. It would be too late."

The Rebel finished his briefing, his flashlight still shining on the map spread over the hood of the Mercedes. "As I told you, this is the original layout we got from the Zoning Commission in Cuxhaven. Those Nazis sure were particular when it came to specifics – I figure everyone was justifyin' a salary or a rank. We get over the ocean radar and head to the old strip that was used for supplies, then do our number. Now mind you, there are still a lot of lights out there, still a lot of people, but a hell of a lot less than there were two days ago. There are some walls but we got grappling hooks and a few boys who know how to use them."

"Who are they?" asked Converse.

"No one you'd ask into your mother's parlour, my friend, but five of the meanest hornets you could find. I tell you they have absolutely no redeeming social qualities. They're perfect."

"What's the aircraft?"

"The best Petey could get, and it's *the* best. A Fairchild Scout. It holds nine people."

"With a glide-ratio of nine to one at four thousand feet," said Joel. "I'm flying."

41

Converse inched the half-wheel forward as he cut the engines and entered a left bank glide over the small airstrip 2,400 feet below. It was erratically visible through the tails of low-flying North Sea clouds, but Joel guessed it could be seen clearly at 500 feet. He would then start his final circle for the short approach, his touchdown heading away from the old U-boat base, minimizing whatever sound the outsized balloon tyres made while braking. The manoeuvre itself was the nearest thing to a carrier landing he could imagine, and he noted with satisfaction that his hands were as steady as his concentration. The fear he had anticipated did not materialize; it was strangely absent. The anxiety and the anger were another matter.

Valerie and LeFevre – over the Frenchman's strenuous objections – remained behind on a deserted pier in Cuxhaven where Johnny Reb had managed to install a primitive but functional relay station. It was Val's job to stay in radio contact with the team – either The Rebel or Converse operating the powerful hand- held equipment on Scharhörn – and the former sergeant from Algiers was to stand guard, letting no one on that pier. The five "recruits" Johnny Reb had hired for apparently large amounts of money were difficult to appraise for they said very little and wore dark wool-knit caps pulled down above their eyes and black turtleneck sweaters pulled up around their throats. The same clothing was provided for Joel and the British computer expert, Geoffrey Larson; The Rebel had his in the Mercedes. Each man, except Larson, carried a pistol with an attached silencer that was held firmly in an extended holster strapped to his waist. On the left side of the black leather belt was a long-bladed hunting knife, and beside it a coil of thin wire. At the back, above the kidneys, and held in place by clips, were two canisters of a mace-like gas that rendered their victims helpless and silent. The fact that each, including the aging Johnny Reb, wore his equipment with such casual authority made Converse feel out of place, but the degree of concentration they gave to the installation's plans and the curt suggestions they had for gaining entry and subsequent explorations also made him feel The Rebel had hired well.

Joel circled slowly, delicately into his final approach, silently gliding over the darkened U-boat base, his eyes on both the strip ahead and the instrument-guidance altimeter. He struck the flaps and dropped; the heavy tyres absorbed the jarring shock of contact. *Touchdown.*

"We're down," said Johnny Reb into the radio. "And with a little luck we'll stop, won't we, son?"

"We'll stop," said Converse. They did, no more than forty feet from the end of the airstrip. Joel removed the knit hat, breathing deeply; his hairline and forehead were drenched with sweat.

"We're going out." The Rebel snapped off the radio and pressed it into the front of his chest; it stayed in place. "Oh," he added, seeing that Converse was watching him. "I forgot to mention it. There's heavy-duty Velcro around the case and on your sweater."

"You're full of surprises."

"You had a fair share yourself during the past few weeks. Let's go catfishin'," boy." Johnny Reb opened his door; Joel did the same, both of them climbing out followed by Larson and the five men, three of them carrying rubberized grappling hooks attached to coils of rope. The second man who had said nothing during the strategy session stood in front of Converse and spoke quietly, startling Joel with his American accent.

"I'm a pilot, Mister, and that was supposed to be part of my job. I'm glad it wasn't. You're good, man."

"Where did you fly? With whom?"

"Let's say a new kind of Peruvian airline. The scenic Florida run."

"Come *on!*" The Rebel ordered, starting for the overgrown borders of the airstrip.

They approached the high walls of the old U-boat base all crouching in the tall grass, studying what was before them. Converse was struck by the sheer immensity of the unending, thick concrete. It was like a fortress with no fort inside, no treasured structure that warranted the protection of the impenetrable walls. The only break was over on the left, in a section that faced the airstrip. A pair of steel double doors layered with plates of bolted, reinforced iron stood ominously in the erratic moonlight. They were also impenetrable.

"This place has quite a history," whispered Johnny Reb beside Joel. "Half the German High Command had no idea it was here and the Allies never got a smell of it. It was Doenitz's private base. Some said he was going to use it as a threat if Hitler didn't turn things over to him."

"It was also going to be used for something else," said Converse, remembering Leifhelm's incredible story of the rising of the Fourth Reich a generation after the war. *Operation Sonnenkinder.*

One of the men with a grappling hook crawled over and spoke to The Rebel in German. The Southerner replied angrily, looking pained, but finally nodding as the man crawled away. He turned to Joel.

"Son of a no-account hound dog *bitch!*" he exclaimed under his breath. "He stole me blind! He said he'd make the first assault on the east flank – which you

511

know damn well that mother studied – if I guaranteed him an additional five thousand American!"

"And you'll pay, of course."

"Of course. We're honourable men. If he's killed, every penny goes to his wife and children. I know the lad; we took a building once with the Meinhof inside. He scaled eight storeys, dropped down through an elevator shaft, kicked a door open and shot the bastards cold with his Uzzi on rapid fire."

"I don't *believe* all this," whispered Converse.

"Believe," said The Rebel softly, as he looked at Joel. "We do it because no one else will. And somebody has to do it. We may be rogues, son, but there are times we're on the side of the angels – for a price."

The muted sound of the rubberized grappling hook split the air, and took hold on top of the wall, the rope stretched taut. In seconds the black-clothed man could be seen climbing hand over hand, his feet bracing, racing up the dark concrete. He reached the ledge, his left hand disappearing over the top, his right leg swinging up as he vaulted into a prone position, his body level with the ledge of concrete. Suddenly, he held out his left arm, waving it back and forth twice, a signal. Then bracing himself, he reached for his holstered weapon with his right hand, pulling it out slowly.

A single spit was heard and once more there was silence as the man's left arm shot out for a second time. A second signal.

The two other men with grappling hooks raced out of the grass, flanking the first man, swinging their hooks in circles and heaving them up, each accurately as the ropes were yanked taut and the two figures began scaling the wall. Joel knew it was his turn; it was part of the plan if he was up to it and he was determined to be. He rose and walked out, joining the remaining two men hired by The Rebel; the American pilot who had spoken to him pointed to the centre rope. He gripped it and started the painful climb to the top of the wall.

Only in the last extremity were the elderly Johnny Reb and the slender, professorial Geoffrey Larson expected to use the ropes. By his own admission the Southerner might not be capable, and the risk of injury to the computer expert was unacceptable.

Arms and legs aching, Converse was hauled up the final inches by his German companion. "Pull up the rope!" ordered the man in a heavily accented whisper. "Drop it slowly down the other side and reverse the hooks."

Joel did as he was told, seeing for the first time the interior of the strange fortress – and a uniformed man below on the ground, dead, blood trickling down the centre of his forehead from the incredibly accurate shot. In the moonlit darkness he could make out a series of huge watery slips in the distance broken up by concrete piers on which there were giant winches, black wheels of immense machinery, long out of use, relics of a violent past. In a semi-circle facing the U-boat docks and the sea were five low, concrete one-storey buildings with small windows, the first two with dim lights on inside. The buildings were joined by cement walkways, wide steps where they were necessary as the central structures were higher off the ground, no doubt once the officers' quarters, commanders of the behemoths that prowled the deep waters of the Atlantic, killers for an abominable cause.

Directly below the wall where the three ropes now dangled were more wide steps that led up both sides of what appeared to be a concrete podium or platform, the area in front some kind of courtyard, perhaps 200 feet wide, that led to the rear of the buildings facing the U-boat slips. A parade ground, thought Converse, visualizing rows of submarine crews, standing at attention, receiving orders and listening to the exhortations of their officers as they prepared once more to enter the deep in search of tonnage and carnage.

"Follow me!" said the German, tapping Joel's shoulder and grabbing the rope as he slid over the wall and lowered himself to the concrete platform beneath. On both sides, the four men were on their way down, one after the other. Converse, less gingerly than the professionals, rolled over the ledge, his hands gripping the rope and slid to the ground.

The two men on Joel's left raced silently across the platform and down the steps toward the huge steel doors. The two men on his right, as if by instinct, ran down the opposing steps, returning below to crouch in front of the platform, their weapons drawn. Converse, following the German, swiftly joined the pair at the doors. Both men were studying the bolts and the layers of plating and the complicated lock with tiny flashlights.

"Fuse it and blow it," said the American. "There's no alarm."

"Are you sure?" asked Joel. "From what I gathered this whole place is wired."

"The trips are down there," explained the second pilot, pointing toward the concrete sides of the parade ground, a three-foot-high wall on both sides.

"Trips?"

"Trip lights. Intersecting beams."

"Which means there are no animals," said the German, nodding. "*Keine Hunde. Sehr gut!*"

The fourth man had finished stuffing wads of a soft, putty-like substance into the lock mechanism, using his knife to finish the job. He then took out a small circular device no larger than a 50-cent coin from his pocket, layered another mound of the substance directly over the lock and plunged the coin into it. "Move back," he ordered.

Converse watched, mesmerized. There was no explosion, no detonation whatsoever, but there was intense heat and a glowing blue-white flame that literally melted the steel. Then a series of clicks could be heard and, hearing them, the American quickly slid back the triple bolts. He pushed the right door open and blinked his flashlight outside. Moments later Johnny Reb and Geoffrey Larson walked through the door into the strange compound.

"Trips," repeated the American to The Rebel. "They're all along those two walls," he said, pointing. "See them?"

"I can," replied the Southerner. "And that means there'll be a few shooting straight up on top for tip-toeing feet. All right, boys, let's do a little crawling. Bellies down with knees and asses wiggling." The six at the door joined the two crouched in front of the platform. Johnny whispered in German, then turned to Larson. "My English friend, I want you to stay right here until us old timers give you the high sign to catch up with us." He looked at Joel. "Sure you want to come?"

"I won't bother to answer that. Let's go."

One by one, with the German who was $5,000 richer in the lead, the seven men snaked their way across the old parade ground. Barely breathing, trousers torn, knees and hands scraped by the rough, cracked concrete. The German headed for the break between buildings 2 and 3, counting from the right. It was a connecting cement path with gradually rising steps on the left. He reached the open space and stood up.

Suddenly, he snapped his fingers once – not very loud but loud enough. Everyone froze where he was under the field of intersecting alarm beams. Converse angled his head on the ground to get what vision he could manage. The German was crouched in the shadows as a man came into view, a guard with a rifle slung over his shoulder. Aware of another presence, the guard whipped his head around; the German lunged out of the shadows, his long-bladed knife arcing in mid-air toward the man's head. Joel closed his eyes, the sound of savagely expelled air telling him more than he cared to know.

The movement began again, and again one by one each member of the unit reached the path. Converse was soaked with sweat. He looked at the row of U-boat slips beyond and the sea beyond them and wished to God he could fall into the water. His brief musings were interrupted by The Rebel touching his elbow, indicating that Joel should take out his gun as the Southerner had done. It was now Johnny Reb who took the lead; he crept out to the front of building 2 and turned right, crouching close to the ground, heading toward the lighted windows. His fingers snapped; all movement stopped, bodies now prone. Diagonally to the left, by the edge of a giant slip, were the glow of cigarettes and the sound of men talking quietly—three men, guards with rifles.

As if on a silent order, three of the five men hired by The Rebel – which ones Converse could not tell – broke away and started crawling in a wide arc toward the opposite side of the old U-boat berth. Approximately a minute and a half later – the longest ninety seconds Joel could remember – a barrage of muted reports punctured the night breezes off the sea. The subsequent sounds were minimal, as hands clutched at heads and bodies snapped, falling to the concrete ground. The hired guns returned and Johnny Reb waved them forward, Converse forced to be the last as men grabbed his shoulders and passed him. They reached the only lighted window in building 2; The Rebel stood up, inching his way to the glass. He turned and shook his head; the unit proceeded.

They came to the open space between buildings 1 and 2. Cautiously each one ran across, crouching the instant he reached the opposite edge then racing ahead. It was Joel's turn; he got to his knees, then to his feet.

"*Horst? Bist das du?*" said a man harshly, walking out of a door and up the cement path.

Converse stood motionless. The rest of the unit was well past the edge of building 1 as the sounds of the North Sea crashing on the rocks in the distance blocked out the intruder's voice. Joel tried not to panic. He was alone and he alone could blow the operation apart, destroy the complex at Scharhörn, killing

514

everyone including Connal Fitzpatrick, if, indeed, the young commander was there.

"*Ja,*" he heard himself saying as he turned away into the shadow, his right hand reaching across his waist for the hunting knife. He could not trust his gun in the darkness.

"*Warten Sie einen Augenblick! Sie sind nicht Horst!*"

Joel shrugged, and waited. The footsteps approached; a hand grabbed his shoulder. He spun round, gripping the handle of the knife with such force it nearly blocked out the terrible thing his mind told him he had to do. He grabbed the man's hair and brought the razor-sharp blade across the throat beneath.

Wanting to vomit, he pulled the man into the darker shadows; the head was all but severed from the body. He raced across the open space and caught up with the others. No one had missed him; each man was taking his turn peering into one of the four lighted windows in a row. Johnny Reb was beyond the first, gesturing as each man ducked away, pointing in successive directions firmly, rapidly, receiving nods of acceptance. Commands were being given, an assault planned for immediate execution. Converse raised himself to the edge of the last window and looked inside. Instantly he understood why The Rebel had to act quickly. There were ten guards in what could only be described as para-military uniforms belonging to no recognizable army. Each was either strapping on a weapon, looking at his watch, or crushing out a cigarette. Then, more ominously, they checked the ammunition clips in their rifles and automatics. Several laughed, raising their voices as if making demands or requests at the expense of the others. Joel could not understand the words. He ducked away from the window only to be confronted by Johnny Reb close to the ground.

"It's a patrol going out, isn't it?" whispered Converse.

"No, son," replied the Southerner. "It's a firing squad. They just got their orders."

"My *God!*"

"We follow them, staying low and out of sight. You may find your old buddy Fitzpatrick after all."

The next minutes were insanely out of Kafka, thought Joel. The ten men lined up and walked out of the door leading to building 2. Suddenly floodlights erupted throughout the parade ground, the trip lights obviously turned off as the squad walked out on the concrete. Two men with automatics in their hands ran over to building 4; they unlocked then unbolted the heavy door and raced inside shouting orders, as lights were turned on.

"*Aufwachen! Aufstehen! Raus antreten! Macht schnell! Eilt Euch!*"

Seconds later, gaunt, manacled figures began straggling out, blinking at the harsh lights in their ragged clothes, some barely able to walk, supported by others who were stronger. Ten, twenty, twenty-five, thirty-two, forty . . . forty-three. Forty-three prisoners of Aquitaine about to be executed! They were marched toward the concrete wall fronting the platform at the far end of the parade ground.

It happened with the hysterical force of a crowd gone mad! The condemned men suddenly bolted in all directions, those nearest the two guards with the automatics crashing the chains of their manacled hands into the stunned faces. Shots rang out, three prisoners fell, writhing on the ground. The firing squad raised its rifles.

"Now, you mother-lovin' catfish hunters!" shouted Johnny Reb, as the Scharhörn unit, as one, raced into the mêlée, pistols firing, muted spits mingling with the ear-shattering explosions of the unsilenced weapons.

It was over in less than twenty seconds. The ten men of Aquitaine lay on the ground. Six were dead, three wounded, one on his knees trembling in fear. Two men of the Scharhörn unit sustained minor wounds – the American pilot and one other.

"*Connal!*" roared Joel, racing about the scattered prisoners, relieved that most were moving. "*Fitzpatrick!* Where the hell *are* you?"

"Over here, Lieutenant," said a weak voice on Converse's right. Joel threaded his way through the fallen bodies and knelt down beside the frail, bearded Navy lawyer. "You took your sweet time getting here," continued the commander. "But then junior grade officers usually have deficiencies."

"What *happened* back there?" asked Converse. "You could all have been killed!"

"That was the point, wasn't it? It was made clear to us last night, so we figured what the hell?"

"But why *you?* Why *all* of you?"

"We talked and we couldn't figure it out. Except one thing – we were all senior officers on thirty-to forty-day leaves, most of them summer leaves. What did it mean?"

"It was meant to throw people off if they began to see a pattern. There are ninety-seven men out in hit teams—all on summer leaves. Numerically you were nearly fifty per cent of that number, presumably above suspicion. You were a bonus and it saved your life."

Suddenly, Connal whipped his head to the left. A man was running out of building 5, racing down the concrete path. "That's the warden!" shouted Fitzpatrick as loud as he could. "*Stop him!* If he gets into the second barracks he'll blow the whole place up!"

Joel got to his feet and started after the racing figure as fast as his painful legs would carry him, his gun in his hand. The man had reached the mid-point of building 3; he had less than thirty yards to go to the door of 2. Converse fired; the bullet was way off its mark, ricocheting off a steel window frame. The man reached the door, smashing it open and slamming it shut. Joel raced into it crashing the full weight of his body into the heavy wood. It gave way, swinging violently back into the wall. The man was running to a metal-encased panel; Converse fired wildly, frantically, again and again. The man spun, wounded in the legs, the panel open. He reached up for a bank of switches. Joel lunged, gripping the man's hand, smashing his head into the stone floor.

Gasping for breath, Converse crawled away from the man, his hands covered with warm blood, his empty pistol on the floor. One of the Scharhörn team burst through the door.

"Are you fine?" he asked in an accent Joel could not place.

"Splendid," said Converse, feeling weak and sick.

The hired man walked past Joel, glancing at the still figure on the floor on his way to the open panel. He studied it and reached into his pocket for some kind of small, multifaceted tool. In seconds, he was taking out screws and pulling off the interior metal plating. Moments later, with another part of the instrument, he was cutting wires far back into their receptacles, leaving nothing but stubs of copper.

"You are not to worry," said the man, finished. "I am best of Norwegian demolitions. Now we do not concern ourselves that a stray pig can do damage. Come, there is much work left to do." The team member stopped and stood above Converse. "We owe you our lives. We will pay."

"It's not necessary," said Joel, getting up.

"It is the custom," replied the man, heading for the door.

Out on the parade ground, Aquitaine's prisoners were sitting up against the wall – all but five whose bodies were covered with sheets, apparently obtained from one of the buildings. Converse went over to Fitzpatrick.

"We lost them," said the naval officer, no strength in his voice, only sorrow.

"Look to the things you believe in, Connal," said Joel. "It may sound banal, but it's the only thing I can think of to say."

"It's good enough." Fitzpatrick looked up, a wan smile on his lips. "Thanks for reminding me. Go on. They need you over there."

"*Larson!*" shouted Johnny Reb, standing above the trembling, unhurt guard. "Get in here!"

The professorial Englishman walked hesitantly through the steel door at the base of the airstrip into the floodlights. He came over to The Rebel, his eyes wandering about the parade ground, his expression one of awe and consternation. "Good *God!*" he uttered.

"I guess that says it," said the Southerner, as two members of the Scharhörn team came running out of buildings. "What'd you *find?*" yelled Johnny Reb.

"Seven others!" shouted one of the men. "They're in a toilet which is an appropriate place."

"I *say!*" said Geoffrey Larson, raising his voice. "Would any by chance be the computer chap?"

"We did not ask, *Mein Herr!*"

"Go *ask!*" ordered The Rebel. "Time's run out!" He turned to Converse. "I've been in touch with your lady. The word out of Israel and Rome is downright awful some of the hit teams eluded Stone's men. The demonstrations began an hour ago and already twelve government people have been killed. In Jerusalem and Tel Aviv they're screaming for Abrahms to take over. In Rome the police can't handle the riots and the panic; the army's moved in."

Joel felt the sharp, hollow pain in his lower chest and for the first time noticed the early light in the sky beyond the walls. The day had come, and so had the killing. Everywhere. "Oh, *Jesus,*" he said, feeling helpless.

"The computer, *boy!*" roared Johnny Reb, his pistol jammed into the temple of the guard beneath him. "You don't have any choices left, *catfish!*"

"*Baracke vier!*"

"*Danke!* It's in building 4. Come on, Brit, let's *go! Move!*"

The enormous, glistening machine stood in an air-filtered room, covering the length of the 15-foot wall. Larson spent nine agonizing minutes studying it. turning dials, punching the keyboard and flipping switches on the console, Joel's notepad in front of him. Finally he announced, "There's a lock on the inner reels. They can't be released without an access code."

"What in *goddamned catfish hell* are you talkin' about?!" screamed The Rebel.

"There's a pre-designed set of symbols that when inserted releases the springs that permit the locked reels to be activated. It's why I asked if there was a computer man about."

Johnny Reb's radio hummed and Converse grabbed it, ripping it off the Southerner's velcroed chest.

"*Val?*"

"*Darling!* You're all right?"

"Yes. What's happening?"

"Radio-France. Bombs set off in the Elysée Palace. Two deputies were shot riding to the dawn rallies. The government's calling in the armed forces."

"*Christ! Out!*"

A man was brought into the room by two members of the Scharhörn team, who were gripping him by the arms. "He did not care to admit his function," said the hired gun on the left. "But when all were against the wall, the others were not so secretive."

The Rebel went to the man, grabbing him by the throat, but Joel rushed forward, pushing the Southerner aside, the hunting knife in his hand.

"I've been through a lot because of you bastards," he said, raising the blood-stained blade to the man's nose. "And now it's the *end!*" He shoved the point into the man's nostrils; the computer expert screamed as blood erupted, streaming downward. Then Converse raised the blade again, the point now in the corner of the man's right eye. "The codes, or it goes in!" he roared.

"*Zwei, eins, null, fünf!*" Again the technician screamed.

"Process it!" yelled Joel.

"They're *free!*" said the Englishman.

"Now the *symbols!*" cried Converse, shoving the man back into the hands of the Scharhörn hornets.

They all looked in astonishment at the green letters on the black television screen. Name after name, rank after rank, position after position. Larson had punched the print-out button and the curling, unending ream of paper spewed out with hundreds of identities.

"It won't do any good!" shouted Joel. "We can't get them *out!*"

"Don't be so antediluvian, old chap," said the Englishman, pointing to a strange-looking telephone recessed in the console. "This is splendid equipment. There are those lovely satellites in the sky and I can send this to anyone anywhere with compatible machinery. This is the age of technology, no longer Aquarius."

"Get it *out*," said Converse, his back against the wall, sliding down to the floor in exhaustion.

The world watched, stunned by the eruption of widespread assassinations and random homicidal violence. Everywhere people cried out for protection, for leadership, for an end to the savagery that had turned whole cities into battlegrounds as panicked, polarized groups of citizens hurled rocks and gas and finally bullets at one another because bullets were being fired at them. Few could tell who their enemies were, therefore anyone who attacked was an enemy and the attackers were everywhere, the orders issued from unseen, unmarked command posts. The police were helpless; then militias and state troops appeared but it was soon evident that they and their leaders were inadequate. The chaos was out of control; stronger measures would have to be implemented. Martial law was pronounced. Everywhere. And military commanders would assume control. *Everywhere.*

In Palo Alto, California, former general of the army, George Marcus Delavane, sat strapped to his wheelchair, watching the recorded hysteria erupting from three television sets. The set on the left went blank, preceded by the screams of a mobile crew as their truck came under sudden attack, the entire unit blown up by grenades. On the centre screen, a woman newscaster was weeping, her barely controlled voice angry, tears of tragedy and outrage streaming down her face as she read the reports of wholesale destruction and wanton murder. The screen on the right showed a Marine colonel being interviewed on a barricaded street in New York's financial district. His .45 Marine issue Colt automatic was in his hand as he tried to answer questions while shouting orders to his subordinates. The screen on the left pulsated with new light, as a familiar anchorman came into focus, his voice numbed, his eyes glassy. He started to speak, but could not; he pivoted in his chair and vomited as the camera swung away to an unsuspecting newsroom editor screaming into a phone. "Goddamned *shit-bastards!* What the fuck *happened?*" He, too, wept, as the woman in the centre screen was weeping; he pounded the desk with his fist, finally collapsing, his head in his arms, his body in spasms as the screen again went dark.

A slow smile emerged on Delavane's lips. Abruptly he reached for two remote controls, switching off the sets on the right and left, as he concentrated on the centre screen. A helmeted army lieutenant general was picked up by the camera as he strode into a press room somewhere in Washington. The soldier removed his helmet, went to a lectern, and spoke harshly into the microphone.

"We have sealed off all roads leading to Washington and my words are to serve as a warning to unauthorized personnel and civilians everywhere! Any attempts to cross the check points will be met by immediate force. My orders are brief and clear. Shoot to kill. My authority is derived by the emergency powers just granted to me by the Speaker of the House in the absence of the President and the Vice President who have been flown out of the capital for security purposes. The military is now in charge, the Army its spokesman, and martial law is in full effect until further notice."

Delavane snapped off the set with a gesture of triumph. "We *did* it, Paul!" he

519

said, turning to his uniformed aide who stood next to the fragmented map on the wall. "Not even the whining pacifists want that law reversed! And if they *do* . . ." The general of Aquitaine raised his right hand, his index finger extended, thumb upright, and mimed a series of pistol shots.

"Yes, it's done," agreed the aide reaching down to Delavane's desk and opening a drawer.

"What are you doing?"

"I'm sorry, General. This also must be done." The aide pulled out a ·357 Magnum revolver.

Before he could raise it, however, Delavane's left hand shot up out of the inside cushion of the wheelchair. In it was a short-barrelled automatic. He shouted as he fired four times in rapid succession.

"You think I haven't been *waiting* for this? Scum! Coward! *Traitor!* You think I trust *any* of you? The way you *look at me!* The way you talk in whispers in the hallways! None of you can stand the fact that *without* legs I'm better than *all* of you! Now you know, scum! And soon the others will know because they'll be shot! Executed for treason against the founder of Aquitaine! . . . You think any of you are worth trusting? You've all tried to be what I am and you *can't do it!*"

The uniformed aide had crashed back into the wall, into the fragmented map. Gasping, blood flowing from his neck, his wide eyes stared at the raving general. From some inner core of strength he raised the powerful Magnum and fired once as he collapsed.

George Marcus Delavane was blown across the room, a massive haemorrhage in his chest, as the wheelchair spun and fell on its side, its strapped-in passenger dead.

No one knew when it started to happen, but gradually, miraculously, the gunfire slowly began to diminish. It was accompanied by squads of uniformed men, many units having broken away from their commanders, racing through the streets and buildings, confronting other men. It was soldier against soldier, the eyes of the interrogators filled with anger and disgust, staring at faces consumed with arrogance and defiance. The commanders of Aquitaine were adamant. They were *right!* Could not their inferiors *understand?* In many cases lives were lost by refusals to surrender and by biting into cyanide capsules.

In Palo Alto, California, a legless legend named George Marcus was found shot to death, but apparently not before he had been able to kill his assailant, an obscure army colonel. No one knew what had happened. In southern France, the bodies of two other legendary heroes were found in a mountain ravine; each of whom, upon leaving a château in the Alps, had been given a weapon with his clothing. Generals Bertholdier and Leifhelm had lost. General Chaim Abrahms disappeared. On military bases throughout the Middle East, all Europe, Great Britain, Canada and the United States, officers of high rank and responsibilities were challenged by subordinates with levelled weapons. *Were they members of an organization called Aquitaine? Their names were on a list! Answer!* In Norfolk,

Virginia, an admiral named Scanlon threw himself out of a sixth-storey window; and in San Diego, California, another admiral named Hickman was ordered to arrest a 4-striper who lived in La Jolla – the charge: murder of a legal officer in the hills above that elegant suburb. Colonel Alan Metcalf personally made the call to the Chief Operations Officer of Nellis Air Force Base; the order was blunt – throw into a maximum security cell the major who was in charge of all aircraft maintenance. In Washington, a venerated senator of Italian descent was called out of the cloakroom by a Captain Guardino of Army G-2 and taken away; while over at State and the Pentagon, eleven men in armaments controls and procurements were placed under guard.

In Tel Aviv, Israeli Army Intelligence rounded up twenty-three aides and fellow officers of General Chaim Abrahms, as well as one of the Mossad's most brilliant analysts. In Paris, thirty-one associates – military and non-military – of General Jacques Louis Bertholdier, including deputy directors of both the *Sûreté* and Interpol, were held in isolation, and in Bonn no fewer than fifty-seven colleagues of General Erich Leifhelm, among them former *Wehrmacht* commanders and current officers of the Federal Republic's Army and its Luftwaffe, were seized. Also in Bonn, the Marine Corps Guard at the American Embassy, on orders from the State Department, arrested four attachés including the military *chargé d'affaires*, Major Norman Anthony Washburn, IV.

And so it went on. Everywhere. The fever of madness that was Aquitaine was broken by legions of the very military the Generals assumed would carry them to absolute global power. By nightfall the guns were still and people began to come out from behind their barricades— from cellars, subways, boarded-up buildings, railroad yards, wherever sanctuary could be found. They wandered out on the streets, numbed, bewildered, wondering what had happened, as trucks with loudspeakers roamed the cities everywhere telling the citizens that the crisis was over. In Tel Aviv, Rome, Paris, Bonn, London, and across the Atlantic in Toronto, New York, Washington and points west, the lights were turned on but certainly the world had not returned to normal. A terrible force had struck in the midst of a universal cry for peace. What was it? What had *happened?*

It would be explained on the following day, blared the sound trucks in a dozen different languages, pleading for patience on the part of citizens everywhere. The hour chosen was 3.00 P.M. Greenwich Mean Time; 10.00 A.M. Washington; 7.00 A.M. Los Angeles. Throughout the night and the morning hours in all the time zones, heads of state conferred over telephones until the texts of all the statements were essentially the same. At 10.03 A.M. the President of the United States went on the air.

"Yesterday an unprecedented wave of violence swept through the Free World taking lives, paralysing governments, creating a climate of terror that very nearly cost free nations everywhere their freedom and might have led them to look for solutions where no solutions should be sought in democratic societies – namely turning ourselves into police- states, handing over controls to men who would subjugate free people to their collective will. It was an organized conspiracy led by demented and deluded men who

521

sought power for its own sake, willing even to sacrifice their own fellow conspirators to achieve it, and to deceive others who were seduced into believing it was the way of the future, the answer to the serious ills of the world. It is not, nor can it ever be.

"As the days and weeks go by – as this terrible thing is put behind us – the facts will be placed before you. For this has been our warning, the toll taken in blood and in the shaken confidence of our institutions. I remind you, however, that our institutions have prevailed. They will prevail.

"In an hour from now a series of meetings will start taking place involving the White House, the Departments of State and Defense, the majority and minority leaders of the House and the Senate, and the National Security Council. Beginning tomorrow, in concert with other governments, reports will be issued on a daily basis until all the facts are before you.

"The nightmare is over. Let the sunlight of truth guide us and clear away the darkness."

On the following morning, Deputy Director Peter Stone of the Central Intelligence Agency, accompanied by Captain Howard Packard and Lieutenant William Landis, were brought to the Oval Office for a private ceremony. The specific honours awarded them were never made public as there was no reason to do so. Each man, with deep respect and gratitude – but with no regrets – declined to accept, each stating that whatever honours were involved belonged to a man not currently residing in the United States.

A week later, in Los Angeles, California, an actor named Caleb Dowling stunned the producers of a television show called *Santa Fe* by giving them his notice effective before the start of the new season. He refused all inducements, claiming simply that there was not enough time to spend with his wife. They were going to travel. Alone. And if the residuals ever ran out, hell, she could always type and he could always teach. Together. *Ciao, friends.*

Epilogue

Geneva. City of bright reflections and inconstancy.

Joel and Valerie Converse sat at the table where it all began, by the glistening brass railing in the *Chat Botté*. The traffic on the lakeside Quai du Mont Blanc was disciplined, unhurried – purpose mixed with civility. As the pedestrians passed by, both were aware of the glances directed at Joel. *There he is*, the eyes were saying. *There is . . . the man.* It was rumoured he was living in Geneva, at least for a while.

By agreement, the second report issued across the Free World made a direct but – on Converse's insistence – brief reference to his role in the tragedy that was Aquitaine. He was exonerated of all charges. The labels were removed and refuted, the debt to him acknowledged without specifics on the basis of NATO security. He refused all interviews although the media dredged up his experiences in South-east Asia, speculating on correlations to the drama of the generals. He was consoled by the fact that as the interest in him had dwindled years ago, it would do so again – faster in Geneva, city of purpose.

They had leased a house on the lake, an artist's house with a studio built on the slope leading to the water, the skylight catching the sun from early morning to dusk. The beach house in Cape Ann was closed, the lease paid in full and returned to the realtor in Boston. Val's friend and neighbour had packed her clothes and all her paints, brushes and favourite easel, sending everything air freight to Geneva. Valerie worked for several hours each morning, happier than she had ever been in her life, permitting her husband to evaluate her progress daily. He judged it to be eminently acceptable, wondering out loud whether there was a market for "lakescapes" as opposed to seascapes. It took him two days to remove the last dabs of paint from his hair.

Nor was Joel without employment; he was Talbot, Brooks and Simon's European branch all by himself. The income, itself, however, was not a vital factor, as Converse never remotely considered himself in the mould of those attorneys in films and on television who rarely if ever collected fees. Since his legal talents had been called upon for crucial evidence, he billed the major governments a reasonable $400,000 apiece; the minor ones, $250,000. No one argued. The total came to something over $2.5 million, safely deposited in an interest-bearing Swiss account.

"What are you thinking about?" asked Valerie, reaching for his hand.

"About Chaim Abrahms and Derek Belamy. They haven't been found – they're still out there and I wonder if they ever will be found. I hope so, because until they are it really isn't over."

"It's over, Joel, you've got to believe it. But that's not what I meant. I meant you. How do you feel?"

523

"I'm not sure. I only knew I had to come here and find out." He looked into her eyes, and at the cascading dark hair that fell to her shoulders, framing the face he loved so very much. "Empty, I think. Except for you."

"No anger? No resentment?"

"Not against Avery, or Stone or any of the others. That's past. They did what they had to do; there wasn't any other way."

"You're far more generous than I am, my darling."

"I'm more realistic, that's all. The evidence had to be obtained by penetrating the outside – by an outsider wanting to get inside. The core was too tight, too lethal."

"I think they were bastards. And cowards."

"I don't. I think they should all be canonized, immortalized, bronzed and with poems written about them for the ages."

"That's absolute rubbish! How can you possibly say such a thing?"

Joel again looked into his wife's eyes. "Because you're here. I'm here. And you're painting lakescapes, not seascapes. And I'm not in New York and you're not in Cape Ann. And I don't have to worry about you, hoping that you're worrying about me."

"If only there'd been another woman or another man. It would have been so much easier, so much more logical, darling."

"There was always you. Only you."

"Try to get away from me again, Converse."

"No way, Converse."

Their hands gripped, unashamed tears in their eyes. The nightmare was over.

The Chancellor Manuscript

For Mary.

The reasons increase every day.
Above all, there is Mary.

Prologue

3 June 1968

The dark-haired man stared at the wall in front of him. His chair, like the rest of the furniture, was pleasing to the eye but not made for comfort. The style was Early American, the theme Spartan, as if those about to be granted an audience with the occupant of the inner office should reflect on their awesome opportunity in stern surroundings.

The man was in his late twenties, his face angular, the features sharp, each pronounced and definite as if carved by a craftsman more aware of details than of the whole. It was a face in quiet conflict with itself, striking and yet unsettled. The eyes were engaging, deep set, and very light blue, with an open, even questioning quality about them. They seemed at the moment to be the eyes of a blue-eyed animal, swift to level in any direction, steady, apprehensive.

The young man's name was Peter Chancellor, and the expression on his face was as rigid as his posture in the chair. His eyes were angry.

There was one other person in the outer office: a middle-aged secretary whose thin, colourless lips were set in constant tension, her grey hair stretched and spun into a bun that took on the appearance of a faded flaxen helmet. She was the Praetorian Guard, the attack dog who protected the sanctuary of the man behind the oak door beyond her desk.

Chancellor looked at his watch; the secretary glanced at him disapprovingly. Any indication of impatience was out of place in this office; the audience itself was everything.

It was a quarter to six; all the other offices were closed. The small Midwest campus of Park Forest University was preparing for another late-spring evening, the controlled revelry heightened by the proximity of graduation day.

Park Forest strove to remain outside the unrest that had swept across the university campuses. In an ocean of turbulence it was an undisturbed sandbar. Insular, rich, at peace with itself, essentially without disruption. Or brilliance.

It was this fundamental lack of external concerns, so the story went, that brought the man behind the oak door to Park Forest. He sought inaccessibility, if not anonymity, which of course could never be granted. Munro St Claire had been undersecretary of state for Roosevelt and Truman; ambassador-extraordinary for Eisenhower, Kennedy and Johnson. He had flown about the globe with an open portfolio, bringing his Presidents' concerns and his own expertise to the world's troubled areas. That he had elected to spend a spring semester at Park Forest as visiting professor of government – while organizing the data that would form the basis of his memoirs – was a coup that had stunned the trustees of this wealthy but minor university. They had swallowed their disbelief and guaranteed

St Claire the isolation he could never have found in Cambridge, New Haven or Berkeley.

So the story went.

And Peter Chancellor thought about the salient points of St Claire's story to keep his mind off his own. But not entirely. At the moment, the salient points of his own immediate existence were as discouraging as one could imagine. Twenty-four months lost, thrown away into academic oblivion. Two years of his life!

His doctoral thesis had been rejected by the vote of eight to one by the honours college at Park Forest. The one dissenting vote was, naturally, that of his adviser and, as such, without influence on the others. Chancellor had been accused of frivolousness, of wanton disregard of historical fact, of slovenly research and ultimately of irresponsibly inserting fiction in lieu of provable data. It was not at all ambiguous. Chancellor had failed; there was no appeal, for the failure was absolute.

From an exhilarating high he had sunk into a deep depression. Six weeks ago the *Foreign Service Journal* of Georgetown University had agreed to publish fourteen excerpts from the thesis. A total of some thirty pages. His adviser had managed it, sending a copy to academic friends in Georgetown, who thought the work was both enlightening and frightening. The *Journal* was on a par with *Foreign Affairs*, its readership among the country's most influential. Something was bound to result; somebody had to offer something.

But the *Journal's* editors made one condition: due to the nature of the thesis, the doctoral acceptance was mandatory before they would publish the manuscript. Without it they would not.

Now, of course, publishing any part was out of the question.

"The Origins of a Global Conflict" was the title. The conflict was World War II, the origins an imaginative interpretation of the men and the forces that collided during the catastrophic years from 1926 to 1939. It did no good to explain to the history committee of the honours college that the thesis was an interpretative analysis, not a legal document. He had committed a cardinal sin: he had attributed invented dialogue to historical figures. Such nonsense was unacceptable to the groves of academe at Park Forest.

But Chancellor knew there was another more serious flaw in the eyes of the committee. He had written his thesis in outrage and emotion, and outrage and emotion had no place in doctoral dissertations.

The premise that financial giants stood passively by while a band of psychopaths shaped post-Weimar Germany was ludicrous. As ludicrous as it was patently false. The multinational corporations could not feed the Nazi wolf pack fast enough; the stronger the pack, the more rapacious the appetites of the market-place.

The German wolf pack's objectives and methods were conveniently obscured, in the interests of an expanding economy. Obscured, hell! They were tolerated, ultimately *accepted*, along with the swiftly rising lines on profit-and-loss charts. Diseased Nazi Germany was given an economic clean bill of health by the financiers. And among the colossi of international finance who fed the Wehrmacht eagle were a number of the most honoured industrial names in America.

There was the problem. He could not come out and identify those corporations because his proof was not conclusive. The people who had given him the information, and led him to other sources, would not allow their names to be used. They were frightened, tired old men, living on government and company pensions. Whatever had happened in the past was past; they would not risk losing the largesse of their benefactors. Should Chancellor make public their private conversations, they would deny them. It was as simple as that.

But it *wasn't* as simple as that. It *had* happened. The story had *not been* told, and Peter wanted very much to tell it. True, he did not want to destroy old men who had merely carried out policies they had not understood, conceived by others so far up the corporate ladders they'd rarely met them. But to walk away from unrecorded history was wrong.

So Chancellor took the only option open to him: he had changed the names of the corporate giants but in such a way as to leave no doubt as to their identities. Anyone who read a newspaper would know who they were.

This was his unforgivable error. He had raised provocative questions few wished to recognize as valid. Park Forest University was looked upon favourably when corporations and corporate foundations issued grants; it was not a dangerous campus. Why should that status be threatened – even remotely – by the work of a single doctoral candidate?

Christ! Two *years*. There were alternatives, of course. He could transfer his credits to another university and resubmit "Origins". But what then? Was it worth it? To face another form of rejection? One that lay in the shadows of his own doubts? For Peter was honest with himself. He had not written so unique or brilliant a work. He had merely found a period in recent history that infuriated him because of its parallels with the present. Nothing had changed; the lies of forty years ago still existed. But he did not want to walk away from it; he *would* not walk away. He would tell it. Somehow.

However, outrage was not a substitute for qualitative research. Concern for living sources was hardly an alternative for objective investigation. Reluctantly Peter acknowledged the validity of the committee's position. He was neither academic fish nor fowl; he was part fact, part fantasy.

Two years! Wasted!

The secretary's telephone hummed, it did not ring. The hum reminded Chancellor of the rumour that special communications had been installed so men in Washington could reach Munro St Claire at any time of day or night. These installations, so the story went, were St Claire's only departure from his self-imposed inaccessibility.

"Yes, Mr Ambassador," said the secretary, "yes, sir, I'll send him in . . . That's perfectly all right. If you need me I can stay." Apparently she was not needed, and Peter had the impression that the secretary was not happy about it. The Praetorian Guard was being dismissed. "You're scheduled to be at the dean's reception at six-thirty," she continued. There was brief silence; then the woman replied, "Yes, sir. I'll telephone your regrets. Good night, Mr St Claire."

She glanced at Chancellor. "You may go in now," she said, her eyes questioning.

"Thank you." Peter rose from the uncomfortable straight-backed chair. "I don't know why I'm here, either," he said.

Inside the oak-panelled office with the cathedral windows, Munro St Claire got up from behind the antique table that served as his desk. He was an old man, thought Chancellor as he approached the extended right hand held over the table. Much older than he appeared at a distance, walking across the campus with a sure stride. Here in this office his tall slender body and aquiline head with the faded blond hair seemed to struggle to stay erect. Yet erect he stood, as if refusing to give in to infirmities. His eyes were large, but of no discernible colour, intense in their steadiness, but not without humour. His thin lips were stretched into a smile beneath his well-groomed white moustache.

"Come in, come in, Mr Chancellor. It's a pleasure to see you again."

"I don't think we've met."

"Good for you! Don't let me get away with that." St Claire laughed and indicated a chair in front of the table.

"I didn't mean to contradict you, I just – " Chancellor stopped, realizing that no matter what he said, it would sound foolish. He sat down.

"Why not?" asked St Claire. "Contradicting me would be minor compared to what you've done to a legion of contemporary scholars."

"I beg your pardon?"

"Your dissertation. I read it."

"I'm flattered."

"I was most impressed."

"Thank you, sir. Others weren't."

"Yes, I understand that. It was rejected by the honours college, I'm told."

"Yes."

"A damned shame. A lot of hard work went into it. And some very original thinking."

Who are you, Peter Chancellor? Have you any idea what you've done? Forgotten men have dredged up memories and whisper in fear. Georgetown is rife with rumour. An explosive document has been received from an obscure university in the Midwest. An insignificant graduate student has suddenly reminded us of that which no one cares to remember. Mr Chancellor, Inver Brass cannot permit you to go on.

Peter saw that the old man's eyes were at once encouraging and yet noncommittal. There was nothing to be lost in being direct. "Are you implying that you might – ?"

"Oh, no," interrupted St Claire sharply, raising the palm of his right hand. "No, indeed. I wouldn't presume to question such a decision: it's hardly my place. And I suspect the rejection was based on certain applicable criteria. No, I wouldn't interfere. But I'd like to ask you several questions, perhaps offer some gratuitous advice."

Chancellor leaned forward. "What questions?"

St Claire settled back in his chair. "First, yourself. I am merely curious. I have spoken with your adviser, but that is secondhand. Your father is a newspaperman?"

Chancellor smiled. "He'd say *was*. He retires next January."

"Your mother's also a writer, isn't she?"

"Of sorts. Magazine articles, women's-page columns. She wrote short stories years ago."

"So the written word holds no terror for you."

"What do you mean?"

"A mechanic's son approaches a malfunctioning carburettor with less trepidation than the offspring of a ballet master. Generally speaking, of course."

"Generally speaking, I'd agree."

"Precisely." St Claire nodded his head.

"Are you telling me my dissertation's a malfunctioning carburettor?"

St Claire laughed. "Let's not get ahead of ourselves. You took your master's degree in journalism, obviously intending to be a newspaperman."

"Some form of communications, at any rate. I wasn't sure which."

"Yet you prevailed upon this university to accept you for a doctorate in history. So you changed your mind."

"Not really. It was never made up." Again Peter smiled, now with embarrassment. "My parents claim I'm a professional student. Not that they mind, particularly. A scholarship saw me through the master's. I served in Vietnam, so the government's paying my way here. I do some tutoring. To tell you the truth, I'm nearly thirty and I'm not sure what I want to do. But I don't suppose that's unique these days."

"Your graduate work would seem to indicate a preference for the academic life."

"If it did, it doesn't any more."

St Claire glanced at him. "Tell me about the dissertation itself. You make startling insinuations, rather frightening judgements. Essentially, you accuse many of the free world's leaders – and their institutions – of either closing their eyes to the menace of Hitler forty years ago, or worse: directly and indirectly financing the Third Reich."

"Not for ideological reasons. For economic advantage."

"Scylla and Charybdis?"

"I'll accept that. Right now, today, there's a repetition – "

"*Despite* the honours college," interrupted St Claire quietly, "you must have done a fair amount of research. How much?"

What started you? That's what we have to know, because we know you will not let it go. Were you directed by men seeking vengeance after all these years? Or was it – far worse – an accident that primed your outrage? We can control sources; we can countermand them, show them to be false. We cannot control accidents. Or an outrage born of an accident. But you cannot go on, Mr Chancellor. We must find a way to stop you.

Chancellor paused; the aged diplomat's question was unexpected. "Research? A lot more than the committee believes and a lot less than certain conclusions warrant. That's as honest as I can put it."

"It's honest. Will you give me specifics? There's very little documentation of sources."

Suddenly Peter felt uneasy. What had begun as a discussion was turning into an interrogation. "Why is it important? There's very little documentation because that's the way the people I spoke to wanted it."

"Then honour their wishes, by all means. Don't use names." The old man smiled; his charm was extraordinary.

We don't need names. Names can be uncovered easily, once areas are discerned. But it would be better not to pursue names. Much better. The whispers would start again. There is a better way.

"All right. I interviewed people who were active during the period from '23 to '39. They were in government – mainly the State Department – and in industry and banking. Also I spoke with about half a dozen former senior officers attached to the War College and the intelligence community. None, Mr St Claire, *none* would allow me to use his name."

"They provided you with so much material?"

"A great deal lay in what they would not discuss. And odd phrases, offhand remarks that were often non sequiturs, but just as often applicable. They're old men now, all – or nearly all – retired. Their minds wandered; so did their memories. They're kind of a sad collection; they're – " Chancellor stopped. He was not sure how to continue.

St Claire did. "By and large, embittered minor executives and bureaucrats living on inadequate pensions. Such conditions breed angry, all too often distorted memories."

"I don't think that's fair. What I learned, what I wrote, is the truth. That's why anyone who reads the thesis will know which those companies were, how they operated."

St Claire dismissed the statement as though he had not heard it. "How did you reach these people? What led you to them? How did you get appointments to see them?"

"My father started me off, and from those few came others. Sort of a natural progression; people remembered people."

"Your father?"

"In the early fifties he was a Washington correspondent for Scripps-Howard – "

"Yes." St Claire interrupted softly. "So, through his efforts, you obtained an initial list."

"Yes. About a dozen names of men who had dealings in pre-war Germany. In government and out. As I said, these led to others. And, of course, I read everything Trevor-Roper and Shirer and the German apologists wrote. *That's all* documented."

"Did your father know what you were after?"

"A doctorate was enough." Chancellor grinned. "My father went to work with a year and half of college. Money was tight."

"Then, shall we say, is he aware of what you found? Or thought you found."

"Not really. I figured my parents would read the thesis when it was finished. Now, I don't know if they'll want to; this is going to be a blow to the homefront." Peter smiled weakly. "The ageing, perpetual student comes to nothing."

"I thought you said *professional* student," corrected the diplomat.

"Is there a difference?"

"In approach, I think there is." St Claire leaned forward in silence, his large eyes levelled at Peter. "I'd like to take the liberty of summarizing the immediate situation as I see it."

"Of course."

"Basically, you have the materials for a perfectly valid theoretical analysis. Interpretations of history, from doctrinaire to revisionist, are never-ending topics of debate and examination. Would you agree?"

"Naturally."

"Yes, of course. You wouldn't have chosen the subject in the first place if you didn't." St Claire looked out the window as he spoke. "But an unorthodox interpretation of events – especially of a period in such recent history – based solely on the writings of others, would hardly justify the unorthodoxy, would it? I mean, certainly historians would have pounced on the material long before now if they had thought a case could be made. But it couldn't, really, so you went beyond the accepted sources and interviewed embittered old men and a handful of reluctant former intelligence specialists and came away with specific judgements."

"Yes, but – "

"Yes, *but*," broke in St Claire, turning from the window.

"By your own telling, these judgements were often based on 'offhand remarks' and 'non sequiturs'. And your sources refuse to be listed. In your own words your research did not justify numerous conclusions."

"But they did. The conclusions *are* justified."

"They'll never be accepted. Not by any recognized authority, academic or judicial. And quite rightly so, in my judgement."

"Then you're wrong, Mr St Claire. Because I'm *not* wrong. I don't care how many committees tell me I am. The facts are there, right below the surface, but nobody wants to talk about them. Even now, forty years later. Because it's happening all over again! A handful of companies are making millions all over the world by fuelling military governments, calling them our *friends*, our 'first line of defence'. When their eyes are on profit-and-loss sheets; that's what they care about . . . All right, maybe I can't come up with documentation, but I'm not going to throw away two years' work. I'm not going to stop because a committee tells me I'm academically unacceptable. Sorry, but *that's* unacceptable."

And that's what we had to know. At the last, would you cut your losses and walk away? Others thought you would, but I didn't. You knew you were right, and that's too great a temptation in the young. We must now render you impotent.

St Claire looked down at Peter and held his eyes. "You're in the wrong arena. You sought acceptance from the wrong people. Seek it elsewhere. Where matters of truth and documentation are not important."

"I don't understand."

"Your dissertation is filled with some rather splendidly imagined fiction. Why not concentrate on that?"

"*What?*"

"Fiction. Write a novel. No one cares whether a novel is accurate, or has historical authenticity. It's simply not important." St Claire sat down, once again leaning forward, his eyes steady on Chancellor. "Write fiction. You may still be ignored, but at least there's a chance of a hearing. To pursue your present course is futile. You'll waste another year, or two, or three. Ultimately, for what? So write a novel. Spend your outrage there, then go about your life."

Peter stared at the diplomat; he was at a loss, uncertain of his thoughts, so he merely repeated the single word. "Fiction?"

"Yes. I think we're back to that malfunctioning carburettor, although the analogy may be terrible." St Claire settled back in his chair. "We agreed that words hold no great fear for you; you've seen blank pages filled with them most of your life. Now, repair the work you've done with other words, a different approach that eliminates the necessity of academic sanction."

Peter exhaled softly; for several moments he had held his breath, numbed by St Claire's analysis. "A *novel?* It never crossed my mind . . ."

"I submit it may have unconsciously," interjected the diplomat. "You didn't hesitate to invent actions – and reactions – when it served you. And God knows you have the ingredients of a fascinating story. Farfetched, in my opinion, but not without merit for a Sunday afternoon, in a hammock. Fix the carburettor; this is a different engine. One of less substance, perhaps, but conceivably quite enjoyable. And someone may listen to you. They won't in this arena. Nor, frankly, should they."

"A novel. I'll be damned."

Munro St Claire smiled. His eyes were still strangely noncommittal.

The afternoon sun disappeared below the horizon; long shadows spread across the lawns. St Claire stood at the window, gazing out on the quadrangle. There was no arrogance in the serenity of the scene; it was out of place in a world so locked in turbulence.

He could leave Park Forest now. His job was finished, the carefully orchestrated conclusion not perfect but sufficient unto the day.

Sufficient unto the limits of deceit.

He looked at his watch. An hour had passed since the bewildered Chancellor had left the office. The diplomat crossed back to his desk, sat down, and picked up the telephone. He dialled the area code 202 and then seven additional digits. Moments later there were two clicks over the line, followed by a whine. For any but those aware of the codes the sound would have simply signified a malfunctioning instrument.

St Claire dialled five more digits. A single click was the result, and a voice answered.

"Inver Brass. Tape is rolling." In the voice was the flat *a* of Boston, but the rhythm was Middle-European.

"This is Bravo. Patch me through to Genesis."

"Genesis is in England. It's past midnight over there."

"I'm afraid I can't be concerned with that. Can you patch? Is there a sterile location?"

"If he's still at the embassy, there is, Bravo. Otherwise it's the Dorchester. No guarantees there."

"Try the embassy, please."

The line went dead as the Inver Brass switchboard linked up communications. Three minutes later another voice was heard; it was clear, with no distortions, as though it were down the street, not 4,000 miles away. The voice was clipped, agitated, but not without respect. Or a degree of fear.

"This is Genesis. I was just leaving. What happened?"

"It's done."

"Thank God!"

"The dissertation was rejected. I made it clear to the committee, quite privately of course, that it was radical nonsense. They'd be the laughing-stock of the university community. They're sensitive; they should be. They're mediocre."

"I'm pleased." There was a pause from London. "What was his reaction?"

"What I expected. He's right and he knows it; therefore he's frustrated. He had no intention of stopping."

"Does he now?"

"I believe so. The idea's firmly planted. If need be, I'll follow up indirectly, put him in touch with people. But I may not have to. He's imaginative; more to the point, his outrage is genuine."

"You're convinced this is the best way?"

"Certainly. The alternative is for him to pursue the research and dredge up dormant issues. I wouldn't like that to happen in Cambridge or Berkeley, would you?"

"No. And perhaps no one will be interested in what he writes, much less publish it. I suppose we could bring that about."

St Claire's eyes narrowed briefly. "My advice is not to interfere. We'd frustrate him further, drive him back. Let things happen naturally. If he does turn it into a novel, the best we can hope for is a minor printing of a rather amateurish work. He'll have said what he had to say, and it will turn out to be inconsequential fiction, with the usual disclaimers as to persons living or dead. Interference might raise questions; that's not in our interest."

"You're right, of course," said the man in London. "But then you usually are, Bravo."

"Thank you. And good-bye, Genesis. I'll be leaving here in a few days."

"Where are you going?"

"I'm not sure. Perhaps back to Vermont. Perhaps far away. I don't like what I see on the national landscape."

"All the more reason to stay in touch," said the voice in London.

"Perhaps. And then again, I may be too old."

"You can't disappear. You know that, don't you?"

"Yes. Good night, Genesis."

St Claire replaced the telephone without waiting for a corresponding good-bye from London. He simply did not want to listen further.

He was swept by a sense of revulsion; it was not the first time, nor would it be the last. It was the function of Inver Brass to make decisions others could not make, to protect men and institutions from the moral indictments born of hindsight. What was right forty years ago was anathema today.

Frightened men had whispered to other frightened men that Peter Chancellor had to be stopped. It was wrong for this obscure doctoral candidate to ask questions that had no meaning forty years later. The times were different, the circumstances altogether dissimilar.

Yet there were certain grey areas. Accountability was not a limited doctrine. Ultimately, they were all accountable. Inver Brass was no exception. Therefore, Peter Chancellor had to be given the chance to vent his outrage, and in a way that removed him from consequence. Or catastrophe.

St Claire rose from the table and surveyed the papers on top of it. He had removed most of his personal effects during the past weeks. There was very little of *him* in the office now; and that was as it should be.

Tomorrow he would be gone.

He walked to the door. Automatically he reached for the light switch, and then he realized no lights were on. He had been standing, pacing, sitting, and thinking in shadows.

The New York Times Book Review
10 May 1969, Page Three

Reichstag! is at once startling and perceptive, awkward and incredible. Peter Chancellor's first novel would have us believe that the early Nazi party was financed by nothing less than a cartel of international bankers and industrialists – American, British, and French – apparently with the acknowledged, though unspoken, approval of their respective governments. Chancellor forces us to believe him as we read. His narrative is breathless; his characters leap from the page with a kind of raw power that illuminates their strengths and weaknesses in a manner that might be vitiated by more disciplined writing. Mr Chancellor tells his tale in outrage, and far too melodramatically, but withal the book is a marvellous "read". And finally, you begin to wonder: could it have happened this way? . . .

The Washington Post Book World
22 April 1970, Page Three

In *Sarajevo!* Chancellor does for the guns of August what he did for the Führer's *Blitzkrieg* last year.

The forces that collided in the July crisis of 1914, preceded by the June assassination of Ferdinand by the conspirator Gavrilo Princip, are abstracted, rearranged, and put back on a fast track by Mr Chancellor, so that no one emerges on the side of the angels and all is a triumph of evil. Throughout, the author's protagonist – in this case a British infiltrator of a Serbo-Croat clandestine organization called, melodramatically, *The Unity of Death* – peels away the layers of deceit as they've been spread by the provocateurs of the Reichstag, the Foreign Office and the Chamber of Deputies. The puppets are revealed; the strings lead back to the industrial vested interests on all sides.

As with so much else, these rarely discussed coincidences go on and on.

Mr Chancellor has a conspiracy complex of a high order. He deals with it in a fascinating manner and with a high readability quotient. *Sarajevo!* should prove to be even more popular than *Reichstag!*

The Los Angeles Times Daily Review of Books
4 April 1971, Page Twenty

Counterstrike! is Chancellor's best work to date, although for reasons that escape this reader, its serpentine plot is based on an extraordinary error of research that one does not expect of this author. It concerns the clandestine operations of the Central Intelligence Agency as they pertain to a spreading reign of terror imposed on a New England university city by a foreign power. Mr Chancellor should know that all domestic involvements are specifically prohibited to the CIA in its 1947 charter.

This objection aside, *Counterstrike!* is a sure winner. Chancellor's previous books have shown that he can spin a yarn with such pace that you can't turn the pages fast enough, but now he's added a depth of character not mined previously.

Chancellor's extensive knowledge of counter-espionage is, according to those who are supposed to know, on zero target. The CIA error notwithstanding.

He gets into the minds as well as the methods of all those involved in an absolutely frightening situation drawing an explicit parallel to the racial disturbances that led to a series of murders in Boston several years ago. Chancellor has arrived as a first-rate novelist who takes events, rearranges the facts, and presents startling new conclusions.

The plot is deviously simple: a man is chosen to perform a task for which he would seem to be ill equipped. He is given extensive CIA training, but nowhere in this training is there an attempt to strengthen his basic flaw. Soon we understand: that flaw is meant to bring about his death. Circles within circles of conspiracy. And once again, as with his previous books, we wonder: is it true? Did this happen? Is this the way it was? . . .

Autumn. The Bucks County countryside was an ocean of yellow, green and gold. Chancellor leaned against the bonnet of a silver Mark IV Continental, his arm casually around a woman's shoulder. His face was fuller now, the distinct features less in conflict with one another, softened yet still sharp. His eyes were focused on a white house that stood at the foot of a winding drive cut out of the gently sloping fields. The drive was bordered on each side by a high white fence.

The girl with Chancellor, holding the hand draped over her shoulder, was as engrossed by the sight in front of them as he was. She was tall; her brown hair fell softly, framing her delicate but curiously strong face. Her name was Catherine Lowell.

"It's everything you described," she said, gripping his hand tightly. "It's beautiful. Really very beautiful."

"To coin a phrase," said Chancellor, glancing down at her, "that's one hell of a relief."

She looked up at him. "You've bought it, haven't you? You're not just 'interested', you've bought it!"

Peter nodded. "I had competition. A banker from Philadelphia was ready to put down a binder. I had to decide. If you don't like it, I'm sure he'll take it from me."

"Don't be silly, it's absolutely gorgeous!"

"You haven't seen the inside."

"I don't have to."

"Good. Because I'd rather show it to you on the way back. The owners'll be out by Thursday. They'd better be. On Friday afternoon I've got a large delivery from Washington. It's coming here."

"The transcripts?"

"Twelve cases from the Government Printing Office. Morgan had to send down a truck. The whole story of Nuremberg as recorded by the Allied tribunals. Do you want to guess what the title of the book's going to be?"

Catherine laughed. "I can see Tony Morgan now, pacing around his office like a disjointed cat in grey flannels. Suddenly he pounces on his desk and shouts, frightening everyone within earshot, which is most of the building: 'I've got it! We'll do something different! We'll use *Nuremberg* with an exclamation mark.' "

Peter joined her laughter. "You're vilifying my sainted editor."

"Never. Without him we'd be moving into a five-flight walk-up, not a farm built for a country squire."

"And the squire's wife."

"And the squire's wife." Catherine squeezed his arm. "Speaking of trucks, shouldn't there be moving vans in the drive?"

Chancellor smiled; it was an embarrassed smile. "Except for odd items, specifically listed, I had to buy it furnished. They're moving to the Caribbean. You can throw it all out if you like."

"My, aren't we grand?"

"Aren't we rich," replied Peter, not asking a question. "No comments, please. Come on, let's go. We've got about three hours on the turnpike, another two and a half after that. It'll be dark soon."

Catherine turned to him, her face tilted up, their lips nearly touching. "With every mile I'm going to get more and more nervous. I'll develop twitches and arrive a babbling idiot. I thought the ritual dance of meeting parents went out ten years ago."

"You didn't mention it when I met yours."

"Oh, for heaven's sake! They were so impressed just being in the same room as you, you didn't have to do anything but sit there and gloat!"

"Which I did not do. I like your parents. I think you'll like mine."

"Will they like me? That's the imponderable."

"Not for a second," said Peter, pulling her to him. "They'll love you. Just as I love you. Oh *God*, I *love* you!"

It's accurate, Genesis. This Peter Chancellor has the Government Printing Office reprinting everything relative to Nuremberg. The publisher has arranged transportation to an address in Pennsylvania.

It does not affect us, Banner. Venice and Christopher agree. We will take no action. That is the decision.

It's a mistake! He's going back to the German theme.

Long after the errors were made. There's no association. Years before Nuremberg we saw clearly what we did not see at the beginning. There's no connection with us. Any of us, including you.

You can't be sure.

We are sure.

What does Bravo think?

Bravo's away. He has not been appraised, nor will he be.

Why not?

For reasons that don't concern you. They go back several years. Before you were called to Inver Brass.

It's wrong, Genesis.

And you're overwrought unnecessarily. You would never have been summoned if your anxieties had merit, Banner. You're an extraordinary man. We've never doubted that.

Nevertheless, it's dangerous.

The traffic on the Pennsylvania Turnpike seemed to move faster as the sky grew darker. Pockets of fog intruded abruptly, distorting the glare of onrushing headlights. A sudden cloudburst of slashing, diagonal rain splattered against the windscreen too rapidly. The wipers were useless against it.

There was a growing mania on the highway, and Chancellor felt it. Vehicles raced by, throwing up sprays of water; drivers seemed to sense several storms converging on western Pennsylvania, and instincts born of experience propelled them home.

The voice on the Continental's radio was precise, commanding.

The highway department urges all motorists to stay off the roads in the Jamestown Warren area. If you are currently en route, drive into the nearest service areas. We repeat: storm warnings out of Lake Erie have now been confirmed. The storms have winds of hurricane force . . .

"There's a turnoff about four miles up," said Peter, squinting at the windscreen. We'll take it. There's a restaurant two or three hundred yards out of the exit."

"How can you tell?"

"We just passed a Pittsfield sign; it used to be a landmark for me. It meant I was an hour from home."

Chancellor never understood how it happened; it was a question that would burn into his mind for the rest of his life. The steep hill was an opaque blanket of torrential rain, which fell in successive, powerful gusts that literally caused the heavy car to sway on its axis, like a small boat in terrible seas.

And suddenly there were headlights blinding through the rear window, reflecting harshly off the mirror. White spots appeared in front of his eyes, obscuring even the torrents of rain against the glass. He saw only the glaring white light.

Then it was beside him! An enormous trailer truck was overtaking him on the dangerous incline of rushing water! Peter screamed at the driver through the closed window; the man was a maniac. Couldn't he see what he was doing?

Couldn't he see the Mark IV in the storm? Was he out of his mind?

The unbelievable happened. The huge truck veered towards him! The impact came; the steel chassis of the carriage crashed into the Continental. Metal smashed against metal. The maniac was forcing him off the road! The man was drunk or panicked by the storm! Through the blanket of slashing rain Chancellor could see the outline of the driver high up in the perch of his seat. He was *oblivious* to the Mark IV! He did not know what he was doing!

A second crunching impact came with such a force that Peter's window shattered. The Mark IV's wheels locked; the car whipped to the right, towards a vacuum of darkness that lay beyond the ridge of the embankment.

The car rose up in the rain; then lurched over the shoulder of the highway, plunging downwards.

Catherine's screams pierced the sounds of shattering glass and crushing steel as the Continental rolled over and over and over. Metal now screeched against metal as if each strip, each panel were fighting to survive the successive impacts of car against earth.

Peter lunged towards the source of the scream – towards Catherine – but he was locked in place by a shaft of steel. The automobile twisted, rolled, plunged down the embankment.

The screams stopped. Everything stopped.

1

The fifth limousine drove slowly through the dark, tree-lined streets of Georgetown. It stopped in front of marble steps that led up through sculptured foliage to a porticoed entrance sixty feet away. The entrance, like the rest of the house, had a quiet grandeur heightened by the muted lighting beyond the pillars that supported the balcony above it.

The four previous limousines had arrived three to six minutes apart; all were deliberately paced. They had been hired from five separate leasing agencies from Arlington to Baltimore.

Should an observer in that quiet street wish to learn the identities of the single passenger within each vehicle, he would not be able to do so. For none could be traced through the leasing arrangements, and all were unseen by the chauffeurs. A pane of opaque glass separated each driver from his charge, and none was permitted to leave his seat behind the wheel while his passenger entered or left the vehicle. These chauffeurs had been selected with care.

Everything had been timed, orchestrated. Two limousines had been driven to private airfields, where for an hour they had been left locked and unattended in designated areas of the parking lots. At the end of that hour the drivers had returned, knowing their passengers would be there. The other three vehicles had been left in the same manner in three different locations: Washington's Union Station; the shopping complex in McLean, Virginia; and the country club in Chevy Chase, Maryland – to which the specific passenger did not belong.

Finally, should any observer in that quiet street in Georgetown try to interfere with the emerging passengers, a blond-haired man stood in the shadows on the balcony above the portico at the top of the marble staircase to prevent him. Around the man's neck was strapped a transistorized, high-impedance microphone through which he could relay commands to others on the block, using a language that was not English. In his hands was a rifle, a silencer attached to the barrel.

The fifth passenger got out of the limousine and walked up the marble steps. The car drove quietly away; it would not return. The blond-haired man on the balcony spoke softly into the microphone; the door beneath was opened.

The conference room was on the first floor. The walls were dark wood, the lighting indirect. Placed at the centre of the east wall was an antique Franklin stove, and in spite of the fact that it was a balmy spring evening, a fire glowed from within the iron casement.

In the centre of the room was a large circular table. Around it sat six men, their ages ranging from mid-fifties to eighties. Two fell into the first category: a greying, wavy-haired man with Hispanic features; and a man with very pale skin, Nordic face, and dark, straight hair combed smoothly back above his wide forehead. The latter sat to the left of the group's spokesman, the focal point of the table. The spokesman was in his late seventies; a fringe of hair extended around his balding head, and his features were tired – or ravaged. Across from the spokesman was a slender, aristocratic-looking man with thinning white hair and a perfectly groomed white moustache; he was also in the indeterminate seventies. On his right was a large Negro with an immense head and face that could have been chiselled from Ghanaian mahogany. On his left, the oldest and frailest man in the room; he was a Jew, a yarmulke on his hairless, gaunt skull.

All their voices were soft, their speech erudite. Their eyes steady and penetrating. Each man had a quiet vitality born of extraordinary power.

And each was known by a single name that had specific significance to all at the table; no other name was ever used among them. In several cases the name had been held by the member for nearly forty years; in other cases it had been passed on, as predecessors died and successors were elected.

There were never more than six men. The spokesman was known as Genesis – he was, in fact, the second man to hold the name. Previously, he had been known as Paris, the identity now held by the Hispanic man with the greying wavy hair.

Others were known as Christopher, Banner, Venice. And there was Bravo.

These were the men of Inver Brass.

In front of each was an identical manila folder, a single page of paper on top. Except for the name in the upper left-hand corner of the page, the remaining typewritten words would have been meaningless to any but these men.

Genesis spoke. "Above all, at all costs, the files must be taken and destroyed. In this there can be no disagreement. We've finally established that they're stored in an upright safe, built into the steel wall of the walk-in closet, behind and to the left of the office desk."

"The closet lock is controlled by a switch in the centre drawer," said Banner quietly. "The safe is protected by a series of electronic releases, the first of which must be triggered from his residence. Without the first release none of the others will activate. It would take ten sticks of dynamite to break in; the estimated time of operation for an acetylene torch is roughly four hours, with alarms sounding at the first touch of heat."

Across the table, his black face obscured in the dim light, Venice asked, "Has the location of this first release been confirmed?"

Yes," answered Banner. "In the bedroom. It's in the shelf of the headboard."

"Who confirmed it?" asked Paris, the Hispanic member of Inver Brass.

"Varak," was Genesis' reply from the south end of the table.

Several heads nodded slowly. The elderly Jew, to the right of Banner, addressed him. "What of the rest?"

"The subject's medical records were obtained from La Jolla, California. As you know, Christopher, he refuses to be examined at Bethesda. The most recent cardioanalysis indicates minor hypochloraemia, a low potassium condition in no way dangerous. The fact in itself, however, might be sufficient to warrant administering the required dosage of digitalis, but there's risk of exposure through autopsy."

"He's an old man." The statement was made by Bravo, a man older than the subject in question. "Why would an autopsy be considered?"

"Because of who he is," said Paris, the Hispanic member, his voice evidence of his early years in Castile. "It might be unavoidable. And the country cannot tolerate the turmoil of another assassination. It would give too many dangerous men the excuse to move, to implement a series of horrors in the name of patriotism."

"I submit," interrupted Genesis, "that should these same dangerous men – and I refer without equivocation to Sixteen hundred Pennsylvania Avenue – should these men and the subject reach an accommodation, the horrors you speak of will be minuscule by comparison. The key, gentlemen, is in the subject's files. They're held out like raw meat to hungry jackals. Those files in the hands of Sixteen hundred would usher in government by coercion and blackmail. We all know what's taking place right now. We *must* act."

"Reluctantly I agree with Genesis," said Bravo. "Our information shows that Sixteen hundred has gone beyond the unattractive limits experienced in previous administrations. It's approaching the uncontrollable. There's hardly an agency or a department that has not been contaminated. But an Internal Revenue investigation, or a DIA surveillance report, pales beside those files. Both in nature and – far more seriously – in the stature of those they concern. I'm not sure we have an alternative."

Genesis turned to the younger member at his side. "Banner, would you summarize, please?"

"Yes, of course." The slender, fiftyish man nodded, paused, and placed his hands in front of him on the table. "There's very little to add. You've read the report. The subject's mental processes have disintegrated rapidly; one intern suspects arteriosclerosis, but there's no way to confirm the diagnosis. The La Jolla records are controlled by the subject. At the source. He screens the medical data. Psychiatrically, however, there's complete agreement: the manic-depressive condition has advanced to the state of acute paranoia." The man stopped, his head turned slightly to Genesis but not excluding anyone else at the table. "Frankly that's all I have to know to cast my vote."

"Who reached this agreement?" asked the old Jew known as Christopher.

"Three psychiatrists, unknown to each other, retained by remote and asked to submit independent reports. These were collectively interpreted by our own man. Acute paranoia was the only conceivable judgement."

"How did they go about their diagnosis?" Venice leaned forward, his large black hands folded as he asked the question.

"Infra-red, telescopic motion-picture cameras were used over a thirty-day period in every possible situation. In restaurants, the Presbyterian Church, in arrivals and departures at all formal and private functions. Two lip-readers provided texts of everything said; the texts were identical. There are also extensive, I should say exhaustive, reports from our own sources within the Bureau. There can be no dispute with the judgement. The man's mad."

"What of Sixteen hundred?" Bravo stared at the younger man.

"They're getting closer, making progress every week. They've gone so far as to suggest a formal, internal association, the objective obviously the files. The subject's wary; he's seen them all, and those at Sixteen hundred aren't the best. But he admires their arrogance, their *macho*, and they stroke him. That's the word that's used, incidentally. *Stroke*."

"How appropriate," replied Venice. "Is their progress substantive?"

"I'm afraid so. There's hard evidence that the subject has delivered several dossiers – or the most damaging information contained in them – to the Oval Office. Understandings are being reached both in the area of political contributions and the election itself. Two contenders for the opposition's presidential nomination have agreed to withdraw – one by exhausted finances, the other by an act of instability."

"Please explain that," instructed Genesis.

"A gross mistake by words or action that eliminates him from the presidential stakes but is not serious enough to threaten his congressional standing. In this case, a display of unreasonable behaviour during the primaries. These things are well thought out."

"They're frightening," said Paris angrily.

"They stem from the subject," said Bravo. "May we touch once again on an autopsy. Can it be controlled?"

"It may not have to be," answered Banner, his hands now separated, the palms face down on the table. "We've flown in a man from Texas, an expert in cardiovascular research. He thinks he's dealing with a prominent family on Maryland's Eastern Shore. A patriarch going insane, capable of extraordinary damage, organic and psychiatric symptoms indistinguishable. There's a chemical derivative of digitalis that, when combined with an intravenous injection of air, may be untraceable."

"Who's overseeing this aspect?" Venice was unconvinced.

"Varak," said Genesis. "He's the source control of the entire project."

Once more there was a nodding of heads.

"Are there further questions?" asked Genesis. Silence.

"Then, we vote," continued Genesis, removing a small pad from beneath the manila envelope. He tore six pages and passed five to his left. "The Roman numeral one signifies affirmative; two, negative. As is customary a tie vote is negative."

The men of Inver Brass made their marks, folded the papers, and returned them to Genesis. He spread them out.

"The vote is unanimous, gentlemen. The project is on." He turned to Banner. "Please bring in Mr Varak."

The younger man got out of his chair and crossed to the door. He opened it, nodded his head to the figure standing outside in the hall, and returned to the table.

Varak walked in, closing the door behind him. He was the man who had stood guard on the dark balcony above the entrance at the top of the marble steps. The rifle was no longer in his hands, but the transistorized microphone was still strapped around his neck, and a thin wire led to his left ear. He was of indeterminate age, somewhere between thirty-five and forty-five – those years so well obscured in active men with strong, muscular bodies. His hair was light blond and cut short. His face was broad with high cheekbones that, together with his gently sloping eyes, were evidence of a Slavic heritage. In contrast to his appearance, however, his speech was soft, the accent faintly Bostonian, the rhythm Middle-European.

"Is there a decision?" he asked.

"Yes," replied Genesis. "Affirmative."

"You had no choice," said Varak.

"Have you projected a schedule?" Bravo leaned forward, his eyes steady, noncommittal.

"Yes. In three weeks. The night of May the first; the body will be discovered in the morning."

"The news will break on the second of May, then." Genesis looked at the members of Inver Brass. "Prepare statements where you think they'll be solicited. Several of us should be out of the country."

"You're assuming the death will be reported in a normal fashion," said Varak, raising his soft voice slightly to imply the contrary. "Without controls I wouldn't guarantee that."

"Why?" asked Venice.

"I think Sixteen hundred will panic. That crowd would put the corpse on ice inside the President's wardrobe if they thought it would buy them time to get the files."

Varak's imagery gave rise to reluctant smiles around the table. Genesis spoke.

"Then, guarantee it, Mr Varak. *We* will have the files."

"Very well. Is that all?"

"Yes."

"Thank you," said Genesis with a nod of his head. Varak left quickly. Genesis got out of his chair and picked up his single page of paper with the coded words typewritten on it. Then he reached down and gathered up the six small notepad pages, all clearly marked with the Roman numeral *I*. "The meeting is adjourned, gentlemen. As usual, will each of you be responsible for your own disposals? If any notes were made, dispense with them as well."

One by one the men of Inver Brass approached the Franklin stove. The first member to reach it removed the cover with the tongs hung on the wall. He dropped the page of paper deliberately into the well of burning coals. The others followed suit.

The last two men to perform the ritual were Genesis and Bravo. They stood away from the others. Genesis spoke quietly.

"Thank you for coming back."

"You told me four years ago I couldn't disappear, replied Munro St Claire. "You were right."

"There's more, I am afraid," Genesis said. "I'm not well. I have very little time."

"Oh, Lord – "

"Please. I'm the lucky one."

"What? How? . . ."

"The doctors said two or three months. Ten weeks ago. I insisted on knowing, of course. They're uncannily accurate; I can feel it. I assure you, there's no other feeling like it. It's an absolute, and there's a certain comfort in that."

"I'm sorry. More than I can say. Does Venice know?" St Claire's eyes strayed to the large black man talking softly in the corner with Banner and Paris.

"No. I wanted nothing to interfere – or influence – our decision tonight." Genesis dropped the typewritten page into the yellow glow of the stove. Then he crumpled the six votes of Inver Brass into a ball and let it too drop into the flame.

"I don't know what to say," whispered St Claire compassionately, watching Genesis' strangely peaceful eyes.

"I do," replied the dying man, smiling. "You're back now. Your resources are beyond those of Venice. Or any other man here tonight. Say that you'll see this through. In the event that I'm removed from the premises, as it were."

St Claire looked at the page in his hand. At the name in the upper left-hand corner. "He tried to destroy you once. He nearly succeeded. I'll see it through."

"Not that way," Genesis' voice was firm and disapproving. "There must be no rancour, no vengeance. That is not our way; it can *never* be our way."

"There are times when differing objectives are compatible. Even moral objections. I'm merely recognizing the fact. The man's a menace."

Munro St Claire looked once more at the page in his hand. At the name in the upper left-hand corner.

John Edgar Hoover.

He crushed the page in his hand and let it drop into the fire.

2

Peter Chancellor lay in the wet sand, the waves slapping gently over his body. He stared at the sky; the grey was receding, the blue emerging. Dawn had come to Malibu beach.

He pressed his elbows into the sand and sat up. His neck hurt, and within moments he would feel the pain in his temples. He had got drunk last night. And the night before, goddamn it.

His eyes strayed to his left leg below his underpants. The thin scar that curved from his calf through his kneecap up into his lower thigh was a twisting white line surrounded by suntanned flesh. It was still sensitive to the touch, but the complicated surgery beneath had been successful. He could walk almost normally now, and the pain had been replaced by a numb stiffness.

His left shoulder was something else; the pain was never completely absent, just dulled at times. The doctors said he had torn most of the ligaments and crushed assorted tendons; it would take longer for them to heal.

Absently he raised his right hand and felt the slightly swollen rivulet of skin that extended from his hairline over his right ear and down to the base of his skull. His hair covered most of the scar now, the break in his forehead only noticeable at close range. During the past weeks more women had remarked about it than he cared to remember. The doctors told him that his head had been sliced as though by a razor blade through a soft melon; a quarter of an inch above or below would have killed him. There had been weeks when he devoutly wished it had. He knew the desire would pass. He did not want to die; he merely was not sure he wanted to live without Cathy.

Time would heal the injuries, inside and outside; he never doubted it. He just wished the process were faster. So the restless energy would return and the early hours of the day could be filled with work, not pounding temples and vague, uneasy concerns about the previous night's behaviour.

But even if he remained sober, the concerns would still be there. He was out of his element; the tribes of Beverly Hills and Malibu confused him. In his agent's wisdom it was the positive thing for him to come to Los Angeles – Hollywood, why didn't he just say it, think it? Hollywood – to co-author the screenplay of *Counterstrike!* The fact that he did not know the first thing about screenwriting apparently did not matter. The redoubtable Joshua Harris, the only agent he had ever known, told him it was a minor deficiency that would be compensated for by major money.

The logic had escaped Peter. But then so had his coauthor. The two men had met three times for a total of about forty-five minutes, of which, again perhaps, ten had been devoted to *Counterstrike!* And, of course, nothing had been written down. Not in his presence, at any rate.

Yet here he was in Malibu, staying in a hundred-thousand-dollar beach house, driving a Jaguar, and charging to the studio tabs from Newport Beach to Santa Barbara.

One did not have to get drunk to feel hints of guilt in a situation like that. Certainly not Mrs Chancellor's little boy, who had been told early in life that you earn what you get just as surely as you are what you live.

On the other hand, *living* was what was uppermost in Joshua Harris's mind when he negotiated the contract. Peter had not been living at the house in Pennsylvania; he had been barely existing.

In the three months after his release from the hospital, he had done almost nothing on the Nuremberg book.

Nothing. When would there be something? Anything?

His head hurt now. His eyes watered with the pain, and his stomach sent up alarms. Peter got to his feet and walked unsteadily into the surf. A swim might help.

He ducked beneath the surface, then sprang up and looked back towards the house. What the hell was he doing on the beach in the first place? He'd brought a girl home last night. He was sure of it. Almost.

He limped painfully over the sand to the steps of the beach house. He paused at the railing, breathing hard, and looked up at the sky. The sun had broken through, burning away the mist. It was going to be another hot, humid day. He turned and saw that two residents were walking their dogs about a quarter-mile away at the water's edge.

It would not do for him to be seen in wet underpants on the beach. What remained of propriety ordered him back to the house.

Propriety and curiosity. And the vague feeling that something unpleasant had happened last night. He wondered what the girl would look like. Blonde, he remembered, large-breasted. And how did they manage to drive from wherever it was in Beverly Hills to Malibu? The vague memory of the unpleasant incident was somehow related to the girl, but he could not remember how or why.

He gripped the railing and pulled himself up the steps to the redwood deck. Redwood and white stucco and heavy wooden beams – that was the beach house. It was an architect's version of Malibu Tudor.

The glass doors on the far right were partially open. It was the bedroom entrance; on the table by the door was a half-empty bottle of Pernod. The deckchair nearest the bottle was overturned. A pair of strapless sandals lay toe to heel beside it, in contradictory neatness.

Things were coming back to him. He had made love to the girl with the dramatic breasts – inadequately, he recalled – and in disgust or self-defence had wandered out to the porch and sat by himself, drinking Pernod without the benefit of a glass.

Why had he done that? Where had the Pernod come from? What the hell difference did it make to him whether he performed acceptably or unacceptably with an accommodating body recruited from Beverly Hills? He could not remember so he held on to the railing and walked towards the overturned chair and the open glass door.

There were dead flies floating in the Pernod; a live one hesitantly circled the rim of the bottle. Chancellor considered righting the fallen chair, but decided otherwise. His head was in pain; not just the temples, but the winding corridor of skin between his hairline and the base of his skull. The pain was undulating, as though guided by an unseen beam.

A warning signal. He had to move slowly.

He limped cautiously through the door. The room was a mess. Clothes were strewn about the furniture, ashtrays were overturned, their contents scattered about the floor; a glass was smashed in front of the bedside table; the telephone was ripped out of its socket.

The girl was in bed, lying on her side, her breasts pressed together. Her blonde hair fell over her face, which was buried in a pillow. The top sheet was draped across the lower half of her body; one leg protruded, displaying the sun-darkened flesh of her inner thigh. Looking at her, Peter could feel the provocative stirring in his groin. He inhaled deeply for a few moments, excited by the sight of the girl's breasts, her exposed leg, her hidden face beneath the fallen blonde hair.

He was still drunk. He knew that, because he realized he did not want to see the girl's face. He merely wanted to make love to an object; he did not want to acknowledge the existence of a person.

He took a step towards the bed and stopped. Fragments of glass were in his path; they explained the sandals outside. At least he'd had the presence of mind to wear them. And the telephone. He remembered yelling into the telephone.

The woman rolled on to her back. Her face was pretty in that innocuous California way. Pert, suntanned, the features too small and co-ordinated for character. Her large breasts separated, the sheet fell away, revealing her pubic hair and the swell of her thighs. Peter moved to the foot of the bed and pulled down his wet underpants. He could feel sand on the tips of his fingers. He placed his right knee on the bed, careful to keep his left leg straight, and lowered himself on the sheets.

The woman opened her eyes. When she spoke, it was with a soft, modulated voice filled with sleep.

"Come on up, honey. You feeling better?"

Chancellor crawled beside her. She moved her hand to his half-swollen erection, cupping it gently.

"Do I owe you an apology?" he asked.

"Hell, no. Maybe to yourself, not me. You banged like a ram, but I don't think it did you any good. You just got mad and stormed out."

"I'm sorry." He reached for her left breast; the nipple was taut under the pressure of his fingers. The girl moaned and began pulling him in short swift movements. She was either a good performer or a highly developed sexual partner who needed very little priming.

"I still feel warm all over. You just didn't stop. You just went on and on and

550

nothing happened for you. But *Jesus*, it did for me! . . . Fuck me, lamb. Come on, fuck me," she whispered.

Peter buried his face between her breasts. Her legs parted, inviting him into her. But the ache in his head increased; shafts of pain pulsed through his skull.

I can't. I can't." He could barely talk.

Don't you worry. Now, don't you worry about a thing," said the girl. She eased him back so his shoulders again touched the sheets. "You just hold on, honey. Hold on and let me do the work."

The moment blurred. He could feel himself waning, then the swift movements of the girl's two hands and the wet moisture of her lips, caressing, provoking. He was becoming alive again. There was need.

Goddamn it. He had to be good for something.

He pulled her head into his groin. She moaned and spread her legs; all was sweet wetness and soft flesh. He grabbed her under her arms, pulling her parallel to him. Her breath came in quick, loud, throated groans.

He could not stop now. He could not allow the pain to interfere. Goddamn it!

"Oh, Peter, you're something. Oh, Christ, you're the fucker of all time! Come on, lamb! Now! *Now!*"

The girl's whole body began to writhe. Her whispers now bordered on shouts.

"Oh, Jesus! Jesus *Christ!* You're driving me crazy, lover! You're the best there ever was! There was never anyone like you! . . . Oh, *my!* Oh, my *God!*"

He exploded inside her, draining himself; his body limp, the ache in his temples receding. At least he was good for *something*. He had aroused her, made her want him.

And then he heard her voice, all professionalism.

"There, lamb. That wasn't so difficult, was it?"

He looked at her. Her expression was that of a well-applauded performer. Her eyes were plastic death.

"I owe you," he said softly, coldly.

"No, you don't." She laughed, "I don't take money from you. He pays me plenty."

Chancellor remembered everything. The party, the argument, the drunken trip from Beverly Hills, his anger on the telephone.

Aaron Sheffield, motion-picture producer, owner of *Counterstrike!*

Sheffield had been at the party, his young wife in tow. In fact, it was Sheffield who had called him, asking him to come along. There was no reason not to accept, and there was a very good reason to do so: his elusive co-author of the *Counterstrike!* screenplay was the host.

Not to worry. You wrote a winner, sweetheart.

But last night there was something to worry about. They wanted to tell him in pleasant surroundings. More than pleasant. Quite a bit more.

The studio had received several "very serious" calls from Washington about the filming of *Counterstrike!* It was pointed out that there was a major error in the book: the Central Intelligence Agency did not operate domestically. It did not involve itself in operations within the borders of the United States. The CIA's 1947 charter had specifically prohibited this. Therefore, Aaron Sheffield had agreed to change that aspect of the script. Chancellor's CIA would become an elite corps of disaffected former intelligence specialists acting outside government channels.

What the hell, Aaron Sheffield had said. *It's better dramatically. We've got two types of villains, and Washington's happy.*

But Chancellor was furious. He knew what he was talking about! He had spoken with truly disaffected men who had worked for the agency and was appalled at what they had been called upon to do. Appalled because it was illegal and appalled because there were no alternatives. A maniac named J. Edgar Hoover had severed all intelligence conduits between the FBI and the CIA. The men of the CIA themselves would have to go after the domestic information withheld from them. Who were they going to complain to? Mitchell? Nixon?

Most of whatever power *Counterstrike!* had was in the specific use of the agency. To eliminate it was to vitiate a great part of the book. Peter had objected strenuously, and the more angry he became, the more, it seemed, he drank. And the more he drank, the more provocative had the girl beside him become.

Sheffield had driven them home. Peter and the girl were in the backseat, her skirt above her waist, her blouse unbuttoned, her enormous breasts exposed in racing shadows driving him wild. Drunken wild.

And they'd gone inside together while Sheffield drove off. The girl had brought two bottles of Pernod, a gift from Aaron, and the games began in earnest. Wild games, drunken, naked games.

Until the shooting pains in his skull stopped him, providing a few moments of clarity. He had lurched for the telephone, thumbed insanely through his notes on the bedside table for Sheffield's number, and punched the buttons furiously.

He had roared at Sheffield, calling him every obscenity he could think of, screaming his objections – and his guilt – at having been manipulated. There'd be *no* changes in *Counterstrike!*

As they lay there on the bed, the blonde girl beside him, Chancellor remembered Sheffield's words over the phone.

"Easy, kid. What difference does it make to you? You don't have script approval. We were just being polite. Get down from your sky-high perch. You're just a lousy little home–maker–fucker like the rest of us."

The blonde girl beside Peter on the bed was Sheffield's wife.

Chancellor turned to her. The vacuous eyes were brighter, but still dead. The mouth opened, and an experienced tongue slid sensuously out and then back and forth, conveying an unmistakable message.

The well–applauded performer was ready to perform again.

Who gave a shit? He reached for her.

3

The man whose face was among the most recognized in the nation sat alone at table ten in the Mayflower Restaurant on Connecticut Avenue. The table was by a window, and the occupant kept glancing through the glass absently, but not without a certain vague hostility, at the passers-by on the street.

He had arrived at precisely eleven thirty-five; he would finish his lunch and depart at twelve-forty. It had been an unbroken custom for over twenty years. The hour and five minutes was the custom, not the Mayflower. The Mayflower was a recent change, since the closing of Harvey's, several blocks away.

The face, with its enormous jaws, drawn-out mouth, and partially thyroid eyes, had disintegrated. The jaws were sagging jowls; creased, blemished flesh overlapped the slits that had been eyes; the touched-up strands of hair attested to the ferocious ego that was intrinsic to the aggressively negative expression.

His usual companion was not in evidence. Declining health and two strokes prevented his elegantly dressed presence. The soft, pampered face – struggling for masculinity – had for decades been the flower to the bristled cactus. The man about to have lunch looked across the table as if he expected to see his attractive alter ego. That he saw no one seemed to trigger a periodic tremor in his fingers and a recurrent twitching of his mouth. He seemed enveloped in loneliness; his eyes darted about, alert to real and imagined ills surrounding him.

A favourite waiter was indisposed for the day; it was a personal affront. He let it be known. Fruit salad with a dome of cottage cheese in the centre was marked for table ten. It was processed from the open, stainless steel shelf in the kitchen to the service counter. The blond-haired second assistant chef, temporarily employed, marked off the various trays, appraising their appearance with a prac-tised eye. He stood over table ten's fruit salad, a clipboard in his hand, his gaze directed at the trays in front of it.

Underneath the clipboard a pair of thin silver tongs were held horizontally. In the tongs' teeth was a soft white capsule. The blond-haired man smiled at a harassed waiter coming through the dining-room door; at the same moment he plunged the silver tongs into the mound of cottage cheese beneath the clipboard, removed them, and moved on.

Seconds later he returned to the order for table ten, shook his head, and touched up the dome of cottage cheese with a fork.

Within the inserted capsule was a mild dose of lysergic acid. The capsule would disintegrate and release the narcotic some seven to eight hours after the moment of ingestion.

The minor stress and the disorientation that resulted would be enough. There would be no traces in the bloodstream at the time of death.

The middle-aged woman sat in a windowless room. She listened to the voice coming out of the wall speakers, then repeated the words into the microphone of a tape recorder. Her objective was to duplicate as closely as possible the now familiar voice from the speakers. Every sliding tone, every nuance; the idiosyncratic short pauses that followed the partially sibilant *s*'s.

The voice coming from the speakers was that of Helen Gandy, for years the personal secretary of John Edgar Hoover.

In the corner of the small studio stood two suitcases. Both were fully packed. In four hours the woman and the suitcases would be on a transatlantic flight bound for Zurich. It was the first leg of a trip that would eventually take her south to the Balearic Islands and a house on the sea in Majorca. But first there was Zurich, where the Staats-Banque would pay upon signature a negotiated sum into Barclay's, which would in turn transfer the amount in two payments to an account at its branch in Palma. The first payment would be made immediately, the second in eighteen months.

Varak had hired her. He believed that for every job there was a correct, skilled applicant. The computerized data banks at the National Security Agency had been programmed in secret, by Varak alone, until they produced the applicant he sought.

She was a widow, a former radio actress. She and her husband had been caught in the crosscurrents of the Red Channels madness of 1954 and had never recovered. It was a madness sanctioned and aided by the Federal Bureau of Investigation. Her husband, considered by many to have been a major talent, did not work for seven years. At the end of that time, his heart had burst in anguish. He had died in an underground station on his way to a clerical job at a downtown bank. By now the woman had been finished professionally for eighteen years; the pain and the rejection and the loneliness had robbed her of the ability to compete.

There was no competition now. She was not told why she was doing what she was doing. Only that her brief conversation had to result in a "yes" on the other end of the line.

The recipient of the call was a man the woman loathed with all her being. A basic accessory to the madness that had stolen her life.

It was shortly past nine in the evening, and the telephone van was not an uncommon sight on Thirtieth Street Place in north-west Washington. The short street was a cul-de-sac, ending with the imposing gates of the Peruvian ambassador's residence, the national shield prominently displayed on the stone pillars. Two-thirds of the way down the block, on the left, was the faded red brick house belonging to the director of the Federal Bureau of Investigation. One or both residences were continuously upgrading communications facilities.

And every once in a while unmarked vans patrolled the area, antennae protruding from their roofs. It was said that John Edgar Hoover ordered such patrols to check out any unwanted electronic surveillance that might have been planted there by inimical foreign governments.

Frequently complaints were registered with the State Department by the

Peruvian ambassador. It was embarrassing; there wasn't anything State could do about the situation. Hoover's private life was an extension of his professional barony.

Peru wasn't very important anyway.

The telephone van drove down the street, made a U-turn, and retraced its route back to Thirtieth Street, where it turned right for fifty yards, then right again into a row of garages. At the end of the garage complex was a stone wall that bordered the rear grounds of 4936 Thirtieth Street Place, Hoover's residence. Above and beyond the garages were other houses with windows overlooking the Hoover property. The man in the telephone van knew that at one of those windows was an agent from the bureau, one of a team assigned to twenty-four-hour surveillance. The teams were secret and were rotated every week.

The driver of the van was also aware that whoever was at one of those windows beyond the garage would place a routine call to a special number at the telephone company. The inquiry would be simple, asked above a strange hum on the line: what was the problem that brought a repair van into the area at that hour?

The operator would check her call sheet and reply with the truth as it had been given to her.

There was a short in a junction box. Suspect: an inquisitive squirrel invading rotted insulation. The damage was responsible for the noticeable buzz on the line. Didn't the caller hear it?

Yes, he hear it.

Varak had learned years ago, in his early days with the National Security Agency, never to give too simple an answer to questions raised by area surveillance. It would not be accepted, any more than an overly complicated one would be accepted. There was always a middle ground.

The high-frequency radio phone in the van hummed: a signal. An inquiring call had been made to the telephone company by an alert FBI man. The driver stopped the small van, once more turned around, and drove thirty-five yards back to the telephone pole. His sightlines to the residency were clear. He parked and waited, blueprints spread on the front seat as if he were studying them.

Agents often took late-night walks in the vicinity. All contingencies had to be covered.

The telephone van was now eighty yards northwest of 4936 Thirtieth Street Place. The driver left his seat, crawled back into the rear of the van, and switched on his equipment. He had precisely forty-six minutes to wait. During that time he had to lock on the flows of current being received in Hoover's residence. The heavier loads defined the circuits of the alarm system; the lesser ones were lights and radios and television sets. Defining the alarm system was crucial, but no less important was the knowledge that current was being used in the lower right area. It meant that electrical units were switched on in the maid's room. It was vital to know that. Annie Fields, Hoover's personal housekeeper for as long as anyone could remember, was there for the night.

The limousine made a right turn off Pennsylvania Avenue into Tenth Street and slowed down in front of the far west entrance to the FBI. The limousine was identical to the one that daily brought the director to his offices – even to the slightly dented chrome bumper Hoover had left as it was, a reminder to the chauffeur, James Crawford, of the man's carelessness. It was not, of course, the same car; that particular vehicle was guarded night and day. But no one, not even Crawford, could have told the difference.

The driver spoke the proper words into the dashboard microphone, and the huge steel doors of the entrance parted. The night guard saluted as the limousine passed through the concrete structure, with its three succeeding concrete doorways, into the small circular drive. A second Justice Department guard leapt out of the south entranceway, reached for the handle of the right rear door, and pulled it open.

Varak got out quickly and thanked the astonished guard. The driver and a third man – seated next to the driver – also stepped out and offered pleasant but subdued greetings.

"Where's the director?" asked the guard. "This is Mr Hoover's private car."

"We're here on his instructions," said Varak calmly. "He wants us taken directly to Internal Security. They're to call him. IS has the number; it's on a scrambler. I'm afraid it's an emergency. Please hurry."

The guard looked at the three well-dressed, well-spoken men. His concern diminished; these men knew the highly classified gate codes that changed every night; beyond that, they carried instructions to call the director himself. On the scrambler phone at the Internal Security desk. That telephone number was *never* used.

The guard nodded, led the men inside to the security desk in the corridor, and returned to his post outside. Behind the wide steel panel with the myriad wires and small television screens, sat a senior agent dressed not unlike the three men who approached him. Varak took a laminated identification card from his pocket and spoke.

"Agents Longworth, Krepps and Salter," he said, placing his ID on the counter. "You must be Parke."

"That's right," replied the agent, taking Varak's identification and reaching for the other two IDs as they were handed to him. "Have we met, Longworth?"

"Not for ten or twelve years. Quantico."

The agent looked briefly at the IDs, returned them to the counter, and squinted in recollection. "Yeah, I remember the name. Al Longworth. Long time." He extended his hand; Varak took it. "Where've you been?"

"La Jolla."

"Christ, you've got a friend!"

"That's why I'm here. These are my two best men in southern Cal. *He* called me last night." Varak leaned ever so slightly over the counter. "I've got bad news, Parke. It's not good at all," he said, barely above a whisper. "We may be getting near 'open territory'."

The expression on the agent's face changed abruptly; the shock was obvious. Among the senior officers at the bureau the phrase *open territory* meant the

556

unthinkable: the director was ill. Seriously, perhaps fatally, ill.

"Oh, my God . . ." muttered Parke.

"He wants you to call him on the scrambler."

"Oh, Christ!" Under the circumstances it was obviously the last thing the agent wanted to do. "What does he want? What am I supposed to say, Longworth? Oh, *Jesus!*"

"He wants us taken up to Flags. Tell him we're here; verify his instructions and clear one of my men for the relays."

"The relays? What for?"

"Ask him."

Parke stared at Varak for a moment, then reached for the telephone.

Fifteen blocks south, in the cellar of a telephone–company complex, a man sat on a stool in front of a panel of interlocking wires. On his jacket was a plastic card with his photograph and, in large letters beneath it, the word *Inspector*. In his right ear was a plug attached to an amplifier on the floor; next to the amplifier was a small cassette recorder. Wires spiralled up to other wires in the panel.

The tiny bulb on the amplifier lighted up. The scrambler phone at the FBI security desk was in use. The man's eyes were riveted on a button in the cassette recorder; he listened with the ears of an experienced professional. Instantly he pushed the button; the tape rolled, and almost immediately he shut it off. He waited several moments and once again pushed the button, and once again the reels spun.

Fifteen blocks north Varak listened to Parke. The words had been lifted, edited, and refined from a number of tapes. As planned, the voice on the other end of the line would be louder than a normal voice; it would be the voice of a man wanting to not acknowledge illness, fighting to appear normal, and in so doing, speaking abnormally. It not only fitted the subject psychiatrically, it had a further value. The volume lent authority, and the authority reduced the possibility that the deception would be spotted.

"Yes, what is it?" The gruff voice could be heard clearly.

"Mr Hoover, this is senior agent Parke at Internal Security. Agents Longworth, Krepps and – " Parke stopped, forgetting the name, his expression bewildered.

"Salter," whispered Varak.

"Salter, sir. Longworth, Krepps and Salter. They've arrived, and they said I was to call you to verify your instructions. They said they're to be cleared for the relays – "

"Those men," came the harsh, unrhythmic interruption, "are there at my personal orders. Do as they say. They are to be given complete co–operation, and nothing is to be said to anyone. Is that understood?"

"Yes, sir."

"What's your name again?"

"Senior Agent Lester Parke, sir."

There was a pause; Varak tensed his stomach muscles and held his breath. The pause was too long!

"I'll remember that," came the word finally. "Good night, Parke." A concluding click was heard on the line.

Varak breathed again. Even the use of the name worked; it had been lifted from a conversation the subject had had during which he had complained about the crime rate in Rock Creek Park.

"He sounds awful, doesn't he?" Parke replaced the telephone and reached underneath the counter for three night passes.

"He's a very courageous man," said Varak. "He asked for your name?"

"Yeah," replied the agent, inserting the passes into the automatic timer. "If the worst happens, you might find yourself with a bonus," added Varak, turning his head away from his two companions.

"What?" Parke looked up.

"A personal bequest. Nothing official."

"I don't understand."

"You're not supposed to. But you heard the man; I heard him, too. Keep your own counsel, as the book says. You'll answer to me if you don't . . . The director's the best friend I've ever had."

Parke stared at Varak. "La Jolla," he said.

"La Jolla," answered Varak.

A great deal more was conveyed than the name of a California seaside town. Stories had circulated for years – the grand designs of a retired monarch, a mansion overlooking the Pacific, a clandestine government housing the secrets of a nation.

The sad-faced middle-aged woman watched the second hand of the clock on the wall in the small studio. Fifty-five seconds to go. The telephone was on the table, in front of the tape recorder she had used to rehearse the words. Over and over again, a full week of rehearsals aimed for a single performance that would last no more than a minute.

Rehearsal. Performance.

Terms of a nearly forgotten lexicon.

She was no fool. The strange, blond-haired man who had hired her had explained very little, but enough to let her know that what she was about to do was a *good* thing. Desired by far better men than the man she would talk to on the telephone in . . . forty seconds.

The woman reminisced as she watched the hand on the clock move slowly towards the mark. They had once said her husband was a fine talent; that's what everyone had said. He was on his way to becoming a star, a *real* star, not a photogenic accident. Everyone had said so.

And then other people came along and said he was on a list. A very important list that meant he was not a good citizen. And those on the list were given a label.

Subversive.

And the label was given legitimacy. Tight-lipped young men in dark suits began to show up in studios and producers' offices.

Federal Bureau of Investigation.

Then they went behind closed doors and held private conversations.

Subversive. It was a word associated with the man she was about to speak to. She reached for the telephone.

"This is for you, my darling," she whispered. She was primed; the adrenalin was flowing as it used to flow. Then a calm swept over her. She was confident, a professional again. It would be the performance of her life.

John Edgar Hoover lay in bed, trying to focus on the television set across the room. He kept changing channels on the remote control; none of the pictures was clear. He was further aggravated by a strange hollowness in his throat. He'd never experienced the feeling before; it was as though a hole had been drilled in his neck, allowing too much air into his upper chest. But there was no pain, just an uncomfortable sensation that was somehow related to the distortion in the sound now coming from the television set.

In and out. Louder, then softer.

And oddly enough, he felt hungry. He had never been hungry at that hour; he had trained himself not to be.

It was all very annoying, the annoyance heightened by the dull ring of his private telephone. No more than ten people in Washington had the number; he was not feeling up to a crisis. He reached for the phone and spoke angrily.

"Yes? What is it?"

"Mr Hoover. I'm sorry to disturb you, but it's urgent."

"Miss Gandy?" What was wrong with his hearing? Gandy's voice seemed to float, in and out, louder, then softer. "What's the matter, Miss Gandy?"

"The President phoned from Camp David. He's en route to the White House and would like you to see Mr Haldeman tonight."

"Tonight? Why?"

"He told me to tell you it was a matter of the utmost importance, related to information the CIA has gathered during the past forty-eight hours."

John Edgar Hoover could not help the scowl that crossed his face. The Central Intelligence Agency was an abomination, a band of sycophants led by the liberal orthodoxy. It was not to be trusted.

Neither was the present occupant of the White House, but if he had data that rightfully belonged to the bureau and it was sufficiently vital to send out a man – *that* man – in the middle of the night to deliver it, there was no point in refusing.

Hoover wished the hollowness in his throat would go away. It was most irritating. And something else bothered him.

"Miss Gandy, the President has this number. Why didn't he call himself?"

"He understood you were having dinner out. He knows you dislike being disturbed in a restaurant. I was to coordinate the meeting."

Hoover squinted through his glasses at the bedside clock. It was not the middle of the night; it was barely ten-fifteen. He should have realized that. He had left Tolson's at eight, claiming a sudden weariness. The President's intelligence was not very accurate, either. He was not at a restaurant, he had been with Clyde.

He was so tired he had gone to bed much earlier than usual. "I'll see Haldeman. Out here."

"I assumed that, sir. The President suggested that you might wish to dictate several memoranda, instructions to a number of field offices. I volunteered to drive out with Mr Haldeman. The White House car is picking me up."

"That's very thoughtful, Miss Gandy. They must have something interesting."

"The President wants no one to know that Mr Haldeman is coming to see you. He said it would be terribly embarrassing."

"Use the side entrance, Miss Gandy. You have a key. The alarms will be shut off. I'll notify surveillance."

"Very well, Mr Hoover."

The middle-aged woman replaced the phone in front of the tape recorder and sat back in the chair.

She had done it! She had really done it! She'd fallen into the rhythm, every tonal nuance, the imperceptible pauses, the slightly nasal inflections. Perfect!

The remarkable thing was that there had never been an instant of hesitation. It was as if the terrors of twenty years had been erased in a matter of moments.

She had one more call to make. Here she could use any voice she liked, the blander the better. She dialled.

"The White House," said the voice on the line.

"FBI, honey," said the middle-aged actress in a faintly southern accent. "This is just information for the logs, nothing urgent. At nine o'clock this evening the director received Mr Haldeman's message. This is to confirm the receipt, that's all."

"Okay, it's confirmed. I'll list it. Muggy day, isn't it?"

"It's a beautiful night, though," replied the actress. "The most beautiful night ever."

"Someone's got a heavy date."

"I've got something better than that. Much better. Good night, White House."

"Good night, Bureau."

The woman got up from the chair and reached for her purse. "We did it, my darling," she whispered. Her last performance had been her finest. She was revenged. She was free.

The driver in the telephone van studied the graph of the electrical field scope closely. There were breaks in the heavier circuits in the lower left and left central areas. It meant that the alarm devices had been shut down in those sections: the drive entrance, the door in the stone wall, and the path beyond it that led to the rear of the house.

Everything was on schedule. The driver looked at his watch; it was nearly time to climb the telephone pole. He checked the rest of his equipment. When he threw a switch, the electrical current throughout Hoover's residence would be interrupted. Lights, television sets, and radios would fade and return in a quick series of disturbances. The disruptions would last for twenty seconds, no more. The length of time was sufficient, the momentary distraction enough.

But before that switch was thrown, there was another job to be done. If a custom unchanged for years was repeated tonight, an obstacle would be removed efficiently. He looked at his watch again.

Now.

He opened the rear doors of the van and jumped to the pavement. He crossed rapidly to the pole, unhooked one end of the long safety belt, and whipped it around the wood, snapping the hook into his waist lamp. He lifted his boots one at a time and kicked the spikes into place.

He looked around. There was no one. He slapped the safety belt above him on the pole and began to climb. In less than thirty seconds he was near the top.

The spill of the streetlight was too bright, too dangerous. It hung suspended from a short metal brace just above him. He reached into his pocket and pulled out an air pistol loaded with lead pellets. He scanned the ground, the alley, the windows above the row of garages. He angled the air gun up at the lighted glass sphere and pulled the trigger.

There was a spit, instantly followed by the static of electric filaments. The light went out.

He waited silently; there was no sound. In the darkness he opened the flap of the equipment case and slid out a metal cylinder eighteen inches long. It was the barrel of an odd-looking rifle. From another compartment he withdrew a heavy steel rod and attached it to the cylinder; at the end was a curved brace. From a third pocket in the leather toolcase the driver extracted a twelve-inch infra-red telescope that had been precision-tooled for the top of the cylinder; it was self-locking and once locked, accurate. Finally, the man reached into his jacket and pulled out the trigger-housing unit. He snapped it into the opening on the underside of the barrel and tested the silent bolt action; all was ready, only the ammunition remained.

Cradling the strange rifle in his left arm, he slid his right hand into his pocket and took out a steel dart, the flared end dipped in luminous paint. He inserted it into the chamber and slid the bolt back into place. The hammer was cocked, the rifle ready to fire.

His watch read ten forty-four; if the longstanding habit was going to be observed this night, he'd know it shortly. Suspended thirty-five feet above the ground, the man stretched himself and tightened the safety strap until his body was pressed against the pole. He raised the rifle and jammed the curved brace into his shoulder.

He looked through the luminous green circle that was the sight and moved it carefully until he had the rear door of the director's house clearly in view. In spite of the darkness, the picture was clear; the cross hairs of zero aim were focused directly on the steps of the entrance.

He waited. Minutes passed slowly. He stole a glance at the dial of his watch; it was ten fifty-three. He could not wait much longer; he had to return to the van to throw the switch.

Of all nights! Routine was not going to be observed!

Then he saw the porch light! The door opened; the driver felt a wave of relief.

Through his infra-red scope the huge animal came into focus. It was Hoover's enormous bull mastiff, rumoured to be among the most vicious of dogs. It was said the director enjoyed the comparisons made between the faces of master and animal.

The custom of years was being carried out. Every evening between ten forty-five and eleven Hoover or Annie Fields let the dog out to wander in the enclosed grounds of the residence, its waste picked up in the morning.

The door closed, the porch light remained on. The man on the pole moved his weapon with his quarry. The cross hairs were now on the animal's enormous throat.

The driver squeezed the trigger; there was a slight metallic click. Through the sight he could see the mastiff's eyes widen in shock; the huge jaws sprang open, but no sound came.

The animal fell to the ground, narcotized.

A nondescript grey automobile coasted to a stop a hundred feet past the driveway of 4936 Thirtieth Street Place. A tall man in a dark suit got out through the passenger door and looked up and down the block. Near the grounds of the Peruvian ambassador's residence a woman walked a dalmatian. In the other direction, perhaps two hundred yards away, a couple were strolling up a path towards a lighted doorway.

Otherwise there was nothing.

The man looked at his watch and felt the small bulge in his coat pocket.

He had exactly half a minute, thirty seconds, and after that he would have precisely twenty seconds. He nodded to the driver and walked rapidly back towards the driveway, the crepe soles of his shoes noiseless on the pavement. He swung into the shadowed drive without breaking his stride, approached the door in the wall, and removed a small air pistol from his belt, shifting it to his left hand. The dart was in place; he hoped he would not have to use it.

He looked again at his watch. Eleven seconds; he could allow an additional three for safety. He checked the position of the key in his right hand.

Now.

He inserted the key, turned the lock, opened the door, and entered the grounds, leaving the door six inches open. The huge dog was on the grass, its jaws slack, its enormous head pressed against the earth. The driver of the telephone van had done his job efficiently. He would remove the dart on his way out; there would be no trace of the narcotic in the morning. He returned the dart gun to his pocket.

He walked rapidly to the door on the ground floor, his mind ticking off the seconds. He could see the intermittent dimming of lights throughout the house. By his estimate nine seconds remained as he inserted the second key.

The lock would not turn! The mechanism was jammed. He manipulated the key furiously.

Four seconds, three.

His fingers – his surgeon's fingers encased in surgical gloves – delicately, swiftly manoeuvred the jagged metal within the jagged orifice as if were a scalpel in flesh.

Two seconds, one.

It opened!

The tall man stepped inside, leaving this door, too, ajar.

He stood in the hall and listened. The lights were steady again. There was the sound of a television set from the housekeeper's room at the other side of the house. Upstairs the sounds were fainter but discernible; it was the eleven o'clock news. The doctor wondered briefly what tomorrow's eleven o'clock news would be like. He wished he could be in Washington to hear it.

He crossed to the staircase and began to climb. At the top he stood in front of the door to the right of the staircase, in the centre of the landing. The door that led to the man he had waited over two decades to see.

Waited in hatred. Deep hatred, never to be forgotten.

He turned the knob cautiously and opened the door. The director had dozed off, his enormous head angled down, the jowls falling over his thick neck. In his fat, feminine hands were the spectacles his vanity rarely allowed him to use in public.

The doctor went to the television set and turned it up so that the sound filled the room. He crossed back to the front of the bed and stared down at the object of his loathing.

The director's head snapped down, then abruptly up. His face was contorted. "What?"

"Put on your glasses," said the doctor above the noise of the television set.

"What's this? Miss Gandy? . . . Who are you? You're not – " Shaking, Hoover put on his glasses.

"Look closely. It's been twenty-two years."

The bulging eyes within the folds of flesh beyond the lenses focused. The sight they saw caused their possessor to gasp. "You! How – ?"

"Twenty-two years," continued the doctor mechanically but loud enough to be heard above the sound of sirens and music from the television set. He reached into his pocket and took out a hypodermic needle. "I have a different name now. I practise in Paris, where my patients have heard the stories but don't concern themselves. *Le médecin américain* is considered one of the finest in the hospital – "

Suddenly the director swung his arm out towards the night table. The doctor lunged forward at the side of the bed, pinning the soft wrist against the mattress. Hoover began to scream; the doctor jammed his elbow into the jowls, cutting off all sound. He raised the naked, trembling arm.

With his teeth the doctor took off the rubber tip of the needle. He plunged the hypodermic into the rubbery flesh of the exposed armpit.

"This is for my wife and my son. Everything you stole from me."

The driver of the grey car turned in his seat, his eyes directed at the first-floor windows of the house. The lights were extinguished for five seconds, then turned on again.

The unknown doctor had done his work; the release in the headboard had been found and activated. There were no seconds to be lost. The driver removed the microphone from the radio unit, pressed the button, and spoke.

"Phase One completed," he said tersely in a pronounced British accent.

The office stretched for nearly forty feet. The large mahogany desk at one end was slightly elevated, facing low overstuffed leather chairs, forcing visitors to raise their eyes to its occupant. Beyond the desk, obscuring the wall beyond, was a row of flags, the Federal Bureau of Investigation's banner sharing the centre position with the nation's.

Varak stood motionless in front of the desk, his eyes on the two telephones. One instrument had its receiver out of the cradle, the open line connected to a phone in the cellar of the building, to a man in the relay room where all alarms were controlled. The other telephone was intact; it was an outside line that bypassed the bureau's switchboard. There was no number printed on the circular tab in the middle of the dial.

The centre drawer of the desk was open. Beside it stood a second man, the spill of the desk lamp illuminating his right hand, which was angled, palm up, in the open space of the drawer. His fingers touched a small toggle switch recessed in the roof of the desk.

The telephone began to ring. Varak picked it up at the first hint of sound. He said one word quietly.

"Flags."

"Phase One completed," was the relayed reply over the line.

Varak nodded. The man in front of him snapped the unseen switch in his fingers.

Four storeys below, in a concrete room, a third man watched a panel of dark squares built into the wall. He heard the whistle from the open telephone that lay within arm's reach on the steel table beside him.

Suddenly a bell shattered the stillness of the enclosure. A red light in the centre of the panel shone brightly.

The man pushed the square beneath the bright red light.

Silence.

A uniformed guard burst through the corridor door, his eyes wild.

564

"We're testing," said the man in front of the panel, calmly replacing the telephone. "I told you that."

"*Christ!*" exploded the guard, inhaling deeply. "You night-crawlers will give me a heart attack."

"Don't let us do that," said the man, smiling.

Varak watched Salter open the door of the closet beyond the flags and switch on the light inside. Both telephones were back in their cradles; there would be one more call. From Varak to Bravo.

Not Genesis. Genesis was dead.

The man was Bravo now. He would be told the job was done.

Several feet in front of the row of flags were two webbed metal baskets on wheels. They were a familiar sight in the bureau's hallways, through which scores like them moved mountains of paper from one office to another. In a few minutes they would be filled with hundreds, perhaps several thousand, dossiers and taken downstairs past a senior agent named Parke to a waiting limousine. The files of John Edgar Hoover would be consigned to a blast furnace.

And a growing Fourth Reich would be crippled.

"Varak! *Quick!*"

The shout came from the closet beyond the flags. Varak raced inside.

The steel safe was open, the locks on the cabinets sprung. The four drawers were pulled out.

The two drawers on the left were thick with papers, bulging. Files *A* to *L* were intact.

The two drawers on the right were empty. The metal dividers fell against each other, holding nothing.

Files *M* to *Z* were missing. One half of Hoover's cabinets of filth was gone.

4

Chancellor lay in the hot sun and read the *Los Angeles Times*. The headlines seemed almost unreal, as if the event were not really possible, rooted somehow in fantasy.

The man at last was dead. J. Edgar Hoover had died insignificantly in his bed, the way millions of old men die. Without drama, without consequence. Just the failure of the heart to keep pace with the years. But with that death a relief swept over the country; it was apparent even in the newspaper copy reporting the death.

The statements issued by Congress and the administration were, as could be expected, sanctimonious and dripping with obsequious praise, but even in these well-chosen words the tears of the crocodiles could be clearly seen. The relief was everywhere.

Chancellor folded the paper and shoved it into the sand to anchor it. He did not want to read any more.

Far more to the point, he did not want to write, either. Oh, Christ! When would he want to? Would he ever want to? If there were such a thing as a sybaritic vegetable, he would be it.

What made it ironic was that he was getting rich. Joshua Harris had called from New York a half-hour ago to report that another payment had been made by the studio on schedule.

Peter was making a great deal of money by doing absolutely nothing. Since the episode with Sheffield's wife he had not bothered to go to the studio or call anyone concerned with *Counterstrike!*

Not to worry. You wrote a winner, sweetheart.

So be it.

He raised his wrist and looked at his watch. It was almost eight-thirty, the morning at Malibu had come quickly. The air was moist, the sun too bright, the sand already too hot. Slowly he got to his feet. He'd go inside and sit in an air-conditioned room and have a drink.

Why not? What was the old phrase? *I never drink before five in the afternoon. Thank God, it's five o'clock somewhere!*

Was it past five – in the morning – back East? No, he always got that mixed up; it was the other way around. Back East it was barely eleven-thirty.

The sky was overcast, the air heavy and oppressive. A steady, humid drizzle threatened to become a downpour. The crowds in the Capitol Plaza were quiet; muted chants of war resisters behind barricades intruded on the hum of the throngs, threatening, as the drizzle threatened, to grow louder as the rain grew louder.

Here and there an umbrella snapped; ribbed circles of black cloth sprung open, stretching over passive faces. Eyes were dull, resentful; expressions lifeless. The day was angry. There was an undercurrent of fear, the final legacy, perhaps, of the man whose body was being transported in the enormous hearse that was twenty-five minutes late arriving. Suddenly it was there, efficiently swinging off the tree-lined drive on to the concrete grounds of the plaza.

Stefan Varak noted that the crowds seemed to move back, although none had been in the hearse's path. Further proof of the legacy, he thought.

Ranks of servicemen stood at attention at either side of the rotunda steps; uniforms were darkened with rain, eyes stared straight ahead. It was eleven twenty-five. The body of John Edgar Hoover was to lie in state throughout the day and night. It was an honour accorded to no civil servant before in the nation's history.

Or was it a desire on the nation's part to prove to itself and to the world that he was really dead – this man who had sprung giantlike out of the morass of corruption that had been the original Bureau of Investigation to fashion an efficient, extraordinary organization, only to disintegrate with the passing years, still believing in his own infallibility. If he had only stopped before the fever gripped him, thought Varak.

Eight servicemen had solemnly broken away from the ranks and were at the rear door of the hearse, four on either side. The heavy panel swung back; the flag-wrapped coffin slid out, dipping slightly as fingers gripped protruding steel handles and pulled it free of the vehicle. In a tortuously slow march the soldiers moved towards the steps through the thickening drizzle.

They began the agonizing climb up the thirty-five steps to the entrance of the rotunda. Lifeless eyes were focused forward, at nothing; faces were drenched with sweat and rain; veins close to bursting could be seen below the cuffs of the uniforms; collars were black from the rivulets of perspiration that rolled down straining necks.

The crowds seemed to suspend their collective breathing until the casket reached the top of the steps. The soldiers paused at attention; then they started again and carried their burden through the great bronze doors of the rotunda.

Varak turned to the cameraman at his side. Both stood on a small, raised platform. The metal initials below the thick lens of the camera were those of a television station in Seattle, Washington. The station was part of a West Coast pool; it had no personnel in the Capitol Plaza that morning.

"Are you getting everything?" asked Varak in French.

"Every group, every row, every face the zoom can reach," replied the Frenchman.

"Will the dim light – the rain – be a problem?"

"Not with this film. Nothing faster."

"Good. I'm going upstairs."

Varak, his NSA photo-identification prominent on his lapel, threaded his way through the crowds to an entrance and walked past the guards to the security desk. He spoke to the uniformed man on duty.

"Is the staircase from Documents sealed off yet?"

"I don't know, sir." The guard's eyes riveted on the page of instructions in front of him. "There's nothing here about closing it."

"Goddamn it, there should be," said Varak. "Make a note of it, please."

Varak walked away. There was no vital reason for that particular staircase to be closed, but by so ordering it, Varak had established his authority with the guard. If their communications equipment broke down, he would need access to a telephone, without seconds wasted for identification purposes. Those precious moments would not be lost now; the guard would remember.

He climbed the staircase, two steps at a time, and stood behind the crowd filling the House entrance to the rotunda. A perspiring congressman was trying to make his way through; he was drunk and twice stumbled. A younger man, obviously an aide, reached him, grabbed his left elbow, and pulled him back out of the crowd. The congressman pivoted unsteadily and his shoulders slammed into the wall.

As Varak looked at the bewildered, sweating face, he remembered that the congressman had publicly accused the FBI of tapping his phone; he had embarrassed the director. Then abruptly the accusations had stopped. Suddenly, the evidence that had been promised did not materialize, the man had no more to say.

His is one of the missing files, Varak guessed as he walked down the corridor to a door. He nodded to the guard, who scrutinized the NSA identification and opened the door for him. Inside were the twisting, narrow steps that led to the dome of the rotunda.

Three minutes later Varak knelt beside a second cameraman 160 feet above the rotunda floor. They were on the upper walk, closed for years to tourists. The quiet hum of the camera was barely heard; it was packed with triple insulation, the telescopic lens screwed in and locked with reinforced clamps. There was no way that camera or the man operating it could be seen from the floor. Several feet away were three cartons of film.

Below on the rotunda floor, the bearers had placed the coffin on the catafalque. Beyond the ropes, crowded in with little dignity, were the leaders of the nation competing for solemn recognition. The guard of honour took up its positions, each branch of the military represented. From somewhere far away in the great hall a telephone rang twice. Instinctively Varak reached into his pocket and pulled out the small radio unit that was his link to others. He held it to his ear, flipped on the switch, and listened. There was nothing and he breathed again.

A voice floated up; Edward Elson, the Senate chaplain and minister of the Presbyterian Church, delivered the opening prayer. He was followed by Warren Burger, who began his eulogy. Varak heard the words; the muscles of his jaw tensed.

" . . . a man of quiet courage, who would not sacrifice principle to public clamour . . . who served his country and earned the admiration of all who believed in ordered liberty."

Whose principles? What is ordered liberty? mused Varak as he watched the scene far below. There was no time for such thoughts. He whispered to the cameraman; the language he spoke was Czech. "Is everything all right?"

"Yes, if I don't get cramps."

"Stretch out every now and then, but don't get up. I'll relieve you for thirty minutes every four hours. Use the room off the second walk; I'll bring food."

"Through the night as well?"

"It's what you're being paid for. I want every face that walks through those bronze doors. Every goddamned face."

Beyond the echoing, bass-toned words that filled the dome he could hear another sound. Far in the distance, outside, behind barricades in the rain across the plaza, the war resisters had begun their own particular chant for the dead. Not for the body in the rotunda, but for thousands halfway across the world. A liturgical drama was being played out in bitter ecclesiastical irony.

"Every face," repeated Varak.

The spray of the fountain cascaded down into the waters of the circular pool in the gardens in front of the Presbyterian Church. Beyond the fountain the white marble tower rose in constricted splendour. To the right was the double-laned drive that passed under a stone portico, with doors on the left that led into the church. The effect was one of tollbooths, not a protected entrance into the house of God.

Varak had his cameras positioned, the two exhausted operators filled with coffee and Benzedrine. In a few hours it would all be over. Both would be far richer than they had been a few days ago; both would be flying home. One to Prague, one to Marseilles.

The limousines started arriving at nine forty-five: the funeral service was scheduled for eleven. The Czech was outside. The Frenchman was the one now cramped; he was on his knees – not in supplication – in a raised doorway to the far left of the altar. He and his camera were concealed by heavy drapes; the official-looking identification pinned to his breast pocket was stamped with the seal of the Department of Archives.

No one questioned it; no one knew what it meant.

The mourners left their cars and filed inside; the cameras were rolling. The sombre tones of the organ filled the church. An army chorus of twenty-five men in gold-ribbed black tunics marched like sleepwalkers into the chancel.

The service began. Unending words, delivered by those who loved and those who hated. Prayer and psalm, selection and recital. Somehow cold, too controlled, thought Varak. Not that he cared; the cameras were rolling.

And then he heard the familiar, sanctimonious voice of the President of the United States, its peculiar cadence fashioned to the occasion. A breathless, hollow echo.

"The trend of permissiveness, a *trend* which has *dangerously* eroded our national heritage as law-abiding people, is now being *reversed*. American people today are *tired* of a *disrespect* for law. America wants to come *back* to the *law* as a way of life . . ."

Varak turned and walked out of the church.

There were better things to do. He crossed over the manicured lawn, past a row of spring flowers to a flagstone path that led to the fountain. He sat on the ledge, feeling the spray on his face. He pulled a road map from his pocket and studied it.

Their last stop was the Congressional Cemetery. They would arrive before the cortège and set up their cameras out of sight. They would photograph the final moments when the body of J. Edgar Hoover was consigned to the ground, his remains interred beneath the earth.

But not his presence. His presence would be felt for as long as the files were missing.

Files *M* to *Z*. Estimated number: 3,000. Three thousand dossiers that could shape the government, alter the laws and attitudes of the country.

Who had them? Who *was it*?

Whoever it was was recorded on film. It had to be so; there was no other conclusion. No stranger to Washington could have broken through the complex security and stolen them.

Somewhere in the tens of thousands of feet they had taken was a face. And a name that went with the face. He would find that face and that name, thought Varak angrily. He had to.

To fail was unthinkable.

5

The film rolled through the machine, projecting images on the wall. Magnified faces appeared one after another. Varak rubbed his eyes in weariness; he'd seen the film perhaps fifty times in the past three months.

M to *Z.* Fourteen letters. More than likely it was a face with a name that began with one of those letters. The man who had stolen the files would not have overlooked the possibility that his dossier was among them. But which man? The mathematical possibilities seemed infinite, compounded by the realization that code names were not ruled out. A man with a name that began with a *K* or a *G* – Kleindienst or a Grey – could be known to the bureau as "Nelson' or "Stark". In point of fact, "Nelson' and "Stark" *were* Kleindienst and Grey.

The cellar of the Georgetown house had been converted into a studio with an adjacent office and sitting room. The films, the photographs, the cartons of paper – personnel and medical records, government dossiers, interviews, telephone and credit-card charges – it was all overwhelming. And there could be no staff to sort out and correlate. Only one man could have access to the materials. Any more than one squared, then cubed, the possibilities of discovery.

It could *not* have begun with a stranger! In the beginning there had to be a friend, a close friend, an associate. It did not make sense otherwise; there were too many barriers for a stranger to surmount. No stranger could trigger the releases: no stranger could throw unseen switches and abort alarms in restricted rooms guarded day and night.

But which friends? Which associates? Thirteen weeks of going through an accumulation of voluminous records, dossiers, motion-picture film, and photographs led him nowhere. Every unusual face, *M* to *Z*, every abnormal scrap of information in a dossier or an interview or a credit check had been cause for an exhaustive examination of the subject. And all had led nowhere.

Varak walked into the small, windowless office. It seemed that he never saw the sun any more, or smelled fresh air. He looked over at the corkboard on the wall; the desk lamp was angled up at a photographic enlargement of Hoover's Last Will and Testament.

The sum total of the estate was written in the upper right-hand corner in the wide strokes of a felt-tipped marker. It was $551,500.

Included were the real estate on Thirtieth Street Place, bank accounts, stocks, bonds, and Civil Service benefits in the amount of $326,500. A family house in Georgetown had an estimated value of $100,000, and there was $125,000 worth of oil, gas and mineral leases in Texas and Louisiana. Total: $551,500.

The chief beneficiary was his friend of nearly fifty years and second in command at the bureau, Clyde Tolson. Nearly everything was left to him; upon *his* death the estate was to be divided between the boys' clubs and the Damon Runyon Fund. A blank wall.

Minor bequests of $2,000, $3,000, and $5,000 were assigned respectively to his chauffeur, James Crawford; his housekeeper, Annie Fields; and the redoubtable Helen Gandy, his secretary. Three people who had spent their lives in his service were dismissed with penny candy. It said something unattractive, but still it was another blank wall.

And there were those who were not mentioned at all, eight survivors of the "close-knit" Hoover family. Four nieces and four nephews, including one nephew who had spent ten years in the bureau. Most had come to the graveside.

None was mentioned in Hoover's will. Another blank wall behind which might be a room filled with rage and condemnation, but certainly it held no files.

So much for the Last Will and Testament of John Edgar Hoover, giant and myth. So much for everything else!

Damn!

Varak moved to the sitting room. Sitting room, bedroom, dining room, *cell*. Actually, Bravo had provided him with more than he needed. Bravo had also given him specific instructions in the event of the diplomat dying. Inver Brass was to be protected at all costs.

Strange, he never thought of Bravo as Munro St Claire. He never thought of any of them by their rightful names. Bravo was simply Bravo.

His telephone rang; the outside line.

"Mr Varak?" It was Bravo.

"Yes, sir?"

"I'm afraid it's begun. I'm in town. Stay where you are. I'll be there as soon as I can."

St Claire settled back in the leather armchair and took several deep breaths. It was his way of approaching a crisis: in calm.

"Within the past twenty-four hours there have been two astonishing resignations," he said. "Lieutenant General Bruce MacAndrew at the Pentagon, and Paul Bromley at GSA. Do you know either of them?"

"Yes. MacAndrew. I don't know Bromley."

"What's your opinion of the general?"

"I'm high on him. He expresses opinions often at odds with a lot of people over there."

"Exactly. He's a moderating influence and yet very respected. But suddenly, just when he's at the top of his career, he chucks it all away."

"What makes you think his resignation has anything to do with the files?"

"Because Bromley's did. I've just come from seeing him. Paul Bromley's a sixty-five-year-old bureaucrat with the General Services Administration. He takes his job seriously."

"I do know him," interrupted Varak. "Or at least *of* him. A year or so ago he testified before a Senate hearing on cost overruns. He criticized the C-40 payments."

"For which he was soundly rebuked. He was reduced to auditing congressional cafeterias, or some such equally vital statistic. But the powers of the GSA made a mistake a month ago. They filed an unsatisfactory-service report that precluded a grade raise. Bromley sued them. He based the suit on his C-40 testimony . . . That's finished now. His resignation's effective immediately."

"Did he tell you why?"

"Yes. He received a telephone call." Bravo paused. He closed his eyes. "Bromley has a daughter. She's in her early thirties, married, lives outside Milwaukee. It's her second marriage, and apparently it's a good one. Her first was something else. She was still in her teens, her husband barely twenty. They were both into drugs, living in the streets. She sold herself to pay for narcotics. Bromley didn't see his daughter for nearly three years. Until a man came to his house one day and said she'd been arrested for the murder of her husband."

Varak did not have to be told the rest. A plea of temporary insanity had been entered by the girl's lawyer. It was followed by several years of rehabilitation and psychiatric care. There was a felony record, complete with the ugly details. Bromley's wife took their daughter to her parents' home in Wisconsin. Some sort of normality returned. The girl got her head back, met and married an engineer who worked for a concern in the Midwest, and started having babies.

Now, ten years later, a telephone call meant the past could surface. Loudly, publicly. It would not only destroy the daughter but stigmatize a family. Unless Paul Bromley dropped his lawsuit and resigned from the General Services Administration.

Varak leaned forward in the couch. "Does the current husband know?"

"In substance, yes; perhaps not every detail. Of course, he's not the only issue. They'd have to move, start over again. But it would be futile. They'd be found."

"Naturally," agreed Varak. "Did Bromley describe the voice on the telephone?"

"Yes. It was a whisper – "

"For effect," interjected Varak quietly. "It never fails."

"Or for disguise. He couldn't tell whether it was a man's voice or a woman's."

"I see. Was there anything unusual in the speech pattern?"

"No. Bromley looked for that. He's an accountant; the unusual attracts him. He said the oddest thing was the mechanical quality."

"Could the voice have been recorded? A tape?"

"No. It responded to his statements. They could not have been anticipated."

Varak sat back. "Why did he come to you?"

Bravo paused. When he spoke, there was a sadness in his voice, as if for some abstract reason he were holding himself responsible. "After Bromley's C-40 testimony, I wanted to meet him. This middle-level bureaucrat who was willing to take on the Pentagon. I asked him to dinner."

"Here?"

"No, of course not. We met at a country inn in Maryland." Bravo stopped.

"You still haven't told me why he got in touch with you."

"Because I told him to. I never thought for a minute he'd get away with interfering with the Pentagon. I told him to contact me if there were reprisals."

"Why are you convinced whoever called Bromley has the Hoover files? His daughter's problems are a matter of court record."

"Something the voice said. He told Bromley that he had all the 'raw meat' there was to have on him and his family. Do you know the significance of 'raw meat'?"

"Yes," replied Varak, his contempt apparent. "It was one of Hoover's favourite expressions. Still, there's an inconsistency. Bromley's name begins with B."

"Bromley explained that, although of course I didn't tell him about the files. At both the Pentagon and the bureau he had a code name: Viper."

"As though he were an enemy agent."

"Exactly."

"What about MacAndrew? Do we have anything?"

"I think so. We've been interested in him for a number of years. He was one of the few soldiers who believed utterly in the civilian control of the military. Frankly, one day he might have been a candidate for Inver Brass. We studied him; it was before you arrived. There was a lapse in his service record. The symbols indicated that the period in question – eight months in 1950 – has been removed to G-Two, PSA."

"Psychiatric Systems Analyses," said Varak. "On his level that's usually reserved for defectors."

"Yes. We were stunned, naturally. We traced the G-Two abstract and found that it, too, had been removed. All that remained was the phrase 'Courier Delivered, FBI DS'. Domestic Security. I'm sure you can guess the rest."

"Yes," said Varak. "You got his FBI file, and there was nothing there. You cross-checked with Domestic Security. Still nothing. 'Raw meat'."

"Precisely. Every paper, every insert, every addendum related to Security crossed Hoover's desk. And as we know, 'Security' took on the widest possible range. Sexual activities, drinking habits, marriages and family confidences, the most personal details of the subjects' lives – none were too remote or insignificant. Hoover pored over those dossiers like Croesus over his gold. Three Presidents wanted to replace him. None did."

Varak leaned forward. "The question is, what was in MacAndrew's service record? There's nothing to prevent us from asking him now."

"*Us?*"

"It can be arranged."

"Through an intermediary?"

"Yes. A blind. There'll be no connection."

"I'm sure of that," said Bravo. "But then what? Assuming you find some character flaw, sexual or otherwise, what have you got? MacAndrew wouldn't still have his maximum clearance if it were a permanent condition."

"It's more information. Somewhere the data will pinpoint the weakness in the chain. It'll break."

"That's what you've been counting on, isn't it?"

"Yes. It'll happen. Whoever stole the files has a first-rate mind, but it will happen."

Both men fell silent, Varak waiting for approval, Bravo deep in thought.

"That chain won't be broken easily," St Claire said. "You're the best there is, and you're no closer now than you were three months ago. You say a 'first-rate mind', but we don't know that. We don't know if we're dealing with a mind or minds. One man or many."

"If it's one," agreed Varak, "we're not even sure it's a man."

"But whoever it is the first moves have been made."

"Then, let me put someone on MacAndrew."

'Wait . . .' Bravo clasped his hands beneath his chin. "An intermediary? A blind?"

"Yes. Untraceable."

"Bear with me for a moment. I haven't really thought it out; you can help. Basically, it's your strategy."

Varak glanced at St Claire. The diplomat continued. "Am I correct in assuming that a blind, as you use the term with respect to interrogation or surveillance, is someone who finds out what you have to know without your being involved?"

"That's right. The blind has his or her own reasons for wanting the same information. The trick is to get it from him without his knowing what you're doing."

"The blind, then, is chosen with extreme care." It was a statement.

"More often than not, it's a question of finding someone with the same interests," answered Varak. "It can be difficult."

"But we could enlist the aid of an investigatory agency. I mean, it's within our capability to alert the authorities – or even a newspaper – to the possibility that Hoover's files survived his death."

"Certainly. The result would be to drive whoever has them further under-ground."

Bravo rose from the chair and paced aimlessly. "There's been almost no mention of those files in the newspapers. It's odd, because their existence was known. It's as though no one wants to talk about them."

"Out of print, out of mind, out of danger," said Varak.

"Yes, exactly. All Washington. Even the media. No one knows whether he's part of the files or not. So there's silence. And when men are silent, the triumph of evil follows. Burke was right about that. We can see it happening."

"On the other hand," countered the intelligence man, "breaking the silence isn't always the answer."

"That depends on who breaks it." Bravo stopped his pacing. "Tell me, under the harshest, most professional microscope could any of those involved in Hoover's death be unearthed?"

"None," was the firm reply.

"Where are they? I mean, specifically."

"Both telephone men are in Australia. The Kimberly bush; they'll never come back. They face indictments for homicide in the Marine Corps. The man who used the cover of 'Salter' is in Tel Aviv; nothing takes precedence over the Holy

Land or the holy war. We feed him data on the Palestinian terrorists. He lives only for his cause, and we make it practical. The actress is in Majorca; she settled a debt and wants nothing more than what she's got. The Englishman who handled the car and the Phase One relay is back with MI6. He made money from the Russians as a double courier in East Berlin; he knows I have the facts that could lead to his execution. You know about the doctor in Paris, the least of our concerns. Each had a motive, none can be traced. They're thousands of miles away."

St Claire stared at Varak. "You left out someone. What about the man in the alarm room? The one who used the cover of 'Krepps'?"

Varak returned Bravo's look. "I killed him. The decision was mine, and I'd make it again."

St Claire nodded. "Then, what you're saying is that all personnel, all the *facts*, are submerged beyond discovery. Hoover's death could never be attributed to anything but natural causes."

"Precisely. Natural causes."

"So, if we used a blind, there would be no chance of that man discovering the truth. Hoover's assassination is beyond reach."

"Beyond reach."

Bravo began to pace again. "I've never asked you why there was no autopsy."

"Orders from the White House. Relayed very quietly, I understand."

"The White House?"

"They had a reason. I gave it to them."

St Claire did not probe; he knew Varak had studied the White House structure and could surmise his strategy, which would be totally professional. "Beyond reach," repeated Bravo. "That's vitally important."

"To whom?"

"To a blind not restricted by fact. To a man interested only in a concept. A theory that did not have to be proven at every turn. Such a man could raise alarms, quite possibly provoke whoever had the files into revealing themselves."

"I don't follow you. Without traceable facts there's no motive for a blind. What could he hope to learn? What could we learn?"

"Perhaps a great deal. The key word is *fact*." St Claire stared at the wall above Varak. It was strange, he reflected. He had not thought of Peter Chancellor in a long time. When he had thought of him – when he'd seen his name in a newspaper or a book supplement – it had always been with a bemused memory of a bewildered graduate student grappling for words six years ago. Chancellor had found the words since. A great many of them.

"I'm afraid I don't understand you," said Varak.

Bravo lowered his gaze. "Have you ever heard of a writer named Peter Chancellor?"

"*Counterstrike!*" said Varak. "I read it. It frightened a lot of people over at Langley."

"Still, it was fiction."

"It was too close. This Chancellor used a lot of wrong terms and incorrect procedures but on the bottom line, he described what happened."

"Because he wasn't restricted by fact. Chancellor approaches a concept, finds a basic situation, and extracts *selected* facts and rearranges them to suit the reality as he perceives it. He is not bound by cause and effect; he *creates* it. You say he frightened a lot of people over in Langley. I believe that; he has a wide readership. And he researches in depth. Suppose it was known that he was researching a book on Hoover, on his last days."

"On the *files*," added Varak, sitting forward. "Use Chancellor as the blind. Tell him the files disappeared. When he starts probing, he'll set off alarms, and we'll be there."

"Go to New York, Mr Varak. Find out everything you can about him. The people around him, his life-style, his methods of work. Everything current. Chancellor has a conspiracy complex. We're going to program him with a conspiracy he'll find irresistible."

6

"Mr Peter Chancellor?" asked the operator.

Peter lifted his hand above the covers and tried to focus on his wristwatch. It was nearly ten o'clock; the morning breezes were billowing the curtains through the open doors of the porch.

"Yes?"

"Long distance from New York. Mr Anthony Morgan calling. One moment, please."

"Sure." There was a click and a hum on the line. It stopped.

"Hi, Mr Chancellor?"

Peter would know that voice anywhere. It belonged to his editor's secretary. If she ever had a discouraging day, no one ever knew about it. "Hello, Radie? How are you?" Chancellor hoped she was better than he was.

"Fine. How's California these days?"

"Bright, humid, shiny, green. Take your choice." The girl laughed. It was a pleasant laugh. "We didn't wake you, did we? You're always up so early."

"No, Radie, I was in the surf," lied Chancellor for no reason.

"Hold on. Here's Mr Morgan." There were two clicks.

"Hello, Peter?"

"How are you, Tony?"

"Christ, forget about me, how are *you*? Marie said you called last night. Sorry, I wasn't home."

Chancellor remembered. "I apologize. I was drunk."

"She didn't mention that, but she said you were mad as hell."

"I was. I am. I was also drunk. Apologize to Marie for me."

"No need to. What you told her made her angry, too. I was greeted at the door with a lecture about protecting my authors. Now, what's this about *Counterstrike!?*"

Peter adjusted his head on the pillow and cleared his throat. He tried to rid his voice of bitterness. "At four-thirty yesterday afternoon a studio messenger brought me the completed first draft of the screenplay. I didn't know we'd started."

"And?"

"It's been turned around. It's the opposite of what I wrote."

Morgan paused, then replied gently. "Wounded ego, Peter?"

"Good God, no. You know better than that. I didn't say it was badly written; a lot of it's pretty damned good. It's effective. I'd feel better if it wasn't. But it's a lie."

"Josh told me they were changing the agency's name – "

"They've changed everything!" interrupted Chancellor, his eyes blinking in pain with the rush of blood to his head. "The government people are all on the side of the angels. They don't have an impure thought in their heads! The manipulators are . . . 'them'. Weird exponents of violence and revolution and – so help me God – with 'faintly European accents'. Whatever the book said has been turned inside out. Why the hell did they buy it in the first place?"

"What does Josh say?"

"As I remember, and I do vaguely, I reached him around midnight my time. I guess it was about three this morning in New York."

"Stay around the house. I'll speak to Josh. One of us'll get back to you."

"All right." Peter was about to offer a last apology to Morgan's wife when he realized the editor was not finished. It was one of those silences between them that meant there was more to say.

"Peter?"

"Yes?"

"Suppose Josh can work things out. I mean with your studio contract."

"There's nothing to work out," interrupted Chancellor again. "They don't need me; they don't want me."

"They may want your name. They're paying for it."

"They can't have it. Not the way they're doing the film. I'm telling you, it's the opposite of what I said."

"Is it that important to you?"

"As literature – hell, no. As my own personal statement – hell, yes. Nobody else seems to be making it."

"I just wondered. I thought you might be ready to start the Nuremberg book."

Peter stared at the ceiling. "Not yet, Tony. Soon, not yet. I'll talk to you later."

He hung up the phone, the apology gone from his mind. He was thinking about Morgan's question and his own answer.

If only the pain would disappear. And the numbness. Both had lessened, but they were still there, and when he felt either or both, the memories returned. The shattering glass, the blinding light, the crunching metal. The screams. And his hatred of a man high up in a truck who had disappeared in the storm. Leaving one dead, one almost dead.

Chancellor swung his legs over the edge of the bed on to the floor. He stood up naked and looked around for his bathing suit. He was late for his morning swim; the dawn had turned into day. He felt guilty somehow, as if he had broken an important ritual. Worse, he understood that the ritual took the place of work.

He saw his bathing suit draped over a chair and started towards it. The telephone rang again. He reversed direction and answered it.

"It's Joshua, Peter. I've just spent an hour talking with Aaron Sheffield."

"He's a winner. Incidentally, sorry about last night."

"This morning," corrected the agent, not unkindly. "Don't worry about it. You were overwrought."

"I was drunk."

"That, too. Let's get to Sheffield."

"I suppose we have to. I gather you got the drift of what I told you last night."

"I'm sure most of Malibu Beach could repeat the better phrases word for word."

"What's his position? I won't budge."

"Legally that doesn't make any difference to him. You have no case. You have no script approval."

"I understand that. But I can talk. I can give interviews. I can demand that my name be removed. I might even try to get the courts to change the title. I'll bet a case can be made for that."

"It's unlikely."

"Josh, they've changed the whole meaning!"

"The courts might see the money you've been paid and not be impressed."

Chancellor blinked again and rubbed his eyes. He exhaled wearily. "I think you're saying they wouldn't be impressed. Period. I'm not Solzhenitsyn with the Siberian camps or Dickens on the death of children in the sweatshops. All right, what can I do?"

"Do you want it put plainly?"

"When you begin like that, the news isn't good."

"Some good can come out of it."

"Now I know it's terrible. Go ahead."

"Sheffield wants to avoid discord; so does the studio. They don't want you giving those interviews or going on talk shows. They know you can do that, and they don't want the embarrassment."

"I see. We reach the heart of the matter: gross receipts at the box office. Their essential pride, their manhood."

Harris was silent for a moment. When he continued, it was in a soft voice. "Peter, that kind of controversy wouldn't affect gross receipts one iota of a percentage point. If anything, it would hype them."

"Then, why are they concerned?"

"They really want to avoid embarrassment."

"They live in a perpetual state of embarrassment out here. They can't even recognize it. I don't believe that."

"They're willing to pay your contract in full, remove your name from the screen credits if you wish – not the title of course – and deliver a bonus equal to fifty per cent of the book purchase."

"*Jesus* . . ." Chancellor was stunned. The figure Joshua Harris alluded to was in the range of a quarter-million dollars. "For what?"

"For you to walk away and not make waves over the adaptation."

Peter stared at the billowing curtains in front of the glass doors. There was something very inconsistent, terribly wrong.

"Are you still there?" asked Harris.

"Wait a minute. You say controversy could only help the receipts. Yet Sheffield's willing to pay all that money to avoid controversy. He's got to lose. It doesn't make sense."

"I'm not his analyst. I just heard the money. Maybe he wants to keep his balls intact."

"No. I know Sheffield, believe me. I know the way he operates. His balls are expendable." Suddenly, Chancellor understood. "Sheffield has a partner, Josh. And it's not the studio. It's the government. It's Washington! They're the ones who don't want the controversy. To quote from a far better writer than I'll ever be, they 'can't stand the light of day'! Goddamn it, that's it."

"It crossed my mind," admitted Harris.

"You tell Sheffield to shove his bonus. I'm not interested!"

Again the agent paused. "I may as well tell you the rest. Sheffield's collected statements from all over Los Angeles and points north and south. The picture isn't pleasant. You're described as a wild alcoholic and something of a menace."

"Good for Sheffield! Controversy hypes the gross receipts. We'll sell twice as many books!"

"He says he has more," continued Harris. "He claims he has sworn affidavits from women who accuse you of rape and physical abuse. He has photographs – police photographs – that show the damage you've inflicted. One's a kid from Beverly Hills who's fourteen years old. He has friends who'll swear they removed narcotics from you when you passed out in their homes. He says you even attacked his wife, which is something he'd rather not make public but will if he has to. He says they've been cleaning up after you for weeks."

"They're lies! Josh, that's crazy! There's no truth in any of that!"

"That may be the problem. There're probably a few grains of truth. I don't mean the rape or the abuse or the narcotics: that stuff's easily manufactured. But you've been drinking, you haven't returned calls, there've been women. And I know Sheffield's wife. I don't rule her out, but I'm sure you weren't the cause of it."

Chancellor lurched from the bed. His head was spinning, the pain in his temples throbbed. "I don't know what to say! I don't believe this!"

"I know what to say; I know what to believe," said Joshua Harris. "They're not playing by any rules I've ever heard of."

Varak leaned forward in the velvet sofa and opened his briefcase on the coffee table. He withdrew two file folders, placed them in front of him, and moved the case to one side. The morning sun was streaming through the windows overlooking Central Park South, filling the elegant hotel suite with shafts of yellowish white light.

Across the room Munro St Claire had poured himself a cup of coffee from a carafe on a silver tray. He sat opposite the intelligence man.

"Are you sure I can't get you a cup?" asked Bravo.

"No, thanks. I've gone through several pots this morning. Incidentally, I appreciate your flying up. It saves time."

"Every day is vital," replied St Claire. "Every hour those files are missing is an hour we can't afford. What have you got?"

"Just about everything we need. My primary sources were Chancellor's editor, Anthony Morgan, and his literary agent, a man named Joshua Harris."

"They co-operated so easily?"

"It wasn't difficult. I convinced them it was standard procedure for a minimum-security clearance."

Varak separated a page in the left file folder. "Before his accident Chancellor had the Government Printing Office send him the transcripts from the Nuremberg tribunals. He's writing a novel on the trials. He thinks Nuremberg was rife with judicial conspiracies. That thousands of Nazis went unaccountable, free to emigrate all over the world, transferring huge sums of money wherever they went."

"He's wrong. It was the exception, not the rule by any means," said Bravo.

"Regardless, some of those transcripts still have a security classification. He didn't get those, but he doesn't know that. I implied that he did, and my job was simply a routine follow-up. Nothing serious. Also, I said that I was a fan of Chancellor's. I enjoyed talking to people who knew him."

"Has he written this Nuremberg book?"

"He hasn't even started it."

"I wonder why."

Varak scanned another page as he spoke. "Chancellor was nearly killed in a road accident last autumn. The woman with him was killed. According to the medical records another ten minutes of internal bleeding and pathogenic toxemia, he would have died. He was in the hospital for five months. He's been patched up; eighty-five to ninety per cent recovery is anticipated. That's the physical part." Varak paused and turned a page.

"Who was the woman?" asked Bravo quietly.

Varak shifted his attention to the folder on his right. "Her name was Catherine Lowell; they'd been living together for nearly a year and planned to get married. They were on their way to meet his parents in northwest Pennsylvania. Her death was a terrible shock to Chancellor. He went into a long period of depression. It's still with him to some degree, according to both his editor and his agent."

"Morgan and Harris," added Bravo for his own clarification.

"Yes. They sweated out his recovery; first the physical injuries, then the depression. Both men admitted that during the past months there were times they thought he was finished as a writer."

"A reasonable assumption. He hasn't written anything."

"He's supposed to be now. He's in California co-authoring the screenplay of *Counterstrike!*, although nobody expects him to do very much. He has no experience in films."

"Then, why was he hired?"

"The value of his name, according to Harris. And the fact that the studio could have an advantage over others for his next book. Actually, that's the way Harris engineered the contract."

"Which means he wanted Chancellor involved. Since he wasn't working on anything. In Harris's opinion, his house in Pennsylvania and his memories were holding Chancellor back. It's why he wanted him in California." Varak turned several pages. "Here it is. Harris's words. He wanted his client to 'experience the perfectly normal Gargantuan excesses of a temporary Malibu resident'."

Bravo smiled. "Are they having a positive effect?"

"There's progress. Not much, but some." Varak looked up from the paper. "That's something we can't allow."

"What do you mean?"

"Chancellor will be infinitely more valuable to us in a weakened psychological condition." The intelligence man gestured at both folders. "The rest of this describes a fairly normal man before the accident. Whatever hostilities or excesses he had were transferred to his writing. He didn't display them in his life-style. If he returns to that normality, he'll be naturally cautious, he'll retreat when we don't want him to. I want to keep him off-balance, in a state of anxiety."

St Claire sipped his coffee without comment. "Go on, please. Describe this life-style."

"There's not much, really. He has an apartment on East Seventy-first Street. He gets up early, usually before dawn, and works. He doesn't use a typewriter; he writes on yellow pads, Xeroxes the pages, and uses a typing service in Greenwich Village." Varak again looked up. "That could be an advantage to us in his research. We can intercept the originals and make our own copies."

"Suppose he works in Pennsylvania and has them driven in. Delivered by messenger."

"Then, we'll get inside the Village offices."

"Of course. Go on."

"There's very little left that's important. He has favourite restaurants where he's known. He skis, plays tennis – neither of which he may be able to do again. His friends, apart from Morgan and Harris, are generally found among other writers and newspapermen and, oddly enough, several lawyers in New York and Washington. That's about it." Varak closed the folder on his right. "Now, I'd like to bring up something."

"Yes?"

"Along the lines we've discussed, I think I know how to program Chancellor, but I need a back-up. I'll use the Longworth cover; it's unbreakable. Longworth is in Hawaii and stays in hiding. We look enough alike – even to the duplication of the scar. His FBI record can be traced. Still, we should have one more piece of bait Chancellor can't walk away from."

"Please clarify."

Varak paused, then said with conviction: "We have a crime but no conspiracy. None we can identify. He's got to follow his own speculations. We have none to give him. If we had, we wouldn't be using him in the first place."

"What are you proposing?" asked St Claire, seeing the hesitation in Varak's eyes.

"I want to bring in a second member of Inver Brass. In my opinion the only other man with your public stature. You call him Venice. Judge Daniel Sutherland. I want to be able to send Chancellor to him."

The diplomat was silent for several moments. "To lend weight to what you tell Chancellor? The irresistible confirmation?"

"Yes. To substantiate our story of the missing files. That's all I need. Sutherland's voice will be the bait Chancellor *has* to take."

"It's dangerous," said Bravo quietly. "No member of Inver Brass should ever be overt in any strategy."

"Time requires it. I ruled you out because of your previous relationship with Chancellor."

"I understand. The coincidence would raise questions. I'll talk with Venice . . . Now, if you please, I want to return to something you said. Chancellor's psychological condition. If I understood you correctly – "

"You did," interrupted Varak quietly. "Chancellor cannot be allowed to recover. He can't be permitted to function at his previous rational level. He's got to draw attention to himself, to his research. If he remains volatile, he becomes a threat. If that threat is dangerous enough, whoever has those files will be compelled to eliminate it. When he does – or they do – we'll be there."

Bravo sat forward, his expression one of sudden concern. "I think that goes beyond the parameters we established."

"I wasn't aware we'd established any."

"They were intrinsic. There are limits to our use of Peter Chancellor. They don't include putting his life in jeopardy."

"I submit it's a logical extension of the strategy. Quite plainly put, the strategy may be useless without that factor. I think we'd willingly exchange Chancellor's life for those files. Don't you?"

St Claire said nothing.

7

Chancellor stood by the doors overlooking the beach and parted the curtains again. The blond-haired man was still there. He'd been there for over an hour, walking back and forth in the hot afternoon sun, his shoes sinking into the warm sand, his shirt open at the collar, his jacket slung over his shoulder.

He was pacing up and down the short area of the beach fifty yards away, between the redwood porch and the water, every now and then glancing up at Peter's house. He was medium-sized, perhaps a shade under six feet, and muscular. His shoulders were broad and thick and stretched the cloth of his shirt.

Chancellor had first seen him around noon. He had stood motionless in the sand, staring up at the redwood porch; staring, Peter was sure, at him.

The sight of the man was no longer merely disconcerting, it was irritating. The first thought that came to Chancellor was that Aaron Sheffield had decided to put a watchdog on him. A great deal more had been offered under circumstances that raised disturbing questions.

Peter did not like watchdogs. Not this kind. He pulled back the curtains, slid open the door, and stepped out on the porch. The man stopped his pacing and again stood motionless in the sand.

They looked at each other and Peter's doubts vanished. The man was there for him, waiting for him. Peter's irritation turned into anger. He walked to the steps and down on to the beach. The man remained where he was, making no move towards him.

Goddamn you, thought Chancellor. There were very few people on this private area of Malibu; but if any were watching, the sight of the limping figure in slacks, naked above the waist, approaching a fully clothed man standing immobile in front of a beach house must have seemed odd. It was odd; the blond-haired stranger had a curious quality about him. He was pleasant-looking, the face clean-cut, even gentle in appearance. Yet there was something menacing about him. As he drew nearer, Chancellor realized what it was: the man's eyes were aware. They were not the eyes of a subordinate watchdog hired by an anxious studio executive.

"It's warm out here," began Peter bluntly. "I can't help asking myself why you're walking around in the heat. Especially since you keep looking up at my house."

"At your rented house, Mr Chancellor."

"Then, I think you'd better explain," replied Peter, "since you know my name and, obviously, the conditions of my lease. It wouldn't be because those who hired you are paying the rent?"

"No."

"Score one for me. I didn't think so. Now, you've got a choice. Either you satisfy my curiosity, or I call the police."

"I want you to do more than that. You have sources in Washington. I want you to call one of them and check out my name in the personnel records of the Federal Bureau of Investigation."

"The *what*!" Peter was stunned. The man's words were spoken quietly, yet there was an undercurrent of urgency.

"I'm retired," added the man quickly. "I'm not here in any official capacity. But my name's in the bureau's personnel records. Check it out."

Chancellor stared at the man, apprehensive. "Why would I do that?"

"I've read your books."

"That's you, not me. It's no reason."

"I think it is. It's why I went to a lot of trouble to find you." The man hesitated, as if unsure of how to continue.

"Go on."

"In each of your books you show that certain events may not have happened the way people think they did. An event took place less than a year ago that falls into that category."

"What was it?"

"A man died. A very powerful man. They said he died of natural causes. He didn't. He was assassinated."

Peter stared at the stranger. "Go to the police."

"I can't. If you check me out, you'll understand."

"I'm a novelist. I write fiction. Why come to me?"

"I told you. I've read your books. I think that maybe the only way the story can be told is in a book. The kind you write."

"Novels." Peter was not asking a question.

"Yes."

"Fiction." Again it was a statement.

"Yes."

"But you say it isn't fiction. It's fact; you imply it's fact."

"That's what I believe. I'm not sure I can prove it."

"And you can't go to the police."

"No."

"Go to a newspaper. Find an investigative reporter. There are dozens of good ones."

"No newspaper would handle this. Take my word for it."

"Why the hell should I?"

"You might after you checked me out. My name is Alan Longworth. For twenty years I was a special agent for the FBI. I retired five months ago. My field office was in San Diego . . . and points north. I live now in Hawaii. On the island of Maui."

"Longworth? Alan Longworth? Should the name mean anything to me?"

"That's not remotely possible. Check me out. It's all I ask."

"Suppose I do. Then what?"

"I'll come by tomorrow morning. If you want to talk further, fine. If not I'll leave." Again the blond-haired man hesitated, the urgency now in his eyes as he spoke softly. "I've travelled a long way to find you. I've taken risks I shouldn't have taken. I may have broken an agreement that could cost me my life. So I've got one more thing to ask you. I want your word on it."

"Or else what?"

"Don't check on me. Don't do anything; forget I came out here, forget we spoke."

"But you did come out here. We have spoken. It's a little late for conditions."

Longworth paused. "Haven't you ever been frightened?" he asked. "No, I don't imagine you have. Not this way. Strange, but you write about fear; you seem to understand it."

"You don't look like you frighten easily."

584

"I don't think I do. My record at the bureau might even confirm that."

"What's this condition?"

"Ask about me. Find out everything you can, say anything you want. But please don't say we met; don't repeat what I've told you."

"That's crazy. What am I supposed to say?"

"I'm sure you can think of something. You're a writer."

"That doesn't necessarily mean I'm a good liar."

"You travel a lot. You could say you heard about me in Hawaii. *Please.*"

Peter shifted his feet in the hot sand. Common sense told him to walk away from this man; there was something unhealthy about the controlled, intense face and the too-alert eyes. But his instincts would not permit his common sense its right of decision. "Who's this man who died? The one you say was assassinated."

"I won't tell you that now. I will tomorrow if you want to talk further."

"Why not now?"

"You're a well-known writer. I'm sure a lot of people come up and tell you things that sound insane. You probably dismiss them quickly, as you should. I don't want you to dismiss me. I want you convinced that I have a certain reasonable stature of my own."

Peter listened. Longworth's words made sense. During the past three years – since *Reichstag!* – people had pulled him over into corners at cocktail parties or slid into chairs across from him at restaurants to impart weird information they *knew* was right up his alley. The world was filled with conspiracies. And would-be conspirators.

"Fair enough," said Chancellor. "Your name is Alan Longworth. You spent twenty years as a special agent; you retired five months ago, and you live in Hawaii."

"Maui."

"That would be listed in your file."

At the mention of the word *file*, Longworth drew back. "Yes, it would be. In my file."

"But then anyone might be able to learn the contents of a specific file. Give me something to identify you."

"I wondered if you'd ask."

"In my books I try to be convincing; it's just step-by-step logic, with no spaces. You want me to be convinced, so fill the space."

Longworth shifted his jacket from his right shoulder to his left, and with his right hand he undid the buttons of his shirt. He pulled his shirt open. Across his chest, descending below the belt, was an ugly, curving scar. "I don't think any of your blemishes can match this."

Peter reacted to the words with a brief rush of anger. There was no point pursuing the statement. If Longworth was who he said he was, he had taken the time to gather his facts together. Undoubtedly, they included a great deal about the life of Peter Chancellor.

"What time will you be round in the morning?"

"What time's convenient?"

"I get up early."

"I'll be here early."

"Eight o'clock."

"See you at eight." Longworth turned and began walking down the beach.

Peter stood where he was and watched him, aware that the pain in his leg had disappeared. It had been there all day, but it was gone now. He would call Joshua Harris in New York. It was around four-thirty in the East; there was still time. There was a lawyer in Washington, a mutual friend, who could get the information on Alan Longworth. Josh once jokingly said that the attorney should demand royalties for *Counterstrike!*, so helpful had he been in Chancellor's research.

As Peter climbed up the porch steps, he found himself hurrying. It was a strangely gratifying sensation, and he could not really account for it.

An event took place less than a year ago . . . A man died. A very powerful man. They said he died of natural causes. He didn't. He was assassinated . . .

Peter rushed across the porch towards the glass doors and the telephone inside.

The morning sky was angry. Dark clouds hung over the ocean; the rain would come soon. Chancellor was dressed for it, had been dressed for over an hour; he wore a nylon jacket above his khaki trousers. It was seven forty-five – ten forty-five in New York. Joshua had promised to call by seven-thirty – ten-thirty back East. What was the delay? Longworth would be there by eight.

Peter poured himself another cup of coffee, his fifth of the morning.

The telephone rang.

"You picked a strange one, Peter," said Harris in New York.

"Why do you say that?"

"According to our friend in Washington, this Alan Longworth did what no one expected him to do. He retired at the wrong time."

"Did he have his twenty years?"

"Just barely."

"That's enough for a pension, isn't it?"

"Sure. If you supplement it with another salary. He hasn't, but that's not the point."

"What is?"

"Longworth had an exceptional record. Most important, he was singled out by Hoover himself for high-echelon advancement. Hoover personally attached a handwritten favourable recommendation to his file. You'd think he'd want to stay on."

"On the other hand, with that kind of record he could probably get a hell of a job on the outside. A lot of FBI men do. Maybe he's working for someone, and the bureau doesn't know it."

"Not likely. They keep extensive files on retired agents. And if he was, why does he live on Maui? There's not much activity there. At any rate, there's no listing of a current employer. He doesn't do anything."

Peter stared out the window; a light rain began to fall from the dark sky. "Do the other items check out?"

"Yes," answered Harris. "His field office was San Diego. Apparently, he was Hoover's personal liaison with La Jolla."

"La Jolla? What does that mean?"

"It was Hoover's favourite retreat. Longworth was in charge of all communications."

"What about the scar?"

"It's listed under identifying marks, but there's no explanation, and that's where we come to the strangest part of his file. His last medical records are missing, the last two annual check-ups. It's very unusual."

"It's very incomplete," mused Peter out loud. "The whole thing."

"Exactly," agreed Joshua.

"When did he retire?"

"Last May. On the second."

Chancellor paused, struck by the date. Over the past several years, dates had come to have special meanings for him. He had trained himself to look for consistencies and inconsistencies where dates were concerned. What was it now? Why did the date bother him?

Through the kitchen windows he saw the figure of Alan Longworth walking across the beach in the rain towards the house. For some reason the sight triggered another image. Of himself. On the sand in bright sunlight. And a newspaper.

The second of May. J. Edgar Hoover had died on the second of May.

A man died. A very powerful man. They said he died of natural causes. He didn't. He was assassinated.

"Jesus Christ," said Peter quietly into the telephone.

They walked along the beach by the water through the drizzle. Longworth would not talk inside the house, nor within any enclosure that might contain electronic surveillance. He was too experienced for that.

"Did you check me out?" asked the blond-haired man.

"You knew I would," said Peter. "I just got off the phone."

"Are you satisfied?"

"That you are who you say you are, yes. That you had a good record, your abilities personally recognized by Hoover himself, and that you retired five months ago – yes to all that, too."

"I didn't mention any personal endorsements from Hoover."

"They're there."

"Of course they are. I worked directly for him."

"You were based in San Diego, as you said. You were his liaison to – or with – La Jolla."

Longworth smiled grimly, with no humour. "I spent more time in Washington than I ever spent in San Diego. Or La Jolla. You won't find that in my bureau record."

"Why not?"

"Because the director didn't want it known."

"Again, why not?"

"I told you. I worked for him. Personally."

"In what way?"

"With his files. His private files. I was a messenger. La Jolla meant a lot more than a name of a village of the Pacific coast."

"That's too cryptic for me."

The blond man stopped. "That's the way it's going to remain. Anything more you find out will have to come from someone else."

"Now you're arrogant. What makes you think I'll look'?"

"Because you can't understand why I retired. Nobody could; it didn't make sense. I have a minimum pension with no additional income. Had I remained with the bureau, I might have become an assistant, even an associate, director."

Longworth started walking again. Peter kept pace, no pain whatsoever in his leg. "All right, why did you retire? Why don't you have a job?"

"The truth is that I didn't retire. I was transferred to another government post and given certain guarantees. My employer of record – a record you'll never find in any file – is the State Department. Foreign Service, Pacific Operations. Six thousand miles from Washington. If I had stayed in Washington, I would have been killed."

"All right, hold it!" Chancellor stopped. "I've got a damned good idea what you're leading up to, and I'm getting sick of the bullshit. You're implying that J. Edgar Hoover was murdered. He's the 'powerful man' you meant."

"You pieced it together, then," said the agent.

"It's a pretty logical conclusion, and I don't believe it for a minute. It's ridiculous."

"I didn't say I could prove it."

"I would hope not. It's preposterous. He was an old man with a history of heart trouble."

"Maybe. Maybe not. I never knew anyone who ever saw his medical records. The originals were sent directly to him, and no copies were allowed. He had ways of enforcing those demands. No autopsy was permitted on his body."

"He was over seventy." Peter shook his head in disgust. "You've got one hell of an imagination."

"Isn't that what novels are all about? Don't you start with a concept? An idea?"

"Granted. But the kind I write have got to be at least credible. There's got to be some basic reality, or the appearance of it."

"If by reality you mean facts, there are several."

"Name them."

"The first is myself. Last March I was approached by a group of people who wouldn't be identified but who were influential enough to move the highest, most classified, wheels at the State Department and effect a transfer that Hoover would never have permitted. Even I don't know how they did it. They were concerned with certain information Hoover had compiled. Dossiers on several thousand subjects."

"These were the same people who gave you the guarantees? For those services rendered you won't elaborate on?"

"Yes. I think – I can't be sure – but I think I know the identity of one of

588

them. I'm willing to give it to you." Longworth stopped; he was, again, as he had been yesterday, uncertain. The urgency returned to his eyes.

"Go ahead," said Chancellor impatiently.

"I have your word that you'll never use my name with him?"

"Goddamn it, yes. To be honest with you, I have an idea we'll say good-bye in a few minutes and I won't even *think* of you."

"Have you ever heard of Daniel Sutherland?"

Peter's expression conveyed his astonishment. Daniel Sutherland was a giant, both figuratively and literally. A huge Black man whose extraordinary accomplishments matched his enormous size. A man who had crawled his way out of the squalor of the Alabama fields a half-century ago, and climbed to the highest circles of the nation's judicial system. He had twice refused presidential appointments to the Supreme Court, preferring the more active bench. "The judge?"

"Yes."

"Of course. Who hasn't? Why do you think he was one of the group who made contact with you?"

"I saw his name on a State Department tracer about me. I wasn't supposed to see it, but I did. Go to him. Ask him if there was a group of men concerned about the last two years of Hoover's life."

The request was irresistible. The stories about Sutherland were legend. Peter now took Alan Longworth far more seriously than he had only seconds ago.

"I may do that. What are the other facts?"

"There's only one that really counts. The rest are minor compared to it. Except perhaps for one other man. A general named MacAndrew. General Bruce MacAndrew."

"Who's he?"

"Until recently, a man very high at the Pentagon. He had everything going for him; Chairman of the Joint Chiefs was probably his for a nod of the head. Suddenly, without any apparent reason he threw it all away. Uniform, career, Joint Chiefs, everything."

"Not unlike you in a way," ventured Chancellor. "On a somewhat grander scale, perhaps."

"Very unlike me," replied Longworth. "I have information about MacAndrew. Let's say it goes back to those services rendered. Something happened to him twenty-one, twenty-two years ago. No one apparently knows what – or if they do, they're not saying – but it was serious enough to have been removed from his service record. Eight months in 1950 or '51, that's all I remember. It could be tied in with that one single overriding fact – your basic fact, Chancellor – and that scares the hell out of me."

"What is it?"

"Hoover's private files. MacAndrew could be part of them. Over three thousand dossiers, a cross-section of the country. Government, industry, the universities, the military; from the most powerful to those lower down. You may hear otherwise, but I'm telling you the truth. Those files are missing, Chancellor. Since Hoover's death they've never been found. Someone's got them, and now that someone's using them."

Peter stared at Longworth. "Hoover's files? That's insane."

"Think about it. That's my theory. Whoever has those files killed Hoover to get them. You've checked me out; I've given you two names to reach. I don't care what you say to MacAndrew, but you've given your word not to mention me to the judge. And I don't want anything from you. I just want you to think about it, that's all. Think about the possibilities."

Without indicating he had finished, without a nod or a gesture, Longworth turned and, as he had the day before, walked away across the beach. Stunned, Peter stood in the light rain and watched as the retired FBI man broke into a run towards the road.

8

Chancellor stood at the bar in the restaurant on East Fifty-sixth Street. It strove to be an uprooted English chophouse, and Peter liked it. The atmosphere was conducive to long lunches given to volubility.

He had phoned Tony Morgan and Joshua Harris and had asked them to meet him there. Then he'd taken the late afternoon flight out to Los Angeles. For the first time in months he slept in his own apartment – how sane it felt. He should have come back much sooner. His false Californian sanctuary had become a very real prison.

It was happening. Something inside his head had snapped, a barricade had been shattered, freeing stored-up energy. He had no idea whether anything Longworth told him made any sense at all. No, it was too preposterous! The fact of assassination was in and of itself beyond reason. But the premise was fascinating. And every story began with a premise. The possibilities were as provocative as anything he had approached. Would an extraordinary man named Sutherland concede there was even a remote chance Hoover had been killed? Could a long-missing insert in a military record of a general named MacAndrew be tied in with the concept?

A momentary flash of light shot through the windows that fronted the street, drawing his eyes to the outside. Then he smiled as he saw the figures of Anthony Morgan and Joshua Harris walking together towards the entrance. The two men were arguing, but only those who knew them well would have understood that. To the casual observer they were two people talking quietly, oblivious of their surroundings and, conceivably, each other.

Tony Morgan was the physical embodiment of the Ivy League postgraduate turned New York publisher. He was slender and tall with shoulders slightly stooped from too many years of courteously feigning interest in the opinions of lesser mortals; his face was thin, the features clean, the brown eyes always a little distant but never vacant. Single-breasted charcoal suits and English-style tweed jackets above inevitable grey flannel trousers were his uniforms. He and Brooks Brothers had gone together for most of his forty-one years, and neither saw any reason to change.

But clothes and appearances did not capture the mercurial essence of Anthony Morgan. That was found in his explosions of enthusiasm and his infectious proselytizing of a manuscript-in-progress or the discovery of an exciting new talent. Morgan was the complete publisher and an editor of rare perception.

And if Morgan the man was somehow sprung from within the cloistered walls of academic New England, Joshua Harris seemed to float through the centuries from some elegant royal court of the 1700s. Generous of girth, Harris's posture was erect, his bearing imperial. His large body moved gracefully, each step taken with deliberateness as if he were part of a baronial procession. He too was in his early forties, the years further disguised by a black chin beard that lent a slightly sinister quality to an otherwise pleasant face.

Peter knew there were scores of editors and agents in New York of equal, perhaps more than equal, stature, and he realized that neither Morgan nor Harris was universally loved. He'd heard the criticisms: Tony's arrogance and often misplaced enthusiasms, Josh's relish for uncomfortable confrontations based frequently on unfounded charges of abuse. But the detractions did not matter to Chancellor. For him these men were the best. Because they cared.

Peter signed his bar bill and made his way to the foyer. Josh walked through the front door held by Tony, who, quite naturally, allowed an intervening couple to enter in front of him. The greetings were too loud, too casual. Peter saw the concern in both men's eyes; each looked at him as though studying a disoriented brother.

The table was the usual table. In the corner, slightly separated from the others. The drinks were the usual drinks, and Chancellor was both amused and irritated to see Josh and Tony watch him closely when the whisky arrived.

"Call off the alert. I promise not to dance on the table."

"Really, Peter . . ." began Morgan.

"Come on, now . . ." completed Harris.

They cared. That was the important thing. And the moment passed, the recognition of the unspoken accepted. There was business to be discussed; Chancellor began.

"I met a man; don't ask me who, I won't tell you. Let's say I met him on the beach, and he told me the outlines of a story that I don't for a minute believe, but I think it could be the basis for one hell of a book."

"Before you go on," interrupted Harris, "did you make any agreement with him?"

"He doesn't want anything. I gave my word I'd never identify him." Peter stopped, his eyes on Joshua Harris. The literary agent had made the enquiries; he had placed the call to Washington. "As a matter of fact, you're the only one who could. By name. But you can't. I'll hold you to it."

"Go on," said Joshua Harris.

"Several years ago a few men in Washington became alarmed over what they considered a very dangerous situation. Maybe more than dangerous, maybe catastrophic. J. Edgar Hoover had compiled a couple of thousand dossiers on the most influential people in the country. In the House, the Senate, the Pentagon, the White House. Presidential and congressional advisers, leading authorities in a dozen different fields. The older Hoover got, the more concerned they became. Stories began to leak out of the bureau that Hoover was actually *using* those files to intimidate those who opposed him."

"Wait a minute, Peter," broke in Morgan. "That story – and variations of it – has been around for years. What's the point?"

Chancellor levelled his eyes on Morgan. "I'll jump. Hoover died four months ago, and no autopsy was permitted. And those files were missing."

There was silence at the table. Morgan leaned forward, revolving his glass slowly, the ice cubes circling in the whisky. "That's quite a jump. Hoover was damned near eighty years old; he had a heart condition."

"Who says those files are missing?" asked Harris. "They could have been destroyed, shredded. Or buried."

"Of course, they could," agreed Peter.

"But you're implying that someone killed Hoover for them," said Morgan.

"I'm not implying, I'm stating it. As a fictional premise, not as fact. I didn't say I believed it, but I think I could make it believable."

Again there was silence. Morgan looked at Harris, and then at Peter. "It's a sensational idea," he said cautiously. "A powerful hypothesis. Perhaps too powerful, too current. You'd have to build a solid foundation, and I don't know if that's possible."

"This man on the beach," said Joshua. "This man neither of us will identify. Does he believe it?"

Chancellor stared at his drink. He realized that when he answered Harris, his voice was as tentative as his judgement. "I don't really know. I have an idea – and it's just an idea – that he thinks the killing was on a drawing board somewhere. That was enough for him. Enough for him to give me two sources to check out."

"Connected with Hoover?" asked Morgan.

"No, he didn't go so far as to claim that. He said it "was only speculation. One name's related to that group in Washington who were nervous about the files, and Hoover's use of them. The other's pretty far-fetched. It concerns lost information over twenty years old."

Morgan held Peter's attention. "They could be your foundation."

"Sure. But if there's any truth at all about that group, I'd have to fictionalize completely. He's that kind of man. The other I don't know anything about."

"Do you want to tell us who they are?" asked Joshua.

"Not yet. I just want your reaction to the idea. To a novel about Hoover's assassination. Killed by people who knew of those files and wanted them for their own purposes."

"It's sensational," repeated Morgan.

"It's going to cost you," said Harris, looking at the editor.

9

Congressman Walter Rawlins of the Roanoke Rawlinses, dynasty without substance, political manipulators of the Commonwealth of Virginia, sat in the library of his suburban Arlington home. It was past midnight; the single source of light was a brass stirrup lamp on the desk beneath enlarged photographs of various Rawlinses astride various horses in various stages of the hunt.

He was alone in the house. His wife had gone to Roanoke for the weekend, and it was the maid's day off, which meant night out; the black bitch couldn't wait for Thursday night to hustle her black ass. Rawlins grinned and raised a glass to his lips, taking several deep swallows of sour mash. It was goddamned sweet nigger ass, and he would have told her to stay except that he didn't trust the other bitch in the house. His wife had *said* she was taking the Cessna to Roanoke, but she could just as easily tell the pilot to turn around and head back to the field in McLean. His goddamned bitch wife could right now be down the street in a car, waiting for just the right moment to walk back into the house.

She'd love to catch him humping away on the nigger.

Rawlins blinked. Then he focused his eyes towards the desk, at the telephone on the desk. The goddamned thing was ringing. It was his office line, the private Washington tie. Goddamn!

The phone kept ringing. It would not stop. Goddamn! He hated to talk on the telephone after he had a little juice in him. He lurched out of the chair, holding on to his glass, and walked unsteadily to the desk.

"Yes? What is it?"

"Good evening."

The voice on the telephone was a whisper, high-pitched and flat. He couldn't tell whether it was a man or a woman.

"Who the hell is this? How did you get this number?"

"Neither question is relevant. What I'm about to say to you is, however."

"You're gonna say nuthin' to me. I don't talk to – "

"*Newport News*, Rawlins!" The whispered voice spat out the words. "I wouldn't hang up if I were you."

Rawlins froze. He stared through the haze at the telephone in his hand. Slowly he brought it up to his ear, his breath suspended. "Who are you? What do you mean? Newport . . ." His voiced trailed off; he could not finish the name.

"Three years ago, Congressman. I'm sure if you think very hard, you'll remember. The Newport News coroner estimated the death to be twelve-thirty in the morning. Just about now as a matter of fact. The date was 22 March."

"Who the hell are you?" Rawlins felt sick to his stomach.

"I told you it's not important. No more important than that little black girl in Newport News. How old was she, Congressman? Fourteen? Was that it? It was grotesque, wasn't it? They said she was cut up, beaten rather badly."

"I don't know what you're talkin' about! It's got nuthin' to do with me!"

Rawlins brought the glass swiftly to his mouth and drank. Most of the sour mash rolled down his chin. "I wasn't anywheres *near* – "

"Newport News?" interrupted the high-pitched whisper. "On the night of 22 March 1969? I think you were. As a matter of fact, I have in front of me a detailed flight plan of a Cessna aircraft flying in and out of a private field ten miles north of Newport News. There's a description of the passenger: bloodstained clothes, drunk. Shall I read it to you?"

Rawlins dropped the glass. It shattered on the floor. "You . . . *stop* . . . *it!*"

There's nothing to worry about. You see, you're chairing a committee in the House that interests me. It's just that I don't approve of your opposition to the bill H.R. Three-seven-five. You're going to change that position, Rawlins. You're going to throw your full support behind that bill. . ."

Phyllis Maxwell walked past the front desk in the Hay-Adams towards the Lafayette Room. There was the usual luncheon crowd waiting to be seated; it did not concern her. The Lafayette captain would spot her and usher her past the others to her table. She was fifteen minutes late; that was good. Her lunch date would be nervous, worried, wondering if she had forgotten; that was very good. He would be on the defensive.

She stopped by a full-length mirror, pleased with what she saw. Rather not bad, she thought. Not bad at all for a once plain, overweight girl named Paula Mingus from Chillicothe, Ohio, who was a good forty-seven. She was . . . well, elegant was the appropriate word. She was slender, the legs tapered, the breasts firm, the neck long – almost Grecian, really – nicely accentuated by the pearl choker. And it was a good face. Again the word *elegant* was quite applicable. Her eyes, of course, were striking; everyone remarked on them. Speckled, curious, the eyes of an experienced newspaperwoman. She used her eyes well, boring into whomever she interviewed, carrying the message: *I don't believe you for a second. You'll have to do better than that.*

She had pried a lot of truth from a lot of liars with her eyes. More than once she'd stunned Washington with a confirmed story many knew existed but never thought to see in print. She had forced confirmations, often by remaining silent, letting her eyes do the work.

Of course, there were times when the eyes did more than doubt; they often promised. But she did not fool herself. Forty-seven was not twenty-seven, elegant or no. As the years went by, there were far more probes than promises. For a number of reasons.

Phyllis Maxwell was the name, not Paula Mingus of the Chillicothe Minguses; the first editor who let her have a byline had changed that a quarter century before. And she was good; she took her job seriously. She went after the hard news.

Like today. There was something rotten, deeply rotten, in the ongoing election campaign. Money was being gathered in staggering sums from reluctant contributors. Threats undefined and assurances impossible to guarantee were being used as weapons.

"Miss Maxwell! So good of you to join us." It was the Lafayette captain.

"Thank you, Jacques."

"Right this way, Miss Maxwell. Your party is here." He was. A cherub-faced, bland-looking young man with scrubbed skin and eager eyes sprang to obsequious attention at the booth. Another clean-cut liar; they were everywhere. *Stroke her.* Phyllis could hear the instructions.

"Sorry I'm late," she said.

"Who's late? I just got here." He smiled.

"Then, you were late, weren't you." It was a statement, accepted with a clumsy smile. "Never mind, Paul. Have a drink. You need one, and I won't snitch."

He did. Three. And he barely touched his eggs Benedict. Instead, he could not bear the waiting. "I'm telling you, Phyl, you're barking up the wrong tree! You don't want to saw yourself off the limb!"

"You're mixing your metaphors. You people do that a lot, Paul. Usually when you've got something to hide."

"We've got nothing to hide."

"Then let's get to business," she interrupted. Small talk irritated her; plunging in was one of her most effective techniques. "My information is as follows: two airlines seeking new routes were told – not very subtly – that the CAB might look unfavourably, et cetera, et cetera, unless sizeable contributions, et cetera. A major road transport firm was reached by the Teamsters. Contribute heavily or face a possible strike. The largest pharmaceutical company in the East was threatened with an investigative inquiry from the FDA two days after it was solicited. They paid up. There'll be no inquiry. Four banks. Four *leading* banks, Paul. Two in New York, one in Detroit, one in Los Angeles – all seeking mergers – were told their petitions might be tied up for years unless they reached sympathetic people. Contributions were made; favourable responses were received. Now, this is all documented. I've got names, dates, and figures. I intend to blow a very shrill whistle unless you've got answers that isolate – and I mean *isolate* – these eight examples from the rest of the campaign. You're not going to buy this or any other election. My God, you damn fools! You don't have to!"

The cherub paled. "You've got it all wrong! The radical posture expressed by the opposition would tear this nation apart. Weaken its very foundations, its fundamental liberties – "

"Oh, stop it, you ass!"

"Miss Maxwell?" It was Jacques. A telephone was in his hand. "A call for you. Shall I connect it?"

"Please."

The captain inserted plug into socket. He bowed and left.

"This is Phyllis Maxwell."

"I'm sorry to disturb your lunch."

"I beg your pardon. I can't hear you."

"I'll try to speak more clearly."

"Who is this?" The voice on the telephone was a whisper. Eerily flat and in an upper register. "Is this a joke?"

"Most emphatically not, Miss Mingus."

"Maxwell's my byline. The fact that you know my given name doesn't shock me. It's on my passport."

"Yes, I know," came the oddly horrible, whispered reply. "I've seen it registered at Immigration on the island of Saint Vincent. In the Grenadines, *Miss Mingus*."

The blood drained from Phyllis Maxwell's face, a terrible pain shot through her head. Her hand trembled. She thought she was going to be sick.

"Are you still there?" asked the horrible whisper.

"Who are you?" She could barely speak.

"Someone you can trust. Be assured of that."

Oh, *God!* The island! How was it possible? Who could *care* that much? What filthy mentality would take the trouble? . . . In defence of righteousness! But the righteous were wrong. It was freedom. From furtiveness and suspicion. Whom did they hurt?

Every year, for three weeks only, Phyllis Maxwell left Washington ostensibly for total seclusion at a retreat in Caracas. But Paula Mingus did not stay in Caracas; she – and others – flew to the Grenadines to *their* island. And there they were themselves. Women who found the fullest expressions of love. With other women.

Paula Mingus was a lesbian. Phyllis Maxwell – in the interests of professionalism and at great, *great* cost to her well-being – did not acknowledge that word.

"You're obscene," she whispered to the terrible whisper.

"Most people would apply that word to you. You'd become your own dirty joke, your career destroyed. If the undeniable story were released."

"What do you want?"

"You must assure that very sincere young man with you that you will no longer pursue the topics you've obviously discussed by now. You will publish nothing."

Phyllis Maxwell replaced the telephone. Tears welled in her speckled, professional eyes. She was barely audible as she spoke.

"Is there nothing you won't do?"

"Phyl, I swear to you – "

"Oh, God! Steal the country!"

She got up and ran out of the restaurant.

Carroll Quinlan O'Brien, known as Quinn to his colleagues at the bureau, walked into his office and sat down behind his desk. It was nearly eight o'clock, the night force was well into its shift, which meant half the offices were empty.

But sixty-four per cent of all violent crimes took place between the hours of seven-thirty P.M. and six A.M., reflected O'Brien, and the country's major law-enforcement instrument was half-staffed during that time.

It was not a valid criticism. The bureau wasn't a field agency, it was a fact-finding house; and data was most obtainable when the rest of the country was awake. No, it was not a valid point to make, although vast reorganization was taking place; that's what everyone said.

They might start with Hoover's ridiculous term *Seat of Government*. S.O.G. It was just as definitive to say FBI and far less pretentious.

There was so much that was antediluvian, thought O'Brien. Confused organization charts. Contradictory and overlapping areas of assignment; strength where it was unnecessary, weakness where strength was mandatory. Dress codes, parameters of behaviour – social, sexual, and meditative. Punishments meted out for inconsequential misbehaviour, valid reprimands avoided by flattery and obsequiousness. Fear, fear, *fear*. It had run the bureau for as long as Quinn had been in Washington.

For four years he had kept his mouth shut. He and a few others who honestly believed they brought a touch of sanity to the upper levels of the Federal Bureau of Investigation. They were also in a position to keep their eyes open for the truly irregular, the conceivably dangerous. And let others know when they *had* to know.

He himself had funnelled information to the intelligence community on a fairly regular basis when the director's fury over real or imagined insults prohibited liaison. He was reminded of the practice as his eyes fell on the small silver shamrock that hung on a chain around his pen set. It was a gift from Stefan Varak over at NSA. He had first met Varak two years before, when Hoover had refused to deliver profile data on Eastern-bloc UN personnel. The National Security Council needed that information. O'Brien had simply walked into Section I, made copies, and given them to Varak during their first dinner together. There'd been a great many dinners since. He had learned a lot from Varak.

Now Hoover was dead, and things were going to change. That's what everyone said. Quinn would believe it when he saw the directives. Then, perhaps, the decision of four years ago would make sense.

He had never fooled himself or his wife. His appointment to the FBI was a political cosmetic. He had been an assistant prosecutor in Sacramento when he'd been swept into the Vietnam War because of his reserve-officer status. He had not been assigned to legal work; he had been put into G2 for reasons vaguely related to criminal prosecution. A forty-plus-old lawyer suddenly transformed into an investigator for Army Intelligence. That was in 1964. Finally, unexpected combat in the northern sectors, capture, two years of survival under the most primitive conditions, and escape.

He had escaped in January 1968 and had made his way through the torrential rains southwest across enemy lines, into UN territory. He had lost fifty pounds; his body was ravaged. And he had returned a hero.

It was a time when heroes were sought. They were needed desperately. Discontent had spread, myths were decaying. The FBI was not exempt, and Quinn's investigatory talents were noted; Hoover was impressed with heroes. So an offer had been made. And the hero had accepted.

His reasoning had been simple. If he could start fairly high up the ladder and learn fast and well, there would be other fine opportunities within the Justice Department. Far more than in Sacramento. Now he was a forty-nine-year-old ex-hero who had learned very well indeed and had kept his mouth shut. He had learned *very* well, and that was what bothered him now.

Something was wrong. Something had not happened that should have happened. A vitally important element of Hoover's dictatorial reign had neither been revealed nor explained.

J. Edgar Hoover had had in his personal possession hundreds – perhaps thousands – of highly inflammatory dossiers. Files that contained devastating information about many of the nation's most influential and powerful men and women.

Since Hoover's death, however, nothing had been said about those files. There were neither demands to acknowledge their existence nor outcries for their destruction. It was as if no one wanted to be associated with bringing them to light. The fear of inclusion was too great; if nothing were said, perhaps they would fade into oblivion.

But that was not realistic; those files had to be somewhere. So Quinn had begun asking questions. He had started with the shredding rooms. Nothing had come down from Hoover's office for months. He had checked the microfilm and microdot laboratories. There had been no reductions of dossiers made within memory. Then he'd scrutinized the entry ledgers – anything related directly to Hoover in the areas of authorized deliveries or pick-ups. Nothing.

He'd found his first clue in the security logs. It was a late entry, authorized by scrambler, on the night of 1 May, the night before Hoover's death. It had stunned him. Three field agents – Salter, Krepps and a man named Longworth – had been admitted at eleven fifty-seven, but there had been no departmental clearance. Just authorization by way of the director's private scrambler. From Hoover's *home*.

It had not made sense. Quinn had then contacted the senior agent who had admitted the trio, Lester Parke. It hadn't been easy. Parke had retired a month after Hoover's death, drawing a minimum pension, but with enough money to buy a fair-sized condominium in Fort Lauderdale. That hadn't made a hell of a lot of sense either.

Parke had clarified nothing. The senior agent had told Quinn that he had spoken with Hoover himself that night. Hoover, himself, had given specific and confidential instructions to admit the field agents. Anything else would have to come from them.

So Quinn had tried to find three field agents named Salter, Krepps and Longworth. But "Salter' and "Krepps' were floating covers, names with biographies used by various agents at various times for clandestine operations. There was *no* record of the names having been assigned during the month of May; or if there was a record, Quinn was not cleared for it.

The information on Longworth had come in a little over an hour ago. It was so startling that Quinn had called his wife, telling her he would not be home for dinner.

Longworth had retired from the bureau two months before Hoover's death! He was now living in the Hawaiian Islands. Since this was the confirmed information, what was Longworth doing in Washington, at the west entry desk, on the night of 1 May?

O'Brien knew he had found serious, unexplained discrepancies in official logs,

598

and he was convinced they were related to the files no one talked about. Tomorrow morning he would go to the attorney general.

His telephone rang, startling him. He reached for it. "O'Brien," he said, conveying his surprise; his telephone rarely rang after five in the evening.

"*Han Chow!*" The whisper seared over the line. "Remember the dead of Han Chow."

Carroll Quinlan O'Brien lost his breath. His eyes had gone blind; darkness and white light replaced familiar images. "What? Who's this?"

"They begged you. Do you remember how they begged you?"

"*No!* I don't know what you're talking about! Who is this?"

"Of course you know," continued the cold whisper. "The Cong commander threatened reprisals – executions – if anyone at Han Chow escaped. Very few were capable of trying. They agreed not to for the sake of the others. But not you, Major O'Brien. Not you."

"That's a lie! There were no agreements! None!"

"You know perfectly well there were. And you disregarded them. There were nine men in your compound. You were the healthiest. You told them you were going, and they begged you not to. The next morning, when you were gone, they were taken out in the fields and shot."

Oh, Christ! Oh, Holy Mary, Mother of God! It wasn't the way it was meant to be! They could hear the artillery through the rain in the distance. They'd never get another chance like that! So close! All he had to do was get through to the guns! To the American guns! Once he got through, he would pinpoint the Han Chow compound on the map, and it could be taken. The men – the dying men – would be freed! But the rain and the sickness and the night played horrible tricks on him. He never found the guns. And the men died.

"Are you remembering?" The whisper was soft now. "Eight men executed so the major could have a parade in Sacramento. Did you know Han Chow was taken less than two weeks later?"

Don't, O'Brien! Don't do it! If they're this close, Charlie will run and leave us! They won't move us. We'd slow them down! They won't kill us either! Unless you give them an excuse. Don't give it to them! Not now! That's an order, Major!

The words had been spoken in the darkness by a half-starved lieutenant colonel, the only other officer in the hut.

"You don't understand," he said into the telephone. "You've twisted everything. It's not the way it was!"

"Yes it is, Major," countered the whisper slowly. "A paper was found on a dead Viet Cong months later. On it was written the last testimony of a lieutenant colonel who knew what faced the prisoners of Han Chow. Eight men were shot because you disobeyed a direct order from your superior officer."

"Nothing was ever said . . . Why?"

"The parades had taken place. That was enough."

Quinn O'Brien brought his hand up to his forehead. There was a hollowness in his chest. "Why are you telling me this?"

"Because you've involved yourself in matters that are no concern of yours. You will pursue them no further."

10

The immense figure of Daniel Sutherland stood at the far end of his chambers, in front of the bookshelves. He was in profile, tortoise-shell glasses on his enormous head, a heavy book in his massive black hands. He turned and spoke; his voice deep, resonant, and warmly pleasant.

"Precedents, Mr Chancellor. The law is all too often governed by precedents, which in themselves are all too often imperfect." Sutherland smiled, closed the book, and replaced it carefully in the shelf. He walked to Peter, his hand extended. In spite of his age he moved with assurance, with dignity. "My son and granddaughter are avid readers of yours. They were most impressed that you were coming to see me. It's my loss that I haven't yet had the opportunity to read your books."

"I'm the one who's impressed, sir," replied Peter, meaning it, his hand enveloped. "Thank you for granting me an appointment. I won't take up much of your time."

Sutherland smiled, releasing Peter's hand, putting him immediately at ease. He indicated one chair among several around a conference table. "Please sit down."

"Thank you." Peter waited until the judge had selected his own chair three places away at the end of the table. They both sat.

"Now, what can I do for you?" Sutherland leaned back, the expression on his dark face kind and not without a tinge of humour. "I admit to being fascinated. You told my secretary it was a personal matter, yet we've never met."

"It's difficult to know where to begin."

"At the risk of offending your writer's sense of cliché, why not at the beginning?"

"That's just it. I don't know the beginning. I'm not sure there is one. And if there is, you may feel strongly that I have no right to know about it."

"Then, I'll tell you, won't I?"

Peter nodded. "I met a man. I can't say who he is or where we met. He mentioned your name with respect to a small group of influential people here in Washington. He said this group had been formed several years ago for the express purpose of monitoring the activities of J. Edgar Hoover. He said he believed you were the man responsible for this group's existence. I'd like to ask you if it's true."

Sutherland did not move. His large dark eyes, magnified by the lenses of his glasses, were expressionless. "Did this man mention any other names?"

"No, sir. Not related to the group. He said he didn't know of anyone else."

"May I ask how my name surfaced?"

"Are you saying it's true, then?"

"I'd appreciate your answering my question first."

Peter thought for a moment. As long as he did not name Longworth, he could

600

answer the question. "He saw it on something he called a tracer. Apparently it meant that you were to receive specific information."

"About what?"

"About him, I imagine. Also about those people known to have been placed under negative surveillance by Hoover."

The judge breathed deeply. "The man you spoke with is named Longworth. A former field agent, Alan Longworth, currently listed as an employee of the State Department."

Chancellor tensed the muscles of his stomach in an effort to conceal his astonishment. "I couldn't comment on that," he said inadequately.

"You don't have to," replied Sutherland. "Did Mr Longworth also tell you that he was the special agent in charge of this negative surveillance?"

"The man I spoke with made reference to that. But only a reference."

"Then, let me amplify." The judge shifted his position in the chair. "To answer your initial question. Yes, there was such a group of concerned individuals, and I stress the tense. *Was.* As to my participation, it was minor and limited to certain legal aspects of the issue."

"I don't understand, sir. What issue?"

"Mr Hoover had a regrettable fecundity when it came to making unsubstantiated charges. Worse, he often cloaked them in innuendo, using provocative generalities against which there was little legal recourse. It was an unforgivable lapse of judgement, considering his position."

"So this group of concerned men – "

"And women, Mr Chancellor," interrupted Sutherland.

"And women," continued Peter, "was formed to protect the victims of Hoover's attacks."

"Basically, yes. In his later years, he could be vicious. He saw enemies everywhere. Good men would be let go, the reasons obscured. Later, often months later, the director's hand was revealed. We were trying to stem this tide of abuse."

"Would you tell me who else was in this group?"

"Of course not." Sutherland removed his glasses and held a stem delicately between the fingers of his hand. "Suffice it to say, they were people capable of raising strong objections, voices that could not be overlooked."

"This man you spoke of, this retired field agent – "

"I didn't say *retired*." Again Sutherland interrupted. "I said *former.*"

Peter hesitated, accepting the rebuke. "You said this former field agent was in charge of surveillance?"

"Certain specific surveillances. Hoover was impressed with Longworth. He placed him in the position of co-ordinating the data on individuals with proven or potential antipathy to the bureau, or Hoover himself. The list was extensive."

"But he obviously stopped working for Hoover." Once more Chancellor paused. He was not sure how to ask the question. "You just said he was now employed by the State Department. If so, he was separated from the bureau under very unusual circumstances."

Sutherland replaced his glasses, letting his hand drop to his chin. "I know what you're asking. Tell me, what's the point of your visit this afternoon?"

"I'm trying to make up my mind whether there's a basis for a book on Hoover's last year. On his death, frankly."

The judge's hand dropped to his lap; he sat completely still, looking at Peter. "I'm not sure I understand. Why come to me?"

It was Peter's turn to smile. "The kind of novels I write require a certain credibility. They're fiction, of course, but I try to use as much recognizable fact as I can. Before I start a book, I talk to a great many people; I try to get a feeling for the conflicts."

"Obviously you're very successful with the approach. My son approves of your conclusions; he was very firm about that last night." Sutherland leaned forward, his forearms on the conference table. The trace of humour returned to his eyes. "And I approve of my son's judgement. He's a fine lawyer, albeit a little strident in the courtroom. You *do* respect confidences, don't you, Mr Chancellor?"

"Of course."

"And identities. But of course again. You won't admit you talked to Alan Longworth."

"I would never use a person's name unless lie gave me permission."

"Legally I'd suggest that you didn't." Sutherland smiled. "I feel as though I'm part of a creation."

"I wouldn't go that far."

"Neither would the Bible." Again, the judge leaned back in his chair. "Very well. It's past history now. And not particularly extraordinary; it's done every day in Washington. An inherent part of the checks and balances of our government, I sometimes think." Sutherland stopped and raised his right palm delicately towards Peter. "Should you use any part of what I tell you, you must do so with discretion, remembering that the objective was a decent one."

"Yes, sir."

"Last March Alan Longworth was offered early retirement from one branch of the government, and under cover he was shifted to another. The shift took place in such a way as to remove him from the bureau's scrutiny altogether. The reasons were self-evident. When we learned that Longworth was the co-ordinator of this negative surveillance – a very apt phrase, by the way – we showed him the dangers of Hoover's abuses. He co-operated; for two months he pored over hundreds of names, recalling which were included and what the damaging information was. He travelled extensively, alerting those we thought should be warned. Until Hoover's death Longworth was our deterrent, our defensive weapon, as it were. He was very effective."

Peter was beginning to understand the strange, blond-haired man in Malibu. There had to be conflicting loyalties in the man; the agent must have been torn with guilt. It explained his odd behaviour, the sudden accusations, the abrupt retreats.

"When Hoover died, this man's job was finished, then?"

"Yes. With Hoover's sudden, and I must say, unexpected death there was no further need for such a defensive operation. It ended with his funeral."

"What's happened to him?"

It's my understanding that he's been compensated handsomely. The State Department transferred him to what I believe is referred to as soft duty. He's living out his tenure in pleasant surroundings with a minimum work load."

Peter watched Sutherland closely. He had to ask the question; there was no reason not to now. "What would you say if I told you my informant questioned Hoover's death?"

"Death is death. How can it be questioned?"

'The way he died. By natural causes."

"Hoover was an old man. A sick man. I'd say Longworth – you won't use his name, but I will – might be suffering from intense psychological pressures. Remorse, guilt – it wouldn't be unusual. He had a personal relationship with Hoover. Perhaps he now feels he betrayed him."

"That's what I was thinking."

"Then, what troubles you?"

"Something this man I talked with said. He said Hoover's private files were never found. They disappeared with Hoover's death."

There was a flash of something – Chancellor did not know what; anger, perhaps – in the Negro's eyes. "They were destroyed. All of Hoover's personal papers were shredded and burned. We've been assured of that."

"By whom?"

"That information I can't possibly give you. We are satisfied; that much I can tell you."

"But what if they weren't destroyed?"

Daniel Sutherland returned Peter's gaze. "It would be an extraordinary complication. One I would not care to dwell on," he said firmly. Then the smile returned. "But it's hardly a possibility."

"Why not?"

"Because we'd know about it, wouldn't we?"

Peter was disturbed. For the first time Sutherland did not sound convincing.

He had to be careful, Peter reminded himself as he walked down the steps of the courthouse. He was not looking for concrete facts, merely credibility. That's what he was after. Supportive events ripped out of context and used to bridge the inevitable gap between reality and fantasy.

He could do it now. Daniel Sutherland had given him the answer to the basic enigma: Alan Longworth. The judge had explained the federal agent with perceptive simplicity. It was contained in the single word *remorse*. Longworth had turned against his mentor, the director who had awarded him the most confidential of assignments and written personal commendations on his service record. It was natural for Longworth to feel guilty, to want to strike back at those who had induced his betrayal. What better way than to question that death?

Knowing this freed Peter's imagination. It removed whatever obligation he might have felt towards Longworth. The concept could be accepted for what it was: a fascinating idea for a book. Nothing more was needed. It was a game, a goddamned game; and the writer in Chancellor was beginning to enjoy it.

He stepped off the kerb and hailed a passing cab. "The Hay-Adams Hotel," he directed.

"I'm sorry, sir, it's an unlisted number," said the telephone operator with that peculiar condescension the Bell System reserved for such information.

"I see. Thank you." Peter hung up and leaned back on the pillows. He was not surprised; he had not been able to find MacAndrew's name in the Rockville, Maryland, directory. A Washington reporter he knew had told him the retired general lived in a rented house far out in the country, had lived there for several years.

But Chancellor was not a newspaperman's son for nothing. He sat up and opened the telephone book at his side. He found the name he was looking for and dialled nine and then the number.

"United States Army, Pentagon Operations," said the male voice on the other end of the line.

"Lieutenant General Bruce MacAndrew, please." Peter spoke the rank and name in clipped cadence.

"Just one minute, sir," came the reply, followed seconds later by the obvious. "There's no listing for General MacAndrew, sir."

"There was a month ago, soldier," said Chancellor authoritatively. "Let me have Directory."

"Yes, sir."

"Pentagon Directory. Good afternoon." The voice was female.

"There seems to be a foul-up somewhere. This is Colonel Chancellor. I've just returned from Command Saigon and I'm trying to reach General MacAndrew, Lieutenant General B. MacAndrew. I have a letter from the general dated twelve August. Arlington. Has he been transferred?"

The operator took less than half a minute to find the information. "No, Colonel. Not transferred. Retired."

Peter allowed himself the proper moment of silence. "I understand; his wounds were extensive. Do I find him at Walter Reed?"

"I have no idea, Colonel."

"Then, let me have his telephone number and address, please."

"I'm not sure I can . . ."

"Young lady," interrupted Peter. "I've just flown ten thousand miles. The general is a close friend; I'm very concerned. Do I make myself clear?"

"Yes, sir. There is no address listed. The number on the print sheet is area code . . ."

Chancellor wrote as the woman spoke. He thanked her, pressed down the telephone button, released it, and dialled.

"General MacAndrew's residence." The drawl on the line obviously belonged to a maid.

"May I speak to the general, please?"

"He's not here. He's expected back in an hour. May I take your name?"

604

Peter thought swiftly. There was no point in wasting time. "This is the Pentagon Messenger Service. We have a delivery for the general but the PMS address is unclear. What's the street number in Rockville?"

"RFD Twenty-three, the Old Mill Pike."

"Thank you."

He hung up and once again leaned back on the pillows, recalling Longworth's statements about MacAndrew. The agent had said the general had thrown away a brilliant career, including perhaps the chairmanship of the Joint Chiefs, for no apparent reason. Longworth had suggested there could be a connection between some missing information in MacAndrew's service record and the general's resignation.

A thought struck him. Why had Longworth even brought up MacAndrew? What was MacAndrew to him?

Chancellor sat up suddenly. Had Longworth, in wanting to strike back at those who had manipulated him, manipulated the general? Had the agent himself used damaging information about MacAndrew?

If so, Longworth was playing a serious game. One that went way beyond the bounds of remorse. It depended on the general; what kind of man was he?

He was of medium height, with broad shoulders and a stocky build; he was dressed in khaki slacks and a white shirt, open at the collar. His face was the face of a professional soldier; the skin was taut, the wrinkles deeply etched, the eyes noncommittal. He stood in the doorway of the old house on the country road, a middle-aged man somewhat startled by a stranger whose features seemed vaguely familiar.

Peter was used to the reaction. His occasional appearances on television talk shows produced it. People rarely knew who he was but were sure they'd seen him somewhere.

"General MacAndrew?"

"Yes?"

"We haven't met," he said, extending his hand. "My name's Peter Chancellor. I'm a writer. I'd like to talk to you."

Was it fear he saw in the general's eyes? "Of course I've seen you. On television, your photograph. I read one of your books, I think. Come in, Mr Chancellor. Forgive my astonishment, but I – well – as you said, we've never met."

Peter stepped into the hall. "A mutual friend gave me your address. But your telephone's unlisted."

"A mutual friend? Who's that?"

Chancellor watched the general's eyes. "Longworth. Alan Longworth."

There was no reaction whatsoever.

"Longworth? I don't think I know him. But obviously I must. Was he in one of my commands?"

"No, General. I think he's a blackmailer."

"I beg your pardon?"

It *was* fear. The eyes darted briefly towards the staircase, then towards Peter.

"May we talk?"

"I think we'd better. It's either that, or I throw you out on your ass." MacAndrew turned and gestured through an archway. "In my study," he said curtly.

The room was small with a dark leather chair, a solid pine desk, and mementoes of the general's career on the walls. "Sit down," said MacAndrew, indicating a chair in front of the desk. It was an order. The general remained standing.

"I may have been unfair," said Peter.

"You were something," replied MacAndrew. Now, what's this all about?"

"Why did you retire?"

"None of your damned business."

"Maybe you're right; maybe it's not mine. But it's somebody's besides yours."

"What the hell are you talking about?"

"I heard of you through a man named Longworth. He suggested that you were forced to resign. That something happened a number of years ago, the information removed from your military record. He implied that this information became part of a collection of missing files. Dossiers that contained suppressed facts that could destroy the subjects in question. He led me to believe that you were threatened with exposure. Told to get out of the Army . . ."

For a long moment MacAndrew stood silently, frozen into position, his eyes a curious mixture of hatred and fright. When he spoke, his voice was flat. "Did this Longworth say what the information was?"

"He claimed not to know. The only conclusion I can draw is that it was of such a damaging nature that you had to follow instructions. If I may say so, your reaction would seem to bear out that assumption."

"You prick bastard." The contempt was absolute. "You don't know what you're talking about."

Peter met his eyes. "Whatever's troubling you is none of my business, and perhaps I shouldn't have come here. I was curious; curiosity's a writer's disease. But I don't want to know your problem; believe me, I don't want that burden. I only wanted to know why your name was given to me, and now I think I do. You're a substitute. You make a pretty scary example."

MacAndrew's look grew less hostile.

"Substitute for what?"

"For someone under the gun. If those files really were missing, in the hands of a fanatic, and this fanatic wanted to use the information against another person – well, you're what that other person would be like."

"I don't follow you. Why would my name be given to you?"

"Because Longworth wants me to believe something to the degree that I'll write a book about it."

"But why me?"

"Because something did happen years ago, and Longworth had access to the information. I know that now. You see, General, I think he used both of us. He gave me your name, and before he gave it to me, he threatened to expose you. He wanted a victim. I think – "

It was as far as Chancellor got. With the speed born of a hundred combat assaults MacAndrew sprang across the space between them. His hands were

606

curved into claws that dug into the cloth of Peter's jacket, pressing down, then pulling up, yanking Chancellor to his feet.

"*Where is he?*"

"Hey! For Christ's sake – "

"Longworth! Where is he? Tell me, you prick bastard!"

"You crazy son of a bitch. Let me *go!*" Peter was larger than the soldier but no match for MacAndrew's strength. "Goddamn it, be careful of my head!"

It was a silly thing to say, but it was all that came to mind. The soldier pinned him against the wall, the hard face with the furious eyes inches from his.

"I asked you a question. Now, you answer me! Where can I find Longworth?"

"I don't know! I met him in California."

"Where in California?"

"He doesn't live there. He lives in Hawaii. Damn it, let go of me!"

When you tell me what I want to know!" MacAndrew pulled Chancellor forward, then slammed him back into the wall. "Is he in Honolulu?"

"No!" Peter's head ached beyond endurance, the pain spreading across his right temple, shooting down to the back of his neck. "He's in Maui. For Christ's sake, you've got to let *go* of me! You don't understand – "

"The hell I don't! Thirty-five years down the chute. When I'm needed. *Needed.* Can you understand that!" It was not a question.

"Yes . . ." Peter grabbed the soldier's wrists with all the strength he had left. The pain was awful. He spoke slowly. "I asked you to listen to me. I don't care what happened; it's not my business. But I *do* care that Longworth used you to get to me. No book's worth it. I'm sorry."

"*Sorry?* It's a little late for that!" The soldier exploded again, smashing Peter back into the wall. "This happened because of a goddamned book?"

"Please! You can't – "

There was a crash beyond the door. From the living room. It was followed by a terrible moaning – half chant, half mad, a toneless singsong. MacAndrew froze, his eyes on the door. He released Peter, throwing him into the desk as he reached for the doorknob. He pulled the door open and disappeared into the living room.

Chancellor supported himself on the edge of the desk. The room was spinning. He inhaled deeply, repeatedly, to regain his focus, to lessen the pain in his head.

He heard it again. The moaning, crazy singsong. It grew louder; he could distinguish the words.

" . . . *outside is frightful but the fire is so delightful and since we've no place to go,* . . . *Let it snow! Let it snow! Let it snow!* . . ."

Peter limped unsteadily to the study door. He looked into the living room – and wished he hadn't.

MacAndrew was on the floor, cradling a woman in his arms. She wore a torn, dishevelled negligee that barely covered a faded nightgown, itself old and worn. All around were fragments of shattered glass. The tulip stem of a smashed wine goblet rolled silently on a small rug.

MacAndrew was suddenly aware of his presence. "Now you know what the damaging information is."

Peter did know. It explained the old house way out in the country, the unlisted telephone, and the absence of an address at the Pentagon Directory. General Bruce MacAndrew lived in isolation because his wife was mad.

"I see," said Chancellor quietly. "But I don't understand. Is this why?"

"Yes." The soldier hesitated, then looked back at his wife, lifting her face to his. "There was an accident; the doctors said she had to be sent away. I wouldn't do that."

Peter understood. High-ranking generals in the Pentagon were not permitted certain tragedies. Other varieties, yes. Death and mutilation on the battlefield, for instance. But not this, not a tormented wife. Wives were to remain deep in the shadows of a soldier's life, interference denied.

" . . . *when we finally kiss good night, how I'll hate going out in the storm . . .*"

MacAndrew's wife was staring at Peter. Her eyes grew wide, her thin, pale lips parted, and she screamed. The scream was followed by another. And another. She twisted her neck and arched her back, the screams wilder, uncontrollable.

MacAndrew held her tightly in his arms and stared up at Chancellor. Peter backed further into the study.

"No!" roared the general. "Come back out! Go to the light! Get by the light; put your face above the shade. In the *light*, goddamn you!"

Simply, blindly, Peter did as he was told. He edged his way towards a lamp on a low table and let the spill wash up into his face.

"It's all right, Mal. It's all right. Everything's all right." MacAndrew swayed back and forth on the floor, his cheek hard against his wife's face, calming her. Her screams subsided.

They were replaced with sobs. Deep and painful.

"Now, get out of here," he said to Chancellor.

11

Old Mill Pike swung west out of Rockville before turning south into the Maryland highway that led to Washington. The highway was nearly twenty miles from MacAndrew's house, the old road to it cut out of the countryside, twisting and turning around massive boulders and rock-dotted hills. It was not rich country. But it was remote, isolated.

How MacAndrew must have searched for such a location! thought Chancellor. The setting sun was directly in front of him now, filling the windscreen with blinding light. He pulled down the visor; it didn't help much. His thoughts returned to the scene he had just left.

Why had the disturbed woman reacted so hysterically to the sight of him? He had been in shadow when she'd first seen him. She calmed down when he followed MacAndrew's command to go into the light. Could he have resembled someone so completely? Impossible. The windows of the old house were small, and the trees outside were full and tall, blocking the late afternoon sun. The general's wife could not have seen him that clearly. So perhaps it wasn't his face. Yet what else could it have been? And what nightmares had he evoked?

Longworth was despicable, yet he had made his point. What better way than to offer the pathetic figure of MacAndrew as the object of the most ruthless type of extortion? Taking Longworth's premise that Hoover's private files survived and could be used viciously, the general was the perfect subject. The man in Chancellor was outraged, the writer primed. The concept was valid; there was a novel in the premise. He had a beginning based in recent events, Daniel Sutherland had provided the facts. And an example of what might have been; he himself had observed it.

He felt his energy flowing. He wanted to write again.

A silver car pulled alongside; Peter slowed down, allowing it to pass in the blinding yellow sunlight. The driver must know the road, thought Chancellor. Only someone familiar with the curves would overtake, especially with the sun filling the windscreen.

The silver car, however, did not pass. It stayed parallel; and if Peter's eyes were not playing tricks on him, it narrowed the space between them. Chancellor looked across the diminishing gulf. Perhaps the driver was trying to signal him.

He was not – she was not. The driver was a woman. Her dark hair, crowned by a wide-brimmed hat, fell over her shoulders. She wore sunglasses, and her mouth was a splash of red lipstick emphasizing her pale white skin. An orange scarf billowed out from the top of her jacket. She stared straight ahead as if oblivious of the vehicle beside her.

Peter pressed his horn repeatedly; the cars were inches from each other. The woman did not respond. A sharp downhill curve to the right appeared in the road. If he braked, he knew he would slide into the silver car. He held the wheel firmly to negotiate the turn; his eyes switching back and forth from the road to the automobile perilously close to him. He could see more clearly; the sunlight was blocked by trees.

It was an S curve; he swung the wheel to the left, his foot cautiously on the brake. The blinding light returned to the windscreen; on his right he could barely make out the gully that lay beyond the road's shoulder. He remembered seeing it when he'd driven out an hour before.

The impact came! The silver car collided with the side of his. It was trying to force him off the road. The woman was trying to send him into the gully! She was trying to kill him!

It was Pennsylvania all over again! The silver car was a Mark IV Continental. The same make of car he had driven that terrible night in the storm. With Cathy.

There was a flat stretch of road at the bottom of the hill. He stabbed at the accelerator with his foot, sending his car forward in a burst of speed.

The Continental kept pace; his rented Chevrolet was no match for it. They reached the foot of the hill, the flat road now the course. Chancellor's panic prohibited clear thought and he knew it. He should simply stop the car . . . *stop the goddamned car* . . . but he could not. He had to get away from the horrible silver apparition.

His breath came erratically as he held the pedal against the floorboard. He drew slightly ahead of the Continental, but the silver mass of steel surged forward, its gleaming grill pounding the side of his door.

The dark-haired woman stared straight ahead impassively as if unaware of the terrible game she played.

"Stop it! What are you doing?" Peter screamed through the open window. She acknowledged nothing.

But the Mark IV dropped back again. Had his screams got through? He gripped the wheel with all his strength; perspiration covered his hands and rolled down his forehead, adding to the blindness caused by the sunlight.

He was jolted; his head snapped back, crashed forward into the windscreen. The impact came from behind. Through the rearview mirror he could see the glistening bonnet of the Continental. It crashed again and again into the body of the Chevrolet. He swung to the left side of the road; the Mark IV did the same. The pounding continued. Peter weaved back and forth. If he stopped now, the larger, heavier car would plough into him.

There was nothing else he could do. He spun the wheel violently to the right; the Chevrolet lurched off the road. A final crash propelled the rented car into a lateral spin; it swerved, the tail swinging to the forward left side, causing it to smash sideways into a barbed-wire fence.

But he was off the road!

He slammed his foot back on to the accelerator. *He had to get away.* The car bolted into the field.

The sickening thud of a collision came. Peter ducked, hovering over the wheel, his whole body lifted off the seat. The motor raced thunderously, but the Chevrolet had stopped.

He had crashed into a large rock in the field. Involuntarily, his neck arched back on the seat; blood ran down his nostrils profusely, mingling with the perspiration on his face.

Through the open window he saw the silver Continental racing away to the west down the flat stretch of road in the sunlight. It was the last thing he saw before his eyes closed.

He could not tell how long he'd been there, slumped in his own darkness. In the distance he heard the sound of a siren. Then soon a uniformed figure was outside the window. An arm reached in and turned off the ignition.

"Can you respond?" the patrolman asked.

Peter nodded. "Yes. I'm all right."

"You're a mess."

"It's just a nosebleed," replied Chancellor, fumbling for a handkerchief.

"Do you want me to radio for an ambulance?"

"No. Help me out. I'll walk around."

The officer did. Peter limped into the field, blotting his face, finding his sanity again.

"What happened, mister? I'll need your licence and registration."

"It's a rented car," said Chancellor, taking his wallet from his pocket, and taking out his licence. "How come you're here?"

"Headquarters got a call from the owner of the property. Over there. That farmhouse." The patrolman gestured towards a house in the distance.

"They just called? They didn't come out?"

"It was a woman. Her husband's not home. She heard the crash and the racing motor. The circumstances were suspicious, so headquarters told her to stay inside."

Chancellor shook his head, bewildered. "The driver was a woman, too."

"What driver?"

Peter told him. The officer listened; he pulled a notebook from his pocket and wrote it all down.

When Chancellor had finished, the patrolman studied his notes. "What are you doing in Rockville?"

Peter did not want to mention MacAndrew. "I'm a writer. I often take long drives when I'm working. It clears the head."

The officer looked up from his notebook. "Wait here. I'll radio in."

Five minutes later, the man returned from the patrol car, shaking his head. "Jesus! What they let on the road these days! They got her, Mr Chancellor. Everything you said checked out."

"What do you mean?"

"Crazy bitch was spotted outside of Gaithersburg. She played chicken with a goddamned mail truck! Can you beat that? With a mail truck! They've got her in the drunk tank. Her husband's been called."

"Who is she?"

"Wife of some Lincoln–Mercury dealer in Pikesville. Got a record of drunken driving; her licence was revoked a couple of months ago. She'll get off with probation and a fine. Her husband's a wheel."

The irony was not lost on Peter. Ten miles back a broken man, a career soldier with no future, cradled a tormented woman in his arms. Ten or twenty miles ahead a car salesman was racing down the motorway, the fix already begun.

"I'd better get to a phone and call the rental agency about the car," said Chancellor.

"No sweat," replied the patrolman, reaching into the Chevrolet. "I'll take the keys. Give them my name, and I'll meet the tow van. Tell them to ask for Donnelly. Officer Donnelly in Rockville."

"That's very nice of you."

"Come on. I'll drive you into Washington."

"Can you do that?"

"Headquarters cleared it. The accident took place within our municipal limits."

Peter looked at the patrolman. "How did you know I was staying in Washington?"

For an instant the officer's eyes went blank. "You're pretty shook up. You mentioned it a few minutes ago."

The silver Continental came to a stop beyond the bend in the road. The wail of the siren diminished in the distance. Soon it would fade, and the man in uniform would do his job. A man hired to impersonate a non-existent police officer named Donnelly, to provide Peter Chancellor with erroneous information. It was part of the plan – as was the silver Continental, the sight of which was meant to terrify the novelist, evoking memories of the night he had nearly been killed.

Everything had to be orchestrated swiftly, thoroughly; each thread of truth, half-truth, and lie woven quickly throughout the net so that Chancellor would not be capable of distinguishing one from the other. All had to be accomplished within a matter of days.

Chancellor's mind was the key. His life was expendable. The files were everything.

The driver removed the wide-brimmed hat and the sunglasses. Hands swiftly unscrewed the top of a cold-cream jar; Kleenex was pulled from a box on the seat, dipped into the cream, and scrubbed over the mouth until the lipstick faded. The scarf and the jacket were taken off and thrown to the floor of the car. Finally Varak removed the dark brown shoulder-length wig. And it, too, was deposited on the floor of the car. He checked his watch; it was ten minutes past six.

Word had reached Bravo. The high-pitched whisper might have made contact with another subject of Hoover's private files. There was a congressman named Walter Rawlins, chairman of the powerful House Subcommittee on Reapportionment. Within the past week his behaviour on the Hill had shocked his colleagues. Rawlins was a closet racist whose intransigence on several bills – one especially – had collapsed without explanation. He had absented himself during a number of crucial meetings, voting sessions he had sworn to attend.

If Rawlins had been reached, another name would be fed to Peter Chancellor.

As Peter approached the lifts, he saw his image in a lobby mirror. He was, as Officer Donnelly had so aptly put it, a mess. His jacket was torn, his shoes filthy, his face streaked with dirt and dried blood. He was not exactly the picture of respectability the Hay-Adams was used to; he had the impression the desk clerks wanted him out of the lobby just as rapidly as possible, which was all right with him. He wanted a hot shower and a cold drink.

He saw a woman approaching as he waited for the elevator. It was the news-paperwoman Phyllis Maxwell, her face familiar from scores of televised press conferences.

"Mr Chancellor? Peter Chancellor?"

"Yes. Miss Maxwell, isn't it?"

"I'm flattered," she said.

"So am I," he replied.

"What in heaven's name has happened? Were you mugged?"

612

Peter smiled. "No, not mugged. Just in a minor accident."

"You're a mess."

"There seems to be general agreement about that. I'm going to my room to clean up."

The lift arrived; its doors opened. Phyllis Maxwell spoke quickly. "Afterwards would you agree to an interview?"

"Good lord, why?"

"I'm a newspaperwoman."

"I'm not news."

"Of course you are. You're a best-selling author, probably in Washington to research another book like *Counterstrike!* I find you limping across the Hay-Adams lobby, looking as though a truck had run over you. That's potential news."

"The limp's not new, and the accident was minor." Peter smiled. "If I were working on something, I wouldn't talk about it."

"Even if you did and you didn't want it public, I wouldn't print it."

Peter knew she was telling the truth. He'd heard his father call her one of the best correspondents in Washington. Which meant she was a *student* of Washington; she might tell him things he wanted to know. "Okay," he said. "Give me an hour, will you?"

"Fine. In the lounge?"

Chancellor nodded. "Okay. See you in an hour." He entered the lift, feeling foolish. He was about to suggest that she could wait upstairs in his suite. Phyllis Maxwell was a striking woman.

He showered for nearly twenty minutes, far longer than usual. It was part of his recovery process when he was agitated or depressed. He'd learned little tricks over the past months, small indulgences that helped restore whatever equilibrium he had temporarily lost. He lay down naked on the bed and stared at the ceiling, breathing deeply.

The time passed; his calm was restored. He dressed in a brown leisure suit and went downstairs.

She was at a small table in the corner. The lounge was so dimly lit he could barely see her, but the flickering candles picked up the features of her handsome face. If not the youngest, Phyllis Maxwell was the best-looking woman there.

The opening conversation was relaxed and comfortable. Peter ordered a round of drinks, and then a second. They talked about their respective careers from Erie, Pennsylvania, and Chillicothe, Ohio, to New York and Washington. Peter ordered a third drink.

"I shouldn't," said Phyllis firmly, but not firmly enough. "I can't remember when I've had three drinks at one sitting. It gets in the way of my imprecise shorthand. But then I can't remember interviewing a most attractive . . . young novelist before." Her voice slipped into a low register. Somewhat nervously, thought Chancellor.

"Not that attractive and, God knows, not so young."

"The point is, neither am I. My days of irreverent youth took place when you were learning algebra."

"That's downright condescending, as well as false. Look around you, lady. There's no one here in your league."

"Thank God it's dark, or I'd have to describe you as a charming liar." The drinks came; the waitress left. Phyllis took out a small notepad. "You don't want to discuss whatever you're working on. That's all right. Tell me what you think of today's fiction. Has entertainment returned to the modern novel?"

Peter looked across the table at the speckled, anxious eyes. The candlelight made them appear larger and softened the lines on her face. "I didn't know you wrote for the comics section. Or am I categorized?"

"Are you offended? I think it's an interesting subject. What does a well-paid, well-received storyteller think? God knows you make your theories clear. They're hardly comic."

Chancellor grinned. Phyllis Maxwell was succinct; she was no doubt devastating to any storyteller who took himself too seriously. Peter answered carefully, eager to get to another subject. She jotted down notes as he talked. She was an expert interviewer, as he had expected.

Their drinks were finished. Peter nodded at the glasses. "Another?"

"No thanks! I've just misspelled *the*."

"Do you use *the* in shorthand?"

"Another reason I should refuse."

"Where are you having dinner?"

Phyllis hesitated. "I have an engagement."

"I don't believe you."

"Why not?"

"You haven't looked at your watch. Organized women check their watches if they have dinner engagements."

"Not all women are alike, young man."

Peter reached across the table, covering her wrist. "What time's your dinner date?"

At his touch she stiffened. Then quickly resumed the game. "That's not fair."

"Come on, what time?"

She smiled, blinking her eyes. "Eight-thirty?"

"Forget it," he said, removing his hand. "He's given up and left. It's ten past nine. You'll have to have dinner with me."

"You're incorrigible."

"We'll eat here, okay?"

Again she hesitated. "All right."

"Would you rather go somewhere else?"

"No, this is fine."

Peter grinned. "We may not be able to tell the difference." He signalled to the waitress, indicating a refill. "I know, I know. I'm incorrigible," he said. "May I ask *you* a couple of questions? You know Washington as well as anyone I can think of."

"Where's your notebook?" She put hers away in her purse.

"I've got a running tape in my head."

"That's not reassuring. What do you want to know?"

"Tell me about J. Edgar Hoover."

At the sound of the name, Phyllis's eyes made sharp, angry contact with his. And yet there was more than anger, thought Chancellor.

"He was a monster. I speak ill of the dead without the slightest compunction."

"All bad?"

"Within recent memory, yes. I've been in Washington sixteen years. I can't remember a year when he didn't destroy someone of extraordinary value."

"You put it strongly."

"I feel strongly. I despised him. I saw what he did. If ever there was an example of terror by fiat, he personified it. The story hasn't been told. I don't think it ever will be."

"Why not?"

"The bureau will protect him. He was the monarch. The heirs apparent won't let the image be tarnished. They fear infected bloodlines, and they damned well should."

"How can they stop it?"

Phyllis coughed a derisive laugh. "Not can, did. The furnaces, dear; little dark-suited robots went through the whole damn building burning anything and everything remotely damaging to their deceased progenitor. They're after canoniz-ation; it's their best protection. Then it's business as usual."

"Are you sure about that?"

"The word – and I grant you it's hearsay – is that Clyde showed up at Eddie's house before the body was cold. They say he and a few courtiers went from room to room with portable shredders."

"That Tolson?"

"The Tulip himself. What he didn't burn, he banked."

"Are there witnesses?"

"I suppose so." Phyllis stopped. The waitress was at the table; she removed the empty glasses, replacing them with new drinks.

Peter looked up at the girl. "Should we reserve a table in the dining room?"

"I'll take care of it, sir," replied the waitress, backing away.

"The name is – "

"I know, sir. Maxwell." The waitress left.

"I'm impressed," said Chancellor, smiling, seeing the satisfaction in Phyllis's eyes. "Go on. Were there witnesses?"

Instead of answering, she leaned forward. The open space at the top of her blouse swelled as her breasts rose. Peter was drawn to them; she seemed oblivious to his interest.

"You're working on a book about Hoover, aren't you?"

"Not the man himself. Not his story as such, although it's a vital part. I have to know as much as I can learn. Tell me what you know. Then I'll explain, I promise."

She began in the lounge and continued at dinner. It was an angry narrative, the anger heightened by her professionalism. Phyllis would not print what she could not document, and the documentation was impossible, regardless of the existing truth.

She spoke of senators and congressmen and cabinet members made to toe the Hoover line or face the Hoover wrath. She described powerful men weeping, remaining silent when silence was abhorrent to them. She detailed Hoover's actions following the assassinations of both Kennedys and Martin Luther King. His behaviour had been obscene, his joy apparent, his responsibility denied.

"The press is convinced he withheld damaging information from the Warren Commission. God knows how devastating it was; it might have altered the judgements at Dallas. And Los Angeles, *and* Memphis. We'll never know."

She outlined Hoover's use of electronic and telephone surveillance; it was worthy of the Gestapo. No one had been sacrosanct; enemies and potential enemies had been held at bay. Tapes had been spliced and edited; guilt had come by remote association, innuendo, hearsay, and manufactured evidence.

As she talked, Peter sensed a fury beyond mere contempt. She drank wine during the meal; she drank brandy afterwards. When she was finished, she was silent for several moments, then forced a smile. Her anger had burned up much of the alcohol; she was in control of herself, but she was not quite sober.

"Now, you promised. And I promised not to print it. What are you working on? Another *Counterstrike!?*"

"There's a parallel, I suppose. It's a novel based on the theory that Hoover was assassinated."

"Fascinating. But not credible. Who would dare?"

"Someone who had access to his private files. That's why I asked you if there were any witnesses to the burning or shredding of Hoover's papers. Anyone who actually saw them destroyed."

Phyllis was transfixed, her eyes riveted on him. "And if they weren't destroyed . . ."

"That's the assumption I'll work under. Fictionally."

"What do you mean?" Her voice was flat, abruptly cold.

"That whoever – fictionally – killed Hoover now has those files and is capable of extortion just as Hoover was. Not only capable, but actively operating. Reaching influential people, forcing them to do what he wants them to do. Hoover was obsessed with sex, so that'll be a primary weapon. It's always effective. Simple, very powerful blackmail."

Phyllis moved back in her chair, her hands flat on the table. Peter could hardly hear her. "With a whisper over the telephone, Mr Chancellor? Tell me, is this some kind of terrible joke?"

"Is it a what?"

She stared at him, her eyes wide, filled with an odd dread. "No, it couldn't be," she continued in that same cold, distant tone. "I was here in the lobby; it was my choice to be here. I saw you; you didn't see me."

"Phyllis, what's the matter?"

"Oh, dear God, I'm losing my *mind* . . ."

He reached across the table for her hand. It was cold, trembling. "Hey, come on." He smiled reassuringly. "I think the last brandy was doctored against you."

Her eyes blinked. "Do you really find me attractive?"

616

extreme stress, but nevertheless an act of such impropriety – even indecency – that its revelation would discredit the soldier and destroy his reputation, his career, his wife and his family.

The stranger demands that the soldier destroy the Saigon report, make no charges, remain silent. In essence, he is to let the military status quo continue – and thus, intrinsically, the slaughter. Failure to do so will result in the exposure of the damaging information. He is given twenty-four hours to decide.

The soldier's frustration is climaxed by the longest casualty list forwarded from Saigon for months. The moment of decision comes. He is tormented, but ultimately he cannot destroy the stranger's command.

In his living room he takes a file of papers from his briefcase (the incriminating evidence he brought back from South-east Asia), he crumples the pages and burns them in the fireplace.

There is a change of scene. We see the stranger walk in to an enormous vault in the Federal Bureau of Investigation. He goes to a cabinet, opens it, and replaces the soldier's file. He closes the drawer and locks it.

Printed in the centre of the drawer's index tab is:

AL – Property of the Director

Peter sat back on the couch and scanned what he had written. He wondered if MacAndrew would recognize himself. From what he had learned about him the fictionalized portrait was applicable. The general's influence would be sorely missed at the Pentagon. But not *by* the Pentagon.

In the opening chapter four or five influential, very different people – in government and out – are shown in the grip of various stages of extortion. The blackmailers are concerned only with silencing dissent. Leaders of legitimate organizations representing the disaffected, the underprivileged and the minorities are attacked. Accusations based on remote association, innuendo, hearsay and manufactured evidence are hurled at the dissenters, crippling their effectiveness. The country is on its way to becoming a police state.

Peter stopped, struck by the words. *Remote association, innuendo, hearsay and manufactured evidence.* They were Phyllis Maxwell's words.

He went back to his writing.

The main character will be different from the usual suspense novel hero. I see him as an attractive middle-forties lawyer with a wife and two or three children. His name is *Alexander Meredith.* He is a late bloomer, just beginning to recognize his capacities. He has come to Washington for an interim appointment with the Justice Department. His field is criminal law. He's a detail man with broad knowledge.

He has been hired to evaluate the procedures used by certain departments of the Federal Bureau of Investigation – a job created by the alarming increase of questionable methods used by the bureau's field offices. Unsubstantiated charges have been made public; illegal searches and seizures have multiplied. Prosecutors at Justice are concerned that legitimate cases will be thrown out of court due to constitutional violations.

Meredith has been at the Washington job for a year, and what began as a relatively routine professional assignment has exploded into a series of staggering revelations.

Within the Federal Bureau of Investigation there is an ongoing covert operation designed to gather inflammatory information on a wide spectrum of public and private figures. Meredith makes the connection between several newspaper stories about influential men doing the astonishingly unexpected, and names he has unearthed at the bureau. These are, of course, the victims described in the first chapter. Two are startling. The first is a Supreme Court justice – a man Hoover is known to loathe – who suddenly resigns from the bench. The second is a black civil rights leader publicly condemned by Hoover, who is found dead, a suicide.

Alarmed, Meredith begins a search for concrete evidence of illegal practices carried out within the FBI. He ingratiates himself with executive personnel close to Hoover. He feigns sympathies he does not have. He digs deeper and deeper, and what he discovers frightens him even more.

At the highest level of the bureau there is a small corps of fanatics blindly devoted to Hoover. They implement policies and carry out orders issued by the director with the full knowledge that many are grossly illegal. Meredith finds that there is one man, assigned to the field office in La Jolla, California, who acts as Hoover's gunslinger. He consistently appears on the scene when the unexpected action of a national figure takes place. His description will match that of the *stranger* in the prologue.

Chancellor put down the pencil and finished his coffee. He thought about Alan Longworth, Hoover's "gunslinger" in reality. Longworth remained an enigma. Assuming the premise that it was remorse over his betrayal of Hoover that had brought the agent to Malibu, why would he jeopardize his current situation in Hawaii? Why had he broken an agreement that could cost him his life? Why, ultimately, had he sent Peter to Daniel Sutherland, who instantly identified the former FBI man?

Was Longworth's guilt so pervasive that there was nothing left of self-interest? Was his need for revenge so intense that nothing else mattered? Apparently, that was the case. He had not hesitated to destroy MacAndrew in the process. And because Longworth had done that, Chancellor felt no compunction in including a portrait of the man in his novel.

Meredith gathers in his evidence; it is appalling. J. Edgar Hoover has compiled several thousand dossiers on the nation's most influential people. They contain all manner of rumours, half-truths, and lies. Also, since few humans are saints, the files are rife with documented facts of the most damaging nature. Sexual appetites and aberrations are dwelled upon at length, the public exposure of which would destroy hundreds of men and women who otherwise conduct themselves responsibly, often brilliantly.

The existence of these files constitutes a threat to the country. What's terrifying is that Hoover is actually using them. He is systematically making contact with scores of subjects he believes are in opposition to policies he favours, threatening to expose their private weaknesses if they do not retreat from their positions.

Meredith knows that the most alarming question of all must be answered: is Hoover acting alone or has he allies? For if he has made a pact with his ideological counterparts in the intelligence community, the Congress, or the White House, the republic may well be near a state of collapse.

Meredith decides to take his evidence to an assistant attorney general. From that moment on, his life becomes virtually unbearable. The assistant A.G. is a decent man, although frightened. He is, however, the weapon; members of his staff have leaked

Portions of Alex's report back to the bureau. The assistant attorney general removed it and, in his one courageous move, delivered it secretly to the office of a senator.

Peter leaned back on the couch and stretched. He had a prototype for his senator. Less than a year ago the man had been his party's leading contender for the presidential nomination. He had held millions transfixed with the fiery integrity of his eyes. The incumbent President was no match for the senator's clarity of thought, the depth of his vision, and his ability to communicate. His reasoned, calm exposition of the issues had evoked a sweeping acceptance across the land. And then something had happened to him. In a brief few minutes during a snowy winter morning the contest had been aborted. An intemperate speech had suicidally been delivered by an exhausted campaigner; the senator was effectively disqualified.

Chancellor leaned forward and took a fresh pencil from the tankard.

A pattern of psychological harassment is implemented against Meredith. His every move is watched; he is placed under continuous surveillance: Telephone calls – some obscene, some threats of physical abuses – are made to his wife. His children are questioned about their father by FBI agents during and after school hours. Cars wait outside the Meredith house at night; torches shine into darkened windows. Every day becomes a nightmare; the nights themselves are still worse.

The point is to cast doubt upon Meredith's credibility by discrediting his life. He goes to the authorities; he tries to confront the men at the bureau as well as those following him; he approaches his congressman. All efforts to escape his own personal trial by terror fail. He is driven to the brink of resignation. Even the assistant attorney general will have no more to do with him. The man has been warned. Hoover's insidious controls are everywhere. You'll note that *I* have used Hoover's name. As they say, I speak ill of the dead without the slightest compunction –

It was not "they" who said that, thought Chancellor, pausing for a second. It was Phyllis Maxwell who said it.

– and, Mean Person, I intend to use it in the book. I see no reason to disguise the identity or cloak it in some nonsense like J. Edwin Haverford, praetor of the Federated Branch of Intelligence. I want to call him what he was: a dangerous megalomaniac who should have been forced from office twenty years ago. A monster –

Phyllis Maxwell again. When he thought about it, the newspaperwoman had painted such a memorable – and grotesque – portrait that she was as much a springboard as Longworth had been. Her fury was contagious.

– whose tactics were more in tune with the policies of the Third Reich than those of a democratic society. I want people to be outraged by J. Edgar Hoover's manipulations. (So you'd better show this to the legal department – Steve will probably have apoplexy and start some kind of estate search to see if there are relatives around who might sue.)

The preceding material will require six chapters, or roughly one third of the book. At this juncture, the focus will shift from Meredith to the victims of Hoover's extortions. Primarily to the senator who is revealed to have been a target of Hoover's.

Since these victims are men of considerable influence in the government, it's credible that two of them would make contact. Here it will be the senator and an outspoken member of the cabinet who has opposed the President and is forced to resign. I envision a scene in which two strong figures admit to being helpless under Hoover's assault. They are worthwhile giants brought to bay by an ageing jackal.

However, a positive result comes from their meeting. They recognize the obvious: if Hoover can silence them, he can silence others. So they gather together a small group of men –

Peter lifted the pencil from the paper. He remembered Daniel Sutherland's words about the Washington group: "And women, Mr Chancellor." But what kind of women would be recruited? Or selected? He smiled to himself. Why not a newspaperwoman? A character patterned after Phyllis Maxwell. However, unlike her; in the book the woman had to be a victim before becoming a member of the group. That was vital.

– and women for the purpose of mounting a defence against Hoover's insidious attacks. They have a starting point: Hoover's gunslinger. They go to the intelligence community and are covertly given every scrap of information that can be unearthed about the man. Dossiers, service records, bank statements, credit references – everything available.

Chancellor stopped writing. There it was again, the enigma named Longworth. Sutherland said that they had appealed to the agent's conscience and had rewarded him with a soil job in Maui, his safety guaranteed. All that was, perhaps, credible, but what had Hoover been doing in the meantime? Had he just sat on his arse and said, "Sure, Alan, my boy. Your twenty years are up and you deserve your pension, and you have my best wishes for a pleasant retirement"?

Not likely. The Hoover that had been described to him would have had Longworth killed before cutting him loose.

There had to be another explanation.

The gunslinger is reached by the senator's group. Through a combination of pressures he is recruited, and a medical deception is mounted. The man complains of prolonged abdominal pains and is sent to Walter Reed Hospital. The "report" is forwarded to Hoover: the agent is riddled with duodenal cancer. It has spread beyond surgery; his life expectancy is no more than a few months at best.

Hoover has no alternative. He releases the man, believing the agent is going home to die.

Thus, the anti-Hoover Nucleus is formed. The "retired" field agent is isolated and put to work. It will be established that he not only had access to the files but, being less a saint than an opportunist, pored over the dossiers with an appetite worthy of a KGB bureaucrat in the middle of a purge.

He provides the anti-Hoover group with hundreds of names and biographies. Names and facts trigger off other names and additional facts. A master list of potential victims is prepared.

Its scope is frightening. Included are not only powerful men in the three branches of government but leaders of industry, labour, the academic world and the news media.

The Nucleus – the name of the Washington group – must act immediately.

Confidential appointments are arranged. The agent is sent to scores of subjects, warning them of Hoover's dossiers.

Their strategy will be described in rapid scenes. I won't dwell on the specific information. It would be too confusing to introduce a whole new set of characters.

Speaking of the characters, I'll get to them shortly. I want to carry out the plot line first.

Peter took a new pencil.

The turning point comes with two events: the first is when Alexander Meredith is contacted by the Nucleus. The second is the decision on the part of two or three of the Nucleus to assassinate Hoover.

This decision will be arrived at gradually, for these men are not killers. They come to regard assassination as an acceptable solution, and that is their unacceptable flaw. When Meredith learns of this, knowing that it is the decision of superior minds, all his values are put to a final test. For him murder cannot be a solution. He now struggles against opposing forces: the fanatics of the bureau and those of the Nucleus.

His attempts to stop the assassination and expose the illegalities of the bureau supply the momentum to carry the book to its conclusion.

Fictionally, the most difficult aspect of the narrative will be precisely what horrifies Alex Meredith: the decision on the part of two or three extraordinary people to accept murder as the solution.

The blocks of logic here will have to be built carefully, so that no other solution appears to be at hand. I think the acceptance of assassination will come with two events "rearranged" from recent history: the withdrawal of the most qualified man from the presidential race, and the resignation of an innovative justice of the Supreme Court.

The Nucleus recognizes both of these catastrophes as the work of J. Edgar Hoover. Irreparable damage is being done to the body politic.

The pencil broke, its point shattered under the force of his pressure. He was getting angry again, and the rage should be used later, when he was writing the novel itself. Now was the time to think.

History had provided a peaceful solution. A madman's death and the destruction of his recorded poisons had allowed the Nucleus – if Sutherland was right – to disband. The alert was over.

These were the facts. But he was not dealing with historical reality. What would such a group of concerned, decent people do if faced with the collapse of the checks and balances so vital to the open form of government? Would such a group consider execution? Assassination?

In one sense they would have no alternative. Yet in taking that action, they would be plunging themselves down to the same level as the murdered man. Therefore, not all would subscribe to such a solution, and no such solution would be openly proposed.

But two, or perhaps three, might consider it the only decision that could be made. And here would be the Nucleus's flaw. Murder is murder, its definition altered only by specific conditions of war. Those who employ murder as a solution are ultimately no better than their targets. The Nucleus would harbour two or three members who would become committed killers.

As Peter conceived it fictionally.

In the Nucleus are two men; and perhaps a woman (the dramatic possibilities here are interesting), of stature, dedicated to the principles espoused by the rest of the group. What we see, however, is a gradual change in their perspectives. It is born of frustration and anguish, a genuine detestation of Hoover's progress and the Nucleus's apparent ineffectiveness. It is brought to a head by the manipulation of a presidential election and the repressive shaping of the court. They have been pushed to the wall: no alternatives remain. There is only assassination.

But that would remove only half the cancer, the other half being Hoover's files. They must be taken. They cannot be allowed to fall into the hands of his successor after his death.

These rebels within the Nucleus conceive of a plan of execution and theft. I think it should be written in a crosscut documentary style, the suspense heightened by the ingeniousness of the plan itself and the realization that at any moment an error of timing or reaction could blow it all apart.

This is as far as I want to go with the plot line at the moment.

Peter stretched his arms, wincing as a sharp pain shot through the muscles of his left shoulder. He did not give it an instant's thought. His concentration was on the page in front of him. Now it would begin. The people.

He started with shadows, formless shapes slowly coming into focus. And then names. As was his custom, he would sketch out his cast of characters, restricting each to a couple of pages, knowing that each in turn would lead to his or her own friends and enemies, known and unknown. Characters gave birth to other characters; it was often as simple as that.

In addition to those he had already considered – the soldier in the prologue, Alexander Meredith, Hoover's gunslinger, the senator, and the cabinet member – he would flesh out the group – the Nucleus – first. There would be several from outside the government: a scholar, a lawyer, perhaps. And unquestionably a judge, but not a Negro judge – that he could not do. There was only one Daniel Sutherland. And the women: they would have to be thought about carefully. The temptation to invent too close a fictional counterpart of Phyllis Maxwell had to be resisted. But some aspects of her would go into the book.

He leaned forward and began.

There is a man in his seventies, an attorney named . . .

He could not tell how long he had been writing. Time was blurred, his concentration absolute. The sun was three-quarters of its way down the sky, its rays streaming through the north window.

He looked at the pages next to the yellow pad; he had sketched no fewer than nine characters. His energy was flowing; he was grateful beyond words because the words were there at last.

The telephone rang, disorienting him. He walked across the room to answer it.

624

"Hello?"

"Is this here a writer by the name of Chancellor? A Peter Chancellor?" The man on the line spoke with a thick southern accent.

"Yes. This is Peter Chancellor."

"What are you tryin' to *do to me?* You got no right – "

"Who is this?"

"You know goddamned well who ah am."

"I'm afraid I don't."

"Fun-*nee.* Your friend Longworth come to see me in Washington."

"*Alan* Longworth?"

"You got it. And you're huntin' in the wrong fields! You want to start a Nigra version of 1861 all over again, you go right ahead. But you better know what you're doin'."

"I haven't the vaguest idea what you're talking about. Now, who the hell is this?"

"Congressman Walter Rawlins. Today's Wednesday. I'll be in New York on Sunday. We're goin' to meet."

"Are we?"

"Yes. Before we both get our goddamned heads shot off."

13

He had done something he'd never done before: he had started writing the book before Morgan approved the outline. He could not help himself. The words kept leaping from head to paper. With a twinge of guilt Peter admitted to himself that it did not matter. The story was everything. Through the story, a monster named Hoover was being revealed. It was important to Chancellor – somehow more important than anything he had ever tried to do before – that the Hoover myth be shown for what it was. Just as quickly as possible, so that it would never happen again.

But the work had to be interrupted for a day. He had agreed to meet Rawlins. He did not want to meet him; he had told Rawlins that whatever Alan Longworth had said to him, whatever threats he had made, Longworth was no friend of his. Peter wanted nothing further to do with him.

Still, Longworth had been in Washington four days ago when Rawlins telephoned. He was not back in the Hawaiian Islands. The enigma had reappeared. Why?

Chancellor decided to stay the night in his New York apartment. He had promised to have dinner with Joshua Harris.

He drove north on the old road parallel to the banks of the Delaware, through the town of Lambertville, and swung west up the long hill into Route 202. If he hit a minimum of country traffic, he'd reach the turnpike in forty-five minutes; from Exit 14 it was another half-hour into New York.

There was almost no traffic. A few hay and milk trucks came cautiously out of dirt roads on to the highway, and speeding cars overtook him intermittently: salesmen who had covered the day's territory, racing to the next motel. If he cared to, he could outrun just about anything on the road, he thought, fingering the thick steering wheel. His car was a Mercedes 450 SEL.

Fear had determined his selection of a car. He chose the heaviest he could find. As it happened, the car immediately available was a dark blue. That was fine; anything as long as it was not . . .

Silver?

Silver! He could not believe what he saw!

Behind him! In the wide convex mirror outside the window, the image magnified by the curvature, the shining radiator immense! It was a silver car! The silver Continental!

His eyes were playing tricks on him. They had to be! He was almost afraid to look at the driver; he didn't have to. The silver car pulled alongside him, the driver in his direct line of sight.

It was the woman! The same woman! *Two hundred miles away!* The wide hat, the long dark hair, the sunglasses, the pale white skin punctuated by bright red lips above an orange scarf. It was insane!

He jammed his foot on the accelerator; the Mercedes lunged forward. Nothing on the road could keep up with him!

But the Continental did. Effortlessly. *Effortlessly!* And the macabre driver was staring straight ahead. As if nothing were unreal, nothing out of the ordinary. Straight ahead. At nothing!

Peter glanced at the speedometer. The needle wavered over a hundred. It was a dual carriageway; cars on the other side were blurs. Cars. *Trucks!* There were two trucks up ahead! They followed one another around a long curve in the road. Chancellor moved his foot off the accelerator; he would wait till he was closer.

Now! He pressed the brake pedal; the Continental shot ahead, pulling to the right side of the highway to block him.

Again, now! He stabbed the accelerator, turning the wheel counterclockwise, swinging to the left side of the road, the engine thundering as he sped past the terrible silver thing and the insane woman who drove it.

He raced past the two trucks in the curve, stunning the drivers, the Mercedes's wheels half in the centre island of autumn grass, its tyres screaming.

Ringos. The sign on the road said *Ringos!*

There was a Ringo years ago, at a place where death had occurred, a gunslinger firing in a burst of fury.

Gunfight at the O.K. Corral.

Why did he think of such things? Why did his head ache so?

Buffalo Bill's defunct . . . Jesus he was a handsome man . . . e e cummings. Why did he think of e e cummings? What the hell was *happening?*

His head was splitting.

In the distance, perhaps a mile away, he could see an amber circle of light suspended in the air. For a moment he did not know what it was.

It was a traffic light at a road intersection. Three cars up ahead were slowing down, one on the left, two on the right. He could not overtake. They were half a mile away now. He slowed the Mercedes.

Oh, *God!* It was there again!

The Continental was approaching rapidly, its radiator growing larger in the rearview mirror. But the traffic light was directly ahead; both cars would have to stop.

He had to control himself, control the pain in his head, and do what he had to do! The madness had to stop!

He pulled to the right side of the road behind the two cars and waited to see what the Continental would do. It swung into the left lane behind the single car but stopped directly alongside his Mercedes.

Chancellor snapped up the handle and leaped out. He raced over to the Continental and grabbed the door handle, pulling with all his strength.

The door was locked. He pounded on the window.

"*Who are you?* What are you *doing?*"

The impassive face – a macabre mask of a face – stared straight ahead behind the glass. There was no acknowledgement whatsoever.

Peter shook the handle and smashed his hand against the window. "You can't do this to me!"

The drivers in the other cars peered out their windows. The light had turned green, but no one drove away.

Chancellor ran around the bonnet to the driver's window, yanking the handle, hitting the glass.

"You crazy bitch! Who are you? What do you want?" The terrible pale face, concealed by the hair and the glasses and the hat, turned and stared up at him. It *was* a mask, horrible and totally impassive. White powder and set, tight lips outlined in fiery red lipstick. He was studying some obscene giant insect made up to look like a ghastly clown.

"Goddamn it, answer me! *Answer me!*"

Nothing. Nothing but that terrible stare from the mask of that terrible face.

The cars ahead started to move. Peter heard the revving of engines. He held on to the door, mesmerized by the macabre sight behind the window; he pounded the glass again.

"*Who –?*"

The Continental's motor roared. His hand loosened its grip, and the Mark IV lurched forward, speeding through the intersection and up the highway.

"You crazy bastard! I'll break your head open. Motherfucker!"

The words, roared in anger, were not his words. The first of the two trucks he had insanely passed in the curve of the highway had come to a stop twenty yards away. Above the step to the driver's cabin, a door opened and a barrel-chested driver climbed out, a wrench in his hand.

"You son of a bitch! You damned near ran me off the road!"

Peter limped to the Mercedes. He threw himself into the seat and slammed the door, his fingers slapping down the lock. The driver was within feet now, the wrench held high.

The Mercedes's motor was still running. Chancellor reached for the gear lever and pulled it back, his foot hard on the accelerator, his hand on the wheel. The 450 SEL exploded in a burst of power; Peter gripped and swung the wheel to prevent the car from jumping the kerb. He straightened it out and sped up the road.

It was a nightmare. A goddamned *nightmare!*

He sat alone in the living room of his apartment for over an hour. The lamp on top of the piano was the only source of light; sounds of the New York night came through the partially opened window. He wanted the air, and the sounds were reassuring. He was still perspiring, and the room was cool.

He had to control his panic. He had to think. Someone was trying to drive him out of his mind. He had to fight back; he had to trace the terrible mask of a face. He had to go back – to a country road in Maryland where the terrible face had first appeared.

What was the name of the patrolman in Rockville? Connelly? Donovan? He'd given it to the rental agency at Dulles Airport; he would call them and find out. Then he would call the patrolman and ask –

The telephone rang. He winced and got up from the chair. The caller had to be the congressman from Virginia. No one else knew he was in town. Rawlins had said he'd telephone during the evening and they would set up a time and a place to meet.

"Hello?"

"Peter?"

It was Joshua Harris, Chancellor had forgotten completely about him. "Hey, I'm sorry, old friend. I had some problems. I just got in."

"What's the matter?" Alarm was apparent in Harris's voice.

"I – " No, he would not tell Joshua. Not now. Everything was too confused. "Nothing serious. Car repairs. It took longer than I thought. Where are you?"

"I was about to leave for the restaurant. The Richelieu, remember?"

Yes, he remembered. But he could not sit through the leisurely pace of a meal at an elegant restaurant. He'd go out of his mind, wanting and not wanting to confide in his literary agent.

"Would you mind if we postponed it for a day if that's convenient? To tell you the truth, I worked from four-thirty this morning till four this afternoon. Then the drive . . . I'm whacked."

"The Hoover book's coming along, then?"

"Better and faster than I ever thought possible."

"That's fine, Peter. I'm happy for you. Strange, Tony didn't tell me."

Chancellor interrupted quietly. "He doesn't know. It's the longest outline I've ever turned in; it'll take him days to read it."

Why didn't he just say he'd started the damned book? "You'll bring me a copy, of course," Harris said. "I don't always trust you two, left alone with all those words."

"Tomorrow night, I promise."

"Tomorrow night, then. I'll switch the reservation. Good night, Peter."

"Good night." Chancellor hung up and walked to the window overlooking Seventy-first Street. It was a quiet, tree-lined block, the sort of block that people associated with another time in the city.

As he looked out the window, he was aware of an image coming into focus. He knew it was not real, but he was incapable of stopping it. It was the macabre face in the Continental. He was looking at that terrible mask of a face! It was in the glass, staring out at him, unseen eyes behind the enormous dark glasses, the bright red lipstick painted with precision in a sea of caked white powder.

Peter shut his eyes and brought his hand up to his forehead. What had he been about to do before Josh called? It had something to do with that horrible image in the glass. And the telephone. He was going to use the telephone.

The telephone rang. But it had just rung a few moments ago. It could not be ringing again.

It was ringing. Oh, Christ! He had to lie down; his temple ached, and he was not sure – *Answer the telephone*. He limped across the room.

"Chancellor?"

"Yes."

"Rawlins. How good are you in the morning?"

"Is that supposed to be a funny joke?"

"Huh?"

"I work in the morning."

"That don't concern me. You know a place here in New York called the Cloisters?"

"Yes." Peter held his breath. Was that, too, a horrible joke? The Cloisters had been a favourite of Cathy's. How many summer Sundays had they walked over its lawns? But Rawlins could not know that. Or could he?

"Be there at five-thirty tomorrow morning. Use the west entrance; the gate will be open. There's a path about four hundred feet north that leads to an open courtyard. I'll see you there." The phone went dead.

The southerner had chosen a strange location, a stranger hour. They were the choices of a frightened man. Alan Longworth had once more triggered off the fear; he would have to be stopped, this "retired" agent, this gunslinger filled with remorse.

But it was no time to think about Longworth. Peter knew he had to rest. Four-thirty would come quickly.

He walked into the bedroom, kicked off his shoes, and unbuttoned his shirt. He sat nearly at the edge of the bed. Involuntarily, his body slowly fell backward, his head sinking into the pillow.

And the dreams came. The nightmares.

* * *

The grass was moist with dew, the early light breaking in the eastern sky. Relics and statuary were everywhere, and gnarled trees that seemed transported through the centuries. The only thing missing was the music of a lute or gentle voices singing madrigals.

Chancellor found the path. It was bordered by flowers and led up a small hill towards stone walls that turned out to be a rebuilt garth of a thirteenth-century French monastery. He approached it and stood in front of an ancient archway. Inside the courtyard were marble benches and miniature trees in artistic isolation. It was eerily still. He waited.

The minutes went by; the early morning light grew faintly brighter, enough to pick up the glistening white of the marble. Peter looked at his wristwatch. It was ten minutes to six. Rawlins was twenty minutes late.

Or had the congressman decided not to come after all? Was the fear so great?

"*Chancellor.*"

Peter turned, startled by the whisper. It came from a cluster of bushes about thirty feet away, foliage that surrounded a wide pedestal on the grass. On top of the stand was the sculptured head of a mediaeval saint. Coming out of the shadows was the figure of a man.

"Rawlins? How long have you been there?"

"Bout three quarters of an hour." Rawlins walked towards Peter. No handshake was offered.

"Why did you wait so long to come out?" Peter asked. "I've been here since five-thirty."

"Five thirty-three," said the southerner. "I waited to see if you were alone."

"I am. Let's talk."

"Let's *walk.*" They started down the path that led away from the pedestal. "Something wrong with your leg?" asked Rawlins.

"It's an old football injury. Or a war wound. Take your choice. I don't want to walk. I want to hear what you have to say. I didn't ask for this meeting, and I've got work to do."

Rawlins's face reddened. "There's a bench over there."

"There were benches inside the courtyard."

"And maybe microphones."

"You're crazy. So is Longworth."

The congressman did not reply until they reached the white wrought-iron bench. "Longworth's your partner, ain't he? In this here extortion." Rawlins sat down as he spoke. The dim light washed over his face; the bravado of seconds ago was fading.

"No," answered Peter. "I have no partner and I'm not an extortionist."

"But you're writin' a book."

"That's how I make my living. I write novels."

"Sure. That's why the Central Intelligence boys had a lot of soiled underwear in a 'round-the-clock laundry. I heard about that one. Thing called *Counterstrike!*"

"I think you're exaggerating. What did you want to tell me?"

"Leave it alone, Chancellor." The congressman spoke in a flat voice. "The information you got ain't worth a thimble of piss. Oh hell, you can ruin me, but I'll save my butt legally; I can do that. Then you gotta answer for what follows."

What information? Whatever Longworth told you is a lie. I have no information about you."

"Don't bullshit me. I don't deny I got problems. I know what people like you think of me. I use the word *nigger* in private more than you'd like to hear; I got a fondness for pretty black arse when I'm juiced up – though, goddamn it, I suppose that could be in my favour; I'm married to a bitch whore who can blow the whistle on me any time and take just about everything I got north of Roanoke. I may live with all that, boy, but I do my job on that Hill! And I ain't no killer! Do you understand?"

"Sure. Just your normal, everyday plantation family. Very quaint and lovable. You've said enough. I'm leaving."

"No, you're not!" Rawlins was on his feet, blocking Peter's path. "Please. Listen to me. I'm a lot of things, but you can't label me a redneck. No one with the brains to get naked out of the rain is any longer. 'Cause the numbers and the motives ain't what they used to be. The whole world's changin', and to be blind to that is to invite a goddamned bloodbath. Nobody wins; everybody loses."

"Motives?" Chancellor studied the southerner's face. It was devoid of artifice. "What are you driving at?"

"I never blocked responsible change. But I fight like a trapped fox when that change is irresponsible. To turn over million-dollar decisions to folks who ain't qualified, who *don't* have the brains to get out of the rain, that only sets *everybody* back."

Peter was fascinated, as he always was when the image and the substance clashed. "What has this got to do with whatever it is you think I've got?"

I was *set up* in Newport News! I was fed a barrel of sour mash and taken down dark alleys I never saw. I may have humped that little girl, but I didn't kill her! I wouldn't know how to do what *they* did to her! But I know who did do it. And those black bastards know I know. They're worse than scum; they're nigger Nazis, killin' their own, hidin' *behind* – "

There was a spit of air behind them, somewhere in the distance. And then the unbelievable – the *inconceivable* – happened. Chancellor stared in terror, unable to move.

Rawlins's mouth had sprung open. A circle of red had formed above his right eyebrow. Blood spewed out, gushing at first, then rolling down in rivulets over the ashen skin and unblinking eye. Still, the body *stood*, frozen in death. And then, slowly, as if in some horrible ballet, Rawlins's legs gave way and his corpse fell over, collapsing in the wet grass.

A muted expulsion of breath came from Peter's throat; a scream had been born, but no sound came, his shock beyond any cry of terror.

There was another spit; the air waves shattered above him. And another; there was a *ping*, and the earth exploded beneath him. A bullet had ricocheted off the bench! Whatever remained of his instincts propelled him off his feet; he dived to his left, rolling on the grass and lunging out of the target area. There were more spits, more furious explosions of grass and dirt. A fragment of stone whipped past his ear; inches closer and he would have been blinded or killed. Suddenly his

631

forehead scraped a hard surface, the palm of his hand stinging as it pressed against jagged rock. He had lurched into a monument of some kind, a medallion of stone surrounded by bushes.

He spun over on his back. He was hidden, but all around were the sickening thumps of bullets.

Then there were shouts, half crazed, hysterical. They came from over *there*, and *there*, and *there!* Moving, racing, fading. And finally one voice, one roar, hard and guttural, commanding obedience.

"*Get out of here!*"

A powerful hand gripped the front of his jacket, bunching his shirt and the skin beneath in its grasp, pulling him up from the stone shield. A second hand held a large automatic, a thick cylinder on its barrel. It was levelled in the direction where the shots were coming from; bursts of fire and smoke spat out of its bore.

Peter was beyond speech, beyond protest. Above him was the blond-haired Longworth. The despised Alan Longworth was saving his life!

He crashed through the bushes, his body low, diving through sharp nettles to the grass beyond. He scratched the earth with his feet and hands, propelling himself forward. The air was gone from his lungs, but only escape mattered. He raced down through the gardens.

14

He walked the streets like a man who wanders in deep sleep. Time and place were lost; disorientation had swept over him. His first thought was to find help, find the police, find *someone* who could impose order on the chaos he had barely lived through. But there was no one. He approached several pedestrians; they looked at his odd appearance and shook him off, hurrying away. He stumbled into the street; horns blew, cars skirted around him angrily. There were no police to be seen, no patrol cars in this quiet section of the city.

His temples throbbed, his left shoulder ached, his forehead felt as though it had been scraped with a file. He looked at the palm of his right hand; the skin was red; specks of blood had been forced to the surface.

Slowly, after he had walked for miles, Chancellor began to find part of his mind. It was a strange realization, a stranger process. Knowing and not knowing, aware of his very dangerous mental state, he vaguely understood that his defences were not capable of repelling the assaults on his mind, so he tried to force the images from his consciousness. He was a man desperately trying to regain control. He had decisions to make.

He looked at his watch, feeling like a lost traveller in a foreign land who was told that if he had not reached a certain destination by a specific time, he had taken a wrong turn. He had taken a great many wrong turns. He looked up at the street sign; he'd never heard of the name.

The sun told him it was morning. He was grateful for that. He had wandered the streets for four hours.

Four hours. Oh my God, I need help.

His car! The Mercedes was back at the Cloisters, parked on the street in front of the west entrance. He put his hand in his trouser pocket and pulled out his wallet. He had enough for a taxi.

"Here's the west gate, Mac," said the driver with the florid face. "I don't see no Mercedes. What time did you leave it?"

"Early this morning."

"Didn't you look at the sign?" The driver pointed out the window. "This is a busy street."

He had parked in a towaway zone.

"It was dark," said Peter defensively. He gave the driver his address in Manhattan.

The cab turned left on to Seventy-first Street from Lexington Avenue; Chancellor stared in astonishment. His Mercedes was parked in front of the block of flats, directly in front of the steps to his apartment. It stood there in eerie splendour, the dark blue glistening in the sunlight. There was no other vehicle like it on the block.

For an insane moment Peter wondered how it had been moved from across the street, where he had parked it the night before. Cathy must have moved it. She often did that because of the sidestreet parking regulations. Cars had to be removed by eight o'clock.

Cathy? Oh, Jesus, what was wrong with him?

He waited on the kerb until the taxi disappeared. He approached the Mercedes, looking at it carefully, as if inspecting an object he had not seen for years. It had been washed and polished, the interior vacuumed, the dashboard cleaned, the metal parts gleaming.

He took out his key case; the climb up the steps seemed interminable. There was a typewritten note on the outside door, stapled to the wood.

Things got out of control. It won't happen again. And you will not see me again.

Longworth

Chancellor ripped the note from the door. Then he looked carefully at the paper. The *o*'s of the script were slightly raised; the paper was a thick bond, cut off at the top.

The note had been typed on his typewriter. The paper was his stationery, his name removed.

"His name is Alan Longworth. Josh found out about him." Peter leaned against the window, staring down at the Mercedes in the street.

Anthony Morgan sat in a leather armchair across the room, his long slender frame uncharacteristically rigid.

"You look like hell. Did you do much drinking last night?"

"No. I didn't sleep well. What sleep I had was filled with nightmares. That's another story – "

"But not booze," interrupted Morgan.

"I told you, no!"

"And Josh is in Boston?"

"Yes. The office said he was taking the four o'clock shuttle back. We're supposed to have dinner tonight."

Morgan got out of the chair; apparently convinced, he spoke emphatically. "Then for Christ's sake, why haven't you called the police? What the hell do you think you're doing? You saw a man killed. A congressman was murdered in front of you!"

"I know, I know. You want to hear something worse? I blanked out. I walked around for damned near four hours in a fog. I don't even know where I was."

"Have you heard anything on the radio? The news must have hit by now."

"I haven't turned it on."

Tony walked to the bookcase radio and tuned in to a news station, keeping the volume low. Then he went to his author, forcing Chancellor to turn from the window "Listen to me. There's no one I'd rather have you call than me. Except right now, the police. I want to know why you haven't!"

Chancellor groped for words. "I don't know, I'm not sure I can tell you."

"All right, all right," said Morgan gently.

"I'm not talking about hysteria. I'm learning to live with that. It's something else." He displayed his injured palm. "I drove my car to Fort Tryon. Look at my hand. My fingerprints, maybe specks of blood, should be on the steering wheel. The grass was wet and there was mud. Look at my shoes, my jacket. Traces should be in the car. But the car was washed clean; it looks as though it had just come out of the showroom. I don't even know how it got back here. And the note on the door. It was typed with my typewriter, on my stationery. And for hours after the . . . madness, the insanity, I can't account for myself!"

"Peter stop it!" Morgan grabbed Chancellor's shoulders, raising his voice. "This isn't fiction. You're not one of your characters! This is real. It happened." He lowered his voice. "I'm calling the police."

Two detectives from the twenty-second precinct interrupted Peter's story with sporadic questions. The older man was in his fifties, with wavy grey hair, the younger about Chancellor's age, and black. They were both alert, experienced professionals and made an effort to put Peter at ease.

When Chancellor finished, the older man went to use the telephone, the younger talked about *Sarajevo!* He had liked it very much.

It was only when the older man rejoined them that Chancellor realized that the black had prevented him from listening to the phone conversation. Peter admired the professionalism. He would remember it.

"Mr Chancellor," began the grey-haired detective cautiously, "there seems to be a problem. When Mr Morgan called us, we dispatched a team to Fort Tryon.

To save time, we included forensic; to make sure the area wasn't tampered with, we called the Bronx precinct and had them post street patrolmen. There's no evidence of gunfire at the scene. There's no disturbance of the grounds."

Peter stared at the man in disbelief. "That's crazy. That's wrong! I was there!"

"Our men are very thorough."

"They weren't thorough enough! You think I'd make up a story like that?!"

"It's a pretty good one," said the black, smiling. "Maybe you're trying out some material."

"Hey, wait just a minute!" Morgan stepped forward. "Peter wouldn't do that."

"It would be a foolish thing to do," said the older man, nodding without agreeing. "It's against the law to falsely report a crime. Any crime, to say nothing of homicide."

"You *are* crazy . . .", Peter's voice trailed off. "You really don't believe me. You get your little report over the telephone, take it as gospel, and conclude I'm a lunatic. What kind of police officers *are* you?"

"Very good ones," said the black.

"I don't think so. I don't think so at all, goddamn it!" Chancellor limped to the phone. "There's a way to settle this; it's been five, six hours now." He dialled and within seconds spoke. "Washington Information? I want the office number of Congressman Walter Rawlins, House of Representatives."

He called out the number as the operator gave it to him; Tony Morgan nodded. The detectives watched without comment.

He dialled again. The wait was interminable; his pulse raced. In spite of his own undeniable knowledge he had to prove himself to the two professionals.

A woman's voice came on the line, subdued and obviously southern. He asked for the congressman.

And when he heard her words, the ache returned to his temples and his eyes momentarily lost focus.

"It's simply terrible, sir. The bereaved family released the news just minutes ago. The congressman passed away last night. He died of a coronary in his sleep."

"No. *No!*"

"We all feel that way, sir. The funeral arrangements will be announced – "

"No! That's a lie! Don't tell me that! It's a lie! Five, six hours ago – in New York! A *lie!*"

Peter felt the restraining arms around his shoulders, hands on hands, taking the telephone from him, pulling him back. He kicked out, shoving his elbows viciously into the policeman behind him. His right hand was free; he grabbed the head nearest him, lashed out his hand, and wrenched the hair half out of the skull. He yanked the head up; the man had fallen to his knees.

Tony Morgan's face was in front of his, wincing in pain, but he made no move to protect himself.

Morgan, Morgan, his *friend*. What was he doing?

Peter slumped; he was still. Arms lowered him to the floor.

* * *

"There won't be any charges," said Morgan, coming into the bedroom, carrying drinks. "They were very understanding."

"Which means I'm a lunatic," added Chancellor from the bed, an icebag on his forehead.

"Hell, no. You're exhausted. You've been working much too hard. The doctors advised you against that – "

"For God's sake, Tony, not with me!" Peter sat up. "Everything I said was true!"

"Okay. Here's your drink."

Chancellor took the glass but did not drink. He placed it on the bedside table. "No you don't, old friend." He pointed to a chair. "Sit down. I want to get some things very clear."

"All right." Morgan ambled to the chair and fell into it. He stretched his long legs out in front of him; the casualness did not fool Peter. The editor's eyes betrayed his concern.

"Calmly, rationally," continued Chancellor. "I think I know what happened. And it won't happen again, which explains Longworth's note. He wants me to believe that; otherwise he's convinced I'll howl like a banshee."

"When have you had time to do any thinking?"

"Those four hours in the street. I didn't realize it, but the pieces were falling together. And when you and the police were having your conference downstairs, I saw the pattern."

Morgan looked up from his glass. "Don't talk like a writer. 'Patterns', 'pieces falling together'. That's bullshit."

"No, it's not. Because Longworth is forced to think like a writer. He has to think as I do, don't you see?"

"No, but go ahead."

"Longworth has to be stopped; he knows I know it. He got me started with scraps of information and one pathetic example of what might have happened if Hoover's files still existed. Remember, he knew those files; he retained a hell of a lot of damaging information. Then to make sure I was really hooked, he provided one more example: a southern congressman with problems, mixed up with the rape of a black girl and a killing he didn't commit. Longworth put the forces in motion and me in the middle. But when he got everything going, he realized he'd gone too far. The trap was murder; he hadn't figured on that. When he found out, he saved my life."

"Thus saving the book?"

"Yes."

"*No!*" Morgan got to his feet. "You're talking like a kid around a campfire. And why not? It's your job; all storytellers are kids around campfires. But for heaven's sake, don't confuse it with what *is*."

Chancellor studied Morgan's face. The realization was painfully obvious. "You don't believe me, do you?"

"You want the truth?"

"Since when have we changed the rules?"

"All right." Tony drained his glass. "I think you did go to the Cloisters. How

636

you got in I don't know; you probably climbed a wall. I know how much you love the early morning, and the Cloisters at dawn must be something else . . . I think you heard about Rawlins's death – "

"How could I? His office said the news was just released!"

"Forgive me. You heard that, I didn't."

"Oh, Christ!"

"Peter, I'm not trying to hurt you. A year ago no one knew whether you'd live or die; you were that close to death. You suffered a terrible loss; Cathy was everything to you, we all knew it . . . Six months ago we thought – I honestly believed – you were finished as a writer. It had gone out of you; the desire had died; the kid around the fire was killed on the Pennsylvania Turnpike. Even when you got out of the hospital, there were entire days – weeks – when you didn't say a word. *Nothing.* Then the drinking began. And then less than three weeks ago your personal volcano erupts. You fly in from the Coast more excited than I've ever seen you, filled with energy, wanting to go back to work with a vengeance. And I mean vengeance . . . Don't *you* see?"

"See what?"

"The mind's funny. It can't take going from zero miles an hour to Mach one so quickly. Something's bound to snap. You yourself said you didn't know where you were for nearly four hours."

Chancellor did not move. He watched Morgan, conflicting thoughts going through his head. He was angry with the editor for not believing him, yet he was strangely relieved. Perhaps it was better this way. Morgan was protective by nature; the events of the past year had magnified that natural instinct. If he believed Peter, there was no question in Peter's mind what the editor would do. Morgan would stop the book.

"Okay, Tony. Let's forget it. It's over. I'm not entirely well. I can't pretend that I am. I don't know."

"I do," replied Morgan gently. "Let's have a drink."

Munro St Claire studied Varak as he came through the door of the diplomat's library in Georgetown. The agent's right arm was in a sling, and there was a strip of gauze on the left side of his neck. Varak closed the door and approached the desk where Bravo sat, the ambassador's expression grim.

"What happened?"

"It's taken care of. His Cessna was at the Westchester airport. I flew him to Arlington and contacted a doctor we use at NSA. His wife had no choice, nor did she want any. Rawlins didn't have assassin insurance. Besides, she's a dirty book. I read her several episodes."

"What about the others?" asked Bravo.

"There were three; one was killed. Once Chancellor was out, I stopped firing and concealed myself on the far side of the area. Rawlins was dead; what more did they want? They fled, taking their colleague's body with them. I threaded the zone, picked up shells, replaced grass; there were no signs of any disturbance."

Bravo rose from the chair, his wrath apparent. "What you've done is beyond anything we sanctioned! You made decisions you knew I would not condone, took action that cost the lives of two men, and nearly killed Chancellor."

"One of those men was a killer himself," replied Varak simply. "And Rawlins was marked. It was only a question of time. As to Chancellor, I nearly lost my own life saving his. I think I paid for my error of judgement."

"Error of judgement? Who gave you the right?"

"You did. You all did."

"There were intrinsic prohibitions! You understood that."

"I understood there are hundreds of missing files that could be used to take this country right into a police state! Please remember that."

"And I ask you to remember this is not Czechoslovakia. Not Lidice in 1942. You are not a thirteen-year-old boy crawling over corpses, killing anyone who might be your enemy. You were not brought here thirty years ago to be turned into your own Sturm und Drang."

"I was brought here because my father worked for the Allies! My family was massacred because he worked for you." His eyes clouded. Off guard, he couldn't hold back the tears when he thought of the sunny morning of 10 June 1942. A morning of death everywhere, of succeeding nights hiding in the mines, of subsequent days and nights when, aged thirteen, he made X marks on a mine shaft, each symbol representing another dead German. A child had turned killer of consequence. Until the British brought him out.

"You were given everything," said Bravo, lowering his voice. "Obligations were acknowledged, nothing was spared. The finest schools, all the advantages – "

"And the memories, Bravo. Don't forget those."

"And the memories," agreed Munro St Claire.

"You misunderstand me," said Varak quickly. "I'm not looking for sympathy. What I'm saying to you is that I do remember." Varak took a step closer to the edge of the desk. "I've spent eighteen years paying for the privilege of that memory. Paid willingly. I'm the best in NSA, I'll seek out the Nazi in any form he is revived in and go after him. And if you think there's any difference between what those files represent and the objectives of the Third Reich, you're very much mistaken."

Varak stopped. The blood had risen to his face; he was close to shouting, but of course that was out of the question. Munro St Claire watched the agent in silence, his own anger subsiding.

"You're very persuasive. I'll convene Inver Brass. It must be kept apprised."

"No. Don't call a meeting. Not yet."

"A meeting's already scheduled for this month. We have to choose a new Genesis. I'm too old; so are Venice and Christopher. That leaves Banner and Paris. It's an awesome – "

"Please." Varak pressed his fingers on the edge of the desk. "Don't call that meeting."

St Claire narrowed his eyes. "Why not?"

"Chancellor's begun the book. The first part of the manuscript was delivered the day before yesterday. I broke into the office of the typing firm. I've read it."

"And?"

"Your theory may be more accurate than you thought. Chancellor's conceived of several things that never occurred to me. And Inver Brass is in the book."

15

The cold snap came, turning autumn into winter. The election was over, the results as predictable as the frost that covered the Pennsylvania countryside. Mendacity and Madison Avenue had prevailed. Over vacillating amateurs. Nobody won anything of value, least of all the republic.

Peter had not paid much attention to politics. Once the players were fielded, there wasn't much that interested him. Instead, he was consumed by the novel. Each morning was his personal adventure. He had refined the plot; the characters had sprung to life.

He was into the seventh chapter, the point where decent men were gradually reaching an indecent decision: murder. The assassination of J. Edgar Hoover.

Before the actual writing of a chapter he outlined it; then he put the outline aside, barely if ever referring to it. It was a technique suggested by Anthony Morgan years ago:

Know where you're going, give yourself a direction so you're not floundering, but don't restrict the natural inclination to wander.

It was strange about Tony, thought Chancellor as he bent over the table. They had talked several times since the incredible madness at the Cloisters several weeks before, but Morgan had never mentioned it. It was as though it had not happened.

Still Morgan had read the first hundred pages of the novel. He said it was the best writing Peter had ever done. That was all that mattered. The book was everything.

Chapter 7 – Outline

A rainy afternoon in a Washington hotel suite. The senator sits in front of a window watching the rain splattering against the glass. He is thinking back thirty years ago, to his days in college when the incident had taken place that when revealed three decades later would take him out of the presidential race. It was the indiscretion Hoover's messenger had confronted him with. He couldn't recall how or when it had happened. His emotions had run high and wild and indiscreet. But there it was: his youthful signature on the card of an organization later revealed to be part of the Communist apparatus. Innocuous, of course; defensible, certainly – laughable, actually. But not in terms of the presidency. It was enough to disqualify him. It would not have been, of course, had his present political philosophy been in tune with the director of the Federal Bureau of Investigation's.

The senator's thoughts are interrupted by the arrival of the newspaperwoman, the columnist silenced by Hoover, now part of the Nucleus. The senator rises and offers her a drink.

The woman replies that if she could accept, she would not be there in the first place. She explains she is an alcoholic; she had not had a drink in over five years, but prior to that she was often drunk for days at a time. It was Hoover's hook into her. During one such binge, photographs were taken.

"Committing unnatural acts with various unsavoury gentlemen is the easiest way to describe them. But for the life of me, I don't remember. Good God, how could I?"

Hoover has the photographs. Her dissent has been effectively muted.

The third member of the Nucleus arrives. The third person is the former cabinet member described in the first chapter, whose indiscretion is the fact that he's a closet homosexual.

He brings alarming news. Hoover has made a temporary pact with the White House. Every viable candidate in the opposition will be reached and eliminated. Where facts do not exist, conjecture under the FBI imprimatur will be used. The bureau's name is sufficient to wreak havoc among politicians. By the time defences are mounted, the damage has been done.

The opposition will field its weakest candidate; the election of the incumbent is assured. Inherent in this agreement is that Hoover has no less damaging weapons to use against the White House. In essence, the director will soon control the pressure points of the country; he'll be running it.

"He's gone too far. The corpses are piling up too fast, too dead. He has to be removed, I don't care how. Even if it means killing him."

The senator is appalled at the cabinet officer's words. He knows what it is to feel Hoover's knife, but there are legitimate ways to fight him. He takes Meredith's report from his briefcase.

The decision is made to reach the messenger, the man who deals with Hoover's private files. Whatever's required will be used to recruit him; above all, the files must be taken.

"First the files. If they can be used the way Hoover uses them, they can be turned around. They can be used for good! Then the execution. There is no other way." The cabinet officer will not waver.

The senator will not listen further; he refuses to acknowledge the statement. He leaves, saying only that he is going to arrange a meeting with Meredith.

Peter stopped. There was enough to start with; he could begin the actual writing.

He picked up his pencil and began.

He was oblivious to time, lost in the accumulated pages. He leaned back on the couch and looked up at the windows, mildly astonished to see tiny flakes of snow drifting downward. He had to remind himself it was late in December. Where had the months gone?

Mrs Alcott had brought him the newspaper an hour ago and he felt like taking a break. It was ten-thirty; he had been writing since quarter to five. He reached for the paper on the edge of the coffee table and snapped it open.

The headlines were the usual headlines. The Paris negotiations were stalled —

whatever that meant. People were dying; he certainly knew what *that* meant.

Suddenly Peter stared at the one-column item in the lower right-hand corner of the front page. A sharp pain shot through his temples.

GEN. BRUCE MACANDREW
APPARENT MURDER VICTIM
Body Washed Up on Waikiki Beach

Waikiki! Oh, my God! Hawaii!

The story was macabre. MacAndrew's body had two bullet holes in it, the first piercing his throat, the second entering his skull below the left eye. Death had been instantaneous and had occurred some ten to twelve days before.

Apparently no one knew the general had been in Hawaii. Hotels and airlines showed no reservations in his name. Interrogations within the island's military establishment produced no information; he had not contacted anyone.

Reading further, Peter was startled again by a paragraph heading near the bottom of the page.

Wife Died Five Weeks Ago

The information was scarce. She had simply died "after a prolonged illness that restricted her activities in recent years". If the reporter knew anything more, he had charitably omitted it.

The story then took a strange twist. If the reporter had been charitable to Mrs MacAndrew, he impugned the general in terms worthy of the Hoover novel.

The Hawaii police are reportedly looking into rumours that a former high-ranking American Army officer was involved with criminal elements operating out of the Malay Peninsula through Honolulu. There are many retired military men and their families in the Hawaiian Islands. Whether or not these rumours are in any way related to the homicide victim could not be established.

Then why include the information? thought Peter angrily, remembering the pathetic sight of the soldier cradling his wife. He flipped the pages to find the continuation of the article.

There was a brief biography devoted to MacAndrew's military record, culminating in mention of the general's sudden and unexpected resignation and his differences with the Joint Chiefs, speculations as to the extra-military cost of his wife's illness, and the subtle insinuation that the maverick general had been subjected to extreme psychological pressures. The connection between these "pressures" and the previously mentioned "rumours" was for the reader to draw, and no reader could help doing so.

The last part of the article took another turn, surprising Peter. He had not realized that MacAndrew had a grown daughter. From the description in the paper she was an angry, independent woman.

Reached at her New York apartment, the general's daughter, Alison MacAndrew, 31, an illustrator for the Welton Greene Agency, an advertising firm at 950 Third Avenue, responded angrily to the speculations surrounding her father's death. "They drove him out of the Army, and now they're trying to destroy his reputation. I've been on the phone to the authorities in Hawaii for the past twelve hours. They've concluded my father was killed fighting off an attack by armed muggers. His wallet, wristwatch, signet ring and money were stolen."

Asked if she could explain why there were no records of airline or hotel reservations, Miss MacAndrew replied, "That's not unusual. He and my mother generally travelled under another name. If the Army people in Hawaii knew he was vacationing there, they would have hounded him."

Peter understood what she was saying. If MacAndrew travelled anywhere with his mentally ill wife, he would of course use an assumed name to protect her. But MacAndrew's wife was dead. And Chancellor knew the general had not gone to Hawaii for a vacation. He had gone to find a man named Longworth.

And Longworth had killed him.

Peter let the newspaper drop from his hands. Revulsion swept over him, part fury, part guilt. What had he done? What had he let happen? A decent man killed! For what?

A book.

In his messianic drive to assuage his own guilt Longworth had killed again. *Again.* For he was responsible for Rawlins's death at the Cloisters as surely as if he had pulled the trigger that took the congressman's life. And now half a world away, there was another death, another murder.

Chancellor got up unsteadily from the couch and walked aimlessly about the room, the protected sanctuary where fiction took place, life and death only products of the imagination. But outside that room life and death were real. And they touched him because they were a part of his fiction; the marks on paper had sprung from the motives that drove other lives, brought about other deaths. *Real* life and *real* death.

What was happening? A nightmare, more realistic and grotesque than anything he might have dreamed, was being played out in front of a backdrop of fiction. A *nightmare*.

He stopped at the telephone as if somebody had commanded him to remain still. Thoughts of MacAndrew triggered images of a silver Mark IV Continental and a mask of a face behind the wheel.

Suddenly, Peter remembered what he had been about to do months ago, before the telephone call from Walter Rawlins that culminated in the madness in Fort Tryon. He had been about to telephone the Rockville, Maryland, police! He had never done so; he had never made that call! He had protected himself by forgetting. He remembered now. Even the name of the patrolman. It was Donnelly.

He dialled Information for the Rockville area code. Thirty seconds later he was speaking to a desk sergeant named Manero. He described the incident on the back road, gave the date, and identified Officer Donnelly.

Manero hesitated. "Are you sure you want Rockville, sir?"

"Of course I am."

"What colour was the patrol car, sir?"

"Colour? I don't know. Black and white, or blue and white. What difference does it make?"

"There's no Officer Donnelly in Rockville, sir. Our vehicles are green with white stripes."

"Then, it was green! The patrolman said his name was Donnelly. He drove me back to Washington."

"Drove you into – Just one minute, sir."

There was the click of a hold button. Chancellor stared out of the window at the wind-blown flakes of snow and wondered whether he was losing his mind. Manero came back on the line.

"Sir, I've got the police entry book for the week of the tenth. There's no record of any accident involving a Chevrolet and a Lincoln Continental."

"It was a silver Mark Four! Donnelly told me it was picked up! A woman driver in dark glasses hit a mail van."

"I repeat, sir. There's no Officer Donnelly – "

"Goddamn it, there is!" Peter could not help shouting.

Perspiration broke out on his forehead; the pain in his temples increased. His memory raced back. "I remember! He said she was a drunk! With a record of violations, that was it. She was the wife of a Lincoln-Mercury dealer in – Pikesville!"

"Just a minute!" The desk sergeant raised his voice. "Is this some kind of joke? My in-laws live in Pikesville. There's no Lincoln dealer there. Who the hell could afford one? And there's no police officer named Donnelly in this station. Now, get off the line. You're interfering with official business!"

The phone went dead. Chancellor stood immobile, not believing the words he'd heard. They were trying to tell him he had lived a fantasy!

The car rental agency at Dulles Airport! He had telephoned from the Hay-Adams and spoken to the manager. The manager had assured him that everything would be taken care of; the agency would simply bill his account. He dialled.

"Yes, of course, I remember our conversation, Mr Chancellor. I enjoyed your last book very – "

"Did you get the car back?"

"Yes, we did."

"Then someone had to take a tow truck out to Rockville. Did he see a police officer named Donnelly? Can you find out for me?"

"It won't be necessary. The next morning the car was back in our parking depot. You said you thought there might be damage, but there wasn't. I remember the dispatcher saying that it was about the cleanest vehicle ever returned."

Peter tried to control himself. "Did whoever bring back the car have to sign anything?"

"Yes, of course."

"Who was it?"

"If you'll hold on, I can find out."

"I'll hold." Peter gripped the phone with all his strength; the muscles in his forearms ached. His mind went blank. Outside, the snowflakes fell.

"Mr Chancellor?"

"Yes?"

"There was a mistake, I'm afraid. According to the depot, the signature on the invoice was yours. Obviously there was a misunderstanding. Because the car was leased to you, the man who returned it probably thought – "

"There was no mistake," interrupted Peter quietly.

"I beg your pardon?"

"Thank you," he said, hanging up the telephone.

It was suddenly clear. Everything. The terrible mask of a face. The silver Continental. A clean, repaired Chevrolet in a Washington parking depot. A spotless Mercedes in front of his New York apartment. A note on the door.

It was Longworth. It was all Longworth. The grotesque, powdered face, the long dark hair, the black glasses . . . and memories of a horrible night of death a year ago in a rainstorm. Longworth had done his research; he was trying to drive him mad. But *why?*

Chancellor walked back to the couch; he had to sit down and let the pain in his temples pass. His eyes fell on the newspaper, and he knew what he had to do.

Alison MacAndrew.

16

He found her name in the New York telephone directory he kept in Pennsylvania, but the number had been disconnected. Which was to say a new, unlisted number had been assigned.

He called the Welton Greene Agency; a secretary told him Miss MacAndrew would be away from the office for several days. No explanation was offered, none sought.

Still, he had the address. It was a block of flats on East Fifty-fourth Street. He knew the one; it was on the river. There was nothing else to do. He had to see this woman, talk with her.

He threw a few clothes into the Mercedes, putting his manuscript into his briefcase, and drove into the city.

She opened the door, her large brown eyes conveying both intelligence and curiosity. Curiosity tinged, perhaps, with anger, in spite of the sadness in her face. She was tall and seemed to have her father's reserve, but her features were her mother's. Fragile, etched in definition, the bone structure elegant, even aloof. Her light brown hair was casually shaped. She wore beige slacks and a yellow blouse, open at the neck. There were dark circles under her eyes; the effects of grief were evident but not for display.

"Mr Chancellor?" she asked directly, no hand extended.

"Yes," he nodded. "Thank you for seeing me."

"You were very persuasive on the lobby phone. Come in, please."

He walked inside the small apartment. The living room was modern and functional, given to swift, sharp lines of glass and chrome. It was a designer's room, ice-like and cool, yet somehow made comfortable by the owner's presence. Beyond her quality of directness Alison MacAndrew had a warmth about her she could not conceal. She gestured towards an armchair; he sat down. She sat on the couch opposite him.

"I'd offer you a drink, but I'm not really sure I want you to stay that long."

"I understand."

"Still, I'm impressed. Even a bit awestruck, I guess."

"Good heavens, why?"

"Through my father, I 'discovered' your books several years ago. You've got a fan, Mr Chancellor."

"I hope for my publisher's sake there are two or three others. But that's not important. It's not why I'm here."

"My father was one," said Alison. "He had your three books; he told me you were very good. He read *Counterstrike!* twice. He said it was frightening and quite possibly true."

Peter was startled. The general hadn't conveyed any such feeling. No admiration beyond vague – very vague – recognition. "I didn't know that. He didn't say anything."

"He wasn't given to flattery."

"We talked about other things. Things much more important to him."

"So you said on the phone. A man gave you his name and implied my father was forced out of the Army. Why? How? I think it's ridiculous. Not that there weren't any number who wanted him out, but they couldn't force him."

"What about your mother?"

"What about her?"

"She was ill."

"She was ill," agreed the girl.

"The Army wanted your father to send her away. He wouldn't do it."

"That was his choice. It's a moot point whether she would have received more professional care if he had. God knows he chose the most difficult way for him. He loved her, that was the important thing."

Chancellor watched her closely. The hard patina, the clipped, precise words were only part of the surface. Beneath, he felt there was a vulnerability she was doing her utmost to hide. He could not help himself; he had to probe. "You sound as if you didn't. Love her, that is."

Anger flashed briefly in her eyes. "My mother became . . . ill when I was six years old. I never really knew her. I never knew the woman my father married, the one he remembered so vividly. Does that explain anything to you?"

645

Peter was silent for a moment. "I'm sorry. I'm a damned fool. Of course it does."

"Not a damned fool. A writer. I lived with a writer for nearly three years. You play with people; you can't help it."

"I don't mean to," he protested.

"I said you couldn't help it."

"Would I know your friend?"

"You might. He writes for television; he lives in California now." She offered no name. Instead, she reached for a pack of cigarettes and a lighter on the table next to her.

"Why do you think my father was forced out of the Army?"

Chancellor was confused. "I just told you. Your mother."

She replaced the lighter on the table, her eyes locked with his. "What?"

"The Army wanted him to send her away. To an institution. He refused."

"And you think that's why?"

"Yes, I do."

"Then, you're wrong. As I'm sure you've gathered, I disliked many things about the Army, but its attitude towards my mother wasn't one of them. For over twenty years the men around my father were very sympathetic, those above him and below. They helped him whenever they could. You look astonished."

Peter was. The general had spelled it out. *Now you know what the damaging information is . . . doctors said she had to be sent away . . . I wouldn't do that.* Those were his words! "I guess I am." He leaned forward. "Then, why did your father resign? Do you know?"

She inhaled on her cigarette. Her eyes strayed, seeing things Peter could not see. "He said he was finished, that he didn't care any more. When he told me that, I realized a part of him had given up. I think I knew the rest of him would go soon. Not the way it happened, of course, but somehow. And even that. Shot in a hold-up – I've thought about it. It fits so well. A last protest. At the end, proving something to himself."

"What do you mean?"

Alison brought her eyes back to him. "To put it in its simplest terms, my father lost his will to fight. At that moment, when he said the words to me, he was the saddest man I ever saw."

At first Peter did not reply. He was disturbed. "Are those the words he used? That he 'didn't care any more'?"

"Essentially, yes. He was sick of it all. Pentagon infighting is very cruel. There's never any let-up. Get the hardware, always more hardware. My father used to say it was understandable. The men who run the Army now were once young officers in a war that really mattered, where hardware had won it. If we had lost that war, there would have been nothing."

"When you say a war that 'really mattered', do you mean – ?"

"I mean, Mr Chancellor," interrupted the girl, "that for five years my father opposed our policy in South-east Asia. He fought it every chance he could get. It was a very lonely position. I think the word is *pariah.*"

"Good lord . . ." Peter's mind spun back involuntarily to the Hoover novel. To the prologue. The general he had invented was the pariah Alison MacAndrew had just described.

"My father wasn't political; his judgement had nothing to do with politics. It was purely military. He knew the war couldn't be won in any conventional way, and to use the unconventional was unthinkable. We couldn't win it because there was no real commitment among those we supported. There were more lies coming out of Saigon than in all the court martials in military history – that's what he said. He considered the whole thing an enormous waste of life."

Chancellor sat back in the couch. He had to clear his head. He was hearing words he had written. Fiction. "I knew the general was opposed to certain aspects. I never thought he dwelt on the corruption, the lies."

"It was almost all he dwelt on. And he was vehement about it. He was in the process of cataloguing hundreds of contradictory reports, logistical misrepresentations, body counts. He once told me that if the body counts were only fifty per cent accurate, we would have won the war in '68."

"What did you say?" asked Peter incredulously. These were *his words*.

"What's the matter?" asked Alison.

"Nothing. Go ahead."

"There's nothing more to tell. He was barred from attending conferences he knew he should be a part of, ignored in staff meetings. The more he fought, the more they disregarded him. Finally he saw it was all futile."

"What about the reports he was cataloguing? The misrepresentations? The lies out of Saigon?"

Alison looked away. "They were the last things we talked about," she said quietly. "I'm afraid it wasn't my finest hour. I was angry. I called him names I now deeply regret. I didn't realize how beaten he was."

"What about the reports?"

Alison raised her head and looked at him. "I think they became a symbol for him. They represented months, maybe years, of further agony, turning against men he'd served with. He wasn't up to it any more. He couldn't face it. He quit."

Peter again leaned forward. Consciously, he spoke with a hard edge in his voice. "That doesn't sound like the professional I spoke with."

"I know it doesn't. That's why I yelled at him. You see, I could argue with him. We were more than father and daughter. We were friends. Equals in a way. I had to grow up fast; he didn't have anyone else to talk to."

The moment was filled with anguish. Chancellor let it pass. "A few minutes ago you said I was wrong. Now it's my turn. The last thing your father wanted to do was resign. And he didn't go to Hawaii for a vacation. He went there to find the man who forced him out of the Army."

"*What?*"

"Something happened to your father years ago. Something he didn't want anyone to know about. This man found out and threatened him. I liked your father very much. I liked what he stood for, and I feel guilty as hell. That's as honestly as I can put it. And I want to tell you about it."

Alison MacAndrew sat motionless, her large eyes level with his. "Would you care for that drink now?" she asked.

He told her the story, everything he could remember. From the blond-haired stranger on the beach at Malibu to the astonishing phone call that morning to the Rockville police. He omitted only the killing at Fort Tryon; if there was a connection, he did not want to burden her with it.

In the telling he felt cheap; the commercial novelist in search of a grand conspiracy. He fully expected her to he outraged, to damn him for being the means to her father's death. In a very real sense he wanted her condemnation, so deep was his own guilt.

Instead, she seemed to understand the depth of his feelings. Remarkably, she tried to lessen his guilt, telling him that if what he told her was true, he was no villain; he was a victim. But regardless of what *he* believed, *she* would not accept the theory that there was an incident in her father's past so damaging that threats of exposure could force him to resign.

"It doesn't make sense. If anything like that existed, it would have been used against him years ago."

"In the newspaper, you said he was driven out."

"Yes, but not that way. By wearing him down, ignoring his decisions. That was the method. I saw it."

Chancellor remembered his prologue; he was almost afraid to ask the question. "What about his report on the corruption in Saigon?"

"What about it?"

"Isn't it possible they tried to stop him?"

"I'm sure they did. But it wasn't the first time he'd done something like that. His field reports were always very critical. He loved the Army; he wanted it to be the best it could be. He would never have made it public, if that's what you're driving at."

"It was."

"Never. He wouldn't do that."

Peter did not understand nor did he press for an explanation. But he had to ask the obvious. "Why did he go to Hawaii?"

She looked at him. "I know what you think. I can't refute you. But I know what he told me. He said he wanted to get away, go on a long trip. There was nothing to prevent him. Mother was gone."

It was no answer; the question remained suspended. And so they talked. For hours, it seemed. Finally, she said it. The next afternoon her father's body was arriving in New York, flown in on a commercial jet-liner from Hawaii. An Army escort would meet the plane at Kennedy Airport, the coffin transferred to a military aircraft and taken to Virginia. The funeral was the day after in Arlington. She was not sure she could face the ordeal.

"Isn't anyone going to be with you?"

"No."

"Will you let me?"

"There's no reason – "

"I think there is," said Peter firmly.

They stood together on the enormous field of concrete that was the cargo area. Two Army officers remained at attention several yards to their left. The wind was strong, swirling odd pieces of paper and leaves from faraway trees into the air in circles. The huge DC-10 taxied to a stop. Shortly, the large panel underneath the giant fuselage slid back; an electric freight dolly approached and was centred beneath. Seconds later the coffin was lowered.

And Alison's face was suddenly ashen, her body rigid. The trembling began at her lips, then reached her hands; her brown eyes stared, unblinking; tears started to roll down her cheeks. Peter put his arm around her shoulders.

She held back as long as she could – far longer, in far greater pain, than made sense. Chancellor could feel the spasms that shot through her arms; he held her tighter. Finally she could take no more. She turned and fell against him, her head buried in his coat, the sobs muffled, the agony complete.

"I'm sorry . . . I'm so sorry," she whispered. "I promised myself I wouldn't."

He held her close and spoke softly. "Hey, come on. It's allowed."

17

Peter had made up his mind, but she changed it for him. He was going to abandon the book; he had been manipulated, and the price of that manipulation was symbolized for him by the dead MacAndrew. He had implied as much to Alison the night before.

"Say you're right," she had said to him. "I don't think you are, but say it's true. Isn't that all the more reason to go on?"

It was.

He sat across the aisle from her on the air force plane. She wanted to be alone; he sensed that and understood. Below them, in the cargo area of the aircraft, was the body of her father. She had a great deal to think about, and he could not help her. Alison was a private person; he understood that, too.

And she was unpredictable as well. He had learned that when he picked her up in the taxi earlier in the afternoon. He told her he had phoned the Hay-Adams in Washington and made reservations for them.

"Don't be silly. There's plenty of room in the Rockville house. We'll stay there. I think we should."

Why should they? He did not pursue the question.

Chancellor opened his briefcase and took out the leatherbound notebook that travelled with him wherever he went. It had been a gift from Joshua Harris two years before. There was a row of sharpened pencils in the inside pocket of the cover. He removed one and wrote on the attached pad.

Chapter 8 Outline

Before he began he thought about Alison's remark the night before.
. . . *say it's true. Isn't that all the more reason to go on?*
He looked at the words he had just written: *Chapter 8 Outline.* The coincidence was mildly startling. This was the chapter in which Meredith is driven to the point of madness because of a terrible secret of his own.

Alex leaves his office at the Federal Bureau of Investigation earlier than usual. He knows he's being followed, so he tries to lose himself in the crowds, walking up short streets and alleys, through several buildings, going in one entrance, emerging from another. He dashes on to a bus; it takes him to within a block of the apartment where the assistant attorney general lives. They have agreed to meet.

At the apartment house the doorman hands him a note from the assistant attorney general. He will not see Alex. He does not want any further association. If Meredith persists, the man will be forced to report his odd behaviour to others. In his judgement, Alex is unbalanced, paranoid over imagined abuses.

Meredith is stunned, the lawyer in him furious. The evidence is there. The assistant attorney general has been reached as so many others have been reached. Hoover's forces have succeeded in blocking Meredith's every move. The raw power of the FBI is all-pervasive.

Outside the apartment house he sees the bureau vehicle that has picked up his trail. There is a driver and a man beside him; they stare at Alex silently. It is part of the strategy of fear aroused when a man knows he is being watched, especially at night. It fits Hoover's methods.

Meredith takes a cab to the garage where his car is parked. We see him speeding down Memorial Parkway, weaving in and out of traffic, aware of the FBI car behind him.

On impulse he changes direction, taking an unfamiliar exit off the highway into the Virginia countryside. The husband and father in him has rebelled. He will not lead those following him back to his house again, back to his wife and his children. His fear is turning into fury.

There's a chase through the back roads. The speed. the rushing scenery, the screeching tyres around sharp curves, all contribute to Alex's growing panic. He is a man alone racing in a maze for survival. We understand that the disorientation produced by the events of the past weeks is heightened by the madness of the chase. Meredith is beginning to crack.

In the growing darkness Alex miscalculates a sudden curve. He slams on the brakes; the car swerves, jumps the road and plunges through the fence into the field.

Bruised, his forehead bleeding from the impact with the windscreen, Meredith climbs out of the car. He sees the FBI vehicle back on the road. He races towards it, screaming. His state of mind demands violence, physical confrontation.

He does not get it in the way that he seeks it. Instead, the two FBI men get out of the car and swiftly subdue him. They feign professional procedures by searching him for a weapon.

The driver speaks coldly. "Don't press us, Meredith. We don't have much use for

650

people like you. Men who put on a uniform and work for the other side."

Alex collapses. It is the secret that is buried in his past. Years ago, during the Korean War, as a young lieutenant barely in his twenties, Meredith had been captured and broken by his captors. He was not alone; there were hundreds. Men driven mad by physical and psychological tortures unknown in modern warfare. The Army understood; the Geneva covenants had been violated. The broken men were assured that all records of their nightmare would be expunged. They had served honourably; they had faced things for which the Army had never prepared them. Each could pick up his life without punishment.

Now Alex realizes that the darkest moment of his life is known by men who will use it ruthlessly against him, and even his wife and children.

The FBI agents release him. He wanders down the country road in the twilight.

Peter closed the notebook and looked over at Alison. She was staring straight ahead, her eyes wide, unblinking. The two-man military escort sat in the front of the plane, where their attentions could not fall on private grief.

She felt his gaze on her and turned to him, forcing a smile. "You working?"

"I was. Not now."

"I'm glad you were. It makes me feel better. Less like I was interrupting you."

"That's hardly the case. You made me go on, remember?"

"We'll be there soon," she said mechanically.

"No more than ten or fifteen minutes, I think."

"Yes." She went back to her thoughts, looking out the window at the bright blue sky beyond.

The aircraft began its descent into Andrews Field.

They taxied to a stop, disembarked, and were instructed to wait in the officers' lounge at terminal six.

The only person in the lounge was a young Army chaplain, obviously ordered to be in attendance. He was both relieved and somewhat startled to find his presence superfluous.

"It's kind of you to be here," said Alison with authority, "but my father died several days ago. The shock's worn off."

The minister shook hands solemnly and left. Alison turned to Peter. "They've scheduled the service for ten tomorrow morning at Arlington. I've requested the minimum; just the officer's cortège within the grounds. It's nearly six. Why don't we have an early dinner somewhere and get out to the house?"

"Fine. Shall I rent a car?"

"No need to. They'll have one for us."

"That means a driver, doesn't it?"

"Yes." Alison frowned again. "You're right. That's a complication. Have you got your licence with you?"

"Of course."

"You can sign for the vehicle. Do you mind?"

"Not at all."

"It'll be simpler without a third person," she said. "Army drivers are notorious scouts for superior officers. Even if we didn't ask him in, I'm sure his orders would be to remain on the premises until relieved."

Alison's words could be taken on several levels. "What do you mean?" he asked.

Alison saw his caution. "If something did happen to my father years ago, something he considered so terrible it could change his life, then there might be a clue to what it was in the Rockville house. He kept mementoes from his posts. Photographs, roster sheets, things that were important to him. I think we should go through them all."

"I see. Better done by two than three," added Peter, curiously satisfied that this was what Alison meant. "Perhaps you'd rather look by yourself. I can stand by and take notes for you."

She searched his eyes in that strange noncommittal way that reminded him of her father. But there was warmth in her voice. "You're very considerate. It's a quality I admire. I'm not. I wish I were, but I don't think it went, as they say, with the territory."

"I've got an idea," he said. "I have one solid talent: I can cook a hell of a meal. You're anxious to get to Rockville. So am I. Why don't we stop at a supermarket and I'll pick up some things? Like steaks and potatoes and scotch."

She smiled. "We'd save a lot of time."

"Done."

They took the eastern roads north and west into the Maryland countryside, stopping at a store in Randolph Hills for groceries and whisky.

It was growing dark. The December sun was below the hills; elongated shadows shot across the windscreen of the Army car, creating odd shapes that came and went swiftly. As he swung off the highway into the twisting road that led to the general's house, he reached the flat stretch of farmland and saw the outlines of the barbed-wire fence and the field beyond, where three months before he'd thought he would lose his life.

The road turned sharply. He held his foot on the accelerator, afraid to lessen the pressure. He had to get away. The ache was at his right temple now, spreading downward, curving in his neck, throbbing at the base of his skull. Faster!

"Peter! For God's sake!"

The tyres screeched; he held the wheel firmly as they rounded the turn and came out of it. He braked the car, reducing speed.

"Is anything the matter?" she asked.

"No," he lied. "I'm sorry. I just wasn't thinking." He could feel her looking at him; he had not fooled her for an instant. "That's not true," he continued. "I was remembering when I was here before, when I saw your father and mother."

"I was thinking about my last visit, too," she said. "It was this past summer. I came down for a few days. I was supposed to stay a week, but it didn't work out that way. I upped and left with a number of choice words I wish to God I'd never said."

"Was that when he told you he was resigning?"

"Had resigned. I think that bothered me as much as anything. We'd always discussed important things. And then the most important decision of his life arose, and I was cut off. I said terrible things."

"He made an extraordinary decision without explaining it to you. Your reaction was natural."

They fell silent; neither said anything of consequence for the final ten miles. The night had come quickly; the moon had risen.

"There it is. The white letterbox," said Alison.

Chancellor slowed down and turned into the concealed driveway, hidden by the profuse foliage on either side and the low-hanging branches of the trees beyond. Had it not been for the letterbox, the entrance could have easily been missed.

The house stood in eerie isolation, ordinary and alone and still. Moonlight filtered through the trees, speckling the front with shadows. The windows were smaller than Peter remembered, the roof lower. Alison got out of the ear and walked slowly up the narrow path to the door. Chancellor followed, carrying the groceries and the whisky from the store in Randolph Hills. She unlocked the door.

They both smelled it at once. It was not overpowering, or even unpleasant, but it pervaded the area. A musk-like odour, faintly aromatic, a dying fragrance escaping closed quarters into the night air. Alison squinted her eyes in the moonlight, her head angled in thought. Peter watched her; for a moment she seemed to shiver.

"It's Mother's," she said.

"Perfume?"

"Yes. But she died over a month ago."

Chancellor remembered her words in the car. "You said you were here last summer. Didn't you come down – "

"For the funeral?"

"Yes."

"No. Because I didn't know she'd died. My father called me when everything was over. There was no announcement, no service to speak of. It was a private burial, just he and the woman he remembered as no one else remembered her." Alison walked into the dark hall and turned on the light. "Come on, we'll put the bags in the kitchen."

They walked through the small dining room to a swinging door that led to the kitchen. Alison switched on the lights, revealing oddly old-fashioned counters and cabinets in contrast to the modern refrigerator. It was as if a 1930s kitchen had been intruded upon by a futuristic appliance. Peter was struck by his memory of the house. Except for the general's study, what he had seen of it was old-fashioned, as if deliberately decorated for a different era.

Alison seemed to read his thoughts. "My father reconstructed wherever possible the type of surroundings she associated with her childhood."

"It's an extraordinary love story." It was all he could say.

"It was an extraordinary sacrifice," she said.

"You resented her, didn't you?"

She did not flinch from the question. "Yes, I did. He was an exceptional man. He happened to be my father, but that is irrelevant. He was a man of ideas. I read once that an idea was a greater monument than a cathedral, and I believe that. But his cathedral – or cathedrals – never got built. His commitments were always sidetracked. He was never allowed the time to see them through. He had *her* in his footlocker!"

Chancellor did not let her angry eye waver from his. "You said the men around him were sympathetic. They helped him in every way they could."

"Of course they did. He wasn't the only one with a whacked-out woman. It's pretty standard, according to the West Point underground. But he was different. He had something original to say. And when they didn't want to hear it, they killed him with kindness. 'Poor Mac! Look what he has to live with!' "

"You were his daughter, not his wife."

"I *was* his wife! In everything but the bed! And sometimes I wondered whether that – It doesn't matter. I got out." She gripped the edge of the counter. "I'm sorry. I don't know you that well. I don't know anyone that well." She bent over the counter, trembling.

Peter resisted the instinct to hold her. "Do you think you're the only girl in the world who's felt that way? I don't think so, Alison."

"It's cold." She pushed herself partially up; still he did not touch her. "I can feel the cold. The furnace must have gone off." She stood erect and wiped away the tears with the back of her hand. "Do you know anything about furnaces?"

"Gas or oil?"

"I don't know."

"I'll find out. Is that the door to the basement?" He pointed to a door in the right wall.

"Yes."

He found the light switch and walked down the narrow stairs, pausing at the bottom. The furnace was in the centre of a low-ceilinged room; an oil tank was against the left wall. It *was* cold; a damp chill permeated the basement as though an outside door had been left open.

But the outside door was bolted. He checked the oil-tank gauge; it registered half full, but could very well be inaccurate. Why else would the furnace be off? MacAndrew was not the sort of man to leave a house in the country without heat in the winter. He tapped the side of the tank. Hollow above, full lower down. The gauge was accurate.

He lifted the plate of the firing mechanism and saw the cause of the problem. The pilot light had gone out. Under normal circumstances it would take a strong gust of wind to extinguish it. Or a blockage in the line. But the furnace had been checked recently. There was a small strip of plastic adhesive dating the last inspection. It was six weeks old.

Peter read the instructions. They were nearly identical to those of his parents' furnace.

Press red button for sixty seconds. Hold match beneath . . .

He heard a sudden, sharp clattering; the sound caused him to gasp. The muscles of his stomach tensed; he angled his head, frozen by the *rat-tat-tat* somewhere behind him. It stopped.

654

Then started again! He spun around and moved towards the stairs. He looked up.

On the top of the basement wall a window was open. It was at ground level; the wind outside was hammering against it.

That was the explanation. Wind from the window had extinguished the pilot light. Chancellor walked to the wall, suddenly afraid again.

The pane of glass had been shattered. He could feel the crunching of glass beneath his feet. Someone had broken into MacAndrew's home!

It happened too quickly. For an instant, he could not send commands from his mind to his body.

Screams came from upstairs. Again and again! Alison! He raced up the narrow steps to the kitchen. Alison was not there, but her screams continued, animal-like and terrified.

"Alison! Alison!"

He ran into the dining room.

"Alison!"

The screaming subsided abruptly, replaced by low moans and sobs. They came from across the house, through the hall and the living room. From MacAndrew's study!

Peter raced through the rooms, kicking one chair out of the way, sending another crashing to the floor. He burst through the study door.

Alison was on her knees, holding a faded, bloodstained nightgown in her hands. All around her were smashed bottles of perfume, the odour overpowering now and sickening.

And on the wall, painted in blood-red enamel, were the words:

MAC THE KNIFE. KILLER OF CHASŎNG

18

The paint on the walls was soft to the touch but not wet. The blood on the tattered nightgown was moist. The general's study had been searched thoroughly by professionals. The desk had been pried apart, the leather upholstery carefully slit. The boxed windowsills and weight sashes had been separated and exposed, the bookcase emptied of its contents, the bindings precisely cut.

Peter led Alison back into the kitchen, where he poured two glasses of straight scotch. He returned to the basement, started the furnace, and plugged the broken window with rags. Upstairs in the living room he discovered that the fireplace worked; more than a dozen logs were in a large wicker bin to the right of the screen. He built a fire and sat with Alison on the couch in front of it. The horror was fading, but the questions remained.

"What's Chasŏng?" he asked.

"I don't know. I think it's a place in Korea, but I'm not sure."

"When we find out, we may learn what it was that happened. What it was they were looking for."

"Anything could have happened. It was war, and – " She stopped, watching the flames.

"And he was a soldier who sent other soldiers into combat. It might be as simple as that. Someone who lost a son or a brother; someone out for vengeance. I've heard of such things."

"But why him? There were hundreds like him. And he was known for leading his men, not staying behind. No one ever questioned any of his commands. Not that way."

"Someone did," said Peter. "Someone very sick."

She looked at him for several moments, not answering. "You know what you're saying, don't you? Whether sick or not, whatever the person knows, or thinks he knows, it's true."

"I haven't thought it out that far. I'm not sure it follows."

"It has to. My father wouldn't have turned his back on everything he believed in if it were anything else." She shuddered. "What could he have *done?*"

"It had something to do with your mother."

"Impossible."

"Is it? I saw that nightgown the afternoon I was here. She was wearing it then. She'd fallen down. There was broken glass around her."

"She was always breaking things. She could be very destructive. The gown is a last cruel joke. I suppose it signifies my father's impotence. That wasn't a secret."

"Where was your mother during the Korean War?"

"In Tokyo. We both were."

"That was in fifty or fifty-one?"

"Around then, yes. I was very young."

"About six years old?"

"Yes."

Peter sipped his scotch. "Is that when your mother became ill?"

"Yes."

"Your father said there was an accident. Do you remember what happened?"

"I *know* what happened. She drowned. I mean, really drowned. They brought her back with electric shock, but the loss of oxygen was too prolonged. It was enough to cause the brain damage."

"How did it happen?"

"She was caught in the undertow at Funabashi Beach. She was swept out. The lifeguards couldn't reach her in time."

They were both silent for a while. Chancellor finished his scotch, got up from the sofa, and poked the fire. "Shall I fix us something to eat? Then afterwards we can – "

"I'm *not* going back in there!" she said harshly, staring at the fire, interrupting him. Then she looked up. "Forgive me. You're the last person I should yell at."

"I'm the only one here," he answered. "If you feel like yelling – "

"I know," she broke in, "it's allowed."

"I think it is."

"Are there no limits to your tolerance?" She asked the question softly, gentle humour in her eyes. He could feel her warmth. And vulnerability.

"I don't think I'm particularly tolerant. It's not a word often associated with me."

"I may test that judgement." Alison rose from the sofa and approached him, putting her hands on his shoulders. With the fingers of her right hand she delicately outlined his left cheek, his eyes, and, finally, his lips. "I'm not a writer. I draw pictures; they're my words. And I'm not capable of drawing what I think, or feel, right now. So I ask your tolerance, Peter. Will you give it to me?"

She leaned into him, her fingers still on his lips, and pressed her mouth against his, removing her fingers only when her lips widened.

He could feel the trembling in her body as she thrust herself against him. Her needs were born of exhaustion and sudden, overwhelming loneliness, thought Peter. She desperately wanted the expression of love, for a love had been taken away. Something – anything, perhaps – had to replace it, if only for a while, for a moment.

Oh, *God*, he understood! And because he understood he wanted her. It was in a way a confirmation of his own agonies. They had been born of the same exhaustion, the same manner of loneliness and guilt. It suddenly occurred to him that for months he'd had no one to talk to, no one had been permitted near him.

"I don't want to go upstairs," she whispered, her breath coming rapidly against his mouth, her fingers digging into his back as she clung to him.

"We won't," he answered softly, reaching for the buttons of her blouse.

She turned partially away from him and brought her right hand to her throat. In one gesture she tore her blouse away; with a second she opened his shirt. Their flesh met.

He was aroused in a way he had not been for months. Since Cathy. He led her to the couch and gently unhooked her brassiere. It fell away, revealing soft, sloping breasts, the nipples taut, awakened. She pulled his head down, and as his mouth roamed over her skin, she reached for the buckle of his belt. They lay down and the comfort was splendid.

Alison fell into a deep sleep, and Peter knew it was pointless to try to get her upstairs into a bed. Instead, he brought down blankets and pillows. The fire had subsided. He lifted Alison's head, placing the softest pillow beneath her, and draped a blanket over her naked body. She did not move.

He arranged two blankets on the floor in front of the fireplace, only feet from the couch, and lay down. He had understood a number of things during the past few hours, but not the state of his own exhaustion. He was asleep immediately.

He awoke with a start, unsure for a moment where he was, jolted by the sound of a log settling into its cradle of embers. There was dim light coming from the small front windows; it was early morning. He looked over at Alison on the couch. She was still asleep, the deep breathing had not changed. He lifted his wrist to see his watch. It was twenty to six. He had slept nearly seven hours.

He got up, put on his trousers, and wandered into the kitchen. The groceries were still there unopened, and he put them away. Rummaging in the old-fashioned cabinets, he found a coffeepot. It was a percolator, in keeping with the decor; it must have been made forty years ago. There was coffee in the refrigerator, and Peter tried to remember how to manipulate the pot and the grounds. He did the best he could and left the percolator over a small flame on the stove.

He walked back to the living room. Quietly, he put on the rest of his clothes, returned to the hall, and let himself out the front door. Their two suitcases and his briefcase weren't going to do them any good in the Army staff car parked in the small driveway.

It was cold and damp. The Maryland winter could not make up its mind whether to produce snow or stay on the edge of freezing mist. As a result the dampness was penetrating. Peter opened the car door and reached into the back seat for their luggage.

His eyes were abruptly riveted in shock; he was unable to control the gasp that emerged from his throat. The sight was appalling, grotesque.

And it explained the blood on the walls of MacAndrew's study and on the nightgown.

On his suitcase, which lay flat on the seat above Alison's on the floor, were the severed hind legs of an animal carcass, its ugly tendons extended beyond its blood-soaked fur. And on the leather of the case, finger-painted in blood was the word:

Chasŏng

Peter's shock was replaced by a shudder of fear and revulsion. He backed out of the car, darting his eyes into the thick foliage and towards the road beyond. He walked cautiously around the car. He knelt down and picked up a rock, not sure why he did so, yet strangely, only slightly comforted by the primitive weapon.

There was the snap of a branch! A twig had been broken somewhere. *There*, or *there*, or – *footsteps*.

Someone was running. Suddenly *running!* On gravel.

Peter did not know whether his fear was suspended by the sound or by the fact that the racing footsteps were running away, but he ran as fast as he could after them. Then the footsteps were muted; the racing feet were now on a hard surface, not gravel. The road!

He crashed through the foliage, branches snapping back into his face, roots and trunks impeding his progress. He reached the road; fifty yards away a figure was running in the dim, early light towards a car. Vapour mingled with the morning mist; the car's engine was being gunned. The right door was opened by an unseen hand from inside the car; the figure leaped in, and the car sped away into the progressive darkness.

Peter stood in the road, perspiration rolling down his forehead. He let the rock drop and wiped his face.

The words came back to him, spoken by an angry woman over candlelight at the Hay-Adams in Washington.

Terror by fiat.

It was what he was witnessing now. Someone wanted to frighten Alison MacAndrew out of her mind. But *why?* Her father was dead. What was to be gained by terrifying the daughter?

He decided to keep part of the horror away from Alison. He *wanted* to keep it from her. Everything had happened too quickly, but he knew a void was being filled for him. Alison had come into his life.

He wondered if it would last. That question was suddenly very important to him. He turned and walked back to the car, removed the blood-soaked animal legs and threw them into the woods. He took out the two suitcases and his briefcase and carried them back into the house. He was thankful that Alison was still asleep.

He left Alison's suitcase in the hall, picked up his own and his briefcase, and carried the two pieces into the kitchen. He remembered from somewhere that cold water removed blood more easily than hot. He turned on the tap, found paper towels, and for fifteen minutes rubbed the stained leather clean. What marks were left he scraped with the blade of a bread knife, roughing the surface until the outline of the letters disappeared.

And then, for reasons he could not explain to himself, he opened the briefcase, removed his notebook, and placed it on the table in the old-fashioned kitchen. The percolator bubbled. He poured a cup of coffee and returned to the table. He opened the notebook and stared at the yellow page half filled with words. It was not merely a compulsion of the morning; it was somehow fitting that he should try to examine his thoughts and put them down through another's mind. For he had just lived through an experience he had attributed to a character he had created. He had been followed in darkness.

The FBI agents release Meredith. He wanders down the country road in the twilight.

There is a lapse of time.

Meredith has returned home. He tells his wife he was in an accident on Memorial Parkway, the car towed away for repairs. She does not believe him.

"Truth is not spoken here any more," she screams. "I can't stand it any longer! What's happening to us?"

Alex knows what's happened to them. Hoover's strategy of fear is too effective. The tensions have become unbearable; even their very strong marriage is in danger of coming apart. He is beaten. He accepts his wife's ultimatum: they will leave Washington. He will leave the Justice Department and go back to private practice, a part of him dead. The most professional part. Hoover has won.

It is past midnight. Alex's family are in bed. He has remained downstairs in his living room, a single table lamp on, the light dim, shadows everywhere. He has been drinking heavily. Mingled with his fear is the realization that everything he has believed in is meaningless.

In his drunken state he passes a window. Frightened, he parts the curtains and peers outside. He sees an FBI car parked down the block. Men are watching his house.

His mind snaps. The alcohol, the fear, the depression and the anxiety combine to produce hysteria. He rushes to the front door and goes outside. He does not yell or scream; instead he imposes a grotesque silence on himself, a *conspiratorial* silence. In his drunkenness he wants to reach his tormentors and surrender, to throw himself at their mercy, to become one of them. His panic is identical with his psychological collapse in wartime years ago.

He runs down the block. The car is gone; he hears voices in the darkness, but he can see no one. He races around the streets after the unseen voices, a part of him wondering if he's gone mad, another part desperately wanting only to surrender, to give up to the victors and plead for their forgiveness.

He doesn't know how long he's been running, but the night air, the heavy breathing, and the physical strain reduce the effects of the alcohol. He begins to take hold of himself. He starts back towards his house, unsure of the streets. He must have run several miles.

As he walks, he spots the FBI car. It is around a corner, in shadows. There's no one inside; the men who have followed him, watched him, abused him, are walking too, in the dark, quiet streets.

He hears footsteps in the darkness. Behind him, in front of him, to the right, to the left. They fall into the rhythm of his heartbeat, becoming louder, until they're like kettledrums; menacing, deafening.

He recognizes a street sign; he knows where he is. He begins to run again; the footsteps keep pace, producing the panic once more. He races in the middle of the street, turning corners, running like a maniac.

He sees his house. He is suddenly alarmed further, filled with a new fear that is overpowering. He had left the front door open. And there is an unfamiliar car parked in front of the kerb.

He runs faster towards the strange car, prepared to kill if need be.

But the man inside the car arrived only minutes ago. He has been there waiting, thinking that perhaps Alex had taken a dog for a walk, carelessly leaving the door open.

"At five-thirty tomorrow afternoon, go to the Carteret Hotel. Room 1201. Take the lift to the top floor, then walk down the stairs to the twelfth floor. We'll have men watching. If you're followed, we'll throw them off."

"What is all this? Who are you?"

"A man wants to meet you. He's a senator."

"Peter, where are you?" It was Alison, her startled voice carried from the living room. The sound brought him back to the other world, the real one.

"In the kitchen," he called out, his eyes on his suitcase; the leather was still damp, the scraping obvious. "I'll be right there," he said.

"Don't bother," Alison replied, her relief clear. "There should be coffee in the fridge, and the pot's in the upper right cabinet."

"I found them," he answered, picking up the suitcase, turning it around, and placing it in the corner. "The coffee didn't turn out so well. I'll try again."

He went quickly to the table, brought the pot back to the sink, and began dismantling the antiquated mechanism. He threw the used grounds into an empty grocery bag and turned on the tap.

Seconds later Alison came through the door, a blanket wrapped around her.

Their eyes met, the message – the communication – clear. At the sight of her Peter ached; the ache was pleasant and warm.

"You've come into my life," she said softly. "I wonder if you'll stay."

"I wondered the same about you. In my life."

"We'll see, won't we?"

19

Varak came through the door of Bravo's study without the usual knock.

"It's more than one man," he said. "Or if it's one man, he's commanding others. They've made their first overt move. Chancellor thinks it's directed at the girl. It's not, of course; it's meant for him."

"They want to stop him, then." Bravo did not ask a question.

"And if he won't be stopped," added Varak, "throw him off the scent. Decoy him."

"Please explain."

"I've run the tapes. You can hear them if you like. And see them – both audio and video. They tore apart MacAndrew's study, searching for something ... or giving the illusion of searching. I tend to favour the latter. The decoy was in the name. *Chasŏng.* They want him to think it's a key."

"Chasŏng?" said Bravo, reflecting. "That goes back a long time, if I'm not mistaken. I remember Truman exploding over it. The Battle of Chasŏng, Korea."

"Yes. Five minutes ago I got a computer print-out from G-Two archives. Chasŏng was our worst defeat north of the thirty-eighth parallel. It was an unauthorized attack – "

"For minor real estate," interrupted St Claire. "A few meaningless hills. It was the first in a series of debacles that eventually led to MacAndrew's dismissal."

"The print-out doesn't put it quite that way, of course."

"Of course. So?"

"MacAndrew was a colonel then. He was one of the commanders."

Bravo reflected. "Does Chasŏng correspond in time with the missing data in MacAndrew's service record?"

"Approximately. If it's the decoy, it would have to. Whoever has Hoover's files can't know precisely what MacAndrew told Chancellor. A panicked man under the stress of being discovered will often base his cover on accurate chronology and false information."

" 'While the bank was being robbed ten days ago, I was at the movies.' "

"Exactly."

"Lifted to this level, it becomes quite cerebral, doesn't it?"

"The chess tournament's begun. I think you should hear and see the tapes."

"Very well."

The two men walked quickly out of Bravo's study to the brass-grilled lift at the rear of the front hall. A minute later St Claire and Varak walked into the small studio in the basement complex. The equipment was set to run.

"We'll start at the beginning. It's the videotape." Varak switched on the video projector. The blank lead-in tape produced a white square on the wall. "The camera was too obvious to place inside the house. Incidentally, it's tripped electronically. Please remember that."

The image of MacAndrew's house was thrown on the wall. But the light was not that of early evening, the time when Chancellor and the girl had arrived. Instead, there was bright sunlight.

The agent snapped a switch. The tape stopped; a still picture remained on the wall. "Yes," said Varak. "The camera was tripped. It's very sensitive. The timer tells us it was three o'clock in the afternoon. Someone has entered the house, obviously from the rear, out of camera range." He snapped the switch again; the tape continued. Then it stopped again. The projector shut off automatically. Again, St Claire looked quizzically at Varak.

"They're in the house now. The trip's deactivated. We go to audio." The agent pressed a button on his audiotape machine.

There were the sounds of footsteps, a door being opened, the squeak of a hinge, more footsteps, the opening of a second door. "There are two men," said Varak. "Or possibly one man and a heavy woman. According to the decibel count, each weighs over a hundred and fifty pounds." There was an indistinguishable series of rustling sounds and then a strange, eerie bleat. It came again, now more pronounced and, in its way, quite terrible. Varak spoke. "It's an animal. Sheep family, I think. But perhaps a pig. I'll refine it later."

The next minutes were taken up with harsh, swift sounds. Paper cut, leather and fabric sliced, drawers opened. Finally there was the smashing of glass, interspersed with the strident squeals of the unknown animal, squeals that suddenly erupted into a screech.

"The animal is being killed." Varak spoke simply.

"Good God!" said St Claire.

Then from the speakers came a human voice. Two words.

Let's go.

The tape stopped. Varak turned off the machine. "We'll pick up approximately three hours later. With the arrival of Chancellor and MacAndrew's daughter. There's a twenty-second video still of the house; that's the intruders leaving – again out of range, so we have no picture of them." The agent paused as if unsure of how to explain something. "I've edited out a particular section, and with your permission I'll destroy it. It's irrelevant. It merely establishes the fact that Chancellor and the girl have formed a relationship. Temporarily, probably."

"I understand and I thank you," said Bravo.

The house once again appeared briefly on the wall. It was night now. A car was seen driving up to the stone path leading to the front door. Alison emerged and stood for a moment looking at the house. She proceeded up the path.

Chancellor came into view carrying grocery bags. They paused on the small porch, talked briefly, and then the girl opened her purse and searched for a key. Taking it out, she opened the door.

The two seemed startled at something. A further discussion ensued, more animated than before, and then they went inside. With the closing of the door the videotape stopped. Without speaking, Varak reached over and pressed the audio button.

Come on, we'll put the bags in the kitchen. The girl. Footsteps, the rustling of paper, the metallic squeak of a hinge, and then a prolonged silence followed. The woman finally spoke again.

My father reconstructed wherever possible the type of surroundings she associated with her childhood.

Chancellor: It's an extraordinary love story.

It was an extraordinary sacrifice. The girl.

You resented her, didn't you. Chancellor.

Yes, I did. He was an exceptional man. . .

Suddenly Varak reached over and snapped the switch. "That's the key. The *mother*. I'd stake everything I know on it. Chasŏng's a decoy. For the next half hour, listen, very, *very* carefully. The writer in Chancellor homed in on her instinctively, but she dissuaded him. Not intentionally, because I don't think she knows."

"I shall listen most carefully, Mr Varak."

They both did. Several times Bravo was forced to dart his eyes away, at nothing, in response to the unexpected: at the girl's scream from inside her father's study, at the sobs and the tears that followed, at Chancellor's compassion and sharp interrogation. The writer's imagination would not be stopped. His original premise was right, St Claire reflected. In less than nine weeks Chancellor had made extraordinary progress. Neither he nor Varak knew how or why, but the murder of Walter Rawlins was related to the files somehow, and now there was this maverick general, his outspoken daughter, and a "decoy" called Chasŏng. Above all, the overt move had been made. Men had come out of the dark, the sounds of their actions recorded.

St Claire did not know where Chancellor was taking them. Only that Hoover's files were closer.

The images appeared once again on the wall: Chancellor coming out of the house, opening the car door, and recoiling. Then cautiously walking around the car, picking up a rock, running into the foliage, returning, throwing two indistinguishable objects out of the car, removing the suitcases, and going back into the house.

Sound then: running water and scraping.

"An hour ago I stopped the tape and studied the picture. He's removing the name Chasŏng from the suitcase," Varak explained. "He doesn't want the girl to see it."

Silence ensued. The microphones picked up the scratching of a pencil against paper. Varak jumped the tape to the sound of recorded voices.

Peter, where are you?

In the kitchen . . .
A discussion about making coffee, rapid footsteps, obscure movement.

You've come into my life. I wonder if you'll stay. Spoken softly by Alison MacAndrew.

I wondered the same about you. In my life.

We'll see, won't we?

It was over. Varak turned off the machine and stood up. Bravo remained in the chair, his aristocratic fingers joined together under his chin.

"That scratching we heard," he said. "Can we presume he was writing?"

"I think so. It fits his habits."

"Remarkable, isn't it? In the midst of it all, he turned to his novel."

"Unusual, perhaps. I don't know how remarkable. If we're doing things right, his novel is becoming very real to him."

Bravo disengaged his fingers and placed his hands on the arms of the chair. "Which brings us to that novel and your interpretation of it. As inconceivable as I find it, do you still believe our quarry is a member of Inver Brass?"

"First, let me ask a question. When I asked you to call a meeting the night before last, did you give the members the information I thought advisable? That Chancellor had met the girl?"

"I would have told you if I hadn't."

"I knew you disapproved."

"My disapproval was based on my conviction. That same conviction led me to follow your instructions, if only to prove you wrong." Bravo's speech was clipped, bordering on the disagreeable. "Now, what's your answer? Are you still convinced a member of Inver Brass has those files?"

"I'll know within a day or two."

"Which is no answer."

"It's the best I can do. Frankly I think I'm right; everything points to it."

St Claire sat up. "Because I told them about Chancellor and the girl and gave them MacAndrew's name?"

"Not just the name," replied Varak. "The fact that eight months are missing from his service record."

"Inconclusive! Whoever has Hoover's files knows it."

"Precisely. That decoy – the diversionary Chasŏng occurred during those eight months. I think we can assume that whatever happened at Chasŏng, whatever military decisions MacAndrew made or refused to make, could not have been sufficiently damaging to cause him to resign. If they had, there were enough men at the Pentagon who would have forced him out long ago."

"A disagreeable incident, perhaps," Bravo agreed, "but not a disastrous one. A part of the file, but not the vital part."

"A cover for it," agreed Varak. "Something else happened, possibly related, possibly not. Assuming there's a primary connection – which we must assume – it's that something else that can lead us to whoever has Hoover's files."

'Then, what you're telling me is' – St Claire's eyes strayed – "that given the twenty-four-hour period between Inver Brass's meeting and Chancellor's arrival at MacAndrew's house, the decoy was culled from the files. The other night was the first Inver Brass had heard of Chancellor, to say nothing of MacAndrew."

"The first Inver Brass – as a *group* – had heard of Chancellor. But not whoever has the files. He knew because Chancellor made contact with two of the victims. MacAndrew and Rawlins. I don't think there's any question that they were victims."

"All right, I'll accept that." Bravo got out of the chair. "So then, it boils down to one specific piece of information: Peter Chancellor had made contact with the general's daughter. They were on their way to the Rockville house. And rather than have the encounter lead to a blank wall, the Chasŏng ruse is planted. To send Chancellor off in another direction."

"That's it," said Varak firmly. "Otherwise, why use Chasŏng at *all?*"

"Still," said St Claire, "why does it have to be a member of Inver Brass?"

"Because no one else knew that Chancellor had made contact with the girl. I can assure you of that. Except for our taps his phones are sterile; there is no surveillance on him but our own. Yet, within twelve hours of Inver Brass's meeting MacAndrew's house is broken into and an elaborate deception is mounted for Chancellor. Those twelve hours were enough to examine MacAndrew's dossier and come up with the Chasŏng decoy."

St Claire nodded sadly. "You're very convincing."

"The facts are convincing. I wish they weren't."

"God knows, so do I. A member of Inver Brass! The most honoured men in the nation. You speak of probability. That's one I would have considered non-existent."

"Chancellor didn't. For him it was defined at the outset. You said it yourself when we began: he's not restricted by fact or conditioning. Incidentally, he calls *his* Inver Brass the Nucleus."

St Claire stared at the wall where minutes before the images had been projected. "The reality and the fantasy. It's extraordinary." He let the words trail off.

"It's what we wanted," said Varak. "What we hoped for."

"Yes, of course. You'll know for certain within a day or two, you say?"

"I'll guarantee it if you'll call another meeting. After MacAndrew's funeral. I want two more names fed to Inver Brass."

"Oh? Who?"

"The first is a newspaper columnist, Phyllis Maxwell. She's – "

"I know who she is. Why?"

"I'm not sure – she hasn't surfaced before. But Chancellor's met her, and he's written a character into his novel that bears a striking resemblance to her."

"I see. Who's the other?"

Varak hesitated. It was obvious he expected resistance. "Paul Bromley. The man from General Services Administration."

"No!" The diplomat reacted emphatically. "I won't permit it. Bromley has my word! For one thing, it doesn't make sense. Bromley begins with *B*. We're after names from *M* to *Z*!"

"Remember, Bromley's code name is Viper," replied Varak. "It's been in continuous use at the Pentagon, G2, and the bureau for over twenty months.

He's been out of sight since August; he's virtually disappeared. He's dangerous to a lot of people in Washington, but no one's heard from him. Viper's the forgotten man, and thus he is ideal for our purpose."

Bravo paced slowly. "The man's suffered so much. You're asking a lot."

"Minor compared to our objective. From what I know about Bromley, I believe he'd be the first to agree."

St Claire closed his eyes, thinking of the anguish Bromley had lived through. The ageing, irascible accountant who had had the courage to take on the Pentagon by himself. His reward was an addicted daughter, who, missing for three years, had returned as an unbalanced killer; and now that his world was stable again, the nightmare promised to return. He was to be used as bait.

But in his field, in the dark corners of his exotic profession, Stefan Varak was brilliant. And he was right.

"Go to work," St Claire said. "I'll convene Inver Brass tonight."

The drum rolls were soft. Muted intrusions of thunder carried on the December wind. The grave was in the north section of Arlington Cemetery. The guard of honour stood on the west flank. The rigid phalanx carried the Army's unspoken command: *The coffin will be taken this far, and no further. It will then be lowered beneath the earth. We are here in military splendour to demand respect. It shall be rendered. But silently. There will be no signs of private grief, for these are not seemly. This is Army ground. We are men. Dead men.*

It was frightening, thought Chancellor, standing several feet behind Alison, who was seated on a single, plain black chair at the foot of the cordoned-off area. One did not touch, one did not relate. To anything except the ritual.

We are put to rest by the numbers. Count off!

Around the square grave-site, beyond the chains, stood the senior officers of the Pentagon. A dozen or so had come up to Alison, speaking softly, holding her hands. She was the Greek chorus that told Peter who the players were in relation to her father. And he kept his eyes alert. It was entirely possible that someone there held the secret of Chasŏng. He could only study the faces and allow his imagination free rein.

There was one man, roughly the same age as MacAndrew, who caught Peter's attention. He was a major, and he was dark-complexioned. Mediterranean heritage, Chancellor thought. He stood silently throughout the brief service, talking to no one. When the coffin was carried from the hearse across the lawn to the grave, the man's eyes remained to the front; he did not acknowledge the presence of the deceased.

It was only during the chaplain's eulogy that the major showed any sign of emotion. It was brief – barely a flash – in his eyes, at the corners of his mouth. The expression was one of hatred.

Peter kept looking at him. For a moment the major seemed aware that he was being watched, and for an instant he locked eyes with Chancellor. The hatred flashed again and disappeared. He looked away.

When the service was over and the flag given to the daughter of the buried soldier, the officers came up one by one to utter the expected words.

But the dark-complected major turned and walked away without saying anything. Peter watched him. He reached the slope of a small hill, beyond the serrated ranks of graves, and stopped. Slowly he turned and looked back, an isolated figure standing above the headstones.

Chancellor had the instinctive feeling that the major wanted a last look at MacAndrew's grave, as though to convince himself that the object of his loathing was really dead. It was a bleakly curious moment.

"I could feel your eyes behind me," said Alison as they settled back in the limousine that would take them out of Arlington Cemetery into Washington. "I glanced at you once. You were studying the crowd. And I know you heard every word said to me. Did you find anyone – or anything – interesting?"

"Yes," replied Peter. "A major. An Italian-looking fellow, or Spanish. He didn't come up to you. He was the only one of the officers who didn't."

Alison looked out of the window at the passing rows of graves. She kept her voice low so as not to be heard by the Army chauffeur and the escort. "Yes, I saw him."

"Then, you had to see the way he acted It was strange."

"It was normal. For him. He wears his resentments like decorations. They're *part* of his decorations."

"Who is he?"

"His name is Pablo Ramirez. He's from San Juan, one of the first appointments to West Point from the territory. I guess you'd call him the token Hispanic, before anyone knew what the term meant."

"Did he know your father?"

"Yes. They served together. Ramirez was two years behind him at the Point."

Peter touched her arm. "Did they serve together in Korea?"

"You mean Chasŏng?"

"Yes."

I don't know. Korea, yes, Also in North Africa in World War Two, and several years ago in Vietnam. But I don't know about Chasŏng."

"I'd like to find out. Why did he resent your father?"

"I'm not sure he did. Any more than he resented anyone else. I said *resentments*. Plural."

"Why?"

"He's still a major. Most of his contemporaries are lieutenant colonels, full colonels, or brigadiers."

"Is his resentment justified? Did he get passed over because he's Puerto Rican?"

"Oh, I suppose, partly. It's a pretty closed society in those regions. And I've heard the jokes: 'Be careful if you take Ramirez to a fleet cocktail party. They'll put a jacket on him.' In the navy the Puerto Ricans are houseboys. That sort of thing."

"That sort of thing justifies a lot of resentment."

"I'm sure it does, but it's not the whole picture. Ramirez was given a great many opportunities – more than most – perhaps because he *was* a member of a minority. He hasn't done much with them."

Peter glanced out the window, vaguely troubled. The look he had seen in Ramirez's eyes was specific hatred, directed at specific objects. MacAndrew's coffin. MacAndrew's grave. MacAndrew.

"What did your father think of him?" he asked.

"About what I just told you. He was a lightweight, hot-headed and too emotional. Not at all reliable. Dad refused to second two field promotions for him. Beyond that, he didn't say much."

"What did he mean, 'not at all reliable'?"

Alison frowned. "I'd have to think. It was in the areas of recap and recon, I believe."

"That's nice. I haven't the vaguest idea what you're talking about."

She laughed. "Sorry. They're written reports to field headquarters. Combat summaries and reconnaissance."

"That doesn't help much, but I think I know what you mean. Your father was saying that Ramirez was a liar. Either emotionally or by design."

"I guess so. He's not important, Peter." Alison placed her hand on his. "It's over. Finished, past, *over*. Thank you, thank you more than I can ever say."

"We're not 'over'," he said.

She held his eyes. "I hope not." Then she smiled. "A hotel's a beautiful idea. We'll luxuriate for a whole day and not think about anything. I'm sick of thinking. Then tomorrow I'll go see the lawyer and take care of things. I don't want you to feel you have to stay. I'll be back in New York in a few days."

Chancellor was startled; he wondered if she'd forgotten. So abruptly, so completely. He held her hand, not wanting her to pull away. "But there's the house in Maryland. Men broke in and – "

"Oh, God! Let it go! He's dead. They made their point, whatever it was."

"We'll talk about it later," he said.

"All right."

Peter understood. Alison had faced the agony of her father's death and the further anguish of examining that death. At the burial she had confronted the men who had tried to destroy him. The service at Arlington was a symbol for her: the Gordian knot had been severed; she was free to find her own world. And now he was asking her to go back.

He had to. Because it wasn't over. He knew it and so did she.

Chancellor knew something else, too. Alison had said that Ramirez was not important.

He was.

20

Once again the limousines arrived at the Georgetown house at different times, from different points of origin. Once again silent drivers had met their passengers sight unseen. Inver Brass convened.

It had been an unspoken agreement for many weeks between the elders – Bravo, Venice, and Christopher – that the choice of a new Genesis was between the two remaining younger men: Banner and Paris.

Beyond doubt, both were qualified, each brilliant, each extraordinary in several fields.

Banner had come to Inver Brass six years ago. He had been the youngest president in the history of a major eastern university, but he had left to assume chairmanship of the international Roxton Foundation. His name was Frederick Wells, and his expertise was in global finance. And yet, in spite of the worldwide impact of his decisions, Wells had never lost sight of the fundamental human need for dignity, respect and the freedoms of choice and expression. Wells believed deeply in human beings, with all their flaws, and those who sought to repress human beings or shape them or dominate them felt his wrath.

As John Edgar Hoover had unknowingly felt it.

Paris was the newest recruit; he had joined Inver Brass barely four years before. He was a scholar. His ancestral roots were in Madrid, but his own were fervently planted in America, where his family had fled to escape the Falangists. His name was Carlos Montelén. Presently, he occupied the Maynard Chair of International Relations at Harvard and was considered the country's most perceptive analyst of twentieth-century geopolitical thought. For a dozen years succeeding administrations had tried to recruit Montelén into the State Department, but he had demurred. He was a scholar, not an activist. He knew the intrinsic dangers that existed when theoreticians moved into the swift world of pragmatic negotiations.

Yet Montelén never stopped probing, never ceased his questioning of men and their motives – whether personal or related to a larger cause. And when he found one or both without merit, or destructive, he did not hesitate to make an active decision.

As he had not hesitated in the case of John Edgar Hoover.

Bravo had put off the selection of either contender, in spite of Christopher's urging. Christopher was Jacob Dreyfus, a banker, the last of the Jewish patriarchs, whose house rivalled the Baruchs' and the Lehmans'. Christopher was eighty and knew his time was short; it was important to him that Inver Brass instal its leader. A house without a man to give it direction was no house at all. And for Jacob Dreyfus there was no "house" in this beloved land as vital as the one he had helped found – Inver Brass.

He had said as much to Bravo, and Munro St Claire knew that no one said it better than Jacob. St Claire had been there at the beginning, too, as had Daniel

Sutherland, the black giant whose extraordinary intellect had carried him from the fields of Alabama to the highest judicial circles in the country. But neither Bravo nor Venice could summon the words that defined Inver Brass as well as Christopher could.

As Jacob Dreyfus expressed it, Inver Brass had been born in chaos, at a time when the nation was being torn apart, on the edge of self-destruction. The market had collapsed, business had ground to a halt; factories had been closed, storefronts boarded up, farms allowed to fall into disuse as cattle died and machinery rusted. The inevitable explosions of violence had begun to take place.

In Washington inept leaders had been incapable of action. So in the last months of 1929 Inver Brass had been formed. The first Genesis had been a Scotsman, an investment banker who'd followed the advice of Baruch and Dreyfus and had got out of the market. It had been he who had given the group its name, after a small marshland lake in the Highlands that was not on any map. For Inver Brass had to exist in secrecy. It operated outside the government bureaucracy because it had to operate swiftly, without encumbrances.

Massive sums of money had been transferred to countless distressed areas where violence – born of need – had erupted. Throughout the country the sharp edges of that violence had been dulled by the wealth of Inver Brass; the fires had been dampened, contained within acceptable limits.

But mistakes had been made, corrected as soon as they'd been understood. Some had gone beyond repair. The Depression had been worldwide; infusions of capital had been required beyond the nation's shores.

There was Germany. The economic devastations of the Versailles Treaty, the inadequacy of the Locarno pacts, the impracticality of the Dawes Plan – they were all misunderstood, the men of Inver Brass had thought. And that had been their most calamitous mistake. One that thirty-five years later a graduate student named Peter Chancellor began to perceive as the one thing it was *not*. A conspiracy of global politics.

He had to be stopped, this young man Chancellor. Inver Brass was in the shadows of his imagination, and he did not know it.

But the mistake had led the men of Inver Brass into new territory. They had entered the realm of national policy. At first beginning it was to try to rectify the errors they had made. But later it was because they could contribute. Inver Brass had the wisdom and the resources. It could act and react swiftly, without interference, answerable to no one but its collective conscience.

Munro St Claire and Daniel Sutherland had listened to Jacob's impassioned plea for the quick appointment of a new Genesis. Neither replied with any passion at all. Each had agreed without conviction, essentially saying nothing. St Claire knew that Sutherland could not know what he knew: there was the possibility that Inver Brass harboured a traitor. So Sutherland's doubts had to lie elsewhere. St Claire thought he knew what those doubts were: the days of Inver Brass were coming to a close. Perhaps, they would end with the elders, and maybe it was better that way. Time mandates change; they were from another era.

St Claire's doubts were much more specific. It was why he could not permit the elevation of a new Genesis. Not from either contender. For if there was a traitor in Inver Brass, it was either Banner or Paris.

They sat around the circular table, the empty Genesis chair a reminder of their essential impermanence. There was no need for a fire in the Franklin stove. No papers would have to be burned; none was on the table, nor would there be any. No coded reports had been delivered, for there were no decisions to make, only information to be imparted and comments to be heard.

A trap was to be set. First, developments had to be described in such a way that St Claire would observe the reaction of each man at the table. And then two names would be given: Phyllis Maxwell, journalist; Paul Bromley – code: Viper – vanished critic of the Pentagon. Vanished, but easily traced by any man at the table.

"Our meeting will be short this evening," said Bravo. "The purpose is to bring you up to date and hear anything you might have to say regarding the new developments."

"I trust that includes a comment on past decisions," said Paris.

"It includes anything you like."

"Good," continued Paris. "Since the other evening, I've picked up two books by Peter Chancellor. I'm not sure why you chose him. True, he has a quick mind and a flair for prose, but he's hardly a writer of literary distinction."

"We weren't looking for literary merit."

"Neither am I. And I don't discount the popular novel. I merely refer to this specific writer. Is he as capable as perhaps a dozen others? Why him?"

"Because we knew him," interjected Christopher. "We don't know a dozen others."

"I beg your pardon?" Banner, on Christopher's right, leaned forward.

"Christopher's point is well taken," said Bravo. "We know a great deal about Chancellor. Six years ago we had reason to learn. You both know the history of Inver Brass; we've concealed nothing from you. Our contributions, our errors. In the late sixties Chancellor was writing . . . ' – Bravo paused and addressed Paris – "an analytical dissertation on the Weimar collapse and the emergence of militant Germany. He came very close to identifying Inver Brass. He had to be stopped."

There was silence around the table. St Claire knew that the Negro and, more profoundly, the Jew were thinking about those days. Each in his own anguish.

"That dissertation," clarified Banner, staring at Paris, "became the novel *Reichstag!*"

"Wasn't that dangerous?" asked Paris.

"It was fair," replied Venice.

"It was also fiction," added Christopher disagreeably.

"That answers my question," said Paris. "It was a matter of familiarity as much as anything. Better a known entity with its limitations than an unknown one with greater promise."

"Why do you persist in discrediting Chancellor?" asked Venice. "We're after Hoover's files, not literary distinction."

"Subjective comparisons," answered the scholar. "He's the type of writer that annoys me. I know something about the events of Sarajevo and the conditions prevalent at the time. I read his book. He bases his conclusions on intentionally misinterpreted facts and on exaggerated associations. Yet I'm sure thousands of readers accept what he writes as authentic history."

Bravo leaned back in his chair. "I read that book too, and I know something about the events leading up to Sarajevo. Would you say that Chancellor's inclusion of the industrial conspiracy was in error?"

"Of course not. It's been established."

"Then, regardless of how he arrived at it, he was correct."

Paris smiled. "If you'll forgive me, I'm relieved that you don't teach history. But as I said, my question is answered. What are the new developments?"

"The developments constitute authentic progress; they can be termed nothing else." Bravo proceeded to describe Chancellor's meeting with Alison at Kennedy Airport, their meeting with the military escort, and the arrival of the plane bearing the general's coffin. As Varak had suggested, St Claire spoke slowly, watching for any reaction that would indicate that someone at the table anticipated his words because the events were known to him. It would be in the eyes, Varak had said. A brief, clouded response that was recognition. Certain chemical changes could not be concealed; the eyes were the microscope.

St Claire found no such reactions. No such responses. Only total absorption from each member at the table.

He proceeded to describe what had been heard on the tape. what had been seen on film.

"Without Varak's preparation we wouldn't have learned of the extraordinary action taken against Chancellor. And it *was* against Chancellor, not MacAndrew's daughter. We believe it's an attempt to throw him off course; to convince him MacAndrew's resignation was the result of command decisions made years ago in Korea, at a place called Chasŏng."

Paris's eyes widened; he reacted visibly. Then he spoke. "The killers of Chasŏng. . ."

A sharp pain shot through St Claire's chest; he lost his breath, unable for a moment to find it. He struggled for control as he looked sharply at Carlos Montelán.

The words Paris spoke were chilling to him. There was no way Paris could have known them! Nowhere on the tapes had the phrase been employed, and St Claire had not used it!

"What does that mean?" asked Venice, shifting his large frame in the chair.

"As any military historian will tell you, it was an epithet used to characterize the officers at the Battle of Chasŏng," said Paris. "It was suicidal madness. Troops revolted up and down the lines; many were shot by their own officers. It was a disastrous strategy, in some ways the political turning point of the war. If MacAndrew was there, it's quite possible a long dormant victim may have surfaced. It *could* be his motive for resigning."

St Claire watched Paris closely, relieved by the academic's explanation.

"Could it be related to his death in Hawaii?" asked Christopher, his gnarled hands trembling as he spoke.

"No," replied Bravo slowly. "MacAndrew was shot by Longworth."

"You mean Varak?" asked an incredulous Wells.

"No," said Bravo. "The real Longworth. In Hawaii."

It was as though a loud whip had been cracked. Eyes were riveted on St Claire.

"How? *Why?*" Anger was in Venice's voice. Daniel Sutherland was outraged.

"It was unpredictable and therefore uncontrollable. As you know, Varak used Longworth's name with Chancellor. It was a source he could check, a springboard. Chancellor gave the name to MacAndrew, told him that Longworth had access to the files. After his wife died, the general flew halfway across the world to find Longworth. He found him."

"Then MacAndrew presumed that only Longworth knew what happened at Chasŏng," said Frederick Wells thoughtfully. "That the information was in Hoover's files and nowhere else."

"And *that* leads us nowhere. Except back to the files." Once again Christopher spoke disagreeably.

"It does help," added Banner, looking at Bravo. "It confirms what you say. Chasŏng is a diversion."

"Why?" asked Venice.

Wells turned to the judge. "Because there was no reason for it. Why was it used at all?"

"I agree." St Claire leaned forward, his composure regained. The first part of Varak's trap had produced nothing. It was the moment for the second, the two names. "As I told you the other night, Chancellor is well into his novel. Varak managed to get his hands on the manuscript. There are two rather startling developments. I should say, two people have surfaced, neither of whom was considered previously. We don't know why. One is a thinly disguised character in the book, the other a man in Chancellor's notes – a man he is trying to find. The first is the newspaper columnist, Phyllis Maxwell. The second, an accountant named Bromley, Paul Bromley. He used to be with General Services. Do any of you have any particular information on either of these people?"

None did. But the names were planted, the second trap set. If there was substance in Varak's conclusions, St Claire wondered which of them would be caught. Banner or Paris? Frederick Wells or Carlos Montelán?

The conversation trailed off. Bravo indicated that Inver Brass's meeting was over. He pushed back his chair but was stopped by Wells's voice.

"Is Varak outside in the hallway?"

"Yes, of course," answered the diplomat. "He's made arrangements for your departures, as usual."

"I'd like to ask him a question. I'll address it first to all of you. There were microphones inside the Rockville house. You describe the sounds of men breaking in and ransacking MacAndrew's study but no words to accompany these sounds. Outside, a camera is triggered off but shows nothing because the intruders were out of visual range. It's almost as if they knew about the equipment."

"What's your question?" asked Montelán, a sharp edge to his voice. "I'm not sure I like the implication."

Banner looked at Paris. It was unmistakable, thought St Claire. Lines were drawn. Lines? Lions, perhaps. The young standing up against the ageing and each other, growling for leadership of the pride.

"I find it curious. The files were taken in such a way – at such a time – as to indicate that the thieves anticipated Hoover's death. Months of intensive investigation led nowhere; one of the best intelligence specialists in this country reports that he's made no progress. Bravo conceives of the idea of using this writer Chancellor to probe. Our intelligence specialist expedites the plan; the writer is programmed and begins his work. As expected, he creates a disturbance. Those who have Hoover's files are alarmed and make their move against him. A move, I submit, that should have been sufficient for them to be trapped. But we have no one on film, no voices on a tape."

Montelán leaned forward in his chair. "Are you suggesting – ?"

"I'm suggesting," interrupted Banner, "that although our specialist is known for his thoroughness, there was a conspicuous absence of it yesterday."

"Too much!" Christopher exploded. His gaunt features were pinched, his bony fingers trembled. "Have you any idea who Varak *is*? What he's *seen* in his life? What *drives* him?"

"I know he's filled with hatred," replied Banner softly. "And that frightens me."

There was silence at the table. The essential truth of Frederick Wells's statement had its effect. It was possible that Stefan Varak had operated on a different level from them, motivated by a hatred unknown to anyone in that room.

St Claire remembered Varak's words; *I'll seek out the Nazi in any form he is revived in and go after him. If you think there's any difference between what those files represent and the objectives of the Third Reich, you're very much mistaken.*

Once the Nazi was found and destroyed, what better way to control his disciples than to control the files?

Bravo pushed his chair back and rose from the table. He went to a cabinet in the wall, unlocked it, and took out a short-barrelled ·38-calibre pistol. He closed the cabinet, returned to his chair, and sat down. The weapon was in his hand, out of sight.

"Will you ask Mr Varak to come in, please,?"

Stefan Varak stood behind the empty Genesis chair studying the members of Inver Brass. St Claire watched him closely, until Varak's eyes met his.

"Mr Varak, we have a question to ask you. We would appreciate a concise answer. Proceed, if you will, Banner."

Wells did so. "Mr Varak, through Chancellor you anticipated an event that could have led us to Hoover's files," he concluded. "One identification, visually or by a voice print. You set the trap, which presumes you understand its importance. Yet your acknowledged thoroughness, your professionalism, was not in evidence. I ask myself why. It would have been a simple matter to have positioned two, three, six cameras, if necessary. Had you done so, the hunt might have been over now, the files in our possession. Why, Mr Varak? Or why not?"

The blood rushed to Varak's blond head; he was flushed with anger. All the signs he had taught Bravo to look for were apparent in the teacher. Did anger, like fear, produce the uncontrollable chemical changes Varak had spoken of? St Claire moved the pistol on his lap and inserted his finger over the trigger.

And then the moment passed. Varak imposed self-control. "It's a fair question," he said calmly. "I'll answer it as concisely as I can. As you know, I work alone except in rare instances where I employ others who can never trace my identity. A case in point was a taxi driver in New York. He picked up Chancellor and the girl and drove them to the airport; their conversation was taped. The driver reached me in Washington and played it over the telephone. It was the first I heard about their staying in Rockville. I had very little time to get my equipment, drive out to the house, and instal it. I was fortunate to mount even one camera with the proper infrared film. That's my answer."

Again the silence as the members of Inver Brass studied Varak. Beneath the table St Claire removed his finger from the trigger. He had spent a lifetime learning to discern the truth when he heard it. In his judgement he had just heard the truth.

He hoped to God he was right.

21

Habit caused Peter to wake up at half past four in the morning. Custom willed him to get out of bed, go to his briefcase on a bedroom chair, and remove his leather notebook.

They were in a suite at the Hay-Adams, and it was Alison's introduction to his odd hours of work.

Alison heard him and bolted upright in the bed.

"Is there a fire?"

"I'm sorry. I didn't think you'd hear me."

"I know I can't see you. It's dark out. What happened?"

"Nothing happened. It's morning. It's when I like to work. Go back to sleep. I'll be in the next room."

Alison fell back into the pillow, shaking her head. Peter smiled and carried his notebook into the sitting room. To the coffee table and the couch.

Three hours later he had finished the eighth chapter. He had not referred to the outline; it was not necessary. He knew the emotions he was defining for Alexander Meredith. He had been gripped with fear; he had panicked. He knew what it was to be the object of a violent chase; he had heard racing footsteps in the darkness.

Alison awoke shortly before eight. He joined her and they made love. Slowly, enfolded in each other, each awakened response more lovely, more exciting than the last, until they were caught in the desperate rhythm of their combined hunger, neither allowing the other to lessen the intensity.

And they fell asleep in each other's arms, the comfort each sought found in the other.

They awoke at half past ten, had breakfast in the room, and began thinking about the rest of the day. Peter had promised her a day of "luxuriating"; he wanted to provide it. She deserved it. As he watched her across the breakfast table, he was struck by something that he should have noticed before. In spite of the strain and the sadness, Alison had a quality of quiet humour within her; it was never far away.

Cathy had had that quality.

Peter reached across the table for her hand. She took it smiling, her eyes searching his with kindness.

The telephone rang. It was her father's lawyer. There were various papers to sign and government forms to be filled out and legal rights to be understood. The general's will was simple, but the Army's death procedures were not. Would Alison please be at his office at two o'clock? If there were no complications, she'd be finished by five.

Chancellor promised that they would luxuriate tomorrow. Actually they would start at one minute after five.

Because the next day, Peter thought to himself, he would bring up the subject of the Rockville house.

Alison left at half past one for the lawyer's office. Chancellor returned to his leather notebook.

Peter tore off the page and folded it. He'd mail it to Morgan later. Right now he wanted to work.

Chapter 9 – Outline

The chapter's objective is the meeting of Alex Meredith and the senator. It will take place in the hotel room after a harrowing chase during which Alex *must* elude those following him. In meeting the senator, Alex becomes aware that there is a group of powerful men willing to fight Hoover. He is not alone. It is the beginning of his journey back to sanity.

He accepts the dangers that will face him now, for there are people he can turn to; his dependence on them is established immediately. His relief given added impact by the senator's revelation of the identities of his two closest associates: the former cabinet officer and the newspaperwoman. They, too, want to meet with Meredith.

There is a plan. Alex does not know what it is, but the fact that one exists is enough. He is committed without fully understanding his own commitment.

The hours passed; the words were compulsively there. He had reached the point where the senator explains the conversion of Hoover's messenger. Chancellor read the words, which he'd use virtually intact in the actual chapter, with satisfaction.

For reasons of survival Alan Long (Longworth) has seen the error of his ways. His past is no more immune to scrutiny than anyone else's. An isolated fact can be twisted here, taken out of context there. It's only the source that matters, the damning imprimatur – like the letters F-B-I. Long is about to retire from the bureau because of a terminal illness. A report has been sent to the Director to that effect. In truth, however, Long is going to work for us. Although one could not exactly say he's been washed in the blood of the lamb, he *is* less inclined towards the archangel of darkness. He's afraid. And fear is a weapon he knows well.

It was not a bad day's work, thought Peter, looking at his watch. It was nearly half past four. The late afternoon sun created blocks of shadows on the buildings outside the hotel window. The December wind was harsh; every now and then a leaf spiralled up beyond the glass.

Alison would be back soon. He would take her to a small restaurant he knew in Georgetown, where they would have a quiet dinner and look at each other and touch each other. There would be the laughter in her eyes, and in her voice, and he would be grateful for her nearness. And they would come back to the hotel and make love. So wondrously. With meaning. There had been no meaning in his bed for so long. Peter got up from the couch and stretched, revolving his neck. It was habit; when the pain came to his temples, it helped to move his head in circles. Yet there was no pain now. In spite of the stress of the past forty-eight hours, there had been only a few brief moments when he'd felt the alarms. Alison MacAndrew had come into his life. It was really as simple as that.

The telephone rang. He smiled, reacting like an adolescent. It had to be Alison; no one else knew he was there. He picked up the phone, expecting her to tell him with her own particular brand of laughter that all the cabs in Washington were avoiding her; she was marooned in a concrete zoo and the animals were snarling.

It was a woman's voice, but it was not Alison's. Only the hard strained tones of a frightened human being.

"What in God's name have you *done?* How could you put me in your book? Who gave you the *right?*"

It was Phyllis Maxwell.

It was the beginning of the madness.

He left a note for Alison, a second message at the desk in case she overlooked the note. He had no time to explain; there was an emergency, and he had to leave for an hour or so. He'd call her at the first opportunity. And he loved her.

Phyllis Maxwell. It was insane! What she had said was crazy. And Peter had had to give a lot of rapid explanations. Yes, there was a character in his book that some might – only might – think was possibly – only possibly – reminiscent of her. But it could just as easily be reminiscent of half a dozen others!

No! He hadn't set out to destroy her. Or anyone or anything! Except the reputation of J. Edgar Hoover, and for that there would be no apologies! For Christ's sake, *no!* He worked alone! Whatever research he did, whatever sources he used, none of it had anything to do with her!

Or . . . Paula Mingus . . . whoever the hell *she* was.

There was no reasoning with the voice on the other end of the line – one moment faint and inaudible, the next shrill and hysterical. Phyllis Maxwell was losing her mind. And somehow he was responsible.

He tried speaking rationally; it was useless. He tried shouting at her; it was chaos. Finally, he extracted her promise to meet him.

She would not come to the Hay-Adams. She had been with him at the Hay-Adams. Didn't he remember that? Was it so repulsive?

Jesus Christ! Stop it!

She would not meet him anywhere of his choosing. She did not trust him; for God's sake, how could she? And she would not meet any place where they might be seen together. There was a house on Thirty-fifth Street Northwest, near the corner of Wisconsin, behind Dumbarton Oaks. It belonged to friends who were out of the country; she had a key. She was not sure of the number; it didn't matter, there was a white porch with a stained-glass window over the door. She'd be there in half an hour.

She hung up with the words: "You were working with them all along, weren't you? You must be very proud of yourself."

A taxi swerved up to the kerb. Chancellor jumped in, gave the address to the driver, and tried to collect his thoughts.

Someone had read his manuscript; that much was clear. But who? *How?* It was the *how* that frightened him because it meant that whoever it was had gone to extraordinary lengths to get it. He knew the precautions the typing service took; they were a part of the service, one of its strongest recommendations. The typing service had to be ruled out.

Morgan! Neither by design nor permission, but by accident! Tony had the aristocrat's carelessness. His peripatetic mind crashed about, overseeing dozens of projects simultaneously. It was entirely possible that Morgan had absent-mindedly left the manuscript on someone's desk. Or, God forbid, the men's room.

The taxi reached the intersection of Pennsylvania Avenue and Twentieth Street. There was an empty telephone booth on the corner. Peter looked at his watch; it was ten minutes to five. Tony would still be in the office.

"Pull up to that telephone, will you please?" he said. "I have to make a call. I won't be long."

"Take your time, mister. The meter's running." Peter closed the door of the glass booth and dialled Morgan's private number.

"It's Peter, Tony. I've got to ask you a question."

"Where the hell *are* you? I spoke to Mrs Alcott this morning, and she said you were in town. I called the apartment, but all I got was the machine."

"I'm in Washington. I haven't time to explain. Listen to me. Someone's read the Hoover manuscript. Whoever it was has done a terrible thing, made an awful mistake – "

"Hey, *wait* a minute," broke in Morgan. "That's impossible. First things first. What terrible thing? What mistake?"

"Told someone she – he – was in the book."

"He or she?"

678

"What *difference* does it make? The point is someone read it and is using the information to scare the hell out of somebody else!"

"Was it a mistake? Is there such a character'?"

"Not really. It could be half a dozen different people, but that doesn't matter." There was no time for Morgan's questions.

"I only meant that several of our characters are loosely based on people down there. That general, for one."

"Oh, God . . ." In the convoluted process of inventing a character he had taken one aspect of Phyllis Maxwell's life – her career as a newspaperwoman – and built another person.

Another person, not *her!* Not Phyllis. The person he created was the victim of extortion; that wasn't Phyllis! It was fiction! But the voice on the Hay-Adams telephone was not a product of fiction. "Have you let anyone else read the manuscript?"

"Of course not. Do you think I want people to know how unpublishable you are before my editorial hand goes to work?"

It was the usual joke between them, but Chancellor did not laugh. "Then, where's your copy?"

"Where? As a matter of fact it's in the drawer of my bedside table, and we haven't been robbed in over six months. I think it's a record."

"When did you last look?"

Morgan paused, suddenly serious, obviously recognizing the depth of Peter's concern. "The other night. And the drawer's locked."

"Did you make a Xerox for Joshua?"

"No, he'll get one when the editing's finished. Could anyone have read your copy?"

"No. It's in my suitcase." Chancellor stopped. *The suitcase.* His briefcase was in the car with the suitcases! The night in Rockville! The early morning, the racing footsteps; the horrible, severed legs of an animal; the bloodstained suitcase. It could have happened then. "Never mind, Tony. I'll phone you in a day or so."

"What are you doing in Washington?"

"I'm not sure. I came down to learn something. Now I don't know . . ." He hung up before Morgan could speak.

He saw the white porch and the dim light shining through the stained-glass window above the front door. The block was lined with old homes, once stately, now beyond their time.

"That's the house," he said to the driver. "Thanks a lot, and keep the change."

The driver hesitated. "Hey, mister," he said. "I could be wrong, and it's none of my business. Maybe you expected it, maybe it's why you telephoned. But I think you were followed out here."

"What? Where's the car?" Peter spun around and looked out the rear window of the taxi.

"Don't bother looking. He waited until we slowed down; then he made a left turn at the corner back there. He slowed down pretty good himself. To see where you stopped, maybe."

"Are you sure?"

"Like I said, I could be wrong. Headlights at night, they're all just a little bit different. You play games."

"I know what you mean." Peter thought for a moment. "Do you want to wait here for me? I'll pay."

"Hey, no thanks. This trip took me way the hell out. My old lady's gonna be groaning as it is. Wisconsin's just down the way. Plenty of cabs heading back into town."

Chancellor got out and closed the door. The cab sped off down the street; Peter turned towards the house. Except for the dim light in the hall there were no other lamps turned on. Yet it was almost an hour since he'd talked to Phyllis Maxwell. She should be here by now. He wondered if she was in a sane enough frame of mind to follow her own instructions. He started up the path to the porch.

He reached the top step and heard the metallic click of a lock. In front of him the door opened, but no one came into view.

"Phyllis?"

"Come in quickly," was the whispered reply.

She was standing against the wall to the left of the door, her back pressed against the faded wallpaper. In the dim light she looked much older than she had over the candles in the Hay-Adams dining room. Her face was pale, fear. Lines of strain were pronounced at the edges of her mouth. Her eyes were penetrating but devoid of the flair he remembered; there was no curiosity in them now, only dread. He closed the door.

"You don't have to be afraid of me. You never did. I mean that, Phyllis."

"Oh, young man, you're the worst kind," she said, her whisper filled with sadness and contempt. "You kill sweetly."

"That's utter nonsense. I want to talk to you. And not standing where I can't see you."

"There'll be no lights turned on!"

"At last now I can hear you." Suddenly, Peter's thoughts were on the cab driver's alarming information. There was a car outside on the streets. Watching, waiting. "All right, no lights. May we sit down?"

Her answer was a glare followed by a sudden movement away from the wall. He walked behind her through an archway into a dark living room. In the wash of hall light he could see overstuffed chairs and a large sofa. She went directly to the chair opposite the sofa, the rustle of her skirt the only sound. He took off his topcoat, throwing it on the arm of the couch, and sat down across from her. Her face caught the light from the hallway better than if she'd been sitting next to him.

"I'm going to tell you something," he began. "If I tell it awkwardly, it's because I've never had to explain anything like this before; maybe I've never analysed what is dubiously called the creative process." He shrugged, denigrating the term. "I was awfully impressed with you," he said.

"You're too kind."

'Please. You know what I mean. My father's been a newspaperman all his life. When we met, I'm sure I was more impressed than you were. The fact that you wanted to interview me struck me as kind of foolish. You gave me a lift when it didn't hurt, and it had nothing to do with my books. You're part of something very important, with a significance I don't have. I was *damned* impressed, and it was a terrific evening. I drank too much and so did you, but what of it?"

"Kill sweetly, young man," she whispered.

Peter held his breath, controlling himself. "I went to bed with a great lady. If that's my crime, I'm guilty."

"Go on." Phyllis closed her eyes.

"I asked you a lot of questions about Hoover that night. You gave me answers, told me things I didn't know. Your vehemence was electric. Your morality had been deeply offended, and you showed me an anger in person that I'd never read in anything you'd written."

"What are you driving at?"

"It's part of my awkward explanation. I was in Washington getting background; a few days later I started work. Your anger was very much on my mind. Besides that, it was a woman's anger. An articulate, successful woman. So it was a logical step to invent a variation of that woman, someone possessing the same characteristics. That's what I did. That's my explanation. You gave me the idea for the character, but you're *not her*. She's only an invention."

"Did you also invent a general who was buried yesterday at Arlington?"

Chancellor sat motionless, stunned. Her dead eyes stared at him through the dim spill of light. "No, I didn't invent him," he answered quietly. "Who told you about him?"

"Surely you know. A horrible, flat, high-pitched whisper over the telephone. It's frighteningly effective for something so basic. Surely you know." Phyllis spaced her words out, as if afraid to hear herself say them.

"I don't know," replied Peter, indeed not knowing but beginning to perceive the spreading of a terrible pattern. He struggled to remain calm, to sound reasonable, but he knew his anger showed. "I think this has all gone far enough. Whispers over a telephone. Words painted on walls! Houses broken into. Animals cut up! Enough." He got up and turned around. "It's going to stop." He saw what he was looking for: a large lamp on a table. Deliberately he went to it, put his hand beneath the shade, and pulled the chain. The light went on. "There's not going to be any more hiding, no more dark rooms. Someone's trying to drive you crazy, drive Alison crazy, drive me out of my goddamned mind! I've *had* it. I'm not going to let – "

It was as far as he got. A pane in one of the front windows exploded. Simultaneously there was a harsh splitting of wood; a bullet imbedded itself somewhere in a moulding. Then another pane shattered; glass fragments shot through the air, cracks of plaster sliced the wall like the jagged edges of black lightning.

Instinctively, Peter lashed out his hand, sending the lamp spiralling off the table on to the floor. It landed on the side of its shade, the bulb still lit, eerily projecting light across the room along the floor.

"Get down!" screamed Phyllis.

Chancellor realized as he dived to the floor, that there were bullets, but there were no gunshots! And terrifying images came back to him.

Dawn at the Cloisters! A man killed in front of his eyes; a circle of blood abruptly, without warning, formed on a white forehead. A body in spastic contortion before it fell. *There had been no gunshots then!* Only sickening spits that had disturbed the stillness and filled it with death.

Move! For Christ's sake, *move!* In his panic he had lunged towards Phyllis, pulling her to the floor with him.

Another pane of glass exploded, another bullet cracked the plaster. Then another, this one ricocheting off stone somewhere, smashing the glass of a photograph on the wall.

Move! There is *death!*

He had to get the light. They were sitting targets with it on. He pushed Phyllis away, holding her down, hearing her moans of fear. He darted his eyes to his right, then his left. Stone! There had to be a fireplace! It was directly behind him and he saw what he wanted. A poker leaning against the brick. He lurched for it.

Glass erupted; twin cracks appeared on the walls, partly obscured by shadows. Phyllis screamed, and for an instant Peter thought she might be heard, but then he remembered the house was on the corner, the nearest house at least a hundred feet away. The night was cold; windows and doors were shut. Her screams would bring no help.

He crawled towards the lamp, raised the poker, and smashed it down on the shade as if killing a deadly animal.

There was still the light in the hall! It took on the intensity of a searchlight, the spill probing corners, washing the room with a brightness he never thought possible. He lunged up, racing to the archway, and heaved the poker towards the fixture in the ceiling. It spun through the air like a whirling crossbar and crashed into the teardrops of glass. All went dark.

He dived back on to the floor and crawled towards Phyllis. "Where's the phone?" he whispered.

He could feel her trembling; she could not answer.

"The phone? *Where is it?*"

She understood him. In the dark shadows produced by faraway streetlamps he could see her eyes grasping what he said, barely audible between her sobs. "Not here. A socket in here, no phone."

"*What?*" What was she trying to tell him? A socket? No telephone?

One more explosion of glass filled the room, the bullet cracking inches over their heads, snapping into the wall above them. Suddenly from outside there was a loud gunshot in counterpoint to the muted firing, and a guttural shout, muffled quickly. It was followed by the sounds of screeching tyres and metal against metal. Another roar of a furious voice. A car door opened and closed.

"Kitchen," whispered Phyllis, pointing in the darkness to her right.

"The telephone's in the kitchen? *Where?*"

"Through there."

"Stay down!" Peter crawled like a panicked insect over the floor, through an archway to a doorway. He felt kitchen tiles beneath him. The phone! Where was it? He tried to adjust his eyes to the new darkness.

He scraped his hands along the walls in panic. Kitchen telephones were usually on the wall, cords spiralling below . . . He found it! His hand shot up; he tore the instrument from its cradle and brought it to his ear, his free hand reaching up for the dial. The last circle. *O.*

The phone was dead.

There was a deafening crash. Glass shattered on the opposite side of the pitch black kitchen. The top of the outside door had been smashed; a brick bounced off the wall. A brick had been thrown through the glass.

A brick! The fireplace! He'd seen it at the corner of the slate, to the right of the grate. He was sure of it. It was the answer! The only one left.

He propelled himself on all fours – half crawling, half lunging – back into the darkness of the living room. Phyllis was crouching next to the sofa, frozen in shock. There it was! Now, if only the owners of the house had meant it when they'd put it there.

Some people called it a New England fire lighter; in the Midwest it was known as a Lake Erie starter. A round porous stone at the end of a brass rod soaking in a pot of paraffin. Held under logs, it acted as kindling.

He reached for the pot and took off the metal lid. There was liquid inside. Paraffin!

A fusillade of gun spits erupted. Bullets cracked the air, some breaking new glass, others having a clear path through previously shattered windowpanes. The walls and ceiling absorbed them; he could hear the *pings* as the deadly missiles ricocheted off metallic objects, deflected in their flights.

Perspiration rolled down Peter's face. He was sure he had his answer, but he did not know how to construct it. And then the words came back to him, rooted in his own fiction. He had *invented* the answer before.

Dobric tore off his shirt and plunged it into the vat of petrol. The harvest was finished; there were stacks of hay in the field. The nearest would go up in flames, and the wind would carry the fire. Soon the grasslands would be ablaze, and platoons of soldiers would be diverted from their search . . .
Sarajevo!

Sarajevo! An incident like that had happened after the assassination of the Archduke Ferdinand.

Peter tore off his jacket and shirt. He lurched over the floor to the table where the lamp had been. He yanked the tablecloth off and returned to the fireplace. He spread his shirt on the floor, placed the tablecloth over it, and poured the paraffin over both, saving only a little. He sprang towards the couch and pulled off a sectional cushion; he poured the remaining paraffin on it.

There were more sickening spits from outside, more shattering of glass; Chancellor thought he would vomit in fear. The pain in his temples had returned with such force he could barely focus his eyes. He closed them for an instant, wanting to scream but knowing he could not.

He placed the empty iron pot in the centre of the tablecloth and proceeded to wrap the tablecloth and the shirt around it. He tied the sleeves together until the pot was securely bedded inside, one sleeve extended. He reached into his trouser pocket and took out a book of matches.

He was ready. He crawled towards the windows on the left, to the wall, pulling the pot behind him, pushing the cushion in front. Slowly he rose to his feet, out of sight, one hand clutching the extended sleeve, the soaked cushion on the floor. He manipulated the book of matches awkwardly between both hands, tore off a match, and struck it. He dropped the flame on the saturated fabric; it exploded in a burst of fire.

In two motions he swung the sleeve behind him, then brought it forward with all his strength, letting go at the last instant. The flaming pot crashed through the remaining glass, whirling out over the lawn like the fireball it was. The outside rush of air intensified the flames; dripping liquid caught fire, leaving a wake of jagged, leaping yellow.

Peter heard footsteps, then incomprehensible shouts. And more footsteps, these coming from the side of the house. Men were trying to put out the fireball. It was the moment for his second weapon. He struck another match, holding the flame in his left hand. With his right he picked up the cushion and brought the lighted match to it.

Again a burst of fire, singeing the hairs on his arm. He raced to the far right window and propelled the flaming cushion through the glass. It landed where he hoped it would: at the base of the white porch.

The old wood and the wind and the paraffin fire were compatible. The porch began to burn.

Again there were shouts, words screamed in some un known tongue. What was it? What language? He'd never heard it before.

A last barrage of muted gunshots were levelled at the windows, fired aimlessly into the house. He heard the racing of a powerful engine. Car doors were opened and closed, tyres screeched, spinning on the street. The car sped away.

Peter ran back to Phyllis. He pulled her to her feet, holding her close, feeling the trembling body in his arms.

"It's over. It's all over. It's all right. We have to get outside. Through the back door. This place is going to go up like – like a haystack."

"Oh, God! Oh, my God . . ." She buried her face in his naked chest; her tears would not stop.

"Come on, let's go! We'll wait outside for the police. Someone'll see the fire and call them. Come *on!*"

Slowly Phyllis looked up at him. A strange, pathetic panic in her eyes, seen clearly in the reflection of the spreading flames outside the windows. "No," she said in the harsh whisper she had used before. "No. Not the police!"

"For Christ's sake! People tried to *kill* us! You'd better goddamned well believe we're going to see the police!"

She pushed him away. An odd passivity seemed to grip her; she was trying, he thought, to find a moment of sanity. "You have no shirt . . ."

"I've got a jacket. And a coat. Come on."

"Yes, I see . . . My purse. Can you get my purse? It's in the hall."

Chancellor looked over at the hall. Smoke was streaming in through the cracks in the front door; the porch was blazing, but no fire had yet penetrated the house.

"Sure." He released her and reached down for his jacket by the fireplace.

"It's on the staircase, I think. Or perhaps I left it in the cupboard. I'm not sure."

"It's okay. I'll get it. You go on outside. Through the kitchen."

Phyllis turned and started out. Peter put on his jacket and went quickly towards the hall, picking his topcoat off the couch on his way.

It was over. There would be conversations with the police, with the authorities, with anyone who wanted to listen. But tonight was the end of it. There would be no book at this cost.

The purse was not on the stairs. He walked halfway up to the landing; it was nowhere in sight. The smoke was thicker now. He had to hurry; the front door had caught fire. He ran down the steps and turned left at the bottom of the staircase, looking for the cupboard. It was in the far right corner of the hall. He walked over quickly and opened the door. There were coats, two fedoras, and various scarves on the hooks and hangers, but no purse.

He had to get out. The smoke was becoming impenetrable. He began to cough, and his eyes were tearing. He raced back through the living room, through the arch to the dining room, into the kitchen, and out the open door.

In the distance he could hear the wail of sirens.

"Phyllis?"

He ran along the side of the house to the front. She was not there. He continued around to the other side, down the driveway to the backyard again.

"Phyllis! *Phyllis!*"

She was nowhere. And then he knew. There was no purse on the staircase or in the cupboard. She had fled.

The sirens were louder, no more than a few blocks away. The old house was going quickly. The whole front section was on fire, the flames spreading rapidly inside.

Peter was not sure why, but he knew he would not talk to the police alone. Now now, not yet.

He raced away into the night.

22

The pain in his temples made him want to drop to the ground and smash his head on the cement kerb, but he knew it would not help.

Instead, he kept walking, his eyes on the traffic heading into downtown Washington. He was looking for a taxi.

He should have remained at the burning house on Thirty-fifth Street and told the incredible story there to the police. And yet a part of him told him that to do so without Phyllis would raise questions to which he was not sure there were answers. Answers that excluded the destruction of Phyllis Maxwell. The shadow of responsibility fell across his thoughts; there were things he did not know, and *had* to know. He owed her that much. Perhaps no more, but at least that.

At last there was a cab; the lighted yellow rooftop sign was like a beacon. He stepped off the kerb and waved his arms. The taxi slowed down; the driver peered cautiously out of the window before he stopped.

"The Hay–Adams Hotel, please," said Chancellor.

"Good Lord! What's *happened?*" asked Alison, stunned as she opened the door.

"There's a bottle of pills in my suitcase. In the back flap. Get them quickly, please."

"Peter, my darling! What *is* it?" Alison held him as he leaned against the door. "I'll call a doctor."

"No! Do as I say. I know exactly what it is. Just the pills. Quickly." He could feel himself falling. He grabbed her arms, and with her help he stumbled into the bedroom. He lay back and gestured towards the suitcase, still on the luggage rack in the corner. She raced to it.

He did what he rarely did: he took two tablets.

She ran into the bathroom, emerging seconds later with a glass of water. She sat next to him, holding his head as he drank.

"Please, Peter. A doctor!"

He shook his head. "No," he replied weakly, trying to smile a semblance of reassurance. "He couldn't do anything. It'll pass in a few minutes." The darkness was closing in, his eyelids terribly heavy. He could not allow that dark to fall until he had calmed her. And prepared her for what might happen when the darkness was complete. "I may sleep for a while. Not long, it's never long. I may talk, even yell a little. Don't worry. It doesn't mean anything. Just rambling, just nonsense."

The dark filled his mind, his personal night had fallen. There was nothingness, and he floated, suspended in calm, gentle breezes.

He opened his eyes, not knowing how long he had been in bed. Looking down at him was Alison's lovely face, her eyes made more beautiful by the tears that filled them.

"Hey," he said, reaching up to touch her moist cheek. "It's all right."

She took his hand, holding it against her lips. "Her name was Cathy, wasn't it?"

He had done what he'd hoped he would not do, said what he had not wanted to say. There was nothing for it. He nodded. "Yes."

"She died, didn't she?"

"Yes."

"Oh darling. So much hurt, so much love – "

"I'm sorry."

"Don't be."

"It can't be very nice for you."

She reached down and touched his eyes, and then his cheek and lips. "It was a gift," she said. "A beautiful gift."

"I don't understand."

"After you spoke her name, you called for me."

He told Alison what had happened at the house on Thirty-fifth Street. He minimized the physical danger, calling the erratic gunfire a strategy of fear, designed to terrify, not to injure or to kill.

It was clear she did not believe him, but she was a soldier's daughter. In one form or another she had heard such false reassurances before. She accepted the watered-down explanation without comment, letting her eyes convey her disbelief.

When he finished, he stood by the window looking down at the Christmas decorations on Sixteenth Street; across the street muted church bells played in an agonizing cadence. Christmas was only days away; he had not thought about it. He wasn't really thinking about it now. His only thoughts were on what he had to do: go to the Federal Bureau of Investigation, to the source of the madness, and let it put the madness to a stop. But private property had been destroyed, lethal weapons fired. Phyllis Maxwell had to go with him.

"I've got to reach her," he said softly. "I've got to make her understand she has to come with me."

"I'll get the number for you." Alison took the phone book from the bedside table. Peter continued to stare out the window. "It's not here. She's not listed."

Chancellor remembered. Alison's father had not been listed, either. He wondered if he could unearth the number as easily as he had MacAndrew's. It would be a variation of the same ploy, a newsman's ruse. An old reporter friend, in town for the night, anxious to make contact.

But the ploy did not work; the man at the city desk had probably used it too often himself. The paper would not give out Maxwell's number.

"Let me try," said Alison. "There's a press officer on duty at all times in the Pentagon. Bad news and casualties don't have business hours. Filtered-down rank still has its privileges. I'll know somebody, or someone'll know me."

The Pentagon had two numbers for Phyllis Maxwell. One was her private phone, the other the switchboard of the apartment house in which she lived.

There was no answer on her private line. The apartment switchboard gave out no information on its tenants; it would only take messages. But because the caller was not absolutely sure of the correct address, the operator gave it.

"I want to go with you," Alison said.

"I don't think you should," Peter replied. "She mentioned your father, not by name, but she spoke of a burial yesterday at Arlington. She's frightened out of her mind. All I want to do is persuade her to come with me. If she saw you, it might stop her."

"All right." Alison nodded. The soldier's daughter understood. "But I worry about you. Suppose you have another attack?"

"I won't." He paused for a moment and then reached out, pulling her to him. "There's something else," he said, looking down into her eyes. "I don't want to involve you. It's over, finished. You said it yourself, remember? I didn't agree with you then. I do now."

"Thank you for that. I guess what I'm saying is that whatever he did, it's done and can't be changed. He stood for something. I don't want that damaged."

"I have something important in mind too, and that won't be changed, either. Or damaged. Us." He kissed her lightly. "When tonight's over, we can start living our own lives. I find that prospect very exciting."

She smiled and returned his kiss. "I was shameless. I caught you at a weak moment and seduced you. I should be branded." And then her smile waned; she held his eyes, the vulnerability in her own. "Everything's happened so fast. I don't require commitments, Peter."

"I do," he answered.

"If you'll take a seat inside the lobby, sir, I'll be with you shortly," said the doorman at Phyllis Maxwell's apartment house. The man did not hesitate for an instant; it was almost as though he expected him.

Peter sat down in a green plastic chair and waited. The doorman simply stood outside, rocking back and forth on his heels, his gloved hands clasped behind his uniformed overcoat.

It was very odd.

Five minutes went by. The doorman made no move to come inside the lobby. Was it possible he'd forgotten? Chancellor got out of the chair and looked around. He had spoken to an operator; where was the apartment switchboard?

There was a small glass panel at the rear of the lobby, sandwiched between rows of letterboxes and a line of lifts. He walked over to it and peered inside. The operator was talking into a mouthpiece attached to her single-eared headset. She spoke rapidly, with emphasis; the conversation was between friends, not switchboard and inquirer. Peter tapped on the glass; the operator suspended her conversation and slid the panel open.

"Yes, sir?"

"I'm trying to reach Phyllis Maxwell. Will you ring her apartment and let me speak with her, please? It's urgent."

The operator's reaction was as odd as the doorman's. Different, but nevertheless strange. She hesitated, embarrassed.

"I don't believe Miss Maxwell is in," she said.

"You won't know until you ring her, will you?"

"Have you checked with the doorman?"

"What the hell *is* this?" Peter understood. These people were following instructions. "Ring her apartment!"

As he could have predicted, there was no answer on the switchboard telephone and no point in wasting any more time. He walked rapidly back outside and confronted the doorman.

"Let's cut the crap, shall we? You've got something to tell me. What is it?"

"It's touchy."

"What is'?"

"She described you, said your name was Chancellor. If you'd arrived, say, an hour ago, I was to tell you to come back at eleven o'clock. That Miss Maxwell had called in saying she'd be back then."

Peter looked at his watch. "All right. It's almost eleven. What happens then?"

"Just a little while longer, okay?"

"Not okay. Now. Or you can say whatever it is to me and the police."

"Okay, okay. What the hell, it's only a few minutes." The doorman reached into his inside overcoat pocket and took out an envelope. He gave it to Chancellor.

Peter looked at the man, then the envelope. His name was written on it. Moving back inside to the light, he ripped open the envelope and took out the letter.

My dear Peter:

I'm sorry I ran, but I knew you would follow me. You saved my life – and to some degree my sanity – and you deserve an explanation. I'm afraid it will be limited.

By the time you read this, I'll be on a plane. Don't try to trace me. It would be impossible. For several years I've had a false passport, knowing that someday I might have to use it. Apparently the time is now.

This afternoon, after that horrible call telling me I was a character in your novel, I informed my paper that I might be taking an extended leave for reasons of health. In truth, my editor did not argue very much. My work hasn't been particularly outstanding in recent months.

The decision to leave is not sudden. I've considered it for quite a while. Tonight simply made it irreversible. Whatever my transgressions, they do not warrant the loss of life. Mine, yours or anyone's. Nor should they compromise the responsibilities I have professionally.

This last has been accomplished. My work *is* compromised. Truths are suppressed when they should be told. The loss of life was avoided – for how long, who knows? – because of you. I cannot continue any longer.

Thank you for my life. And my deepest apologies for my thinking you were part of something you were not.

A part of me says, for God's sake, give up your book! It is balanced by another voice that says you *can't!*

You will not hear from me again, my dear young, young man. But you will always have a part of my love. And my gratitude.

Phyllis

689

Peter reread the letter, trying to grasp the meaning behind the words. Phyllis had chosen her phrases with a deliberateness born of extraordinary fear. But of what? What were her "transgressions"? What could she have done – or not done – that would cause her to throw away a lifetime of accomplishments? It was insane!

It was *all* insane. Everything! And the insanity was going to stop! He started for the door. From somewhere he heard a prolonged buzzing. It stopped as he had his hand on the glass bar of the door. And then he heard the words, accompanied by the sliding of a glass panel.

"Mr *Chancellor?*" The operator was calling him, her head halfway through the switchboard opening. "There's a call for you."

Phyllis. Perhaps she'd changed her mind! He ran across the lobby and took the phone.

It was not Phyllis Maxwell. It was Alison.

"Something dreadful's happened. You had a telephone call from a man in Indianapolis. He was out of his mind. He was at the airport, catching a plane for Washington – "

"Who was it?"

"A man named Bromley. He said he was going to kill you."

Carroll Quinlan O'Brien took the security logs from the guard and thanked him. The Pennsylvania Avenue doors were closed; the list of names of those who had entered and exited would be processed and sent down to the main desk. At all times every person in the FBI complex was accounted for; at no time was anyone permitted to leave without surrendering his pass.

It was a security-logs entry that had started it all four months before, O'Brien thought. Started his rapid decline in the eyes of the bureau. Four months ago he had found three names on the 1 May P.M. logs: Salter, Krepps and Longworth. Two names were unassigned field covers, the third belonged to a retired agent living on the island of Maui in the Pacific. These three unknown men had gained entrance that night. The next morning Hoover was dead, and all traces of the director's files had vanished. The dossiers themselves had become a quickly forgotten legacy from hell that no one cared to exhume or examine.

So Quinn O'Brien had asked questions, keeping his voice down, seeking counsel from those he knew would listen because they cared. Men liked him within the bureau whose sensibilities had been offended during the past years – theirs more than his, mostly. At least over a longer time. He had arrived only four and a half years before, the war hero from Sacramento, the cosmetic from Army G2, the forty-year-old lawyer who had escaped from a Viet Cong prison camp and later had been given parades in California. Washington had summoned him, the President had decorated him, Hoover had employed him. It was good public relations. He lent a much-needed air of dignity to the bureau. It was supposed to be good for Quinn, too. He could have had a future at the Justice Department.

Could have had. No longer. Because he had asked questions. A whisper over

690

a telephone had ordered him to stop. A flat, terrible, high-pitched whisper that told him they knew. *They* had a deposition written by a captured lieutenant colonel who faced execution with seven other men because of the actions of one Major Carroll Quinlan O'Brien. The major had disobeyed a direct order. Eight American soldiers had been executed as a result.

Of course, it was only half of the story. There was another half. It told of this same major looking after the sick and the wounded of the compound with far greater concern than the executed lieutenant colonel. It told how this major had taken others' work details, how he had stolen food and medicine from the guards to help sustain the men, how in the last analysis he had made his escape as much for the other prisoners as for himself.

He was a lawyer, not a soldier. It was the lawyer's logic that had guided him, not a soldier's strategy. Nor a soldier's willingness to accept the unbearable cruelties of war – and therein, he realized, was the weakness of his argument. Did he do what he did for the combined concerns of all? Or did he do what he did for himself alone?

O'Brien was not sure there was a clear-cut answer. It was the question itself that could destroy him. An exposed "war hero" was the most despicable of citizens. People had been fooled; they were embarrassed – that was the part that made them furious.

These were the things the terrible whisper had made clear. And all because he had asked questions. Three unknown men without accountability had gained entrance the night before Hoover's death. And the next morning Hoover's files had disappeared.

If O'Brien needed proof of his continuing decline within the bureau, he had only to look at his own assignment sheet. He had been removed from several committees; he no longer received classified reports dealing with the newly re-established liaisons with NSA and CIA. And he was suddenly drawing continuous night duty assignments. Night duty! It was the Washington equivalent of the Omaha field office. It forced an agent to re-evaluate a lot of things, primarily his own future.

It also forced O'Brien to wonder who within the bureau was after him. Whoever it was knew something about three unidentified men using improper covers to infiltrate the building the night before Hoover died. And whoever it was perhaps knew a great deal more about hundreds and hundreds of dossiers that had been Hoover's private files.

One other consideration was forced on Quinn O'Brien. It was not one he relished thinking about. Since that whispered voice on the telephone four months ago the will to resist, to fight, had gone out of him. It was entirely possible that his decline at the bureau was due to himself. To his own performance.

The ring of the telephone interrupted his thoughts, bringing him back to the minor realities of night duty. He looked at the lighted button; it was an inside call from one of the two entrance desks.

"This is the Tenth Street desk. We've got a problem. There's a man down here who insists on seeing someone in authority, whoever's in charge. We told him to come back in the morning, but he refuses."

"Is he drunk? Or a nut?"

"Can't say that he's either. As a matter of fact, I *know* who he is. I read a book he wrote. A thing called *Counterstrike!* His name's Chancellor. Peter Chancellor."

"I've heard of him. What's he want?"

"He won't say. Only that it's an emergency."

"What do you think?"

"I think he'll stay here all night until somebody sees him. I figure that's you, Quinn."

"All right. Check him for weapons, assign an escort, and send him up."

23

Peter walked into the office, nodding his thanks to the uniformed guard, who closed the door and left. Behind the desk in front of the window a stocky man with reddish brown hair got to his feet and extended his hand. Chancellor approached and took it, the grip was strange. It was cold, physically cold, and abrupt.

"I'm Senior Agent O'Brien, Mr Chancellor. I'm sure I don't have to tell you that your coming here at this hour is highly irregular."

"The circumstances are irregular."

"You sure you don't want the police? Our jurisdiction is limited."

"I want you."

"Whatever it is can't wait until morning?" asked O'Brien, still standing.

"No."

"I see. Sit down, please." The agent gestured to one of the two chairs in front of the desk.

Peter hesitated. "I'd prefer to stand, at least for now. To tell you the truth, I'm very nervous."

"Suit yourself." O'Brien returned to his chair. "At least take your overcoat off. That is, if you intend to be here long."

"I may be here for the rest of the night," said Chancellor removing his coat and draping it over a chair.

"I wouldn't count on it," said O'Brien, watching him.

"I'll let you decide. Is that fair?"

"I'm a lawyer, Mr Chancellor. Elliptical responses, especially when phrased as questions, are pointless and irritating. They also bore me."

Peter stopped and looked at the man. "A lawyer? I thought you said you were an agent. A senior agent."

"I did. Most of us are lawyers. Or accountants."

"I forgot."

"Now I've reminded you. But I can't imagine it's pertinent."

"No, it isn't," replied Chancellor, forcing his concentration back to the issue. "I've got a story to tell you, Mr O'Brien. When I'm finished, I'll go with you to whoever you think should hear it, and repeat it. But I have to start at the beginning; it won't make sense otherwise. Before I do, I'd like to ask you to make a telephone call."

"Wait a minute," interrupted the agent. "You came here voluntarily and refused our suggestion that you return in the morning for a formal appointment. I won't accept any preconditions, and I won't make any phone calls."

"I've a good reason for asking you to."

"If it's a precondition, I'm not interested. Come back in the morning."

"I *can't*. Among other reasons, there's a man flying in from Indianapolis who says he's going to kill me."

"Go to the police."

"Is that all you can say? That, and 'come back in the morning'?"

The agent leaned back in his chair; his eyes conveyed his growing suspicion. "You wrote a book called *Counterstrike!*, didn't you?"

"Yes, but that's not – "

"I remember now," interrupted O'Brien. "It came out last year. A lot of people thought it was true; a lot of other people were upset. You said the CIA was operating domestically."

"I happen to think it's true."

"I see," continued the agent warily. "Last year it was the agency. Is it the FBI this year? You come off the street in the middle of the night trying to provoke us into doing something you can write about?"

Peter gripped the back of the chair. "I won't deny it started with a book. With the *idea* of a book. But it's gone way beyond that. People have been killed. Tonight *I* was nearly killed; so was the person with me. It's all connected."

"I repeat emphatically. Go to the police."

"I want *you* to call the police."

"Why?"

"So you'll believe me. Because it concerns people here at the Federal Bureau of Investigation. I think you're the only ones who can stop it."

O'Brien leaned forward, still wary, but aroused. "Stop what?"

Chancellor hesitated. He had to appear rational to this suspicious man. If the agent thought he was a lunatic – even half a lunatic – he'd thrown him to the police. Peter did not reject the police; they were protection and he welcomed them. But the solution did not lie with the police. It lay within the bureau. He spoke as calmly as he could.

"Stop the killing, that's first, of course. Then stop the terror tactics, the extortion, the blackmail. People are being destroyed."

"By whom?"

"By others who think they have information that could irreparably damage the FBI."

O'Brien remained motionless. "What's the nature of this irreparable damage?"

"It's founded in the theory that Hoover was assassinated."

O'Brien stiffened. "I see. And this phone call to the police. What's that about?"

"An old house on Thirty-fifth Street North-west, near Wisconsin, behind Dumbarton Oaks. It was burning when I left several hours ago. I set it on fire."

The agent's eyes widened, his voice urgent. "That's quite an admission. As a lawyer I think you should – "

"If the police look," continued Peter, overriding O'Brien's urgency, "they'll find shells on the front lawn, bullet holes in the walls and woodwork as well as the furniture, and the upper half of the kitchen door smashed. Also, the telephone wires were cut."

The FBI man stared at Chancellor. "What the hell are you saying?"

"It was an ambush."

"Weapons were fired in the middle of a residential neighbourhood?"

"The gunshots were muffled by silencers. No one heard anything. There were periods of quiet – probably for passing cars. That's why I thought of the fire. The flames would be spotted by someone."

"You left the scene?"

"I ran away. Now I'm sorry I did."

"Why did you?"

Again Peter hesitated. "I was confused. Frightened."

"That person with you?"

"That's part of it, I imagine." Chancellor paused, seeing the obvious question in the agent's eyes. For a hundred reasons he could not protect her. As Phyllis herself had put it, whatever her transgressions, they did not warrant the loss of life. "Her name is Phyllis Maxwell."

"The newspaperwoman?"

"Yes. She ran first. I tried to find her. I couldn't."

"You said this all happened several hours ago. Do you know where she is now?"

"Yes. On a plane." Peter reached into his jacket pocket and took out Phyllis's letter. Reluctantly, but knowing he had to, he handed it to O'Brien.

As O'Brien read, Peter had the distinct impression that something was happening to the FBI man. For a moment the colour seemed to drain from his face. At one point he raised his eyes and stared at Peter; the look he conveyed Chancellor knew well, but he did not understand it coming from this stranger. It was a look of fear.

When he was finished, the agent put the letter face down, reached for a booklet on his desk, opened it to a specific page, and picked up his telephone. He pressed a button and dialled.

"This is the FBI, one of the night-duty officers, emergency code, seven-five-sparrow. There was a fire at a house on Thirty-fifth North-west. Near Wisconsin. Do you have anyone on the scene? . . . Can you put me through to the officer in charge? Thank you." O'Brien looked up at Peter. He spoke curtly; it was not a request but an order. "Sit down."

Chancellor did so, vaguely realizing that in spite of the agent's commanding tone, the strange fear he had seen in O'Brien's eyes was now in his voice.

"Sergeant, this is the FBI." The agent shifted the phone to his right hand. Bewildered, Peter saw that the palm of O'Brien's left hand, the hand that had been holding the telephone, was moist with sweat. "You've received my clearance. I want to ask you a couple of questions. Is there any evidence as to how the fire was started, and are there any signs of gunshots? Cartridge shells in front or bullet holes inside?"

The agent listened, his eyes riveted on the desk, staring at nothing, really, but staring intently. Chancellor watched him, mesmerized. O'Brien's forehead broke out in small beads of perspiration. Absently, his breath suspended, the FBI man raised his left hand and wiped the sweat away. When finally he spoke, he was barely audible.

"Thank you, Sergeant. No, it's not our basket. We don't know anything, just following up an anonymous lead. It's got nothing to do with us."

O'Brien hung up. He was profoundly disturbed; there was a sudden sadness in his eyes.

"As near as can be determined," O'Brien said, "the fire was deliberately started. Remnants of fabric soaked with paraffin were found. There were shells on the lawn, windows shot out; there's every reason to expect bullets impacted throughout the interior – what's left of it. Everything will be sent to the laboratories."

Peter sat forward. Something was wrong. "Why did you tell the sergeant you didn't know anything?"

The agent swallowed. "Because I want to hear what you have to say. You've told me it concerns the bureau; some crazy theory about Hoover being murdered. That's enough for me. I'm a career man. I want to hear it first. I can always pick up the phone and call that precinct back."

O'Brien gave his explanation in a flat, quiet voice. It was reasonable, thought Chancellor. Everything he had learned about the bureau pointed to the fact that the bottom line was public relations. Avoid embarrassment at all costs. Protect the Seat of Government. Phyllis Maxwell's words came back to him.

The story hasn't been told. I don't think it ever will be . . . The bureau will protect him . . . The heirs apparent won't let the image be tarnished. They fear infected bloodlines, and they damned well should.

Yes, reflected Chancellor. O'Brien fitted the mould. His burden was the heaviest because he was the first to hear the extraordinary news. Something was very rotten in the bureau, and this agent would have to carry the message of that rot to his superiors. His dilemma was understandable: messengers were often held accountable for their reports of catastrophe; the bloodlines could be infected after all. It was no wonder that this career man perspired.

But nothing in his imagination prepared Peter for what followed.

To go back to the beginning," said Chancellor. "I was on the West Coast four, five months ago, living in Malibu. It was late afternoon; a man was on the beach staring up at my house. I went out and asked him why. He knew me; he said his name was Longworth."

O'Brien bolted forward in his chair, his eyes locked with Peter's. His lips formed the name, but only a shadow of sound emerged. "Longworth!"

"Yes, Longworth. You know who he is, then."

"Go on," the agent whispered.

Peter sensed the cause of O'Brien's shock. Alan Longworth had betrayed Hoover, defected from the bureau. Somehow the word had got out. But Hoover was dead, the defector half a world away – the stain removed. Now Senior Agent O'Brien had to bear the news that the vanished Longworth had surfaced. In a strange way Chancellor felt sorry for this middle-aged career man.

"Longworth said he wanted to talk to me because he'd read my books. He had a story to tell, and he thought I was the one to write it. I told him I wasn't looking for anything. Then he made that extraordinary statement about Hoover's death, linking it with some private files of Hoover's that were missing. He told me to check out his name; I have sources to do that, and he knew it. I know it sounds crazy, but I bit. God knows I didn't believe it; Hoover was an old man with a history of heart disease. But the concept fascinated me. And the fact that this Longworth would go to the trouble of – "

O'Brien got out of his chair. He stood behind the desk looking down at Peter, his eyes burning. "Longworth. The files. Who sent you to me? Who *are* you? Who the hell am I to *you?*"

"What?"

"You expect me to believe this? You walk off the street in the middle of the night and tell me this! For Christ's sake, what do you want from me? What more do you want?"

"I don't know what you're talking about," said Chancellor, stunned. I've never seen you before in my life."

"Salter and Krepps! Go on, say it! *Salter and Krepps!* They were there, too!"

"Who are Salter and Krepps? Where were they?"

O'Brien turned away. He was breathing rapidly. "You know where they were. Unassigned field covers. Longworth in the Hawaiian Islands."

"He lives in Maui," agreed Peter. "They paid him off that way. I don't know the other two names; he never mentioned them. Were they working with Longworth?"

O'Brien stood motionless, his body rigid. Slowly he turned back to Chancellor, his eyes narrowed. "Working with Longworth?" he asked, barely above a whisper. "What do you mean, 'working with Longworth'?"

"Just that. Longworth was transferred from the bureau. His cover was an assignment with the State Department. But it was never true. It was only an accommodation. I've learned that much. What amazes me is that you people even know about Longworth."

The senior agent continued to stare in silence. His frightened eyes widened. "You're clean . . ."

"What?"

"You're *clean*. You walk off the goddamned streets and you're clean!"

"What do you mean, I'm clean?"

"Because you wouldn't have told me what you just did. You'd be crazy to. A deep-cover accommodation that's false. With *State* . . . Oh, Christ." O'Brien was like a man in a trance, aware of his state of suspension but incapable of shaking it. He braced himself against the desk, the fingers of both hands pressed into the wood. He closed his eyes.

Peter was alarmed. "Maybe you'd better take me to someone else."

"No. Wait a minute. Please."

"I don't think so." Peter got out of the chair. "As you said, this isn't your 'basket'. I want to talk to one of the other night-duty officers."

"There aren't any others."

"You said on the phone – "

"I know what I said! Try to understand. You *have* to talk to me. You've got to tell me everything you know. Every detail!"

Never, thought Peter. There'd be no mention of Alison; she was not going to be touched. Nor was he yet sure he wanted to talk further with this strangely disturbed man. "I want others to hear what I have to say."

O'Brien blinked several times. The trance was broken; he walked swiftly to a shelf on the other side of the room, pulled out a cassette recorder, and returned to the desk. He sat down and opened a bottom drawer. When his hands emerged, it held a small plastic box in which there was a cassette tape.

"The seal's unbroken; the tape is unused. I'll play it through if you like." The agent snapped the box open, removed the cassette, and inserted it. "You have my word. Others will hear what you have to say."

"A tape won't do."

"You've got to trust me," said O'Brien. "Whatever you think of my behaviour these past few minutes, you've got to trust me. You can only tell your story on tape. And don't identify yourself. Describe yourself as a writer, that's all. Use all the other names involved except those associated with you personally or professionally. If that becomes impossible, if those people are intrinsic to the events, hold up your hand; I'll stop the tape, and we'll talk about it. Have you got that?"

"*No.*" Chancellor balked. "Now *you* just wait a minute. This isn't what I came here for."

"You came here to put a stop to it! That's what you told me. Stop the killing, stop the terror, stop the blackmail. Well, I want the same thing! You're not the only one who's been pushed to the fucking wall! Or this Maxwell woman or *any* of you. Christ, I've got a wife and family!"

Peter recoiled, stung by O'Brien's words. "What did you say?"

Self-consciously, the FBI man lowered his voice. "I have a family. It's not important, forget it."

"I think it's very important," said Peter. "I don't think I can ever tell you how important it is to me right now."

"Don't bother," interrupted O'Brien. He was abruptly the complete professional. "Because I'm doing the telling. Remember what I said: don't identify yourself, but use the names of everyone else who approached you or you were sent to – people *not* known to you previously. Give the other names to me later, but not on the tape. I don't want you traced. Speak slowly; think about what you're saying. If you have any doubts, just look at me; I'll know. I'm going to start now. Give me a moment to identify myself and the circumstances."

O'Brien depressed two buttons on the small recorder and spoke in a clipped, hard voice.

"This tape is being prepared by Senior Agent C. Quinlan O'Brien, Eyedent clearance seventeen-twelve, on the night of December the eighteenth at approximately twenty-three hundred hours. The man you will hear was escorted to the night-duty office. I have removed his name from the security logs and informed the desk agent to report to me any and all inquiries, under the aforementioned seventeen-twelve in-house clearance." O'Brien paused, picked up a pencil, and scribbled a note to himself on a pad. "I consider the information on this tape to be of the highest priority of classification and for reasons of security can accept no interference. I fully understand the irregularity of the methods I employ and – for personal reasons – fully assume responsibility."

The agent stopped the machine and looked at Peter. "Ready? Start last summer. At Malibu and your meeting with Longworth." He pressed the buttons; the tape rolled.

Through the mists of disbelief Chancellor began, speaking slowly, trying to follow the instructions of this man he suddenly, strangely knew so well. This man who was somehow a part of his own invention. C. Quinlan O'Brien, *Alexander Meredith*. Attorney. *Attorney*. The bureau. *The bureau*. A wife and family . . . *A wife and family* . . .

Frightened men.

O'Brien was visibly shaken as the story unfolded, both stunned and disturbed by the incidents Peter described. Whenever he mentioned Hoover's private files, the agent grew tense and his hands shook.

When Peter came to Phyllis's description of the horrible, flat, high-pitched whisper over the telephone, O'Brien could not conceal his reaction. He gasped, his neck arched back, his eyes closed.

Peter stopped; the tape continued rolling. There was silence. O'Brien opened his eyes, staring at the ceiling. Slowly he turned to Chancellor.

"Go on," he said.

"There isn't much more. You read her letter."

"Yes. Yes, I read the letter. Describe what happened. The gunshots, the fire. Why you ran away."

Peter did. And then it was over. He had said it all. Or nearly all. He had not mentioned Alison.

O'Brien stopped the tape, rewound it for several seconds, and played the last words back for clarity. Satisfied, he switched off the machine.

"All right. You've put down what you wanted to. Now, tell me the rest."

"What?"

"I asked you to trust me, but you haven't told it all. You were writing in Pennsylvania; suddenly you came to Washington. Why? According to you, your research was completed. You ran away from a burning house on Thirty-fifth Street nearly five hours ago. You got here two hours ago. Where were you for three hours? With whom? Fill in the gaps, Chancellor. They're important."

"No. That's not part of our bargain."

"What bargain? Protection'?" Angrily, O'Brien got to his feet. "You damned fool, how can I offer protection if I don't know whom to protect? And don't kid yourself, protection *is* the bargain. Besides, it would take me – or anyone who really wanted to – roughly an hour to trace every move you made since you left Pennsylvania."

The agent's logic was undeniable. Chancellor had the feeling that he was an ill-equipped amateur facing a hardened professional. "I don't want her part of this. I want your word on that. She's been through enough."

"So have we all," replied O'Brien. "Did she receive a telephone call?"

"No. But you did, didn't you?"

"I'm asking the questions." The agent sat down again. "Tell me about her."

Peter told the dark, sad story of Lieutenant General Bruce MacAndrew, his wife, and the daughter who was forced to grow so early in her life. He described the isolated house on the backcountry road in Maryland. And the words sprayed in blood-red paint on a wall: *Mac the Knife. Killer of Chasŏng.*

Quinlan O'Brien closed his eyes and said softly "Han Chow."

"Is that Korea'?"

"Different war. Same method of extortion. military records that never reached the Pentagon. Or if they did, were removed. And now someone else has them."

Peter held his breath. "Are you talking about Hoover's files?"

O'Brien stared at him without replying. Chancellor felt torn apart; the insanity was complete.

"They were shredded," whispered Peter, unsure of his own mind. "They were destroyed! What the hell are you trying to tell me? This is a book! None of it's real! You have to protect your goddamned bureau! But not *this!* Not the *files!*"

O'Brien stood up, raising the palms of his hands. It was a reassuring gesture, a father calming an hysterical child. "Take it easy. I didn't say anything about Hoover's files. You've been through a lot tonight, and you're making assumptions. For a second I did, too. But it's wrong. Two isolated incidents involving military records hardly constitute a pattern. Those files were destroyed. We know that."

"What's Han Chow?"

"Not pertinent."

"A minute ago you thought it was."

"A minute ago a lot of thoughts went through my head. But things are clear now. You're right. Someone's using you. And me and probably a couple of dozen others to tear the bureau apart. Someone who knows us, knows the working structure. Very possibly it's one of us. It wouldn't be the first time."

Peter studied the FBI man. Since Hoover's death there had been rumours, many reported in the newspapers, that factions within the bureau were fighting among themselves. And Quinn's intelligence and sincerity were convincing.

"I'm sorry," he said. "You scared hell out of me."

"You've got every right to be scared. Much more than I have. Nobody's fired a gun at me." O'Brien smiled reassuringly. "But that's all over with. I'll find men to stay with you around the clock."

Chancellor returned the smile weakly. "Whoever they are, I hope they're the best you've got. I don't mind telling you, I've never been so frightened in my life."

The smile disappeared from O'Brien's face. "Whoever they are, they won't be from the bureau."

"Oh? Why not?"

"I don't know who to trust."

"Then, apparently you know there are people you can't trust. Anyone in particular?"

"More than one. There's a pack of extremists here. We know some of them, not all. They're loosely called the Hoover Group. When Hoover died, they thought they'd take over. They didn't and they're angry. Some are as paranoid as Hoover was."

Again Chancellor was struck by O'Brien's words; it was confirmation of Peter's original thinking. Everything that had happened – from Malibu to Rockville to the old house on Thirty-fifth Street – was the result of violent infighting within the FBI. And Longworth had reappeared.

"We have a bargain," he said. "I want protection. For the woman and myself."

"You'll have it."

"From where? Who?"

"You mentioned Judge Sutherland. A couple of years ago he was instrumental in repairing a severed connection between the bureau and the rest of the intelligence community. Hoover had cut off the flow of information to the CIA and NSA."

"I know that," interrupted Chancellor quietly. "I wrote a book about it."

"That was *Counterstrike!*, wasn't it? I guess I'd better read it."

"I'll send you a copy. You send protection. I repeat: who? Where from?"

"There's a man named Varak. Sutherland's man. He owes me a debt."

O'Brien collapsed in the chair. His head fell back, his breath fast and erratic as if he could not let sufficient air into the lungs. He brought his face forward into his hands; he could feel the trembling in his fingers.

He had not been sure he could carry it off. A number of times during the past two hours he thought he was going to fall apart.

It was the writer's panic that had got him through the last minutes. The realization that Chancellor had to be controlled; he could not be allowed to learn the truth.

Hoover's files were not destroyed, as Quinn *knew* they had not been. That much seemed certain. And now someone else knew it, too. How many? How many phone calls had been made? How many others had been reached by that terrible high-pitched whisper? A dead general, a murdered congressman, a vanished newspaperwoman – how many more?

Things were not the same as they had been two hours ago. Peter Chancellor's revelation meant there was work to do quickly, and to his great relief, O'Brien began to think he was again capable of doing it.

He picked up the phone and dialled the National Security Agency. But Stefan Varak could not be traced.

Where was Varak? What kind of assignment would cut the NSA agent off from the bureau? Especially from *him?* Varak and he were friends. Two years ago Quinn had taken an enormous risk for Varak. He had provided him with profile data Hoover had restricted; it could have cost him his career.

Now he needed Varak. Of all the men in the intelligence community Varak was the best. His range of expertise and the sheer numbers and depth of his contacts were extraordinary. He was the man Quinn wanted to hear Chancellor's tape first. Varak would know what to do.

In the meantime the writer had temporary protection. His name had been removed from the security logs, all inquiries directed to O'Brien. There were a couple of men at CIA Quinn had fed print information to during Hoover's embargo. When O'Brien told them the subject to be guarded was the author of *Counterstrike!*, they damned near refused. But, of course, they did not refuse. Reasonable men in the most unreasonable of professions had to help each other. Otherwise unreasonable men would assume control, and that way lay disaster.

Perhaps they had. Perhaps disaster had already come.

24

The FBI escort made his delivery to the Hay-Adams lobby. Chancellor was the package. He was signed for by a nod and a corresponding "Okay . . . Good night," spoken politely by the man from the Central Intelligence Agency.

In the lift Peter tried to make conversation with this stranger who had volunteered to protect him. "My name's Chancellor," he said foolishly.

"I know," replied the man. "I read your book. You did quite a job on us."

It was not the most reassuring of greetings. "It wasn't meant that way. I have several friends in the CIA."

"Want to bet?"

Not reassuring at all. "There's a man named Bromley flying in from Indianapolis."

"We know. He's sixty-five years old and in poor health. He had a weapon on him at the Indie airport. He has a permit, so it's supposed to be returned to him at the National terminal, but it won't be. It'll be lost."

"He could pick up another."

"Not likely. O'Brien'll put a man on him."

They reached the floor; the lift door opened. The CIA man blocked Peter's exit with his arm and walked out first, his right hand in his overcoat pocket. He glanced up and down the corridor, turned and nodded to Chancellor.

"What about the morning?" asked Peter, coming out of the lift. "Bromley could walk into any gun shop – "

With an Indianapolis permit? No retailer would sell him a firearm."

"Some would. There are ways."

"There are better ways to prevent it."

They were at the door of the suite. The CIA man removed his right hand from his coat pocket; he held a small automatic. With his left hand he undid the two middle buttons of his overcoat and shoved the weapon out of sight. Peter knocked.

He could hear Alison's racing footsteps. She opened the door and moved to embrace him, stopping at the sight of the stranger. "Alison, this is – I'm sorry, I don't know your name."

"Tonight I don't have one," the CIA man said, nodding to Alison. "Good evening, Miss McAndrew."

"Hello?" Alison was understandably bewildered. "Please come in."

"No, thank you." The agent looked at Chancellor. "I'll be right out here in the corridor at all times. My relief comes on at eight in the morning, which means I'll have to wake you up so you know who he is."

"I'll be up."

"Fine. Good night."

"Wait a minute . . ." An idea struck Peter. "If Bromley shows up, and you're sure he's not armed, maybe I should talk to him. I don't know him. I don't know why he's after me."

"That's up to you. Let's play it as it comes." He closed the door.

"You were gone so long!" Alison threw her arms around him, her face next to his. "I nearly went out of my mind!"

He held her gently. "That's finished with. Nobody's going out of his mind. Not any more."

"You told them everything?"

"Yes." He moved her back so he could look at her face. "Everything. About your father, too. I had to. The man I talked to knew I was holding back. He made it clear that they could trace every move we made. They wouldn't have to go very far; just across the river to the Pentagon."

She nodded and took his arm, leading him away from the door into the sitting room. "How do you feel?"

"Fine. Relieved. How about a drink?"

"My man's been working. I'll make them," she said, heading for the bar stocked by the hotel's room service. Peter fell into an armchair, his body limp, his feet stretched out. "I've been meaning to ask you," said Alison, pouring whisky and opening the ice bucket. "Do you always have a bar set up for you wherever you go? You don't drink that much."

"A few months ago I drank that much." Chancellor laughed; it was good to remember, knowing things had changed, he thought. "To answer your question, it's an indulgence that came with the first large advance. I remembered all those movies. Writers in hotel rooms always had fancy bars and wore smoking jackets. I don't have a smoking jacket."

It was Alison's turn to laugh. She brought his drink to him and sat in the chair opposite his. "I'll buy you one for Christmas."

"Next Christmas," he said, holding her eyes with his. "This Christmas give me a plain gold ring. It'll go on the third finger of my left hand. Just as yours will."

Alison drank from her glass and glanced away. "I meant what I said a few hours ago. I don't require any commitments."

Chancellor looked at her, alarmed. He put his drink down and went to her. He knelt by her side and touched her face. "What am I supposed to say? 'Thank you, Miss MacAndrew, it's been a nice interlude'? I won't say it, and I can't think it. I don't think you can, either."

She stared at him, her eyes vulnerable. "There's a great deal you don't know about me."

Peter smiled. "What? You're the daughter of the regiment? The whore of battalion twelve? Virgin you're not, but the other doesn't fit, either. You're not the type. You're too damned independent."

"You make judgements too quickly."

"God! I'm glad you think so. I'm very decisive, a quality that's been noticeably absent for a long time . . . before I met you."

"You were recovering from a very painful experience. I was here. And in trouble of my own."

"Thank you, Madame Freud. But you see, I *am* recovered, and I *am* decisive. Try this decision out. I realize marriage isn't in fashion this year, it's so middle class." He moved closer to her. "But you see, I meant what I said before, too. I do require a commitment. I believe in marriage, and I want to live with you for the rest of my life."

Her eyes filled with tears. She shook her head and held his face. "Oh, Peter. Where were you for so many years?"

"In a different life."

"So was I. What's that silly poem? 'Come live with me and be my love . . .' "

"Marlowe. Not so silly."

"And I'll come live with you, Peter. And be your love.

For as long as it makes sense for both of us. But I won't marry you."

He moved back, again alarmed. "I want more than that."

"I can't give you any more. I'm sorry."

"I know you can! I feel it! So completely, so much like – " He stopped.

"Like her? Like your Cathy?"

"Yes! I can't bury that."

"I'd never want you to bury it. Maybe we can have something just as beautiful. But not marriage."

"Why?"

Tears rolled down her cheeks. "Because marriage means – I won't have children, Peter."

She was saying something obliquely, and Chancellor knew it. He was just not sure what it was. "You're jumping ahead. I hadn't thought one way or the other about – " Suddenly it was clear to him. "It's your mother. Her madness."

Alison closed her eyes, her faced streaked with tears. "My darling, try to understand."

Peter did not move; he remained at her side and forced her to look at him. "Listen to me. I understand something else, too. You never believed what they told you, what your father told you. That your mother's illness came about because she nearly drowned. You never accepted that. Why not?"

The look in her eyes was pathetic. "I couldn't be sure. I'm not sure why. That's the awful, awful thing."

"Why couldn't you be sure? Why would your father lie to you?"

"I don't know! I knew him so well, every inflection of his voice, every gesture. He must have told me the story fifty times, always compulsively, as if he wanted me to love her as he once loved her. But there was always something false, something missing. Finally I understood. She was simply a crazy woman. She had gone insane naturally. *Naturally*. And he never wanted me to know. Do you understand now?"

Chancellor reached for her hand. "He could have been hiding something else from you."

"What? Why would – ?"

The telephone rang. Peter looked at his watch. It was past three in the morning. Who the hell would call him now? It had to be O'Brien. He picked up the phone.

"You think you've stopped me, but you haven't!" The voice on the line was strident, the breathing heavy.

"*Bromley?*"

"You animal. You rotten, filthy scum!" Age was in the voice now. The hysterical voice belonged to an old man.

"Bromley, who *are* you? What have I ever done to you? I've never met you before in my life!"

"That wasn't necessary, was it? You don't have to know a person to destroy him. Or her. Destroy a child! And her children!"

Phyllis Maxwell had used the same word! *Destroy*. Did Bromley mean Phyllis? Was he talking about *her*? It couldn't be; she had no children.

"I swear I don't know what you're talking about. Somebody's lied to you. They've lied to others."

"No one lied. They read it to me! You dug out the court transcripts, the confidential transcripts, the psychiatric reports. You wrote it all down, every filthy thing! You used our names, where we live, where *she* lives!"

"None of that's true! I haven't used any court transcripts or psychiatric reports! There's nothing like that in the manuscript! I haven't the vaguest idea what it all means!"

"*Scum. Liar.*" The old man drew out his words in hatred. "Do you think I'm a fool? Do you think they didn't give me proof? I've been responsible for printing thousands of audits." The voice exploded. "They gave me a number and I *checked* that number and I *called* that number! Bedford Printers! I spoke with the typographer. He read me what you'd written! What he'd set in type a week ago!"

Peter was stunned. Bedford was the printing house his publisher used for its books. "That's impossible! The manuscript's not with Bedford. It couldn't be. It's nowhere near finished!"

There was a momentary silence. Chancellor could only hope he was getting through to the old man. But Bromley's next words told him he was not.

"You go to such lengths to lie! The publication date is set for April. Your publication date's always April."

"Not this year."

"Your book's printed. And I don't care any more. You weren't satisfied with destroying me. Now you go after *her*. But I'll stop you, Chancellor. You can't hide from me. I'll find you, and I'll kill you. Because I don't care. My life is over."

Peter thought quickly. "Listen to me! What's happened to you has happened to others. Let me ask you. Did someone call you, whisper over the telephone? A high-pitched whisper – "

The phone went dead. Chancellor looked at it and then turned to Alison, her face still damp with tears. "He's insane."

"It's the season for it."

"I won't listen to that," he said, reaching into his pocket for the page of notepaper with O'Brien's number on it. He dialled. "It's Chancellor. Bromley called me. He's desperate. He thinks my book's coming out in April. Like Phyllis Maxwell, he's convinced there's damaging information in it."

"Is there?" asked O'Brien.

"No. I've never heard of him before in my life."

"I'm surprised. He's the GSA accountant who took on the Defense Department over the C-40 cargo plane. He said there was collusion in the over-runs."

"I remember . . ." Peter's mind raced back, picturing the newspaper stories. "There were Senate hearings. He was a pretty lonely guy, if I recall. The superpatriots painted him pale red and into a corner."

"That's the one. His code name over here was Viper."

"It would be. What happened to him?"

"They removed him from 'sensitive' audits – that's what they called it. Then some damned fool at GSA tried to make points with the administration and withheld a rating. He instituted a civil suit."

"And?"

"We don't know. The suit was dropped and he disappeared."

"But we do know, don't we?" said Chancellor. "He received a telephone call with a high-pitched whisper on the other end of the line. And he's just received another. With enough scraps of accurate information to convince him he was hearing the truth."

"Easy. He can't touch you. Whatever he thinks you did to him – "

"Not him," interrupted Peter. "He talked about 'her', 'a child', 'her children'."

O'Brien paused. Chancellor knew what the FBI man was thinking: *I've got a wife and family.*

Alexander Meredith.

"I'll try to find out," said the agent finally. "He's checked into a hotel downtown. I've got him under surveillance."

"Does your man know why? Couldn't he be – ?"

"Of course not," interrupted Quinn. "Code Viper was enough. The fact that a weapon was picked up on him in Indianapolis was more than enough. He's immobilized. Get some sleep."

"O'Brien?"

"What?"

"Tell me something. Why him? Why a sick old man?"

Again the agent paused before answering. When he spoke, a cold pain formed in Peter's stomach. "Old men move around freely. Very few people stop them or suspect them; not much importance is accorded them. My guess is that an old man who's desperate could be programmed into a killer."

"Because he doesn't care any more?"

"That's part of it, I imagine. Don't worry. He won't get near you."

Chancellor hung up. He needed sleep. There were many things to think about, but he was incapable of thinking. The strain of the night had caught up with him; the pills had worn off.

He could sense Alison watching him, waiting for him to say something. He turned and their eyes met. Deliberately, he walked over to her, with each step more sure of himself. He spoke calmly, with deep concern.

"I'll accept whatever conditions you want to make, whatever way of living you choose, as long as we can be together. I don't want ever to lose you. But there's one condition I insist on. I'm not going to let you torment yourself over something that may not exist. I think something happened to your mother to drive her mad. I've never heard of a person normal one minute and mentally wasted the next unless he or she was pushed. I want to find out what happened. It may be painful, but I think you've got to know. Will you accept my condition?" Peter held his breath.

Alison nodded. A half smile appeared on her face. "Maybe we both have to know."

"Good." Peter resumed breathing. "Now the decision's made, I don't want to talk about it for a while. We don't have to; we've got all the time in the world. As a matter of fact, I don't want to talk about anything vaguely unpleasant for days."

Alison remained in the chair, looking up at him. "Is your novel unpleasant?"

"The blackest. Why?"

"Are you going to stop writing it?"

He paused. It was odd, but once he'd made the decision, actually *gone* to the bureau and told his story, the pressure had been lifted, and his mind was clearer. The professional in him was emerging again. "It'll be a different book. I'll take out people, put in new ones, change the circumstances. But I'll keep a lot, too."

"Can you do that?"

"It'll happen. The premise is still strong. I'll find a way. I'll go slowly for a while; it'll come to me."

Alison smiled. "I'm glad."

"That's the last decision for the night. Anyway, I want to go back to the first one."

"Which is?"

He smiled. "You. Come live with me and be my love."

He heard rapid tapping through the mists of sleep. Alison stirred beside him, burying her head deeper into her pillow. He slid out of the bed and grabbed his trousers from the chair where he had draped them. Naked, he walked into the sitting room, closing the bedroom door behind him. Awkwardly pulling on his trousers, he hopped towards the foyer.

"Who is it?" he asked.

"It's eight o'clock," said the voice of the CIA man beyond the door.

Peter remembered. At eight o'clock the guard changed; it was time for identifications, his and the new sentry's.

And it was all he could do to conceal his shock. He blinked and stifled a yawn and rubbed his eyes to further hide his astonishment. The new man was the CIA "domestic" who had given Peter material for *Counterstrike!* Given it freely. In anger. Deeply concerned over the illegalities the agency was forced to perpetrate.

"Names aren't necessary," said the agent initially assigned to Chancellor. "He'll take over from me."

Peter nodded. "Okay. No names, no handshakes. I wouldn't want you to catch anything."

"What you've got jumps," said the second man quietly, with an offensive tone worthy of his companion. He turned to the first agent. "He stays in the hotel, right?"

"That's what we've agreed to. No outside work."

Both men turned, dismissing him, and walked towards the lifts. Peter went inside and closed the door. He listened for the faint sounds of the lift. When they came, he waited an additional ten seconds before he opened the door.

The CIA man slid past Chancellor into the small foyer of the suite. Peter closed the door. "Christ!" said the agent. "I nearly had a cardiac arrest when I got the call last night."

"You? I damned near fell over when I saw you standing there!"

"You carried it off. Sorry. I couldn't take the chance of phoning you."

"How did it happen?"

"O'Brien. He's one of our contacts at the bureau. When Hoover shut down communications, O'Brien and several others worked with us, got us information we had to have. It wouldn't make sense for him to call anyone else; they'd probably refuse him. He knew we wouldn't."

"You owed him a debt," said Chancellor.

"More than you realize. O'Brien and his friends put their necks as well as their careers on the line for us. If they'd ever been found out, Hoover would have gone berserk. He'd have made sure they were sent to some choice prisons for ten to twenty years apiece."

Peter winced. "He could do that, couldn't he?"

"Could and did. There are several unadvertised carcasses rotting away in Mississippi cells even now. It was his last Siberia. O'Brien's owed; we can't forget that."

"But Hoover's dead."

"Maybe somebody's trying to bring him back. Isn't that what this is all about? Why else would O'Brien call us in?"

Chancellor wondered. It was as valid a possibility as he had heard. O'Brien spoke of the Hoover group – some known, others not, none to be trusted. Did they have Hoover's files? Were they trying to regain control of the bureau? If so, men like Quinn O'Brien had to be destroyed for that control to be taken. "You could be right," he said.

The man nodded. "It starts all over again. Not that it's ever really stopped. When I heard your name last night, I wondered what had taken you so long."

"What does that mean?" Peter was confused.

"The information I gave you. You used it pretty exclusively against us. Why? There were a lot of people at fault, not just us."

"I'll say now what I said two years ago. The agency used the failings of other people as an excuse. Too damned quickly and with too much enthusiasm. I thought we'd agreed. I thought that's why you gave me the information."

The man shook his head. "I guess I thought you'd spread the guilt around a little more. Then I figured you were saving it for another book. That *is* what this is all about, isn't it? You're writing a book about the bureau."

Chancellor was stunned. "Where did you hear that?"

"I didn't hear it, I read it. In this morning's paper. Phyllis Maxwell's column."

25

She had done it. The column was short, ominous in its brevity as well as its content, and centred on the editorial page with a black border around it. It would be read widely, raising startling questions and no less startling alarms. Chancellor could picture the distraught Phyllis Maxwell at the airport, clinging to her sanity, reaching the inevitable decision and calling her newspaper's night desk. No editor would cut the copy; she had a sure reputation for documenting her facts. But beyond this, it was a last gesture, a final testament, and recognizable as such. She owed it to her profession, and that profession would not turn its back on her.

Washington, 19 December – Information from an unimpeachable source reveals that the Federal Bureau of Investigation will soon be confronted with extraordinary charges of malfeasance, extortion, suppression of criminal evidence and illegal surveillance of citizens in flagrant violation of their constitutional rights. These allegations will be made in a forthcoming novel by Peter Chancellor, author of *Counterstrike!* and *Sarajevo!* Although the work has been written as fiction, Chancellor has developed his material from fact. He has traced victims and observed their paralyses. Due only to his own sense of morality has he withheld identities and fictionalized the events. This book is long overdue. Throughout this magnificent city with its symbols everywhere of a people's unique struggle for freedom, men and women are afraid. For themselves, their loved ones, their very thoughts, and often their sanity. They lived with their fears because a giant squid has reached its tentacles into every corner, spreading its terror. The head of this monster is somewhere within the FBI.

This reporter has been touched by these tactics. Therefore, in conscience, I will be absent from these pages for an indeterminate period of time. It is my hope to return one day, but it will only be when I can dispatch my responsibilities in a manner to which you, the reader, are entitled.

A final word. Too many good and powerful men in this government have been compromised by the working methods of the Federal Bureau of Investigation. These assaults must stop. Perhaps Mr Chancellor's fiction will bring about that reality. If so, a part of our system will be cleansed.

It was a bombshell, its crater was smouldering, defined by the black border. Peter looked at his watch; it was twenty minutes past eight. He was surprised O'Brien had not phoned him. Surely he'd seen the paper; surely there was chaos at the FBI. Perhaps the agent was being exceptionally careful. A telephone was suddenly an instrument of danger.

And then, as if his thoughts had willed it, the phone rang and O'Brien was there.

"I knew they were waking you at eight," said Quinn. "Have you seen the paper?"

"Yes, I wondered when you'd call."

"I'm in a phone booth. Obviously. I didn't want to call from home."

"I got off at four this morning. I drove around just thinking for a while, then managed a couple of hours' sleep. Did you expect her to do this?"

"It's the last thing I expected. But I can understand. Maybe it was the only thing she thought she could do."

"It's an unnecessary complication, that's what it is. They'll be looking for her. God help her if she's found. One side will want her life, the other her testimony."

Peter thought for a moment. "She wouldn't have done what she did if she believed she'd be found. She meant what she said in her letter: she'd planned this for a long time."

"Which means a dead skip. I know something about dead skips. All too often they end up more dead than skipped. But that's her problem; we've got enough of our own."

"Your compassion is touching. Did you reach your man Varak?"

"I've put out an emergency defector code for him. He'll have to respond. It's his speciality."

"What do we do until then?"

"Stay where you are. We'll move you later. Varak will know where."

"*I* know where," said Peter angrily. O'Brien was treating them like fugitives. "My house in Pennsylvania. We'll go there. You just get us – "

"No," interrupted the FBI man firmly, "for the time being you stay away from that house and your apartment. You go where I tell you to go. I want you alive, Chancellor. You're very important to me."

The words had their effect; memories of gunfire returned. "All right. We sit and wait."

"Does anyone in New York or Pennsylvania know where you are?"

"Not specifically. They know I'm in Washington."

"Would they know where to look?"

"Probably this hotel. I stay here a lot."

"You're no longer registered there," said O'Brien. "You checked out late last night; the manager made that clear to the front desk."

It was a chilling piece of news. That it could be effected so easily, that it was even necessary in the agent's judgement, caused Peter to swallow involuntarily. Then he remembered. "I called room service. I gave my name and room number. I signed the bill."

"Goddamn it!" O'Brien exploded. "I didn't consider that."

"I'm glad you're not perfect."

"Less so than I want to think about. It's the kind of mistake Varak wouldn't make. We'll handle it, though. It's only for a few hours. You simply want to be incognito."

"What's my new name?"

"Peters. Charles Peters. It's not very original, but it doesn't matter. I'll be the only one calling you. Now, as soon as you can, telephone anyone in New York who knows you're in Washington. Tell them you and Miss MacAndrew have decided to take a couple of days off. You're driving down through Virginia, the Fredericksburg route, towards the Shenandoah. Have you got that?"

"I've got it, but I don't know what I've got. Why?"

"There are a limited number of hotels and motels where you could stay overnight. I want to see who shows up."

Chancellor felt a knot in his stomach. For a moment he was speechless. "What the hell are you saying?" he whispered. "You think Tony Morgan or Joshua Harris are a part of this? You're out of your mind!"

"I told you," replied O'Brien. "I drove around last night just thinking. Everything that's happened to you has happened because of this book you're writing. Most of the places you've been to – not all, but most – have been known by those men because you told them."

"I won't listen to this! They're my friends!"

"They may have no choice," said O'Brien. "I know the recruitment methods better than you do. And I'm not saying they *are* involved, I'm only saying they could be. I guess what I'm telling you is not to trust anyone. Not for the moment; not until we learn more." O'Brien lowered his voice. "Perhaps not even me. I say I'm ready to be tested, and I think I am. But I haven't been tested yet. I can only give you my word that I'll try like hell. I'll be in touch."

Quinn hung up abruptly, as if he could not bring himself to talk a second longer. The fact that he was able to express his own self-doubt was remarkable. He was a brave man because he was so obviously frightened, accepting his fear in a loneliness that Chancellor did not have to know.

Peter sat down to breakfast. Only vaguely aware that he was eating, he went through juice, eggs, bacon, and toast. His thoughts were on what O'Brien had said to him: *I guess what I'm telling you is not to trust anyone.*

There was the echo of unreality about it. A once-removed quality too couched in melodrama to be part of life. Abnormal, false.

Fiction.

Without his thinking about it, his eyes strayed beyond the coffeepot to his notebook on the table in front of the couch. He got out of the chair, carrying his coffee, and sat down on the couch. He opened the notebook, staring at the words he had written yesterday before the madness had begun. The madness that had led him to Quinn O'Brien.

The compulsion was there. He recognized it for what it was: a need to translate the madness he had experienced into a reality he could communicate. Because he *had* experienced it. He had always imagined what it would be like to be hunted, to be trapped, to be frightened and confused and face death – to strain every fibre and brain cell in a search for escape and survival. He had never before lived those feelings, until now. The changes in the book could come later, but for now he'd follow the story line he had developed and complete the chapter tomorrow. He had to put it down, this new, firsthand madness.

Chapter 10 – Outline

Meredith has joined the Nucleus. He is to develop undeniable evidence that within the FBI there is a group of *specific* men who are involved in grossly illegal activities. Not words on paper but voices on tape.

The method will be entrapment, and Alex is tutored by Alan Long. The converted Hoover gunslinger tells Meredith that the only approach is to feign total capitulation to the fanatics inside the bureau. He has the motive: he cannot take the harassment any longer.

The trap will be in the form of a miniaturized tape recorder, placed in his handkerchief pocket, activated by touch.

There is a series of short, emotional confrontations in which Alex is seen abjectly "surrendering" to the Hoover forces. It is not difficult for him to be convincing, for he is reflecting a state of mind he has experienced.

There is a scene at night in which Meredith overhears – in detail – a plan to "eliminate" an FBI informant who has threatened to expose the bureau's involvement in the killing of five black radicals in Chicago. The massacre was the direct result of FBI provocation. The informant is marked for death; the method will be an untraceable weapon in a crowded subway.

Alex has activated the miniaturized equipment. He has the voices on tape. The evidence is now undeniable: conspiracy to commit murder.

The enormity of the charge is enough to drive Hoover from office. It will lead to the uncovering of additional abuses, for it is only one incident in a network of conspiracies. Hoover is finished.

Alex is seen leaving, but the Hoover men sense his duplicity.

Meredith races out of the bureau to his car. He has been given an address in McLean, Virginia, to reach in emergencies. There has never been an emergency like this; he has in his pocket the evidence that will destroy the Man and the men who would turn the country into their own personal police state.

As he drives out of the parking lot, he spots a car behind him he believes to be an FBI vehicle.

A wild chase ensues through the streets of Washington. At a traffic light the man beside the driver of the FBI car rolls down the window shouting "There!" He then leaps out for Meredith's door. Alex jumps the light, careering down the street, pressing his horn, dodging other cars.

He recalls a tactic: lose a car, lose surveillance. He stops in front of a government building, leaves the engine running, gets out, and races up the steps inside.

Only a uniformed guard is there. Meredith flashes his FBI identification; and runs across the marble floor past rows of lifts, pressing the buttons, looking for another exit. He sees a pair of glass doors leading to an open-air corridor that connects the building to another. He races out; from behind a pillar a man emerges. It is one of the two men following him. He holds a gun in his hand. Alex touches the recorder, activating it.

"It's an old trick, Meredith. You're not very good at it."

You're executioners! You're Hoover's executioners!" screams Alex in panic.

The screams are enough to cause the man to lose his concentration; screams can be heard. In that brief instant Meredith does what he never believed he'd be capable of doing. He rushes at the man with the gun.

A violent struggle takes place; two shots are fired.

The first wounds Alex in the shoulder. The second kills the FBI fanatic.

Meredith stumbles through the corridor holding his wound. The second FBI man is seen running towards the glass doors at the other end.

He gets through to the other building and out on to the street. He hails a taxi, falls back into the seat, and gives the driver the address in McLean.

He reaches McLean, barely conscious. He struggles up the path to the door and holds his hand on the bell. The former cabinet officer answers; it is his residence.

"I've been shot. In my pocket. The recorder. Everything's on it."

He falls into unconsciousness.

He awakes in a darkened room; he is on a couch, bandages across his chest and shoulder. He hears voices beyond the closed door; he gets up and edges his way along the wall to the door and opens it an inch. Beyond, around a dining room table, sit the cabinet officer, the newspaperwoman, and Alan Long. The senator is not there.

Alex's tape recorder is by the ex-member of the President's cabinet. He is speaking to Long.

"Did you know about these . . . execution squads?"

"There've been rumours, replies Long cautiously. "I was never involved."

"You wouldn't be trying to save your own neck?"

"What's there to save?" asks Long. "If anyone found out what I've done – what I'm doing – I'm dead."

"Which brings us back to these squads," says the woman. "What did you hear?"

"Nothing specific," answers Long. "No proof. Hoover departmentalizes everything. He does it all secretly; no one really knows what the man in the next office does. That way everyone stays in line."

"Gestapo!" says the woman.

"What *did* you hear?" The cabinet officer.

"Only that there were final solutions if everything fell apart on a project."

The woman stares at Long, then briefly closes her eyes. "Final – oh, my God."

"If ever we needed a last, overwhelming justification," says the balding man, "I think we have it. Hoover will be killed two weeks from Monday, the files taken."

"No!" Alex has yanked the door open with such force that it crashes into the wall. "You can't do it! You have everything you need. Bring him to trial. Let him face the judgment of the courts! Of the country!"

"You don't understand," says the cabinet officer. "There's not a court in the land, not a judge, not a member of the House or of the Senate, not the President or any of his cabinet, who can bring him to trial. It's beyond that."

"No, it isn't! There are laws!"

"There are the files," says the newspaperwoman softly. "People would be reached . . . by others who have to survive."

Meredith sees the eyes staring at him. The eyes are cold, without sympathy.

"Then, you're no better than he is," says Alex, knowing that, if he ever gets out of that house, he will be hunted again.

Chancellor let the pencil drop. He was suddenly aware of Alison in the doorway. She stood in her blue bathrobe, looking down at him. He was grateful for the warmth in her eyes and the smile on her lips.

"Do you know I've been standing here for nearly three minutes and you didn't see me."

"I'm sorry."

"Don't be. I was fascinated. You were so far away."

"I was in McLean, Virginia."

"That's not so far."

"It'd better be." Peter got up from the couch and took her in his arms. "You're adorable and I love you and let's go to bed."

"I've just got out of bed. Let me have some coffee; it'll wake me up."

"Why wake up?"

"So I can enjoy you. Is that too lascivious?" She kissed him.

"The coffee's cold," he said. "I'll order more."

"That's okay. I don't mind."

"I want to post something anyway."

"What?"

"The work I've done during the past couple of days. I should get it up to the typists."

"Now?"

Peter nodded. "I should reread it, have it Xeroxed, send it by messenger. But I don't want to look at it for a while. I just want to get rid of it. I've got some manila envelopes in my briefcase." He walked to the phone across the room, remembering O'Brien's instructions. "Operator? This is Mr Peters in five-eleven. I'd like room service, but I'd also like to post something special delivery. May I give it to the waiter to bring to the desk?"

"Certainly, Mr Peters." There seemed to be a smile in the operator's voice.

They lay naked in each other's arms, warmed by the moment and the desire each felt growing again.

The afternoon sun was reflected from unseen windows outside. From somewhere down in the streets the faint strains of a Christmas carol drifted up from a shopfront down the block. It occurred to Peter that most of the day was gone.

The telephone rang. Chancellor reached for it.

"Mr Peters?" It was the operator; he recognized the voice.

"Yes?"

"Mr Peters, I know this is very improper. I realize you don't want it known you're registered, and I can assure you I didn't say anything to the contrary – "

"What is it?" interrupted Peter, his heart racing.

"There's a man on the line. He says it's an emergency and that he has to talk to a Mr Chancellor. He sounds quite ill, sir."

"Who is it?"

"He says his name is Longworth. Alan Longworth."

The pain in Peter's temples made him shut his eyes.

26

"Get out of my life, Longworth! It's over! I've gone to the bureau and told them everything!"

"You damned fool. You don't know what you've done."

It was Longworth's voice, yet it was more guttural than Peter remembered, more pronounced in its Middle-European accent.

"I know exactly what I've done, and I know what you're trying to do. You and your friends want control of the FBI. You think it's yours by some kind of right or inheritance. Well, it isn't. And now they'll stop you."

"You're wrong, all wrong. It's we who want to stop it. Always *we*." Longworth coughed; it was a horrible sound. "I can't talk on the phone. We must meet."

Again there was the strange echo of an accent. "Why? So you can set up a firing squad like you did on Thirty-fifth Street?"

"I was there. I tried to stop it."

"I don't believe you."

"Listen to me." Longworth went into another spasm of coughing. "There were silencers. Everywhere. Weapons with silencers, as there were in Fort Tyron."

"I remember. I'll never forget."

"But one shot last night was *not* fired through a silencer! Can you remember that?"

Longworth's words triggered off a memory. There *had* been a shot, a loud explosion in counterpoint to the spits. And one shout of anger. He hadn't thought of it then; there had been far too much going on. But now it seemed clear. A gunman had forgotten to employ a silencer.

"Do you remember?" continued Longworth. "You must."

"Yes. What's your point?"

"It was I!" There was that *tone* again. And the proper grammar. Most men in panic would say: It was *me*.

"You?"

"Yes. I followed you. I'm always near you. When those men appeared, I wasn't prepared for what happened. I did what I could. Frankly, I don't know how you got out alive . . ." Longworth coughed again.

Chancellor had never heard a death rattle, but in his imagination he was hearing one now. And if he was, Longworth was telling the truth. "I have a question," he said. "Maybe an accusation, I don't know. You say you're always near me. I know you ride in a silver Continental, that'll come later – "

"*Quickly!*"

"If you're always near me, it means you've been waiting for someone to reach me."

"Yes."

"Who?"

"Not on the telephone! Especially not now."

"I've been *bait!*"

"You were never to be hurt," said Longworth.

"But I was, wasn't I? I was damned near killed. You say you weren't prepared. In New York and down here. Why not?"

Longworth paused. "Because what happened was contrary to everything we knew, everything we projected."

"Inconceivable?" asked Peter sarcastically.

"Yes. That such chances would be taken – there's no more time. I'm very weak, calls can be traced. You must come and see me for your own safety. For the girl's safety."

"There's a CIA man in the corridor. He'll stay here. I'll come with the police!"

"You do and they'll kill you on sight. The girl will be next." Chancellor knew it was true. It was in Longworth's voice. A dying man's voice. "What happened? Where are you?"

"I escaped. Listen to me; do as I tell you. I'll give you three telephone numbers. Do you have a pencil?"

Peter turned. "There's a pencil and paper – " He did not have to finish. Alison got out of bed and brought them rapidly to him. "Go ahead."

Longworth gave three telephone numbers, repeating each. "Take coins with you. In precisely thirty minutes call each of these numbers from a telephone booth. One you'll recognize as being part of something you've written. You'll know where to find me."

"What? Something I've *written?* I've written three books!"

"It is a short paragraph, but I believe you thought deeply about it when you wrote it. Expect to be followed. Take the man in the corridor with you. You've got thirty minutes. Lose those who follow you. The agent in the corridor will know what to do."

"*No,*" said Peter firmly. "He stays here. With MacAndrew's daughter. Unless he's replaced by another man."

"There's no time!"

"Then, you'll just have to trust that I know what I'm doing."

"You don't."

"We'll see. I'll call in thirty minutes." Chancellor hung up and stared at the telephone.

Alison touched his arm. "Who stays with me and where are you going?"

"The CIA man. I'm going out."

"Why?"

"Because I have to."

"That's no answer. I thought you said it was over!"

"I was wrong. But it will be soon, I promise you that." He got out of bed and began dressing.

"What are you going to do? You can't just leave without telling me." Her voice was shrill.

Chancellor turned, buttoning his shirt. "Longworth's hurt, I think pretty seriously."

"Why do you *care?* Look what he's done to you! What he's done to us."

"You don't understand. It's the way I want him, the only way I can force him to go with me." From his suitcase Peter pulled out a dark brown sweater and put it on.

"Go where?"

"To O'Brien. I don't give a damn what Longworth says, I trust him. Quinn won't tell me everything, but he knows what's going on. I heard him on that tape. He's risking his career, maybe his life. This whole goddamned thing started inside the bureau, and that's where it's going to end. Longworth's the key. I'm going to deliver him to O'Brien. Let O'Brien unravel it."

Alison put her hands on his arms. Her grip was firm. "Why deliver him? Why not call O'Brien now? Let *him* find him."

"It wouldn't work; Longworth's an expert – I've seen that. He'll take precautions. If he even suspected what I intend to do, he'd run." Chancellor left unspoken the thought that Longworth might die before O'Brien could get the answers, the identities, from him. If that happened, the insanity would continue.

"Why did he give you three telephone numbers?"

"He'll be at one of them. It's part of the precautions; he's not taking chances."

"When you talked to him, you mentioned your books – "

"More of the same," interrupted Peter, going to the wardrobe for his jacket. "He's going to quote something he says I'll recognize. It'll tell me specifically where he is. It's another reason O'Brien would be useless right now."

"*Peter!*" Alison confronted him, her eyes concerned and angry. "He wanted that man in the hallway to go with you, didn't he?"

"It doesn't make any difference what he wants." Chancellor walked into the sitting room. He went to the coffee table, tore pages of blank paper from his notebook, and picked up a pencil. Alison followed.

"Take him with you," she said.

"No," he answered simply. "There's no time."

"For what?"

He turned and faced her. "To talk any more. I have to go."

She would not let him. "You told him you were going to call the police, bring them with you. Why won't you?"

It was the question he'd hoped she would not ask. The answer was found in threats of death, threats he knew were based in truth. "For the same reason I can't call O'Brien. Longworth would run. I have to find him, take him, and deliver him. I can't let him get away." He held her by the shoulders. "I'll be fine. Trust me. I know what I'm doing."

He kissed her, went to the foyer without looking back, and stepped outside into the corridor. The agency man snapped his head up, startled.

"I have to go out," Peter said.

"No way," replied the CIA man. "That's not part of the rules."

"There are no rules. For instance, you and I have an agreement. Two years ago I needed information, and you gave it to me. I swore to you I'd never say where I got it. But I'm changing that. If you don't help me, I'll go back inside that room, pick up the phone, call the agency, and reveal every source I had for *Counterstrike!* Do I make myself clear?"

"You rotten son of a bitch – "

"You'd better believe it." Chancellor did not raise his voice. "Now there are men watching this hotel who are going to try to follow me. If I can get out without their seeing me, I've got a fair chance. I want that chance, and you're going to tell me how to get it; you'd better be good. If I'm caught, so are you. But you're not going to leave this hallway. Because ii you do, if anything happens to that girl, you're hung."

The agency man said nothing. Instead, he pressed the wall button; the lift on the right arrived first, but there were passengers in it. He let it go by. The second lift came from the lobby; it was empty. The CIA man stepped inside, pressed the stop button, and picked up the emergency telephone. When maintenance got on the phone, he identified himself as a building inspector, but he made light of it, joking with the man on the line. He needed help, he said. Would his new friend please send up a repairman right away? He had loused up the panel box and did not have his tools. He hung up and turned to Chancellor.

"Have you got money?"

"Some."

"Let me have twenty dollars."

Peter gave it to him. "What are you going to do?"

"Get you out of here."

In less than a minute the door of the lift on the left opened, and the repairman came out. He wore overalls and a large tool belt. The agency man greeted him, flashed his CIA identification, and asked him to step into the car. They talked so quietly Chancellor could not hear them, but he could see the agent hand the man the twenty dollars. He came out and motioned Peter inside.

"Do what he says. He thinks it's an agency training exercise."

Chancellor walked into the lift. The repairman was taking off his overalls. Peter watched him, astonished. Underneath the work clothes the repairman wore a soiled undershirt and a pair of white shorts with blue and red polka dots, not unlike a Wonder bread wrapper.

"I can't give you the tool belt, you understand. That's personal property."

"I understand," said Chancellor. He put on the overalls and the repairman's cap.

They took the lift directly to the basement. The repairman led Chancellor around a corner and up a short flight of cement steps into a locker room.

Two hotel employees were dressed and ready to leave. The repairman talked quietly with them.

"Come on, mister," said the man on the right. "You've practically got a union card."

"What do you know?" said his companion. "The super spies play games."

The basement door opened into an alley, which in turn led to the street. The alley was narrow and lined with dustbins. Peter could see the figure of a man in a raincoat at the street entrance, silhouetted against the dull yellowish twilight beyond. The streets would be dark soon. He would use the darkness and the crowds, thought Chancellor. But first he had to get past the man in the raincoat. The man wasn't there by coincidence. He walked between the two hotel employees, and nodded at the figure ahead; the two men understood. They entered the game, enjoying it. Each began talking at once, directing their conversation at Peter as they walked past the man in the main entrance.

"You!" said the man in the raincoat.

Chancellor froze. A hand was clamped on his shoulder. He shrugged it off angrily. The man spun Peter around, ripping the repairman's cap off his head.

Chancellor rushed at the man, body checking him back into the alleyway. The two hotel employees looked at each other, suddenly concerned.

"You guys play rough," said the man on the left.

"I don't think they're playing," said his companion, moving away.

Peter heard no more. He ran, dodging the pedestrians on the pavement. He reached the corner; the light was red and traffic filled the street. He turned to his right, aware of a racing figure behind him, and started running again down the block. He dashed into the street, glancing off the fender of a car, and reached the other side. There was a crowd in front of a shop window; beyond the glass a marionette show depicted Santa Claus and his elves. Chancellor forced his way between bodies like a man possessed. He looked back over the heads of the crowd.

The man in the raincoat was on the other side of the street, but he was making no move to cross over. Instead, he held a rectangular case against his face, angled from cheek to mouth. He was talking into a radio.

Peter edged his way along the side of the building, away from the crowd. Before he realized it, he was in front of another window, this one a jeweller's. Suddenly the glass splintered; it was like no other sound he had ever heard.

An alarm went off, filling the air with a deafening bell. People turned to stare at him. Petrified, he looked at the window. Only inches from him a small circle in the glass. A bullet hole! *An unseen hand was firing at him!*

The crowds on the sidewalk began yelling. He raced to the corner; a man ran after him.

"Stop! I'm a police officer!"

Peter lunged into the crowd; if the policeman had his pistol levelled, he dared not fire it. He tugged and pulled and crashed his way to the kerb, where he started racing along the edge of the street. The intersection was jammed, the rush-hour traffic at a standstill.

There was an empty taxi up the block, halfway towards the next corner. Chancellor ran towards it, hoping no one would reach it first. It was more than a means of travel, it was sanctuary.

"I'm off duty, buddy. No more fares."

"Your light's on!"

"A mistake. Now it's off." The driver looked at him, shaking his head in disgust.

Peter was suddenly aware that the repairman's overalls had split; he looked dishevelled, maybe worse. Without thinking, he began taking them off in the middle of the street.

"A pret-ty girl . . . is like . . . a mel-ody . . ."

A drunk on the kerb was watching him, clapping in the rhythm of the strip. The traffic moved; the taxi drove forward. Chancellor stepped out of the overalls and hurled them at the drunk on the kerb.

The cars in the street jerked to a stop. Peter leaped between bumpers and trunks and ran into the crowds. He looked at his watch. It was twenty-seven minutes since he had talked to Longworth. He had to get to a telephone.

In the next block, diagonally across the street, he could see the reflection of coloured lights off the glass of a booth. It was no longer twilight, it was evening. Above, the Washington sky was dark.

He threaded his way through the traffic in the street. The booth was occupied. A teen-aged girl in dungarees and a red flannel shirt was talking animatedly. Peter looked at his watch; twenty-nine minutes had passed. Longworth had said to call in precisely thirty minutes. How crucial was it? Would a minute or two make any difference?

Chancellor knocked on the glass. The girl shot him a hostile glance. He pushed the door and shouted. "I'm a police officer! I need that phone!" It was the only thing that came to mind.

It was enough. The girl dropped the phone. "Sure." She started to slide out; then she thrust her head down towards the dangling instrument. "I'll call ya", Jennie!" She ran out into the crowds.

Peter replaced the phone, took out the paper with the numbers written on it, inserted a coin, and dialled.

"Manfriedie's," announced the voice on the line. There was music in the background; it was a restaurant.

"Peter Chancellor. I was told to call this number." It was going to be one of the decoys, Peter was sure of it.

"There was a strange occurrence in Munich in the year 1923. It was a portent of things to come, but no one recognized it. What was it, describe it, name the book of yours in which it appeared."

"It took place in the Marienplatz. Thousands of men held a rally. They were dressed in identical uniforms, and each carried a shovel. They called themselves the Army of shovellers. The *Schutzstaffel*. It was the beginning of the Nazis. The book was *Reichstag!*"

There was a brief silence, then the voice came back again. "Disregard the next telephone number given you. Use the same exchange, but the last four digits are now five, one, seven, seven. Fifty-one, seventy-seven. Have you got that?"

"Yes. Five, one, seven, seven. Same exchange."

The man hung up. Peter dialled the new number.

"Arts and Industries," said a woman's voice.

"My name is Chancellor. Do you have a question for me?"

"Yes, I do," answered the woman pleasantly. "There was an organization in Serbia, established during the second decade of the century and headed by a man –"

"Let me save you time," interrupted Peter. "The organization was called the Unity of Death. It was formed in 1911, and its leader was known as Apis. His real name was Dragutin and he was the director of Serbia's military intelligence. The book was *Sarajevo!*"

"Very good, Mr Chancellor." The woman sounded as though she were in a classroom, commending a well-prepared student. "Now, here's a new telephone number for you."

She gave it to him; he dialled it. Again the exchange was the same.

"History and Technology, Laboratories Division." The speaker was male. Peter identified himself and was told to wait a moment. Another voice came on the line, this time a woman's, the accent foreign.

"I should like you to tell me what moves a man to separate himself from all he has known and accepted, and to risk becoming a pariah in the eyes of his peers. For to refuse that risk, to continue as he has, is to die within himself."

Chancellor stared at the white casing on the telephone. Those were his words, from *Counterstrike!* One short paragraph among thousands, but for Peter it was the key to that entire book. If Longworth had the capacity to discern that, there was, perhaps, more to the man than he had considered.

"The knowledge that the administration of justice and fairness no longer mattered to the country's leaders The people must be shown this, the leaders confronted." Chancellor felt foolish; he quoted himself.

"Thank you, Mr Chancellor," said the woman with the accent. "Please analyse your reply and the telephone calls you have just made. The combination will tell you what you want to know."

720

Peter was bewildered. "It tells me nothing! I've got to reach Longworth! Now, you tell me where he is!"

"I don't know any Mr Longworth; I'm only reading what was given me over the phone by an old friend."

There was a click and then the whine of the dialling tone. Peter slammed his hand on the phone. It was crazy! Three unconnected phone calls involving books he'd written over – Unconnected? No, not actually. The exchanges were identical. That meant the locations – Where was the telephone book?

It was on a chain on the right side of the booth. He found Manfriedie's Restaurant. The address was on Twelfth Street North-west. The second call was taken by a woman who said the words *Arts and Industries*. The third was *History and Technology*. Where was the connection?

It was suddenly very obvious. They were buildings in the Smithsonian complex! Manfriedie's was near the Mall. Near the Smithsonian! Probably the only restaurant in the area.

But where in the Smithsonian? It was immense.

Analyse your reply.

The knowledge that the administration of justice and fairness . . .

Administration!

The administration building at the Smithsonian! One of Washington's landmarks.

That was it! Longworth was there!

Peter let the telephone book swing back into place. He turned and yanked the door open.

He stopped. In front of him stood the man in the raincoat. In the darkness, illuminated by the flashing colours of the Christmas lights, Chancellor saw the gun in the man's hand. On its barrel was the perforated tube of a silencer. The weapon was pointing at his stomach.

27

There was no time for thought. So Peter screamed. As loudly and as maniacally as he could.

He swung his left hand down towards the obscene perforated cylinder. There were two vibrations, shots; a piece of cement exploded. Only yards away a man and a woman cried out hysterically. The woman grabbed her stomach, collapsing on the pavement, writhing; the man reeled, holding his face, blood rolling through his fingers.

There was chaos. The man in the raincoat pulled the trigger again. Chancellor heard the spit, his hand felt the white heat of the cylinder, and glass shattered behind him. Peter would not let go of the deadly thing; he kicked at the man's legs, brought his knees up into the man's groin and pushed him backward into the street. The traffic was moving; the man crashed into the fender of an onrushing car, the impact hurling him back on to the kerb.

Peter's hand was burned, the skin blistered, but his fingers were still gripped around the cylinder, stuck to it. The gun was his.

With the strength born of panic the man in the raincoat staggered up; a knife was in his hand, the long blade whipping out from its recess. He lunged at Chancellor.

Peter fell against the booth, avoiding the knife. He pulled the cylinder from his left hand; some of the blistered skin of his palm came off with it. He pointed the barrel at the man in the raincoat.

He could not pull the trigger! He could not fire the gun!

The man slashed the knife up in a backhand lunge, the blade meant to sever Chancellor's throat. Peter lurched away, the blade's point entering his sweater. He brought his right foot up, catching the man in the chest and hammering him backward. The man fell on his shoulder. For an instant he lay stunned.

Sirens wailed in the distance now. Shrill whistles blew as the police converged. Chancellor followed his physical instincts. Holding the pistol in his hand, he sprang at this stunned attacker and brought the barrel down on the man's head.

Then he ran through the hysterical crowds to the intersection, out into the street, against the traffic. He kept running.

He turned into a narrow side street; the cacophony of sirens and screams receded behind him. The street was darker than those of the shopping district; it was a street that housed small offices in old two- and three-storey brick buildings.

Peter fell into the shadows of a doorway. His chest and legs and temples were in pain. His breath was so spent he thought he would vomit; so he went limp and let air fill his lungs.

Somehow he would have to get to the Smithsonian. To Alan Longworth. He did not want to think about it, not for a few minutes. He had to find a moment of quiet, a void where the pounding in his head would cease because there would be no –

Oh, Jesus! At the entrance of the narrow street, in the dim spill of the streetlights, two men were stopping pedestrians, asking questions. They had followed him. His scent was no less than that left by a fugitive tracked down by bloodhounds.

Chancellor crept out of the shadows into other shadows on the sidewalk. He could not run; he would be seen too easily. He spun around behind the iron grillwork of a railing that rose above a stone staircase and looked back between the fluting. The men were talking to each other now, the man on the right holding a walkie-talkie next to his ear.

There was the sound of a horn. A car was turning into the street, and the two men were in its path. They moved to their left to let the vehicle go by; they were blocked from sight. If they were blocked, so was he! But it would only be for seconds – two or three at most.

Chancellor stepped out from behind the grillwork and started running to his right down the sidewalk. If he could pace himself somehow with the approaching car, he could stretch out the time he would be out of sight; three or four more seconds would be enough. He listened for the engine behind him. The manoeuvre worked! He was at the corner. He ducked behind the edge of the building and pressed his back against the stone. He inched his face forward and looked around into the narrow street. The two men were moving cautiously from doorway to doorway, their caution itself bewildering Peter. Then he understood. In his panic he had forgotten, but the weight in his jacket pocket reminded him: he had the gun. The gun he could not fire.

Strollers looked at him; a couple hurried past, a mother and child crossed to the curb edge of the sidewalk to avoid him. Chancellor raised his eyes to the street sign. New Hampshire Avenue; diagonally across was the intersection of T Street. He had been in the shopping district north of Lafayette Square; he had run between fifteen and twenty blocks, perhaps more if he took into account the various cutoffs and alleyways. He had to double back somehow and head south-east towards the Mall.

The two men were no more than fifty yards away. To his right, a half block north of where he was, the traffic light turned green. Chancellor started to run again. He reached the corner, crossed the street, turned left, and stopped. A policeman stood beneath the traffic signal; he was looking at Peter.

It was, thought Chancellor, perhaps the only opportunity he'd have. He could go up to the police officer, identify himself, and say that men were hunting him. The officer could call in and learn of the chaos twenty blocks away, hear for himself how a gun had been fired and shoppers wounded. He could say all this to the officer and plead for assistance.

But even as he considered the idea, he realized that there would be questions, and forms to fill in, and statements to be made. Longworth would wait only so long. And there were men with radios and weapons looking for him; back at the hotel Alison was alone, with only one man to protect her. The madness would not be stopped by going to the police. It would only be prolonged.

The light changed. Peter walked rapidly across the intersection, past the police officer, and into T Street. He stepped into a doorway, into the shadows, and looked back. A block and a half south a black limousine heading north had pulled to a stop at the corner of the narrow street and New Hampshire Avenue. Directly in front of the car was a streetlamp. He could see the two men approaching the car; a rear window slid down.

A taxi headed south on New Hampshire. The light was red; the cab stopped. Chancellor raced to it from the doorway. In the back seat was an elderly, well-dressed man. Peter opened the door.

"*Hey!*" yelled the driver. "I've got a fare!"

Chancellor addressed the passenger. He tried to sound reasonable, a man doing his best to remain calm in a crisis. "Please forgive me, but there's an emergency. I have to get downtown. My – my wife is very ill. I've just heard – "

"Come in, come in," said the elderly man without hesitation. "I'm only going as far as Dupont Circle. Is that convenient? I can – "

"That's fine, sir. I'm very grateful." Peter stepped in as the light changed. He slammed the door; the taxi bolted forward.

Whether it was the door slam or the driver's loud voice, Chancellor would never know, but as they passed the limousine on the other side of New Hampshire, he could see that the two men spotted him. Peter looked out the rear window. The man on the right had his walkie-talkie against his face.

They reached Dupont Circle; the elderly man got out. Chancellor instructed the driver to go south on Connecticut Avenue. The traffic was heavier, guaranteed to become worse as they headed into the centre of Washington. It was both an asset and a liability. The congested streets allowed him to look in all directions carefully to see if anyone had picked up his trail. Conversely, the heavy traffic allowed others to find him, to catch up with him on foot if necessary.

They reached K Street; to the right was Seventeenth. Peter tried to visualize a Washington map, the main intersecting thoroughfares south of the Ellipse.

Constitution Avenue! He could have the driver turn left on Constitution and head for the Smithsonian through the Mall's entrance. Was there an entrance in that stretch of block?

There had to be. In the chapter outline that morning, he had envisioned Alexander Meredith driving – racing – out of the Mall. Had he written that? Or was it only – ?

Chancellor saw it through the rear window. A grey car had swung out of the traffic and sped forward in the left-turn lane. It drew parallel with the taxi; suddenly a beam of light shot through the window, crisscrossing with the shafts of headlights behind. Peter edged forward, keeping his face obscured by the car frame, and looked out. Across the short distance a man next to the driver had the window rolled down. His torch was aimed at the cab's identification on the door panel. Chancellor heard him speak.

"There! That's it!"

It was madness within madness. In his imagination that morning two men had careered through the Washington streets after Alexander Meredith. A car had pulled alongside Meredith's car; a window had been rolled down, and a voice had exclaimed.

"There!"

The man got out of his car. He jumped across the narrow space between the two vehicles, his hand thrust forward, gripping the handle of the taxi door. The traffic light changed and Chancellor yelled at the driver.

"Go down Seventeenth! Hurry!"

The cab lurched forward, the driver only vaguely aware there was a problem he wanted none of. Behind them horns blared. Peter looked out the window. The man was still in the street – confused, angry, blocking traffic.

The taxi sped south on Seventeenth Street, past the Executive Office Building to New York Avenue and the Corcoran Gallery. A traffic light was red; the cab stopped. There were lights still on in the gallery; he had read something in the newspaper about a new exhibition from a museum in Brussels.

The traffic light was taking too long! The grey car would be beside them any moment. Peter reached into his pocket for his wallet. There were a number of singles and two ten-dollar notes. He took them out and leaned forward.

"I want you to do something for me. I have to go inside the Corcoran Gallery, but I want you to wait for me outside the door with your engine running and roof light off. If I'm delayed more than ten minutes, forget it, you're paid."

The driver saw the tens and took them. "I thought your wife was sick. Who the hell was that back there? He tried to open the door – "

"It doesn't matter," interrupted Chancellor. "The light's changing; please do as I say."

"It's your money. You've got ten minutes."

"Ten minutes," agreed Peter. He climbed out. Above the short flight of steps, the glass doors were closed; beyond them a uniformed guard stood casually beside a small desk. Chancellor walked swiftly up the steps and opened the door. The guard glanced at him but made no move to interfere.

"May I see your invitation, sir?"

"For the exhibition?"

"Yes, sir."

"I'm embarrassed, officer," said Peter quickly, reaching for his wallet. "I'm from the *New York Times*. I'm supposed to cover the exhibition for next Sunday's paper. I was in a traffic accident a few minutes ago, and I can't find. . ."

He hoped to God he had it in his wallet. A year ago he'd written several pieces for the *Times Magazine*; the editors had given him a temporary press pass.

He found it between credit cards. He held it out for the guard, his thumb covering the expiration date. His hand trembled; he wondered if the guard noticed.

"Okay, okay," said the guard. "Take it easy. Just sign the register."

Chancellor leaned over the desk, picked up the chained ballpoint pen and scribbled his name. "Where's the exhibition?"

"Take one of the lifts on the right to the second floor."

He walked rapidly to the row of lifts and pressed the buttons. He looked back at the guard; the man was paying no attention. A lift door opened, but Peter had no intention of taking it. He wanted the sound to cover his steps as he ran to an exit on the other side of the building.

There was another sound. Behind him the glass doors opened. Chancellor saw the figure of the man from the grey car. The decision was made for him. He went swiftly into the empty lift, his hand pressing the first buttons he could reach on the panel. The door closed; the lift started up.

He walked out into a milling crowd and the pools of light that shot down from the ceiling. Waiters in red jackets carrying silver trays mingled among the guests. Paintings and sculptures were everywhere, illuminated by spotlights. The guests were the diplomatic corps and those who travelled with that crowd, including members of the Washington press. He recognized several.

Peter stopped a waiter for champagne. He drank it quickly so he could hold the empty glass up, partly concealing his face, and look around.

"You're Peter Chancellor! I'd know you anywhere!" The greeter was a Brunhilde, her Valkyrie helmet a flowery hat set squarely above her Wagnerian face. "When's your new novel being published?"

"I'm not working on anything right now."

"Why are you in Washington?"

Peter looked at the wall. "I'm partial to Flemish art."

Brunhilde had a small spiral pad in her left hand, a pencil in her right. She wrote as she talked. "Invited by the Belgian Embassy . . . a connoisseur of Flemish art."

"I didn't say that," protested Chancellor. "I'm not."

Through the crowd he saw the lift door slide open. Out walked the man who moments ago had rushed through the glass doors downstairs in the lobby.

Brunhilde was saying something; he had not been listening. "I'd much rather you were having an affair with an embassy wife. Anybody's wife."

"Is there a staircase up here?"

"What?"

"A *staircase*. An exit!" Chancellor took her elbow and manoeuvred her ample body between himself and the man's line of sight.

"I *thought* I recognized you!" The thin, high-pitched woman's voice belonged to a blonde-haired columnist Peter vaguely recognized. "You're Paul Chancellor, the writer."

"Close enough. Do you know where an exit is? I have to get downstairs in a hurry."

"Use the lift," said the columnist. "Look, there's one now." She stepped back to gesture.

The movement attracted the man's attention. He started towards Peter. Chancellor backed away.

The man made his way through the crowd. In the far corner of the room, beyond an hors d'oeuvres table, a waiter came through a swinging door. Chancellor dropped his glass and grabbed the arms of the two astonished newspaperwomen, propelling them towards the door.

The man was only yards behind them, the swinging door just beyond the table. Peter lurched to the side, still holding on to the columnists. As the man broke free of the crowd, Chancellor spun the women around and pushed them as hard as he could towards the onrushing figure. The man yelled; the obese woman's pencil pierced his lower lip. Blood trickled from his mouth. Pete swung his hands under the wide table filled with food and two huge punch bowls and heaved it up, sending the mass of silver, glass, liquid and food crashing to the floor.

Shouts became screams; someone blew a whistle. Chancellor raced through the swinging door into a pantry.

On the left wall he saw a red Exit sign. He grabbed a serving cart, rolling it behind him with such force a wheel came off. Bowls of salad crashed in front of the swinging door. He ran to the exit and shouldered it open. He looked behind him; there was chaos at the pantry entrance and no sign of the man chasing him.

The staircase was empty. He took the steps three at a time to the landing and swung himself around by the railing.

His feet slammed to a stop, his left knee smashed into the iron post. Below

726

him, in front of the lobby door, stood the man he had last seen on Connecticut Avenue. The man who had jumped out of the car. He was not part of a novel now; he was real. As the gun in his hand was real.

The madness! The insane thought came to Peter that he must have a tape recorder in his handkerchief pocket. Involuntarily, he raised his left arm to press the cloth. To start the recorder. A non-existent recorder! What was *happening* to him?

"What do you want with me? Why are you following me?" he whispered, not sure what was fact any more.

"We just want to talk to you. Make sure you understand – "

"No!" His mind exploded. He sprang from the landing, conscious only of empty space. Somewhere deep in the sound waves of that space he heard the sickening spit of a bullet, but he was not affected; his disbelief was complete.

Suddenly his hands clamped on to skin and hair. The thrust of his flying body made contact; he slammed the man's head into the metal door.

The real man with the real gun collapsed, his hair and face covered with blood. Peter rose and stood for an instant in shock, trying to separate fantasy and reality.

He had to run. There was nothing left but running. He crashed open the door and started across the marble floor. The guard was at the entrance to the street, his hand on his holster, a walkie-talkie next to his ear.

As Peter approached, the guard spoke. "Some trouble up there, huh?"

"Yes. Couple of drunks, I think."

"Did the two guys find you? They told me you're with the bureau."

Peter stopped, gripping the entrance door in his hand. "*What?*"

"Your back-up? The other two guys. They came in right after you. They showed me their IDs. They're with the FBI, too."

Chancellor did not wait to hear more. The madness was now complete. The FBI! He ran down the short flight of steps, his eyes blurred, his breath gone.

"You've still got time on the meter, mister."

Not eight feet away from him at the kerb was the taxi. He ran to the door and got inside.

"Drive down to Ellipse Road! For God's sake, hurry! Go around to the Smithsonian Park. I'll tell you where to let me off."

The cab accelerated. "It's still your money."

Peter spun around and looked out the rear window at the Corcoran. A man came running down the steps on to the pavement, one hand on his face, the other holding a walkie-talkie. It was the man from the second floor reception, the man whose lip had been pierced by the obese columnist's pencil. He had seen the taxi. Others would be waiting. Somewhere.

They entered the curve around the Ellipse. To the south was the Washington Monument, floodlights washing the alabaster needle. "Slow down," instructed Peter, "near the edge of the grass. But don't stop. I'm going to jump out, but I don't want . . ." Peter's voice faded; he did not know how to say it.

The driver helped him. "But you don't want whoever might be watching my cab to see you jump, is that it?"

"Yes."

"You in trouble?"

"Yes."

"Is it the cops?"

"Jesus, no! It's . . . personal."

"You sound okay to me. You were fair with me. I'm fair with you." The driver slowed down. "About fifty yards ahead, at the farthest point in the curve before it swings straight, jump. Then I'll go like a bat outta hell for a couple of blocks. Nobody'll see you. Got it?"

"Yes. I've got it. Thanks."

"*Now!*"

The cab had slowed. Chancellor opened the door and jumped over the edge of the kerb, the force of his leap and the curve of the road propelling him on to the grass.

The driver held the horn down in one continuous blast. Other cars swung to the right, allowing the taxi to pass. The sound was the sound of emergency; someone was in trouble.

Peter watched the scene from his concealed position in the grass. One did not stop or hesitate or swing to the right as the others did in front of and behind the screaming cab. It was not affected by the sound of panic. Instead, it fell in line with the taxi and raced after it.

It was the black limousine he had seen on New Hampshire Avenue.

Peter lay motionless for a moment. Tyres screeched in the distance. From across the Ellipse road, in the direction of Continental Hall, another automobile was careering into the circular drive. Looking for him? He got to his feet and started running over dirt and grass.

He felt concrete beneath him; he was in the street. Buildings were in front of him, cars alongside him, driving slowly. He kept running, knowing that beyond the dark buildings and the scattered trees stood the Smithsonian.

He fell suddenly and rolled over on the pavement. Behind him he heard the unmistakable sounds of racing footsteps. They'd found him!

He scrambled to his feet, lurching forward, the overanxious sprinter jumping the gun. He kept racing where instinct directed him, and suddenly he saw it! Its parapets were silhouetted against the sky! The outlines of the Smithsonian! He ran as fast as he could across an unending lawn, jumping over low, sagging chains that bordered paths, until he stood, breathless, in front of the enormous building.

He was there, but where was Longworth?

For an instant he thought he heard sounds behind him. He turned; there was no one.

Suddenly, two tiny specks of light flashed from somewhere in the darkness, beyond the steps that led to the road in front of the entrance. They came from ground level, to the left of the statue that stood at the top of the steps. They flashed again, as if aimed at him! He walked rapidly towards the source of the light. Nearer, nearer; thirty feet, twenty feet. He was walking towards a dark corner of the massive museum; there was a shrubbery in front of the stone.

"Chancellor! Get down!"

Peter threw himself to the ground. Two flashes came from the darkness: muted pistol shots.

Behind him he heard a body fall. In the dull grey of the night he saw the gun in the slain figure's hand. It had been aimed at him.

"Drag him back here!" It was a whispered command from the darkness.

All thought dulled, Chancellor did as he was told. He pulled the body over the grass into the shadows, and then he crawled over to Alan Longworth.

The man was dying. His back was against the Smithsonian stone. In his right hand was the gun that had saved Peter's life; his left hand held his stomach. His fingers were covered with blood.

"I haven't got time to thank you," said Chancellor, barely able to hear himself. "Maybe I shouldn't. He was one of your men."

"I haven't got any men," replied the blond-haired killer.

"We'll talk about that later. You're coming with me. *Now*." Angrily, Peter struggled to his feet.

"I'm not going anywhere, Chancellor. If I stay still and keep things in place, I've got a few minutes. Not if I move."

There was that strange, guttural sound in Longworth's voice again. "Then, I'll go find someone!" said Peter, his answer now mixed with fear. He could not let Longworth die. Not *now*. "I'll get an ambulance!"

"An ambulance won't help. Take my word for it. But you have to be told. You have to understand."

"I understand everything. A group of fanatics is trying to tear the FBI apart so that they can take control. And you're one of them."

"That's not true. It goes beyond the bureau. We're trying to stop them; I've tried. And now you're the only one who can. You're closest to the core; no one else has your advantage."

"Why?"

Longworth seemed to ignore the question. He took a deep breath. "The missing files. Hoover's private dossiers – "

"There *are* no missing files!" broke in Peter, furiously. "There are only men like you and the man you just killed. You made a mistake, Longworth. He was following me, chasing me. He used his identification; he's FBI! He's one of you!"

Longworth stared at the body of the man he had killed. "So the maniacs found out about the files. I imagine it was unavoidable. They can be used by the one who has them. They're the perfect foils! They'll be blamed for everything."

Chancellor was not listening. The only thing that mattered was to deliver Longworth to Quinn O'Brien. "I'm not interested in any more of your observations."

"You say you love that girl," said Longworth, breathing hard. "If you do, you'll listen to me."

"You bastard! You leave her out of this!"

"Her mother, her father . . . it's them. Something happened to the mother."

Peter knelt closer. "What do you know about her mother?"

"Not enough. But you can learn. Bear with me. To begin with, my name isn't Longworth."

Chancellor stared in disbelief, yet he knew he was hearing the truth. Circles within circles. Reality and fantasy, but which was which? The moon came out of the grey night sky. For the first time he was able to see Longworth's face clearly. The dying man had no eyebrows, no lashes. There was only raw scraped flesh around the sockets and blisters everywhere. He had been beaten, tortured.

28

"My name is Stefan Varak. I'm a code specialist for the National Security Agency, but I also perform certain functions for a group of – "

"*Varak?*" It took several seconds for the name to register, but when it did, the shock made Peter grow cold. "You're the man O'Brien's looking for!"

"Quinn O'Brien?" asked Varak, wincing in pain.

"Yes. He's the man I talked to, the one I told the story to. He's been trying to reach you!"

"I was in no position to receive messages. You were lucky. Quinn's one of the quickest and cleanest men over there. Trust him." Varak coughed, pain visible in his face. "If the maniacs have surfaced, O'Brien will stop them."

"What have you got to tell me? What do you know about MacAndrew's wife?"

Varak held up his bloody hand. "I have to explain. As quickly as possible. You've got to understand . . . From the beginning you were programmed. Part truth, part lie. We had to get you involved, get you started, force the enemy to react, show themselves." Varak was gripped by a spasm.

Chancellor waited till it passed; then he asked: "Part lie, part truth. Which was which?"

"I told you. The files. They disappeared."

"There was no assassination, then?"

"Inconceivable." Varak stared at Peter, his breath coming fast. "The men who fought Hoover were honourable. They protected Hoover's victims by the law, not outside of it."

"But the files were taken."

"Yes. That part's true. Dossiers with the letters *M* to *Z*. Remember that." Again a spasm took hold of Varak. Peter held his shoulders; it was all he could think of to do. The shivering ran its course; Varak continued. "And now I must elaborate. I use your words."

His words? Varak's eyes were glazed; the accent was there once more. "My words? What do you mean?"

"In your fourth chapter – "

"My what?"

"Your manuscript."

"You've read it?"

"Yes."

"How?"

"It doesn't matter. There's no time . . . Your Nucleus. You concentrate on three people. A senator, a newspaperwoman, a cabinet member . . ." Varak's eyes lost control; his voice faded.

"What about them?" pressed Chancellor, not understanding.

"Use the files for good . . ." The dying man inhaled suddenly. "You said that."

Peter remembered. The *files*. In the manuscript he had given the words to the former cabinet officer. *If they can be used the way Hoover uses them, they can be turned around. They can be used for good!* It was the false reasoning that would lead to tragedy.

"What if I did! What are you talking about?"

"It's what happened . . ." Varak's eyes came briefly into focus; his concentration all-consuming. "One man turned into a killer. A killer who hires killers."

"*What?*"

"Five men. One of four . . . not Bravo. Never Bravo."

"What did you say? Who's Bravo?"

"A splendid temptation. To use the files for good."

"*Splendid?* . . . There's nothing splendid. It's extortion!"

"That's the tragedy."

Oh, *Christ!* His words! "What five men? What do you mean?"

"Venice you know . . . Bravo, too, but *not* Bravo! *Never* Bravo!" Varak struggled with his bloodied right hand; he inched it away from the wound in his stomach to his jacket pocket. He drew out a piece of paper, white paper soiled with blood. "One of four men. I thought it was Banner or Paris. Now I'm not sure."

He pushed the paper into Chancellor's palm. "Code names. Venice, Christopher, Banner, Paris. It's one of them. Not Bravo."

" 'Venice' . . . 'Bravo' . . . who are they?"

"The group. Your Nucleus." Varak pulled his hand down to his wound. "One of them knows."

"Knows what?"

"The meaning of *Chasŏng*. The mother."

"MacAndrew? His *wife?*"

"Not him. *Her!* He's the decoy."

"Decoy? You've got to be clearer."

"The slaughter. The meaning behind the slaughter of Chasŏng!"

Peter looked at the bloodstained paper in his hand. Names were written on it. "One of these men?" he asked the dying man, unsure what he meant by his own question.

"Yes."

"Why?"

"You and the daughter. *You!* It was to throw you off. To make you think it was the answer. It isn't."

"*What* answer?"

"Chasŏng. Something *beyond* it."

"*Stop* it! What are you saying?"

"Not Bravo . . ." Varak's eyes swam in their sockets.

"Who is Bravo? Is he one of them?"

"No. *Never* Bravo."

"Varak, what *happened?* Why are you so certain about Chasŏng?"

"There are others who'll help . . ."

"What about *Chasŏng?*"

"Thirty-fifth Street. The house. They took me and taped my eyes, my face. I never saw them. They needed a hostage. They know what I've done . . . I didn't see them, but I heard them. They spoke a language I didn't know, which means they knew I didn't know it. But they used the name *Chasŏng*. Each time . . . fanatically. It has another meaning. Find what it was behind the killing at Chasŏng. It will lead you to the files."

Varak fell forward. Chancellor grabbed him, pulling him back. "There's got to be more!"

"There's very little." Varak's whisper faded. Peter had to put his ear next to the agent's lips to hear him. "They drove me through a town; they thought I was unconscious. I heard cars. I crashed through the door with the tapes on my face. They fired at me but drove away. I had to get you alone. I could not talk on the telephone. I was right. The two false numbers I gave you were tapped. If I had told you on the phone what I'm telling you now, you'd have been killed. Protect the girl. Find the meaning behind the slaughter of Chasŏng."

Chancellor felt panic swell inside him; his head was about to explode. Varak was nearly dead. He'd be gone in moments! In seconds! "You said there were others! Who can I go to? Who'll *help?*"

"O'Brien," whispered Varak. Then he stared at Peter, a strange smile on his bloodless lips. "Look to your manuscript. There's a senator. He might have been – Go to him. He's not afraid."

Varak's eyes closed. He was dead.

And Chancellor's mind was filled with white light and thunder. The detonations shook the earth; there was no sanity left. A senator . . . He had crossed a line no one should cross. He let Varak's head fall back on to the stone and slowly got to his feet, backing away, filled with a terror so personal, so absolute, he could not think.

But he could run. And so, blindly, he ran.

He was near water. The reflections of light shimmered on the surface like thousands of miniature candles flickering in an unfelt wind. How long he had been running he could not tell. As his mind began to clear, he thought for a moment he was back in New York, at dawn, within the sculptured confines of Fort Tryon, where a blond-haired man named Longworth had just saved his life.

But his name was not Longworth. It was Varak, and he was dead.

Peter closed his eyes. The void he had sought for so long swept over him. He slowly lowered himself to the ground; his knees touched the grass, and he trembled.

He heard the sound of an engine approaching. Gravel crunched beneath wheels. He opened his eyes and looked around.

A motor scooter parked, its single headlight angled diagonally down. A police officer got off. He shot the beam of his torch over at Peter.

"You all right, mister?"

"Yes. Yes, I'm all right."

The officer approached. Chancellor rose unsteadily, noting that behind the beam of the light, the man's hand had un-snapped his pistol holder. "What are you doing down here?"

"I'm – I'm not sure. To tell you the truth, I had a little too much to drink, so I went for a walk. I do that; it's better than getting into a car."

"It certainly is," replied the officer. "You're not thinking about doing anything foolish though, are you?"

"What? What do you mean?"

"Like taking a swim, not figuring to come out?"

"What?"

The officer was standing in front of him, scrutinizing him carefully. "You're pretty messed up."

"I fell. I told you, I had – "

"I know. Booze. Funny, I don't smell any."

"Vodka."

"You depressed? Family problems? In trouble? You want to see a priest or a rabbi? Or a lawyer?"

Peter understood. "I see. You think I want to drown myself."

"It's happened. We've pulled bodies out of the Basin."

"We're at the Tidal Basin?" asked Chancellor.

"South-west point." The officer gestured to his right. "That's Ohio Drive over there. Across the water's the Jefferson Memorial."

Peter looked at his watch, at the radium dial. It was a little after nine-thirty. He had lost nearly two hours; he'd drawn a blank for *two hours*. And there were things to do. The first was to mollify a concerned policeman. He struggled for the words.

"Look, I'm fine, officer. I really am. As a matter of fact I've got to get to a telephone. Is there a booth around here?"

The officer reached down and snapped his holster shut. "Over on Ohio, about a hundred yards south, maybe less. You can probably get a cab there, too. But if you're stopped again, watch out. Other cops may be rougher than I am."

"Thanks for the warning." Peter smiled. "And thanks for your concern."

"Part of the job. Take care, now."

Chancellor nodded and started across the lawn towards Ohio Drive. Someone had tapped his hotel phone; he could call Alison, but he could not say anything. Instead, he must reach Quinn O'Brien.

"Where the hell *are* you? My orders were for you to stay in that hotel! Goddamn you – "

"The maniacs tried to kill me," broke in Chancellor quickly, remembering Varak's description.

"The *maniacs?*" It was as if O'Brien had been struck. "Where did you hear that term?"

"That's what we're going to talk about. That and other things. I just got out of the Corcoran Gallery."

"The *Corcoran* . . . *You* were there?"

"Yes."

"Oh, my God!" O'Brien sounded frightened.

"I'm down at – "

"Shut *up!*" yelled the FBI man suddenly. "Don't say another thing! Wait a minute . . . stay on the line." Peter could hear O'Brien's breathing; the agent was thinking. "Our conversation last night. Think carefully. You told me you made three phone calls to New York from telephone booths. You used your credit card."

"But I – "

"I said shut up! Think. They were made before and after the fire on Thirty-fifth Street."

"I – "

"Listen to me! There was one call in particular – I think it was after, I'm not sure. Get to the booth you made that call from. Now, do you understand me? Don't answer right away. Filter it."

Peter tried to understand what O'Brien was telling him. There had not been three phone calls, there had only been one. He had called Tony Morgan before the insanity on Thirty-fifth Street. He had made no calls after.

Filter it. Eliminate. That was it! The agent referred to that one call, that one booth. "I understand," he said.

"Good. It was after, wasn't it? After Thirty-fifth Street."

"Yes," said Chancellor, knowing it was a lie.

"Somewhere on Wisconsin, I think."

"Yes." Again, the deception.

"Good. Get there. I'll call every ten minutes. Pick out a phrase I'd remember from our talk and say it when you answer. Have you got that?"

"Yes."

Peter hung up the phone and went out of the booth. He continued walking south towards the bridge lights extending over the Potomac, looking for a cab. As he walked, he tried to remember the exact location of the phone booth where he had called Morgan. It was near George Washington University.

A cab came. They found the phone booth easily. There were crowds again, and coloured lights and Christmas carols coming from unseen speakers. He asked the driver to wait; the only money he had was two fifty-dollar notes in his wallet. He would need to change them, and he would need the taxi.

He knew exactly what he was going to do.

Find the meaning of Chasŏng.

He closed the door of the booth and took the phone off its cradle, making sure his finger held the lip down. The ringing had barely started when he released the tab and spoke.

" 'I may be here for the rest of the night . . . I'll let you decide . . .' " It was

734

one of the first things he had said to the agent when they met.

"Good enough," said O'Brien. "I'm ten blocks away on Twentieth Street. I may have been followed, so we can't meet. Now, tell me what happened. Where did you hear the term *maniacs?*"

"Why? Is it special?"

"Don't joke. You don't have time."

"I'm not joking. I'm being careful. If I see anyone paying attention to me, or see a car stop, I'm going to run. I think you're clean, O'Brien; that's what I was told. But I want to make sure. Now, you tell *me* what the term means. Who are the maniacs?"

O'Brien exhaled audibly. "Five or six special agents who worked secretly, closely with Hoover. They were in his confidence. They want the old regime back; they want to control the bureau. I implied as much to you last night. Still, I didn't use the word *maniacs.*"

"But they're not part of this, are they? They don't have the missing files."

O'Brien fell silent, his shock evident to Peter over the phone. "You know then?"

"Yes. You said those files were destroyed; that there was no pattern, but you lied. There is a pattern: they *weren't* destroyed. Whoever has them thinks I'm close to learning who he is . . . who they are. It was the whole idea behind everything. I was the snare. It nearly worked, but the man who programmed me was killed in his own trap. Now, you tell me what you know, and tell it straight!"

O'Brien replied calmly, his urgency controlled. "I think the maniacs *do* have those files. They operated with them; they had access. That's why I couldn't talk to you from my office; they've tapped my line. They had to. Now, for Christ's sake, tell me what happened."

"Fair enough. I found your man Varak."

"What?"

"I knew him as Longworth."

"*Longworth?* May first . . . the security logs! He has the *files!*" O'Brien involuntarily shouted into the phone.

"That doesn't make *sense!*" said Peter, bewildered. "He's dead. He threw away his life to find those files." Chancellor told the agent everything that had happened from Varak's phone call through Varak's death and the dying man's conviction that O'Brien would stop the maniacs. But he did not mention Chasŏng. For the time being, that was private.

"Varak gone," O'Brien said softly. "I can't believe it. He was one of the ones we counted on. There aren't many left."

"The guy from CIA – we knew each other. He said a number of you people work together. All over Washington. That you had to."

"We do. The hell of it is, there's no one to go to for legal advice. There's not a lawyer I'd trust."

"There may be someone. A senator. Varak told me. But not yet. Not now . . . You're good at giving orders, O'Brien. How are you at taking them?"

"Not good. They have to make sense."

"Are those files sense enough?"

"A stupid question."

"Then, do two things for me. Get Alison MacAndrew out of the Hay-Adams, stay with her, and take her some place where she'll be safe. They want me. They'll use her to get me."

"All right. I can do that. What's the other?"

"I need the address of a major named Pablo Ramirez. He's stationed at the Pentagon."

"Wait a minute."

Suddenly Peter was alarmed. Over the telephone he could hear the rustling of paper. *Paper!* He put his hand up to the cradle of the telephone, about to break the connection and run.

"O'Brien! I thought you said you were ten blocks away. In a phone booth!"

"I am. I'm looking in the phone book."

"Oh, *Christ* . . ." Chancellor swallowed.

"Here it is. Ramirez, P. He lives in Bethesda." The agent read the address; Peter memorized it. "Is that all?"

"No. I'm going to want to see Alison later tonight, or in the morning. How do I find out where you are, where you've taken her? Do you have any ideas?"

Silence. Five seconds later O'Brien spoke. "Do you know Quantico?"

"The marine base?"

"Yes, but not the camp. There's a motel on the bay. It's called the Pines. I'll take her there."

"I'll rent a car."

"Don't do that. Rental agencies are too easily covered. There's a machine that can scan every one in the city. They'd pick you up. That goes for cab companies, too; no one withholds destinations. They'd know where you went."

"What the hell am I going to do? Walk?"

"There are trains to Quantico every hour or so. That's your best bet."

"All right. I'll see you later."

"Wait a minute." O'Brien's tone was urgent, but again controlled. "You're holding back again, Chancellor. It's MacAndrew."

Peter's head snapped back; he stared at the crowds through the glass booth. "You're making assumptions."

"You're making a fool of yourself. It doesn't take any powers of deduction. Ramirez works at the Pentagon; so did MacAndrew."

"Don't push it, O'Brien. *Please.*"

"Why shouldn't I? You haven't told me the most important thing Varak said: why he had to see you."

"I *did*. He explained his strategy. How I was programmed."

"He wouldn't waste his time, not when he was dying. He learned something, and he told you what it was."

Chancellor shook his head; perspiration rolled down his brow. O'Brien could not be told the significance of Chasŏng – until Peter found out what it was. For the deeper he went, the more Peter was convinced that Alison's survival was at stake.

736

"Give me till tomorrow morning," he said.

"Why?"

"Because I love her."

Paul Bromley stared into the cracked mirror on top of the dresser with knobs missing from the middle drawers. What he saw saddened him: the pallid face of a sick old man. The stubble of his grey beard was obvious; he had not shaved in over forty-eight hours. The wide space between the dirty starched collar and his throat was further evidence of his illness. He had very little time left. But it would be enough. It had to be.

He turned away from the mirror and walked over to the bed. The spread was filthy. His eyes swept over the walls and ceiling. There were cracks everywhere and peeling paint.

They thought they had him trapped, but their arrogance was misplaced. He was owed favours. A lifetime in Washington overseeing vast expenditures left many people in his debt. Everything was a trade-off: you can do this if you give me that. Most of the time it worked very well. By and large, he was proud of his Washington record; he had done many fine things.

He had done several things he was not very proud of, too. One in particular for a scoundrel who had provided him with the data he needed to go after the thieves at Defense. That was the debt he was going to call in. If the man refused, a phone call would be made to the *Washington Post*. The man would not refuse.

Bromley picked up his jacket from the bed, put it on, and went out of the door into the filthy hallway, then down a flight of steps to the lobby. The FBI agent who had been assigned to him stood awkwardly in the corner, a clean-cut manikin among the human debris. At least the man did not have to wait in the upstairs hallway. The hotel's only exit was its front door – testimony to the trust placed in its clientele.

Bromley walked to the pay telephone on the wall, inserted the coin, and dialled.

"Hello?" The voice was nasal and unattractive.

"This is Paul Bromley."

"Who?"

"Three years ago. Detroit. The project."

There was a pause before the voice replied. "What do you want?"

"What I'm owed. Unless you'd rather I call friends at the *Post*. They almost got you three years ago. They could do it now. I've also prepared a letter. It will be posted if I don't return home."

Again there was a pause. "Spell it out."

"You send a car for me. I'll tell you where. And when you do, send one of your thugs with it. There's a federal man here watching me. I want him temporarily sidetracked. It's the sort of thing you do very well."

Bromley waited on the pavement outside the Hay-Adams. He would wait all night if need be. And when daylight came, he could hide in the church doorway across the avenue. Sooner or later Chancellor would emerge. When he did, Bromley would kill him.

The gun in his pocket had cost him five hundred dollars. He doubted it was worth more than twenty. But he had only asked his Detroit contact for help, not for charity.

Bromley kept raising his eyes to the right front windows on the fifth floor of the hotel. They were Chancellor's rooms. Expensive rooms. Last night he had asked a then unsuspecting switchboard operator the number of the suite before he had called the writer. The despicable novelist lived well.

He would not live long.

Bromley heard the sound of a car racing south on Sixteenth Street. It pulled into the hotel driveway. A red-haired man got out, spoke to the doorman, and went inside the lobby.

The accountant recognized the unmarked automobile. He had routinely approved scores of such purchases whenever the rubber stamp was requested. It was the FBI, come for Chancellor!

Bromley went back across the street and walked up the driveway, staying in the shadows by the wall of the building, to the right of the entrance next to the FBI car. The doorman had walked down the path to whistle for a cab. A couple followed him to the kerb since the driveway was blocked.

Everything was perfect! Chancellor would die!

Moments later a woman came out with the red-haired man. But there was no Chancellor!

He had to be there!

"Are you sure?" the woman asked, concerned.

"He'll take the train down later tonight," said the red-haired man. "Or in the morning. Don't worry."

A train.

Bromley pulled up the collar of his overcoat and began the long walk to Union Station.

29

In a taxi headed for Ramirez's house, Peter took out the page of bloodstained paper with the dead Varak's handwriting on it. Once again he was awed by the names. Awed and frightened, for they were extraordinary men – each renowned, each brilliant, each immensely powerful. And one of them had Hoover's files.

For God's sake, why? Peter looked at each name; each evoked an image.

The lean, sharp-featured Frederick Wells – code name: Banner. University president, dispenser of millions through the huge Roxton Foundation, one of the brightest architects of the Kennedy years. A man who was known never to compromise on principle, even when his stand incurred the wrath of all Washington.

Daniel Sutherland – Venice – perhaps the most honoured Black in the country. Honoured not only for his accomplishments, but for the wisdom of his judicial decisions. Peter had felt the judge's compassion in his brief half-hour conversation with him months ago. It was in his eyes.

Jacob Dreyfus – Christopher. Dreyfus's face was less clear than the others in Peter's mind. The banker shunned public attention, but he could never be ignored by the financial community, which meant the financial press. His influence often formed the basis of national monetary policy; the Federal Reserve rarely made decisions without consulting him. His charity was known throughout the world, his generosity limitless.

Carlos Montelán – Paris – was the tutor of Presidents, a force at the Department of State, an academic giant whose analyses of global politics were discriminating and audacious. Montelán was a naturalized American; his family was Spanish, intellectual Castilians who had fought a compromising church and Franco alike. He was an arch-enemy of oppression in any form.

One of these four exceptional men had betrayed the beliefs he professed to hold. Was it Varak's "splendid temptation"? The commission of dreadful acts for an idealistic reason? It was impossible to accept. From lesser men perhaps. Not these.

Unless one of the four was not what he appeared to be. And that was the most frightening thing of all. That a man could be raised to such height concealing such fundamental corruption.

Chasŏng.

Varak knew he was dying, and so he had selected his words carefully. He had at first narrowed his options down to Wells and Montelán – Banner and Paris – and then reversed himself and expanded the possibilities to include Sutherland and Dreyfus – Venice and Christopher. His change of mind had been related to a language he did not know and the fanatic repetition of the name Chasŏng. But why these? What had led Varak to single out an unfamiliar language and a reported cry? What had been his reasoning? He had not had time to explain.

The meaning behind the slaughter of Chasŏng. The slaughter! Peter remembered Ramirez's expression of cold loathing at MacAndrew's burial. Ramirez hated MacAndrew. But was it connected to Chasŏng? Or just the passions of jealousy that found no comfort in a rival's death? That was possible, but there was something too specific in Ramirez's eyes.

He would know soon; the taxi had crossed into Bethesda. And if the connection *was* there, to which of the four extraordinary men would Chasŏng lead? And how?

Peter folded Varak's scrap of paper and shoved it into his jacket pocket. There was a fifth man, unidentified – code name: Bravo. Who was he? And had Varak mistakenly protected him? Could the unknown Bravo have the files? Suddenly Peter remembered something else. *Venice you know . . . Bravo, too . . .* How would he know such a man, Peter wondered. Who *was* Bravo?

There were too many questions, too few answers. Only one stood out: Alison MacAndrew. She was his answer to so much.

The house was small and made of brick. The neighbourhood was one of those middle-class developments that had proliferated in the Washington area – plots of equal size, frontages identical. Chancellor told the driver the truth: he had no idea how long he'd be. He did not even know if Ramirez was home. Or if he was married, or had children. It was possible he had made the trip to Bethesda for nothing, but if he had phoned first, Major Ramirez doubtless would have refused to see him.

The door opened. To Peter's relief Pablo Ramirez stood in the frame, his expression quizzical.

"Major Ramirez?"

"Yes. Have we met?"

"No, but we were both at Arlington Cemetery the other morning. My name's – "

"You were with the girl," interrupted the major. "His daughter. You're the writer."

"Yes. My name's Peter Chancellor. I'd like to talk with you."

"What about?"

"MacAndrew."

Ramirez paused before replying, studying Peter's face. He spoke quietly, with the slightest trace of an accent, but to Chancellor's surprise there was no hostility in his voice. "I really haven't anything to say about the general. He's dead. Leave him in peace."

"That wasn't what you had in mind at the burial. If the dead could be killed twice, your looks would have done just that."

"I apologize."

"Is that all you'll say?"

"I believe it's sufficient. Now, if you don't mind, I have work to do."

Ramirez stepped back, his hand on the doorknob. Peter spoke quickly.

"Chasŏng. The *slaughter* at Chasŏng."

The major stopped, his body rigid. The connection *was* there. "That goes back a long time. The 'slaughter', as you call it, was thoroughly investigated by the Inspector-General. The heavy losses were attributed to unexpected and overwhelming Chincom firepower."

"And perhaps overzealousness in command," added Peter swiftly. "For instance, in the command of Mac the Knife, killer of Chasŏng."

The major remained immobile, his eyes clouded in that odd, noncommittal way peculiar to the military.

"I think you'd better come inside, Mr Chancellor."

Peter had a sense of déjà vu. Once again he had stepped up to a stranger's door – that stranger an Army officer – and demanded an audience through the use of information he was not supposed to have. There was even a similarity between Ramirez's and MacAndrew's studies. The walls were lined with photographs and mementoes of a career. Chancellor glanced at the open study door,

740

his mind wandering back for a moment to the isolated house in the countryside. Ramirez misinterpreted his look.

"There's no one else here," he said curtly – as curtly as MacAndrew had spoken months before. "I'm a bachelor."

"I didn't know that. I know very little about you, Major. Except that you went to West Point around the same time MacAndrew did. Also that you served with him in North Africa and later in Korea."

"I'm sure you've learned other things. You couldn't know even that much without having been told more."

"Such as?"

Ramirez sat down in the armchair opposite Peter. "That I'm discontented, if not a certified malcontent. A troublemaker from Puerto Rico who feels he's been passed over because of his race."

"I heard a tasteless navy joke I didn't like."

"Oh, the fleet cocktail party? The one where they put a busboy's jacket on me?" A mechanical smile appeared on the major's face. Chancellor nodded. "That's not bad. I made that one up myself."

"What?"

"I work in a very specialized, extremely sensitive department of the Pentagon. But it has nothing to do with orthodox intelligence. For lack of a better phrase, we call it minority relations."

"Major, what are you saying? . . ."

"I'm not a major. My permanent rank is brigadier-general. I will undoubtedly receive my second star in June. You see, a major – especially one of my age – can go into many areas and have better communication with the men than can a colonel or a general."

"You have to go to those extremes?" asked Peter.

"Today's military faces an extraordinary problem. Nobody likes to put it into words, but no one can bury it, either. The ranks are being filled with unemployables, the outcasts. Do you know what can be the result when that happens?"

"Sure. The quality of the services diminishes."

"That's the first stage. We get the My Lais, and we get spaced-out troops trading in narcotics like C-rations. Then there's another step, and it's not far down the road. By simple attrition, the lack of quality recruitment, *and* a superiority of numbers, the quality of leadership deteriorates. Historically, that's frightening. Forget Genghis Khan and even the latter-day Cossacks; their environments were barbarian. There's a more recent example. The criminals took over the German army, and the Nazi Wehrmacht was the result. Do you begin to understand?"

Peter shook his head slowly. The soldier's evaluations seemed exaggerated; there were too many controls. "I can't buy some kind of Black terrorist junta."

"Neither can we. Statistics – base demographics, actually – confirm what we've suspected for a long time. The average Black drawn to the military is more highly and properly motivated than his white counterpart. Those that aren't motivated run with the wild packs anyway. It's a very democratic filtering system: rubbish attracts rubbish. And they *are* minorities: Spanish Harlem, Slovak Chicago, Chicano Los Angeles. The words are *unemployment, poverty* and *ignorance*."

"And you're the Army's solution?"

"I'm a beginning. We try to reach them, upgrade them, make them better than they are. Educational programmes, lessening of resentments, installing self-respect. All the concepts the liberals think we're incapable of practising."

There was something missing, something that did not make sense. "This is all very enlightening," Peter said, "but what's it got to do with General MacAndrew? With what I saw at Arlington?"

"What's your reason for going back to Chasŏng?" countered the brigadier.

Peter looked away, at the photographs and decorations that were so reminiscent of MacAndrew's study. "I won't tell you how, but the name Chasŏng came up after MacAndrew resigned. I think it had something to do with his resignation."

"Highly unlikely."

"Then I saw you at Arlington," continued Chancellor, ignoring Ramirez's comment. "I'm not sure why, but I thought there might be a connection. I was right; there was. A few minutes ago you were closing the door in my face; I mention Chasŏng and you ask me in."

"I was curious," said the soldier. "It was a highly inflammatory issue."

"But before we talk about it," said Peter, again ignoring the interruption, "you make damned sure I hear about this sensitive department you work in. You're preparing me for something. What is it? Why did you hate MacAndrew?"

"All right." The brigadier shifted his position in the chair. Peter knew he was stalling, allowing himself a brief moment to consider how much to hide. Part truth, part lie. Peter had described many characters doing the same thing. "We all function best in those areas we feel deeply about. Although I'm not malcontent, I am discontented. I have been, throughout my career. I've been an angry man. And in many ways MacAndrew represented the reason for my anger. He was an elitist, a racist. Strangely enough, he was a fine commander because he truly believed he was superior and thought of everyone else as inferior. All the faults of middle command were the result of inferior human beings being given responsibilities beyond their capabilities. He would study roster sheets and equate last names with ethnic origins; too often those associations formed the basis of his decisions."

Ramirez stopped. Peter remained silent for a moment, too disturbed to speak. The soldier's explanation had both the ring of truth and the ring of falsehood to it. It *was* part truth, part lie. "You knew him very well, then," he finally said.

"Well enough to understand the insidiousness."

"Did you know his wife?"

There it was again. The rigidity in Ramirez's bearing. It passed as rapidly as it appeared.

"She was a sad case. Unfortunate, unstable. A vacuous woman with too many servants, too little to do, and too much to drink. She went off the deep end."

"I didn't know she was an alcoholic."

"Terms are unimportant."

"Was there an accident? A near drowning?"

"She was involved in a number of 'accidents'. A few rather unsavoury, I

742

understand. But in my opinion the larger accident was inactivity. I really know very little about her."

Again Peter sensed the lie in Ramirez's words. This major-brigadier knew a great deal about Alison's mother, but he was determined to say nothing. So be it. Chancellor thought. *Not him. Her! He's the decoy.* Varak's words. "There's nothing more?" Peter asked.

"No. Now, I've been honest with you. What have you heard about Chasŏng?"

"That there was an unnecessary slaughter and maiming of thousands of men."

"Chasŏng is only one of many battles represented in scores of veterans' hospitals. To repeat, it was investigated."

Chancellor sat forward. "Okay, General. I'll be honest with you. I don't think it was investigated anywhere near thoroughly enough. Or if it was, the results were shoved under a rug so fast the dust flew. There are a lot of things I don't know, but the picture's getting clearer. You hated MacAndrew; you freeze at the name Chasŏng; you give me a sermon, saying what a great guy you are; and then you freeze again when MacAndrew's wife is mentioned, telling me that you don't know much about her. A lie – you're filled with lies and evasions. I'll tell you what I think. I think Chasŏng is tied in with MacAndrew, his resignation, his murder, a gap in his service record and missing files from the Federal Bureau of Investigation. And somewhere in this mess is MacAndrew's wife. How much more there is, I haven't the vaguest idea, but you'd better tell me. Because I'm going to find out. There's a woman involved, and I love her, and I won't let any of you go on any longer. Cut the bullshit, Ramirez! Tell me the truth!"

The brigadier reacted as though suddenly pinned down by gunfire. His body tensed; his whisper was strained. "The gap in his service record. How did you know? You didn't mention it. You had no right – you tricked me." He began to shout. "You had no right to do that! You can't understand! We *did*. We *tried!*"

"What happened at Chasŏng?"

Ramirez closed his eyes. "Only what you think. The slaughter was unnecessary. The command decisions faulty . . . It was so long ago. Let it *be!*"

Chancellor got up from the chair and looked down at the brigadier. "No. Because I'm beginning to understand. I think Chasŏng was the biggest military cover-up in this country's history. And somewhere, somehow, it's in those files. I think after all these years, MacAndrew couldn't live with it any more. At long last he was going to talk about it. So you all got together and went after him because you couldn't live with that."

Ramirez opened his eyes. "That's not true. For God's sake, leave it alone!"

"Not true?" said Peter quietly. "I'm not sure you'd know the truth. You're so guilty, you're running standing still. Your righteousness is very suspect, General. I liked you better at Arlington; your anger was genuine then. You're hiding something – maybe from yourself, I don't know. But I know I'm going to find out what Chasŏng means."

"Then, may God have mercy on your soul," whispered Brigadier General Pablo Ramirez.

Chancellor hurried through Union Station towards the Amtrak gate. It was past two in the morning: the cavernous doomed enclosure was nearly deserted. There was a scattering of old men slumped on the long benches, gathering warmth, escaping the December chill of the Washington night. One old man seemed to sit up and take notice as Peter rushed past towards the gate. A lonely dream of what never could be had been disturbed, perhaps.

He had to hurry. The train to Quantico was the last until six. He wanted to reach Alison; he had to talk to her, make her remember. He also had to sleep; there was so much to do that to go on without rest would diminish whatever capabilities he had left. A plan was coming into focus. The beginnings of it were found in Ramirez's offhand remark: *Chasŏng* . . . is represented in scores of veterans' hospitals.

Peter walked to the centre of a deserted carriage and slid into the seat by the window, noting his reflection in the spotted glass. Although the image was dark and filmy, there was no mistaking the haggard, drawn expression on his face. From somewhere outside on the platform a mechanical voice blared through a loudspeaker. Chancellor closed his eyes and sank into weariness as the wheels gathered speed, the rhythm quickly hypnotic.

He heard muted footsteps behind him in the aisle, heard them over the sounds of rolling metal against metal. He presumed it was the conductor, so he kept his eyes shut, expecting to be asked for his ticket.

No request came. The footsteps had stopped. Peter opened his eyes and turned in the seat.

It all happened so fast. The sick, pale maniacal face behind him, the muffled report, the explosion of fabric beside him.

The seat had been blown apart! The man not three feet away had tried to kill him! Chancellor spun out of the seat, his body arching in the air, his hands lunging downward for the bony white fingers that held the weapon. The old man tried to get up, tried to force the barrel of the gun into Peter's stomach. Chancellor crashed the thin wrist against the metal arm of the seat; the weapon fell into the aisle, and Peter spun round again, throwing himself between the seats, covering the gun, reaching under his body until it was in his grasp. He lurched to his feet; the old man started to run towards the end of the car. Chancellor sprang after him, grabbing him with one hand. He forced him to stop, pressing him against the rim of an aisle seat.

"Bromley!"

"Child killer!"

"You're a goddamned lunatic!" Peter turned, pinning Bromley fiercely against the seat in the deserted car. Where was the conductor? The conductor could stop the train and summon the police! Then Chancellor balked; did he want the police?

"How could he have done it?" The old man was whimpering, the words spoken bitterly between his tears. "How could he have told you?"

"What are you talking about?!"

"Only one man knew. St Claire . . . Munro St Claire. I thought he had such greatness, such honour." Bromley broke down and wept uncontrollably.

Peter released him, unable to control his own shock. *Munro St Claire*. A name out of the past, but always a part of the present. The man responsible for all that had happened since the days of rejection and indecision at Park Forest.

All?

Oh, my God . . .

Venice you know . . . Bravo, too, but not Bravo! Never Bravo! Stefan Varak.

Such greatness, such honour. Paul Bromley.

The fifth man. Bravo.

Munro St Claire.

Clouds swirled in Chancellor's mind; the pain returned to his temples. He watched, helpless, unable to move, unable to stop him, as the old man rushed to the metal door between the cars and pulled it back. And then there was the crash of another door and a terrible rush of wind above the amplified sounds of the wheels hammering against the tracks below.

There was a scream of anguish, or of courage – whatever, it was of death. Bromley had hurled himself into the night.

There was no peace for Peter Chancellor.

Munro St Claire.

Bravo.

30

The Quantico cab turned off the bay highway and drove through the stone gateposts of the Pines Motel and Restaurant. It was isolated from any other structure in that section of the bay area. There were no buildings on either side – only tall brick walls – and the motel itself appeared to be directly on the water.

Peter got out and paid the driver in the bright light of the motel's entrance. There were floodlights everywhere. The cab sped away; Chancellor turned and started towards the large colonial doors.

"Stop where you are! Don't move your hands!"

Chancellor froze; the biting commands had come from the darkness beyond the floodlights, to the left of the entrance.

"What do you want?"

"Turn this way," ordered the man in shadows. "Slowly! It *is* you. I wasn't sure."

"Who are you?"

"Not one of the maniacs. Go on inside and ask for Mr Morgan."

"*Morgan?*"

"Mr Anthony Morgan. You'll be taken to the room."

The insanity again. *Anthony Morgan!* Numbly, he followed the incomprehensible instructions and walked into the lobby. He approached the front desk; a tall, muscular clerk sprang to attention behind the counter. Bewildered, Chancellor asked for Mr Anthony Morgan.

The clerk nodded. There was more than intelligence behind the man's clear eyes; there was conspiracy. He tapped a bell on the counter. Seconds later a uniformed bellhop arrived; he, too, was tall and powerfully built.

"Take this gentleman to room seven, please."

Peter followed the uniformed man down a carpeted hallway. A window at the far end of the corridor overlooked the waters of the bay. Chancellor thought he saw iron grillwork beyond the glass. They reached a door with the number seven on it; the bellhop rapped lightly.

"Yes?" said the voice behind the door.

"Needle one," said the tall bellhop softly.

"Four," replied the voice behind the door.

"Eleven."

"Thirteen."

"Ten."

"Terminate," said the unseen man. A bolt slid back; the door opened. O'Brien was silhouetted in the dim light of a comfortable sitting room. He nodded to the bellhop and motioned Chancellor inside. Peter saw him put a pistol back in its holster.

"Where is she?" Peter asked instantly.

"Shhh." The FBI man closed the door, a finger against his lips. "She dozed off about twenty minutes ago. She hasn't been able to sleep; she's worried sick."

"Where is she?"

"In the bedroom. Don't worry, there's a set of electronically tripped windows on the water side, with grillwork and bullet-proof glass. No one can touch her. Let her be; we'll talk."

"I want to see her!"

O'Brien nodded. "Sure. Go ahead. Just be quiet."

Chancellor opened the door a crack. A lamp was on. Alison lay on the bed, a blanket draped over her. Her head was angled back, her strong, lovely face caught the light. She was breathing deeply. She'd been asleep for twenty minutes. He would let her rest only a little while longer. What he had to do would be best done when Alison was close to exhaustion.

He closed the door. "There's a breakfast alcove back here," O'Brien said.

The sitting room was larger than Peter realized. At the east end, beyond a slatted room divider, was a round table by a window overlooking the water. Peter could now clearly see the grillwork behind the glass. The area contained a small kitchenette. There was coffee on the stove; O'Brien took two cups from a shelf and poured.

Peter sat down. "Not exactly a regular motel, is it?"

O'Brien smiled. "It's a good restaurant, though. Very popular with the social set."

"A proprietary? CIA?"

"Yes to the first. No to the second. It belongs to Naval Intelligence."

"Those men outside. The clerk, the bellboy. Who are they?"

"Varak told you. There aren't many of us, but we know who we are. We help each other." O'Brien drank from his cup. "Sorry to throw you with Morgan's name. I had a reason."

"What was it?"

"You and the girl will be out of here in the morning, but Morgan will still be registered. If anyone picks up your trail and it leads them here, the name Morgan in the register will mean something. They'll come to room seven. We'll know who they are."

"I thought you knew who the maniacs were." Peter drank his coffee, watching O'Brien carefully.

"Only some of them," replied the agent. "You ready to talk?"

"In a minute." The pain in his head was subsiding, but it was not gone. He needed a few moments; he wanted to think clearly. "Thanks for taking care of her."

"You're welcome. I have a niece about her age – my brother's daughter. They're very much alike. Strong, good faces. Not just pretty, you know?"

"I know." The pain was nearly gone. "What were all those numbers about at the door?"

The FBI man smiled. "Corny but effective. Not much different from what you read in spy novels: progressions and timing, mainly. That's what you writers don't seem to know about."

"What are they?"

"A basic code with a number. As the respondent I add a number, and the contact is trained to associate that number with another figure – plus or minus. He has to reply pretty damned quickly."

"What happens if he doesn't?"

"You saw my gun out. I've never used it that way, but I wouldn't have hesitated. I would have shot him through the door."

Chancellor put the coffee cup down on the table. "We'll talk now."

"Good. What happened?"

"Bromley followed me on the train. He tried to kill me. I was lucky, but he wasn't. He ran from me and threw himself off the train."

"Bromley? It's impossible!"

Peter reached into his pocket and pulled out the revolver he had recovered on the train. "This was fired through a seat in the middle of the third or fourth car on the two o'clock train from Washington. I didn't fire it."

O'Brien got out of the chair and walked to a telephone in the alcove. He spoke as he dialled. "The man we placed with Bromley was on official assignment. We can check him out right away." The agent became the executive. "Security. Surveillance, D.C. area, Duty Officer O'Brien . . . Yes, Chet, it's me. Thanks. Clear me, please . . . This is O'Brien. There's a special agent covering a subject named Bromley. The Olympic Hotel, downtown area. Raise him, please. Right away." O'Brien held his hand over the mouthpiece and turned to Chancellor. "Did you go back to the hotel? Did you tell anybody – Ramirez, *anyone* – that you were taking the train?"

"No."

"Taxi drivers?"

"I've taken one cab since nine-thirty. He drove me to Bethesda and waited for me. He didn't know I would be going back to Union Station."

"Jesus, it doesn't – Yes, yes, what is it? You can't?" The agent's eyes squinted as he spoke into the phone. "There's no response at all? Send a back-up squad down to the Olympic immediately. Get clearance from the D.C. police, and let them help. That man may be in trouble. I'll check with you later." O'Brien hung up; he was bewildered and showed it.

"What do you think happened?" asked Peter.

"I don't know. Only two people knew. The girl and myself." The agent stared at Chancellor.

"Now *wait* a minute. If you're – "

"I'm not," broke in O'Brien. "She's been with me every moment. She hasn't used the telephone; she'd have had to go through the switchboard here."

"What about the men outside? The ones who are so good with progressions."

"No way. I waited until the last train before I told anyone you might show up. And even then I never mentioned your means of travel. Don't mistake me, I'd trust them with our lives. It was just easier, less responsibility spread around." The agent walked slowly back to the table; then he suddenly brought his hand to his forehead. "Mother of Christ, it could have been me! Outside the Hay-Adams, when we were getting into the car. She was upset; I told her then. He could have been waiting in the drive by the wall. In the shadows."

"What are you talking about?"

O'Brien sat down in weary disgust. "Bromley knew where you were; he could have been waiting for you outside the hotel, hoping to get you in close range. If he was, he could have overheard me. I think I have to apologize for nearly getting you killed."

"That's an apology I find hard to accept."

"I don't blame you. What about this Ramirez? Why did you go see him?"

The transition from Bromley to Ramirez was too rapid for Peter. It took him several moments to clear the image of the sick old man from his mind. But he had made his decision. He would tell the FBI man everything. He reached into his pocket and withdrew the bloodstained scrap of paper with the names written on it.

"Varak was right. He said the key was Chasŏng."

"That's what you held back on the phone, wasn't it?" O'Brien asked. "Because of MacAndrew and his daughter. Ramirez was at Chasŏng?"

Chancellor nodded. "I'm sure of it. They're all hiding something. I think it's a massive cover-up. Even after twenty-two years they're frightened out of their minds. But that's only the beginning. Whatever's behind Chasŏng will lead to one of these four men." Chancellor handed O'Brien the scrap of paper. "Whoever he is, he has Hoover's private files."

The agent read the names; the blood drained from his face. "My God! Have you any idea who these people are?"

"Of course. There's a fifth man, but Varak didn't want him identified. He thought a great deal of him and didn't want him hurt. Varak was convinced the fifth man was used, that he was not involved."

"I wonder who he is."

"I know who he is."

"You're full of surprises."

"I found out through Bromley, but he didn't know he told me. You see, I knew the man. Years ago. He resolved a personal quandary I was in. I owe him a great deal. If you insist, I'll give you his name, but I'd rather see him first myself."

O'Brien considered. "All right. Fair enough. But only if you'll let me have a support option."

"Speak English."

"Write out the name and give it to an attorney who will hand it over to me after a reasonably short period of time."

"Why?"

"In case this fifth man kills you."

Chancellor studied the agent's eyes. O'Brien meant precisely what he said. "Fair enough."

"Let's talk about Ramirez. Tell me everything he said; describe every reaction you recall. What was his relationship to MacAndrew? To Chasŏng? How did you know it? What took you to him in the first place?"

"Something I saw at Arlington Cemetery and something Varak said. I put the two together; call it an educated guess . . . or perhaps it fitted something I might have written. I don't know. I just didn't think I could be too far wrong. I wasn't."

It took Chancellor less than ten minutes to tell it all. During his narrative Peter could see Quinn O'Brien making mental notes, just as he had done the night before in Washington. "Let's leave Ramirez on a burner and go back to Varak for a minute. He built his connection between Chasŏng and one of those four men on the list because specific information was leaked that couldn't have come from any other source but one of them. Is that right?"

"Yes. He worked for them. He fed them the information."

"And the fact that a language was spoken that he didn't know."

"Apparently he knew several."

"Six or seven, I imagine," agreed O'Brien.

His point was that the men who took him at the Thirty-fifth Street house had to know he wouldn't be able to understand what they said. They had to know *him*. Again, one of those four men. They all knew him, knew his background."

"Another link in the connection. Could he at least identify the root of the language? Like Oriental or Middle Eastern?"

"He didn't say. He only said that when the name Chasŏng was used, it was spoken fanatically, repeated fanatically."

"What he might have meant was that Chasŏng has become a kind of cult."

"A cult?"

"Let's go back to Ramirez. He confirmed the slaughter, admitted the command foul-up?"

"Yes."

"But he'd already told you Chasŏng was investigated by the Inspector-General, that the losses were attributed to unexpected enemy forces who were superior in numbers and firepower."

"He was lying."

"About the I.G. investigation? I doubt that." O'Brien got up and poured more coffee.

"About the findings, then," said Peter.

"I doubt that, too. You could research them too easily."

"What are you driving at?"

"The sequence. I'm a lawyer, remember?" The agent put the pot back on the stove and returned to the table. "Ramirez told you about the I.G. investigation without any hesitation. He just assumed you'd accept the findings if you checked them out. Then moments later he reverses himself. He's suddenly not sure you're going to accept them; and that concerns him. He actually pleads with you to leave it alone. You had to give him a reason to change his mind. It had to be something you said."

"I accused him. I told him it was a cover-up."

"But accused him of what? What were they covering up? You didn't say because you don't know. Hell, charges like that are the reason the I.G. steps in to begin with. He wasn't afraid of those. It was something else. Think."

Chancellor tried. "I told him he hated MacAndrew; that he froze at the name Chasŏng, that it was tied in with MacAndrew's resignation, with a gap in his service record, with the missing files. That he – Ramirez, I mean – was filled with lies and evasions. That he and the others had got together because they were frightened to death – "

"Of Chasŏng," completed Quinn O'Brien. "Now go back. What specifically did you say about Chasŏng?"

"That it involved MacAndrew! It was why he resigned, because he was going to expose it. That the information, the cover-up, was in the missing FBI files. It was why he was murdered."

"That's everything? That's *everything* you said?"

"Christ, I'm *trying*."

"Calm down." He put his hand on Peter's arm. "Sometimes the most relevant evidence is right in front of us and we don't see it. We dig so hard for details, we miss the obvious."

The obvious. Words – it was always words. The uncanny way they could provoke a thought, gave rise to an image, prod a memory – the memory of a brief flash of recognition in a frightened general's eyes. Of a dying man's statement: *Not him. Her! He's the decoy.* Peter looked through the thin, delicately woven slats of the room divider. His eyes were focused on the door of Alison's room. He turned to O'Brien.

"Oh God, that's it," he said quietly.

"What?"

"MacAndrew's wife."

31

Senior Agent Carroll Quinlan O'Brien agreed to leave. He understood. Things were going to be said behind that door that were terribly private.

Also, he had work to do. There were four celebrated men to learn about and a remote stretch of hills in Korea that two decades ago had been a killing ground. Wheels had to start turning, knowledge had to be unearthed.

Peter entered the bedroom, unsure of how he would begin, sure only that he had to. At the sound Alison stirred, moving her head from one side to the other. She opened her eyes as if startled, and for an instant she stared at the ceiling.

"Hello," said Chancellor gently.

Alison gasped and sat up. "Peter! You're here!"

He walked swiftly to the bed and sat on the edge, embracing her. "Everything's all right," he said, and then he thought of her father and mother. How many times had Alison heard her father say those words to the madwoman who was her mother? "I was frightened." Alison held his face with both her hands. Her wide brown eyes searched his for evidence of pain. Her whole face was alive and concerned. She was the most intensely beautiful woman he had ever known, and much of that beauty came from within her.

"There's nothing to be frightened about," he said, knowing the lie was preposterous, sensing she knew it, too. "It's almost all over. I've just got to ask you some questions."

"Questions?" Slowly she took her hands from his face.

"About your mother."

Alison blinked. For a moment he felt her resentment. It was always there when her mother was mentioned.

"I've told you what I can. She became ill when I was very young."

"Yet she remained in the same house with you. You had to know her even in her illness."

Alison leaned against the headboard. She was not relaxing, however; she was wary, as if afraid of the conversation. "That's not entirely right. There was always someone caring for her, and I learned early to keep my distance. And there were the boarding schools from the time I was ten. Whenever my father was sent to a new post, the first thing he did was to find me a school. For two years when we were in Germany, I went to school in Switzerland. When he was in London, I was at the Gateshead Academy for Girls; that's in the north country, near Scotland. So you see, I wasn't in the same house very often."

"Tell me about your mother. Not after she became ill, but before."

"How can I? I was a child."

"What you know about her. Your grandparents, her home, where she lived. How she met your father."

"Is this necessary?" She reached for a packet of cigarettes on the bedside table.

Chancellor looked at her, his eyes steady. "I agreed to your condition last night. You said you'd accept mine. Remember?"

He took the matches from her and lighted her cigarette, the flame flickering between them.

She returned his look and nodded. "I remember. All right. My mother, as she was before I knew her. She was born in Tulsa, Oklahoma. Her father was a bishop in the Church of Heavenly Christ. It's a Baptist denomination, very rich, very strict. As a matter of fact both her parents were missionaries. She travelled almost as much as I did when she was young. Remote places. India, Burma, Ceylon, the Po Hai Gulf."

"Where was she educated?"

"Missionary schools mainly. That was part of the upbringing. All God's children were the same in Jesus' eyes. It was also fake. You went to school with them – probably because it helped the teachers – but damned if you could eat with them or play with them."

"I don't understand something." Peter leaned sideways, across her covered legs, his elbow resting on the bed, his head in his hand.

"What?"

"That kitchen in Rockville. The 1930s decor. Even the goddamned coffeepot. You said your father had it designed to remind her of her childhood."

"The happier moments, I said. Or should have said. As a child my mother was happiest when she was back in Tulsa. When her parents returned for spiritual R and R. It wasn't often enough. She hated the Far East, hated the travelling."

"Strange she should wind up marrying an Army man."

"Ironic, perhaps – not so strange. Her father was a bishop; her husband became a general. They were strong, decisive men and very persuasive." Alison avoided his eyes; he did not try to re-engage them.

"When did she meet your father?"

Alison drew on her cigarette. "Let me think. God knows he told me often enough, but there were always variations. As if he constantly, purposely, exaggerated or romanticized."

"Or left something out?"

She had been looking across the room at the wall. She shifted her eyes quickly to him. "Yes. That, too. Anyway, they met during World War II, right here in Washington. Dad was recalled after the North African campaign. He was being transferred to the Pacific, which meant briefing and training in D.C. and Benning. He met her at one of those Army receptions."

"What was the daughter of a Baptist bishop doing at an Army reception in wartime Washington?"

"She worked for the Army as a translator. Nothing dramatic – pamphlets, manuals. 'I am an American pilot who has parachuted into your beautiful country, and I am your ally' – that sort of thing. She could read and write several Far Eastern languages. She could even work her way through basic Mandarin."

Chancellor sat up. "Chinese?"

"Yes."

"She was in China?"

"I told you. The provinces of the Po Hai Gulf. She spent four years there, I think. Her father operated – if that's the word – between Tientsin and Tsingtao."

Peter looked away, trying to conceal his sudden apprehension. A dissonant chord had been struck, its abrasive sound disturbing. He let the moment pass as quickly as possible and turned back to Alison. "Did you know your grandparents?"

"No. I vaguely recall Dad's mother, but his father – "

"Your mother's parents."

"No." Alison reached over and crushed out her cigarette. "They died proselytizing."

"Where?"

Alison held her extinguished cigarette against the glass of the ashtray and replied softly without looking at Peter. "In China."

They were silent for several moments. Alison sat back against the headboard. Chancellor remained motionless and held her gaze. "I think we both know what we're saying. Do you want to talk about it?"

"About what?"

"Tokyo. Twenty-two years ago. Your mother's accident."

"I don't remember."

"I think you do."

"I was so young."

"Not that young. You said you were five or six, but you shaved a couple of points. You were nine. Newspapermen are usually accurate in matters of age; it's easy to check. That article on your father gave your right age – "

"*Please–*"

"Alison, I love you. I want to help you, help us. At first only I had to be stopped. Now you're involved because you're part of the truth. Chasŏng is part of it."

"What truth are you talking about?"

"Hoover's files. They were stolen."

"No! That's in your book. That's not real!"

"It's been real from the beginning. Before he died, they were taken. They're being used right now. And the new owners are tied in with Chasŏng. That's all we know. Your mother's tied in, and your father's protected that connection throughout her life. Now we've got to find out what it was. It's the only thing that will lead us to the man who has those files. And we've got to find him."

"But that doesn't make sense! She was a sick woman, getting worse. She wasn't important!"

"She was to somebody. She still is. For God's sake, stop running away from it! You couldn't lie to me, so you skimmed over it, then you circled it, and finally you said it: *China*. The Po Hai provinces are *China*. Your mother's parents died in *China*. At Chasŏng we were fighting *China!*"

"What does it mean?"

"I don't know! I may be so far off base, but I can't help thinking. *Nineteen fifty* . . . Tokyo. Korea. The Chinese Nationalists thrown out of the mainland;

they wandered about pretty freely, I would think. And if they did, they could be infiltrated. Orientals can tell one another apart; Westerners can't. Was it possible your mother was reached? The wife of one of the top commanders in Korea reached and somehow compromised – because she had parents in China. Until something snapped. What happened twenty-two years ago?"

The words came painfully to Alison. "It started several months before, I think. When we first got to Tokyo. She just gradually began to slip away."

"What do you mean, 'slip away'?"

"I'd say something to her and she'd simply stare at me, not hearing. Then she'd turn without answering and walk out of the room, singing bits and pieces of tunes."

"I heard one in the Rockville house. She was singing an old tune. 'Let It Snow'."

"That sort of thing came later. She'd get attached to a song, and it would last for months. Over and over again."

"Was your mother an alcoholic?"

"She drank, but I don't think so. At least, not then."

"You remember her quite well," said Peter softly.

Alison looked at him. "More than my father knew, and less than you think."

He accepted the rebuke. "Go on," he said gently. "She began slipping away. Did anybody know? Was anything done for her?"

Alison reached nervously for another cigarette. "I suppose I was the reason something was done. You see, there was no one to talk to. The servants were all Japanese. What few visitors we had were Army wives; you don't talk to Army wives about your mother."

"You were alone, then. A child."

"I was alone. I didn't know how to cope. Then the telephone calls started coming late at night. She'd get dressed and go out, sometimes with that dazed look in her eyes, and I didn't know if she'd ever come back. One night my father called from Korea. She was always home when he called; he would write and tell her the day and the time beforehand. But that night she wasn't, so I told him everything. I guess I just blurted it out. A few days later he flew back to Tokyo."

"How did he react?"

"I don't remember. I was so happy to see him. I just knew everything would be all right."

"Was it?"

"It was stabilized for a while; that's the word I'd use now. An Army doctor began coming to the house. Then he brought others, and they'd take her away for several hours, every few days. The phone calls stopped, and she stopped going out at night."

"Why do you say 'stabilized for a while'? Did things come unglued?"

Tears formed in her eyes. "There was no warning. She just suddenly went. It happened late one bright, sunny day; I'd just come home from school. She was screaming. She'd chased the servants out of the house; she was raving, smashing things. Then she stared at me. I've never seen such a look. As though she loved me one moment, then hated me, then was terrified of me." Alison brought her hand to her mouth; it was trembling. She stared down at the blanket, her eyes frightened. She whispered the rest. "Then mother came at me. It was horrible. She had a kitchen knife in her hand. She grabbed me by the throat; she tried to plunge the knife into my stomach. She kept trying to stab me. I held her wrist and screamed and screamed. She wanted to kill me! Oh, *God!* She wanted to *kill me!*"

Alison fell forward on her side, her whole body convulsed, her face ashen. Peter reached for her and held her, rocking her back and forth.

He could not let her stop now. "Please, try to remember. When you came in the house, when you saw her, what was she screaming? What was she saying?"

Alison pushed herself away from him and leaned back on the headrest, her eyes shut tight, her face wet with tears. But the crying had stopped. "I don't know."

"*Remember!*"

"I *can't!* I didn't *understand* her!" Her eyes opened; she stared at him. They both understood.

"Because she was speaking a foreign language." He said the words firmly, not asking a question. "She was screaming in Chinese. Your mother, who spent four years in the Po Hai provinces, who was fluent in Mandarin, was screaming at you in Chinese."

Alison nodded. "Yes."

The real question was not answered; Chancellor understood that. Why would mother attack daughter? For a few seconds Peter let his mind wander, recalling vaguely the hundreds of pages he had written in which irrational conflicts led to terrible acts of violence. He was no psychologist; he had to think in simpler terms. Schizophrenic infanticide, Medea complex – these were not the areas to probe even if he were capable. The answer lay elsewhere. In more obvious descriptions . . . Descriptions? A madwoman in a rage, unbalanced, unfocused. *Unfocused.* Late afternoon. Bright sunshine. Most houses in Japan were light and airy. Sun streaming through the windows. A child walks through the door. Peter reached for the child's hand.

"Try very hard to remember what you were wearing."

"It's not hard. We wore the same thing every day. Dresses were considered immodest. We wore light, loose-fitting little slacks and jackets. It was the school uniform."

Peter looked away. A *uniform.* He turned back.

"Was your hair long or short?"

"During those days?"

"During that day. When your mother saw you coming through the door that afternoon."

"I was wearing a cap. We all wore caps, and we usually kept our hair short."

That was it! thought Peter. An unbalanced woman in a rage, sun streaming through the windows, perhaps through the door; a figure comes in wearing a *uniform.*

He reached for Alison's other hand. "She never saw you."

"What?"

"Your mother never saw you. That's what Chasŏng's all about. It explains the broken glass, the old nightgown underneath the words on the wall in your father's study, the look in Ramirez's eyes when your mother was mentioned."

"What do you mean, she never saw me? I was there!"

"But she didn't see *you*. She saw a uniform. That's *all* she saw."

Alison brought her hand to her mouth, curiosity and fear intermingled. "A uniform? Ramirez? You went to see Ramirez?"

"There's a lot I can't tell you because I don't know myself, but we're getting nearer. Officers were rotated back and forth from the Korean combat centres to the command centres in Tokyo. That's common knowledge. You say your mother went out frequently at night. There's a pattern, Alison."

"You're saying she was a whore. That she whored to get information!"

"I'm saying it's possible she was forced into acts that tore her apart. Husband and father. On the one hand, her husband, a brilliant commander at the front; on the other, an adored father held captive in China. What could she do?"

Alison raised her eyes to the ceiling. Again she understood; it was a conflict with which she could identify. "I don't want to go on. I don't want to know any more."

"We have to. What happened after the attack?"

"I ran outside. One of the servants was there; he had called the police from the house nearest ours. He took me there, and I waited . . . waited while the Japanese family stared at me as if I were diseased. Then an MP came and took me to the base. I stayed with a colonel's wife for several days until my father came back."

"Then what? Did you see your mother?"

"About a week or so later, I think. It's hard to remember precisely. When she came home, a nurse was with her. She was never without a nurse or a companion ever again."

"How was she?"

"Withdrawn."

"Permanently damaged?"

"That's difficult to say. It was more than a breakdown; that's obvious to me now. But she might have recovered sufficiently to function then."

"Then?"

"When she came home from the hospital the first time. With the nurse. Not after the second time."

"Tell me about it. The second time."

Alison blinked. The memory was obviously as painful to her as the violent image of her mother's attack. "Arrangements had been made for me to go back to the States, to Dad's parents. As I said, Mother was quiet, withdrawn. Three nurses were on eight-hour shifts; she was never alone. My father was needed back in Korea. He left, believing everything was under control. Other officers' wives would come to the house to see Mother, take us both out for picnics, take her shopping for an afternoon – that sort of thing. Everyone was very kind. Too kind, really. You see, mentally ill people are like alcoholics. If they're gripped by an obsession, if they want to break away, they'll suddenly pretend normality; they'll smile and laugh and lie convincingly. Then when you least expect it, they're gone. That's what I think happened."

"You think? You don't know?"

"No. They told me that she'd been pulled out of the surf. That she'd been underwater so long, they thought she was dead. I was a child, and it was an explanation I could accept. It made sense; Mother was taken out for the day to Funabashi Beach. It was a Sunday, but I had a cold, so I stayed home. Then some time in the afternoon the phone started ringing. Was my mother there? Had she come back? The first few calls were from the women who had taken her to Funabashi, but they didn't want me to know that. They pretended to be other people, so as not to alarm me, I guess. Two Army officers drove out to the house. They were nervous and agitated, but they didn't want me to know it, either. I went to my room; I knew something was wrong, and all I could think of was that I wanted my father."

The tears came again. Peter held both her hands; he spoke gently. "Go on."

"It was awful. At night, quite late, I heard screams. Then shouts and people running outside. Then there were the sounds of cars and sirens and tyres screeching in the street. I got out of bed and went to the door and opened it. My room was on the landing above the hall. Downstairs the house seemed to be filling up with Americans – Army mostly, but civilians, too. There probably weren't more than ten men, but everyone was walking around rapidly, talking into the telephone, using hand radios. Then the front door opened, and she was brought inside. On a stretcher. She was under a sheet, but there were bloodstains on the cloth. And her face – it was white. Her eyes were wide, staring blankly as if she were dead. At the corners of her mouth were trickles of blood that rolled down over her chin on to her neck. As the stretcher passed beneath a light, she suddenly lurched up screaming, her head wrenching back and forth, her body writhing but held in place by the straps. I cried out and ran down the stairs, but a major – a handsome Black major, I'll never forget – stopped me and picked me up and held me, telling me that everything was going to be all right. He didn't want me to go to her, not then. And he was right – she was in hysterics, she wouldn't have known me. They lowered the stretcher to the floor, unstrapped her and held her down. A doctor tore some cloth. He had a hypodermic needle in his hand; he administered it, and within seconds she was quiet. I was crying. I tried to ask questions, but nobody would listen to me. The major carried me back to my room and put me to bed. He stayed with me for a long time, trying to reassure me, telling me there'd been an accident and my mother would be all right. But I knew she wouldn't be, not ever again. I was taken to the base and stayed there until Dad came back for the next to last time before we were flown home to America. His tour of duty had only a few months left."

Chancellor pulled her to him. "The only thing that's clear is that the accident didn't have anything to do with being caught in an undertow and pulled out to sea. For one thing, she was brought to the house, not to a hospital. It was an elaborate hoax that you pretended to believe but never did. You don't believe it now. Why did you pretend all these years?"

Alison whispered. "It was easier, I think."

"Because you thought she tried to kill you? Because she screamed at you in Chinese, and you didn't want to think about that? You didn't want to consider the alternatives?"

Alison's lips trembled. "Yes."

"But now you've got to face it – you understand that, don't you? You can't run away from it any more. It's what is in Hoover's files. Your mother worked for the Chinese. She was responsible for the slaughter at Chasŏng."

"Oh, *God* . . . "

"She didn't do anything *willingly*. Maybe not even knowingly. Months ago, when I was with your father, and your mother came downstairs, she saw me and began screaming. I started to back away into the study, but your father yelled at me and told me to get by a lamp. He wanted her to see my face, my features. She stared at me, then calmed down and just sobbed. I think your father wanted her to realize I wasn't an Oriental. I think the accident that Sunday afternoon was no accident at all. I believe she was caught and tortured by the people who had been using her, forcing her to work for them. It's possible your mother was a much braver woman than anyone's given her credit for. She may have finally stood up to them and taken the consequences. That's not congenital madness, Alison. That's a person who's been *driven* out of her mind."

He stayed with her for nearly an hour, until exhaustion made her finally close her eyes. It was past five; the sky outside the window was growing brighter. It would be morning soon. In a few hours Quinn O'Brien would move them to some other place of safety. Peter knew that he, too, had to sleep.

But before he could allow himself sleep, he had to know if what he believed was true. It had to be confirmed, and one man could do that. Ramirez.

He let himself out the bedroom door and walked to the telephone. He rummaged through his pockets until he found the scrap of paper on which he'd written Ramirez's number. No doubt O'Brien's man would be listening at the switchboard, but it did not matter. Nothing mattered any more but the truth.

He dialled. The phone was answered almost immediately.

"Yes, what is it?" The voice was slurred with sleep.

"Ramirez?"

"Who's this?"

"Chancellor. I've got the answer now, and you're going to confirm it for me. If you hesitate, if you lie, I'm going right to my publisher. He'll know what to do."

"I told you to stay out of it!"

"MacAndrew's wife. There was a Chinese connection, wasn't there? Twenty-two years ago she was carrying information to the Chinese. She was responsible for Chasŏng!"

"No! Yes. You don't understand. Let it alone!"

"I want the truth!"

Ramirez was momentarily silent. "They're both dead."

"Ramirez!"

"They had her on drugs. She was totally dependent; she couldn't go two days without a needle. We found out. We helped her. We did our best for her. Things were going badly. It made sense . . . to do what we did. Everyone agreed."

Peter's eyes narrowed. The dissonant chord was there again, louder and more jarring than before. "You *helped* her because it made sense? Things were going badly, so it made some sort of goddamned *sense?*"

"Everyone agreed." The soldier's voice was nearly inaudible.

"Oh, my God! You didn't help her, you *maintained* her! You *kept* her on drugs so you could transmit the information you wanted to get through."

"Things were going badly. The Yalu was – "

"Wait a minute! Are you telling me MacAndrew was a part of this? He let his wife be used this way?"

"MacAndrew never knew."

Chancellor felt sick. "Yet in spite of everything you did to her, Chasŏng still happened," he said. "And all these years MacAndrew thought his wife was responsible. Drugged, tortured, nearly beaten to death, made a traitor by an enemy that held her parents captive. You bastards!"

Ramirez screamed into the telephone. "He was a bastard, too! Don't you ever forget it! He was a *killer!*"

32

He was a bastard, too! Don't you ever forget it! He was a killer! He was a bastard, too! . . . a killer! The words rang in Chancellor's ears. He watched the swiftly passing countryside, Alison in the back seat of the government car with him, and tried to understand.

He was a bastard, too! It did not make sense. MacAndrew and his wife were victims. They had been manipulated by *both* antagonists – the woman destroyed, the general living out his life with a terrible fear of exposure.

He was a bastard, too! . . . a killer! If Ramirez meant that MacAndrew had become irrational, a commander who did not care about the cost of destroying an enemy that had destroyed his wife, *bastard* was hardly the right term. Mac the Knife had hurled hundreds, perhaps thousands, to their death in a futile attempt at vengeance. Reason had deserted him; vengeance was everything.

If these were the things that caused Ramirez to judge MacAndrew a bastard, so be it. But what bothered Peter, and it bothered him deeply, was the unclear picture of this new MacAndrew, this bastard, this killer. It conflicted with the man Chancellor had met, the soldier who truly hated war because he knew it so well. Or had Alison's father merely lapsed momentarily – a matter of months in a lifetime – into a madness of his own?

So now the secret of Chasŏng was known. But where did it lead them? How could MacAndrew's betrayed, manipulated wife lead to one of the four men on Varak's list? Varak was convinced that whatever was behind Chasŏng would take them directly to the man who had Hoover's files. But how? Perhaps Varak was wrong. The secret was known, and it led nowhere.

The government car reached an intersection. A lone petrol station stood on the right; a single car was parked by a pump. The driver beside O'Brien turned the wheel, and they drove up to it. He nodded to O'Brien and got out of the car; the FBI man slid over behind the wheel. The driver walked to the parked car. He greeted the man inside and climbed in the front seat.

"They'll stay with us until we reach Saint Michael's," said Quinn from behind the wheel.

A minute later they were on the road again, the car behind them following at a discreet distance.

"Where's Saint Michael's?" asked Alison.

"South of Annapolis, on the Chesapeake. We can use a house there. It's sterile. Do you want to talk now? The radio's off; there are no tapes. We're alone."

Peter knew what Quinn meant. "Was a tape made of what was said between Ramirez and me?"

"No. Only a shorthand transcript. One copy; it's in my pocket."

"I haven't had time to explain everything to Alison, but she knows some of it." He turned to her. "Your mother was strung out on narcotics – probably heroin – by the Chinese. She became dependent; that was the 'slipping away' you described. She was used to gather bits and pieces of information. Troop movements, combat strength, supply routes – a hundred things she might overhear from the officers she met at night. Besides the drugs, her mother and father were being held in a Chinese prison. The combination was overpowering."

"How horrible . . ." Alison looked out the window.

"I doubt that she was the only one," said Peter. "I'm sure there were others."

"I know damned well there were," added O'Brien.

"I'm afraid that doesn't help," Alison said. "Did my father know? It must have killed him – "

"Your father knew only what the Army wanted him to know. It was only part of the truth, the Chinese part. He was never told the rest of it."

Alison turned from the window. "What rest of it?"

Peter took her hand. "There was another connection. The Army's. She was manipulated to transmit selected, misleading intelligence back to the Chinese."

Alison stiffened, her eyes boring in on his. "How?"

"There are a number of ways to do it. Keep her spaced out on narcotics or administer chemicals that heighten the withdrawal pains. Probably that was it; the agony would drive her right back to her original connection. With the information the Army wanted carried."

Alison pulled her hand away in anger. She closed her eyes, breathing deeply, in an agony of her own. Chancellor did not touch her; the moment was hers alone.

She turned back to Peter. "Make them pay," she said.

"We know what Chasŏng means now," said Quinn O'Brien from the front seat. "But where does it take us?"

"To one of four men, Varak believed." Chancellor saw O'Brien's head jerk up, his eyes looking at Peter in the rearview mirror. "I've told her there are four men," he explained, "I haven't used names."

"Why not?" asked Alison.

"For your own protection, Miss MacAndrew," answered the FBI man. "I'm working on those. I'm not sure what to look for."

"Something to do with China," Peter said. "Anything Chinese."

"You mentioned that you wanted to reach a fifth man. How soon?"

"Before the day's over."

Quinn was silent behind the wheel. Several moments went by before he spoke. "You agreed to leave the name with a lawyer."

"I don't need a lawyer. I'll leave it with Morgan in New York. Get me to a phone. There should be one on a road around here somewhere."

O'Brien frowned. "You're not experienced making these kind of contacts. I don't want you taking unnecessary risks. You don't know what you're doing."

"You'd be surprised how many secret meetings I've invented. You just get me an unmarked car and give me a few hours. And don't go back on your word. I'll know if you have me followed. Believe that."

"I'm forced to. Mother of God. *A writer.*"

"Goddamn it, where are you?" Tony shouted the question, his next words only slightly less strident. "The hotel said you'd checked out, and the night manager told me you were on your way to the Shenandoah Valley! And your doctor phoned, asking me if I expected you in New York. Would you please explain – ?"

"There isn't time. Except that he wasn't the hotel's night manager, he was an FBI man. And I doubt my doctor called you. It was someone else looking for me."

"What are you *doing?*"

"Trying to find the man who has Hoover's files."

"Stop that! We had this out a couple of months ago. You're crossing the line again; you're not someone in one of your goddamned books!"

"But the files *are* missing. They've been missing from the beginning; that's what it's all about. I'll come back to New York, I promise, but first I want you to phone someone for me. I want you to tell him to meet me in a car at the precise location and time I give you. He's in Washington and probably very difficult to get through to. But you'll be able to do it if you say your name is Varak. Stefan Varak. Write that down; you mustn't use your own name."

"And I suppose," said Morgan sarcastically, "that I should place the call from a pay phone."

"Exactly. On the street, not in the building."

"Come on. This is – "

"The man you're calling is Munro St Claire."

The name had its effect; Morgan was stunned. "You're not joking, are you." It was not a question.

"I'm not joking. When you get St Claire on the line, tell him you're a contact from me. Tell him Varak is dead. He may know it by now, but he may not. Have you got a pencil?"

"Yes."

"Write this down. St Claire uses the name Bravo . . ."

Peter waited in the unmarked car on the back road that led to the edge of the Chesapeake; it was a dead end that stopped at the water. The banks were marshland, the wild reeds tall and swaying in the December winds. It was shortly past two in the afternoon; the sky was overcast, the air cold, and the dampness penetrating.

Alison and O'Brien were several miles north in the sterile house in Saint Michael's. The FBI man had agreed to give him three hours – until five o'clock – before he telephoned Morgan for Bravo's identity. If Chancellor had not returned by then, Quinn made it clear that Peter was to be presumed dead and appropriate measures would be taken.

Chancellor remembered Varak's words. There was a senator. A man who was not afraid, who among all men in Washington could be sought out for help. For Peter it had been another part of the madness. He had invented a senator for his Nucleus. The parallel was once again too close; the fictional character had its basis in a living man.

He gave the senator's name to Quinn in case he did not return.

In the distance a black limousine had rounded a bend in the road and was approaching slowly. He opened the door of the car and got out. The limousine came to a stop twenty feet away. The chauffeur's window was lowered.

"Mr Peter Chancellor?" asked the man.

"Yes," answered Peter, alarmed. There was no one in the rear seat of the car. "Where's Ambassador St Claire?"

"If you'll get in, sir, I'll take you to him."

"That wasn't part of my instructions!"

"It has to be this way."

"No, it doesn't!"

"The ambassador told me to tell you it was for your own protection. He asked me to remind you of a conversation four and a half years ago. He did not mislead you then."

Peter's breathing stopped for a moment. Munro St Claire had *not* misled him four and a half years before. He had given him his life. Chancellor nodded and got into the limousine.

The enormous Victorian house stood on the waterfront. A long dock protruded into the bay at the centre point of the large front lawn. The house itself was three storeys high. On the ground level was a wide screened-in porch that ran along the side of the building that faced the Chesapeake.

The chauffeur preceded Chancellor up the steps to the entrance. He unlocked the door and motioned Peter inside.

"Turn to the right, through the archway, and into the sitting room. The ambassador is waiting for you."

Chancellor stepped into the hall; he was alone. He walked through an archway into a high-ceilinged room and adjusted his eyes. At the far end a lone figure stood in front of a pair of glass French doors overlooking the porch and the waters of the Chesapeake. His back was to Chancellor; he was looking out at the ever-changing surface of the bay.

"Welcome," said Munro St Claire, turning to face Peter. "This house belonged to a man named Genesis. He was Bravo's friend."

"I've heard of Banner and Paris, Venice and Christopher. And, of course, Bravo. I haven't heard of Genesis."

St Claire had obviously been testing. He controlled his astonishment, but it was there. "There would be no reason for you to. He's dead. I find it incredible that Varak gave you my name."

"He didn't. As a matter of fact, he refused to. A man named Bromley did, but he didn't know he did. His code name at the Bureau was Viper. The *B* becomes *V* and thus one of the missing files. Part truth, part lie. That's how I was programmed."

St Claire narrowed his eyes as he moved away from the glass doors towards Chancellor. " 'Part truth, part lie'; Varak said that?"

"Yes. He died in front of me. But not before he told me everything."

"Everything?"

"From the beginning. From Malibu to Washington. How I was provoked into getting involved; how I was the snare for provoking others into showing themselves. He didn't say so directly, but it really didn't matter whether I lived or died, did it? How could you do it?"

"Sit down."

"I'd prefer standing."

"Very well. Are we two gladiators circling each other?"

"Perhaps."

"If so, you've lost the battle. My chauffeur is watching us from the porch."

Chancellor turned towards the windows. The chauffeur stood motionless, a gun in his hand. "You think I've come to kill you?" Peter asked.

"I don't know what to think. I only know that nothing can stand in the way of retrieving those files. I'd willingly *give* my life if that would be accomplished."

"Letters *M* to *Z*. The man who has them whispers over the telephone, threatens his victims. And he's one of four men: Banner, Paris, Venice, or Christopher. Or perhaps he's Bravo; that's possible, I guess. He's reached Phyllis Maxwell, Paul Bromley, and Lieutenant General Bruce MacAndrew. The general was about to expose a twenty–two–year–old cover-up that he couldn't live with any more when he was forced out. Its name was Chasŏng. How many others this man has reached, no one knows. But if he's not found, if the files aren't found – and destroyed – he'll control the pressure points of the government."

Peter made the statements flatly, but they had their effect. "You know things that could cost you your life," said St Claire.

"Since I've nearly lost it several times, thanks to you, that doesn't surprise me. It just frightens me. I want it to stop."

"I wish I could stop it. I wish to God it was over and the files brought back. I wish with all my heart that I was convinced it would end that way."

"There's a way to bring it about. To ensure it, as a matter of fact."

"How?"

"Make public the names of your group. Acknowledge Hoover's missing files. Force the issue."

"You're out of your mind."

"Why?"

"The issue is far more complex than you seem to understand." St Claire moved to an armchair. He placed his hands on the rim of the back, his long fingers extended delicately over the fabric. His hands trembled. "You say Bromley gave you my name," he said. "How?"

"He tracked me down on a train and tried to kill me. He had been told that my manuscript was finished, that it included information about his family. I gather that information could only have come from you. He used your name; suddenly everything was clear. From the beginning, the very beginning. All the way back to Park Forest. I owed you a debt, and you took your payment. The debt's cancelled."

St Claire looked up. "Your debt to me? It was never owed. But I submit you have a debt to your country."

"I'll accept that. I just want to know how I'm paying." Peter raised his voice. "Make public the names of your group! Tell the country – since debts are owed – that Hoover's private files are missing!"

"*Please!*" St Claire held up one hand. "Try to understand. We came together under extraordinary circumstances – "

"To stop a maniac," interrupted Chancellor.

Bravo nodded. "To *try* to stop a maniac. In doing so, we exceeded the limits of authority in a number of areas. We bent the machinery of government because we thought it was justified. We could be ruined, everything we stand for destroyed; we understood that. Our only motive was fairness, our only protection anonymity."

"Change the rules! One of you already has!"

"Then, he must be found. But the others can't be made to pay!"

"I'm not getting through to you. The debt's cancelled, Mr St Claire. You've *used* me. I've been manipulated, kept off balance until I was damned near out of my mind. For what? So *you*, the Pentagon, the Federal Bureau of Investigation – for all I know, the White House, the Justice Department, the Congress . . . half the goddamned government – can go on lying? Telling people those files were destroyed when they weren't? I'm not asking; I'm demanding! Either you go public, or I will!"

St Claire could control his trembling but not conceal it. The long, thin fingers were pressed into the chair. "Tell me about Varak," he said softly. "I'm entitled to that; he was a friend."

Chancellor told him, omitting Varak's conclusion that Chasŏng was the key. Alison was too intrinsic to that key; he did not trust St Claire with her name.

"He died," said Peter, "convinced it wasn't you, but one of the other four. 'Never Bravo.' He said that over and over."

"And what about you? Are you convinced?"

"Not yet, but you can convince me. Go public."

"I see." St Claire turned from the chair and looked out at the waters of the Chesapeake. "Varak told you you were programmed with part truth, part lie. Did he explain that?"

"Of course. The missing files were the truth; the assassination was the lie. I never believed it anyway. It was only a concept for a book . . . We've talked long enough. I want your answer. Will you go public with the story, or shall I?"

St Claire turned around slowly. Gone was the anxiety of seconds ago; it was replaced by a gaze so cold Peter was frightened. "Don't threaten me. You're in no position to do that."

"You can't be sure. You don't know what precautions I've taken."

"Do you think you're a character in one of your novels? Don't be foolish." Bravo glanced at the window. The chauffeur was watching them closely, the gun held steady in his hand. "You're not important, and neither am I."

Chancellor felt on the edge of panic. "There's a man in New York who knows I've come to see you. If anything happened to me, he'd identify you. As a matter of fact you spoke with him."

"I listened to him," replied Claire. "I didn't agree to anything. You drove your car to a dead-end road on the banks of the Chesapeake. I am listed in the State Department logs as being in conference at this moment with an undersecretary who will swear I was there. But an alibi isn't necessary. We could kill you anytime. Tonight, tomorrow, next week, next month. But no one wants to do that. It was never part of the plan . . . Four and a half years ago I steered you into the world of fiction. Go back to that world; leave this one to others."

Peter was stunned. Their roles had reversed. St Claire's fears had evaporated, as though the news an outraged young man had brought him were no longer vital. It didn't make sense. What caused the change? His eyes strayed to the window. The chauffeur seemed to sense the tension inside; he had moved closer to the glass. St Claire saw Peter's concern and smiled.

"I said you could go back. That man's there only for my protection. I didn't know the state of your mind."

"You still don't. How can you be sure that I won't leave here and tell the story?"

"Because we both know that isn't the right way. Too many people could lose their lives; neither of us wants that to happen."

"I should tell you I know who Banner, Paris, Venice and Christopher are! Varak wrote out their names for me!"

"I presumed he had. And you must do what you have to."

"Goddamn it, I *will* tell the story! The killing's going to stop! The lying's going to stop!"

"In my judgement," said St Claire icily, "if you do, Alison MacAndrew will be dead before the day is over."

Peter tensed, then took a step towards Bravo.

There was a crash of glass as a single windowpane was smashed; the chauffeur's gun protruded through the open space.

"Go home, Mr chancellor. Do what you have to do."

Peter turned and ran out of the room.

Munro St Claire opened the glass doors and stepped out on to the porch. The air was cold, the winds off the bay growing stronger. The sky was dark now. Soon it would rain.

It was remarkable, St Claire reflected. Even in death Varak orchestrated events. He understood that only one option remained: Peter Chancellor had to take Varak's place. The writer was now the *provocateur*. He had no choice but to go after Banner, Paris, Venice, and Christopher.

Chancellor had said he had been manipulated. What he did not know was that he still was. It was a question now of watching the novelist very closely, keeping track of his every move, until he led them to the one who had the files. Banner, Paris, Venice or Christopher.

There would be a final tragedy, and like the assassination of John Edgar Hoover, it could not be avoided. Two men would die. The betrayer of Inver Brass and, unquestionably, Peter Chancellor.

To the last Stefan Varak had been a professional. With Chancellor's death all avenues would be closed. And Inver Brass disbanded, for ever unknown.

33

"You still won't tell me who he is?" asked O'Brien, across from Peter at the kitchen table. Each had a half-empty glass of whisky in front of him.

"No. Varak was right. He doesn't have the files."

"How can you be sure?"

"Because he would never have let me come back alive."

"Okay, then. I won't probe. I think you're crazy, but I won't probe."

Chancellor smiled. "It wouldn't do you any good. What have you found out about our four candidates? Is there a China connection? Anything remotely possible?"

"Yes. Two possibilities. Two mostly negative. One of the possibilities is pretty dramatic. I'd say a probable."

"Who is it?"

"Jacob Dreyfus. Christopher."

"How?"

"Money. He arranged heavy financial backing for several multinationals operating out of Taiwan."

"Openly?"

"Yes. His public posture was to help create a viable Formosan economy. There was a lot of resistance; most of the banks thought Taiwan would fall, but Dreyfus was a tiger. Apparently he got assurance from Eisenhower and Kennedy. He rallied the institutions and single-handedly brought in new industry."

Peter's doubts were aroused; it was too obvious. A man like Dreyfus would not be obvious. "There was nothing secret? No undercover deals or anything?"

"Not that we can find. Why are they necessary? Money means involvement. That's what we're looking for."

"If money's the bottom line, we are. I'm not convinced it is. Who's the other possibility?"

"Frederick Wells – Banner."

"What's his relationship to the Nationalists?"

"To China, not necessarily the Chinese government. He's a Sinophile. His hobby is early Oriental history. He has one of the most extensive Chinese art collections in the world. They're lent to museums all the time."

"An art collection? What's that got to do with anything?"

"I don't know. We're looking for a connection. It's a connection."

Chancellor frowned. Actually Wells might be a more logical contender than Dreyfus, he considered. A man steeped in the culture of a nation was more apt to be caught up in the mystique of that culture than someone who dealt merely in money. Was it possible that beneath Frederick Wells's pragmatism there was an Oriental mystic in conflict with the Western shell? Or was it preposterous?

Anything was possible. Nothing could be overlooked.

"You said the other two were *mostly* negative. What did you mean?"

"Neither could be construed as having any tangible Chinese sympathies *per se*. Still, Sutherland – Venice ruled against the government in a suit brought by three New York journalists who'd been refused passports to the mainland by the State Department. Essentially he contended that as long as Peking was willing to let them in, it was an abridgement of the First Amendment to prohibit them."

That sounds logical."

"It was. There was no appeal."

"What about Montelán?"

"Paris has been an active anti-Nationalist for a long time. He tagged Chiang Kai-shek as a corrupt warlord years ago. He was outspoken in his support for Red China's admission to the UN."

"So were a lot of people."

"That's what I mean by mostly negative. Both Venice and Paris took positions that might have been unpopular, but they weren't very unusual."

"Unless there were other reasons for those positions."

"Unless anything. I'm going by probabilities at this point. I think we should concentrate on Dreyfus and Wells."

"They can be first, but I'm going to reach all four. Confront each one." Peter finished his whisky.

O'Brien leaned back in his chair. "Would you mind repeating that?"

Peter got out of the chair and carried his glass to the counter, where there was a bottle of scotch. They'd had one drink; Chancellor hesitated, then poured a second. "How many men can you count on? Like those at the motel in Quantico and the ones who followed us here."

"I asked you to repeat what you just said."

"Don't fight me," said Peter. "Help me, but don't fight me. I'm the connecting link between all four men. Each knows how I've been manipulated. One knows – or will *think* he knows – that I've zeroed in on him."

"And then?"

Chancellor poured his drink. "He'll try to kill me."

"That crossed my mind," said O'Brien. You think I'm going to be responsible? Forget it."

"You can't stop me. You can only help me."

"The hell I can't stop you! I can formalize a dozen charges against you that will put you in isolation!"

"Then what? *You* can't confront them."

"Why not?"

Chancellor walked back to the table and sat down. "Because you've been reached. Han Chow, remember?"

O'Brien remained motionless, returning Peter's stare. "What do you know about Han Chow?"

"Nothing, Quinn. And I don't want to know. But I can guess. That first night we talked, when I mentioned Longworth's name, when I told you what happened to Phyllis Maxwell . . . when I said the word Chasŏng. Your face, your eyes; you were frightened. You said the name *Han Chow* as if it was killing you. You looked at me the way you're looking now; you started to accuse me of things I couldn't understand. You may not want to believe this, but I invented you before I met you."

"What kind of crap is that?" O'Brien asked, his voice strained.

Peter drank self-consciously. He took his eyes away from Quinn's and looked at the glass. "You were my cleansing process. My good guy who has to face his vulnerabilities and surmount them."

"I don't understand you."

"Every story about corruption has to have a foil. The person on the side of the angels. I think the difference between a fair novel and a cartoon is that no one in a novel begins as a hero. If he becomes one, it's only because he forces himself to overcome his own fear. I'm not good enough to write a tragedy, so you can't call that fear a tragic flaw. But you can call it a weakness. Han Chow was your weakness, wasn't it? You're part of the files."

Quinn swallowed involuntarily, his eyes still on Chancellor. "Do you want to hear about it?"

"No. I mean that. But I do want to know why you were reached. It had to be before I came to see you."

O'Brien's words were clipped, as if he were afraid of them. "The night before Hoover died, the names of three men were recorded in the security logs at the bureau. Longworth, Krepps and Salter."

"Longworth was *Varak!*" interrupted Peter harshly.

"Or was he?" replied Quinn. "*You* told me Varak died trying to get the files back. A man doesn't kill himself trying to find what he's already got. It was someone else."

"Go on."

"There was no way the real Longworth could have been there. Krepps and Salter were unassigned covers. I couldn't establish any identities. Three unknown men, in other words, were cleared for admittance into Hoover's office that night. I began asking questions. I got a phone call – "

"A high-pitched whisper?" asked Peter.

"A whisper. Very courteous, very precise. I was told to stop. Han Chow was the lever."

Chancellor leaned forward. Two nights ago O'Brien had been the interrogator; now it was his turn. The amateur was leading the professional. Because the professional was frightened.

"What's an unassigned cover?"

"An identity prepared in advance for emergencies. Biographical data. Parents, schools, friends, occupation, service records – that sort of thing."

"In ten minutes a man has a personal history."

"Let's say a couple of hours. He's got to memorize a number of things."

"What led you to the security logs in the first place?"

"The files," said O'Brien. "A few of us wondered what had happened to them; we talked about it. Quietly, just among ourselves."

"But why the security logs?"

"I'm not sure. Process of elimination, I imagine. I checked the shredding rooms, the furnaces, computerized inputs – there were no loads to speak of. I even made inquiries about the cartons of personal effects taken from Flags."

"Flags?"

"Hoover's office. He didn't like the name. It was never used in his presence."

"Were there a lot of cartons?"

"Nowhere near enough to contain the files. To me, that meant they'd been removed. And that scared the hell out of me. Remember, I'd seen them in use."

"Alexander Meredith . . . I've been here before."

"Who's this Meredith?"

"Someone you should meet. Only he doesn't exist."

"Your books?"

"Yes. Go on."

"Since physical removal was a possibility, I began researching the logs. Everyone had known Hoover was dying; there'd even been a code name for his death: 'open territory'. The meaning, I think, is clear. After the director, who?"

"Or what?"

"Right. I pored over the records, going back several months before he died, concentrating on the night entries because skips filled with cartons from Flags would be a little awkward to remove during the day. There was nothing out of order – everything and everyone checked out – until I noticed the logs for the night of 1 May. That's where I found the three names. Two of them were meaningless, without identities." Quinn paused and sipped his whisky.

"What was your theory then? When you realized there were no identities."

"Then, and in part now." O'Brien lit a cigarette. "I think Hoover died a day before they said he did." The agent inhaled deeply.

"That's quite a statement."

"It's logical."

"How?"

"The unassigned covers. Whoever appropriated them had to be familiar with clandestine operations, had to be able to come up with authentic IDs. The agent at the desk that night, a man named Parke, won't discuss what happened. He claims only that the three men were cleared personally on Hoover's scrambler. That checks out; it was used. But I don't think he talked with Hoover. He talked with someone else at Hoover's house. It was enough for him. That phone was sacred."

"So he talked with someone at Hoover's house. So what?"

"Someone whose authority he wouldn't question. Someone who found Hoover dead and wanted those files removed before it was known that Hoover had died and everything was shut up tight. I think the files were taken the night of 1 May."

"Any ideas?"

"Up until two hours ago, yes. I thought it was Hoover's second-in-command, Tolson, and the maniacs. But thanks to you, that's no longer realistic."

"Thanks to me?"

"Yes. You damned near killed a man at the Corcoran Gallery. He was found in a stairwell – one of the maniacs. He was confronted in the hospital and given a choice: name the others in a deposition and resign, or face prosecution, loss of pension, and one hell of a long jail sentence. He chose the first, naturally. Two hours ago I got word from one of our people. All the maniacs have resigned. They wouldn't do that if they had the files."

Chancellor watched O'Brien closely. "Which leads us back to our four candidates. Banner, Paris, Venice and Christopher."

"And Bravo," added O'Brien. "I want you to use him. Follow your own advice: make him force the issue. If he's the man you think he is – or Varak thought he was – he won't refuse. Go back to him."

Chancellor shook his head slowly. "You're missing the point. He's tired; he can't do it any more. Varak knew that. It's why he came to me. It's you and me, O'Brien. Don't look for anyone else."

"Then we'll force the issue! We'll name them!"

"Why? Whatever we said would be denied. I'd be dismissed as a hack writer promoting a book, and far worse, you have to live with Han Chow." Peter pushed his drink away. "And it wouldn't stop there. Bravo was very clear about that. Sooner or later there'd be a couple of accidents. We have to face that. We're expendable."

"Goddamn it, they can't deny the missing files!"

Chancellor watched the angry, frustrated agent. Alex Meredith lived in Quinn O'Brien. Peter decided to tell him everything.

"I'm afraid they might deny it very successfully. Because only half the files are missing. Letters *M* to *Z*. The rest were recovered."

O'Brien was stunned. "Recovered? By whom?"

"Varak didn't know."

Quinn crushed out his cigarette. "Or wouldn't say!"

"Peter! Quinn!"

It was Alison shouting from the living room. O'Brien reached the door first. All was dark. Alison stood by the window, her hand on the curtains.

"What is it?" asked Chancellor, going to her. "What's wrong?"

"Up the road," she answered flatly. "The rise between the gates. I saw someone, I know I did. He stood there, just watching the house. Then he moved back."

Quinn walked rapidly to a panel in the wall partly concealed by the curtains. There were two rows of convex white discs barely distinguishable in the shadows. They looked like two columns of blankly staring eyes. "None of the photo–electric cells was tripped," he said as if he were discussing sameness in the weather.

Peter wondered what precisely made a "sterile' house, besides the radio sets, the heavy glass, and the grillwork everywhere. "Are there electronic beams all around the place? I assume that's what those lights are."

"Yes. All around, infrared and crisscrossed. And there are auxiliary generators underground if the electricity goes off; they're tested every week."

"This place is like the motel in Quantico, then?"

"Same architect designed it, same construction firm built it. Everything is steel, even the doors."

"The front door's wood," interrupted Chancellor.

"Panelling," replied Quinn calmly.

"Could it have been a neighbour out for a walk?" asked Alison.

"Possible, but not likely. The houses here are on three-acre lots. The homes on both sides are owned by State personnel, diplomatic level, very high up. They've been alerted to stay away."

"Just like that?"

"It's nothing unusual. This place is used to house defectors during periods of debriefing."

"There he is!" Alison held the curtain back.

Silhouetted in the distance, between the stone gateposts, was the figure of a man in an overcoat. He was on the rise in the road, outlined against the night sky. "He's just standing there," said Peter.

"Not making any move to go through the gate," added Quinn. "He knows they're tripped. And he wants us to know he knows it."

"Look," whispered Alison. "He's moving now!"

The figure took a step forward and raised his right arm. As though it were a ritualistic gesture, he brought it slowly down in front of him, cutting the air. Instantly there was a hum from the panel. A white disc turned bright red.

The man moved to his left and disappeared into the darkness.

"What was that all about?" O'Brien asked, more of himself than of the others.

"You just said it," answered Chancellor. "He wants us to know he knows the posts are wired."

"That's not so impressive. Most of these houses have alarm systems."

A second hum abruptly shot out of the panel; another white disc turned red.

Then in rapid succession hum followed hum, red light followed red light. The cacophony was all-encompassing, the alarms actually painful to the ears. Within thirty seconds every disc was bright red, every hum activated. The room was washed in magenta.

O'Brien stared at the panel. "They know each vector point! Every damned one!" He ran across the room to a cabinet in the wall. It contained a radio set. O'Brien pressed a button and spoke; there was no mistaking his urgency. "This is Saint Michael's One, come in, please! Repeat, Saint Michael's One, emergency!"

The only response was continuous static.

"Come in, please! This is Saint Michael's One. Emergency!"

Nothing. Only the static, which seemed to grow louder. Peter glanced about the room, adjusting his eyes to the red light and the shadows. "The phone!" he said.

"Don't bother." O'Brien stepped back from the radio. "They wouldn't leave it; they'd cut the wires. It's dead."

It was.

"What about the radio?" asked Alison, trying to speak calmly. "Why can't you get through?"

Quinn looked at them. "They've jammed the frequency, which means they must have known which one it was. It's changed daily."

"Then, try another frequency!" said Chancellor.

"It's no use. Somewhere outside, within fifty to a hundred yards, there's a computerized scanner. By the time I raised anybody, before I could get our message across, they'd jam that, too."

"Goddamn you, try!"

"No," replied O'Brien, looking back up at the panel. "That's exactly what they want us to do. They want us to panic; they're counting on it."

"Why shouldn't we panic? What difference does it make? You said nobody could trace us here. Well, someone did trace us, and the radio's useless! I'm not about to trust your steel constructions and your two-inch glass! They're no match for a couple of blowtorches and a sledgehammer! For Christ's sake, do something!"

"I'm doing nothing, which is what they don't expect. In two or three minutes

I'm going back on that frequency to deliver a second message." Quinn looked over at Alison. "Go upstairs and check the windows front and rear. Call down if you see anything. Chancellor, get back in the dining room. Do the same."

Peter held his place. "What are you going to do?"

"I haven't got time to explain." He walked to the front window and peered out. Peter joined him. Between the gateposts, once more silhouetted against the night sky, stood the figure. He stood motionless for ten or fifteen seconds, and then he seemed to raise both his hands in front of him.

And now a searchlight of several thousand candlepower shot out, slicing through the darkness.

"In the front!" Alison yelled from upstairs. "There's a — "

"We see it!" roared O'Brien. He turned to Chancellor. "Check the rear of the house!"

Peter ran across the room towards the small archway that led to the dining room. A second blinding beam of light hit the much smaller network of windows in the dining room's rear wall. He looked away, closing his eyes; the light made his forehead ache. "There's another back here!" he yelled.

"And on *this* side!" shouted O'Brien, his voice coming from an alcove at the far end of the living room. "Check the kitchen! On the north side!"

Peter raced into the kitchen. As Quinn had anticipated, there was a fourth beam shooting through the grilled windows at the north end of the house. Peter shielded his eyes again. It was a nightmare! Wherever they looked outside, they were blinded by the hot white light. They were being attacked by blinding white light!

"Chancellor!" screamed O'Brien from somewhere outside the kitchen. "Go upstairs! Get Alison and stay away from the windows! Get in the centre of the house. Move!"

Peter could not think, he could only obey. He reached the staircase, grabbed the railing, and swung himself around. As he started up the steps, he heard O'Brien's voice. In spite of the madness it was controlled, precise. He was back at the radio.

"If I'm getting through, emergency is cancelled. Saint Michael's One, repeat. Emergency is cancelled. We've raised Chesapeake on the alternate equipment. They're on their way. They'll be here in three or four minutes. Repeat. Stay out of the area. Emergency cancelled."

"What are you doing?" Chancellor screamed.

"Goddamn it, get upstairs! Get the girl and stay in the centre of the house!"

"Whose side are you *on*?"

"Those ghouls are trying to trick us! They're drawing us to the windows, then blinding us!"

"What are you saying? . . ."

"It's our only hope!" roared the agent. "Now get to Alison and do as I tell you!" He turned back to the radio and again depressed the microphone button.

Peter did not wait to hear O'Brien's words; he saw only that the agent had crouched below the cabinet, behind a chair, as near the floor as possible, his hand extended up to the radio. Chancellor raced up the steps. "Alison!"

"In here! In the front room."

Peter dashed through the upper hall into the bedroom. Alison was at the window, hypnotized by the sight below. "Someone's running!"

"Get away from there!" He pulled her out of the room and into the hall.

The first thing he heard was a metallic sound – an object striking the glass or the grillwork of the bedroom window. And then it happened.

The explosion was thunderous, the force of the vibrations hurling them to the floor. The thick glass of the bedroom window blew out in all directions, fragments embedded themselves in the walls and the floor; pieces of grillwork rang as they struck solid objects.

The entire house shook; plaster cracked as beams were twisted. And Peter realized, as he held Alison in his arms, that there must have been two or three explosions, so closely timed as to be indistinguishable.

No. There had been *four* explosions, one at each side of the house from each source of blinding light. O'Brien had been right. The strategy had been based on luring them to the windows and then throwing explosives. If they were in front of the windows, the sharp fragments of glass would be embedded all over their bodies. Veins and arteries would be severed, heads sliced as his had been sliced so many months ago on the Pennsylvania Turnpike. The similarities were too painful. Even the plaster dust brought back images of the dirt mud inside the reeling car; the woman in his arms another woman.

"Chancellor! Are you all right? Answer me!"

It was Quinn, his voice strident, in pain, from somewhere downstairs. Peter could hear cars racing away in the distance.

"Yes."

"They're gone." O'Brien's voice was weaker now. "We've got to get out of here! Now!"

Peter crawled to the edge of the staircase and reached for the hallway light switch. He snapped it on. O'Brien was bent over the bottom step, his hand gripped on the railing. He looked up at Chancellor.

His face was covered with blood.

Chancellor drove; Alison cradled O'Brien in her arms in the back seat of the unmarked car. The FBI man had fragments of glass embedded in his right arm and shoulder and numerous lacerations about his face and neck, but the wounds were not severe, merely painful.

"I think we should take you home," said Peter, his breath still coming rapidly, accelerated by fear, "to your wife and your own doctor."

"Do as I tell you," replied Quinn, suppressing the effects of his pain. "My wife thinks I'm in Philadelphia; my doctor would ask questions. There's another man we use."

"I think questions are in order right now!"

"No one would listen to the answers."

"You can't do this," said Alison, wiping O'Brien's face with a handkerchief. "Peter's right."

"No, he's not." O'Brien winced. "We're closer to those files than we've ever been. We have to find them. Take them. It's the only answer. For us."

"Why?" asked Peter.

"The Saint Michael's house is restricted territory. A four-million-dollar piece of real estate that's out of reach."

"You reached it," interrupted Chancellor.

"Strangely enough, I didn't." Quinn inhaled audibly. The pain passed, and he continued. "If the State Department or the bureau ever found out how I lied or what I divulged, I'd spend twenty years in a federal prison. I've violated every oath I took."

Peter felt a rush of affection for him. "What happened?" he asked.

"I used Varak's name with the State Department. He was a defector specialist, and I knew the clearance procedures to obtain the use of a sterile house. The bureau's been involved with defectors before. I said it was a joint operation between my office and NSA. Varak's name ensured acceptance. My office could be questioned. Not Varak."

Chancellor swung the car around a long curve to the right. Even in death Varak was part of everything. "Wasn't it dangerous using Varak? He was dead. His body would be found."

"But his prints were burned off years ago. I'd guess that even his dental work was done under an assumed name. With the number of homicides in this city and the procedures the police have to follow, it could be a week before his identity is known."

"What's your point? You used Varak's name to gain access to the Saint Michael's house. So what? Why are we closer to the files?"

"You'd never make a lawyer. Whoever attacked us tonight had to know two specific things. One: the clearing process at State that made the house available. And two: that Varak was dead. Those four men you're going to see. *Banner, Paris, Venice* or *Christopher.* One of them knew both."

Peter gripped the wheel. He remembered the words he had heard only hours ago.

I am listed in the State Department logs as being in conference at this moment . . .

Munro St Claire, ambassador-extraordinary with access to the secrets of the nation, knew Varak was dead.

"Or *Bravo,*" said Chancellor angrily. "The fifth man."

34

There were no further sterile locations available to O'Brien. His resources had come to an end. Even the most sympathetic of his associates would not help him. Saint Michael's One had been destroyed; a four-million-dollar piece of government property had been blown up.

There might have been explanations for that disaster, explanations that could conceivably have been in O'Brien's favour. But there was no explanation in the intelligence community that covered the shocking revelation of a certain killing.

Varak's corpse had been found on the scene, his body riddled with bullets. *Outside* the sterile house. Treason had to be considered.

Peter understood, but his understanding was of no consequence. Varak's body had been found by the men following him, chasing him over the lawns of the Smithsonian, and it had been brought to Saint Michael's to add an insidious complication.

No consequence. Who would listen?

The word was out. A senior agent, Carroll Quinlan O'Brien, had disappeared. The urgent request for Saint Michael's One had been relayed to the State Department from O'Brien's office at the bureau. The clearance procedures included Varak's name and the statement that the request was a joint operation between the FBI and NSA. The statement was false, and O'Brien was nowhere to be found.

And a secret debriefing centre had been destroyed.

Phone calls made by O'Brien from booths along the highways and the back roads revealed a government net closing in with alarming swiftness. Quinn's wife was frantic. Men had come to see her, saying terrible things – men who only days ago had been their friends. O'Brien could only try to reassure her. Quickly. He could say nothing of substance. Undoubtedly their telephone was tapped. Besides, he and Peter and Alison had to get out of each area where a phone call had been made. Phone booths could be traced.

Chancellor called Tony Morgan in New York. The editor was frightened: government people had been in touch with him. And with Joshua Harris. They had made startling accusations. Peter had given false statements to a night-duty officer at the Federal Bureau of Investigation that had resulted in the deaths of Justice Department personnel. Further, he had assaulted an FBI agent in the Corcoran Gallery. The man was in critical condition; if he died, the charge would be murder. Beyond these charges there was evidence linking him to the destruction of highly classified government property, the value of which was four million dollars.

"Lies!" Peter cried. "The man I assaulted tried to kill me! He was a maniac; he was forced to resign. Did they tell you that?"

"No. Who told *you*? An agent named O'Brien?"

"Yes!"

"Don't believe him. O'Brien's an embittered career man, an incompetent. The government people made that clear. He was being eased out when you came along."

"He saved my life!"

"Maybe he just wanted you to think so. Come back, Peter. We'll get you the best lawyers. There are legitimate explanations, the government people realize that. My God, you've been under a terrible strain; last year you were barely alive. Your head was sliced half off; no one knows the extent of the damage."

"That's bullshit and you know it!"

"I don't know it. I'm trying to find reasons." Morgan's voice cracked. He cared.

"Tony, listen to me. I haven't much time. Don't you see what they're doing? They can't admit the truth. They'll try to correct the situation, but they can't admit that the situation exists! Hoover's files are missing!"

"*Get away from the campfire!* You're killing yourself!" Morgan's explosion came from deep within him.

Chancellor understood. Now Tony was being used, manipulated, too. "Did you mention the files?"

"Yes . . ." Morgan could barely speak.

"Did they deny that the files were missing?"

"Of course. They were never missing because they were destroyed. Hoover himself gave the instructions."

The lying was total. Phyllis Maxwell's words came back to Peter. *They fear infected bloodlines.* Were they Phyllis's? Or had he invented them? He was not sure any longer. Fact and fantasy had converged and were one. The only certainty was Quinn O'Brien's judgement:

The files had to be found and produced. There was no other way. Until then, the three of them were fugitives.

"You've been lied to, Tony. I wish to God it weren't so, but it is." He replaced the phone and ran from the booth to the car.

They found an almost deserted motel on the beach at Ocean City. Winter, two days before Christmas; there was a dearth of reservations. A doctor ministered to Quinn, taking the money but no other interest. A transient had fallen through a glass door. It was explanation enough.

On Christmas Eve the rogue agent came close to breaking. Quinn's wife and children were less than two hours away, but they might as well have been on the other side of the world behind fences of barbed wire, crisscrossed by searchlights. He could give them no words of comfort, not even words of hope. There was only the separation and the knowledge of the pain it was causing. Peter watched as O'Brien struggled with his fear and his guilt and his loneliness, knowing that one day his words and his emotions would be put in the mind of another. On paper, Peter was watching a man of reluctant courage whose panic was consuming him and whose heart was breaking, and it both touched and outraged him.

One professional. Two amateurs. Three fugitives. It was up to them now. There wasn't anyone else. Alison could no longer be excluded; she was needed. Together they had to solve the riddle, or the destruction would continue. They would be destroyed themselves in the process. The unfairness of it all was appalling.

It was as painful a Christmas as he and Alison would ever spend, if indeed they should be allowed others. The three of them shared what the motel manager called his Upper South Suite. It was a second-floor complex with windows facing the side of the building as well as the beach. The entrance was below them in plain sight. There was a bedroom and a sitting room with a sofa bed, along with a small kitchenette. The decor was Middle Plastic.

They waited, knowing the wait was necessary. The radio and the television set were kept on to pick up any sudden breaks in the news, any hints that one hundred miles away in Washington someone had decided to acknowledge their disappearance. They bought newspapers from the metal machine in the lobby and read thoroughly. One article caught their attention.

Saint Michael's Md. – An explosion caused by a malfunctioning gas furnace wrought considerable damage to a suburban home in this exclusive section of the Chesapeake. Fortunately there was no one in residence at the time. The owners, Mr and Mrs Chancellor O'Brien, are abroad. They are being contacted . . .

"What does it mean?" asked Peter.

"They want us to know they have proof we were there," replied Quinn. "Subtle, aren't they?"

"How could they know?"

"Easy. Fingerprints. You were in the service; mine are in any number of records."

"But they don't know about Alison." Chancellor felt a surge of relief. It was quickly blunted.

"I'm afraid they do," said O'Brien. "That's why they used the 'Mr and Mrs'."

"I don't care!" Alison was angry. "I *want* them to know. They think they can threaten whomever they please! They won't threaten me. I've got a great deal to say!"

"They'll tell you they have, too," said Quinn softly, walking to the window overlooking the beach and the ocean. "My guess is they'll give you a choice – for reasons of national security. Keep silent about everything you've seen and heard, or face the disclosure of your mother's activities twenty years ago. Activities recently come to light that cost upwards of a thousand American lives in a single day. Inevitably this will raise questions regarding your father."

"Mac the Knife?" said Peter coldly. "Killer of Chasŏng?"

O'Brien turned from the window. "That's too ambiguous. Traitor of Chasŏng would be more like it. Whose drug addict wife whored for an enemy twenty-two years ago and killed American soldiers."

"They wouldn't dare," said Alison.

"It's pretty far-fetched," added Chancellor. "They'd be in dangerous territory. It could snap back in their faces."

"Revelations of this kind," said O'Brien with a quiet conviction Peter recognized as being intensely personal, are always the most dramatic. They go on page one. Later, whatever explanations there are don't seem to be so important. The damage has been done; it's not easily undone."

"I don't believe that," countered Alison nervously. "I don't want to believe it."

"Take my word for it. It's the story of Hoover's files."

"Then, let's get the files," said Peter, folding the newspaper. "We'll start with Jacob Dreyfus."

"He's Christopher, isn't he?" asked Alison.

"Yes."

"It's appropriate," she said, turning her head to look at O'Brien. "I can't believe there's no one we can turn to."

"There's a senator," interrupted Peter. "We can go to him!"

"But even he'll want more than the case I built," said Quinn. "Perhaps not two days ago, but now he will."

"What do you mean?" Chancellor was alarmed. The other evening O'Brien had been so sure of himself. The files were missing; Quinn had the evidence. Things were desperate now.

"I mean we can't go to him."

"Why not?"

"Saint Michael's happened. Destruction of government property, violations of security procedures. He's bound by oath to report it if we make contact. If he doesn't, it's obstruction of justice."

"Shit! Words."

"Law. He may offer to help; if Varak was right, he probably will. But it'll be after the fact. He'll insist we surrender ourselves. Legally that's the only position he can take."

"And if we do, that's where they want us! It's no good!"

Alison touched his arm. "Who are 'they', Peter?"

Chancellor paused. The answer to her question was as appalling as the circumstances in which they found themselves. "Everyone. The man who has the files wants to kill us; we know that now. The people who know the files are missing refuse to acknowledge it and want us quiet. They're willing to sacrifice us to get that silence. Yet, they want the same thing we do." Peter walked slowly across the room past O'Brien to the window. He looked out at the ocean. "You know, Bravo said something to me. He said that four and a half years ago he steered me into a world I hadn't considered. He told me to go back to that world, leave the real one to others. To him and people like him." He turned from the window. "But they're not good enough. I don't know if we are, but I know they're not."

Jacob Dreyfus rose from the breakfast table, not a little annoyed. The butler said the White House was on the line. The damned fool was probably calling to wish him Merry Christmas. *Merry Christmas!* It would not have occurred to the President to call on the first day of Chanukah. That was on the twenty-fifth day of Kislev, and not exactly a date commemorating the birth of Christ.

The word was that the man was drinking heavily. It was not surprising. There had been no administration in the history of the republic like this one. The venality was unsurpassed, the lust for power the essential evil. Of course, the man drank heavily. It was his balm of Gilead.

Jacob considered not taking the call, but respect for the office demanded that he do so.

"Good morning, Mr Pres – "

"I'm not the President," a voice said. "I'm someone else. Just as you are someone else, Christopher."

The blood drained from Jacob's face. It was suddenly difficult to breathe. His gaunt legs were weak; he thought he might fall to the floor. The secret of a lifetime was known. It was beyond belief. "Who's speaking?"

"A man who's been working for you. My name is Peter Chancellor, and I've done my job too well. I've learned things I'm sure you never intended me to learn. And because of that we have to meet. Today. Early this afternoon."

"This afternoon? . . ." Dreyfus felt faint. Peter Chancellor, the writer? How in the name of God could the writer have done this? "I don't make appointments on such short notice."

"You'll make this one," said Chancellor.

The writer was nervous; Jacob could sense it. "I don't take orders. Nor have I ever heard of a Christopher. You used a clever ruse in reaching me. However, I enjoy your little entertainments. If you'd care to lunch with me one day next week."

"This afternoon. No lunch."

"You don't listen – "

"I don't have to. It's possible the 'little entertainments' aren't important any more. Maybe I'm interested in other things. Perhaps you and I can reach an understanding."

"I can't imagine there being an understanding between us."

"There won't be if you talk to the others. Any of them."

"The others?"

"Banner, Paris, Venice or Bravo. Don't talk to them."

Jacob's body trembled. "What are you saying?"

"I'm saying they don't understand you. I think I do. That's the writer's job – to try to understand people. That's why you people used me, isn't it? I believe I understand you. The others can't."

"What are you talking about?" Dreyfus could not control his hands.

"Let's call it a splendid temptation. Anyone familiar with Chasŏng would grasp the logic. But the others, they'd kill you for it."

"Chasŏng? Kill me?" Jacob's eyes blurred. A terrible error had been made! "Where do you want to meet?"

"There's a stretch of beach north of Ocean City in Maryland; any cab driver can find it. So take a cab, and come alone. Get a pencil, Christopher. I'll give you the directions. Be there by one-thirty."

Perspiration poured down Peter's forehead. He leaned against the glass panel of the telephone booth. He had done it; he had actually *done* it. An idea born of fiction worked in fact!

The strategy was to present Christopher – as he would present the others – with options. If Christopher had the files, he could draw only one conclusion: he had been found out. If so, he would agree to meet for the sole purpose of killing the man who had unearthed him. It was doubtful in that case he would come alone.

If Christopher did not have the files, there were two alternatives: dismiss the caller, refusing to meet. Or agree to meet on the dreadful possibility that one or all of the others had betrayed their cause. In this case he would come alone.

Only the middle option – dismissal – exonerated the candidate. And Christopher had not chosen it. Peter wondered if any of them would choose it.

Alison tapped on the door. For a second he simply looked at her through the glass, struck once again by her lovely face, and the intelligent eyes that conveyed love in the midst of anxiety.

He pulled the door open. "One down."

"How did it go?"

"It depends on how you look at it. He'll be here."

The love and the anxiety remained in Alison's eyes. But now there was an added element.

Fear.

35

Frederick Wells looked up from the Christmas breakfast table, astonished. He was not at all sure he had heard the maid's words accurately through the shouts of the children.

"Be quiet!" he ordered; the table was silent. "What did you say?"

"The White House is on the telephone, sir," replied the maid.

The squeals that accompanied the statement served only to remind Wells that he had married too late in life. At least, too late to have young children. If the truth were known, he did not really like children; they were fundamentally uninteresting.

He rose from the table, his eyes briefly locking with his wife's. She seemed to be reading his thoughts.

Why in heaven's name would the White House be calling? Short of blatantly insulting the President and his corps of incompetents Frederick Wells had made his position clear. He did not approve of the man in the White House.

Was it possible the President was using the pretext of Christmas greetings to offer olive branches to his enemies? The man had an embarrassment of embarrassments.

Wells closed the door of his study and walked to his desk, his eyes falling on the row of Yüan and Ming vases locked behind the glass in the case. They were exquisite; he never tired of looking at them. They reminded him that there was peace and beauty in the midst of ugliness.

He picked up the phone.

"Mr Frederick Wells?"

Sixty seconds later his personal world had collapsed. The writer had done it! How was immaterial, the fact was everything!

Inver Brass could protect itself. Instant dissolution, non-existent records . . . If need be, a second justifiable assassination, removing Peter Chancellor from this world.

But what about *him?* Banner had all the weapons save one. And that remaining weapon was exposure. Exposure of a name over which he had absolutely no control. To Wells, exposure was tantamount to destruction.

A lifetime wasted!

Still he could fight. This time on a country road west of Baltimore. An accommodation had to be reached. For everyone's good.

His eyes fell once again on the Chinese vases behind the glass. They did nothing for him.

Carlos Montelán sat back in the church pew and watched with a certain detached hostility as the priest went through the incantations of the Christmas mass. He would not kneel; there were limits to the hypocrisy he indulged in for his wife and family.

Boston was not Madrid, but the memories were too sharp still. The Spanish church had been a sworn companion of the political winds, concentrating on its own survival without compassion for its brutalized flocks.

Montelán felt a vibration an instant before he heard the hum. The worshippers in the immediate vicinity were startled; several turned towards him, their faces angry. The Lord's house was being intruded upon by an alien phone call, but the recipient of the call was a great man, an adviser to Presidents. The Lord's house was not immune to the emergencies of this man's world.

Carlos thrust his hand inside his jacket, shutting off the sound. His wife and children turned; he nodded to them, got out of the pew, and walked up the marble aisle past flickering candles. He went outside, found a telephone booth, and called his service.

The White House was trying to find him, but he was not to return the call. It had to be made on a special telephone. He was to leave a number where he could be reached.

The conspiracies of *idiotas!* thought Montelán. He gave the number of the telephone booth.

The telephone rang, its strident bell echoing harshly within the booth. Swiftly Carlos removed the instrument and brought it to his face.

The words had the effect of sharp knives entering his stomach; the pain was ice cold. The writer had found him out! Everything he had done, everything he had agreed to, was exploded in the accusations of Peter Chancellor.

The agreement, his pact, had been necessary! It was the final preservation of Inver Brass's integrity! There could be no other way!

The writer had to be made to understand! Yes, of course, he'd meet him. A golf course, east of Annapolis, the tenth green? Yes, he'd find it. The hour did not matter; he would be there shortly past midnight.

His hand trembling, Montelán hung up the phone. For several moments he stood in the cold, staring at the instrument. He wondered briefly whether he should pick it up again and call Jacob Dreyfus.

No, he could not do that. Christopher was a very old man. A coronary was not out of the question.

Daniel Sutherland drank his sherry and listened to his son, Aaron, hold forth to his two sisters and their husbands. The couples had flown in from Cleveland for Christmas; the children were in the sun-room with their grandmother and Aaron's wife, wrapping presents. Aaron, as usual, held his audience mesmerized.

The judge watched his son with profoundly mixed emotions. Love was paramount, of course, but close to it was disapproval. The newspapers called Aaron a firebrand, the brilliant lawyer of the legitimate Black left. Still, Daniel wished he weren't so fiery, so sure that only he had the answers to the problems of race.

There was such hatred in his son's eyes, and hatred was not the way; there was no essential strength in it. One day his son would learn that. And one day he would also learn that his ill-conceived loathing of all whites was not only fruitless but often misplaced.

His name said something about that. It had been given him by the dearest friend Daniel had ever had. Jacob Dreyfus.

His name must be Aaron, Jacob had said. *The older brother of Moses, the first priest of the Hebrews. It is a beautiful name, Daniel. And he is a beautiful son.*

The telephone rang.

Aaron's wife, Abby, came through the door. As always Daniel looked at her lovingly, and not without a certain awe. Alberta Wright Sutherland was, perhaps, the finest Black actress in the country. Tall, erect, with a magnificent presence that could, when necessary, subdue her own husband. Her audience, unfortunately, was limited by her taste. She would not accept roles that exploited either her sex or her race.

"I'll try to deliver the line with a straight face, all right?" she said.

"All right, my dear."

"The White House is on the telephone."

"It's bewildering, to say the least," said Daniel, getting out of the chair. "I'll take it in the dining room."

It *was* bewildering. His last four appellate decisions had infuriated the administration, its disapproval expressed in print.

"This is Judge Sutherland."

"You're also Venice," said the flat, hard voice on the phone.

The writer had done it! The commitment of a lifetime was suddenly, awesomely suspended. If it was destroyed, there was nothing, for nothing was worth the loss. The deceivers would inherit the earth.

Daniel listened carefully, weighing each word the writer spoke, each inflection.

There might be a way. It was a desperate strategy, one he was not sure he could survive, much less execute. But it had to be attempted.

Deception.

"Tomorrow morning, Mr Chancellor. At sunrise. The inlet east of Deal Island, the trawler moorings. I'll find it. I'll find you."

Sutherland's eyes were focused absently over the telephone, through the hallway arch into the distant living room. His daughter-in-law came into view. She stood erect and proud.

She had been a superb Medea, Daniel recalled. He remembered her final words in the last act, a cry to the heavens.

Here are my babes, bloodied and slain for the love of a god named Jason.

Sutherland wondered why those words came back to him. Then he knew.

They had been in the corner of his mind only seconds ago.

36

The winter wind came in gusts off the water, bending the wild grass on the dunes. The sun kept breaking through the fast-moving clouds above, intensely bright when it did so but carrying no warmth in its rays. It was early afternoon on Christmas day, and it was cold on the beach.

Chancellor looked down at his footprints. He had been pacing back and forth between the boundaries prescribed by Quinn O'Brien. From within that ten-yard space he had a clean sightline to the clump of foliage above the dunes to the left of the planked path that led from the road. O'Brien was stationed there, concealed from any view but Peter's.

According to O'Brien the tactic was basic. He would wait in the cluster of wild bushes as Jacob Dreyfus arrived. He would make sure that Dreyfus dismissed the cab as he'd been instructed to do; in the event Christopher betrayed them – either by not dismissing the cab or by having his own men in nearby vehicles – Quinn would signal Peter, and they would race to a concealed area above an adjacent beach, where Alison waited in the unmarked car.

This aspect of self-protection Quinn called "up front". The more immediate and less controllable protection was up to Peter. In his jacket pocket was the short-barrelled ·38-calibre revolver he had taken from Paul Bromley on the train. The gun that had been meant to kill him. He was to use it if he had to.

Peter heard a short, piercing whistle: the first signal. The taxi was in sight.

He could not tell how many minutes passed before the gaunt figure came into view. Each second was interminable; the pounding in his chest unbearable. He watched the small, frail Dreyfus unsteadily inch his way over the planks towards the open beach. He was so much *older* than Peter had pictured him, older and infinitely more fragile. The wind off the ocean buffeted him, sand whipped against him, causing him to bow and twist his head; his cane kept slipping on the planks.

He came to the end of the boarded path to the beach and poked his cane into the sand before stepping off. Chancellor could sense the question in the eyes behind the thick glasses. The racked body did not want to make the rest of the journey; could not the younger man come to him?

But Quinn had been adamant. Position was everything; rapid escape had to be considered. Peter held his place, and Dreyfus painfully continued over the wind-swept beach.

Dreyfus fell. Chancellor started across the sand but was stopped by the waving arms of O'Brien beyond. The FBI agent was firm, his message clear.

Dreyfus was within thirty feet, his face seen clearly now. Somehow the banker understood; his expression turned to one of determination. Using his cane, he struggled to his feet. Unsteadily, blinking against the wind and the sand, he walked up to Chancellor; no hand was offered.

"We meet," said Dreyfus simply. "I have things to say to you, and you have things to say to me. Which of us shall begin?"

"Did you follow my instructions?" asked Peter, as he had been instructed to ask.

"Of course I did. We have information to exchange; we both want to know what the other knows. Why add complications? You're wanted, you know."

"Yes. For the wrong reasons."

"The people hunting you don't think so. However, that's irrelevant. If you're not guilty, your innocence can be established."

"The only thing I'm guilty of is being a goddamned fool! Besides, we're not here to discuss me."

"We're here to discuss certain events that affect both of us." Dreyfus brought his hand up to shield his face from a sudden gust of wind. "We must reach an understanding."

"I don't have to reach anything with you! I've been manipulated, lied to, shot at. Four men were killed — four that I know about. Three I watched die. God knows how many people have been driven out of their minds by a whisper over the telephone! You know who they are. I know several." Peter looked away briefly at the water, then turned back to Dreyfus. "I've written it all down. It's not what you expected me to write, but I wrote it. Now, you either reach an understanding with me, or I let the world know who you really are."

Dreyfus stared at him in silence for several moments, the sound of the wind the only intrusion between them. His eyes were devoid of fear. "And who do you think I am? *What* do you think I am?"

"You're Jacob Dreyfus, known as Christopher."

"I concede that. I don't know how you unearthed it, but it's a name I carry with pride."

"Maybe you deserved it until you turned on them."

"Turned on whom?"

"The others. Banner, Paris, Venice, Bravo. You betrayed them."

"Betrayed them? Betrayed Paris? Venice? You don't know what you're talking about."

"Chasŏng! Chasŏng's in Hoover's files, and you've got them!"

Jacob Dreyfus stood motionless, his skull-like face a mirror of shock. "Almighty God, you believe that?"

"You've worked with the State Department!"

"On many occasions."

"You could easily trace a sterile location if you knew where to look!"

"Perhaps. If I knew what it was."

"You knew Varak was dead!"

"Varak dead? That can't be!"

"You're lying!"

"You're a madman. And dangerous. Whatever you've written down must be destroyed. You don't know what you've done. Over forty years of service to the country, countless millions spent. You must understand. I must *make* you understand!"

The unbelievable was happening! Dreyfus reached into his overcoat, his bony hand trembling. Peter knew he was reaching for a gun.

"Don't do that! For Christ's sake, *don't!*"

"I have no choice."

Behind Dreyfus, on the mountain of sand in the cluster of wild bushes, Chancellor could see the figure of O'Brien suddenly stand up. He was seeing what Peter saw: the old man was going to take out a gun. He had come alone, but he had come armed. At the last he was prepared to kill.

Chancellor gripped the weapon in his own pocket, his finger on the trigger. He could not squeeze it! He could not *pull* the trigger!

A shot was heard above the wind. Dreyfus's head snapped back, his throat a mass of blood and shattered bone. His body arched, then fell on its side in the sand. Beyond, O'Brien lowered the gun and raced over the dunes.

Christopher was dead, killed on a deserted stretch of wind-swept beach.

And then Peter saw what was in his hand.

It was a folded page of paper. Not a gun. A letter.

He knelt down, overwhelmed by a sense of revulsion, and removed the paper. He stood up, his breathing erratic, the pain in his temple robbing him of thought. O'Brien was beside him; the FBI man took the paper and unfolded it. Chancellor stared at it, and together they read it. It was a Xeroxed copy of a handwritten letter. The addressee was a single name: Paris.

I.B. must be dissolved. Venice and Bravo agree with this conclusion. I can see it in their eyes, although we have not discussed it among ourselves. We are consumed with memories. But we are old and have very little time left. What concerns me deeply is that the end may come for one or all of us without the proper means for dissolution. Or worse, that our faculties will desert us, and our old tongues will rattle. This can never be allowed. Therefore, I beg you, should age destroy reason, do for one or all of us what we cannot do for ourselves. Under separate cover the tablets have been sent to you by messenger. Place them in old men's mouths and pray for us.

If this is impossible for you, show this letter to Varak. He will understand and carry out what must be done.

Lastly, to Banner, whose weakness is his commitment to his own extraordinary capabilities. He will be tempted to carry on I.B. This also cannot be allowed. Our time is past. If he insists, Varak again will know what to do.

The above is our covenant.

Christopher

"He said he didn't know what a sterile location was," said Peter weakly.

"He didn't know Varak was dead," added O'Brien softly, re-reading the letter. "He wasn't the one."

Chancellor turned away and wandered aimlessly towards the water. He fell to his knees in the lapping waves and vomited.

They buried the body of Jacob Dreyfus in the sand beneath the dunes. The question of responsibility was not considered; time was needed. Desperately. Responsibility would come later.

Frederick Wells would not be met on an expanse of abandoned breach. Instead, the man known as Banner was to walk into a field south of a stretch of road off Route 40 west of Baltimore. O'Brien had used the location for an informer drop less than six months before. He knew it well.

If was a curving section of the highway removed from all-night diners and filling stations; it was bordered by fields that looked like marshland in the darkness.

Peter waited in the field several hundred feet beyond the embankment where Wells was to park his car. He looked up at headlights racing down the highway, flickering and magnified in the rain that drenched the field and sent chills throughout his body. O'Brien had concealed himself halfway down the embankment, his weapon drawn, waiting. Again, Chancellor had his instructions: at the first sign of the unexpected he was to immobilize Frederick Wells with his gun. Fire it if need be.

For added precaution O'Brien had a torch. Should Wells bring others with him, Quinn would switch on the light, covering the lens with his fingers, and wave it in circles. It was the signal for Peter to run across the field and up the road, where Alison waited in the car.

There were two blasts of an impatient horn from the road. A car slowed down and pulled over on the shoulder; the car behind swung around it, accelerating in anger.

The car stopped by the embankment, and a lone figure climbed out. It was Frederick Wells; he walked to the railing overlooking the field and peered through the rain.

The beam of light shot down briefly from the far end of the embankment. It was O'Brien's first signal. Wells was alone; there were no overt signs of a weapon. Peter did not move; it was up to Banner to come to him.

Wells climbed over the railing and made his way down the incline. Chancellor crouched in the wet grass and withdrew the .38.

"Take your hands out of your pockets!" he shouted as he'd been instructed to shout. "Walk forward slowly with your hands at your sides."

Wells stopped and stood motionless in the rain, then did as he was told. His bare hands held out at his sides, he walked into the darkness of the field. When he was within five feet, Peter rose from the ground.

"Stop right here!"

Wells gasped, his eyes wide. "Chancellor?" He took several deep breaths, blinking as the rain pounded down on his face, saying nothing until his breathing was steady – an Oriental exercise to suspend thought to restore calm.

"Listen to me, Chancellor," Wells said at last. "You're beyond your depth. You've made friends with the wrong people. I can only appeal to whatever feeling you have for this country to give me their names. I know one, of course. Give me the rest."

Peter was stunned. Wells had taken the initiative. "What are you talking about?"

"The files! Files *M* to *Z*! They have them, and they're using you. I don't know what they've promised you – what *he's* promised you. If it's your life, I'll guarantee it far better than he could. The girl's too."

Chancellor stared at the shadowed, wet face of Frederick Wells. "You think somebody sent me. You think I'm a messenger. I never mentioned the files to you over the phone."

"Did you think you had to? For God's sake, stop it! Destroying Inver Brass is no answer! Don't let them do it!"

"Inver Brass?" Peter's mind raced back to the handwritten letter in a dead man's hand, the covenant between Christopher and Paris. I. B. *must be dissolved . . . I.B. . . .* Inver Brass.

"You can't become a part of it, Chancellor! Don't you see what he's done? He programmed you too well; you learned much too quickly. You were closing in on *him!* He can't kill you now; he knows we'd know he did it. So he tells you things, reveals Inver Brass, feeds you lies so you'll set us against one another!"

"Who?"

"The man who has the files. Varak!"

"Oh, *Christ . . .*" Peter's stomach knotted.

It was not Frederick Wells.

"I have the answer." Wells was speaking in his sharp, nasal voice; Peter barely listened, so futile did everything suddenly seem. "It will extricate you and get the files back. They *must* be taken! You tell Varak there's no way he can connect Inver Brass with the events of last May. There are no records, no transactions that can be traced. Varak was the killer, not Inver Brass. He did his job too well; there are no links. But I can and will raise disturbing questions about his every move from April to the night of 10 May. I'll do it in a way that will leave no doubt; he'll be exposed. And we remain unknown. Carry that message back."

It was all too much for Peter. Truths, half-truths, and lies piled on abstractions; dates woven into a fabric of accusations. "You think Varak betrayed the others?"

"I know it! It's why you must work with me. The country needs me now. Varak has those files!"

The rain came down in torrents. "Get out of here," Peter said.

"Not until I have your word."

"*Get out of here!*"

"You don't *understand!*" Wells could not tolerate the dismissal. His arrogance gave way to desperation. "The country needs me! I must lead Inver Brass. The others are old, weak! Their time is finished. I'm the one! I must have those files. I'm *in them!*"

Chancellor raised the revolver. "Get out of here before I kill you."

"You want that excuse, don't you? That's what you *really* want!" Banner's words were rushed, his voice again strident, now panicked. "Varak told you it was *me*, didn't he? I had nothing to do with it! It was *him!* I asked him to intercede with Bravo, that's all I asked him to do! He was closest to St Claire; everyone knew that. He was sworn to protect us all, each one of us . . . You were going back to Nuremberg! We couldn't allow you to do that! Varak understood!"

"Nuremberg . . ." Peter felt the rain on his skin. It had been raining the night his silver Continental was hit, the night Cathy had died. There was a highway in the distance now, as there was then; and an embankment. And the rain.

"But good *God!* I never wanted him to kill you! Or the girl! That was *his* decision; he was never afraid to act."

Varak. Longworth. The horrible mask of a face behind the wheel. A driver at night oblivious to the storm, staring straight ahead as he killed.

Varak, the professional, who used vehicles as weapons.

The pain in his temple was unendurable. Peter raised the gun, pointing it at Banner's head. He squeezed the trigger.

Banner's life was saved by the inexperience of an amateur. The safety catch prevented the hammer from exploding the shell.

Frederick Wells ran through the rain towards the road.

East of Annapolis, several miles beyond the Severn River, were the rolling hills of the Chanticlaire. It was a patrician golf club formed in the thirties by the proper aristocrats, thus given to exclusivity, and by extension, it was a gathering place for executives of the Central Intelligence Agency, an organization prone to the old school tie.

It was also used as an information drop between agents of the FBI and the CIA during those times when J. Edgar Hoover stopped the flow of data from the former to the latter. O'Brien knew it well; it was to be the meeting ground for Carlos Montelán. Paris was to be there no sooner than midnight, no later than twelve-thirty. On the tenth tee; the instructions were clear.

Quinn took the wheel; he knew the back roads from Route 40 to the Chanticlaire. Alison and Peter sat in the back. Chancellor did his best to dry off, his mind still numbed by the shock of Banner's revelation.

"He killed her," said Peter, drained, absently watching the headlights in the diminishing rain. "Varak killed Cathy. What kind of man was he?"

Alison gripped his hand. O'Brien spoke from behind the wheel.

"I can't answer that. But I don't think he thought in terms of life and death.

In certain situations he thought only of eliminating problems."

"He wasn't human."

"He was a specialist."

"Which is the coldest thing I've ever heard."

O'Brien found an out-of-the-way country inn. They went inside for warmth and coffee.

"Inver Brass," said Quinn at the table in the dimly lit dining room. "What is it?"

"Frederick Wells assumed I knew," replied Peter. "Just as he assumed Varak had sent me to him."

"You're sure he wasn't feeding you false information? Trying to throw you off?"

"I'm sure. His panic was genuine. He's in the files. Whatever's there could ruin him."

"Inver Brass," repeated O'Brien quietly. "The *inver* is Scottish, the *brass* could be anything. What does the combination mean?"

"I think you're overcomplicating things," said Peter. "It's the name they've given their nucleus."

"Their what?"

"Sorry. *My* 'Nucleus'."

"Your book?" asked Alison.

"Yes."

"I'd better read that damned manuscript," said O'Brien.

"Is there any way," asked Chancellor, "that we can trace Varak's movements from 10 April to 2 May of this year?"

"Not now there isn't," O'Brien answered.

"We know Hoover died on 2 May," continued Peter. "So the implication – "

"The implication won't stand scrutiny," interrupted Quinn. "Hoover died of heart failure. That's been established."

"By whom?"

"Medical records. They were fragmentary but complete enough."

"So we're back at the beginning," concluded Peter wearily.

"No, we're not," said Quinn, looking at his watch. "We've eliminated two candidates. It's time for the third."

It was the most secure contact location the FBI man had engineered, and for that reason he was particularly cautious. They arrived at the Chanticlaire an hour before Montelán was due to appear; the agent explored the area thoroughly. When he had finished, he told Peter to walk out to the tenth tee while Alison remained in the car at the far end of the drive near the gates and he concealed himself in the grass off the fairway.

The ground was wet, but the rain had stopped. The moon struggled to penetrate the passing clouds, its light progressively getting brighter. Chancellor waited in the shadows of an overhanging tree.

He heard the sound of a car driving through the open gate and looked at the radium dial of his wristwatch. It was five minutes past midnight; Montelán was anxious. Yet no more filled with anxiety than he was, reflected Peter. He felt the handle of the gun in his jacket pocket.

In less than a minute he saw the figure of Carlos Montelán walking rapidly around the corner of the clubhouse. The Spaniard was walking too fast, Peter thought. A frightened man was a cautious man; the figure coming towards him was not cautious.

"Mr Chancellor?" Paris began calling fifty yards from the tee. He stopped and put his left hand into his overcoat pocket. Peter took out his ·38 and levelled it in front of him, watching in silence.

Montelán pulled his hand from his pocket. Chancellor lowered the gun. Paris held a torch; he turned it on, shooting the beam in several directions. The shaft of light hit Peter.

"Turn off the light!" yelled Chancellor, crouching.

"As you wish." The shaft of light disappeared.

Remembering O'Brien's instructions, Peter ran several yards away from his former position, keeping his eyes on Montelán. The Spaniard made no extraneous moves; he had no weapon. Chancellor stood up, knowing he could be seen in the moonlight.

"I'm over here," he said.

Montelán turned, adjusting his eyes. "Sorry about the light. I won't do that again." He approached Peter. "I had no trouble coming here. Your directions were excellent."

In the pale yellow light Peter could see Montelán's face. It was strong, the features Latin, the dark eyes searching. Peter realized there was no fear in the man. In spite of the fact that he had been told to meet a stranger, known to him by name only, on an isolated golf course in the middle of the night – a stranger he had to at least consider might do him violence – Paris behaved as though their meeting were merely a mutually desirable business conference.

"This is a gun in my hand," said Chancellor, raising the barrel. Montelán squinted. "Why?"

"After what you've done to me – what Inver Brass has done to me – can you even ask?"

"I don't know what's been done to you."

"You're lying."

"Let me put it this way. I know that you were given misinformation on the premise that you might write a novel based on that false information. It was hoped this might alarm certain individuals who are part of a conspiracy and force them to reveal themselves. In all candour I've doubted the wisdom of the exercise since I first heard of it."

"That's all you've learned?"

"I gather there's been some unpleasantness, but we were given assurance that no harm would come to you."

"Who are the 'certain individuals'? What's the 'conspiracy'?"

Paris paused for a moment as if resolving a conflict within himself. "If no

791

one's told you, perhaps it's time someone did. There *is* a conspiracy. A very real and dangerous one. An entire section of J. Edgar Hoover's private files is missing. They've disappeared."

"How do you know that?"

Again Montelán fell briefly silent, then having made the decision, continued. "I can't give you specifics, but since you mentioned the name and – more to the point – referred to the others in your telephone call this morning, I must assume you've learned more than was intended for you to learn. It doesn't matter; it's coming to an end. Inver Brass managed to get hold of the remaining files."

"How?"

"I can't tell you that."

"Can't or won't?"

"A little of both, perhaps."

"That's not good enough!"

"Do you know a man named Varak?" asked Paris softly, as if Chancellor had not shouted.

"Yes."

"Ask him. He may tell you, he may not."

Peter studied the Spaniard's face in the moonlight. Montelán was not lying. He did not know of Varak's death. Chancellor felt a hollowness in his throat; a third contender had been eliminated. Questions remained, but the most vital issue was resolved. Paris did not have the files.

"What did you mean when you said it didn't matter what I'd learned? That it was 'coming to an end'?"

"The days of Inver Brass are over."

"What exactly is Inver Brass?"

"I presumed you knew."

"Don't presume anything!"

Again the Spaniard paused before he spoke. "A group of men dedicated to the well-being of this nation."

"A nucleus," said Peter.

"I imagine it could be called that," replied Montelán. "It's made up of outstanding men, men of extraordinary character and great love for their country."

"Are you one of them?"

"I was privileged to be asked."

"This is the group that was formed to warn Hoover's victims?"

"It has had many functions."

"How many weeks ago were you asked to join? Or was it months?"

For the first time Paris seemed bewildered. "Weeks? Months? I've been a member for four years."

"Four years?!" There was the dissonant chord again. As far as Peter knew, the group – St Claire's nucleus, this Inver Brass – had been formed to combat Hoover's final and most vicious tactic: the exploitation of fear through his private files. It was a late-in-the-day defence born of necessity. A year, a year and a half, two years at the most, had been the span of its existence. Yet Paris spoke of four years. . .

792

And Jacob Dreyfus had used the phrase "forty years of service"; then he'd followed it with a reference to countless millions spent". At the time, during those moments of panic on the beach, Chancellor had thought Dreyfus had somehow been referring to himself. But now... *forty years... countless millions.*

Frederick Wells's biting words suddenly came back to Peter. *The country needs me. I must lead Inver Brass. The others are old, weak! Their time is finished. I'm the one!*

Four years... *forty* years! Countless *millions.*

And finally Peter remembered Dreyfus's letter to Montelán. The covenant between Christopher and Paris.

We are consumed with memories.

Memories of what?

"Who are you people?" he asked, staring at Montelán.

"Beyond what I've said, I'll say no more. You were right, Mr Chancellor. I presumed. In any event, I'm not here to discuss such matters. I came to try to convince you not to interfere any longer. Your inclusion was an error of judgement by a brilliant but frustrated man. There was no great harm as long as you remained in the background, poking among the ruins, but should you surface and be asked questions publicly, in that way there's disaster."

"You're frightened," said Chancellor, surprised. "You pretend to be very cool, but underneath you're frightened out of your wits."

"I most certainly am. For you as well as all of us."

"Does 'us' mean Inver Brass?"

"And many others. There's a rift in the country between the people and its leaders. There is corruption at the highest levels of government; it goes beyond mere power politics. The Constitution has been seriously assaulted, our way of life threatened. I'm not being melodramatic, I'm telling you the truth. Perhaps a person not born here, who has seen it happen before, understands more clearly what these things mean."

"What's the answer? Or is there one?"

"There certainly is. The rigid, dispassionate application of the legal process. I repeat, dispassionate. The people must be awakened to the real dangers of abuse. Clearly, reasonably, not propelled by emotional accusations and demands for recrimination. The system will work if it's given the chance; the process has begun. It's *no* time for explosive disclosures. It's a time for intensive examination. And reflection."

"I see," said Peter slowly. "And it's not the time for the exposure of Inver Brass, is it?"

"No," said Montelán firmly.

"Perhaps it will never be."

"Perhaps. I told you. Its time has passed."

"Is that why you have your covenant with Jacob Dreyfus? With Christopher?"

It was as though Paris had been struck in the face. "I wondered," he said softly. "I nearly phoned him but thought better of it. So you reached him."

"I reached him."

"I'm sure he spoke as I have. His devotion to this country is infinite. He understands."

"I don't. I don't understand any of you people."

"Because your knowledge is limited. And you'll learn no more from me. I can only beg you again to go away. If you continue, I think you'll be killed."

"That's been suggested. One last question: what happened at Chasŏng?"

"Chasŏng? The Battle of Chasŏng?"

"Yes."

"A terrible waste. Thousands lost over an inconsequential stretch of barren territory. Megalomania superseded civilian authority. It's on the record."

Peter realized he still held the gun in his hand. It was meaningless; he put it back in his pocket.

"Go back to Boston," he said.

"You'll consider carefully everything I've said?"

"Yes." But he knew he would have to go on.

For Daniel Sutherland, O'Brien had chosen an inlet east of Deal Island on the Chesapeake. The rendezvous was a commercial marina where fishing boats were moored, primarily oyster craft that would of necessity stay in shore for another week or two. The beds were poor; the ocean was not hospitable at this point in December.

The waves lapped incessantly against the pilings beneath the docks. The creaking of the boats at their moorings kept up a steady, snapping tattoo as the gulls cawed in the sky above in the early light.

Venice. The last of the candidates, thought Peter as he sat on an oily railing of a trawler at the end of the dock. The last, that is, unless Bravo . . . That Peter would go back to Munro St Claire seemed certain. The possibility that Sutherland was the betrayer of Inver Brass, the whispering killer who had the files, was remote. But then nothing was as it seemed to be. Anything was conceivable.

Sutherland had told him that the committee formed to combat Hoover's viciousness had been disbanded. Too, Sutherland had maintained that the files had been destroyed. As a member of Inver Brass he knew both were lies.

But why would Sutherland want the files? Why would he kill? Why would he belie the law he championed?

Peter could barely distinguish the entrance to the dock, beyond the hoist pulleys and the engine winches. They formed a strange, silhouetted archway, sharp black lines against a background of grey. He looked across the short span of water to his right where he knew O'Brien lay concealed on the deck of a scow. He turned his head to the left, trying to make out the car sandwiched between dry-docked oyster boats pulled out of the water for repairs. Alison was in the car. In her hand was a book of matches, a single match torn off, ready to strike. It was to be struck and held in the window, its flame shielded from the front, should there be anyone but the judge in Sutherland's car.

Suddenly, Peter heard the low tones of a powerful engine approaching in the distance. Moments later dual headlight beams shot through the fenced entrance into the shipyard, reflecting off the dry-docked hulls. The car continued on, turning right down a wide space between the boats towards the water's edge.

The headlights were shut off, leaving a lingering residue of light in Chancellor's eyes. He crouched below the gunwale of the trawler, and kept watching the base of the dock. Lapping waves slapped against pilings in erratic rhythms; the creaking of boats continued ceaselessly.

A car door opened and closed, and moments later Sutherland's immense figure emerged from the darkness and filled a large area under the arch of steel and the taut metal coils of the winches. He walked out on the dock towards Peter, his footsteps heavy and cautious but without hesitation.

He reached the end of the dock and stood motionless, looking across the bay, a giant Black man at dawn by the water's edge. Daniel Sutherland looked as if he were the last man on earth, contemplating the end of the universe. Or waiting for a barge to dock and men to order a huge buck to start unloading.

Peter stood up, pushing himself away from the trawler's railing, his hand in his pocket, gripping the gun. "Good morning, Judge. Or should I call you Venice?"

Sutherland turned and looked towards the trawler's slip where Chancellor stood on the narrow walkway. He said nothing.

"I said good morning," continued Chancellor softly, even courteously, unable to shut out the respect he felt for this man who had achieved so much in a lifetime. "I heard you," replied Sutherland in his resonant voice, itself a weapon. "You called me Venice."

"That's the name you're known by. That's the name Inver Brass gave you."

"You're only half right. It's a name I gave myself."

"When? Forty years ago?"

Sutherland did not at first reply. He seemed to absorb Peter's statement with equal degrees of ire and astonishment, equally controlled. "When's not important. Neither's the name."

"I think both are. Does Venice mean what I think it means?"

"Yes. The Moor."

"Othello was a killer."

"This Moor is not."

"That's what I'm here to find out. You lied to me."

"I misled you for your own good. You should never have been involved at the start."

"I'm sick of hearing that. Why was I, then?"

"Because other solutions had failed. You seemed worth a try. We faced a national catastrophe."

"Hoover's missing files?"

Sutherland paused, his large dark eyes locked with Chancellor's. "You've learned then," he said. "It's true. Those files had to be found and destroyed, but all attempts to locate them had failed. Bravo was desperate and sought desperate measures. You were one of them."

"Then, why did you tell me the files had been destroyed?"

"I was asked to confirm certain aspects of the story given you. However, I didn't want you to take yourself too seriously. You're a novelist, not an historian. To allow you greater latitude would have placed you in danger. I couldn't permit that."

"Bait me in, but not all the way in, was that it?"

"It'll do."

"No, it won't. There's more. You were protecting a group of men who call themselves Inver Brass. You're one of them. You told me a few concerned men and women got together to fight Hoover and then disbanded after his death. You lied about that, too. This group goes back forty years."

"You've let your imagination run away with you." The judge was breathing harder.

"No, I haven't. I've spoken to the others."

"You've *what!*" Gone was the control, the sense of judicial propriety that underscored his every phrase. Sutherland's head trembled in the early light. "What in the name of God have you done?"

"I listened to the words of a dying man. And I think you know who that man was."

"Oh God! *Longworth!*" The Black giant froze.

"You *know!*" The shock caused Peter to lose his breath. His muscles tensed, his foot slipped; he steadied himself. It *was* Sutherland. None of the others had made the connection. Sutherland had! He would not have made it, *could* not have made it, without following Varak, without tapping the Hay-Adams's switchboard!

"I know it now," said the judge in a flat, ominous monotone. "You found him in Hawaii, you brought him back and broke him. You may have touched off a chain of events that could drive the fanatics over the edge! Send them screaming into the streets with their charges of conspiracy and worse! What Longworth did was necessary. It was *right!*"

"What the hell are you talking about? Longworth was Varak, and you damned well know it! He found me! He saved my life, and I watched him die."

Sutherland seemed to lose his equilibrium. His breathing stopped, his immense body wavered as if he might fall. He spoke softly, in deep pain. "So Varak was the one. I had considered it but didn't want to believe it. He worked with others; I thought it was one of them. Not Varak. The wounds of his childhood never healed; he couldn't resist the temptation. He had to have all the weapons."

"Are you telling me he took the files? It won't wash. He didn't have them."

"He delivered them to someone else."

"He what?" Chancellor took a step forward, stunned by Sutherland's words.

"His hatred ran too deep. His sense of justice was twisted; all he wanted was revenge. The files could give him that."

"Whatever you're saying, it's wrong! Varak gave his life to find those files! You're lying! He told me the truth! He said it was one of four men!"

"It is . . ." Sutherland looked away across the water. The awful silence was broken by the sounds of the boat basin. "Almighty God," he said, turning back to Peter. "If he had only come to me. I might have convinced him there was a better way. If he'd only come to me – "

"Why should he? You weren't above suspicion. I've spoken to the others; you're still not. You're one of the four!"

"You arrogant young fool!" thundered Daniel Sutherland, his voice echoing throughout the bay. Then he spoke quietly, with enormous intensity. "You say I lie. You say you've spoken to the others. Well, let me tell you, you've been lied to far more expeditiously by someone else."

"What does that mean?"

"It means that I know who has those files! I've known for weeks! It is, indeed, one of four men, but it's not I. The discovery was not so difficult. What will be difficult is getting them back! Convincing a man who's gone mad to seek help. You and Varak may have made that impossible!"

Peter stared at the Black giant. "You've never said anything to anyone – "

"I couldn't!" interrupted the judge. "The situation had to be contained; the risks were too great. He hires killers. He has a thousand hostages in those files." Sutherland took a step towards Chancellor. "Did you tell anyone you were coming here? Did you watch to see if you were followed?"

Chancellor shook his head. "I travel with my own protection. No one followed me."

"You travel with what?"

"I'm not alone," said Peter quietly.

"Others are *with* you?"

"It's all right," said Chancellor, frightened by the old man's sudden dread. "He's *with* us."

"*O'Brien?*"

"Yes."

"Oh, my God!"

There was a sudden loud splash of water. It could not be mistaken for an anxious fish. There was a human being beneath the dock. In darkness. Peter ran to the edge.

Two rapid explosions of gunfire came from behind him. From the direction of Quinn's boat! Chancellor dived to the wood, flattening himself against the planks. The whole area erupted; shots came from the surface of the water, from the railings of other boats. Spits cracked in the air: bullets fired from weapons equipped with silencers. Peter rolled to his left, instinctively seeking the cover of adjacent pilings. Wood splintered in front of his face; he covered his eyes, opening them in time to see a flash of gunfire from an opposing dock. He brought his own gun up and pulled the trigger repeatedly in panic.

There was a scream, followed by the sounds of a falling body, crashing into unseen objects and rolling over the dock into water.

Chancellor heard a grunt to his left. He turned. A man in a black wet suit was climbing over the edge of the pier. Peter aimed and fired; the man-monster arched his back, then fell forward in a last attempt to reach out at him.

Alison! He had to get to her! He lunged backward and came in startled contact with human flesh. It was Sutherland's body, his face covered with blood, his overcoat stained throughout the upper section; splotches of deep red were everywhere.

The Black giant was dead.

"Chancellor!" O'Brien was yelling at him, his voice penetrating the explosions and the spits of gunfire. For what purpose? To kill him? Who was O'Brien? *What* was O'Brien?

He would not answer; he would not become a target. Survival forced him to move. He lurched over the slain Daniel Sutherland towards the mass of steel machinery at the foot of the dock. He scrambled on all fours, diving, twisting, zig-zagging as fast as he could over the filthy planks.

There was the ping of a ricocheting bullet. He had been *seen!* He had no choice; he rose partially off the ground, his legs aching in fear, and sped towards the black iron objects. He was in front of them; he plunged between the arch of cascading coils, twisting to his right behind a shield of steel.

"Chancellor! *Chancellor!*" Still O'Brien's shouts punctuated the gunfire. Still Peter would not heed him. For there was only one explanation. The man he had pitied, admired, given his life to, had led him into a trap!

There was a sudden fusillade, followed by an explosion. Flames leapt up from the stern of the trawler two docks away. Then a second detonation; another boat erupted in fire. There were shouts, orders; men ran over the docks and jumped from railings into the water. The gunfire seemed to diminish in the confusion. Then there was a single loud report, and a third boat burst into flames. Another shot followed; a man screamed. He screamed *words*.

The words were unintelligible. All but one: Chasŏng.

Chasŏng!

A man was hit, his last words a roar of defiance before death; no other motive could cause the fanatic sound. It was the language Varak had not understood! Chancellor now heard it for himself; it was like no other he had ever heard.

The noise abated. Two men in wet suits climbed over the end of the short pier where Daniel Sutherland lay dead. Across the water on the opposing dock three shots came in rapid succession; a ricocheting bullet glanced harshly off a gearbox above Peter and imbedded itself in the wood beside him. A figure raced towards the shore, jumping between the boats, over railings, on to decks, around wheelhouses. More shots; Chancellor ducked beneath the shield of steel. The figure of the racing man reached the muddy shore and dived beyond a beached rowboat. He stayed there only seconds, then rose and ran into the darkness.

O'Brien! Peter watched in disbelief as he disappeared into the woods that bordered the boat basin.

The gunfire stopped. From the water beyond the docks came the sound of a motor launch. Chancellor could not wait any longer. He crawled out of his sanctuary, got to his feet, and raced between the boats towards the automobile.

Alison lay prostrate on the ground next to the car. Her eyes were glazed, her body trembled. Peter sank beside her and held her in his arms.

"I never thought I'd see you alive!" she whispered, her fingers digging into him, her moist cheek against his.

"Come on. Quickly!" He pulled her to her feet. He yanked the car door open and pushed Alison inside.

There was a commotion on the dock. The motor launch he had heard in the distance had pulled alongside. There was an argument; men turned, several started towards the shore.

It was the moment to move. In seconds it would be too late. He looked through the windshield and turned the ignition key. The motor groaned but did not start.

The morning dampness! The car had not run for hours!

He heard shouts from the base of the dock. Alison heard them, too; she grabbed for his gun from the seat where he had dropped it. Automatically, with the swiftness born of experience, she cracked out the magazines.

"You've only got two bullets left! Do you have others?"

"Bullets? No!" Peter turned the key again, pressing the accelerator.

The figure of a man in a wet suit loomed between the hulls of the beached trawlers. He started towards them.

"Watch your eyes!" shouted Alison.

She fired the weapon, the explosion thunderous inside the car. The side window blew open. The motor started.

Chancellor yanked the gear lever and plunged his foot on to the accelerator. The car lurched forward wildly. He swung the wheel to his right; the car skidded sideways, throwing up sprays of mud and dust. He straightened the wheel out and sped towards the exit turn.

They could hear shots behind them; the back window exploded.

Chancellor pushed Alison to the floor of the car as he whipped the steering wheel to the left. She would not stay down but lunged up, levelling the second and last bullet. Briefly the gunshots behind them stopped.

Then they resumed firing, the bullets wild, without effect. Peter reached the entrance of the boat basin and raced down the road cut out of the forest towards the highway.

They were alone. An hour before there had been three fugitives; now there were two.

They had given their trust to Quinn O'Brien; he had betrayed them.

Whom would they turn to now?

They had only each other. Houses and office buildings were watched. Friends, acquaintances, placed under surveillance. Telephones were tapped, their car known. The highways and side roads would soon be patrolled.

Peter began to feel a remarkable change within him. He wondered for a moment whether it was real or merely another aspect of his imagination; whatever, he decided he was grateful for it.

The fear – the sense of utter helplessness – was replaced by anger.

He gripped the wheel and drove on, the scream of death he had heard only minutes before echoing in his ears.

Chasŏng!

After everything was said, it was still the key.

37

The average citizen was not aware of their flight. No radio broadcasts described them; no photographs appeared on television or in the newspapers. And yet they ran, for ultimately there would be no protection; laws had been broken, men had been killed. To turn themselves in would lead to a dozen traps. The unknown men were everywhere among the authorities.

Hoover's private files were their only vindication, their only hope of survival.

Death had brought them nearer to the answer. Varak had said it was one of four men. Peter had added a fifth. Now Sutherland was dead and Dreyfus was dead and that left three. Banner, Paris and Bravo.

Frederick Wells, Carlos Montelán, Munro St Claire.

You've been lied to far more expeditiously by someone else.

But there was the key. *Chasŏng.* It was not a lie. One of the three remaining members of Inver Brass was somehow deeply, irrevocably associated with the waste at Chasŏng twenty-two years ago. Whoever he was, he had the files.

Peter recalled Ramirez's words. *Chasŏng is . . . represented in scores of veterans' hospitals.*

There was only a remote chance that something might be learned from the survivors. Their memories would be vague, but it was the only step he could think of. Perhaps the last one.

His thoughts turned to Alison. She had developed an anger matching his own, and in that anger was a remarkable sense of inventive determination. The general's daughter had resources, and she used them; her father had accumulated favours during a lifetime of service. She approached only those she knew were far removed from the centres of Pentagon influence and control. Men she had not spoken to for years received telephone calls asking for help – tactful assistance to be rendered privately, without questions.

And so that no complete picture be traced to a single source, the requests were divided.

An air force colonel attached to NASA Ordnance met them across the Delaware line in Laurel and gave them his car. O'Brien's vehicle was hidden in the woods near the banks of the Nanticoke River.

An artillery captain at Fort Benning made reservations for them in his name at a Holiday Inn outside Arundel Village.

A lieutenant commander in the Third Naval District, once a skipper on an LCI at Omaha Beach, drove to Arundel and brought three thousand dollars to their room. He accepted – without question – a note from Chancellor addressed to Joshua Harris instructing the literary agent to pay the borrowed sum.

The last thing they needed was the hardest to get: the casualty records of Chasŏng. In particular, the whereabouts of the permanently disabled survivors. If there was a single focal point that might be under round-the-clock surveillance, it was Chasŏng. They had to work on the assumption that unseen men were watching, waiting for an interest to be shown.

It was nearly eight in the evening. The lieutenant commander had left minutes ago, the three thousand dollars dropped casually on the night table. Peter reclined wearily on the bed, leaning against the headboard. Alison was across the room at the desk. In front of her were her notes. Dozens of names, most crossed out for one reason or another. She smiled.

"Are you always so nonchalant about money?"

"Are you always so handy with a gun?" he replied.

"I've been around weapons most of my life. It doesn't mean I approve of them."

"I've been around money for about three and a half years. I approve of it very much."

"My father used to take me out to the pistol and rifle ranges several times a month. When nobody was around, of course. Did you know I could dismantle a carbine and a regulation ·45 blindfolded by the time I was thirteen? God, how he must have wished I were a boy!"

"God, how he must have been out of his mind," said Chancellor, imitating her cadence. "What are we going to do about the casualty lists? Can you pull another string?"

"Maybe. There's a doctor at Walter Reed. Phil Brown. He was a medic in Korea when my father found him. He flew helicopter runs to the front lines and treated the wounded when the doctors said no thank you. Later, Dad got him started in the right direction, including medical school, courtesy of the Army. He was from a poor family; it wouldn't have been possible otherwise."

"That was a long time ago."

"Yes, but they stayed in touch. We stayed in touch. It's worth a try. I can't come up with anyone else."

"Can you get him here? I don't want to talk on the phone."

"I can ask," said Alison.

Within the hour a slender forty-three-year-old Army doctor walked through the door and embraced Alison. There was a good-natured quality about the man, thought Chancellor; he liked him, although he had an idea that when Alison had said they'd "stayed in touch", she meant precisely that. They were good friends; they had once been better friends.

"Phil, it's so good to see you!"

"I'm sorry I didn't make Mac's burial," said the doctor, holding Alison by the shoulders. "I figured you'd understand. All those sanctimonious words from all those bastards who wanted his stars impounded."

"You haven't lost your directness, Charlie Brown."

The major kissed her on the forehead. "I haven't heard that name in years." He turned to Peter. "She's a *Peanuts* freak, you know. We used to wait up for the Sunday papers – "

"This is Peter Chancellor, Phil," interrupted Alison.

The doctor focused on Peter and offered his hand. "You've upgraded your friends, Ali. I'm impressed. I enjoy your books, Peter. May I call you Peter?"

"Only if I can call you Charlie."

"Not in the office. They'd think I was an intellectual; that's frowned upon . . . Now, what's this all about? Ali sounded like a fugitive from a narc raid."

"Right to the first," said Alison. "Far worse than the second. May I tell him, Peter?"

Chancellor looked at the major, at the abrupt concern in his eyes, at the strength veiled in pleasantness. "I think you can tell him everything."

"I think you'd better," said Brown. "This girl means a lot to me. Her father was an important part of my life."

They told him. Everything. Alison began; Peter filled in. The telling was cathartic; there was someone they could trust at last. Alison started to explain the events in Tokyo twenty-two years before. She stopped when she got to her mother's attack on her; further words would not come.

The doctor knelt in front of her. "Listen to me," he said professionally. "I want to hear it all. I'm sorry, but you have to tell it."

He did not touch her, but in his voice was the soft, firm command.

When she had finished, Brown nodded to Peter and got up to make himself a drink. Chancellor went to Alison and held her as the doctor poured himself a drink.

"The bastards," said Brown, revolving the glass in his hand. "Hallucinogens – that's what they plateaued her on. They may have strung her out on a morphine derivative or cocaine, but the hallucinogens provoke visual displacement; that's the prime symptom. Both sides were into heavy experiments in those days. The *bastards!*"

"What difference does it make which narcotics were used?" asked Chancellor, his arm around Alison.

"Maybe none at all," answered Brown. "But there could be. Those experiments were very restricted, very secret. Somewhere there are records – God knows where – but they exist. They could tell us the strategy, give us names and dates, tell us how wide the net spread."

"I'd rather talk to the men who were at Chasŏng," Peter said. "A few of the survivors, the higher the rank the better. Those in the VA hospitals. But there's no time to chase all over the country looking for them."

"You think you'll find the answer there?"

"Yes. Chasŏng's become a cult. I heard a dying man scream the name as if his own death were a willing sacrifice. There was no mistaking it."

"All right." Brown nodded in agreement. "Then why couldn't the sacrifice be based in revenge? Retribution for the activities of Mac's wife, her mother?" The doctor looked at Alison, his expression apologetic. "Actions she had no control over, but whoever's looking for revenge wouldn't know that."

"That's the point," interrupted Peter. "The kind of people involved in this are followers, willing to die – rank and file – not command personnel. They wouldn't know anything about her mother. You just said it. Ramirez confirmed it. Those experiments were restricted, very secret. Only a few people knew. There's no connection."

"*You* found it. With Ramirez."

"I was *expected* to find it, expected to settle for it. But something else happened at Chasŏng. Varak sensed it, but he couldn't put a label on it, so he called it a decoy."

"A decoy?"

"Yes. Same pond, wrong duck. 'Mac the Knife' had nothing to do with his wife's manipulation. The torn nightgown on the floor of the study in Rockville, the smashed glasses, the perfume – they were all signposts pointing in the wrong direction. Pointing towards a wreck of a woman destroyed by the enemy, and I was supposed to leap at it. I did, too, but I was wrong. It's something else."

"How do you know all this? How can you be so sure?"

"Because, goddamn it, I've invented this sort of thing myself. In books."

"In *books?* Come on, Peter, this is real."

"I could answer that, but you'd tie me up and take me in for observation. Just get me as many names as you can of the Chasŏng survivors."

Major Philip Brown, M.D., looked at the memorandum that resulted from the morning's conference. He was pleased with himself. The memo had just the right portentous ring to it without raising alarms that might be too shrill.

It was the sort of paper he could use to gain access to those thousands of microfilmed records that specified the location and brief medical histories of the disabled men residing in veterans' hospitals throughout the country.

Essentially the memorandum theorized that in a number of older disabled soldiers certain internal tissues were deteriorating at a somewhat faster pace than the normal ageing process allowed for. These men had served in Korea, in and around Chagang Province. It was quite possible that a virus had infected their bloodstreams, and though it had appeared dormant, it was in fact molecularly active. The memo theorized that it was the *Hynobius*, a microscopic antigen carried by insects indigenous to Chagang Province. Further study was recommended as priorities allowed.

It was effective nonsense. The major had no idea if a *Hynobius* antigen existed. He reasoned that if he invented it, there could be no one to dispute him.

Memorandum in hand, Brown walked into the microfilm depository. He did not use the name Chasŏng with the staff sergeant in charge. Instead, he let the sergeant arrive at the selections. The enlisted man took his detective work seriously; he went back to the metal stacks and returned with the microfilms.

Three hours and twenty-five minutes later, Brown stared at the last projection on the screen. His tunic had been removed long ago, draped over a chair. His tie had been loosened, his collar unbuttoned. He sat back stunned.

In the hundreds of feet of microfilm there was not one mention of Chasŏng. Not one.

It was as though Chasŏng had never existed. Nothing had ever happened there according to the microfilm depository of the Walter Reed Hospital.

He stood up and carried the rolls back to the sergeant. Brown knew he had to be cautious, but whatever the risk, it had to be taken. He had reached a dead end.

"I've extracted a lot of what we need," he said, "but I think there's more. *Hynobius* in the Ss subgroupings turned up in the mobile labs around P'yŏngyang. A number of these records refer to a Chasŏng district or province. I wondered if you had an index on it."

There was an immediate response from the sergeant, a speck of recognition in his eyes. "Chasŏng? Yes sir, I know the name, I saw it recently. I'm trying to think where."

Brown's pulse accelerated. "It could be important, Sergeant. It's just another line in the spectrograph, but it could be the one we need. The *Hynobius* is a bitch. Try to remember, please."

The sergeant got out of his chair and came to the counter, still frowning. "I think it was an entry on another shift, the insert in the far right column. That's always a little unusual, so it sort of stands out."

"Why is it unusual?"

"That column's for removals. The films are signed out. Generally people use the equipment here like you did."

"Can you pinpoint the time?"

"Couldn't have been more than a day or so ago. Let me look." The clerk pulled a metal-bound ledger from a shelf. "Here it is. Yesterday afternoon. Twelve strips were signed out. All Chasŏng. At least signing them out makes sense."

"Why is that?"

"It'd take someone two days in here to go through all that material. I'm surprised it was even collated the way it was."

"What way was that?"

"Coded indexes. National-security classification. You need the master schedule to locate the films. Even though you're a doctor, you couldn't see them."

"Why not?"

"Your rank isn't high enough, sir."

"Who did sign them out?"

"A Brigadier General Ramirez?"

Brown turned his TR-6 into the drive of the enormous data-processing centre in McLean, Virginia. There was a guardhouse on the left. Across the roadway was a barrier with the inevitable Authorized Government Personnel Only sign affixed to the metal strips.

It hadn't taken much pressure to convince the staff sergeant at the depository that if men died because a general named Ramirez had removed the means of tracing the *Hynobius*, the sergeant could well be responsible.

Besides, Brown was perfectly willing to take full responsibility – rank and medical – and sign for the microfilm identification numbers under his own name. The sergeant was not giving him the film, only the numbers; Reed Security would clear him for the duplicates in McLean.

The doctor reasoned that he had a personal score to settle with Ramirez. The brigadier had destroyed General MacAndrew, and MacAndrew had given Phil

Brown, farm boy from Gandy, Nebraska, a very decent chance in life. If Ramirez didn't like it, he could always file charges.

Somehow Brown didn't think the brigadier would do that.

Breaching the security desk at Walter Reed was not very difficult. It was a question of using the memorandum to browbeat a non-medical security officer into giving him a general clearance for McLean.

Brown showed his clearance to the civilian behind the entrance desk at McLean. The man punched the buttons of a computer; small green numbers appeared on the miniature screen, and the doctor was directed to the proper floor.

The main point, reflected Brown as he walked through the doors into Section M, Data Processing, was that since he had the serial numbers for the material signed out by Ramirez, he needed nothing else. Each strip of microfilm had its own individual identification. The medical clearance was accepted; the obstacles fell, and ten minutes later he sat in front of a very complicated machine that, weirdly enough, looked like a shiny new version of an old-time Movieola.

And ten minutes after that he realized the staff sergeant at the depository was wrong when he said it would take someone two days to go through these records. It would take less than an hour; Brown was not sure what he had found, but whatever it was, it caused him to stare in disbelief at the information flashed on the small screen in front of him.

Of the hundreds of men who had engaged in the Battle of Chasŏng, only thirty-seven had survived. If that were not startling enough, the disposition of the thirty-seven was appalling. It was in contradiction to every accepted psychological practice. Men severely maimed or crippled in the same combat operation were rarely separated. Since they would spend the rest of their lives in institutions, their comrades were often all they had left, families and friends visiting them less and less frequently until they were only uncomfortable, unseemly shadows in far distant wards.

Yet the thirty-seven survivors of Chasŏng had been meticulously isolated from one another. Specifically, thirty-one had been separated, in thirty-one different hospitals from San Diego to Bangor, Maine.

The remaining six were together, but their close association was next to meaningless. They were in a maximum-security psychiatric ward ten miles west of Richmond. Brown knew the place. The patients were certifiably insane – all dangerous, most homicidal.

Still, they were together. It was not a pleasant prospect, but if Chancellor believed he could learn something, here were the names of six survivors of Chasŏng. From the writer's point of view the circumstances might be advantageous. As long as communication was possible, these men whose mental capacities had been destroyed at Chasŏng might be capable of revealing a great deal. Unconsciously perhaps, but without the inhibiting strictures imposed by rational thought. The causes of their insanity rarely left the minds of the insane.

Something he could not define bothered the doctor, but he was too stunned to analyse it. His mind was too packed with the inexplicable to think any more.

Also, he wanted to get out of the data-processing centre into the cold fresh air.

They were not entering a hospital, Peter felt. They were going inside a prison. A sanitized version of a concentration camp.

"Remember, your name is Conley, and you're an MN subgroup specialist," said Brown. "I'll do the talking."

They walked down the long white corridor lined with white metal doors on both sides. There were small, thick observation windows in the walls beside the doors, behind which Chancellor could see the inmates. Grown men lay curled up on bare floors, many soiled by their own wastes. Others paced like animals, when, suddenly catching sight of strangers in the corridor, they thrust contorted faces against the glass. Still others stood at their windows, staring blankly at the sunlight outside, lost in silent fantasies.

"You never get used to it," said the psychiatrist accompanying them. "Human beings reduced to the lowest primates. Yet they were once men. We must never forget that."

It took Peter a moment or two to realize the man was speaking to him. At the same time he knew his face reflected the impact of the emotions he was experiencing: equal parts of compassion, curiosity, revulsion.

"We'll want to talk to the Chasŏng survivors," said Brown, relieving Chancellor of the need to reply. "Will you arrange that, please?"

The staff doctor seemed surprised but did not object. "I was told you wanted blood samples."

"Those, too, of course. But we'd also like to talk to them."

"Two can't talk, and three usually won't. The first are catatonic, the others are schizophrenic. Have been for years."

"That's five," said Brown. "What about the sixth? Would he remember anything?"

"Nothing you'd want to hear. He's homicidal. And anything can set off his rage – a gesture of your hand or the light from a bulb. He'll be the one in the jacket."

Chancellor felt ill; the pain shot through his temples. They'd made the trip for nothing, for nothing could be learned. He heard Brown ask a question, his tone reflecting an equal sense of despair.

"Where are they? Let's make it quick."

"They're all together in one of the south-wing labs. They're prepped for you. Right this way."

They reached the end of the hallway and turned into another, wider corridor. It was lined with separate enclosed cubicles, some with benches against the walls, others with examination tables in the centre. Each cubicle was fronted by an observation window made of the same thick glass as in the hallway they had just left. The psychiatrist led them to the last cubicle and gestured through the window.

Chancellor stared through the glass, his breath suspended, his eyes wide. Inside

806

were six men in green buttonless fatigues. Two sat immobile on benches, their eyes distant. Three were sprawled on the floor, moving their bodies in horrible, tortured motions – giant insects imitating one another. One stood in the corner, his neck and shoulders twitching, his face a series of unending contortions, his trapped arms straining against the tight fabric that bound his upper body.

But what caused Peter's sudden and profound terror was not merely the sight of the pathetic half-humans beyond the glass but the sight of their skin.

All were Blacks.

"That's *it*," he heard Brown whisper. "The letter *n*."

"What?" asked Chancellor, barely able to be heard, so intense was his fear.

"It was there. Everything," said the major quietly. "It didn't register because I was looking for other things. The small letter *n* after the names. Hundreds of names. Negro. All the troops at Chasŏng were Black. All Negroes."

"Genocide," said Peter softly, the fear total, the sickness complete.

38

They raced north on the highway in silence, each with his own thoughts, each consumed with a horror neither had ever before experienced. Yet both knew precisely what had to be done; the man they had to confront had been identified: Brigadier-General Pablo Ramirez.

"I *want* that son of a bitch," Brown had said as soon as they left the hospital.

"Nothing makes sense," answered Peter, knowing it was no reply. "Sutherland was Black. He was the only connection. But he's dead."

Silence.

"I'll make the call," said Brown finally. "You can't; he'd never see you. And there are too many ways for a general to be suddenly transferred halfway around the world."

They drove into one of those Colonial-style restaurants that seem to breed in the Virginia countryside. There was a telephone booth at the end of a dimly lit hallway. Chancellor waited by the open door; the doctor went inside and dialled the Pentagon.

"Major Brown?" asked the irritated Ramirez over the phone. "What's so urgent you can't discuss it with my secretary?"

"It's more than urgent, General. And you *are* a general according to the microfilm depository at Walter Reed. I'd say it's an emergency."

A momentary silence conveyed the brigadier's shock. "What are you talking about?" he asked, barely audible.

"A medical accident, I think, sir. I'm a doctor assigned to trace a viral strain that had its origins in Korea. We isolated the districts; one of them was Chasŏng. All the casualty records were removed under your name."

"Chasŏng has a national-security classification."

"Not medically, General," interrupted Brown. "We have controlled priority. I received clearance to check the duplicates at data processing . . ." He let his voice trail off, suspended, as if he had more to say but did not know how to say it.

Ramirez couldn't stand the tension. "What are you driving at?"

"That's it, sir. I don't know how to put it, but as one military man to another, I'm scared to death. Hundreds of men killed at Chasŏng; hundreds missing with no postwar resolutions. All Negro troops. Thirty-seven survivors; except for six insane men, thirty-one in thirty-one separate hospitals. All Black, all isolated. That's against every accepted practice. I don't care if it *is* twenty-two years ago, if all this comes out – "

"Who else knows about these records?" broke in Ramirez.

"At this juncture no one but me. I called you because your name – "

"Keep it that way!" said the brigadier curtly. "That's an order. It's seventeen-thirty hours. Come to my house in Bethesda. Be there at nineteen hundred." Ramirez gave him the address and hung up.

Brown stepped out of the booth. "We're here; we've got time. Let's get something to eat."

They ate mechanically, with a minimum of conversation. The coffee came; Brown leaned forward. "How do you explain O'Brien?" he asked.

"I can't. Any more than I can explain a man like Varak. They take lives, they risk their own lives, and for what? They live in a world I can't understand." Chancellor paused, remembering. "Maybe O'Brien explained it himself. Something he said in the car when I asked him about Varak. He said there were times when life and death weren't the issues; times when all that mattered was the elimination of a problem."

"That's incredible."

"It's inhuman."

"It still doesn't explain O'Brien."

"Something else might. He was part of the files. He told me he thought he was ready to be tested, but he wasn't sure. We know the answer now."

Peter's eyes were drawn to a slight movement at the window overlooking the porch of the restaurant. The front lights had been switched on, the day having turned into early evening. Suddenly he froze. His hand stayed where it was, the glass at his lips, his eyes riveted on the window, on the figure of a man on the porch.

For an instant he wondered if he were going mad, if his mind had cracked under the strain of the swiftly disintegrating line between the real and the unreal. Then he knew he was seeing someone he had seen before. Outside another window, standing on another porch. A man with a gun!

The *same man*. Through the window, on the walkaround porch of the old Victorian house on Chesapeake Bay: Munro St Claire's chauffeur. He was waiting for them, checking to make sure they were still there!

"We've been followed," he said to Brown.

"What?"

"There's a man on the porch. He's looking inside. Keep your eyes on me! . . . He's walking away now."

"Are you sure?"

"Positive. He's St Claire's man. Which means if he's followed us here, he's been following us the whole time. He knows Alison's in Arundel!" Peter got to his feet, doing his best to conceal his fear. "I'm going to phone her."

Alison answered.

"Thank God you're there," he said. "Now listen to me, and do as I tell you. That lieutenant commander from the Third District, the one who gave us the money. Get hold of him and ask him to come out and stay with you. Tell him to bring a gun. Until he gets there call the hotel's security and say I telephoned and insisted you be taken to the dining room. There are crowds there; stay in the dining room until he arrives. Now, do as I say."

"Of course I will," said Alison, sensing his panic. "Now tell me why."

"We've been followed. I don't know for how long."

"I understand. Are you all right?"

"Yes. Which means, I think, they're following us to see where we lead them. Not to harm us."

"Are you leading them somewhere?"

"Yes. But I don't want to. I don't have time to talk, just do as I tell you. I love you." He hung up and walked back to the table.

"Is she there?" Brown asked. "Everything all right?"

"Yes. Someone's coming to stay with her. Another friend of the general's."

"He had a lot of them. I feel better. As you surmised, I'm fond of that girl."

"I surmised."

"You're a lucky man. She passed on me."

"I'm surprised."

"I wasn't. She didn't want anything permanent with a uniform. She pictured it on you even when – What are we going to do?"

The abrupt shift would have amused Peter any other time. "How strong are you?"

"That's a hell of a question. What do you mean?"

"Can you fight?"

"I'd rather not. You're not challenging me, so you must mean our friend outside."

"There could be more than one."

"Then, I like the prospects even less. What did you have in mind?"

"I don't want them following us to Ramirez."

"Neither do I," Brown said. "Let's find out if it's a 'them' or a 'him'."

It was a "him". The man stood leaning against a sedan at the far end of the car park, under the branches of a tree, his eyes focused on the front entrance. Chancellor and Brown had come out of a side door; St Claire's man did not see them.

"Okay," Brown whispered. "There's only one. I'll go back inside and walk out the front. You'll see me swing the car around. Good luck."

"I hope you know what you're doing."

"It's better than fighting. We could lose. Just hold on tight. I only need a second."

Peter remained in the shadows by the side door until he saw St Claire's man move away from the bonnet of the sedan and walk quietly around to the tree side, out of sight. The chauffeur had spotted Brown coming out the front entrance. Why didn't the man get into his car?

Several seconds passed. Brown sauntered casually across the parking lot towards the Triumph under the restaurant's floodlights.

Peter moved. Crouched, he made his way along the border of the paved area, hidden by the parked cars, towards St Claire's man. The ground beyond the border consisted of unkempt shrubbery and uncut grass. When Chancellor was within thirty feet of the chauffeur, he stepped over the kerb and into the foliage. As quietly as he could, he crept nearer, counting on the sound of the Triumph's engine to cover whatever noise he made.

In the parking lot Brown backed his car out of its slot and pointed it towards the exit; then he suddenly yanked the gears into reverse and gunned the motor furiously. The Triumph lurched backward towards the tree.

Chancellor was within fifteen feet of St Claire's chauffeur, hidden by darkness and the shrubbery. The man was confused, astonishment seen clearly on his face. He ducked beneath the windows of the sedan; he had no other choice. Brown had slammed on the brakes of the Triumph within inches of the sedan's front bumper and climbed out. The chauffeur stepped back, his concentration totally on Brown.

Chancellor sprang out of the shadows, his hands outstretched towards St Claire's man. The chauffeur heard the sounds from the darkness to his right. He whipped round, reacting instantly to the attack. Peter grabbed his coat, swinging him around against the metal of the sedan. The chauffeur's foot lashed out, striking Chancellor's kneecap. A sharp punch caught Peter in the throat. An elbow crashed into his chest, the pain excruciating; a knee hammered into his groin with the swift, harsh impact of a piston.

In the sudden, stinging agony Chancellor found himself pitched into a frenzy. He could feel outrage welling up inside him. There was only the violence, the brute force he hated remaining to him.

Peter clenched his right fist, he kept his left hand open, a claw soaring in to grab flesh. He threw his weight against the thrashing man, crashing him into the steel of the sedan, his fist pummelling the chauffeur's stomach and below, hammering the man's testicles. His open hand found the chauffeur's face; he dug his fingers into the man's eyes, his thumb ripping up into a nostril. He yanked with all his strength, sending the skull sideways, smashing it into the roof of the car. Blood poured out of the chauffeur's mouth, eye sockets, and nostrils. Still he would not stop; his fury matched Chancellor's.

Peter yanked the man's head again, twisting away from the chauffeur's knees. He crashed the skull again into the metal; his hands were slippery, covered with blood. He smashed the chauffeur against the window with such force that the glass shattered.

"For Christ's sake!" screamed Brown. "Just hold him!"

But Chancellor could not control himself. His rage had found an outlet, brutal and satisfying. He was avenging so much!

He ripped at the chauffeur's neck, his hand sliding around to the throat. He pushed suddenly upward, catching the man's chin, sending the head back once more into steel as he brought his own knee up into the dark trousers of the chauffeur's uniform and slammed his upper leg with surging impact into the man's groin.

The chauffeur screamed and began to go limp.

"Shit!" exploded Brown.

"What is it?" gasped Chancellor, no breath left in his lungs.

"The goddamned needle broke!"

In his hand the doctor held a hypodermic; he had plunged it into the chauffeur's shoulder. Suddenly the man fell forward against Peter. Brown stepped back and spoke again.

"Son of a bitch . . . Enough got through."

A crowd had gathered on the restaurant porch. Someone had heard the chauffeur's scream and had gone back for help.

"Let's get out of here!" Brown said, grabbing Chancellor's arm.

At first Peter did not respond; his mind was filled with mist and light. He could not think.

Brown seemed to understand. He pulled Chancellor away from the sedan, propelling him to the door of the Triumph. He opened it and shoved Chancellor inside, then he ran around the bonnet and climbed in behind the wheel.

They raced out of the car park, into the darkness of the highway, and drove in silence for several minutes. Brown reached behind him into the well of the back seat and pulled up his medical bag.

"There's a bottle of alcohol and some surgical gauze," he said. "Clean yourself up."

Still dazed, Chancellor did as he was told.

The major spoke again. "What the hell were you? A Green Beret?"

"Nothing."

"I beg to differ. You were something! I'd never have believed it. You just don't seem the type."

"I'm not."

"Well, if I ever raise my voice to you, I apologize in advance. I'll also run like hell. You're the best street fighter I've seen."

Peter looked at Brown. "Don't talk like that," he said simply.

They fell quiet again. The major slowed as they approached an intersection, then swung the Triumph to the left, into the road that would take them to Bethesda.

Chancellor touched the doctor's arm. "Wait a minute." The obscure question that had bothered him when Brown walked out of the restaurant had formed in his mind. *Why hadn't the chauffeur got into his car?*

Peter's memory raced back in time nearly two and a half years, when he was researching *Counterstrike!* To the disaffected men he had spoken to and the technology they had described.

"What's the matter?" asked Brown.

"If we've been followed, how come we never realized it? God knows we were watching."

"What are you talking about?"

"Pull over!" interrupted Chancellor, alarm in his voice. "Do you have a torch?"

"Sure. In the glove compartment." Brown pulled off the road on to the shoulder.

Peter took the torch, jumped out of the car, and ran back to the boot, lowering himself to the ground. He switched on the light and crawled under the chassis.

"I've got them!" he yelled. "Get me your tool kit. The wrench!"

Brown got it for him. Chancellor stayed beneath the car, working furiously with the iron instrument. Crunching, prying sounds came from the rear axle area, then Peter slid out, holding two small metal objects in his left hand.

"Transmitters," he said. "A primary and a back-up! That's why we never saw anyone. They could stay three to five miles behind and still follow us. Wherever we went, whomever we met, they just waited for the right moment." He paused for a second, his face grim. "But I found them. They're cut off. Let's go to Bethesda."

"I've changed my mind. I think I should go with you," said Brown as they drove down Ramirez's tree-lined street.

"No," replied Peter. "Let me off at the next corner. I'll walk back."

"Has it occurred to you he might try to kill you? He's expecting me. I wear the same uniform as he does."

"That's why he won't kill me. I'll tell him the truth. I'll make it clear that you're waiting for me. A fellow officer. If I don't come out, you'll go somewhere else, and Chasŏng will blow up in their faces."

They approached the comer; Brown slowed the Triumph. "That might work with a rational person. It may not with Ramirez. If Chasŏng's what we think it is – "

"*Know* it was," broke in Chancellor.

"All right, say it's true. He may not want to face the consequences. He's Army, don't forget that. He may decide to take you out, then go with you."

"Kill himself?" asked Peter incredulously.

"The incidence of military suicide," said the doctor, stopping the car, "isn't discussed much, but it's sky high. Some say it goes with the terrain. I didn't ask you before. Do you have a gun?"

"No. I had one; ran out of bullets. Never tried to get more."

Brown reached into his medical bag, rummaged inside a flap, and pulled out a small revolver. "Here, take this. We're issued these because we carry drugs. Good luck. I'll be waiting."

Chancellor reached the flagstone path. Ramirez was at the window, staring outside, his face reflecting his astonishment at seeing Peter. Astonishment, but not shock, not panic. He let the curtain fall back and disappeared. Chancellor walked down the path and up the steps; he rang the bell.

The door opened. The brigadier's Latin eyes looked harshly at Peter.

"Good evening, General. Major Brown sends his regrets. The Chasŏng records disturbed him so much he didn't want to talk to you. But he's waiting for me down the block."

"I thought so," replied Ramirez noncommittally. "The doctor has a short memory, or he thinks others do. The enlisted man, the medic from Korea MacAndrew made a doctor. The one who had an affair with his daughter." He looked past Chancellor, raised his hand, and chopped the night air twice.

It was a signal.

From behind him in the street, Peter heard an engine start. He turned. The headlights of a military police car were switched on. It pulled out swiftly, gathering speed, and raced to the corner, stopping barely in sight, near the spill of a streetlight, the brakes screeching. Two soldiers jumped out and ran towards a third figure. He, in turn, started to run but was not quick enough.

Chancellor watched as Major Philip Brown was taken, no match for the military police. He was led back to the Army car and thrown inside.

"No one's waiting for you now," said Ramirez. Peter turned in fury, his hand going for the gun.

Then he stopped. Levelled at his chest was a .45 automatic.

"You can't do this!"

"I think I can," said Ramirez. "The doctor will be held in isolation, allowed no visitors, no calls, no outside communication whatsoever. That's standard for officers who violate national security. Come inside, Mr Chancellor."

39

They were in Ramirez's study. The brigadier's eyes grew wide, his lips parted, and slowly he lowered the gun.

Look to the fiction, always the fiction, thought Peter. *In fiction lies reality, the devices of the imagination more powerful than any weapon.*

"Where is this letter?" asked the general.

Chancellor had lied to Ramirez, telling him he had written a letter detailing the cover-up and the racial character of Chasŏng. It had been posted to New York, copies to be sent to major newspapers, the Senate Armed Services Committee and the secretary of the Army if the general did not co-operate.

"Out of my control," replied Peter. "Out of yours, too. You couldn't intercept it. Unless I show up in New York by noon tomorrow, it'll be opened. The story of Chasŏng will be read by a very aggressive editor."

"He'd trade your life for it," said Ramirez cautiously. The threat was hollow; his voice lacked conviction.

"I don't think so. He'd weigh the priorities. I think he'd take the risk."

"There are other priorities! They go way beyond us!"

"I'm sure you've convinced yourself of that."

"It's true! An accident of command, a coincidence that could not occur again in a thousand years must not be given a label it doesn't deserve!"

"I see." Chancellor looked down at the gun. The brigadier hesitated, then placed the weapon on the table beside him. He did not move from the table, however. The gun was within a swift hand's reach. Peter acknowledged the gesture with a nod. "I see," he repeated. "That's the official explanation. An accident. A coincidence. All the troops at Chasŏng just happened to be Black. Over six hundred men killed, God knows how many hundreds missing – all Black."

"That's the way it was."

"That's the way it *wasn't!*" contradicted Chancellor. "There were no segregated battalions then."

Ramirez's expression was contemptuous. "Who told you that?"

"Truman gave the order in '48. All the branches of the service were integrated."

"With all deliberate speed. The services were no faster than anyone else."

"Are you saying you were caught by your own delay? Your resistance to a policy order resulted in wholesale slaughter of Black troops? Is that it?"

"Yes." The brigadier took a step forward. "Resistance to an impossible policy! But Christ, you can see how it would be twisted by the radicals of this country! Beyond the country!"

"I can understand that." Peter saw a flicker of hope in Ramirez's eyes. The soldier had reached out for an elusive lifeline, and for a brief moment he believed he had it in his grasp. Chancellor altered the tone of his voice just enough to take advantage of the brigadier's false hope. "Let's leave the casualties for a minute. What about MacAndrew? Where does he fit in with Chasŏng?"

"You know the answer to that. When you called, I said things I should never have told you."

It was all so pat. The lie was deep, thought Peter. There were two fears of exposure, one more terrifying to Ramirez than the other, so the lesser – the transmitting of erroneous intelligence to an enemy – was put forward to avoid the more damaging. What was that other fear?

"MacAndrew's wife?"

The general nodded, guilt accepted in humility. "We did what we believed was right at the time. The objective was to save American lives."

"She was used to send back false information," said Peter.

"Yes. She was the perfect conduit. The Chinese operated extensively in Japan; some Japanese fanatics helped them. For many it came down to Oriental against white."

"I never heard that before."

"It was never given much coverage. It was a constant thorn in MacArthur's side; it was played down."

"What kind of information did you feed MacAndrew's wife?"

"The usual. Troop movements, supply routes, concentration of ordnance, and tactical options. Mainly troop movements and tactics, of course."

814

"She was the one who relayed the tactical information about Chasŏng?"

Ramirez paused; his eyes strayed to the floor. There was something artificial in the brigadier's reaction, something rehearsed. "Yes," he said reluctantly.

"But that information wasn't false. It wasn't inaccurate. It resulted in a massacre."

"No one knows how it happened," continued Ramirez. "To understand, you must realize how these reverse conduits operate. How compromised people like MacAndrew's wife are used. They're not given blanket lies; outright misinformation would be rejected, the conduit suspect. They're provided with variations of the truth, subtle alterations of the possible. 'The Sixth Engineer Battalion will enter Combat Sector Baker on 3 July.' Only it's not the Sixth Engineers, it's the Sixth Tank Artillery, and it reaches Combat Baker on 5 July, outflanking the positioned enemy. With the Chasŏng operation the variation given MacAndrew's wife was not, in fact, the variation at all. It was the actual strategy. Somehow the orders were fouled up in G-Two command. She carried back information that resulted in wholesale slaughter." The soldier levelled his eyes with Peter's and stood erect. "Now you know the truth."

"Do I?"

"You have the word of a general officer."

"I wonder if it's any good."

"Don't press me, Chancellor. I've told you more than you have any right to know. To make you see the anguish that would result if the tragedy of Chasŏng were made public. Facts would be misinterpreted, the memory of fine people dragged through filth."

"Wait a minute," interrupted Peter. In his sanctimonious rendering of the obvious, Ramirez had *said* it. *The memory of . . . those close to you.* Alison's *memories.* Her mother's parents held prisoners in the Po Hai Gulf; that was the first Chinese connection, but that wasn't it. It was something Alison said that happened *after* the night her mother had been carried in on the stretcher. Something about her father . . . Her father had flown back to Tokyo for the next to last time. That was it: the *next* to last time! Between his wife's final collapse and his return to the States, MacAndrew had gone back to Korea! The Battle of Chasŏng took place *then*. Weeks after Alison's mother was hospitalized. She couldn't have relayed information, accurate or otherwise.

"What's the matter?" asked the brigadier.

"You. Goddamn it, *you!* The *dates!* It couldn't have happened! What did you say a few minutes ago? Some battalion or other is expected on the third of July but doesn't get there until the fifth, and anyway, it's a different battalion. What did you call it? Some bullshit phrase . . . 'subtle alteration of the possible'. Wasn't that it? Well, General, you've just blown it! The massacre at Chasŏng took place weeks after MacAndrew's wife was hospitalized! She couldn't have carried that information to anyone! Now, you son of a bitch, you tell me what happened! Because if you don't, there won't be any waiting until tomorrow. That letter I sent to New York will be read tonight!"

Ramirez's eyes bore into his; his mouth twitched. "*No!*" he roared. "You won't! You can't! I won't let you!"

He was reaching for the gun!

Chancellor rushed forward, throwing himself at the general. His shoulder crashed into Ramirez's back, propelling the soldier against the wall. Ramirez gripped the gun by its barrel; he swung it up viciously. The handle of the gun caught Chancellor on the temple. Searing shafts of pain caused a thousand white spots to converge in front of him.

His left hand was dug into Ramirez's tunic, the fabric clutched against the soldier's chest. His right hand lashed out in thrust and counterthrust, trying to grab and hold the heavy weapon.

He felt the handle! He brought his knee up into the general's stomach, smashing him against the wall. He had the handle of the gun, and he would not let go! Ramirez kept punching hysterically at Peter's kidney. Chancellor thought he might collapse, so intense was the pain.

His finger was near the trigger! In the slashing movements of both their arms, Peter felt the rim of the trigger enclosure.

But he could not let it fire! An explosion would bring neighbours! The police! If that happened, nothing could be learned!

Chancellor took a half step back, then crashed his left leg up, pulling the soldier's tunic down with all his strength. His knee smashed into Ramirez's face, sending his head back. The general expelled a chestful of air; the gun left his hand; his fingers straightened in agony. The weapon flew across the room, crashing into the marble pen set on top of the desk. Peter released the tunic. Ramirez collapsed, unconscious, blood pouring out of his nostrils.

It took Peter a minute to find his thoughts again. He knelt in front of the soldier and waited until his breathing was steadier, until the white spots faded and the pain in his temples began to subside. Then he picked up the gun.

There was a bottle of Evian water on a silver tray in a bookshelf. He opened the bottle and poured the water into his palm, splashing it over his face. It helped. He was finding his sanity again.

He poured what was left in the bottle on the soldier's unconscious face. The water mingled with blood on the floor from the general's nosebleed, producing a sickening pink.

Slowly, Ramirez regained consciousness. Peter yanked a loose cushion from an easy chair and threw it over to him. The general blotted his face and neck with the pillow and stood up, supporting himself against the wall.

"Sit down," ordered Peter, waving the barrel of the gun towards the leather armchair.

Ramirez sank into the chair. He let his head fall back. "Slut. Whore," he whispered.

"That's progress," said Chancellor softly. "A few nights ago she was 'unfortunate', 'unstable'."

"That's what she was."

"What she was or what you turned her into?"

"The material has to be there to work with," replied the general. "She sold out."

"She had a mother and father in China."

"I have two brothers who emigrated to Cuba. You think the *Fidelistas* haven't tried to reach *me?* Right now they're rotting in jail. But I won't be compromised!"

"You're stronger than she was. You've been trained not to be compromised."

"She was the wife of an American combat officer! His Army was *her* Army."

"Then, she wasn't up to it, was she? Instead of helping her you *used* her. You filled her full of lethal junk and sent her right back into a fight she couldn't win. Brown said it best. You *bastards!*"

"The strategy was optimum!"

"Cut that Army bullshit! Who gave you the right?"

"No one! *I* saw the tactic. *I* created the strategy. *I* was the source control!" Ramirez blanched. He had gone too far.

"*You?*" Alison's words came back to Peter; he had asked her after the funeral what MacAndrew had thought of Ramirez. *A lightweight, hotheaded and too emotional. Not at all reliable. Dad refused to second two field promotions for him.*

"There were many such operations. Others were involved, naturally." Ramirez retreated.

"No, they weren't! Not with this one!" broke in Chancellor. "It was all yours! What better way to get at the man who pegged you for what you were. A hothead! A liar! Who refused to let them give you a rank you weren't qualified for! You got revenge through his wife!"

"*I got* the rank! He couldn't stop me; that whore couldn't stop me!"

"Of course not! You immobilized him through her! How did you begin? By sleeping with her?"

"It wasn't difficult. She was a slut!"

"And you had the candy! Oh, you're a thoroughbred! And when you got your goddamned rank, you didn't have the stomach for it because you knew you'd got it. You invented reasons to hide it because you knew you weren't qualified for it. You don't pretend to be a major so you can talk to the men. You don't give a damn for anybody! You're afraid of the rank! You're a fraud!"

Ramirez sprang up from the chair, his face on fire. Chancellor caught him in the stomach with his foot; the general fell back into the chair.

"You filthy liar!" screamed the soldier.

"Hits a nerve, doesn't it." It was not a question. Suddenly Peter stopped. *Whore?* It didn't make sense. An enormous contradiction was apparent. "Wait a minute. You couldn't have compromised MacAndrew that way. He would have killed you! He never knew his wife was a *reverse* conduit because you couldn't tell him! Any of you. He had to be told something else; he had to believe something else. He never knew!"

"He knew his wife was a whore! He knew that!"

A sharp image sprang to Peter's mind. A strong but broken man cradling a madwoman on the floor of an isolated house. Cradling her lovingly, telling her that everything would be all right. It was too great an inconsistency. Regardless of the personal anguish a whoring wife would have been ripped out of MacAndrew's life.

"I don't believe you," said Chancellor.

"He saw for himself! He *had* to know!"

"He saw *something* for himself. He was *told* something. Or maybe it was just hinted at. You people are terrific at indicating something but never coming out and saying it. I don't think MacAndrew thought his wife was a whore. I don't think he'd put up with that for minute."

"All the symptoms were there! The slut's mentality."

Symptoms. Peter stared down at Ramirez. He was getting closer, he could sense it. *Symptoms.* According to Alison her mother had begun to "slip away" several months before the explosion came. Alison's father did not know why, so he ascribed it to a progressive deterioration of her faculties, using an accident at a beach to pin the final breakdown on. Used it so often he came to believe it himself.

In the recesses of his mind such a man would continue to love, continue to protect, because his wife was not to blame. No matter what she did. Conflicting forces – parents in the hands of an enemy, a husband fighting that enemy every day – had driven that woman out of her mind.

And all the while trusted friends hinted at promiscuous behaviour in order to cover their own actions.

What those colleagues did not understand was that MacAndrew was a far better man than they could imagine. Far better and far more compassionate. Whatever the manifestations of an illness it was the illness that was to be despised, not the actions of the human being afflicted.

And this maggot with his bloody face perspiring in the chair, this "source control" who had held out the lethal candy until he'd slept with the wife of the man he hated, could only repeat the words whore and slut.

Those words were the screen that concealed the truth. "What's a 'slut's mentality', General?"

Ramirez's eyes were wary; he suspected a trap. "She hung around the Ginza," he said. "In the off limits bars. She picked up men."

"Those bars were in the south-west district of the Ginza, weren't they? I've been in Tokyo; those bars were still there in '67."

"A number of them, yes."

"They trafficked in narcotics."

"It's possible. More to the point, they sold sex."

"What did they sell it for, General?"

"What it's always sold for."

"Money?"

"Naturally. And kicks."

"No! Not naturally. MacAndrew's wife didn't need money. Or kicks. She was looking for drugs! You strung her out, and she tried to find junk by herself! Without going to the Chinese! That's what you found out! And by her doing that your whole strategy would blow up in your faces! Just one arrest, one Tokyo bust investigated by an outside agency, and you were finished! *Exposed!* You had the most to hide, you motherfucker! But others were involved, too. What did you say a few minutes ago? 'There were many such operations.' You were all running

818

for cover, trying to protect yourselves!" Again Peter stopped, the realization there. "Which means you had to *control* what happened – "

"It happened!" screamed Ramirez, interrupting. "We weren't responsible! She was found down an alley in the Ginza! We didn't put her there! She was found. She would have died!"

The images and the phrases wove swiftly in and out of Chancellor's mind. Alison's words came back like the echoes of kettle drums. Her mother had been taken on a Sunday afternoon to Funabashi Beach. *The phone started ringing. Was my mother there? . . . Two Army officers drove out to the house. They were nervous and agitated . . .*

Was my mother there? Was my mother there?

At night, quite late, I heard screams . . . Downstairs . . . men . . . walking around rapidly, using hand radios. Then the front door opened, and she was brought inside. On a stretcher . . . her face – it was white. Her eyes were wide, staring blankly . . . blood that rolled down over her chin on to her neck. As the stretcher passed beneath a light, she suddenly lurched up screaming . . . her body writhing but held in place by the straps.

Christ! thought Peter. Alison's next words!

I cried out and ran down the stairs, but a . . . Black major . . . stopped me and picked me up and held me.

A Black major!

The Black soldier had to be at the bottom of the stairs, near the light! He was what Alison's mother had seen!

Chancellor remembered other words. A command barked at him by a man in agony twenty-two years later in the late afternoon, still protecting a loved one who'd been driven out of her mind by an event so horrible she could never forget it.

Get by the light; put your face above the shade. It was not to show that his features were Western and not Oriental. It wasn't that at all! It was to show he was not a Black!

Alison's mother had *not* been tortured by Chinese agents sending back a message to Army Intelligence. She had been raped! At an off limits bar in the filthiest district of the Ginza, where she'd come for a connection, she had been dragged down an alley and raped!

"Oh, my *God*," whispered Peter in revulsion. "That's what you told him. That's what you kept hammering at; that's what you used. She was raped by Blacks. She was trying to find a connection in a bar, and she got raped."

"It was the truth!"

"In one of those places it could have been anybody! *Anybody!* But it wasn't, so you *used* it! You blamed the Blacks! Oh, *Christ!*" It was all Chancellor could do to restrain himself. He wanted to kill or maim, so complete was his abhorrence of this man. "You don't have to spell out the rest. It's goddamned clear! It's the information missing in MacAndrew's record. It's what's in Hoover files! After his wife had been put in the hospital, you made sure he was sent back to Korea. But not to his *own* outfit! To another! To a Black command! And somehow you relayed the battle plans – the *actual* strategy – back to the Chinese! It was so obvious! An officer's wife is raped, driven insane, by Blacks, so he subjects Black troops to murderous gunfire, willing to die with them if he has to, but above all, vengeance! A trap set by men in his own army! Hundreds of men killed, hundreds missing, so the truth of what you did to his wife and probably dozens like her would never be known! Your experiments hidden! That's what you held over him: rape and genocide! The first he wouldn't talk about, the second he didn't understand. But he saw the connection between them! It must have paralysed him!"

"Lies." Ramirez's head moved back and forth convulsively. "That's not what happened. You've built a terrible lie!"

Peter stood over the brigadier in the last extremity of loathing. "You *look* like a man who's heard a lie," he said sarcastically. "No, General, you've just heard the truth. You've been running from it for twenty-two years."

Ramirez's head moved faster, the denial more emphatic.

"There's no proof!"

"There are questions. They lead to other questions. That's how it works. People in high places betray the rest of us who put them there. *Bastards!*" Chancellor thrust his left hand down and grabbed Ramirez by the shirt, pulling him forward, the gun inches from the general's eyes. "I don't want to talk to you any more. You disgust me. I think I could pull this trigger and kill you, and that scares the hell out of me. So you do exactly what I tell you, or you won't live to do anything else. You go over to the telephone on your desk and you call wherever you had that major taken and you tell them to release him. Now!"

"No!"

In a single, swift movement Peter whipped the barrel of the Colt automatic across Ramirez's face. The skin broke; a trickle of blood rolled down the soldier's cheek. Chancellor felt nothing. There was something frightening in that absence of feeling. "Make that call."

Slowly Ramirez got to his feet, his eyes on the weapon, his hand touching the blood on his face. He picked up the phone and dialled.

"This is General Ramirez. I called for a special detail to be at my residence at eighteen-hundred for an arrest. The prisoner is a Major Brown. Release him."

Ramirez listened as the voice on the line spoke. Peter pressed the barrel of the automatic into the brigadier's temple.

"Do as I tell you," said Ramirez. "Return the major to his vehicle." He replaced the telephone, his hand still on the instrument. "He'll be here soon. The MP depot's ten minutes away."

"I just told you I didn't want to talk to you any more, but I've changed my mind. We're going to wait for Brown, and you're going to tell me everything you know about Hoover's files."

"I know nothing."

"The hell you don't. You people are into this thing like it was a pocket of quicksand. You're choking in it. You removed eight months' worth of material from MacAndrew's service record."

"That's all we did."

"Eight months! And the dates corresponded to the events leading up to Chasŏng. All the incriminating material. Then the massacre where MacAndrew sent waves of Black troops into suicidal gunfire. Everything but the truth! You knew where that material ended up!"

"Not at first." The general could barely be heard. "At first it was standard procedure. All compromising information about candidates for the Joint Chiefs is removed and placed in G-Two archives. Someone thought it was dangerous; it was routed to PSA."

"What's that?"

"Psychiatric Systems Analyses. Until recently certain people at the bureau had access. PSA deals with defectors, potential blackmail of high-ranking officers, espionage. Lots of things."

"Then, you knew it was in Hoover's files!"

"We found out."

"How?"

"A man named Longworth. He was a retired FBI agent living in Hawaii. He came back – for only a day, maybe two, I don't remember – and warned Hoover that he was going to be killed. For his files. Hoover went out of his mind. He combed through them, looking for anything that might lead to the identity of the killers. He came across Chasŏng, and we got a phone call. We swore we were not involved; we offered guarantees, protection, *anything*. Hoover just wanted us to know what he knew. Then, of course, he was killed."

Peter dropped the gun. The crash of metal against wood was loud and abrasive, but he did not hear it. He heard only the echo of the brigadier's last words.

Then, of course, he was killed . . . Then, of course, he was killed . . . Then, of course, he was killed.

Spoken as if the incredible information were neither electrifying nor even shocking, neither appalling nor even, perhaps, out of the ordinary. Instead, as though it were routine, common knowledge – data recorded and accepted and so entered into the books.

But it was not *real*. Other things were real, but not that. Not the assassination. That was the fantasy, the fiction that had propelled him into the nightmare, but it was the one thing that had never happened!

"What did you say?"

"Nothing you didn't know," said Ramirez, staring at the gun on the floor next to his shoes.

"Hoover died of heart failure. The medical examiner called it a cardiovascular disease. That's how he died. He was an old man." Chancellor spoke without breathing.

The brigadier looked up into Peter's eyes. "Are you playing games? There was no autopsy. You know why and so do I."

"You tell me. Don't assume I know anything. Why wasn't there an autopsy?"

"Orders from Sixteen hundred."

"Who?"

"The White House."

"Why?"

"They killed him. If they didn't, they think they did. They think someone there did it. Or had it done. They give oblique orders over there, very ambiguous. You're either on the team or you're not; you learn how to read what's said. He had to be killed. What's the difference who did it?"

"Because of the files?"

"Partly. But they're records; they can be burned, destroyed. It was the dispatch units. They'd gone too far."

"Dispatch units? What are you talking about?"

"For God's sake, Chancellor! You know what I'm talking about, or you wouldn't be here! You wouldn't have done what you did!"

Peter grabbed Ramirez by the cloth of his shirt. "What are dispatch units? What were Hoover's dispatch units?"

The general's eyes were flat. It was as if he did not care any longer. "Assassination teams," he said. "Men assigned to engineer situations in which specific people were killed. Either by provoking violence resulting in local police or national-guard action, or by hiring psychopaths, known killers, or potential killers, to do the work and cutting them down when it was done. It was all once removed, divided secretly inside the bureau. No one knows how far it went. How far it was going. What assassinations could be attributed to Hoover. Or who would be called an enemy next."

Slowly, staring in disbelief as the throbbing in his temples increased, Chancellor released the brigadier. Blinding white spots converged again in front of his eyes.

Dispatch units! *Execution squads!*

His own words came back to him. He saw the page and read it in his mind's eye with terrible pain.

"Did you know about these . . . execution squads?"

"There've been rumours.' . . ."

"What did you hear?"

"Nothing specific. No proof . . . Hoover departmentalizes everything. Everybody. He does it all secretly . . . That way everyone stays in line."

"Gestapo!"

"What did you hear?"

"Only that there were final solutions . . ."

"Final – Oh, my God."

"If we ever needed a last, overwhelming justification, I think we have it. Hoover will be killed two weeks from Monday, the files taken."

It was all true. It had been true from the beginning. God in heaven, it was never fiction; it was fact!

J. Edgar Hoover had not died the natural death of a sick old man. He had been assassinated.

And with sudden clarity Peter knew who had called for that assassination. It had not been the White House. Instead, it had been a group of men above reproach who made decisions of such impact that they were often the unseen, unelected force that ran the nation.

"You can't do it! You have everything you need. Bring him to trial! Let him face the judgment of the courts! Of the country!"

"You don't understand . . . There's not a court in the land, not a judge, not a member of the House or of the Senate, not the President or any of his cabinet, who can bring him to trial. It's beyond that."

"No, it isn't! There are laws!"

"There are the files . . . People would be reached . . . by others who have to survive . . ."

"Then, you're no better than he is."

All true.

Inver Brass had demanded the death of J. Edgar Hoover, and the order had been carried out.

It happened so fast Chancellor could only react with a twisting, lurching movement of his body. He felt hands on his chest, then Ramirez's shoulder against his ribs. He fell, turning sideways to avoid a second blow, but he was too late.

The brigadier had fallen to one knee, his right hand shooting out for the gun on the floor. He grabbed it, twisting it firmly in his grip, his fingers expertly around the handle, his thumb flicking upward instinctively to check the safety. He raised it.

Peter understood that if he had to die at this moment, he had to die trying to avoid that death. He sprang off his feet, hurling himself at the general.

Again he was too late. The thunderous explosion filled the room. Blood and tissue slapped against the nearby wall. The smoke from the barrel billowed in an acrid cloud.

Below him the soldier was dead. Brigadier General Ramirez, source control of Chasŏng, had blown off most of his head.

40

The gunshot – the explosion – was so shattering it had to have been heard blocks away. Someone would have called the police. He could not be seen leaving the house. He had to get out the back way *quickly*, into the darkness, into the shadows.

He ran in blind panic through a narrow hall into a small kitchen. He lurched across the tiled floor to the back door, stood up, opened it cautiously, and let himself out, spinning around the door frame, pressing his back against the wall.

The house that faced him was separated from Ramirez's by a tall hedge; he could see a drive beyond the garage. Peter leaped off the small back porch on to the lawn and ran towards the hedge, shouldering his way though the thick branches until he was on the other side. He raced down the drive into the street, turned left and kept running. Brown's Triumph was in the next block, back on Ramirez's street. At the corner he turned left again; a siren was whining harshly in the distance, coming closer. He slowed down and tried to walk casually; the police would not overlook a running man after the reports of a gunshot.

He reached the Triumph and climbed inside. Through the rear window he could see that a small, excited crowd had gathered on Ramirez's lawn. The flashing lights of a patrol car accompanied the approaching siren.

He heard the sound of another engine, this from the opposite direction. He turned; it was the military police vehicle. It stopped by the side of the Triumph. Brown got out, taking his keys from one of the soldiers.

They saluted the major; he did not return their salutes. The Army car started up.

"Good. You're back," said Brown, opening the door.

"We've got to get out of here! Right away!"

"What's the matter? What's the crowd – ?"

"Ramirez is dead."

Brown said nothing. He climbed behind the wheel and started the Triumph's engine. They sped off down the block, when suddenly coming towards them was a limousine, its headlights blinding, its outlines those of a giant killer shark slicing through dark waters. Peter could not help himself; he stared into the windows as the car raced past.

The driver was intent only on reaching his destination. Through the rear window, Chancellor saw what that destination was: Ramirez's house.

The driver was Black. Peter closed his eyes, trying to think.

"What happened?" asked Brown, turning the Triumph west towards the highway. "Did you kill him?"

"No. I might have, but I didn't. You were right; he shot himself. He couldn't face Chasŏng. He was responsible for the massacre. It was engineered to keep the wraps on what they'd done to MacAndrew's wife."

Brown was silent for a moment. When he spoke, it was with loathing as well as disbelief. "*Bastards!*"

"If the story of MacAndrew's wife had been broken," Peter continued, "it would have led to the exposure of dozens of other such operations. Other experiments. They knew what they were doing."

"Ramirez admitted it?"

Peter looked at Brown. "Let's say it came out. What's mind-blowing is the rest. I'm not sure I can even say the words. It's that crazy."

"Hoover's files?"

"No. Hoover. He was killed. He was assassinated! It was true all along! It was never a lie!"

"Take it easy. I thought you said Varak told you it *was* a lie."

"*He* was lying! He was protecting – " Peter stopped. *Varak.* The *specialist.* The man of a hundred weapons, a dozen faces . . . assorted names. Good God! It had been there all the time, and he hadn't seen it! *Longworth.* Varak *had* assumed the name of an agent named Longworth on the night of 1 May. It wasn't someone else. Varak masquerading as Longworth had been one of the three men, without accountability, who had entered the bureau the night before Hoover died – which meant they *knew* that death was certain! They found half the files missing; that part was true. And Varak had given his life to trace them, then protected Bravo, protected with his life the extraordinary diplomat known to the world as Munro St Claire.

Varak had been Hoover's assassin! What had Frederick Wells said? *Varak was the killer, not Inver Brass ... I can and will raise disturbing questions ... from the tenth of April to the night of May first ... Varak has those files!*

Which meant Munro St Claire had the files. Varak *himself* had been lied to, manipulated!

By his mentor Bravo.

And now the cult of Chasŏng had zeroed in on Ramirez. The cult given influence and power by Munro St Claire, who had used Varak as he had used everyone else. Including one Peter Chancellor.

It was all coming to an end. The forces were closing in, colliding, as Carlos Montelán had said they would collide. It would be finished this night, one way or the other.

"I'm going to tell you everything I know," he said. "Drive to Arundel; they can't follow us. I'll tell you on the way. I want you to stay with Alison. When we get there, I want to take your car. I want you to wait a while, then phone Munro St Claire in Washington. Tell him I'll be waiting for him at Genesis' house on the bay. He's to come alone. I'll be watching; he won't find me if he's not alone."

41

The sound of waves slapping against rocks drifted up from the water's edge. Peter lay in the wet grass. The air was cold as the ground was cold, the wind from the bay carried in gusts, whistling through the tall trees that bordered the winter lawn. A man who had betrayed him, a man he had believed was his friend, had taught him things in the midst of that betrayal. That was why he was where he was, his eyes on the stone gates of the entrance fifty yards away and on the road beyond.

When making a contact, position was everything. Protect yourself by being able to observe all approaching vehicles; keep rapid, undetectable escape available.

Friends were enemies, and enemies taught one strategies with which to fight them. It was part of the insanity that was all too real.

He saw headlights in the distance, about half a mile away. Peter could not be sure, but the lights seemed to sway back and forth. Every now and then they appeared to be stationary, as if the car had stopped, only to start swaying again. Had the circumstances been different, Chancellor thought, he might have been watching a drunken driver trying to find his way home. Was it possible this powerful manipulator of men and governments had been drinking? Ramirez had blown his own head off because he could not face Chasŏng. Were the revelations about Inver Brass more than St Claire wanted to hear in a stable frame of mind?

The car came haltingly through the gates. Peter momentarily suspended his breath, his eyes riveted on the terrible sight. It was the silver Mark IV Continental! That St Claire would drive it to their confrontation was confirmation that the man, like the vehicle, was a monster.

He watched as the silver obscenity rolled around the circular drive to the wide steps of the front entrance; then he focused his eyes back on the road beyond the gates. He peered into the darkness, his concentration total. There were no headlights on the road, nor any black shape against grey darkness that would be a vehicle travelling with its headlights off.

He remained in the grass for nearly five minutes, watching St Claire. The diplomat had left the car, climbed the steps, and walked to the end of the porch. He was standing by the railing, staring out at the water.

Another man, a compassionate man, had stood on a fisherman's dock staring out an another stretch of water twelve hours before. At dawn. That man was dead, led into a trap by an enemy, cut down by fanatics who obeyed the instructions of a monster.

Chancellor was satisfied: Munro St Claire had come alone.

Peter rose from the grass and walked across the lawn towards the Victorian porch. St Claire remained at the railing; Chancellor approached him from behind. He reached into his pockets with both hands and pulled out Brown's automatic in his right, the torch in his left. When he was within eight feet, he levelled both up at St Claire and snapped on the light.

"Keep your right arm above you," he ordered. "With your left reach into your pocket and throw me the keys to your car."

It took the ambassador several seconds to answer. He seemed shaken. The suddenness of Chancellor's appearance, the blinding beam of light, the curt instructions barked from the darkness momentarily paralysed him. Peter was grateful for an enemy's training.

"I don't have the keys, young man. They're in the car."

"I don't believe you," said Chancellor angrily. "Give me those keys!"

"I suggest we return to the car, and you can see for yourself. I'll keep both hands above me if you wish."

"I wish."

The keys were in the ignition of the Mark IV. Chancellor held the old man against the bonnet as he checked the diplomat's pockets and chest. St Claire carried no weapon. The realization was bewildering, as bewildering as the keys left in the Mark IV. A car was an escape; the leader of Inver Brass would know that.

The torch off, Peter shoved the automatic into St Claire's back. They walked up the steps and out to the front of the porch. He spun the old man around against the railing and stood facing him.

"If I was late, forgive me," said the ambassador. "I haven't driven in nearly twelve years. I tried to explain that to your unidentified friend on the telephone, but he wouldn't listen."

St Claire's statement made sense. It explained the swaying headlights. It also proved that St Claire was frightened. He would never have taken such risks at night on the highways and side roads if he had been anything else. "But you came anyway, didn't you?"

"You knew I couldn't refuse. You found my man. You discovered the transmitters. I imagine they could be traced to me."

"Could they?"

"I'm not an expert at such things. Varak was, but I'm not. I'm not even sure how they were obtained."

"I can't accept that. The man who runs Inver Brass is much more resourceful."

St Claire drew himself up in the darkness. The sound of the name seemed to pain him. "You've been told, then."

"Does it surprise you? You already knew I knew the identities of Venice, Christopher, Paris and Banner. And Bravo. Why not Inver Brass?"

"How much have you learned since?"

"Enough to frighten me to death. Forty years, countless millions. Unknown men who ran the country."

"You're exaggerating. We came to the aid of the country during periods of crisis. That's far more accurate."

"Who determined what a crisis was? You?"

"Crises have a way of being apparent."

"Not always. Not to everybody."

"We had access to information not available to 'everybody'."

"And you acted on it rather than making the information public."

"They were essentially acts of charity. Ultimately for the good of that 'everybody' you refer to. We never acted for ourselves." St Claire's voice rose, his defence of Inver Brass deeply felt.

"There are ways to provide charity openly. Why didn't you use them?"

"That sort of charity is always temporary. It doesn't attack root causes."

"And root causes can't be left to the judgements of those elected to understand them, is that it?"

"You're oversimplifying our viewpoint, and you know it, Mr Chancellor."

"I know I'd rather take my chances with an imperfect system I can follow than one I can't see."

"That's sophistry. It's quite easy for you to argue civics, but while you're arguing, a thousand pockets of frustrations are inexorably spreading. If they touch, there'll be an eruption of violence beyond your imagination. When that happens, freedom of choice will be eliminated in the cause of adequate diet. It's as simple as that. Over the years we've tried to control that spread. Would you want to stop us?"

Peter conceded the logic of St Claire's reasoning, knowing that this brilliant, devious man, masked in such goodness, was forcing him on the defensive, veering him away from the point of their confrontation. He had to remind himself that St Claire was a monster; there was blood on his hands.

"There are other ways," he said. "Other solutions."

"There may be, but I'm not sure we'll find them in our lifetimes. Certainly not mine. Perhaps in the act of seeking solutions there's the prevention of violence we hope for."

Peter attacked suddenly. "You found one solution that was rooted in violence, though, didn't you? The bait was the truth, after all."

"What?"

"You killed Hoover! Inver Brass ordered his assassination!"

At the words St Claire stiffened; a short stifled cry came from his throat. His confidence vanished. He was suddenly an old man accused of a terrible crime.

"Where did – ? . . . Who – ?" He could not articulate the question.

"For the moment it doesn't matter. What matters is that the order was given and carried out. You executed a man without a trial, without the judgement of an open court. That's what is supposed to separate us from a large part of this world, Mr Ambassador. From that violence you hate so."

"There were reasons!"

"Because you believed he was a killer? Because you'd heard he had his assassination teams, his 'dispatch units'?"

"In large measure, yes!"

"Not good enough. If you knew it, you should have said it! All of you."

"It couldn't have been done that way! I told you, there were reasons."

"*Other* reasons, you mean?"

"Yes!"

"The files?"

"For God's sake, yes! The files!"

"*You can't do it! You have everything you need. Bring him to trial! Let him face the judgment of the courts! Of the country!*"

"*You don't understand . . . There's not a court in the land, not a judge, not a member of the House or of the Senate, not the President or any of his cabinet, who can bring him to trial. It's beyond that.*"

"*No, it isn't! There are laws!*"

"*There are the files . . . People would be reached . . . by others who have to survive.*" Then, you're no better than he is."

"You're better than he was," said Chancellor quietly.

"We believed with all our hearts and souls that we were." St Claire was passing through the first shock waves; he was finding part of the control he had lost. "I can't believe this. I misread Varak so completely."

"Don't try that," replied Peter coldly. "I despise everything he was, but Varak gave his life for you. The truth is you misled him."

"Wrong! Never!"

"The whole time! Varak was 'Longworth', and 'Longworth' got into the bureau the night Hoover was killed. Varak got those files! He gave them to *you!*"

"*A* to *L*, yes! We've never denied it. They were destroyed. Not *M* to *Z*! They were missing. They are missing!"

"*No!* Varak thought they were missing because that's what you wanted him to think!"

"You're insane!" St Claire whispered.

"There were two other men with Varak that night! One of them – maybe both working together – emptied and switched the folders, or combined them, or just lied. I don't know how, but that's where it was done. You knew Varak wouldn't be compromised about the files, so you went around him."

St Claire shook his head, his expression tortured. "No. You're wrong. The theory is plausible, even ingenious, I admit that. But it simply *is not true.*"

"Those two men disappeared! Their names were covers, their identities impossible to trace!"

"For a different purpose! Hoover had to be eliminated. The country couldn't stand even the hint of another assassination. There would have been chaos; it would have fuelled the fanatics who want to run this government in violation of every constitutional principle. We couldn't allow any traces. You must believe that!"

"You've lied and lied and lied! There's no way you can make me believe anything."

St Claire paused, reflective. "Perhaps there is. By explaining why, then going one step further: putting my life and everything I've stood for for over fifty years of service in your hands."

"The purpose first," said Peter harshly. "Why was Hoover murdered?"

"He was the absolute ruler of a government unto itself. There was no clear-cut chain of command. His government was amorphous, without structure; he kept it that way. He had gone way beyond the severest illegalities. No one really knew how far, but there was sufficient evidence pointing to the killings you spoke of; we knew about the blackmail. It reached as far as the Oval Office. All this might, in itself, have justified the decision, but there was a further consideration that made it irrevocable. An amorphous chain of command was organizing; both within and outside the bureau. Viciously unprincipled men were circling around Hoover, flattering, cajoling, pretending to worship. They had only one objective: his private files. With them they could rule the country. He had to be eliminated before any pacts were made."

St Claire stopped. He was becoming tired; his own doubts showed on his face.

"I don't agree with you," said Peter, "but things are clearer. How are you going to put fifty years of service in my hands?"

St Claire took a deep breath. "I believe in man's instinct at certain moments to perceive the truth no matter what. I think this is one of those moments. Only two men on the face of the earth knew every step of Hoover's assassination. The man who created the plan and myself. That man is dead; he died in front of you. I'm left. That plan is your final proof, for no strategy conceived by human beings is perfect; something is always left undone if others know where to look. By telling you I not only place my life in your hands, but far more important, I place the work of a lifetime at your disposal. What you do with it means more to me than whatever time I have left. Will you accept this moment? Will you let me *try* to convince you?"

"Go ahead."

As St Claire spoke, Peter understood the devastating nature of what was being given him. The ambassador was right on two points. Chancellor knew instinctively that he was hearing the truth, and beyond that certainty, he realized that Hoover's murder was within reach of being confirmed. St Claire would not use names – other than Varak's – but it was reasonable to assume that identities could be uncovered.

An actress whose husband had been destroyed during the McCarthy madness; two former Marine communications specialists, both experienced in electronics and telephone interceptions, one an expert marksman; an operative from Britain's MI6, known to have worked closely with the National Security Agency during the Berlin crisis; an American surgeon living in Paris, an expatriate socialist whose wife and son had been killed in an accident with an FBI vehicle that had been involved in illegal, unwarranted surveillance. These had been the team. The threads were uncut; they could be followed to their sources. The plan itself was the work of an intelligence genius, even to the subtle inclusion of a White House adviser's name.

It accounted for Ramirez's judgement: *There was no autopsy. . . . Orders from Sixteen hundred . . . The White House . . . killed him. If they didn't, they think they did. They think someone over there did it. Or had it done.*

What an incredible mind Varak had possessed!

St Claire finished, exhausted. "Have I told you the truth? Do you believe me now?"

"As far as we've gone, yes. There's one step further. If I sense a lie, it's all a lie. Is that fair?"

"There are no more lies. Not where you are concerned. It's fair."

"What's the meaning of Chasŏng?"

"I don't know."

"It's not significant?"

"Quite the contrary. Varak called it a 'decoy'. He believed it was the key to the identity of the man in Inver Brass who betrayed us."

"Explain that."

Once again St Claire breathed deeply, his exhaustion even more apparent. "It concerned MacAndrew. Something happened at Chasŏng to discredit his command. Thus the phrase 'Mac the Knife, killer of Chasŏng'. There was an enormous loss of life; MacAndrew was held responsible. Once his guilt was established, it was expected to stop there. Varak thought that it shouldn't. He felt there was something else, something that involved MacAndrew's wife."

"Did you ever learn the composition of the troops at Chasŏng?"

"The composition?"

"The racial composition." Chancellor watched the old man closely.

"No. I wasn't aware that there was any such thing as a 'racial composition'."

"Suppose I told you that the casualty records of Chasŏng are among the most

830

closely guarded secrets in the Army archives; hundreds were killed and listed as missing. Only thirty-seven survived, six of whom are incapable of communicating. That the thirty-one remaining survivors are in thirty-one separate hospitals across the country. Would all this mean anything to you?"

"It would be further confirmation of the paranoia that exists in the Pentagon. Not unlike the Hoover regime at the bureau."

"That's all?"

"We're speaking of wasted lives. Perhaps *paranoia* is too vague a term."

"I'd say so. Because it wasn't an unnecessary loss of life due to MacAndrew. It was a trap set by our own Army. It was a conspiracy of command. Those troops – to the last soldier – were Black. It was racial murder."

St Claire held his position by the railing, his expression frozen. Seconds passed; the only sounds were the waves against the rocks and the gusts of wind off the water. The ambassador found his voice.

"In the name of God, why?"

Peter stared at the diplomat, feeling both relief and bewilderment. The old man was not lying; his shock was genuine. St Claire was many things that were unforgivable, but he was not the betrayer of Inver Brass. He did not have the files. Peter returned the gun to his pocket.

"To cover an intelligence operation that involved MacAndrew's wife. To stop MacAndrew from asking questions. If it had been unearthed, it would have led to the exposure of dozens of similar operations. Men and women placed on drugs, on hallucinogens. Experiments that would have blown up in the faces of those who conceived them, destroyed their careers, and probably got several of them killed by the man they had led into the trap: MacAndrew."

"And for *those* reasons they *sacrificed* – Oh, my *God!*"

"That's what Chasŏng means," said Peter quietly. "Everything else was Varak's decoy."

St Claire stepped forward, his legs unsteady, his features contorted. "Do you realize what you're saying? Inver Brass – Only one member of Inver Brass is – "

"He's dead."

The breath left St Claire's lungs. For an instant his whole body was contorted. Chancellor continued softly.

"Sutherland's dead. So is Jacob Dreyfus. And you don't have the files. That leaves two men. Wells and Montelán."

The news of Dreyfus's death was almost more than St Claire could absorb. His eyes seemed to float in their sockets. He held the railing, gripping it awkwardly in his hands.

"Gone. They're gone." The words were whispered in sorrow.

Peter approached the old man, feeling compassion and relief. At last there was an ally! A powerful man who could end the nightmare.

"Mr Ambassador?"

At the sound of the title, St Claire looked up at Peter. There was an unmistakable flash of gratitude in his eyes. "Yes?"

"I should leave you alone for a while, but I can't do that. People have traced me. I think they've found out what I've learned. MacAndrew's daughter is in hiding; two people are with her, but that's no guarantee she's safe. I can't go to the police, I can't get protection. I need your help."

The diplomat was finding what was left of his strength. "You'll have it, of course," he began. "And you're quite right, there's no time for remorse. Thoughts can come later. Not now."

"What can we do?"

"Cut out the cancer in the full knowledge that the patient may die. And in this case the patient is dead already. Inver Brass is gone."

"May I take you to my friends? To MacAndrew's daughter?"

"Yes, of course." St Claire pushed away from the railing. "No, it would be a waste of time. The telephone is faster. In spite of what you think, there are people in Washington who can be trusted. The vast majority, in fact. You'll have your protection." St Claire gestured toward the front entrance; he reached into his pocket for a key.

They had to step in quickly. The diplomat explained: the alarm system was suspended by a key for ten seconds while they entered, reactivated with the closing of the door.

Inside, St Claire went through the arch into the huge sitting room, turning on the lights. He walked to a telephone, picked up the receiver, stopped and replaced it in its cradle. He turned to Chancellor.

"The best protection," he said, "is to stop the attackers. Wells or Montelán, either or both."

"My guess would be Wells."

"Why? What did he say to you?"

"That the country needed him."

"He's right. His arrogance in no way vitiates his brilliance."

"The files panicked him. He said he was part of them."

"He was. Is."

"I don't understand."

"Wells is his middle name, his mother's. The files make that clear. It was legally assumed shortly after his parents were divorced. He was an infant. His name at birth was Reisler. It's in the missing files, *M* to *Z*. Does the name mean anything to you?"

"Yes." Peter remembered. The name evoked an image of a strutting, vicious figure of thirty-five years ago. "Frederick Reisler. One of the leaders of the German-American Bund. I used him as the basis for a character in *Reichstag!* He was a stockbroker."

"A genius on the Street. He funnelled millions to Hitler. Wells has been running from that stigma all his life. More important, he's served his country selflessly to make amends. He's terrified the files will expose a legacy that's tortured him."

"Then, I think it's him. The heritage fits."

"Perhaps, but I doubt it. Unless his cunning is beyond anything I can conceive of, why would he fear exposure if he has the files? What did the *hidalgo* say?"

"What?"

"Montelán. Paris. Far more attractive than Banner, yet infinitely more arrogant. Generations of Castilian wealth, immense family influence, stolen and stripped by the Falangists. Carlos has a hatred in him. He despises all sources of absolute control. I sometimes think he searches the world for deposed aristocrats – "

"What did you just say?" broke in Chancellor. "He despises what?"

"Absolutists. The fascist mentality in all forms."

"No. You said *control. Sources of control!*"

"Yes, I did."

Ramirez! thought Peter. The source control of Chasŏng. Was that it? Was that the connection? Ramirez. Montelán. Two aristocrats of the same blood. Both filled with hatred. Appealing to – using – the same minorities they held in such contempt?

"I haven't got time to explain," Peter said, suddenly sure. "But it's Montelán! Can you reach him?"

"Of course. Each member of Inver Brass can be contacted within minutes. There are codes he can't ignore."

"Montelán might."

The ambassador arched his eyebrows. "He won't know why I'm calling. His own fear of exposure will force him to respond. But, of course, exposure isn't enough, is it?" St Claire paused; Chancellor did not interrupt. "He must be killed. A final life demanded by Inver Brass. How tragically it's all turned out." St Claire picked up the telephone. Instantly, he stopped, his ashen face now white. "It's dead."

"It *can't* be!"

"It wasn't a moment ago."

Without warning, the shattering sound of a bell filled the cavernous room.

Chancellor spun towards the archway, his right hand lunging into his pocket, gripping the small automatic, pulling it out.

A gunshot accompanied the smashing of glass from a window on the porch. Quick, iced pain spread throughout Peter's arm and shoulder; blood appeared on his jacket. He dropped the gun to the floor.

There was the crash of wood against wood from the hallway. The front door was slammed back into the wall. Two slender men – Black men in tight-fitting trousers and dark shirts – raced into the room with cat-like speed and crouched, still standing, gripping weapons levelled at Chancellor.

Behind them an immense figure walked out of the darkness of the hall into the eerie light of the room.

It was Daniel Sutherland.

He stood motionless, staring at Peter, his eyes contemptuous. He held out his huge hand and opened the palm. In it was a capsule. He closed his fist and turned his hand downward; his fingers ground against his palm.

A dark red fluid burst from his fist, covering his skin and dripping to the floor.

"The theatre, Mr Chancellor. The art of deception."

42

Everything happened in rapid, crisp movements that were marks of professionals. Other Blacks entered; the house was surrounded. Munro St Claire was held by the table. Peter was pulled away, a strip of cloth strapped tightly over his shoulder wound. A man was dispatched to the gates to await the local police with the proper explanation of why the alarm went off.

Daniel Sutherland nodded, turned, and walked back into the darkness of the hall. Again, without warning, the inconceivable happened. The man holding Bravo released him and stepped away; sounds of explosions filled the room.

Munro St Claire was impaled against the wall, riddled by gunfire, his body host to a fusillade of bullets. He slumped to the floor, his wide eyes dead and unbelieving.

"Oh, my *God* . . ." Chancellor heard the terrified words, unaware that they were his. Aware only of the horror he had witnessed.

In seconds Sutherland returned from the dark hall. His eyes were sad, his erect bearing somehow burdened with grief.

He spoke softly as he looked down at the fallen St Claire. "You would never have understood. Nor would the others. Those files must not be destroyed. They must be used to right a great many wrongs." The judge raised his eyes and looked at Peter. "We gave Jacob a more proper burial than you accorded him. His death will be announced in time. As will the others."

"You've killed them all," whispered Chancellor.

"Yes," replied Sutherland. "Banner two nights ago, and Paris last night."

"You'll be caught."

"Mrs Montelán believes her husband has been sent to the Far East by the State Department. We have men at State; the proper documents will be recorded, and Montelán will be reported killed by terrorists. It's not so unusual these days. Wells had a fatal accident on a wet country road off the highway. You were of considerable help in his case. His car was found in the morning."

Sutherland spoke matter-of-factly, as if killing and violence were perfectly natural phenomena, neither unusual nor to be dwelt upon.

"You have men at the State Department?" said Peter, bewildered. "Then you were able to trace the sterile house in Saint Michael's."

"We could and did."

"But you didn't have to. You had O'Brien."

"I don't think you should try to deceive us, Mr Chancellor. We're not in the pages of a book. We're all real here."

"What do you mean?"

"You know precisely what I mean. We never had O'Brien. We had others. Not him."

"Not him . . ." Chancellor could only repeat Sutherland's words.

"A resourceful man, Mr O'Brien," continued Sutherland. "A very brave man.

He fired into the fuel tanks, setting the boats on fire, then risked his life to lead us away from your car. Courage matching ingenuity, an estimable combination."

Peter could not repress the sound of the sharp intake of breath that escaped from his throat. O'Brien had not betrayed them!

Sutherland was talking, but the words had no meaning. Nothing had meaning any longer.

"What did you say?" asked Peter, looking around at the scrubbed, clean faces of the Blacks. There were five men now, each with a weapon in his hand.

"I said as gently as possible that your death can't be avoided."

"Why didn't you kill me before?"

"In the beginning we tried to. Then I reconsidered. You'd begun your manuscript. We had to prove you were mad. People have read what you've written; we have no way of knowing how many. You've come remarkably close to the truth. We couldn't allow that. The country must believe those files were destroyed. You wrote otherwise. Fortunately, your behaviour has been questioned, and there are some who think you've gone out of your mind. You sustained head injuries in an accident that nearly killed you. You lost a loved one, and your recovery has been abnormally slow. Your paranoid sense of conspiracy is displayed in each of your books, progressively more acute. The final proof of your instability – "

"Final proof?" interrupted Peter, dazed by Sutherland's argument.

"Yes," continued the judge. "The final proof of your instability would come when you swore I was dead. Needless to say, my reaction would be one of amusement. I had met you once, the memory of that meeting dim. It wasn't particularly memorable. You'd be dismissed as a maniac."

"A maniac," Peter said. "The bureau had 'maniacs'. Hoover's inheritors. They worked with you."

"Three did. They didn't understand it was to be a short-lived association. We had the same objective: Hoover's files. What they did not know was that we had half of them, the half that weren't destroyed. We wanted known fanatics who would be caught and killed, the entire files presumably having disappeared with their deaths. Their other function was to drive you to the precipice. If they killed you, it was on their heads. You were a harmless meddler, but they took you seriously."

"You *are* going to kill me. You wouldn't tell me these things if you weren't." Peter made the observation calmly, almost clinically.

"I'm not without feeling. I don't wish to take your life; I derive no pleasure from it. But I have to. The least I can do is try to satisfy your curiosity. And I do have an offer to make."

"What offer?"

"The girl's life. There's no reason for Miss MacAndrew to die. Whatever she thinks she knows will have been told her by a writer who recognized his own madness and killed himself. The pathology is classic for creative people. Depression sets in when the lines of reality are blurred."

Peter wondered at his own calm. "Thank you. You put me in company I'm not sure I deserve. What's the exchange? I'll do anything you say."

"Where's O'Brien?"

"What? . . ." Chancellor drew out the word, bewildered.

"Where's O'Brien? Did you speak with him while you were with Ramirez? He can't go to the bureau or the police. We'd know about it if he did. Where is he?"

Peter watched Sutherland's eyes closely. *Look to the fiction*, he thought. Something was better than nothing, no matter how remote the possibilities. And there was a possibility.

"If I tell you, what guarantees do I have that you'll let her live?"

"Ultimately, none. Only my word."

"Your *word*? You're the one who's crazy! Accept the word of the man who betrayed his friends, betrayed Inver Brass?"

"There's no inconsistency. Inver Brass was formed to give extraordinary aid to the country in times of desperate need – to *all* the men and women of this country, because this nation was for all its people. What has become apparent is that the country is *not* for all its people. It never will be. It must be *forced* to include those it would prefer to overlook. The nation has betrayed me, Mr Chancellor. And millions like me. That fact does not alter who *I* am. It may change *what* I am, but not my values. My word is one of them. You have it."

Peter's mind raced, remembering, selecting. O'Brien had only one place to go after the Chesapeake marina, one place where they had not been followed. The motel in Ocean City. It would be there he would wait – a day at least for Alison and Peter to make contact. Quinn had nowhere else to go.

Look to the fiction; there is nothing else left.

In *Counterstrike!* a telephone call was made to enlist help in an escape. The method was simple: a false message was given, logical to those who overheard it but virtually meaningless to the receiver. In it was hidden a clue to a specific location. It was up to the receiver to figure out where.

"A trade, then," said Peter. "O'Brien for MacAndrew's daughter."

"That does not include Major Brown. He's not part of the exchange. He's our property."

"You know about him?"

"Of course. From the data-processing centre in McLean. Within minutes of the Chasŏng records being pulled, we were aware of it."

"I see. You're going to kill him?"

"That depends. We don't know him. It may well be he'll be assigned to a base hospital thousands of miles away. We do not indiscriminately take life."

You'll kill him, thought Chancellor. *Once you know him, you'll kill him.*

"You're telling me you know where Brown and Alison are," said Peter.

"We do. In Arundel Village. We have a man there, outside the hotel."

"I want her driven into Washington where I can speak with her."

"Demands, Mr Chancellor?"

"If you want O'Brien."

"She won't be harmed. You have my word."

"Let's call it the initial proof that you'll keep it. For God's sake, don't push me. I don't want to die. I'm frightened." Peter kept his voice low; it was not difficult to be convincing.

"What guarantee do I have?" asked the judge. "How will you deliver O'Brien?"

"We'll have to get to a telephone. This one's dead, but you know that. I only have a number and a room. I have no idea where." Chancellor raised his arm to look at his watch. The movement caused a sharp pain in his wounded shoulder. "O'Brien should be there for another twenty to thirty minutes. After that he's to call me."

"What's the telephone number?"

"That won't do you any good; he's fifty miles away. He knows my voice. He worked out a code for me to use and one of several places to meet during specific times." Peter's mind raced as he spoke. Several nights ago O'Brien had used a fictitious pay telephone on Wisconsin Avenue as a cover for a second location, a second phone booth, where Peter was to go to take his call. There was a pay phone at a petrol station outside of Salisbury. Quinn and Alison had been there with him when he'd called Morgan in New York. O'Brien would remember that booth.

"It's two-fifteen. Where could you meet at this hour?" Sutherland stood motionless, his voice wary.

"A petrol station near Salisbury; I'm to confirm it. He'll want me to describe the car I'm driving. And I don't think he'll show himself if he sees people in the car with me. You'll have to conceal yourselves."

"It's not a problem. What are the words of the code?" asked the judge. "The precise words."

"They don't mean anything. He was reading a newspaper."

"What are they?"

" 'The senator called a last-minute quorum on the defence expenditures.' "

Chancellor winced and reached across his chest to hold his wounded shoulder. The gesture diminished any importance Peter might have given to the meaning of the code. They were merely words chosen at random from a newspaper.

"We'll use the ambassador's car," said Sutherland finally. "You'll drive the last few miles. Until then you'll ride in the back with me. Two of my men will accompany us. When you take the wheel, they'll conceal themselves. I'm sure you'll co-operate fully."

"I expect your co-operation, too. I want your man away from Arundel. I want Alison driven to Washington. Brown can do that; you can go after him later. How far's the nearest telephone?"

"On the table, Mr Chancellor. Or will be in a matter of minutes." The judge turned to the muscular Black on his left. He spoke quietly in an unfamiliar language.

It was the language shouted at the Chesapeake marina! Shouted in defiance at the moment of death. The language Varak had not understood.

The slender Black man nodded and ran quickly into the hall and out through the front door.

"The telephone will be reconnected," Sutherland explained. "The wires were not severed, only placed on an intermediate circuit that does not break the terminal line." The judge paused, then continued. "I spoke in Ashanti. It was the language of the African Gold Coast in the seventeenth and eighteenth centuries. It's not easy to learn; there's no language like it. We can converse anywhere, among anyone; relay instructions, issue orders without being understood."

Sutherland turned to the two men across the room. Again he spoke in the strange-sounding Ashanti. The two Blacks put their weapons in their belts and walked rapidly to St Claire's dead body. They picked it up and carried it out.

The telephone rang once. "It's fixed," Sutherland said. "Call O'Brien. Our man is listening on the line. If you say anything unacceptable, the connection will be broken, the woman killed."

Peter walked to the telephone. St Claire's blood formed jagged blots and streaks on the wall next to the table. He could feel it beneath the soles of his shoes. He picked up the phone.

He dialled the number of the motel in Ocean City and asked the switchboard for Upper South Suite. The room phone rang; the wait was unbearable; *O'Brien wasn't there!*

Then he heard the click and a quiet "Yes?"

"Quinn?"

"Peter! My God, where *are* you? I've been – "

"There's no time!" interrupted Chancellor, speaking in uncharacteristic anger in the hope that O'Brien would look for a message in his words. "You asked for a goddamned code, so I'm giving it to you. 'The senator called a last-minute quorum over the defence expenditures.' Wasn't that it? If it isn't, it's close enough. Stupid fucking games!"

"What the hell – ?"

"I want to meet as soon as possible!" Again the interruption was abrasive, discourteous, on the edge of contempt. *So out of character, so inconsistent.* "It's between two and three in the morning. According to your schedule that's the petrol station on the road to Salisbury. I'll be driving a light-coloured Continental. A silver Mark IV. Be sure you're alone!"

There was a brief silence on the line. Peter stared at the blood-soaked wallpaper and closed his eyes, his face turned away from Sutherland. When he heard Quinn's words, he felt like crying. Tears of relief. "All *right*," said O'Brien, his voice as hostile as Chancellor's. "A Mark IV. I'll be there. And for your information, a code isn't stupid. By using it I know you're not under pressure. And with you, you son of a bitch, that's rare. See you in an hour."

O'Brien hung up. *He had understood. Quinn's final words confirmed it. They were as out of character as his own. The false message had carried the right meaning.*

Peter faced the judge. "Now it's your turn. Call Arundel."

Sutherland sat beside him in the back seat of the Continental, the two Blacks in front. They sped south over country roads, across the Choptank River, past signs that proclaimed the townships of Bethlehem, Preston, and Hurlock. Towards Salisbury. The judge had kept his word. Alison was in Washington; she'd arrive at the Hay-Adams long before they reached Salisbury. Peter would telephone her from a roadside booth once O'Brien was taken. It was to be his good-bye, his death to follow, mercifully quick, at an unexpected moment – that, too, was part of the agreement.

Chancellor turned to the judge. The huge black head reflected racing flashes of light and shadow.

"How did you get the files?" Peter asked.

"*M* to *Z*, Mr Chancellor," said Sutherland. "That's what we have. *A* to *L* were destroyed by Inver Brass. I could only get half."

"I'm going to die; that's not easy for me to say. I'd like to know how you got them."

The judge looked at Peter, his dark eyes magnified in the dim light. "There's no harm in telling you. It wasn't difficult. As you know, Varak assumed Longworth's name. The real Alan Longworth is exactly what I told you he was in my office several months ago: one of Hoover's closest associates, persuaded to work against Hoover. His reward was to spend the rest of his life in the Hawaiian Islands, his wants supplied, beyond the reach of those who might try to kill him. Hoover was told he died of natural causes: a disease. In fact, a memorial service was held for Longworth. Hoover himself gave the eulogy."

Chancellor thought of the outline for his novel.

. . . *A medical deception is mounted, the report forwarded to Hoover. The agent is riddled with cancer, it's spread beyond surgery. His life expectancy no more than a few months. Hoover has no alternative. He releases the man, believing the agent is going to die . . .*

"Hoover never questioned Longworth's death?" asked Peter.

"There was no reason to," replied Sutherland. "The surgeon's report was sent to him. It left no doubts."

The fiction.

The judge continued. "I brought Alan Longworth back to life. From Hawaii. For one day. It was most dramatic. A man returned from the dead for only a single day, but it was a day J. Edgar Hoover nearly stopped the wheels of government; his fury was intense. And his fear." A slow smile came to Sutherland; it could be seen in the swiftly moving shadows. He went on, staring straight ahead. "Longworth told Hoover the truth as far as he knew it, as much as we told him. He was psychologically ready to do this, so deep was his own guilt. Hoover had been his mentor – in a way his god – and he had been forced to betray him. There was a conspiracy to murder him, Longworth told Hoover. For his private files. The conspirators were unknown men inside and outside the bureau. Men with access to every code, every release of a vault in an emergency. Hoover panicked, as we knew he would panic. Phone calls were made all over Washington – including one to Ramirez, incidentally – and Hoover learned nothing. There was only one person he felt he could trust: his closest friend, Clyde Tolson. He began systematically removing the files to Tolson's house – to his basement, to be precise. But he fell behind the schedule we had projected; not all the files were removed. We couldn't press him; we couldn't take the risk of doing that. We could get inside Tolson's home. We had enough. We *have* enough. Files *M* to *Z* will give us the leverage we never had before."

"For what?"

"To shape the concerns of government," said Sutherland emphatically.

"What happened to Longworth?"

"You killed him, Mr Chancellor. MacAndrew pulled the trigger, but you killed him. You sent MacAndrew after him."

"And your people killed MacAndrew."

"We had no choice. He'd learned too much. He had to die, at any rate. Although he wasn't responsible, he was the symbol of Chasŏng. Hundreds of Black soldiers murdered, led to their deaths by their own commanders. The most heinous crime of which man is capable."

"Racial murder," said Peter quietly.

"A form of genocide. The most despicable form," said Sutherland, his eyes filled with hatred. "For *convenience*. To stop one man from learning the truth because that truth would expose a network of crimes – experiments – that civilized men should never have sanctioned but did."

Chancellor let the moment pass. The silence was electric. "The phone calls. The killing. Why? What did Phyllis Maxwell or Bromley or Rawlins have to do with Chasŏng? Or O'Brien, for that matter? Why did you go after them?"

The judge answered rapidly. The victims mentioned were not of consequence. "Chasŏng was not involved. Phyllis Maxwell had uncovered information we wished to use ourselves; it led to the Oval Office. Bromley deserved no less. He had the courage to take on the Pentagon, but he crippled an urban-renewal project in Detroit that would have benefited thousands of destitute slum dwellers. Black people, Mr Chancellor. He sold out to criminal elements who provided him with information that augmented his headline-gathering crusade against the military. At the expense of Black people! Rawlins was the most dangerous example of the false New South. He gave lip service to emerging 'new values' and privately in committee thwarted every congressional attempt to give teeth to the laws. And he abused Black women, don't forget that. The parents of those children can't."

Sutherland had finished.

"What about O'Brien?" Peter asked. "Why do you want him now?"

"Once again, you're responsible. He's the only one who pieced together the theft of the remaining files. If that were all, he might have lived. His silence could be counted on; he had no viable proof. However, no longer. He knows Venice's identity. You gave it to him."

Peter looked away. He was surrounded by death; he was the precursor of death.

"Why you?" asked Peter softly. "Of all men, why *you*?"

"Because I can," replied Sutherland, his eyes on the road ahead.

"That's not an answer."

"It's taken me a lifetime to understand what the young see every day of their lives. I was too filled with doubts; it's not complicated at all. This nation has forsaken its Black citizens. The Black man must no longer interfere. America is bored with his dreams; the Black man's attainments are suspect. It was fashionable to support him while he was an achieving oddity, but not when he becomes a challenge and moves into the neighbourhood."

"You weren't forsaken."

"The extraordinary man never is. I say that with no sense of false pride. My gifts were from God, and they were extraordinary. But what of the ordinary man? The ordinary woman, the ordinary child, who grow up to be less than ordinary because they're marked at birth? No change of name can alter that stigma; no certificate can lighten the skin. I'm no revolutionary in the accepted sense, Mr Chancellor. I know very well that such a course would result in a holocaust unknown to the Jews. Quite simply, the numbers and the hardware are against us. I'm merely using the tools of the society in which we live. *Fear*. The most common weapon known to man. It has no prejudice; it respects no racial barriers. That's what those files represent – nothing more, nothing less. We can do so much with them, influence so much legislation, enact so many laws, give teeth to statutes that are violated daily. That's what those files can accomplish. I seek no violence that would certainly ensure our annihilation. I want none of that. I seek only what rightfully belongs to us, what's been withheld from us. And providence has given me the weapon. I intend to lead the *ordinary* Black man out of his sorrow and embarrassment."

"But you do use violence. You kill."

"Only those who would take our lives!" Sutherland's voice thundered; it filled the car. "As our lives were taken! Only those who would interfere!"

Sutherland's explosion caused Peter to react in kind, with his own intensity, his own anger. "An eye for an eye? Is that where you're at? Is that what you came away with after a lifetime of law? For Christ's sake, not *you! Why?*"

Sutherland turned in the seat, his eyes furious. "I'll tell you why. It wasn't the judgement of a lifetime. It was the result of a brief half hour five years ago. I had rendered a decision that was not particularly popular with the Justice Department. It prohibited further abuses of Miranda and upheld the conviction of a well-known superintendent of police."

"I remember," said Peter, and he did. It had been called the Sutherland decision, an anathema to the law-and-order crowd. Had any other judge but Sutherland rendered it, there would have been an appeal to the Supreme Court.

"I received a call from J. Edgar Hoover, requesting me to come to his office. More from curiosity than anything else, I bowed to his arrogance and accepted the invitation. During that meeting I listened to the unbelievable. On the desk of the highest law-enforcement officer in the country were spread the dossiers of every major Black civil rights leader: King, Abernathy, Wilkins, Rowan, Farmer. They were volumes of filth – scurrilous rumour, unsubstantiated gossip, transcripts of telephone and electronic taps. Words taken out of context made to appear inflammatory – morally, sexually, legally, philosophically! I was enraged, appalled! That it could happen in *that office!* Blackmail! Blatant extortion! But Hoover had been through it many times before. He let me vent my rage, and when I had finished, he viciously said that were I to continue to be an obstruction, those files would be put to use. Men and their families destroyed! The Black movement *crippled!* At the very last, he said to me, "We don't want another Chasŏng, do we, Judge Sutherland?'

"Chasŏng," said Peter, repeating the name softly. "That's where you heard it first."

"It took me nearly two years to learn what happened at Chasŏng. When I did, I reached the decision. The children had been right all along. In their simplicity they saw what I did not see. As a people we were expendable. But then I saw what the young did not see. The answer was not indiscriminate violence and protests. It was to use the weapon Hoover used; make the system work from within. By *fear!* . . . We'll talk no more. You should have silence. Make peace with your God."

The man beside the driver studied a map with the aid of a pencil torch. He turned his head slightly to speak with the judge in Ashanti.

Sutherland nodded and replied in the strange African tongue. He looked at Peter. "We're within a mile and a half of the petrol station. We'll stop a quarter of a mile short of it. These men are efficient scouts. They learned the expertise of night patrol in South-east Asia. Those patrols were usually the province of Black soldiers; the casualty rates were the highest. If O'Brien's brought anyone with him, if there's any hint of a trap, they'll come back, and we'll drive away. The girl will die in front of you."

Chancellor's throat went dry. *It's over.* He should have known. Sutherland would never settle for words over a telephone. Peter had sentenced Alison to death. He had loved two women in his life, and he had killed them both.

He thought of overpowering Sutherland when they were alone. It was something to keep him from screaming.

"How could O'Brien do that?" Peter asked. "You said he couldn't go to anyone, that you'd know if he did."

"On the surface it would appear impossible. He's isolated."

"Then, why are we stopping? Why are we wasting time?"

"I saw what O'Brien did at the marina yesterday morning. Courage and ingenuity are to be respected. It's a simple precaution."

The car stopped. Whatever thoughts Peter had of attacking Sutherland were dispelled quickly. The man beside the driver leaped out of the car, opened the door next to Chancellor, and grabbed his arm. A pair of handcuffs were snapped to his wrist and the metal clasp below the window. The movement put his shoulder in agony. He winced and held his breath.

The judge climbed out of the back seat. "I leave you to your thoughts, Mr Chancellor."

The two young Black men disappeared into the darkness.

It was the longest forty-five minutes Peter could imagine. He tried to think of the various tactics O'Brien might conceive, but the more he thought about them, the more bleak were his conclusions. If Quinn had managed to get help, as surely he must have done, the additional men would be seen by Sutherland's scouts. Death. If for some reason O'Brien had decided to come alone, then he would die. But at least Alison would live. There was a bleak comfort in that.

The scouts returned, drenched with sweat. They had been running hard; they'd covered a great deal of ground.

The Black on the left opened the door and Sutherland climbed in. "It would appear that Mr O'Brien keeps the rendezvous. He is sitting in an automobile with the motor running, in the centre of the road where he can observe all sides. There is no one else within three miles of the station."

Chancellor was too numb and too sick to think clearly. His last amateurish gesture had been to lead Quinn into the trap.

It's over.

The Mark IV started. They approached the intersection; the driver braked the Continental slowly, and they came to a stop. The Black on the driver's right got out and opened Chancellor's door. He unlocked the cuffs; Peter shook his wrist trying to restore the circulation. His wounded shoulder began to hurt again. It did not matter.

"Get behind the wheel, Mr Chancellor. You'll drive now. My two friends will be crouched behind you in the back seat, their guns drawn. The girl dies if you disregard instructions."

Sutherland got out of the car with Peter, and stood by the door, facing him.

"You're wrong. You know that, don't you?" said Chancellor.

"You look for absolutes. As with precedents, they're all too often imperfect, and much of the time they don't apply. There's no right and wrong between us. We're products of a long-standing crisis neither of us is responsible for but both are swept up in."

"Is that a judicial opinion?"

"No, Mr Chancellor. It's the opinion of a Negro. I was a Negro before I was a judge." Sutherland turned and walked away.

Peter watched him, then climbed in behind the wheel and slammed the door. *It's over. Dear God, if you exist, let it come quickly, furiously. I have no courage.*

Peter turned right at the intersection and drove down the road. The petrol station was on the left, a single naked lightbulb in a bracket above the pumps.

"Slow down," came the quiet command from the back.

"What's the difference?" said Chancellor.

"Slow *down!*"

The barrel of a gun was shoved into the base of his skull. He pressed the brake of the Mark IV and coasted towards the station. He approached the rear of O'Brien's car; it had to be Quinn's. Vapour from the exhaust curled in the night air; the headlights illuminating the distant country road beyond.

Peter was alarmed. The lights from the Mark IV shone directly into the rear window of O'Brien's car. It was empty.

"He's not there," whispered Chancellor.

"He's below the seat," said the low voice on his right.

"Get out and walk to the car," said the other man.

Peter turned off the engine, opened the door and stepped out into the road. He closed his eyes briefly, wondering if a gun would fire at him the instant Quinn appeared. He was not fooled. Sutherland would spare Alison, but there'd be no conversation over the telephone. The judge would take no such risk.

O'Brien did not appear. He did not get out of the car.

"Quinn," called Chancellor. There was no answer.

What are you doing, O'Brien? It's over!

Nothing.

Peter walked towards the car, his temples throbbing, the pain in his throat agonizing. The sound of the idling engine mingled with the night noises; a breeze swirled dry leaves across the roadway. Any second now, Quinn would show himself; gunshots would follow. Would he hear them as his life ended? He approached the driver's window.

There was no one there.

"*Chancellor! Get down!*"

The scream came from out of the darkness. The sudden roar of a powerful engine filled the night. Blinding headlights shot out from the left, from the petrol station! A car came racing out of the dim light, speeding directly at the silver Mark IV. The driver's door of the racing car swung open; a figure lunged out, rolling on to the tarmac.

The impact came, a thunderous collision, the crunching of metal, the shattering of glass, the screams of the two men inside . . . all came at once, and at once Peter knew the last fury he had hoped for had arrived.

Gunshots followed, as he knew they would. He closed his eyes and gripped the hard surface of the road; the searing, ice-like pain would come. The darkness would come.

The firing continued; Chancellor rolled his face to the side. It did not come from the Mark IV. It came from Quinn O'Brien!

Peter raised his head. Smoke and dust billowed in the air. In front of him he saw O'Brien throw himself into the side of the idling car; he was only feet from Chancellor. The agent crouched, both hands extended over the boot, his pistol levelled.

"Get over here!" he roared to Peter.

Chancellor lunged forward, knees and hands pounding the tar beneath, until he reached the car.

He saw O'Brien hesitate, then raise his head and take careful aim.

The explosion came. The petrol tanks of the Continental erupted. Peter crouched in front of Quinn. Through a blanket of flames one of Sutherland's scouts lurched out of the burning car, firing at the source of O'Brien's gunshots.

But the man could be seen clearly in the light of the spreading fires; flames had ignited the fabric of his clothes. O'Brien aimed again. There was a scream; the scout fell to the ground behind the burning car.

"Quinn!" yelled Peter. "*How?*"

"I understood you! When you used 'senator' in your code, you meant it was our last hope. You meant there was a crisis. You said I had to be alone; that meant you weren't. But you were in one car, *that* car, so I needed two. One a decoy!" O'Brien shouted as he inched forward around Chancellor towards the bonnet.

"A *decoy?*"

"A diversion! I paid a guy to follow me and leave his car. If, could hit and run, we had a chance. What the hell, there was nothing left!" He raised his gun over the bonnet and levelled it.

844

"Nothing left . . ." Peter echoed the phrase, suddenly aware of its ultimate truth.

Quinn fired three shots in rapid succession. Chancellor's mind went blank for a moment, then was brought back to the madness by a second explosion from the Continental.

O'Brien spun around towards Chancellor. "Get inside!" he yelled. "We'll get out of here."

Peter rose to his feet; he grabbed O'Brien's jacket, stopping him. "Quinn! Quinn, wait! There are no others! Just *him!* Back in the road. He's *alone!*"

"Who?"

"Sutherland. It's Daniel Sutherland."

O'Brien's wild eyes stared at Peter for a brief instant. "Get in," he commanded. He swung the idling car around in a U-turn and sped towards the intersection.

In the distance the headlights showed the immense figure of Daniel Sutherland, standing in the middle of the road. The Black giant had seen what had happened. He raised his hand to his head.

There was a final gunshot.

Sutherland fell.

Venice was dead. Inver Brass was gone.

Epilogue

Morning. Peter stood by the table in his study, holding the telephone, listening to the words spoken in quiet anger from Washington. The sun streamed through the windows. Outside, the snow was deep, pure white; sharp reflections of sunlight bounced continuously up into the glass. Proof of the earth's movement. As the voice on the telephone was proof of one aspect of the human condition; ultimately there was to be found a sense of morality.

The caller was Daniel Sutherland's son, Aaron. Firebrand, brilliant lawyer for the Black movement, a man Chancellor wanted to call a friend but knew he never could.

"I will *not* fight you that way! I won't lower myself to use your weapons. And I won't let others use them. I found the files. I *burned* them! You'll have to take my word."

"I was willing to take your father's when I thought I was going to die. I believed him. I believe you."

"You don't have a choice." The lawyer hung up.

Chancellor walked back to his couch and sat down. Through the north window he could see Alison, bundled in a coat, laughing, her arms folded, warding off the winter chill. She was between Mrs Alcott and the taciturn grounds keeper, Burrows, who today seemed positively voluble. Mrs Alcott was smiling at Alison.

Mrs Alcott approved. The lady of the house was in residence. The home needed that lady.

The three of them turned towards the barn and started down the shovelled path that was bordered by shrubs, a green and white colonnade. In the distance, beyond the fence, a colt raced freely, then stopped and cocked his head at the threesome. He pranced towards them, his mane flowing.

Peter looked down at the pages of his manuscript. At the fiction. The fantasy that was his reality. He had made his decision.

He would start at the beginning, knowing it would be much better now. The invention would be there: thoughts and words put in the minds of others. But for himself no invention was needed. The experience was whole and never to be forgotten.

The story would be written as a novel.

His reality. Let others find other meanings.

He leaned forward and picked up a pencil from the tankard. He began on a fresh yellow pad.

The dark-haired man stared at the wall in front of him. His chair, like the rest of the furniture, was pleasing to the eye but not made for comfort. The style was Early American, the theme Spartan, as if those about to be granted an audience with the occupant of the inner office should reflect on their awesome opportunity in stern surroundings.

The man was in his late twenties, his face angular, the features sharp, each pronounced and definite as if carved by a craftsman more aware of details than of the whole. It was a face in quiet conflict with itself . . .